MW00809177

"*The Orc King* finds Drizzt's whirling scimitar blades tackling both familiar foes and refreshingly ambiguous moral challenges . . . The story line marks the continuation of Salvatore's maturation as a writer, introducing more complex themes into a frequently black-and-white fantasy landscape."

—*Kirkus*

"Salvatore's fight scenes are probably the best I've ever read. His description, though detailed, is very fast paced. Every time I read one, my heart races and my hands shake. It is pure brilliance . . ."

—SFFWorld on *The Legacy*

"The story is superb . . . taking unexpected turns, as always, but this time Salvatore has included something that has made the book even better, half the book is from the point of view of Drizzt's most hated enemy: Artemis Entreri . . ."

—candlekeep.com on *The Silent Blade*

"This one delivers everywhere you could expect! Really, if you have read *The Crystal Shard* and *Streams of Silver*, don't abuse yourself by not reading this! This is vintage material."

—fantasy-fan.org on *The Halfling's Gem*

The Legend of Drizzt®

Homeland

Exile

Sojourn

The Crystal Shard

Streams of Silver

The Halfling's Gem

The Legacy

Starless Night

Siege of Darkness

Passage to Dawn

The Silent Blade

The Spine of the World

Sea of Swords

A Reader's Guide to R.A. Salvatore's The Legend of Drizzt

The Collected Stories

The Hunter's Blades Trilogy

The Thousand Orcs

The Lone Drow

The Two Swords

Transitions

The Orc King

The Pirate King

The Ghost King

The Sellswords

Servant of the Shard

Promise of the Witch-King

Road of the Patriarch

FORGOTTEN REALMS

R. A. SALVATORE

THE LEGEND OF DRIZZT® COLLECTOR'S EDITION · BOOK III

THE LEGACY

STARLESS NIGHT

SIEGE OF DARKNESS

PASSAGE TO DAWN

D&D

THE LEGEND OF DRIZZT®
COLLECTOR'S EDITION, BOOK III

©2009 Wizards of the Coast LLC

All characters in this book are fictitious. Any resemblance to actual persons, living or dead, is purely coincidental.

This book is protected under the copyright laws of the United States of America. Any reproduction or unauthorized use of the material or artwork contained herein is prohibited without the express written permission of Wizards of the Coast LLC.

Published by Wizards of the Coast LLC. Hasbro SA, represented by Hasbro Europe, Stockley Park, UB11 1AZ. UK.

FORGOTTEN REALMS, DUNGEONS & DRAGONS, D&D, Wizards of the Coast, their respective logos, and THE LEGEND OF DRIZZT are trademarks of Wizards of the Coast LLC in the U.S.A. and other countries. All other trademarks are the property of their respective owners.

All Wizards of the Coast characters and their distinctive likenesses are property of Wizards of the Coast LLC.

PRINTED IN THE U.S.A.

Cover art by Todd Lockwood
Map by Todd Gamble
Hardcover Edition First Printing: January 2009
This Edition First Printing: September 2010

This book collects the complete text from the April 2008 edition of *The Legacy,* the May 2008 edition of *Starless Night,* the June 2008 edition of *Siege of Darkness,* and the August 2008 edition of *Passage to Dawn.*

9 8 7 6 5 4 3 2
ISBN: 978-0-7869-5573-2
620-21446000-001-EN

For customer service, contact:

U.S., Canada, Asia Pacific, & Latin America: Wizards of the Coast LLC, P.O. Box 707, Renton, WA 98057-0707, +1-800-324-6496, www.wizards.com/customerservice

U.K., Eire, & South Africa: Wizards of the Coast LLC, c/o Hasbro UK Ltd., P.O. Box 43, Newport, NP19 4YD, UK, Tel: +08457 12 55 99, Email: wizards@hasbro.co.uk

Europe: Wizards of the Coast p/a Hasbro Belgium NV/SA, Industrialaan 1, 1702 Groot-Bijgaarden, Belgium, Tel: +32.70.233.277, Email: wizards@hasbro.be

Visit our websites at www.wizards.com
www.DungeonsandDragons.com

DEDICATIONS

THE LEGACY

TO DIANE,
SHARE THIS WITH ME

STARLESS NIGHT

AND ON THE FIRST DAY,
ED CREATED THE
FORGOTTEN REALMS® WORLD
AND GAVE MY IMAGINATION
A PLACE TO LIVE

TO ED GREENWOOD
WITH ALL MY THANKS
AND ADMIRATION

SIEGE OF DARKNESS

TO LUCY SCARAMUZZI
THE TRUEST OF TEACHERS,
WHO TAUGHT ME HOW TO MAKE A BOOK—
EVEN THOUGH ALL OF MY IDEAS
BACK IN HER SECOND-GRADE CLASSROOM
WERE STOLEN FROM SNOOPY!

THE LEGACY

THE LEGEND OF DRIZZT® BOOK VII

The rogue Dinin made his way carefully through the dark avenues of Menzoberranzan, the city of drow. A renegade, with no family to call his own for nearly twenty years, the seasoned fighter knew well the perils of the city, and knew how to avoid them.

He passed an abandoned compound along the two-mile-long cavern's western wall and could not help but pause and stare. Twin stalagmite mounds supported a blasted fence around the whole of the place, and two sets of broken doors, one on the ground and one beyond a balcony twenty feet up the wall, hung open awkwardly on twisted and scorched hinges. How many times had Dinin levitated up to that balcony, entering the private quarters of the nobles of his house, House Do'Urden?

PRELUDE

House Do'Urden. It was forbidden even to speak the name in the drow city. Once, Dinin's family had been the eighth-ranked among the sixty or so drow families in Menzoberranzan; his mother had sat on the ruling council; and he, Dinin, had been a Master at Melee-Magthere, the School of Fighters, at the famed drow Academy.

Standing before the compound, it seemed to Dinin as if the place were a thousand years removed from that time of glory. His family was no more, his house lay in ruins, and Dinin had been forced to take up with Bregan D'aerthe, an infamous mercenary band, simply to survive.

"Once," the rogue drow mouthed quietly. He shook his slender shoulders and pulled his concealing *piwafwi* cloak around him, remembering how vulnerable a houseless drow could be. A quick glance toward the center of the cavern, toward the pillar that was Narbondel, showed him that the hour was late. At the break of each day, the Archmage of Menzoberranzan went out to Narbondel and infused the pillar with a magical, lingering heat that would work its way up, then back down. To sensitive drow eyes, which could look into the infrared spectrum, the level of heat in the pillar acted as a gigantic glowing clock.

Now Narbondel was almost cool; another day neared its end.

Dinin had to go more than halfway across the city, to a secret cave within the Clawrift, a great chasm running out from Menzoberranzan's northwestern wall. There Jarlaxle, the leader of Bregan D'aerthe, waited in one of his many hideouts.

The drow fighter cut across the center of the city, passed right by Narbondel, and beside more than a hundred hollowed stalagmites, comprising a dozen separate family compounds, their fabulous sculptures and gargoyles glowing in multicolored faerie fire. Drow soldiers, walking posts along house walls or along the bridges connecting multitudes of leering stalactites, paused and regarded the lone stranger carefully, hand-crossbows or poisoned javelins held ready until Dinin was far beyond them.

That was the way in Menzoberranzan: always alert, always distrustful.

Dinin gave one careful look around when he reached the edge of the Clawrift, then slipped over the side and used his innate powers of levitation to slowly descend into the chasm. More than a hundred feet down, he again looked into the bolts of readied handcrossbows, but these were withdrawn as soon as the mercenary guardsmen recognized Dinin as one of their own.

Jarlaxle has been waiting for you, one of the guards signaled in the intricate silent hand code of the dark elves.

Dinin didn't bother to respond. He owed commoner soldiers no explanations. He pushed past the guardsmen rudely, making his way down a short tunnel that soon branched into a virtual maze of corridors and rooms.

Several turns later, the dark elf stopped before a shimmering door, thin and almost translucent. He put his hand against its surface, letting his body heat make an impression that heat-sensing eyes on the other side would understand as a knock.

"At last," he heard a moment later, in Jarlaxle's voice. "Do come in, Dinin, my *Khal'abbil*. You have kept me waiting far too long."

Dinin paused a moment to get a bearing on the unpredictable mercenary's inflections and words. Jarlaxle had called him *Khal'abbil*, "my trusted friend," his nickname for Dinin since the raid that had destroyed House Do'Urden (a raid in which Jarlaxle had played a prominent role), and there was no obvious sarcasm in the mercenary's tone. There seemed to be nothing wrong at all. but why, then, had Jarlaxle recalled him from his critical scouting mission to House Vandree, the Seventeenth House of Menzoberranzan? Dinin wondered. It had taken Dinin nearly a year to gain the trust of the imperiled Vandree house guard, a position, no doubt, that would be severely jeopardized by his unexplained absence from the house compound.

There was only one way to find out, the rogue soldier decided. He held his breath and forced his way into the opaque barrier. It seemed as if he were passing through a wall of thick water, though he did not get wet, and after several long steps across the flowing extraplanar border of two planes of existence, he forced his way through the seemingly inch-thick magical door and entered Jarlaxle's small room.

The room was alight in a comfortable red glow, allowing Dinin to shift his eyes from the infrared to the normal light spectrum. He blinked as the transformation completed, then blinked again, as always, when he looked at Jarlaxle.

The mercenary leader sat behind a stone desk in an

exotic cushioned chair, supported by a single stem with a swivel so that it could rock back at a considerable angle. Comfortably perched, as always, Jarlaxle had the chair leaning way back, his slender hands clasped behind his clean-shaven head (so unusual for a drow!).

Just for amusement, it seemed, Jarlaxle lifted one foot onto the table, his high black boot hitting the stone with a resounding thump, then lifted the other, striking the stone just as hard, but this boot making not a whisper.

The mercenary wore his ruby-red eye patch over his right eye this day, Dinin noted.

To the side of the desk stood a trembling little humanoid creature, barely half Dinin's five-and-a-half-foot height, including the small white horns protruding from the top of its sloping brow.

"One of House Oblodra's kobolds," Jarlaxle explained casually. "It seems the pitiful thing found its way in, but cannot so easily find its way back out."

The reasoning seemed sound to Dinin. House Oblodra, the Third House of Menzoberranzan, occupied a tight compound at the end of the Clawrift and was rumored to keep thousands of kobolds for torturous pleasure, or to serve as house fodder in the event of a war.

"Do you wish to leave?" Jarlaxle asked the creature in a guttural, simplistic language.

The kobold nodded eagerly, stupidly.

Jarlaxle indicated the opaque door, and the creature darted for it. It had not the strength to penetrate the barrier, though, and it bounced back, nearly landing on Dinin's feet. Before it even bothered to get up, the kobold foolishly sneered in contempt at the mercenary leader.

Jarlaxle's hand flicked several times, too quickly for Dinin to count. The drow fighter reflexively tensed, but knew better than to move, knew that Jarlaxle's aim was always perfect.

When he looked down at the kobold, he saw five daggers sticking from its lifeless body, a perfect star formation on the scaly creature's little chest.

Jarlaxle only shrugged at Dinin's confused stare. "I could not allow the beast to return to Oblodra," he reasoned, "not after it learned of our compound so near theirs."

Dinin shared Jarlaxle's laugh. He started to retrieve the daggers, but Jarlaxle reminded him that there was no need.

"They will return of their own accord," the mercenary explained, pulling at the edge of his bloused sleeve to reveal the magical sheath enveloping his wrist. "Do sit," he bade his friend, indicating an unremarkable stool at the side of the desk. "We have much to discuss."

"Why did you recall me?" Dinin asked bluntly as he took his place beside the desk. "I had infiltrated Vandree fully."

"Ah, my *Khal'abbil*," Jarlaxle replied. "Always to the point. That is a quality I do so admire in you."

"*Uln'hyrr,*" Dinin retorted, the drow word for "liar."

Again, the companions shared a laugh, but Jarlaxle's did not last long, and he dropped his feet and rocked forward, clasping his hands, ornamented by a king's hoard of jewels—and how many of those glittering items were magical? Dinin often wondered—on the stone table before him, his face suddenly grave.

"The attack on Vandree is about to commence?" Dinin asked, thinking he had solved the riddle.

"Forget Vandree," Jarlaxle replied. "Their affairs are not so important to us now."

Dinin dropped his sharp chin into a slender palm, propped on the table. Not important! he thought. He wanted to spring up and throttle the cryptic leader. He had spent a whole year . . .

Dinin let his thoughts of Vandree trail away. He

looked hard at Jarlaxle's always calm face, searching for clues, then he understood.

"My sister," he said, and Jarlaxle was nodding before the word had left Dinin's mouth. "What has she done?"

Jarlaxle straightened, looked to the side of the small room, and gave a sharp whistle. On cue, a slab of stone shifted, revealing an alcove, and Vierna Do'Urden, Dinin's lone surviving sibling, swept into the room. She seemed more splendid and beautiful than Dinin remembered her since the downfall of their house.

Dinin's eyes widened as he realized the truth of Vierna's dressings; Vierna wore her robes! The robes of a high priestess of Lolth, the robes emblazoned with the arachnid and weapon design of House Do'Urden! Dinin did not know that Vierna had kept them, had not seen them in more than a decade.

"You risk . . ." he started to warn, but Vierna's frenzied expression, her red eyes blazing like twin fires behind the shadows of her high ebony cheekbones, stopped him before he could utter the words.

"I have found again the favor of Lolth," Vierna announced.

Dinin looked to Jarlaxle, who only shrugged and quietly shifted his eye-patch to his left eye instead.

"The Spider Queen has shown me the way," Vierna went on, her normally melodic voice cracking with undeniable excitement.

Dinin thought the female on the verge of insanity. Vierna had always been calm and tolerant, even after House Do'Urden's sudden demise. Over the last few years, though, her actions had become increasingly erratic, and she had spent many hours alone, in desperate prayer to their unmerciful deity.

"Are you to tell us this way that Lolth has shown to you?" Jarlaxle, appearing not at all impressed, asked after many moments of silence.

"Drizzt." Vierna spat the word, the name of their sacrilegious brother, with a burst of venom through her delicate lips.

Dinin wisely shifted his hand from his chin to cover his mouth, to bite back his retort. Vierna, for all her apparent foolhardiness, was, after all, a high priestess, and not one to anger.

"Drizzt?" Jarlaxle calmly asked her. "Your brother?"

"No brother of mine!" Vierna cried out, rushing to the desk as though she meant to strike Jarlaxle down. Dinin didn't miss the mercenary leader's subtle movement, a shift that put his dagger-launching arm in a ready position.

"Traitor to House Do'Urden!" Vierna fumed. "Traitor to all the drow!" Her scowl became a smile suddenly, evil and conniving. "With Drizzt's sacrifice, I will again find Lolth's favor, will again . . ." Vierna broke off abruptly, obviously desiring to keep the rest of her plans private.

"You sound like Matron Malice," Dinin dared to say. "She, too, began a hunt for our broth—for the traitor."

"You remember Matron Malice?" Jarlaxle teased, using the implications of the name as a sedative on over-excited Vierna. Malice, Vierna's mother and Matron of House Do'Urden, had ultimately been undone by her failure to recapture and kill the traitorous Drizzt.

Vierna did calm down, then she began a fit of mocking laughter that went on for many minutes.

"You see why I summoned you?" Jarlaxle remarked to Dinin, taking no heed of the priestess.

"You wish me to kill her before she can become a problem?" Dinin replied equally casually.

Vierna's laughter halted; her wild-eyed gaze fell over her impertinent brother. "*Wishya!*" she cried, and a wave of magical energy hurled Dinin from his seat, sent him crashing into the stone wall.

"Kneel!" Vierna commanded, and Dinin, when he regained his composure, fell to his knees, all the while looking blankly at Jarlaxle.

The mercenary, too, could not hide his surprise. This last command was a simple spell, certainly not one that should have worked so easily on a seasoned fighter of Dinin's stature.

"I am in Lolth's favor," Vierna, standing tall and straight, explained to both of them. "If you oppose me, then you are not, and with the power of Lolth's blessings for my spells and curses against you, you will find no defense."

"The last we heard of Drizzt placed him on the surface," Jarlaxle said to Vierna, to deflect her rising anger. "By all reports, he remains there still."

Vierna nodded, grinning weirdly all the while, her pearly white teeth contrasting dramatically with her shining ebony skin. "He does," she agreed, "but Lolth has shown me the way to him, the way to glory."

Again, Jarlaxle and Dinin exchanged confused glances. By all their estimates, Vierna's claims—and Vierna herself—sounded insane.

But Dinin, against his will and against all measures of sanity, was still kneeling.

PART ONE

Nearly three decades have passed since I left my homeland, a small measure of time by the reckoning of a drow elf, but a period that seems a lifetime to me. All that I desired, or believed that I desired, when I walked out of Menzoberranzan's dark cavern, was a true home, a place of friendship and peace where I might hang my scimitars

THE INSPIRING FEAR

above the mantle of a warm hearth and share stories with trusted companions.

I have found all that now, beside Bruenor in the hallowed halls of his youth. We prosper. We have peace. I wear my weapons only on my five-day journeys between Mithral Hall and Silverymoon.

Was I wrong?

I do not doubt, nor do I ever lament, my decision to leave the vile world of Menzoberranzan, but I am beginning to believe now, in the (endless) quiet and peace, that my desires at that critical time were founded in the inevitable longing of inexperience. I had never known that calm existence I so badly wanted.

I cannot deny that my life is better, a thousand

times better, than anything I ever knew in the Underdark. And yet, I cannot remember the last time I felt the anxiety, the inspiring fear, of impending battle, the tingling that can come only when an enemy is near or a challenge must be met.

Oh, I do remember the specific instance—just a year ago, when Wulfgar, Guenhwyvar, and I worked the lower tunnels in the cleansing of Mithral Hall—but that feeling, that tingle of fear, has long since faded from memory.

Are we then creatures of action? Do we say that we desire those accepted cliches of comfort when, in fact, it is the challenge and the adventure that truly give us life?

I must admit, to myself at least, that I do not know.

There is one point that I cannot dispute, though, one truth that will inevitably help me resolve these questions and which places me in a fortunate position. For now, beside Bruenor and his kin, beside Wulfgar and Catti-brie and Guenhwyvar, dear Guenhwyvar, my destiny is my own to choose.

I am safer now than ever before in my sixty years of life. The prospects have never looked better for the future, for continued peace and continued security. And yet, I feel mortal. For the first time, I look to what has passed rather than to what is still to come. There is no other way to explain it. I feel that I am dying, that those stories I so desired to share with friends will soon grow stale, with nothing to replace them.

But, I remind myself again, the choice is mine to make.

—Drizzt Do'Urden

I

SPRING DAWNING

Drizzt Do'Urden walked slowly along a trail in the jutting southernmost spur of the Spine of the World Mountains, the sky brightening around him. Far away to the south, across the plain to the Evermoors, he noticed the glow of the last lights of some distant city, Nesmé -probably, going down, replaced by the growing dawn. When Drizzt turned another bend in the mountain trail, he saw the small town of Settlestone, far below. The barbarians, Wulfgar's kin from faraway Icewind Dale, were just beginning their morning routines, trying to put the ruins back in order.

Drizzt watched the figures, tiny from this distance, bustle about, and he remembered a time not so long ago when Wulfgar and his proud people roamed the frozen tundra of a land far to the north and west, on the other side of the great mountain range, a thousand miles away.

Spring, the trading season, was fast approaching, and the hardy men and women of Settlestone, working as dealers for the dwarves of Mithral Hall, would soon know more wealth and comfort than they ever would have believed possible in their previous day-by-day existence. They had come to Wulfgar's call, fought valiantly beside the dwarves in the ancient halls, and would soon reap the rewards of their labor, leaving behind their desperate nomadic ways as they had left behind the endless, merciless wind of Icewind Dale.

"How far we have all come," Drizzt remarked to the chill emptiness of the morning air, and he chuckled at the double-meaning of his words, considering that he had just returned from Silverymoon, a magnificent city far to the east, a place where the beleaguered drow ranger never before dared to believe that he would find acceptance. Indeed, when he had accompanied Bruenor and the others in their search for Mithral Hall, barely two years before, Drizzt had been turned away from Silverymoon's decorated gates.

"Ye've done a hundred miles in a tenday alone," came an unexpected answer.

Drizzt instinctively dropped his slender black hands to the hilts of his scimitars, but his mind caught up to his reflexes and he relaxed immediately, recognizing the melodic voice with more than a little of a Dwarvish accent. A moment later, Catti-brie, the adopted human daughter of Bruenor Battlehammer, came skipping around a rocky outcropping, her thick auburn mane dancing in the mountain wind and her deep blue eyes glittering like wet jewels in the fresh morning light.

Drizzt could not hide his smile at the joyous spring in the young girl's steps, a vitality that the often vicious battles she had faced over the last few years could not diminish. Nor could Drizzt deny the wave of warmth that rushed over him whenever he saw Catti-brie, the young woman who knew him better than any. Catti-brie had understood Drizzt and accepted him for his heart, and not the color of his skin, since their first meeting in a rocky, wind-swept vale more than a decade before, when she was but half her present age.

The dark elf waited a moment longer, expecting to see Wulfgar, soon to be Catti-brie's husband, follow her around the bluff.

"You have come out a fair distance without an escort," Drizzt remarked when the barbarian did not appear.

Catti-brie crossed her arms over her chest and leaned on one foot, tapping impatiently with the other. "And ye're beginning to sound more like me father than me friend," she replied. "I see no escort walking the trails beside Drizzt Do'Urden."

"Well spoken," the drow ranger admitted, his tone respectful and not the least bit sarcastic. The young woman's scolding had pointedly reminded Drizzt that Catti-brie could take care of herself. She carried with her a short sword of dwarven make and wore fine armor under her furred cloak, as fine as the suit of chain mail that Bruenor had given to Drizzt! Taulmaril the Heartseeker, the magical bow of Anariel, rested easily over Catti-brie's shoulder. Drizzt had never seen a mightier weapon. and even beyond the powerful tools she carried, Catti-brie had been raised among the sturdy dwarves, by Bruenor himself, as tough as the mountain stone.

"Is it often that ye watch the rising sun?" Catti-brie asked, noticing Drizzt's east-facing stance.

Drizzt found a flat rock to sit upon and bade Catti-brie to join him. "I have watched the dawn since my first days on the surface," he explained, throwing his thick forest-green cloak back over his shoulders. "Though back then, it surely stung my eyes, a reminder of where I came from, I suppose. Now, though, to my relief, I find that I can tolerate the brightness."

"And well that is," Catti-brie replied. She locked the drow's marvelous eyes with her intense gaze, forced him to look at her, at the same innocent smile he had seen those many years before on a windswept slope in Icewind Dale.

The smile of his first female friend.

"'Tis sure that ye belong under the sunlight, Drizzt Do'Urden," Catti-brie continued, "as much as any person of any race, by me own measure."

Drizzt looked back to the dawn and did not answer. Catti-brie went silent, too, and they sat together for a long while, watching the awakening world.

"I came out to see ye," Catti-brie said suddenly. Drizzt regarded her curiously, not understanding.

"Now, I mean," the young woman explained. "We'd word that ye'd returned to Settlestone, and that ye'd be coming back to Mithral Hall in a few days. I've been out here every day since."

Drizzt's expression did not change. "You wish to talk with me privately?" he asked, to prompt a reply.

Catti-brie's deliberate nod as she turned back to the eastern horizon revealed to Drizzt that something was wrong.

"I'll not forgive ye if ye miss the wedding," Catti-brie said softly. She bit down on her bottom lip as she finished, Drizzt noted, and sniffled, though she tried hard to make it seem like the beginnings of a cold.

Drizzt draped an arm across the beautiful woman's strong shoulders. "Can you believe for an instant, even if all the trolls of the Evermoors stood between me and the ceremony hall, that I would not attend?"

Catti-brie turned to him—fell into his gaze—and smiled widely, knowing the answer. She threw her arms around Drizzt for a tight hug, then leaped to her feet, pulling him up beside her.

Drizzt tried to equal her relief, or at least to make her believe that he had. Catti-brie had known all along that he would not miss her wedding to Wulfgar, two of his dearest friends. Why, then, the tears, the sniffle that was not from any budding cold? the perceptive ranger wondered. Why had Catti-brie felt the need to come out and find him only a few hours from the entrance to Mithral Hall?

He didn't ask her about it, but it bothered him more than a little. Anytime moisture gathered in Catti-brie's deep blue eyes, it bothered Drizzt Do'Urden more than a little.

✕ ✕ ✕ ✕ ✕

Jarlaxle's black boots clacked loudly on the stone as he made his solitary way along a winding tunnel outside of Menzoberranzan. Most drow out alone from the great city, in the wilds of the Underdark, would have taken great care, but the mercenary knew what to expect in the tunnels, knew every creature in this particular section.

Information was Jarlaxle's forte. The scouting network of Bregan D'aerthe, the band Jarlaxle had founded and taken to greatness, was more intricate than that of any drow house. Jarlaxle knew everything that happened, or would soon happen, in and around the city, and armed with that information, he had survived for centuries as a houseless rogue. So long had Jarlaxle been a part of Menzoberranzan's intrigue that none in the city, with the possible exception of First Matron Mother Baenre, even knew the sly mercenary's origins.

He was wearing his shimmering cape now, its magical colors cascading up and down his graceful form, and his wide-brimmed hat, hugely plumed with the feathers of a *diatryma*, a great flightless Underdark bird, adorned his clean-shaven head. A slender sword dancing beside one hip and a long dirk on the other were his only visible weapons, but those who knew the sly mercenary realized that he possessed many more than that, concealed on his person, but easily retrieved if the need arose.

Pulled by curiosity, Jarlaxle picked up his pace. As soon as he realized the length of his strides, he forced himself to slow down, reminding himself that he wanted to be fashionably late for this unorthodox meeting that crazy Vierna had arranged.

Crazy Vierna.

Jarlaxle considered the thought for a long while, even stopped his walk and leaned against the tunnel wall to recount the high priestess's many claims over the last few tendays. What had seemed initially to be a desperate, fleeting hope of a broken noble, with no chance at all of success, was fast becoming a solid plan. Jarlaxle had gone along with Vierna more out of amusement and curiosity than any real beliefs that they would kill, or even locate, the long-gone Drizzt.

But something apparently was guiding Vierna—Jarlaxle had to believe it was Lolth, or one of the Spider Queen's powerful minions. Vierna's clerical powers had returned in full, it seemed, and she had delivered much valuable information, and even a perfect spy, to their cause. They were fairly sure now where Drizzt Do'Urden was, and Jarlaxle was beginning to believe that killing the traitorous drow would not be such a difficult thing.

The mercenary's boots heralded his approach as he clicked around a final bend in the tunnel, coming into a wide, low-roofed chamber. Vierna was there, with Dinin, and it struck Jarlaxle as curious (another note made in the calculating mercenary's mind) that Vierna seemed more comfortable out here in the wilds than did her brother. Dinin had spent many years in these tunnels, leading patrol groups, but Vierna, as a sheltered noble priestess, had rarely been out of the city.

If she truly believed that she walked with Lolth's blessings, however, then the priestess would have nothing to fear.

"You have delivered our gift to the human?" Vierna asked immediately, urgently. Everything in Vierna's life, it seemed to Jarlaxle, had become urgent.

The sudden question, not prefaced by any greeting or even a remark that he was late, caught the mercenary off guard for a moment, and he looked to Dinin, who responded with only a helpless shrug. While hungry fires burned in Vierna's eyes, defeated resignation lay in Dinin's.

"The human has the earring," Jarlaxle replied.

Vierna held out a flat, disc-shaped object, covered in designs to match the precious earring. "It is cool," she explained as she rubbed her hand across the disc's metallic surface, "thus our spy has already moved far from Menzoberranzan."

"Far away with a valuable gift," Jarlaxle remarked, traces of sarcasm edging his voice.

"It was necessary, and will further our cause," Vierna snapped at him.

"If the human proves to be as valuable an informant as you believe," Jarlaxle added evenly.

"Do you doubt him?" Vierna's words echoed through the tunnels, causing Dinin further distress and sounding clearly as a threat to the mercenary.

"It was Lolth who guided me to him," Vierna continued with an open sneer, "Lolth who showed me the way to regain my family's honor. Do you doubt—"

"I doubt nothing where our deity is concerned," Jarlaxle promptly interrupted. "The earring, your beacon, has been delivered as you instructed, and the human is well on his way." The mercenary swept into a respectfully low bow, tipping his wide-brimmed hat.

Vierna calmed and seemed appeased. Her red eyes flashed eagerly, and a devious smile widened across her face. "And the goblins?" she asked, her voice thick with anticipation.

"They will soon make contact with the greedy dwarves," Jarlaxle replied, "to their dismay, no doubt. My scouts are in place around the goblin ranks. If your brother makes an appearance in the inevitable battle, we will know." The mercenary hid his conniving smile at the sight of Vierna's obvious pleasure. The priestess thought to gain only the confirmation of her brother's whereabouts from the unfortunate goblin tribe, but Jarlaxle had much more in mind. Goblins and dwarves shared a mutual hatred as intense as that between the drow and their surface elf cousins, and any meeting between the groups would ensure a fight. What better opportunity for Jarlaxle to take an accurate measure of the dwarven defenses?

And the dwarven weaknesses?

For, while Vierna's desires were focused—all that she wanted was the death of her traitorous brother—Jarlaxle was looking at the wider picture, of how this costly exploration up near the surface, perhaps even onto the surface, might become more profitable.

Vierna rubbed her hands together and turned sharply to face her brother. Jarlaxle nearly laughed aloud at Dinin's feeble attempt to imitate his sister's beaming expression.

Vierna was too obsessed to notice her less-than-enthusiastic brother's obvious slip. "The goblin fodder understand their options?" she asked the mercenary, but she answered her own question before Jarlaxle could reply. "Of course, they have no options!"

Jarlaxle felt the sudden need to burst her eager bubble. "What if the goblins kill Drizzt?" he asked, sounding innocent.

Vierna's face screwed up weirdly and she stammered unsuccessfully at her first attempts at a reply. "No!" she decided at length. "We know that more than a thousand dwarves inhabit the complex, perhaps two or three times that number. The goblin tribe will be crushed."

"But the dwarves and their allies will suffer some casualties," Jarlaxle reasoned.

"Not Drizzt," Dinin unexpectedly answered, and there was no compromise in his grim tone, and no argument forthcoming from either of his companions. "No goblin will kill Drizzt. No goblin weapon could get near his body."

Vierna's approving smile showed that she did not understand the sincere terror behind Dinin's claims. Dinin alone among the group had faced off in battle against Drizzt.

"The tunnels back to the city are clear?" Vierna asked Jarlaxle, and on his nod, she swiftly departed, having no more time for banter.

"You wish this to end," the mercenary remarked to Dinin when they were alone.

"You have not met my brother," Dinin replied evenly, and his hand instinctively twitched near the hilt of his magnificent drow-made sword, as though the mere mention of Drizzt put him on the defensive. "Not in combat, at least."

"Fear, *Khal'abbil?*" The question went straight to Dinin's sense of honor, sounded more like a taunt.

Still, the fighter made no attempt to deny it.

"You should fear your sister as well," Jarlaxle reasoned, and he meant every word. Dinin donned a disgusted expression.

"The Spider Queen, or one of Lolth's minions, has been talking with that one," Jarlaxle added, as much to himself as to his shaken companion. At first glance, Vierna's obsession seemed a desperate, dangerous thing, but Jarlaxle had been around the chaos of Menzoberranzan long enough to realize that many other powerful figures, Matron Baenre included, had held similar, seemingly outrageous fantasies.

Nearly every important figure in Menzoberranzan, including members of the ruling council, had come to power through acts that seemed desperate, had squirmed their way through the barbed nets of chaos to find their glory.

Might Vierna be the next to cross that dangerous terrain?

2

TOGETHER

The River Surbrin flowing in a valley far below him, Drizzt entered the eastern gate of Mithral Hall early that same afternoon. Catti-brie had skipped in some time before him to await the "surprise" of his return. The dwarven guards welcomed the drow ranger as though he were one of their bearded kin. Drizzt could not deny the warmth that flowed through him at their open welcome, though it was not unexpected since Bruenor's people had accepted him as a friend since their days in Icewind Dale.

Drizzt needed no escort in the winding corridors of Mithral Hall, and he wanted none, preferring to be alone with the many emotions and memories that always came over him when he crossed this section of the upper complex. He moved across the new bridge at Garumn's Gorge. It was a structure of beautiful, arching stone that spanned hundreds of feet across the deep chasm. In this place Drizzt had lost Bruenor forever, or so he had thought, for he had seen the dwarf spiral down into the lightless depths on the back of a flaming dragon.

He couldn't avoid a smile as the memory flowed to completion; it would take more than a dragon to kill mighty Bruenor Battlehammer!

As he neared the end of the long expanse, Drizzt noticed that new guard towers, begun only ten days before, were nearly completed, the industrious dwarves having gone at their work with absolute devotion. Still, every one of the busy dwarven workers looked up to regard the drow's passing and give Drizzt a word of greeting.

Drizzt headed for the main corridors leading out of the immense chamber south of the bridge, the sound of even more hammers leading the way. Just beyond the chamber, past a small anteroom, he came into a wide, high corridor, practically another chamber in itself, where the best craftsmen of Mithral Hall were hard at work, carving into the stone wall the likeness of Bruenor Battlehammer, in its appropriate place beside sculptures of Bruenor's royal ancestors, the seven predecessors of his throne.

"Fine work, eh, drow?" came a call. Drizzt turned to regard a short, round dwarf with a short-clipped yellow beard barely reaching the top of his wide chest.

"Well met, Cobble," Drizzt greeted the speaker. Bruenor recently had appointed the dwarf Holy Cleric of the Halls, a valued position indeed.

"Fitting?" Cobble asked as he indicated the twenty-foot-high sculpture of Mithral Hall's present king.

"For Bruenor, it should be a hundred feet tall," Drizzt replied, and the good-hearted Cobble shook with laughter. The continuing roar of it echoed behind Drizzt for many steps as he again headed down the winding corridors.

He soon came to the upper level's hall area, the city above the wondrous Undercity. Catti-brie and Wulfgar roomed in this area, as did Bruenor most of the time, as he prepared for the spring trading season. Most of the other twenty-five hundred dwarves of the clan were far below, in the mines and in the Undercity, but those in this region were the commanders of the house guard and the elite soldiers. Even Drizzt, so welcomed in Bruenor's home, could not go to the king unannounced and unescorted.

A square-shouldered rock of a dwarf with a sour demeanor and a long brown beard that he wore tucked into a wide, jeweled belt, led Drizzt down the final corridor to Bruenor's upper-level audience hall. General Dagna, as he was called, had been a personal attendant of King Harbromme of Citadel Adbar, the mightiest dwarven stronghold in the northland, but the gruff dwarf had come in at the head of Citadel Adbar's forces to help Bruenor reclaim his ancient homeland. With the war won, most of the Adbar dwarves had departed, but Dagna and two thousand others had remained after the cleansing of Mithral Hall, swearing fealty to clan Battlehammer and giving Bruenor a solid force with which to defend the riches of the dwarven stronghold.

Dagna had stayed on with Bruenor to serve as his adviser and military commander. He professed no love for Drizzt, but certainly would not be foolish enough to insult the drow by allowing a lesser attendant to escort Drizzt to see the dwarf king.

"I told ye he'd be back," Drizzt heard Bruenor grumbling from beyond the open doorway as they approached the audience hall. "Th' elf'd not be missing such a thing as yer wedding!"

"I see they are expecting me," Drizzt remarked to Dagna.

"We heard ye was about from the folks o' Settlestone," the gruff general replied, not looking back to Drizzt as he spoke. "Figerred ye'd come in any day."

Drizzt knew that the general—a dwarf among dwarves, as the others said—had little use for him, or for anyone, Wulfgar and Catti-brie included, who was not a dwarf. The dark elf smiled, though, for he was used to such prejudice and knew that Dagna was an important ally for Bruenor.

"Greetings," Drizzt said to his three friends as he entered the room. Bruenor sat on his stone throne, Wulfgar and Catti-brie flanking him.

"So ye made it," Catti-brie said absently, feigning disinterest. Drizzt smirked at their running secret; apparently Catti-brie hadn't told anyone that she had met him just outside the eastern door.

"We had not planned for this," added Wulfgar, a giant of a man with huge, corded muscles, long, flowing blond locks, and eyes the crystal blue of the northland's sky. "I pray that there may be an extra seat at the table."

Drizzt smiled and bowed low in apology. He deserved their chiding, he knew. He had been away a great deal lately, for tendays at a time.

"Bah!" snorted the red-bearded Bruenor. "I told ye he'd come back, and back to stay this time!"

Drizzt shook his head, knowing he soon would go out again, searching for . . . something.

"Ye hunting for the assassin, elf?" he heard Bruenor ask.

Never, Drizzt thought immediately. The dwarf referred to Artemis Entreri, Drizzt's most hated enemy, a heartless killer as skilled with the blade as the drow ranger, and determined—obsessed!—to defeat Drizzt. Entreri and Drizzt had battled in Calimport, a city far to the south, with Drizzt luckily winning the upper hand before events drove them apart. Emotionally Drizzt had brought the unfinished battle to its conclusion and had freed himself from a similar obsession against Entreri.

Drizzt had seen himself in the assassin, had seen what he might have become had he stayed in Menzoberranzan. He could not stand the image, hungered only to destroy it. Catti-brie, dear and complicated Catti-brie, had taught Drizzt the truth, about Entreri and about himself. If he never saw Entreri again, Drizzt would be a happier person indeed.

"I've no desire to meet that one again," Drizzt answered. He looked to Catti-brie, who sat impassively. She shot Drizzt a sly wink to show that she understood and approved.

"There are many sights in the wide world, dear dwarf," Drizzt went on, "that cannot be seen from the shadows, many sounds more pleasant than the ring of steel, and many smells preferable to the stench of death."

"Cook another feast!" Bruenor snorted, hopping up from his stone seat. "Suren the elf has his eyes fixed on another wedding!"

Drizzt let the remark pass without reply.

Another dwarf rushed into the room, then exited, pulling Dagna out behind him. A moment later, the flustered general returned.

"What is it?" Bruenor grumbled.

"Another guest," Dagna explained and even as he spoke, a halfling, round in the belly, bopped into the room.

"Regis!" cried a surprised Catti-brie, and she and Wulfgar rushed over to greet their friend. Unexpectedly, the five companions were together again.

"Rumblebelly!" Bruenor shouted his customary nickname for the always hungry halfling. "What in the Nine Hells—"

What indeed, Drizzt thought, curious that he had not spotted the traveler on the trails outside Mithral Hall. The friends had left Regis behind in Calimport, more than a thousand miles away, at the head of the thieves guild the companions had all but decapitated in rescuing the halfling.

"Did you believe I would miss this occasion?" Regis huffed, acting insulted that Bruenor even doubted him. "The wedding of two of my dearest friends?"

Catti-brie threw a hug on him, which he seemed to enjoy immensely.

Bruenor looked curiously at Drizzt and shook his head when he realized that the drow had no answers for this surprise. "How'd ye know?" the dwarf asked the halfling.

"You underestimate your fame, King Bruenor," Regis replied, gracefully dipping into a bow that sent his belly dropping over his thin belt.

The bow made him jingle as well, Drizzt noted. When Regis dipped, a hundred jewels and a dozen fat pouches tinkled. Regis had always loved fine things, but Drizzt had never seen the halfling so garishly bedecked. He wore a gem-studded jacket and more jewelry than Drizzt had ever seen in one place, including the magical, hypnotic ruby pendant.

"Might ye be staying long?" Catti-brie asked.

"I am in no hurry," Regis replied. "Might I have a room," he asked Bruenor, "to put my things and rest away the weariness of a long road?"

"We'll see to it," Catti-brie assured him as Drizzt and Bruenor exchanged glances once more. They both were thinking the same thing: that it was unusual for a master of a back-stabbing, opportunistic thieves' guild to leave his place of power for any length of time.

"And for yer attendants?" Bruenor asked, a loaded question.

"Oh," stammered the halfling. "I . . . came alone. The Southerners do not take well to the chill of a northern spring, you know."

"Well, off with ye, then," commanded Bruenor. "Suren it be me turn to set out a feast for the pleasure of yer belly."

Drizzt took a seat beside the dwarf king as the other three scooted out of the room.

"Few folk in Calimport have ever heared o' me name, elf," Bruenor remarked when he and Drizzt were alone. "And who south o' Longsaddle would be knowing of the wedding?"

Bruenor's sly expression showed that the experienced dwarf agreed exactly with Drizzt's feeling. "Suren the little one brings a bit of his treasure along with him, eh?" the dwarf king asked.

"He is running," Drizzt replied.

"Got himself into trouble again—" Bruenor snorted "—or I'm a bearded gnome!"

⚔ ⚔ ⚔ ⚔ ⚔

"Five meals a day," Bruenor muttered to Drizzt after the drow and the halfling had been in Mithral Hall for a tenday. "And helpings bigger than a half-sized one should hold!"

Drizzt, always amazed by Regis's appetite, had no answer for the dwarf king. Together they watched Regis from across the hall, stuffing bite after bite into his greedy mouth.

"Good thing we're opening new tunnels," Bruenor grumbled. "I'll be needing a fair supply o' mithral to keep that one fed."

As if Bruenor's reference to the new explorations had been a cue, General Dagna entered the dining hall. Apparently not interested in eating, the gruff, brown-bearded dwarf waved away an attendant and headed straight across the hall, toward Drizzt and Bruenor.

"That was a short trip," Bruenor remarked to Drizzt when they noticed the dwarf. Dagna had gone out just that morning, leading the latest scouting group to the new explorations in the deepest mines far to the west of the Undercity.

"Trouble or treasure?" Drizzt asked rhetorically, and Bruenor only shrugged, always expecting—and secretly hoping for—both.

"Me king," Dagna greeted, coming in front of Bruenor and pointedly not looking at the dark elf. He dipped in a curt bow, his rock-set expression giving no clues about which of Drizzt's suppositions might be accurate.

"Mithral?" Bruenor asked hopefully.

Dagna seemed surprised by the blunt question. "Yes," he said at length. "The tunnel beyond the sealed door intercepted a whole new complex, rich in ore, from what we can tell. The legend of yer gem-sniffing nose'll continue to grow, me king." He dipped into another bow, this one even lower than the first.

"Knew it," Bruenor whispered to Drizzt. "Went down that way once, afore me beard even came out. Killed me an ettin . . ."

"But we have trouble," Dagna interrupted, his face still expressionless.

Bruenor waited, and waited some more, for the tiresome dwarf to explain. "Trouble?" he finally asked, realizing that Dagna had paused for dramatic effect, and that the stubborn general probably would stand quietly for the remainder of the day if Bruenor didn't offer that prompt.

"Goblins," Dagna said ominously.

Bruenor snorted. "Thought ye said we had trouble?"

"A fair-sized tribe," Dagna went on. "Could be hundreds."

Bruenor looked up to Drizzt and recognized from the sparkle in the drow's lavender eyes that the news had not disturbed his friend any more than it had disturbed him.

"Hundreds of goblins, elf," Bruenor said slyly. "What do ye think o' that?"

Drizzt didn't reply, just continued to smirk and let the gleam in his eye speak for itself. Times had become uneventful since the retaking of Mithral Hall; the only metal ringing in the dwarven tunnels was the miner's pick and shovel and the craftsman's sledge, and the trails between Mithral Hall and Silverymoon were rarely dangerous or adventurous to the skilled Drizzt. This news held particular interest for the drow. Drizzt was a ranger, dedicated to defending the good races, and he despised spindly-armed, foul-smelling goblins above all the other evil races in the world.

Bruenor led the two over to Regis's table, though every other table in the large hall was empty. "Supper's done," the red-bearded dwarf king huffed, sweeping the plates from in front of the halfling to land, crashing, on the floor.

"Go and get Wulfgar," Bruenor growled into the halfling's dubious expression. "Ye got a count of fifty to get back to me. Longer than that, and I put ye on half rations!"

Regis was through the door in an instant.

On Bruenor's nod, Dagna pulled a hunk of coal from his pocket and sketched a rough map of the new region on the table, showing Bruenor where they had encountered the goblin sign, and where further scouting had indicated the main lair to be. Of particular interest to the two dwarves were the worked tunnels in the region, with their even floors and squared walls.

"Good for surprising stupid goblins," Bruenor explained to Drizzt with a wink.

"You knew the goblins were there," Drizzt accused him, realizing that Bruenor was more thrilled, and less surprised, by the news of potential enemies than of potential riches.

"Figured there might be goblins," Bruenor admitted. "Seen 'em down there once, but with the coming of the dragon, me father and his soldiers never got the time to clean the vermin out. Still, it was a long, long time ago, elf"—the dwarf stroked his long red beard to accentuate the point—"and I couldn't be sure they'd still be there."

"We are threatened?" came a resonant baritone voice behind them. The seven-foot-tall barbarian moved to the table and leaned low to take in Dagna's diagram.

"Just goblins," Bruenor replied.

"A call to war!" Wulfgar roared, slapping Aegis-fang, the mighty warhammer Bruenor had forged for him, across his open palm.

"A call to play," Bruenor corrected, and he exchanged a nod and chuckle with Drizzt.

"By me own eyes, don't ye two seem eager to be killing," Catti-brie, standing behind with Regis, put in.

"Bet on it," Bruenor retorted.

"Ye found some goblins in their own hole, not to bothering anybody, and ye're planning for their slaughter," Catti-brie went on in the face of her father's sarcasm.

"Woman!" Wulfgar shouted.

Drizzt's amused smile evaporated in the blink of an eye, replaced by an expression of amazement as he regarded the towering barbarian's scornful mien.

"Be glad for that," Catti-brie answered lightly, without hesitation and without becoming distracted from the more important debate with Bruenor. "How do ye know the goblins want a fight?" she asked the king. "Or do ye care?"

"There's mithral in those tunnels," Bruenor replied, as if that would end the debate.

"Would that make it the goblins' mithral?" Catti-brie asked innocently. "Rightfully?"

"Not for long," Dagna interjected, but Bruenor had no witty remarks to add, taken aback by his daughter's surprising line of somewhat incriminating questions.

"The fight's more important to ye, to all of ye," Catti-brie went on, turning her knowing blue eyes to regard all four of the group, "than any treasures to be found. Ye hunger for the excitement. Ye'd go after the goblins if the tunnels were no more than bare and worthless stone!"

"Not me," Regis piped in, but nobody paid much attention.

"They are goblins," Drizzt said to her. "Was it not a goblin raid that took your father's life?"

"Aye," Catti-brie agreed. "And if ever I find that tribe, then be knowing that they'll fall in piles for their wicked deed. But are they akin to this tribe, a thousand miles and more away?"

"Goblins is goblins!" Bruenor growled.

"Oh?" Catti-brie replied, crossing her arms before her. "And are drow drow?"

"What talk is this?" Wulfgar demanded as he glowered at his soon-to-be bride.

"If ye found a dark elf wandering yer tunnels," Catti-brie said to Bruenor, ignoring Wulfgar altogether—even when he stormed over to stand right beside her—"would ye draw up yer plans and cut the creature down?"

Bruenor gave an uncomfortable glance Drizzt's way, but Drizzt was smiling again, understanding where Catti-brie's reasoning had led them—and where it had trapped the stubborn king.

"If ye did cut him down, and if that drow was Drizzt Do'Urden, then who would ye have beside ye with the patience to sit and listen to yer prideful boasts?" the young woman finished.

"At least I'd kill ye clean," Bruenor, his blustery bubble popped, muttered to Drizzt.

Drizzt's laughter came straight from his belly. "Parley," he said at length. "By the well-spoken words of our wise young friend, we must give the goblins at least a chance to explain their intentions." He paused and looked wistfully at Catti-brie, his lavender eyes sparkling still, for he knew what to expect from goblins. "Before we cut them down."

"Cleanly," Bruenor added.

"She knows nothing of this!" Wulfgar griped, bringing the tension back to the meeting in an instant.

Drizzt silenced him with a cold glare, as threatening a stare as had ever passed between the dark elf and the barbarian. Catti-brie looked from one to the other, her expression pained, then she tapped Regis on the shoulder and together they left the room.

"We're gonna talk to a bunch o' goblins?" Dagna asked in disbelief.

"Aw, shut yer mouth," Bruenor answered, slamming his hands back to the table and studying the map once more. It took him several moments to realize that Wulfgar and Drizzt had not finished their silent exchange. Bruenor recognized the confusion underlying Drizzt's stare, but in looking at the barbarian, he found no subtle undercurrents, no hint that this particular incident would be easily forgotten.

$$\times \quad \times \quad \times \quad \times \quad \times$$

Drizzt leaned back against the stone wall in the corridor outside Catti-brie's room. He had come to talk to the young woman, to find out why she had been so concerned, so adamant, in the conference about the goblin tribe. Catti-brie had always brought a unique perspective to the trials facing the five companions, but this time it seemed to Drizzt that something else was driving her, that something other than goblins had brought the fire to her speech.

Leaning on the wall outside the door, the dark elf began to understand.

"You are not going!" Wulfgar was saying—loudly. "There will be a fight, despite your attempts to put it off. They are goblins. They'll take no parley with dwarves!"

"If there is a fight, then ye'll be wanting me there," Catti-brie retorted.

"You are not going."

Drizzt shook his head at the finality of Wulfgar's tone, thinking that never before had he heard Wulfgar speak this way. He changed his mind, though, remembering when he first had met the rough young barbarian, stubborn and proud and talking nearly as stupidly as now.

Drizzt was waiting for the barbarian when Wulfgar returned to his own room, the drow leaning against the wall casually, wrists resting against the angled hilts of his magical scimitars and his forest-green cloak thrown back from his shoulders.

"Bruenor sends for me?" Wulfgar asked, confused as to why Drizzt would be in his room.

Drizzt pushed the door closed. "I am not here for Bruenor," he explained evenly.

Wulfgar shrugged, not catching on. "Welcome back, then," he said, and there was something strained in his greeting. "Too oft you are out of the halls. Bruenor desires your company—"

"I am here for Catti-brie," Drizzt interrupted.

The barbarian's ice-blue eyes narrowed immediately and he squared his broad shoulders, his strong jaw firm. "I know she met with you," he said, "outside on the trails before you came in."

A perplexed look crossed Drizzt's face as he recognized the hostility in Wulfgar's tone. Why would Wulfgar care if Catti-brie had met with him? What in the Nine Hells was going on with his large friend?

"Regis told me," Wulfgar explained, apparently misunderstanding Drizzt's confusion. A superior look came into the barbarian's eye, as though he believed his secret information had given him some sort of advantage.

Drizzt shook his head and brushed his thick white mane back from his face with slender fingers. "I am not here because of any meeting on the trails," he said, "or because of anything Catti-brie has said to me." Wrists still comfortably resting against his weapon hilts, Drizzt strolled across the wide room, stopping opposite the large bed from the barbarian.

"Whatever Catti-brie does say to me, though," he had to add, "is none of your affair."

Wulfgar did not blink, but Drizzt could see that it took all of the barbarian's control to stop from leaping over the bed at him. Drizzt, who thought he knew Wulfgar well, could hardly believe the sight.

"How dare you?" Wulfgar growled through gritted teeth. "She is my—"

"Dare I?" Drizzt shot back. "You speak of Catti-brie as if she were your possession. I heard you tell her, command her, to remain behind when we go to the goblins."

"You overstep your bounds," Wulfgar warned.

"You puff like a drunken orc," Drizzt returned, and he thought the analogy strangely fitting.

Wulfgar took a deep breath, his great chest heaving, to steady himself. A single stride took him the length of the bed to the wall, near the hooks holding his magnificent warhammer.

"Once you were my teacher," Wulfgar said calmly.

"Ever was I your friend," Drizzt replied.

Wulfgar snapped an angry glare on him. "You speak to me like a father to a child. Beware, Drizzt Do'Urden, you are not the teacher anymore."

Drizzt nearly fell over, especially when Wulfgar, still eyeing him dangerously, pulled Aegis-fang, the mighty warhammer, from the wall.

"Are you the teacher now?" the dark elf asked.

Wulfgar nodded slowly, then blinked in surprise as the scimitars suddenly appeared in Drizzt's hands. Twinkle, the magical blade the wizard Malchor Harpel had given Drizzt, glowed with a soft blue flame.

"Remember when first we met?" the dark elf asked. He moved around the bottom of the bed, wisely, since Wulfgar's longer reach would have given him a distinct advantage with the bed between them. "Do you remember the many lessons we shared on Kelvin's Cairn, looking out over the tundra and the camp-fires of your people?"

Wulfgar turned slowly, keeping the dangerous drow in front of him. The barbarian's knuckles whitened for lack of blood as he tightly clutched his weapon.

"Remember the verbeeg?" Drizzt asked, the thought bringing a smile to his face. "You and I fighting together, winning together, against an entire lair of giants?

"And the dragon, Icingdeath?" Drizzt went on, holding his other scimitar, the one he had taken from the defeated wyrm's lair, up before him.

"I remember," Wulfgar replied quietly, calmly, and Drizzt started to slide his scimitars back into their sheaths, thinking he had sobered the young man.

"You speak of distant days!" the barbarian roared suddenly, rushing forward with speed and agility beyond what could be expected from so large a man. He launched a roundhouse punch at Drizzt's face, clipping the surprised drow on the shoulder as Drizzt ducked.

The ranger rolled with the blow, coming to his feet in the far corner of the room, the scimitars back in his hands.

"Time for another lesson," he promised, his lavender eyes gleaming with an inner fire that the barbarian had seen many times before.

Undaunted, Wulfgar came on, putting Aegis-fang through a series of feints before turning it down in an overhead chop that would have crushed the drow's skull.

"Has it been too long since last we saw battle?" Drizzt asked, thinking this whole incident a strange game, perhaps a ritual of manhood for the young barbarian. He brought his scimitars up in a blocking cross above him, easily catching the descending hammer. His legs nearly buckled under the sheer force of the blow.

Wulfgar recoiled for a second strike.

"Always thinking of offense," Drizzt scolded, snapping the flat sides of his scimitars out, one-two, against the sides of Wulfgar's face.

The barbarian fell back a step and wiped a thin line of blood from his cheek with the back of one hand. Still he did not blink.

"My apology," Drizzt said when he saw the blood. "I did not mean to cut—"

Wulfgar came over him in a rush, swinging wildly and calling out to Tempus, his god of battle.

Drizzt sidestepped the first strike—it took out a fair-sized chunk from the stone wall beside him—and stepped forward toward the warhammer, locking his arm around it to hold it in place.

Wulfgar let go of the weapon with one hand, grabbed Drizzt by the front of the tunic, and easily lifted him from the floor. The muscles on the barbarian's bare arm bulged as he pressed his arm straight ahead, crushing the drow against the wall.

Drizzt could not believe the huge man's strength! He felt as if he would be pushed right through the stone and into the next chamber—at least, he hoped there was a next chamber! He kicked with one leg. Wulfgar ducked back, thinking the kick aimed for his face, but Drizzt hooked the leg over the barbarian's stiffened arm, inside the elbow. Using the leg for leverage, Drizzt slammed his hand against the outside of Wulfgar's wrist, bending the arm and freeing him from the wall. He punched out with his scimitar hilt as he fell, connecting solidly on Wulfgar's nose, and let go his lock on the barbarian's warhammer.

Wulfgar's snarl sounded inhuman. He took up the hammer for a strike, but Drizzt had dropped to the floor by then. The drow rolled onto his back, planted his feet against the wall, and kicked out, slipping right between Wulfgar's widespread legs. Drizzt's foot snapped up once, stinging the barbarian's groin, and then, when he was behind Wulfgar, snapped both feet straight out, kicking the barbarian behind the knees.

Wulfgar's legs buckled and one of his knees slammed into the wall.

Drizzt used the momentum to roll again. He came back to his feet and leaped, grabbing the overbalanced Wulfgar by the back of his hair and tugging hard, toppling the man like a cut tree.

Wulfgar groaned and rolled, trying to get up, but Drizzt's scimitars came whipping in, hilts leading, to connect heavily on the big man's jaw.

Wulfgar laughed and slowly rose. Drizzt backed away.

"You are not the teacher," Wulfgar said again, but the line of blood-filled spittle rolling from the edge of his torn mouth weakened the claim considerably.

"What is this about?" Drizzt demanded. "Speak it now!"

Aegis-fang came hurling at him, end over end.

Drizzt dove to the floor, narrowly avoiding the deadly hit. He winced when he heard the hammer hit the wall, no doubt blasting a clean hole in the stone.

He was up again, amazingly, by the time the charging barbarian got anywhere near him. Drizzt ducked under the lumbering man's reach, spun, and kicked Wulfgar in the rump. Wulfgar roared and spun about, only to get hit again in the face with the flat of Drizzt's blade. This time the line of blood was not so thin.

As stubborn as any dwarf, Wulfgar launched another roundhouse punch.

"Your rage defeats you," Drizzt remarked as he easily avoided the blow. He couldn't believe that Wulfgar, so finely trained in the art—and it was an art!—of battle had lost his composure.

Wulfgar growled and swung again, but recoiled immediately, for this time, Drizzt put Twinkle, or more particularly, put Twinkle's razor-edged blade, in line to catch the blow. Wulfgar retracted the swing too late and clutched his bloodied hand.

"I know your hammer will return to your grasp," Drizzt said, and Wulfgar seemed almost surprised, as though he had forgotten the magical enchantment of his own weapon. "Would you like to have fingers remaining so you might catch it?"

On cue, Aegis-fang came into the barbarian's grasp.

Drizzt, stunned by the ridiculous tirade and tired of this whole episode, slipped his scimitars back into their sheaths. He stood barely four feet from the barbarian, well within Wulfgar's reach, with his hands out wide, defenseless.

Somewhere in the fight, when he had realized that this was no game, perhaps, the gleam had flown from his lavender eyes.

Wulfgar remained very still for a long moment and closed his eyes. To Drizzt, it seemed as if he was fighting some inner battle.

He smiled, then opened his eyes, and let the head of his mighty warhammer dip to the floor.

"My friend," he said to Drizzt. "My teacher. It is good you have returned." Wulfgar's hand reached out toward Drizzt's shoulder.

His fist balled suddenly and shot for Drizzt's face.

Drizzt spun, hooked Wulfgar's arm with his own, and pulled along the path of the barbarian's own momentum, sending Wulfgar headlong. Wulfgar got his other hand up in time to grab the drow, though, and took Drizzt along for the tumble. They came up together, propped side by side against the wall, and shared a heartfelt laugh.

For the first time since before the meeting in the dining hall, it seemed to Drizzt that he had his old fighting companion beside him.

Drizzt left soon after, not mentioning Catti-brie again—not until he could sort out what, exactly, had just happened in the room. Drizzt at least understood the barbarian's confusion about the young woman. Wulfgar had come from a tribe dominated by men, where women spoke only when they were told to speak, and did as their masters, the males, bade. It appeared as if, now that he and Catti-brie were to be wed, Wulfgar was finding it difficult to shake off the lessons of his youth.

The thought disturbed Drizzt more than a little. He now understood the sadness he had detected in Catti-brie, out on the trails beyond the dwarven complex.

He understood, too, Wulfgar's mounting folly. If the stubborn barbarian tried to quench the fires within Catti-brie, he would take from her everything that had brought him to her in the first place, everything that he loved—that Drizzt, too, loved, in the young woman.

Drizzt dismissed that notion summarily; he had looked into her knowing blue eyes for a decade, had seen Catti-brie turn her stubborn father in submissive circles.

Neither Wulfgar, nor Drizzt, nor the gods themselves could quench the fires in Catti-brie's eyes.

3

PARLEY

The Eighth King of Mithral Hall, leading his four friends and two hundred dwarf soldiers, was more appropriately arrayed for battle than for parley. Bruenor wore his battered, one-horned helmet, the other horn having long ago been broken away, and a fine suit of mithral armor, vertical lines of the silvery metal running the length of his stout torso and glittering in the torchlight. His shield bore the foaming mug standard of Clan Battlehammer in solid gold, and his customary axe, showing the nicks of a thousand battle kills (and a fair number of them goblins!) was ready in a loop on his belt, within easy reach.

Wulfgar, in a suit of natural hide, a wolf's head set in front of his great chest, walked behind the dwarf, with Aegis-fang, his warhammer, angled out across the crook of his elbow in front of him. Catti-brie, Taulmaril over her shoulder, walked beside him, but the two said little, and the tension between them was obvious.

Drizzt flanked the dwarf king on his right, Regis scampering to keep up beside him, and Guenhwyvar, the sleek, proud panther, muscles rippling with every stride, moved to the right of the two, darting off into the shadows whenever the low and uneven corridor widened. Many of the dwarves marching behind the five friends carried torches, and the flickering light created monsterlike shadows, keeping the companions on their guard—not that they were likely to be surprised marching beside Drizzt and Guenhwyvar. The dark elf's black panther companion was all too adept at leading the way.

And nothing would care to surprise this group. The whole of the force was bedecked for battle, with great, sturdy helms and armor and fine weapons.

Every one of the dwarves carried a hammer or axe for distance shots and another nasty weapon in case any enemies got in close.

Four dwarves in a line near the middle of the contingent supported a great wooden beam across their stocky shoulders. Others near them carried huge, circular slabs of stone with the centers cut out. Heavy rope, long notched poles, chains, and sheets of pliable metal all were evident among this section of the brigade as the tools for a "goblin toy," as Bruenor had explained to his nondwarven companions' curious expressions. In looking at the heavy pieces, Drizzt could well imagine how much fun the goblins would get from this particular contraption.

At an intersection where a wide passage ran to their right they found a pile of giant bones, with two great skulls sitting atop it, each of them large enough for the halfling to crawl completely into.

"Ettin," Bruenor explained, for it was he, as a beardless lad, who had felled the monsters.

At the next intersection they met up with General Dagna and the lead force, another three hundred battle-hardened dwarves.

"Parley's set," Dagna explained. "Goblins're down a thousand feet in a wide chamber."

"Ye'll be flanking?" Bruenor asked him.

"Aye, but so're the goblins," the commander explained. "Four hundred of the things if there's a one. I sent Cobble and his three hundred on a wide course, around the backside o' the room to cut off any escape."

Bruenor nodded. The worst that they could expect was roughly even odds, and Bruenor would put any one of his dwarves against five of the goblin scum.

"I'm going straight in with a hundred," the dwarf king explained. "Another hundred're going to the right, with the toy, and the left's for yerself. Don't ye let me down if I'm needin' ye!"

Dagna's chuckle reflected supreme confidence, but then his expression turned abruptly grave. "Should it be yerself doing the talking?" he asked Bruenor. "I'm not for trusting goblins."

"Oh, they've got a trick for me, or I'm a bearded gnome," Bruenor replied, "but this goblin crew ain't seen the likes o' dwarves in hunnerds o' years, unless I miss me guess, and they're sure to think less of us than they should."

They exchanged a heavy handshake, and Dagna stormed off, the hard boots of his three hundred soldiers echoing through the corridors like the rumbling of a gathering thunderstorm.

"Stealth was never a dwarven strong point," Drizzt remarked dryly.

Regis let his stare linger for many moments on the departing host's crack formations, then turned the other way to regard the other group, bearing the beam, stone disks, and other items.

"If ye've not got the belly for it . . ." Bruenor began, interpreting the halfling's interest as fear.

"I am here, aren't I?" Regis came back sharply, rudely actually, and the uncustomary edge to his voice made his friends regard him curiously. But then, in a peculiarly Regis-like movement, the halfling straightened his belt under his prominent paunch, squared his shoulders, and looked away.

The others managed a laugh at Regis's expense, but Drizzt continued to stare at him curiously. Regis was indeed "here," but why he had come, the drow did not know. To say that Regis was not fond of battle was as much an understatement as to say that the halfling was not fond of missing meals.

A few minutes later the hundred soldiers remaining behind their king entered the appointed chamber, coming in through a large archway onto a raised section of stone, several feet up from the wide floor of the huge main area, wherein stood the goblin host. Drizzt noted with more than passing curiosity that this particular raised section held no stalagmite mounds, which seemed to be common throughout the rest of the chamber. Many stalactites leered down from the not-too-high ceiling above Drizzt's head; why hadn't their drippings left the commonplace stone mounds?

Drizzt and Guenhwyvar moved to one side, out of the range of the torches, which the drow, with his exceptional vision, did not need. Slipping into the shadows of a grouping of low-hanging stalactites, the two seemed to disappear.

So did Regis, not far behind Drizzt.

"Gave up the high ground afore we ever started," Bruenor whispered to Wulfgar and Catti-brie. "Ye'd think even goblins'd be smarter than that!" That notion gave the dwarf pause, and he glanced around to the edges of the raised section, taking note that this slab of stone had been worked—worked with tools—to fit into this section of the cavern. His dark eyes narrowed with suspicion as Bruenor looked to the area where Drizzt had disappeared.

"I'm thinking that it's a good thing we're up high for the parley," Bruenor said, too loudly.

Drizzt understood.

"The whole section is trapped," Regis, right behind the drow, remarked.

Drizzt nearly jumped, amazed that the halfling had gotten so close to him and wondering what magical item Regis carried to make his movements so silent. Following the halfling's leading gaze, Drizzt regarded the nearest edge of the platform and a pillar half out from under the stone, a slender stalagmite that had been recently decapitated.

"A good hit would bring it down," Regis reasoned.

"Stay here," Drizzt instructed, agreeing with the crafty halfling's estimate. Perhaps the goblins had spent some time in preparing this battlefield. Drizzt moved out into view of the dwarves, gave Bruenor some signals to indicate that he would check it out, then slipped away, Guenhwyvar moving parallel to him, not far to the side.

All the dwarves had entered the chamber by then, with Bruenor cautiously keeping them back, lined end to end against the back edge of the semicircular platform.

Bruenor, with Wulfgar and Catti-brie flanking him, came out a few steps to regard the goblin host. There were well over a hundred—maybe two hundred—of the smelly things in the darker area of the chamber, judging from the many sets of red-shining eyes staring back at the dwarf.

"We came to talk," Bruenor called out in the guttural goblin tongue, "as agreed."

"Talk," came a goblin reply, surprisingly in the Common tongue. "Whats will dwarfses offer to Gar-yak and his thousands?"

"Thousands?" Wulfgar remarked.

"Goblins cannot count beyond their own fingers," Catti-brie reminded him.

"Get on yer toes," Bruenor whispered to them both. "This group's looking for a fight. I can smell it."

Wulfgar gave Catti-brie a positively superior look, but his juvenile bluster was lost, for the young woman was paying him no heed.

⚔ ⚔ ⚔ ⚔ ⚔

Drizzt slipped from shadow to shadow, around boulders, and finally, over the lip of the raised platform. As he and Regis had expected, this section, supported along its front end by several shortened stalagmite pillars, was not a solid piece, but a worked slab propped in place. and as expected, the goblins planned to drop the front end of the platform and spill the dwarves. Great iron wedges had been driven partway through the front supporting line of pillars, waiting for a hammer to drive them through.

It was no goblin poised underneath the stone to spring the trap, however, but another two-headed giant, an ettin. Even lying flat, it was nearly as tall as Drizzt; he guessed it would tower at least twelve feet high if it ever got upright. Its arms, as thick as the drow's chest, were bare, it held a great spiked club in either hand, and its two huge heads stared at each other, apparently holding a conversation.

Drizzt didn't know whether the goblins intended to honestly parley, dropping the stone slab only if the dwarves made move to attack, but with the appearance of the dangerous giant, he wasn't willing to take any chances. Using the cover of the farthest pillar, he rolled under the lip and disappeared into the blackness behind and to the side of the waiting giant.

When a cat's green eyes stared back at Drizzt from across the breadth of the prone giant, he knew that Guenhwyvar, too, had moved silently into position.

✕ ✕ ✕ ✕ ✕

A torch went up among the goblin ranks, and three of the four-foot-tall, yellow-skinned creatures ambled forward.

"Well," Bruenor grumbled, already tired of this meeting. "Which one of ye dogs is Gar-yak?"

"Gar-yak back with others," the tallest of the group answered, looking over his sloping shoulder to the main host.

"A sure sign there's to be trouble," Catti-brie muttered, unobtrusively slipping her great bow from her shoulder. "When the leader's safely back, the goblins mean to fight."

"Go tell yer Gar-yak that we don't have to kill ye," Bruenor said firmly. "Me name's Bruenor Battlehammer—"

"Battlehammer?" The goblin spat, apparently recognizing the name. "Yous is king dwarf?"

Bruenor's lips did not move as he mumbled to his companions, "Be ready." Catti-brie's hand came to rest on the quiver at her side.

Bruenor nodded.

"King!" the goblin hooted, looking back to the monster host and pointing excitedly Bruenor's way. The ready dwarves understood the cue for the onslaught faster than the stupid goblins, and the next calls from the chamber were dwarven battle cries.

✕ ✕ ✕ ✕ ✕

Drizzt took the call to action faster than the dim-witted ettin. The creature swung its clubs back, then yelped in pain and surprise as the six-hundred-pound panther clamped onto one wrist and a wickedly edged scimitar dove into its armpit on the other side.

The monster's huge heads turned outward in a weird, synchronous movement, one to regard Drizzt, one toward Guenhwyvar.

Before the ettin ever knew what was happening, Drizzt's second scimitar slashed across its bulging eyes. The giant tried to squirm about to get to the stinging elf, but the agile Drizzt slipped under its arm and came in hard and fast at the monster's vulnerable heads.

Across the way, Guenhwyvar dug teeth into flesh and set claws into stone, holding fast the monster's arm.

⚔ ⚔ ⚔ ⚔ ⚔

"Drizzt got him!" Bruenor reasoned when the floor bucked beneath him. With the failure of the simple, if not clever, trap, the goblins had indeed surrendered the favorable high ground. The stupid creatures hooted and whooped and came on anyway, launching crude spears, most of which never reached their targets.

More effective was the dwarven response. Catti-brie led it, putting the Heartseeker up in an instant and loosing a magical, silver-shafted arrow that seemed to trail lightning in its deadly flight. It blasted a clean, smoking hole through one goblin, did likewise to a second farther back, and drove into the chest of a third. All three dropped to the floor.

A hundred dwarves roared and charged forward, heaving axes and warhammers into the charging goblin throng.

Catti-brie fired again, and then again, and with just the three shots, her kill count was up to eight. Now it was her turn to give Wulfgar a superior stare, and the barbarian, humbled, promptly looked away.

The floor bucked wildly; Bruenor heard the roars of the wounded giant beneath him.

"Down!" the dwarf king commanded above the sudden roar of battle.

The ferocious dwarves needed little encouragement, for the leading goblins were close to the platform by then. Out came living dwarven missiles, crushing into the goblin ranks, flailing away with fists and boots and weapons before they even stopped bouncing.

⚔ ⚔ ⚔ ⚔ ⚔

A supporting pillar cracked in half as the ettin inadvertently struck it, trying to bring its club around to get at Drizzt. Down came the platform, pinning the stupid beast.

Drizzt, crouched safely below the level of the giant's girth, could not believe how badly the goblins—and the ettin—had thought out their plan. "How did you ever mean to get out of here?" he asked, though, of course, the ettin could not understand him.

Drizzt shook his head, almost in pity, then his scimitars went to work on the monster's face and throat. A moment later, Guenhwyvar sprang onto the other head, claws raking deep gouges.

In mere seconds, the ranger and his feline companion sprinted out from under the low-riding platform, their business finished. Knowing that his unique talents could be of better use in other ways, Drizzt avoided the wild melee of battle and moved to the side along the cavern wall.

A dozen corridors led into this main chamber, he could see, and goblins were pouring in through nearly every one. Of more concern were the unexpected allies of the goblin forces, though, for, to Drizzt's surprise, he noticed several more gigantic ettins standing still and quiet behind stalagmites, waiting for the moment when they might join the fray.

×　×　×　×　×

Catti-brie, still on the platform and firing into the goblin horde, was the first to spot Drizzt, halfway up a stalagmite mound to the left-hand side of the cavern and motioning back for her and Wulfgar.

A goblin came up out of the fighting mass and charged the young woman, but Wulfgar stepped in front of her and whaled on it with his great hammer, sending it flying a dozen feet over the edge. The barbarian spun about as fast as he could, trying to ready a defense, for another goblin had come up to the side, closing with a spear point leading the way.

It nearly got the spear in for a strike, but its head exploded under the impact of a silver-streaking arrow.

"Drizzt is needing us," Catti-brie explained, and she led the barbarian to their left along the tilting platform, Wulfgar running along the edge and pounding any goblins that tried to scramble up.

When they were clear of the main fighting, Drizzt motioned for Catti-brie to hold her position and for Wulfgar to come forward cautiously.

"He has found some giants," Regis, hidden below the pair, explained to them, "behind those mounds."

Drizzt leaped down around the stalagmite, then came diving back out, turning defensive somersaults with an ettin in close pursuit, twin clubs ready to squash the drow.

The giant jerked upright when Catti-brie's arrow thudded into its chest, scorching the filthy animal hide it wore.

A second arrow knocked it off balance, then Wulfgar's hurled hammer, flying to the barbarian's resounding cries of "Tempus!" blasted the creature away.

Guenhwyvar, still on the side of the mound, leaped atop the second ettin as it came barreling out, muscled claws raking viciously, blinding both the monster's heads until Drizzt got in close enough to put his scimitars to work.

The next giant came around the other side of the mound, but Catti-brie was ready for it, and arrow after arrow slammed it, spun it around, and finally dropped it, dead, to the ground.

Wulfgar charged forward, catching his magical warhammer back in his grasp. Drizzt had finished with the giant by the time the barbarian caught up to him, and the dark elf joined his friend as they met the next of the charging monsters side by side.

"Like old times," Drizzt remarked. He didn't wait for an answer, but dove into a roll in front of Wulfgar.

Both of them winced, blinded for an instant, as Catti-brie's next arrow sliced between them, slamming into the nearest giant's belly.

"She did that to make a point, you know," Drizzt remarked, and he didn't wait for an answer, but dove into a roll in front of Wulfgar.

Understanding Drizzt's diversionary tactics, the barbarian heaved Aegis-fang right over the rolling form, and the ettin, stooping for a hit at Drizzt, caught the warhammer squarely on the side of one head. The other head remained alive, but dazed and disoriented for the split second it took to take control of the entire body.

A split second was far too long when dealing with Drizzt Do'Urden. The agile drow came up in a leap, easily avoiding a lumbering swing, and sent his scimitars in a crossing swipe that drew two parallel lines along the giant's throat.

The ettin dropped both its clubs and clutched at the mortal wound.

An arrow blew it to the ground.

Two more ettins remained behind the mound, but they—all four heads—had seen quite enough of the fighting companions. Out a side tunnel the beasts went.

Right into Dagna's rambling force.

One wounded ettin stumbled back into the main chamber, a dozen hurled hammers bouncing off its stooped back for every lumbering step it took. Before Drizzt, Wulfgar, or even Catti-brie with her bow, could make a move at the beast, a multitude of dwarves rushed out of the tunnel and leaped upon it, bore it to the ground, and hacked and pounded away with battle-crazed abandon.

Drizzt looked at Wulfgar and shrugged.

"Fear not, my friend," the barbarian replied, smiling. "There are many more enemies to hit!" With another bellow to his battle god, Wulfgar turned about and charged for the main fight, trying to pick out Bruenor's one-horned helmet amidst a writhing sea of tangled goblins and dwarves.

Drizzt didn't follow, though, for he preferred single combat to the wildness of general melee. Calling Guenhwyvar to his side, the drow made his way along the wall, eventually exiting the main chamber.

After only a few steps and a warning growl from his trusted panther ally, he came to realize that Regis wasn't far behind.

✕ ✕ ✕ ✕ ✕

Bruenor's estimates of the dwarven prowess seemed on target as the battle soon became a rout. In trading hits with the armored dwarves, the goblins found their crude swords and puny clubs to be no match against the tempered weapons of their enemies. Bruenor's people, too, were better trained, holding tight formations and keeping their nerves, which was difficult amidst all the chaos and the cries of the dying.

Goblins fled by the dozen, most finding the line of Dagna and his charges eagerly waiting to kill them.

With all the confusion, Catti-brie had to pick her shots carefully, particularly since she couldn't be certain that a skinny goblin torso would stop her flying arrows. Mostly, the young woman concentrated on those goblins breaking ranks, fleeing into the open ground between the main fight and Dagna's line.

For all her talk of parley and all the accusations she had leveled at Bruenor and the others, the young woman could not deny the tingle, the adrenaline rush, that swept over her every time she lifted Taulmaril the Heartseeker.

Wulfgar's eyes, too, gleamed with a luster that indicated the fine edge of survival. Raised among a warlike people, he had learned the battle-lust at an early age, a rage that had been tempered only when Bruenor and Drizzt had taught him the worth of his perceived enemies and the many sorrows his tribe's wars had caused.

There was no guilt in this fight, though, not against evil goblins, and Wulfgar's charge from the dead ettins to the larger battle was accompanied by a hearty song to Tempus. Wulfgar found no target clear enough for him to chance a throw with his hammer, but he was not dismayed, particularly when a group of several goblins broke clear of the fighting and fled his way.

The leading three hardly realized that the barbarian was there when Wulfgar's first sidelong cut with Aegis-fang swept them aside, killing two. The goblins behind stumbled in surprise, but came on anyway, flowing around the barbarian like a river around a rock.

A goblin head exploded under Aegis-fang's next heavy blow; Wulfgar snapped the hammer across one-handed to deflect a sword, then followed with a punching left hook that shattered his would-be attacker's jaw and sent the creature flying.

The barbarian felt a sting in his side, and he flinched before the sword could dig in deeply. His free hand whipped back across, clamping atop his attacker's head and lifting the squirming creature from the ground. It still had its sword, and Wulfgar realized that he was vulnerable. He found his only possible defense in sheer savagery, jerking the lifted goblin back and forth so violently that the creature could not get its bearings for a strike.

Wulfgar spun around to drive his many attackers back, using his momentum to aid in his one-handed hammer swipe. An advancing goblin tried to back-track, and lifted its arm in a pitiful defense, but the warhammer blasted through the skinny limb and crushed on, knocking the creature's head so powerfully that when the goblin fell to the ground, it landed on its back. Its face, too, was squarely against the stone.

The stubborn, stupid goblin in the air nicked Wulfgar's huge biceps. The barbarian brought the creature down hard, squeezed and twisted, and heard the satisfying crack of neck bone. Seeing a coming charge from the corner of his eye, he hurled the dead thing at its companions, scattering them.

"Tempus!" the barbarian roared. He took up his warhammer in both hands and rushed into the bulk of the surrounding group, whipping Aegis-fang back and forth repeatedly. Any goblin that could not flee that furious charge, could not get out of deadly range, found a piece of its body utterly destroyed.

Wulfgar pivoted and came back at the group he knew was behind him. The goblins had indeed begun an advance, but when the mighty warrior spun about, his face contorted in wild-eyed frenzy, the goblins turned about and ran away. Wulfgar heaved his hammer, crushing one, then pivoted again and rushed back the other way, at the other group.

These, too, fled, apparently not caring that the wild human was unarmed.

Wulfgar caught one of them by the elbow, spun it about to face him, and clamped his other hand over its face, bending it over backward to the ground. Aegis-fang reappeared in his hand, and the barbarian's fury doubled.

✕ ✕ ✕ ✕ ✕

Bruenor had to plant a boot solidly to free his many-notched axe from the chest of his latest victim. When the blade pulled free, a burst of blood followed it, showering the dwarf. Bruenor didn't care, sure that the goblins were evil things, that the results of his savage attacks bettered the world.

Smiling with abandon, the dwarf king darted this way and that in the tight press, finally finding another target. The goblin swung first, its club smashing apart when it connected with Bruenor's fine shield. The stupid goblin stared at its broken weapon in disbelief, then looked at the dwarf just in time to see the axe dive between its eyes.

A flash cut right by the dwarf, frightening the pleasure from him. He realized it was Catti-brie's doing, though, and saw the victim a dozen feet away, pinned to the stone floor by the quivering silver-shafted arrow.

"Damn good bow," the dwarf muttered, and in looking back to his daughter, he noticed a goblin scrambling up onto the platform.

"No, ye don't!" the dwarf cried, rushing to the slab and diving into a roll atop it. He came up beside the creature, ready to exchange blows, when another flash forced him to jump back.

The goblin still stood, looking down to its chest as though it expected to find an arrow sticking there. It found a hole instead, right through both lungs.

The goblin poked a finger in, in a ridiculous attempt to stem the blood flow, then it fell dead.

Bruenor planted his hands on hips and stared hard at his daughter. "Hey, girl," he scolded. "Ye're stealing all me fun!"

Catti-brie's fingers began to pull on her bowstring, but she relaxed it immediately.

Bruenor considered the woman's curious action, then understood as a goblin club connected heavily with the back of his head.

"I left that one for yerself," Catti-brie said with a shrug, a lame movement when weighed against the glower of Bruenor's dark eyes.

Bruenor wasn't listening. He threw his shield up, blocking the next predictable attack, and whirled, his axe leading the way. The goblin sucked in its belly and hopped back to its tiptoes.

"Not far enough," the dwarf told it, politely using its own tongue, and his words were proven true as the goblin's guts spilled out.

The horrified creature regarded them in disbelief.

"Ye shouldn't be hitting me when I'm not looking," was all the apology it would get from Bruenor Battlehammer, and his second swipe, angled in at the

goblin's neck, took the creature's head from its shoulders.

With the platform clear of enemies, both Bruenor and Catti-brie turned to regard the general battle. Catti-brie brought her bow up, but then didn't see the point of releasing any more arrows. Most of the goblins were in flight, but with Dagna's troops lined across the chamber, they had nowhere to go.

Bruenor leaped down and put his forces into an organized pursuit, and like a great, snapping maw, the dwarven hosts closed over the goblin horde.

4

DWARVEN TOY

Drizzt slipped down a quiet passageway, the clamor of the wild battle lost behind him. The drow was not worried, for he knew that his shadow, his Guenhwyvar, was padding along silently not too far ahead. Of more concern to Drizzt was Regis, still stubbornly close to his back. Fortunately, the halfling moved as silently as the drow, keeping equally well to the shadows, and did not seem to be a liability to Drizzt.

The need for silence was the only thing that kept Drizzt from questioning the halfling then and there, for if they stumbled on a number of goblins, Drizzt did not know how Regis, who was not skilled in battle, would keep out of harm's way.

Ahead, the black panther paused and looked back at Drizzt. The cat, darker than the darkness, then slipped through an opening and moved to the side into a chamber. Beyond the opening Drizzt heard the unmistakable snarling voices of goblins.

Drizzt looked back to Regis, to the red dots that showed the halfling's heat-sensing infravision. Halflings, too, could see in the dark, but not nearly as well as drow or goblins. Drizzt held one hand up, motioned for Regis to wait in the corridor, then slipped ahead to the entrance.

The goblins, at least six or seven, were huddled near the center of the small chamber, milling about many natural, toothlike pillars.

To the right, along the wall, Drizzt sensed a slight movement and knew it was Guenhwyvar, patiently waiting for him to make the first move.

How wondrous a fighting companion that panther was, Drizzt reminded himself. Always, Guenhwyvar let Drizzt determine the course of battle, then discerned the best way to fit in.

The drow ranger moved to the nearest stalagmite, belly-crawled to another, and rolled behind yet another, ever closer to his prey. He made out nine goblins now, apparently discussing their best course of action.

They had no guard posted, had no clue that danger was near.

One rolled around to put its back against a stalagmite, separated from the others by a mere five feet. A scimitar sliced up through its belly, into its lungs before it could utter a sound.

Eight remained.

Drizzt eased the corpse to the ground and took its place, putting his back to the stone.

A moment later, one of the goblins called to him, thinking he was the dead goblin. Drizzt grunted in reply. A hand reached around to pat his shoulder, and the drow couldn't hide his smile.

The goblin tapped him once, then again, more slowly, then the thing began feeling around the drow's thick cloak, apparently noticing Drizzt's taller stature.

A curious expression on its ugly face, the goblin peeked around the mound.

Then there were seven, and Drizzt leaped out into their midst, scimitars flashing in a flurry that took the two nearest goblins down in the blink of an eye.

The remaining five shrieked and ran about, some colliding with stalagmites, others slapping and falling all over each other.

A goblin came straight for Drizzt, its mouth flapping a steady stream of undiscernible words and its hands held wide, as though in a gesture of friendship. Apparently the evil creature only then recognized this dark elf was no potential comrade, for it began to frantically back away. Drizzt's scimitars crossed in a downward slash, drawing an **X** of hot blood on the creature's chest.

Guenhwyvar streaked beside the drow and attacked a goblin fleeing toward the far side of the cavern. With a single swipe of the panther's huge claw, the count was down to three.

Finally, two goblins regained their senses enough to come at the drow in a coordinated fashion, weapons drawn. One launched its club in a roundhouse swing, but Drizzt slapped the weapon wide before it ever got close.

His scimitar, the same he had used to deflect the blow, darted left, then right, left and right, and again a third time, leaving the stunned creature with six mortal wounds. It stared dumbfounded as it fell backward to the floor.

All the while, Drizzt's second scimitar easily parried the other goblin's many desperate attacks.

When the drow turned to face this creature fully, it knew it was doomed. It hurled its short sword at Drizzt, again with little effect, and darted behind the nearest stone pillar.

The last of the confused creatures crossed behind it, startling the drow, and securing the other's escape. Drizzt cursed the goblin's apparent luck. He wanted none to get away, but these two were, either wisely or fortunately, fleeing in opposite directions. A split second later, though, the drow heard a resounding crack from behind the pillar, and the goblin that had thrown its short sword toppled back out from behind the mound, its skull shattered.

Regis, holding his little mace, peeked around the pillar and shrugged.

Drizzt was at a loss and simply returned the stare, then spun about to pursue the remaining goblin, which was fast weaving its way around the cavern teeth toward a corridor at the chamber's far end.

The drow, faster and more agile, gained steadily. He noticed Guenhwyvar, the panther's maw glowing hot with the blood of a fresh kill, loping along a parallel course and gaining on the goblin with every long stride. Drizzt was confident then that the creature had no chance of escape.

At the corridor's entrance, the goblin jolted to a stop. Drizzt skidded aside, as did Guenhwyvar, both diving for the cover of pillars, as a series of snapping and sparking explosions ignited all about the goblin's body. It shrieked and jerked wildly, this way and that; pieces of its clothing and its flesh blew away.

The continuing explosions held the goblin up long after it was dead. Finally, they ended and the creature fell to the floor, trailing thin lines of smoke from several dozen blasted wounds.

Drizzt and Guenhwyvar held steady, perfectly silent, not knowing what new monster had arrived.

The chamber lit up suddenly with a magical light.

Drizzt, fighting hard to bring his eyes into focus, clutched his scimitars tightly.

"All dead?" he heard a familiar dwarven voice say. He blinked his eyes open just in time to see the cleric Cobble enter the room, one hand in a large belt pouch, the other holding a shield out before him.

Several soldiers came in behind, one of them muttering, "Damn good spell, priest."

Cobble moved to inspect the shattered body, then nodded his agreement. Drizzt slipped out from behind the mound.

The surprised cleric's hand came whipping out, launching a score of small objects—pebbles?—at the drow. Guenhwyvar growled, Drizzt dove, and the pebbles hit the rock where he had been standing, initiating another burst of small explosions.

"Drizzt!" Cobble cried, realizing his mistake. "Drizzt!" He rushed to the drow, who was looking back to the many scorch marks on the floor.

"Are you all right, dear Drizzt?" Cobble cried.

"Damn good spell, priest," Drizzt replied in his best imitation-dwarf voice, his smile wide and admiring.

Cobble clapped him hard on the back, nearly knocking him over. "I like that one, too," he said, showing Drizzt that he had a pouch full of the bomblike pebbles. "Ye want to carry some?"

"I do," replied Regis, coming around a stalagmite, closer to the tunnel entrance than Drizzt had been.

Drizzt blinked his lavender orbs in amazement at the halfling's prowess.

⚔ ⚔ ⚔ ⚔ ⚔

Another force of goblins, more than a hundred strong, had been positioned in corridors to the right of the main chamber, to come in at the flank after the fighting had begun. With the trap's failure and Bruenor's ensuing charge (led by the horrible, silver-streaking arrows), the ettin force's miserable failure and Dagna's dwarven troops' subsequent arrival, even the stupid goblins had been wise enough to turn the other way and run.

"Dwarfses," one of the front-running goblins cried out, and the others soon echoed him in calls that shifted from terror to hunger when the creatures came to believe they had stumbled on a small band of the bearded folk, perhaps a scouting party.

Whatever the case, these dwarves apparently had no intentions of stopping to fight, and the chase was on.

A few twists and turns put the fleeing dwarves and the goblins near a wide, smoothly worked, torchlit tunnel, one that had been cut by the dwarves of Mithral Hall several hundred years before.

For the first time since that long-ago day, the dwarves were there again, waiting.

Powerful dwarven hands eased great disks onto a wooden beam, one after another until the whole resembled a solid, cylindrical wheel as tall as a dwarf and nearly as wide as the worked corridor, weighing well over a ton. Completing the structure's main frame were a few well-placed pegs, a wrapping of sheet metal (with sharp, nasty ridges hammered into it), and two notched handles that ran from the wheel's side to behind the contraption, where dwarves could man them and push the thing along.

A cloth with the full-sized likenesses of charging dwarves painted on it was hung out in front as a finishing touch that would keep the goblins in line until it was too late to retreat.

"Here they come," one of the forward scouts reported, returning to the main battle group. "They'll turn the corner in a few minutes."

"Are the baiters ready?" asked the dwarf in charge of the toy brigade.

The other dwarf nodded, and the haulers took up the poles, setting their hands firmly behind the appropriate notches. Four soldiers got out in front of the contraption, ready for their wild run, while the rest of the hundred-dwarf contingent fell into lines behind the haulers.

"The cubbies are a hunnerd feet down," the boss dwarf reminded the lead soldiers. "Don't ye miss the mark! Once we get this thing a-rolling, we're not likely to be stopping it!"

Feigned cries of fear came from the fleeing dwarves at the other end of the long corridor, followed by the whooping of the pursuing goblins.

The boss dwarf shook his bearded face; it was so easy to bait goblins. Just let them believe they had the upper hand, and on they'd come.

The lead soldiers began a slow trot, the haulers behind them took up the easy pace, and the army plodded along behind the thunder of the slow-rolling wheel.

Another series of shouts sounded, and mixed in was the unmistakable cry of "Now!"

The lead soldiers roared and broke into a run. The massive toy came right behind, pumping dwarven legs setting the devilish wheel into a great roll. Above the thunder, the dwarves began their growling song:

> *Tunnel's too tight,*
> *Tunnel's too low,*
> *Better run, goblin,*
> *'Cause here we go!*

Their charge sounded like an avalanche, rumbling undertones to the goblins' cries. The baiters waved to their approaching kin, then stopped beside the cubbies and turned to hurl insults at their goblin pursuers.

The boss dwarf smiled grimly at the knowledge that he, that the toy, would pass the small alcoves, the only safe places in front of the contraption, a split second before the goblin hosts arrived there.

Just as the dwarves had planned.

With no way to turn back, thinking that they had encountered a simple dwarven expedition, the long lines of goblins hooted their battle cries and continued their charge.

The leading dwarven soldiers joined the baiters; together they dove aside into the alcoves, and the toy rumbled by, its disguising canopy making the front goblins slow their pace and wonder.

Howls of terror replaced battle cries and echoed down the goblin line. The closest goblin bravely hacked at the bouncing dwarven image, taking the painted canopy down and revealing the disaster an instant before the creature was squashed.

The fearsome dwarves called their war toy, "the juicer," and the puddle of goblin fluid that came out the back side of the crushing wheel showed it was a fitting title.

"Sing, my dwarves!" commanded the boss, and they took their chant to great crescendos, their rumbling voices echoing above the goblin howls.

> *Every bump's a goblin's head,*
> *Pools of blood from the goblin dead.*
> *Run, good dwarves, push that toy,*
> *Squish the little goblin boys!*

The brutal contraption bounced and bumped; the haulers stumbled on goblin piles. But if any dwarf fell away, a dozen more were ready to take up his part of the pole, powerful legs pumping feverishly.

The army behind the contraption began to stretch out, dwarves stopping to finish off those broken goblins that still squirmed. The main host stayed close to the bouncing contraption, though, for as it came farther along the tunnel, it began to pass side tunnels. Predetermined brigades of dwarven soldiers turned down these, right behind the passing toy, slaughtering any goblins still in the area.

"Tight turn!" the boss dwarf yelled, and sparks flew from the side of the steel-covered outer stone wheels as they screeched along. The dwarves had counted on this region to stop the rolling monstrosity.

It didn't, and around the bend loomed the end of the corridor, a dozen goblins scratching at the unyielding stone, trying to find escape.

"Let it go!" cried the boss, and the wild-rushing dwarves did, falling all over each other as they continued to bounce along.

With a tremendous explosion that shook the bedrock, the juicer collided with the wall. It wasn't hard for the cheering dwarves to figure out what had happened to the unfortunate creatures caught in between.

"Oh, good work!" the boss dwarf said to his charges as he looked back around the bend to the long line of crushed goblins. The dwarven soldiers were still battling, but now they badly outnumbered their enemies, for more than half the goblin force had been squashed.

"Good work!" the boss reiterated heartily, and by a goblin-hating dwarf's estimation, it certainly was.

⚔ ⚔ ⚔ ⚔

Back in the main chamber, Bruenor and Dagna exchanged victorious and wet hugs, "sharing the blood of their enemies," as the brutal dwarves called it. A few dwarves had been killed and many others lay wounded, but neither of the leaders had dared to hope that the rout would be so complete.

"What do ye think o' that, me girl?" Bruenor asked Catti-brie when she came over to join him, her long bow comfortably over one shoulder.

"We did as we had to do," the woman replied. "And the goblins were, as expected, a treacherous bunch. But I'll not back down on me words. We did right in trying to talk first."

Dagna spat on the floor, but Bruenor, the wiser of the two, nodded his agreement with his daughter.

"Tempus!" they heard Wulfgar cry in victory, and the barbarian, spotting the group, began bounding over to them, his mighty warhammer held high above his head.

"I'm still for thinking that ye're all taking a bit too much pleasure in it all," Catti-brie remarked to Bruenor. Apparently not wanting to talk with Wulfgar, she moved away, back to help the wounded.

"Bah!" Bruenor snorted behind her. "Suren ye set yer own bow to some sweet singing!"

Catti-brie brushed her auburn locks out of her face and did not look back. She didn't want Bruenor to see her smile.

The juicer brigade entered the main chamber a half hour later, reporting the right flank clear of goblins. Only a few minutes after them, Drizzt, Regis, and Guenhwyvar came in, the drow telling Bruenor that Cobble's forces were finishing up in the corridors to the left and the rear.

"Did ye get a few for yerself?" the dwarf asked. "After the ettins, I mean?"

Drizzt nodded. "I did," he replied, "as did Guenhwyvar . . . and Regis." Both Drizzt and the dwarf turned curious eyes on the halfling, who stood easily, his bloodied mace in hand. Noticing the looks, Regis slipped the weapon behind his back as though he were embarrassed.

"I did not even expect ye to come, Rumblebelly," Bruenor said to him. "I thought ye'd be staying up, helping yerself to more food, while the rest of us did all the fighting."

Regis shrugged. "I figured that the safest place in all the world would be beside Drizzt," he explained.

Bruenor wasn't about to argue with that logic. "We can set to digging in a few tendays," he explained to his ranger friend. "After some expeditionary miners come through and name the place safe."

By this point, Drizzt was hardly listening to him. He was more interested in the fact that Catti-brie and Wulfgar, moving about the ranks of wounded, obviously were avoiding each other.

"It's the boy," Bruenor told him, noticing his interest.

"He did not think a woman should be at the battle," Drizzt replied.

"Bah!" snorted the red-bearded dwarf. "She's as fine a fighter as we've got. Besides, five dozen dwarf women came along, and two of 'em even got killed."

Drizzt's face twisted with surprise as he regarded the dwarf king. He shook his white shock of hair helplessly and started away to join Catti-brie, but stopped and looked back after only a few steps, shaking his head yet again.

"Five dozen of 'em," Bruenor reiterated into his doubting expression. "Dwarf women, I tell ye."

"My friend," Drizzt answered, moving off once more, "I never could tell the difference."

⚔ ⚔ ⚔ ⚔ ⚔

Cobble's forces joined the other dwarves two hours later, reporting the rear areas clear of enemies. The rout was complete, as far as Bruenor and his commanders could discern, with not a single enemy left alive.

None of the dwarven forces had noticed the slender, dark forms—dark elves, Jarlaxle's spies—floating among the stalactites near critical areas of battle, watching the dwarven movements and battle techniques with more than passing interest.

The goblin threat was ended, but that was the least of Bruenor Battlehammer's problems.

YE OF LITTLE FAITH

Dinin watched Vierna's every move, watched how his sister went through the precise rituals to honor the Spider Queen. The drow were in a small chapel Jarlaxle had secured for Vierna's use in one of the minor houses of Menzoberranzan. Dinin remained faithful to the dark deity Lolth and willingly had agreed to accompany Vierna to her prayers this day, but in truth, the male drow thought the whole thing a senseless facade, thought his sister a ridiculous mockery of her former self.

"You should not be so doubting," Vierna remarked to him, still going about her ritual and not bothering to look over her shoulder to regard Dinin.

At the sound of Dinin's disgusted sigh, though, Vierna did spin about, an angry red glower in her narrow-set eyes.

"What is the purpose?" Dinin demanded, facing her wrath bravely. Even if she was out of Lolth's favor, as Dinin stubbornly believed, Vierna was larger and stronger than he and armed with some clerical magic. He gritted his teeth, firmed his resolve, and did not back down, fearful that Vierna's mounting obsession again would lead those around him down a path to destruction.

In answer, Vierna produced a curious whip from under the folds of her clerical robes. While its handle was unremarkable black adamantite, the instrument's five tendrils were writhing, living snakes. Dinin's eyes widened; he understood the weapon's significance.

"Lolth does not allow any but her high priestesses to wield these," Vierna reminded him, affectionately petting the heads.

"But we lost favor . . ." Dinin started to protest, but it was a lame argument in the face of Vierna's demonstration.

Vierna eyed him and laughed evilly, almost purred, as she bent to kiss one of the heads.

"Then why go after Drizzt?" Dinin asked her. "You have regained the favor of Lolth. Why risk everything chasing our traitorous brother?"

"That is how I regained the favor!" Vierna screamed at him. She advanced a step, and Dinin wisely backed away. He remembered his younger days at House Do'Urden, when Briza, his oldest and most vicious sister, often tortured him with one of those dreaded, snake-headed whips.

Vierna calmed immediately, though, and looked back to her dark, (both live and sculpted) spider-covered altar. "Our family fell because of Matron Malice's weakness," she explained. "Malice failed in the most important task Lolth ever gave her."

"To kill Drizzt," Dinin reasoned.

"Yes," Vierna said simply, looking back over her shoulder to regard her brother. "To kill Drizzt, wretched, traitorous Drizzt. I have promised his heart to Lolth, have promised to right the family's wrong, so that we—you and I—might regain the favor of our goddess."

"To what end?" Dinin had to ask, looking around the unremarkable chapel with obvious scorn. "Our house is no more. The name of Do'Urden cannot be spoken anywhere in the city. What will be the gain if we again find Lolth's favor? You will be a high priestess, and for that I am glad, but you will have no house over which to preside."

"But I will!" Vierna retorted, her eyes flashing. "I am a surviving noble of a destroyed house, as are you, my brother. We have all the Rights of Accusation."

Dinin's eyes went wide. Vierna was technically correct; the Rights of Accusation was a privilege reserved for surviving noble children of destroyed houses, wherein the children named their attackers and thus brought the weight of drow justice upon the guilty party. In the continuing back-room intrigue of chaotic Menzoberranzan, though, justice was selectively meted out.

"Accusation?" Dinin stammered, barely able to get the word out of his suddenly dry mouth. "Have you forgotten which house it was that destroyed our own?"

"It is all the sweeter," purred his stubborn sister.

"Baenre!" Dinin cried. "House Baenre, First House of Menzoberranzan! You cannot speak against Baenre. No house, alone or in alliance, will move against them, and Matron Baenre controls the Academy. Where will your force of justice be garnered?

"And what of Bregan D'aerthe?" Dinin reminded her. "The very band of mercenaries that took us in helped defeat our house." Dinin stopped abruptly, considering his own words, ever amazed by the paradox, the cruel irony, of drow society.

"You are a male and cannot understand the beauty of Lolth," Vierna replied. "Our goddess feeds from this chaos, considers this situation all the sweeter simply because of the many furious ironies."

"The city will not wage war against House Baenre," Dinin said flatly.

"It will never come to that!" Vierna snapped back, and again came that wild flash in her red-glowing orbs. "Matron Baenre is old, my brother. Her time has long past. When Drizzt is dead, as the Spider Queen demands, I will be granted an audience in House Baenre, wherein I . . . we will make our accusation."

"Then we will be fed to Baenre's goblin slaves," Dinin replied dryly.

"Matron Baenre's own daughters will force her out so that the house might regain the Spider Queen's favor," the excited Vierna went on, ignoring her doubting brother. "To that end, they will place me in control."

Dinin could hardly find the words to rebut Vierna's preposterous claims.

"Think of it, my brother," Vierna went on. "Envision yourself standing beside me as I preside over the First House of Menzoberranzan!"

"Lolth has promised this to you?"

"Through Triel," Vierna replied, "Matron Baenre's oldest daughter, herself Matron Mistress of the Academy."

Dinin was beginning to catch on. If Triel, much more powerful than Vierna, meant to replace her admittedly ancient mother, she certainly would claim the throne of House Baenre for herself, or at least allow one of her many worthy sisters to take the seat. Dinin's doubts were obvious as he half-sat on one bench, crossing his arms in front of him and shaking his head slowly, back and forth.

"I have no room for disbelievers in my entourage," Vierna warned.

"Your entourage?" Dinin replied.

"Bregan D'aerthe is but a tool, provided to me so that I might please the goddess," Vierna explained without hesitation.

"You are insane," Dinin said before he could find the wisdom to keep the thought to himself. To his relief, though, Vierna did not advance toward him.

"You shall regret those sacrilegious words when our traitorous Drizzt is given to Lolth," the priestess promised.

"You'll never get near our brother," Dinin replied sharply, his memories of his previous disastrous encounter with Drizzt still painfully clear. "And I'll not go along with you to the surface—not against that demon. He is powerful, Vierna, mightier than you can imagine."

"Silence!" The word carried magical weight, and Dinin found his next planned protests stuck in his throat.

"Mightier?" Vierna scoffed a moment later. "What do you know of power, impotent male?" A wry smile crossed her face, an expression that made Dinin squirm in his seat. "Come with me, doubting Dinin," Vierna bade. She started for a side door in the small chapel, but Dinin made no move to follow.

"Come!" Vierna commanded, and Dinin found his legs moving under him, found himself leaving the single stalagmite mound of the lesser house, then leaving Menzoberranzan altogether, faithfully following his insane sister's every step.

✕ ✕ ✕ ✕ ✕

As soon as the two Do'Urdens walked from view, Jarlaxle lowered the curtain in front of his scrying mirror, dispelling the image of the small chapel. He thought he should speak with Dinin soon, to warn the obstinate fighter of the consequences he might face. Jarlaxle honestly liked Dinin and knew that the drow was heading for disaster.

"You have baited her well," the mercenary remarked to the priestess standing beside him, giving her a devious wink with his left eye—the uncovered one this day.

The female, shorter than Jarlaxle but carrying herself with an undeniable strength, snarled at the mercenary, her contempt obvious.

"My dear Triel," Jarlaxle cooed.

"Hold your tongue," Triel Baenre warned, "or I will tear it out and give it to you, that you might hold it in your hand."

Jarlaxle shrugged and wisely shifted the conversation back to the business at hand. "Vierna believes your claim," he remarked.

"Vierna is desperate," Triel Baenre replied.

"She would have gone after Drizzt on the simple promise that you would take her into your family," the mercenary reasoned, "but to bait her with delusions of replacing Matron Baenre . . ."

"The greater the prize, the greater Vierna's motivation," Triel replied calmly. "It is important to my mother that Drizzt Do'Urden be given to Lolth. Let the fool Do'Urden priestess think what she will."

"Agreed," Jarlaxle said with a nod. "Has House Baenre prepared the escort?"

"A score and a half will slip out beside the fighters of Bregan D'aerthe," Triel replied. "They are only males," she added derisively, "and expendable." The first daughter of House Baenre cocked her head curiously as she continued to regard the wily mercenary.

"You will accompany Vierna personally with your chosen soldiers?" Triel asked. "To coordinate the two groups?"

Jarlaxle clapped his slender hands together. "I am a part of this," he answered firmly.

"To my displeasure," the Baenre daughter snarled. She uttered a single word and with a flash, disappeared.

"Your mother loves me, dear Triel," Jarlaxle said to the emptiness, as if the Matron Mistress of the Academy were still beside him. "I would not miss this," the mercenary continued, thinking out loud. By Jarlaxle's estimation, the hunt for Drizzt could be only a good thing. He might lose a few soldiers, but they were replaceable. If Drizzt was indeed brought to sacrifice, Lolth would be pleased, Matron Baenre would be pleased, and Jarlaxle would find a way to be rewarded for his efforts. After all, on a simpler level, Drizzt Do'Urden, as a traitorous renegade, carried a high bounty on his head.

Jarlaxle chuckled wickedly, reveling in the beauty of it all. If Drizzt managed somehow to elude them, then Vierna would take the fall, and the mercenary would continue on, untouched by it all.

There was another possibility that Jarlaxle, removed from the immediate situation and wise in the ways of the drow, recognized, and if, by some remote chance, it came to pass, he again would be in a position to profit greatly, simply from his favorable relationship with Vierna. Triel had promised Vierna an unbelievable prize because Lolth had instructed her, and her mother, to do so. What would happen if Vierna fulfilled her part of the agreement? the mercenary wondered. What ironies did conniving Lolth have in store for House Baenre?

Surely Vierna Do'Urden seemed insane for believing Triel's empty promises, but Jarlaxle knew well that many of Menzoberranzan's most powerful drow, Matron Baenre included, had seemed, at one time in their lives, equally crazy.

✕ ✕ ✕ ✕ ✕

Vierna pressed through the opaque doorway to Jarlaxle's private chambers later that day, her crazed expression revealing the anxiety for the coming events.

Jarlaxle heard a commotion in the outer corridor, but Vierna merely continued to smile knowingly. The mercenary rocked back in his comfortable chair, tapping his fingers together in front of him and trying to discern what surprise the Do'Urden priestess had prepared for him this time.

"We will need an extra soldier to complement our party," Vierna ordered.

"It can be arranged," Jarlaxle replied, beginning to catch on. "But why? Will Dinin not be accompanying us?"

Vierna's eyes flashed. "He will," she said, "but my brother's role in the hunt has changed."

Jarlaxle didn't flinch, just continued to sit back and tap his fingers.

"Dinin did not believe in Lolth's destiny," Vierna explained, casually taking a seat on the edge of Jarlaxle's desk. "He did not wish to accompany me in this critical mission. The Spider Queen has demanded this of us!" She hopped back to the floor, suddenly ferocious, and stepped back toward the opaque door.

Jarlaxle made no move, except to flex the fingers on his dagger-throwing hand, as Vierna's tirade continued. The priestess swept about the small room, praying to Lolth, cursing those who would not fall to their knees before the goddess, and cursing her brothers, Drizzt and Dinin.

Then Vierna calmed again suddenly, and smiled wickedly. "Lolth demands fealty," she said accusingly.

"Of course," replied the unshakable mercenary.

"Justice is for a priestess to deal."

"Of course."

Vierna's eyes flashed—Jarlaxle quietly tensed, fearing that the unsteady female would lash out at him for some unknown reason. She instead went back to the door and called loudly for her brother.

Jarlaxle saw the unremarkable, veiled silhouette beyond the portal, saw the opaque material bend and stretch as Dinin started in from the other side.

A huge spider leg slipped into the room, then another, then a third. The mutated torso came through next, Dinin's unclothed and bloated body transmuted from the waist down into the lower torso of a giant black spider. His once fair face now seemed a dead thing, swollen and expressionless, his eyes showing no luster.

The mercenary fought hard to keep his breathing steady. He removed his great hat and ran a hand over his bald, sweating head.

The disfigured creature moved into the room fully and stood obediently behind Vierna, the priestess smiling at the mercenary's obvious discomfort.

"The quest is critical," Vierna explained. "Lolth will not tolerate dissent."

If Jarlaxle had held any doubts about the Spider Queen's involvement with Vierna's quest, they were gone now.

Vierna had exacted the ultimate punishment of drow society on trouble-some

Dinin, something only a high priestess in the highest favor of Lolth could ever accomplish. She had replaced Dinin's graceful drow body with this grotesque and mutated arachnid form, had replaced Dinin's fierce independence with a malevolent demeanor that she could bend to her every whim.

She had turned him into a drider.

PART TWO

PERCEPTIONS

There is no word in the drow language for love. The closest word I can think of is ssinssrigg, but that is a term better equated with physical lust or selfish greed. The concept of love exists in the hearts of some drow, of course, but true love, a selfless desire often requiring personal sacrifice, has no place in a world of such bitter and dangerous rivalries.

The only sacrifices in drow culture are gifts to Lolth, and those are surely not selfless, since the giver hopes, prays, for something greater in return.

Still, the concept of love was not new to me when I left the Underdark. I loved Zaknafein. I loved both Belwar and Clacker. Indeed, it was the capacity, the need, for love that ultimately drove me from Menzoberranzan.

Is there in all the wide world a concept more fleeting, more elusive? Many people of all the races seem simply not to understand love, burden its beauteous simplicity with preconceived notions and unrealistic expectations. How ironic that I, walking from the darkness of loveless Menzoberranzan, can better grasp the concept than many of those who have lived with it, or at least with the very real possibility of it, for all of their lives.

Some things a renegade drow will not take for granted.

My few journeys to Silverymoon in these past tendays have invited good-hearted jests from my friends. "Suren the elf has his eyes fixed on another wedding!" Bruenor has often crooned, regarding my relationship with Alustriel, the Lady of Silverymoon. I accept the taunts in light of the sincere warmth and hopes behind them, and have not dashed those hopes by explaining to my dear friends that their notions are misguided.

I appreciate Alustriel and the goodness she has shown me. I appreciate that she, a ruler in a too-often unforgiving world, has taken such a chance as to allow a dark elf to walk freely down her city's wondrous avenues. Alustriel's acceptance of me as a friend has allowed me to draw my desires from my true wishes, not from expected limitations.

But do I love her?

No more than she loves me.

I will admit, though, I do love the notion that I could love Alustriel, and she could love me, and that, if the attraction were present, the color of my skin and the reputation of my heritage would not deter the noble Lady of Silverymoon.

I know now, though, that love has become the most prominent part of my existence, that my bond of friendship with Bruenor and Wulfgar and Regis is of utmost importance to any happiness that this drow will ever know.

My bond with Catti-brie runs deeper still.

Honest love is a selfless concept, that I have already said, and my own selflessness has been put to a severe test this spring.

I fear now for the future, for Catti-brie and Wulfgar and the barriers they must, together, overcome.

Wulfgar loves her, I do not doubt, but he burdens his love with a possessiveness that borders on disrespect.

He should understand the spirit that is Catti-brie, should see clearly the fuel that stokes the fires in her marvelous blue eyes. It is that very spirit that Wulfgar loves, and yet he will undoubtedly smother it under the notions of a woman's place as her husband's possession.

My barbarian friend has come far from his youthful days roaming the tundra. Farther still must he come to hold the heart of Bruenor's fiery daughter, to hold Catti-brie's love.

Is there in all the world a concept more fleeting, more elusive?

—Drizzt Do'Urden

A PATH, STRAIGHT
AND SMOOTH

I'll not accept the group from Nesmé!" Bruenor growled at the barbarian emissary from Settlestone.

"But, king dwarf . . ." the large, red-haired man stammered helplessly.

"No!" Bruenor's severe tone silenced him.

"The archers of Nesmé played a role in reclaiming Mithral Hall," Drizzt, who stood at Bruenor's side in the audience hall, promptly reminded the dwarf king.

Bruenor shifted abruptly in his stone seat. "Ye forgotten the treatment the Nesmé dogs gave ye when first we passed through their land?" he asked the drow.

Drizzt shook his head, the notion actually bringing a smile to his face. "Never," he replied, but his calm tones and expression revealed that, while he had not forgotten, he apparently had forgiven.

Looking at his ebon-skinned friend, so at peace and content, the huffy dwarf's rage was soon deflated. "Ye think I should let them come to the wedding, then?"

"You are a king now," answered Drizzt, and he held out his hands as though that simple statement should explain everything. Bruenor's expression showed clearly that it did not, though, and so the equally -stubborn dark elf promptly elaborated. "Your responsibilities to your people lie in diplomacy," Drizzt explained. "Nesmé will be a valuable trading partner and a worthwhile ally. Besides, we can forgive the soldiers of an oft-imperiled town for their reaction to the sight of a dark elf."

"Bah, ye're too soft-hearted, elf," Bruenor grumbled, "and ye're taking me along with ye!" He looked to the huge barbarian, obviously akin to Wulfgar, and nodded. "Send out me welcome to Nesmé, then, but I'll be needing a count o' them that's to attend!"

The barbarian cast an appreciative look at Drizzt, then bowed and was gone, though his departure did little to stop Bruenor's grumbling.

"A hunnerd things to do, elf," the dwarf complained.

"You try to make your daughter's wedding the grandest the land has ever seen," Drizzt remarked.

"I try," Bruenor agreed. "She's deserving it, me Catti-brie. I've tried to give her what I could all these years, but . . ." Bruenor held his hands out, inviting a visual inspection of his stout body, a pointed reminder that he and Catti-brie were not even of the same race.

Drizzt put a hand on his friend's strong shoulder. "No human could have given her more," he assured Bruenor.

The dwarf sniffled; Drizzt did well to hide his chuckle.

"But a hunnerd damned things!" Bruenor roared, his fit of sentimentality predictably short-lived. "King's daughter has to get a proper wedding, I say, but I'm not for getting much help in doing the damned thing right!"

Drizzt knew the source of Bruenor's overblown frustration. The dwarf had expected Regis, a former guildmaster and undeniably skilled in etiquette, to help in planning the huge celebration. Soon after Regis had arrived in the halls, Bruenor had assured Drizzt that his troubles were over, that "Rumblebelly'll see to what's needin' seein' to."

In truth, Regis had taken on many tasks, but hadn't performed as well as Bruenor had expected or demanded. Drizzt wasn't sure if this came from Regis's unexpected ineptitude or Bruenor's doting attitude.

A dwarf rushed in, then, and handed Bruenor twenty different scrolls of possible layouts for the great dining hall. Another dwarf came in on the first one's heels, bearing an armful of potential menus for the feast.

Bruenor just sighed and looked helplessly to Drizzt.

"You will get through this," the drow assured him. "And Catti-brie will think it the grandest celebration ever given." Drizzt meant to go on, but his last statement gave him pause and a concerned expression crossed his brow that Bruenor did not miss.

"Ye're worried for the girl," the observant dwarf remarked.

"More for Wulfgar," Drizzt admitted.

Bruenor chuckled. "I got three masons at work to fixing the lad's walls," he said. "Something put a mighty anger in the boy."

Drizzt only nodded. He had not revealed to anyone that he had been

Wulfgar's target on that particular occasion, that Wulfgar probably would have killed him blindly if the barbarian had won.

"The boy's just nervous," Bruenor said.

Again the drow nodded, though he wasn't certain he could bring himself to agree. Wulfgar was indeed nervous, but his behavior went beyond that excuse. Still, Drizzt had no better explanations, and since the incident in the room, Wulfgar had become friendly once more toward Drizzt, had seemed more his old self.

"He'll settle down once the day gets past," Bruenor went on, and it seemed to Drizzt that the dwarf was trying to convince himself more than anyone else. This, too, Drizzt understood, for Catti-brie, the orphaned human, was Bruenor's daughter in heart and soul. She was the one soft spot in Bruenor's rock-hard heart, the vulnerable chink in the king's armor.

Wulfgar's erratic, domineering behavior had not escaped the wise dwarf, it seemed. but while Wulfgar's attitude obviously bothered Bruenor, Drizzt did not believe the dwarf would do anything about it—not unless Catti-brie asked him for help.

And Drizzt knew that Catti-brie, as proud and stubborn as her father, would not ask—not from Bruenor and not from Drizzt.

"Where ye been hiding, ye little trickster?" Drizzt heard Bruenor roar, and the dwarf's sheer volume startled Drizzt from his private contemplations. He looked over to see Regis entering the hall, the halfling looking thoroughly flustered.

"I ate my first meal of the day!" Regis shouted back, and he got a sour look on his cherubic face and put a hand on his grumbling tummy.

"No time for eating!" Bruenor snapped back. "We got a—"

"Hunnerd things to do," Regis finished, imitating the dwarf's rough accent and holding up his chubby hand in a desperate plea for Bruenor to back off.

Bruenor stomped a heavy boot and stormed over to the pile of potential menus. "Since ye're so set on thinking about food, . . ." Bruenor began as he gathered up the parchments and heaved them, showering Regis. "There'll be elves and humans aplenty at the feast," he explained as Regis scrambled to put the pile in order. "Give 'em something their sensitive innards'll take!"

Regis shot a pleading look at Drizzt, but when the drow only shrugged in reply, the halfling picked up the parchments and shuffled away.

"I'd've thought that one'd be better at this wedding planning stuff," Bruenor remarked, loudly enough for the departing halfling to hear.

"And not so good at fighting goblins," Drizzt replied, remembering the halfling's remarkable efforts in the battle.

Bruenor stroked his thick red beard and looked to the empty doorway through which Regis had just passed. "Spent lots of time on the road beside the likes of us," the dwarf decided.

"Too much time," Drizzt added under his breath, too quietly for Bruenor to hear, for it was obvious to the drow that Bruenor, unlike Drizzt, thought the surprising revelations about their halfling friend a good thing.

⚔ ⚔ ⚔ ⚔ ⚔

A short while later, when Drizzt, on an errand for Bruenor, neared the entrance to Cobble's chapel, he found that Bruenor was not the only one flustered by the hectic preparations for the upcoming wedding.

"Not for all the mithral in Bruenor's realm!" he heard Catti-brie emphatically shout.

"Be reasonable," Cobble whined back at her. "Yer father's not asking too much."

Drizzt entered the chapel to see Catti-brie standing atop a pedestal, hands resolutely on her slender hips, and Cobble down low before her, holding out a gem-studded apron.

Catti-brie regarded Drizzt and gave a curt shake of her head. "They're wanting me to wear a smithy's apron!" she cried. "A damned smithy's apron on the day o' me wedding!"

Drizzt prudently realized that this was not the time to smile. He walked solemnly to Cobble and took the apron.

"Battlehammer tradition," the cleric huffed.

"Any dwarf would be proud to wear the raiment," Drizzt agreed. "Must I remind you, though, that Catti-brie is no dwarf?"

"A symbol of subservience is what it is," the auburn-haired woman spouted. "Dwarven females are expected to labor at the forge all the day. Not ever have I lifted a smithy's hammer, and . . ."

Drizzt calmed her with an outstretched hand and a plaintive look.

"She's Bruenor's daughter," Cobble pointed out. "She has a duty to please her father."

"Indeed," Drizzt, the consummate diplomat, agreed once more, "but remember that she is not marrying a dwarf. Catti-brie has never worked the forge—"

"It's symbolic," Cobble protested.

"—and Wulfgar lifted the hammer only during his years of servitude to Bruenor, when he was given no choice," Drizzt finished without missing a beat.

Cobble looked to Catti-brie, then back to the apron, and sighed. "We'll find a compromise," he conceded.

Drizzt threw a wink Catti-brie's way and was surprised to realize that his efforts apparently had not brightened the young woman's mood.

"I have come from Bruenor," the drow ranger said to Cobble. "He mentioned something about testing the holy water for the ceremony."

"Tasting," Cobble corrected, and he hopped all about, looking this way and that. "Yes, yes, the mead," he said, obviously flustered. "Bruenor's wanting to settle the mead issue this day." He looked up at Drizzt. "We're thinking that the dark stuff'll be too much for the soft-bellied group from Silverymoon."

Cobble rushed about the large chapel, scooping buckets from the various fonts that lined the walls. Catti-brie offered Drizzt an incredulous shrug as he silently mouthed the words, "Holy water?"

Priests of most religions prepared their blessed water with exotic oils; it should have come as no surprise to Drizzt, after many years beside rowdy Bruenor, that the dwarven clerics used hops.

"Bruenor said you should bring a generous amount," Drizzt said to Cobble, instructions that were hardly necessary given that the excited cleric already had filled a small cart with flasks.

"We're done for the day," Cobble announced to Catti-brie. The dwarf ambled quickly to the door, his precious cargo bouncing along. "But don't ye be thinking that ye've had the last word in all of this!" Catti-brie snarled again, but Cobble, rambling along at top speed, was too far gone to notice.

Drizzt and Catti-brie sat side by side on the small pedestal in silence for some time. "Is the apron so bad?" the drow finally mustered the nerve to ask.

Catti-brie shook her head. "'Tis not the garment, but the meaning of the thing I'm not liking," she explained. "Me wedding's in two tendays. I'm thinking that I've seen me last adventure, me last fight, except for those I'm doomed to face against me own husband."

The blunt admission struck Drizzt profoundly and alleviated much of the weight of keeping his fears private.

"Goblins across Faerûn will be glad to hear that," he said facetiously, trying to bring some levity to the young woman's dark mood. Catti-brie did manage a slight smile, but there remained a profound sadness in her blue eyes.

"You fought as well as any," Drizzt added.

"Did ye not think I would?" Catti-brie snapped at him, suddenly defensive, her tone as sharp as the edges of Drizzt's magical scimitars.

"Are you always so filled with anger?" Drizzt retorted, and his accusing words calmed Catti-brie immediately.

"Just scared, I'm guessing," she replied quietly.

Drizzt nodded, understanding and appreciating his friend's growing dilemma. "I must go back to Bruenor," he explained, rising from the pedestal. He would have left it at that, but he could not ignore the pleading look Catti-brie then gave him. She turned away immediately, staring straight ahead under the cowl of her thick auburn locks, and that despondence struck Drizzt even more profoundly.

"It is not my place to tell you how you should feel," Drizzt said evenly. Still the young woman did not look back to him. "My burden as your friend is equal to the one you carried in the southern city of Calimport, when I had lost my way. I say to you now: The path before you turns soon in many directions, but that path is yours to choose. For all our sakes, and mostly yours, I pray that you consider your course carefully." He bent low, pushed back the side of Catti-brie's hair and kissed her gently on the cheek.

He did not look back as he left the chapel.

✕ ✕ ✕ ✕ ✕

Half of Cobble's cart was already empty by the time the drow entered Bruenor's audience hall. Bruenor, Cobble, Dagna, Wulfgar, Regis, and several other dwarves argued loudly over which pail of the "holy water" held the finest, smoothest taste—arguments that inevitable produced further taste tests, which in turn created further arguments.

"This one!" Bruenor bellowed after draining a pail and coming back up with his red beard covered in foam.

"That one's good for goblins!" Wulfgar roared, his voice dull. His laughter ended abruptly, though, when Bruenor plopped the pail over his head and gave it a resounding backhand.

"I could be wrong," Wulfgar, suddenly sitting on the floor, admitted, his voice echoing under the metal bucket.

"Tell me what ye think, drow," Bruenor bellowed when he noticed Drizzt. He held out two sloshing buckets.

Drizzt put up a hand, declining the invitation. "Mountain springs are more to my liking than thick mead," he explained.

Bruenor threw the buckets at him, but the drow easily stepped aside, and the dark, golden liquid oozed slowly across the stone floor. The sheer volume of the ensuing protests from the other dwarves at the waste of good mead astounded Drizzt, but not as much as the fact that this probably was the first time he had ever seen Bruenor scolded without finding the courage to fight back.

"Me king," came a call from the door, ending the argument. A rather plump dwarf, fully arrayed in battle gear, entered the audience hall, the seriousness of his expression deflating the mirth in the tasting chamber.

"Seven kin have not returned from the newer sections," the dwarf explained.

"Taking their time, is all," Bruenor replied.

"They missed their supper," said the guard.

"Trouble," Cobble and Dagna said together, suddenly solemn.

"Bah!" snorted Bruenor as he waved his thick hand unsteadily in front of him. "There be no more goblins in them tunnels. The groups down there now're just hunting mithral. They found a vein o' the stuff, I tell ye. That'd keep any dwarf, even from his supper."

Cobble and Dagna, even Regis, Drizzt noted, wagged their heads in agreement. Given the potential danger whenever traveling the tunnels of the Underdark (and the deepest tunnels of Mithral Hall could be considered nothing less), the wary drow was not so easily convinced.

"What're ye thinking?" Bruenor asked Drizzt, seeing his plain concern.

Drizzt considered his response for a long while. "I am thinking that you are probably right."

"Probably?" Bruenor huffed. "Ah, well, I never could convince ye. Go on, then. It's what ye want. Take yer cat and go find me overdue dwarves."

Drizzt's wry smile left no doubt that Bruenor's instructions had been his intention all along.

"I am Wulfgar, son of Beornegar! I will go!" Wulfgar proclaimed, but he sounded somewhat ridiculous with his head still under the bucket. Bruenor leveled another backhand to silence his spouting.

"And elf," the king called, turning Drizzt back to him. Bruenor offered a wicked smile to all of those about him, then dropped it fully over Regis. "Be taking Rumblebelly with ye," the dwarf king explained. "He's not doing me much good about here."

Regis's big, round eyes got even bigger and rounder. He ran plump, soft fingers through his curly brown hair, then tugged uncomfortably at the one dangling earring he wore. "Me?" he asked meekly. "Go back down there?"

"Ye went once," Bruenor reasoned, making his argument more to the other dwarves than to Regis. "Got yerself a few goblins, if me memory's right."

"I have too much to—"

"Get ye going, Rumblebelly," Bruenor growled, leaning forward in his seat and nearly overbalancing in the process. "For the first time since ye come running back to us—and know that we're knowing ye're running!—do what I ask of ye without yer back talk and excuses!"

The seriousness of Bruenor's grim tone surprised everyone in the room, apparently even Regis, for the halfling offered not another word, just got up and walked obediently to stand beside Drizzt.

"Can we stop by my room?" Regis quietly asked the drow. "I would like my mace and pack, at least."

Drizzt draped an arm over his three-foot-tall companion's slumping shoulders and turned him about. "Fear not," he said under his breath, and to accentuate the point he dropped the onyx figurine of Guenhwyvar into the halfling's eager hands.

Regis knew he was in fine company.

QUIET IN THE
DARKNESS

Even with burning lamps lining all the walls and the paths clear and well marked, it took Drizzt and Regis the better part of three hours to cross the miles of the great Mithral Hall complex to the new tunnel areas. They passed through the wondrous, tiered Undercity, with its many levels of dwarven dwellings that resembled gigantic steps on two sides of the huge cavern. The dwellings overlooked a central work area on the cavern floor that bustled with the activities of the industrious race. This was the hub of the entire complex; here the majority of Bruenor's people lived and worked. Great furnaces roared all day, every day. Dwarven hammers rang out in a continual song, and though the mines had been opened for only a couple of months, thousands of finished products—everything from finely crafted weapons to beautiful goblets— already filled many pushcarts, which waited along the walls for the onset of the trading season.

Drizzt and Regis entered from the eastern end on the top tier, crossed the cavern along a high bridge, and weaved down the many stairways to exit the city's lowest level, heading west into Mithral Hall's deepest mines. Low-burning lamps lined the walls, though these were fewer now and farther between, and every now and then the companions came to a dwarven work crew, bleeding precious silvery mithral from the tunnel wall.

Then they came to the outer tunnels, where there were no lamps and no dwarves. Drizzt pulled off his pack, thinking to light a torch, but noticed the halfling's eyes glowing with the telltale red of infravision.

"I do prefer the light of a torch," Regis commented when the drow started to replace the pack without striking a light.

"We should save them," Drizzt answered. "We do not know how long we will have to remain in the new areas."

Regis shrugged; Drizzt took amusement in the fact that the halfling was already holding his small but undeniably effective mace, though they hadn't yet passed beyond the secured regions of the complex.

They took a short break, then started on again, putting another two or three miles behind them. Predictably, Regis soon began to complain about his sore feet and quieted only when they heard the sound of dwarven chatter somewhere up ahead.

A few twists and turns in the tunnel took them to a narrow stair that emptied into the final guardroom of this section. Four dwarves were in there, playing bones (grumbling with every throw) and paying little attention to the great, iron-barred stone door that sealed off the new areas.

"Well met," Drizzt said, interrupting the game.

"We got some kin down there," a stocky, brown-bearded dwarf replied as soon as he noticed Drizzt. "King Bruenor sending yerselves to find them?"

"Lucky us," Regis remarked.

Drizzt nodded. "We are to remind the missing dwarves that the mithral will be gotten in proper time," he said, trying to keep this encounter lighthearted, wanting to not alarm the dwarven guards by telling them that he believed there might be trouble in the new section.

Two of the dwarves took up their weapons while the other two walked over to remove the heavy iron bar that locked the door.

"Well, when ye're ready to come back out, tap the door three, then two," the brown-bearded dwarf explained. "We're not for opening it unless the signal's right!"

"Three, then two," Drizzt agreed.

The bar came off and the door fell inward with a great sucking sound. Nothing but the blackness of an empty tunnel was apparent beyond it.

"Easy, my little friend," Drizzt said, seeing the sudden gleam in the halfling's eye. They had been down here just a couple of tendays before, for the goblin fight, but though they had seen that threat eradicated, the hushed tunnel seemed no less imposing.

"Hurry ye up," the brown-bearded dwarf said to them, obviously not happy with keeping the door open.

Drizzt lighted a torch, and led the way into the gloom, Regis close on his heels. The dwarves shut the door immediately when the companions were clear, and Drizzt and Regis heard the clanging of the iron bar being set back into place.

Drizzt handed Regis the torch and drew out his scimitars, Twinkle glowing a soft blue. "We should get done as quickly as we can," the drow reasoned. "Bring in Guenhwyvar and let the cat lead us."

Regis set down his mace and torch and fumbled around to find the onyx figurine. He placed it on the ground before him and took up his other items, then looked to Drizzt, who had moved a few steps farther down the tunnel.

"You may call the panther," Drizzt said, somewhat surprised, when he looked back to see the halfling waiting for him, a curious sight given Regis's close relationship with the great cat. Guenhwyvar was a magical entity, a denizen of the Astral Plane, that came to the summons of the figurine's possessor. Bruenor always had been a bit shy around the cat (dwarves didn't generally like magic other than the magic of fine weapons), but Regis and Guenhwyvar had been close friends. Guenhwyvar had even saved the halfling's life once by taking Regis along on an astral ride, getting the halfling out of a collapsing tower in the process.

Now, though, Regis stood above the figurine, torch and mace in hand, apparently unsure of how to proceed.

Drizzt walked back the few steps to join his diminutive friend. "What is the problem?" he asked.

"I . . . I just think you should call Guenhwyvar," the halfling replied. "It's your panther, after all, and yours is the voice Guenhwyvar knows best."

"Guenhwyvar would come to your call," Drizzt assured Regis, patting the halfling's shoulder. Not wanting to delay and argue the point, though, the drow softly called out the panther's name. A few seconds later, a grayish mist, seeming darker in the dim light, gathered about the figurine and gradually shaped itself into the panther form. The mist subtly transformed, became something more substantial, then it was gone, leaving in its stead Guenhwyvar's muscled feline form. The panther's ears went flat immediately—Regis took a prudent step back—then Drizzt grabbed Guenhwyvar by a jowl and gave a playful shake.

"Some dwarves are missing," Drizzt explained to the cat, and Regis knew that Guenhwyvar understood every word. "Find their scent, my friend. Lead me to them."

Guenhwyvar spent a long moment studying the immediate area, turned back to stare at Regis for a bit, then issued a low growl.

"Go on," Drizzt bade the cat, and the sleek muscles flexed, propelling Guenhwyvar easily and in perfect silence into the darkness beyond the torchlight.

Drizzt and Regis followed at an easy pace, the drow confident that the panther would not outdistance them and Regis glancing nervously, this way and that, with every passing inch. They came through the intersection with the giant ettin's bones, Bruenor's first kill, a short while later, and Guenhwyvar joined them once more when they entered the low cavern where the main goblin force had been routed.

Little evidence remained of that recent battle, save the many bloodstains and a diminishing pile of goblin bodies in the center of the place. Ten-foot-long wormlike creatures swarmed all about these, long tendrils feeling the way as they feasted on the bloated corpses.

"Keep close," Drizzt warned, and Regis didn't have to be told twice. "Those are carrion crawlers," the drow ranger explained, "the vultures of the Underdark. With food so readily available, they likely will leave us alone, but they are dangerous foes. A sting from their tendrils can steal the strength from your limbs."

"Do you think the dwarves got too close to them?" Regis asked, squinting in the dim light to see if he could make out any nongoblin bodies among the pile.

Drizzt shook his head. "The dwarves know the crawlers well," he explained. "They welcome the beasts to be rid of the stench of goblin corpses. I would hardly expect seven veteran dwarves to be taken down by crawlers."

Drizzt started down from the angled platform, but the halfling grabbed his cloak to stop him. "There's a dead ettin under here," Regis explained. "Lots of meat."

Drizzt cocked his head curiously as he regarded the quick-thinking halfling, the drow thinking that maybe Bruenor had been wise in sending the little one along. They skirted the lip of the raised stone and came down far to the side. Sure enough, several carrion crawlers worked over the huge ettin body; Drizzt's original course would have taken him dangerously close to the beasts.

They were into the empty tunnels again in a few seconds, Guenhwyvar drifting silently into the darkness to lead them.

The torch soon burned low; Regis shook his head when Drizzt reached for another one, reminding Drizzt that they should save their light sources.

They went on, in the quiet, in the dark, with only the soft glow of Twinkle to mark their passing. To the drow it seemed like old times, traversing the Underdark with his feline companion, his senses heightened in the knowledge that danger might well lurk around any bend.

✕ ✕ ✕ ✕ ✕

"The disk is warm?" Jarlaxle asked, seeing Vierna's pleasurable expression as she rubbed her delicate fingers across the metallic surface. She sat atop the drider, her mount for the journey, Dinin's bloated face expressionless and unblinking.

"My brother is not far," the priestess replied, her eyes closed in concentration.

The mercenary leaned against the wall, peering down the long tunnel filled with flattened goblin corpses. All about him dark forms, his quiet band of killers, slipped silently about their way.

"Can we know that Drizzt is here at all?" the mercenary dared to ask, though he was not anxious to dispel volatile Vierna's anticipation—especially not with the priestess sitting atop so poignant a reminder of her wrath.

"He is here," Vierna replied calmly.

"And you are sure our friend will not kill him before we find him?" the mercenary asked.

"We can trust this ally," Vierna replied calmly, her tone a relief to the edgy mercenary leader. "Lolth has assured me."

So ends any debate, Jarlaxle told himself, though he hardly felt secure in trusting any human, particularly the wicked one to whom Vierna had led him. He looked back to the tunnel, back to the shifting forms as the mercenary band cautiously made its way.

What Jarlaxle did trust was his soldiers, drow-for-drow as fine a force as any in the dark elf world. If Drizzt Do'Urden was indeed wandering about these tunnels, the skilled killers of Bregan D'aerthe would get him.

"Should I dispatch the Baenre force?" the mercenary asked Vierna.

Vierna considered the words for a moment, then shook her head, her indecision revealing to Jarlaxle that she was not as certain of her brother's whereabouts as she claimed. "Keep them close a while longer," she instructed. "When we have found my brother, they will serve to cover our departure."

Jarlaxle was all too glad to comply. Even if Drizzt was down here, as Vierna believed, they did not know how many of his friends might have accompanied him. With fifty drow soldiers about them, the mercenary was not too worried.

He did wonder, though, how Triel Baenre might welcome the news that her soldiers, even if they were only males, had been used as no more than fodder.

⚔ ⚔ ⚔ ⚔

"These tunnels are endless," Regis moaned after two more hours of unremarkable twists and turns in the goblin-enhanced natural passageways. Drizzt allowed a break for supper—even lit a torch—and the two friends sat in a small natural chamber on a flat rock, surrounded by leering stalactites and monster-like mounds of piled stone.

Drizzt understood just how unintentionally perceptive the halfling's words might prove. They were far underground, several miles, and the caverns continued aimlessly, connecting chambers large and small and meeting with dozens of side passages. Regis had been in the dwarven mines before, but he had never entered that next lower realm, the dreaded Underdark, wherein lived the drow elves, wherein Drizzt Do'Urden had been born.

The stifling air and inevitable realizations of thousands of tons of rock over his head inevitably led the dark elf to thoughts of his past life, of the days when he had lived in Menzoberranzan, or walked with Guenhwyvar in the seemingly endless tunnels of Toril's subterranean world.

"We'll get lost, just like the dwarves," Regis grumbled, munching a biscuit. He took tiny bites and chewed them a thousand times to savor each precious crumb.

Drizzt's smile didn't seem to comfort him, but the ranger was confident that he and more particularly, Guenhwyvar knew exactly where they were, making a systematic circuit with the chamber of the main goblin battle as their hub. He pointed behind Regis, his motion prompting the halfling to half-turn in his rocky seat.

"If we went back through that tunnel and branched at the first right-hand passage, we would come, in a matter of minutes, to the large chamber where Bruenor defeated the goblins," Drizzt explained. "We were not so far from this spot when we met Cobble."

"Seems like farther, that's all," Regis mumbled under his breath.

Drizzt did not press the point, glad to have Regis along, even if the halfling was in a particularly grumpy mood. Drizzt hadn't seen much of Regis in the tendays since he had returned to Mithral Hall; no one had, actually, except perhaps the dwarven cooking staff in the communal dining halls.

"Why have you returned?" Drizzt asked suddenly, his question making Regis choke on a piece of biscuit. The halfling stared at him incredulously.

"We are glad to have you back," Drizzt continued, clarifying the intentions of his rather blunt question. "And certainly all of us are hoping you will stay here for a long time to come. but why, my friend?"

"The wedding . . ." Regis stammered.

"A fine reason, but hardly the only one," Drizzt replied with a knowing smile. "When last we saw you, you were a guildmaster and all of Calimport was yours for the taking."

Regis looked away, ran his fingers through his curly brown hair, fiddled with several rings, and slipped his hand down to tug at his one dangling earring.

"That is the life the Regis I know always desired," Drizzt remarked.

"Then maybe you really didn't understand Regis," the halfling replied.

"Perhaps," Drizzt admitted, "but there is more to it than that. I know you well enough to understand that you would go to great lengths to avoid a fight. Yet, when the goblin battle came, you remained beside me."

"Where safer than with Drizzt Do'Urden?"

"In the higher complex, in the dining halls," the drow replied without hesitation. Drizzt's smile was one of friendship; the luster in his lavender eyes showed no animosity for the halfling, whatever falsehoods Regis might be playing. "Whatever the reason you have come, be sure that we are all glad you are here," Drizzt said honestly. "Bruenor more than any, perhaps. But if you have found some trouble, some danger, you would be well advised to state it openly, that we might battle it together. We are your friends and will stand beside you, without blame, against whatever odds we are offered. By my experience, those odds are always better when I know the enemy."

"I lost the guild," Regis admitted, "just two tendays after you left Calimport."

The news did not surprise the drow.

"Artemis Entreri," Regis said grimly, lifting his cherubic face to stare at Drizzt directly, studying the drow's every movement.

"Entreri took the guild?" Drizzt asked.

Regis nodded. "He didn't have such a hard time of that. His network reached to my most trusted colleagues."

"You should have expected as much from the assassin," Drizzt replied, and he gave a small laugh, which made Regis's eyes widen with apparent surprise.

"You find this funny?"

"The guild is better in Entreri's hands," Drizzt replied, to the halfling's continued surprise. "He is suited for the double-dealing ways of miserable Calimport."

"I thought you . . ." Regis began. "I mean, don't you want to go and . . ."

"Kill Entreri?" Drizzt asked with a soft chuckle. "My battle with the assassin is ended," he added when Regis's eager nod confirmed his guess.

"Entreri might not think so," Regis said grimly.

Drizzt shrugged—and noticed that his casual attitude seemed to bother the halfling more than a little. "As long as Entreri remains in the southland, he is of no concern to me." Drizzt knew that Regis didn't expect Entreri to remain in the south. Perhaps that was why Regis would not stay in the upper levels during the goblin fight, Drizzt thought. Perhaps Regis feared that Entreri might sneak into Mithral Hall. If the assassin found both Drizzt and Regis, he probably would go after Drizzt first.

"You hurt him, you know," Regis went on, "in your fight, I mean. He's not the type to forgive something like that."

Drizzt's look became suddenly grave; Regis shifted back, putting more distance between himself and the fires in the drow's lavender eyes. "Do you believe he has followed you north?" Drizzt asked bluntly.

Regis shook his head emphatically. "I arranged things so it would look like I had been killed," he explained. "Besides, Entreri knows where Mithral Hall is. He could find you without having to follow me here.

"But he won't," Regis went on. "From all I have heard, he has lost the use of one arm, and lost an eye as well. He would hardly be your fighting equal anymore."

"It was the loss of his heart that stole his fighting ability," Drizzt remarked, more to himself than to Regis. Despite his casual attitude, Drizzt could not easily dismiss his long-standing rivalry with the deadly assassin. Entreri was his opposite in many ways, passionless and amoral, but in fighting ability he had proven to be Drizzt's equal—almost. Entreri's philosophy maintained that a true warrior be a heartless thing, a pure, efficient killer. Drizzt's beliefs went in exactly the opposite direction. To the drow, who had grown up among so many warriors holding similar ideals as the assassin, the passion of righteousness enhanced a warrior's prowess. Drizzt's father, Zaknafein, was unequaled in Menzoberranzan because his swords rang out for justice, because he fought with the sincere belief that his battles were morally justified.

"Do not doubt that he will ever hate you," Regis remarked grimly, stealing Drizzt's private contemplations.

Drizzt noted a sparkle in the halfling's eye and took it as an indication of Regis's burning hatred of Entreri. Did Regis want, expect, him to go back to Calimport and finish his war with Entreri? the drow wondered. Did Regis expect Drizzt to deliver the thieves' guild back to him, deposing its assassin leader?

"He hates me because my way of life shows his to be an empty lie," Drizzt remarked firmly, somewhat coldly. The drow would not go back to Calimport, would not go back to do battle with Artemis Entreri, for any reason. To do so would put him on the assassin's moral level, something the drow, who had turned his back on his own amoral people, feared more than anything in all the world.

Regis looked away, apparently catching on to Drizzt's true feelings. Disappointment was obvious in his expression; the drow had to believe that

Regis really did hope he would regain his precious guild at the end of Drizzt's scimitars. And Drizzt didn't really take much hope in the halfling's claims that Entreri would not come north. If the assassin, or at least agents of the assassin, would not be about, then why had Regis remained tight to Drizzt's side when they went down to fight the goblins?

"Come," the drow bade, before his mounting anger could take hold of him. "We have many more miles to cover before we break for the night. We must soon send Guenhwyvar back to the Astral Plane, and our chances of finding the dwarves are better with the panther beside us."

Regis stuffed his remaining food in his small pack, doused the torch, and fell in step behind the drow. Drizzt looked back at him often, somewhat amazed, somewhat disappointed, by the angry glow in the red dots that were the halfling's eyes.

8

SPARKS A-FLYING

Beads of glistening sweat rolled along the barbarian's sculpted arms; shadows of the flickering hearth drew definitive lines along his biceps and thick forearms, accentuating the enormous, corded muscles.

With astounding ease, as though he were swinging a tool made for slender nails, Wulfgar brought a twenty-pound sledge down repeatedly on a metal shaft. Bits of molten iron flew with every ringing hit and spattered the walls and floor and the thick leather apron he wore, for the barbarian had carelessly overheated the metal. Blood surged in Wulfgar's great shoulders, but he did not blink and he did not tire. He was driven by the certainty that he had to work out the demon emotions that had grabbed his heart.

He would find solace in exhaustion.

Wulfgar had not worked the forge in years, not since Bruenor had released him from servitude back in Icewind Dale, a place, a life, that seemed a million miles removed.

Wulfgar needed the iron now, needed the unthinking, instinctual pounding, the physical duress to overrule the confusing jumble of emotions that would not let him rest. The rhythmic banging forced his thoughts into a straight line pattern; he allowed himself to consider only a single complete thought between each interrupting bang.

He wanted to resolve so many things this day, mostly to remind himself of those qualities that initially had drawn him to his soon-to-be bride. At each interval, though, the same image flashed to him: Aegis-fang twirling dangerously close to Drizzt's head.

He had tried to kill his dearest friend.

With suddenly renewed vigor, he sent the sledge pounding home on the metal and again sent lines of sparks flying throughout the small, private chamber.

What in the Nine Hells was happening to him?

Again, the sparks flew wildly.

How many times had Drizzt Do'Urden saved him? How empty would his life have been without his ebon-skinned friend?

He grunted as the hammer hit home.

But the drow had kissed Catti-brie—Wulfgar's Catti-brie!—outside Mithral Hall on the day of his return!

Wulfgar's breathing came in labored gasps, but his arm pumped fiercely, playing his fury through the smithy hammer. His eyes were closed as tightly as the hand that clenched the hammer; his muscles swelled with the strain.

"That one for throwin' around corners?" he heard a dwarf's voice ask.

Wulfgar's eyes popped open and he spun about to see one of Bruenor's kinfolk shuffling past the partly opened doorway, the dwarf's laughter echoing as he made his way along the stone-worked corridor. When the barbarian looked back to his work, he understood the dwarf's mirth, for the metal spear he had been shaping was now badly bowed in the middle from the too-hard slams on the overheated metal.

Wulfgar tossed the ruined shaft aside and let the hammer drop to the stone floor.

"Why did you do it to me?" he asked aloud, though, of course, Drizzt was too far away to hear him. His mind held a conjured image of Drizzt and his beloved Catti-brie embraced in a deep kiss, an image the beleaguered Wulfgar could not let go, even though he had not actually seen the two in the act.

He wiped a hand across his sweaty brow, leaving a line of soot on his forehead, and slumped to a seat on the edge of a stone table. He hadn't expected things to become this complicated, hadn't anticipated Catti-brie's outrageous behavior. He thought of the first time he had seen his love, when she was barely more than a girl, skipping along the tunnels of the dwarven complex in Icewind Dale—carelessly skipping, as though all the ever-present dangers of that harsh region, and all the memories of the recent war against Wulfgar's people simply fell away from her delicate shoulders, bounced off her as surely as did her lustrous auburn tresses.

It didn't take young Wulfgar long to understand that Catti-brie had captured his heart with that carefree dance. He had never met a woman like her; in his male-dominated tribe, women were virtual slaves, cowering to the often unreasonable demands of the menfolk. Barbarian women did not dare to question their men, certainly did not embarrass them, as Catti-brie had done to

Wulfgar when he had insisted that she not accompany the force sent to parley with the goblin tribe.

Wulfgar was wise enough now to admit his own shortcomings, and he felt a fool for the way he had spoken to Catti-brie. Still, there remained in the barbarian a need for a woman—a wife—that he could protect, a wife that would allow him his rightful place as a man.

Things had become so very complicated, and then, just to make matters worse, Catti-brie, his Catti-brie, had shared a kiss with Drizzt Do'Urden!

Wulfgar bounced up from his seat and rushed to retrieve the hammer, knowing that he would spend many more hours at the forge, many more hours transferring the rage from his knotted muscles to the metal. For the metal had yielded to him as Catti-brie would not, had complied to the undeniable call of his heavy hammer.

Wulfgar sent the hammer down with all his might, and a newly heated metal bar shuddered with the impact. *Pong!* Sparks whipped across Wulfgar's high cheekbones, one nipping at the edge of his eye.

Blood surging, muscles corded, Wulfgar felt no pain.

⚔ ⚔ ⚔ ⚔ ⚔

"Put up the torch," the drow whispered.

"Light will alert our enemies," Regis argued in similarly hushed tones.

They heard a growl, low and echoing, down the corridor.

"The torch," Drizzt instructed, handing Regis a small tinderbox. "Wait here with the light. Guenhwyvar and I will circle about."

"Now I am bait?" the halfling asked.

Drizzt, his senses tuned outward for signs of danger, did not hear the question. One scimitar drawn, Twinkle and its telltale glow waiting poised in its sheath, he slipped silently ahead and disappeared into the gloom.

Regis, still grumbling, struck flint to steel and soon had the torch blazing. Drizzt was out of sight.

A growl spun the halfling about, mace at the ready, but it was only Guenhwyvar, ever alert, doubling back down a side passage. The panther padded past the halfling, following Drizzt's course, and Regis quickly shuffled behind, though he could not hope to keep pace with the beast.

He was alone again in seconds, his torch casting elongated, ominous shadows along the uneven walls. His back to the stone, Regis inched on, as quiet as death.

The black mouth of a side passage loomed just a few feet away. The halfling continued walking, holding the torch straight out behind him, his mace leading the way. He sensed a presence around that corner, something inching up to the edge at him from the other direction.

Regis carefully laid the torch on the stone and brought his mace in close to his chest, gently sliding his feet to perfectly balance his weight.

He went around the corner in a blinding rush, chopping with the mace. Something blue flashed to intercept; there came the ring of metal on metal. Regis instantly brought his weapon back and sent it whipping in sidelong, lower.

Again came the distinctive ring of a parry.

Out came the mace, and back in, deftly along the same course. The halfling's skilled adversary was not fooled, though, and the blocking blade was still in place.

"Regis!"

The mace twirled above the halfling's head, ready to dart ahead, but Regis swung it down at arm's length instead, suddenly recognizing the voice.

"I told you to remain back there with the light," Drizzt scolded him, stepping out of the shadow. "You are fortunate I did not kill you."

"Or that I did not kill you," Regis replied without missing a beat, and his calm, cold tone made Drizzt's face contort with surprise. "Have you found anything?" the halfling asked.

Drizzt shook his head. "We are close," he replied quietly. "Both Guenhwyvar and I are certain of that."

Regis walked over and picked up his torch, then tucked his mace into his belt, within easy reach.

Guenhwyvar's sudden growl echoed at them from farther down the long corridor, launching them both into a run. "Don't leave me behind!" Regis demanded, and he grabbed hold of Drizzt's cloak and would not let go, his furry feet skipping, jumping, even skidding along as he tried to keep pace.

Drizzt slowed when Guenhwyvar's yellow-green, glassy eyes reflected back at him from just beyond the leading edge of the torchlight, at a corner where the passageway turned sharply.

"I think we found the dwarves," Regis muttered grimly. He handed Drizzt the torch and let go of the cloak, following the drow up to the bend.

Drizzt peeked around—Regis saw him wince—then brought the torch into the open, casting light on the dreadful scene.

They had indeed found the missing dwarves, sliced and slaughtered, some lying, some propped against the walls at irregular intervals along a short expanse of worked stone corridor.

⚔ ⚔ ⚔ ⚔ ⚔

"If ye're not for wearing the apron, then don't ye be wearing it!" Bruenor said in frustration. Catti-brie nodded, finally hearing the concession she had wanted from the beginning.

"But, me king, . . ." protested Cobble, the only other one in the private chamber with Bruenor and Catti-brie. Both he and Bruenor sported severe holy water headaches.

"Bah!" the dwarf king snorted to silence the good-intentioned cleric. "Ye're not knowing me girl as well as meself. If she's saying she won't be wearing it, then all the giants o' the Spine of the World couldn't be changing her mind."

"Bah yerself!" came an unexpected call from outside the room, followed by a tremendous knock. "I know ye're in there, Bruenor Battlehammer, who calls himself king o' Mithral Hall! Now be opening yer door and meet your better!"

"Do we know that voice?" asked Cobble, he and Bruenor exchanging confused glances.

"Open it, says me!" came another cry, followed by a sharp rap. Wood splintered as a glove nail, a large spike set into the face of a specially constructed metal gauntlet, wedged itself through the thick door.

"Aw, sandstone," came a quieter call.

Bruenor and Cobble looked to each other in disbelief. "No," they said in unison, wagging their heads back and forth.

"What is it?" Catti-brie asked, growing impatient.

"It cannot be," Cobble replied, and it seemed to the young woman that he hoped with all his heart that his words were true.

A grunt signaled that the creature beyond the door had finally extracted his spike.

"What is it?" Catti-brie demanded of her father, her hands planted squarely on her hips.

The door burst open, and there stood the most curious-looking dwarf Catti-brie had ever seen. He wore a spiked steel gauntlet, open-fingered, on each hand, had similar spikes protruding from his elbows, knees, and the toes of his heavy boots, and wore armor (custom-fitted to his short, barrellike form) of parallel, horizontal metal ridges half an inch apart and ringing his body from neck to midthigh and his arms from shoulder to forearm. His gray helmet was open-faced, with thick leather straps disappearing under his monstrous black beard, and sported a gleaming spike atop it, nearly half again as tall as the four-foot-high dwarf.

"It," Bruenor answered, his tone reflecting his obvious disdain, "is a battlerager."

"Not just 'a battlerager,'" the curious, black-bearded dwarf put in. "*The* battlerager! The most wild battlerager!" He walked toward Catti-brie and smiled widely with his hand extended toward her. His armor, with every movement, issued grating, scraping noises that made the young woman's hair stand straight up on the back of her neck.

"Thibbledorf Pwent at yer service, me good lady!" the dwarf introduced himself grandly. "First fighter o' Mithral Hall. Yerself must be this Catti-brie I've heard so much tell of back in Adbar. Bruenor's human daughter, so they told me, though still I'm a bit shaken at seeing any Battlehammer woman without a beard to tickle her toes!"

The smell of the creature nearly overwhelmed Catti-brie. Had he taken that armor off anytime this century? she had to wonder. "I'll try to grow one," she promised.

"See that ye do! See that ye do!" Thibbledorf hooted, and he hopped over to stand before Bruenor, the noise of his armor scraping at the marrow of Catti-brie's bones.

"Me king!" Thibbledorf bellowed. He fell to a bow—and nearly halved Bruenor's long, pointy nose with his helmet spike as he did.

"What in the Nine Hells is yerself doing here?" Bruenor demanded.

"Alive, anyway," Cobble added, then he returned Bruenor's incredulous stare with a helpless shrug.

"It was me belief that ye fell when the dragon Shimmergloom took the lower halls," Bruenor went on.

"His breath was death!" Thibbledorf shouted.

Look who's talking, Catti-brie thought, but she kept silent.

Pwent roared on, dramatically waving his arms about and turning a spin on the floor, his eyes staring at nothing in particular, as though he was recalling a scene from his distant past. "Evil breath. A deep blackness that fell over me and stole the strength from me bones.

"But I got out and got away!" Thibbledorf cried suddenly, spinning at Catti-brie, one stubby finger pointing her way. "Out a secret door in the lower tunnels. Even the likes o' that dragon couldn't stop the Pwent!"

"We held the halls for two more days afore Shimmergloom's minions drove us into Keeper's Dale," Bruenor put in. "I heared no words o' yer return to fight beside me father and his father, the then king o' Mithral Hall."

"It was a tenday afore I got me strength back and got back around the mountain passes to the western door," Pwent explained. "By then the halls were lost.

"Sometime later," Pwent continued, parting his impossibly thick beard with one of his glove nails, "I heared that a bunch of the younger folk, yerself included, had gone to the west. Some said ye were to work the mines o' Mirabar, but when I got there, I heared not a word."

"Two hunnerd years!" Bruenor growled in Pwent's face, stealing his seemingly perpetual smile. "Ye had two hunnerd years to find us, but not once did we hear a word that ye was even alive."

"I came back to the east," Pwent explained easily. "Been living—living well, doing mercenary work, mostly—in Sundabar and for King Harbromme of Citadel Adbar. It was back there, three tendays past—I'd been off to the south for some time, ye see—that I first heared o' yer return, that a Battlehammer had taken back the halls!

"So here I be, me king," he said, dipping to one knee. "Point me at yer enemies." He gave Catti-brie a garish wink and poked a dirty, stubby finger toward the tip of his helmet spike.

"Most wild?" Bruenor asked, somewhat derisively.

"Always been," Thibbledorf replied.

"I'll call ye an escort," Bruenor said, "so ye can get yerself a bath and a meal."

"I'll take the meal," Pwent replied. "Keep yer bath and yer escort. I know me way around these old halls as well as yerself, Bruenor Battlehammer. Better, I say, since ye was but a stubble-chinned dwarfling when we was pushed out." He put his hand out to pinch Bruenor's chin and had it promptly slapped away. His shrieking laughter like a hawk's cry, his armor squealing like talons on slate, the battlerager stomped away.

"Pleasant sort," Catti-brie remarked.

"Pwent alive," Cobble mused, and Catti-brie could not tell if that was good news or not.

"Ye've never once mentioned that one," Catti-brie said to Bruenor.

"Trust me, girl," Bruenor replied. "That one's not worth mentioning."

⚔ ⚔ ⚔ ⚔ ⚔

Exhausted, the barbarian fell onto his cot and sought some needed sleep. He felt the dream returning before he had even closed his eyes. He bolted upright, not wanting to see again the images of his Catti-brie entwined with the likes of Drizzt Do'Urden.

They came to him anyway.

He saw a thousand thousand sparkles, a million reflected fires, spiraling downward, inviting him along.

Wulfgar growled defiantly and tried to stand. It took him several moments to realize that the attempt had been futile, that he was still on his cot, and that he was descending, following the undeniable trail of glittering sparkles down to the images.

9

TOO CLEAN CUTS

"Goblins?" Regis asked. Drizzt bent low over one of the dwarven corpses, shaking his head even before he got close enough to fully inspect the wounds. Goblins would not likely have left the dwarves in this condition, the drow ranger knew, certainly not with all of their valuable armor and equipment intact. Besides, goblins never recovered the bodies of their own dead, yet the only kills in this corridor were dwarves. No matter how large the goblin force, and how great their advantage of surprise, Drizzt did not think it likely that they could have killed this sturdy party without a single loss.

The wounds on the nearest dwarf seemed to confirm the drow's instincts. Slender and precise, these cuts were not made by crude, jagged goblin weapons. A fine edge, razor sharp and probably enchanted, had sliced this particular dwarf's throat. The line was barely visible, even after Drizzt had wiped away the blood, but ultimately deadly.

"What killed them?" Regis asked, growing impatient. He shifted about from foot to foot, moving the torch alternately from one hand to the other.

Drizzt's mind refused to accept the obvious conclusion. How many times in his years in Menzoberranzan, fighting beside his drow kin, had Drizzt Do'Urden witnessed wounds similar to these? No other race in all the Realms, with the possible exception of the surface elves, used weapons so finely edged.

"What killed them?" Regis asked again, a notable tremor in his voice.

Drizzt shook his white locks. "I do not know," he replied honestly. He moved to the next body, this one slumped, half-sitting against the wall. Despite the abundance of blood, the only wound the drow found was a single clean, diagonal slash along the right side of the unfortunate dwarf's throat, a cut paper thin but very deep.

"It could be Duergar," Drizzt said to Regis, referring to the evil race of gray dwarves. The thought made sense, since Duergar had served as minions to Shimmergloom the dragon, and had inhabited these halls until just a few months before, when Bruenor's forces had chased them out. Still, Drizzt knew that his reasoning was based more in hope than in truth. Greedy Duergar would have stripped these victims clean, particularly of the valuable mining equipment, and Duergar, like mountain dwarves, favored heavier weapons, such as the battle-axe. No such weapon had hit this dwarf.

"You don't believe that," Regis said behind him. Drizzt didn't turn to regard the halfling; staying in a crouch, he shuffled over to the next unfortunate dwarf.

Regis's voice fell away behind him, but Drizzt heard the halfling's last statement as clearly as he had ever heard anything in his life.

"You think Entreri did it."

Drizzt did not think that, did not think that any lone warrior, however skilled, could possibly have done such a complete and precise job. He glanced back at Regis, standing impassively under his upheld torch, his eyes searching Drizzt for some clue of a reaction. Drizzt thought the halfling's reasoning curious indeed, and the only explanation he could think of was that Regis was terribly frightened that Entreri had followed him out of Calimport.

Drizzt shook his head and turned back to his investigation. On the body of the third dwarf he found a clue that narrowed the list of potential killers to one race.

A tiny dart protruded from the body's side, under its cloak. Drizzt had to take a steadying breath before he mustered the nerve to pull it out, for he recognized it, and it explained the ease with which these toughened dwarves had been slaughtered. The quarrel, made for a hand-held crossbow, undoubtedly had been coated with sleep poison and was a favored missile of dark elves.

Drizzt came up from his low crouch; his scimitars leaped into his slender hands. "We must leave this place," he whispered harshly.

"What is it?" Regis asked.

Drizzt, his keen senses attuned to the darkness farther along the corridor, did not answer.

From somewhere back behind the halfling, Guenhwyvar issued a low growl.

Drizzt eased one foot behind him and slid slowly backward, somehow understanding that any abrupt movement would trigger an attack. Dark elves in Mithral Hall! Of all the horrors Drizzt could think of—and in Faerûn, these were countless—not one came near to the disaster of the drow.

"Which way?" Regis whispered.

Twinkle's blue light seemed to flare.

"Go!" Drizzt cried, understanding the scimitar's warning. He spun about and saw Regis for just a moment, then the halfling disappeared under a ball of conjured darkness, the magic snuffing out the light of the halfling's torch in the blink of an eye.

Drizzt rolled to the side of the corridor and spun back around behind the propped body of a dead dwarf. He closed his eyes, forcing them into the infrared spectrum, and felt the dwarf's body jerk slightly, once and then again. Drizzt knew it had been hit with quarrels.

A black streak emerged from the globe of darkness behind him; the corridor brightened just a bit as Regis apparently went out the back side of the darkened area, his torch shedding some light around the edge of the unyielding globe.

The halfling did not cry out, though. This surprised Drizzt and made him fear that Regis had been taken.

Guenhwyvar padded by him and darted left, then right. A poison-coated quarrel skipped off the stone floor, inches from the panther's fast-moving paws. Another struck Guenhwyvar with a thud, but the cat hardly slowed.

Drizzt saw the heated outlines of two slender forms many yards away, each with a single arm extended, as though they were again taking aim with their wicked weapons. Drizzt called upon his own innate magical abilities and dropped a globe of darkness into the corridor ahead of Guenhwyvar, offering some cover. Then he, too, was up and running, following the cat, hoping that Regis somehow had escaped.

He went into his own area of darkness without slowing, sure-footed, remembering the layout of the corridor perfectly and deftly skipping over yet another dwarven body. When he emerged, Drizzt noticed the black mouth of a side passage to his left. Guenhwyvar had flown right past it, and now was bearing down on the two drow forms, but Drizzt, trained in the tactics of the dark elves, knew in his heart that the side passage could not be clear.

He heard a scuttling noise, as of many hard-edged legs, and then he fell back, stunned and afraid, as an eight-legged monstrosity, half drow and half arachnid, clambered around the bend, its legs catching hold with equal ease on both floor and wall. Twin axes waved ominously in its hands, which once had been the delicate hands of a drow.

In all the wide world, there was nothing more repulsive to any dark elf, Drizzt Do'Urden included, than a drider.

Guenhwyvar's roar, accompanied by the sounds of several clicking crossbows, brought Drizzt back to his senses in time to deflect the drider's first attack. The monster came straight in with its front legs raised and kicking—to keep Drizzt off balance—and launched its axes in a quick double chop at Drizzt's head.

Drizzt spun back out of range of the legs in time to avoid the slicing axes, but instead of continuing his retreat, he hooked an arm on one spidery leg and rolled around it, rushing back in. Twinkle whipped across, blasting aside a second leg and giving Drizzt enough of an opening to slide down to his knees, right under the beast.

The drider reared and hissed, both of its axes chopping at Drizzt's backside.

Drizzt's other scimitar was already in place, though, leveled horizontally in back of his vulnerable neck. It deflected one axe harmlessly wide and caught the other where its head met its handle. Drizzt put his feet under him and turned sideways as he rose, both his blades turning point up. With his parrying scimitar, he continued the movement, twisting the trapped axe right over in the drider's hand, then tugging it free. With Twinkle he thrust straight up, finding a ridge in the creature's armored exoskeleton and sinking the blade deep into spidery flesh. Hot fluids gushed over Drizzt's arm; the drider shrieked in agony and twitched violently.

Legs buffeted Drizzt from every side. He nearly lost his grip on Twinkle and had to pull the blade out to keep hold of it. Through his prison bars of spider legs Drizzt noticed more dark forms emerging from the side corridor, drow elves, he knew, each with one arm extended his way.

He spun frantically as the first one fired. His thick cloak luckily floated out behind him and caught the quarrel harmlessly in its heavy folds. When he ended his desperate maneuver, though, Drizzt found that he was half out from under the drider, and the creature had turned about enough to line him up with its remaining axe. Even worse, the second drow had him solidly targeted in crossbow sights.

The axe came down curiously—flat end leading, Drizzt noted—forcing Drizzt to parry. He expected to hear the click of a firing crossbow, but Drizzt heard instead a muffled groan as six hundred pounds of black panther buried his dark elf attacker.

Drizzt slapped the axe aside with one blade, then the other, buying himself enough time to get out the rest of the way. He came up, instinctively spinning away from the drider, just in time to get his weapons up to block a sword thrust from the closest drow enemy.

"Drop your weapons and it will go easier on you!" the drow, holding two fine swords, cried in a language that Drizzt had not heard in more than a decade, a language that sent images of beautiful, twisted, terrible Menzo-berranzan flowing back into his mind. How many times had Zaknafein, his father, stood before him, similarly armed, awaiting their inevitable sparring tournament?

A growl that he was not even cognizant of escaped Drizzt's lips; he went into a series of offensive combinations that left his opponent dazzled and off balance in a split second. A scimitar came in low to the side, the second came in high, straight ahead, and the first chopped in again, angled downward at shoulder level.

The enemy drow's eyes widened as if he had suddenly realized his doom.

Guenhwyvar shot by them both, hit the drider full on, and went tumbling in a black ball of raking claws and flailing spider legs.

More dark elves were coming, Drizzt knew, from farther ahead and from the side passage. Drizzt's fury did not relent. Twinkle and his other blade worked fiercely, preventing the other drow from beginning an offensive counter.

He found an opening level with the drow's neck but had no heart for a kill. This was no goblin he faced, but a drow, one of his own race, one like Zaknafein, perhaps. Drizzt remembered a vow he had made when he had left the dark elf city. Ignoring the opening for the drow's neck, he whipped his blade low instead, banging one of his opponent's swords. Twinkle followed the attack immediately, slamming at the same sword, then Drizzt's first blade whipped back the other way, hitting the weapon on the opposite side and sending the battered thing flying away. The evil drow fell back, then came in low, hoping to counter quickly enough with his remaining sword to push Drizzt back, that he might recover his lost weapon.

A blinding backhand from Twinkle sent that remaining sword flying out wide, and Drizzt, never doubting the effectiveness of his strike, was moving forward before Twinkle ever connected.

He could have hit the drow anywhere he chose, including a dozen critical areas, but Drizzt Do'Urden recalled again the vow he had made when he had left Menzoberranzan, a promise to himself and a justification of his departure, that he would never again take the life of one of his people.

His scimitar jabbed downward, angling in above his opponent's kneecap. The evil drow howled and fell back, rolling to the stone and grasping at his torn joint.

Guenhwyvar was under the standing drider, the muscles of the panther's flank exposed from under a loose-hanging piece of the cat's black-furred skin.

"Go, Guenhwyvar!" Drizzt shouted as he ran along the wall, leaping wildly, hacking away, into the jumble of drider legs on that side. He heard the monstrosity shriek again as a scimitar blasted deep into one leg, nearly severing it, and then he tumbled free, out the back side.

Guenhwyvar took another axe hit but did not respond, did not follow Drizzt or counter the attack.

"Guenhwyvar!" Drizzt called, and the panther's head turned slowly to regard him. Drizzt understood the panther's delay when Guenhwyvar flinched several more times from continued crossbow hits.

Drizzt's instincts told him to send the panther away before any more punishment could be leveled upon it—but he did not have the figurine!

"Guenhwyvar!" he cried again, seeing many forms closing quickly from beyond the drider. Truly torn, Drizzt decided to rush back in and fight beside the panther to the bitter end.

The eight-legged creature hissed victoriously as its axe lined up for a stroke on the helpless and quivering panther's neck. Down came the blade, but it hit only insubstantial mist, and the drider's cry turned to one of frustration.

"Come on!" Drizzt heard Regis say behind him. The ranger understood then and was relieved.

But then the drider turned on him fully, and for the first time, with the torchlight returned to this area of the tunnel, Drizzt got a good look at the creature's unnervingly familiar face.

He had not the time to stop to consider it, though. He swept about, exaggerating the movement to send his cloak flying wide (and it took yet another quarrel that had been diving for his back), and rushed away.

The corridor darkened immediately, then lightened a bit, then darkened again, as Regis went into and through the two globes of darkness. Drizzt dove to the side as soon as he went into the cover of his own globe, and he heard a quarrel skip off the stone not far away. In full stride, he caught Regis just beyond the second globe, and the two flew past the dwarven bodies, cut around the bend in the corridor, and kept on running, Drizzt leading the way.

In the Facets of a
Wondrous Gem

Regis and Drizzt pulled up in a small side chamber, its ceiling relatively clear of the persistent stalactites common in this region of caves, and its entryway low and defensible.

"Should I put out the torch?" the halfling asked. He stood behind Drizzt as the drow crouched in front of the entryway, listening for sounds of movement in the main tunnel beyond.

Drizzt thought for a long moment, then shook his head, knowing that it really did not matter, that he and Regis had no chance of escaping these tunnels without further confrontation. Soon after they had fled the battle, Drizzt discovered other enemies paralleling them down side corridors. He knew the dark elf hunting techniques well enough to understand that the trap would not be set with any obvious openings.

"I fight better in the light than my kin, I would guess," Drizzt reasoned.

"At least it wasn't Entreri," Regis said lightly, and Drizzt thought the reference to the assassin a strange thing indeed. Would that it were Artemis Entreri! the drow mused. At least then he and Regis would not be surrounded by a horde of drow warriors!

"You did well in dismissing Guenhwyvar," Drizzt remarked.

"Would the panther have died?" Regis asked.

Drizzt honestly did not know the answer, but he did not believe that Guenhwyvar had been in any mortal peril. He had seen the panther dragged into the stone by a creature of the elemental plane of earth and plunged into a magically created lake of pure acid. Both times the panther had returned to him and eventually all of Guenhwyvar's wounds had healed.

"If the drow and the drider had been allowed to continue," he added, "it is likely that Guenhwyvar would have needed more time to mend wounds on the Astral Plane. I do not believe the panther can be killed away from its home, however, not as long as the figurine survives." Drizzt looked back to Regis, sincere gratitude on his handsome face. "You did well in sending Guenhwyvar away, though, for certainly the panther was suffering at the hands of our enemies."

"I'm glad Guenhwyvar would not die," Regis commented as Drizzt looked back to the entryway. "It would not do to lose so valuable a magical item."

Nothing Regis had said since his return from Calimport, nothing Regis had ever said to Drizzt, seemed so very out of place. No, it went further than that, Drizzt decided as he crouched there, stunned by his halfling companion's callous remark. Guenhwyvar and Regis had been more than companions, had been friends, for many years. Regis would never refer to Guenhwyvar as a magical item.

Suddenly, it all began to make sense to the dark elf: the halfling's references to Artemis Entreri now, back with the dead dwarves, and back when they had talked of what had happened in Calimport after Drizzt's departure. Now Drizzt understood the eager way in which Regis measured his responses to remarks about the assassin.

And Drizzt understood the viciousness of his fight with Wulfgar—hadn't the barbarian mentioned that it was Regis who had told him about Drizzt's meeting with Catti-brie outside Mithral Hall?

"What else did you tell Wulfgar?" Drizzt asked, not turning around, not flinching in the least. "What else did you convince him of with that ruby pendant that hangs about your neck?"

The little mace skipped noisily across the floor beside the drow, coming to rest several feet to the front and side of him. Then came another item, a mask that Drizzt himself had worn on his journey to the southern empires, a mask that had allowed Drizzt to alter his appearance to that of a surface elf.

⚔ ⚔ ⚔ ⚔ ⚔

Wulfgar eyed the outrageous dwarf curiously, not quite sure what to make of this unorthodox battlerager. Bruenor had introduced Pwent to the barbarian just a minute before, and Wulfgar had gotten the distinct impression that Bruenor wasn't overly fond of the black-bearded, smelly dwarf. The dwarf king, to take his seat between Cobble and Catti-brie, had then rushed across the audience hall, leaving Wulfgar awkwardly standing by the door.

Thibbledorf Pwent, though, seemed perfectly at ease.

"You are a warrior, then?" Wulfgar asked politely, hoping to find some common ground.

Pwent's burst of laughter mocked him. "Warrior?" the bawdy dwarf bellowed. "Ye mean, one who's for fighting with honor?"

Wulfgar shrugged, having no idea of where Pwent was leading.

"Is yerself a warrior, big boy?" Pwent asked.

Wulfgar puffed out his great chest. "I am Wulfgar, son of Beornegar . . ." he began somberly.

"I thinked as much," Pwent called across the room to the others. "And if ye was fighting another, and he tripped on his way in and dropped his weapon, ye'd stand back and let him pick it up, knowing that ye'd win the fight anyway," Pwent reasoned.

Wulfgar shrugged, the answer obvious.

"Ye realize Pwent will surely insult the boy," Cobble, leaning on the arm of Bruenor's chair, whispered to the dwarf king.

"Gold against silver on the boy, then," Bruenor offered quietly. "Pwent's good and wild, but he ain't got the strength to handle that one."

"Not a bet I'd take," Cobble replied, "but if Wulfgar lifts a hand against that one, he's to get stung, not to doubt."

"Good," Catti-brie put in unexpectedly. Both Bruenor and Cobble turned incredulous looks on the young woman. "Wulfgar's needing some stinging," she explained with uncharacteristic callousness.

"Well, there ye have it then!" Pwent roared in Wulfgar's face, leading the barbarian across the room as he spoke. "If I was fighting anyone, if I was fighting yerself, and ye dropped yer weapon, I'd let ye bend and pick it up."

Wulfgar nodded in agreement, but jumped back as Pwent snapped his dirty fingers right under Wulfgar's nose. "And then I'd put me spike right through the top o' yer thick head!" the battlerager finished. "I ain't no damned stupid warrior, ye durned fool! I'm a battlerager, *the* battlerager, and don't ye ever forget that the Pwent plays to win!" He snapped his fingers again Wulfgar's way, then stormed past the stunned barbarian, stomping over to stand before Bruenor.

"Ye got some outrageous friends, but I'm not surprised," Pwent roared at Bruenor. He regarded Catti-brie with his broken-toothed smile. "But yer girl'd be a cute one if ye could find a way to put some hair on her chin."

"Take it as a compliment," Cobble quietly offered to Catti-brie, who only shrugged and smiled with amusement.

"Battlehammers always kept a soft spot in their hearts for them that wasn't dwarf-kin," Pwent went on, directing his remarks at Wulfgar as the tall man moved beside him. "And we let 'em be our kings anyway. Never could figure that part out."

Bruenor's knuckles whitened under the strain as he grabbed hard on the arms of his chair, trying to control himself. Catti-brie dropped a hand over his, and when he looked at her tolerant eyes, the storm quickly passed.

"Speaking of that," Pwent went on, "there's an ugly rumor making the rounds that ye've got a drow elf standing beside ye. There be any truth o' that?"

Bruenor's first reaction was one of anger—always the dwarf had been defensive about his oft-maligned drow friend.

Catti-brie spoke first, though, her words directed more to her father than to Pwent, a reminder to Bruenor that Drizzt's skin had thickened and that he could take care of himself. "Ye'll be meeting the drow soon enough," she told the battlerager. "Suren that one's a warrior to fit yer description, if ever there was one."

Pwent roared in derisive laughter, but it faded as Catti-brie continued.

"If ye came at him to start a fight, but dropped yer pointy helm, he'd pick it up for ye and put it back on yer head," she explained. "Of course, then he'd take it back off and stuff it down the back of yer pants, and give ye a few boots, just so ye'd get 'the pwent.'"

The battlerager's lips seemed to tie themselves up in a neat knot. For the first time in many days, Wulfgar seemed to approve completely of Catti-brie's reasoning, and the nod of his head, and of Bruenor's and of Cobble's, was certainly appreciative when Pwent made no move to answer.

"How long will Drizzt be gone?" the barbarian asked, to change the subject before Pwent could find his irritating voice.

"The tunnels are long," Bruenor replied.

"He will return for the ceremony?" Wulfgar asked, and there seemed to Catti-brie to be some ambivalence in his tone, an uncertainty of which answer he would prefer.

"Be sure that he will," the young woman put in evenly. "For be sure that there'll be no wedding until Drizzt is back from the tunnels." She looked at Bruenor, thoroughly squashing his protests before he ever uttered them. "And I'm not for caring if all the kings and queens of the North are kept waiting a month!"

Wulfgar seemed on the verge of an explosion, but he was wise enough to direct his mounting anger away from volatile Catti-brie. "I should have gone with him!" he growled at Bruenor. "Why did you send Regis along? What good might the halfling do if enemies are found?"

The ferocity of the lad's tone caught Bruenor off his guard.

"He's right," Catti-brie snapped in her father's ear, not that she wanted to agree with Wulfgar on any point, but that she, like Wulfgar, saw the opportunity to vent her anger openly.

Bruenor sank back in his chair, his dark eyes darting from one to the other. "Dwarves're lost, is all," he said.

"Even if that is true, what will Regis do but slow down the drow?" Catti-brie reasoned.

"He said he'd find a way to fit in!" Bruenor protested.

"Who said?" Catti-brie demanded.

"Rumblebelly!" shouted her flustered father.

"He did not even wish to go!" Wulfgar shot back.

"Did too!" Bruenor roared, leaping up from his seat and pushing the leaning Wulfgar back two steps with a sturdy forearm slam to the lad's chest. "'Twas Rumblebelly that told me to send him along with the drow, I tell ye!"

"Regis was here with yerself when ye got the news o' the missing dwarves," Catti-brie reasoned. "Ye didn't say a thing about Regis telling ye to send him."

"He told me before that," Bruenor answered. "He told . . ." The dwarf stopped, realizing the illogic of it all. Somehow, somewhere in the back of his mind, he remembered Regis explaining that he and Drizzt should go after the missing dwarves, but how could that be, since Bruenor had made the decision as soon as they all learned that dwarves were missing?

"Have ye been tasting the holy water again, me king?" Cobble asked respectfully but firmly.

Bruenor held his hand out, motioning for them all to be quiet while he sought his recollections. He remembered Regis's words distinctly and knew he was not imagining them, but no images accompanied the memory, no scene where he could place the halfling and thus straighten out the apparent time discrepancy.

Then an image came to Bruenor, a swirling array of shining facets, spiraling down and drawing him with them into the depths of a wondrous ruby.

"Rumblebelly told me that the dwarves'd be missing," Bruenor said slowly and clearly, his eyes closed as he forced the memory from his subconscious. "He told me I should send himself, and Drizzt, to find them, that them two alone'd get me dwarves back to the halls safely."

"Regis could not have known," Cobble reasoned, obviously doubting Bruenor's words.

"And even if he did, the little one would not have wished to go along to find them," Wulfgar added, equally doubtful. "Is this a dream—?"

"Not a dream!" Bruenor growled. "He told me . . . with that ruby of his." Bruenor's face screwed up as he tried to remember, tried to call upon his dwarven resistance to magic to fight past the stubborn mental block.

"Regis would not—" Wulfgar started to say again, but this time it was Catti-brie, knowing the truth of her father's claims, who interrupted him.

"Unless it wasn't really Regis," she offered, and her own words made her mouth drop open with their terrible implications. The three had been through much beside Drizzt, and they all knew well that the drow had many evil and powerful enemies, one in particular who would have the wiles to create such an elaborate deception.

Wulfgar looked equally stricken, at a loss, but Bruenor was fast to react. He jumped down from the throne and blasted between Wulfgar and Pwent, nearly knocking them both from their feet. Catti-brie went right behind, Wulfgar turning to follow.

"What in the head of a goblin are them three talking about?" Pwent demanded of Cobble as the cleric, too, rambled past.

"A fight," Cobble replied, knowing well how to deflect any of Pwent's demands for a lengthy explanation.

Thibbledorf Pwent dropped to one knee and rolled his burly shoulder, punching his fist triumphantly out in front of him. *"Yeeeeeah!"* he cried in glee. "Suren it's good to be back serving a Battlehammer!"

⚔ ⚔ ⚔ ⚔ ⚔

"Are you in league with them, or is this all a terrible coincidence?" Drizzt asked dryly, still refusing to turn about and give Artemis Entreri the satisfaction of viewing his torment.

"I do not believe in coincidence," came the predictable answer.

Finally, Drizzt did turn around, to see his dreaded rival, the human assassin Artemis Entreri, standing easily at the ready, fine sword in one hand, jeweled dagger in the other. The torch, still burning, lay at his feet. The magical transformation from halfling to human had been complete, clothing included, and this fact somewhat confused Drizzt. When Drizzt had used the mask, it had done no more than alter the color of his skin and hair, and his amazement now was obvious on his face.

"You should better learn the value of magical items before you so casually toss them aside," the assassin said to him, understanding the look.

There was a note of truth in Entreri's words, apparently, but Drizzt had never regretted leaving the magical mask in Calimport. Under its protective camouflage, the dark elf had walked freely, without persecution, among the other races. But under that mask, Drizzt Do'Urden had walked in a lie.

"You could have killed me in the goblin fight, or a hundred other times since your return to Mithral Hall," Drizzt reasoned. "Why the elaborate games?"

"The sweeter comes my victory."

"You wish me to draw my weapons, to continue the fight we began in Calimport's sewers."

"Our fight began long before there, Drizzt Do'Urden," the assassin chided. He casually poked his blade at Drizzt, who neither flinched nor reached for his scimitars as the fine sword nicked him on the cheek.

"You and I," Entreri continued, and he began to circle to Drizzt's side, "have been mortal enemies from the day we learned of each other, each an insult to the other's code of fighting. I mock your principles, and you insult my discipline."

"Discipline and emptiness are not the same," Drizzt answered. "You are but a shell that knows how to use weapons. There is no substance in that."

"Good," Entreri purred, tapping Drizzt's hip with his sword. "I feel your anger, drow, though you try so desperately to hide it. Draw your weapons and let it loose. Teach me with your skills what your words cannot."

"You still do not understand," Drizzt replied calmly, his head cocked to the side and a smug, sincere grin widening on his face. "I would not presume to teach you anything. Artemis Entreri is not worth my time."

Entreri's eyes flared in sudden rage and he leaped forward, sword high as if to strike Drizzt down.

Drizzt didn't flinch.

"Draw your weapons and let us continue our destiny," Entreri growled, falling back and leveling his sword at the drow's eye level.

"Fall on your own blade and meet the only end you'll ever deserve," Drizzt replied.

"I have your cat!" Entreri snapped. "You must fight me, or Guenhwyvar will be mine."

"You forget that we are both soon to be captured—or killed," Drizzt reasoned. "Do not underestimate the hunting skills of my people."

"Then fight for the halfling," Entreri growled. Drizzt's expression showed that the assassin had hit a nerve. "Had you forgotten about Regis?" Entreri teased. "I have not killed him, but he will die where he is, and only I know of that place. I will tell you only if you win. Fight, Drizzt Do'Urden, if for no better reason than to save the life of that miserable halfling!"

Entreri's sword made a lazy thrust at Drizzt's face again, but this time it went flying wide to the side as a scimitar leaped out and banged it away.

Entreri sent it right back in, and followed it closely with a dagger strike that nearly found a hole in Drizzt's defenses.

"I thought you had lost the use of an arm and an eye," the drow said.

"I lied," Entreri replied, stepping back and holding his weapons out wide. "Must I be punished?"

Drizzt let his scimitars answer for him, rushing in quickly and chopping repeatedly, left and right, left and right, then right a third time as his left blade twirled up above his head and came straight ahead in a blinding thrust.

Sword and dagger countering, the assassin batted aside each attack.

The fight became a dance, movements too synchronous, too much in perfect harmony for either to gain an advantage. Drizzt, knowing that time was running out for him, and more particularly for Regis, maneuvered near the low-burning torch, then stomped down on it, rolling it about and smothering the flames, stealing the light.

He thought his racial night vision would gain him the edge, but when he looked at Entreri, he saw the assassin's eyes glowing in the telltale red of infravision.

"You thought the mask gave me this ability?" Entreri reasoned. "Not true, you see. It was a gift from my dark elf associate, a mercenary, not so unlike myself." His words ended at the beginning of his charge, his sword coming high and forcing Drizzt to twist and duck to the side. Drizzt grinned in satisfaction as Twinkle came up, the scimitar ringing as it knocked Entreri's dagger aside. A subtle twist put Drizzt back on the offensive, Twinkle coming around Entreri's dagger hand and slicing at the assassin's exposed chest.

Entreri already had begun to roll, straight backward, and the blade never got close.

In the dim light of Twinkle's glow, their skin colors lost in a common gray, they seemed alike, brethren come from the same mold. Entreri approved of that perception, but Drizzt surely did not. To the renegade drow, Artemis Entreri seemed a dark mirror of his soul, an image of what he might have become had he remained in Menzoberranzan beside his amoral kin.

Drizzt's rage led him now in another series of dazzling thrusts and cunning, sweeping cuts, his curved blades weaving tight lines about each other, hitting at Entreri from a different angle with every attack.

Sword and dagger played equally well, blocking and returning cunning counters, then blocking the countering counters that the assassin seemed to anticipate with ease.

Drizzt could fight him forever, would never tire with Entreri standing opposite him. But then he felt a sting in his calf and a burning, then numbing, sensation emanating throughout his leg.

In seconds, he felt his reflexes slowing. He wanted to shout out the truth, to steal the moment of Entreri's victory, for surely the assassin, who so desired to beat Drizzt in honest combat, would not appreciate a win brought on by the poisoned quarrel of hidden allies.

Twinkle's tip dipped to the floor and Drizzt realized he was dangerously vulnerable.

Entreri fell first, similarly poisoned. Drizzt sensed the dark shapes slipping in through the low door and wondered if he had time to bash in the fallen assassin's skull before he, too, slumped to the ground.

He heard one of his own blades, then the other, clang to the floor, but he was not aware that he had dropped them. Then he was down, his eyes closed, his dimming consciousness trying to fathom the extent of this disaster, the many implications for his friends and for him.

His thoughts were not eased with the last words he heard, a voice in the drow language, a voice from somewhere in his past.

"Sleep well, my lost brother."

What dangerous paths I have trod in my life; what crooked ways these feet have walked, in my homeland, in the tunnels of the Underdark, across the surface Northland, and even in the course of following my friends.

I shake my head in wonderment— is every corner of the wide world possessed of people so self-absorbed that they cannot let others cross the paths of their lives? People so filled with hatred that they must take up chase and vindicate themselves against perceived wrongs, even if those wrongs were no more than an honest defense against their own encroaching evils?

LEGACY

I left Artemis Entreri in Calimport, left him there in body and with my taste for vengeance rightfully sated. Our paths had crossed and separated, to the betterment of us both. Entreri had no practical reason to pursue me, had nothing to gain in finding me but the possible redemption of his injured pride.

What a fool he is.

He has found perfection of the body, has honed his fighting skills as perfectly as any I have known. But his need to pursue reveals his weakness. As we uncover the mysteries of the body, so too must we unravel the harmonies of the soul. But Artemis Entreri, for all his physical prowess, will never know what songs his spirit might sing. Always will he listen jealously for the harmonies of others, absorbed with bringing down anything that threatens his craven superiority.

So much like my people is he, and so much like many others I have met, of varied races: barbarian warlords whose positions of power hinge on their ability to wage war on enemies who are not enemies; dwarf kings who hoard riches beyond imagination, while when sharing but a pittance of their treasures could better the lives of all those around them and in turn allow them to take down their ever-present military defenses and throw away their consuming paranoia; haughty elves who avert their eyes to the sufferings of any who are not elven, feeling that the "lesser races" somehow brought their pains unto themselves.

I have run from these people, passed these people by, and heard countless stories of them from travelers of every known land. And I know now that I must battle them, not with blade or army, but by remaining true to what I know in my heart is the rightful course of harmony.

By the grace of the gods, I am not alone. Since Bruenor regained his throne, the neighboring peoples take hope in his promises that the dwarven treasures of Mithral Hall will better all the region. Catti-brie's devotion to her principles is no less than my own, and Wulfgar has shown his warrior people the better way of friendship, the way of harmony.

They are my armor, my hope in what is to come for me and for all the world. And as the lost chasers such as Entreri inevitably find their paths linked once more with my own, I remember Zaknafein, kindred of blood and soul. I remember Montolio and take heart that there are others who know the truth, that if I am destroyed, my ideals will not die with me. Because of the friends I have known, the honorable people I have met, I know I am no solitary hero of unique causes. I know that when I die, that which is important will live on.

This is my legacy; by the grace of the gods, I am not alone.

—Drizzt Do'Urden

11

FAMILY BUSINESS

Clothing flew wildly, bric-a-brac smashed against the wall across the room, assorted weapons spun up into the air and twirled back down, some bouncing off Bruenor's back. The dwarf, top half buried in his private locker, felt none of it, didn't even grunt when, as he rose for a moment, the flat side of a throwing axe struck and dislodged his one-horned helmet.

"It's in here!" the dwarf growled stubbornly, and a half-completed suit of chain mail whipped over his shoulder, nearly clobbering the others in the room. "By Moradin, the damned thing's got to be in here!"

"What in the Nine—" Thibbledorf Pwent began, but Bruenor's ecstatic cry cut him short.

"I knowed it!" the red-bearded dwarf proclaimed, spinning up and turning away from the dismantled chest. In his hand he held a small, heart-shaped locket on a golden chain.

Catti-brie recognized it instantly as the magical gift Lady Alustriel of Silverymoon had given Bruenor, that he might find his friends who had gone into the Southland. Inside the locket was a tiny portrait of Drizzt, and the item was attuned to the drow, would give its possessor general information about Drizzt Do'Urden's whereabouts.

"This'll lead us to the elf," Bruenor proclaimed, holding the locket up high before him.

"Then give it over, me king," said Pwent, "and let me find this strange . . . friend o' yers."

"I can work it well enough," Bruenor growled in reply, replacing his one-horned helm atop his head and taking up his many-notched axe and golden shield.

"Ye're king of Mithral Hall!" Pwent protested. "Ye cannot be running off into the danger of unknown tunnels."

Catti-brie ripped off an answer before Bruenor got the chance.

"Shut yer mouth, battlerager," the young woman insisted. "Me Dad'd throw the halls to the goblins afore he'd be letting Drizzt stay in trouble!"

Cobble grabbed Pwent's shoulder (and got a nasty cut on one finger from the many-ridged armor in the process) to confirm the woman's observation and silently warn the wild battlerager not to press this point.

Bruenor wouldn't have listened to any arguments anyway. The red-bearded dwarf king, fires aglow in his dark eyes, again blasted past Pwent and Wulfgar and led the charge out of the room.

⚔ ⚔ ⚔ ⚔ ⚔

The image came into focus slowly, surrealistically, and by the time Drizzt Do'Urden fully awakened, he clearly recognized his sister Vierna, bending low to regard him.

"Purple eyes," the priestess said in the drow tongue.

A sense that he had played out this identical scene a hundred times in his youth nearly overwhelmed the trapped dark elf.

Vierna! The only member of his family that Drizzt had ever cared for, besides the dead Zaknafein, stood before him now.

She had been Drizzt's wean-mother, assigned to bring him, as a prince of House Do'Urden, into the dark ways of drow society. But thinking back to those distant memories, to times of which he had few, if any, recollections, Drizzt knew there was something different about Vierna, some underlying tenderness buried beneath the wicked robes of a priestess of the Spider Queen.

"How long has it been, my lost brother?" Vierna asked, still using the language of the dark elves. "Nearly three decades? And how far you have come, and yet so close again to where you began, and where you belong."

Drizzt steeled his gaze, but had no practical retort—not with his hands bound behind him and a dozen drow soldiers milling about the small chamber. Entreri was there, too, talking to a most curious dark elf who wore an outrageously plumed hat and a short, open-front vest that showed the rippling muscles of his slender stomach. The assassin had the magical mask tied to his belt, and Drizzt feared the mischief Entreri might cause if he were allowed to return to Mithral Hall.

"What will you think when you walk again into Menzoberranzan?" Vierna asked Drizzt, and though the question was again rhetorical, it drew his attention fully back to her.

"I will think as a prisoner thinks," Drizzt replied. "And when I am brought before Matr—before wicked Malice—"

"Matron Malice!" Vierna hissed.

"Malice," Drizzt repeat defiantly, and Vierna slapped him hard across the face. Several dark elves turned to regard the incident, then gave quiet chuckles and went back to their conversations.

Vierna, too, erupted in laughter, long and wild. She threw her head back, her flowing white tresses flipping back from her face.

Drizzt regarded her silently, having no idea of what had precipitated the explosive reaction.

"Matron Malice is dead, you fool!" Vierna said suddenly, snapping her head forward to within an inch of Drizzt's face.

Drizzt did not know how to react. He had just been told that his mother was dead, and he had no idea of how the information should affect him. He felt a sadness, distantly, but dismissed it, understanding that it came from a sense of never knowing a mother, not from the loss of Malice Do'Urden. As he settled back, digesting the news, Drizzt came to feel a calmness, an acceptance that brought not an ounce of grief. Malice was his natural parent, never his mother, and by all of Drizzt Do'Urden's estimation, her death was not a bad thing.

"You do not even know, do you?" Vierna laughed at him. "How long you have been gone, lost one!"

Drizzt cocked a curious eye, suspecting that some further, even greater, revelation was yet to be spoken.

"By your own actions House Do'Urden was destroyed, and you do not even know!" Vierna cackled hysterically.

"Destroyed?" Drizzt asked, surprised but again, not overly concerned. In truth, the renegade drow felt no more for his own house than for any other in Menzoberranzan. In truth, Drizzt felt nothing at all.

"Matron Malice was charged with finding you," Vierna explained. "When she could not, when you slipped through her grasp, so, too, did the favor of Lolth."

"A pity," Drizzt interjected, his voice dripping with sarcasm. Vierna hit him again, harder, but he held firm to his stoic discipline and did not blink.

Vierna spun away from him, clenched her delicate but deceptively strong hands in front of her and found breath hard to come by.

"Destroyed," she said again, suddenly obviously pained, "taken down by the will of the Spider Queen. They are dead because of you," she cried, spinning back at Drizzt and pointing accusingly. "Your sisters, Briza and Maya, and your mother. All the house, Drizzt Do'Urden, dead because of you!"

Drizzt gave no outward expression, an accurate reflection of his absence of feelings, for the incredible news Vierna had just thrown at him. "And what of our brother?" he asked, more to discern information about this raiding force than for any sincere cares about Dinin's well-deserved demise.

"Why, Drizzt," Vierna said with obviously feigned confusion, "you have met him yourself. You nearly took one of his legs."

Drizzt's confusion was genuine—until Vierna finished the thought.

"One of his eight legs."

Again Drizzt managed to keep his features expressionless, but the stunning information that Dinin had become a drider certainly had caught him by surprise.

"Again the blame is yours!" Vierna snarled, and she watched him for a long moment, her smile gradually fading as he did not react.

"Zaknafein died for you!" Vierna cried suddenly, and though Drizzt knew she had said it only to evoke a reaction, this time he could not remain calm.

"No!" he shouted back in rage, lurching forward from the floor, only to be easily pushed back to his seat.

Vierna smiled evilly, knowing she had found Drizzt's weak spot.

"Were it not for the sins of Drizzt Do'Urden, Zaknafein would live still," she prodded. "House Do'Urden would have known its highest glories and Matron Malice would sit upon the ruling council."

"Sins?" Drizzt spat back, finding his courage against the painful memories of his lost father. "Glories?" he asked. "You confuse the two."

Vierna's hand shot up as though to lash out again, but when stoic Drizzt did not flinch, she lowered it.

"In the name of your wretched deity, you revel in the evilness of the drow world," the indomitable Drizzt went on. "Zaknafein died . . . no, was murdered, in pursuit of false ideals. You cannot convince me to accept the blame. Was it Vierna who held the sacrificial dagger?"

The priestess seemed on the verge of an explosion, her eyes glowing intensely and her face flushed hot to Drizzt's heat-seeing eyes.

"He was your father, too," Drizzt said to her, and she winced in spite of her efforts to sustain her rage. It was true enough. Zaknafein had sired two, and only two, children with Malice.

"But you do not care about that," Drizzt reasoned immediately. "Zaknafein was just a male, after all, and males do not count in the world of the drow.

"But he was your father," Drizzt had to add. "And he gave more to you than you will ever accept."

"Silence!" Vierna snarled through gnashing teeth. She slapped Drizzt again, several times in rapid succession. He could feel the warmth of his own blood oozing down his face.

Drizzt remained quiet for the moment, caught in private reflections of Vierna, and of the monster she had become. She now seemed more akin to Briza, Drizzt's oldest and most vicious sister, caught up in the frenzy that the Spider Queen always seemed ready to promote. Where was the Vierna that had secretly shown mercy to young Drizzt? Where was the Vierna who went along with the dark ways, as did Zaknafein, but never seemed to fully accept what Lolth had to offer?

Where was Zaknafein's daughter?

She was dead and buried, Drizzt decided as he regarded that heat-flushed face, buried beneath the lies and the empty promises of twisted glory that perverted everything about the dark world of the drow.

"I will redeem you," Vierna said, calm again, the heat gradually leaving her delicate, beautiful face.

"More wicked ones than you have tried," Drizzt replied, misunderstanding her intent. Vierna's ensuing laughter revealed that she recognized the error of his conclusions.

"I will give you to Lolth," the priestess explained. "And I will accept, in return, more power than even ambitious Matron Malice ever hoped for. Be of cheer, my lost brother, and know that you will restore to House Do'Urden more prestige and power than it ever before knew."

"Power that will wane," Drizzt replied calmly, and his tone angered Vierna more than his insightful words. "Power that will raise the house to another precipice, so that another house, finding the favor of Lolth, might push Do'Urden down once more."

Vierna's smile widened.

"You cannot deny it," Drizzt snarled at her, and it was he who now faltered in the war of words, he who found his logic, however sound, to be inadequate. "There is no constancy, no permanence, in Menzoberranzan beyond the Spider Queen's latest whim."

"Good, my lost brother," Vierna purred.

"Lolth is a damned thing!"

Vierna nodded. "Your sacrilege cannot harm me any more," the priestess explained, her tone deathly calm, "for you are not of me anymore. You are nothing more than a houseless rogue whom Lolth has deemed suitable for sacrifice.

"So do continue to spit your curses at the Spider Queen," Vierna went on.

"Do show Lolth how proper this sacrifice will be! How ironic it is, for if you repented your ways, if you came back to the truth of your heritage, then you would defeat me."

Drizzt bit his lip, realizing that he would do well to hold his silence until he better fathomed the depth of this unexpected meeting.

"Do you not understand?" Vierna asked him. "Merciful Lolth would welcome back your skilled sword, and my sacrifice would be no more. Thus would I live as an outcast, like you, a houseless rogue."

"You do not fear to tell me this?" Drizzt asked her coyly.

Vierna understood her renegade brother better than he believed. "You will not repent, foolish, honorable Drizzt Do'Urden," she replied. "You would not utter such a lie, would not proclaim your fealty to the Spider Queen, even to save your very life. What useless commodities are these ideals you hold so precious!"

Vierna slapped him one more time, for no particular reason that Drizzt could discern, and she twirled away, her hot form blurred by the shielding flow of her clerical robes. How fitting that image seemed to Drizzt, that the true outline of his sister should be hidden beneath the garments of the perverting Spider Queen.

The curious-looking drow that had been conversing with Entreri walked over to Drizzt then, his high boots clacking loudly on the stone. He gave Drizzt an almost sympathetic look, then shrugged.

"A pity," he remarked, as he produced the glowing Twinkle from under the folds of his shimmering cape.

"A pity," he said again, and he walked away, this time his boots making not a whisper of sound.

⚔ ⚔ ⚔ ⚔ ⚔

The amazed guards snapped to rigid attention when their king unexpectedly entered their chamber, accompanied by his daughter, Wulfgar, Cobble, and a strangely armored dwarf that they did not know.

"Ye heared from the drow?" Bruenor asked the guards, the dwarf king going straight for the heavy bar on the stone door as he spoke.

Their silence told Bruenor all he needed to know. "Get to General Dagna," he instructed one of the guardsmen. "Tell him to gather together a war party and get down the new tunnels!"

The dwarven guard obediently kicked up his heels and darted away.

Bruenor's four companions came beside him as the bar clanged to the stone, Wulfgar and Cobble bearing blazing torches.

"Three, then two, is the drow's signal," the remaining guard explained to Bruenor.

"Three, then two, it is," Bruenor replied, and he disappeared into the gloom, forcing the others, particularly Thibbledorf, who still did not think it a good thing that the king of Mithral Hall was even down there, to scamper quickly just to keep pace.

Cobble and even hardy Pwent glanced back and grimaced as the stone door slammed shut, while the other three, bent forward with the weight of their fears for their missing friend, did not even hear the sound.

12

THE TRUTH BE KNOWN

Blood," Catti-brie muttered grimly, holding a torch and bending low over the line of droplets in the corridor, near the entryway of a small chamber.

"Could be from the goblin fight," Bruenor said hopefully, but Catti-brie shook her head.

"Still wet," she replied. "The blood from the goblin fight'd be long dried by now."

"Then from them crawlers we seen," Bruenor reasoned, "tearing apart the goblin bodies."

Still Catti-brie was not convinced. Stooping low, torch held far in front of her, she went through the short doorway of the side chamber. Wulfgar clambered in behind and pushed past her as soon as the passage widened again, coming up defensively in front of the young woman.

The barbarian's action did not sit well with Catti-brie. Perhaps, from Wulfgar's point of view, he was merely following a prudent course, getting his battle-ready body in front of one encumbered with a torch and whose eyes were on the floor. But Catti-brie doubted that possibility, felt that Wulfgar had come in so urgently because she had been in the lead, because of his need to protect her and stand between her and any possible danger. Proud and able, Catti-brie was more insulted than flattered.

And worried, for if Wulfgar was so fearful of her safety, then he might well make a tactical mistake. The companions had survived many dangers together because each had found a niche in the band, because each had played a role complementary to the abilities of the others. Catti-brie understood clearly that a disruption of that pattern could be deadly.

She pushed back ahead of Wulfgar, batting aside his arm when he held it out to block her progress. He glared at her, and she promptly returned the unyielding stare.

"What d'ye got in there?" came Bruenor's call, deflecting the imminent showdown. Catti-brie looked back to see the dark form of her father crouched in the low doorway, Cobble and Pwent, who held the second torch, out in the corridor behind him.

"Empty," Wulfgar answered firmly, and turned to go.

Catti-brie kept on crouching and looking about, though, as much to prove the barbarian wrong as in an honest search for clues.

"Not empty," she corrected a moment later, and her superior tone turned Wulfgar back around and lured Bruenor into the chamber.

They flanked Catti-brie, who bent low over a tiny object on the floor: a crossbow quarrel, but far too small for any of the crossbows Bruenor's fighters carried, or any similar weapon the companions had ever seen. Bruenor picked it up in his stubby fingers, brought it close to his eyes, and studied it carefully.

"We got pixies in these tunnels?" he asked, referring to the diminutive but cruel sprites more common to woodland settings.

"Some type of—" Wulfgar began.

"Drow," Catti-brie interrupted. Wulfgar and Bruenor turned on her, Wulfgar's clear eyes flashing with anger at being interrupted, but only for the moment it took him to understand the gravity of what Catti-brie had announced.

"The elf had a bow that'd fit this?" Bruenor balked.

"Not Drizzt," Catti-brie corrected grimly, "other drow." Wulfgar and Bruenor screwed up their faces in obvious doubt, but Catti-brie felt certain of her guess. Many times in the past, back in Icewind Dale on the empty slopes of Kelvin's Cairn, Drizzt had told her of his homeland, had told her of the remarkable accomplishments and exotic artifacts of the dark elf nation. Among those artifacts was the most favored weapon of the dark elves, hand-held crossbows, with quarrels usually tipped in poison.

Wulfgar and Bruenor looked to each other, each hopeful that the other would find some logic to defeat Catti-brie's grim assertions. Bruenor only shrugged, tucked the quarrel away, and started for the outside passage. Wulfgar looked back to the young woman, his face flushed with concern.

Neither of them spoke—neither had to—for they both knew well the horror-filled tales of marauding dark elves. The implications seemed grave indeed if Catti-brie's guess proved correct, if drow elves had come to Mithral Hall.

There was something more in Wulfgar's expression that troubled Catti-brie, though, a possessive protectiveness that the young woman was beginning to believe would get them all in trouble. She pushed past the huge man, dipping low and exiting the chamber, leaving Wulfgar in the dark with his inner turmoil.

✕ ✕ ✕ ✕ ✕

The caravan made its slow but steady way through the tunnels, the passageways becoming ever more natural. Drizzt still wore his armor but had been stripped of his weapons and had his hands tightly bound behind his back by some magical cord that would not loosen in the least, no matter how he managed to twist his wrists.

Dinin, eight legs clicking on the stone, led the troupe, with Vierna and Jarlaxle a short way behind. Several in the twenty-drow party had fallen into formation behind them, including the two keeping watch over Drizzt. They intersected once with the larger, flanking band of House Baenre soldiers, Jarlaxle issuing quiet orders and the second drow force slipping, melting, away into the shadows.

Only then did Drizzt begin to understand the import of the raid on Mithral Hall. By his count, somewhere between two and three score dark elves had come up from Menzoberranzan, a formidable raiding party indeed.

And it had all been for him.

What of Entreri? Drizzt wondered. How did the assassin fit into this? He seemed to mesh so well with the dark elves. Of similar build and temperament, the assassin moved along with the drow ranks easily, inconspicuously.

Too well, Drizzt thought.

Entreri spent some time with the shaven-headed mercenary and Vierna, but then dropped back rank by rank, making his way inevitably toward his most-hated enemy.

"Well met," he said coyly when he at last fell into step beside Drizzt. A look from the human sent the two closest dark elf guards moving respectfully away.

Drizzt eyed the assassin closely for a moment, looking for clues, then pointedly turned away.

"What?" Entreri insisted, grabbing the obstinate drow's shoulder and turning him back. Drizzt stopped abruptly, drawing concerned looks from the drow flanking him, particularly Vierna. He started moving again immediately, though, not liking the attention and gradually, the other dark elves settled into their comfortable pace around him.

"I do not understand," Drizzt remarked offhandedly to Entreri. "You had the mask, had Regis, and knew where I could be found. Why then did you ally with Vierna and her gang?"

"You presume that the choice was mine to make," Entreri replied. "Your sister found me—I did not seek her out."

"Then you are a prisoner," Drizzt reasoned.

"Hardly," Entreri replied without hesitation, chuckling as he spoke. "You said it correctly the first time. I am an ally."

"Where my kin are concerned, the two are much the same."

Again Entreri chuckled, apparently seeing the bait for what it was. Drizzt winced at the sincerity in the assassin's laughter, because he then realized the strength in the bonds of his enemies, ties he had hoped, in a fleeting moment of any hope, he might stretch and exploit.

"I deal with Jarlaxle, actually," the assassin explained, "not your volatile sister. Jarlaxle, the pragmatic mercenary, the opportunist. That one, I understand. He and I are much alike!"

"When you are no longer needed—" Drizzt began ominously.

"But I am and shall continue to be!" Entreri interrupted. "Jarlaxle, the opportunist," he reiterated loudly, drawing an approving nod from the mercenary, who apparently understood well the Common tongue of the surface. "What gain would Jarlaxle find in killing me? I am a valuable tie to the surface, am I not? The head of a thieves' guild in exotic Calimport, an ally that might well prove useful in the future. I have dealt with Jarlaxle's kind all my life, guildmasters from a dozen cities along the Sword Coast."

"Drow have been known to kill for the simple pleasure of killing," Drizzt protested, not willing to let go of this one loose strand so easily.

"Agreed," Entreri replied, "but they do not kill when they stand to gain by not killing. Pragmatic. You will not shake this alliance, doomed Drizzt. It is of mutual benefit, you see, to your inevitable loss."

Drizzt paused a long while to digest the information, to find some way to regain that potentially unwinding strand, that loose end that he believed always existed when treacherous individuals came together on any cause.

"Not mutual benefit," he said quietly, noting Entreri's curious glance his way.

"Explain," Entreri bade him after a long moment of silence.

"I know why you came after me," Drizzt reasoned. "It was not to have me killed, but to kill me yourself. And not just to kill me, but to defeat me in even combat. That possibility seems less likely now, in these tunnels beside merciless Vierna and her desires for simple sacrifice."

"So formidable even when all is lost," Entreri remarked, his superior tones pulling that elusive strand from Drizzt's reach once more. "Defeat you in combat, I will—that is the deal, you see. In a chamber not so far from here, your kin and I will part company, but not until you and I have settled our rivalry."

"Vierna would not let you kill me," Drizzt retorted.

"But she would allow me to defeat you," Entreri answered. "She desires that very thing, desires that your humiliation be complete. After I have settled our business, then she will give you to Lolth . . . with my blessings."

"Come now, my friend," Entreri purred, seeing no response coming from Drizzt, seeing Drizzt's face screwed up in an uncharacteristic pout.

"I am not your friend," Drizzt growled back.

"My kindred, then," Entreri teased, his delight absolute when Drizzt turned an angry glower at him.

"Never."

"We fight," Entreri explained. "We both fight so very well, and fight to win, though our purposes for battle may vary. I have told you before that you cannot escape me, cannot escape who you are."

Drizzt had no answer for that, not in a corridor surrounded by enemies and with his hands tied behind his back. Entreri had indeed made these claims before, and Drizzt had reconciled them, had come to terms with the decisions of his life and with the path he had chosen as his own.

But seeing the obvious pleasure on the evil assassin's face disturbed the honorable drow nonetheless. Whatever else he might do in this seemingly hopeless situation, Drizzt Do'Urden determined then not to give Entreri his satisfaction.

They came to an area of many side passages, winding, scalloped tunnels, worm holes, they seemed, meandering and rolling about in every direction at once. Entreri had said that the room, the parting of ways, was close, and Drizzt knew he was running out of time.

He dove headlong to the floor, tucked his feet in tight, and slipped his arms over them, then brought them back in front, as he rolled to a standing position. By the time he turned back, the ever-alert Entreri already had his sword and dagger in hand, but Drizzt charged him anyway. Weaponless, the drow had no practical chance, but he guessed that Entreri would not strike him down, guessed that the assassin would not so impulsively destroy the even challenge he desperately craved, the very moment Entreri had worked so very hard to achieve.

Predictably, Entreri hesitated, and Drizzt was beyond his half-hearted defenses in a moment, leaping into the air and landing a double-footed kick on Entreri's face and chest that sent the man flying away.

Drizzt bounced back to his feet and rushed toward the entrance to the nearest side tunnel, blocked by a single drow guard. Again Drizzt came on fearlessly, hoping that Vierna had promised incredible torments to anyone who stole her sacrifice—a hope that seemed confirmed when Drizzt glanced back to Vierna, to see her hand holding back Jarlaxle's, the mercenary's fingers clutching a throwing dagger.

The blocking drow fighter, as agile as a cat, punched out at the charging Drizzt, hilt first. But Drizzt, quicker still, snapped his hands straight up, and the ties binding his wrists hooked the fighter's weapon hand and threw his sword harmlessly high. Drizzt slammed into him, body to body, lifting his knee as they came together, and connecting cleanly on his opponent's abdomen. The fighter doubled over and Drizzt, with no time to spare, pushed past him, throwing him down to trip up the next soldier, and Entreri, coming in fast.

Around a bend, down a short expanse, then diving into yet another side passage, Drizzt barely managed to keep ahead of the pursuit—so close were his enemies in fact, that as he turned into the next passage, he heard a quarrel skip along the wall to the side.

Even worse, the drow ranger noted other forms slipping in and out of the openings to the sides of the tunnel. There had been no more than seven dark elves in the corridor with him, but he knew that more than twice that number had accompanied Vierna, not to mention the larger force that had been left behind not so long ago. The missing soldiers were all about, Drizzt knew, flanking and scouting, feeding reports along prescribed routes in silent codes.

Around another bend he went, then another, turning back opposite the first. He scrambled up a short wall, then cursed his luck when the branching corridor atop it sloped back down to the previous level.

Around another bend he saw a flash of heat glowing fiercely and knew it was a signal speculum, a metal plate magically heated on one side, which the dark elves used for signaling. The heated side glowed like a mirror in sunlight to beings using infravision. Drizzt cut down a side passage, realizing that the webs were tightening about him, knowing that his attempt would not succeed.

Then the drider reared up in front of him.

Drizzt's revulsion was absolute, and he backpedaled in spite of the dangers he knew were behind him. To see his brother in such a state! Dinin's bloated torso moved in harmony with the eight scrabbling legs, his face an expressionless death mask.

Drizzt quieted his churning emotions, his need to scream out, and looked for a practical way to get past this obstacle. Dinin had turned his twin axes to their blunt sides, waving them wildly, and his eight legs kicked and bucked, giving Drizzt no obvious opening.

Drizzt had no choice; he spun about, intending to flee back the other way. Vierna, Jarlaxle, and Entreri turned the corner to greet him.

They conversed quietly in the Common tongue. Entreri said something about settling his score then and there, but apparently changed his mind.

Vierna advanced instead, her whip of five living snake heads waving ominously before her.

"If you defeat me, then you can have back your freedom," she teased in the drow tongue, as she tossed Twinkle to the floor at Drizzt's feet. He went for the weapon and Vierna struck, but Drizzt had expected as much and he fell back short of his dropped scimitar, leaving Twinkle just out of reach.

The drider scrambled ahead, an axe clipping Drizzt's shoulder, knocking him backward toward Vierna. The ranger had no other choice now, and dove headlong for his blade, his fingers barely reaching it.

Snake fangs dug into his wrist. Another bite took him on the forearm and three more dove at his face or at his other hand, which was twisted over his grasping hand in a feeble defense. The sting of the bites was vicious, but it was the more insidious poison that defeated Drizzt. He had Twinkle in his grasp, he thought, but he couldn't be certain, since his numbed fingers could no longer feel the weapon's metal.

Vierna's cruel whip lashed out again, five heads biting eagerly into Drizzt's flesh, spreading the waves of numbness throughout his battered form. The merciless priestess of a merciless goddess beat the helpless prisoner a dozen times, her face twisted in absolute, evil glee.

Drizzt stubbornly held consciousness, eyed her with utter contempt, but that only prodded Vierna on, and she would have beaten him to death then and there had not Jarlaxle, and more pointedly, Entreri, come beside her and calmed her.

For Drizzt, his body racked with agony and all hope of survival long flown, it seemed less than a reprieve.

✕ ✕ ✕ ✕ ✕

"Aaargh!" Bruenor wailed. "Me kinfolk!"

Thibbledorf Pwent's reaction to the gruesome scene of seven slaughtered dwarves was even more dramatic. The battlerager floundered to the side of the tunnel and began slamming his forehead against the stone wall. Undoubtedly he would have knocked himself cold had not Cobble quietly reminded him that his hammering could be heard a mile away.

"Killed clean and fast," Catti-brie commented, trying to keep rational and make some sense of this newest clue.

"Entreri," Bruenor growled.

"By all our guesses, if he's truly wearing the face and body of Regis, these dwarves were missing afore he went into these tunnels," Catti-brie reasoned. "Seems the assassin might have bringed some helpers along." The image of the small crossbow bolt played in her mind and she hoped her suspicions would prove false.

"Dead helpers when I get me hands around their murdering throats!" Bruenor promised. He fell to his knees then, hunched over a dead dwarf who had been a close friend.

Catti-brie could not bear the sight. She looked away from her father, to Wulfgar, standing quietly and holding the torch.

Wulfgar's scowl, aimed at her, caught her by surprise.

She studied him for a few moments. "Well, say yer thoughts," she demanded, growing uncomfortable under his unrelenting glare.

"You should not have come down here," the barbarian answered calmly.

"Drizzt is not me friend, then?" she asked, and she was surprised again at how Wulfgar's face crinkled in barely explosive rage at her mention of the dark elf.

"Oh, he is your friend, I do not doubt," Wulfgar replied, his tone dripping with venom. "But you are to be my wife. You should not be in this dangerous place."

Catti-brie's eyes opened wide in disbelief, in absolute outrage, showing the reflections of the torchlight as though some inner fire burned within them. " 'Tis not yer choice to be making!" she cried loudly—so loudly that Cobble and Bruenor exchanged concerned looks and the dwarf king rose from his dead friend and moved toward his daughter.

"You are to be my bride!" Wulfgar reminded her, his volume equally disturbing.

Catti-brie didn't flinch, didn't blink, her determined stare forcing Wulfgar back a step. The resolute young woman almost smiled in spite of her rage, with the knowledge that the barbarian was finally beginning to catch on.

"You should not be here," Wulfgar said again, renewing his strength in his declaration.

"Get yerself to Settlestone, then," Catti-brie retorted, poking a finger into Wulfgar's massive chest. "For if ye're thinking I should not be here to help in finding Drizzt, then ye cannot call yerself a friend of the ranger!"

"Not as much as you can!" Wulfgar snarled back, his eyes glowing angrily, his face twisted and one fist clenched tightly at his side.

"What're ye saying?" Catti-brie asked, sincerely confused by all of this, by Wulfgar's irrational words and erratic behavior.

Bruenor had heard enough. He stepped between the two, pushing Catti-brie gently back and turning to squarely face the barbarian who had been like a son to him.

"What are ye saying, boy?" the dwarf asked, trying to keep calm, though he wanted nothing more than to punch Wulfgar in the blabbering mouth.

Wulfgar didn't look at Bruenor at all, just reached over the sturdy but short dwarf to point accusingly at Catti-brie. "How many kisses have you and the drow shared?" he bellowed.

Catti-brie nearly fell over. "What?" she shrieked. "Ye've lost yer senses. I never—"

"You lie!" Wulfgar roared.

"Damn yer words!" howled Bruenor and out came his great axe. He whipped it across, forcing Wulfgar to leap back and slam hard against the corridor wall, then chopped with it, forcing the barbarian to dive aside. Wulfgar tried to block with the torch, but Bruenor slapped it from his hand. Wulfgar tried to get to Aegis-fang, which he had slipped under his backpack when they had found the dead dwarves, but Bruenor came at him relentlessly, never actually striking, but forcing him to dodge and dive, to scramble across the hard stone.

"Let me kill him for ye, me king!" Pwent cried, rushing up and misunderstanding Bruenor's intentions.

"Get ye back!" Bruenor roared at the battlerager, and all the others were amazed, Pwent most among them, at the sheer force of Bruenor's voice.

"I been playing along with yer stupid actions for tendays now," Bruenor said to Wulfgar, "but I've no more time for ye. Ye speak out whatever's got yer hair up here and now, or shut yer stupid mouth and keep it shut until we find Drizzt and get us outta these stinking tunnels!"

"I have tried to remain calm," Wulfgar retorted, and it seemed more a plea, since the barbarian was still on his knees from dodging Bruenor's dangerously close swings. "But I cannot ignore the insult to my honor!" As though realizing his subservient appearance, the proud barbarian leaped to his feet. "Drizzt met with Catti-brie before the drow returned to Mithral Hall."

"Who telled ye that?" Catti-brie demanded.

"Regis!" Wulfgar shouted back. "And he told me that your meeting was filled with more than words!"

"It's a lie!" Catti-brie cried.

Wulfgar started to respond in kind, but he saw Bruenor's wide smile and heard the dwarf's mocking laughter. The head of the dwarf's axe dropped to the floor, Bruenor placing both hands on his hips and shaking his head in obvious disbelief.

"Ye stupid . . . ," the dwarf muttered. "Why don't ye use whatever part o' yer body's not muscle and think o' what ye just said? We're here because we're guessing that Regis ain't Regis!"

Wulfgar scrunched his face up in confusion, realizing only then that he had not reconsidered the halfling's volatile accusations in light of the recent revelations.

"If ye're feeling as stupid as ye look, then ye're feeling the way ye ought to feel," Bruenor remarked dryly.

The sudden revelations hit Wulfgar as surely as Bruenor's axe ever could. How many times had Regis spoken with him alone these last few days? And what, he considered carefully, had been the content of those many meetings? For the first time, perhaps, Wulfgar realized what he had done in his chamber against the drow, truly realized that he would have killed Drizzt if the drow had not won the battle. "The halfling . . . Artemis Entreri, tried to use me in his evil plans," Wulfgar reasoned. He remembered a swirling myriad of sparkling reflections, the facets of a gemstone, inviting him down into its depths. "He used his pendant on me—I cannot be sure, but I think I remember . . . I believe he used . . ."

"Be sure," Bruenor said. "I knowed ye a long time, lad, and never have I knowed ye to act so durned stupid. And meself as well. To send the halfling along with Drizzt into this unknown region!"

"Entreri tried to get me to kill Drizzt," Wulfgar went on, trying to fathom it all.

"Tried to get Drizzt to kill yerself, ye mean," Bruenor corrected. Catti-brie snorted, unable to contain her pleasure and her gratitude that Bruenor had put the boastful barbarian in his place.

Wulfgar scowled at her from over Bruenor's shoulder.

"You did meet with the drow," he stated.

"That's me own business," the young woman replied, not giving in an inch to Wulfgar's lingering jealousy.

The tension began to mount again—Catti-brie could see that while the revelations about Regis had taken some of the bite from Wulfgar's growl, the protective man still did not wish her there, did not wish his bride-to-be in a dangerous situation. Stubborn and proud, Catti-brie remained more insulted than flattered.

She didn't get the chance to vent her rage, though, not then, for Cobble came shuffling back to the group, begging them all to be silent. Only then did Bruenor and the others notice that Pwent was no longer present.

"Noise," the cleric explained quietly, "somewhere farther along in the deeper tunnels. Let us pray to Moradin that whatever is down there did not hear the clamor of our own stupidity!"

Catti-brie looked to the fallen dwarves, looked to see Wulfgar do likewise, and knew that the barbarian, like her, was reminding himself that Drizzt was in serious danger. How petty their arguments seemed to her then, and she was ashamed.

Bruenor sensed her despair, and he came over to her and draped his arm across her shoulders. "Had to be said," he offered comfortingly. "Had to be brought out and cleared afore the fighting begins."

Catti-brie nodded her agreement and hoped that the fighting, if there was to be any, would begin soon.

She hoped, too, with all her heart, that the next battle would not be fought as vengeance for the death of Drizzt Do'Urden.

13

BROKEN VOWS

A single torch was lit; Drizzt realized it was part of the deal. Entreri probably was not yet comfortable enough with his newly acquired infravision to battle Drizzt without any light source at all.

When his eyes shifted into the normal spectrum of light, Drizzt studied the medium-sized chamber. While its walls and ceiling were quite naturally formed, curving and with jutting angles and small stalactites hanging down, it had two wooden doors—recently constructed, Drizzt believed, most probably arranged by Vierna as part of the deal with Entreri. A drow soldier flanked the doors on each side and a third stood between them, right in front of each portal.

Twelve dark elves were in the room now, including Vierna and Jarlaxle, but the drider was nowhere to be found. Entreri was talking with Vierna; Drizzt saw her give the assassin the belt holding Drizzt's two scimitars.

There also was a curious alcove in the room, a single step in from the back wall of the main area and with a waist-high ledge, the top covered by a blanket and a soldier leaning on it, his sword and dagger drawn.

A chute? Drizzt wondered.

Entreri had said this was the place where he and the dark elves would part company, but Drizzt doubted that the assassin, his business finished, meant to go back the way they had come, anywhere near Mithral Hall. With only one other door apparent in the chamber, perhaps there did indeed loom a chute under that blanket, a way to the open and twisted corridors of the deeper Underdark.

Vierna said something that Drizzt did not hear, and Entreri came over to him, bearing his weapons. A drow soldier moved behind Drizzt and released his bonds, and he slowly brought his hands back in front of him, his shoulders aching from their long stay in the awkward position and from the residual pain of Vierna's vicious beating.

Entreri dropped the scimitar belt at Drizzt's feet and took a cautious step backward. Drizzt looked down to his weapons curiously, unsure of what he should do.

"Pick them up," Entreri instructed.

"Why?"

The question seemed to slap the assassin across the face. A great scowl flashed for just an instant, then was replaced by Entreri's typically emotionless expression.

"That we might learn the truth," he answered.

"I know the truth," Drizzt replied calmly. "You wish to distort it, that you might keep hidden, even from yourself, the folly of your wretched existence."

"Pick them up," the assassin snarled, "or I will kill you where you stand."

Drizzt knew the threat was a hollow one. Entreri would not kill him, not until the assassin had tried to redeem himself in honest battle. Even if Entreri did strike to slay him, Drizzt figured Vierna would intervene. Drizzt was too important to Vierna; sacrifices to the Spider Queen were not readily accepted unless given by drow priestesses.

Drizzt finally did bend and retrieve his weapons, feeling more secure as he belted them on. He knew that the odds in this room were impossible, whether he had the scimitars or not, but he was experienced enough to realize that opportunities were fleeting and often came when least expected.

Entreri drew his slender sword and jeweled dagger, then crouched low, his thin lips widening into an eager smile.

Drizzt stood easily, shoulders slumped, scimitars still in their sheaths.

The assassin's sword cut across, nicking Drizzt on the tip of his nose, forcing his head to flinch to the side. He reached up casually with his thumb and index finger, pinching the flow of blood.

"Coward," Entreri teased, feigning a straightforward lunge and still circling.

Drizzt turned to keep him directly in front, not bothered at all by the ridiculous insult.

"Come now, Drizzt Do'Urden," Jarlaxle intervened, drawing looks from both Drizzt and Entreri. "You know you are doomed, but will you not gain any pleasure in killing this human, this man who has done you and your friends so many wrongs?"

"What have you to lose?" Entreri asked. "I cannot kill you, only defeat you—that is my deal with your sister. But you may kill me. Surely Vierna would not intervene, and might even be amused, at the loss of a simple human life."

Drizzt remained impassive. He had nothing to lose, they claimed. What they apparently did not understand was that Drizzt Do'Urden did not fight when he had nothing to lose, only when he had something to gain, only when the situation necessitated that he fight.

"Draw your weapons, I beg," Jarlaxle added. "Your reputation is considerable and I would dearly love to see you at play, to see if you are truly the better of Zaknafein."

Drizzt, trying to play it calm, trying to hold fast to his principles, could not hide his grimace at the mention of his dead father, reputably the finest weapons master ever to draw swords in Menzoberranzan. In spite of himself, he drew his scimitars, Twinkle's angry blue glow -sincerely reflecting the welling rage that Drizzt Do'Urden could not fully suppress.

Entreri came on suddenly, fiercely, and Drizzt reacted with warrior instincts, scimitars ringing against sword and dagger, defeating every attack. Taking the offensive before he even realized what he was doing, acting solely on instinct, Drizzt began turning full circles, his blades flowing around him like the edging of a screw, every turn bringing them in at his opponent from different heights and different angles.

Entreri, confused by the unconventional routine, missed as many parries as he hit, but his quick feet kept him out of reach. "Always a surprise," the assassin admitted grimly, and he winced jealously at the approving sighs and comments from the dark elves lining the room.

Drizzt stopped his spin, ending perfectly squared to the assassin, blades low and ready.

"Pretty, but to no avail," Entreri cried and rushed forward, sword flying low, dagger slicing high. Drizzt twisted diagonally, one blade knocking the sword aside, the other forming a barrier that the dagger could not get through as it cut harmlessly high.

Entreri's dagger hand continued a complete circuit—Drizzt noticed that he flipped the blade over in his fingers—while his sword darted and thrust, this way and that, to keep Drizzt busy.

Predictably, the assassin's dagger hand came about, dipping down to the side, and he whipped the dagger free.

Ringing like a hammer on metal, Twinkle darted into the missile's path and batted it away, knocking it across the room.

"Well done!" Jarlaxle congratulated, and Entreri, too, backed off and nodded his sincere approval. With just a sword now, the assassin came in more cautiously, loosing a measured strike.

His surprise was absolute when Drizzt did not parry, when Drizzt missed not one deflection, but two and the thrusting weapon slipped past the scimitar defense. The sword quickly recoiled, never reaching its vulnerable mark. Entreri came in again, feigning another straightforward thrust, but snapping the weapon back and around instead.

He had Drizzt beaten, could have ripped the drow's shoulder, or neck, apart with that simple feint! Drizzt's knowing smile stopped him, though. He turned his sword to its flat edge and smacked it against the drow's shoulder, doing no real damage.

Drizzt had let him through, both times, was now mocking the assassin's precious fight with a pretense of inability!

Entreri wanted to scream out his protests, let all the other dark elves in on Drizzt's private game. The assassin decided that this battle was too personal, though, something that should be settled between himself and Drizzt, and not through any intervention by Vierna or Jarlaxle.

"I had you," he teased, using the rocky Dwarvish language in the hopes that those drow around him, except, of course, for Drizzt, would not understand it.

"You should have ended it, then," Drizzt replied calmly, in the Common surface language, though he spoke the Dwarvish tongue perfectly well. He wouldn't give Entreri the satisfaction of removing this to a personal level, would keep the fight public and ridicule it openly with his actions.

"You should have fought better," Entreri retorted, reverting to the Common tongue. "For the sake of your halfling friend, if not for yourself. If you kill me, then Regis will be free, but if I walk from here . . ." He let the threat hang in the air, but it grew less ominous indeed when Drizzt laughed at it openly.

"Regis is dead," the drow ranger reasoned. "Or will be, whatever the outcome of our battle."

"No—" Entreri began.

"Yes," Drizzt interrupted. "I know you better than to fall prey to your unending lies. You have been too blinded by your rage. You did not anticipate every possibility."

Entreri came in again, easily, not making any blatant strikes that would make this continuing charade obvious to the gathered dark elves.

"He is dead," Drizzt asked as much as stated.

"What do you think?" Entreri snapped back, his snarling tone making the answer seem obvious.

Drizzt realized the shift in tactics, understood that Entreri now was attempting to enrage him, to make him fight in anger.

Drizzt remained impassive, let fly a few lazy attack routines that Entreri had little trouble defeating—and that the assassin could have countered to devastating effect if he had so desired.

Vierna and Jarlaxle began to speak in whispers, and Drizzt, thinking they might grow tired of the charade, came on more forcefully, though still with measured and ineffective strikes. Entreri gave a slight but definite nod to show that he was beginning to understand. The game, the subtle and silent undercurrents and communications, were getting personal, and Drizzt, as much as Entreri, did not want Vierna intervening.

"You will savor your victory," Entreri promised uncharacteristically, a leading phrase.

"It will come as no gain," Drizzt replied, a response the assassin was obviously fully beginning to expect. Entreri wanted to win this fight, wanted to win it even more badly because Drizzt did not seem to care. Drizzt knew that Entreri was not stupid, though, and while he and Drizzt were of similar fighting skills, their motivations surely separated them. Entreri would fight with all his heart against Drizzt just to prove something, but Drizzt honestly felt that he had nothing to prove, not to the assassin.

Drizzt's failings in this fight were not a bluff, were not something that Entreri could call him on. Drizzt would lose, taking more satisfaction in not giving Entreri the enjoyment of honest victory.

And, as his actions now revealed, the assassin was not completely surprised by the turn of events.

"Your last chance," Entreri teased. "Here, you and I part company. I leave through the far door, and the drow go back *down* to their dark world."

Drizzt's violet eyes flicked to the side, to the alcove, for just a moment, his movement revealing to Entreri that he had not missed the emphasis on the word "down," had not missed the obvious reference to the cloth—covered chute.

Entreri rolled to the side suddenly, having worked himself around close enough to retrieve his lost dagger. It was a daring maneuver, and again a revealing move to his opponent, for with Drizzt's fighting so obviously lacking, Entreri had no need to take the risk of going for his lost weapon.

"Might I rename your cat?" Entreri asked, shifting his waist to reveal a large belt pouch, the black statuette obvious through the open edges of its bulging top.

The assassin came in fast and hard with a four-strike routine, any of which could have slipped through, had he pressed them, to nick at Drizzt.

"Come now," Entreri said loudly. "You can fight better than that! I have witnessed your skills too many times—in these very tunnels even—to think you might be so easily defeated!"

At first, Drizzt was surprised that Entreri had so obviously let their private communication become so public, but Vierna and the others probably had figured by that point that Drizzt was not fighting with all his heart. Still, it seemed a curious comment—until Drizzt came to understand the hidden meanings of the assassin's words, the assassin's bait. Entreri had referred to their fighting in these tunnels, but those battles had not been against each other. On that unusual occasion, Drizzt Do'Urden and Artemis Entreri had fought together, side by side and back-to-back, out of simple desire to survive against a common enemy.

Was it to be that way again, here and now? Was Entreri so desperate for an honest fight against Drizzt that he was offering to help him defeat Vierna and her gang? If that happened, and they won, then any following battle between Drizzt and Entreri would certainly give Drizzt something to gain, something to honestly fight for. If together he and Entreri could win out, or get away, the ensuing battle between them would dangle Drizzt's freedom before his eyes with only Artemis Entreri standing in his way.

"*Tempus!*" The cry stole the contemplations from both opponents, forced them to react to the obvious forthcoming distraction.

They moved in perfect harmony, Drizzt whipping his scimitar across and the assassin dropping his defenses, falling back and turning his hip to stick out his belt pouch. Twinkle cut through the pouch cleanly, spilling the figurine of the enchanted panther onto the floor.

The door, the same door through which they had entered the chamber, blew apart under the weight of flying Aegis-fang, hurling the drow standing before it to the floor.

Drizzt's first instinct told him to go to the door, to try to link up with his friends, but he saw that possibility blocked by the many scrambling dark elves. The other door, too, offered no hope, for it opened immediately with the onset of commotion, the drider Dinin leading the drow charge into the room.

The chamber flashed bright with magical light; groans erupted from every corner. A silver-streaking arrow sizzled in through the blasted portal, catching the same unfortunate dark elf in midstep as he rose from beneath the blasted door. It hurtled him backward against the far wall, where he stuck in place, arrow through chest and stone.

"Guenhwyvar!"

Drizzt could not wait and see if his call to the panther had been heard, could not wait for anything at all. He rushed for the alcove, the single drow holding guard near it raising his weapons in surprised defense.

Vierna cried out; Drizzt felt a dagger cut into his wide-flying cloak and knew it was hanging just an inch from his thigh. Straight ahead he ran, dipping one shoulder at the last moment as though he meant to dive sidelong.

The drow guard dipped right along with him, but Drizzt came back up straight before his adversary, his scimitars crossing high, at neck level.

The guarding drow couldn't get his sword and dirk up fast enough to deflect the lightning-fast attack, couldn't reverse his momentum and fall back to the side out of harm's way.

Drizzt's fine-edged weapons crossed over his throat.

Drizzt winced, tucked his bloodied blades in close and dove headlong for the cloth, hoping that there was indeed an opening under it and hoping that it was a chute, not a straight drop.

14

OVERMATCHED

Thibbledorf Pwent rushed along a side passage, running parallel and twenty feet to the right of the tunnel where he had split from his companions to go out on a prudent flanking maneuver. He heard the crash of the warhammer-blasted door, the sizzle of Catti-brie's arrows, and cries from several places, even a growl or two, and cursed his luck for being caught out of fun's way.

Torch leading, the battlerager eagerly spun around a sharp left-hand corner, hoping to get back with the others before the fighting was through. He pulled up short, considering a curious figure, apparently as surprised to see him as he was to see it.

"Hey, now," the battlerager asked, "is yerself Bruenor's pet drow?"

Pwent watched the slender elf's hand come up and heard the *click* as a hand-held crossbow fired, the quarrel striking Pwent's sturdy armor and slipping through one of the many cracks to draw a drop of blood on the dwarf's shoulder.

"Guess not!" the happy Pwent cried, charging wildly with every word and tossing his torch aside. He dipped his head, putting his helmet spike in line, and the dark elf, seeming amazed at the sheer viciousness of this one's attack, fumbled to get his sword out and ready.

Pwent, barely able to see but fully expecting the defense, whipped his head from side to side as he neared the target, parrying the sword away. He stood up straight again without slowing and launched himself at his opponent, barreling into the stunned dark elf with abandon.

They crashed against the wall, the drow still holding his balance, and holding Pwent up in the air, not knowing what to make of this unusual, hugging battle style.

The dark elf shook his sword hand free, while Pwent simply began to shake, his sharp-ridged armor digging lines in the drow's chest. The elf squirmed frantically, his own desperate actions only aiding the battlerager's convulsive attack. Pwent freed one arm and punched wildly, glove nail poking holes in the smooth ebony skin. The dwarf kneed and elbowed, bit the drow on the nose, and punched him in the side.

"Aaaaaargh!" The growling scream erupted all the way from Pwent's belly, reverberating unsteadily from his flapping lips as he furiously whipped himself about. He felt the warmth of his enemy's flowing blood, the sensation only driving him, driving the most wild battlerager, to further heights of ferocity.

"*Aaaaaargh!*"

The drow went down in a heap, Pwent atop him, still convulsing wildly. In a few moments, his enemy no longer squirmed, but Pwent did not relinquish his advantage.

"Ye sneaky elven thing!" he roared, repeatedly slamming his forehead into the dark elf's face.

Quite literally, the battlerager, with his sharpened armor and spiked joints, shook the unfortunate drow apart.

Pwent finally let go and hopped to his feet, pulling the limp body to a sitting position and leaving it slumped against the wall. The battlerager felt the pain in his back and realized that the drow's sword had hit him at least once. Of more concern, though, was the numbness flowing down Pwent's arm, poison spreading from the crossbow wound. Rage mounting once more, Pwent dipped his pointy helmet, scraped a boot across the stone several times for traction, and rushed ahead, spearing the already dead foe through the chest.

When he jumped back this time, the dead drow toppled to the floor, warm blood spreading out under the body's ripped torso.

"Hope ye wasn't Bruenor's pet drow," the battlerager remarked, suddenly realizing that the whole incident might have been an honest mistake. "Oh, well, can't be helped now!"

⚔ ⚔ ⚔ ⚔ ⚔

Cobble, magically inspecting for traps ahead, instinctively winced as another arrow zipped past his shoulder, its silver shine diminishing into the brightly lit chamber beyond. The dwarven cleric forced himself back to his work, wanting to be done quickly, that he might loose the charge of Bruenor and the others.

A crossbow quarrel dove into his leg, but the cleric wasn't too concerned about its buglike sting or its poison, for he had placed enchantments upon himself to slow the drug's effects. Let the dark elves hit him with a dozen such bolts; it would be hours before Cobble fell to sleep.

His scan of the corridor complete, with no immediate traps discerned, Cobble called back to others, who were impatient and already moving toward him. When the cleric looked back, though, in the dim light emanating from the enemies' chamber, he noticed something curious across the floor: metallic shavings.

"Iron?" he whispered. Instinctively his hand went into his bulging pouch, filled with enchanted pebble bombs, and he went into a defensive crouch, holding his free hand out behind him to warn the others back.

When he focused within the general din of the sudden battle, he heard a female drow voice, chanting, spell-casting.

The dwarf's eyes widened in horror. He turned back, yelling for his friends to be gone, to run away. He, too, tried to run, his boots slipping across the smooth stone, so fast did his little legs begin to move.

He heard the drow spell-caster's crescendo.

The iron shavings immediately became an iron wall, unsupported and angled, and it fell over poor Cobble.

There came a great gush of wind, the great explosion of tons of iron slamming against the stone floor, and flying spurts of pressure-squeezed blood and gore whipped back into the faces of the three stunned companions. A hundred small explosions, a hundred tiny sparkling bursts, rang hollowly under the collapsed iron wall.

"Cobble," Catti-brie breathed helplessly.

The magical light in the distant chamber went away. A ball of darkness appeared just outside the chamber door, blocking the end of the passageway. A second ball of darkness came up, just ahead of the first, and a third after that, covering the back edge of the fallen iron wall.

"Get charging!" Thibbledorf Pwent cried at them, coming back into the corridor and rushing past his hesitating friends.

A ball of darkness appeared right in front of the battlerager, stopping him short. Handcrossbow after handcrossbow clicked unseen behind the blackness, sending stinging little darts whipping out.

"Back!" Bruenor cried. Catti-brie loosed another arrow; Pwent, hit a dozen times, began to slump to the stone. Wulfgar grabbed him by the helmet spike and started away after the red-bearded dwarf.

"Drizzt," Catti-brie moaned quietly. She dropped low to one knee, firing another arrow and another after that, hoping that her friend would not come running out of the room into danger's path.

A quarrel, oozing poison, clicked against her bow and bounced harmlessly wide.

She could not stay.

She fired one more time, then turned and ran after her father and the others, away from the friend she had come to rescue.

⚔ ⚔ ⚔ ⚔ ⚔

Drizzt fell a dozen feet, slammed against the sloping side of the chute, and careened along a winding and swiftly descending way. He held tightly to his scimitars; his greatest fear was that one of them would get away from him and wind up cutting him in half as he bounced along.

He did a complete loop, managed to somersault to put his feet out in front of him, but inadvertently got turned back around at the next vertical drop, the ending slam nearly knocking him unconscious.

Just as he thought he was gaining control, was about to turn himself about once more, the chute opened up diagonally into a lower passageway. Drizzt rifled out, though he kept the presence of mind to hurl his scimitars to their respective sides, clear of his tumbling body.

He hit the floor hard, rolled across, and slammed his lower back into a jutting boulder.

Drizzt Do'Urden lay very still.

He did not consider the pain—fast changing to numbness—in his legs; he did not inspect the many scrapes and bruises the tumbling ride had given him. He did not even think of Entreri, and at that agonizing moment, one notion overruled even the loyal dark elf's compelling fears for his friends.

He had broken his vow.

When young Drizzt had left Menzoberranzan, after killing Masoj Hun'ett, a fellow dark elf, he had vowed that he would never again kill a drow. That vow had held up, even when his family had come after him in the wilds of the Underdark, even when he had battled his eldest sister. Zaknafein's death had been fresh in his mind and his desire to kill the wicked Briza as great as any desire he had ever felt. Half mad from grief, and from ten years of surviving in the merciless wilds, Drizzt still had managed to hold to his vow.

But not now. There could be no doubt that he had killed the guardsman at the top of the chute; his scimitars had cut fine lines, a perfect **X** across the dark elf's throat.

It had been a reaction, Drizzt reminded himself, a necessary move if he meant to be free of Vierna's gang. He had not precipitated the violence, had not asked for it in any way. He could not reasonably be blamed for taking whatever action necessary to escape from Vierna's unjust court, and to aid his friends, coming in against powerful adversaries.

Drizzt could not reasonably be blamed, but as he lay there, the feeling gradually returning to his bruised legs, Drizzt's conscience could not escape the simple truth of the matter.

He had broken his vow.

⚔ ⚔ ⚔ ⚔ ⚔

Bruenor led them blindly through the twisting maze of corridors, Wulfgar right behind and carrying the snoring Pwent (and getting a fair share of cuts from the battlerager's sharp-ridged armor!). Catti-brie slipped along at his side, pausing whenever pursuit seemed close behind to launch an arrow or two.

Soon the halls were quiet, save the group's own clamor—too quiet, by the frightened companions' estimation. They knew how silent Drizzt could move, knew that stealth was the dark elves' forte.

But where to run? They could hardly figure out where they were in this little known region, would have to stop and take time to get their bearings before they could make a reasonable guess on how to get back to familiar territory.

Finally, Bruenor came upon a small side passage that branched three ways, each fork branching again just a short way in. Following no predetermined course, the red-bearded dwarf led them in, left then right, and soon they came into a small chamber, goblin worked and with a large slab of stone just inside the low entryway. As soon as they all were in, Wulfgar leaned the slab against the portal and fell back against it.

"Drow!" Catti-brie whispered in disbelief. "How did they come to Mithral Hall?"

"Why, not how," Bruenor corrected quietly. "Why are the elf's kin in me tunnels?

"And what?" Bruenor continued grimly. He looked to his daughter, his beloved Catti-brie, and to Wulfgar, the proud lad he had helped mold into so fine a man, a sincerely grave expression on the dwarf's bristling cheeks. "What have we landed ourself into this time?"

Catti-brie had no answer for him. Together the companions had battled many monsters, had overcome incredible obstacles, but these were dark elves, infamous drow, deadly, evil, and apparently with Drizzt in their clutches, if indeed he still drew breath. The mighty friends had gone in fast and strong to rescue Drizzt, had struck the dark elves by surprise. They had been simply overmatched, driven back without catching more than a fleeting glimpse of what might have been their lost friend.

Catti-brie looked to Wulfgar for support, saw him staring her way with the same helpless expression Bruenor had placed over her.

The young woman looked away, having neither the time nor the inclination to berate the protective barbarian. She knew that Wulfgar continued to be worried more for her than for himself—she could not chastise him for that—but Catti-brie, the fighter, knew, too, that if Wulfgar was looking out for her, his eyes would not be focused on the dangers ahead.

In this situation, she was a liability to the barbarian, not for any lack of fighting skills or survival talents, but because of Wulfgar's own weakness, his inability to view Catti-brie as an equal ally.

And with dark elves all about them, how badly they needed allies!

⚔ ⚔ ⚔ ⚔ ⚔

Using innate powers of levitation, the pursuing drow soldier eased himself out of the chute, his gaze immediately locking on the slumped form under the thick cloak across the corridor.

He pulled out a heavy club and rushed across, crying out with joy for the rewards that certainly would come his way for recapturing Drizzt. The club came down, sounding unexpectedly sharp as it banged off the solid stone under Drizzt's cloak.

As silent as death, Drizzt came down from his perch above the chute exit, right behind his adversary.

The evil drow's eyes widened as he realized the deception, remembered then the stone lying opposite the chute.

Drizzt's first instincts were to strike with the hilt of his scimitar; his heart asked him to honor his vow and take no more drow lives. A well-placed blow might drop this enemy and render him helpless. Drizzt could then bind him and strip him of his weapons.

If Drizzt were alone in these tunnels, if it simply were a matter of his desire to escape Vierna and Entreri, he would have followed the cry of his merciful heart. He could not ignore his friends above, though, no doubt struggling against those enemies he had left behind. He could not chance that this soldier, recovered, would bring harm to Bruenor or Wulfgar or Catti-brie.

Twinkle came in point first, slicing through the doomed drow's backbone and heart, driving out the front of his chest, the blade's blue glow showing a reddish tint.

When he pulled the scimitar back out, Drizzt Do'Urden had more blood on his hands.

He thought again of his imperiled friends and gritted his teeth, determined, if not confident, that the blood would wash away.

What turmoil I felt when first I broke my most solemn, principle-intentioned vow: that I would never again take the life of one of my people. The pain, a sense of failure, a sense of loss, was acute when I realized what wicked work my scimitars had done.

The guilt faded quickly, though—not because I came to

CAT AND MOUSE

excuse myself for any failure, but because I came to realize that my true failure was in making the vow, not in breaking it. When I walked out of my homeland, I spoke the words out of innocence, the naivete of unworldly youth, and I meant them when I said them, truly. I came to know, though, that such a vow was unrealistic, that if I pursued a course in life as defender of those ideals I so cherished, I could not excuse myself from actions dictated by that course if ever the enemies showed themselves to be drow elves.

Quite simply, adherence to my vow depended on situations completely beyond my control. If, after leaving Menzoberranzan, I had never again met a dark elf in battle, I never would have broken my vow. But that, in the end, would not have made me any more honorable. Fortunate circumstances do not equate to high principles.

When the situation arose, however, that dark elves threatened my dearest friends, precipitated a state of warfare against people who had done them no wrong, how could I, in good conscience, have kept my scimitars tucked away? What was my vow worth when weighed against the lives of Bruenor, Wulfgar, and Catti-brie, or when weighed against the lives of any innocents, for that matter? If, in my travels, I happened upon a drow raid against surface elves, or against a small village, I know beyond any doubts that I would have joined in the fighting, battling the unlawful aggressors with all my strength.

In that event, no doubt, I would have felt the acute pangs of failure and soon would have dismissed them, as I do now.

I do not, therefore, lament breaking my vow— though it pains me, as it always does, that I have had to kill. Nor do I regret making the vow, for the declaration of my youthful folly caused no subsequent pain. If I had attempted to adhere to the unconditional words of that declaration, though, if I had held my blades in check for a sense of false pride, and if that inaction had subsequently resulted in injury to an innocent person, then the pain in Drizzt Do'Urden would have been more acute, never to leave.

There is one more point I have come to know concerning my declaration, one more truth that I believe leads me farther along my chosen road in life. I said I would never again kill a drow elf. I made the assertion with little knowledge of the many other races of the wide world, surface and Underdark, with little understanding that many of these myriad peoples even existed. I would never kill a drow, so I said, but what of the svirfnebli, the deep gnomes? Or the halflings, elves, or dwarves? And what of the humans?

I have had occasion to kill men, when Wulfgar's barbarian kin invaded Ten-Towns. To defend those innocents meant to battle, perhaps to kill, the aggressor humans. Yet that act, unpleasant as it may have been, did not in any way affect my most solemn vow, despite the fact that the reputation of human-kind far outshines that of the dark elves.

To say, then, that I would never again slay a drow, purely because they and I are of the same physical heritage, strikes me now as wrong, as simply racist. To place the measure of a living being's worth above that of another simply because that being wears the same color skin as I belittles my principles. The false values embodied in that long-ago vow have no place in my world, in the wide world of countless physical and cultural differences. It is these very differences that make my journeys exciting, these very differences that put new colors and shapes on the universal concept of beauty.

I now make a new vow, one weighed in experience and proclaimed with my eyes open: I will not raise my scimitars except in defense: in defense of my principles, of my life, or of others who cannot defend themselves. I will not do battle to further the causes of false prophets, to further the treasures of kings, or to avenge my own injured pride.

And to the many gold-wealthy mercenaries, religious and secular, who would look upon such a vow as unrealistic, impractical, even ridiculous, I cross my arms over my chest and declare with conviction: I am the richer by far!

—Drizzt Do'Urden

THE PLAY'S THE THING

Silence! Vierna's delicate fingers signaled the command repeatedly in the intricate drow hand code.

Two handcrossbows clicked as their bowstrings locked into a ready position. Their drow wielders crouched low, staring at the broken door.

From behind them, across the small chamber, there came a slight hiss as an arrow magically dissolved, releasing its dark elf victim, who slumped to the floor at the base of the wall. Dinin, the drider, shifted away from the fallen drow, his hard-skinned legs clacking against the stone.

Silence!

Jarlaxle crawled to the edge of the blasted door, cocked an ear to the impenetrable blackness of the conjured globes. He heard a slight shuffling and drew out a dagger, signaling to the crossbowmen to stand ready.

Jarlaxle stood them down when the figure, his scout, crawled out of the darkness and entered the room.

"They have gone," the scout explained as Vierna rushed over to join the mercenary leader. "A small group, and smaller still with one crushed under your most excellent wall." Both Jarlaxle and the guard bowed low in respect to Vierna, who smiled wickedly in spite of the sudden disaster.

"What of Iftuu?" Jarlaxle asked, referring to the guard they had left watching the corridor where the trouble had begun.

"Dead," the scout replied. "Torn and ripped."

Vierna turned sharply on Entreri. "What do you know of our enemies?" she demanded.

The assassin eyed her dangerously, remembering Drizzt's warnings against alliances with his kin. "Wulfgar, the large human, hurled the hammer that broke the door," he answered with all confidence. Entreri looked to the two fast-cooling forms splayed out across the stone floor. "You can blame the deaths of those two on Catti-brie, another human, female."

Vierna turned to Jarlaxle's scout and translated what Entreri had told her into the drow tongue. "Were either of these under the wall?" the priestess asked of the scout.

"Only a single dwarf," the drow replied.

Entreri recognized the drow word for the bearded folk. "Bruenor?" he asked rhetorically, wondering if they had inadvertently assassinated the king of Mithral Hall.

"Bruenor?" Vierna echoed, not understanding.

"Head of Clan Battlehammer," Entreri explained. "Ask him," he bade Vierna, indicating the scout, and he grabbed at his clean-shaven chin with his hand, as though stroking a beard. "Red hair?"

Vierna translated, then looked back, shaking her head. "There was no light out there. The scout could not tell."

Entreri silently cursed himself for being so foolish. He just couldn't get used to this heat-sight, where shapes blurred indistinctly and colors were based on amount of heat, not reflecting hues.

"They are gone and are no longer our concern," Vierna said to Entreri.

"You would let them escape after killing three in your entourage?" Entreri started to protest, seeing where this line of reasoning would take them—and not so sure he liked that path.

"Four are dead," Vierna corrected, her gaze leading the assassin to Drizzt's victim lying beside the revealed chute.

"Ak'hafta went after your brother," Jarlaxle quickly put in.

"Then five are dead," Vierna replied grimly, "but my brother is below us and must get through us to rejoin his friends."

She began talking to the other drow in their native tongue, and though he had not come close to mastering the language, Entreri realized that Vierna was organizing the departure down the chute in pursuit of Drizzt.

"What of my deal?" he interrupted.

Vierna's reply was to the point. "You have had your fight. We allow you your freedom, as agreed."

Entreri acted pleased by that reply; he was worldly enough to understand that to show his outrage would be to join the other fast-cooling forms on the floor. But the assassin was not about to accept his losses so readily. He looked around frantically, searching for some distraction, some way to alter the apparently done deal.

Entreri had planned things perfectly to this point, except that, in the commotion, he hadn't been able to get into the chute behind Drizzt. Alone down below, he and his arch-rival would have had the time to settle things once and for all, but now the prospect of getting Drizzt alone for a fight seemed remote and moving farther away with every second.

The wily assassin had wormed his way through more precarious predicaments than this—except, he prudently reminded himself, that this time he was dealing with dark elves, the masters of intrigue.

⚔ ⚔ ⚔ ⚔ ⚔

"Shhh!" Bruenor hissed at Wulfgar and Catti-brie, though it was Thibbledorf Pwent, deep in sleep and snoring as only a dwarf can snore, who was making all the noise. "I think I heared something!"

Wulfgar angled the battlerager's helmet point against the wall, slapped one hand under Pwent's chin, closing the battlerager's mouth, then clamped his fingers around Pwent's wide nose. Pwent's cheeks bulged weirdly a couple of times, and a strange squeaky-smacking type of noise came out from somewhere. Wulfgar and Catti-brie exchanged looks; Wulfgar even bent to the side, wondering if the outrageous dwarf had just snored out of his ears!

Bruenor cringed at the unexpected blast, but was too intent to turn and scold his companions. From down the corridor there came another slight shuffling noise, barely perceptible, and then another, still closer. Bruenor knew they soon would be found; how could they escape when both Wulfgar and Catti-brie needed torchlight to navigate the twisting tunnels?

Another scuffle came, just outside the small chamber.

"Well, come on out, ye pointy-eared orc kisser!" the frustrated and frightened dwarf king roared, hopping through the small opening around the slab Wulfgar had used to partially block the passageway. The dwarf lifted his great axe high above his head.

He saw the black form, as expected, and tried to chop, but the form was by him too quickly, springing into the small chamber with hardly a whisper of noise.

"What?" the startled dwarf, axe still high, balked, swinging himself around and nearly spinning to the floor.

"Guenhwyvar!" he heard Catti-brie call from beyond the slab.

Bruenor rambled back into the chamber just as the mighty panther opened its maw wide and let drop the valuable figurine—along with the ebon-skinned hand of the unfortunate dark elf who had grabbed for it when Guenhwyvar had made the break.

Catti-brie gave a sour look and kicked the disembodied hand far from the figurine.

"Damn good cat," Bruenor admitted, and the rugged dwarf was truly relieved that a new and powerful ally had been found.

Guenhwyvar roared in reply, the mighty growl reverberating off the tunnel walls for many, many yards in every direction. Pwent opened his weary eyes at the sound. Wide those dark orbs popped indeed when the battlerager caught sight of the six-hundred-pound panther sitting only three feet away!

Adrenaline soaring to new heights, the wild battlerager flubbed out sixteen words at once as he scrambled and kicked to regain his footing (inadvertently kneeing himself in the shin and drawing some blood). He almost got there, until Guenhwyvar apparently realized his intent and absently slapped a paw, claws retracted, across his face.

Pwent's helmet rung out a clear note as he rebounded off the wall, and he thought then that another nap might do him good. But he was a battlerager, he reminded himself, and by his estimation, a most wild battle was about to be fought. He produced a large flask from under his cloak and took a hearty swig, then whipped his head about to clear the cobwebs, his thick lips flapping noisily. Somehow seeming revived, the battlerager set his feet firmly under him for a charge.

Wulfgar grabbed him by the helmet point and hoisted him off the floor, Pwent's stubby legs pumping helplessly.

"What're ye about?" the battlerager snarled in protest, but even Thibbledorf Pwent had his bluster drained, along with the blood in his face, when Guenhwyvar looked to him and growled, ears flattened and pearly teeth bared.

"The panther is a friend," Wulfgar explained.

"The wh—who is . . . the damn cat?" Pwent stuttered.

"Damn good cat," Bruenor corrected, ending the debate. The dwarf king went back to watching the hall then, glad to have Guenhwyvar beside them, knowing that they would need everything Guenhwyvar could give, and perhaps a little bit more.

⚔ ⚔ ⚔ ⚔ ⚔

Entreri noticed one wounded drow propped against the wall, being tended by two others, the bandages they applied quickly growing hot with spilling blood. He recognized the injured dark elf as one that had reached for the statuette soon after Drizzt had called for the cat, and the reminder of Guenhwyvar gave the assassin a new ploy to try.

"Drizzt's friends will pursue you, even down the chute," Entreri remarked grimly, interrupting Vierna once more.

The priestess turned to him, obviously concerned about his reasoning—as was the mercenary standing beside her.

"Do not underestimate them," Entreri continued. "I know them, and they are loyal beyond anything in the dark elf world—except of course for a priestess's loyalty to the Spider Queen," he added, in deference to Vierna because he didn't want his skin peeled off as a drow trophy. "You plan now to go after your brother, but even if you catch him at once and head with all speed for Menzoberranzan, his loyal friends will chase you."

"They were but a few," Vierna retorted.

"But they will be back with many more, especially if that dwarf under the wall was Bruenor Battlehammer," Entreri countered.

Vierna looked to Jarlaxle for confirmation of the assassin's claims, and the more worldly dark elf only shrugged and shook his head in helpless ignorance.

"They will come better equipped and better armed," Entreri went on, his new scheme formulating, his banter building momentum. "With wizards, perhaps. With many clerics, surely. And with that deadly bow"—he glanced at the body near the wall—"and the barbarian's warhammer."

"The tunnels are many," Vierna reasoned, seemingly dismissing the argument. "They could not follow our course." She turned, as if her argument had satisfied her, to go back to formulating her initial plans.

"They have the panther!" Entreri growled at her. "The panther that is the dearest friend of all to your brother. Guenhwyvar would pursue you to the Abyss itself if there you carried Drizzt's body."

Again distressed, Vierna looked to Jarlaxle. "What say you?" she demanded.

Jarlaxle rubbed a hand across his pointy chin. "The panther was well known among the scouting groups when your brother lived in the city," he admitted. "Our raiding party is not large—and apparently five fewer now."

Vierna turned back sharply on Entreri. "You who seem to know the ways of these people so well," she prompted with more than a bit of sarcasm, "what do you suggest we do?"

"Go after the fleeing band," Entreri replied, pointing to the blackened corridor beyond the blasted door. "Catch them and kill them before they can get back to the dwarven complex and muster support. I will find your brother for you."

Vierna eyed him suspiciously, a look Entreri most certainly did not like.

"But I am awarded another fight against Drizzt," he insisted, baiting the plan with some measure of believability.

"When we are rejoined," Vierna added coldly.

"Of course." The assassin swept into a low bow and leaped for the chute.

"And you will not go alone," Vierna decided. She gave a look to Jarlaxle, and he motioned for two of his soldiers to accompany the assassin.

"I work alone," Entreri insisted.

"You die alone," Vierna corrected, "against my brother in the tunnels, I mean," she added in softer, teasing tones, but Entreri knew that Vierna's promise had nothing at all to do with her brother.

He saw little point in continuing to argue with her, so he just shrugged and motioned for one of the dark elves to lead the way.

Actually, having a drow with the levitational powers beneath him made the ride down the dangerous chute much more comfortable for the assassin.

The leading dark elf came out into the lower corridor first, Entreri landing nimbly behind him and the second drow coming in slowly behind the assassin. The first drow shook his head in apparent confusion and kicked lightly at the prone body, but Entreri, wiser to Drizzt's many tricks, pushed the dark elf aside and slammed his sword down onto the apparent corpse. Gingerly, the assassin turned the dead drow over, confirming that it was not Drizzt in a clever disguise. Satisfied, he slipped his sword away.

"Our enemy is clever," he explained, and one of his companions, understanding the surface language, nodded, then translated for the other drow.

"That is Ak'hafta," the dark elf explained to Entreri. "Dead, as Vierna predicted." He led his drow companion toward the assassin.

Entreri was not at all surprised to find the slain soldier right below the chute. He, above anyone else in Vierna's party, understood how deadly their opponent might be, and how efficient. Entreri did not doubt that the two accompanying him, skilled fighters but inexperienced concerning the ways of their enemy, would have little chance of catching Drizzt. By Entreri's estimation, if these unknowing dark elves had come through the chute alone, Drizzt might well have cut them down already.

Entreri smiled privately at the thought, then smiled even more widely as he realized that these two didn't understand their ally, let alone their enemy.

His sword jabbed to the side as the trailing drow passed by him, neatly skewering both of the unfortunate elf's lungs. The other drow, quicker than Entreri had expected, wheeled about, handcrossbow leveled and ready.

A jeweled dagger came first, nicking the drow's weapon hand hard enough to deflect the shot harmlessly wide. Undaunted, the dark elf snarled and produced a pair of finely edged swords.

It never ceased to amaze Entreri how easily these dark elves fought so well with two weapons of equal length. He whipped his thin leather belt from his breeches and looped it double in his free left hand, waving it and his sword out in front to keep his opponent at bay.

"You side with Drizzt Do'Urden!" the drow accused.

"I do not side with you," Entreri corrected. The drow came at him hard, swords crossing, going back out wide, then crossing in close again, forcing Entreri to bat them with his own sword, then promptly retreat. The attack was skilled and deceptively quick, but Entreri immediately recognized the primary difference between this drow and Drizzt, the subtle level of skill that elevated Drizzt—and Entreri, for that matter—from these other fighters. The double crossing attack had been launched as finely as any Entreri had ever seen, but during the few seconds he had taken to execute the maneuver, the dark elf's defenses had not been aligned. Like so many other fine fighters, this drow was a one-way warrior, perfect on the attack, perfect on defense, but not perfect on both at the same time.

It was a minor thing; the drow's quickness compensated so well that most fighters would never have noticed the apparent weakness. But Entreri was not like most fighters.

Again the drow pressed the attack. One sword darted straight for Entreri's face, only to be swatted aside at the last moment. The second sword came in low, right behind, but Entreri reversed his weapon's momentum and batted the thrusting tip to the ground.

Furiously the drow came on, swords flying, diving for any apparent opening, only to be intercepted by Entreri's sword or hooked and pulled wide by the leather belt.

And all the while the assassin willingly retreated, bided his time, waited for the sure kill.

The swords crossed, went out wide, and crossed again as they charged for Entreri's midsection, the dark elf repeating his initial attack.

The defense had changed, the assassin moving with sudden, terrifying speed.

Entreri's belt looped around the tip of the sword in the drow's right hand, which was crossed under the other, and then the assassin jerked back to his left, pulling the swords tightly together and forcing them both to the side.

The doomed dark elf started backing at once, and both swords easily came free of the awkward belt, but the drow, his defensive balance forfeited in the offensive routine, needed a split second to recover his posture.

Entreri's flashing sword didn't take that split second. It dove hungrily into the drow's exposed left flank, tip twisting as it weaved its way into the soft flesh beneath the rib cage.

The wounded warrior fell back, his belly wickedly torn, and Entreri did not pursue, instead falling into his balanced battle stance.

"You are dead," he said matter-of-factly as the drow struggled to stand and keep his swords level.

The drow could not dispute the claim, and could not hope, through the blinding and burning agony, to stop the assassin's impending attack. He dropped his weapons to the floor and announced, "I yield."

"Well spoken," Entreri congratulated him, then the assassin drove his sword into the foolish dark elf's heart.

He cleaned the blade on his victim's *piwafwi*, retrieved his precious dagger, then turned to regard the empty tunnel, running fairly straight both ways beyond the range of his somewhat limited infravision. "Now, dear Drizzt," he said loudly, "things are as I had planned." Entreri smiled, congratulating himself for so perfectly manipulating such a dangerous situation.

"I have not forgotten the sewers of Calimport, Drizzt Do'Urden!" he shouted, his anger suddenly boiling over. "Nor have I forgiven!"

Entreri calmed at once, reminding himself that his rage had been his weakness on that occasion when he had battled Drizzt in the southern city.

"Take heart, my respected friend," he said quietly, "for now we can begin our play, as it was always meant to be."

⚔ ⚔ ⚔ ⚔ ⚔

Drizzt circled back to the chute area soon after Entreri had departed. He knew at once what had transpired when he saw the two new corpses, and he realized that none of this had occurred by accident. Drizzt had baited Entreri in the chamber above, had refused to play the game the way the assassin had desired. But Entreri apparently had anticipated Drizzt's reluctance and had prepared, or improvised, an alternative plan.

Now he had Drizzt, just Drizzt, in the lower tunnels, one against one. Now, too, if it came to combat, Drizzt would fight with all his heart, knowing that to win was to at least have some chance of freedom.

Drizzt nodded his head, silently congratulating his opportunistic enemy.

But Drizzt's priorities were not akin to Entreri's. The dark elf's main concern was to find his way through, to circle back around, that he might rejoin his friends and aid them in their peril. To Drizzt, Entreri was no more than another piece of the larger threat.

If he happened to encounter Entreri on his way, though, Drizzt Do'Urden meant to finish the game.

16
DRAWING LINES

I am not pleased," Vierna remarked, standing with Jarlaxle in the tunnel near the conjured iron wall, with poor Cobble's squashed body underneath.

"Did you believe it would be so easy?" the mercenary replied. "We have entered the tunnels of a fortified dwarven complex with a contingent of barely fifty soldiers. Fifty against thousands.

"You will recapture your brother," Jarlaxle added, not wanting Vierna to get overly anxious. "My troops are well-trained. Already I have dispatched nearly three dozen, the entire Baenre complement, to the single corridor leading out of Mithral Hall proper. None of Drizzt's allies shall enter that way, and his trapped friends shall not escape."

"When the dwarves learn we are about, they will send an army," Vierna reasoned grimly.

"If they learn," Jarlaxle corrected. "The tunnels of Mithral Hall are long. It will take our adversaries some time to muster a significant force—days perhaps. We will be halfway to Menzoberranzan, with Drizzt, before the dwarves are organized."

Vierna paused for a long while, considering her next course of action. There were only two ways up from the bottom level: the chute in the nearby room and winding tunnels some distance to the north. She looked to the room and moved into it to regard the chute, wondering if she had done wrong in sending only three after Drizzt. She considered ordering her entire force—a dozen drow and the drider—down in pursuit.

"The human will get him," Jarlaxle said to her, as though he had read her mind. "Artemis Entreri knows our enemy better than we; he has battled Drizzt across the wide expanses of the surface world. Also, he wears still the earring, that you might track his progress. Up here we have Drizzt's friends, only a handful by my scouts' reckoning, to deal with."

"And if Drizzt eludes Entreri?" Vierna asked.

"There are only two ways up," Jarlaxle reminded her again.

Vierna nodded, her decision made, and walked across to the chute. She took a small wand out of a fold in her ornamental robes and closed her eyes, beginning a soft chant. Slowly and deliberately, Vierna traced precise lines across the opening, the tip of the wand spewing sticky filament. Perfectly, the priestess outlined a spiderweb of thin strands, covering the opening. Vierna stepped back to examine her work. From a pouch she produced a packet of fine dust, and beginning a second chant, she sprinkled it over the web. Immediately the strands thickened and took on a black and silvery luster. Then the shine faded and the warmth of the enchantment's energy cooled to room temperature, leaving the strands practically invisible.

"Now there is one way up," Vierna announced to Jarlaxle. "No weapon can cut the strands."

"To the north, then," Jarlaxle agreed. "I have sent a handful of runners ahead to guard the lower tunnels."

"Drizzt and his friends must not join," Vierna instructed.

"If Drizzt sees his friends again, they will already be dead," the cocky mercenary replied with all confidence.

⚔ ⚔ ⚔ ⚔

"There may be another way into the room," Wulfgar offered. "If we could strike at them from both sides—"

"Drizzt is gone from the place," Bruenor interrupted, the dwarf fingering the magical locket and looking to the floor, sensing that his friend was somewhere below them.

"When we've killed all our enemies, yer friend'll find us," Pwent reasoned.

Wulfgar, still holding the battlerager off the ground by his helmet spike, gave him a little shake.

"I've no heart for fighting drow," Bruenor replied, and he gave both Catti-brie and Wulfgar concerned sidelong glances, "not like this. We're to keep away from them if we can, hit at 'em only when we find the need."

"We could go back and get Dagna," Wulfgar offered, "and sweep the tunnels clean of dark elves."

Bruenor looked to the maze of corridors that would bring him back to the dwarven complex, considering the path. He and his friends could lose perhaps an hour in working their roundabout way to Mithral Hall, and several hours more in rounding up a sizable force. Those were several hours that Drizzt probably didn't have to spare.

"We go for Drizzt," Catti-brie decided firmly. "We got yer locket to point us right, and Guenhwyvar will take us to him."

Bruenor knew Pwent would readily agree to anything that opened the possibility for a fight, and Guenhwyvar's fur was ruffled, the panther anxious, sleek muscles tense. The dwarf looked to Wulfgar and nearly spat at the lad for the worried, condescending expression splayed across his face as he studied Catti-brie.

Without warning, Guenhwyvar froze in place, issuing a low, quiet growl. Catti-brie immediately doused the low-burning torch and crouched low, using the red-glowing dots of dwarven eyes to keep her bearings.

The group came closer together, Bruenor whispering for the others to remain in the side chamber while he went out to see what the cat had sensed.

"Drow," he explained when he returned a moment later, Guenhwyvar at his side, "just a handful, moving fast and to the north."

"Handful o' dead drow," Pwent corrected. The others could hear the battlerager eagerly rubbing his hands together, the shoulder joints of his armor scraping too noisily.

"No fighting!" Bruenor whispered as loudly as he dared, and he grabbed Pwent's arms to stop the motion. "I'm thinking that this group might have an idea of where to find Drizzt, that they're out looking for him, but we got no chance of keeping up with them without light."

"And if we put up the torch, we'll find ourselves fighting soon enough," Catti-brie reasoned.

"Then light the damned torch!" Pwent said hopefully.

"Shut yer mouth," Bruenor answered. "We're going out slow and easy—and ye keep the torch, make it two torches, ready for lighting at the first signs of a fight," he told Wulfgar. Then he motioned to Guenhwyvar to lead them, bidding the cat to keep the pace slow.

Pwent shoved his large flask into Catti-brie's hand as soon as they exited the tunnel. "Take a hit o' this," he instructed, "and pass it about."

Catti-brie blindly moved her hands about the item, finally discerning it to be a flask. She gingerly sniffed the foul-smelling liquid and started to hand it back.

"Ye'll think the better of it when a drow elf puts a poisoned dart into yer backside," the crude battlerager explained, patting Catti-brie on the rump. "With this stuff flowing about yer blood, no poison's got a chance!"

Reminding herself that Drizzt was in trouble, the young woman took a deep draw on the flask, then coughed and stumbled to the side. For a moment, she saw eight dwarf eyes and four cat eyes staring at her, but the double vision soon went away and she passed the flask on to Bruenor.

Bruenor handled it easily, offering a sigh and a profound, though quiet, belch when he had finished. "Warms yer toes," he explained to Wulfgar when he passed it along.

After Wulfgar had recovered, the group set off, Guenhwyvar's padded paws quietly marking the way, and Pwent's armor squealing noisily with every eager stride.

⚔ ⚔ ⚔ ⚔ ⚔

Forty battle-ready dwarves followed the stomping boots of General Dagna through the lower mines of Mithral Hall to the final guardroom.

"We'll make right for the goblin hall," the general explained to his charges, "and branch out from there." He went on to instruct the door guards, setting up a series of tapping signals and leaving directions for any subsequent troops that came in, explicitly commanding that no dwarves in groups less than a dozen were to be allowed into the new sections.

Then stern Dagna put his soldiers in line, placed himself bravely and proudly at their lead, and moved through the opened door. Dagna really didn't believe that Bruenor was in peril, figured that perhaps a pocket of goblin resistance or some other minor inconvenience remained to be cleared. But the general was a conservative commander, preferring overkill to even odds, and he would take no chances where Bruenor's safety was concerned.

The heavy footsteps of hard boots, clanking armor, and even a grumbling war chant now and then heralded the approach of the force, and every third dwarf held a torch. Dagna had no reason to believe that this formidable force would need stealth, and hoped that Bruenor and any other allies who might be wandering about down here would be able to find the boisterous troupe.

Dagna didn't know about the dark elves.

The dwarves' rolling pace soon got them near the first intersection, in sight of the piled ettin bones from Bruenor's long-ago kill. Dagna called for "side watchers" and started forward, meaning to continue straight ahead, straight for the main chamber of the goblin battle. Before he even reached the side passage, Dagna slowed his troops and called for a measure of quiet.

The general glanced all about curiously, nervously, as he began to cross through the wider intersection. His warrior instincts, honed over three centuries of fighting, told him that something wasn't right; the thick layers of hair on the back of his neck tingled weirdly.

Then the lights went out.

At first, the dwarf general thought something had extinguished the torches, but he quickly realized, from the clamor arising behind him and from the fact that his infravision, when he was able to refocus his eyes, was utterly useless, that something more ominous had occurred.

"Darkness!" cried one dwarf.

"Wizards!" howled another.

Dagna heard his companions jostle about, heard something whistle by his ear, followed by the grunt of one of his undercommanders standing immediately behind him. Instinctively, the general began to backtrack, and only a few short strides later, he emerged from the globe of conjured darkness to find his charges rushing all around. A second globe of darkness had split the dwarven force almost exactly in half, and those in front of the spell were calling out to those caught within it and to those behind, trying to muster some organization.

"Wedge up!" Dagna cried above the tumult, demanding the most basic of dwarven battle formations. "It's a spell of darkness, nothing more!" Beside the general, a dwarf clutched at his chest, pulled out some small type of dart that Dagna did not recognize, and tumbled to the ground, snoring before he ever hit the stone.

Something nicked at Dagna's shin, but he ignored it and continued his commands, trying to orient the group into a single and unified fighting unit. He sent five dwarves rushing out to the right flank, around the darkness globe and into the beginning of the intersecting passage.

"Find me that damned wizard!" he ordered them. "And find out what in the Nine Hells we're fighting against!"

Dagna's frustration only fueled his ire, and soon he had the remaining dwarven force in a tight wedge formation, ready to punch through the initial darkness globe.

The five flanking dwarves rambled into the side passage. Once convinced that no enemies lurked down that way, they quickly looped about the blackness globe, heading for the narrow opening between the sphere and the entryway farther along the main corridor.

Two dark forms emerged from the shadows, dropping to one knee before the dwarves and leveling small crossbows.

The leading dwarf, hit twice, stumbled but still managed to call for the charge. He and his four companions launched themselves at their enemy in full flight, taking no notice until it was too late that other enemies, other dark elves, were levitating above and dropping down all about them.

"What the . . ." a dwarf gasped as a drow nimbly landed beside him, smashing in the side of his skull with a powerfully enchanted mace.

"Hey, yerself ain't Drizzt!" another dwarf managed to remark a split second before a drow sword sliced his throat.

The group leader wanted to call for a retreat, but even as he started to yell, the floor rushed up and swallowed him. It was a fine bed for a sleeping dwarf, but from this slumber, the vulnerable soldier would never awaken.

In the span of five seconds, only two dwarves remained. "Drow! Drow!" they cried out in warning.

One went down heavily, three arrows in his back. He struggled to get back to his knees, but two dark elves fell over him, hacking with their swords.

The remaining dwarf, rushing back to rejoin Dagna, found himself facing only a single opponent. The drow poked forward with his slender sword; the dwarf accepted the hit and returned it with a vicious axe chop to the side, blasting the drow's arm and rending his fine suit of chain mail.

Past the falling drow and into the darkness the terrified dwarf ran, bursting out the other side of the enchanted globe, right into the front ranks of Dagna's slow-moving wedge.

"Drow!" the frightened dwarf cried once more.

A third globe of darkness came up, connecting the other two. A volley of handcrossbow bolts whipped through, and behind it came the dark elves, skilled at fighting without the use of their eyes.

Dagna realized that clerics would be needed to battle this dark elven magic, but when he tried to call for a retreat, it came out instead as a most profound yawn.

Something hard hit him on the side of the head, and he felt himself falling.

Amidst the chaos and the impenetrable darkness, the wedge could not be maintained, and the surprised dwarves had little chance against a nearly even number of skilled and prepared dark elves. The dwarves wisely broke ranks, many keeping the presence of mind to reach down and grab a fallen kin, and rushed back the way they had come.

The rout was on, but the dwarves were not novices to battle, and there was not a coward among them. As soon as they got out of the darkened areas of tunnel, several took it upon themselves to reorganize the band. Pursuit was hot—there could be no thoughts of turning back to do full battle—but burdened by nearly ten snoozing dwarves, Dagna among them, the slower force could not hope to outrun the quicker drow.

A call went up for blockers and there came no shortage of volunteers. When it sorted out a moment later, the dwarves ran on, leaving six brave soldiers standing shield to shield in the corridor to cover the retreat.

"Run on or those who've fallen will have died in vain!" cried one of the new commanders.

"Run on for the sake of our missing king!" cried another.

Those in the back ranks of the fleeing troupe looked often over their stocky shoulders to view their blocking comrades—until a globe of darkness enveloped the defensive line.

"Run on!" came a common cry, from those fleeing and from the brave blockers alike.

The fleeing dwarves heard the joining of battle as the dark elves hit their stubborn, blocking comrades. They heard the clang of steel against steel, heard the grunts of solid hits and glancing blows. They heard the shriek of a wounded drow and smiled grimly.

They did not look back, but bowed their heads forward and ran on, each vowing silently to toast the lost companions. The blockers would not break ranks and join them in their flight; they would hold the line, hold the enemy back until their lifeless bodies fell to the stone. It was all done in loyalty to their fleeing kin, an act of supreme, valiant sacrifice, dwarf for dwarf.

On ran the dwarves, and if one tripped on the stone, four others paused to help him get back up again. If one's burden of a sleeping kinsman became too cumbersome, another willingly took over the load.

One younger dwarf sprinted ahead of the main host and began tap-tapping his hammer against the stone walls in the appointed signal for the door guards. By the time he arrived at the tunnel's end, the great barrier was already cracked open, and it spread wide when the truth of the rout became apparent.

The dwarven force piled into the guardroom, some remaining just inside the doorway to coax on any possible stragglers. They kept the door open until the last minute, until a globe of darkness blocked the very end of the tunnel and a handcrossbow quarrel cut through it and took down another soldier.

The tunnel was shut and sealed, and the count showed that twenty-seven of the original forty-one had escaped, with more than a third of them sleeping soundly.

"Get the whole damned army!" one of the dwarves suggested.

"And the clerics," added another, lifting Dagna's limp head to accentuate his point. "We're needing clerics to stop the poisons and to keep the damned lights on!"

The resourceful dwarves soon determined a pecking order and an order of business. Half the force stayed with the sleepers and the guards; the other half ran to the far corners of Mithral Hall, shouting the call to arms.

FRIENDLY BURDEN

He felt so very vulnerable with his scimitars tucked away, and often paused to tell himself that he was being incredibly foolhardy. The potential cost—the lives of his friends—prodded Drizzt on, though, and he cautiously, quietly, placed hand over hand, inching his way up the winding and treacherous chute. Years ago, when he, too, was a creature of the Underdark, Drizzt had been able to levitate and could have managed the chute much more easily. But that ability, apparently somehow linked to the strange magical emanations of the deepest regions, had flown from Drizzt soon after he had stepped onto Toril's surface.

He hadn't realized how far he had fallen and silently thanked his goddess, Mielikki, that he had survived the plummet! He put a hundred crawling feet behind him, some of the going easy along sloping stretches, other parts nearly vertical. As nimble as any thief, the drow stubbornly climbed on.

What had happened to Guenhwyvar? Drizzt worried. Had the panther come to his hurried call? Had one of the drow, the opportunistic Jarlaxle, perhaps, simply scooped up the dropped figurine to claim the panther as his own?

Scaling hand over hand, Drizzt neared the chute opening. The blanket had not been replaced, and the room above was eerily quiet. Drizzt knew the silence meant little where his dark elf kin were concerned. He had led drow scouting parties that had covered fifty miles of rough tunnel without a whisper of noise. Rightly fearful, Drizzt imagined a dozen dark elves encircling the small chute, weapons drawn, awaiting their prisoner's foolish return.

But Drizzt had to go up. For the sake of his imperiled friends, Drizzt had to block his fear that Vierna and the others were still in the room.

He sensed danger as his hand inched upward, reaching for the lip. He saw nothing, had no practical, plausible warning, save the silent shouts of his warrior instincts.

Drizzt tried to dismiss them, but his hand inevitably moved more slowly. How many times had his insight—he could call it luck—saved him?

Sensitive fingers slid gingerly up the stone; Drizzt resisted his anxious urge to shoot his hand up, grab the lip and hoist himself over, forcing the play of whatever peril awaited him. He stopped, felt something, barely perceptible, against the tip of his middle digit.

He could not retract his hand!

As soon as the initial moment of fear passed, Drizzt realized the truth of the spiderweb trap and held himself steady. He had witnessed the many uses of magical webs in Menzoberranzan; the First House of the city was actually encircled by a weblike fence of unbreakable strands. And now, though only a single finger was barely touching the magical strands, Drizzt was caught.

He remained perfectly still, perfectly quiet, concentrating his muscle movements so that his weight came more fully against the nearly vertical wall. Gradually he maneuvered his free hand to his cloak, first going for a scimitar, then wisely changing his mind and reaching instead for one of the tiny quarrels he had taken from the dead dark elf in the corridor below.

Drizzt froze at the sound of drow voices above, in the room.

He couldn't make out half their words, but he discerned that they were talking about him—and about his friends! Catti-brie, Wulfgar, and whoever else was with them apparently had escaped.

And the panther was running free; Drizzt heard several remarks, fearful warnings, about the "devil cat."

More determined than ever, Drizzt inched his free hand back toward Twinkle, thinking that he must try to cut through the magical barrier, must get up from the chute and rush to his friends' aid. The moment of desperation was fleeting, however, lasting only as long as it took Drizzt to realize that if Vierna had sealed this chute with the bulk of her force still above it, then there must be another path, not too far, from level to level.

The drow voices receded, and Drizzt took another moment to solidify his precarious perch. He then worked the quarrel free of his cloak, rubbing it against the stone, then against his clothing in an effort to get all of the insidious sleeping poison from its tip. Gingerly he reached his hand up toward the trapped finger, bit his lip to keep from crying out, and jabbed the quarrel under the skin and worked a tear.

Drizzt could only hope he had removed all of the poison, that he would not fall asleep and tumble, probably to his death, back down the chute. Finding a solid grip with his free hand, bracing himself for the jolt and the pain, he jerked his arm hard, tearing the top, trapped skin clean of his finger.

He nearly swooned for the pain, nearly lost his balance, but somehow he held on, brought the finger to his mouth to suck out and spit out the possibly poisoned blood.

He came back into the lower corridor five minutes later, scimitars in hand, eyes darting this way and that in search of his archenemy and in an effort to make some guess about which way he should travel. He knew that Mithral Hall was somewhere back to the east, but realized that his captives had been taking him primarily north. If there was indeed a second way up, it likely was beyond the chute, farther to the north.

He replaced Twinkle in its sheath—not wanting its glow to reveal him—but held his other scimitar out in front of him as he made his stealthy way along the corridor. There were few side passages, and Drizzt was glad for that, realizing that any direction choice he might make at this point, with no feasible landmarks to guide him, would be mere guesswork.

Then he came to an intersection and caught a glimpse of a fleeting, shadowy figure darting along an apparently parallel tunnel to his right flank.

Drizzt knew instinctively that it was Entreri, and it seemed obvious that Entreri would know the other way out of this level.

To the right Drizzt went, in crouched, measured steps, now the pursuer, not the pursued.

He paused when he got to the parallel tunnel, took a deep breath, and peeked around. The shadowy figure, moving quickly, was far ahead, turning unexpectedly right once more.

Drizzt considered this course change with more than a little suspicion. Shouldn't Entreri have kept to the left, kept close to the course he thought Drizzt was taking?

Drizzt suspected then that the assassin knew he was being followed and was leading Drizzt to a place Entreri considered favorable. Drizzt couldn't afford the delay of heeding his suspicions, though, not while the fate of his overmatched friends lay in the balance. To the right he went, quickly, only to find that he had not gained any ground, that Entreri's course had led them both into quite a maze of crisscrossing passageways.

With the assassin no longer in sight, Drizzt concentrated on the floor. To his relief, he was close enough behind so that the residual heat of Entreri's passing footsteps was still visible, though barely, to his superior infravision. He realized that he was vulnerable, head down, with little idea of how many seconds ahead of him the assassin might be, or how many seconds behind, Drizzt knew, for he felt certain that Entreri had led him to this region so that he could double back and come at Drizzt from the back.

His pace barely matched Entreri's as the narrow tunnels gave way to wider natural chambers. The footsteps remained obscure and fast cooling, but Drizzt somehow managed.

A small cry ahead gave him pause. It wasn't Entreri, Drizzt knew, but he believed he was not yet close enough to link up with his friends.

Who had it been, then?

Drizzt used his ears instead of his eyes and sorted through the tiny echoes to follow a barely audible whimpering. He was glad then for his drow warrior training, for years of studying echo patterns in winding tunnels.

The whimpering grew louder; Drizzt knew its source was just around the bend, in what appeared to him from his angle to be a small, oval side chamber.

One scimitar drawn, another hand on Twinkle's hilt, the drow dashed around the corner.

Regis!

Battered and torn, the plump halfling lay sprawled against the far wall, his hands tightly bound, a thin gag pulled tightly across his mouth, and his cheeks caked with blood. Drizzt's first instincts sent him running forward for his injured friend, but he skidded to a halt, fearing another of clever Entreri's many tricks.

Regis noticed him, looked desperately to him.

Drizzt had seen that expression before, recognized its sincerity beyond anything a disguised Entreri, mask or no mask, could hope to duplicate. He was at the halfling's side in a moment, cutting the bonds, tearing free the tight gag.

"Entreri . . ." the halfling began breathlessly.

"I know," Drizzt said calmly.

"No," Regis retorted sharply, demanding the drow's attention. "Entreri . . . was just . . ."

"He passed through here no more than a minute ahead of me," Drizzt finished, not wanting Regis to struggle any more than necessary for his labored breath.

Regis nodded, his round eyes darting about as though he expected the assassin to charge back in and slay them both.

Drizzt was more concerned with an examination of the halfling's many wounds. Taken individually, each of them appeared superficial, but together they added up to a severe condition indeed. Drizzt let Regis take a few moments to get the blood circulating through his recently untied hands and feet, then tried to get the halfling to stand.

Regis shook his head immediately; a great wave of dizziness knocked him from his feet, and he would have hit the stone floor hard had not Drizzt been there to catch him.

"Leave me," Regis said, showing an unexpected measure of altruism.

Indomitable, the drow smiled comfortingly and hoisted Regis to his side.

"Together," he explained casually. "I would not leave you any more than you would leave me."

The assassin's trail was, by then, too cool to follow, so Drizzt had to go on blindly, hoping he would stumble on some clue as to the location of the passage to the higher level. He drew out Twinkle now, instead of his other blade, and used the light to help him avoid any small jags in the floor, that he might keep Regis's walk more comfortable. All measure of stealth had been lost anyway, with the groaning halfling held at his side, Regis's feet more often scraping than stepping as Drizzt pulled him along.

"I thought he would . . . kill . . . me," Regis remarked after he had caught and held enough of his hard-to-find breath to utter a complete sentence.

"Entreri kills only when he perceives it to his advantage," Drizzt replied.

"Why did he . . . bring me along?" Regis honestly wondered. "And why . . . did he let you find me?"

Drizzt looked at his little friend curiously.

"He led you to me," Regis reasoned. "He . . ." The halfling slumped heavily, but Drizzt's strong arm continued to hold him upright.

Drizzt understood exactly why Entreri had led him to Regis. The assassin knew that Drizzt would carry Regis along—by Entreri's measure, that was exactly the difference between him and Drizzt. Entreri perceived that very compassion to be the drow's weakness. In all truth, the stealth had been lost, and now Drizzt would have to play this game of cat and mouse by Entreri's rules, showing as much attention to his burdening friend as to the game. Even if luck showed Drizzt the way up to the next level, he would have a difficult time getting to his friends before Entreri caught up to him.

Even more important than the physical burden, Drizzt realized, Entreri had given Regis back to him to ensure an honest fight. Drizzt would play out their inevitable battle wholeheartedly, with no intention of running away, with Regis lying helpless somewhere nearby.

Regis slipped in and out of consciousness over the next half hour, Drizzt uncomplaining and carrying him along, every now and then switching arms to balance the load. The drow ranger's skill in the tunnels was considerable, and he felt confident that he was making headway in sorting through the maze.

They came into a long, straight passage, a bit higher-roofed and wider than the many they had crossed. Drizzt placed Regis down easily against a wall and studied the patterns in the rock. He noticed a barely perceptible incline in the floor, rising to the south, but the fact that they, traveling north, were going slightly down did not disturb the drow at all.

"This is the main corridor of the region," he decided at length. Regis looked to him, puzzled.

"It once ran fast with water," Drizzt explained, "probably cutting through the mountain to exit at some distant waterfall to the north."

"We're going down?" Regis asked.

Drizzt nodded. "But if there is a passageway back up to the lower levels of Mithral Hall, it will likely lie along this route."

"Well done," came a reply from somewhere in the distance. A slender form stepped out of a side passage, just a few dozen feet ahead of Drizzt and Regis.

Drizzt's hand went instinctively inside his cloak, but putting more trust in his scimitars, he retracted it immediately as the assassin approached.

"Have I given to you the hope you so desired?" Entreri teased. He said something under his breath—a call to his weapon probably, for his slender sword began glowing fiercely in bluish-green hues, revealing the assassin's graceful form in dim outline as he sauntered toward his waiting enemy.

"A hope you will come to regret," Drizzt replied evenly.

The whiteness of Entreri's teeth gleamed in the aqua light as he answered through a wide smile. "Let us see."

18

COMMON DANGER

His noise will bring the whole of the Underdark on our heads," Catti-brie whispered to Bruenor, referring to the battlerager's continually squealing armor. Pwent, realizing the same, had gone far ahead of the others and was gradually outpacing them, for Catti-brie and Wulfgar, human and not blessed with eyes that could see in the infrared spectrum, had to nearly crawl along, one hand on Bruenor at all times. Only Guenhwyvar, sometimes leading, more often moving as a silent emissary between Bruenor and the battlerager, maintained any semblance of communication between the principals of the small troupe.

Another grating squeal from ahead brought a grimace to Bruenor's face. He heard Catti-brie's resigned sigh and agreed with it. Even more so than his daughter, the experienced Bruenor understood the futility of it all. He thought of making Pwent remove the noisy armor but dismissed the notion immediately, realizing that even if all four of them walked naked, their footfalls would sound as clearly as a marching drumbeat to the sensitive ears of the enemy dark elves.

"Put up the torch," he instructed Wulfgar.

"Surely ye cannot," Catti-brie argued.

"They're all about us," Bruenor replied. "I can sense the dogs, and they'll see us as well without the light as with. We've no chance of getting through without another fight—I'm knowing that now—so we might as well fight 'em on terms better suited for our side."

Catti-brie turned her head about, though she could see nothing at all in the pitch blackness. She sensed the truth of Bruenor's observations, though, sensed that dark and silent shapes were moving all about them, closing a noose about the doomed party. A moment later she had to blink and squint when Wulfgar's torch came up in a fiery blaze.

Flickering shadows replaced absolute blackness; Catti-brie was surprised at how uncut this tunnel was, much more natural and rough than those they had left. Soil mixed with the stone along the ceiling and walls, giving the young woman less confidence in the stability of the place. She became acutely aware of the hundreds of tons of earth and rock above her head, aware that a slight shift in the stone could instantly crush her and her companions.

"What're ye about?" Bruenor asked her, seeing her obvious anxiety. He turned to Wulfgar and saw the barbarian growing similarly unnerved.

"Unworked tunnels," the dwarf remarked, coming to understand. "Ye're not so used to the wild depths." He put a gnarly hand on his beloved daughter's arm and felt beads of cold sweat.

"Ye'll get used to it," the dwarf gently promised. "Just remember that Drizzt is alone down here and needing our help. Keep yer mind on that fact and ye'll fast forget the stone above yer head."

Catti-brie nodded resolutely, took a deep breath, and determinedly wiped the sweat from her brow. Bruenor moved ahead then, saying that he was going to the front edge of the torchlight to see if he could locate the leading battlerager.

"Drizzt needs us," Wulfgar said to Catti-brie as soon as the dwarf had gone.

Catti-brie turned to him, surprised by his tone. For the first time in a long while, Wulfgar had spoken to her without a hint of either protective condescension or mounting rage.

Wulfgar walked up to her, put his arm gently against her back to move her along. She matched his slow stride, all the while studying his fair face, trying to sort through the obvious torment in his strong facial features.

"When this is through, we have much to discuss," he said quietly.

Catti-brie stopped, eyeing him suspiciously—and that seemed to wound the barbarian even more.

"I have many apologies to offer," Wulfgar tried to explain, "to Drizzt, to Bruenor, but mostly to you. To let Regis—Artemis Entreri—fool me so!" Wulfgar's mounting excitement flew away when he took the moment to look closely at Catti-brie, to see the stern resolve in her blue eyes.

"What happened over the last few tendays surely was heightened by the assassin and his magical pendant," the young woman agreed, "but I'm fearing that the problems were there afore Entreri ever arrived. First thing, ye got to admit that to yerself."

Wulfgar looked away, considered the words, then nodded his agreement. "We will talk," he promised.

"After we're through with the drow," Catti-brie said.

Again the barbarian nodded.

"And keep yer place in mind," Catti-brie told him. "Ye've a role to play in the group, and it's not a role of looking out for me own safety. Keep yer place."

"And you keep yours," Wulfgar agreed, and his ensuing smile sent a burst of warmth through Catti-brie, a poignant reminder of those special, boyish qualities, innocent and unjudging, that had so attracted her to Wulfgar in the first place.

The barbarian nodded again and still smiling, started away, Catti-brie at his side—but no longer behind him.

⚔ ⚔ ⚔ ⚔ ⚔

"I have given you all of this," Entreri prodded, moving slowly toward his rival, his glowing sword and jeweled dagger held out wide as though he were guiding a tour around some vast treasure hoard. "Because of my efforts, you have hope once more, you can walk these very dark tunnels with some belief that you will again see the light of day."

Drizzt, jaw set firm, scimitars in hand, did not reply.

"Are you not grateful?"

"Please kill him," Drizzt heard battered Regis whisper, possibly the most pitifully sounding plea the drow ranger had ever heard. He looked to the side to see the halfling trembling with unbridled fright, gnawing his lips and twisting his still-swollen hands about each other. What horrors Regis must have experienced at Entreri's hands, Drizzt realized.

He looked back to the approaching assassin; Twinkle flared angrily.

"Now you are ready to fight," Entreri remarked. He curled his lips up in his customary evil smile. "And ready to die?"

Drizzt flipped his cloak back over his shoulders and boldly strode ahead, for he did not want to fight Entreri anywhere near Regis. Entreri might just flick that deadly dagger of his into the halfling, for no better reason than to torment Drizzt, to raise Drizzt's rage.

The assassin's dagger hand did pump as if he meant to throw, and Drizzt instinctively dropped into a crouch, his blades coming up defensively. Entreri didn't release the blade, though, and his widening smile showed that he never intended to.

Two more strides brought Drizzt within sword's reach. His scimitars began their flowing dance.

"Nervous?" the assassin teased, pointedly slapping his fine sword against Twinkle's reaching blade. "Of course you are. That is the problem with your tender heart, Drizzt Do'Urden, the weakness of your passion."

Drizzt came in a cunning cross, then swiped at a low angle for Entreri's belt, forcing the assassin to suck in his belly and leap back, at the same time snapping his dagger across to halt the scimitar's progress.

"You have too much to lose," Entreri went on, seeming unconcerned for the close call. "You know that if you die, the halfling dies. Too many distractions, my friend, too many items keeping your focus from the battle." The assassin charged as he spoke the last word, sword pumping fiercely, ringing from scimitar to scimitar, trying to open some hole in Drizzt's defenses that he might slip his dagger through.

There were no holes in Drizzt's defenses. Each maneuver, skilled as it might have been, left Entreri back where he had started, and gradually Drizzt worked his blades from defense to offense, driving the assassin away, forcing another break.

"Excellent!" Entreri congratulated. "Now you fight with your heart. This is the moment I have awaited since our battle in Calimport."

Drizzt shrugged. "Please do not let me disappoint you," he said, and came ahead viciously, spinning with his scimitars angled like the edging of a screw, as he had done in the chamber above. Again Entreri had no practical defense against the move—except to keep out of the scimitars' shortened reach.

Drizzt came out of the spin angled slightly to the assassin's left, Entreri's dagger hand. The drow dove ahead and rolled, just out of Entreri's lunging strike, then came back to his feet and reversed momentum immediately, rushing around Entreri's back side, forcing the assassin to spin on his heels, his sword whipping about in a frantic effort to keep the thrusting scimitars at bay.

Entreri was no longer smiling.

He managed somehow to avoid being hit, but Drizzt pressed the attack, kept him on his heels.

They heard the soft click of a handcrossbow from somewhere down the hall. In unison, the mortal enemies jumped back and fell into rolls, and the quarrel skipped harmlessly between them.

Five dark forms advanced steadily, swords drawn.

"Your friends," Drizzt remarked evenly. "It seems our fight will wait once more."

Entreri's eyes narrowed in open hatred as he regarded the approaching dark elves.

Drizzt understood the source of the assassin's frustration. Would Vierna give Entreri another battle, especially with other powerful enemies in the tunnels, searching for Drizzt? And even if she did, Entreri had to realize that, as with the fight before, he would not coax Drizzt into this level of battle, not with Drizzt's hopes for freedom extinguished.

Still, the assassin's next words caught the drow ranger somewhat by surprise.

"Do you remember our time against the Duergar?"

Entreri came in again at Drizzt as the dark elf soldiers continued their advance. Drizzt easily parried the swift but not well-aimed attacks.

"Left shoulder," Entreri whispered. His sword came up behind his words, darting for Drizzt's shoulder. Twinkle crossed over from the right to block, but missed, and the assassin's sword nicked in, driving clean holes in the drow's cloak.

Regis cried out; Drizzt dropped one scimitar and lurched to the side, openly revealing his agony. Entreri's sword came tip in, barely five inches from his throat, and Twinkle was too far down for a parry.

"Yield!" the assassin cried. "Drop your weapon!"

Twinkle clanged to the floor and Drizzt continued his exaggerated lean, appearing as though he might tumble over at any moment. From behind, Regis groaned loudly and tried to shuffle away, but his weary, bruised limbs would not support him, would not even afford him the strength to crawl along.

The dark elves came tentatively into the torchlit area, talking among themselves and nodding appreciatively at the assassin's fine work.

"We will take him back to Vierna," one of them said in halting Common.

Entreri began to nod his agreement, then whirled about suddenly, driving his sword right through the speaker's chest.

Drizzt, low to begin with and not at all wounded, snatched up his blades and came up in a spin, one scimitar following the other in a clean slash across the nearest drow's belly. The wounded dark elf tried to fall away, but Drizzt was too quick, reversing his grip on his trailing blade and thrusting it ahead with an upward backhand, its tip cutting under the dark elf's ribs and puncturing his chest cavity.

Entreri was full out against a third drow by this time, the dark elf's twin swords working frantically to keep the assassin's sword and dagger at bay. The assassin wanted the battle over quickly, and his routines were purely offensive, designed to score a fast kill. But this drow, a longtime soldier of Bregan

D'aerthe, was no novice to battle and he half-twisted and spun complete circles, fell into a backward roll and pumped his swords hand over hand in a blinding wall of defense.

Entreri growled in dismay but kept up the pressure, hoping his adversary would make even the slightest mistake.

Drizzt found himself squared off against two, and one of these smiled wickedly as he lifted a small crossbow in his free hand. Drizzt proved the quicker, though, angling his scimitar right in front of the weapon so that when the drow fired, the quarrel skipped off the blade and flew harmlessly high.

The drow threw the handcrossbow at Drizzt, forcing the ranger back long enough so that he could draw a dirk to complement the slender sword he carried.

The other drow seized the apparent advantage as Drizzt ducked away, his broadsword and short sword weaving viciously.

Metal rang against metal a dozen times, two dozen, as Drizzt impossibly defeated each attack. Then the second drow joined the melee and Drizzt, as skilled as he was, found himself sorely pressed. Twinkle snapped across to block the short sword, darted farther ahead and low to knock down the tip of the thrusting broadsword, then rifled back the other way, barely deflecting the darting dirk.

So it went for several long and frantic moments, with the two soldiers of Bregan D'aerthe working in harmony, each measuring his attacks in light of the other's, each raising appropriate defenses whenever his companion seemed vulnerable.

Drizzt was not so sure he could win against these two, and knew that even if he did, this battle would take a long time to turn his way. He glanced over his shoulder, to see Entreri beginning to back off from his attack routines, falling into a more mundane rhythm against his skilled opponent.

The assassin noticed Drizzt, and apparently noted Drizzt's predicament. He gave a slight nod, and Drizzt caught a subtle shift in the way Entreri was holding his jeweled dagger.

Drizzt went forward in a sudden burst, driving back the sword and dirk wielder, then spun to the other drow, scimitars starting low and sweeping upward, forcing the drow's broadsword high.

Drizzt released the move immediately, snapped his scimitar from the blade of the broadsword, and skipped two steps backward.

The enemy drow, not understanding, kept his broadsword high for another instant—an instant too long—before he began his countering advance.

The jewels of Entreri's dagger gave a multicolored flicker as the weapon cut through the air, thudding into the vulnerable drow's ribs, below his raised sword arm. He grunted and hopped to the side, crashed against the wall, but kept his balance and kept both his swords defensively out in front.

His comrade came ahead immediately, understanding what Drizzt would do. Long sword darted low, darted high, then came up in a twirl for a high slice.

Drizzt blocked, blocked again, then ducked under the predictably high third attack and veered to the side, both his blades working in sudden, short snaps that opened the defenses of the slumping, wounded drow. One scimitar jabbed into drow flesh just beside the dagger; the other followed at once, sinking deeper, finishing the job.

Instinctively, Drizzt threw his retracted blade out horizontally and up high, the metal singing a perfect note as it stopped the overhead chop from the second drow's descending sword.

The dark elf battling Entreri went on the offensive as soon as the assassin relinquished his dagger. Twin swords worked Entreri's remaining blade high and low, to one side, then the other. When he had prepared the assassin's stance to his liking, thinking the end at hand, the drow came with a straight double-thrust, both swords parallel and knifing in at the assassin.

Entreri's sword hit one, then the other, impossibly fast, knocking both attacks wide. He hit the sword on his right a second time with a backhand, nearly sending the blade from the drow's hand, then a third time, his sword driving his enemy's high.

Drizzt's second scimitar came free of the dead drow's chest, but Drizzt did not bring the blade to bear on his present opponent. Rather, he angled the tip under the crosspiece of the stuck dagger and when he saw Entreri prepared to receive it, he jerked his blade around, sending the dagger flying across the way.

Entreri caught it with his free hand and redirected its momentum, sticking it into his opponent's exposed ribs under the high-riding swords. The assassin jumped back; the dying drow stared at him in disbelief.

What a pitiful sight, Entreri thought, watching his enemy try to lift swords with arms that no longer had any strength. He shrugged callously as the drow toppled to the floor and died.

One against one, the remaining drow soon realized that he was no match for Drizzt Do'Urden. He kept his movements defensive, angling around to Drizzt's side, then noticed a desperate opportunity. Sword working furiously to keep the darting scimitars at bay, he flipped his dirk over in his hand as if to throw.

Drizzt immediately went into defensive maneuvers, one scimitar flashing across any possible missile path while the other kept the pressure on.

But the enemy warrior glanced to the side, to the halfling, sprawled helpless on the floor not so far away.

"Surrender or I kill the halfling!" the evil dark elf cried in the drow tongue.

Drizzt's lavender eyes flared wickedly.

A scimitar hit the evil drow's wrist, taking the dirk from his grasp; Drizzt's other blade batted the sword once, then darted low, slicing against his enemy's knee. Twinkle came across in a blue flash, batting aside the descending sword, and straight ahead came the free, low-riding scimitar, taking the drow in the thigh.

The doomed dark elf grimaced and wobbled, trying to back away, trying to utter something, some word of surrender, to call off his attacker. But his threat against Regis had put Drizzt past the point of reasoning.

Drizzt's advance was slow and deadly even. Scimitars low to his side, he still got one or the other up to destroy any attempted strikes long before they got near his body.

All that Drizzt's opponent could watch was Drizzt's simmering eyes, and nothing this drow had ever before seen, neither the snake-headed whips of merciless priestesses nor the rage of a matron mother, had promised death so completely.

He ducked his head, screamed aloud, and giving in to his terror, threw himself forward desperately.

Scimitars hit him alternately in the chest. Twinkle took his biceps cleanly, keeping his sword arm helplessly pinned back, and Drizzt's other blade came up fast under his chin, lifting his face, that he might, at the moment of his death, look once more into those lavender eyes.

Drizzt, his chest heaving with the rush of adrenaline, his eyes burning from inner fires, shoved the corpse away and looked to the side, eager to be done with his business with Entreri.

But the assassin was nowhere to be seen.

19

SACRIFICE

Thibbledorf Pwent stood at the end of the narrow tunnel, scanning the wide cavern beyond with his infravision, registering the shifting gradations of heat, that he might better understand the layout of the dangerous area ahead. He made out the many teeth of the ceiling, stalactites long and narrow, and saw two distinctly cooler lines indicating ledges on the high walls—one directly ahead, the other along the wall on his right. Dark holes lined the walls at floor level in several places; Pwent knew that one immediately to his left, two directly across from where he stood, and another diagonally ahead and to the right, under the ledge, likely were long tunnels, and figured several others to be smaller side chambers or alcoves.

Guenhwyvar was at the battlerager's side, the cat's ears flattened, its low growl barely perceptible. The panther sensed the danger, too, Pwent realized. He motioned for Guenhwyvar to follow him—suddenly he was not so upset at having so unusual a companion—and he skittered back down the corridor into the approaching torchlight to stop the others short of the room.

"There be at least three or four more ways in or out," the battlerager told his companions gravely, "and lots of open ground across the place." He went on to give a thorough description of the chamber, paying particular attention to the many obvious hiding spots.

Bruenor, sharing Pwent's dark fears, nodded and looked to the others. He, too, felt that their enemies were near, were all about them, and had been steadily closing in. The dwarf king looked back the way they had come, and it was obvious to the others that he was trying to figure out some other way around this region.

"We can turn their hoped-for surprise against them," Catti-brie offered, knowing the futility of Bruenor's hopes. The companions had precious little time to spare and few of the side tunnels they had passed offered little promise of bringing them to the lower regions, or to wider tunnels where they might find Drizzt.

A sparkle of battle-lust came into Bruenor's dark eyes, but he frowned a moment later when Guenhwyvar plopped down heavily at Catti-brie's feet.

"The cat's been about too long," the young woman reasoned. "Guenhwyvar's needing a rest soon." Wulfgar's and the dwarves' expressions showed that they did not welcome the news.

"More the reason to go straight ahead," Catti-brie said determinedly. "Guen's got a bit of the fight left, don't ye doubt!"

Bruenor considered the words, then nodded grimly and slapped his many-notched axe across his open palm. "Got to get in close to this enemy," he reminded his friends.

Pwent produced his bitter potion. "Take another hit," he offered to Catti-brie and Wulfgar. "Got to make sure the stuff's fresh in yer belly."

Catti-brie winced, but she did take the flask, then handed it to Wulfgar, who similarly frowned and took a brief draw.

Bruenor and Pwent squatted to the floor between them, Pwent quickly scratching a rough map of the chamber. They had no time for detailed plans, but Bruenor sorted out areas of responsibility, assigning each person the task best suited to his or her battle style. The dwarf could give no specific directions to Guenhwyvar, of course, and didn't bother to include Pwent in much of the discussion, knowing that once the fighting began, the battlerager would go off on his wild, undisciplined way. Catti-brie and Wulfgar, too, realized Pwent's forthcoming role, and neither complained, understanding that, against skilled and precise opponents such as drow elves, a little chaos could well be a good thing.

They kept the torch burning, even lit a second one, and started cautiously ahead, ready to put the fight on their own terms.

As the torchlight breached the room, a darting black form cut through, going into the darkness in full flight. Guenhwyvar broke to the right, cut left toward the center of the chamber, then darted right again, toward the back wall.

From somewhere ahead there came the sound of firing crossbows, followed by the skip of quarrels hitting the stone, always one step behind the dodging, leaping panther.

Guenhwyvar veered again at the last moment, leaped, and turned sidelong, paws running along the vertical wall for several strides before the panther had to come back to the floor. The cat's target, the high ledge on the right-hand wall was now in sight, and Guenhwyvar ran full out, speeding for it recklessly.

At the base, in full stride, and apparently soaring toward a headfirst collision, the panther's muscles subtly shifted. Guenhwyvar's direction change was almost perpendicular, the panther flying, seeming to run, straight up the twenty-foot expanse to the ledge.

The three dark elves atop the ledge could not have expected the incredible maneuver. Two fired their crossbows Guenhwyvar's way and fell back into a tunnel; the third, having the misfortune to be directly in the leaping panther's path, could only throw his arms up as the panther fell over him.

Torches flew into the room, lighting the battle area, followed by the leading charge of Bruenor, flanked on his right by Wulfgar and on his left by Thibbledorf Pwent. Catti-brie quietly filtered in behind them, slipping to the side along the same general course Guenhwyvar had taken, her bow readied and in hand.

Again the crossbows of unseen dark elves clicked, and all of the leading companions took hits. Wulfgar felt the venom streaming into his leg, but felt the tingling burn as Pwent's potent potion counteracted its sleepy effects. A darkness spell fell over one of the torches, defeating its light, but Wulfgar was ready, lighting a third and tossing it far to the side.

Pwent noticed an enemy drow in the tunnel to the left, and off he went, predictably, roaring with every charging stride.

Bruenor and Wulfgar slowed but kept their course straight across the room, for the largest tunnel entrances across the way. The barbarian caught sight of the flicker of drow eyes along the remaining ledge, farther ahead and above the tunnels. He stopped, twirled, and heaved his warhammer with a cry to his god. Aegis-fang went in low, crushing the lip of the walkway, smashing stone apart. One dark elf leaped away to another point on the long ledge; the other tumbled down, his leg blasted, and barely caught the stone halfway down the crumbling wall.

Wulfgar did not follow the throw forward. He got hit again by a stinging quarrel and rushed instead to the side, to the remaining tunnel, along the right-hand wall, wherein crouched a pair of dark elves.

Eager to join in close combat, Bruenor veered behind the barbarian. The dwarf looked back before he had even completed the turn, though, as an eight-legged monster, the drider, came out of the tunnel directly ahead, other dark forms shifting about behind it.

With a whoop of delight, never considering the odds now that he and his friends were committed to the battle, the fiery dwarf veered again to his initial course, determined to meet the enemy, however many there might be, head on.

⚔ ⚔ ⚔ ⚔ ⚔

It took all the discipline Catti-brie could muster to hold her first shot in check. She really didn't have a good angle for either those that Pwent had pursued or the ledge where Guenhwyvar had gone, and she didn't think it worth the trouble to spike the wounded drow hanging helplessly below the blasted ledge—not yet. Bruenor had bade her to make certain that her first shot, the one shot she might get before she was fully noticed, counted.

The eager young woman watched the split between Bruenor and Wulfgar and found her opportunity. A drow, crouching behind a four-foot diagonal jag in the back wall, almost exactly halfway between her rushing companions, leaned out, crossbow in hand. The dark elf fired, then fell back in surprise as a silver arrow streaked past him, skipped off the stone, and left a smoldering scorch in its wake.

Catti-brie's second shot was in the air an instant later. She could no longer see the drow, fully covered by the stone, but she did not believe his cover so thick.

The arrow hit the jutting slab two feet from its edge, two feet from where it joined the wall. There came a sharp crack as the rock split, followed by a grunt as the arrow blasted deep into the dying drow's skull.

⚔ ⚔ ⚔ ⚔ ⚔

The prone dark elf on the high ledge scrambled and kicked, kept his buckler above him, and managed, somehow, to get his dagger out with his other hand. Only his fine mesh armor kept Guenhwyvar's raking claws somewhat at bay, kept his mounting wounds serious but not mortal.

He brought the dagger to bear on the panther's flank, but the weapon seemed small against such a foe, seemed only to further enrage the cat. His buckler arm was batted aside, back up over his head with enough force to dislocate his shoulder. He tried to get it back to block but found it would not respond to his mind's frantic call. He scrambled to put his other hand in the great paw's way, a futile defense.

Guenhwyvar's claws hooked his scalp line just above his forehead. The drow plunged the dagger in again, praying for a quick kill.

The panther's claws sheared off his face.

Crossbows clicked again from down the tunnel at the back of the narrow ledge. Not really hurt, the panther came off its victim and loped ahead in pursuit.

The two dark elves summoned globes of darkness between them and the cat, turned, and fled.

If they had looked back, they might have rejoined the fight, for Guenhwyvar's pursuit was not dogged. With the dagger and quarrel wounds, the insidious sleep poison, and the simple duration of the panther's visit to the plane, Guenhwyvar's energy was no more. The cat did not wish to leave, wanted to stay and fight beside the companions, to stay to hunt for its missing master.

The magic of the figurine would not support the desires, though. A few strides into the darkened area, Guenhwyvar stopped, barely holding a tentative balance. Panther flesh dissolved into gray smoke. The planar tunnel opened and beckoned.

He got hit again as he exited the chamber, but the tiny quarrel did no more than bring a smile to the most wild battlerager's contorted face. A darkness globe blocked his flight, but he roared and barreled through, smiling even when he collided full force with the winding wall out the other side.

The amazed dark elf, watching ferocious Pwent's progress, spun away, darting along the tunnel, then turned a sharp corner. Pwent came right behind, armor squealing and drool running from his fat lips in lines down his thick black beard.

"Stupid!" he yelled, ducking his head as he spun the corner right behind the fleeing drow, fully expecting the ambush.

Pwent's darting helmet spike intercepted the sword cut, impaling his enemy through the forearm. The battlerager didn't slow, but hurled himself into the air and lay out flat, body-blocking his opponent across the chest and driving the drow to the ground under him.

Glove nails dug for the dark elf's groin and face; Pwent's ridged armor creased the fine mesh mail as he went into a series of violent convulsions. With each of the battlerager's movements, waves of searing agony ran up the drow's impaled arm.

Bruenor noticed the slender form of a drow, wearing an outrageously wide-brimmed and plumed hat, moving about the entrance to the tunnel. Then came the flicker of objects cutting into the torchlight from behind the monstrous drider, and Bruenor threw his shield up defensively. A dagger banged against the metal, then another, and a third behind that. The fourth throw came in low, scraping the dwarf's shin; the fifth dipped over the leaning shield as Bruenor inevitably bent forward, cutting a line across the dwarf's scalp under the edge of his one-horned helmet.

But minor wounds would not slow Bruenor, nor would the sight of the bloated drider, axes waving, eight legs clacking and scrabbling. The dwarf came in hard, took a hit on the shield, and returned with a smash against the drider's second descending axe. Much smaller than his opponent, Bruenor worked low, his axe smacking the hard exoskeleton of the drider's armored legs. All the while, the dwarf remained a blur of frenzied motion, his shield above him, as fine a shield as was ever forged, deflecting hit after hit from the wickedly edged, drow-enchanted weapons.

Bruenor's axe dove into the wedge between two legs, cracking through to the drider's fleshy interior. The dwarf's smile was short-lived, though, for the drider's responses banged hard on the shield, twisting it about on Bruenor's arm, and the creature put a leg in line and kicked hard into the dwarf's belly, throwing Bruenor back before his axe could do any real damage.

He squared off, his breath lost and his arm aching. Again came a series of dagger throws from the corridor behind the drider, forcing Bruenor off balance. He barely got his shield up to stop the last four. He looked down to the first, jutting from the front of his layered armor, a trickle of blood oozing from behind its tip, and knew he had escaped death by a hair's breadth.

He knew, too, that the distraction would cost him dearly, for he was no longer squared up for melee and the drider was upon him.

⋈ ⋈ ⋈ ⋈ ⋈

Wulfgar's flying hammer led the way to the corridor, his one throw more than matching the crossbow darts that struck the roaring barbarian. He aimed high, for the stalactite teeth hanging above the entryway, and his mighty hammer did its work perfectly, smashing apart several of the hanging rocks.

One dark elf fell back—Wulfgar could not tell if the falling stone had crushed him or not—and the other dove forward, drawing sword and dagger and coming up in the chamber to meet the unarmed barbarian's charge.

Wulfgar skidded to a stop short of the flashing blades, skipped to the side, and kicked out, punched out, doing anything to keep the dangerous and quick opponent at bay for the few seconds the barbarian needed.

The drow, not understanding the magic of Aegis-fang, took his time, seemed in no hurry to chance the grasp of the obviously mighty human. He came with a measured combination, sword, dagger, and dagger again, the last thrust painfully nicking the barbarian's hip.

The drow smiled wickedly.

Aegis-fang appeared in Wulfgar's waiting hands.

With one hand, grasping low on the warhammer's handle, Wulfgar sent the weapon into a flowing circular motion in front of him. The drow took careful measure of the weapon's speed—Wulfgar carefully appraised the drow's examination.

In darted the dagger, behind the flowing hammer. Wulfgar's other hand clapped against the handle just under his weapon's head and abruptly reversed the direction, parrying the drow's attack aside.

The drow was quick, snapping his sword in a downward angle for Wulfgar's shoulder even as his dagger hand was knocked wide. Wulfgar's huge forearm flexed with the strain as he halted the heavy hammer's flow, snapping it back up in front of him. He caught Aegis-fang halfway up the handle with his free hand and jabbed diagonally up, the warhammer's solid head intercepting the sword and driving it harmlessly away.

The end of the parry left the drow with one arm wide and low, the other wide and high, and left Wulfgar standing before his opponent in perfect balance, both hands grasping Aegis-fang. Before the dark elf could recover his wide-flying blades, before he could set his feet to dive away, Wulfgar chopped him, the hammer crunching under his shoulder and driving down toward his opposite hip. The drow fell back from the blow, then, as though the full weight of the incredible hit had not immediately registered, went into an involuntary backward hop that slammed him against the wall.

One leg buckling, one lung collapsed, the drow brought his sword horizontally before his face in a meager defense. Hands low on the handle, Wulfgar brought the hammer up behind him and slammed it home with all his strength, through the blade and into the drow's face. With a sickening crack, the drow's skull exploded, crushed between the unyielding stone of the wall and the unyielding metal of the mighty Aegis-fang.

A blinding streak of silver halted the drider's attacks and saved Bruenor Battlehammer. The arrow didn't hit the drider, however. It soared high, pegging the wounded drow (who had just about climbed back to the blasted ledge) to the stone wall.

The distraction, the moment to recover from the daggers, was all Bruenor needed. He came in hard again, his many-notched axe smashing the drider's closest leg, his shield up high to block the now off-balance axe swipes. The dwarf pressed right into the beast, using its bulk to offer him some cover from the enemies in the corridor, and bulled it backward before it could set its many legs against the charge.

Another of Catti-brie's arrows whipped past him, sparking as it ricocheted along the stone of the corridor.

Bruenor grinned widely, thankful that the gods had delivered to him an ally and friend as competent as Catti-brie.

The first two arrows enraged Vierna; the third, coming down the corridor, nearly took off her head. Jarlaxle raced back from his position near the chamber's entrance to join her.

"Formidable," the mercenary admitted. "I have dead soldiers in the room."

Vierna raced forward, focusing on the dwarf battling her mutated brother. "Where is Drizzt Do'Urden?" she demanded, using magic to focus her voice so that Bruenor would hear her through the drider.

"Ye hit me and ye're meaning to talk?" the dwarf howled, finishing his sentence with an exclamation point in the form of a chopping axe. One of Dinin's legs fell free, and the dwarf barreled on, pushing the unbalanced drider back another few strides.

Vierna hardly had the chance to begin her intended spell before Jarlaxle grabbed her and hauled her down. Her instinctive anger toward the -mercenary was lost in the blast of yet another streaking arrow, this one driving a hole into the stone wall where the priestess had been standing.

Vierna remembered Entreri's warning about this group, had the evidence right before her as the battle continued to sour. She trembled with rage, growled indecipherably as she considered what the defeat might cost her. Her thoughts fell inward, followed the path of her faith toward her dark deity, and cried out to Lolth.

"Vierna!" Jarlaxle called from someplace remote.

Lolth could not allow her to fail, had to help her against this unexpected obstacle, that she might deliver the sacrifice.

"Vierna!" She felt the mercenary's hands on her, felt the hands of a second drow helping Jarlaxle put her back on her feet.

"Wishya!" came her unintentional cry, then she knew only calm, knew that Lolth had answered her call.

Jarlaxle and the other drow slammed against the tunnel's walls from the force of Vierna's magical outburst. Each looked at her with trepidation.

The mercenary's features relaxed when Vierna bade him to follow her farther along the corridor, out of harm's way.

"Lolth will help us finish what we have started here," the priestess explained.

⚔ ⚔ ⚔ ⚔ ⚔

Catti-brie put another arrow into the corridor for good measure, then glanced about, searching for a more apparent target. She studied the battle between Bruenor and the monstrous drider, but she knew that any shots she made at the bloated monster would be too risky given the furious melee.

Wulfgar apparently had his situation under control. A drow lay dead at his feet as he peeked about the rubble of the collapsed corridor in search of the enemy who had not come in. Pwent was nowhere to be found.

Catti-brie looked up to the blasted ledge above Bruenor and the drider for the drow who had not fallen, then to the other ledge, where Guenhwyvar had disappeared. In a small alcove below that area the young woman saw a curious sight: a gathering of mists similar to that heralding the panther's approach. The cloud shifted colors, became orange, almost like a swirling ball of flames.

Catti-brie sensed an evil aura, gathering and overwhelming, and put her bow in line. The hairs on the back of her neck tingled; something was watching her.

Catti-brie dropped the Heartseeker and spun about, snapping her short sword from its sheath with her turn, barely in time to bat aside the thrusting sword of a levitating drow that had silently descended from the ceiling.

Wulfgar, too, noticed the mist, and he knew that it demanded his attention, that he must be ready to strike out at it as soon as its nature was revealed. He could not ignore Catti-brie's sudden cry, though, and when he looked at her, he found her hard pressed, nearly sitting on the floor, her short sword working furiously to keep her attacker at bay.

In the shadows some distance behind the young woman and her attacker, another dark shape began its descent.

✕ ✕ ✕ ✕ ✕

The warm blood of his torn enemy mingled with the drool on Thibbledorf Pwent's beard. The drow had stopped thrashing, but Pwent, reveling in the kill, had not.

A crossbow quarrel pierced his ear. His head came up as he roared, the impaled helmet spike lifting the dead drow's arm weirdly. There stood another enemy, advancing steadily.

Up leaped the battlerager, snapping his head from side to side, whipping the caught drow back and forth until the ebony skin ripped apart, freeing the helmet spike.

The approaching dark elf stopped his advance, trying to make some sense of the gruesome scene. He was moving again—back the other way—when indomitable Pwent took up the roaring charge.

The drow was truly amazed at the stubby dwarf's frantic pace, amazed that he could not easily outdistance this enemy. He wouldn't have run too far anyway, though, preferring to bait this dangerous one away from the main battle.

They went through a series of twisting corridors, the dark elf ten strides ahead. His graceful steps barely seemed to alter as he leaped, landing and spinning about, sword ready and smile wide.

Pwent never slowed. He merely ducked his head to put his helmet spike in line. With his eyes to the stone, the battlerager realized the trap, too late, as he crossed the rim of a pit the drow had subtly leaped across.

Down went the battlerager, crashing and bouncing, the many points of his battle armor throwing sparks as he skidded along the stone. He cracked a rib against the rounded top of a stalagmite mound some distance down, bounced completely over, and landed flat on his back in a lower chamber.

He lay there for some time, admiring the cunning of his enemy and admiring the curious way the ceiling—tons of solid rock—continued to spin about.

✕ ✕ ✕ ✕ ✕

No novice with the sword, Catti-brie worked her blade marvelously, using every defense Drizzt Do'Urden had shown her to gain back some measure of equal footing. She was confident that the drow's initial advantage was fading, confident that she could soon get her feet under her and come back up evenly against this opponent.

Then, suddenly, she had no one to fight.

Aegis-fang twirled by her, its windy wake bringing her thick hair about, and hit the surprised dark elf full force, blasting him away.

Catti-brie spun about, her initial appreciation lost as soon as she recognized Wulfgar's protectiveness. The mist near the barbarian was forming by then, taking on the substantial, corporeal body of a denizen of some vile lower plane, some enemy far more dangerous than the dark elf Catti-brie had been battling.

Wulfgar had come to her aid at the risk of his own peril, had put her safety above his own.

To Catti-brie, confident that she could have taken care of her own situation, that act seemed more stupid than altruistic.

Catti-brie went for her bow—she had to get to her bow.

Before she even had her hands on it, though, the monster, the yochlol, came fully to the plane. Amorphous, it somewhat resembled a lump of half-melted wax, showing eight tentaclelike appendages and a central, gaping maw lined with long, sharp teeth.

Catti-brie sensed danger behind her before she could call out to Wulfgar. She spun, bow in hand, and looked up to her enemy, to a drow's sword fast descending for her head.

Catti-brie shot first. The arrow jolted the drow several inches from the floor and passed right through the dark elf to explode in a shower of sparks against the ceiling. The drow was still standing when he came back to the floor, still holding his sword, his expression revealing that he was not quite sure what had just happened.

Catti-brie grabbed her bow like a club and jumped up to meet him, pressing him fiercely until his mind registered the fact that he was dead.

She looked back once, to see Wulfgar grabbed by one of the yochlol's tentacles, then another. All the barbarian's incredible strength could not keep him from the waiting maw.

⚔ ⚔ ⚔ ⚔ ⚔

Bruenor could see nothing but the black of the drider's torso as he continued to bull in, continued to drive Dinin backward. He could hear nothing except the sounds of flying blades, the clang of metal against metal, or the sound of cracking shell whenever his axe struck home.

He knew instinctively that Catti-brie and Wulfgar, his children, were in trouble.

Bruenor's axe finally caught up with the retreating creature with full force as the drider slammed against the wall. Another spider leg fell away; Bruenor planted his feet and heaved with all his strength, launching himself several feet back.

Dinin, weirdly contorted, two legs lost, did not immediately pursue, glad for the reprieve, but ferocious Bruenor came back in, the dwarf's savagery overwhelming the wounded drider. Bruenor's shield blocked the first axe; his helmet blocked the following strike, a blow that should have dropped him.

Straight across whipped the dwarf's many-notched axe, above the hard exoskeleton to cut a jagged line across the bloated drider's belly. Hot gore spewed out. Fluids ran down the drider's legs and Bruenor's pumping arms.

Bruenor went into a frenzy, his axe smacking repeatedly, incessantly, into the crook between the drider's two foremost legs. Exoskeleton gave way to flesh; flesh opened to spill more gore.

Bruenor's axe struck hard yet again, but he took a hit atop the shoulder of his weapon arm. The drider's awkward angle stole most of the strength from the blow, and the axe did not get through Bruenor's fine mithral mail, but a blast of hot agony assaulted Bruenor.

His mind screamed that Catti-brie and Wulfgar needed him!

Grimacing against the pain, Bruenor whipped his axe in an upward backhand, its flat back cracking against the drider's elbow. The creature howled and Bruenor brought the weapon to bear again, angled up the other way, catching the drider in the armpit and shearing the creature's arm off.

Catti-brie and Wulfgar needed him!

The drider's longer reach got its second axe around the dwarf's blocking shield, its bottom edge drawing a line of blood up the back of Bruenor's arm. Bruenor tucked the shield in close and shoulder-blocked the monster against the wall. He bounced back, drove his axe in hard at the monster's exposed side, then shoulder-blocked again.

Back bounced the dwarf, in chopped his axe, and Bruenor's stubby legs twitched again, sending him hurtling forward. This time, Bruenor heard the drider's other axe fall to the floor, and when he bounced back, he stayed back, chopping wildly with his axe, driving the drider to the stone, splitting flesh and breaking ribs.

Bruenor turned about, saw Catti-brie in command of her situation, and took a step toward Wulfgar.

"Wishya!"

Waves of energy hit the dwarf, lifting his feet from the ground and launching him a dozen feet through the air, to slam against the wall.

He rebounded in a redirected run, and he cried a single note of rage as he bore down on the entrance to the distant tunnel, the eyes of several drow watching him from farther within.

"*Wishya!*" came the cry once more, and Bruenor was moving backward suddenly.

"How many ye got?" the tough dwarf roared, shrugging off this newest hit against the wall.

The eyes, every set, turned away.

A globe of darkness fell over the dwarf, and he was, in truth, glad for its cover, for that last slam had hurt him more than he cared to admit.

⚔ ⚔ ⚔ ⚔ ⚔

A fourth soldier joined Vierna, Jarlaxle, and their one bodyguard as they again moved deeper into the tunnels.

"Dwarf to the side," the newcomer explained. "Insane, wild with rage. I put him down a pit, but I doubt he is stopped!"

Vierna began to reply, but Jarlaxle interrupted her, pointing down a side passage, to yet another drow signaling to them frantically in the silent hand code.

Devil cat! the distant drow signaled. A second form rushed by him, followed by a third a few seconds later. Jarlaxle understood the movements of his troops, knew that these three were the survivors of two separate battles, and understood that both the ledge and the side passage below it had been lost.

We must go, he signaled to Vierna. *Let us find a more advantageous region where we might continue this fight.*

"Lolth has answered my call!" Vierna growled at him. "A handmaiden has arrived!"

"More the reason to be gone," Jarlaxle replied aloud. "Show your faith in the Spider Queen and let us be on with the hunt for your brother."

Vierna considered the words for just a moment, then, to the worldly mercenary's relief, nodded her agreement. Jarlaxle led her along at a great pace, wondering if it could be true that only seven of his skilled Bregan D'aerthe force, himself and Vierna included, remained.

⚔ ⚔ ⚔ ⚔ ⚔

Wulfgar's arms slapped wildly at the waving tentacles; his hands clasped over those appendages wrapping him, trying to break free of their iron grip. More tentacles slapped in at him, forcing his attention.

He was jerked out straight, yanked sidelong into the great maw, and he understood these newest slapping attacks to be merely diversions. Razor-edged teeth dug into his back and ribs, tore through muscle, and scraped against bone.

He punched out and grabbed a handful of slimy yochlol skin, twisting and tearing a hunk free. The creature did not react, continued to bite bone, razor teeth working back and forth across the trapped torso.

Aegis-fang came back to Wulfgar's hand, but he was twisted awkwardly for any hits against his enemy. He swung anyway, connecting solidly, but the fleshy, rubbery hide of the evil creature seemed to absorb the blows, sinking deep beneath the weight of Aegis-fang.

Wulfgar swung again, twisted about despite the searing pain. He saw Catti-brie standing free, the second drow lying dead at her feet, and her face locked in an expression of open horror as she stared at the white of Wulfgar's exposed ribs.

Still, the image of his love, free from harm, brought a grimace of satisfaction to the barbarian's face.

A bolt of silver flashed right below, startling Wulfgar, blasting the yochlol, and the barbarian thought his salvation at hand, thought that his beloved Catti-brie, the woman he had dared to underestimate, would strike his attacker down.

A tentacle wrapped around Catti-brie's ankles and jerked her from her feet. Her head hit the stone hard, her precious bow fell from her grasp, and she offered little resistance as the yochlol began to pull her in.

"No!" Wulfgar roared, and he whacked again and again, futilely, at the rubbery beast. He cried out for Bruenor; out of the corner of his eye, he saw the dwarf stumble out of a dark globe, far away and dazed.

The yochlol's maw crunched mercilessly; a lesser man would have long since collapsed under the force of that bite.

Wulfgar could not allow himself to die, though, not with Catti-brie and Bruenor in danger.

He began a hearty song to Tempus, his god of battle. He sang with lungs fast filling with blood, with a voice that came from a heart that had pumped mightily for more than twenty years.

He sang and he forgot the waves of crippling pain; he sang and the song came back to his ears, echoing from the cavern walls like a chorus from the minions of an approving god.

He sang and he tightened his grip on Aegis-fang.

Wulfgar struck out, not against the beast, but against the alcove's low ceiling. The hammer chopped through dirt, hooked about stone.

Pebbles and dust fell all around the barbarian and his attacker. Again and again, all the while singing, Wulfgar slammed at the ceiling.

The yochlol, not a stupid beast, bit fiercely, shook its great maw wildly, but Wulfgar had passed beyond the admission of pain. Aegis-fang chopped upward; a chunk of stone followed its inevitable descent.

As soon as she recovered her wits, Catti-brie saw what the barbarian was doing. The yochlol was no longer interested in her, was no longer pulling her in, and she managed to claw her way back to her bow.

"No, me boy!" she heard Bruenor cry from across the way.

Catti-brie nocked an arrow and turned about.

Aegis-fang slammed against the ceiling.

Catti-brie's arrow sizzled into the yochlol an instant before the ceiling gave way. Huge boulders toppled down; any space between them quickly filled with piles of rock and soil, spewing clouds of dust into the air. The chamber shook violently; the collapse resounded through all the tunnels.

Neither Catti-brie nor Bruenor still stood. Both huddled on the floor, their arms defensively over their heads as the cave-in slowly ended. Neither could see amid the darkness and the dust; neither could see that both the monster and Wulfgar had disappeared under tons of collapsing stone.

PART FIVE

END GAME

When I die . . .

I have lost friends, lost my father, my mentor, to that greatest of mysteries called death. I have known grief since the day I left my homeland, since the day wicked Malice informed me that Zaknafein had been given to the Spider Queen.

It is a strange emotion, grief, its focus shifting. Do I grieve for Zaknafein, for Montolio, for Wulfgar? Or do I grieve for myself, for the loss I must forever endure?

It is perhaps the most basic question of mortal existence, and yet it is one for which there can be no answer. . . .

Unless the answer is one of faith.

I am sad still when I think of the sparring games against my father, when I remember the walks beside Montolio through the mountains, and when those memories of Wulfgar, most intense of all, flash through my mind like a summary of the last several years of my life. I remember a day on Kelvin's Cairn, looking out over the tundra of Icewind Dale, when young Wulfgar and I spotted the campfires of his nomadic people. That was the moment when

Wulfgar and I truly became friends, the moment when we came to learn that, for all the other uncertainties in both our lives, we would have each other.

I remember the white dragon, Icingdeath, and the giant-kin, Biggrin, and how, without heroic Wulfgar at my side, I would have perished in either of those fights. I remember, too, sharing the victories with my friend, our bond of trust and love tightening—close, but never uncomfortable.

I was not there when he fell, could not lend him the support he certainly would have lent me.

I could not say "Farewell!"

When I die, will I be alone? If not for the weapons of monsters or the clutch of disease, I surely will outlive Catti-brie and Regis, even Bruenor. At this time in my life I do firmly believe that, no matter who else might be beside me, if those three were not, I would indeed die alone.

These thoughts are not so dark. I have said farewell to Wulfgar a thousand times. I have said it every time I let him know how dear he was to me, every time my words or actions affirmed our love. Farewell is said by the living, in life, every day. It is said with love and friendship, with the affirmation that the memories are lasting if the flesh is not.

Wulfgar has found another place, another life—I have to believe that, else what is the point of existence?

My very real grief is for me, for the loss I know I will feel to the end of my days, however many centuries have passed. But within that loss is a serenity, a divine calm. Better to have known Wulfgar and shared those very events that now fuel my grief, than never to have walked beside him, fought beside him, looked at the world through his crystal-blue eyes.

When I die . . . may there be friends who will grieve for me, who will carry our shared joys and pains, who will carry my memory.

This is the immortality of the spirit, the ever-lingering legacy, the fuel of grief.
But so, too, the fuel of faith.

—Drizzt Do'Urden

SUÐÐENLY

Dust continued to settle in the wide chamber, dulling the flickering light; one of the torches had been extinguished beneath a falling chunk of stone, its glow snuffed out in the blink of an eye.

Snuffed out like the light in Wulfgar's eyes.

When the rumbling finally stopped, when the larger pieces of collapsed ceiling settled, Catti-brie turned herself about and managed to sit up, facing the rubble-filled alcove. She wiped the dirt from her eyes, blinked through the gloom for several long moments before the grim truth of the scene registered fully.

The monster's one visible tentacle, still wrapped about the young woman's ankle, had been cleanly severed, its back edge, near the rubble, twitching reflexively.

Beyond it there was only piled rock. The enormity of the situation overwhelmed Catti-brie. She swayed to the side, nearly swooned, finding her strength only when a burst of anger and denial welled up within her. She tore her feet free of the tentacle and scrambled ahead on all fours. She tried to stand, but her head throbbed, keeping her low. Again came the wave of weak nausea, the invitation to fall back into unconsciousness.

Wulfgar!

Catti-brie crawled on, slapped aside the twitching tentacle, and began digging into the stone pile with her bare hands, scraping her skin and tearing a fingernail painfully. How similar this collapse seemed to the one that had taken Drizzt on the companions' first crossing of Mithral Hall. But that had been a dwarf-designed trap, a rigged fall that dropped out the floor as it had dropped out a ceiling block, sending Drizzt careening safely into a lower corridor.

This was no rigged trap, Catti-brie reminded herself; there was no chute to a lower chamber. A soft groan, a whimper, escaped her lips and she clawed on, desperate to get Wulfgar from the crushing pile, praying that the rocks had collapsed in an angle that would allow the barbarian to survive.

Then Bruenor was beside her, dropping his axe and shield to the floor and going at the pile with abandon. The powerful dwarf managed to move several large stones aside, but when the outer rim of the cave-in had been cleared, he stopped his work and stood staring blankly at the pile.

Catti-brie kept digging, didn't notice her father's frown.

After more than two centuries of mining, Bruenor understood the truth. The collapse was complete.

The lad was gone.

Catti-brie continued to dig, and to sniffle, as her mind began to tell her what her heart continued to deny.

Bruenor put his hand on her arm to stop her from her pointless work, and when she looked up at him, her expression broke the tough dwarf's heart. Her face was grime-covered. Blood was caked on one cheek, and her hair was matted to her head. Bruenor then saw only Catti-brie's eyes, doelike orbs of deepest blue, glistening with moisture.

Bruenor slowly shook his head.

Catti-brie fell back to a sitting position, her bleeding hands limp in her lap, her eyes unblinking. How many times had she and her friends come so close to this final point? she wondered. How many times had they escaped Death's greedy clutches at the last instant?

The odds had caught up to them, had caught up to Wulfgar, here and now, suddenly, without warning.

Gone was the mighty fighter, leader of his tribe, the man Catti-brie had intended to marry. She, Bruenor, even mighty Drizzt Do'Urden, could do nothing to help him, nothing to change what had happened.

"He saved me," the young woman whispered.

Bruenor seemed not to hear her. The dwarf continually wiped at the dust in his eyes, at the dust that collected in the large teardrops that gathered and then slipped down, streaking his dirty cheeks. Wulfgar had been like a son to Bruenor. The tough dwarf had taken the young Wulfgar—just a boy back then—into his home after a battle, ostensibly as a slave but in truth to teach the lad a better way. Bruenor had molded Wulfgar into a man who could be trusted, a man of honest character. The happiest day in the dwarf's life, even happier than the day Bruenor had reclaimed Mithral Hall, was the day Wulfgar and Catti-brie had announced they would wed.

Bruenor kicked a heavy stone, the force of his blow shifting it aside.

There lay Aegis-fang.

The brave dwarf's knees went weak at the sight of the marvelous warhammer's head, etched with the symbols of Dumathoin, a dwarven god, the Keeper of Secrets Under the Mountain. Bruenor forced deep breaths into his lungs and tried to steady himself for a long while before he could manage the strength to reach down and work the hammer free of the rubble.

It had been Bruenor's greatest creation, the epitome of his considerable smithing abilities. He had put all of his love and skill into forging the hammer; he had made it for Wulfgar.

Catti-brie's semistoic front collapsed like the ceiling at the sight of the weapon. Quiet sobs made her shoulders bob, and she trembled, seeming frail in the dim, dusty light.

Bruenor found his own strength in watching her display. He reminded himself that he was the Eighth King of Mithral Hall, that he was responsible for his subjects—and for his daughter. He slipped the precious warhammer into the strap of his traveling pack and hooked an arm under Catti-brie's shoulder, hoisting her to her feet.

"We can't do a thing for the boy," Bruenor whispered. Catti-brie pulled away from him and moved back to the pile, growling as she tossed several smaller stones aside. She could see the futility of it all, could see the tons of dirt and stones, many of them too large to be moved, filling the alcove. But Catti-brie dug anyway, simply incapable of giving up on the barbarian. No other apparent course offered any hope.

Bruenor's hands gently closed about her upper arms.

With a snarl, the young woman shrugged him away and resumed her work.

"No!" Bruenor roared, and he grabbed her again, forcefully, lifting her from the ground and hauling her back from the pile. He put her down hard, with his wide shoulders squared between her and the pile, and whichever way Catti-brie went to get around him, Bruenor shuffled to block her.

"Ye can't do a thing!" he shouted into her face a dozen times.

"I've got to try!" she finally pleaded with him, when it became obvious to her that Bruenor was not going to let her back to the digging.

Bruenor shook his head—only the tears in his dark eyes, his obvious distress, prevented Catti-brie from punching him in the face. She did calm down then, stopped trying to slip past the stubborn dwarf.

"It's over," Bruenor said to her. "The boy . . . me boy, choosed his course. He gave himself for us, yerself and me. Don't ye do him the dishonor of letting stupid pains keep ye here, in danger."

Catti-brie's body seemed to slump at the undeniable truth of Bruenor's reasoning. She did not move back to the pile, to Wulfgar's burial cairn, as Bruenor retrieved his shield and axe. The dwarf came back to her and draped one arm about her back.

"Say yer good-byes," he offered, and he silently waited a moment before leading Catti-brie away, first to her bow, then from the chamber, toward the same entrance through which they had come.

Catti-brie stopped beside him and regarded him and the tunnel curiously, as if questioning their course.

"Pwent and the cat'll have to find their own way about," Bruenor answered her blank stare, misunderstanding her confusion.

Catti-brie wasn't worried about Guenhwyvar. She knew that nothing could bring the panther serious harm while she still possessed the magical figurine, and she wasn't worried about the missing battlerager at all.

"What about Drizzt?" she asked simply.

"Me guess is that th'elf's alive," Bruenor answered with confidence. "One of them drow asked me about him, asked me where he was at. He's alive, and he's got away from them, and by me own figuring, Drizzt's got a better chance o' getting clear of these tunnels than the two of us. Might be that the cat's with him even now."

"And it might be that he needs us," Catti-brie argued, pulling free of Bruenor's gentle touch. She flipped the bow over her shoulder and crossed her arms over her chest, her face grim and determined.

"We're going home, girl," Bruenor ordered sternly. "We're not for knowing where Drizzt might be. I'm only guessing, and hoping, that he really is alive!"

"Are ye willing to take the chance?" Catti-brie asked simply. "Are ye willing to risk that he's needing us? We lost one friend, maybe two if the assassin finished off Regis. I'm not for giving up on Drizzt, not for any risk." She winced as another memory flashed through her mind, a memory of being lost on Tarterus, another plane of existence, when Drizzt Do'Urden had bravely faced unspeakable horrors to bring her home.

"Ye remember Tarterus?" she said to Bruenor, and the thought made the helpless-feeling dwarf blink and turn away.

"I'm not giving up," Catti-brie said again, "not for any risk." She looked to the tunnel entrance across the way, where the escaping dark elves apparently had taken flight. "Not for any damned dark elves and their hell-spawned friends!"

Bruenor stayed quiet for a long while, thinking of Wulfgar, milling over his daughter's determined words. Drizzt might be about, might be hurt, might be caught again. If it was Bruenor lost down there, and Drizzt up here, the dwarf had no doubt which course Drizzt would choose.

He looked again at Catti-brie and at the pile behind her. He had just lost Wulfgar. How could he risk losing Catti-brie as well?

Bruenor looked more closely at Catti-brie, saw the seething determination in her eyes. "That's me girl," the dwarf said quietly.

They retrieved the remaining torch and left through the exit on the opposite side of the chamber, moved deeper into the tunnels in search of their missing friend.

⚔ ⚔ ⚔ ⚔ ⚔

One who had not been raised in the perpetual gloom of the Underdark would not have noticed the subtle shift in the depth of the darkness, the slight tingling breeze of fresher air. To Drizzt the changes came as obviously as a slap across the face, and he picked up his pace, hoisting Regis tight to his side.

"What is it?" the scared halfling demanded, glancing about as if he expected Artemis Entreri to jump out of the nearest shadows and devour him.

They passed a wide but low side passage, sloping upward. Drizzt hesitated, his direction sense screaming to him that he had just passed the correct tunnel. He ignored those silent pleas, though, and continued on, hopeful that the opening to the outside world would be accessible enough for him and Regis to get a welcome breath of fresh air.

It was. They rounded a bend in the tunnel and felt the chilly burst of wind in their faces, saw a lighter opening ahead, and saw beyond it towering mountains . . . and stars!

The halfling's profound sigh of relief echoed Drizzt's sentiments perfectly as he carried Regis on. When they came out of the tunnel, both of them were nearly overcome by the splendor of the mountainous scene spread wide before them, by the sheer beauty of the surface world under the stars, so removed from the starless nights of the Underdark. The wind, rushing past them, seemed a vital and alive entity.

They were on a narrow ledge, two-thirds of the way to the bottom of a steep, thousand-foot cliff. A narrow path wound up to their right, down to the left, but at only a slight angle, which offered little hope that it would continue long enough to get them either up or down the cliff.

Drizzt considered the towering wall. He knew he could easily manage the few hundred feet to the bottom, could probably get up to the top without too much trouble, but he didn't think he'd be able to bring Regis with him and didn't like the prospect of being in an unknown stretch of wilderness, not knowing how long it might take him to get back to Mithral Hall.

His friends, not so far away, were in trouble.

"Keeper's Dale is up there," Regis remarked hopefully, pointing to the northwest, "probably no more than a few miles."

Drizzt nodded but replied, "We have to go back in."

While Regis did not seem pleased by that prospect, he did not argue, understanding that he could not get off this ledge in his present condition.

"Well done," came Entreri's voice from up around the bend. The assassin's dark silhouette came into sight, the jewels of his belted dagger glimmering like his heat-seeing eyes. "I knew you would come to this place," he explained to Drizzt. "I knew you would sense the clean air and make for it."

"Do you congratulate me or yourself?" the drow ranger asked.

"Both!" Entreri replied with a hearty laugh. The white of his teeth disappeared, replaced by a cold frown, as he continued to approach. "The tunnel you passed fifty yards back will indeed take you to the higher level, where you'll likely find your friends—your dead friends, no doubt."

Drizzt didn't take the bait, didn't let his rage send him charging ahead.

"But you cannot get there, can you?" Entreri teased. "You alone could keep ahead of me, could avoid the fight I demand. but alas for your wounded companion. Think of it, Drizzt Do'Urden. Leave the halfling and you can run free!"

Drizzt didn't justify the absurd thought with a reply.

"I would leave him," Entreri remarked, dropping his cold glare over Regis as he spoke. The halfling gave a curious whimper and slumped under the strong hold of Drizzt's arm.

Drizzt tried not to imagine the horrors Regis had suffered at Entreri's vile hands.

"You will not leave him," Entreri continued. "We long ago established that difference between us, the difference you call strength, but that I know to be weakness." He was only a dozen strides away; his slender sword hissed free of its scabbard, illuminating him in its blue-green glow. "And so to our business," he said. "And so to our destiny. Do you like the battlefield I have prepared? The only way off this ledge is the tunnel behind you, and so I, like yourself, cannot flee, must play it out to the end." He looked over the cliff as he spoke. "A deadly drop for the loser," he explained, smiling. "A fight with no reprieve."

Drizzt could not deny the sensations that came over him, the heat in his breast and behind his eyes. He could not deny that, in some repressed corner of his heart and soul, he wanted this challenge, wanted to prove Entreri wrong, to prove the assassin's existence to be worthless. Still, the fight would never have happened if Drizzt Do'Urden had been given a reasonable choice. The desires of his ego, he understood and fully accepted, were no valid reason for mortal combat. Now, with Regis helpless behind him and his friends somewhere above, facing dark elf enemies, the challenge had to be met.

He felt the hard metal of his scimitar hilts in his hands, let his eyes slip back fully into the normal spectrum of light as Twinkle flared its angry blue.

Entreri halted, sword at one side, dagger at the other, and motioned for Drizzt to approach.

For the third time in less than a day, Twinkle slapped hard against the assassin's slender blade; the third time, and as far as both Drizzt and Entreri were concerned, the very last time.

They started easily, each measuring his steps on the unorthodox arena. The ledge was perhaps ten feet wide at this point, but narrowed considerably just behind Drizzt and just behind Entreri.

A backhand slash with the sword led Entreri's routine, dagger thrust following.

Two solid parries sounded, and Drizzt snapped one scimitar for the opening between Entreri's blades, an opening that was closed by a retreating sword in the blink of an eye, with Drizzt's attack slapped harmlessly aside.

They circled, Drizzt inside and near the wall, the assassin moving easily near the drop. Entreri slashed low, unexpectedly leading with the dagger this time.

Drizzt hopped the shortened cut, came with a two-chop combination for the ducking assassin's head. Entreri's sword darted left and right, worked horizontally above his head to block ensuing blows, and shifted its angle slightly to poke ahead, to keep the drow at bay while the assassin came back to equal footing.

"It will not be a quick kill," Entreri promised with an evil smile. As if to disprove his own claim, he leaped ahead furiously, sword leading.

Drizzt's hands worked in a blur, his scimitars hitting the deftly angled weapon repeatedly. The dark elf worked to the side, kept his back from flattening against the wall.

Drizzt agreed fully with the assassin's estimate—this would not be a quick kill, whoever might win. They would fight for many minutes, for an hour, perhaps. And to what end? Drizzt wondered. What gain could he expect? Would Vierna and her cohorts show up and bring the challenge to a premature conclusion?

How vulnerable Drizzt and Regis would be then, with nowhere to run and a drop of several hundred feet just inches away!

Again the assassin pressed the attack, and again Drizzt worked his scimitars through the proper, perfectly balanced defenses, Entreri getting nowhere near to hitting him.

Entreri went into a spin then, imitating Drizzt's movements in their previous two encounters, working his two blades like the edge of a screw to force Drizzt back to a narrower position on the ledge.

Drizzt was surprised that the assassin had learned the daring and difficult maneuver so completely after only two observations, but it was a move Drizzt had designed, and he knew how to counter it.

He, too, went into a spinning rotation, scimitars flowing, up and down. Blades connected repeatedly with each turn, sometimes lighting sparks in the dark night, metal screeching, green and blue mixing in an indistinct blur. Drizzt moved right by Entreri—the assassin reversed his spin suddenly, but Drizzt saw the shift and came to a stop, both blades blocking the reversed cut of sword and dagger.

Drizzt began once more, counter to Entreri, and this time, when Entreri again turned his rotation back the other way, the drow anticipated it so fully that he actually reversed direction first.

For Regis, staring helplessly, not daring to intervene, and for any of the region's nocturnal creatures that might have been watching, there were no words to describe the amazing dance, the interweaving of colors as Twinkle and the assassin's glowing blade passed, the violet sparkle of Drizzt's eyes, the red heat of Entreri's. The scrape of blades became a symphony, a myriad of notes playing to the dance, evoking a strange sense of harmony between these most bitter enemies.

They stopped in unison, a few feet apart, both understanding that there would be no end to that spinning dance, no advantage by either player. They stood like matching bookends of identical weight.

Entreri laughed aloud at the realization, laughed so that he might savor this moment, this many act play that perhaps would see the dawn, and perhaps would never be resolved.

Drizzt found no humor, and his private eagerness at the beginning of the challenge had flown, leaving him with the weight of responsibility—for Regis and for his friends back in the tunnels.

The assassin came in low and hard, sword darting, climbing with each strike as Entreri gradually straightened his stance, taking a full measure of Drizzt's defenses from a variety of cunning angles.

Entreri settled him into a parrying rhythm, then broke the melody with a vicious dagger cut. The assassin howled in glee, thinking for a moment that his blade had slipped through.

Twinkle's hilt had intercepted it cleanly, had caught it and held it, barely an inch from Drizzt's side. The assassin grimaced and stubbornly tried to push on as he came to understand the truth.

Drizzt's expression was colder still; the dagger did not move.

A twist of the drow's wrist sent both blades flying wide. Entreri was wise enough to push off and break the clench, to circle back and wait for the next opportunity to present itself.

"I almost had you," he teased. He hid his frown well as Drizzt in no way responded, not with words, not with body movements, not with the unyielding set of his ebony-skinned features.

A scimitar snapped across, ringing loudly through the breeze as Entreri brought his blocking sword in its path.

The sudden sound assaulted Drizzt, reminded him that Vierna might not be far away. He pictured his friends in dire trouble, captured or dead, felt a special twinge of remorse for Wulfgar that he could not explain. He locked stares with Entreri, reminded himself that this man had been the one to cause it all, that this enemy had tricked him into the tunnels, had separated him from his friends.

And now Drizzt could not protect them.

A scimitar snapped across; the other came slashing in the other way. Drizzt repeated the routine, then a third time, each movement, each ring of metal against metal, bringing his thoughts more in line with this task, lifting his emotional preparations, heightening his warrior senses.

Each strike was perfectly aimed, and each parry intercepted the attacking blades perfectly, yet neither Drizzt nor Entreri, locked through their staring eyes into mental combat, watched their hands through the physical movements. Neither one blinked, not when the breeze of Drizzt's high slice moved the hair atop the assassin's head, not when Entreri's sword thrust came to a parried stop a hairsbreadth from Drizzt's eye.

Drizzt felt his momentum building, felt the give and take of the battle coming quicker, strike and parry. Entreri, as consumed as the ranger, paced him.

The movements of their bodies began to catch the blur of hands and weapons. Entreri dipped a shoulder, sword lashing out straight ahead; Drizzt spun a complete circle, parrying behind his back as he flitted out of reach.

Images of Bruenor and Catti-brie captured by Vierna tormented the ranger; he pictured Wulfgar, wounded or dying, a drow sword at his throat. He imagined the barbarian atop a funeral pyre, a conjured image that, for some reason Drizzt could not understand, would not be easily dismissed. Drizzt accepted the images, gave the mental assault his full attention, let the fears for his friends fuel his passion. That had been the difference between him and the assassin, he told himself, told that part of himself that argued for him to keep his mind clear and his movements precise and well considered.

That was how Entreri played the game, always in control, never feeling anything beyond the enemy at hand.

A slight growl escaped Drizzt's lips; his lavender eyes simmered in the starlight. In his mind Catti-brie screamed out in pain.

He came at Entreri in a wild rush.

The assassin laughed at him, sword and dagger working furiously to keep the two scimitars at bay. "Give in to the rage," he chided. "Let go of your discipline!"

Entreri didn't understand; that was precisely the point.

Twinkle chopped in, to be predictably parried by Entreri's sword. It wouldn't be that easy for the assassin this time, though. Drizzt retracted and struck again, and again, repeatedly, willingly slamming his blade against the assassin's already poised weapon. His other blade came in furiously from the other side; Entreri's dagger turned it aside.

Drizzt's ensuing flurry, sheer madness, it seemed, kept the assassin back on his heels. A dozen hits, two dozen, sounded like one long cry of ringing steel.

Entreri's expression betrayed his laughter. He had not expected this wild an offensive routine, had not expected Drizzt to be so daring. If he could get one of his blades free for just an instant, the drow would be vulnerable.

But Entreri could not free up sword or dagger. Fires drove Drizzt on, kept his pace impossibly fast and his concentration perfect. To the Nine Hells with his own life, he decided, for his friends needed him to prevail.

On and on the offensive routine continued; Regis covered his ears at the horrid wail and screech of the blades, but the halfling could not, for all his terror, take his gaze from the fighting masters. How many times Regis expected one or both to pitch over the cliff! How many times he thought a sword or scimitar thrust had struck home! But they somehow kept on fighting, each attack just missing, each defense in line at the last possible instant.

Twinkle hit the sword; Drizzt's following strike from the other side was not parried but went in short as Entreri shifted his foot and fell back a step.

The assassin's dagger arm shot forward. Entreri released a primal scream of victory, thinking Drizzt had slipped up.

Twinkle came across from its high perch faster than Entreri expected, faster than the assassin believed possible, gashing his forearm an instant before he got the dagger to Drizzt's exposed belly. Back flew the scimitar, backhanding the sword away. Entreri leaped ahead to get in close, realizing his vulnerability.

His sudden charge saved his life, but while Drizzt could not angle the tip of his free blade for a killing thrust, he could, and did, punch out with the hilt, connecting solidly with Entreri's face, sending the man staggering backward.

On came the dark elf, blades flashing relentlessly, driving Entreri back to within an inch of the cliff. The assassin tried to go to his right, but one scimitar knocked aside his blocking sword while the other's maneuvering kept Drizzt directly in front of him. The assassin started left, but with his wounded dagger arm slow to react, he knew he could not get beyond the drow's reach in time. Entreri held his ground, parrying furiously, trying to find a countering routine that would drive this possessed enemy back.

Drizzt's breath came in short puffs as he found a rhythm to his frantic pace. His eyes flared, unrelenting, as he reminded himself over and over that his friends were dying—and that he could not protect them!

He fell too far into the rage, hardly registered the movement as the dagger flew at him. At the very last instant, he ducked aside, the skin above his cheekbone slashed in a three-inch-long cut. More importantly, Drizzt's forward rhythm was shattered. His arms ached from the exertion; his momentum had played itself out.

On came the snarling assassin, sword poking, even scoring a slight hit, as he drove Drizzt back and around. By the time the ranger had regained his balance somewhat, his toes, not Entreri's, were squarely facing the mountain wall, his heels feeling the free-flowing emptiness of the mountain winds.

"I am the better!" Entreri proclaimed, and his ensuing attack almost proved his claim. Sword slashing and darting, he drove Drizzt's heel over the edge.

Drizzt dropped to one knee to keep his weight forward. He felt the wind keenly, heard Regis scream his name.

Entreri could have leaped back and retrieved his dagger, but he sensed the kill, sensed he would never again have a better opportunity to end the game. His sword banged down with fury; Drizzt seemed to buckle under its weight, seemed to slip even farther over the cliff edge.

Drizzt reached to his inner self, to the innate magic of his heritage . . . and produced darkness.

Drizzt dove to the side in a roll, came up several feet along the ledge, beyond the darkness globe he had created near Regis.

Incredibly, Entreri was still in front of him, pressing him wickedly.

"I know your tricks, drow," the skilled assassin declared.

A part of Drizzt Do'Urden wanted to give in then, to simply lie back and let the mountains take him, but it was a fleeting moment of weakness, one from which Drizzt recoiled, one that fueled his indomitable spirit and lent strength to his weary arms.

But so, too, was hungry Entreri fueled.

Drizzt slipped suddenly and had to grab for the ledge, releasing his grip on his blade. Twinkle toppled over the cliff, skipping down along the stones.

Entreri's sword slammed down, blocked by only the remaining scimitar. The assassin howled and jumped back, coming right back with a thrust.

Drizzt could not stop it, Entreri knew, his eyes going wide as the moment of victory finally presented itself. The twisted drow's angle was all wrong; Drizzt couldn't possibly get his remaining blade down and turned in line in time.

He couldn't stop it!

Drizzt didn't try to stop it. He had quietly coiled one leg under him for a roll, and he went to the side and ahead as the sword dived in, narrowly missing. Drizzt spun his prone body about, one foot kicking against the front of Entreri's ankle, the other hooking and slamming the assassin behind the knee.

Only then did Entreri realize that the drow's slip, and the lost scimitar, had been a ruse. Only then did Artemis Entreri realize that his own hunger for the kill had defeated him.

His momentum forward with the eager thrust, he pitched toward the ledge. Every muscle in his body snapped taut; he drove his slender sword through Drizzt's foot and somehow managed to catch a hold on the drow's impaled boot with his free hand.

The momentum was too great for Drizzt, still sidelong on the smooth ledge, to hold them both back. The drow was pulled out straight as he went over, right above Entreri, skidding down the stone, the agony in his foot fading as more pains, bruises and cuts from the jagged ride became evident.

Drizzt held tightly to his second scimitar, jammed its hilt into a nook, and found a grasp with his other hand.

He shuddered to a stop, and Entreri stretched out below him, over an inverted section that offered the assassin no chance of a handhold. Drizzt thought his entire insides would be ripped out through his impaled foot. He glanced down to see one of Entreri's hands waving wildly; the other clutched desperately to the sword hilt, a macabre and tentative lifeline.

Drizzt groaned and grimaced, nearly fainted from the pain, as the blade slipped out several inches.

"No!" he heard Entreri deny, and the assassin went very still, apparently understanding the precariousness of his position.

Drizzt looked down at him, hanging in midair, still well over two hundred feet from the ground.

"This is not the way to claim victory!" Entreri called to him in a desperate burst. "This defeats the purpose of the challenge and dishonors you."

Drizzt reminded himself of Catti-brie, got the strange sensation once more that Wulfgar was lost to him.

"You did not win!" Entreri cried.

Drizzt let the fires in his lavender eyes speak for him. He set his hands and squared his jaw and turned his foot, feeling every deliciously agonizing inch as the long sword slipped through.

Entreri scrambled and kicked, almost got a hold on Drizzt with his free hand, as the blade came free.

The assassin tumbled away into the blackness of night, his cry swallowed by the mourn of the mountain wind.

MOUNTAIN VALLEY
WINDS

Drizzt slowly doubled over and managed to get a hand to his ripped boot, where he somehow stemmed the blood flow. The wound was clean, at least, and after a few tries, Drizzt found that he still had use of the foot, that it would still support his weight, though painfully.

"Regis?" he called up the cliff face. The dark shape of the halfling's head peered out over the ledge.

"Drizzt?" Regis called back tentatively. "I . . . I thought . . ."

"I am all right," the drow assured him. "Entreri is gone." Drizzt couldn't make out Regis's cherubic features from that distance, but he could well imagine the joy the news brought his tormented friend. Entreri had chased Regis for many years, had caught him twice, and neither time had been a pleasant experience for the halfling. Regis feared Artemis Entreri more than anything else in the world, and now, it seemed, the halfling could put that fear to rest.

"I see Twinkle!" the halfling called excitedly, the silhouette of his arm coming over the lip in a downward point. "It's glowing down at the bottom, to your right."

Drizzt peered that way, but he could not see the bottom of the cliff since the stone sloped out directly beneath him. He inched his way to the side, and as Regis had claimed, the magical scimitar came into sight, its blue glow stark against the dark stone of the valley floor. Drizzt cautiously considered this revelation for a few moments. Why would the scimitar, out of his grasp, flare so? Always he had considered the blade's fire a reflection of himself, a magically empathetic reaction to the fires within him.

He winced at the notion that perhaps Artemis Entreri had retrieved the blade. Drizzt pictured the assassin grinning up at him, holding Twinkle out as ironic bait.

Drizzt dismissed the dark notion immediately. He had seen Entreri fall, down across the face of an inverted slope with nothing to grab on to, the wall moving farther away from him as he plummeted. The best the assassin could have hoped for was a bouncing skid after a thirty- or forty-foot free-fall. Even if he was not dead, he certainly was not standing on the valley floor.

What, then, was Drizzt to do? He thought he should go back immediately to Regis and hunt on, to find out the fate of his friends. He could get back to the valley easily enough from Keeper's Dale when the trouble had passed, and with any luck, no goblin or mountain troll would have scooped up the blade.

When he considered the possibility of battling Vierna's charges once more, though, Drizzt realized he would feel better with Twinkle in hand. He looked down again, and the scimitar called out to him—he felt its call in his mind and could not be sure if he had imagined it or if Twinkle possessed some abilities that Drizzt did not yet understand. Something else called to Drizzt, too, he had to admit to himself if not to anyone else. His curiosity over Entreri's fate would not be easily sated. Drizzt would rest easier if he found the assassin's broken form at the base of the mountain wall.

"I am going for the blade," the drow yelled up to Regis. "I'll not be gone long. Cry out for any trouble."

He heard a slight whimper from above, but Regis only called, "Hurry!" and did not argue the decision.

Drizzt sheathed his remaining scimitar and picked his way carefully around the inverted region, catching firm handholds and trying as best he could to keep the pressure from his wounded foot. After fifty feet or so, he came to a steeply pitched but not sheer region of loose stone. There were no handholds here, but Drizzt didn't need any. He lay flat against the wall and slid slowly down.

He saw the danger from the corner of his eye, bat-winged and man-sized and cutting sharp angles in its flight along the mountain valley winds. Drizzt braced himself as it veered in, saw the greenish-blue glow of a familiar sword.

Entreri!

The assassin cackled with taunting glee as he soared past, scoring a slight hit on the drow's shoulder. Entreri's cloak had transformed, had sprouted to form bat wings!

Drizzt now understood the true reason the devious assassin had chosen to fight on the ledge.

The assassin made a second pass, closer, smacking the drow with the side of his sword and kicking out with his boot into Drizzt's back.

Drizzt rolled with the hits, then began to slide dangerously, the loose rubble shifting under him. He drew his scimitar and somehow parried the next passing strike.

"Have you a cloak like mine?" Entreri teased, cutting a sharp turn some distance away and seeming to hover in midair. "Poor little drow, with no net to catch him." Another gleeful cackle sounded, and in swooped the assassin, still keeping a respectable distance, knowing he held every advantage and could not let his eagerness betray him.

The sword, carrying the momentum of the assassin's swift flight, slammed hard against Drizzt's scimitar, and while the ranger managed to keep the slender blade clear of his body, the assassin clearly had won the pass.

Drizzt was sliding once more. He turned back to face the stone, clutched at it, put one arm under him, and hooked his fingers, using his weight to dig them deeply enough into the loose gravel to slow the descent. Drizzt seemed helpless at that awful moment, as concerned with holding his precarious perch as in parrying the assassin's strikes.

A few more passes likely would send him to his death.

"You cannot begin to know my many tricks!" the assassin cried in victory, swooping back toward his prey.

Drizzt rolled over to face Entreri as the killer dove in, the drow ranger's free hand coming up and out straight, holding something Entreri did not expect.

"As you cannot know mine!" Drizzt retorted. He sorted through the assassin's suddenly evasive spins and fired the handcrossbow, the weapon he had taken from the drow he had felled at the base of the chute.

Entreri slapped a hand against the side of his neck, tore the quarrel free just an instant after it had stung him. "No!" he wailed, feeling the poison burn. "Damn you! Damn you, Drizzt Do'Urden!"

He swooped for the wall, knowing that flying while sleeping would be less than wise, but the insidious poison, already coursing through a major artery, blurred his vision.

He bounced off the wall twenty feet to Drizzt's right, the light of his sword dying immediately as it fell from his grasp.

Drizzt heard the groan, heard another curse, this one interrupted by a profound yawn.

Still the cloak's bat wings beat, holding the assassin aloft. He could not focus his weary mind to guide his way, though, and he flitted and darted on the mountain winds, hitting the wall again, and then a third time.

Drizzt heard the crack of bone; Entreri's left arm fell limp beneath his horizontal form. His legs, too, drooped, his strength stolen by the poison.

"Damn you," he said again, groggily, obviously slipping in and out of consciousness. The cloak caught an air current then, apparently, for Entreri soared off down the valley and was swallowed by the darkness, silently, like death.

Drizzt's descent from that point was not too difficult or dangerous for the agile drow. The hike became a reprieve, a few moments in which he could allow his defenses to slip away and he could reflect on the enormity of what had just occurred. His fight with Entreri had not spanned so many months, particularly by a drow elf's reckoning, but it had been as brutal and vital as anything Drizzt had ever known. The assassin had been his antithesis, the dark mirror image of Drizzt's soul, the greatest fears Drizzt had ever held for his own future.

Now it was over. Drizzt had shattered the mirror. Had he really proven anything? he wondered. Perhaps not, but at the very least, Drizzt had rid the world of a dangerous and evil man.

He found Twinkle easily, the scimitar flaring brightly when he picked it up, then its inner light died away to show the reflections of starlight on its silvery blade. Drizzt approved of the image and reverently slid the scimitar back into its sheath. He considered searching for Entreri's lost sword, then reminded himself that he had not the time to spare, that Regis, and probably his other friends, needed him.

He was back beside the halfling in a few minutes, hoisting Regis to his side and heading back for the tunnel entrance.

"Entreri?" the halfling asked tentatively, as though he could not bring himself to believe that the assassin was finally gone.

"Lost on the mountain winds," Drizzt replied confidently, but with no hint of superiority in his even-toned voice. "Lost on the winds."

⚔ ⚔ ⚔ ⚔ ⚔

Drizzt could not know how accurate his cryptic answer had been. Drugged and fast fading from consciousness, Artemis Entreri meandered along the rising currents of the wide valley. His mind could not focus, could not issue telepathic commands to the animated cloak, and without his guidance, the magical wings kept beating.

He felt the rush of air increase with his speed. He hurtled along, barely aware that he was in flight.

Entreri shook his head violently, trying to be rid of the sleeping poison's nagging grasp. He knew, somewhere in the back of his mind, that he had to wake up fully, had to regain control and slow himself.

But the rushing air felt good as it washed over his cheeks; the sound of the wind in his ears gave him a sensation of freedom, of breaking free of mortal bonds.

His eyes blinked open and saw only starless, ominous blackness. He could not realize that it was the end of the valley, a mountain wall.

The rush of air beckoned him to fall into his dreams. He hit the wall head-on. Fiery explosions erupted in his head and body; the air gushed from his lungs in one great burst.

He was not aware that the impact had torn his magical cloak, had broken its winged enchantment, was not aware that the wind in his ears was now the sound of falling, or that he was two hundred feet off the ground.

22
CHARGE OF THE HEAVY BRIGADE

Twelve armored dwarves led the procession, their interlocking shields presenting a solid wall of metal to enemy weapons. The shields were specially hinged, allowing the dwarves on the outside edges to turn back behind the front rank whenever the corridor tightened.

General Dagna and his elite cavalrylike force came in the following ranks, riding, not marching, each warrior armed with a readied heavy crossbow fitted with special darts tipped in a silver-white metal. Several torchbearers, each holding two of the flaming brands out far for easy access to the riders, wandered between the tusked mounts of Dagna's twenty troops. The remainder of the dwarven army came behind, wearing grim expressions, different from those looks they had worn when they had come down this way to battle the goblins.

Dwarves did not laugh about the presence of dark elves, and by all their reckoning, their king was in dire trouble.

They came to the side passage, clear once more since the darkness spells had long since expired. The ettin bones sat facing them, across the way, somehow undisturbed through all the tumult of the previous encounter.

"Clerics," Dagna whispered, a quiet call that was repeated down the dwarven lines. Somewhere in the closest ranks behind Dagna's elites, half a dozen dwarven priests, wearing their smithy apron vestments and holding mithral warhammer holy symbols tight in upraised fists, sighted their targets, two to the side, two in front, and two above.

"Well," Dagna said to the shield-bearing dwarves in the front rank, "give 'em something worth shooting at."

The blocking wall of shields broke apart, twelve dwarves stringing out along the wide intersection.

Nothing happened.

"Damn," Dagna pouted after a few uneventful moments, realizing that the dark elves had moved back to another ambush spot. In a minute, the battle formation was rejoined and the force tromped off, at a greater pace, with just a small group slipping down the side passage to make sure their enemies would not come out at their backs.

Grumbling whispers ran the length of the ranks, eager dwarves frustrated by the delay.

Some time later, the growl of one of the war dogs, leashed and held in the middle ranks of the army, came as the only warning.

Crossbows clicked from up ahead, most of the quarrels banging harmlessly off the interlocked shields, but some, coming from higher angles, soaring down to strike the dwarves in the second and third ranks. One torchbearer went down, his flaming brands causing minor havoc with the mounts of the nearest two riders. But the dwarves and their mounts were well trained and the situation did not deteriorate into chaos.

Clerics went into their chants, reciting the proper magical syllables; Dagna and his riders put the tips of their crossbows against the flaming torches; the front row counted in unison to ten, then fell straight to their backs, shields defensively atop them.

On came the cavalry, armored war pigs grunting, magnesium-tipped quarrels flaring to intense white light. The calvary charge took the dwarves beyond the area of torchlight quickly, but the clerical spells popped into the corridor ahead of them, magical lights stealing the darkness.

Dagna and every other member of his eager band whooped with delight, seeing the dark elves scrambling this time, apparently caught by surprise with the sudden ferocity and speed of the dwarven attack. The drow had been confident that they could outrun the short-legged dwarves, and so they could, but they couldn't outrun the sturdy, tusked mounts.

Dagna saw one dark elf turn and reach out, as if to throw, and instinctively, the worldly and wise general understood the creature to be using his darkness ability, trying to counter the stinging magical lights.

When the magnesium quarrel lit up the inside of the drow's belly, his focus predictably shifted.

"Sandstone!" cried the rider right beside Dagna, a dwarven curse if ever there was one. The general saw his companion lurch backward, angling his weapon above. He jerked—obviously hit by some missile—but managed to fire his own crossbow before he tumbled from his saddle, bouncing along the stone.

The flaring quarrel missed, but it doomed the drow floating among the rafters anyway, serving as a tracer for the many dwarven foot soldiers rushing in behind.

"Ceiling!" cried one dwarf, and two dozen crossbowmen skidded to their knees, eyes going up. They caught a shifting motion among the few stalactites and fired, practically in unison.

More dwarves rushed by them as they reloaded, war dogs sounding anxious cries. Dagna's band charged on in hot pursuit, caring little that they had passed beyond the lighted area. The tunnels were fairly flat, and the fleeing drow were not far ahead.

One cleric stopped to aid the kneeling crossbowmen. They showed him the general direction of their quarry, and he put a light spell up there.

The dead drow, his torso ripped by a score of heavy bolts, hung motionless in the air. As if on cue to the revealing light, his levitation spell gave out and he plummeted the twenty feet to the floor.

The dwarves were not even watching him. The light in the ceiling had revealed two of the drow's hidden companions. These new dark elves worked fast to counter the spell with their innate powers of darkness, but it did them little good, for the skilled crossbowmen had picked them out and no longer needed to see them.

Groans and a scream of agony accompanied a frantic explosion of clicking sounds as the host of quarrels skipped and ricocheted off the many stalactites. The two drow dropped, one writhing about as he hit the floor, not quite dead.

The fierce dwarves fell over him, bludgeoning him with the butts of their heavy weapons.

⚔ ⚔ ⚔ ⚔ ⚔

The one tunnel became several as the riders, in hot pursuit, came into a region of snaking side passages. Dagna picked out his target easily enough, despite the growing maze and the gloom. Actually the dimness aided Dagna, for the drow he was chasing had been hit in the shoulder, the white-flaring magnesium serving as a beacon for the charging dwarf.

He gained with every stride, saw the drow turn to face him, the dark elf's shoulder glowing red when viewed from the front. Dagna dropped his crossbow aside and whipped out a heavy mace, angling the boar as if to make a close pass by the drow's wounded flank.

The drow, taking the bait, turned sidelong, getting his one working weapon hand in line.

At the last moment, Dagna lowered his head and veered the tusked boar, and the drow's eyes widened when he realized the wild dwarf's new course. He tried to leap aside, but got hit solidly, tusks catching him just above the knee, Dagna's iron helmet slamming his belly. He hurtled through the air for perhaps fifteen feet, and would have gone farther if the tunnel wall hadn't abruptly stopped him.

Crumpled in a broken heap at the base of the wall, the barely conscious drow saw Dagna pull his mount up before him and saw Dagna's mace go up.

The explosion in his head flared as brightly as the magnesium in his shoulder, then there was only darkness.

⚔ ⚔ ⚔ ⚔ ⚔

Bloodhounds led a large contingent of the dwarven army down to the left of the main chamber, into a region of looping, more natural caverns. Soldiers rumbled straight in, clerics among their ranks, while other dwarves, armed not with weapons, but with tools, went to work behind them and among the passages to the sides.

They came to the four-way intersection, the bloodhounds straining against their leads both left and right. The sneaky dwarves forced the dogs straight ahead, though, and predictably, more than a dozen dark elves slipped into the central corridor behind them, firing their nasty bolts.

The army swung about, the clerics called upon their spells to light up the area, and the drow, outnumbered four to one, wisely turned and fled. They had no reason to fear their way back blocked, not with so many tunnels before them. They had a good idea of the dwarven numbers and were certain that fewer than half of their options would be blocked.

Down the very first path they chose, they came to understand their error, though, running up against a freshly constructed iron door, barred from the other side. The dark elves could see around the edges of the portal—the dwarves hadn't had the time to fit it perfectly into the oddly shaped tunnel—but there was no way to slip through.

The next tunnel seemed more promising, and by the hopes of the fleeing drow, it had to be, for the dwarven force, dogs barking wildly, was right on their heels again. Turning a corner, the dark elves found a second door, heard the hammers of the working dwarves behind it, putting in the finishing touches.

The desperate dark elves dropped spells of darkness on the other side of the door, slowing the work. They found the widest cracks along the jam and fired their crossbows blindly at the workers, adding to the confusion. One drow got his hand around and located the locking bar.

Too late. The dogs rounded the corner, and the dwarven force fell over them.

Darkness descended over the area of battle. A dwarven cleric, his powers nearly exhausted, countered it, but then another drow blackened the area once more. The brave dwarves fought blindly, matching drow skill with sheer fury.

One dwarf felt the hot burn as an unseen enemy's sword slipped between his ribs, slashing through his lung. The dwarf knew the wound would prove mortal, felt the blood filling his lungs and choking off his breathing. He could have retreated, hoped to fall out of the darkened area close enough to a cleric with curative spells to treat the wound. In that critical instant, though, the dwarf knew his opponent was vulnerable, knew that if he retreated, one of his comrades might next feel the dark elf's cruel sword. He lunged ahead, the drow's sword impaling him further, and chopped with his warhammer, connecting once, then again on his enemy.

He went down atop the dead drow and died with a grim smile of satisfaction splayed across his bearded face.

Two dwarves, driving in deeply side by side, felt their intended target dive between them, but turned too late to avoid a collision on the iron door. Disoriented but sensing movement to the side, each of them launched mighty swings with his hammer, each connecting on the other.

Down they went in a heap, and they felt the rush of air as the dark elf came back over them—this time at the end of a dwarven spear—to be slammed hard against the door. The drow fell wounded atop the two dwarves, and they had enough wits and strength remaining to grab on to the gift. They kicked and bit, punched out with their weapon hilts or with their gauntleted hands. In mere seconds, they ripped the unfortunate dark elf apart.

More than a score of dwarves died at the end of drow weapons in that narrow corridor, but so, too, did fifteen dark elves, half of the force that had stood to block the way into the new sections.

⚔ ⚔ ⚔ ⚔ ⚔

A handful of drow kept ahead of their pig-riding pursuers long enough to make their way into the back chambers, into the very room where Drizzt and Entreri had fought for the enjoyment of Vierna and her minions. The blasted door and several dead companions told the soldiers that Vierna's group had been hit hard, but they nevertheless believed their salvation at hand when the first of them leaped for the chute—leaped and got stuck on the webbing barring the way.

The stuck drow flailed helplessly, both his arms fully trapped. His companions, with no thoughts of aiding their doomed friend, looked to the room's other door for their salvation.

War pigs grunted; a dozen dwarven riders whooped in joy as they kicked their mounts across the blasted wooden door.

General Dagna came into the room barely five minutes later to see five dark elves, two dwarves, and three pigs lying dead on the floor.

Satisfied that no other enemies were about, the general ordered an inspection of the remarkable area. Grief stung their hearts when they found Cobble's crushed form under the conjured wall of iron, but it was mixed with some measure of hope, for Bruenor and the others obviously had hit the enemy hard in this place, and apparently, with the exception of poor Cobble, had survived.

"Where are ye, Bruenor?" the general asked down the empty corridors. "Where are ye?"

✕ ✕ ✕ ✕ ✕

Sheer determination, pure denial of defeat, was their only strength as Catti-brie and Bruenor, weary and wounded and leaning on each other for support, made their way through the winding tunnels, deeper into the natural corridors. Bruenor held the torch in his free hand. Catti-brie kept her bow ready. Neither of them believed they would stand a chance if they again encountered the dark elves, but in their hearts, neither of them believed that they could possibly lose.

"Where's that damned cat?" Bruenor asked. "And the wild one?"

Catti-brie shook her head, having no definite answers. Who knew where Pwent might have gotten to? He had flown from the chamber in typical blind rage and could have run all the way back to Garumn's Gorge by this time. Guenhwyvar was a different story, though. Catti-brie dropped her hand into her pouch, sensitive fingers tracing the intricate work of the figurine. She sensed that the panther was no longer about, and trusted the feeling, for if Guenhwyvar had not left the material plane, the panther would have made contact with them by this time.

Catti-brie stopped, and Bruenor, after a few steps, turned back curiously and did likewise. The young woman, on one knee, held the figurine in both hands, studying it intently, her bow on the floor by her side.

"Gone?" Bruenor asked.

Catti-brie shrugged and placed the statue on the floor, then called softly to Guenhwyvar. For a long moment, nothing happened, but just as Catti-brie was about to retrieve the item, the familiar gray mist began to gather and take shape.

Guenhwyvar looked haggard indeed! The panther's muscles drooped, slack from exhaustion, and the black-furred skin of one shoulder hung out, torn, revealing sinew and cordlike tendons underneath.

"Oh, go back!" Catti-brie cried, horrified by the sight. She scooped up the figurine and moved to dismiss the panther.

Guenhwyvar moved faster than either Catti-brie or the dwarf would have believed possible, given the cat's desperate state. A paw slashed up at Catti-brie, batting the figurine to the ground. The panther flattened its ears and issued an angry growl.

"Let the cat stay," Bruenor said.

Catti-brie gave the dwarf an incredulous look.

"Ain't no worse than the rest of us," Bruenor explained. He walked over and dropped a gentle hand on the panther's head, easing the tension. Guenhwyvar's ears came back up, and the cat stopped growling. "And no less determined."

Bruenor looked back to Catti-brie, then to the corridor beyond. "The three of us, then," the dwarf said, "beat up and ready to fall down—but not afore we take them stinking drow down under us!"

✕ ✕ ✕ ✕ ✕

Drizzt could sense that he was getting close, and he drew his second blade, Twinkle, concentrating hard to keep the scimitar's blue light from flaring. To his delight, the scimitar responded perfectly. Drizzt was hardly aware of the halfling he still held at his side. His keen senses were instead trained in all directions for some clue that the enemy was about. He came through a low doorway into an unremarkable chamber, barely a wider section of hallway, with two other exits, one to the side and level, the other straight ahead, ascending once more.

Drizzt suddenly pushed Regis to the ground, fell back against the wall, weapons and eyes trained to the side. It was no drow that came through the side entrance, though, but a dwarf, possibly the most odd-looking creature either of the companions had ever seen.

Pwent was barely three running strides from the dark elf, and his hearty roar showed that he felt confident he had gained the advantage of surprise. He dipped his head, put his spiked helm in line with Drizzt's belly, and heard the little one lying to the side squeak out in alarm.

Drizzt snapped his hands up above his head, feeling grooves in the wall with strong, sensitive fingers. He still held both his blades, and there wasn't much to grab, but the agile drow didn't need much. As the confident battlerager barreled in blindly, Drizzt lifted his legs up, out, and over the spike.

Pwent hit the wall head-on, his spike digging a three-inch-deep gouge in the stone. Drizzt's legs came down, one on either side of the bent battle-rager's head, and down, too, came the drow's scimitars, hilts pounding hard against the back of Pwent's exposed neck.

The dwarf's spike, bent queerly to one side, squealed and scraped as he dropped flat to the stone, groaning loudly.

Drizzt leaped away, allowed the eager scimitar to flare up, bathing the area in a blue glow.

"Dwarf," Regis commented, surprised.

Pwent groaned and rolled over; Drizzt spotted an amulet, carved with the foaming mug standard of Clan Battlehammer, on a chain about his neck.

Pwent shook his head and leaped suddenly to his feet.

"Ye won that one!" he roared, and he started for Drizzt.

"We are not enemies," the drow ranger tried to explain. Regis cried out again as Pwent came in close, launching a one-two punching combination with his glove nails.

Drizzt easily avoided the short punches and took note of the many sharp ridges on his opponent's armor.

Pwent lashed out again, stepping in behind the blow to give it some range. It was a ruse, Drizzt knew, with no chance of hitting. Already the veteran drow understood Pwent's battle tactics, and he knew the phony punch was designed only to put this fearsome dwarf in line, that he might hurl himself at Drizzt. A scimitar flashed out to intercept the punch. Drizzt surprised the dwarf by twirling his second blade above his head and stepping in closer (exactly the opposite course Pwent had expected him to travel), then launching his high-riding weapon out in a wide, arcing, and smoothly descending course as he stepped to the side, bringing the blade to bear at the back of the dwarf's knee.

Pwent momentarily forgot about his impending leap and instinctively bent the vulnerable leg away from the attack. Drizzt pressed on, putting just enough pressure on the dwarf's knee to keep it moving along. Pwent pitched into the air, landed hard on the floor, flat on his back.

"Stop it!" Regis yelled at the stubborn, fallen dwarf, who was again trying to get up. "Stop it. We are not your enemies!"

"He speaks the truth," Drizzt added.

Pwent, up on one knee, paused and looked curiously from Regis to Drizzt. "We came in here to get the halfling," he said to Drizzt, obviously confused. "To get him and skin him alive, and now ye're telling me to trust him?"

"Different halfling," Drizzt remarked, snapping his blades into their sheaths.

An inadvertent grin showed on the dwarf's face as he considered the advantage his enemy apparently had just given him.

"We are not your enemy," Drizzt said evenly, lavender eyes flashing dangerously, "but I've no more time to play your foolish games."

Pwent leaned forward, muscles twitching, eager to leap ahead and rip the drow apart.

Again the drow's eyes flashed, and Pwent relaxed, understanding that this opponent had just read his thoughts.

"Come ahead if you will," Drizzt warned, "but know that the next time you go down, you will never get back up."

Thibbledorf Pwent, rarely shaken, considered the grim promise and his opponent's easy stance, and he remembered what Catti-brie had told him about this drow—if indeed this was the legendary Drizzt Do'Urden. "Guess we're friends," the unnerved dwarf admitted, and he slowly rose.

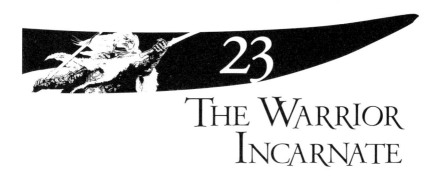

23

THE WARRIOR
INCARNATE

With Pwent backtracking and leading the way, Drizzt was sure he would soon learn the fate of his friends, and would face his evil sister once more. The battlerager couldn't tell him much about Bruenor and the others, only that when he had been separated from them, they were being hard pressed.

The news drove Drizzt on more quickly. Images of Catti-brie, a helpless prisoner being tortured by Vierna, flitted on the edges of his consciousness. He pictured stubborn Bruenor spitting in Vierna's face—and Vierna tearing the dwarf's face off in reply.

Few chambers dotted this region. Long, narrow tunnels dominated, some wholly natural, others worked in places where the goblins apparently had decided that support was needed. The three came into a fully bricked tunnel then, long and straight, angling slightly up and with several side passages running off it. Drizzt didn't see the forms of the dark elves ahead of him, down the long, dark corridor, but when Twinkle flared suddenly, he did not doubt the sword's warning.

The fact was confirmed a moment later when a crossbow quarrel zipped from the darkness and stuck Regis in the arm. The halfling groaned; Drizzt pulled him back and dropped him safely behind the corner of a side passage they had just passed. By the time the drow had turned back to the main corridor, Pwent was in full charge, singing wildly, taking hit after hit from poisoned darts but walking through them without a concern.

Drizzt rushed after him, saw Pwent charge right past the dark hole of another side corridor, and knew instinctively that the dwarf likely had wandered into a trap.

Drizzt lost all track of the battlerager a moment later, when a quarrel shot past the distant dwarf to hit Drizzt. He looked down to it, hanging painfully from his forearm, and felt the burning tingle as Pwent's countering elixir battled the poison. Drizzt thought of slumping where he stood, of inviting his enemies to think that their poison had felled him again, an easy capture.

He couldn't abandon Pwent, though, and he was simply too angry to wait for this encounter any longer. The time had come to end the threat.

He slipped up to the dark hole of the side tunnel, kept Twinkle back a bit so it would not fully give him away. A roar of outrage exploded from up ahead, followed by a steady stream of dwarven curses, which told Drizzt that Pwent's intended victims had slipped away.

Drizzt heard a slight shuffle to the side, knew that the battlerager had piqued the curiosity of whoever was in there. He took one deep breath, mentally counted to three, and leaped around the corner, Twinkle flaring viciously. The closest drow fell back, firing a second crossbow quarrel at Drizzt that nicked his skin through a shoulder crease in his fine armor. He could only hope that Pwent's potion was strong enough to handle a second hit and took some comfort in the fact that Pwent had seemed to be hit repeatedly during his corridor charge.

Drizzt pressed the crossbowman backward in a rush, the evil drow fumbling to draw his melee weapon. He would have had the drow quickly, except that a second drow joined him, this one armed with sword and dirk. Drizzt had come into a small, roughly circular chamber, a second exit off to his right, probably joining the main corridor somewhere farther along. Drizzt hardly registered the physical features of the room, though, hardly took note of the initial swings of battle, parrying aside his opponents' measured strikes. His eyes remained beyond them, to the back of the room, where stood Vierna and the mercenary Jarlaxle.

"You have caused me great pains, my lost brother," Vierna snarled at him, "but the reward will be worth the cost, now that you have returned to me."

Listening to her every word, the distracted Drizzt nearly let a sword slip past his defenses. He slapped it away at the last moment and came on in a flourish, scimitars swirling in a descending, crisscrossing pattern.

The dark elf soldiers worked well together, though, and they fended off the attack, countering one after the other and forcing Drizzt back on his heels.

"I do so love to watch you fight," Vierna continued, now smiling smugly, "but I cannot take the chance that you will be slain—not yet." She began a series of chants then, and Drizzt knew her impending spell would be aimed his way, probably at his mind. He gritted his teeth and accelerated the course of his battle, conjuring images of a tortured Catti-brie, putting up a wall of sheer anger.

Vierna released her spell with a glorious cry, and waves of energy rolled over Drizzt, assaulted him and told him, mind and body, to stop in place, to simply hold still and be captured.

Inside the drow ranger welled a part of him, a primal and savage alter ego that he had not known since his days in the wild Underdark. He was the hunter again, free of emotions, free of mental vulnerability. He shrugged away the spell; his scimitars banged hard against his enemies' blades, hard-pressing his two opponents.

Vierna's eyes went wide with surprise. Jarlaxle, at her side, gave an undeniable snicker.

"Your Lolth-given powers will not affect me," Drizzt proclaimed. "I deny the Spider Queen!"

"You will be given to the Spider Queen!" Vierna shouted back, and she seemed to gain the upper hand once more as another drow soldier entered the chamber from the tunnel to Drizzt's right. "Kill him!" the priestess commanded. "Let the sacrifice be here and now. I'll tolerate no more blasphemy from this outcast!"

Drizzt was fighting magnificently, keeping both his enemies more on their heels than on their toes. If the third skilled soldier came in, however . . .

It never got to that. There came a wild roar from the tunnel on the right, and Thibbledorf Pwent, head bowed in one of his typically frantic charges, plowed through. He hit the surprised drow soldier on the side, his bent helmet spike slicing through the unfortunate elf's slender hip, tearing into his abdomen.

Pwent's powerful legs continued to drive through until he at last got tangled in the impaled drow's feet, and both combatants crashed to the floor right before a stunned Vierna.

The drow thrashed in helpless desperation as Pwent pounded him mercilessly.

Drizzt knew he had to get to his peer's side quickly, understood the danger Pwent faced with Vierna and the mercenary having open shots at him. He brought Twinkle in a flashing downward cross, deflecting both his opponents' swords to the side, and he stepped right in behind the blade, coming with his second blade at his closest opponent, the one who had hit him with the crossbow bolt and who carried no second weapon.

The arm of the other drow shot across, dirk hitting the scimitar just enough to prevent a kill. Still, Drizzt had scored a painful hit on one opponent, slicing the drow's cheek wide.

Out came Vierna's snake-headed whip, the priestess's face an image of pure rage as she beat at the prone battlerager's back. Living snake heads darted about the battlerager's fine armor, finding gaps through which they could bite at his thick hide.

Pwent wriggled his helmet spike free, drove a glove nail through the dying dark elf's face, then turned his attention to his newest attacker and her wicked weapon.

Snap!

A snake head got him on the shoulder. Two others nipped his neck. Pwent threw his arm up as he turned, but got bitten twice on the hand, his limb immediately going numb. He felt his potent elixir fighting back, but he hesitated, near to swooning.

Snap!

Vierna hit him again, all five snake heads finding a target on the dwarf's hand and face. Pwent regarded her a moment longer, formed his lips as if to speak out a curse, then he fell to the stone and flopped about like a grounded fish, his entire body nearly numb, his nerves and muscles unable to function in any coordinated way.

Vierna looked Drizzt's way, her eyes burning with open hatred. "Now all your pitiful friends are dead, my lost brother!" she growled, something she sincerely believed true. She advanced a step, snake whip held high, but paused at the sheer and unbridled rage that suddenly contorted her brother's features.

All your pitiful friends are dead!

The words burned in Drizzt's blood, turned his heart to stone.

All your pitiful friends are dead!

Catti-brie, Wulfgar, and Bruenor, everything Drizzt Do'Urden held dear, were lost to him, taken by a heritage that he had not been able to escape.

He could hardly see his opponent's movements, though he knew his scimitars were intercepting every attack with perfection, moving in a precise blur that offered his enemies no openings.

All your pitiful friends are dead!

He was the hunter again, surviving the wilds of the Underdark. He was beyond the hunter, the warrior incarnate, fighting on perfect instinct.

A sword thrust in from the right. Drizzt's scimitar slapped down across it, driving its tip to the ground. Faster than the agile evil drow could react, Drizzt turned his blade completely over the sword and heaved high, throwing the drow back a step.

Across flashed the scimitar, severing the triceps muscles on the back of the swordsman's arm. The pained drow yelled but somehow held his weapon, though it did him no good as the scimitar came back across, squealing as it cut through the fine mesh armor, drawing a line of blood across the drow's chest.

Drizzt flipped the blade over in his hand in the blink of an eye, and the scimitar flashed back the other way, high. He flipped it again and sent it back a fourth time, and the only reason he missed the mark was that the head that had been his intended target was already flying free.

All the while, the scimitar in Drizzt's other hand had parried the other opponent's attacks.

Vierna gasped, as did the remaining soldier facing Drizzt, and Drizzt would have fallen over him just as easily. He saw Jarlaxle's arm pumping, though, from beyond the opening left by the fallen opponent.

Drizzt's next dance was pure and furious desperation. His first scimitar rang out with a metallic impact. Twinkle came across and batted a second dagger aside.

It was over in a mere second, five daggers knocked away by a dark elf that hadn't even consciously seen them coming.

Jarlaxle fell back on his heels, then began to circle, laughing all the while, amazed and thrilled by the stunning display and the continuing battle.

Drizzt's troubles were not ended, though, for Vierna, crying for Lolth to be with her, leaped ahead to lend support to the soldier, and her snake-headed whip presented more problems by far than had the dead drow soldier's single sword.

⚔ ⚔ ⚔ ⚔ ⚔

Regis huddled back into as small a ball as he could manage when he saw the dark shapes drifting silently past the opening of the side passage. The halfling relaxed when the group had passed, was daring enough to crawl nearer to the entrance and use his infravision to try to discern if these were more evil dark elves.

Those red-glowing eyes gave him away; a sixth soldier was moving behind the first group.

Regis fell back with a squeak. He grabbed a rock in his plump little hand and held it out before him. A pitiful weapon indeed against the likes of a drow elf!

The dark elf considered the halfling and the tunnel all about Regis, carefully, then entered, coming in cautiously. A smile widened as he came to realize Regis's apparent helplessness.

"Already wounded?" he asked in the Common tongue.

It took Regis a moment to sort through the heavy and unfamiliar accent. He lifted the rock threateningly as the drow edged in close, kneeling to Regis's level and holding a long and cruel sword in one hand, a dagger in the other.

The drow laughed aloud. "You will strike me down with your pebble?" he taunted, and he moved his arms out wide, presenting Regis an easy opening for his chest. "Hit me, then, little halfling. Amuse me before my dagger digs a fine line across your throat."

Regis, trembling, moved the rock in a jerking motion, as though he meant to take the drow up on the offer. It was the halfling's other hand which shot forward, though, the hand holding Artemis Entreri's dropped dagger.

The jewels in the deadly blade flared appreciatively, as though the weapon had a life and a hunger of its own, when it ripped past the fine mesh armor and sank deeply into the startled dark elf's soft skin.

Regis blinked in amazement at how easily the dagger had penetrated. It seemed as though his opponent wore thin parchment instead of metallic chain mail. The halfling's hand was nearly thrown from the weapon hilt as a surge of power coursed through the dagger, into his arm. The drow tried to respond, and Regis would have had no defense if he had brought either weapon to bear.

But the drow did not, for some reason could not. His eyes remained wide in shock, his body jerked spasmodically, and it seemed to Regis as if his very life force was being stolen away. His own mouth agape, Regis stared into the most profound expression of horror he had ever seen.

More vital energy surged up the halfling's arm; he heard the drow's weapons fall to the stone. Regis could think only of old tales his papa had told him of frightening night creatures. He felt as he imagined a vampire must feel when feeding on the blood of its victims, felt a perverse warmth wash over him.

His wounds were on the mend!

The drow victim slumped lifelessly to the stone. Regis sat staring blankly at the magical dagger. He shuddered many times, recalling vividly each occasion when he had nearly felt that weapon's wicked sting.

✕ ✕ ✕ ✕ ✕

The two drow moved silently but swiftly through the winding tunnels that would bring them to Vierna and Jarlaxle. They were confident they had out-distanced the outrageous dwarf, did not know that Pwent had sidetracked and had gotten to Vierna first.

Nor did they know that another dwarf had entered the tunnels, a red-bearded dwarf whose teary eyes promised death to any enemy he stumbled upon.

The dark elves turned a bend into the tunnel that would get them to the side room, parallel to the main tunnel. They saw the short but wide form of the dwarf swing about, just a few strides ahead of them, and charge in fearlessly, wildly.

The three opponents intertwined in a confused jumble, Bruenor shield-rushing with abandon, whipping his many-notched axe about him blindly.

"Ye killed me boy!" the dwarf bellowed, and though neither of his opponents could understand the Common tongue, they could discern Bruenor's rage clearly enough. One of the drow regained his footing and slipped his sword over the emblazoned shield, scoring a hit on the dwarf's shoulder that should have stolen the strength from that arm.

If Bruenor even knew he had been hit, he did not show it.

"Me boy!" he growled, slapping aside the other drow's sword with a powerful swipe of his heavy axe. The drow replaced the sword with his second sword, again pressing the dwarf. But Bruenor accepted the hit, didn't even flinch, his thoughts purely aimed for the kill.

He chopped his axe in a low swoop. The drow hopped the blade, but Bruenor stopped the swing and turned it about. The drow tried to hop a second time as soon as he landed, but Bruenor's movement was too quick, the dwarf jerking the axe around the drow's ankle and heaving with all his strength, taking the drow from his feet.

The other dark elf came over the dwarf, trying to shield his downed companion. His sword slashed across, scarring Bruenor's face, blinding the dwarf in one eye. Again Bruenor ignored the searing agony, bulled ahead within striking distance.

"Me boy!" he cried again, and he chopped down with all his strength, his axe blade cracking through the scrambling drow's spine.

Bruenor threw his shield up just in time to stop a sword thrust from the standing drow. Off balance and shuffling backward, the dwarf tugged repeatedly, finally tearing the weapon free.

⚔ ⚔ ⚔ ⚔ ⚔

Snake heads seemed to work independently of each other, assaulting Drizzt from different angles, snapping and coiling to snap again. Spurred on by the sight of Vierna fighting beside him, the male drow pressed Drizzt as well, sword and dirk working furiously, that he might score the kill for the priestess, for the glory of the wicked Spider Queen.

Drizzt kept his composure throughout the assault, worked his scimitars and his feet in harmony to block or dodge, and to keep his opponents, particularly Vierna, back from him.

He knew he was in trouble, though, especially when he noticed Jarlaxle, the devious mercenary, circling behind, finding an opening between Vierna and the male soldier. Drizzt expected another series of flying daggers, did not honestly know how he would escape their bite this time with Vierna's whip demanding his attention.

His fears doubled when he saw the mercenary point out at him, not with a dagger, but a wand.

"A pity, Drizzt Do'Urden," the mercenary said. "I would give many lives to own a warrior of your skills." He began to chant in the drow tongue. Drizzt tried to go to the side, but Vierna and the other drow worked him hard, kept him in line.

There came a flash, a lightning bolt, beginning just ahead of the ducking Vierna and the drow soldier. But there came, too, just as the mercenary uttered the triggering words, a flying black form, from behind Drizzt, that clipped the drow ranger's shoulder as it leaped past him and flew through the opening between Vierna and her male ally.

Guenhwyvar took the blast full force, absorbed the energy of the lightning bolt before it ever got started. The panther soared through its magical force, slamming into the surprised mercenary and driving him to the stone.

The sudden flash, the sudden appearance of the panther, did not distract the veteran Drizzt. Nor did Vierna, so filled with hatred, so obsessed with this kill, turn her attention from the furious battle. The other drow, though, squinted at the sudden flash and turned his head for an instant to look over his shoulder.

In that instant, when the drow turned back to the battle, he found Twinkle's deadly point already passing through his armor and reaching for his heart.

⚔ ⚔ ⚔ ⚔ ⚔

The flash had lasted no more than a split second, and it hadn't brought too much light into the main corridor beyond the entrance of the side chamber, but in that split second, Catti-brie, crouched farther down the hall to watch Guenhwyvar's progress, saw the slender forms of the approaching dark elf band.

She put an arrow into the air and used its silvery light to discern the dark elves' exact positions. Her face locked in a merciless grimace and the battered young woman rose behind the arrow's silvery wake to steadily begin stalking her enemies, nocking another arrow as she went.

Vengeance for Wulfgar dominated her every thought. She knew no fear, did not even flinch as she heard the expected reply from hand-crossbows. Two quarrels stung her.

Another arrow went off, this one catching a dark elf in the shoulder and hurling him to the floor. Before its streaking light had dissipated, Catti-brie fired a third, this one screeching like a banshee as it careened off the worked tunnel's stone walls.

Still the young woman walked on. She knew the dark elves could see her every step, while she caught only silhouetted glimpses of the elves as her arrows streaked past.

Instinct told her to put an arrow up high, and she smiled grimly as it connected with a levitating drow, catching him squarely in the face as he rose, blowing his head apart. The force of the blow spun the body over, and it hung, motionless, in midair.

Catti-brie did not see her next arrow go off, and only then did she realize that the dark elves had put a globe of darkness over her. How foolish! she thought, for now they could not see her as she could not see them.

Still she walked, out of the globe, firing again, killing another of her enemies.

A crossbow quarrel hit the side of her face, scraped painfully against her jawbone.

Catti-brie walked on, jaw set, teeth gritted tightly. She saw the red-glowing eyes of the remaining two drow closing on her fast, knew that they had drawn swords and charged. She put the bow up, using their eyes as beacons.

A globe of darkness fell over her.

Terror welled up inside the young woman, but she fought it back stubbornly, her expression not changing. She knew she had only moments before a drow sword plunged through her. Her mind recalled the last positions in which she had seen her enemies, showed her the angles for her shot.

She put another arrow up, heard the slightest scuffle ahead and to the left, turned, and fired. Then she loosed a third and a fourth, using no guidance beyond her instinct, hoping that she might at least wound the charging dark elves and slow their progress. She fell flat to the floor and fired sidelong, then winced as her arrow soared away in the blackness, apparently not connecting.

Instincts guiding her still, Catti-brie rolled to her back and fired above her, heard a dull thump, then a sharp crack as the missile drove through a floating drow and into the ceiling. Chunks of rubble fell from above, and Catti-brie covered up.

She remained in a defensive position for a long while, expecting the ceiling to fall on her, expecting a dark elf to rush up and slash her apart.

He got his sword near the dwarf far more often than the dwarf's bulky axe came near to hitting him, but the lone drow facing Bruenor knew he could not win, could not stop this enraged enemy. He called upon his innate magic and lined Bruenor with blue-glowing, harmless flames—faerie fire, it was called—distinctively outlining the dwarf's form and presenting the drow with an easier target.

Bruenor didn't even flinch.

The drow came with a vicious, straightforward thrust that forced the dwarf back on his heels, then turned and fled, thinking to put a few feet between him and his enemy, then turn and drop a darkness globe over the dwarf.

Bruenor didn't try to match the drow's long strides. He brought his axe in, clasped it in both hands, and pulled it back over his head.

"Me boy!" the dwarf yelled with all his rage, and with all his strength he hurled the axe, end over end. It was a daring move, a move offered by the desperation of a father who had lost his child. Bruenor's axe would not return to him as Aegis-fang had to Wulfgar. If the axe did not hit the mark . . .

It caught the drow just as he was turning the corner back into the winding side tunnel, diving into his hip and back and hurling him across the way to collide with the opposite corner. He tried to recover, wriggled about on the floor for a few moments, searching for his lost sword and air to breathe.

As his hand neared the hilt of his fallen weapon, a dwarven boot slammed down atop it, crushing the fingers.

Bruenor considered the angle of the sticking axe and the gush of blood pouring all about the weapon's blade. "Ye're dead," he said coldly to the dark elf, and he tore the weapon free with a sickening crackle.

The drow heard the words distantly, but his mind had shut down by that time, his thoughts flowing away from him as surely as was his life's blood.

Vierna did not relent as her companion fell dead, showed no signs that she cared at all for the battle's sudden turn. Drizzt's stomach turned at the sight of his sister, her features locked in the hatred that the Spider Queen so often fostered, a rage beyond reason, beyond consciousness and conscience.

Drizzt did not let his ambivalence affect his swordplay, though, not after Vierna had proclaimed his friends dead. He hit the snapping snake heads often, but couldn't seem to connect solidly enough to seriously damage any.

One got its fangs into his arm. Drizzt felt the numbing tingle and whipped his other blade across to sever the thing.

The movement left his opposite flank open, though, and a second head got him on the shoulder. A third came in for the side of his face.

His backhand slash took the nearest viper's head and drove the other attacking snake away.

Vierna's whip had only three heads remaining, but the hits had staggered Drizzt. He rocked back a few steps, found some support in the solid wall along the side of the entryway. He looked to his shoulder, horrified to see the severed head of the snake still holding fast, its fangs deeply embedded.

Only then did Drizzt notice the familiar silver flashes of Taulmaril, Catti-brie's bow. Guenhwyvar was alive and about; Catti-brie was out in the hall, fighting; and from somewhere far down the other corridor, the one along the right-hand side of the small chamber, Drizzt heard the unmistakable roar of Bruenor Battlehammer's litany of rage.

"Me boy!"

"You said they were dead," Drizzt remarked to Vierna. He steadied himself against the wall.

"They do not matter!" Vierna yelled back at him, obviously as amazed as Drizzt by the revelation. "You are all that matters, you and the glories your death will bring me!" She launched herself forward at her wounded brother, three snake heads leading the way.

Drizzt had found his strength again, had found it in the presence of his friends, in the knowledge that they, too, were involved in this fight and would need him to win.

Instead of lashing out or swiping across, Drizzt let the snake heads come to him. He got bit again, twice, but Twinkle split one viper's rushing head down the middle, leaving its torn body writhing uselessly.

Drizzt kicked off the wall, driving Vierna back in surprise. He worked his blades fast and hard, aiming always for the snakes of Vierna's whip, though more than once he felt as if he could have slipped through his sister's defenses and scored a hit on her body.

Another snake head dropped to the floor.

Vierna came across with the decimated whip, but a scimitar sliced deeply into her forearm before she could snap the remaining snake head forward. The weapon flew to the floor. The writhing snake became a lifeless thong as soon as the whip left Vierna's hand.

Vierna hissed—she seemed an animal—at Drizzt, her empty hands grasping the air repeatedly.

Drizzt did not immediately advance, did not have to, for Twinkle's deadly tip was poised only inches from his sister's vulnerable breast.

Vierna's hand twitched toward her belt, where twin maces, carved in intricate runes of spiderwebs, awaited. Drizzt could well guess the power of those weapons, and he knew firsthand from his days in Menzoberranzan Vierna's skill in using them.

"Do not," he ordered, indicating the weapons.

"We were both trained by Zaknafein," Vierna reminded him, and the mention of his father stung Drizzt. "Do you fear to find out who best learned the many lessons?"

"We were both sired by Zaknafein," Drizzt retorted, tapping Vierna's hand away from her belt with Twinkle's furiously glowing blade. "Do not continue this and dishonor him. There is a better way, my sister, a light you cannot know."

Vierna's cackling laughter mocked him. Did he really believe he could reform her, a priestess of Lolth?

"Do not!" Drizzt commanded more forcefully as Vierna's hand again inched toward the nearest mace.

She lurched for it. Twinkle plunged through her breast, through her heart, its bloody tip coming out her back.

Drizzt was right against her then, holding her arms in tight, supporting her as her legs failed her.

They stared at each other, unblinking, as Vierna slowly slumped to the floor. Gone was her rage, her obsession, replaced by a look of serenity, a rare expression on the face of a drow.

"I am sorry," was all Drizzt could quietly mouth.

Vierna shook her head, refusing any apology. To Drizzt, it seemed as if that buried part of her that was Zaknafein Do'Urden's daughter approved of this ending.

Vierna's eyes then closed forever.

24

THE LONG WALK HOME

Well done." The words came at Drizzt unexpectedly, jerked him into the realization that while Vierna was dead, the battle might not yet be won. He jumped aside, scimitars coming up defensively before him.

He lowered the weapons when he considered Jarlaxle, the mercenary sitting propped against the chamber's far wall, one leg sticking out to the side at a weird angle.

"The panther," the mercenary explained, speaking the Common tongue as fluidly as if he had spent his life on the surface. "I thought I would be killed. The panther had me down." Jarlaxle gave a shrug. "Perhaps my lightning bolt hurt the beast."

The mention of the lightning bolt reminded Drizzt of the wand, reminded Drizzt that this drow was still very dangerous. He went down in a crouch, circling defensively.

Jarlaxle winced in pain and held an empty hand up in front of him to calm the alerted ranger. "The wand is put away," he assured Drizzt. "I would have no desire to use it if I had you helpless—as you believe you have me."

"You meant to kill me," Drizzt replied coldly.

Again the mercenary shrugged, and a smile widened on his face. "Vierna would have killed me if she had won and I had not come to her aid," he explained calmly. "And, skilled as you may be, I thought she would win."

It seemed logical enough, and Drizzt knew well that pragmatism was a common trait among dark elves. "Lolth would reward you still for my death," Drizzt reasoned.

"I do not slave for the Spider Queen," Jarlaxle replied. "I am an opportunist."

"You make a threat?"

The mercenary laughed loudly, then winced again at the throb in his broken leg.

Bruenor rushed into the chamber from the side passage. He glanced at Drizzt, then focused on Jarlaxle, his rage not yet played out.

"Hold!" Drizzt commanded him as the dwarf started for the apparently helpless mercenary.

Bruenor skidded to a stop and put a cold stare on Drizzt, a look made more ominous by the dwarf's ripped face, his right eye badly gouged and a line of blood running from the top of his forehead to the bottom of his left cheek. "We're not for needing prisoners," Bruenor growled.

Drizzt considered the venom in Bruenor's voice and considered the fact that he had not seen Wulfgar anywhere in this fight. "Where are the others?"

"I'm right here," replied Catti-brie, coming into the chamber from the main tunnel, behind Drizzt.

Drizzt turned to regard her, her dirty face and incredibly grim expression revealing much. "Wulf—" he started to ask, but Catti-brie shook her head solemnly, as though she could not bear to hear the name spoken aloud. She walked near Drizzt and he winced, seeing the small crossbow quarrel still sticking from the side of her jaw.

Drizzt gently stroked Catti-brie's face, then took hold of the obscene dart and yanked it free. He brought his hand immediately to the young woman's shoulder, lending her support as waves of nausea and pain swept over her.

"I pray I did not harm the panther," Jarlaxle interrupted, "a magnificent beast indeed!"

Drizzt spun about, his lavender eyes flashing.

"He's baiting ye," Bruenor remarked, his fingers moving eagerly over the handle of his bloody axe, "begging for mercy without the begging."

Drizzt wasn't so sure. He knew the horrors of Menzoberranzan, knew the lengths that some drow would travel to survive. His own father, Zaknafein, the drow Drizzt had loved most dearly, had been a killer, had served as Matron Malice's assassin out of a simple will to survive. Might it be that this mercenary was of similar pragmatism?

Drizzt wanted to believe that. With Vierna dead at his feet, his family, his ties to his heritage, were no more, and he wanted to believe that he was not alone in the world.

"Kill the dog, or we drag him back," Bruenor growled, his patience exhausted.

"What would be your choice, Drizzt Do'Urden?" Jarlaxle asked calmly.

Drizzt considered Jarlaxle once more. This one was not so much like Zaknafein, he decided, for he remembered his father's rage when it was rumored that Drizzt had slain surface elves. There was indeed an undeniable difference between Zaknafein and Jarlaxle. Zaknafein killed only those he believed deserved death, only those serving Lolth or other evil minions. He would not have walked beside Vierna on this hunt.

The sudden rage that welled up in Drizzt almost sent him rushing at the mercenary. He fought the impulse back, though, remembering again the weight of Menzoberranzan, the burden of pervasive evil that bowed the backs of those few dark elves who were not of typical demeanor. Zaknafein had admitted to Drizzt that he had almost lost himself to the ways of Lolth many times, and in his own trek through the Underdark Drizzt Do'Urden often feared what he would, what he had, become.

How could he pass judgment on this dark elf? The scimitars went back into their sheaths.

"He killed me boy!" Bruenor roared, apparently understanding Drizzt's intentions.

Drizzt shook his head resolutely.

"Mercy is a curious thing, Drizzt Do'Urden," Jarlaxle remarked. "Strength, or weakness?"

"Strength," Drizzt answered quickly.

"It can save your soul," Jarlaxle replied, "or damn your body." He tipped his wide-brimmed hat to Drizzt, then moved suddenly, his arm coming free of his cloak. Something small slammed the floor in front of Jarlaxle, exploding, filling that area of the chamber with opaque smoke.

"Damn him!" Catti-brie growled, and she snapped off a streaking shot that cut through the haze and thundered against the stone of the far wall. Bruenor rushed in, axe flailing wildly, but there was nothing there to hit. The mercenary was gone.

By the time Bruenor came out of the smoke, both Drizzt and Catti-brie were standing over the prone form of Thibbledorf Pwent.

"He dead?" the dwarf king asked.

Drizzt bent to the battlerager, remembered that Pwent had been hit viciously by Vierna's snake-headed whip. "No," he replied. "The whips are not designed to kill, just to paralyze."

His keen ears caught the words as Bruenor muttered, "Too bad," under his breath.

It took them a few moments to revive the battlerager. Pwent hopped up to his feet—and promptly fell over once more. He struggled back up, humbled until Drizzt made the mistake of thanking him for his valuable help.

In the main corridor, they found the five dead drow, one still hanging near the ceiling in the area where the globe of darkness had been. Catti-brie's explanation of where this small band had come from sent a shudder through Drizzt.

"Regis," he breathed, and he rushed off down the hallway, to the side passage where he had left the halfling.

There sat Regis, terrified, half-buried under a dead drow, holding the jeweled dagger tightly in his hand.

"Come on, my friend," the relieved Drizzt said to him. "It is time we went home."

✕ ✕ ✕ ✕ ✕

The five beaten companions leaned on each other as they made their way slowly and quietly through the tunnels. Drizzt looked around at the ragged group, at Bruenor with his eye closed and Pwent still having trouble coordinating his muscles. Drizzt's own foot throbbed painfully. The realization of the wound became clearer as the adrenaline rush of battle slowly ebbed. It was not the physical problems that most alarmed the drow ranger, though. The impact of Wulfgar's loss seemed to have fully sunk in for all those who had been his companions.

Would Catti-brie be able to call upon her rage once more, to ignore the emotional battering she had taken and fight with all her heart? Would Bruenor, so wickedly wounded that Drizzt was not certain he would make it back to Mithral Hall alive, be able to guide himself through yet another battle?

Drizzt couldn't be sure, and his sigh of relief was sincere when General Dagna, at the lead of the dwarven cavalry and its grunting mounts, rounded the bend in the tunnel far ahead.

Bruenor allowed himself to collapse at the sight, and the dwarves wasted little time in getting their injured king, and Regis, strapped to war pigs and ushered out of the untamed complex. Pwent went, too, accepting the reins of a pig, but Drizzt and Catti-brie did not take a direct route back to Mithral Hall. Accompanied by the three displaced dwarven riders, General Dagna included, the young woman led Drizzt to Wulfgar's fateful cave.

There could be no doubt, Drizzt realized as soon as he looked at the collapsed alcove, no doubt, no reprieve. His friend was gone forever.

Catti-brie recounted the details of the battle, had to stop for a long while before she mustered the voice to tell of Wulfgar's valiant end.

She finally looked to the pile of rubble, quietly said "Good-bye," and walked out of the room with the three dwarves.

Drizzt stood alone for many minutes, staring helplessly. He could hardly believe that mighty Wulfgar was under there. The moment seemed unreal to him, against his sensibilities.

But it was real.

And Drizzt was helpless.

Pangs of guilt assaulted the drow, realizations that he had caused his sister's hunt, and thus had caused Wulfgar's death. He summarily dismissed the thoughts, though, refusing to consider them again.

Now was the time to bid farewell to his trusted companion, his dear friend. He wanted to be with Wulfgar, to be beside the young barbarian and comfort him, guide him, to share one more mischievous wink with the barbarian and boldly face together whatever mysteries death presented to them.

"Farewell, my friend," Drizzt whispered, trying futilely to keep his voice from breaking. "This journey you make alone."

⚔ ⚔ ⚔ ⚔ ⚔

The return to Mithral Hall was not a time of celebration for the weary, battered friends. They could not claim victory over what had happened in the lower tunnels. Each of the four, Drizzt, Bruenor, Catti-brie, and Regis, held a different perspective on the loss of Wulfgar, for the barbarian's relationship had been very different for each of them—as a son to Bruenor, a fiance to Catti-brie, a comrade to Drizzt, a protector to Regis.

Bruenor's physical wounds were most serious. The dwarf king had lost an eye and would carry an angry reddish blue scar from forehead to jawline for the rest of his days. The physical pains, though, were the least of Bruenor's troubles.

Many times over the next few days the sturdy dwarf suddenly remembered some arrangement yet to be made with the presiding priest, only to recall that Cobble would not be there to help him sort things out, to recall that there would be no wedding that spring in Mithral Hall.

Drizzt could see the intense grief etched on the dwarf's face. For the first time in the years he had known Bruenor, the ranger thought the dwarf looked old and tired. Drizzt could hardly bear to look at him, but his heart broke even more whenever he chanced by Catti-brie.

She had been young and vital, full of life and feeling immortal. Now Catti-brie's perception of the world had been shattered.

The friends kept to themselves mostly as the interminably long hours crawled by. Drizzt, Bruenor, and Catti-brie saw each other rarely, and none of them saw Regis.

None of them knew that the halfling had gone out from Mithral Hall, out the west exit, into Keeper's Dale.

Regis inched out onto a rocky spur, fifty feet above the jagged floor of the southern end of a long and narrow valley. He came upon a limp figure, hanging by the shreds of a torn cloak. The halfling lay atop the garment, hugging close to the exposed stone as the winds buffeted him. To his amazement, the man below him shifted slightly.

"Alive?" the halfling whispered approvingly. Entreri, his body obviously broken and torn, had been hanging for more than a day. "Still you're alive?" Always cautious, especially where Artemis Entreri was concerned, Regis took out the jeweled dagger and placed its razor edge under the remaining seam of the cloak so that a flick of his wrist would send the dangerous assassin falling free.

Entreri managed to tilt his head to the side and groan weakly, though he could not find the strength to form words.

"You have something of mine," Regis said to him.

The assassin turned a little more, straining to see, and Regis winced and pulled back a bit at the grotesque sight of the man's shattered face. His cheekbone blasted to powder, the skin torn from the side of his face, the assassin obviously could not see out of the eye he had turned toward Regis.

And Regis was certain that the man, his bones broken, agony assaulting him from every garish wound, wasn't even aware that he could not see.

"The ruby pendant," Regis said more forcefully, spotting the hypnotic gemstone as it hung low on its chain beneath Entreri.

Entreri apparently comprehended, for his hand inched toward the item but fell limp, too weak to continue.

Regis shook his head and took up his walking stick. Keeping the dagger firm against the cloak, he reached below the spur and prodded Entreri.

The assassin did not respond.

Regis poked him again, much harder, then several more times before he was convinced the assassin was indeed helpless. His smile wide, Regis worked the tip of the walking stick under the chain around the assassin's neck and gently angled it out and around, lifting the pendant free.

"How does it feel?" Regis asked as he gathered in his precious ruby. He poked down with the stick, popping Entreri on the back of the head.

"How does it feel to be helpless, a prisoner of someone else's whims? How many have you put another in the position you now enjoy?" Regis popped him again. "A hundred?"

Regis moved to strike again, but then he noticed something else of value hanging on a cord from the assassin's belt. Retrieving this item would be far more difficult than getting the pendant, but Regis was a thief, after all, and he prided himself (secretly, of course) on being a good one. He looped his silken rope about the spur and swung low, placing his foot on Entreri's back for balance.

The mask was his.

For good measure, the thieving halfling fished his hands through the assassin's pockets, finding a small purse and a fairly valuable gemstone.

Entreri groaned and tried to swing about. Frightened by the movement, Regis was back on the spur in the blink of an eye, the dagger again firmly against the tattered cloak's seam.

"I could show mercy," the halfling remarked, looking up to the vultures circling overhead, the carrion birds that had shown the way to Entreri. "I could get Bruenor and Drizzt to bring you in. Perhaps you have information that might prove valuable."

Regis's memories of Entreri's tortures came flooding back when he noticed his own hand, missing two fingers that the assassin had cut away—with the very dagger Regis now held. How beautifully ironic, Regis thought.

"No," he decided. "I do not feel particularly merciful this day." He looked up again. "I should leave you hanging here for the vultures to pick at," he said.

Entreri in no way reacted.

Regis shook his head. He could be cold, but not to that level, not to the level of Artemis Entreri. "The enchanted wings saved you when Drizzt let you fall," he said, "but they are no more!"

Regis flicked his wrist, severing the cloak's remaining seam, and let the assassin's weight do the rest.

Entreri was still hanging when Regis slid back off the spur, but the cloak had begun to tear.

Artemis Entreri had run out of tricks.

25
IN THE PALM OF HER HAND

Matron Baenre sat back easily in the cushioned chair, her withered fingers tapping impatiently on the hard stone arms of the seat. A similar chair, the only other furnishing in this particular meeting room, rested across from her, and in it sat the most extraordinary mercenary.

Jarlaxle had just returned from Mithral Hall with a report that Matron Baenre had fully expected.

"Drizzt Do'Urden remains free," she muttered under her breath. Oddly enough, it seemed to Jarlaxle as if that fact did not displease the conniving matron mother. What was Baenre up to this time? the mercenary wondered.

"I blame Vierna," Jarlaxle said calmly. "She underestimated the wiles of her younger brother." He gave a sly chuckle. "And paid for her mistake with her life."

"I blame you," Matron Baenre quickly put in. "How will you pay?"

Jarlaxle did not smile, but simply returned the threat with a solid glare. He knew Baenre well enough to understand that, like an animal, she could smell fear, and that smell often guided her next actions.

Matron Baenre matched the stern look, fingers tap-tapping.

"The dwarves organized against us more quickly than we believed possible," the mercenary went on after a few uncomfortable moments of silence. "Their defenses are strong, as is their resolve and apparently, their loyalty to Drizzt Do'Urden. My plan"—he emphasized the personal reference—"worked perfectly. We took Drizzt Do'Urden without much trouble. But Vierna, against my wishes, allowed the human spy his deal before she had put enough distance between us and Mithral Hall. She did not understand the loyalty of Drizzt Do'Urden's friends."

"You were sent to retrieve Drizzt Do'Urden," Matron Baenre said too quietly. "Drizzt is not here. Thus, you have failed."

Jarlaxle went silent once more. There was no sense in arguing Matron Baenre's logic, he knew, for she needed no approval, and sought none, in any of her actions. This was Menzoberranzan, and in the drow city, Matron Baenre had no peer.

Still, Jarlaxle wasn't afraid that the withered matron mother would kill him. She continued with her tongue-lashing, her voice rising into a shriek by the time she was done with the scolding, but through it all, Jarlaxle got the distinct impression that she was enjoying herself. The game was still on, after all; Drizzt Do'Urden remained free and waiting to be caught, and Jarlaxle knew that Matron Baenre would not see the loss of a couple dozen soldiers—male, at that—and Vierna Do'Urden as any great price.

Matron Baenre then began discussing the many ways that she might torture Jarlaxle to death—she favored "skin-stealing," a drow method of taking a victim's skin, one inch at a time, using various acids and specially designed jagged knives.

Jarlaxle had all he could handle in biting back his laughter at that notion.

Matron Baenre stopped suddenly, and the mercenary feared that she had figured out that he was not taking her seriously. That, Jarlaxle knew, could be a fatal mistake. Baenre didn't care about Vierna or the dead males—she apparently was pleased that Drizzt was still on the loose—but to wound her pride was to surely die a slow and agonizing death.

Baenre's pause went on interminably; she even looked away. When she turned back to Jarlaxle, he breathed a sincere sigh of relief, for she was at ease, smiling widely as though something had just come to her.

"I am not pleased," she said, an obvious lie, "but I will forgive your failure this time. You have brought back valuable information."

Jarlaxle knew who she was referring to.

"Leave me," she said, waving her hand with apparent disinterest.

Jarlaxle would have preferred to stay longer, to get some hint at what the beautifully conniving matron mother might be plotting. He knew better than to contradict Baenre when she was in such a curious mood, though. Jarlaxle had survived as a rogue for centuries because he knew when to take his leave.

He pulled himself up from the chair and eased his weight onto a broken leg, then winced and nearly fell over into Baenre's lap. Shaking his head, Jarlaxle picked up his cane.

"Triel did not complete the healing," the mercenary said apologetically. "She treated my wound, as you instructed, but I did not feel that all of her energy was into the spell."

"You deserve it, I am sure," was all the cold Matron Baenre would offer, and she waved Jarlaxle away once more. Baenre had probably instructed her daughter to leave him in pain, and was probably taking great pleasure in watching him limp from the room.

As soon as the door was closed behind the departing mercenary, Matron Baenre enjoyed a heartfelt laugh. Baenre had sanctioned the attempt at capturing Drizzt Do'Urden, but that did not mean that she hoped it would succeed. In truth, the withered matron mother was hoping that things would turn out pretty much as they had.

"You are not a fool, Jarlaxle. That is why I let you live," she said to the empty room. "You must realize by now that this is not about Drizzt Do'Urden. He is an inconvenience, a moss gnat, and hardly worthy of my thoughts.

"But he is a convenient excuse," Matron Baenre went on, fiddling with a wide dwarven tooth, fashioned into a ring and hanging on a chain about her neck. Baenre reached up and undid the clasp on the necklace, then held the item aloft in the palm of her hand and chanted softly, using the ancient Dwarvish tongue.

> *For all the dwarves in all the Realms*
> *Heavy shields and shining helms,*
> *Swinging hammers, hear them ring,*
> *Come forth my prize, tormented King!*

A swirl of bluish smoke appeared at the tip of the dwarf tooth. The mist gained speed and size as the seconds slipped past. Soon a small twister stood up from Matron Baenre's hand. It leaned away from her at her mental bidding, intensifying in speed and in light, growing as it stretched outward. After a few moments, it broke free of the tooth altogether and swirled in the middle of the room, where it glowed a fierce blue light.

Gradually an image formed in the middle of that swirl: an old, gray-bearded dwarf standing very still in the vortex, upraised hands clenched tightly.

The wind, the blue light, died away, leaving the specter of the ancient dwarf. It was not a solid image, merely translucent, but the ghost's distinctive details— the red-tinged gray beard and steel-gray eyes—showed clearly.

"Gandalug Battlehammer," Matron Baenre said immediately, utilizing the binding power of the dwarf's true name to keep the spirit fully under her command. Before her stood the First King of Mithral Hall, the patron of Clan Battlehammer.

The old dwarf looked at his ancient nemesis, his eyes narrowed in hatred.

"It has been too long," Baenre teased.

"I'd walk an eternity o' torment as long as I'd the guarantee that yerself'd not be there, drow witch!" the ghost replied in its gravelly voice. "I'd . . . "

A wave of Matron Baenre's hand silenced the angry spirit. "I did not recall you to hear your complaints," she replied. "I thought to offer you some information that you might find entertaining."

The spirit turned sideways and cocked his hairy head to stare over his shoulder, pointedly looking away from Baenre. Gandalug was trying to appear indifferent, removed, but like most dwarves, the old king was not so good at hiding his true feelings.

"Come now, dear Gandalug," Baenre teased. "How boring the waiting must be for you! Centuries have passed as you have sat in your prison. Surely you care how your descendants fare."

Gandalug turned a pensive pose over the other shoulder, back toward Matron Baenre. How he hated the withered old drow! Her talk of his descendants alarmed him, though, that much he could not deny. Heritage was the most important thing to any respectable dwarf, even above gems and jewels, and Gandalug, as the patron of his clan, considered every dwarf who allied himself with Clan Battlehammer as one of his own children.

He could not hide his worry.

"Did you hope that I would forget Mithral Hall?" Baenre asked teasingly. "It has been only two thousand years, old king."

"Two thousand years," Gandalug spat back disgustedly. "Why don't ye just lay down and die, old witch?"

"Soon," Baenre answered and nodded at the truth of her own statement, "but not before I complete what I began two thousand years ago.

"Do you remember that fateful day, old king?" she went on, and Gandalug winced, understanding that she meant to replay it again, to open old wounds and leave the dwarf in perfect despair.

> *When the halls were new, when the veins ran thick,*
> *Gleaming walls, with silver slick,*
> *When the king was young, the adventure fresh,*
> *And your kinfolk sang as one,*
> *When Gandalug ruled from the mithral throne,*
> *Clan Battlehammer had begun.*

Compelled by the magic within Matron Baenre's continuing chant, Gandalug Battlehammer found his thoughts cascading back along the corridors of the distant past, back to the time of the founding of Mithral Hall, back to when he looked ahead with hope for his children, and their children after them.

Back to the time right before he had met Yvonnel Baenre.

⋈ ⋈ ⋈ ⋈ ⋈

Gandalug stood watching the cutting as the busy dwarves of Clan Battlehammer chipped away at the sloping walls of the great cavern, cutting the steps that would become the Undercity of Mithral Hall. This was the vision of Bruenor, Gandalug's third son, the clan's greatest hero, who had led the procession that had brought the thousand dwarves to this place.

"Ye did well in givin' it to Bruenor," the dirty dwarf beside the aged king remarked, referring to Gandalug's decision to award his throne to Bruenor, and not to Bruenor's older brothers. Unlike many of the races, dwarves did not automatically award their inheritance or titles to the eldest of their children, taking the more pragmatic approach of choosing which they thought most fitting.

Gandalug nodded and was content. He was old, well past four centuries, and tired. The quest of his life had been to establish his own clan, the Battlehammer clan, and he had spent the better part of two centuries seeking the location of a fitting kingdom. Soon after Clan Battlehammer had tamed and settled Mithral Hall, Gandalug had begun to see the truth, had begun to realize that his time and his duty had passed. His ambitions had been met, and thus contented, Gandalug found that he could not muster the energy to match the plans his sons and the younger dwarves laid out before him, plans for the great Undercity, for a bridge spanning the huge chasm at the complex's eastern end, for a city above the ground, south of the mountains, to serve as a trading link with the surrounding kingdoms.

It all sounded wonderful to Gandalug, of course, but he hadn't the yearning to see it through.

The old graybeard, his hair and whiskers still showing hints of their previous fiery red, turned an appreciative look upon his dear companion. Through those two centuries, Gandalug could not have asked for a better traveling companion than Crommower Pwent, and now, with one more journey before him, the king who had stepped down from the throne was glad for the company.

Unlike the regal Gandalug, Crommower was dirty. He wore a beard, black still, and kept his head shaved so that his huge, pointed helm would hold a tight fit. "Can't be runnin' into things with me helm turnin' aside, now can I?" Crommower was fond of saying. And in all truth, Crommower Pwent loved to run into things.

He was a battlerager, a dwarf with a singular view of the world. If it threatened his king or insulted his gods, he'd kill it, plain and simple. He'd duck his head and skewer the enemy, slam the enemy with his glove nails, with his elbow spikes, with his knee spikes. He'd bite an enemy's ear off, or his tongue out, or his head off if he could. He'd scratch and claw and kick and spit, but most of all, he'd win.

Gandalug, whose life had been hard in the untamed world, valued Crommower above all others in his clan, even above his precious and loyal children. That view was not shared among the clan. Some of the dwarves, sturdy as they were, could hardly tolerate Crommower's odor, and the squealing of the battlerager's ridged armor grated as sourly as fingernails scratching a piece of slate.

Two centuries of traveling beside someone, of fighting beside someone, often in desperate straits, tends to make such facts diminish.

"Come, me friend," old Gandalug bade. He had already said his farewells to his children, to Bruenor, the new King of Mithral Hall, and to all his clan. Now was the time for traveling again, with Crommower beside him, as it had been for so many years. "I go to expand the boundaries of Mithral Hall," Gandalug had proclaimed, "to seek greater riches for me clan." And so the dwarves had cheered, but more than one eye had been teary that day, for all the dwarves understood that Gandalug would not be coming home.

"Think we'll get a good fight or two outta this?" Crommower eagerly asked as he skittered along beside his beloved king, his armor squealing noisily every step of the way.

The old graybeard only laughed.

The two spent many days searching the tunnels directly below and west of the Mithral Hall complex. They found little in the way of the precious silvery mithral, though—certainly no hints of any veins to match the huge deposits back in the complex proper. Undaunted, the two wanderers then went lower, into caverns that seemed foreign even to their dwarven sensibilities, into corridors where the sheer pressure of thousands of tons of rock pushed crystals out in front of them in swirling arrays, into tunnels of beautiful colors, where strange lichen glowed eerie colors.

Into the Underdark.

Long after their lamp oils had been exhausted, long after their torches had burned away, Crommower Pwent got his fight.

It started when the myriad of color patterns revealed by heat-sensing dwarven infravision blurred to gray and then disappeared altogether in a cloud of inky blackness.

"Me king!" Crommower called out wildly. "I've lost me sight!"

"As have I!" Gandalug assured the smelly battlerager, and predictably, he heard the roar and the shuffle of anxious feet as Crommower sped off, looking for an

enemy to skewer.

Gandalug ran in the noise of the battlerager's wake. He had seen enough magic to understand that some wizard or cleric had dropped a globe of darkness over them, and that, the old graybeard knew, was probably only the beginning of a more direct assault.

Crommower's grunts and crashes allowed Gandalug to get out of the darkened area with relatively few bruises. He caught a quick look at his adversary before yet another globe dropped over him.

"Drow, Crommower!" Gandalug cried, terror in his voice, for even back then, the reputation of the merciless dark elves sent shivers along the backbones of the hardiest surface dwellers.

"I seen 'em," came Crommower's surprisingly easy reply. "We oughtta kill about fifty o' the skinny things, lay 'em flat out with their hands above their heads, and use 'em for window blinds once they're stiffened!"

The sight of drow and the use of magic told Gandalug that he and the battlerager were in tight straits, but he laughed anyway, gaining confidence and strength from his friend's confident manner.

They came bouncing out of the second globe, and a third went over them, this one accompanied by the subtle clicking sound of hand-held crossbows firing.

"Will ye stop doing that?" Crommower complained to the mysterious enemies. "How am I supp—Ow! Why ye dirty sneaksters!—supposed to skewer ye if I can't see ye?"

When they came out the other side of this globe, into a wider tunnel strewn with tall stalagmite mounds and hanging stalactites, Gandalug saw Crommower yanking a small dart from the side of his neck.

The two slid to a stop; no darkened globe fell over them and no drow were in sight, though both seasoned warriors understood the many hiding places the stalagmite mounds might offer their enemies.

"Was it poisoned?" Gandalug asked with grave concern, knowing the sinister reputation of drow darts.

Crommower looked at the small quarrel curiously, then put its tip to his lips and sucked hard, furrowing his bushy eyebrows contemplatively and smacking his lips as he studied the taste.

"Yup," he announced and threw the dart over his shoulder.

"Our enemies are not far," Gandalug said, glancing all around.

"Bah, they probably runned away," snickered Crommower. "Too bad, too. Me helm's getting rusty. Could use a bit o' skinny elf blood to grease it proper. Ow!" The battlerager growled suddenly and grasped at a new dart, this one sticking from his shoulder. Following its up-angled line, Gandalug understood the trap—drow

elves were not hiding among the stalagmites, but were up above, levitating among the stalactites!

"Separate!" the battlerager cried. He grabbed Gandalug and heaved him away. Normally, dwarves would have stayed together, fought back-to-back, but Gandalug understood and agreed with Crommower's reasoning. More than one friendly dwarf had taken a glove nail or a knee spike when wild Crommower went into his fighting frenzy.

Several of the dark elves descended swiftly, weapons drawn, and Crommower Pwent, with typical battlerager intensity, went berserk. He hopped all around, slamming elves and stalagmites, skewering one drow in the belly with his helmet spike, then cursing his luck as the dying drow got stuck. Bent over as he was, Crommower took several slashing hits across his back, but he only roared in rage, flexed his considerable muscles and straightened, taking the unfortunate, impaled drow along for the ride.

With Crommower's insanity occupying most of the enemy force, Gandalug did well initially. He faced off against two drow females. The old dwarf was quite taken with how beautiful these evil creatures were, their features angled, but not sharp, their hair more lustrous than a well-groomed dwarven lady's beard, and their eyes so very intense. That observation didn't slow Gandalug's desire to gash the skin off the drow faces, though, and he whipped his battle-axe back and forth, battering aside shields and blocking weapons alike, forcing the females back.

But then Gandalug grimaced in pain, once, again, and then a third time, as some unseen missiles scorched into his back. Magical energy slipped through his fine plate armor and bit at his skin. A moment later, the old graybeard heard Crommower growl in rage and sputter, "Damn wizard!" He knew then that his friend had been similarly assaulted.

Crommower spotted the magic-thrower from under the dangling legs of the now-dead drow impaled on his helmet. "I hates wizards," he grumbled and began punching his way toward the distant drow.

The wizard said something in a language that Crommower could not understand, but he should have caught on when the six dark elves he was fighting suddenly parted ranks, opening a direct line between Crommower and the wizard.

Crommower was not in any rational state, though, consumed as he was by the battle rage, the bloodlust. Thinking to get a clear punch at the wizard, he charged ahead, the dead drow flopping atop his helm. The battlerager took no note of the wizard's chanting, no note of the metal rod the drow held out before him.

Then Crommower was flying, blinded by a sudden flash and hurled backward by the energy of a lightning bolt. He slammed a stalagmite hard and slid down to the seat of his pants.

"I hates wizards," the dwarf muttered a second time, and he heaved the dead drow off his head, leaped up, and charged again, smoking and fuming.

He dipped his head, put his helmet spike in line, and thrust forward furiously, bouncing off mounds, his armor scraping and squealing. The other dark elves he had been fighting came in at his sides, slashing with fine swords, banging with enchanted maces as the battlerager plowed through the gauntlet, and blood ran freely from several wounds.

Crommower's single cry continued without interruption; if he felt the wounds at all, he did not show it. Rage, focused directly on the drow wizard, consumed him.

The wizard realized then that his warriors would not be able to stop the insane creature. He called on his innate magic, hoping that these outrageous dwarf-things couldn't fly, and began to levitate from the floor.

Gandalug heard the commotion behind him and winced every time it sounded as though Crommower took a hit. But the old graybeard could do little to help his friend. These drow females were surprisingly good fighters, working in perfect concert and parrying all his attacks, even managing to get in a few hits of their own, one slashing with a cruelly edged sword, the other whipping a fiercely glowing mace. Gandalug bled in several places, though none of the wounds was serious.

As the three settled into a dancing rhythm, the mace-wielder stepped back from the fight and began an incantation.

"No, ye don't," Gandalug whispered, and he drove hard into the sword-wielder, forcing her into a clinch. The slender drow was no physical match for the tough dwarf's sheer strength, and Gandalug heaved her back, to collide with her companion and disrupt the spell.

On came the old graybeard, the First King of Mithral Hall, battering the two with his emblazoned shield, slamming them with the foaming mug standard of the clan he had founded.

Back down the corridor, Crommower turned to the side, virtually ran up a stalagmite, and leaped high, his helmet spike driving into the rising wizard's knee, splintering the kneecap and cutting right out the back of the leg.

The wizard screamed in agony. His levitation was strong enough to hold them both aloft, and in the blur of pain, the frightfully wounded drow couldn't think to release the spell. They hung weirdly in midair, the wizard clutching his leg, his hands weak with pain, and Crommower thrashing from side to side, destroying the leg and punching up with his glove nails. He smiled as he sank them deep into the drow's thighs.

A rain of warm blood descended over the battlerager, feeding his frenzy.

But the other drow were under Crommower, and he was not that high from the ground. He tried to tuck his legs under him as swords slashed his feet. He jerked then, and understood that this would be his final battle, as one drow produced a long lance and stuck it hard into the battlerager's kidney.

The mace-wielder fell back again, around a corner, and Gandalug closed quickly on the female with the sword. He moved as if he would shield rush again, close in tight, and heave her back as he had done before. The crafty old dwarf pulled up short, though, and fell low, his wicked axe coming across and sweeping the drow's feet out from under her. Gandalug fell over her in an instant, accepting one nasty stick from the sword, and dishing out a head-splitting chop in exchange.

He looked up just in time to see a magical hammer appear in midair before him and whack him across the face. Gandalug shifted his thick tongue about curiously, then spit out a tooth, staring incredulously at the young—and this drow was indeed young—female.

"Ye got to be kidding," the old graybeard remarked. He hardly noticed that the female had already launched a second spell, pulling the tooth to her waiting fingers with a magically conjured hand.

The magical hammer continued its assault, scoring a second hit on the side of Gandalug's head as he straightened over the drow. "Ye're dead," he promised the young female, smiling wickedly. His mirth was stolen, though, when a resounding scream split the air. Gandalug had seen many fierce battles; he knew a death cry when he heard it, and he knew that this one had come from a dwarf.

He spent an instant steadying himself, reminding himself that he and old Crommower had fully expected that this would be their last journey. When he focused ahead once more, he saw that the young female had retreated farther around the bend, and he heard her chanting softly. Gandalug knew that other dark elves would soon be at his back, but he determined then that they would find their two female companions dead. The stubborn dwarf stalked ahead, heedless of whatever magic the young drow might have waiting for him.

He spotted her, standing vulnerable in the middle of the passage, eyes closed, hands by her side, as he rounded the corner. In charged the old graybeard—to be intercepted by a sudden whirlwind, a vortex that encircled him, stopped him, and held him in place.

"What're ye about?" Gandalug roared. He fought wildly against the cunning magic, but could not break free of its stubborn grasp, could not even shuffle his feet toward the devious female.

Then Gandalug felt a horrid sensation deep within his breast. He could no longer feel the whipping of the cyclone, but its winds continued, as if they had somehow found a way to pass through his skin. Gandalug felt a tug at his soul, felt as though his insides were being ripped out.

"What're ye . . . ?" he started to ask again, but his words disappeared into blabber *as he lost control of his lips, lost control of all his body. He floated helplessly toward the drow, toward her extended hand and a curious item—what was it? he wondered. What was she holding?*

His tooth.

Then there was only white emptiness. From a great distance Gandalug heard the chatter of dark elves, and he found one last view as he looked back. A body—his body!—lay dead on the floor, surrounded by several dark elves.

His body . . .

✕ ✕ ✕ ✕ ✕

The dwarf ghost teetered weakly as he came out of the dream, the nightmare, that cruel Yvonnel Baenre, that devious young female, had once again forced upon him. Baenre knew that those recollections were the most horrid torture she could exact upon the stubborn dwarf, and she did so often.

Now Gandalug stared at her with utter hatred. Here they were, nearly two thousand years later, two thousand years of an empty white prison and terrible memories that poor Gandalug could not escape.

"When you left Mithral Hall, you gave the throne to your son," Baenre stated. She knew the story, had forced it out of her tormented prisoner many centuries before. "The new king of Mithral Hall is named Bruenor—that was your son's name, was it not?"

The spirit held steady, kept his gaze firm and determined.

Matron Baenre laughed at him. "Contained in your memories are the ways and defenses of Mithral Hall," she said, "not so different now from what they were then, if I properly understand the ways of dwarves. It is ironic, is it not, that you, great Gandalug, the founder of Mithral Hall, the patron of Clan Battlehammer, will aid in the end of the hall and the clan?"

The dwarf king howled with rage and grew in size, gigantic hands reaching out for Baenre's skinny, withered throat. The matron mother laughed at him again. She held out the tooth and the whirlwind came at her bidding, grabbing at Gandalug and banishing him back to his white prison.

"And so Drizzt Do'Urden has escaped," Matron Baenre purred, and she was not unhappy. "He is a fortunate excuse and nothing more!"

Baenre's evil smile widened as she sat comfortably in her chair, thinking of how Drizzt Do'Urden would allow her to cement the alliance she would need, thinking how coincidence and fate had given her the means and the method for the conquest she had desired for nearly two thousand years.

EPILOGUE

Drizzt Do'Urden sat in his private chambers, considering all that had transpired. Memories of Wulfgar dominated his thoughts, but they were not dark images, were not flashes of the alcove wherein Wulfgar had been buried. Drizzt remembered the many adventures, always exciting, often reckless, he had shared beside the towering man. Trusting in his faith, Drizzt placed Wulfgar in that same corner of his heart where he had tucked the memories of Zaknafein, his father. He could not deny his sadness at Wulfgar's loss, didn't want to deny it, but the many good memories of the straight-backed young barbarian could counter that sadness, bring a bittersweet smile to Drizzt Do'Urden's calm face.

He knew that Catti-brie, too, would come to a similar, accepting mind-set. She was young and strong and filled with a lust for adventure, however dangerous, as great as that of Drizzt and of Wulfgar. Catti-brie would learn to smile along with the tears.

Drizzt's only fear was for Bruenor. The dwarf king was not so young, not so ready to look ahead to what was yet to come in his remaining years. But Bruenor had suffered many tragedies in his long and hardy life, and generally speaking, it was the way of the stoic dwarves to accept death as a natural passing. Drizzt had to trust that Bruenor was strong enough to continue.

It wasn't until Drizzt focused on Regis that he considered the many other things that had occurred. Entreri, the evil man who had done grievous wrongs to so many, was gone. How many in the four corners of Faerûn would rejoice at that news?

And House Do'Urden, Drizzt's tie to the dark world of his kin, was no more.

Had Drizzt finally slipped beyond the grasp of Menzoberranzan? Could he, and Bruenor and Catti-brie and all the others of Mithral Hall, rest easier now that the drow threat had been eliminated?

Drizzt wished he could be sure. By all accounts of the battle in which Wulfgar was killed, a yochlol, a handmaiden of Lolth, had appeared. If the raid to capture him had been inspired simply by Vierna's desperation, then what had brought so powerful a minion into their midst?

The thought did not sit well with Drizzt, and as he sat there in his room, he had to wonder if the drow threat was ended, if he might, at long last, finally know his peace with that city he had left behind.

⚔ ⚔ ⚔ ⚔ ⚔

"The emissaries from Settlestone are here," Catti-brie said to Bruenor, entering the dwarf's private chambers without even the courtesy of a knock.

"I'm not for caring," the dwarf king answered her gruffly.

Catti-brie moved over to him, grabbed him by his broad shoulder, and forced him to turn and look her in the eye. What passed between them was silent, a shared moment of grief and understanding that if they did not go on with their lives, did not forge ahead, then Wulfgar's death was all the more pointless.

What loss is death if life is not to be lived?

Bruenor grabbed his daughter around her slender waist and pulled her close in as crushing a hug as the dwarf had ever given. Catti-brie squeezed him back, tears rolling from her deep blue eyes. So, too, did a smile widen on the vital young woman's face, and though Bruenor's shoulders bobbed with unabashed sobs, she felt sure he soon would come to peace as well.

For all he had gone through, Bruenor remained the Eighth King of Mithral Hall, and for all the adventures, joys, and sorrows Catti-brie had known, she had just passed her twentieth year.

There still was much to be done.

STARLESS NIGHT

THE LEGEND OF DRIZZT® BOOK VIII

Drizzt ran his fingers over the intricate carvings of the panther statuette, its black onyx perfectly smooth and unmarred even in the ridged areas of the muscled neck. So much like Guenhwyvar, it looked, a perfect representation. How could Drizzt bear to part with it now, fully convinced that he would never see the great panther again?

"Farewell, Guenhwyvar," the drow ranger whispered, his expression sorrowful, almost pitiful, as he stared at

PROLOGUE

the figurine. "I cannot in good conscience take you with me on this journey, for I would fear your fate more than my own." His sigh was one of sincere resignation. He and his friends had fought long and hard, and at great sacrifice, to get to this point of peace, yet Drizzt had come to know that it was a false victory. He wanted to deny it, to put Guenhwyvar back in his pouch and go blindly on, hoping for the best.

Drizzt sighed away the momentary weakness and handed the figurine over to Regis, the halfling.

Regis stared up at Drizzt in disbelief for a long, silent while, shocked by what the drow had told him and had demanded of him.

"Five tendays," Drizzt reminded him.

The halfling's cherubic, boyish features crinkled. If Drizzt did not return in five tendays, Regis was to give Guenhwyvar to Catti-brie and tell both her and King Bruenor the truth of Drizzt's departure. From the drow's dark and somber tones, Regis understood that Drizzt did not expect to return.

On sudden inspiration, the halfling dropped the figurine to his bed and fumbled with a chain about his neck, its clasp caught in the long, curly locks of his brown hair. He finally got the thing undone and produced a pendant, dangling a large and magical ruby.

Now Drizzt was shocked. He knew the value of Regis's gemstone and the halfling's craven love of the thing. To say that Regis was acting out of character would be an incredible understatement.

"I cannot," Drizzt argued, pushing the stone away. "I may not return, and it would be lost. . . ."

"Take it!" Regis demanded sharply. "For all that you have done for me, for all of us, you surely deserve it. It's one thing to leave Guenhwyvar behind—it would be a tragedy indeed if the panther fell into the hands of your evil kin—but this is merely a magical token, no living being, and it may aid you on your journey. Take it as you take your scimitars." The halfling paused, his soft gaze locking with Drizzt's violet orbs. "My friend."

Regis snapped his fingers suddenly, stealing the quiet moment. He rambled across the floor, his bare feet slapping on the cold stone and his nightshirt swishing about him. From a drawer he produced yet another item, a rather unremarkable mask.

"I recovered it," he said, not wanting to reveal the whole story of how he had acquired the familiar item. In truth, Regis had gone from Mithral Hall and found Artemis Entreri hanging helplessly from a jutting stone far up the side of a ravine. Regis promptly had looted the assassin, then cut the seam of Entreri's cloak. The halfling had listened with some measure of satisfaction as the cloak, the only thing holding the battered, barely conscious man aloft, began to rip.

Drizzt eyed the magical mask for a long time. He had taken it from the lair of a banshee more than a year before. With it, its user could change his entire appearance, could hide his identity.

"This should help you get in and out," Regis said hopefully. Still Drizzt made no move.

"I want you to have it," Regis insisted, misunderstanding the drow's hesitation and jerking it out toward

Drizzt. Regis did not realize the significance the mask held for Drizzt Do'Urden. Drizzt had once worn it to hide his identity, because a dark elf walking the surface world was at a great disadvantage. Drizzt had come to see the mask as a lie, however useful it might be, and he simply could not bring himself to don it again, whatever the potential gain.

Or could he? Drizzt wondered then if he could refuse the gift. If the mask could aid his cause—a cause that would likely affect those he was leaving behind—then could he in good conscience refuse to wear it?

No, he decided at length, the mask was not that valuable to his cause. Three decades out of the city was a long time, and he was not so remarkable in appearance, not so notorious, certainly, that he would be recognized. He held out his upraised hand, denying the gift, and Regis, after one more unsuccessful try, shrugged his little shoulders, and put the mask away.

Drizzt left without another word. Many hours remained before dawn; torches burned low in the upper levels of Mithral Hall, and few dwarves stirred. It seemed perfectly quiet, perfectly peaceful.

The dark elf's slender fingers, lightly touching, making not a sound, traced the grain of a wooden door. He had no desire to disturb the person within, though he doubted that her sleep was very restful. Every night, Drizzt wanted to go to her and comfort her, and yet he had not, for he knew that his words would do little to soothe Catti-brie's grief. Like so many other nights when he had stood by this door, a watchful, helpless guardian, the ranger ended up padding down the stone corridor, filtering through the shadows of low-dancing torches, his toe-heel step making not a whisper of sound.

With only a short pause at another door, the door of his dearest dwarven friend, Drizzt soon crossed out of the living areas. He came into the formal gathering places, where the king of Mithral Hall entertained visiting emissaries. A couple of dwarves—Dagna's troops probably—were about in here, but they heard and saw nothing of the drow's silent passing.

Drizzt paused again as he came to the entrance of the Hall of Dumathoin, wherein the dwarves of Clan Battlehammer kept their most precious items. He knew that he should continue, get out of the place before the clan began to stir, but he could not ignore the emotions pulling at his heartstrings. He hadn't come to this hallowed hall in the two tendays since his drow kin had been driven away, but he knew that he would never forgive himself if he didn't take at least one look.

The mighty warhammer, Aegis-fang, rested on a pillar at the center of the adorned hall, the place of highest honor. It seemed fitting, for to Drizzt's violet eyes, Aegis-fang far outshone all the other artifacts: the shining suits of mail, the great axes and helms of heroes long dead, the anvil of a legendary smith. Drizzt smiled at the notion that this warhammer hadn't even been wielded by a dwarf. It had been the weapon of Wulfgar, Drizzt's friend, who had willingly given his life so that the others of the tight band might survive.

Drizzt stared long and hard at the mighty weapon, at the gleaming mithral head, unscratched despite the many vicious battles the hammer had seen and showing the perfectly etched sigils of the dwarven god Dumathoin. The drow's gaze drifted down the item, settling on the dried blood on its dark adamantite handle. Bruenor, so stubborn, hadn't allowed that blood to be cleaned away.

Memories of Wulfgar, of fighting beside the tall and strong, golden-haired and golden-skinned man flooded through the drow, weakening his knees and his resolve. In his mind, Drizzt looked again into Wulfgar's clear eyes, the icy blue of the northern sky and always filled with an excited sparkle. Wulfgar had been just a boy, his spirit undaunted by the harsh realities of a brutal world.

Just a boy, but one who had willingly sacrificed everything, a song on his lips, for those he called his friends.

"Farewell," Drizzt whispered, and he was gone, running this time, though no more loudly than he had walked before. In a few seconds, he crossed onto a balcony and down a flight of stairs, into a wide and high chamber. He crossed under the watchful eyes of Mithral Hall's eight kings, their likenesses cut into the stone wall. The last of the busts, that of King Bruenor Battlehammer, was the most striking. Bruenor's visage was stern, a grim look intensified by a deep scar running from his forehead to his jawbone, and with his right eye gone.

More than Bruenor's eye had been wounded, Drizzt knew. More than that dwarvish body, rock tough and resilient, had been scarred. Bruenor's soul was the part most pained, slashed by the loss of a boy he had called his son. Was the dwarf as resilient in spirit as in body? Drizzt knew not the answer. At that moment, staring at Bruenor's scarred face, Drizzt felt that he should stay, should sit beside his friend and help heal the wounds.

It was a passing thought. What wounds might still come to the dwarf? Drizzt reminded himself. To the dwarf and to all his remaining friends?

⚔ ⚔ ⚔ ⚔ ⚔

Catti-brie tossed and squirmed, reliving that fateful moment, as she did every night—at least, every night that exhaustion allowed her to find sleep. She heard Wulfgar's song to Tempus, his god of battle, saw the serene look in the mighty barbarian's eye, the look that denied the obvious agony, the look that allowed him to chop up at the loose stone ceiling, though blocks of heavy granite had begun to tumble all about him.

Catti-brie saw Wulfgar's garish wounds, the white of bone, his skin ripped away from his ribs by the sharklike teeth of the yochlol, an evil, extradimensional beast, an ugly lump of waxy flesh that resembled a half-melted candle.

The roar as the ceiling dropped over her love brought Catti-brie up in her bed, sitting in the darkness, her thick auburn hair matted to her face by cold sweat. She took a long moment to control her breathing, told herself repeatedly that it was a dream, a terrible memory, but ultimately, an event that had passed. The torchlight outlining her door comforted and calmed her.

She wore only a light slip, and her thrashing had knocked her blankets away. Goose bumps rose on her arms, and she shivered, cold and damp and miserable. She roughly retrieved the thickest of her covers and pulled them tightly to her neck, then lay flat on her back, staring up into the darkness.

Something was wrong. She sensed that something was out of place.

Rationally, the young woman told herself that she was imagining things, that her dreams had unnerved her. The world was not right for Catti-brie, far from right, but she told herself forcefully that she was in Mithral Hall, surrounded by an army of friends.

She told herself that she was imagining things.

⚔ ⚔ ⚔ ⚔ ⚔

Drizzt was a long way from Mithral Hall when the sun came up. He didn't sit and enjoy the dawn this day, as was his custom. He hardly looked at the rising sun, for it seemed to him now a false hope of things that could not be. When the initial glare had diminished, the drow looked out to the south and east, far across the mountains, and remembered.

His hand went to his neck, to the hypnotic ruby pendant Regis had given him. He knew how much Regis relied on this gem, loved it, and considered again the halfling's sacrifice, the sacrifice of a true friend. Drizzt had known true friendship; his life had been rich since he had walked into a forlorn land called Icewind Dale and met Bruenor Battlehammer and his adopted daughter, Catti-brie. It pained Drizzt to think that he might never again see any of them.

The drow was glad to have the magical pendant, though, an item that might allow him to get answers and return to his friends, but he held more than a little guilt for his decision to tell Regis of his departure. That choice seemed a weakness to Drizzt, a need to rely on friends who, at this dark time, had little to give. He could rationalize it, though, as a necessary safeguard for the friends he would leave behind. He had instructed Regis to tell Bruenor the truth in five tendays, so that, in case Drizzt's journey proved unsuccessful, Clan Battlehammer would at least have time to prepare for the darkness that might yet come.

It was a logical act, but Drizzt had to admit that he had told Regis because of his own need, because he had to tell someone.

And what of the magical mask? he wondered. Had he been weak in refusing that, too? The powerful item might have aided Drizzt and, thus, aided his friends, but he had not the strength to wear it, to even touch it.

Doubts floated all about the drow, hovered in the air before his eyes, mocking him. Drizzt sighed and rubbed the ruby between his slender black hands. For all his prowess with the blade, for all his dedication to principles, for all his ranger stoicism, Drizzt Do'Urden needed his friends. He glanced back toward Mithral Hall and wondered, for his own sake, if he had chosen rightly in undertaking this quest privately and secretly.

More weakness, stubborn Drizzt decided. He let go of the ruby, mentally slapped away the lingering doubts, and slid his hand inside his forest-green traveling cloak. From one of its pockets he produced a parchment, a map of the lands between the Spine of the World Mountains and the Great Desert of Anauroch. In the lower right-hand corner Drizzt had marked a spot, the location of a cave from which he had once emerged, a cave that would take him home.

PART ONE

DUTY BOUND

No race in all the Realms better understands the word vengeance than the drow. Vengeance is their dessert at their daily table, the sweetness they taste upon their smirking lips as though it was the ultimate delicious pleasure. And so hungering did the drow come for me.

I cannot escape the anger and the guilt I feel for the loss of Wulfgar, for the pains the enemies of my dark past have brought to the friends I hold so dear. Whenever I look into Catti-brie's fair face, I see a profound and everlasting sadness that should not be there, a burden that has no place in the sparkling eyes of a child.

Similarly wounded, I have no words to comfort her and doubt that there are any words that might bring solace. It is my course, then, that I must continue to protect my friends. I have come to realize that I must look beyond my own sense of loss for Wulfgar, beyond the immediate sadness that has taken hold of the dwarves of Mithral Hall and the hardy men of Settlestone.

By Catti-brie's account of that fateful fight, the

creature Wulfgar battled was a yochlol, a hand-maiden of Lolth. With that grim information, I must look beyond the immediate sorrow and consider that the sadness I fear is still to come.

I do not understand all the chaotic games of the Spider Queen—I doubt that even the evil high priestesses know the foul creature's true designs—but there lies in a yochlol's presence a significance that even I, the worst of the drow religious students, cannot miss. The handmaiden's appearance revealed that the hunt was sanctified by the Spider Queen. And the fact that the yochlol intervened in the fighting does not bode well for the future of Mithral Hall.

It is all supposition, of course. I know not that my sister Vierna acted in concert with any of Menzoberranzan's other dark powers, or that, with Vierna's death, the death of my last relative, my link to the city of drow would ever again be explored.

When I look into Catti-brie's eyes, when I look upon Bruenor's horrid scars, I am reminded that hopeful supposition is a feeble and dangerous thing. My evil kin have taken one friend from me.

They will take no more.

I can find no answers in Mithral Hall, will never know for certain if the dark elves hunger still for vengeance, unless another force from Menzoberranzan comes to the surface to claim the bounty on my head. With this truth bending low my shoulders, how could I ever travel to Silverymoon, or to any other nearby town, resuming my normal lifestyle? How could I sleep in peace while holding within my heart the very real fear that the dark elves might soon return and once more imperil my friends?

The apparent serenity of Mithral Hall, the brooding quiet, will show me nothing of the future designs of the drow. Yet, for the sake of my friends,

I must know those dark intentions. I fear that there remains only one place for me to look.

Wulfgar gave his life so that his friends might live. In good conscience, could my own sacrifice be any less?

—Drizzt Do'Urden

THE AMBITIOUS ONE

The mercenary leaned against the pillar anchoring the wide stairway of Tier Breche, on the northern side of the great cavern that housed Menzoberranzan, the city of drow. Jarlaxle removed his wide-brimmed hat and ran a hand over the smooth skin of his bald head as he muttered a few curses under his breath.

Many lights were on in the city. Torches flickered in the high windows of houses carved from natural stalagmite formations. Lights in the drow city! Many of the elaborate structures had long been decorated by the soft glow of faerie fire, mostly purple and blue hues, but this was different.

Jarlaxle shifted to the side and winced as his weight came upon his recently wounded leg. Triel Baenre herself, the matron mistress of Arach-Tinilith, among the highest-ranking priestesses in the city, had tended the wound, but Jarlaxle suspected that the wicked priestess had purposely left the job unfinished, had left a bit of the pain to remind the mercenary of his failure in recapturing the renegade Drizzt Do'Urden.

"The glow wounds my eyes," came a sarcastic remark from behind. Jarlaxle turned to see Matron Baenre's oldest daughter, that same Triel. She was shorter than most drow, nearly a foot shorter than Jarlaxle, but she carried herself with undeniable dignity and poise. Jarlaxle understood her powers—and her volatile temperament—better than most, and he certainly treated the diminutive female with the greatest caution.

Staring, glaring, out over the city with squinting eyes, she moved beside him. "Curse the glow," she muttered.

"It is by your matron's command," Jarlaxle reminded her. His one good eye avoided her gaze; the other lay beneath a patch of shadow, which was tied behind his head. He replaced his great hat, pulling it low in front as he tried to hide his smirk at her resulting grimace.

Triel was not happy with her mother. Jarlaxle had known that since the moment Matron Baenre had begun to hint at her plans. Triel was possibly the most fanatic of the Spider Queen's priestesses and would not go against Matron Baenre, the first matron mother of the city—not unless Lolth instructed her to.

"Come along," the priestess growled. She turned and made her way across Tier Breche to the largest and most ornate of the drow Academy's three buildings, a huge structure shaped to resemble a gigantic spider.

Jarlaxle pointedly groaned as he moved, and lost ground with every limping step. His attempt to solicit a bit more healing magic was not successful, though, for Triel merely paused at the doorway to the great structure and waited for him with a patience that was more than a bit out of character, Jarlaxle knew, for Triel never waited for anything.

As soon as he entered the temple, the mercenary was assaulted by myriad aromas, everything from incense to the drying blood of the latest sacrifices, and chants rolled out of every side portal. Triel took note of none of it; she shrugged past the few disciples who bowed to her as they saw her walking the corridors.

The single-minded Baenre daughter moved into the higher levels, to the private quarters of the school's mistresses, and walked down one small hallway, its floor alive with crawling spiders—including a few that stood as tall as Jarlaxle's knee).

Triel stopped between two equally decorated doors and motioned for Jarlaxle to enter the one on the right. The mercenary paused, did well to hide his confusion, but Triel was expecting it.

She grabbed Jarlaxle by the shoulder and roughly spun him about. "You have been here before!" she accused.

"Only upon my graduation from the school of fighters," Jarlaxle said, shrugging away from the female, "as are all of Melee-Magthere's graduates."

"You have been in the upper levels," Triel snarled, eyeing Jarlaxle squarely. The mercenary chuckled.

"You hesitated when I motioned for you to enter the chamber," Triel went on, "because you know that the one to the left is my private room. That is where you expected to go."

"I did not expect to be summoned here at all," Jarlaxle retorted, trying to shift the subject. He was indeed a bit off guard that Triel had watched him so closely. Had he underestimated her trepidation at her mother's latest plans?

Triel stared at him long and hard, her eyes unblinking and jaw firm.

"I have my sources," Jarlaxle admitted at length.

Another long moment passed, and still Triel did not blink.

"You asked that I come," Jarlaxle reminded her.

"I demanded," Triel corrected.

Jarlaxle swept into a low, exaggerated bow, snatching off his hat and brushing it out at arm's length. The Baenre daughter's eyes flashed with anger.

"Enough!" she shouted.

"And enough of your games!" Jarlaxle spat back. "You asked that I come to the Academy, a place where I am not comfortable, and so I have come. You have questions, and I, perhaps, have answers."

His qualification of that last sentence made Triel narrow her eyes. Jarlaxle was ever a cagey opponent, she knew as well as anyone in the drow city. She had dealt with the cunning mercenary many times and still wasn't quite sure if she had broken even against him or not. She turned and motioned for him to enter the left-hand door instead, and, with another graceful bow, he did so, stepping into a thickly carpeted and decorated room lit in a soft magical glow.

"Remove your boots," Triel instructed, and she slipped out of her own shoes before she stepped onto the plush rug.

Jarlaxle stood against the tapestry-adorned wall just inside the door, looking doubtfully at his boots. Everyone who knew the mercenary knew that these were magical.

"Very well," Triel conceded, closing the door and sweeping past him to take a seat on a huge, overstuffed chair. A rolltop desk stood behind her, in front of one of many tapestries, this one depicting the sacrifice of a gigantic surface elf by a horde of dancing drow. Above the surface elf loomed the nearly translucent specter of a half-drow, half-spider creature, its face beautiful and serene.

"You do not like your mother's lights?" Jarlaxle asked. "You keep your own room aglow."

Triel bit her lower lip and narrowed her eyes once more. Most priestesses kept their private chambers dimly lit, that they might read their tomes. Heat-sensing infravision was of little use in seeing the runes on a page. There were some inks that would hold distinctive heat for many years, but these were expensive and hard to come by, even for one as powerful as Triel.

Jarlaxle stared back at the Baenre daughter's grim expression. Triel was always mad about something, the mercenary mused. "The lights seem appropriate for what your mother has planned," he went on.

"Indeed," Triel remarked, her tone biting. "And are you so arrogant as to believe that you understand my mother's motives?"

"She will go back to Mithral Hall," Jarlaxle said openly, knowing that Triel had long ago drawn the same conclusion.

"Will she?" Triel asked coyly.

The cryptic response set the mercenary back on his heels. He took a step toward a second, less-cushiony chair in the room, and his heel clicked hard, even though he was walking across the incredibly thick and soft carpet.

Triel smirked, not impressed by the magical boots. It was common knowledge that Jarlaxle could walk as quietly or as loudly as he desired on any type of surface. His abundant jewelry, bracelets and trinkets seemed equally enchanted, for they would ring and tinkle or remain perfectly silent, as the mercenary desired.

"If you have left a hole in my carpet, I will fill it with your heart," Triel promised as Jarlaxle slumped back comfortably in the covered stone chair, smoothing a fold in the armrest so that the fabric showed a clear image of a black and yellow *gee'antu* spider, the Underdark's version of the surface tarantula.

"Why do you suspect that your mother will not go?" Jarlaxle asked, pointedly ignoring the threat, though in knowing Triel Baenre, he honestly wondered how many other hearts were now entwined in the carpet's fibers.

"Do I?" Triel asked.

Jarlaxle let out a long sigh. He had suspected that this would be a moot meeting, a discussion where Triel tried to pry out what bits of information the mercenary already had attained, while offering little of her own. Still, when Triel had insisted that Jarlaxle come to her, instead of their usual arrangement, in which she went out from Tier Breche to meet the mercenary, Jarlaxle had hoped for something substantive. It was quickly becoming obvious to Jarlaxle that the only reason Triel wanted to meet in Arach-Tinilith was that, in this secure place, even her mother's prying ears would not hear.

And now, for all those painstaking arrangements, this all-important meeting had become a useless bantering session.

Triel seemed equally perturbed. She came forward in her chair suddenly, her expression fierce. "She desires a legacy!" the female declared.

Jarlaxle's bracelets tinkled as he tapped his fingers together, thinking that now they were finally getting somewhere.

"The rulership of Menzoberranzan is no longer sufficient for the likes of Matron Baenre," Triel continued, more calmly, and she moved back in her seat. "She must expand her sphere."

"I had thought your mother's visions Lolth-given," Jarlaxle remarked, and he was sincerely confused by Triel's obvious disdain.

"Perhaps," Triel admitted. "The Spider Queen will welcome the conquest of

Mithral Hall, particularly if it, in turn, leads to the capture of that renegade Do'Urden. But there are other considerations."

"Blingdenstone?" Jarlaxle asked, referring to the city of the svirfnebli, the deep gnomes, traditional enemies of the drow.

"That is one," Triel replied. "Blingdenstone is not far off the path to the tunnels connecting Mithral Hall."

"Your mother has mentioned that the svirfnebli might be dealt with properly on the return trip," Jarlaxle offered, figuring that he had to throw some tidbit out if he wanted Triel to continue so openly with him. It seemed to the mercenary that Triel must be deeply upset to be permitting him such an honest view of her most private emotions and fears.

Triel nodded, accepting the news stoically and without surprise. "There are other considerations," she repeated. "The task Matron Baenre is undertaking is enormous and will require allies along the way, perhaps even illithid allies."

The Baenre daughter's reasoning struck Jarlaxle as sound. Matron Baenre had long kept an illithid consort, an ugly and dangerous beast if Jarlaxle had ever seen one. He was never comfortable around the octopus-headed humanoids. Jarlaxle survived by understanding and outguessing his enemies, but his skills were sorely lacking where illithids were concerned. The mind flayers, as members of the evil race were called, simply didn't think the same way as other races and acted in accord with principles and rules that no one other than an illithid seemed to know.

Still, the dark elves had often dealt successfully with the illithid community. Menzoberranzan housed twenty thousand skilled warriors, while the illithids in the region numbered barely a hundred. Triel's fears seemed a bit overblown.

Jarlaxle didn't tell her that, though. Given her dark and volatile mood, the mercenary preferred to do more listening than speaking.

Triel continued to shake her head, her expression typically sour. She leaped up from the chair, her black-and-purple, spider-adorned robes swishing as she paced a tight circle.

"It will not be House Baenre alone," Jarlaxle reminded her, hoping to comfort Triel. "Many houses show lights in their windows."

"Mother has done well in bringing the city together," Triel admitted, and the pace of her nervous stroll slowed.

"But still you fear," the mercenary reasoned. "And you need information so that you might be ready for any consequence." Jarlaxle couldn't help a small, ironic chuckle. He and Triel had been enemies for a long time, neither trusting the other—and with good reason! Now she needed him. She was a priestess in a secluded school, away from much of the city's whispered rumors. Normally her prayers to the Spider Queen would have provided her all the information she needed, but now, if Lolth sanctioned Matron Baenre's actions—and that fact seemed obvious—Triel would be left, literally, in the dark. She needed a spy, and in Menzoberranzan, Jarlaxle and his spying network, Bregan D'aerthe, had no equal.

"We need each other," Triel pointedly replied, turning to eye the mercenary squarely. "Mother treads on dangerous ground, that much is obvious. If she falters, consider who will assume the seat of the ruling house."

True enough, Jarlaxle silently conceded. Triel, as the eldest daughter of the house, was indisputably next in line behind Matron Baenre and, as the matron mistress of Arach-Tinilith, held the most powerful position in the city behind the matron mothers of the eight ruling houses. Triel already had established an impressive base of power. But in Menzoberranzan, where pretense of law was no more than a facade against an underlying chaos, power bases tended to shift as readily as lava pools.

"I will learn what I may," Jarlaxle answered, and he rose to leave. "And will tell you what I learn."

Triel understood the half-truth in the sly mercenary's words, but she had to accept his offer.

Jarlaxle was walking freely down the wide, curving avenues of Menzoberranzan a short while later, passing by the watchful eyes and readied weapons of house guards posted on nearly every stalagmite mound—and on the ringed balconies of many low-hanging stalactites as well. The mercenary was not afraid, for his wide-brimmed hat identified him clearly to all in the city, and no house desired conflict with Bregan D'aerthe. It was the most secretive of bands—few in the city could even guess at the numbers in the group—and its bases were tucked away in the many nooks and crannies of the wide cavern. The company's reputation was widespread, though, tolerated by the ruling Houses, and most in the city would name Jarlaxle among the most powerful of Menzoberranzan's males.

So comfortable was he that Jarlaxle hardly noticed the lingering stares of the dangerous guards. His thoughts were inward, trying to decipher the subtle messages of his meeting with Triel. The assumed plan to conquer Mithral Hall seemed very promising. Jarlaxle had been to the dwarven stronghold, had witnessed its defenses. Though formidable, they seemed meager against the strength of a drow army. When Menzoberranzan conquered Mithral Hall, with Matron Baenre at the head of the force, Lolth would be supremely

pleased, and House Baenre would know its pinnacle of glory.

As Triel had put it, Matron Baenre would have her legacy.

The pinnacle of power? The thought hung in Jarlaxle's mind. He paused beside Narbondel, the great pillar time clock of Menzoberranzan, a smile widening across his ebon-skinned face.

"Pinnacle of power?" he whispered aloud.

Suddenly Jarlaxle understood Triel's trepidations. She feared that her mother might overstep her bounds, might be gambling an already impressive empire for the sake of yet another acquisition. Even as he considered the notion, Jarlaxle understood a deeper significance to it all. Suppose that Matron Baenre was successful, that Mithral Hall was conquered and Blingdenstone after that? he mused. What enemies would then be left to threaten the drow city, to hold together the tentative hierarchy in Menzoberranzan?

For that matter, why had Blingdenstone, a place of enemies so near Menzoberranzan, been allowed to survive for all these centuries? Jarlaxle knew the answer. He knew that the gnomes unintentionally served as the glue that kept Menzoberranzan's houses in line. With a common enemy so near, the drow's constant infighting had to be kept under control.

But now Matron Baenre hinted at ungluing, expanding her empire to include not only Mithral Hall, but the troublesome gnomes as well. Triel did not fear that the drow would be beaten; neither did she fear any alliance with the small colony of illithids. She was afraid that her mother would succeed, would gain her legacy. Matron Baenre was old, ancient even by drow standards, and Triel was next in line for the house seat. At present, that would be a comfortable place indeed, but it would become far more tentative and dangerous if Mithral Hall and Blingdenstone were taken. The binding common enemy that kept the houses in line would be no more, and Triel would have to worry about a tie to the surface world a long way from Menzoberranzan, where reprisals by the allies of Mithral Hall would be inevitable.

Jarlaxle understood what Matron Baenre wanted, but now he wondered what Lolth, backing the withered female's plans, had in mind.

"Chaos," he decided. Menzoberranzan had been quiet for a long, long time. Some houses fought—that was inevitable. House Do'Urden and House DeVir, both ruling houses, had been obliterated, but the general structure of the city had remained solid and unthreatened.

"Ah, but you are delightful," Jarlaxle said, speaking his thoughts of Lolth aloud. He suddenly suspected that Lolth desired a new order, a refreshing housecleaning of a city grown boring. No wonder that Triel, in line to inherit her mother's legacy, was not amused.

The bald mercenary, himself a lover of intrigue and chaos, laughed heartily and looked to Narbondel. The clock's heat was greatly diminished, showing it to be late in the Underdark night. Jarlaxle clicked his heels against the stone and set out for the Qu'ellarz'orl, the high plateau on Menzoberranzan's eastern wall, the region housing the city's most powerful house. He didn't want to be late for his meeting with Matron Baenre, to whom he would report on in his "secret" meeting with her eldest daughter.

Jarlaxle pondered how much he would tell the withered matron mother, and how he might twist his words to his best advantage.

How he loved the intrigue.

2

FAREWELL RIÐÐLES

Bleary-eyed after yet another long, restless night, Catti-brie pulled on a robe and crossed her small room, hoping to find comfort in the daylight. Her thick auburn hair had been flattened on one side of her head, forcing an angled cowlick on the other side, but she didn't care. Busy rubbing the sleep from her eyes, she nearly stumbled over the threshold and paused there, struck suddenly by something she did not understand.

She ran her fingers over the wood of the door and stood confused, nearly overwhelmed by the same feeling she had felt the night before, that something was out of place, that something was wrong. She had intended to go straight to breakfast, but felt compelled to get Drizzt instead.

The young woman shuffled swiftly down the corridor to Drizzt's room and knocked on the door. After a few moments, she called, "Drizzt?" When the drow didn't answer, she gingerly turned the handle and pushed the door open. Catti-brie noticed immediately that Drizzt's scimitars and traveling cloak were gone, but before she could begin to think about that, her eyes focused on the bed. It was made, covers tucked neatly, though that was not unusual for the dark elf.

Catti-brie slipped over to the bed and inspected the folds. They were neat, but not tight, and she understood that this bed had been made a long while ago, that this bed had not been slept in the previous night.

"What's all this?" the young woman asked. She took a quick look around the small room, then made her way back out into the hall. Drizzt had gone out from Mithral Hall without warning before, and often he left at night. He usually journeyed to Silverymoon, the fabulous city a tenday's march to the east.

Why, this time, did Catti-brie feel that something was amiss? Why did this not-so-unusual scene strike Catti-brie as very out of place? The young woman tried to shrug it away, to overrule her heartfelt fears. She was just worried, she told herself. She had lost Wulfgar and now felt overprotective of her other friends.

Catti-brie walked as she thought it over, and soon paused at another door. She tapped lightly, then, with no response forthcoming—though she was certain that this one was not yet up and about—she banged harder. A groan came from within the room.

Catti-brie pushed the door open and crossed the room, sliding to kneel beside the tiny bed and roughly pulling the bedcovers down from sleeping Regis, tickling his armpits as he began to squirm.

"Hey!" the plump halfling, recovered from his trials at the hands of the assassin Artemis Entreri, cried out. He came awake immediately and grabbed at the covers desperately.

"Where's Drizzt?" Catti-brie asked, tugging the covers away more forcefully.

"How would I know?" Regis protested. "I have not been out of my room yet this morning!"

"Get up." Catti-brie was surprised by the sharpness of her own voice, by the intensity of her command. The uncomfortable feelings tugged at her again, more forcefully. She looked around the room, trying to discern what had triggered her sudden anxiety.

She saw the panther figurine.

Catti-brie's unblinking stare locked on the object, Drizzt's dearest possession. What was it doing in Regis's room? she wondered. Why had Drizzt left without it? Now the young woman's logic began to fall into agreement with her emotions. She skipped across the bed, buried Regis in a jumble of covers—which he promptly pulled tight around his shoulders—and retrieved the panther. She then hopped back and tugged again at the stubborn halfling's blanket shell.

"No!" Regis argued, yanking back. He dived facedown to his mattress, pulling the ends of the pillow up around his dimpled face.

Catti-brie grabbed him by the scruff of the neck, yanked him from the bed, and dragged him across the room to seat him in one of the two wooden chairs resting at opposite sides of a small table. Pillow still in hand, still tight against his face, Regis plopped his head straight down on the table.

Catti-brie took a firm and silent hold on the end of the pillow, quietly stood, then yanked it suddenly, tearing it from the surprised halfling's grasp so that his head knocked hard against the bare wood.

Groaning and grumbling, Regis sat straight in the chair and ran stubby fingers through his fluffy and curly brown locks, their bounce undiminished by a long night's sleep.

"What?" he demanded.

Catti-brie slammed the panther figurine atop the table, leaving it before the seated halfling. "Where is Drizzt?" she asked again, evenly.

"Probably in the Undercity," Regis grumbled, running his tongue all about his cottony-feeling teeth. "Why don't you go ask Bruenor?"

The mention of the dwarvish king set Catti-brie back on her heels. Go ask Bruenor? she silently scoffed. Bruenor would hardly speak to anyone, and was so immersed in despair that he probably wouldn't know it if his entire clan up and left in the middle of the night!

"So Drizzt left Guenhwyvar," Regis remarked, thinking to downplay the whole thing. His words fell awkwardly on the perceptive woman's ears, though, and Catti-brie's deep blue eyes narrowed as she studied the halfling more closely.

"What?" Regis asked innocently again, feeling the heat of that unrelenting scrutiny.

"Where is Drizzt?" Catti-brie asked, her tone dangerously calm. "And why do ye have the cat?"

Regis shook his head and wailed helplessly, dramatically dropping his forehead again against the table.

Catti-brie saw the act for what it was. She knew Regis too well to be taken in by his wily charms. She grabbed a handful of curly brown hair and tugged his head upright, then grabbed the front of his nightshirt with her other hand. Her roughness startled the halfling; she could see that clearly by his expression, but she did not relent. Regis flew from his seat. Catti-brie carried him three quick steps, then slammed his back against the wall.

Catti-brie's scowling visage softened for just a moment, and her free hand fumbled with the halfling's nightshirt long enough that she could determine that Regis was not wearing his magical ruby pendant, an item she knew he never removed. Another curious, and certainly out-of-place, fact that assailed her sensibilities, fed her growing belief that something indeed was terribly wrong.

"Suren there's something going on here that's not what it's supposed to be," Catti-brie said, her scowl returning tenfold.

"Catti-brie!" Regis replied, looking down to his furry-topped feet, dangling twenty inches from the floor.

"And ye know something about it," Catti-brie went on.

"Catti-brie!" Regis wailed again, trying to bring the fiery young woman to her senses.

Catti-brie took up the halfling's nightshirt in both her hands, pulled him away from the wall, and slammed him back again, hard. "I've lost Wulfgar," she said grimly, pointedly reminding Regis that he might not be dealing with someone rational.

Regis didn't know what to think. Bruenor Battlehammer's daughter had always been the levelheaded one of the troupe, the calm influence that kept the others in line. Even cool Drizzt had often used Catti-brie as a guidepost to his conscience. But now . . .

Regis saw the promise of pain set within the depths of Catti-brie's deep blue, angry eyes.

She pulled him from the wall once more and slammed him back. "Ye're going to tell me what ye know," she said evenly.

The back of Regis's head throbbed from the banging. He was scared, very scared, as much for Catti-brie as for himself. Had her grief brought her to this point of desperation? And why was he suddenly caught in the middle of all this? All that Regis wanted out of life was a warm bed and a warmer meal.

"We should go and sit down with Brue—" he began, but he was summarily interrupted as Catti-brie slapped him across the face.

He brought his hand up to the stinging cheek, felt the angry welt rising there. He never blinked, eyeing the young woman with disbelief.

Catti-brie's violent reaction had apparently surprised her as much as Regis. The halfling saw tears welling in her gentle eyes. She trembled, and Regis honestly didn't know what she might do.

The halfling considered his situation for a long moment, coming to wonder what difference a few days or tendays could make. "Drizzt went home," the halfling said softly, always willing to do as the situation demanded. Worrying about consequences could come later.

Catti-brie relaxed somewhat. "This is his home," she reasoned. "Suren ye don't mean Icewind Dale."

"Menzoberranzan," Regis corrected.

If Catti-brie had taken a crossbow quarrel in her back, it would not have hit her harder than that single word. She let Regis down to the floor and tumbled backward, falling into a sitting position on the edge of the halfling's bed.

"He really left Guenhwyvar for you," Regis explained. "He cares for both you and the cat so very much."

His soothing words did not shake the horrified expression from Catti-brie's face. Regis wished he had his ruby pendant, so that he might use its

undeniable charms to calm the young woman.

"You can't tell Bruenor," Regis added. "Besides, Drizzt might not even go that far." The halfling thought an embellishment of the truth might go a long way. "He said he was off to see Alustriel, to try to decide where his course should lead." It wasn't exactly true—Drizzt had only mentioned that he might stop by Silverymoon to see if he might confirm his fears—but Regis decided that Catti-brie needed to be given some hope.

"You can't tell Bruenor," the halfling said again, more forcefully. Catti-brie looked up at him; her expression was truly one of the most pitiful sights Regis had ever seen.

"He'll be back," Regis said to her, rushing over to sit beside her. "You know Drizzt. He'll be back."

It was too much for Catti-brie to digest. She gently pulled Regis's hand off her arm and rose. She looked to the panther figurine once more, sitting upon the small table, but she had not the strength to retrieve it.

Catti-brie padded silently out of the room, back to her own chambers, where she fell listlessly upon her bed.

⚔ ⚔ ⚔ ⚔ ⚔

Drizzt spent midday sleeping in the cool shadows of a cave, many miles from Mithral Hall's eastern door. The early summer air was warm, the breeze off the cold glaciers of the mountains carrying little weight against the powerful rays of the sun in a cloudless summer sky.

The drow did not sleep long or well. His rest was filled with thoughts of Wulfgar, of all his friends, and of distant images, memories of that awful place, Menzoberranzan.

Awful and beautiful, like the dark elves who had sculpted it.

Drizzt moved to his shallow cave's entrance to take his meal. He basked in the warmth of the bright afternoon, in the sounds of the many animals. How different was this from his Underdark home! How wonderful!

Drizzt threw his dried biscuit into the dirt and punched the floor beside him.

How wonderful indeed was this false hope that had been dangled before his desperate eyes. All that he had wanted in life was to escape the ways of his kin, to live in peace. Then he had come to the surface, and soon after, had decided that this place—this place of buzzing bees and chirping birds, of warm sunlight and alluring moonlight—should be his home, not the eternal darkness of those tunnels far below.

Drizzt Do'Urden had chosen the surface, but what did that choice mean? It meant that he would come to know new, dear friends, and by his mere presence, trap them into his dark legacy. It meant that Wulfgar would die by the summons of Drizzt's own sister, and that all of Mithral Hall might soon be in peril.

It meant that his choice was a false one, that he could not stay.

The disciplined drow calmed quickly and took out some more food, forcing it past the angry lump in his throat. He considered his course as he ate. The road before him would lead out of the mountains and past a village called Pengallen. Drizzt had been there recently, and he did not wish to return.

He would not follow the road at all, he decided at length. What purpose would going to Silverymoon serve? Drizzt doubted that Lady Alustriel would be there, with the trading season open in full. Even if she was, what could she tell him that he did not already know?

No, Drizzt had already determined his ultimate course and he did not need Alustriel to confirm it. He gathered his belongings and sighed as he considered again how empty the road seemed without his dear panther companion. He walked out into the bright day, straight toward the east, off the southeastern road.

⚔ ⚔ ⚔ ⚔ ⚔

Her stomach did not complain that breakfast—and lunch—had passed and still she lay motionless on her bed, caught in a web of despair. She had lost Wulfgar, barely days before their planned wedding, and now Drizzt, whom she loved as much as she had the barbarian, was gone as well. It seemed as though her entire world had crumbled around her. A foundation that had been built of stone shifted like sand on the blowing wind.

Catti-brie had been a fighter all of her young life. She didn't remember her mother, and barely recalled her father, who had been killed in a goblin raid in Ten-Towns when she was very young. Bruenor Battlehammer had taken her in and raised her as his own daughter, and Catti-brie had found a fine life among the dwarves of Bruenor's clan. Except for Bruenor, though, the dwarves had been friends, not family. Catti-brie had forged a new family one at a time—first Bruenor, then Drizzt, then Regis, and, finally, Wulfgar.

Now Wulfgar was dead and Drizzt gone, back to his wicked homeland with, by Catti-brie's estimation, little chance of returning.

Catti-brie felt so very helpless about it all! She had watched Wulfgar die, watched him chop a ceiling down onto his own head so that she might escape

the clutches of the monstrous yochlol. She had tried to help, but had failed and, in the end, all that remained was a pile of rubble and Aegis-fang.

In the tendays since, Catti-brie had teetered on the edge of control, trying futilely to deny the paralyzing grief. She had cried often, but always had managed to check it after the first few sobs with a deep breath and sheer willpower. The only one she could talk to had been Drizzt.

Now Drizzt was gone, and now, too, Catti-brie did cry, a flood of tears, sobs wracking her deceptively delicate frame. She wanted Wulfgar back! She protested to whatever gods might be listening that he was too young to be taken from her, with too many great deeds ahead of him.

Her sobs became intense growls, fierce denial. Pillows flew across the room, and Catti-brie grabbed the blankets into a pile and heaved them as well. Then she overturned her bed just for the pleasure of hearing its wooden frame crack against the hard floor.

"No!" The word came from deep inside, from the young fighter's belly. The loss of Wulfgar wasn't fair, but there was nothing Catti-brie could do about that.

Drizzt's leaving wasn't fair, not in Catti-brie's wounded mind, but there was nothing . . .

The thought hung in Catti-brie's mind. Still trembling, but now under control, she stood beside the overturned bed. She understood why the drow had left secretly, why Drizzt had, as was typical, taken the whole burden on himself.

"No," the young woman said again. She stripped off her nightclothes, grabbed a blanket to towel the sweat from her, then donned breeches and chemise. Catti-brie did not hesitate to consider her actions, fearful that if she thought about things rationally, she might change her mind. She quickly slipped on a chain-link coat of supple and thin mithral armor, so finely crafted by the dwarves that it was barely detectable after she had donned her sleeveless tunic.

Still moving frantically, Catti-brie pulled on her boots, grabbed her cloak and leather gloves, and rushed across the room to her closet. There she found her sword belt, quiver, and Taulmaril the Heartseeker, her enchanted bow. She ran, didn't walk, from her room to the halfling's and banged on the door only once before bursting in.

Regis was in bed again—big surprise—his belly full from a breakfast that had continued uninterrupted right into lunch. He was awake, though, and none too happy to see Catti-brie charging at him once more.

She pulled him up to a sitting position, and he regarded her curiously. Lines from tears streaked her cheeks, and her splendid blue eyes were edged by angry red veins. Regis had lived most of his life as a thief, had survived by understanding people, and it wasn't hard for him to figure out the reasons behind the young woman's sudden fire.

"Where did ye put the panther?" Catti-brie demanded.

Regis stared at her for a long moment. Catti-brie gave him a rough shake.

"Tell me quick," she demanded. "I've lost too much time already."

"For what?" Regis asked, though he knew the answer.

"Just give me the cat," Catti-brie said. Regis unconsciously glanced toward his bureau, and Catti-brie rushed to it, then tore it open and laid waste to the drawers, one by one.

"Drizzt won't like this," Regis said calmly.

"To the Nine Hells with him, then!" Catti-brie shot back. She found the figurine and held it before her eyes, marveling at its beautiful form.

"You think Guenhwyvar will lead you to him," Regis stated more than asked.

Catti-brie dropped the figurine into a belt pouch and did not bother to reply.

"Suppose you do catch up with him," Regis went on as the young woman headed for the door. "How much will you aid Drizzt in a city of drow? A human woman might stand out a bit down there, don't you think?"

The halfling's sarcasm stopped Catti-brie, made her consider for the first time what she meant to do. How true was Regis's reasoning! How could she get into Menzoberranzan? And even if she did, how could she even see the floor ahead of her?

"No!" Catti-brie shouted at length, her logic blown away by that welling, helpless feeling. "I'm going to him anyway. I'll not stand by and wait to learn that another of me friends has been killed!"

"Trust him," Regis pleaded, and, for the first time, the halfling began to think that maybe he would not be able to stop the impetuous Catti-brie.

Catti-brie shook her head and started for the door again.

"Wait!" Regis called, begged, and the young woman pivoted about to regard him. Regis hung in a precarious position. It seemed to him that he should run out shouting for Bruenor, or for General Dagna, or for any of the dwarves, enlisting allies to hold back Catti-brie, physically if need be. She was crazy; her decision to run off after Drizzt made no sense at all.

But Regis understood her desire, and he sympathized with her with all his heart.

"If it was meself who left," Catti-brie began, "and Drizzt who wanted to follow . . ."

Regis nodded in agreement. If Catti-brie, or any of them, had gone into apparent peril, Drizzt Do'Urden would have taken up the chase, and taken up the fight, no matter the odds. Drizzt, Wulfgar, Catti-brie, and Bruenor had gone more than halfway across the continent in search of Regis when Entreri had abducted him. Regis had known Catti-brie since she was just a child, and had always held her in the highest regard, but never had he been more proud of her than at this very moment.

"A human will be a detriment to Drizzt in Menzoberranzan," he said again.

"I care not," Catti-brie said under her breath. She did not understand where Regis's words were leading.

Regis hopped off his bed and rushed across the room. Catti-brie braced, thinking he meant to tackle her, but he ran past, to his desk, and pulled open one of its lower drawers. "So don't be a human," the halfling proclaimed, and he tossed the magical mask to Catti-brie.

Catti-brie caught it and stood staring at it in surprise as Regis ran back past her, to his bed.

Entreri had used the mask to get into Mithral Hall, had, through its magic, so perfectly disguised himself as Regis that the halfling's friends, even Drizzt, had been taken in.

"Drizzt really is making for Silverymoon," Regis told her.

Catti-brie was surprised, thinking that the drow would have simply gone into the Underdark through the lower chambers of Mithral Hall. When she thought about it, though, she realized that Bruenor had placed many guards at those chambers, with orders to keep the doors closed and locked.

"One more thing," Regis said. Catti-brie looped the mask on her belt and turned to the bed, to see Regis standing on the shifted mattress, holding a brilliantly jeweled dagger in his hands.

"I won't need this," Regis explained, "not here, with Bruenor and his thousands beside me." He held the weapon out, but Catti-brie did not immediately take it.

She had seen that dagger, Artemis Entreri's dagger, before. The assassin had once pressed it against her neck, stealing her courage, making her feel more helpless, more a little girl, than at any other time in her life. Catti-brie wasn't sure that she could take it from Regis, wasn't sure that she could bear to carry the thing with her.

"Entreri is dead," Regis assured her, not quite understanding her hesitation.

Catti-brie nodded absently, though her thoughts remained filled with memories of being Entreri's captive. She remembered the man's earthy smell and equated that smell now with the aroma of pure evil. She had been so powerless . . . like the moment when the ceiling fell in on Wulfgar. Powerless now, she wondered, when Drizzt might need her?

Catti-brie firmed her jaw and took the dagger. She clutched it tightly, then slid it into her belt.

"Ye mustn't tell Bruenor," she said.

"He'll know," Regis argued. "I might have been able to turn aside his curiosity about Drizzt's departure—Drizzt is always leaving—but Bruenor will soon realize that you are gone."

Catti-brie had no argument for that, but, again, she didn't care. She had to get to Drizzt. This was her quest, her way of taking back control of a life that had quickly been turned upside down.

She rushed to the bed, wrapped Regis in a big hug, and kissed him hard on the cheek. "Farewell, me friend!" she cried, dropping him to the mattress. "Farewell!"

Then she was gone, and Regis sat there, his chin in his plump hands. So many things had changed in the last day. First Drizzt, and now Catti-brie. With Wulfgar gone, that left only Regis and Bruenor of the five friends remaining in Mithral Hall.

Bruenor! Regis rolled to his side and groaned. He buried his face in his hands at the thought of the mighty dwarf. If Bruenor ever learned that Regis had aided Catti-brie on her dangerous way, he would rip the halfling apart.

Regis couldn't begin to think of how he might tell the dwarven king. Suddenly he regretted his decision, felt stupid for letting his emotions, his sympathies, get in the way of good judgment. He understood Catti-brie's need and felt that it was right for her to go after Drizzt, if that was what she truly desired to do—she was a grown woman, after all, and a fine warrior—but Bruenor wouldn't understand.

Neither would Drizzt, the halfling realized, and he groaned again. He had broken his word to the drow, had told the secret on the very first day! And his mistake had sent Catti-brie running into danger.

"Drizzt will kill me!" he wailed.

Catti-brie's head came back around the doorjamb, her smile wider, more full of life, than Regis had seen it in a long, long time. Suddenly she seemed the spirited lass that he and the others had come to love, the spirited young woman who had been lost to the world when the ceiling had fallen on Wulfgar. Even the redness had flown from her eyes, replaced by a joyful inner sparkle. "Just ye hope that Drizzt comes back to kill ye!" Catti-brie chirped, and she blew the halfling a kiss and rushed away.

"Wait!" Regis called halfheartedly. Regis was just as glad that Catti-brie didn't stop. He still thought himself irrational, even stupid, and still knew that he would have to answer to both Bruenor and Drizzt for his actions, but that last smile of Catti-brie's, her spark of life so obviously returned, had settled the argument.

BAENRE'S BLUFF

The mercenary silently approached the western end of the Baenre compound, creeping from shadow to shadow to get near the silvery spiderweb fence that surrounded the place. Like any who came near House Baenre, which encompassed twenty huge and hollowed stalagmites and thirty adorned stalactites, Jarlaxle found himself impressed once more. By Underdark standards, where space was at a premium, the place was huge, nearly half a mile long and half that wide.

Everything about the structures of House Baenre was marvelous. Not a detail had been overlooked in the craftsmanship; slaves worked continually to carve new designs into those few areas that had not yet been detailed. The magical touches, supplied mostly by Gromph, Matron Baenre's elderboy and the archmage of Menzoberranzan, were no less spectacular, right down to the predominant purple and blue faerie fire hues highlighting just the right areas of the mounds for the most awe-inspiring effect.

The compound's twenty-foot-high fence, which seemed so tiny anchoring the gigantic stalagmite mounds, was among the most wonderful creations in all of Menzoberranzan. Some said that it was a gift from Lolth, though none in the city, except perhaps ancient Matron Baenre, had been around long enough to witness its construction. The barrier was formed of iron-strong strands, thick as a drow's arm and enchanted to grasp and stubbornly cling stronger than any spider's web. Even the sharpest of drow weapons, arguably the finest edged weapons in all of Toril, could not nick the strands of Baenre's fence, and, once caught, no monster of any strength, not a giant or even a dragon, could hope to break free.

Normally, visitors to House Baenre would have sought one of the symmetrical gates spaced about the compound. There a watchman could have spoken the day's command and the strands of the fence would have spiraled outward, opening a hole.

Jarlaxle was no normal visitor, though, and Matron Baenre had instructed him to keep his comings and goings private. He waited in the shadows, perfectly hidden as several foot soldiers ambled by on their patrol. They were not overly alert, Jarlaxle noted, and why should they be, with the forces of Baenre behind them? House Baenre held at least twenty-five hundred capable and fabulously armed soldiers and boasted sixteen high priestesses. No other house in the city—no five houses combined—could muster such a force.

The mercenary glanced over to the pillar of Narbondel to discern how much longer he had to wait. He had barely turned back to the Baenre compound when a horn blew, clear and strong, and then another.

A chant, a low singing, arose from inside the compound. Foot soldiers rushed to their posts and came to rigid attention, their weapons presented ceremoniously before them. This was the spectacle that showed the honor of Menzoberranzan, the disciplined, precision drilling that mocked any potential enemy's claims that dark elves were too chaotic to come together in common cause or common defense. Non-drow mercenaries, particularly the gray dwarves, often paid handsome sums of gold and gems simply to view the spectacle of the changing of the Baenre house guard.

Streaks of orange, red, green, blue, and purple light rushed up the stalagmite mounds, to meet similar streaks coming down from above, from the jagged teeth of the Baenre compound's stalactites. Enchanted house emblems, worn by the Baenre guards, created this effect as male dark elves rode subterranean lizards that could walk equally well on floors, walls, or ceilings.

The music continued. The glowing streaks formed myriad designs in brilliant formations up and down the compound, many of them taking on the image of an arachnid. This event occurred twice a day, every day, and any drow within watching distance paused and took note each and every time. The changing of the Baenre house guard was a symbol in Menzoberranzan of both House Baenre's incredible power, and the city's undying fealty to Lolth, the Spider Queen.

Jarlaxle, as he had been instructed by Matron Baenre, used the spectacle as a distraction. He crept up to the fence, dropped his wide-brimmed hat to hang at his back, and slipped a mask of black velvet cloth, with eight joint-wired legs protruding from its sides, over his head. With a quick glance, the mercenary started up, hand over hand, climbing the thick strands as though they were ordinary iron. No magical spells could have duplicated this effect; no spells of levitation and teleportation, or any other kind of magical travel, could have brought someone beyond the barrier. Only the rare and treasured spider mask, loaned to Jarlaxle by Gromph Baenre, could get someone so easily into the well-guarded compound.

Jarlaxle swung a leg over the top of the fence and slipped down the other side. He froze in place at the sight of an orange flash to his left. Curse his luck if he had been caught. The guard would likely pose no danger—all in the Baenre compound knew the mercenary well—but if Matron Baenre learned that he had been discovered, she would likely flail the skin from his bones.

The flaring light died away almost immediately, and as Jarlaxle's eyes adjusted to the changing hues, he saw a handsome young drow with neatly cropped hair sitting astride a large lizard, perpendicular to the floor and holding a ten-foot-long mottled lance. A death lance, Jarlaxle knew. It was coldly enchanted, its hungry and razor-edged tip revealing its deadly chill to the mercenary's heat-sensing eyes.

Well met, Berg'inyon Baenre, the mercenary flashed in the intricate and silent hand code of the drow. Berg'inyon was Matron Baenre's youngest son, the leader of the Baenre lizard riders, and no enemy of, or stranger to, the mercenary leader.

And you, Jarlaxle, Berg'inyon flashed back. *Prompt, as always.*

As your mother demands, Jarlaxle signaled back. Berg'inyon flashed a smile and motioned for the mercenary to be on his way, then kicked his mount and scampered up the side of the stalagmite to his ceiling patrol.

Jarlaxle liked the youngest Baenre male. He had spent many days with Berg'inyon lately, learning from the young fighter, for Berg'inyon had once been a classmate of Drizzt Do'Urden's at Melee-Magthere and had often sparred against the scimitar-wielding drow. Berg'inyon's battle moves were fluid and near-perfect, and knowledge of how Drizzt had defeated the young Baenre heightened Jarlaxle's respect for the renegade.

Jarlaxle almost mourned that Drizzt Do'Urden would soon be no more.

Once past the fence, the mercenary replaced the spider mask in a pouch and walked nonchalantly through the Baenre compound, keeping his telltale hat low on his back and his cloak tight about his shoulder, hiding the fact that he wore a sleeveless tunic. He couldn't hide his bald head, though, an unusual trait, and he knew that more than one of the Baenre guards recognized him as he made his way casually to the house's great mound, the huge and ornate stalagmite wherein resided the Baenre nobles.

Those guards didn't notice, though, or pretended not to, as they had likely

been instructed. Jarlaxle nearly laughed aloud; so many troubles could have been avoided just by his going through a more conspicuous gate to the compound. Everyone, Triel included, knew full well that he would be there. It was all a game of pretense and intrigue, with Matron Baenre as the controlling player.

"Z'ress!" the mercenary cried, the drow word for "strength" and the password for the mound. He pushed on the stone door, which retracted immediately into the top of its jamb.

Jarlaxle tipped his hat to the unseen guards—probably huge minotaur slaves, Matron Baenre's favorites—as he passed along the narrow entry corridor, between several slits, no doubt lined with readied death lances.

The inside of the mound was lighted, forcing Jarlaxle to pause and allow his eyes to shift back to the visible light spectrum. Dozens of female dark elves moved about, their silver-and-black Baenre uniforms tightly fitting their firm and alluring bodies. All eyes turned toward the newcomer—the leader of Bregan D'aerthe was considered a fine catch in Menzoberranzan—and the lewd way the females scrutinized him, hardly looking at his face at all, made Jarlaxle bite back a laugh. Some male dark elves resented such leers, but to Jarlaxle's thinking, these females' obvious hunger afforded him even more power.

The mercenary moved to the large black pillar in the heart of the central circular chamber. He felt along the smooth marble and located the pressure plate that opened a section of the curving wall.

Jarlaxle found Dantrag Baenre, the house weapons master, leaning casually against the wall inside. Jarlaxle quickly discerned that the fighter had been waiting for him. Like his younger brother, Dantrag was handsome, tall—closer to six feet than to five—and lean, his muscles finely tuned. His eyes were unusually amber, though they shifted toward red when he grew excited. He wore his white hair pulled back tightly into a ponytail.

As weapons master of House Baenre, Dantrag was better outfitted for battle than any other drow in the city. Dantrag's shimmering black coat of mesh mail glistened as he turned, conforming to the angles of his body so perfectly that it seemed a second skin. He wore two swords on his jeweled belt. Curiously, only one of these was of drow make, as fine a sword as Jarlaxle had ever seen. The other, reportedly taken from a surface dweller, was said to possess a hunger of its own and could shave the edges off hard stone without dulling in the least.

The cocky fighter lifted one arm to salute the mercenary. As he did so, he prominently displayed one of his magical bracers, tight straps of black material lined with gleaming mithral rings. Dantrag had never told what purpose those bracers served. Some thought that they offered magical protection. Jarlaxle had seen Dantrag in battle and didn't disagree, for such defensive bracers were not uncommon. What amazed the mercenary even more was the fact that, in combat, Dantrag struck at his opponent first more often than not.

Jarlaxle couldn't be sure of his suspicions, for even without the bracers and any other magic, Dantrag Baenre was one of the finest fighters in Menzoberranzan. His principal rival had been Zaknafein Do'Urden, father and mentor of Drizzt, but Zaknafein was dead now, sacrificed for blasphemous acts against the Spider Queen. That left only Uthegental, the huge and strong weapons master of House Barrison Del'Armgo, the city's second house, as a suitable rival for dangerous Dantrag. Knowing both fighters' pride, Jarlaxle suspected that one day the two would secretly meet in a battle to the death, just to see who was the better.

The thought of such a spectacle intrigued Jarlaxle, though he never understood such destructive pride. Many who had seen the mercenary leader in battle would argue that he was a match for either of the two, but Jarlaxle would never play into such intrigue. To Jarlaxle it seemed that pride was a silly thing to fight for, especially when such fine weapons and skill could be used to bring more substantive treasures. Like those bracers, perhaps? Jarlaxle mused. Or would those fabulous bracers aid Dantrag in looting Uthegental's corpse?

With magic, anything was possible. Jarlaxle smiled as he continued to study Dantrag; the mercenary loved exotic magic, and nowhere in all the Underdark was there a finer collection of magical items than in House Baenre.

Like this cylinder he had entered. It seemed unremarkable, a plain circular chamber with a hole in the ceiling to Jarlaxle's left and a hole in the floor to his right.

He nodded to Dantrag, who waved his hand out to the left, and Jarlaxle walked under the hole. A tingling magic grabbed him and gradually lifted him into the air, levitating him to the great mound's second level. Inside the cylinder, this area appeared identical to the first, and Jarlaxle moved directly across the way, to the ceiling hole that would lead him to the third level.

Dantrag was up into the second level as Jarlaxle silently floated up to the third, and the weapons master came up quickly, catching Jarlaxle's arm as he reached for the opening mechanism to this level's door. Dantrag nodded to the next ceiling hole, which led to the fourth level and Matron Baenre's private throne room.

The fourth level? Jarlaxle pondered as he followed Dantrag into place and slowly began to levitate once more. Matron Baenre's private throne room?

Normally, the first matron mother held audience in the mound's third level.

Matron Baenre already has a guest, Dantrag explained in the hand code as Jarlaxle's head came above the floor.

Jarlaxle nodded and stepped away from the hole, allowing Dantrag to lead the way. Dantrag did not reach for the door, however, but rather reached into a pouch and produced some silvery-glowing dust. With a wink to the mercenary, he flung the dust against the back wall. It sparkled and moved of its own accord, formed a silvery spider's web, which then spiraled outward, much like the Baenre gates, leaving a clear opening.

After you, Dantrag's hands politely suggested.

Jarlaxle studied the devious fighter, trying to discern if treachery was afoot. Might he climb through the obvious extradimensional gate only to find himself stranded on some hellish plane of existence?

Dantrag was a cool opponent, his beautiful, chiseled features, cheekbones set high and resolute, revealing nothing to Jarlaxle's usually effective, probing gaze. Jarlaxle did go through the opening, though, finally deciding that Dantrag was too proud to trick him into oblivion. If Dantrag had wanted Jarlaxle out of the way, he would have used weapons, not wizard's mischief.

The Baenre son stepped right behind Jarlaxle, into a small, extradimensional pocket sharing space with Matron Baenre's throne room. Dantrag led Jarlaxle along a thin silver thread to the far side of the small chamber, to an opening that looked out into the room.

There, on a large sapphire throne, sat the withered Matron Baenre, her face crisscrossed by thousands of spidery lines. Jarlaxle spent a long moment eyeing the throne before considering the matron mother, and he unconsciously licked his thin lips. Dantrag chuckled at his side, for the wary Baenre could understand the mercenary's desire. At the end of each of the throne's arms was set a huge diamond of no fewer than thirty carats.

The throne itself was carved of the purest black sapphire, a shining well that offered an invitation into its depths. Writhing forms moved about inside that pool of blackness; rumor said that the tormented souls of all those who had been unfaithful to Lolth, and had, in turn, been transformed into hideous driders, resided in an inky black dimension within the confines of Matron Baenre's fabulous throne.

That sobering thought brought the mercenary from his casing; he might consider the act, but he would never be so foolish as to try to take one of those diamonds! He looked to Matron Baenre then, her two unremarkable scribes huddled behind her, busily taking notes. The first matron mother was flanked on her left by Bladen'Kerst, the oldest daughter in the house proper, the third oldest of the siblings behind Triel and Gromph. Jarlaxle liked Bladen'Kerst even less than he liked Triel, for she was sadistic in the extreme. On several occasions, the mercenary had thought he might have to kill her in self-defense. That would have been a difficult situation, though Jarlaxle suspected that Matron Baenre, privately, would be glad to have the wicked Bladen'Kerst dead. Even the powerful matron mother couldn't fully control that one.

On Matron Baenre's right stood another of Jarlaxle's least favorite beings, the illithid, Methil El-Viddenvelp, the octopus-headed advisor to Matron Baenre. He wore, as always, his unremarkable, rich crimson robe, its sleeves long so that the creature could keep its scrawny, three-clawed hands tucked from sight. Jarlaxle wished that the ugly creature would wear a mask and hood as well. Its bulbous, purplish head, sporting four tentacles where its mouth should have been, and milky-white pupilless eyes, was among the most repulsive things Jarlaxle had ever seen. Normally, if gains could be made, the mercenary would have looked past a being's appearance, but Jarlaxle preferred to have little contact with the ugly, mysterious, and ultimately deadly illithids.

Most drow held similar feelings toward illithids, and it momentarily struck Jarlaxle as odd that Matron Baenre would have El-Viddenvelp so obviously positioned. When he scrutinized the female drow facing Matron Baenre, though, the mercenary understood.

She was scrawny and small, shorter than even Triel and appearing much weaker. Her black robes were unremarkable, and she wore no other visible equipment—certainly not the attire befitting a matron mother. But this drow, K'yorl Odran, was indeed a matron mother, leader of Oblodra, the third house of Menzoberranzan.

K'yorl? Jarlaxle's fingers motioned to Dantrag, the mercenary's facial expression incredulous. K'yorl was among the most despised of Menzoberranzan's rulers. Personally, Matron Baenre hated K'yorl, and had many times openly expressed her belief that Menzoberranzan would be better off without the troublesome Odran. The only thing that had stopped House Baenre from obliterating Oblodra was the fact that the females of the third house possessed mysterious powers of the mind. If anyone could understand the motivations and private thoughts of mysterious and dangerous K'yorl, it would be the illithid, El-Viddenvelp.

"Three hundred," K'yorl was saying.

Matron Baenre slumped back in her chair, a sour expression on her face. "A pittance," she replied.

"Half of my slave force," K'yorl responded, flashing her customary grin, a well-known signal that not-so-sly K'yorl was lying.

Matron Baenre cackled, then stopped abruptly. She came forward in her seat, her slender hands resting atop the fabulous diamonds, and her scowl unrelenting. Her ruby-red eyes narrowed to slits. She uttered something under her breath and removed one of her hands from atop the diamond. The magnificent gem flared to inner life and loosed a concentrated beam of purple light, striking K'yorl's attendant, an unremarkable male, and engulfing him in a series of cascading, crackling arcs of purple—glowing energy. He cried out, threw his hands up in the air, and fought back against the consuming waves.

Matron Baenre, lifted her other hand and a second beam joined the first. Now the male drow seemed like no more than a purple silhouette.

Jarlaxle watched closely as K'yorl closed her eyes and furrowed her brow. Her eyes came back open almost immediately, and she stared with disbelief at El-Viddenvelp. The mercenary was worldly enough to realize that, in that split second, a battle of wills had just occurred, and he was not surprised that the mind flayer had apparently won out.

The unfortunate Oblodran male was no more than a shadow by then, and a moment later, he wasn't even that. He was simply no more.

K'yorl Odran scowled fiercely, seemed on the verge of an explosion, but Matron Baenre, as deadly as any drow alive, did not back down.

Unexpectedly, K'yorl grinned widely again and announced lightheartedly, "He was just a male."

"K'yorl!" Baenre snarled. "This duty is sanctified by Lolth, and you shall cooperate!"

"Threats?" spoke K'yorl.

Matron Baenre rose from her throne and walked right in front of the unflinching K'yorl. She raised her left hand to the Oblodran female's cheek, and calm K'yorl couldn't help but wince. On that hand Matron Baenre wore a huge golden ring, its four uncompleted bands shifting as though they were the eight legs of a living spider. Its huge blue-black sapphire shimmered. That ring, K'yorl knew, contained a living *velsharess orbb*, a queen spider, a far more deadly cousin of the surface world's black widow.

"You must understand the importance," Matron Baenre cooed.

To Jarlaxle's amazement—and he noted that Dantrag's hand immediately went to his sword hilt, as though the weapons master would leap out of the extradimensional spying pocket and slay the impudent Oblodran—K'yorl slapped Matron Baenre's hand away.

"Barrison Del'Armgo has agreed," Matron Baenre said calmly, shifting her hand upright to keep her dangerous daughter and illithid advisor from taking any action.

K'yorl grinned, an obvious bluff, for the matron mother of the third house could not be thrilled to hear that the first two houses had allied on an issue that she wanted to avoid.

"As has Faen Tlabbar," Matron Baenre added slyly, referring to the city's fourth house and Oblodra's most hated rival. Baenre's words were an obvious threat, for with both House Baenre and House Barrison Del'Armgo on its side, Faen Tlabbar would move quickly to crush Oblodra and assume the city's third rank.

Matron Baenre slid back into her sapphire throne, never taking her gaze from K'yorl.

"I do not have many house drow," K'yorl said, and it was the first time Jarlaxle had ever heard the upstart Oblodran sound humbled.

"No, but you have kobold fodder!" Matron Baenre snapped. "And do not dare to admit to six hundred. The tunnels of the Clawrift beneath House Oblodra are vast."

"I will give to you three thousand," K'yorl answered, apparently thinking the better of some hard bargaining.

"Ten times that!" Baenre growled.

K'yorl said nothing, merely cocked her head back and looked down her slender, ebon-skinned nose at the first matron mother.

"I'll settle for nothing less than twenty thousand," Matron Baenre said then, carrying both sides of the bargaining. "The defenses of the dwarven stronghold will be cunning, and we'll need ample fodder to sort our way through."

"The cost is great," K'yorl said.

"Twenty thousand kobolds do not equal the cost of one drow life," Baenre reminded her, then added, just for effect, "in Lolth's eyes."

K'yorl started to respond sharply, but Matron Baenre stopped her at once.

"Spare me your threats!" Baenre screamed, her thin neck seeming even scrawnier with her jaw so tightened and jutting forward. "In Lolth's eyes, this event goes beyond the fighting of drow houses, and I promise you, K'yorl, that the disobedience of House Oblodra will aid the ascension of Faen Tlabbar!"

Jarlaxle's eyes widened with surprise and he looked at Dantrag, who had no explanation. Never before had the mercenary heard, or heard of, such a blatant threat, one house against another. No grin, no witty response, came from K'yorl this time. Studying the female, silent and obviously fighting to keep her features calm, Jarlaxle could see the seeds of anarchy. K'yorl and House Oblodra would not soon forget Matron Baenre's threat, and given Matron Baenre's arrogance, other houses would undoubtedly foster similar

resentments. The mercenary nodded as he thought of his own meeting with fearful Triel, who would likely inherit this dangerous situation.

"Twenty thousand," K'yorl quietly agreed, "if that many of the troublesome little rats can be herded."

The matron mother of House Oblodra was then dismissed. As she entered the marble cylinder, Dantrag dropped out of the end of the spider filament and climbed from the extradimensional pocket, into the throne room.

Jarlaxle went behind, stepping lightly to stand before the throne. He swept into a low bow, the diatryma feather sticking from the brim of his great hat brushing the floor. "A most magnificent performance," he greeted Matron Baenre. "It was my pleasure that I was allowed to witness—"

"Shut up," Matron Baenre, leaning back in her throne and full of venom, said to him.

Still grinning, the mercenary came to quiet attention.

"K'yorl is a dangerous nuisance," Matron Baenre said. "I will ask little from her house drow, though their strange mind powers would prove useful in breaking the will of resilient dwarves. All that we need from them is kobold fodder, and since the vermin breed like muck rats, their sacrifice will not be great."

"What about after the victory?" Jarlaxle dared to ask.

"That is for K'yorl to decide," Matron Baenre replied immediately. She motioned then for the others, even her scribes, to leave the room, and all knew that she meant to appoint Jarlaxle's band to a scouting mission—at the very least—on House Oblodra.

They all went without complaint, except for wicked Bladen'Kerst, who paused to flash the mercenary a dangerous glare. Bladen'Kerst hated Jarlaxle as she hated all drow males, considering them nothing more than practice dummies on which she could hone her torturing techniques.

The mercenary shifted his eye patch to the other eye and gave her a lewd wink in response.

Bladen'Kerst immediately looked to her mother, as if asking permission to beat the impertinent male senseless, but Matron Baenre continued to wave her away.

"You want Bregan D'aerthe to keep close watch on House Oblodra," Jarlaxle reasoned as soon as he was alone with Baenre. "Not an easy task—"

"No," Matron Baenre interrupted. "Even Bregan D'aerthe could not readily spy on that mysterious house."

The mercenary was glad that Matron Baenre, not he, had been the one to point that out. He considered the unexpected conclusion, then grinned widely, and even dipped into a bow of salute as he came to understand. Matron Baenre wanted the others, particularly El-Viddenvelp, merely to think that she would set Bregan D'aerthe to spy on House Oblodra. That way, she could keep K'yorl somewhat off guard, looking for ghosts that did not exist.

"I care not for K'yorl, beyond my need of her slaves," Matron Baenre went on. "If she does not do as she is instructed in this matter, then House Oblodra will be dropped into the Clawrift and forgotten."

The matter-of-fact tones, showing supreme confidence, impressed the mercenary. "With the first and second houses aligned, what choice does K'yorl have?" he asked.

Matron Baenre pondered that point, as though Jarlaxle had reminded her of something. She shook the notion away and quickly went on. "We do not have time to discuss your meeting with Triel," she said, and Jarlaxle was more than a little curious, for he had thought that the primary reason for his visit to House Baenre. "I want you to begin planning our procession toward the dwarvish home. I will need maps of the intended routes, as well as detailed descriptions of the possible final approaches to Mithral Hall, so that Dantrag and his generals might best plan the attack."

Jarlaxle nodded. He certainly wasn't about to argue with the foul-tempered matron mother. "We could send spies deeper into the dwarven complex," he began, but again, the impatient Baenre cut him short.

"We need none," she said simply.

Jarlaxle eyed her curiously. "Our last expedition did not actually get into Mithral Hall," he reminded.

Matron Baenre's lips curled up in a perfectly evil smile, an infectious grin that made Jarlaxle eager to learn what revelation might be coming. Slowly, the matron mother reached inside the front of her fabulous robes, producing a chain on which hung a ring, bone white and fashioned, so it appeared, out of a large tooth. "Do you know of this?" she asked, holding the item up in plain view.

"It is said to be the tooth of a dwarf king, and that his trapped and tormented soul is contained within the ring," the mercenary replied.

"A dwarf king," Matron Baenre echoed. "And there are not so many dwarvish kingdoms, you see."

Jarlaxle's brow furrowed, then his face brightened. "Mithral Hall?" he asked.

Matron Baenre nodded. "Fate has played me a marvelous coincidence," she explained. "Within this ring is the soul of Gandalug Battlehammer, First King of Mithral Hall, Patron of Clan Battlehammer."

Jarlaxle's mind whirled with the possibilities. No wonder, then, that Lolth had instructed Vierna to go after her renegade brother! Drizzt was just a tie to the surface, a pawn in a larger game of conquest.

"Gandalug talks to me," Matron Baenre explained, her voice as content as a cat's purr. "He remembers the ways of Mithral Hall."

Sos'Umptu Baenre entered then, ignoring Jarlaxle and walking right by him to stand before her mother. The matron mother did not rebuke her, as the mercenary would have expected for the unannounced intrusion, but rather, turned a curious gaze her way and allowed her to explain.

"Matron Mez'Barris Armgo grows impatient," Sos'Umptu said.

In the chapel, Jarlaxle realized, for Sos'Umptu was caretaker of the wondrous Baenre chapel and rarely left the place. The mercenary paused for just a moment to consider the revelation. Mez'Barris was the matron mother of House Barrison Del'Armgo, the city's second-ranking house. But why would she be at the Baenre compound if, as Matron Baenre had declared, Barrison Del'Armgo had already agreed to the expedition?

Why indeed.

"Perhaps you should have seen to Matron Mez'Barris first," the mercenary said slyly to Matron Baenre. The withered old matron accepted his remark in good cheer; it showed her that her favorite spy was thinking clearly.

"K'yorl was the more difficult," Baenre replied. "To keep that one waiting would have put her in a fouler mood than usual. Mez'Barris is calmer by far, more understanding of the gains. She will agree to the war with the dwarves."

Matron Baenre walked by the mercenary to the marble cylinder; Sos'Umptu was already inside, waiting. "Besides," the first matron mother added with a wicked grin, "now that House Oblodra has come into the alliance, what choice does Mez'Barris have?"

She was too beautiful, this old one, Jarlaxle agreed. Too beautiful. He cast one final, plaintive look at the marvelous diamonds on the arms of Baenre's throne, then sighed deeply and followed the two females out of House Baenre's great stronghold.

4

THE FIRE IN HER EYES

Catti-brie pulled her gray cloak about her to hide the dagger and mask she had taken from Regis. Mixed feelings assaulted her as she neared Bruenor's private chambers; she hoped both that the dwarf would be there, and that he would not.

How could she leave without seeing Bruenor, her father, one more time? And yet, the dwarf now seemed to Catti-brie a shell of his former self, a wallowing old dwarf waiting to die. She didn't want to see him like that, didn't want to take that image of Bruenor with her into the Underdark.

She lifted her hand to knock on the door to Bruenor's sitting room, then gently cracked the door open instead and peeked in. She saw a dwarf standing off to the side of the burning hearth, but it wasn't Bruenor. Thibbledorf Pwent, the battlerager, hopped about in circles, apparently trying to catch a pesky fly. He wore his sharp-ridged armor—as always—complete with glove nails and knee and elbow spikes, and other deadly points protruding from every plausible angle. The armor squealed as the dwarf spun and jumped, an irritating sound if Catti-brie had ever heard one. Pwent's open-faced gray helm rested in the chair beside him, its top spike half as tall as the dwarf. Without it, Catti-brie could see, the battlerager was almost bald, his remaining thin black strands of hair matted greasily to the sides of his head, then giving way to an enormous, bushy black beard.

Catti-brie pushed the door a little farther and saw Bruenor sitting before the low-burning fire, absently trying to flip a log so that its embers would flare to life again. His halfhearted poke against the glowing log made Catti-brie wince. She remembered the days not so long ago, when the boisterous king would have simply reached into the hearth and smacked the stubborn log with his bare hand.

With a look to Pwent—who was eating something that Catti-brie sincerely hoped was not a fly—the young woman entered the room, checking her cloak as she came in to see that the items were properly concealed.

"Hey, there!" Pwent howled between crunchy bites. Even more than her disgust at the thought that he was eating a fly, Catti-brie was amazed that he could be getting so much chewing out of it!

"Ye should get a beard!" the battlerager called, his customary greeting. From their first meeting, the dirty dwarf had told Catti-brie that she'd be a handsome woman indeed if she could only grow a beard.

"I'm working at it," Catti-brie replied, honestly glad for the levity. "Ye've got me promise that I haven't shaved me face since the day we met." She patted the battlerager atop the head, then regretted it when she felt the greasy film on her hand.

"There's a good girl," Pwent replied. He spotted another flitting insect and hopped away in pursuit.

"Where ye going?" Bruenor demanded sharply before Catti-brie could even say hello.

Catti-brie sighed in the face of her father's scowl. How she longed to see Bruenor smile again! Catti-brie noted the bruise on Bruenor's forehead, the scraped portion finally scabbing over. He had reportedly gone into a tirade a few nights before, and had actually smashed down a heavy wooden door with his head while two frantic younger dwarves tried to hold him back. The bruise combined with Bruenor's garish scar, which ran from his forehead to the side of his jaw, across one socket where his eye had once been, made the old dwarf seem battered indeed!

"Where ye going?" Bruenor asked again, angrily.

"Settlestone," the young woman lied, referring to the town of barbarians, Wulfgar's people, down the mountain from Mithral Hall's eastern exit. "The tribe's building a cairn to honor Wulfgar's memory." Catti-brie was somewhat surprised at how easily the lie came to her; she had always been able to charm Bruenor, often using half-truths and semantic games to get around the blunt truth, but she had never so boldly lied to him.

Reminding herself of the importance behind it all, she looked the red-bearded dwarf in the eye as she continued. "I'm wanting to be there before they start building. If they're to do it, then they're to do it right. Wulfgar deserves no less."

Bruenor's one working eye seemed to mist over, taking on an even duller appearance, and the scarred dwarf turned away from Catti-brie, went back to his pointless fire poking, though he did manage one slight nod of halfhearted agreement. It was no secret in Mithral Hall that Bruenor didn't like talking of Wulfgar—he had even punched out one priest who insisted that Aegis-fang could not, by dwarvish tradition, be given a place of honor in the Hall of Dumathoin, since a human, and no dwarf, had wielded it.

Catti-brie noticed then that Pwent's armor had ceased its squealing, and she turned about to regard the battlerager. He stood by the opened door, looking forlornly at her and at Bruenor's back. With a nod to the young woman, he quietly—for a rusty-armored battlerager—left the room.

Apparently, Catti-brie was not the only one pained by the pitiful wretch Bruenor Battlehammer had become.

"Ye've got their sympathy," she remarked to Bruenor, who seemed not to hear. "All in Mithral Hall speak kindly of their wounded king."

"Shut yer face," Bruenor said out of the side of his mouth. He still sat squarely facing the low fire.

Catti-brie knew that the implied threat was lame, another reminder of Bruenor's fall. In days past, when Bruenor Battlehammer suggested that someone shut his face, he did, or Bruenor did it for him. But, since the fights with the priest and with the door, Bruenor's fire, like the one in the hearth, had played itself to its end.

"Do ye mean to poke that fire the rest o' yer days?" Catti-brie asked, trying to incite a fight, to blow on the embers of Bruenor's pride.

"If it pleases me," the dwarf retaliated too calmly.

Catti-brie sighed again and pointedly hitched her cloak over the side of her hip, revealing the magical mask and Entreri's jeweled dagger. Even though the young woman was determined to undertake her adventure alone, and did not want to explain any of it to Bruenor, she prayed that Bruenor would have life enough within him to notice.

Long minutes passed, quiet minutes, except for the occasional crackle of the embers and the hiss of the unseasoned wood.

"I'll return when I return!" the flustered woman barked, and she headed for the door. Bruenor absently waved her away over one shoulder, never bothering to look at her.

Catti-brie paused by the door, then opened it and quietly closed it, never leaving the room. She waited a few moments, not believing that Bruenor remained in front of the fire, poking it absently. Then she slipped across the room and through another doorway, to the dwarf's bedroom.

Catti-brie moved to Bruenor's large oaken desk—a gift from Wulfgar's people, its polished wood gleaming and designs of Aegis-fang, the mighty warhammer that Bruenor had crafted, carved into its sides. Catti-brie paused a long while, despite her need to be out before Bruenor realized what she was doing, and looked at those designs, remembering Wulfgar. She would never get over that loss. She understood that, but she knew, too, that her time of grieving neared its end, that she had to get on with the business of living. Especially now, Catti-brie reminded herself, with another of her friends apparently walking into peril.

In a stone coffer atop the desk Catti-brie found what she was looking for: a small locket on a silver chain, a gift to Bruenor from Alustriel, the Lady of Silverymoon. Bruenor had been thought dead, lost in Mithral Hall on the friends' first passage through the place. He had escaped from the halls sometime later, avoiding the evil gray dwarves who had claimed Mithral Hall as their own, and with Alustriel's help, he found Catti-brie in Longsaddle, a village to the southwest. Drizzt and Wulfgar had left long before that, on their way south in pursuit of Regis, who had been captured by the assassin Entreri.

Alustriel had then given Bruenor the magical locket. Inside was a tiny portrait of Drizzt, and with this device the dwarf could generally track the drow. Proper direction and distance from Drizzt could be determined by the degrees of magical warmth emanating from the locket.

The metal bauble was cool now, colder than the air of the room, and it seemed to Catti-brie that Drizzt was already a long way from her.

Catti-brie opened the locket and regarded the perfect image of her dear drow friend. She wondered if she should take it. With Guenhwyvar she could likely follow Drizzt anyway, if she could get on his trail, and she had kept it in the back of her mind that, when Bruenor learned the truth from Regis, the fire would come into his eyes, and he would rush off in pursuit.

Catti-brie liked that image of fiery Bruenor, wanted her father to come charging in to her aid, and to Drizzt's rescue, but that was a child's hope, she realized, unrealistic and ultimately dangerous.

Catti-brie shut the locket and snapped it up into her hand. She slipped out of Bruenor's bedroom and through his sitting room—with the red-bearded dwarf still seated before the fire, his thoughts a million miles away—then rushed through the halls of the upper levels, knowing that if she didn't get on her way soon, she might lose her nerve.

Outside, she regarded the locket again and knew that in taking it, she had cut off any chances that Bruenor would follow. She was on her own.

That was how it had to be, Catti-brie decided, and she slipped the chain over her head and started down the mountain, hoping to get to Silverymoon not so long after Drizzt.

⚔ ⚔ ⚔ ⚔ ⚔

He slipped as quietly and unobtrusively as he could along the dark streets of Menzoberranzan, his heat-seeing eyes glowing ruby red. All that he wanted was to get back to Jarlaxle's base, back with the drow who recognized his worth.

"*Waela rivvil!*" came a shrill cry from the side.

He stopped in his tracks, leaned wearily against the pile of broken stone near an unoccupied stalagmite mound. He had heard those words often before—always those two words, said with obvious derision.

"*Waela rivvil!*" the drow female said again, moving toward him, a russet tentacle rod in one hand, its three eight-foot-long arms writhing of their own accord, eagerly, as though they wanted to lash out with their own maliciousness and slap at him. At least the female wasn't carrying one of those whips of fangs, he mused, thinking of the multi-snake-headed weapons many of the higher-ranking drow priestesses used.

He offered no resistance as she moved to stand right in front of him, respectfully lowered his eyes as Jarlaxle had taught him. He suspected that she, too, was moving through the streets inconspicuously—why else would a drow female, powerful enough to be carrying one of those wicked rods, be crawling about the alleys of this, the lesser section of Menzoberranzan?

She issued a string of drow words in her melodic voice, too quickly for this newcomer to understand. He caught the words *quarth,* which meant "command," and *harl'il'cik,* or "kneel," and expected them anyway, for he was always being commanded to kneel.

Down he went, obediently and immediately, though the drop to the hard stone pained his knees.

The drow female paced slowly about him, giving him a long look at her shapely legs, even pulling his head back so that he could stare up into her undeniably beautiful face, while she purred her name, "Jerlys."

She moved as if to kiss him, then slapped him instead, a stinging smack on his cheek. Immediately, his hands went to his sword and dirk, but he calmed and reminded himself of the consequences.

Still the drow paced about him, speaking to herself as much as to him. "*Iblith,*" she said many times, the drow word for "excrement," and finally he

replied with the single word *"abban,"* which meant "ally," again as Jarlaxle had coached him.

"Abban del darthiir!" she cried back, smacking him again on the back of his head, nearly knocking him flat to his face.

He didn't understand completely, but thought that darthiir had something to do with the faeries, the surface elves. He was beginning to figure out then that he was in serious trouble this time, and would not so easily get away from this one.

"Abban del darthiir!" Jerlys cried again, and her tentacle rod, and not her hand, snapped at him from behind, all three tentacles pounding painfully into his right shoulder. He grabbed at the wound and fell flat to the stone, his right arm useless and the waves of pain rolling through him.

Jerlys struck again, at his back, but his sudden movement had saved him from a hit by all three of the tentacles.

His mind raced. He knew that he had to act fast. The female kept taunting him, smacking her rod against the alley walls, and every so often against his bleeding back. He knew for certain then that he had caught this female by surprise, that she was on a mission as secret as his own, and that he would not likely walk away from this encounter.

One of the tentacles slapped off the back of his head, dazing him. Still his right arm remained dead, weakened by the magic of a simultaneous three-strike.

But he had to act. He moved his left hand to his right hip, to his dirk, then changed his mind and brought it around the other side.

"Abban del darthiir!" Jerlys cried again, and her arm came forward.

He spun about and up to meet it, his sword, not of drow make, flaring angrily as it connected with the tentacles. There came a green flash, and one tentacle fell free, but one of the others snaked its way through the parry and hit him in the face.

"Jivvin!" the amused drow cried the word for "play," and she elaborated most graciously, thanking him for his foolish retaliation, for making it all such fun.

"Play with this," he said back at her, and he came forward, straight ahead with the sword.

A globe of conjured darkness fell over him.

"Jivvin!" Jerlys laughed again and came forward to smack with her rod. But this one was no novice in fighting dark elves, and, to the female's surprise, she did not find him within her globe.

Around the side of the darkness he came, one arm hanging limp, but the other flashing this way and that in a marvelous display of swordsmanship. This was a drow female, though, highly trained in the fighting arts and armed with a tentacle rod. She parried and countered, scoring another hit, laughing all the while.

She did not understand her opponent.

He came in a straightforward lunge again, spun about to the left as if to continue with a spinning overhand chop, then reversed his grip on the weapon, pivoted back to the right, and heaved the sword as though it were a spear.

The weapon's tip dived hungrily between the surprised female's breasts, sparking as it sliced through the fine drow armor.

He followed the throw with a leaping somersault and kicked both feet forward so that they connected on the quivering sword hilt, plunging the weapon deeper into the malevolent female's chest.

The drow fell back against the rock pile, stumbling over it until the uneven wall of the stalagmite supported her at a half-standing angle, her red eyes locked in a wide stare.

"A pity, Jerlys," he whispered into her ear, and he softly kissed her cheek as he grasped the sword hilt and pointedly stepped on the writhing tentacles to pin them down on the floor. "What pleasures we might have known."

He pulled the sword free and grimaced as he considered the implications of this drow female's death. He couldn't deny the satisfaction, however, at taking back some of the control in his life. He hadn't gone through all his battles just to wind up a slave!

He left the alley a short while later, with Jerlys and her rod buried under the stones, and with a bounce returned to his step.

OVER THE YEARS

Drizzt felt the gazes on him. They were elven eyes, he knew, likely staring down the length of readied arrows. The ranger casually continued his trek through the Moonwood, his weapons tucked away and the hood of his forest-green cloak back off his head, revealing his long mane of white hair and his ebon-skinned elven features.

The sun made its lazy way through the leafy green trees, splotching the forest with dots of pale yellow. Drizzt did not avoid these, as much to show the surface elves that he was no ordinary drow as for his honest love of the warmth of sunlight. The trail was wide and smooth, unexpected in a supposedly wild and thick forest.

As the minutes turned into an hour and the forest deepened around him, Drizzt began to wonder if he might pass through the Moonwood without incident. He wanted no trouble, certainly, wanted only to be on with, and be done with, his quest.

He came into a small clearing some time later. Several logs had been arranged into a square around a stone-blocked fire pit. This was no ordinary campsite, Drizzt knew, but a designated meeting place, a shared campground for those who would respect the sovereignty of the forest and the creatures living within its sheltered boughs.

Drizzt walked the camp's perimeter, searching the trees. Looking to the moss bed at the base of one huge oak, the drow saw several markings. Though time had blurred their lines, one appeared to be a rearing bear, another a wild pig. These were the marks of rangers, and with an approving nod, the drow searched the lower boughs of the tree, finally discovering a well-concealed hollow. He reached in gingerly and pulled out a pack of dried food, a hatchet, and a skin filled with fine wine. Drizzt took only a small cup of the wine, but regretted that he could not add anything to the cache, since he would need all the provisions he could carry, and more, in his long trek through the dangerous Underdark.

He replaced the stores after using the hatchet to split some nearby deadwood, then gently carved his own ranger mark, the unicorn, in the moss at the base of the trunk and returned to the nearest log to start a fire for his meal.

"You are no ordinary drow," came a melodic voice from behind him before his meal was even cooked. The language was Elvish, as was the pitch of the voice, more melodic than that of a human.

Drizzt turned slowly, understanding that several bows were probably again trained on him from many different angles. A single elf stood before him. She was a young maiden, younger than even Drizzt, though Drizzt had lived only a tenth of his expected life. She wore forest colors, a green cloak, much like Drizzt's, and a brown tunic and leggings, with a longbow resting easily over one shoulder and a slender sword belted on one hip. Her black hair shone so as to be bluish and her skin was so pale that it reflected that blue hue. Her eyes, too, bright and shining, were blue flecked with gold. She was a silver elf—a moon elf, Drizzt knew.

In his years of living on the surface, Drizzt Do'Urden had encountered few surface elves, and those had been gold elves. He had encountered moon elves only once in his life, on his first trip to the surface in a dark elf raid in which his kin had slaughtered an small elf clan. That horrible memory rushed up at Drizzt as he faced this beautiful and delicate creature. Only one moon elf had survived that encounter, a young child that Drizzt had secretly buried beneath her mother's mutilated body. That act of treachery against the evil drow had brought severe repercussions, costing Drizzt's family the favor of Lolth, and, in the end, costing Zaknafein, Drizzt's father, his life.

Drizzt faced a moon elf once more, a maiden perhaps thirty years of age, with sparkling eyes. The ranger felt the blood draining from his face. Was this the region to which he and the drow raiders had come?

"You are no ordinary drow," the elf said again, still using the Elvish tongue, her eyes flashing dangerously and her tone grim.

Drizzt held his hands out to the side. He realized that he should say something, but simply couldn't think of any words—or couldn't get them past the lump in his throat.

The elf maiden's eyes narrowed; her lower jaw trembled, and her hand instinctively dropped to the hilt of her sword.

"I am no enemy," Drizzt managed to say, realizing that he must either speak or, likely, fight.

The maiden was on him in the blink of a lavender eye, sword flashing.

Drizzt never even drew his weapons, just stood with his hands out wide, and his expression calm. The elf slid up short of him, her sword raised. Her expression changed suddenly, as though she had noticed something in Drizzt's eyes.

She screamed wildly and started to swing, but Drizzt, too quick for her, leaped forward, caught her weapon arm in one hand, and wrapped his other arm about her, pulling her close and hugging her so tightly that she could not continue the fight. He expected her to claw him, or even bite him, but, to his surprise, she fell limply into his arms and slumped low, her face buried in his chest and her shoulders bobbing with sobs.

Before he could begin to speak words to comfort, Drizzt felt the keen tip of an elven sword against the back of his neck. He let go of the female immediately, his hands out wide once more, and another elf, older and more stern, but with similarly beautiful features, came from the trees to collect the young maiden and help her away.

"I am no enemy," Drizzt said again.

"Why do you cross the Moonwood?" the unseen elf behind him asked in the Common tongue.

"Your words are correct," Drizzt replied absently, for his thoughts were still focused on the curious maiden. "I mean only to cross the Moonwood, from the west to the east, and will bring no harm to you or the wood."

"The unicorn," Drizzt heard another elf say from behind, from near the huge oak tree. He figured that the elf had found his ranger mark in the moss. To his relief, the sword was taken away from his neck.

Drizzt paused a long moment, figuring that it was the elves' turn to speak. Finally, he mustered the nerve to turn about—only to find that the moon elves were gone, disappeared into the brush.

He thought of tracking them, was haunted by the image of that young elven maiden, but realized that it was not his place to disturb them in this, their forest home. He finished his meal quickly, made sure that the area was cleaned and as he had found it, then gathered up his gear and went on his way.

Less than a mile down the trail, he came upon another curious sight. A black-and-white horse, fully saddled, its bridle lined with tinkling bells, stood quietly and calmly. The animal pawed the ground when it saw the drow coming.

Drizzt spoke softly and made quiet sounds as he eased over to it. The horse visibly calmed, even nuzzled Drizzt when he got near. The animal was fine, the ranger could tell, well muscled and well groomed, though it was not a tall beast. Its coat held black and white splotches, even on its face, with one eye surrounded by white, the other appearing as though it was under a black mask.

Drizzt searched around, but found no other prints in the ground. He suspected that the horse had been provided by the elves, for him, but he couldn't be sure, and he certainly didn't want to steal someone's mount.

He patted the horse on the neck and started to walk past. He had gone only a few steps when the horse snorted and wheeled about. It galloped around the drow and stood again before him on the path.

Curious, Drizzt repeated the movement, going by the beast, and the horse followed suit to stand before him.

"Did they tell you to do this?" Drizzt asked plainly, stroking the animal's muzzle.

"Did you instruct him so?" Drizzt called loudly to the woods around him. "I ask the elves of Moonwood, was this horse provided for me?"

All that came in response was the protesting chatter of some birds disturbed by Drizzt's shout.

The drow shrugged and figured that he would take the horse to the end of the wood; it wasn't so far anyway. He mounted up and galloped off, making great progress along the wide and flat trail.

He came to the eastern end of Moonwood late that afternoon, long shadows rolling out from the tall trees. Figuring that the elves had given him the mount only so that he could be gone of their realm more quickly, he brought the horse to a halt, still under the shadows, meaning to dismount and send it running back into the forest.

A movement across the wide field beyond the forest caught the drow ranger's eye. He spotted an elf atop a tall black stallion, just outside the brush line, looking his way. The elf put his hands to his lips and gave a shrill whistle, and Drizzt's horse leaped out from the shadows and ran across the thick grass.

The elf disappeared immediately into the brush, but Drizzt did not bring his horse up short. He understood then that the elves had chosen to help him, in their distant way, and he accepted their gift and rode on.

Before he set camp that night, Drizzt noticed that the elven rider was paralleling him, some distance to the south. It seemed that there was a limit to their trust.

⚔ ⚔ ⚔ ⚔ ⚔

Catti-brie had little experience with cities. She had been through Luskan, had flown in an enchanted chariot over the splendor of mighty Waterdeep, and had traveled through the great southern city of Calimport. Nothing, though, had ever come close to the sights that awaited her as she walked the wide and curving avenues of Silverymoon. She had been here once before, but at the time, she had been a prisoner of Artemis Entreri and had hardly noticed the graceful spires and free-flowing designs of the marvelous city.

Silverymoon was a place for philosophers, for artists, a city known for tolerance. Here an architect could let his imagination soar along with a hundred-foot spire. Here a poet could stand on the street corner, spouting his art and earning a fair and honest living on the trinkets that passersby happened to toss his way.

Despite the seriousness of her quest, and the knowledge that she soon might walk into darkness, a wide smile grew on Catti-brie's face. She understood why Drizzt had often gone from Mithral Hall to visit this place; she never guessed that the world could be so varied and wonderful.

On impulse, the young woman moved to the side of one building, a few steps down a dark, though clean, alleyway. She took out the panther figurine and set it on the cobblestones before her.

"Come, Guenhwyvar," Catti-brie called softly. She didn't know if Drizzt had brought the panther into this city before or not, didn't know whether she was breaking any rules, but she believed that Guenhwyvar should experience this place, and believed, too, for some reason, that, in Silverymoon, she was free to follow her heart.

A gray mist surrounded the figurine, swirled, and gradually took shape. The great panther, six-hundred pounds of inky black, muscled cat, its shoulders higher than Catti-brie's waist, stood before her. Its head turned from side to side as it tried to fathom their location.

"We're in Silverymoon, Guen," Catti-brie whispered.

The panther tossed its head, as though it had just awakened, and gave a low, calm growl.

"Keep yerself close," Catti-brie instructed, "right by me side. I'm not for knowing if ye should be here or not, but I wanted ye to see the place, at least."

They came out of the alley side by side. "Have ye seen the place before, Guen?" Catti-brie asked. "I'm looking for Lady Alustriel. Might ye know where that'd be?"

The panther bumped close to Catti-brie's leg and moved off, apparently with purpose, and Catti-brie went right behind. Many heads turned to regard the curious couple, the road-dirty woman and her unusual companion, but the gazes were innocuous enough, and not one person screamed or hurried away in fright.

Coming around one sweeping avenue, Guenhwyvar almost ran headfirst into a pair of talking elves. They jumped back instinctively and looked from the panther to the young woman.

"Most marvelous!" one of them said in a singsong voice.

"Incredible," the other agreed. He reached toward the panther slowly, testing the reaction. "May I?" he asked Catti-brie.

She didn't see the harm and nodded.

The elf's face beamed as he ran his slender fingers along Guenhwyvar's muscled neck. He looked to his more hesitant companion, his smile seeming wide enough to take in his ears.

"Oh, buy the cat!" the other agreed excitedly.

Catti-brie winced; Guenhwyvar's ears flattened, and the panther let out a roar that echoed about the buildings throughout the city.

Catti-brie knew that elves were fast afoot, but these two were out of sight before she could even explain to them their mistake. "Guenhwyvar!" she whispered harshly into the panther's flattened ear.

The cat's ears came up, and the panther turned and rose on its haunches, putting a thick paw atop each of Catti-brie's shoulders. It bumped its head into Catti-brie's face and twisted to rub against her smooth cheek. Catti-brie had to struggle just to keep her balance and it took her a long while to explain to the panther that the apology was accepted.

As they went on, pointing fingers accompanied the stares, and more than one person slipped across the avenues ahead to get on the opposite side of the street and let the woman and cat pass. Catti-brie knew that they had attracted too much attention; she began to feel foolish for bringing Guenhwyvar here in the first place. She wanted to dismiss the cat back to the Astral Plane, but she suspected that she couldn't do so without attracting even more attention.

She wasn't surprised a few moments later, when a host of armed soldiers wearing the new silver-and-light-blue uniforms of the city guard, surrounded her at a comfortable distance.

"The panther is with you," one of them reasoned.

"Guenhwyvar," Catti-brie replied. "I am Catti-brie, daughter of Bruenor Battlehammer, Eighth King of Mithral Hall."

The man nodded and smiled, and Catti-brie relaxed with a deep sigh.

"It is indeed the drow's cat!" another of the guardsmen blurted. He blushed at his uncalled-for outburst, looked to the leader, and promptly lowered his eyes.

"Aye, Guen's the friend of Drizzt Do'Urden," Catti-brie replied. "Is he about in the city?" she couldn't help asking, though, logically, she would have preferred to ask the question of Alustriel, who might give her a more complete answer.

"Not that I have heard," replied the guard leader, "but Silverymoon is honored by your presence, Princess of Mithral Hall." He dipped a low bow, and Catti-brie blushed, not used to—or comfortable with—such treatment.

She did well to hide her disappointment about the news, reminding herself that finding Drizzt was not likely to be easy. Even if Drizzt had come into Silverymoon, he had probably done so secretly.

"I have come to speak with Lady Alustriel," Catti-brie explained.

"You should have been escorted from the gate," the guard leader groused, angered by the lack of proper protocol.

Catti-brie understood the man's frustration and realized that she had probably just gotten the unwitting soldiers at the Moonbridge, the invisible structure spanning the great River Rauvin, in trouble. "They did not know me name," she added quickly, "or me quest. I thought it best to come through on me own and see what I might."

"They did not question the presence of such a—" He wisely caught himself before saying "pet." "A panther?" he went on.

"Guen was not beside me," Catti-brie replied without thinking, then her face crinkled up, realizing the million questions she had probably just inspired.

Fortunately, the guards did not belabor the point. They had heard enough descriptions of the impassioned young woman to be satisfied that this was indeed the daughter of Bruenor Battlehammer. They escorted Catti-brie and Guenhwyvar—at a respectful distance—through the city, to the western wall and the graceful and enchanting palace of Lady Alustriel.

Left alone in a waiting chamber, Catti-brie decided to keep Guenhwyvar by her side. The panther's presence would give her tale credibility, she decided, and if Drizzt had been about, or still was, Guenhwyvar would sense it.

The minutes slipped by uneventfully, and restless Catti-brie grew bored. She moved to a side door and gently pushed it open, revealing a decorated powder room, with a wash basin and a small, gold-trimmed table, complete with a large mirror. Atop it was an assortment of combs and brushes, a selection of small vials, and an opened coffer containing many different colored packets of dye.

Curious, the young woman looked over her shoulder to make sure that all was quiet, then moved in and sat down. She took up a brush and roughly ran it through her tangled and thick auburn hair, thinking she should try to appear her best when standing before the Lady of Silverymoon. She scowled when she noticed dirt on her cheek, and quickly dipped her hand in the water basin and rubbed it roughly over the spot, managing a smile when it was gone.

She peeked out of the anteroom again, to make sure that no one had come. Guenhwyvar, lying comfortably on the floor, looked up and growled.

"Oh, shut yer mouth," Catti-brie said, and she slipped back into the powder room and inspected the vials. She removed the tight top of one and sniffed, and her blue eyes opened wide in surprise at the powerful aroma. From outside the door, Guenhwyvar growled again and sneezed, and Catti-brie laughed. "I know what ye mean," she said to the cat.

Catti-brie went through several of the vials, crinkling her nose at some, sneezing at more than one, and finally finding one whose aroma she enjoyed. It reminded her of a field of wildflowers, not overpowering, but subtly beautiful, the background music to a spring day.

She nearly jumped out of her boots, nearly stuffed the vial up her nose, when a hand grasped her shoulder.

Catti-brie spun about, and her breath was stolen away. There stood Alustriel—it had to be!—her hair shining silver and hanging halfway down her back and her eyes sparkling more clearly than any Catti-brie had ever seen—more clearly than any eyes except Wulfgar's sky-blue orbs. The memory pained her.

Alustriel was fully half a foot above Catti-brie's five and a half, and gracefully slender. She wore a purple gown of the finest silk, with many layers that seemed to hug her womanly curves and hide them alluringly all at once. A high crown of gold and gems sat atop her head.

Guenhwyvar and the lady apparently were not strangers, for the panther lay quietly on its side, eyes closed contentedly.

For some reason that she did not understand, that bothered Catti-brie.

"I have wondered when we would at last meet," Alustriel said quietly.

Catti-brie fumbled to replace the cap on the vial and replace it on the table, but Alustriel put her long, slender hands over the young woman's—and Catti-brie felt like a young and foolish girl at that moment!—and eased the vial into her belt pouch instead.

"Drizzt has spoken often of you," Alustriel went on, "and fondly."

That thought, too, bothered Catti-brie. It might have been unintentional, she realized, but it seemed to her that Alustriel was being just a bit condescending. And Catti-brie, standing in road-dusty traveling clothes, with her hair hardly brushed, certainly was not comfortable beside the fabulous woman.

"Come to my private chambers," the lady invited. "There we might speak more comfortably." She started out, stepping over the sleeping panther. "Do come along, Guen!" she said, and the cat perked up immediately, shaking away its laziness.

"Guen?" Catti-brie mouthed silently. She had never heard anyone besides herself, and very rarely Drizzt, call the panther so familiarly. She gave a look to the cat, her expression hurt, as she obediently followed Alustriel out of the room.

What had at first seemed to Catti-brie an enchanted palace now made her feel terribly out of place as Alustriel led her along the sweeping corridors and through the fabulous rooms. Catti-brie kept looking to her own trail, wondering fearfully if she might be leaving muddy tracks across the polished floors.

Attendants and other guests—true nobility, the young woman realized—stared as the unlikely caravan passed, and Catti-brie could not return the gazes. She felt small, so very small, as she walked behind the tall and beautiful Alustriel.

Catti-brie was glad when they entered Alustriel's private sitting room and the lady closed the door behind them.

Guenhwyvar padded over and hopped up on a thickly upholstered divan, and Catti-brie's eyes widened in shock.

"Get off there!" she whispered harshly at the panther, but Alustriel only chuckled as she walked past, dropping a hand absently on the comfortable cat's head and motioning for Catti-brie to take a seat.

Again Catti-brie turned an angry gaze on Guenhwyvar, feeling somewhat betrayed. How many times had Guenhwyvar plopped down on that very same couch? she wondered.

"What brings the daughter of King Bruenor to my humble city?" Alustriel asked. "I wish I had known that you would be coming. I could have better prepared."

"I seek Drizzt," Catti-brie answered curtly, then winced and sat back at the sharper-than-intended tone of her reply.

Alustriel's expression immediately grew curious. "Drizzt?" she echoed. "I have not seen Drizzt in some time. I had hoped that you would tell me that he, too, was in the city, or at least on his way."

Suspicious as she was, thinking that Drizzt would try to avoid her and that Alustriel would undoubtedly go along with his wishes, Catti-brie found that she believed the woman.

"Ah, well." Alustriel sighed, sincerely and obviously disappointed. She perked up immediately. "And how is your father?" she asked politely. "And that handsome Wulfgar?"

Alustriel's expression changed suddenly, as though she had just realized that something must be terribly out of place. "Your wedding?" she asked hesitantly as Catti-brie's lips thinned in a scowl. "I was preparing to visit Mithral Hall . . ."

Alustriel paused and studied Catti-brie for a long while.

Catti-brie sniffed and braced herself. "Wulfgar is dead," she said evenly, "and me father is not as ye remember him. I've come in search of Drizzt, who has gone out from the halls."

"What has happened?" Alustriel demanded.

Catti-brie rose from her chair. "Guenhwyvar!" she called, rousing the panther. "I've not the time for tales," she said curtly to Alustriel. "If Drizzt has not come to Silverymoon, then I've taken too much of yer time already, and too much o' me own."

She headed for the door and noticed it briefly glow blue, its wood seeming to expand and tighten in the jam. Catti-brie walked up to it anyway and tugged on the handle, to no avail.

Catti-brie took a few deep breaths, counted to ten, then to twenty, and turned to face Alustriel.

"I've a friend needing me," she explained, her tone even and dangerous. "Ye'd best be opening the door." In days to come, when she looked back on that moment, Catti-brie would hardly believe that she had threatened Alustriel, the ruler of the northwest's largest and most powerful inland city! She had threatened Alustriel, reputably among the most powerful mages in all the north!

At that time, though, the fiery young woman meant every grim word.

"I can help," Alustriel, obviously worried, offered. "But first you must tell me what has transpired."

"Drizzt hasn't the time," Catti-brie growled. She tugged futilely on the wizard-locked door again, then banged a fist against it and looked over her shoulder to glare at Alustriel, who had risen and was slowly walking her way. Guenhwyvar remained on the divan, though the cat had lifted its head and was regarding the two intently.

"I have to find him," Catti-brie said.

"And where will you look?" replied Alustriel, her hands out defenselessly as she stepped before the young woman.

The simple question took the bluster out of Catti-brie's ire. Where indeed? she wondered. Where to even begin? She felt helpless, standing there, in a

place she did not belong. Helpless and foolish and wanting nothing more than to be back home, beside her father and her friends, beside Wulfgar and Drizzt, with everything the way it had been . . . before the dark elves had come to Mithral Hall.

6

DIVINE SIGN

Catti-brie awoke the next morning on a pillowy soft bed in a plush chamber filled with fine lace draperies that let the filtered sunrise gently greet her sleepy gaze. She was not used to such places, wasn't even used to sleeping above ground.

She had refused a bath the night before, even though Lady Alustriel had promised her that the exotic oils and soaps would bubble around her and refresh her. To Catti-brie's dwarven-reared sensibilities, this was all nonsense and, worse, weakness. She bathed often, but in the chill waters of a mountain stream and without scented oils from far-off lands. Drizzt had told her that the dark elves could track enemies by their scent for miles through the Underdark's twisting caverns, and it seemed silly to Catti-brie to bath in aromatic oils and possibly aid her enemies.

This morning, though, with the sun cascading through the gauzy curtains, and the wash basin filled again with steamy water, the young woman reconsidered. "Suren ye're a stubborn one," she quietly accused Lady Alustriel, realizing that Alustriel's magic was likely the reason that steam once again rose off the water.

Catti-brie eyed the line of bottles and considered the long and dirty road ahead, a road from which she might never return. Something welled inside her then, a need to indulge herself just once, and before her pragmatic side could argue, she had stripped off her clothes and was sitting in the hot tub, the fizzing bubbles thick about her.

At first, she kept glancing nervously to the room's door, but soon she just let herself sink lower in the tub, perfectly relaxed, her skin warm and tingling.

"I told you." The words jolted Catti-brie from her near-slumber. She sat up straight, then sank back immediately, embarrassed, as she noticed not only Lady Alustriel, but a curious dwarf, his beard and hair snowy white and his gowns silken and flowing.

"In Mithral Hall, we've the habit o' knocking before we go into someone's private room," Catti-brie, regaining a measure of her dignity, remarked.

"I did knock," Alustriel replied. "You were lost in the warmth of the bath."

Catti-brie brushed her wet hair back from her face, getting a handful of suds on her cheek. She managed to salvage her pride and ignore the froth for a moment, then angrily slapped it away.

Alustriel merely smiled.

"Ye can be leaving," she snapped at the too dignified lady.

"Drizzt is indeed making for Menzoberranzan," Alustriel announced, and Catti-brie came forward again, anxiously, her embarrassment lost in the face of more important news.

"I ventured into the spirit world last night," Alustriel explained. "There one might find many answers. Drizzt traveled north of Silverymoon, through the Moonwood, on a straight line for the mountains surrounding Dead Orc Pass."

Catti-brie's expression remained quizzical.

"That is where Drizzt first walked from the Underdark," Alustriel went on, "in a cave east of the fabled pass. It is my guess that he means to return by the same route that led him from the darkness."

"Get me there," the young woman demanded, rising from the water, too intent for modesty.

"I will provide mounts," Alustriel said as she handed the younger woman a thick towel. "Enchanted horses will allow you to speed across the land. The journey should take you no more than two days."

"Ye cannot use yer magic to just send me there?" Catti-brie asked. Her tone was sharp, as though she believed that Alustriel was not doing all that she could.

"I do not know cave's location," the silver-haired lady explained.

Catti-brie stopped toweling herself, nearly dropped her clothing, which she had gathered together, and stared blankly, helplessly.

"That is why I have brought Fret," Alustriel explained, holding up a hand to calm the young woman.

"Fredegar Rockcrusher," the dwarf corrected in a strangely melodic, sing-song voice, and he swept his arm out dramatically and dipped a graceful bow. Catti-brie thought he sounded somewhat like an elf trapped in a dwarf's body.

She furrowed her brow as she closely regarded him for the first time; she had been around dwarves all of her life and had never seen one quite like this. His beard was neatly trimmed, his robes perfectly clean, and his skin did not show the usual hardness, rockiness. Too many baths in scented oils, the young woman decided, and she looked contemptuously at the steaming tub.

"Fret was with the party that first tracked Drizzt from the Underdark," Alustriel continued. "After Drizzt had left the area, my curious sister and her companions backtracked the drow's trail and located the cave, the entrance to the deep tunnels.

"I hesitate to point the way for you," the Lady of Silverymoon said after a long pause, her concern for the young woman's safety evident in her tone and expression.

Catti-brie's blue eyes narrowed, and she quickly pulled on her breeches. She would not be looked down upon, not even by Alustriel, and would not have others deciding her course.

"I see," remarked Alustriel with a nod of her head. Her immediate understanding set Catti-brie back.

Alustriel motioned for Fret to retrieve Catti-brie's pack. A sour expression crossed the tidy dwarf's face as he moved near the dirty thing, and he lifted it gingerly by two extended fingers. He glanced forlornly at Alustriel, and when she did not bother to look back at him, he left the room.

"I did not ask ye for any companion," Catti-brie stated bluntly.

"Fret is a guide to the entrance," Alustriel corrected, "and nothing more. Your courage is admirable, if a bit blind," she added, and before the young woman could find the words to reply, Alustriel was gone.

Catti-brie stood silently for a few moments, water from her wet hair dripping down her bare back. She fought away the feeling that she was just a little girl in a big and dangerous world, that she was small indeed beside the tall and powerful Lady Alustriel.

But the doubts lingered.

Two hours later, after a fine meal and a check on provisions, Catti-brie and Fret walked out of Silverymoon's eastern gate, the Sundabar Gate, beside Lady Alustriel, an entourage of soldiers keeping a respectful but watchful distance from their leader.

A black mare and a shaggy gray pony awaited the two travelers.

"Must I?" Fret asked for perhaps the twentieth time since they had left the castle. "Would not a detailed map suffice?"

Alustriel just smiled and otherwise ignored the tidy dwarf. Fret hated anything that might get him dirty, anything that would keep him from his

duties as Alustriel's best-loved sage. Certainly the road into the wilds near Dead Orc Pass qualified on both counts.

"The horseshoes are enchanted, and your mounts will fly like the wind itself," Alustriel explained to Catti-brie. The silver-haired woman looked over her shoulder to the grumbling dwarf.

Catti-brie was not quick to respond, offered no thanks for Alustriel's effort. She had said nothing to Alustriel since their meeting earlier that morning, and had carried herself with an unmistakably cool demeanor.

"With luck, you will arrive at the cave before Drizzt," Alustriel said. "Reason with him and bring him home, I beg. He has no place in the Underdark, not anymore."

"Drizzt's 'place' is his own to decide," Catti-brie retorted, but she was really implying that her own place was hers to decide.

"Of course," Alustriel agreed, and she flashed that smile—that knowing grin that Catti-brie felt belittled her—again.

"I did not hinder you," Alustriel pointed out. "I have done my best to aid your chosen course, whether I think it a wise choice or not."

Catti-brie snickered. "Ye just had to add that last thought," she replied.

"Am I not entitled to my opinion?" Alustriel asked.

"Entitled to it and givin' it to all who'll hear," Catti-brie remarked, and Alustriel, though she understood the source of the young woman's demeanor, was plainly surprised.

Catti-brie snickered again and kicked her horse into a walk.

"You love him," Alustriel said.

Catti-brie pulled hard on the reins to stop her horse and turn it halfway about. Now she wore the expression of surprise.

"The drow," Alustriel said, more to bolster her last statement, to reveal her honest belief, than to clarify something that obviously needed no further explanation.

Catti-brie chewed on her lip, as though seeking a response, then turned her mount roughly about and kicked away.

"It's a long road," Fret whined.

"Then hurry back to me," Alustriel said, "with Catti-brie and Drizzt beside you."

"As you wish, my lady," the obedient dwarf replied, kicking his pony into a gallop. "As you wish."

Alustriel stood at the eastern gate, watching, long after Catti-brie and Fret had departed. It was one of those not-so-rare moments when the Lady of Silverymoon wished that she was not encumbered with the responsibilities of government. Truly, Alustriel would have preferred to grab a horse of her own and ride out beside Catti-brie, even to venture into the Underdark, if necessary, to find the remarkable drow that had become her friend.

But she could not. Drizzt Do'Urden, after all, was a small player in a wide world, a world that continually begged audience at the Lady of Silverymoon's busy court.

"Good speed, daughter of Bruenor," the beautiful, silver-haired woman said under her breath. "Good speed and fare well."

⚔ ⚔ ⚔ ⚔ ⚔

Drizzt eased his mount along the stony trail, ascending into the mountains. The breeze was warm and the sky clear, but a storm had hit this region in the last few days, and the trail remained somewhat muddy. Finally, fearing that his horse would slip and break a leg, Drizzt dismounted and led the beast carefully, cautiously.

He had seen the shadowing elf many times that morning, for the trails were fairly open, and in the up-and-down process of climbing mountains, the two riders were not often far apart. Drizzt was not overly surprised when he went around a bend to find the elf approaching from a trail that had been paralleling his own.

The pale-skinned elf, too, walked his mount, and he nodded in approval to see Drizzt doing likewise. He paused, still twenty feet from the drow, as though he did not know how he should react.

"If you have come to watch over the horse, then you might as well ride, or walk, beside me," Drizzt called. Again the elf nodded, and he walked his shining black stallion up to the side of Drizzt's black-and-white mount.

Drizzt looked ahead, up the mountain trail. "This will be the last day I will need the horse," he explained. "I do not know that I will ride again, actually."

"You do not mean to come out of these mountains?" the elf asked.

Drizzt ran a hand through his flowing white mane, surprised by the finality of those words, and by their truth.

"I seek a grove not far from here," he said, "once the home of Montolio DeBrouchee."

"The blind ranger," the elf acknowledged.

Drizzt was surprised by the elf's recognition. He considered his pale companion's reply and studied him closely. Nothing about the moon elf indicated that he was a ranger, but he knew of Montolio. "It is fitting that the name Montolio DeBrouchee lives on in legend," the drow decided aloud.

"And what of the name Drizzt Do'Urden?" the moon elf, full of surprises, asked. He smiled at Drizzt's expression and added, "Yes, I know of you, dark elf."

"Then you have the advantage," Drizzt remarked.

"I am Tarathiel," the moon elf said. "It was no accident that you were met on your passage through the Moonwood. When my small clan discovered that you were afoot, we decided that it would be best for Ellifain to meet you."

"The maiden?" Drizzt reasoned.

Tarathiel nodded, his features seeming almost translucent in the sunlight. "We did not know how she would react to the sight of a drow. You have our apologies."

Drizzt nodded his acceptance. "She is not of your clan," he guessed. "Or at least, she was not, not when she was very young."

Tarathiel did not reply, but the intrigue that was splayed across his face showed Drizzt that he was on the right track.

"Her people were slaughtered by drow," Drizzt went on, fearing the expected confirmation.

"What do you know?" Tarathiel demanded, his voice taking a hard edge for the first time in the conversation.

"I was among that raiding party," Drizzt admitted. Tarathiel went for his sword, but Drizzt, lightning fast, grabbed hold of his wrist.

"I killed no elves," Drizzt explained. "The only ones I wanted to fight were those who had accompanied me to the surface."

Tarathiel's muscles relaxed, and he pulled his hand away. "Ellifain remembers little of the tragedy. She speaks of it more in dreams than in her waking hours, and then she rambles." He paused and stared Drizzt squarely in the eye. "She has mentioned purple eyes," he said. "We did not know what to make of that, and she, when questioned about it, cannot offer any answers. Purple is not a common color for drow eyes, so say our legends."

"It is not," Drizzt confirmed, and his voice was distant as he remembered again that terrible day so long ago. This was the elf maiden! The one that a younger Drizzt Do'Urden had risked all to save, the one whose eyes had shown Drizzt beyond doubt that the ways of his people were not the ways of his heart.

"And so, when we heard of Drizzt Do'Urden, drow friend—drow friend with purple eyes—of the dwarven king that has reclaimed Mithral Hall, we thought that it would be best for Ellifain to face her past," Tarathiel explained.

Again Drizzt, his mind looking more to the past than to the mountain scenery about him, merely nodded.

Tarathiel let it go at that. Ellifain had, apparently, viewed her past, and the sight had nearly broken her.

The moon elf refused Drizzt's request for him to take the horses and leave and, later that day, the two were riding again, along a narrow trail on a high pass, a way that Drizzt remembered well. He thought of Montolio, Mooshie, his surface mentor, the blind old ranger who could shoot a bow by the guidance of a pet owl's hoots. Montolio had been the one to teach a younger Drizzt of a god figure that embodied the same emotions that stirred Drizzt's heart and the same precepts that guided the renegade drow's conscience. Mielikki was her name, goddess of the forest, and since his time with Montolio, Drizzt Do'Urden had walked under her silent guidance.

Drizzt felt a wellspring of emotions bubbling within him as the trail wound away from the ridge and climbed a steeper incline through a region of broken boulders. He was terrified of what he might find. Perhaps an orc horde—the wretched humanoids were all too common in this region—had taken over the old ranger's wondrous grove. Suppose a fire had burned it away, leaving a barren scar upon the land?

They came into a thick copse of trees, plodding along a narrow but fairly clean trail, with Drizzt in the lead. He saw the wood thinning ahead, and beyond it a small field. He stopped his black-and-white horse and glanced back at Tarathiel.

"The grove," he explained, and he slipped from his saddle, Tarathiel doing likewise. They tethered the horses under the cover of the copse and crept side by side to the wood's end.

There stood Mooshie's grove, perhaps sixty yards across, north to south, and half that wide. The pines stood tall and straight—no fire had struck this grove—and the rope bridges that the blind ranger had constructed could still be seen running from tree to tree at various heights. Even the low stone wall stood intact, not a rock out of place, and the grass was low.

"Someone is living in there," Tarathiel reasoned, for the place had obviously not grown wild. When he looked to Drizzt, he saw that the drow, features set and grim, had scimitars in his hands, one glowing a soft bluish light.

Tarathiel strung his long bow as Drizzt crawled out from the brush and skittered over to the rock wall. Then the moon elf rushed off, joining his drow companion.

"I have seen the signs of many orcs since we entered the mountains," Tarathiel whispered. He pulled back on his bowstring and nodded grimly. "For Montolio?"

Drizzt returned the nod and inched up to peek over the stone wall. He expected to see orcs, and expected to see dead orcs soon after.

The drow froze in place, his arms falling limply at his sides and his breath suddenly hard to come by.

Tarathiel nudged him, looking for an answer, but with none forthcoming, the elf took up his bow and peeked over the wall.

At first he saw nothing, but then he followed Drizzt's unblinking gaze to the south, to a small break in the trees, where a branch was bobbing as though something had just brushed against it. Tarathiel caught a flash of white from the shadows beyond. A horse, he thought.

It came from the shadows then, a powerful steed wearing a coat of gleaming white. Its unusual eyes glowed fiery pink, and an ivory horn, easily half the height of the elf's body, protruded from its forehead. The unicorn looked in the companions' general direction, pawed the ground, and snorted.

Tarathiel had the good sense to duck low, and he pulled the stunned Drizzt Do'Urden down beside him.

"Unicorn!" the elf mouthed silently to Drizzt, and the drow's hand instinctively went under the front collar of his traveling cloak, to the unicorn's-head pendant Regis had carved for him from the bone of a knucklehead trout.

Tarathiel pointed back to the thick copse of trees and signaled that he and Drizzt should be leaving, but the drow shook his head. His composure returned, Drizzt again peeked over the stone wall.

The area was clear, with no indication that the unicorn was about.

"We should be gone," Tarathiel said, as soon as he, too, discerned that the powerful steed was no longer close. "Take heart that Montolio's grove is in the best of care."

Drizzt sat up on the wall, peering intently into the tangle of pines. A unicorn! The symbol of Mielikki, the purest symbol of the natural world. To a ranger, there was no more perfect beast, and to Drizzt, there could be no more perfect guardian for the grove of Montolio DeBrouchee. He would have liked to remain in the area for some time, would have dearly liked to glimpse the elusive creature again, but he knew that time was pressing and that dark corridors awaited.

He looked to Tarathiel and smiled, then turned to leave.

But he found the way across the small field blocked by the mighty unicorn.

"How did she do that?" Tarathiel asked. There was no need to whisper anymore, for the unicorn was staring straight at them, pawing the ground nervously and rolling its powerful head.

"He," Drizzt corrected, noticing the steed's white beard, a trait of the male unicorn. A thought came over Drizzt then, and he slipped his scimitars into their sheaths and hopped up from his seat.

"How did *he* do that?" Tarathiel corrected. "I heard no hoofbeats." The elf's eyes brightened suddenly, and he looked back to the grove. "Unless there are more than one!"

"There is only one," Drizzt assured him. "There is a bit of magic within a unicorn, as this one, by slipping behind us, has proven."

"Go around to the south," Tarathiel whispered. "And I will go north. If we do not threaten the beast, . . ." The moon elf stopped, seeing that Drizzt was already moving—straight out from the wall.

"Take care," Tarathiel warned. "Beautiful indeed are the unicorns, but, by all accounts, they can be dangerous and unpredictable."

Drizzt held a hand up behind him to silence the elf and continued his slow pace from the stone wall. The unicorn neighed and tossed its great head, mane flying wildly. It slammed a hoof into the ground, digging a fair-sized hole in the soft turf.

"Drizzt Do'Urden," Tarathiel warned.

By all reasoning, Drizzt should have turned back. The unicorn could have easily run him down, squashed him into the prairie, and the great beast seemed to grow more and more agitated with each step the drow took.

But the beast did not run off, and neither did it lower its great horn and skewer Drizzt. Soon, the drow was just a few steps away, feeling small beside the magnificent steed.

Drizzt reached out a hand, fingers moving slowly, delicately. He felt the outer strands of the unicorn's thick and glistening coat, then moved in another step and stroked the magnificent beast's muscled neck.

The drow could hardly breathe; he wished that Guenhwyvar were beside him, to witness such perfection of nature. He wished that Catti-brie were here, for she would appreciate this vision as much as he.

He looked back to Tarathiel, the elf sitting on the stone wall and smiling contentedly. Tarathiel's expression turned to one of surprise, and Drizzt looked back to see his hand stroking the empty air.

The unicorn was gone.

Part Two

Not since the day I walked out of Menzoberranzan have I been so torn about a pending decision. I sat near the entrance of a cave, looking out at the mountains before me, with the tunnel leading to the Underdark at my back.

This was the moment in which I had believed my adventure would begin. When I had set out from Mithral Hall, I had given little thought to the part of my

Prayers Unanswered

journey that would take me to this cave, taking for granted that the trip would be uneventful.

Then I had glimpsed Ellifain, the maiden I had saved more than three decades before, when she had been just a frightened child. I wanted to go to her again, to speak with her and help her overcome the trauma of that terrible drow raid. I wanted to run out of that cave and catch up with Tarathiel, and ride beside the elf back to the Moonwood.

But I could not ignore the issues that had brought me to this place.

I had known from the outset that visiting Montolio's grove, the place of so many fond memories, would prove an emotional, even spiritual, experience. He had been my first surface friend, my mentor, the one who had guided me to Mielikki. I can never express the joy I felt in learning that Montolio's grove was under the protective eye of a unicorn.

A unicorn! I have seen a unicorn, the symbol of my goddess, the pinnacle of natural perfection! I might well be the first of my race to have ever touched the soft mane and muscled neck of such a beast, the first to encounter a unicorn in friendship. It is a rare pleasure to glimpse the signs that a unicorn has been about, and rarer still to ever gaze at one. Few in the Realms can say that they have ever been near a unicorn; fewer still have ever touched one.

I have.

Was it a sign from my goddess? In good faith, I had to believe that it was, that Mielikki had reached out to me in a tangible and thrilling way. But what did it mean?

I rarely pray. I prefer to speak to my goddess through my daily actions, and through my honest emotions. I need not gloss over what has occurred with petty words, twisting them to show myself most favorably. If Mielikki is with me, then she knows the truth, knows how I act and how I feel.

I prayed that night in the cave entrance, though. I prayed for guidance, for something that would indicate the significance of the unicorn's appearance. The unicorn allowed me to touch it; it accepted me, and that is the highest honor a ranger can ask. But what was the implication of that honor?

Was Mielikki telling me that here, on the surface, I was, and would continue to be, accepted, and that I should not leave this place? Or was the unicorn's appearance to show me the goddess's approval of my choice to return to Menzoberranzan?

Or was the unicorn Mielikki's special way of saying "farewell?"

That last thought haunted me all through the night. For the first time since I had set out from Mithral Hall, I began to consider what I, Drizzt Do'Urden, had to lose. I thought of my friends, Montolio and Wulfgar, who had passed on from this world, and thought of those others I would likely never see again.

A host of questions assailed me. Would Bruenor ever get over the loss of his adopted son? And would Catti-brie overcome her own grief? Would the enchanted sparkle, the sheer love of life, ever return to her blue eyes? Would I ever again prop my weary head against Guenhwyvar's muscled flank?

More than ever, I wanted to run from the cave, home to Mithral Hall, and stand beside my friends, to see them through their grief, to guide them and listen to them and simply embrace them.

Again I could not ignore the issues that had brought me to this cave. I could go back to Mithral Hall, but so could my dark kin. I did not blame myself for Wulfgar's death—I could not have known that the dark elves would come. And now I could not deny my understanding of the awful ways and continuing hunger of Lolth. If the drow returned and extinguished that—cherished!—light in Catti-brie's eyes, then Drizzt Do'Urden would die a thousand horrible deaths.

I prayed all that night, but found no divine guidance. In the end, as always, I came to realize that I had to follow what I knew in my heart was the right course, had to trust that what was in my heart was in accord with Mielikki's will.

I left the fire blazing at the entrance of that cave. I needed to see its light, to gain courage from it, for as many steps as possible as I walked into the tunnel. As I walked into darkness.

—Drizzt Do'Urden

UNFINISHED BUSINESS

Berg'inyon Baenre hung upside down from the huge cavern's roof, securely strapped to the saddle of his lizard mount. It had taken the young warrior some time to get used to this position, but as commander of the Baenre lizard-riders, he spent many hours watching the city from this high vantage point.

A movement to the side, behind a cluster of stalactites, put Berg'inyon on the alert. He lowered his ten-foot-long death lance with one hand; the other held the lizard's bridle while resting on the hilt of his ready hand-crossbow.

"I am the son of House Baenre," he said aloud, figuring that to be enough of a threat to defeat any possible foul play. He glanced around, looking for support, and moved his free hand to his belt pouch and his signal speculum, a shielded metal strip heated on one side and used to communicate with creatures using infravision. Dozens of other House Baenre lizard riders were about and would come rushing to Berg'inyon's call.

"I am the son of House Baenre," he said again.

The youngest Baenre relaxed almost immediately when his older brother Dantrag, emerged from behind the stalactites, riding an even larger subterranean lizard. Curious indeed did the elder Baenre look with his ponytail hanging straight down from the top of his upside-down head.

"As am I," Dantrag replied, skittering his sticky-footed mount beside Berg'inyon's.

"What are you doing up here?" Berg'inyon asked. "And how did you appropriate the mount without my permission?"

Dantrag scoffed at the question. "Appropriate?" he replied. "I am the

weapons master of House Baenre. I took the lizard, and needed no permission from Berg'inyon."

The younger Baenre stared with red-glowing eyes, but said nothing more.

"You forget who trained you, my brother," Dantrag remarked quietly.

The statement was true; Berg'inyon would never forget, could never forget, that Dantrag had been his mentor.

"Are you prepared to face the likes of Drizzt Do'Urden again?" The blunt question nearly sent Berg'inyon from his mount.

"It would seem a possibility, since we are to travel to Mithral Hall," Dantrag added coolly.

Berg'inyon blew a long and low sigh, thoroughly flustered. He and Drizzt had been classmates at Melee-Magthere, the Academy's school of fighters. Berg'inyon, trained by Dantrag, had gone there fully expecting to be the finest fighter in his class. Drizzt Do'Urden, the renegade, the traitor, had beaten him for that honor every year. Berg'inyon had done well at the Academy, by every standard except Dantrag's.

"Are you prepared for him?" Dantrag pressed, his tone growing more serious and angry.

"No!" Berg'inyon glowered at his brother, sitting astride the hanging lizard, a cocky grin on his handsome face. Dantrag had forced the answer for a reason, Berg'inyon knew. Dantrag wanted to make certain that Berg'inyon knew his place as a spectator if they should happen to encounter the rogue Do'Urden together.

And Berg'inyon knew, too, why his brother wanted the first try at Drizzt. Drizzt had been trained by Zaknafein, Dantrag's principal rival, the one weapons master in Menzoberranzan whose fighting skills were more highly regarded than those of Dantrag. By all accounts, Drizzt had become at least Zaknafein's equal, and if Dantrag could defeat Drizzt, then he might at last come out from under Zaknafein's considerable shadow.

"You have fought us both," Dantrag said slyly. "Do tell me, dear brother, who is the better?"

Berg'inyon couldn't possibly answer that question. He hadn't fought against, or even beside, Drizzt Do'Urden for more than thirty years. "Drizzt would cut you down," he said anyway, just to peeve his upstart sibling.

Dantrag's hand flashed faster than Berg'inyon could follow. The weapons master sent his wickedly sharp sword across the top strap of Berg'inyon's saddle, easily cutting the binding, though it was enchanted for strength. Dantrag's second hand came across equally fast, slipping the bridle from the lizard's mouthpiece as Berg'inyon plummeted from his seat.

The younger brother turned upright as he fell. He looked into that area of innate magic common to all drow, and stronger in drow nobles. Soon the descent had ceased, countered by a levitation spell that had Berg'inyon, death lance still in hand, slowly rising back up to meet his laughing brother.

Matron Baenre would kill you if she knew that you had embarrassed me so in front of the common soldiers, Berg'inyon's hand flashed in the silent code.

Better to have your pride cut than your throat, Dantrag's hands flashed in reply, and the older Baenre walked his mount away, back around the stalactites.

Beside the lizard again, Berg'inyon worked to retie the top strap and fasten together the bridle. He had claimed Drizzt to be the better fighter, but, in considering what Dantrag had just done to him, a perfectly aimed two-hit attack before he could even begin to retaliate, the younger Baenre doubted his claim. Drizzt Do'Urden, he decided, would be the one to pity if and when the two fighters faced off.

The thought pleased young Berg'inyon. Since his days in the Academy, he had lived in Drizzt's shadow, much as Dantrag had lived in Zaknafein's. If Dantrag defeated Drizzt, then the Brothers Baenre would be proven the stronger fighters, and Berg'inyon's reputation would rise simply because of his standing as Dantrag's protegee. Berg'inyon liked the thought, liked that he stood to gain without having to stand toe-to-toe against that devilish purple-eyed Do'Urden again.

Perhaps the fight would come to an even more promising conclusion, Berg'inyon dared to hope. Perhaps Dantrag would kill Drizzt, and then, weary and probably wounded, Dantrag would fall easy prey to Berg'inyon's sword. Berg'inyon's reputation, as well as his position, would rise further, for he would be the logical choice to replace his dead brother in the coveted position as weapons master.

The young Baenre rolled over in midair to find his place on the repaired saddle, smiling evilly at the possibilities afforded him in this upcoming journey to Mithral Hall.

⚔ ⚔ ⚔ ⚔ ⚔

"Jerlys," the drow whispered grimly.

"Jerlys Horlbar?" Jarlaxle asked, and the mercenary leaned against the rough wall of the stalagmite pillar to consider the startling news. Jerlys Horlbar was a matron mother, one of the two high priestesses presiding over House Horlbar, the twelfth house of Menzoberranzan. Here she lay, dead, under a pile of rubble, her tentacle rod ruined and buried beside her.

It is good we followed him, the soldier's flicking fingers remarked, more to placate the mercenary leader than to make any pertinent revelations. Of course it was good that Jarlaxle had ordered that one followed. He was dangerous, incredibly dangerous, but, seeing a matron mother, a high priestess of the Spider Queen, lying dead, sliced by a wicked sword, the mercenary had to wonder if he, too, had underestimated.

We can report it and absolve ourselves of responsibility, another of Bregan D'aerthe's dark band signaled.

At first, that notion struck Jarlaxle as sound advice. The matron mother's body would be found, and there would be a serious inquiry, by House Horlbar if by no one else. Guilt by association was a very real thing in Menzoberranzan, especially for such a serious crime, and Jarlaxle wanted no part of a covert war with the twelfth house, not now, with so many other important events brewing.

Then Jarlaxle let the circumstances lead him down another avenue of possibility. As unfortunate as this event seemed, the mercenary might still turn it to profit. There was at least one wild card in this game that Matron Baenre played, an unknown factor that could take the impending chaos to new levels of glory.

Bury her once more, the mercenary signaled, deeper under the pile, but not completely. *I want the body found, but not for a while.*

His hard boots making not a sound, his ample jewelry quiet, the mercenary leader started from the alley.

Are we to rendezvous? one soldier flashed to him.

Jarlaxle shook his head and continued on, out of the remote alley. He knew where to find the one who had killed Jerlys Horlbar, and knew, too, that he could use this information against him, perhaps to heighten his slavish loyalty to Bregan D'aerthe, or perhaps for other reasons. Jarlaxle had to play the whole thing very carefully, he knew. He had to walk a narrow line between intrigue and warfare.

None in the city could do that better.

⚔ ⚔ ⚔ ⚔ ⚔

Uthegental will be prominent in the days to come.

Dantrag Baenre cringed when the thought drifted into his mind. He understood its source, and its subtle meaning. He and the weapons master of House Barrison Del'Armgo, House Baenre's chief rival, were considered the two greatest fighters in the city.

Matron Baenre will use his skills, the next telepathic message warned. Dantrag drew out his surface-stolen sword and looked at it. It flared a thin red line of light along its impossibly sharp edge, and the two rubies set into the eyes of its demon-sculpted pommel flared with inner life.

Dantrag's hand clasped the pommel and warmed as Khazid'hea, Cutter, continued its communication. *He is strong and will fare well in the raids on Mithral Hall. He lusts for the blood of the young Do'Urden, the legacy of Zaknafein, as greatly as you do—perhaps even more.*

Dantrag sneered at that last remark, thrown in only because Khazid'hea wanted him on the edge of anger. The sword considered Dantrag its partner, not its master, and knew that it could better manipulate Dantrag if he was angry.

After many decades wielding Khazid'hea, Dantrag, too, knew all of this, and he forced himself to keep calm.

"None desire Drizzt Do'Urden's death more than I," Dantrag assured the doubting sword. "And Matron Baenre will see to it that I, not Uthegental, have the opportunity to slay the renegade. Matron Baenre would not want the honors that would undoubtedly accompany such a feat to be granted to a warrior of the second house."

The sword's red line flared again in intensity and reflected in Dantrag's amber eyes. *Kill Uthegental, and her task will become easier,* Khazid'hea reasoned.

Dantrag laughed aloud at the notion, and Khazid'hea's fiendish eyes flared again. "Kill him?" Dantrag echoed. "Kill one that Matron Baenre has deemed important for the mission ahead? She would flay the skin from my bones!"

But you could kill him?

Dantrag laughed again, for the question was simply to mock him, to urge him on to the fight that Khazid'hea had desired for so very long. The sword was proud, at least as proud as either Dantrag or Uthegental, and it wanted desperately to be in the hands of the indisputably finest weapons master of Menzoberranzan, whichever of the two that might be.

"You must pray that I could," Dantrag replied, turning the tables on the impetuous sword. "Uthegental favors his trident, and no sword. If he proved the victor, then Khazid'hea might end up in the scabbard of a lesser fighter."

He would wield me.

Dantrag slid the sword away, thinking the preposterous claim not even worth answering. Also tired of this useless banter, Khazid'hea went silent, brooding.

The sword had opened some concerns for Dantrag. He knew the importance of this upcoming assault. If he could strike down the young

Do'Urden, then all glory would be his, but if Uthegental got there first, then Dantrag would be considered second best in the city, a rank he could never shake unless he found and killed Uthegental. His mother would not be pleased by such events, Dantrag knew. Dantrag's life had been miserable when Zaknafein Do'Urden had been alive, with Matron Baenre constantly urging him to find and slay the legendary weapons master.

This time, Matron Baenre probably wouldn't even allow him that option. With Berg'inyon coming into excellence as a fighter, Matron Baenre might simply sacrifice Dantrag and turn the coveted position of weapons master over to her younger son. If she could claim that the move was made because Berg'inyon was the better fighter, that would again spread doubt among the populace as to which house had the finest weapons master.

The solution was simple: Dantrag had to get Drizzt.

8

OUT OF PLACE

H e moved without a whisper along the lightless tunnels, his eyes glowing lavender, seeking changes in the heat patterns along the floor and walls that would indicate bends, or enemies, in the tunnel. He seemed at home, a creature of the Underdark, moving with typically quiet grace and cautious posture.

Drizzt did not feel at home, though. Already he was deeper than the lowest tunnels of Mithral Hall, and the stagnant air pressed in on him. He had spent nearly two decades on the surface, learning and living by the rules that governed the outer world. Those rules were as different to Underdark precepts as a forest wildflower was to a deep cavern fungus. A human, a goblin, even an alert surface elf, would have taken no note of Drizzt's silent passage, though he might cross just a few feet away, but Drizzt felt clumsy and loud.

The drow ranger cringed with every step, fearing that echoes were resounding along the blank stone walls hundreds of yards away. This was the Underdark, a place negotiated less by sight than by hearing and the sense of smell.

Drizzt had spent nearly two-thirds of his life in the Underdark, and a good portion of the last twenty years underground in the caverns of Clan Battlehammer. He no longer considered himself a creature of the Underdark, though. He had left his heart behind on a mountainside, watching the stars and the moon, the sunrise and the sunset.

This was the land of starless nights—no, not nights, just a single, unending starless night, Drizzt decided—of stagnant air, and leering stalactites.

The tunnel's width varied greatly, sometimes as narrow as the breadth of

Drizzt's shoulders, sometimes wide enough for a dozen men to walk abreast. The floor sloped slightly, taking Drizzt even deeper, but the ceiling paralleled it well, remaining fairly consistent at about twice the height of the five-and-a-half-foot drow. For a long time, Drizzt detected no side caverns or corridors, and he was glad of that, for he didn't want to be forced into any direction decisions yet, and in this simple setup, any potential enemies would have to come at him from straight ahead.

Drizzt honestly believed that he was not prepared for any surprises, not yet. Even his infravision pained him. His head throbbed as he tried to sort out and interpret the varying heat patterns. In his younger years, Drizzt had gone for tendays, even months, with his eyes tuned exclusively to the infrared spectrum, looking for heat instead of reflected light. But now, with his eyes so used to the sun above and the torches lining the corridors of Mithral Hall, he found the infravision jarring.

Finally, he drew out Twinkle, and the enchanted scimitar glowed with a soft bluish light. Drizzt rested back against the wall and let his eyes revert to the regular spectrum, then used the sword as a guiding light. Soon after, he came to a six-way intersection, two crossing horizontal corridors intersected by a vertical shaft.

Drizzt tucked Twinkle away and looked above, up the shaft. He saw no heat sources, but was little comforted. Many of the Underdark's predators could mask their body temperatures, like a surface tiger used its stripes to crawl through thick strands of high grass. Dreaded hook horrors, for example, had developed an exoskeleton; the bony plates shielded the creature's body heat so that they appeared as unremarkable rocks to heat-sensing eyes. And many of the Underdark's monsters were reptilian, cold-blooded, and hard to see.

Drizzt sniffed the stagnant air several times, then he stood still and closed his eyes, letting his ears provide all the external input. He heard nothing, save the beating of his own heart, so he checked his gear to ensure that all was secure and started to climb down the shaft, taking care amid the dangerously loose rubble.

He nearly made it silently down the sixty feet to the lower corridor, but a single stone skidded down before him, striking the corridor's floor with a sharp crack at almost the same instant that Drizzt's soft boots quietly came down from the wall.

Drizzt froze in place, listening to the sound as it echoed from wall to wall. As a drow patrol leader, Drizzt had once been able to follow echoes perfectly, almost instinctively discerning which walls were rebounding the sound, and from which direction. Now, though, he had difficulty sorting through the echo's individual sounds. Again he felt out of place, overmatched by the brooding darkness. And again he felt vulnerable, for many denizens of the dark ways could indeed follow an echo trail, and this particular one led directly to Drizzt.

He swiftly traversed a virtual maze of crisscrossing corridors, some veering sharply and descending to pass beneath others, or climbing along natural stairs to new levels of winding ways.

Drizzt sorely missed Guenhwyvar. The panther could sort through any maze.

He thought of the cat again a short time later, when he came around a bend and stumbled upon a fresh kill. It was some type of subterranean lizard, too mutilated for Drizzt to figure out exactly what. Its tail was gone, as was its lower jaw, and its belly had been gashed open, its innards devoured. Drizzt found long tears in the skin, as though it had been raked by claws, and long and thin bruises, like those made by a whip. Beyond a pool of blood a few feet from the corpse, the drow found a single track, a paw print, in a shape and size very similar to one Guenhwyvar might make.

But Drizzt's cat was hundreds of miles away, and this kill, by the ranger's estimation, was barely an hour old. Creatures of the Underdark did not roam as did creatures of the surface; the dangerous predator was likely not far away.

⚔ ⚔ ⚔ ⚔ ⚔

Bruenor Battlehammer stormed along the passageway, his grief stolen, for the moment, by undeniably mounting rage. Thibbledorf Pwent bounced along beside the king, his mouth flapping one question after another and his armor squealing annoyingly with every movement.

Bruenor skidded to a stop and turned on the battlerager, put his angry scar and angry scowl in line with Pwent's bushy-bearded face. "Why don't ye get yerself a bath!" Bruenor roared.

Pwent fell back and began to choke on the command. By his estimation, a dwarf king ordering a subject to go take a bath was roughly the equivalent of a human king telling his knights to go out and kill babies. There were some lines that a ruler simply did not cross.

"Bah!" Bruenor snorted. "Good enough for ye, then. But go and grease that damned armor! How's a king to think with yer squeakin' and squealin'?"

Pwent's head bobbed his agreement with the compromise, and he bounded away, almost afraid to stay, afraid that the tyrant King Bruenor would again demand the bath.

Bruenor just wanted the battlerager away from him—he didn't really care how he accomplished that task. It had been a difficult afternoon. The dwarf had just met with Berkthgar the Bold, an emissary from Settlestone, and had learned that Catti-brie had never arrived in the barbarian settlement, even though she had been out of Mithral Hall for nearly a tenday.

Bruenor's mind raced over the events of his last meeting with his daughter. He recalled images of the young woman, tried to scrutinize them and remember every word she had said for some clue as to what might be happening. But Bruenor had been too absorbed on that occasion. If Catti-brie had hinted at anything other than her intentions to go to Settlestone, the dwarf had simply missed it.

His first thoughts, when talking with Berkthgar, were that his daughter had met some trouble on the mountainside. He had almost called out a dwarven contingent to scour the area, but, on an impulse, had paused long enough to ask the emissary about the cairn being erected for Wulfgar.

"What cairn?" Berkthgar had replied.

Bruenor knew then that he had been deceived, and if Catti-brie had not been alone in that deception, then Bruenor could easily guess the identity of her coconspirator.

He nearly took the wooden, iron-bound door of Buster Bracer, a highly regarded armorer, off its hinges as he burst in, catching the blue-bearded dwarf and his halfling subject by surprise. Regis stood atop a small platform, being measured so that his armor could be let out to fit his widening girth.

Bruenor bounded up beside the pedestal—and Buster was wise enough to fall back from it—grabbed the halfling by the front of his tunic, and hoisted him into the air with one arm.

"Where's me girl?" the dwarf roared.

"Settle . . ." Regis started to lie, but Bruenor began shaking him violently, whipping him back and forth through the air like some rag doll.

"Where's me girl?" the dwarf said again, more quietly, his words a threatening snarl. "And don't ye play games with me, Rumblebelly."

Regis was getting more than a little tired of being assaulted by his supposed friends. The quick-thinking halfling immediately concocted a ruse about Catti-brie having run off to Silverymoon in search of Drizzt. It wouldn't be a complete lie, after all.

Looking at Bruenor's scarred face, twisted in rage, but so obviously filled with pain, the halfling could not bring himself to fib.

"Put me down," he said quietly, and apparently Bruenor understood the halfling's empathy, for the dwarf gently lowered Regis to the ground.

Regis brushed his tunic straight, then waggled a fist before the dwarf king. "How dare you?" he roared.

Bruenor went back on his heels at the unexpected and uncharacteristic outburst, but the halfling did not relent.

"First Drizzt comes to me and forces me to hold a secret," Regis expounded, "then Catti-brie comes in and pushes me around until I tell her. Now you. . . . What fine friends I have surrounded myself with!"

The stinging words calmed the volatile dwarf, but only a little. What secret might Regis be hinting at?

Thibbledorf Pwent bounded into the room then, his armor squeaking no less, though his face, beard, and hands were certainly smeared with grease. He stopped beside Bruenor, surveying the unexpected situation for just a moment.

Pwent rubbed his hands eagerly in front of him, then ran them down the front of his cruelly ridged armor. "Should I hug him?" he asked his king hopefully.

Bruenor slapped a hand out to hold the eager battlerager at bay. "Where's me girl?" the dwarf king asked a third time, this time quietly and calmly, as though he was asking a friend.

Regis firmed his jaw, then nodded and began. He told Bruenor everything, even his role in aiding Catti-brie, in handing her the assassin's dagger and the magical mask.

Bruenor's face began to twist in rage again, but Regis stood tall—relatively speaking—and dispelled the rising ire.

"Am I to trust in Catti-brie any less than you would?" Regis asked simply, reminding the dwarf that his human daughter was no child, and no novice to the perils of the road.

Bruenor didn't know how to take it all. A small part of him wanted to throttle Regis, but he understood that he would simply be playing out his frustration, and that the halfling was really not to blame. Where else could he turn, though? Both Drizzt and Catti-brie were long gone, well on their way, and Bruenor had no idea of how he could get to them!

Neither did the scarred dwarf, at that moment, have any strength to try. He dropped his gaze to the stone floor, his anger played out and his grief returned, and, without another word, he walked from the room. He had to think, and for the sake of his dearest friend and his beloved daughter, he had to think fast.

Pwent looked to Regis and Buster for answers, but they simply shook their heads.

✕ ✕ ✕ ✕ ✕

A slight shuffle, the padded footsteps of a hunting cat, perhaps, was all that Drizzt could discern. The drow ranger stood perfectly still, all his senses attuned to his surroundings. If it was the cat, Drizzt knew that it was close enough to have caught his scent, that it undoubtedly knew that something had wandered into its territory.

Drizzt spent a moment scrutinizing the area. The tunnel continued haphazardly, sometimes wide, sometimes narrow, and this entire section was broken and uneven, the floor full of bumps and holes and the walls lined by natural alcoves and deep nooks. The ceiling, too, was no longer constant, sometimes low and sometimes high. Drizzt could see the varied gradations of heat on the high walls ahead and knew that those walls were lined by ledges in many places.

A great cat could jump up there, watching its intended prey from above.

The thought was not a settling one, but Drizzt had to press on. To backtrack, he would have to go all the way to the chute and climb to a higher level, then wander about in the hopes that he would find another way down. Drizzt didn't have time to spare; neither did his friends.

He put his back against the wall as he continued, stalking in a crouch, one scimitar drawn and the other, Twinkle, ready in its sheath. Drizzt did not want the magical blade's glow to further reveal his position, though he knew that hunting cats in the Underdark needed no light.

He lightly stepped across the mouth of one wide and shallow alcove, then came to the edge of a second, narrower and deeper. When he was satisfied that this one, too, was unoccupied, he turned back for a general scan of the area.

Shining green eyes, cat eyes, stared back at him from the ledge on the opposite wall.

Out came Twinkle, flaring an angry blue, bathing the area in light. Drizzt, his eyes shifting back from the infrared spectrum, saw the great, dark silhouette as the monster leaped, and he deftly dived out of harm's way. The cat touched down lightly—with all six legs!—and it pivoted about, showing white teeth and sinister eyes.

It was pantherlike, its fur so black as to shimmer a deep blue, and it was nearly as large as Guenhwyvar. Drizzt didn't know what to think. If this had been a normal panther, he would have tried to calm it, tried to show it that he was no enemy and that he would go right past its lair. But this cat, this monster, had six legs! And from its shoulders protruded long, whiplike appendages, waving menacingly and tipped with bony ridges.

Snarling, the beast padded in, ears tight against its head, formidable fangs bared. Drizzt crouched low, scimitars straight out in front, feet perfectly balanced so that he could dodge aside.

The beast stopped its stalk. Drizzt watched carefully as its middle set of legs and its hind legs tamped down.

It came fast; Drizzt started left, but the beast skidded to a stop, and Drizzt did likewise, lurching ahead to cut with one blade in a straight thrust. Right between the panther's eyes went the scimitar, perfectly aligned.

It hit nothing but air, and Drizzt stumbled forward. He instinctively dived to the stone and rolled right as one tentacle whipped just above his head and the other scored a slight hit on his hip. Huge paws raked and swatted all about him, but he worked his scimitars wildly, somehow keeping them at bay. He came up running, quickly putting a few feet between himself and the dangerous cat.

The drow settled back into his defensive crouch, less confident now. The beast was smart—Drizzt would never have expected such a feint from an animal. Worse, the drow could not understand how he had missed. His blade's thrust had been true. Even the incredible agility of a cat could not have gotten the beast out of the way so quickly.

A tentacle came at him from the right, and he threw a scimitar out that way not just to parry, but hoping to sever the thing.

He missed, then barely managed, past his surprise, to twirl to the left, taking another hit on the hip, this one painful.

The beast rushed forward, one paw flying out in front to hook the spinning drow. Drizzt braced, Twinkle ready to block, but the paw caught him fully a foot below the scimitar's blocking angle.

Again Drizzt's ability to react saved him, for instead of fighting the angle of the in-turned paw—which would have ripped large lines in his body—he dived with it, down to the stone, scrambling and kicking his way past the panther's snapping maw. He felt like a mouse running back under a house cat, and, worse, this cat had two sets of legs left to cross!

Drizzt elbowed and batted, jabbed up, and scored a solid hit. He couldn't see in the sudden, wild flurry, and only when he came out the panther's back side did he realize that his blindness was his saving grace. He came up into a running step, then leaped into a headlong roll just ahead of twin snapping tentacles.

He hadn't been able to see, and he had scored his only hit.

The panther came around again, snarling in rage, its green eyes boring like lamplights into the drow.

Drizzt spat at those eyes, a calculated move, for though his aim seemed true and the beast made no move to dodge, the spittle hit only the stone floor. The cat was not where it appeared to be.

Drizzt tried to remember his training in Menzobcrranzan's Academy. He had heard of such beasts once, but they were very rare and hadn't been a source of any major lessons.

In came the cat. Drizzt leaped forward, inside the snapping reach of those painful tentacles. He guessed, aiming his attack a couple of feet to the right of where he perceived the beast.

But the cat was left, and as his scimitar swished harmlessly through the air, Drizzt knew he was in trouble. He leaped straight up, felt a claw slash at his foot—the same foot that had been wounded in his fight with Artemis Entreri on the ledge outside Mithral Hall. Down sliced Twinkle, the magnificent blade gashing the front claw, forcing the cat to retreat. Drizzt landed half-entwined with the beast, felt the hot breath of its drooling maw about his forearm and punched out, twisting his wrist so that his weapon's crosspiece prevented the monster from tearing his hand off.

He closed his eyes—they would only confuse him—and bashed down with Twinkle's hilt, clubbing the monster's head. Then he jerked free and ran off. The bony end of a tentacle flew out behind him, caught up to his back, and he threw himself into a headlong roll, absorbing some of the sting.

Up again, Drizzt ran on in full flight. He came to the wide and shallow alcove and spun in, the monster right behind.

Drizzt reached within himself, into his innate magical abilities, and brought forth a globe of impenetrable darkness. Twinkle's light disappeared, as did the monster's shining eyes.

Drizzt circled two steps and came forward, not wanting the beast to escape the darkened area. He felt the swish of a tentacle, a near hit, then sensed it coming back again the other way. The drow smiled in satisfaction as his scimitar slashed out to meet it, cutting right through.

The beast's pained roar guided Drizzt back in. He couldn't get caught in too tight, he knew, but, with his scimitars, he had an advantage of reach. With Twinkle up to fend against the remaining tentacle, he jabbed the other blade repeatedly, scoring a few minor hits.

The enraged cat leaped, but Drizzt sensed it and fell flat to the floor, rolling to his back and thrusting both his blades straight up, scoring a serious double hit on the monster's belly.

The cat came down hard, skidding heavily into the wall, and, before it could recover, Drizzt was upon it. A scimitar bashed against its skull, creasing its head. The cat whipped about and sprang forward, paws extended, maw opened wide.

Twinkle was waiting. The scimitar's tip caught the beast on the chin and slid down under the maw to dig at its rushing neck. A paw batted the blade, nearly tearing it free from the drow's extended hand, but Drizzt knew that he had to hang on, for all his life. There came a savage flurry, but the drow, backpedaling, managed to keep the beast at bay.

Out of the darkness the two came, the beast pressing on. Drizzt closed his eyes. He sensed that the remaining tentacle would snap at him, and he reversed direction, suddenly throwing all his weight behind Twinkle. The tentacle wrapped his back; he got his opposite elbow up just in time to prevent its end from coming right around and slamming his face.

Twinkle was in the monster halfway to the hilt. A wheezing and gurgling sound came from the beast's throat, but heavy paws battered at Drizzt's sides, shredding pieces of his cloak and scratching the fine mithral armor. The cat tried to turn its impaled neck to the side to bite Drizzt's arm.

Drizzt free hand went to work, furiously pumping up and down, bashing his scimitar repeatedly against the cat's head.

He felt the claws grasp and hold him, biting maw just an inch from his belly. One claw slipped through a chain link in the metal coat, slightly puncturing the drow's side.

The scimitar bashed again and again.

Down they tumbled in a heap. Drizzt, on his side and staring into wicked eyes, thought he was doomed and tried to squirm free. But the cat's grip loosened, and Drizzt realized that the beast was dead. He finally wriggled from the hold and looked down at the slain creature, its green eyes shining even in death.

⚔ ⚔ ⚔ ⚔ ⚔

"Don't ye go in there," one of the two guards outside Bruenor's throne room said to Regis as he boldly approached the door. The halfling considered them carefully—he never remembered seeing a dwarf so pale!

The door banged open, and a contingent of dwarves, fully armed and armored, burst out, falling all over each other as they ran off down the stone corridor. Behind them came a verbal tirade, a stream of curses from their king.

One of the guards started to close the door, but Regis hopped up and pushed his way in.

Bruenor paced about his throne, punching the great chair whenever he

passed close enough. General Dagna, Mithral Hall's military leader, sat in his appointed chair, looking rather glum, and Thibbledorf Pwent hopped about gleefully in Bruenor's shadow, cautiously dodging aside whenever Bruenor spun about.

"Stupid priests!" Bruenor growled.

"With Cobble dead, there are none powerful enough—" Dagna tried to intervene, but Bruenor wasn't listening.

"Stupid priests!" the dwarf king said more forcefully.

"Yeah!" Pwent readily agreed.

"Me king, ye've set two patrols off to Silverymoon, and another north o' the city," Dagna tried to reason. "And ye've got half me soldiers walking the tunnels below."

"And I'll be sending the other half if them that's there don't show me the way!" Bruenor roared.

Regis, still standing unnoticed by the door, was beginning to catch on, and he wasn't displeased by what he was seeing. Bruenor—and it seemed like the old Bruenor once more!—was moving heaven and earth to find Drizzt and Catti-brie. The old dwarf had stoked his inner fires!

"But there are a thousand separate tunnels down there," Dagna argued. "And some may take a tenday to explore before we learn that they're dead ends."

"Then send down a thousand dwarves!" Bruenor growled at him. He stalked past the chair again, then skidded to a stop—and Pwent bounced into his back—as he regarded the halfling.

"What're ye looking at?" Bruenor demanded when he noticed Regis's wide-eyed stare.

Regis would have liked to say, "At my oldest friend," but he merely shrugged instead. For an instant, he caught a flash of anger in the dwarf's one blue-gray eye, and he thought that Bruenor was leaning toward him, perhaps fighting an inner urge to rush over and throttle him. But the dwarf calmed and slid into his throne.

Regis cautiously approached, studying Bruenor and taking little heed of pragmatic Dagna's claims that there was no way to catch up with the two wayfaring friends. Regis heard enough to figure that Dagna wasn't too worried for Drizzt and Catti-brie, and that didn't surprise him much, since the crusty dwarf wasn't overly fond of anyone who wasn't a dwarf.

"If we had the damned cat," Bruenor began, and again came that flash of anger as he regarded the halfling. Regis put his hands behind his back and bowed his head.

"Or me damned locket!" Bruenor roared. "Where in the Nine Hells did I put me damned locket?"

Regis winced at every roaring outburst, but Bruenor's anger did not change his feelings that he had done the right thing in assisting Catti-brie, and in sending Guenhwyvar along with her.

And, though he half expected Bruenor to punch him in the face at any moment, it did not change the halfling's feelings that he was glad to see Bruenor full of life again.

9

CAGED

Plodding along a slow and rocky trail, they had to walk the horses more than ride them. Every passing inch tormented Catti-brie. She had seen the light of a campfire the previous night and knew in her heart that it had been Drizzt. She had gone straight to her horse, meaning to saddle up and head out, using the light as a beacon to the drow, but Fret had stopped her, explaining that the magical horseshoes that their mounts wore did not protect the beasts from exhaustion. He reminded her, too, of the dangers she would likely encounter in the mountains at night.

Catti-brie had gone back to her own fire then, thoroughly miserable. She considered calling for Guenhwyvar and sending the panther out for Drizzt, but shook the notion away. The campfire was just a dot somewhere on the higher trails, many miles away, and she had no way of knowing, rationally, that it was indeed Drizzt.

Now, though, crossing along the higher trails, making their steady but painfully slow way in that very same direction, Catti-brie feared that she had erred. She watched Fret, scratching his white beard, looking this way and that at the unremarkable landscape, and wished they had that campfire to guide them.

"We will get there!" the tidy dwarf often said to her, looking back into her disgusted expression.

Morning turned into afternoon; long shadows drifted across the landscape.

"We must make camp," Fret announced as twilight descended.

"We're going on," Catti-brie argued. "If that was Drizzt's fire, then he's a day up on us already, no matter for yer magical horseshoes!"

"I cannot hope to find the cave in the darkness!" the dwarf retorted. "We could find a giant, or a troll, perhaps, and I'm sure that many wolves will be about, but a cave?" Looking into Catti-brie's deepening scowl, Fret began to ponder the wisdom of his sarcasm.

· "Oh, all right!" the tidy dwarf cried. "We will keep looking until the night is full."

They pressed on, until Catti-brie could hardly see her horse walking beside her and Fret's pony nearly stumbled over the edge of a ravine. Finally, even stubborn Catti-brie had to relent and agree to make camp.

After they had settled in, she went and found a tree, a tall pine, and climbed nearly to its top to keep her vigil. If the light of a campfire came up, the young woman determined, she would set out, or would at least send the panther.

There were no campfires that night.

As soon as the dawn's light permitted, the two set off again. Barely an hour out, Fret clapped his clean hands together excitedly, thinking that he had found a familiar trail. "We are not far," he promised.

Up and down went the trail, into rocky, tree-filled valleys, and up again across bare, windswept stone. Fret tethered his pony to a tree branch and led the way up the steep side of one mound, telling Catti-brie that they had found the place, only to discover, two hours of climbing later, that they had scaled the wrong mountain.

In midafternoon they discovered that Fret's earlier promise that they were "not far," was accurate. When he had made that statement, the cave the dwarf sought was no more than half a mile from their location. But finding a specific cave in mountain territory is no easy task, even for a dwarf, and Fret had been to the place only once—nearly twenty years before.

He found it, finally, as the shadows again grew long in the mountains. Catti-brie shook her head as she examined the entrance and the fire pit that had been used two nights before. The embers had been tended with great care, such as a ranger might do.

"He was here," the young woman said to the dwarf, "two nights ago." Catti-brie rose from the fire pit and brushed her thick auburn locks back from her face, eyeing the dwarf as though he was to blame. She looked out from the cave, back across the mountains, to where they had been, to the location from which they had seen this very fire.

"We could not have gotten here that night," the dwarf answered. "You could have run off, or ridden off, into the darkness with all speed, and—"

"The firelight would've shown us through," Catti-brie interrupted.

"For how long?" the dwarf demanded. "We found one vantage point, one

hole through the towering peaks. As soon as we went into a ravine, or crossed close to the side of a mountain, the light would have been lost to us. Then where would we be, stubborn daughter of Bruenor?"

Again Catti-brie's scowl stopped the dwarf short. He sighed profoundly and threw up his hands.

He was right, Catti-brie knew. While they had gone no more than a few miles deeper into the mountains since that night, the trails had been treacherous, climbing and descending, winding snakelike around the many rocky peaks. She and the dwarf had walked a score of miles, at least, to get to this point, and even if she had summoned Guenhwyvar, there was no way the panther could have caught up to Drizzt.

That logic did little to quell the frustration boiling within Catti-brie. She had vowed to follow Drizzt, to find him and bring him home, but now, standing at the edge of a forlorn cave in a wild place, she faced the entrance to the Underdark.

"We will go back to Lady Alustriel," Fret said to her. "Perhaps she has some allies—she has so many of those!—who will be better able to locate the drow."

"What're ye saying?" Catti-brie wanted to know.

"It was a valiant chase," Fret replied. "Your father will be proud of your effort, but—"

Catti-brie rushed up to the dwarf, pushed him aside, and stumbled down toward the back of the cave, toward the blackness of a descending tunnel entrance. She stubbed her toe hard against a jag in the floor, but refused to cry out, even to grunt, not wanting Fret to think her ridiculous. In fumbling with her pack, though, trying to get to her tinderbox, lantern, and oil, Catti-brie thought herself so just the same.

"Do you know that she likes you?" Fret asked casually.

The question stopped the young woman. She looked back to regard the dwarf, who was just a short, dark silhouette before the lighter gray of the outside night.

"Alustriel, I mean," Fret clarified.

Catti-brie had no answer. She hadn't felt comfortable around the magnificent Lady of Silverymoon, far from it. Intentionally or not, Alustriel had made her feel little, perfectly insignificant.

"She does," Fret insisted. "She likes you and admires you."

"In an orc's thoughts," Catti-brie huffed. She thought she was being mocked.

"You remind her of her sister," Fret went on, without missing a beat, "Dove Falconhand, a spirited woman if ever there was one."

Catti-brie did not reply this time. She had heard many tales of Alustriel's sister, a legendary ranger, and had indeed fancied herself somewhat like Dove. Suddenly the dwarf's claims did not seem so outrageous.

"Alas for Alustriel," Fret remarked. "She wishes that she could be more like you."

"In an orc's thoughts!" Catti-brie blurted, unable to stop herself. The notion that Alustriel, the fabulous Lady of Silverymoon, could be the least bit jealous of Catti-brie seemed absurd.

"In a human's thoughts, I say!" Fret replied. "What is it about your race that none of you can seem to properly weigh your own value? Every human seems to think more of herself than she should, or less of herself than is sensible! Alustriel likes you, I say, even admires you. If she did not, if she thought you and your plans were silly, then why would she go to this trouble? Why would she send me, a valuable sage, along with you? And why, daughter of Bruenor Battlehammer, would she give you this?"

He lifted one hand, holding something delicate that Catti-brie could not make out. She paused a moment to digest what he had said, then walked back over to him.

The dwarf held a fine silver chain, a circlet headdress, with a gemstone set into it.

"It is beautiful," Catti-brie admitted, studying the pale green gem, a line of black running through its center.

"More than beautiful," Fret said, and he motioned for Catti-brie to put it on.

She clasped it in place, the gem set against the middle of her forehead, and then she nearly swooned, for the images around her suddenly blurred and wavered. She could see the dwarf—not just his silhouette, but actually Fret's features! She glanced about in disbelief, focusing on the back of the cave. It seemed as if it was bathed in starlight, not brightly, but Catti-brie could make out the jags and the nooks clearly enough.

Catti-brie could not see it, of course, but the thin black line along the middle of the gemstone had widened like a pupil.

"Walking into the Underdark under a blazing torch is not the wisest move," Fret remarked. "A single candle would mark you as out of place and would leave you vulnerable. And how much oil could you carry, in any case? Your lantern would be useless to you before the first day had ended. The Cat's Eye eliminates the need, you see."

"Cat's eye?"

"Cat's Eye agate," Fret explained, pointing to the gemstone. "Alustriel did

the enchanting herself. Normally a gem ensorcelled such would show you only shades of gray, but the lady does favor starlight. Few in the Realms could claim the honor of receiving such a gift."

Catti-brie nodded and didn't know how to reply. Pangs of guilt accompanied her scrutiny of her feelings for the Lady of Silverymoon, and she thought herself ridiculous for ever doubting—and for ever allowing jealousy to cloud her judgment.

"I was instructed to try to dissuade you from the dangerous course," the dwarf went on, "but Alustriel knew that I would fail. You are indeed so like Dove, headstrong and stubborn, and feeling positively immortal. She knew that you would go, even into the Underdark," Fret said. "And, though Alustriel fears for you, she knows that nothing could or should stop you."

The dwarf's tone was neither sarcastic nor demeaning, and again Catti-brie was caught off guard, unprepared for the words.

"Will you stay the night in the cave?" Fret asked. "I could start a fire."

Catti-brie shook her head. Drizzt was already too far ahead of her.

"Of course," the tidy dwarf muttered quietly.

Catti-brie didn't hear him; she was already walking toward the back of the cave, toward the tunnel. She paused and summoned Guenhwyvar, realizing that she would need the panther's support to get going. As the cat materialized, Catti-brie looked back to the cave entrance to tell the dwarf to relay her thanks to Alustriel, but Fret was already gone.

"Come along, Guen," the young woman said, a strained smile on her face. "We have to find Drizzt." The panther poked about the tunnel entrance for a bit, then started down, apparently on the trail.

Catti-brie paused a long moment, staring back to the cave entrance and the starry sky beyond. She wondered if she would ever see those stars again.

10
OLD FRIENDS

He crossed through narrow tunnels and halls that spread beyond vision to either side and above. He trotted along muddy flats and bare stone, without splashes, without sound. Every step Drizzt Do'Urden took in the deeper tunnels of the Underdark jogged his memory a little bit more, brought him back to the days when he had survived the wilds, when he had been the hunter.

He had to find that inner being, that primal savage within him, that heard the call of his instincts so very well. There was no time for rational calculations in the wilds of the Underdark; there was only time to act.

Drizzt hated the prospect of giving in to that savage element, hated this whole journey, but he had to go on, knowing that if he failed, if he was killed in the wilds before he ever got to Menzoberranzan, his quest would prove detrimental to his friends. Then he would be gone, but the dark elves would not know it and would still go after Mithral Hall. For the sake of Bruenor, Regis, and dear Catti-brie, Drizzt had to go on, and had to become the primal hunter once more.

He climbed to the ceiling of a high corridor for his first break and slept lightly, hanging upside down, his legs wedged up to the knees in a narrow crack, his fingers hooked under his belt, near his scimitars.

An echo down a distant tunnel woke him after only an hour of dozing. It had been a slight sound, a step into sucking mud, perhaps, but Drizzt held perfectly still, sensing the disturbance in the still air, hearing minute residual echoes and correctly guessing the direction.

He pulled out his legs and rolled, dropping the fifteen feet to the ground,

the toes of his soft boots touching first to absorb the impact and bring him down without a whisper. He ran on, taking care to keep far from those echoes, desiring no more conflicts before he got to the drow city.

He grew more confident with every step. His instincts were returning, along with his memories of that time he spent alone in the wilds of the Underdark. He came to another muddy area, where the air was warm, and the sound of hot, aerated water hissed and gurgled. Wet, gleaming stalagmite and stalactites, glowing warm to the drow's heat-seeing eyes, dotted the area, breaking this single tunnel into a virtual maze.

Drizzt knew this place, remembered it from the journey he had taken to the surface. That fact brought both relief and trepidation to the drow. He was glad that he was on course, but he could not deny his fear that he was on course. He let the water sound guide him along, knowing that he would find the proper tunnels just beyond the hot springs.

The air grew steadily warmer, soon uncomfortably so, but Drizzt kept his cloak on and drawn tight, not wanting to get caught up with anything more than a scimitar in his hands in this dangerous area.

And the drow knew that this was indeed a dangerous area. Any number of monsters might be crouched behind one of the ever-present mounds, and it took great effort for Drizzt to move silently through the thickening mud. If he kept his foot in one position for any length of time, the clinging stuff ran up around his boot, and subsequently lifting the gummed foot would inevitably result in a sucking sound. On one such occasion, Drizzt paused as he slowly hoisted his foot, trying to discern the echo patterns. It took only a moment for him to understand that the responding sounds he heard were made by more feet than his own.

Drizzt quickly surveyed the area and considered the air temperature and the intensity of the stalagmites' glow. The footsteps grew louder, and Drizzt realized that a band of more than a few approached. He scanned every side tunnel, quickly coming to the conclusion that this band carried no light source.

Drizzt moved under one narrow spike of a stalactite, its tip hanging no more than four feet from the floor. He tucked his legs under him and knelt beneath the thing. He positioned his cloak about his knees in a conical fashion, taking care so that there were no obvious jags, like a foot sticking out too far, along all his body. Then the drow looked up to the stalactite, studied its form. He lifted his hands to feel its tip, then ran them up and around the stalactite, joining with it smoothly, making sure that its tip remained the smallest taper.

He closed his eyes and tucked his head between his upper arms. He swayed a few times, feeling his balance, smoothing the outer edges of his form.

Drizzt became a stalagmite mound.

He soon heard sucking sounds, and squeaking, croaking voices that he knew to be goblins', all about him. He peeked out only once, and only for an instant, ensuring that they had no light sources. How obvious he would be if a torch passed near him!

But hiding in the lightless Underdark was very different from hiding in a forest, even on a dark night. The trick here was to blur the distinctive lines of body heat, and Drizzt felt confident that the air about him, and the stalagmites, was at least as warm as his outer cloak.

He heard goblin footsteps barely a few feet away, knew that the large troupe—it numbered at least twenty, Drizzt believed—was all about him. He considered the exact movements it would take for him to get his hands most quickly to his scimitars. If one of the goblins brushed against him, the game would be up and he would explode into motion, ripping at their ranks and trying to get beyond them before they even realized that he was there.

It never came to that. The goblin troupe continued on its way through the host of stalactites and stalagmites and the one drow that was not a mound of rock.

Drizzt opened his lavender eyes, which blazed with the inner fires of the hunter. He remained perfectly still for a few moments longer, to ensure that there were no stragglers, then he ran off, making not a sound.

⚔ ⚔ ⚔ ⚔ ⚔

Catti-brie knew immediately that Drizzt had killed this six-legged, tentacled, pantherlike beast. Kneeling over the carcass, she recognized the curving, slashing wounds and doubted that anyone else could have made so clean a kill.

"It was Drizzt," she muttered to Guenhwyvar, and the panther gave a low growl. "No more than two days old."

This dead monster reminded her of how vulnerable she might be. If Drizzt, with all his training in stealth and in the ways of the Underdark, had been forced into combat, then how could she hope to pass unscathed?

Catti-brie leaned against the black panther's muscled flank, needing the support. She couldn't keep Guenhwyvar with her for much longer, she knew. The magical cat was a creature of the Astral Plane and needed to return there often to rest. Catti-brie had meant to spend her first hour in the tunnel alone, had meant to leave the cave without the panther beside her, but her nerve had waned with the first few steps. She needed the tangible support of her feline

ally in this foreign place. As the day had gone on, Catti-brie had become somewhat more comfortable with her surroundings and had planned to dismiss Guenhwyvar as soon as the trail became more obvious, as soon as they found a region with fewer side passages. It seemed that they had found that place, but they had found, too, the carcass.

Catti-brie started ahead quickly, instructing Guenhwyvar to keep close to her side. She knew that she should release the panther then, not tax Guenhwyvar's strength in case she should need the cat in an emergency, but she justified her delay by convincing herself that many carrion monsters, or other six-legged feline beasts, might be about.

Twenty minutes later, with the tunnels dark and quiet around them, the young woman stopped and searched for her strength. Dismissing Guenhwyvar then was among the most courageous things Catti-brie had ever done, and when the mist dissolved and Catti-brie replaced the statuette into her pouch, she was glad indeed for the gift Alustriel had given her.

She was alone in the Underdark, alone in deep tunnels filled with deadly foes. She could see, at least, and the starry illusion—beautiful even here against the gray stone—bolstered her spirits.

Catti-brie took a deep breath and steadied herself. She remembered Wulfgar and spoke again her vow that no other friends would be lost. Drizzt needed her; she could not let her fears defeat her.

She took up the heart-shaped locket, holding it tightly in her hand so that its magical warmth would keep her on the proper path. She set off again, forcing one foot in front of the other as she moved farther from the world of the sun.

⚔ ⚔ ⚔ ⚔ ⚔

Drizzt quickened his pace after the hot springs, for he now remembered the way, and remembered, too, many of the enemies he had to take care to avoid.

Days passed uneventfully, became a tenday, and then two for the running drow. It had taken Drizzt more than a month to get to the surface from Blingdenstone, the gnome city some forty to fifty miles west of Menzoberranzan, and now, with his belief that danger was pressing Mithral Hall, he was determined to shorten that time.

He came into tunnels winding and narrow, found a familiar fork in the trail, one corridor cutting north and one continuing to the west. Drizzt suspected that the northern route would get him more quickly to the drow city, but he stayed the course west, hoping that he might gain more information along that more familiar route, and secretly hoping that he might find some old friends along the way.

He was still running a couple of days later, but he now paused often and put his ear to the stone, listening for a rhythmic tap-tapping sound. Blingdenstone was not far away, Drizzt knew, and deep gnome miners might well be about. The halls remained silent, though, and Drizzt began to realize that he did not have much time. He thought of going straight into the gnome city, but decided against that course. He had spent too long on the road already; it was time to draw near to Menzoberranzan.

An hour later, cautiously rounding a bend in a low corridor that was lined with glowing lichen, Drizzt's keen ears caught a distant noise. At first the drow smiled, thinking that he had found the elusive miners, but as he continued to listen, catching the sounds of metal scraping metal, even a cry, his expression greatly changed.

A battle was raging, not so far away.

Drizzt sprinted off, using the increasingly loud echoes to guide his steps. He came into one dead end and had to backtrack, but soon was on the course again, scimitars drawn. He came to a fork in the corridor, both tunnels continuing on in a similar direction, though one rose sharply, and both resounding with the cries of battle.

Drizzt decided to go up, running, crouching. Around a bend he spotted an opening and knew that he had come upon the fight. He eased out of the tunnel, moving onto a ledge twenty feet above a wide chamber, its floor broken and dotted with stone mounds. Below, svirfnebli and drow forms scrambled all about.

Svirfnebli and drow! Drizzt fell back against the wall, his scimitars slipping down to his sides. He knew that the svirfnebli, the deep gnomes, were not evil, understood in his heart that the drow had been the ones to instigate this fight, probably laying an ambush for the gnome mining party. Drizzt's heart screamed at him to leap down to aid the sorely pressed gnomes, but he could not find the strength. He had fought drow, had killed drow, but never with a clear conscience. These were his kin, his blood. Might there be another Zaknafein down there? Another Drizzt Do'Urden?

One dark elf, in hot pursuit of a wounded gnome, scrambled up the side of a rocky mound, only to find that it had become a living rock, an earth elemental, ally of the gnomes. Great stony arms wrapped about the dark elf and crushed him, the elemental taking no notice of the weapons that nicked harmlessly off its natural rocky armor.

Drizzt winced at the gruesome sight, but was somewhat relieved to see the gnomes holding their own. The elemental slowly turned about, smashing down a blocking stalagmite and tearing its great chunks of feet from the stone floor.

The gnomes rallied behind their giant ally, trying to reform some semblance of ranks amid the general chaos. They were making progress, many of them zigzagging through the rocky maze to link up with their mounting central force, and the dark elves inevitably fell back from the dangerous giant. One burly gnome, a burrow warden, Drizzt guessed, called for a straight march across the cavern.

Drizzt crouched low on the ledge. From his vantage point, he could see the skilled drow warriors fanning out about the gnomes, flanking and hiding behind mounds. Another group slipped toward the far exit, the gnomes' destination, and took up strategic positions there. If the elemental held out, though, the gnomes would likely punch their way through, and, once into the corridor, they could put their elemental behind them to block the way and run on to Blingdenstone.

Three drow females stepped out to confront the giant. Drizzt sighed, seeing that they wore the unmistakable spider-emblazoned robes of Lolth worshipers. He recognized that these were priestesses, possibly high priestesses, and knew then that the gnomes would not escape.

One after another, the females chanted and threw their hands out in front of them, sending forth a spray of fine mist. As the moisture hit the rocky elemental, the giant began to dissolve, streaks of mud replacing the solid stone.

The priestesses kept up their chants, their assaults. On came the rocky giant, growling with rage, its features distorted by the slipping mud.

A blast of mist hit it squarely, sending a thick line of mud running down the monster's chest, but the priestess who had made the assault was too concerned with her attack and did not get back fast enough. A rock arm shot out and punched her, breaking bones and hurling her through the air to crash against a stalagmite.

The remaining two drow hit the elemental again, dissolving its legs, and it crashed helplessly to the floor. It began to reform its appendages immediately, but the priestesses continued their deadly spray. Seeing that the ally was lost, the gnome leader called for a charge, and the svirfnebli rushed on, overwhelming one priestess before the flanking dark elves closed in like a biting maw. The fight was on in full again, this time right below Drizzt Do'Urden.

He gasped for breath as he witnessed the spectacle, saw a gnome slashed repeatedly by three drow, to fall, screaming, dying, to the floor.

Drizzt was out of excuses. He knew right from wrong, knew the significance of the appearance of Lolth's priestesses. Fires simmered in his lavender eyes; out came his scimitars, Twinkle flaring to blue-glowing life.

He spotted the remaining priestess down to the left. She stood beside a tall, narrow mound, one arm out touching a svirfneblin. The gnome made no moves against her, only stood and groaned, trembling from the priestess's magical assaults. Black energy crackled up the drow female's arm as she literally sucked the life force from her unfortunate victim.

Drizzt tucked Twinkle under his other arm and leaped out, hooking the top of that narrow mound and rotating about it as he quickly descended. He hit the floor right beside the priestess and snapped his weapons back to the ready.

The startled drow female uttered a series of sharp commands, apparently thinking Drizzt an ally. Twinkle dived into her heart.

The half-drained gnome eyed Drizzt curiously, then fainted away. Drizzt ran on, calling out warnings to the gnomes, in their own tongue, that dark elves were in position near the far exit. The ranger took care to keep out of the open, though, realizing that any gnome he encountered would likely attack him, and any drow he encountered might recognize him.

He tried not to think of what he had just done, tried not to think of the female's eyes, so similar to his sister Vierna's.

He rushed in hard and put his back against a mound, the cries of battle all about him. A gnome jumped out from behind another stalagmite, waving a hammer dangerously, and before Drizzt could explain that he was no enemy, another drow came around the side, to stand shoulder to shoulder with Drizzt.

The suddenly hesitant gnome looked about, looked for an escape route, but the newest opponent leaped at him.

Purely on instinct, Drizzt slashed the drow's weapon arm, his scimitar drawing a deep gash. The ebon-skinned elf dropped his sword and half-turned to look back in horror at this drow who was not an ally. Stumbling, the surprised drow focused ahead, just in time to catch a gnomish hammer in the face.

The gnome didn't understand it, of course, and as the dark elf fell, all he thought about was readying his hammer for this second enemy. But Drizzt was long gone.

With the priestesses down, a gnome shaman ran over to the felled elemental. He placed a stone atop the pile of rubble and crushed it with his mattock, then began chanting. Soon the elemental reformed, as large as ever, and lumbered

away like a moving avalanche in search of enemies. The shaman watched it go, but he should have been watching his own situation instead, for another dark elf crept out behind him, mace held high for a killing strike.

The shaman realized the danger only as the mace came crashing down . . . and was intercepted by a scimitar.

Drizzt shoved the shaman aside and stood to face the stunned drow.

Friend? the fingers of the drow's free hand quickly asked.

Drizzt shook his head, then sent Twinkle slamming against the drow's mace, batting it aside. The ranger's second scimitar quickly followed the same path, ringing loudly off the metal mace and knocking it far out to Drizzt's left.

Drizzt's advantage of surprise was not as great as he had supposed, though, for the drow's free left hand had already slipped to his belt and grabbed a slender dirk. Out of the folds of the drow's *piwafwi* cloak shot the new weapon, straight for Drizzt's heart, the evil drow snarling in apparent victory.

Drizzt spun to the right, backstepping out of harm's way. He brought his closest scimitar back across and down, hooking the dirk's hilt and pulling the drow's arm out straight. He completed his spin, putting his back tightly against his opponent's chest, wrapping the outstretched arm right about him. The drow tried to work his mace into an angle so that he could strike at Drizzt, but Drizzt was in the better position and was the quicker. He stepped away, then came back in, elbow flying high to smash into his opponent's face, once, twice, and then again in rapid succession.

Drizzt flung the drow's dirk hand out wide, and wisely reversed his spin, getting Twinkle up just in time to catch the swinging mace. Drizzt's other arm shot forward, the hilt of his scimitar crushing the drow's face.

The evil drow tried to hold his balance, but he was clearly dazed. A quick twist and snap of Twinkle sent the mace flying into the air, and Drizzt punched out with his left hand, Twinkle's hilt catching the drow on the side of the jaw and dropping him to the floor.

Drizzt looked to the gnome shaman, who stood open-mouthed, clutching his hammer nervously. All around them, the fight had become a rout, with the revived elemental leading the svirfnebli to a decisive victory.

Two other gnomes joined the shaman and eyed Drizzt with suspicion and fear. Drizzt paused a moment to consider the Svirfneblin tongue, a language that used the melodic inflections similar to surface Elvish alongside the hard consonant sounds more typical of Dwarvish talk.

"I am no enemy," he said, and to prove his point he dropped his scimitars to the ground.

The drow on the floor groaned. A gnome sprang upon him and lined his pickaxe up with the back of the dark elf's skull.

"No!" Drizzt cried in protest, starting forward and bending low to intercept the strike.

Drizzt stood up straight suddenly, though, as a searing flash of pain erupted along his backbone. He saw the gnome finish the dazed drow, but couldn't begin to contemplate that brutal action as a series of minor explosions went off down his spine. The lip of some devious, flat-edged club ran down his vertebrae like a board snapping across a picket fence.

Then it was over and Drizzt stood motionlessly for what seemed like a very long time. He felt his legs tingle, as though they had gone to sleep, then felt nothing at all below his waist. He fought to hold his balance, but wobbled and fell, and lay scratching at the stone floor and trying to find his breath.

He knew that the darkness of unconsciousness—or a deeper darkness still—was fast approaching, for he could hardly remember where he was or why he had come.

He did hear the shaman, but that small flicker of consciousness that Drizzt had remaining was not comforted by the shaman's words.

"Kill him."

FUTILITY

This the place?" the battlerager asked, shouting so that his gruff voice could be heard over the whipping wind. He had come out of Mithral Hall with Regis and Bruenor—had forced the halfling to take him out, actually—in search of the body of Artemis Entreri. "Ye find the clues where ye find them," Pwent had said in typically cryptic explanation.

Regis pulled the cowl of his oversized cloak low to ward off the wind's sting. They were in a narrow valley, a gully, the sides of which seemed to focus the considerable wind into a torrent. "It was around here," Regis said, shrugging his shoulders to indicate that he could not be sure. When he had come out to find the battered Entreri, he had taken a higher route, along the top of the ravine and other ledges. He was certain that he was in the general region, but things looked too different from this perspective to be sure.

"We'll find him, me king," Thibbledorf assured Bruenor.

"For what that's worth," the dejected Bruenor grumbled.

Regis winced at the dwarf's deflated tones. He recognized clearly that Bruenor was slipping back into despair. The dwarves had found no way through the maze of tunnels beneath Mithral Hall, though a thousand were searching, and word from the east was not promising—if Catti-brie and Drizzt had gone to Silverymoon, they were long past that place now. Bruenor was coming to realize the futility of it all. Tendays had passed and he had not found a way out of Mithral Hall that would take him anywhere near his friends. The dwarf was losing hope.

"But, me king!" Pwent roared. "He knows the way."

"He's dead," Bruenor reminded the battlerager.

"Not to worry!" bellowed Pwent. "Priests can talk to the dead—and he might have a map. Oh, we'll find our way to this drow city, I tell ye, and there I'll go, for me king! I'll kill every stinking drow—except that ranger fellow," he added, throwing a wink at Regis, "—and bring yer girl back home!"

Bruenor just sighed and motioned for Pwent to get on with the hunt. Despite all the complaining, though, the dwarf king privately hoped that he might find some satisfaction in seeing Entreri's broken body.

They moved on for a short while, Regis constantly peeking out from his cowl, trying to get his bearings. Finally, the halfling spotted a high outcropping, a branchlike jag of rock.

"There," he said, pointing the way. "That must be it."

Pwent looked up, then followed a direct line to the ravine's bottom. He began scrambling around on all fours, sniffing the ground as if trying to pick up the corpse's scent.

Regis watched him, amused, then turned to Bruenor, who stood against the gully's wall, his hand on the stone, shaking his head.

"What is it?" Regis asked, walking over. Hearing the question and noticing his king, Pwent scampered to join them.

When he got close, Regis noticed something along the stone wall, something gray and matted. He peered closer as Bruenor pulled a bit of the substance from the stone and held it out.

"What is it?" Regis asked again, daring to touch it. A stringy filament came away with his retracting finger, and it took some effort to shake the gooey stuff free.

Bruenor had to swallow hard several times. Pwent ran off, sniffing at the wall, then across the ravine to consider the stone on the other side.

"It's what's left of a web," the dwarf king answered grimly.

Both Bruenor and Regis looked up to the jutting rock and silently considered the implications of a web strung below the falling assassin.

⚔ ⚔ ⚔ ⚔

Fingers flashed too quickly for him to follow, conveying some instructions that the assassin did not understand. He shook his head furiously, and the flustered drow clapped his ebon-skinned hands together, uttered, *"Iblith,"* and walked away.

Iblith, Artemis Entreri echoed silently in his thoughts. The drow word for offal, it was the word he had heard the most since Jarlaxle had taken him to this wretched place. What could that drow soldier have expected from him?

He was only beginning to learn the intricate drow hand code, its finger movements so precise and detailed that Entreri doubted that one in twenty humans could even begin to manage it. And he was trying desperately to learn the drow spoken language as well. He knew a few words and had a basic understanding of drow sentence structure, so he could put simple ideas together.

And he knew the word *iblith* all too well.

The assassin leaned back against the wall of the small cave, this tenday's base of operations for Bregan D'aerthe. He felt smaller, more insignificant, than ever. When Jarlaxle had first revived him, in a cave in the ravine outside of Mithral Hall, he had thought the mercenary's offer—actually more of a command, Entreri realized—to take him to Menzoberranzan a wonderful thing, a grand adventure.

This was no adventure; this was living hell. Entreri was *colnbluth,* "nondrow," living in the midst of twenty thousand of the less-than-tolerant race. They didn't particularly hate humans, no more than they hated everybody else, but because he was *colnbluth,* the once powerful assassin found himself beneath the lowest ranks of Bregan D'aerthe's drow force. No matter what he did, no matter who he killed, in Menzoberranzan, Artemis Entreri could never rank higher than twenty thousand and first.

And the spiders! Entreri hated spiders, and the crawly things were everywhere in the drow city. They were bred into larger, more poisonous varieties, and were kept as pets. And to kill a spider was a crime carrying the punishment of *jivvin quui'elghinn,* "torture until death." In the great cavern's eastern end, the moss bed and mushroom grove near the lake of Donigarten, where Entreri was often put to work herding goblin slaves, spiders crawled about by the thousands. They crawled around him, crawled on him, hung down in strands, dangling inches from the tormented man's face.

The assassin drew his green-gleaming sword and held its wicked edge before his eyes. At least there was more light now in the city; for some reason that Entreri did not know, magical lights and flickering torches had become much more common in Menzoberranzan.

"It would not be wise to stain so marvelous a weapon with drow blood," came a familiar voice from the doorway, easily speaking the Common tongue. Entreri didn't take his gaze from the blade as Jarlaxle entered the small room.

"You presume that I would find the strength to harm one of the mighty drow," the assassin replied. "How could I, the *iblith . . .*" he started to ask, but Jarlaxle's laughter mocked his self-pity. Entreri glanced over at the mercenary and saw the drow holding his wide-brimmed hat in his hand, fiddling with the *diatryma* feather.

"I have never underestimated your prowess, assassin," Jarlaxle said. "You have survived several fights against Drizzt Do'Urden, and few in Menzoberranzan will ever make that claim."

"I was his fighting equal," Entreri said through gritted teeth. Simply uttering the words stung him. He had battled Drizzt several times, but only twice had they fought without a premature interruption. On both those occasions, Entreri had lost. Entreri wanted desperately to even the score, to prove himself the better fighter. Still, he had to admit, to himself, at least, that in his heart he did not desire another fight with Drizzt. After the first time he had lost to Drizzt, in the muddy sewers and streets of Calimport, Entreri had lived every day plotting revenge, had shaped his life around one event, his rematch with Drizzt. But after his second loss, the one in which he had wound up hanging, broken and miserable, from a jag of rock in a windswept ravine . . .

But what? Entreri wondered. Why did he no longer wish to battle that renegade drow? Had the point been proven, the decision rendered? Or was he simply too afraid? The emotions were unsettling to Artemis Entreri, as out of place within him as he was in the city of drow.

"I was his fighting equal," he whispered again, with as much conviction as he could muster.

"I would not state that openly if I were you," the mercenary replied. "Dantrag Baenre and Uthegental Armgo would fight one another simply to determine which of them got to kill you first."

Entreri did not blink; his sword flared, as if reflecting his simmering pride and anger.

Jarlaxle laughed again. "To determine which would get to *fight* you first," the mercenary corrected, and he swept a low and apologetic bow.

Still the out-of-place assassin didn't blink. Might he regain a measure of pride by killing one of these legendary drow warriors? he wondered. Or would he lose again, and, worse than being killed, be forced to live with that fact?

Entreri snapped the sword down and slipped it into its scabbard. He had never been so hesitant, so unsure. Even as a young boy, surviving on the brutal streets of Calimshan's crowded cities, Entreri had brimmed with confidence, and had used that confidence to advantage. But not here, not in this place.

"Your soldiers taunt me," he snapped suddenly, transferring his frustration the mercenary's way.

Jarlaxle laughed and put his hat back on his bald head. "Kill a few," he offered, and Entreri couldn't tell if the cold, calculating drow was kidding or not. "The rest will then leave you alone."

Entreri spat on the floor. Leave him alone? The rest would wait until he was

asleep, then cut him into little pieces to feed to the spiders of Donigarten. That thought broke the assassin's narrow-eyed concentration, forced him to wince. He had killed a female—which, in Menzoberranzan, was much worse than killing a male—and some house in the city might be starving their spiders right now in anticipation of a human feast.

"Ah, but you are so crude," the mercenary said, as though he pitied the man. Entreri sighed and looked away, bringing a hand up to rub his saliva-wetted lips. What was he becoming? In Calimport, in the guilds, even among the pashas and those others that called themselves his masters, he had been in control. He was a killer hired by the most treacherous, double-dealing thieves in all the Realms, and yet, not one had ever tried to cross Artemis Entreri. How he longed to see the pale sky of Calimport again!

"Fear not, my *abbil*," Jarlaxle said, using the drow word for "trusted friend." "You will again see the sunrise." The mercenary smiled widely at Entreri's expression, apparently understanding that he had just read the assassin's very thoughts. "You and I will watch the dawn from the doorstep of Mithral Hall."

They were going back after Drizzt, Entreri realized. This time, judging from the lights in Menzoberranzan, which he now came to understand, Clan Battlehammer itself would be crushed!

"That is," Jarlaxle continued teasingly, "unless House Horlbar takes the time to discover that it was you who slew one of its matron mothers."

With a click of his boot and a tip of his hat, Jarlaxle spun out of the room.

Jarlaxle knew! And the female had been a matron mother! Feeling perfectly miserable, Entreri leaned heavily against the wall. How was he to know that the wicked beast in the alley was a damned matron mother?

The walls seemed to close in on the man, suffocating him. Cold sweat beaded on his normally cool brow, and he labored to draw breath. All his thoughts centered on possible escape, but they inevitably slammed against unyielding stone walls. He was caught by logistics as much as by drow blades.

He had tried to escape once, had run out of Menzoberranzan through the eastern exit, beyond Donigarten. But where could he go? The Underdark was a maze of dangerous tunnels and deep holes filled with monsters the assassin did not know how to fight. Entreri was a creature of the very different surface world. He did not understand the wild Underdark, could not hope to survive there for long. Certainly he would never find his own way back to the surface. He was trapped, caged, stripped of his pride and his dignity, and, sooner or later, he was going to be horribly killed.

12

RISING TO THE OCCASION

W e can drop this whole section," General Dagna remarked as he poked a stubby finger against the map spread on the table.

"Drop it?" bellowed the battlerager. "If ye drop it, then how're we to kill the stinking drow?"

Regis, who had arranged this meeting, looked incredulously to Dagna and the other three dwarven commanders huddled about the table. Then he looked back to Pwent. "The ceiling *will* kill the stinking drow," he explained.

"Bah, sandstone!" huffed the battlerager. "What fun do ye call that? I got to grease up me armor with some drow blood, I do, but with yer stupid plan, I'll have to do a month's digging just to find a body to rub against."

"Lead the charge down here," Dagna offered, pointing to another section of open corridors on the map. "The rest of us'll give ye a hunnerd-foot head start."

Regis put a sour look on the general and moved it, in turn, to each of the other dwarves, who were all bobbing their heads in agreement. Dagna was only half-kidding, Regis knew. More than a few of Clan Battlehammer would not be teary-eyed if obnoxious Thibbledorf Pwent happened to be among the fallen in the potential fight against the dark elves.

"Drop the tunnel," Regis said to get them back on track. "We'll need strong defenses here and here," he added, pointing to two open areas in the otherwise tight lower tunnels. "I'm meeting later this day with Berkthgar of Settlestone."

"Ye're bringin' the smelly humans in?" Pwent asked.

Even the dwarves, who favored the strong smells of soot-covered, sweaty

bodies, twisted their faces at the remark. In Mithral Hall, it was said that Pwent's armpit could curl a hardy flower at fifty yards.

"I don't know what I'm doing with the humans," Regis answered. "I haven't even told them my suspicions of a drow raid yet. If they agree to join our cause, and I have no reason to believe that they won't, I suspect that we would be wise to keep them out of the lower tunnels—even though we plan to light those tunnels."

Dagna nodded his agreement. "A wise choice indeed," he said. "The tall men are better suited to fighting along the mountainsides. Me own guess is that the drow'll come in around the mountain as well as through it."

"The men of Settlestone will meet them," added another dwarf.

$$\times \quad \times \quad \times \quad \times \quad \times$$

From the shadows of a partly closed door at the side of the room, Bruenor Battlehammer looked on curiously. He was amazed at how quickly Regis had taken things into his control, especially given the fact that the halfling did not wear his hypnotic ruby pendant. After scolding Bruenor for not acting quickly and decisively, for falling back into a mire of self-pity with the trails to Catti-brie and Drizzt apparently closed, the halfling, with Pwent in tow, had gone straight to General Dagna and the other war commanders.

What amazed Bruenor now was not the fact that the dwarves had gone eagerly into preparations for war, but the fact that Regis seemed to be leading them. Of course, the halfling had concocted a lie to assume that role. Using Bruenor's resumed indifference, the halfling was faking meetings with the dwarf king, then going to Dagna and the others pretending that he was bringing word straight from Bruenor.

When he first discovered the ruse, Bruenor wanted to throttle the halfling, but Regis had stood up to him, and had offered, more than sincerely, to step aside if Bruenor wanted to take over.

Bruenor wished that he could, desperately wanted to find that level of energy once more, but any thought of warfare inevitably led him to memories of his recent past battles, most of them beside Drizzt, Catti-brie, and Wulfgar. Paralyzed by those painful memories, Bruenor had simply dismissed Regis and allowed the halfling to go on with his facade.

Dagna was as fine a strategist as any, but his experience was rather limited regarding races other than dwarves or stupid goblins. Regis was among Drizzt's best friends, had sat and listened to Drizzt's tales of his homeland and his kin hundreds of times. Regis had also been among Wulfgar's best friends, and so he understood the barbarians, whom the dwarves would need as allies should the war come to pass.

Still, Dagna had never been fond of anyone who wasn't a dwarf, and the fact that he wholeheartedly accepted the advice of a halfling—and one not known for bravery!—surprised Bruenor more than a little.

It stung the king as well. Bruenor knew of the dark elves and the barbarians at least as well as Regis, and he understood dwarven tactics better than anyone. He should be at that table, pointing out the sections on the map; he should be the one, with Regis beside him, to meet with Berkthgar the Bold.

Bruenor dropped his gaze to the floor, rubbed a hand over his brow and down his grotesque scar. He felt an ache in the hollow socket. Hollow, too, was his heart, empty with the loss of Wulfgar, and breaking apart at the thought that Drizzt and his precious Catti-brie had gone off into danger.

The events about him had gone beyond his responsibilities as king of Mithral Hall. Bruenor's first dedication was to his children, one lost, the other missing, and to his friends. Their fates were beyond him now; he could only hope that they would win out, would survive and come back to him, for Bruenor had no way to get to Catti-brie and Drizzt.

Bruenor could never get back to Wulfgar.

The dwarf king sighed and turned away, walking slowly back toward his empty room, not even noticing that the meeting had adjourned.

Regis watched Bruenor silently from the doorway, wishing that he had his ruby pendant, if for no other reason than to try to rekindle the fires in the broken dwarf.

⚔ ⚔ ⚔ ⚔ ⚔

Catti-brie eyed the wide corridor ahead suspiciously, trying to make out distinct shapes among the many stalagmite mounds. She had come into a region where mud mixed with stone, and she had seen the tracks clearly enough— goblin tracks, she knew, and recent.

Ahead loomed the perfect place for an ambush. Catti-brie took an arrow from the quiver strapped behind her hip, then held Taulmaril the Heartseeker, her magical bow, ready in her hands. Tucked under one arm, ready to be dropped, was the panther figurine. She silently debated whether or not she should summon Guenhwyvar from the Astral Plane. She had no real proof that the goblins were about—all the mounds in the corridor seemed natural and benign—but she felt the hairs on the back of her neck tingle.

She decided to hold off calling the cat, her logic overruling her instincts.

She fell against the left-hand wall and slowly started forward, wincing every time the mud sloshed around her lifting boot.

With a dozen stalagmite mounds behind her, the wall still tightly to her left, the young woman paused and listened once more. All seemed perfectly quiet, but she couldn't shake the feeling that her every step was being monitored, that some monster was poised not far away, waiting to spring out and throttle her. Would it be like this all the way through the Underdark? she wondered. Would she drive herself insane with imagined dangers? Or worse, would the false alarms of her misguided instincts take her off guard on that one occasion when danger really did rise against her?

Catti-brie shook her head to clear the thoughts and squinted her eyes to peer into the magically starlit gloom. Another benefit of Lady Alustriel's gift was that Catti-brie's eyes did not glow with the telltale red of infravision. The young woman, though, inexperienced in such matters, didn't know that; she knew only that the shapes ahead seemed ominous indeed. The ground and walls were not firmly set, as in other parts of the tunnels. Mud and open water flowed freely in different areas. Many of the stalagmites seemed to have appendages—goblin arms, perhaps, holding wicked weapons.

Again Catti-brie forced away the unwanted thoughts, and she started forward, but froze immediately. She had caught a sound, a slight scraping, like that of a weapon tip brushing against stone. She waited a long while but heard nothing more, so she again told herself not to let her imagination carry her away.

But had those goblin tracks been part of her imagination? she asked herself as she took another step forward.

Catti-brie dropped the figurine and swung about, her bow coming to bear. Around the nearest stalagmite charged a goblin, its ugly, flat face seeming broader for the wide grin it wore and its rusting and jagged sword held high above its head.

Catti-brie fired, point blank, and the silver-streaking arrow had barely cleared the bow when the monster's head exploded in a shower of multicolored sparks. The arrow blasted right through, sparking again as it sliced a chunk off the stalagmite mound.

"Guenhwyvar!" Catti-brie called, and she readied the bow. She knew she had to get moving, that this area had been clearly marked by the spark shower. She considered the gray mist that had begun to swirl about her, and, knowing the summoning was complete, scooped up the figurine and ran away from the wall. She hopped the dead goblin's body and cut around the nearest stalagmite, then slipped between two others. Out of the corner of her eye she saw another four-foot-tall huddled shape. An arrow streaked off in pursuit, its silvery trail stealing the darkness, and scored another hit. Catti-brie did not smile, though, for the flash of light revealed a dozen more of the ugly humanoids, slinking and crawling about the mounds.

They screamed and hooted and began their charge.

Over by the wall, gray mist gave way to the powerful panther's tangible form. Guenhwyvar had recognized the urgency of the call and was on the alert immediately, ears flattened and shining green eyes peering about, taking full measure of the scene. Quieter than the night, the cat loped off.

Catti-brie circled farther out from the wall, taking a roundabout course to flank the approaching group. Every time she came past another blocking mound, she let fly an arrow, as often hitting stone as goblins. She knew that confusion was her ally here, that she had to keep the creatures from organizing, or they would surround her.

Another arrow streaked away, and in its illumination Catti-brie saw a closer target, a goblin crouched right behind the mound she would soon pass. She went behind the mound, skidded to a stop, and came back out the same way, desperately working to fit an arrow.

The goblin swung around the mound and rushed in, sword leading. Catti-brie batted with her bow, barely knocking the weapon aside. She heard a sucking sound behind her, then a hiss, and instinctively dropped to her knees.

A goblin pitched over her suddenly low form and crashed into its surprised ally. The two were up quickly, though, as quickly as Catti-brie. The woman worked her bow out in front to keep them at bay, tried to get her free hand down to grab at the jeweled dagger on her belt.

Sensing their advantage, the goblins charged—then went tumbling away along with six hundred pounds of flying panther.

"Guen," Catti-brie mouthed in silent appreciation, and she pivoted about, pulling an arrow from her quiver. As she expected, goblins were fast closing from behind.

Taulmaril twanged once, again, and then a third time, Catti-brie blasting holes in the ranks. She used the sudden and deadly explosions of streaking lines and sparks as cover and ran, not away, as she knew the goblins would expect, but straight ahead, backtracking along her original route.

She had them fooled as she ducked behind another mound, wide and thick, and nearly giggled when a goblin leaped out behind her, rubbing its light-stung eyes and looking back the other way.

Just five feet behind the stupid thing, Catti-brie let fly, the arrow blasting

into the goblin's back, snaring on a bone, and sending the creature flying through the air.

Catti-brie spun and ran on, around the back side of the wide mound. She heard a roar from Guenhwyvar, followed by the profound screams of another group of goblins. Ahead, a huddled form was running away from her, and she lifted her bow, ready to clear the path.

Something jolted her on the hip. She released the bowstring, and the arrow zipped wide of the mark, scorching a hole in the wall.

Catti-brie stumbled off balance, startled and hurt. She banged her shin against a jutting stone and nearly pitched headlong, skidding to a stop down on one knee. As she reached down to get another arrow from her quiver, she felt the wet warmth of her lifeblood pouring generously from a deep gash in her hip. Only then did stunned Catti-brie realize the hot waves of agony.

She kept her wits about her and turned as she fitted the arrow.

The goblin was right above her, its breath coming hot and smelly through pointed yellow teeth. Its sword was high above its head.

Catti-brie let fly. The goblin jerked up into the air, but came back to its feet. Behind it, another goblin caught the arrow under the chin, the powerful bolt blowing the back of its skull off.

Catti-brie thought she was dead. How could she have missed? Did the arrow slip under the goblin's arm as it jumped in fright? It made no sense to her, but she could hardly stop to think it over. The moment of death was upon her, she was sure, for she could not maneuver her bow quickly enough to parry the goblin's next strike. She could not block the descending sword.

But the sword did not descend. The goblin simply stopped, held perfectly still for what seemed to Catti-brie an interminable time. Its sword then clanged to the stone; a wheeze issued from the center of its rib cage, followed by a thick line of blood. The monster toppled to the side, dead.

Catti-brie realized that her arrow had indeed hit the mark, had driven cleanly through the first goblin to kill the second.

Catti-brie forced herself to her feet. She tried to run on, but waves rolled over her, and before she understood what had happened, she was back to the floor, back to one knee. She felt a coldness up her side, a swirling nausea in her stomach, and, to her horror, saw yet another of the miserable goblins fast closing, waving a spiked club.

Summoning all of her strength, Catti-brie waited until the very last moment and whipped her bow across in front of her. The goblin shrieked and fell backward, avoiding the hit, but its sudden retreat gave Catti-brie the time to draw her short sword and the jeweled dagger.

She stood, forcing down the pain and the sick feeling.

The goblin uttered something in its annoying, high-pitched voice, something threatening, Catti-brie knew, though it sounded like a typical goblin whine. The wretched creature came at her all of a sudden, whipping the club to and fro, and Catti-brie leaped back.

A jolting flare of agony rushed up her side, nearly costing her her balance. On came the goblin, crouched and balanced, sensing victory.

It continued to talk to her, taunt her, though she could not understand its language. It chuckled and pointed to her wounded leg.

Catti-brie was confident that she could defeat the goblin, but she feared that it would be to no avail. Even if she and Guenhwyvar won out, killed all the goblins or sent them fleeing, what might come next? Her leg would barely support her—certainly she could not continue her quest—and she doubted that she could properly clean and dress the wound. The goblins might not kill her, but they had stopped her, and the waves of pain continued unabated.

Catti-brie's eyes rolled back and she started to sway.

Her eyes blinked open and she steadied herself as the goblin took the bait and charged. When it realized the ruse, it tried to stop, but skidded in the slippery mud.

The goblin whipped its club across frantically, but Catti-brie's short sword intercepted it, locking against one of the spikes. Knowing that she had not the strength to force the club aside, she pressed forward, into the goblin, tucking her sword arm in close as she went, forcing the goblin's arm to hook about her as she turned.

All the while, the jeweled dagger led the way, reaching for the creature's belly. The goblin got its free arm up to block, and only the dagger's tip slipped through its skin.

Catti-brie did not know how long she could hold the clinch. Her strength was draining; she wanted nothing more than to curl up in a little ball and faint away.

Then, to her surprise, the goblin cried out in agony. It whipped its head back and forth, shook its whole body wildly in an effort to get away. Catti-brie, barely holding the dangerous club at bay, had to keep pace with it.

A burst of energy pulsed through the dagger and coursed up her arm.

The young woman didn't know what to make of it, didn't know what was happening, as the goblin went into a series of violent convulsions, each one sending another pulse of energy flowing into its foe.

The creature fell back against a stone, its blocking arm limp, and Catti-brie's momentum carried her closer, the wicked dagger sinking in to the

hilt. The next pulse of energy nearly knocked Catti-brie away, and her eyes widened in horror as she realized that Artemis Entreri's weapon was literally eating away at the goblin's life force and transferring it to her!

The goblin sprawled over the arcing edge of the stalagmite mound, its eyes open and unblinking, its body twitching in death spasms.

Catti-brie fell back, taking the bloodied dagger with her. She worked hard to draw breath, gasping in disbelief and eyeing the blade with sheer revulsion.

A roar from Guenhwyvar reminded her that the battle was not ended. She replaced the dagger on her belt and turned, thinking that she had to find her bow. She had gone two running steps before she even realized that her leg was easily supporting her now.

From somewhere in the shadows, a goblin heaved a spear, which skipped off the stone just behind the running woman and stole her train of thought. Catti-brie skidded down in the mud and scooped up her bow as she slid past. She looked down to her quiver, saw its powerful magic already at work replacing the spent arrows.

She saw, too, that no more blood was coming from her wound. Gingerly, the young woman ran a hand over it, felt a thick scab already in place. She shook her head in disbelief, took up her bow, and began firing.

Only one more goblin got close to Catti-brie. It sneaked around the back side of the thick mound. The young woman started to drop her bow and draw out her weapons for melee, but she stopped—and so did the goblin!—when a great panther's paw slapped down atop the creature's head and long claws dug into the goblin's sloping forehead.

Guenhwyvar snapped the creature backward with sudden, savage force such that one of the monster's shoddy boots remained where it had been standing. Catti-brie looked away, back to the area behind them, as Guenhwyvar's powerful maw closed over the stunned goblin's throat and began to squeeze.

Catti-brie saw no targets, but let fly another arrow to brighten the end of the corridor. Half a dozen goblins were in full flight, and Catti-brie sent a shower of arrows trailing them, chasing them, and cutting them down.

She was still firing a minute later—her enchanted quiver would never run short of arrows—when Guenhwyvar padded over to her and bumped against her, demanding a pat. Catti-brie sighed deeply and dropped a hand to the cat's muscled flank, her eyes falling to the jeweled dagger, sitting impassively on her belt.

She had seen Entreri wield that dagger, had once had its blade against her own throat. The young woman shuddered as she recalled that awful moment, more awful now that she understood the cruel weapon's properties.

Guenhwyvar growled and pushed against her, prodding her to motion. Catti-brie understood the panther's urgency; according to Drizzt's tales, goblins rarely traveled in the Underdark in secluded bands. If there were twenty here, there were likely two hundred somewhere nearby.

Catti-brie looked to the tunnel behind them, the tunnel from which she had come and down which the goblins had fled. She considered, briefly, going that way, fighting through the fleeing few and running back to the surface world, where she belonged.

It was a fleeting thought for her, an excusable instant of weakness. She knew that she must go on, but how? Catti-brie looked down to her belt once more and smiled as she untied the magical mask. She lifted it before her face, unsure of how it even worked.

With a shrug to Guenhwyvar, the young woman pressed the mask against her face.

Nothing happened.

Holding it tight, she thought of Drizzt, imagined herself with ebony skin and the fine chiseled features of a drow.

Biting tingles of magic nipped at her every pore. In a moment, she moved her hand away from her face, the mask holding fast of its own accord. Catti-brie blinked many times, for in the magical starlight afforded her by the Cat's Eye, she saw her receding hand shining perfectly black, her fingers more slender and delicate than she remembered them.

How easy it had been!

Catti-brie wished that she had a mirror so that she could check the disguise, though she felt in her heart that it was true. She considered how perfectly Entreri had mimicked Regis when he had come back to Mithral Hall, right down to the halfling's equipment. With that thought, the young woman looked to her own rather drab garb. She considered Drizzt's tales of his homeland, of the fabulous and evil high priestesses of Lolth.

Catti-brie's worn traveling cloak had become a rich robe, shimmering purple and black. Her boots had blackened, their tips curling up delicately. Her weapons remained the same, though, and it seemed to Catti-brie, in this attire, that Entreri's jeweled dagger was the most fitting.

Again the young woman focused her thoughts on that wicked blade. A part of her wanted to drop it in the mud, to bury it where no one could ever find it. She even went so far as to close her fingers over its hilt.

But she released the dagger immediately, strengthened her resolve, and smoothed her drowlike robes. The blade had helped her; without it she would be crippled and lost, if not dead. It was a weapon, like her bow, and, though

its brutal tactics assaulted her sensibilities, Catti-brie came, in that moment, to accept them. She carried the dagger more easily as the days turned into a tenday, and then two.

This was the Underdark, where the savage survived.

PART THREE

There are no shadows in the Underdark.

    Only after years on the surface have I come to understand the significance of that seemingly minute fact, the significance of the contrast between lightness and darkness. There are no shadows in the Underdark, no areas of mystery where only the imagination can go.

SHADOWS

What a marvelous thing is a shadow! I have seen my own silhouette walk under me as the sun rode high; I have seen a gopher grow to the size of a large bear, the light low behind him, spreading his ominous silhouette far across the ground. I have walked through the woods at twilight, my gaze alternating between the lighter areas catching the last rays of day, leafy green slipping to gray, and those darkening patches, those areas where only my mind's eye could go. Might a monster be there? An orc or a goblin? Or might a hidden treasure, as magnificent as a lost, enchanted sword or as simple as a fox's den, lay within the sheltering gloom?

When I walk the woods at twilight, my imagination walks beside me, heightens my senses, opens my mind to any possibilities. But there are no shadows in the Underdark, and there is no room for fanciful imagining. All, everywhere, is gripped in a brooding, continual, predatory hush and a very real, ever present danger.

To imagine a crouched enemy, or a hidden treasure, is an exercise in enjoyment, a conjured state of alertness, of aliveness. But when that enemy is too often real and not imagined, when every jag in the stone, every potential hiding place, becomes a source of tension, then the game is not so much fun.

One cannot walk the corridors of the Underdark with his imagination beside him. To imagine an enemy behind one stone might well blind a person to the very real enemy behind another. To slip into a daydream is to lose that edge of readiness, and in the Underdark, to be unwary is to die.

This proved the most difficult transition for me when I went back into those lightless corridors. I had to again become the primal hunter, had to survive, every moment, on that instinctual edge, a state of nervous energy that kept my muscles always taut, always ready to spring. Every step of the way, the present was all that mattered, the search for potential hiding places of potential enemies. I could not afford to imagine those enemies. I had to wait for them and watch for them, react to any movements.

There are no shadows in the Underdark. There is no room for imagination in the Underdark. It is a place for alertness, but not aliveness, a place with no room for hopes and dreams.

—Drizzt Do'Urden

13

HUNGRY GODDESS

Councilor Firble of Blingdenstone normally enjoyed his journeys out of the deep gnome city, but not this day. The little gnome stood in a small chamber, but its dimensions seemed huge to him, for he felt quite vulnerable. He kicked his hard boots about the rocks on the otherwise smooth floor, twiddled his stubby fingers behind his back, and every so often ran a hand over his almost-bald head, wiping away lines of sweat.

A dozen tunnels ran into this chamber, and Firble took some comfort in the knowledge that two score svirfnebli warriors stood ready to rush to his aid, including several shamans with enchanted stones that could summon elemental giants from the plane of earth. Firble understood the drow of Menzoberranzan, forty-five miles to the east of Blingdenstone, better than any of his kin, though, and even his armed escort's presence did not allow him to relax. The gnome councilor knew well that if the dark elves had set this up as an ambush, then all the gnomes and all the magic of Blingdenstone might not be enough.

A familiar clicking sounded from the tunnel directly across the small chamber and, a moment later, in swept Jarlaxle, the extraordinary drow mercenary, his wide-brimmed hat festooned with a giant diatryma feather, his vest cut high to reveal rolling lines of muscles across his abdomen. He strode before the gnome, glanced about a couple of times to take in the whole scene, then dipped into a low bow, brushing his hat across the floor with an outstretched hand.

"My greetings!" Jarlaxle said heartily as he came back upright, crooking his arm above him so that the hat tucked against his elbow. A snap of the arm sent

the hat into a short spin, to land perfectly atop the swaggering mercenary's shaved head.

"High soar your spirits this day," Firble remarked.

"And why not?" the drow asked. "It's another glorious day in the Underdark! A day to be enjoyed."

Firble did not seem convinced, but he was amazed, as always, by the conniving drow's command of the Svirfneblin language. Jarlaxle spoke the tongue as easily and fluidly as any of Blingdenstone's deep gnome inhabitants, though the mercenary used the sentence structure more common to the drow language and not the inverted form favored by many of the gnomes.

"Many svirfneblin mining parties have been assaulted," Firble said, his tone verging on that of an accusation. "Svirfneblin parties working *west* of Blingdenstone."

Jarlaxle smiled coyly and held his hands out wide. "Ched Nasad?" he asked innocently, implicating the next nearest drow city.

"Menzoberranzan!" Firble asserted. Ched Nasad was many tendays away. "One dark elf wore the emblem of a Menzoberranzan house."

"Rogue parties," Jarlaxle reasoned. "Young fighters out for pleasure."

Firble's thin lips almost disappeared with his ensuing scowl. Both he and Jarlaxle knew better than to think that the raiding drow were simple young rowdies. The attacks had been coordinated and executed perfectly, and many svirfnebli had been slain.

"What am I to say?" Jarlaxle asked innocently. "I am but a pawn to the events about me."

Firble snorted.

"I thank you for your confidence in my position," the mercenary said without missing a beat. "But, really, dear Firble, we have been over this before. The events are quite out of my hands this time."

"What events?" Firble demanded. He and Jarlaxle had met twice before over the last two months, discussing this very issue, for the drow activity near the svirfneblin city had increased dramatically. At each meeting Jarlaxle had slyly eluded to some great events, but never had he come out and actually told Firble anything.

"Have we come to banter this same issue?" the mercenary asked wearily. "Really, dear Firble, I grow tired of your—"

"A drow we have captured," Firble interrupted, crossing his short but burly arms over his chest, as though that news should carry some weight.

Jarlaxle's expression turned incredulous and he held his hands out wide again, as if to ask, "So?"

"We believe this drow is a native of Menzoberranzan," Firble went on.

"A female?" Jarlaxle asked, thinking that the gnome, apparently viewing his information as vital, must be referring to a high priestess. The mercenary hadn't heard of any missing high priestesses—except, of course, Jerlys Horlbar, and she wasn't really missing).

"A male," Firble replied, and again the mercenary's expression turned dubious.

"Then execute him," the pragmatic Jarlaxle reasoned.

Firble tightened his arms across his chest and began tap-tapping his foot impatiently on the stone.

"Really, Firble, do you believe that a male drow prisoner gives your city some bargaining power?" the mercenary asked. "Do you expect me to run back to Menzoberranzan, pleading for this one male? Do you expect that the ruling matron mothers will demand that all activity in this area be ceased for his sake?"

"Then you admit sanctioned activity in this area!" the svirfneblin retorted, pointing a stubby finger Jarlaxle's way and thinking he had caught the mercenary in a lie.

"I speak merely hypothetically," Jarlaxle corrected. "I was granting you your presumption so that I might correctly mirror your intentions."

"My intentions you do not know, Jarlaxle," Firble assured. It was clear to Jarlaxle, though, that the gnome was growing agitated by the mercenary's cool demeanor. It was always that way with Jarlaxle. Firble met with the drow only when the situation was critical to Blingdenstone, and often his meetings cost him dearly in precious gems or other treasures.

"Name your price, then," the gnome went on.

"My price?"

"Imperiled is my city," Firble said sharply. "And Jarlaxle knows why!"

The mercenary did not respond. He merely smiled and leaned back from the gnome.

"Jarlaxle knows, too, the name of this drow we have taken," Firble went on, in turn trying to be sly. For the first time, the mercenary revealed, albeit briefly, his intrigue.

Firble really hadn't wanted to take the conversation this far. It was not his intent to reveal the "prisoner's" identity. Drizzt Do'Urden was, after all, a friend of Belwar Dissengulp, the Most Honored Burrow Warden. Drizzt had never proven himself an enemy of Blingdenstone, had even aided the svirfnebli a score of years before, when he first had passed through the city. And by all accounts, the rogue drow had helped svirfnebli again on his

return, out in the tunnels against his drow kin.

Still, Firble's first loyalty was to his own people and his city, and if giving Drizzt's name to Jarlaxle might aid the gnomes in their current predicament, might reveal the imposing events that Jarlaxle kept hinting at, then, to Firble, it would be worth the price.

Jarlaxle paused for a long while, trying to figure out where he should take this suddenly meaningful conversation. He figured that the drow was some rogue male, perhaps a former member of Bregan D'aerthe presumed lost in the outer tunnels. Or maybe the gnomes had bagged a noble from one of the higher-ranking houses, a fine prize indeed. Jarlaxle's ruby eyes gleamed at the thought of the profits such a noble might bring to Bregan D'aerthe.

"Has he a name?" the mercenary asked.

"A name that is known to you, and to us," Firble replied, feeling positively superior—a rare occurrence in his dealings with the crafty mercenary.

His cryptic answer, though, had given more information than intended to Jarlaxle. Few drow were known by name to the gnomes of Blingdenstone, and Jarlaxle could check on the whereabouts of most of those few quite easily. The mercenary's eyes widened suddenly, but he quickly regained his composure, his mind reeling down the path of a new possibility.

"Tell me of the events," Firble demanded. "Why are Menzoberranzan drow near Blingdenstone? Tell me, and to you I shall give the name!"

"Give the name if you choose," Jarlaxle scoffed. "The events? I have already told you to look to Ched Nasad, or to playful young males, students, perhaps, out of the Academy."

Firble hopped up and down, fists clenched in front of him as though he meant to jump over and punch the unpredictable mercenary. All feelings that he had gained the upper hand washed away in the blink of a drow eye.

"Dear Firble," Jarlaxle cooed. "Really, we should not be meeting unless we have more important matters to discuss. And, really, you and your escort should not be so far from home, not in these dark times."

The little svirfneblin let out an unintentional groan of frustration at the mercenary's continued hints that something dire was going on, that the increased drow activity was linked to some greater design.

But Jarlaxle, standing with one arm across his belly, his elbow in his hand and his other hand propping his chin, remained impassive, seeming positively amused by it all. Firble would get no pertinent information this day, he realized, so he gave a curt bow and spun about, kicking stones every step of the way out of the chamber.

The mercenary held his relaxed posture for some time after the gnome had left, then casually lifted one hand and signaled to the tunnel behind him. Out walked a human, though his eyes glowed red with the infravision common to Underdark races, a gift from a high priestess.

"Did you find that amusing?" Jarlaxle asked in the surface tongue.

"And informative," Entreri replied. "When we get back to the city, it should be a minor thing for you to discern the identity of the captured drow."

Jarlaxle regarded the assassin curiously. "Do you not already know it?" he asked.

"I know of no missing nobles," Entreri replied, taking time as he spoke to carefully study the mercenary. Had he missed something? "Certainly, their prisoner must be a noble, since his name was known not only to you, but to the gnomes. A noble or an adventurous drow merchant."

"Suppose I told you that the drow in Blingdenstone was no prisoner," Jarlaxle hinted, a wry smile on his ebon-skinned face.

Entreri stared at him blankly, apparently having no clue as to what the mercenary was talking about.

"Of course," Jarlaxle said a moment later. "You do not know of the past events, so you would have no way of putting the information together. There was once a drow who left Menzoberranzan and stopped, for a time, to live with the gnomes, though I hardly expected that he would return."

"You cannot be hinting that . . ." Entreri said, verily losing his breath.

"Precisely," Jarlaxle replied, turning his gaze to the tunnel through which Firble had disappeared. "It seems that the fly has come to the spiders."

Entreri did not know what to think. Drizzt Do'Urden, back in the Underdark! What did that mean for the planned raid on Mithral Hall? Would the plans be dropped? Would Entreri's last chance to see the surface world be taken from him?

"What are we to do?" he asked the mercenary, his tone hinting at desperation.

"Do?" Jarlaxle echoed. He leaned back and gave a hearty laugh.

"Do?" the drow asked again, as though the thought was absurd. "Why, we sit back and enjoy it, of course!"

His response was not totally unexpected to Entreri, not when the assassin took a moment to consider it. Jarlaxle was a lover of ironies—that was why he thrived in the world of the chaotic drow—and this unexpected turn certainly qualified. To Jarlaxle, life was a game, to be played and enjoyed without consideration for consequences or morality.

In other times, Entreri could empathize with that attitude, had even adopted it on occasion, but not now. Too much hung in the balance for

Artemis Entreri, for the poor, miserable assassin. Drizzt's presence so near Menzoberranzan raised important questions for the assassin's future, a future that looked bleak indeed.

Jarlaxle laughed again, long and hard. Entreri stood solemnly, staring at the tunnel that led generally toward the gnome city, his mind staring into the face, the violet eyes, of his most hated enemy.

⚔ ⚔ ⚔ ⚔ ⚔

Drizzt took great comfort in the familiar surroundings about him. He almost felt that he must be dreaming, for the small stone dwelling was exactly as he remembered it, right down to the hammock in which he now found himself.

But Drizzt knew that this was no dream, knew it from the fact that he could feel nothing from his waist down, neither the hammock's cords nor even a tingle in his bare feet.

"Awake?" came a question from the dwelling's second, smaller, chamber. The word struck Drizzt profoundly, for it was spoken in the Svirfneblin tongue, that curious blend of elven melodies and crackling dwarven consonants. Svirfneblin words rushed back to Drizzt's thoughts, though he had neither heard nor spoken the language in more than twenty years. It took some effort for Drizzt to turn his head and see the approaching burrow warden.

The drow's heart skipped a few beats at the sight.

Belwar had aged a bit but still seemed sturdy. He banged his "hands" together when he realized that Drizzt, his long-ago friend, was indeed awake.

Drizzt was pleased to see those hands, works of metallic art, capping the gnome's arms. Drizzt's own brother had cut off Belwar's hands when Drizzt and Belwar had first met. There had been a battle between the deep gnomes and a party of drow, and, at first, Drizzt had been Belwar's prisoner. Dinin came fast to Drizzt's aid, though, and the positions were quickly reversed.

Dinin would have killed Belwar had it not been for Drizzt. But Drizzt wasn't sure how much his attempt to save the svirfneblin's life had been worth, for Dinin had ordered Belwar crippled. In the brutal Underdark, crippled creatures usually did not survive long.

When Drizzt had met Belwar again, when he had come into Blingdenstone as a refugee from Menzoberranzan, he had found that the svirfnebli, so unlike the drow, had come to their wounded friend's aid, crafting him apropos caps for his stubby arms. On the right arm, the Most Honored Burrow Warden—as the deep gnomes called Belwar—wore a mithral hammerhead etched with marvelous runes and sketchings of powerful creatures, including an earth elemental. The double-headed pickaxe Belwar wore on his left arm was no less spectacular. These were formidable tools for digging and fighting, and more formidable still, for the svirfneblin shamans had enchanted the "hands." Drizzt had seen Belwar burrow through solid stone as fast as a mole through soft dirt.

It was so good to see that Belwar had continued to thrive, that Drizzt's first non-drow friend, Drizzt's first true friend, other than Zaknafein, was well.

"Magga cammara, elf," the svirfneblin remarked with a chuckle as he walked past the hammock. "I thought you would never wake up!"

Magga cammara, Drizzt's mind echoed, "by the stones." The curious phrase, one that Drizzt had not heard in twenty years, put the drow at ease, brought his thoughts cascading back to the peaceful time he had spent as Belwar's guest in Blingdenstone.

He came out of his personal thoughts and noticed that the svirfneblin was at his feet, studying his posture.

"How do they feel?" Belwar asked.

"They do not," Drizzt replied.

The gnome nodded his hairless head and brought his pickaxe up to scratch at his huge nose. "You got nookered," he remarked.

Drizzt did not reply, obviously not understanding.

"Nookered," Belwar said again, moving to a cabinet bolted to the wall. He hooked the door with his pickaxe and swung it open, then used both hands to tentatively grasp some item inside and take it out for Drizzt to see. "A newly designed weapon," Belwar explained. "Been around for only a few years."

Drizzt thought that the item resembled a beaver's tail, with a short handle for grasping on the narrow end and with the wide end curled over at a sharp angle. It was smooth all about, with the notable exception of one serrated edge.

"A nooker," Belwar said, holding it up high. It slipped from his tentative grasp and dropped to the floor.

Belwar shrugged and clapped his mithral hands together. "A good thing it is that I have my own weapons!" Belwar banged the hammer and pickaxe together a second time.

"Lucky you are, Drizzt Do'Urden," he went on, "that the svirfnebli in battle recognized you for a friend."

Drizzt snorted; he didn't, at that moment, feel very lucky.

"He could have hit you with the sharp edge," Belwar went on. "Cut your backbone in half, it would have!"

"My backbone feels as if it *has* been cut in half," Drizzt remarked.

"No, no," Belwar said, walking back to the bottom of the hammock, "just nookered." The gnome poked his pickaxe hard against the bottom of Drizzt's foot, and the drow winced and shifted. "See, coming back already is the feeling," Belwar declared, and, smiling mischievously, he prodded Drizzt again.

"I will walk again, Burrow Warden," the relieved drow promised, his tone threatening so that he could play along with the game.

Belwar poked him again. "A while will that be!" he laughed. "And soon you will feel a tickle as well!"

It seemed like old times to Drizzt; it seemed like the very pressing problems that had burdened his shoulders had been temporarily lifted. How good it was to see his old friend again, this gnome who had gone out with him, out of loyalty alone, into the wilds of the Underdark, who had been captured beside Drizzt by the dreaded mind flayers and had fought his way out beside Drizzt.

"It was a coincidence, fortunate for both me and your fellows in the tunnels, that I happened into the area when I did," Drizzt said.

"Not so much a chance of fate," Belwar replied, and a grim demeanor clouded his cheerful expression. "The fights have become too common. One a tenday, at least, and many svirfnebli have died."

Drizzt closed his lavender eyes and tried to digest the unwelcome news.

"Lolth is hungry, so it is said," Belwar went on, "and life has not been good for the gnomes of Blingdenstone. The cause of it all we are trying to learn."

Drizzt took it all in stride, feeling then, more than ever before, that he had done right in returning. More was happening than a simple drow attempt to recapture him. Belwar's description, the assertion that Lolth was hungry, seemed on the mark.

Drizzt got prodded again, hard, and he popped open his eyes to see the smiling burrow warden staring down at him, the cloud of recent events apparently passed. "But enough of the darkness!" Belwar declared. "Twenty years we have to recall, you for me and me for you!" He reached down and hooked one of Drizzt's boots, lifting it up and sniffing at the sole. "You found the surface?" he asked, sincerely hopeful.

The two friends spent the rest of that day trading tales, with Drizzt, who had gone into so different a world, doing most of the talking. Many times Belwar gasped and laughed; once he shared tears with his drow friend, seeming sincerely hurt by the loss of Wulfgar.

Drizzt knew at that moment that he had rediscovered another of his dearest friends. Belwar listened intently, with caring, to Drizzt's every word, let him share the most personal moments of his last twenty years with the silent support of a true friend.

After they dined that night, Drizzt took his first tentative steps, and Belwar, who had seen the debilitating effects of a well-wielded nooker before, assured the drow that he would be running along rubble-filled walls again in a day or so.

That news came as a mixed blessing. Drizzt was glad that he would heal, of course, but a small part of him wished that the process would take longer, that he might extend his visit with Belwar. For Drizzt knew that, the moment his body was able, the time would be at hand for him to finish his journey, to return to Menzoberranzan and try to end the threat.

14

DISGUISE

W ait here, Guen," Catti-brie whispered to the panther, both of whom stared at the wider area, a chamber relatively clear of stalagmites, that loomed up ahead. Many goblin voices came from that chamber. Catti-brie guessed that this was the main host, probably growing nervous since their scouting party hadn't returned. Those few surviving goblins were likely coming fast behind her, the young woman knew. She and Guen had done a fine job in prodding them on their way, had sent them running in the opposite direction down the corridor, but they likely had already turned about. And that fight had occurred less than an hour's hike from this spot.

There was no other apparent way around the chamber, and Catti-brie understood without even seeing the goblin horde that there were simply too many of the wretches to fight or scare off. She looked down to her ebon-skinned hands one last time, took some comfort in their accurate drow appearance, then straightened her thick hair—showing stark white now instead of its normal auburn—and plush robes, and defiantly strode forward.

The closest goblin sentries fell back in terror as the drow priestess casually entered their lair. Numbers alone kept the group from running off altogether, for, as Catti-brie had guessed, more than a hundred goblins were camped here. A dozen spears came up, angled in her direction, but she continued to walk steadily toward the center of the cavern.

Goblins gathered all around the young woman, cutting off any retreat. Others crouched facing the tunnel from which Catti-brie had emerged, not knowing if other drow would come strolling through. Still, the sea of flesh parted before the unexpected visitor; Catti-brie's bravado and disguise had apparently put the creatures off their collective guard.

She reached the chamber's halfway point, could see the corridor continuing on across the way, but the sea closed around her, giving ground more slowly and forcing the woman-turned-drow to slow her pace as well.

Then she was stopped, goblin spears pointing her way from every direction, goblin whispers filling the room. *"Gund ha, moga moga,"* she demanded. Her command of the Goblin tongue was rudimentary at best, and she wasn't quite sure if she had said, "move aside and let me pass," or "move my mother into the ditch."

She hoped it was the former.

"Moga gund, geek-ik moon'ga'woon'ga!" rasped one huge goblin, nearly as large as a man, and it shifted through the horde to stand right before Catti-brie. The young woman forced herself to remain calm, but a large part of her wanted to cry out for Guenhwyvar and run away, and a smaller part wanted to break out in laughter. This was obviously the goblin leader, or the tribe's shaman, at least.

But the creature needed a few fashion tips. It wore high black boots, like those of a nobleman, but with the sides cut out to allow for its wide, duck-like feet. A pair of women's pantaloons, ringed with wide frills, served as its breeches, and, though it was obviously male, the beast wore a woman's underpants and corset, as well, complete with cups for very ample breasts. Several mismatched necklaces, some gold, some silver, and one strand of pearls, circled its skinny neck, and a gaudy ring adorned every crooked finger. Catti-brie recognized the goblin's headdress as religious, though she wasn't quite certain of the sect. It resembled a sunburst trimmed with long gold ribbons, but Catti-brie was fairly sure that the goblin had it on backward, for it leaned forward over the ugly creature's sloping brow, one ribbon dangling annoyingly before the goblin's nose.

No doubt, the goblin thought itself the height of thieving fashion, dressed in the clothing of its tribe's unfortunate victims. It continued to ramble in its high-pitched voice, too fast for Catti-brie to make out more than a single word here or there. Then the creature stopped, abruptly, and pounded a fist against its chest.

"Do ye speak the surface tongue?" Catti-brie asked, trying to find some common ground. She fought hard to hold her nerve, but expected a spear to plunge into her back at any moment.

The goblin leader regarded her curiously, apparently not understanding a word she had said. It scanned the woman up and down, its red-glowing eyes finally coming to rest on the locket that hung about Catti-brie's neck. *"Nying*

so, wucka," it remarked, and it pointed to the locket, then to Catti-brie, then swept its hand about to indicate the far exit.

Had the locket been a normal piece of jewelry, Catti-brie willingly would have given it over in exchange for passage, but she needed the magic item if she was to have any chance of locating Drizzt. The goblin repeated its demand, its tone more urgent, and the young woman knew that she had to think fast.

On sudden inspiration, she smiled and stuck an upraised finger before her. *"Nying,"* she said, thinking that to be the goblin word for "gift." She clapped her hands sharply twice before her and called out, "Guenhwyvar!" without looking back over her shoulder.

A startled cry from the goblins at the back end of the chamber told her that the panther was on its way.

"Come in with calm, Guen," Catti-brie called. "Walk to me side without a fight."

The panther stalked slowly and steadily, head down and ears flattened. Every so often, Guenhwyvar let out a low growl, just to keep the closest goblins on their heels. The crowd parted widely, giving the magnificent cat a large open path to the drow priestess.

Then Guenhwyvar was at Catti-brie's side, nuzzling the woman's hip.

"Nying," Catti-brie said again, pointing from the panther to the goblin. "Ye take the cat and I walk out the passage," she added, motioning as best she could with her hands to convey the message. The ugly goblin fashion king scratched its head, shifting the headpiece awkwardly to the side.

"Well, go over and make nice," Catti-brie whispered to Guenhwyvar. She pushed the cat away with her leg. The panther looked up to her, seemed more than a little annoyed by it all, then padded over to the goblin leader and plopped down at its feet—and the blood drained from the monster's face!).

"Nying," Catti-brie said again, motioning that the goblin should reach down and pet the cat. The creature eyed her incredulously, but gradually, with her coaxing, the goblin mustered the nerve to touch the cat's thick fur.

The goblin's pointy-toothed smile widened, and it dared to touch the cat again, more solidly. Again it dipped, and again, and each stroke went more firmly over the panther's back. Through it all, Guenhwyvar leveled a withering stare at Catti-brie.

"Now, ye're to stay here with this friendly goblin," Catti-brie instructed the cat, making sure that her tones did not give away her true meaning. She patted her belt pouch, the one holding the figurine, and added, "I'll be calling ye, don't ye doubt."

Then Catti-brie straightened and faced the goblin leader squarely. She slapped a hand against her chest, then snapped it straight out and pointed to the far exit, her expression a scowl. "I go!" she declared and took a step forward.

At first, the goblin leader seemed as though it would move to hinder her, but a quick glance to the powerful cat at its feet changed the creature's mind. Catti-brie had played the game perfectly; she had allowed the overly proud goblin leader to retain its dignity, had kept herself appearing as a potentially dangerous enemy, and had strategically placed six hundred pounds of fighting ally right at the goblin leader's feet.

"Nying so, wucka," the goblin said again, pointing to Guenhwyvar, then to the far exit, and it gingerly stepped aside so that the drow could pass.

Catti-brie swept across the rest of the chamber, backhand slapping one goblin that didn't get far enough out of her path. The creature came right back at her, sword raised, but Catti-brie didn't flinch, and a cry from the goblin leader, still with the panther curled about its ankles, stopped the goblin's response.

Catti-brie laughed in its ugly face, showed it that she held her own dagger, a magnificent, jeweled thing, ready under the folds of her beautiful robes.

She made it to the narrower tunnel and continued walking slowly for many steps. Then she stopped, glanced back, and pulled out the panther figurine.

Back in the chamber, the goblin leader was showing off its new acquisition to the tribe, explaining how it had outsmarted a "stupid drow female thing," and had taken the cat as its own. It didn't matter that the other goblins had witnessed the whole affair; in goblin culture, history was recreated almost daily.

The leader's smug smile waned quickly when a gray mist rose up about the panther, and the cat's material form began to melt away.

The goblin wailed a stream of protests and curses and dropped to its knees to grab the fast-fading cat.

A huge paw shot out of the mist, hooked around the leader's head, and yanked the wretch in. Then there was only mist, the surprised and not-too-smart goblin leader going along with the panther on a ride to the Astral Plane.

The remaining goblins hooted and ran all about, bumping into and falling over each other. Some thought to take up the chase for the departing drow, but by the time they began to organize, Catti-brie was long gone, running with all speed along the corridor and thinking herself positively clever.

⚔ ⚔ ⚔ ⚔ ⚔

The tunnels were familiar to him—too familiar. How many times had young Drizzt Do'Urden traveled these ways, usually serving as the point in a drow patrol? Then he had Guenhwyvar with him; now he was alone.

He limped slightly, one of his knees still a bit weak from the svirfneblin nooker.

He couldn't use that as an excuse to remain in Blingdenstone any longer, though. He knew that his business was pressing, and Belwar, though the parting stung the burrow warden, had not argued with Drizzt's decision to be on his way, an indication to Drizzt that the other svirfnebli wished him gone.

That had been two days ago, two days and about fifty miles of winding caverns. Drizzt had crossed the trails of at least three drow patrols on his way, an unusually high number of warriors to be out so far from Menzoberranzan, and that led credence to Belwar's claim that something dangerous was brewing, that the Spider Queen was hungry. On all three of those occasions, Drizzt could have tracked down the drow group and attempted to link up. He thought of concocting some story that he was an emissary from a merchant of Ched Nasad. All three times, Drizzt had lost his nerve, had kept moving instead toward Menzoberranzan, putting off that fateful moment when he would make contact.

Now the tunnels were too familiar, and that moment was nearly upon him.

He measured every step, maintaining perfect silence, as he crossed into one wider way. He heard some noise up ahead, a shuffle of many feet. Not drow feet, he knew; dark elves made no noise.

The ranger scaled the uneven wall and moved along a ledge half a dozen feet up from the main floor. Sometimes he found himself grasping with fingertips and pulling himself forward, his feet dangling, but Drizzt was not hindered, and he did not make a sound.

He froze in place at the din of more movement ahead. Fortunately, the ledge widened once more, freeing his hands, and he gingerly slipped his scimitars free of their sheaths, concentrating to keep Twinkle from flaring with inner light.

Slurping sounds led him around a bend, where he viewed a host of short, huddled humanoids, wearing ragged cloaks with cowls pulled over their faces. They spoke not at all, but milled about aimlessly, and only their floppy feet showed Drizzt that they were goblins.

Goblin slaves, he knew by their movements, by their slumped posture, for only slaves carried such a weight of broken resignation.

Drizzt continued to watch silently for a while, trying to spot the herding drow. There were at least four score goblins in this cavern, lining the edge of a small pond that the drow called Heldaeyn's Pool, scooping water up under their low-pulled cowls as though they had not drunk in many days.

They probably had not. Drizzt spotted a couple of rothé, small Underdark cattle, milling nearby, and he realized that this group probably was out of the city in search of the missing creatures. On such trips, slaves were given little or nothing to eat, though they carried quite a bit of supplies. The accompanying drow guards, though, ate handsomely, usually right in front of their starving slaves.

The crack of a whip brought the goblins back to their feet and shuffling back from the pool's edge. Two drow soldiers, one male, one female, came into Drizzt's view. They talked casually, the female every so often cracking her whip.

Another drow called out some commands from the other side of the cavern, and the goblins began to fall into a rough line, more of an elongated huddle than any organized formation.

Drizzt knew that the most opportune moment was upon him. Slavers were among the least organized and least regimented of Menzoberranzan's extracity bands. Any slaver contingent usually comprised dark elves from several different houses and a complement of young drow students from each of the Academy's three schools.

Drizzt quietly slipped down from the ledge and walked around the jutting wall, flashing the customary hand signal greetings—though his fingers felt awkward going through the intricate routine—to the drow in the cavern.

The female pushed her male escort forward and stepped to the side behind him. Immediately the male's hand came up, holding one of the typical drow hand-crossbows, its dart coated, most likely, with a powerful sleeping potion.

Who are you? the female's hand asked over the male's shoulder.

"All that is left of a patrol group that ventured near Blingdenstone," Drizzt answered.

"You should go in near Tier Breche, then," the female answered aloud. Hearing her voice, so typical of drow females, voices that could be incredibly melodic or incredibly shrill, sent Drizzt's thoughts cascading back to those long years past. He realized then, fully, that he was just a few hundred yards from Menzoberranzan.

"I do not wish to 'go in' at all," Drizzt answered. "At least, not announced." The reasoning made perfect sense, Drizzt knew. If he had indeed been the only survivor of a lost patrol, he would have been vigorously interrogated at

the drow Academy, probably even tortured until the masters were certain that he played no treacherous role in the patrol's fate, or until he died, whichever came first.

"Who is the first house?" the female asked, her eyes locked on Drizzt's lavender-glowing orbs.

"Baenre," Drizzt answered immediately, expecting the test. Spying dark elves from rival cities were not unknown in Menzoberranzan.

"Their youngest son?" the female asked slyly. She curled her lips up in a lewd and hungry smile, Drizzt realized as she continued to stare deeply into his unusual eyes.

By fortunate coincidence, Drizzt had attended the Academy in the same class as House Baenre's youngest son—as long as ancient Matron Baenre had not reared another child in the three decades Drizzt had been gone.

"Berg'inyon," he answered confidently, dropping his hands in a cocky cross at his belt—and putting them near his scimitars).

"Who are you?" the female asked again, and she licked her lips, obviously intrigued.

"No one who matters," Drizzt replied, and he matched her smile and the intensity of her stare.

The female patted her blocking male on the shoulder and her fingers motioned for him to go.

Am I to be off this miserable duty? he responded with his hands, a hopeful expression on his face.

"The *bol* will take your place this day," the female purred, labeling Drizzt with the drow word that described something mysterious or intriguing.

The male smiled widely and moved to put his hand-crossbow away. Noticing that it was cocked and ready, and looking up to take note that a whole herd of goblins stood nearby, he widened his smile instead and lifted the weapon to fire.

Drizzt offered no reaction, though it pained him to see even goblins treated so miserably.

"No," the female said, putting her hand over the male's wrist. She reached up and removed the dart from the hand-crossbow, then replaced it with another. "Yours would put the creature to sleep," she explained, and she cackled in laughter.

The male considered her for just a moment, then apparently caught on. He took aim at a goblin loitering near the water's edge and fired. The goblin jerked as the small dart jabbed into its back. It started to turn about, but toppled instead, into the pool.

Drizzt gnawed at his lips, understanding, by the goblin's futile flopping, that the dart the female had supplied was coated with a paralyzing potion, one that left the doomed creature fully conscious. The goblin had little control of its limbs and would surely drown, and, worse, it would know its cruel fate. It managed to arch its back enough so that its face came above the water level, but Drizzt knew that it would tire long before the wicked potion expired.

The male laughed heartily, replaced the hand-crossbow in its small holster, which lay diagonally across its lower chest, and walked off down the tunnel to Drizzt's left. Before he had gone even a dozen steps, the female began cracking her whip and called for the few drow guards to get the caravan moving, down the tunnel to the right.

After a moment, she turned a cold glare on Drizzt. "Why are you standing there?" she demanded.

Drizzt pointed to the goblin in the pool, floundering badly now, barely able to keep its mouth out of the water. He managed a laugh, as if he was enjoying the macabre spectacle, but he seriously considered rushing over and cutting the evil female down at that moment.

All the way out of the small cavern, Drizzt looked for opportunities to get over to the goblin, to pull the creature out of the water so that it would have a chance to get away. The female drow never stopped eyeing him, though, not for an instant, and Drizzt understood that she had more on her mind than simply including him in the slave caravan. After all, why hadn't *she* taken the break when the new slaver unexpectedly arrived?

The dying goblin's last splashes followed Drizzt out of that place. The renegade drow swallowed hard and fought away his revulsion. No matter how many times he witnessed it, he would never get used to the brutality of his kin.

And Drizzt was glad of that.

MASKS

Catti-brie had never seen such creatures. They somewhat resembled gnomes, at least in stature, being about three feet tall, but they had no hair on their lumpy, ruddy heads, and their skin, in the starlight afforded her by the magical circlet, showed grayish. They were quite stout, nearly as muscular as dwarves, and judging from the fine tools they carried and the well-fitting metal armor they wore, they were, like dwarves, adept at mining and crafting.

Drizzt had told Catti-brie of the svirfnebli, the deep gnomes, and that is what she presumed she was looking upon. She couldn't be sure, though, and was afraid that this might be some offshoot of the evil duergar, gray dwarves.

She crouched amid a cluster of tall, thin stalagmites in an area of many crisscrossing corridors. The deep gnomes, if that's what they were, had come down the opposite way, and were now milling about one wide, flat section of corridor, talking among themselves and paying little heed of the stalagmite cluster twenty feet away.

Catti-brie was not sure of how she should proceed. If these were svirfnebli, and she was fairly sure of that, they could prove to be valuable allies, but how might she approach them? They certainly did not speak the same language and probably were as unfamiliar with humans as she was with them.

She decided that her best course would be simply to sit tight and let the creatures pass. Catti-brie had never experienced the strangeness of infravision, though, and she did not fully appreciate that, sitting among the cool stalagmites, her body temperature fully thirty degrees warmer than the stone, she was practically glowing to the svirfnebli's heat-seeing eyes.

Even as the young woman crouched and waited, deep gnomes fanned out in the tunnels around her, trying to discern if this drow—for Catti-brie still wore the magical mask—was alone or part of a larger band. A few minutes slipped by; Catti-brie looked down to her hand, thinking that she felt something in the stone, a slight vibration, perhaps. The young woman continued to stare at her tingling hand curiously. She did not know that deep gnomes communicated in a method that was part telepathy and part psychokinesis, sending their thought patterns to each other through the stone, and that a sensitive hand could sense the vibrations.

She did not know that the minute tingling was the confirmation from the deep gnome scouts that this drow crouching in the stalagmite cluster was indeed alone.

One of the svirfnebli ahead suddenly burst into motion, chanting a few words that Catti-brie did not understand and hurling a rock her way. She dipped lower behind the stones for cover and tried to decide whether to call out a surrender or take out her bow and try to frighten the creatures away.

The stone bounced harmlessly short and shattered, its flecks spreading in a small area before the stalagmite cluster. Those flecks began to smoke and sizzle, and the ground began to tremble.

Before Catti-brie knew what was happening, the stones before her rose up like a gigantic bubble, then took on the shape of a giant fifteen-foot-tall humanoid, its girth practically filling the corridor. The creature had huge, rocky arms that could smash a building to pieces. Two of the front stalagmites had been caught up in the monstrous formation and now served as dangerous spikes protruding from the front of the monster's massive chest.

Down the passage, the deep gnomes let out battle cries—calls that echoed in corridors all about the frightened woman.

Catti-brie scrambled backward as a gigantic hand swooped in and took the top from one stalagmite. She dropped the onyx figuring and called frantically for Guenhwyvar, all the while fitting an arrow to her bowstring.

The earth elemental shifted forward, its bulky legs melding with, slipping right through, the stony stalagmites in its way. It moved again to grab the woman, but a silver-streaking arrow ripped through its rock face, blowing a clean crevice between the monster's eyes.

The elemental straightened and reeled, then used its hands to push its halved head back into one piece. It looked back to the cluster and saw not the female drow, but a huge cat, tamping down its hind legs.

Catti-brie came out the back of the cluster, thinking to flee, but found deep gnomes coming down every side passage. She ran along the main

corridor, cutting from mound to mound for cover, not daring to glance back at Guenhwyvar and the elemental. Then something hard banged against her shin, tripping her, and she sprawled headlong. She squirmed about to see another of the svirfnebli rising from behind one mound, a pickaxe still angled out as it had been placed to trip her.

Catti-brie pulled her bow around and shifted into a sitting position, but the weapon was batted away. She instinctively rolled to the side, but heard shuffling feet as three gnomes kept pace with her, heavy mauls lifted high to squash her.

Guenhwyvar snarled and soared, thinking to fly right past the behemoth and turn it about. The elemental was faster than the panther suspected, though, and a great rocky hand shot out, catching the cat in midflight and pulling it to its massive chest. Guenhwyvar shrieked as a stalagmite spike dug into a shoulder, and the deep gnomes, running up beside their champion, shrieked as well, in glee that the drow and her unexpected ally were apparently soon to be finished.

A maul descended toward Catti-brie's head. She snapped out her short sword and caught it at the joint between handle and head, deflecting it enough so that it banged loudly off the floor. The young woman scampered and parried, trying to get far enough from the gnomes to regain her footing, but they paced her, every which way, banging their mauls with shortened, measured strokes so that this fast-tiring dark elf had no opportunities for clear counterstrikes.

The sight of the marvelous panther, soon to be fully impaled and crushed, brought victorious thrills to a handful of the trailing svirfnebli, but brought only confusion to two others. Those two, Seldig and Pumkato by name, had played with such a panther as fledglings, and since Drizzt Do'Urden, the drow renegade they had played beside almost thirty years before, had just passed through Blingdenstone, they felt the panther's appearance could not be coincidence.

"Guenhwyvar!" Seldig cried, and the panther roared in reply.

The name, so perfectly spoken, struck Catti-brie profoundly and made those three deep gnomes about her hesitate as well.

Pumkato, who had summoned the elemental in the first place, called for the monster to hold steady, and Seldig quickly used his pickaxe to scale partway up the behemoth. "Guenhwyvar?" he asked, just a few feet from the panther's face. The trapped cat's ears came up, and it put a plaintive look on the somewhat familiar gnome.

"Who is that?" Pumkato demanded, pointing to Catti-brie.

Though she did not understand any of the svirfneblin's words, Catti-brie realized that she would never find a better opportunity. She dropped her sword to the stone, reached up with her free hand and pulled off the magical mask, her features immediately reverting to those of a young human woman. The three deep gnomes near her cried out and fell back, regarding her with less-than-complimentary sour expressions, as though her new appearance was quite ugly by their standards.

Pumkato mustered the courage to shuffle over to her, and he stood right in front of her.

He had known one name, Catti-brie realized, and she hoped that he would recognize another. She pointed to herself, then held her arms out wide and pulled them in as if hugging someone. "Drizzt Do'Urden?" she asked.

Pumkato's gray eyes widened, then he nodded, as though he should not have been surprised. Hiding his disgust at the human's appearance, the gnome extended one hand and helped Catti-brie to her feet.

Catti-brie moved slowly, obviously, as she took out the figurine and dismissed Guenhwyvar. Pumkato, likewise, sent his elemental back into the stone.

✕ ✕ ✕ ✕ ✕

"Kolsen'shea orbb," Jarlaxle whispered, an arcane phrase rarely uttered in Menzoberranzan that roughly translated to "pull the legs off a spider."

The seemingly plain wall before the mercenary reacted to the passwords. It shifted and twisted into a spiderweb, then rotated outward, its strands tucked together, to leave a hole for the mercenary and his human escort to climb through.

Even Jarlaxle, usually one step ahead of other drow, was somewhat surprised—pleasantly surprised—to find Triel Baenre waiting for him in the small office beyond, the private chambers of Gromph Baenre at Sorcere, the school of magic in the drow Academy. Jarlaxle had hoped that Gromph would be about, to witness the return, but Triel was an even better witness.

Entreri came in behind the mercenary and wisely stayed behind at the sight of volatile Triel. The assassin eyed the intriguing room, perpetually bathed in soft-glowing bluish light, as was most of the wizards' tower. Parchments lay everywhere, on the desk, on the three chairs, and on the floor. The walls were lined with shelves that held dozens of large, capped bottles and smaller, hourglass-shaped containers, their tops off and with sealed packets lying next to them. A hundred other curious items, too strange for the surface dweller to even guess at what they might do, lay amid the jumble.

"You bring *colnbluth* to Sorcere?" Triel remarked, her thin eyebrows angling up in surprise.

Entreri took care to keep his gaze to the floor, though he managed a few peeks at the Baenre daughter. He hadn't viewed Triel in so strong a light before, and he thought now that she was not so beautiful by drow standards. She was too short and too stocky in the shoulders for her very angular facial features. It struck the assassin as odd that Triel had risen so high among the ranks of drow, a race that treasured physical beauty. Her station was testament to the Baenre daughter's power, he decided.

Entreri couldn't understand very much of the drow tongue, though he realized that Triel probably had just insulted him. Normally, the assassin responded to insults with weapons, but not here, not so far from his element and not against this one. Jarlaxle had warned Entreri about Triel a hundred times. She was looking for a reason to kill him—the vicious Baenre daughter was always looking for a reason to kill any *colnbluth,* and quite a few drow as well.

"I bring him many places," Jarlaxle answered. "I did not think that your brother would be here to protest."

Triel looked about the room, to the fabulous desk of polished dwarf bones and the cushioned chair behind. There were no connecting rooms, no obvious hiding places, and no Gromph.

"Gromph must be here," Jarlaxle reasoned. "Else, why would the matron mistress of Arach-Tinilith be in this place? That is a violation of the rules, as I remember them, as serious a breach, at least, as my bringing a non-drow to Sorcere."

"Take care how you question the actions of Triel Baenre," the short priestess replied.

"Asanque," Jarlaxle answered with a sweeping bow. It was a somewhat ambiguous word that could mean either "as you wish," or "likewise."

"Why are you here?" Triel demanded.

"You knew I was coming," Jarlaxle stated.

"Of course," Triel said slyly. "I know many things, but I wish to hear your explanation for entering Sorcere, through private doors reserved for headmasters, and into the private quarters of the city's archmage."

Jarlaxle reached into the folds of his black cloak and produced the strange spider mask, the magical item that had gotten him over House Baenre's enchanted web fence. Triel's ruby-red eyes widened.

"I was instructed by your mother to return this to Gromph," the mercenary said, somewhat sourly.

"Here?" Triel balked. "The mask belongs at House Baenre."

Jarlaxle couldn't hide a bit of a smile, and he looked to Entreri, secretly hoping that the assassin was getting some of this conversation.

"Gromph will retrieve it," Jarlaxle answered. He walked over to the dwarf bone desk, uttered a word under his breath, and quickly slipped the mask into a drawer, though Triel had begun to protest. She stalked over to the desk and eyed the closed drawer suspiciously. Obviously Gromph would have trapped and warded it with a secret password.

"Open it," she instructed Jarlaxle. "I will hold the mask for Gromph."

"I cannot," Jarlaxle lied. "The password changes with each use. I was given only one." Jarlaxle knew that he was playing a dangerous game here, but Triel and Gromph rarely spoke to each other, and Gromph, especially in these days, with all the preparations going on in House Baenre, rarely visited his office at Sorcere. What Jarlaxle needed now was to be rid of the mask—openly, so that it could not be tied to him in any way. That spider mask was the only item, spells included, in all of Menzoberranzan that could get someone past House Baenre's magical fence, and if events took the turns that Jarlaxle suspected, that mask might soon be an important piece of property—and evidence.

Triel chanted softly and continued to stare at the closed drawer. She recognized the intricate patterns of magical energy, glyphs and wards, on the drawer, but they were woven too tightly for her to easily unravel. Her magic was among the strongest in Menzoberranzan, but Triel feared to try her hand against her brother's wizardly prowess. Dropping a threatening gaze at the cunning mercenary, she walked back across the room and stood near Entreri.

"Look at me," she said in the common tongue of the surface, which surprised the assassin, for very few drow in Menzoberranzan spoke the language.

Entreri lifted his gaze to peer into Triel's intense eyes. He tried to keep his demeanor calm, tried to appear subjugated, broken in spirit, but Triel was too perceptive for such facades. She saw the strength in the assassin, smiled as though she approved of it.

"What do you know of all this?" she asked.

"I know only what Jarlaxle tells me," Entreri replied, and he dropped the facade and stared hard at Triel. If she wished a contest of wills, then the assassin, who had survived and thrived on the most dangerous streets of Faerûn's surface, would not back down.

Triel matched the unblinking stare for a long while and became convinced that she would garner little of use from this skilled adversary. "Be gone from here," she said to Jarlaxle, still using the surface tongue.

Jarlaxle rushed past the Baenre daughter and scooped up Entreri in his wake. "Quickly," the mercenary remarked. "We should be long out of Sorcere before Triel tries that drawer!" With that, they were through the spidery door, which fast reverted to a plain wall behind them, blocking Triel's inevitable curses.

But the Baenre daughter was not as mad as she was intrigued. She recognized three courses coming together here, her own and her mother's, and now, apparently, Jarlaxle's. The mercenary was up to something, she knew, something that obviously included Artemis Entreri.

When they were safely away from Tier Breche and the Academy, Jarlaxle translated all that had transpired to Entreri.

"You did not tell her of Drizzt's impending arrival," the assassin remarked. He had thought that important bit of information to be the gist of Jarlaxle's brief conversation with Triel, but the mercenary said nothing about it now.

"Triel has her own ways of discerning information," Jarlaxle replied. "I do not wish to make her work easier—not without a clear and agreed upon profit!"

Entreri smiled, then bit his lower lip, digesting the mercenary's words. There was always so much going on in this infernal city, the assassin mused. It was no wonder that Jarlaxle enjoyed the place so! Entreri almost wished that he was a drow, that he could carve out a place such as Jarlaxle had done, playing on the edge of disaster. Almost.

"When did Matron Baenre instruct you to return the mask?" the assassin asked. He and Jarlaxle had been out of Menzoberranzan for some time, had gone into the outer caverns to meet with a svirfneblin informant. They had returned only a short time before their trip to Sorcere, and Jarlaxle, as far as Entreri knew, hadn't gone anywhere near House Baenre.

"Some time ago," Jarlaxle replied.

"To bring it to the Academy?" Entreri pressed. It seemed out of place to him. And why had Jarlaxle taken him along? He had never been invited to that high place before, had even been refused on one occasion, when he had asked to accompany Jarlaxle to Melee-Magthere, the school of fighters. The mercenary had explained that taking a *colnbluth,* a non-drow, there would be risky, but now, for some reason, Jarlaxle had thought it appropriate to take Entreri to Sorcere, by far the more dangerous school.

"She did not specify where the mask was to be returned," Jarlaxle admitted.

Entreri did not respond, though he realized the truth of that answer. The spider mask was a prized possession of the Baenre clan, a potential weak spot in its hardened defenses. It belonged in the secured quarters of House Baenre and nowhere else.

"Foolish Triel," Jarlaxle remarked offhandedly. "The same word, *asanque,* would get her into that drawer. She should know that her brother was arrogant enough to believe that none would ever try to steal from him, and so he would not spend too much time with password tricks."

The mercenary laughed, and Entreri followed suit, though he was more intrigued than amused. Jarlaxle rarely did or said anything without purpose, and the mercenary had told him all of this for a reason.

But why?

16

MENZOBERRANZAN

The raft slid slowly across Donigarten, the small, dark lake on the eastern end of the great cavern that housed Menzoberranzan. Drizzt sat on the prow of the craft, looking west as the cavern opened wide before him, though, with his infravision, the image seemed strangely blurred. Drizzt initially attributed it to the lake's warm currents and gave it little thought. He was preoccupied, his mind looking as much in the past as in the present, reeling with stirring memories.

The rhythmic moaning of the orcan paddlers behind him allowed him to find a calmness, to flow his memories one at a time.

The drow ranger closed his eyes and willed the shift from heat-sensing infravision into the normal spectrum of light. He remembered the splendor of Menzoberranzan's stalagmite and stalactite structures, their intricate and crafted designs highlighted by glowing faerie fire of purple, blue, and red.

He wasn't prepared for what he found when he opened his eyes. The city was filled with light! Not just with faerie fires, but with sparkling dots of yellow and white, the light of torches and bright magical enchantments. For a very brief moment, Drizzt allowed himself to believe that the presence of light might be some remote indication of a changing of the dark elves' dark ways. He had always connected the perpetual gloom of the Underdark to the dark demeanor of drow, or, at least, had thought the darkness a fitting result of his kin's dark ways.

Why the lights? Drizzt was not arrogant enough to think that their presence might be somehow connected to the hunt for him. He did not think that he was that important to the drow, and had little more than the deep gnomes' supposition that things were awry.—He had no idea that plans were being laid for an all-out surface raid.—He wanted to question one of the other drow on the matter—the female, in particular, would likely have some information—but how could he broach the subject without giving away his identity as an outsider?

As if on cue, the female was at his side, sitting uncomfortably close.

"The days are long on the Isle of Rothé," she said coyly, obvious attraction reflected in her red-glowing eyes.

"I will never get used to the light," Drizzt replied, changing the subject and looking back toward the city. He kept his eyes operating in the normal spectrum and hoped that his leading statements might prompt some conversation on the matter. "It stings my eyes."

"Of course it does," the female purred, moving closer, even putting a hand inside Drizzt's elbow. "But you will get used to it in time."

In time? In time for what? Drizzt wanted to ask, for he suspected from her tone that she was referring to some specific event. He had no idea of how to begin the question, though, and, as the female moved ever closer, he found that he had more pressing problems.

In drow culture, males were subservient, and to refuse the advances of a female could invite serious trouble. "I am Khareesa," she whispered in his ear. "Tell me that you wish to be my slave."

Drizzt jumped up suddenly and snapped his scimitars from their sheaths. He turned away from Khareesa, focused his attention on the lake to make sure that she understood he meant no threat against her.

"What is it?" the surprised female demanded.

"A movement in the water," Drizzt lied. "A subtle undercurrent, as though something large just passed under our craft." Khareesa scowled but stood and peered into the gloomy lake. It was common knowledge in Menzoberranzan that dark things resided under the usually still waters of Donigarten. One of the games the slavers played was to make the goblins and orcs swim from the isle to the shore, to see if any of them would be pulled down to terrible deaths.

A few moments passed quietly, the only sound the continual moaning chants of the orcs lining the sides of the raft.

A third drow joined Drizzt and Khareesa on the prow, eyeing Drizzt's blue-flaring scimitar. *You mark us for every enemy in the area,* his hands flashed in the silent code.

Drizzt slid the scimitars away and let his eyes drift back into infravision. *If our enemies are beneath the waters, then the motion of our craft marks us more than any light,* his hands answered.

"There are no enemies," Khareesa added, motioning for the third drow to go back to his station. When he left, she turned a lewd look upon Drizzt. "A warrior?" she asked, carefully regarding the purple-eyed male. "A patrol leader, perhaps?"

Drizzt nodded and it was no lie; he had indeed been a patrol leader.

"Good," Khareesa remarked. "I like males who are worth the trouble." She looked up then, took note that they were fast approaching the Isle of Rothé. "We will speak later, perhaps." Then she turned and swept away, brushing her hands behind her so that her robes rode high on her shapely legs.

Drizzt winced as though slapped. The last thing Khareesa had on her mind was speaking. He couldn't deny that she was beautiful, with sculpted features, a thick mane of well-groomed hair, and a finely toned body. But in his years among the drow, Drizzt Do'Urden had learned to look beyond physical beauty and physical attraction. Drizzt did not separate the physical from the emotional. He was a superb fighter because he fought with his heart and would no sooner battle merely for the sake of battle than he would mate for the sake of the physical act.

"Later," Khareesa said once more, glancing back over her delicate, perfectly squared shoulder.

"When worms eat your bones," Drizzt whispered through a phony smile. For some reason, he thought of Catti-brie then, and the warmth of that image pushed away the chill of this hungry drow female.

⚔ ⚔ ⚔ ⚔ ⚔

Blingdenstone charmed Catti-brie, despite her obvious predicament and the fact that the svirfnebli did not treat her as a long-lost friend. Stripped of her weapons, armor, jewelry, and even her boots, she was taken into the city in just her basic clothes. The gnome escorts did not abuse her, but neither were they gentle. They tightly clasped her arms at the elbows and hoisted her and pulled her around the narrow, rocky ways of the city's defensible anterooms.

When they had taken the circlet from the woman's head, the gnomes had easily come to guess its function, and as soon as the anterooms were past, they gave the precious item back to Catti-brie. Drizzt had told her of this place, of the deep gnomes' natural blending with their environment, but she had never pictured that the drow's words would ring so true. Dwarves were miners, the best in all the world, but the deep gnomes went beyond that description. They were part of the rock, it seemed, burrowing creatures wholly at one with the stone. Their houses could have been the randomly tumbled boulders of a long-past volcanic eruption, their corridors, the winding ways of an ancient river.

A hundred sets of eyes followed Catti-brie's every step as she was led across the city proper. She realized that she was probably the first human the svirfnebli had ever seen, and she did not mind the attention, for she was no less enchanted by the svirfnebli. Their features, seeming so gray and dour out in the wild tunnels, appeared softer now, gentler. She wondered what a smile would look like on the face of a svirfneblin, and she wanted to see it. These were Drizzt's friends, she kept reminding herself, and she took comfort in the drow ranger's judgment.

She was brought into a small, round room. A guard motioned for her to sit in one of three stone chairs. Catti-brie did so hesitantly, for she recalled a tale that Drizzt had told her, of a svirfneblin chair that had magically shackled him and held him fast.

No such thing happened now, though, and a moment later, a very unusual deep gnome entered the room, dangling the magical locket with Drizzt's picture from the end of a hand that was crafted into a mithral pickaxe.

"Belwar," Catti-brie stated, for there could not be two gnomes who so perfectly fit Drizzt's description of his dear svirfneblin friend.

The Most Honored Burrow Warden stopped in his tracks and eyed the woman suspiciously, obviously caught off guard by her recognition.

"Drizzt . . . Belwar," Catti-brie said, again wrapping her arms about her, as though hugging someone. She pointed to herself and said, "Catti-brie . . . Drizzt," and repeated the motion.

They could not speak two words of each other's language, but, in a short time, using hand and body language, Catti-brie had won over the burrow warden, had even explained to him that she was searching for Drizzt.

She did not like the grave face Belwar wore at that remark, and his explanation, a single common name, the name of a drow city, was not reassuring; Drizzt had gone into Menzoberranzan.

She was given a meal of cooked mushrooms and other plantlike growths that she did not recognize, then she was given back her items, including the locket and the onyx panther, but not the magical mask.

She then was left alone, for hours it seemed, sitting in the starlit darkness, silently blessing Alustriel for her precious gift and thinking how perfectly miserable the trek would have been without the Cat's Eye. She would not even have seen Belwar to recognize him!

Her thoughts were still on Belwar when he at last returned, along with two

other gnomes wearing long, soft robes, very unlike the rough, leatherlike, metal-plated outfits typical of the race. Catti-brie figured that these two must be important, perhaps councilors.

"Firble," Belwar explained, pointing to one of the svirfnebli, one that did not look happy.

Catti-brie figured out why a moment later, when Belwar pointed to her, then to Firble, then to the door and spoke a long sentence, the only word of which Catti-brie caught was, "Menzoberranzan."

Firble motioned for her to follow him, apparently anxious to be on their way, and Catti-brie, though she would have loved to stay in Blingdenstone and learn more about the intriguing svirfnebli, thoroughly agreed. Drizzt was too far ahead of her already. She rose from the chair and started out, but was caught at the arm by Belwar's pickaxe hand and turned about to face the burrow warden.

He pulled the magical mask from his belt and lifted it to her. "Drizzt," he said, pointing his hammer hand at her face. "Drizzt."

Catti-brie nodded, understanding that the burrow warden thought it would be wise of her to walk as a drow. She turned to leave, but, on a sudden impulse, turned back and gave Belwar a peck on the cheek. Smiling appreciatively, the young woman walked from the house, and, with Firble leading the way, strode from Blingdenstone.

"How did you get Firble to agree to take her into the drow city?" the remaining gnome councilor asked the burrow warden when they were alone.

"Bivrip!" Belwar bellowed. He clapped his mithral hands together and immediately sparks and arcing lines of energy ran along his crafted hands. He put a wry look on the councilor, who merely laughed in a squeaky svirfneblin way. Poor Firble.

⚔ ⚔ ⚔ ⚔ ⚔

Drizzt was glad to escort a group of orcs from the isle back to the mainland, if only so that he could avoid the eager Khareesa. She watched him go from the shore, her expression caught somewhere between a pout and anticipation, as if to say that Drizzt might have escaped, but only for now.

With the isle behind him, Drizzt put all thoughts of Khareesa from his mind. His task, and dangers, lay ahead, in the city proper, and he honestly did not know where he would begin looking for answers. He feared that it would all come down to his surrender, that he would have to give himself over to protect the friends that he had left behind.

He thought of Zaknafein, his father and friend, who had been sacrificed to the evil Spider Queen in his stead. He thought of Wulfgar, his lost friend, and memories of the young barbarian strengthened Drizzt's resolve.

He offered no explanation to the surprised slavers awaiting the craft on the beach. His expression alone told them not to question him as he walked past their encampment, away from Donigarten.

Soon he moved easily, warily, along the winding ways of Menzoberranzan. He passed close by several dark elves, under the more-than-curious eyes of dozens of house guards, standing watch from their parapets along the sides of hollowed stalactites. Drizzt carried with him an irrational notion that he might be recognized, and had to tell himself many times that he had been out of Menzoberranzan for more than thirty years, that Drizzt Do'Urden, even House Do'Urden, was now part of Menzoberranzan's history.

But, if that were true, why was he here, in this place where he did not want to be?

Drizzt wished that he had a *piwafwi*, the black cloak typical of drow outerwear. His forest-green cloak, thick and warm, was more suited to the environs of the surface world and might connect him, in the eyes of onlookers, to that rarely seen place. He kept the hood up, the cowl low, and pushed on. This would be one of many excursions into the city proper, he believed, as he familiarized himself once more with the winding avenues and the dark ways.

The flicker of light around a bend surprised him, stung his heat-seeing eyes, and he moved tightly against the wall of a stalagmite, one hand under his cloak, grasping Twinkle's hilt.

A group of four drow males came around the bend, talking easily, paying Drizzt no heed. They wore the symbol of House Baenre, Drizzt noted as his vision shifted back to the normal spectrum, and one of them carried a torch!

Little that Drizzt had witnessed in all his life seemed so out of place to him. Why? he asked himself repeatedly, and he felt that this all was somehow related to him. Were the drow preparing an offensive against some surface location?

The notion rocked Drizzt to his core. House Baenre soldiers carrying torches, getting their Underdark eyes desensitized to the light. Drizzt did not know what to think. He would have to go back to the Isle of Rothé, he decided, and he figured that that out-of-the-way place was as good a base as any he could secure in the city. Perhaps he could get Khareesa to tell him the meaning of the lights, so that the next excursion into the city proper might prove fruitful.

He stalked back through the city, cowl low, thoughts inward, and did not notice the movements shadowing his own; few in Menzoberranzan ever noticed the movements of Bregan D'aerthe.

$\times$ $\times$ $\times$ $\times$ $\times$

Catti-brie had never viewed anything so mysterious and wonderful and, in the starlight of her vision, the glow of the stalagmite towers and hanging stalactites seemed more wonderful still. The faerie fires of Menzoberranzan highlighted ten thousand wondrous carvings, some of definite shape—mostly spiders—and others free-flowing forms, surrealistic and beautiful. She would like to come here under different circumstances, Catti-brie decided. She would like to be an explorer that discovered an empty Menzoberranzan, that she might study and absorb the incredible drow workmanship and relics in safety.

For, as overwhelmed as Catti-brie was by the magnificence of the drow city, she was truly terrified. Twenty thousand drow, twenty thousand deadly enemies, were all about her.

As proof against the fear, the young woman tightly clasped Alustriel's magic locket and thought of the picture therein, of Drizzt Do'Urden. He was here, somewhere close, she believed, and her suspicions were confirmed when the locket flared suddenly with warmth.

Then it cooled. Catti-brie moved methodically, turning back to the north, to the secret tunnels Firble had taken her through to get to this place. The locket remained cool. She shifted to her right and faced west, across the chasm near her—the Clawrift, it was called—and past the great, sweeping steppes that led to a higher level. Then she faced south, toward the highest and grandest section of all, judging from the elaborate, glowing designs. Still the locket remained cool, then began to warm as the young woman continued to turn, looking past the nearest stalagmite mounds to the relatively clear section in the east.

Drizzt was there, in the east. Catti-brie took a deep breath then another, to steady her nerves and muster the courage to come fully out of the protected tunnel. She looked to her hands again, and her flowing robes, and took comfort in the apparently perfect drow disguise. She wished that she had Guenhwyvar beside her—remembered the moment in Silverymoon when the panther had loped down the streets beside her—but wasn't sure how the cat would be received in Menzoberranzan. The last thing she wanted to do was call attention to herself.

She moved quickly and quietly, throwing the hood of her robes low over her head. She hunched as she walked, and kept her grasp on the locket to guide her way and bolster her strength. She worked hard to avoid the stares of the many house sentries, and pointedly looked away whenever she saw a drow coming down the avenue toward her from the other direction.

She was almost past the area of stalagmites, could see the moss bed, the mushroom grove, even the lake beyond, when two drow came out of the shadows suddenly, blocking the way, though their weapons remained sheathed.

One of them asked her a question, which she, of course, did not understand. She subconsciously winced and noticed that they were looking at her eyes. Her eyes! Of course, they were not glowing with infravision, as the deep gnomes had informed her. The male asked his question again, somewhat more forcefully, then looked over his shoulder, toward the moss bed and the lake.

Catti-brie suspected that these two were part of a patrol, and that they wanted to know what business she might have on this side of the city. She noted the courteous way they addressed her, and remembered those things that Drizzt had taught her about drow culture.

She was a female; they, only males.

The undecipherable question came again, and Catti-brie responded with an open snarl. One of the males dropped his hands to the hilts of his twin swords, but Catti-brie pointed at them and snarled again, viciously.

The two males looked to each other in obvious confusion. By their estimation, this female was blind, or at least was not using infravision, and the lights in the city were not that bright. She should not have been able to see the movement clearly, and yet, by her pointing finger, she obviously had.

Catti-brie growled at them and waved them away, and to her surprise—and profound relief—the males backed off, eyeing her suspiciously but making no moves against her.

She started to hunch over, thinking to hide again under her cowl, but changed her mind instead. This was Menzoberranzan, full of brash dark elves, full of intrigue, a place where knowing—even *pretending* to know—something your rival did not know could keep you alive.

Catti-brie threw off the hood and stood straight, shaking her head as her thick hair freed itself of the folds. She stared at the two males wickedly and began to laugh.

They ran off.

The young woman nearly toppled with relief. She took another deep breath, clasped the locket in a clenched fist, and headed toward the lake.

Epitome of Enemies

D*o you know who he is?* the drow soldier's fingers asked imperatively in the intricate hand code.

Khareesa rocked back on her heels, not quite understanding any of this. A contingent of well-armed drow had come to the Isle of Rothé, demanding answers, interrogating both the orc and goblin slaves and the few drow slavers on the island. They wore no house emblems and, as far as Khareesa could tell, were exclusively males.

That did not stop them from treating her roughly, though, without the proper protocol typically afforded her gender.

"Do you?" the drow asked aloud. The unexpected noise brought two of the male's comrades rushing to his sides.

"He is gone," the male explained to calm his companions, "into the city."

But he is on his way back, a fourth drow replied in the silent hand code as he rushed to join the others. *We just received the code flashes from the shore.*

The heightening intrigue was more than curious Khareesa could take. "I am Khareesa H'kar," she proclaimed, naming herself a noble of one of the city's lesser houses, but a noble nonetheless. "Who is this male you speak of? And why is he so important?"

The four males looked to each other slyly, and the newcomer turned an evil glare on Khareesa.

"You have heard of Daermon N'a'shezbaernon?" he asked softly.

Khareesa nodded. Of course she had heard of the powerful house, House Do'Urden by its more common name. It had once been the eighth-ranked house in all the city, but had met a disastrous end.

"Of their secondboy?" the male went on.

Khareesa pursed her lips, unsure. She tried to remember the tragic story of House Do'Urden, something about a renegade, when another of the males jogged her memory.

"Drizzt Do'Urden," he said.

Khareesa started to nod—she had heard the name before, in passing—then her eyes went wide as she realized the significance of the handsome, purple-eyed drow that had left the Isle of Rothé.

She is a witness, one of the males reasoned.

She was not, argued another, *until we told her the renegade's name.*

"But now she is," said the first, and they looked in unison at the female.

Khareesa had long caught on to their wicked game and was steadily backing away from them, sword and whip in hand. She stopped as she felt the tip of yet another sword gently prod her fine armor from behind, and she held her hands out wide.

"House H'kar—" she began, but abruptly ended as the drow behind her plunged his fabulous drow-made sword through the fine armor and through a kidney. Khareesa jerked as the male yanked the weapon back out. She slumped to one knee, trying to hold her concentration against the sudden assault of agony, trying to hold fast to her weapons.

The four soldiers fell over her. There could be no witnesses.

⚔ ⚔ ⚔ ⚔ ⚔

Drizzt's gaze remained toward the strangely lighted city as the raft slipped slowly across Donigarten's dark waters.

Torches? The thought hung heavily in his mind, for he had pretty much convinced himself that the drow were preparing a huge excursion to the surface. Why else would they be stinging their sensitive eyes so?

As the raft floated across the weedy bay of the Isle of Rothé, Drizzt noticed that no other craft were docked at the island. He gave it little thought as he climbed over the prow and sprang lightly to the mossy beach. The orcs had barely put up their oars when another drow whisked past Drizzt and sprang into the boat, ordering the slave crew to put back out for the mainland.

Orc rothé herders congregated by the shore, each squatting in the mossy muck, ragged cloaks pulled tight. This was not unusual, for there was really little for them to do. The isle was not large, barely a hundred yards long and less than that in width, but it was incredibly thick with low vegetation, mainly mosses and fungi. The landscape was broken, filled with valleys and steep-

sloping hillocks, and the biggest job facing the orcs, aside from taking rothé from the isle to the mainland and chasing down strays, was simply to make sure that none of the herd fell into any ravines.

So the slaves sat down by the shore, silent and brooding. They seemed somewhat edgy to Drizzt, but, consumed by his fears over what was happening in the city, he again gave it little thought. He did glance about to the drow slaver posts, and took comfort in the fact that all the dark elves were apparently in place, standing quietly and calmly. The Isle of Rothé was not an eventful place.

Drizzt headed straight inland, away from the small bay and toward the highest point on the island. Here stood the isle's lone structure, a small, two-chambered house constructed of gigantic mushroom stalks. He considered his strategy as he moved, thought of how he might get the necessary information from Khareesa without open confrontation. Events seemed to be moving quickly about him, though, and he resolved that if he had to use his scimitars to "convince" her, he would.

Barely ten feet from the structure's door, Drizzt stopped and watched as the portal gently swung in. A drow soldier stepped to the threshold and casually tossed Khareesa's severed head at Drizzt's feet.

"There is no way off the island, Drizzt Do'Urden," the drow remarked.

Drizzt didn't turn his head, but shifted his eyes, trying to get a clear measure of his surroundings. He inconspicuously worked one toe under the soft moss, burying his foot to the ankle.

"I'll accept your surrender," the drow went on. "You cannot—"

The drow stopped abruptly as a wad of moss flew at his face. He snapped out his sword and instinctively threw his hands up before him in defense.

Drizzt's charge followed the moss divot. The ranger sprang across the ten feet to his enemy, then dropped in a deceptive spin, pivoting on one planted knee. Using his momentum, Drizzt sent Twinkle in a wicked, low cut that caught the surprised drow on the side of the knee. The drow turned a complete somersault over that stinging hit, striking the soft ground with a thud and a cry of pain as he clutched at his ripped leg.

Drizzt sensed that other dark elves were in the house behind this one, so he was up and running quickly, around the structure and out of sight of the door, then down the hillock's steep back slope. He dived, skidded, and rolled to build momentum, his thoughts a jumble, his desperation mounting.

Several dozen rothé milled about the mossy bank, and they bleated and grunted as Drizzt scrambled among them. Drizzt heard several clicks behind him, heard a hand-crossbow quarrel slap into one rothé. The creature tumbled, asleep before it hit the ground.

Drizzt kept low, scrambling, trying to figure where he could run. He had been on the island only a short time, had never been here in his earlier years in the city, and wasn't familiar with its landscape. He knew that this hillock dropped into a steep ravine, though, and thought that was his best chance.

More shots came from behind; a javelin joined the quarrels. Muck and divots flew wildly as the rothé, frightened by the rushing dark elf and missiles, kicked about, threatening to stampede. They were not large creatures, only three feet high at the shoulder, but were solidly built. If caught on his hands and knees in the midst of a rothé stampede, Drizzt knew he would be c rushed.

His problems compounded as he neared the back of the rothé herd, for between the legs of one creature he spotted boots. Hardly thinking, Drizzt lifted his shoulder and barreled sidelong into the rothé, pushing it down the slope, into his enemy. One scimitar went up high and sang as it struck a descending sword; another scimitar jabbed low, under the rothé's belly, but the enemy drow hopped back, out of range.

Drizzt coiled his legs under him and heaved with all his strength, using the ground's fairly steep angle to his advantage. The rothé lifted off the ground and skipped sidelong, slamming the drow. He was agile enough to lift a leg over the creature's low back and come cleanly over it, spinning about in an attempt to face Drizzt squarely. But Drizzt was nowhere to be seen.

A bleat to the side was the only warning the drow got as the fierce ranger rushed in, scimitars flashing. The surprised drow threw both his swords out in front as he spun about, barely deflecting the scimitar cuts. One foot skidded out from under him, but he came back up quickly, fire in his eyes and his swords thrusting wildly, holding Drizzt at bay.

Drizzt moved quickly to the right, gained the higher ground again, though he knew that that move would put his back to the archers at the top of the hillock. He kept his scimitars moving, his eyes focused ahead, but listened to sounds from the back.

A sword darted in low, was caught by Twinkle and held down. A second thrust came in parallel to the first but a bit higher, and Drizzt's second scimitar responded, coming unexpectedly straight across, angling the drow's sword right for Drizzt's low arm.

Drizzt heard a slight whistle behind him.

The enemy drow flashed a wicked grin, thinking he was about to score a hit as the blades flashed across, but Drizzt sent Twinkle in motion as well, equally fast, taking the drow's sword arm with him in the wide-flying move. Drizzt swept the scimitars under and up, using their curving blades to keep the

swords moving in line. He turned a complete circuit, moving the blades high above his head and moving himself one step to the side of the enemy drow.

His trust in the unseen archer's skill was not misplaced, and his melee opponent jerked his hips to the side in a frantic effort to dodge the javelin. He took a stinging hit and grimaced in pain.

Drizzt heaved him away, sent him skidding down the slope. The drow caught his balance as the ranger descended over him in a wild rush.

Scimitar batted sword again and again and again. Drizzt's second scimitar worked a more direct and devious pattern, thrusting and angling for the drow's belly.

The wounded drow's parries were impressive against the onslaught, but with one leg numb from pain, he was backing up and inevitably building momentum. He managed to glance back and noticed one spur of stone rising above the ledge of the twenty-foot sheer drop. He thought to make for that spur and put his back against it for support. His allies were rushing down the slope; they would be beside him in a matter of seconds.

Seconds he didn't have.

Both scimitars came in rapid succession, beating against the steel of the drow's swords, forcing him down the hill. Near the drop, Drizzt launched his weapons simultaneously, side-by-side, in crossing cuts, turning the tips of his enemy's swords. Then Drizzt launched himself, slamming against the drow's chest, knocking him off balance to crash against the rocky spur. Explosions went off in the dazed drow's head. He slumped to the moss, knowing that this renegade, Drizzt Do'Urden, and his wicked scimitars would be right behind.

Drizzt hadn't the time or the desire to complete the kill. Before the drow finished collapsing, Drizzt had leaped over the ledge, hoping to find moss and not sharp rocks, below.

What he found was mud, and he hit with a splash, turning an ankle, then turning a somersault. He finally hauled himself out and ran off as fast as he could, zigzagging around stalagmite pillars, keeping low to the cover of the mounds, for he expected that the archers would soon be at the ledge.

Enemies were all about him, and very close, he realized, seeing a form paralleling him along a stalagmite row to his right. Drizzt went behind one mound and, instead of coming out the other side, veered to meet his enemy head-on. He dropped to his knees as he came behind the second mound, slashing across low in the expectation that his enemy would be back there.

Twinkle hit a low-riding sword this time. Drizzt had not gained surprise, not with his maneuver, at least, but the drow was certainly off guard, his second sword high for a strike, when Drizzt snapped his second scimitar straight up, quicker than his enemy could anticipate. The pointed tip punctured the drow's diaphragm, and though Drizzt, as he continued his slide, could not extend his arm enough to complete the move, the drow fell back against the stalagmite, out of the fight.

An ally was right behind him, though, and this soldier fell upon the kneeling Drizzt with abandon, swords hacking fiercely.

Pure instinct kept the darting blades from Drizzt as the ranger worked his scimitars over his head, feeling more than seeing his opponent's moves. Understanding his sudden disadvantage, Drizzt called upon his innate magic and summoned a globe of darkness over himself and his enemy.

Ringing steel continued to sound, weapons meeting and sliding, with both combatants taking nicks. Drizzt growled and increased his intensity, parrying and countering, still slashing up over his head. Gradually, the skilled ranger shifted his weight to get one foot under him.

The enemy drow came with a sudden and fierce double chop—and nearly fell over when his blades caught nothing but air. He spun immediately, whipping his swords across—and nearly lost both blades as they slammed the side of the stony stalagmite mound.

In the heat of battle, he had forgotten the layout of the immediate area, forgotten the mound not so far away. The drow had heard the reputation of Drizzt Do'Urden and suddenly understood the magnitude of his mistake.

Drizzt, perched high on a rounded shoulder of the mound, winced as he heard the swords connect with stone below him, taking little satisfaction in this action. He couldn't see Twinkle's flaring blue light as the scimitar descended through the darkness globe.

He ran free a moment later, his ankle still sore but supporting him. He came out the back side of the ravine and moved up on the ledge opposite the high hillock. The ledge ran toward the more remote eastern end of the isle. There lay a lagoon, Drizzt believed, not so far away, and if he could reach it, he intended to dive right in. Damn the legends of monsters in the water; the enemies about him were all too real!

Catti-brie heard the continuing scuffles from the isle. The sounds drifted clearly across the still, dark waters of Donigarten. From behind the stalk of one mushroom, she called up Guenhwyvar and ran off as the mist took its solid form.

By the lake, the young woman, still not confident of her drow disguise,

avoided the few dark elves that were about and motioned to a nearby orc instead. Then she motioned to a boat, trying to indicate that the creature should take her out to the isle. The orc seemed nervous, or at least confused. It turned away and started to walk off.

Catti-brie punched it in the back of the head.

Cowering, obviously terrified, it turned about to face her. Catti-brie shoved it toward the small boat, and this time the creature got in and took up a paddle.

Before she could join the orc, Catti-brie was intercepted by a male drow, his strong hand closing tightly over her elbow.

She eyed him dangerously and growled, trying to bluff once again, but this determined dark elf was not taking the bait. In his free hand he held a dagger, poised below Catti-brie's elbow, just inches from her ribs.

"Be gone!" he said. "Bregan D'aerthe tells you to be gone!"

Catti-brie didn't understand a word of it, but her enemy's confusion was at least equal to hers as six hundred pounds of black fur flew past, taking the surprised male on a splashing ride many feet from the boat.

Catti-brie turned fiercely on the orc, who pretended not to see a thing and began paddling frantically. The young woman looked back to the shore a moment later, fearful that Guenhwyvar would be left behind and would have to swim the entire distance.

A huge splash beside the boat—nearly overturning it—told her differently, and the panther was now the one leading.

It was simply too much for the terrified orc to take. The pitiful creature shrieked and leaped for the water, swimming desperately for the shore. Catti-brie took up the paddle and never looked back.

⚔ ⚔ ⚔ ⚔ ⚔

The ledge was open to both sides at first, and Drizzt heard the hiss of crossbow quarrels cutting the air over his head and just behind him. Fortunately for Drizzt, the firing drow were back across the ravine, at the base of the tall hillock, and hand-crossbows were not very accurate at long range.

Drizzt wasn't surprised when his running form began to glow in purplish hues, tiny faerie fires igniting along his arms and legs, not burning, but marking him clearly to his enemies.

He felt a sting in his left shoulder and quickly reached over and popped out the small quarrel. The wound was only superficial, the dart's momentum mostly stalled by the dwarf-crafted mithral chain mail that Drizzt wore. He ran on, and could only hope that not enough poison had entered his blood to tire him.

The ledge veered to the right, putting Drizzt's back to his enemies. He felt even more vulnerable then, for just a moment, but soon realized that the turn might be a good thing, putting more distance between him and the stinging crossbows. Soon after, as the quarrels bounced harmlessly behind him, the ledge veered again, back to the left, going around the base of another hillock.

This put the lapping waters of Donigarten at Drizzt's right, a dozen feet below him. He thought of sheathing his blades and jumping in right there, but too many jagged mounds protruded from the water for him to chance it.

The ledge remained mostly open on his right as he sped along, the drop sporadically blocked by only a few anchoring stalagmites. The hillock loomed on Drizzt's left, fully protecting him from the distant archers . . . but not from nearer enemies, he realized. As he came around a slight bend, he discovered at the last instant that beyond the bend lay a hollow, and in the hollow waited an enemy.

The soldier leaped out into Drizzt's path, sword and dirk waving.

A scimitar turned the sword aside, and Drizzt thrust straight ahead, knowing his second weapon would be intercepted by the dirk. When the weapons predictably locked, Drizzt used his momentum to push the dirk out wide and lifted one knee to collide heavily with the drow's belly.

Drizzt clapped his wide-spread hands together, simultaneously snapping his scimitar hilts against his enemy's face. He snapped his weapons back out immediately, fearing that either the sword or dagger would dive at him, but his opponent was past retaliation. The evil drow fell straight to the ground, unconscious, and Drizzt plowed over him and kept on going.

The ranger had hit his stride, literally. Savage instincts churned within Drizzt, and he believed that no single drow could stand against him. He was fast reverting to the hunter again, the embodiment of primal, passionate rage.

A dark elf leaped out from behind the next stalagmite; Drizzt skidded down to one knee and spun, a similar maneuver to the one he had used against the drow at the mushroom house's door.

This time, though, his enemy had more time to react, had his sword down to the stone to block.

The hunter knew that he would.

Drizzt's lead foot caught hold, and he spun up from his slide, his trailing foot flying wide in a circle kick that caught the surprised drow under the chin and dropped him over the side of the ledge. He caught a handhold just a few

feet down, groggy from the blow and thinking that this purple-eyed fiend would surely kill him.

The hunter was already gone, though, running on, running for freedom.

Drizzt saw another drow on the path in front of him, this one's arm held up before him, probably aiming a hand-crossbow.

The hunter was quicker than the quarrel. His instincts told him that, repeatedly, and they were proven correct when a flashing scimitar intercepted the dart.

Then Drizzt was upon the drow, and the drow's ally, who came out from behind the nearest mound. The two enemies worked furiously with their weapons, thinking their numerical advantage more than sufficient.

They didn't understand the hunter—but the red-glowing eyes of Artemis Entreri, watching from a nearby hollow, did.

PART FOUR

IN THE WEB

One of the sects of Faerûn names the sins of humanity as seven, and foremost among them is pride. My interpretation of this had always been to think of the arrogance of kings, who proclaimed themselves gods, or at least convinced their subjects that they spoke with some divine beings, thus conveying the image that their power was god-given.

That is only one manifestation of this most deadly of sins. One does not have to be a king to be taken down by false pride. Montolio DeBrouchee, my ranger mentor, warned me about this, but his lessons concerned a personal aspect of pride. "A ranger often walks alone, but never walks without friends nearby," the wise man explained. "A ranger knows his surroundings and knows where allies might be found."

To Montolio's way of thinking, pride was blindness, a blurring of insight and wisdom, and the defeat of trust. A too-proud man walked alone and cared not where allies might be found.

When I discovered the web of Menzoberranzan growing thick about me, I understood my error, my arrogance. Had I come to think so much of myself and my abilities that I forgot those allies who had, to this point, allowed me to survive? In my anger over the death of Wulfgar and my fears for Catti-brie, Bruenor, and Regis, I never considered that those living friends could help to take care of themselves. The problem that had befallen us all was my own fault, I had decided, and, thus, was my duty to correct, however impossible that might be for a single person.

I would go to Menzoberranzan, discover the truth, and end the conflict, even if that end meant the sacrifice of my own life.

What a fool I had been.

Pride told me that I was the cause of Wulfgar's death; pride told me that I could be the one to right the wrong. Sheer arrogance prevented me from dealing openly with my friend, the dwarven king, who could muster the forces necessary to combat any forthcoming drow attacks.

On that ledge on the Isle of Rothé, I realized that I would pay for my arrogance; later, I would learn that others dear to me might pay as well.

It is a defeat of the spirit to learn that one's arrogance causes such loss and pain. Pride invites you to soar to heights of personal triumph, but the wind is stronger at those heights and the footing, tentative. Farther, then, is the fall.

—Drizzt Do'Urden

18

VALIANT FAILURE

She noticed a dark elf on the isle's dock, waving his arms and motioning for her to go back. He seemed to be alone.

Catti-brie lifted Taulmaril and let fly. The arrow cut the darkness as would a bolt of lightning, slamming into the surprised drow's chest and hurling him back a dozen feet. Catti-brie and Guenhwyvar stepped onto the beach a minute later. The young woman felt the locket and started to tell Guenhwyvar to run around to the right, but the panther had already sensed the nearness of its master, was already in full flight across the broken landscape, veering in from the beach as it ran.

The woman followed as quickly as she could, but lost sight of the speeding cat almost immediately as Guenhwyvar cut a sharp turn around the base of the nearest hillock, claws throwing up moist turf.

Catti-brie heard a startled cry and, when she came around the base of that mound, she saw a dark elf soldier, looking away from her, his gaze apparently following the run of the panther. One of his arms was upraised, steadying a hand-crossbow.

Catti-brie fired on the run, her arrow going high and scorching a hole in the side of the mound, just inches above the drow's head. He spun about immediately and retaliated, the dart clipping the turf near the diving and rolling woman.

Quick to fit another arrow, Catti-brie fired next, driving a hole in the drow soldier's trailing *piwafwi* as he scrambled to the side. He skidded to one knee, fitted a quarrel as he went, and raised his arm again.

Catti-brie fired also, the arrow blasting through the hand-crossbow and the

drow's hand, slicing out his wrist and burying deep in his upper chest.

She had won the duel, but had lost precious time. Disoriented, the young woman needed the locket again to direct her, and off she ran.

His skilled opponents' fierce attacks soon became measured strikes as Drizzt parried every move and often managed an effective counter. One of the drow held just one weapon now, with his dirk arm tucked in close to his side to stem the flow of blood from a curving scimitar gash.

Drizzt's confidence continued to soar. How many enemies were here on the isle? he wondered, and he dared to believe that he might win.

His blood froze when he heard a roar behind him, thinking that some monstrous ally had come to his enemies' aid. The wounded drow soldier widened his eyes in terror and began to backpedal, but Drizzt took little comfort in that. Most drow allies were tentative at best, chaotic creatures of incredible and unpredictable power. If this were indeed some summoned monster, some demonic ally, stalking from behind him, then Drizzt was surely its primary target.

The backpedaling drow broke into a dead run, fleeing along the ledge, and Drizzt used his departure to work around to the side, to try to get a look at what he would face next.

A black feline form whipped past him, pursuing his fleeing enemy. For an instant, he thought that some drow must have a figurine similar to his own, must have summoned a cat similar to Guenhwyvar. But this was Guenhwyvar! Drizzt knew instinctively. This was his Guenhwyvar!

Excitement fast turned to confusion. Drizzt thought that Regis must have called the panther, back in Mithral Hall, and that the cat must have come running out after him. It made no sense, though, for Guenhwyvar could not remain on the Material Plane long enough to make the journey all the way from the dwarven stronghold. The figurine had to have been carried to Menzoberranzan.

A cunning sword thrust slipped through Drizzt's defenses momentarily, the weapon tip nicking into his fine armor and stinging his breast. It brought the distracted ranger from his reverie, reminding Drizzt that he had to take one enemy and one problem at a time.

He came forward in a blinding burst, scimitars waving and rolling, cutting in at the opposing dark elf from many different angles. The drow soldier was up to the test, though, his swords banging away the deadly blades, even smacking the side of Drizzt's boot as the ranger tried to kick out at the drow's knee.

"Patience," Drizzt reminded himself, but with Guenhwyvar's appearance and so many unanswered questions, patience was hard to come by.

⚔ ⚔ ⚔ ⚔ ⚔

The fleeing drow rounded a bend. Then, with the panther quickly gaining, he hooked his good arm around a narrow stalagmite and spun to the right, leaping over the ledge to splash into the muck. He got his feet back under him and was bent over, trying to recover his dropped sword, when Guenhwyvar crashed down, driving him into the water.

He spun and kicked briefly, and when the jumble sorted out, the panther's maw was clamped about the pinned drow's neck, squeezing. He had his face above the water, but could not draw breath, would never again draw breath.

Guenhwyvar came up from the kill, turned to spring back the dozen feet to the ledge, but dropped low and turned its head, snarling suspiciously as a rainbow-hued bubble floated over it. Before Guenhwyvar could react, the strange thing burst, and Guenhwyvar was showered by flecks of tingling material.

Guenhwyvar leaped for the ledge, but felt as though the intended target was getting farther and farther away. The panther roared again, in protest, understanding then the nature of those flecks, understanding that they were sending it back to its own plane of existence.

The roar was soon lost to the gentle lapping of the stirred ripples and the clang of steel from up on the ledge.

Jarlaxle leaned against the stone wall, considering this new development. He put away his valuable metal whistle, the item that had dismissed the dangerous panther, and lifted one of his boots so that he could wipe the muck from it. Casually, the cocky mercenary looked up to the continuing sounds of battle, confident that Drizzt Do'Urden would soon be taken.

⚔ ⚔ ⚔ ⚔ ⚔

Catti-brie was pinned down in the ravine; two dark elves stood sheltered behind twin mounds directly ahead of her, and a third plucked away with his hand-crossbow from the base of the hillock to her left. She squeezed in close to her own stalagmite cover as best she could, but still felt vulnerable as darts ricocheted all about her. Every now and then she managed a shot, but her enemies were well under cover and the streaking arrows skipped and sparked harmlessly off the many stones.

A quarrel nicked the young woman's knee; another forced her to duck deeper into the cubby, forced her to angle her body so that she probably wouldn't be able to fire her bow again. Catti-brie grew scared then, thinking that defeat had caught up with her. There was no way she could win against three well-trained and well-armed drow soldiers.

A quarrel stuck into the heel of her boot, but did not penetrate. The young woman took a long, deep breath. She told herself stubbornly that she had to try to retaliate, that crouching here would prove worthless and would ensure her—and Drizzt's—death.

The thought of her friend gave her courage, and she wriggled about for a shot. She cursed aloud as she fired, for her enemies, again, were well hidden.

Or were they? Catti-brie scrambled suddenly to the back side of the stalagmite cluster, putting as much interference between herself and the drow on the hillock as possible. She was an open target now to the two soldiers ahead of her, but she was only a target if they managed to get off any shots.

Taulmaril hummed repeatedly, continuously, as the woman loosed a mighty barrage. She saw no dark elf forms to shoot at, but went after their cover instead, each enchanted arrow pounding away at the twin stalagmites. Sparks flew all about the target area. Chips of flying stone sizzled as they arced into the air.

Unable to come out long enough to retaliate, the two drow lost their nerve and fled down the ravine. Catti-brie got one in the back, then lifted an arrow for the second.

She felt a sting in her side and turned about to see another enemy barely ten feet away, smiling confidently with his hand-crossbow out in front of him.

Catti-brie whipped about, her deadly bow falling in line. The drow's mouth opened wide in a suddenly terrified scream, and Catti-brie put the arrow right into his face, hurling him head over heels through the air.

The young woman looked to her bleeding side. She grimaced and yanked out the stinging quarrel, then pulled herself up to her feet and looked all about. She couldn't be certain that this last drow had been the one from the hillock, but she felt the insidious poison creeping into her limbs and knew that she couldn't wait around to make sure that no other enemies were creeping behind her. Determinedly, the young woman began to scale the ravine's broken wall and soon she was up on the ledge, trotting along, trying to keep her focus and her balance.

✕ ✕ ✕ ✕ ✕

Twinkle hooked inside the drow's sword, and Drizzt sent it rotating, the two weapons cutting great circles in the air between the combatants. His opponent sneaked a thrust in behind the fast-flying blades, but Drizzt's other scimitar was in line, knocking the second sword harmlessly aside.

Drizzt kept the momentum up, even increased the pressure of the spin. Around went the blades, low and high, and now it was Drizzt who kept his free weapon slipping in through their wake, with cunning strikes that kept his opponent dancing back and off balance. With his superior agility, Drizzt was in control of the circling blades, and both opponents knew that the ranger was gaining the advantage.

The enemy drow tightened his muscles to apply counterpressure against Twinkle—exactly what cunning Drizzt had been waiting for. The instant he felt the pressure on his blade, sword and scimitar coming up again before his eyes, he ended his roundabout cut, reversed direction, and snapped Twinkle in a short loop, striking the drow's sword on the other side. Overbalanced by the sudden release, the drow soldier stumbled and could not reverse his pressure on the sword.

His blade dived low and flew out wide across his body, twisting him to the side. He tried to get his other sword around for a block, but Drizzt's second scimitar was too quick, jabbing hard into the side of his abdomen.

He fell back, reeling, one sword dropping to the stone.

Drizzt heard a call; someone rammed him hard in the shoulder, slamming him against the stone wall. He bounced off and spun, scimitars up.

Entreri! Drizzt's jaw dropped with his guard.

✕ ✕ ✕ ✕ ✕

Catti-brie spotted Drizzt on the ledge, saw the other drow fall away, clutching his side, and she cried out as another dark form rushed from a cranny and barreled into Drizzt. She put her bow up, but realized that if the enemy's body did not stop her arrow, it would drive through to strike Drizzt. Besides, a wave of dizziness assaulted the young woman as the effects of the sleeping poison began to course through her veins.

She kept Taulmaril ready and staggered on, but the fifty-or-so feet to Drizzt seemed like a hundred miles.

Entreri's sword flared a green light, further revealing the assassin. But how could it be? Drizzt wondered. He had defeated this one, had left Entreri for dead in a windy ravine outside Mithral Hall.

Apparently, not everyone had left Entreri for dead.

The sword came in a devilish two-stroke routine, thrusting low at Drizzt's hip, then slashing high, nearly connecting across the drow's eyes.

Drizzt tried to recover his balance, and his sensibilities, but Entreri was all over him, hacking wildly, growling all the while. A snap kick caught the ranger in the knee, and he had to throw himself away from the wall as the green-glowing sword sliced down, igniting a line of sparks.

The snarling assassin spun with Drizzt, sending his dirk in a wide-flying hook. Drizzt's scimitar banged against the shorter weapon and it flew away, but Entreri's hand came on, balling into a fist, now inside the blocking angle of Drizzt's weapon.

A split second before the assassin's fist smacked into his nose, Drizzt realized that Entreri had been one step ahead of him, had expected, even desired, that exact parry.

The stunned ranger tumbled backward. Only a narrow stalagmite mound prevented Drizzt from flying over the ledge. Entreri was on him instantly. Sparks, green and blue, erupted as a brutal swipe of the assassin's sword took Twinkle from Drizzt's hands.

Drizzt's remaining blade parried the ensuing backhand, but before he could begin to bend to retrieve his dropped weapon, Entreri crouched and kicked Twinkle from the ledge.

Still off balance, Drizzt tried a downward chop that was easily foiled, and the assassin countered with another heavy punch, connecting solidly with Drizzt's belly.

Up swooped Entreri, his sword running an outward-circling arc, taking Drizzt's scimitar with it. It was a game of chess, and Entreri was playing white, advantage gained, and not relinquishing the offensive. Sword and scimitar out wide, the enraged assassin hurled himself into the ranger, forearm leading, smashing Drizzt in the face and snapping the drow's head back brutally against the stone. Entreri's sword hit the scimitar again, knocking it straight out, then again, straight up, and Drizzt, with his sword arm high and Entreri's poised to come in at him, recognized his doom. He rolled away to his right as the sword sliced across, slashing through his fine cloak, banging hard against his dwarf-forged armor and cutting a line across his armpit, aiding the momentum of his dive.

Then Drizzt was flying free over the ledge, diving face first into the muck.

Entreri instinctively leaped and rolled as he noticed a flash out of the corner of his eye. A silver-streaking arrow sliced across the jumble of man and cloak, then continued on along the ledge, leaving Entreri prone on the stone, groaning. He managed to slip a hand out from under him, fingers inching to his dropped dirk.

"Drizzt!" Catti-brie called, her grogginess temporarily defeated by the sight of her fallen friend. Drawing her sword, the woozy woman increased her pace, not sure of whether to finish the assassin first or look for the downed drow.

Nearing the spot, she veered for the stalagmite, but the choice was moot, for the assassin sprang to his feet, apparently unhurt. The arrow had missed, cutting only a clean hole in Entreri's flapping cloak.

Catti-brie fought through teary eyes and gritted teeth, smacked aside Entreri's first sword thrust and reached for the jeweled dagger on her belt. Her movements were sluggish, though, for the insidious sleeping poison was fast overwhelming the adrenaline rush, and, as her fingers closed on the dagger, she suddenly found her sword slapped away and a dirk pressing the back of her hand, pinning it in place against the dagger hilt.

Entreri's sword tip was up, dangerously high and dangerously free.

The end was upon her, Catti-brie knew, and all her world had flown away. She felt only the cold steel of Entreri's sword slipping through the tender skin of her neck.

19

FALSE PRIDE

He is alive, the soldier signaled to Jarlaxle as he inspected the downed ranger.

The mercenary leader motioned for the soldier to turn the fallen Drizzt so that his head was out of the water. Jarlaxle looked across the still lake, understanding that the sound of battle had echoed clearly across its waters. The mercenary saw the distinctive, pale blue glow of driftdisks, flying disks of energy typically used to carry matron mothers across the city, floating out from the banks. They held House Baenre soldiers, Jarlaxle knew.

Leave him, the mercenary leader signaled to his soldier, *and his equipment.*

Almost as an afterthought, Jarlaxle pulled his whistle out once more, put it to his lips, and faced Drizzt, then blew a high note. The whistle's dweomer showed him that the ranger wore magical armor, at least as fine as drow make, and Jarlaxle sighed when he saw the intensity of Twinkle's enchantment. He would have loved to add that scimitar to his armory, but it was well known in Menzoberranzan that Drizzt Do'Urden fought with two scimitars, and if one was missing, the mercenary would only be inviting trouble from Matron Baenre.

Drizzt carried little else that was enchanted, except for one item that caught and held the mercenary's attention. Its magic was strong indeed, shining in the hues common to charm enchantments, exactly the type of item that cagey Jarlaxle used to best effect.

His soldier, having shifted the unconscious ranger so that Drizzt's face was above the murky water, started toward Jarlaxle, but the mercenary leader stopped him.

Take the pendant, Jarlaxle's fingers instructed.

The soldier turned about and seemed to notice the approaching driftdisks for the first time. "Baenre?" he asked quietly as he turned back to his leader.

They will find their quarry, Jarlaxle signaled confidently. *And Matron Baenre will know who delivered Drizzt Do'Urden to her.*

⋈ ⋈ ⋈ ⋈ ⋈

Entreri wasn't about to ask what drow female he was killing this time. He was working in concert with Bregan D'aerthe, and this drow, like the one in the mushroom house, had interfered, and was a witness.

A timely glance showed him something that gave him pause, though, showed him a familiar jeweled dagger hanging on this drow's belt.

Entreri studied the female closely, kept his sword tip at her neck, drawing small droplets of blood. He shifted the weapon deftly, and a subtle ridge showed along the female's smooth skin.

"Why are you here?" Entreri asked breathlessly, honestly surprised. He knew that this one had not come to Menzoberranzan beside Drizzt— Councilor Firble of Blingdenstone certainly would have mentioned her. Jarlaxle certainly would have known about her!

Yet, here she was, surprisingly resourceful.

Entreri shifted his sword again from her neck, then delicately tipped it up under the crease beneath her chin and used it to remove the magical mask.

Catti-brie fought hard to sublimate her mounting terror. This was too much like the first time she had been in Artemis Entreri's clutches; the assassin evoked an almost irrational horror in her, a deep fear that no other monster, neither a dragon nor a fiend of Tarterus, could bring.

Here he was again, amazingly alive, with his sword to her vulnerable throat.

"An unexpected bonus," Entreri mused. He chuckled evilly, as though he was trying to sort out the best way to make his prisoner profitable.

Catti-brie thought of leaping over the ledge—if she had been near a cliff a thousand feet in the air, she would have considered it! She felt the hairs on the back of her neck tingle, felt sweat beading on her brow.

"No," she uttered, and Entreri's features twisted with confusion.

"No?" he echoed, not understanding that her remark had been aimed inward.

Catti-brie steeled her gaze at him. "So ye've survived," she remarked matter-of-factly. "To go and live among those who're most akin to ye."

She saw by the assassin's slight grimace that Entreri did not like that description. He confirmed that fact by punching her with his sword hilt, raising a welt on the woman's cheek and bringing a trickle of blood from her nose.

Catti-brie fell back, but straightened immediately, and stared at the assassin with unblinking eyes. She would not give Entreri the satisfaction of terror, not this time.

"I should kill you," Entreri whispered. "Slowly."

Catti-brie laughed at him. "Then do," she replied. "Ye've no hold over me, not since I've seen the proof that Drizzt is yer better."

Entreri, in sudden rage, almost ran her through. "Was," he corrected, then he looked wickedly to the ledge.

"I've seen ye both fall more than once," Catti-brie asserted with as much conviction as she could muster in that dark moment. "I'll not call either of ye dead until I've felt the cold body!"

"Drizzt is alive," came a whisper from behind, spoken in perfect surface Common, as Jarlaxle and two Bregan D'aerthe soldiers moved to join the assassin. One of them stopped to finish off the squirming drow with the wounded side.

His rage taking control, Entreri instinctively swung again at Catti-brie, but this time the woman lifted a stiffened hand and turned her wrist, subtly diverting the blow.

Then Jarlaxle was between them, eyeing Catti-brie with more than a passing interest. "By the luck of a Lolth-blessed spider," the mercenary leader remarked, and he lifted a hand to stroke Catti-brie's bruised cheek.

"Baenre approaches," the soldier behind the mercenary leader reminded, using the Drow tongue.

"Indeed," Jarlaxle replied absently, again in the surface language. He seemed wholly absorbed by this exotic woman standing before him. "We must be on our way."

Catti-brie straightened, as though she expected the killing blow to fall. Jarlaxle reached up instead and removed the circlet from her head, in effect, blinding her. She offered no resistance as Taulmaril and her quiver were taken from her, and knew that it was Entreri's rough grasp that snapped the jeweled dagger from her belt sheath.

A strong but surprisingly gentle hand hooked her upper arm and led her away—away from the fallen Drizzt.

✕ ✕ ✕ ✕ ✕

Caught again, Drizzt thought, and this time he knew that the reception would not be as pleasant as his stay in Blingdenstone. He had walked into the spider's web, had delivered the prized catch to the dinner table.

He was shackled to a wall, standing on his tiptoes to keep from hanging by his sore wrists. He did not remember coming to this place, did not know how long he had hung here, in the dark and dirty room, but both his wrists ached and showed hot welts to his infravision, as though most of the skin had been worn away. Drizzt's left shoulder also hurt, and he felt an uncomfortable stretch along his upper chest and armpit, where Entreri's sword had hit him.

He realized, though, that one of the priestesses must have cleaned the gash and healed him, for the wound had been worse when he had gone off the ledge. That supposition did little to bolster Drizzt's spirits, though, for drow sacrifices were usually in the very best of health before they were given to the Spider Queen.

But, through it all, the pain and the helplessness, the ranger fought hard to find some measure of comfort. In his heart Drizzt had known all along that it would end this way, that he would be taken and killed so that his friends in Mithral Hall might live in peace. Drizzt had long ago accepted death, and had resigned himself to that probability when he had last ventured from Mithral Hall. But why, then, was he so uncomfortable?

The unremarkable room was just a cave with shackles built into the stone along three walls and a cage hanging from the ceiling. Drizzt's survey of the place was cut short as the iron-bound door creaked open and two uni-formed drow female soldiers rushed in, going to rigid attention at either side of the portal.

Drizzt firmed his jaw and set his gaze, determined to face his death with dignity.

An illithid walked through the door.

Drizzt's mouth dropped open, but he quickly regained his composure. A mind flayer? He balked, but when he took the moment to consider the crea-ture, he came to realize that he must be in House Baenre's dungeon. That was not a comforting thought, for either him or his friends.

Two drow priestesses, one small and vicious-looking, her face angular and her mouth tight in a perpetual pout, the other taller, more dignified, but no less imposing, came in behind the illithid. Then came the legendary, withered matron mother, sitting easily on a floating driftdisk, flanked by another female, a younger, more beautiful version of Matron Baenre. At the end of the train came two males, fighters, judging from their attire and weapons.

The glow from Matron Baenre's disk allowed Drizzt to shift his gaze to

the normal spectrum—and he noticed a pile of bones under one of the other pairs of shackles.

Drizzt looked back to the entourage, to the drow males, his gaze settling on the younger of the two for a long moment. It was Berg'inyon, he believed, a classmate of his at the drow Academy, the second-ranking fighter of Drizzt's class—second behind Drizzt.

The three younger females fanned out in a line behind Matron Baenre's driftdisk; the two males stood beside the female soldiers at the door. The illithid, to Drizzt's amazement, and supreme discomfort, paced about the captured drow, its tentacles waving near Drizzt's face, brushing his skin, teasing him. Drizzt had seen such tentacles suck the brains out of a dark elf, and it was all he could do to hold his nerve with the wretched creature so near.

"Drizzt Do'Urden," Matron Baenre remarked.

She knew his name. Drizzt realized that to be a bad sign. That sickly, uncomfortable feeling welled within him again, and he was beginning to understand why.

"Noble fool!" Matron Baenre snapped suddenly. "To come to Menzoberranzan, knowing the price upon your pitiful head!" She came forward, off the driftdisk, in a sudden rush and slapped Drizzt across the face. "Noble, arrogant fool! Did you dare to believe that you could win? Did you think that five thousand years of what has been could be disrupted by pitiful you?"

The outburst surprised Drizzt, but he kept his visage solid, his eyes straight ahead.

Matron Baenre's scowl disappeared, replaced suddenly by a wry smile. Drizzt always hated that typical trait of his people. So volatile and unpredictable, dark elves kept enemies and friends alike off guard, never letting a prisoner or a guest know exactly where they stood.

"Let your pride be appeased, Drizzt Do'Urden," Matron Baenre said with a chuckle. "I introduce my daughter Bladen'Kerst Baenre, second eldest to Triel." She indicated the female in the middle. "And Vendes Baenre," she continued, indicating the smallest of the three. "And Quenthel. Behind stand my sons, Dantrag and Berg'inyon, who is known to you."

"Well met," Drizzt said cheerily to Berg'inyon. He managed a smile with his salutation and received another vicious slap from the matron mother.

"Six Baenres have come to see you, Drizzt Do'Urden," Matron Baenre went on, and Drizzt wished that she would quit repeating his name with every sentence! "You should feel honored, Drizzt Do'Urden."

"I would clasp wrists," Drizzt replied, "but . . ." He looked helplessly up to his chained hands and barely flinched as another stinging slap predictably came against his face.

"You know that you will be given to Lolth," Baenre said.

Drizzt looked her straight in the eye. "In body, but never in soul."

"Good," purred the matron mother. "You will not die quickly, I promise. You will prove a wellspring of information, Drizzt Do'Urden."

For the first time in the conversation, a dark cloud crossed Drizzt's features.

"I will torture him, Mother," Vendes offered eagerly.

"Duk-Tak!" Matron Baenre scolded, turning sharply on her daughter.

"Duk-Tak," Drizzt mouthed under his breath, then he recognized the name. In the Drow tongue, duk-tak meant, literally, unholy executioner. It was also the nickname of one of the Baenre daughters—this one apparently—whose handiwork, in the form of dark elves turned into ebony statues, was often on display at the drow Academy.

"Wonderful," Drizzt muttered.

"You have heard of my precious daughter?" Matron Baenre asked, spinning back to the prisoner. "She will have her time with you, I promise, Drizzt Do'Urden, but not before you provide me with valuable information."

Drizzt cast a doubting look the withered drow's way.

"You can withstand any torture," Matron Baenre remarked. "That I do not doubt, noble fool." She lifted a wrinkled hand to stroke the illithid who had moved to her side. "But can you withstand the intrusions of a mind flayer?"

Drizzt felt the blood drain from his face. He had once been a prisoner of the cruel illithids, a helpless, hapless fool, his mind nearly broken by their overpowering wills. Could he fend such intrusions?

"You thought this would end, O noble fool!" Matron Baenre screeched. "You delivered the prize, stupid, arrogant, noble fool!"

Drizzt felt that sick feeling return tenfold. He couldn't hide his cringe as the matron mother went on, her logic following an inescapable course that tore into Drizzt Do'Urden's heart.

"You are but one prize," she said. "And you will aid us in the conquest of another. Mithral Hall will be ours more easily now that King Bruenor Battlehammer's strongest ally is out of the way. And that very ally will show us the dwarven weaknesses.

"Methil!" she commanded, and the illithid walked directly in front of Drizzt. The ranger closed his eyes, but felt the four octopuslike tentacles of the creature's grotesque head squirm across his face, as if looking for specific spots.

Drizzt cried out in horror, snapped his head about wildly, and even managed to bite one of the tentacles.

The illithid fell back.

"Duk-Tak!" Matron Baenre commanded, and eager Vendes rushed forward, slamming a brass-covered fist into Drizzt's cheek. She hit him again, and a third time, gaining momentum, feeding off the torture.

"Must he be conscious?" she asked, her voice pleading.

"Enough!" Drizzt heard Matron Baenre reply, though her voice seemed far away. Vendes smacked him once more, then he felt the tentacles squirm over his face again. He tried to protest, to move his head about, but he hadn't the strength.

The tentacles found a hold; Drizzt felt little pulses of energy run through his face.

His screams over the next ten minutes were purely instinctive, primal, as the mind flayer probed his mind, sent horrid images careening through his thoughts and devoured every mental counter Drizzt had to offer. He felt naked, vulnerable, stripped of his very emotions.

Through it all, Drizzt, though he did not know it, fought valiantly, and when Methil moved back from him, the illithid turned to Matron Baenre and shrugged.

"What have you learned?" the matron mother demanded.

This one is strong, Methil replied telepathically. *It will take more sessions.*

"Continue!" snapped Baenre.

"He will die," Methil somehow said in a gurgling, watery-sounding voice. *"Tomorrow."*

Matron Baenre thought for a moment, then nodded her accord. She looked to Vendes, her vicious Duk-Tak, and snapped her fingers, sending the wild drow into a fierce rush.

Drizzt's world fell away into blackness.

PERSONAL AGENDA

The female?" Triel asked impatiently, pacing Jarlaxle's private quarters in a secret cave along one wall of the Clawrift, a great chasm in the northeastern section of Menzoberranzan.

"Beheaded," the mercenary answered easily. He knew that Triel was employing some sort of lie detection magic, but was confident that he could dance around any such spells. "She was a youngest daughter, an unimpressive noble, of a lower house."

Triel stopped and focused her glare on the evasive mercenary. Jarlaxle knew well that the angry Baenre was not asking about that female, that Khareesa H'kar creature. Khareesa, like all the slavers on the Isle of Rothé, had been killed, as ordered, but reports filtering back to Triel had suggested another female, and a mysterious great cat as well.

Jarlaxle played the staring game better than any. He sat comfortably behind his great desk, even relaxed in his chair. He leaned back and dropped his booted feet atop the desk.

Triel swept across the room in a rush and slapped his feet away. She leaned over the desk to put her scowl close to the cocky mercenary. The priestess heard a slight shuffle to one side, then another from the floor, and suspected that Jarlaxle had many allies here, concealed behind secret doors, ready to spring out and protect the leader of Bregan D'aerthe.

"Not that female," she breathed, trying to keep things somewhat calm. Triel was the leader of the highest school in the drow Academy, the eldest daughter of the first house of Menzoberranzan, and a mighty high priestess in full favor—as far as she knew—of the Spider Queen. She did not fear Jarlaxle or

his allies, but she did fear her mother's wrath if she was forced to kill the often helpful mercenary, if she precipitated a covert war, or even an atmosphere of uncooperation, between valuable Bregan D'aerthe and House Baenre.

And she knew that Jarlaxle understood her paralysis against him, knew that Jarlaxle grasped it better than anyone and would exploit it every step of the way.

Pointedly throwing off his smile, pretending to be serious, the mercenary lifted his gaudy hat and ran a hand slowly over the side of his bald head. "Dear Triel," he replied calmly. "I tell you in all honesty that there was no other drow female on the Isle of Rothé, or near the isle, unless she was a soldier of House Baenre."

Triel backed off from the desk, gnawed at her lips, and wondered where to turn next. As far as she could tell, the mercenary was not lying, and either Jarlaxle had found some way to counter her magic, or he was speaking the truth.

"If there was, I certainly would have reported it to you," Jarlaxle added, and the obvious lie twanged discordantly in Triel's mind.

Jarlaxle hid his smile well. He had thrown out that last lie just to let Triel know that her spell was in place. By her incredulous expression, Jarlaxle knew that he had won that round.

"I heard of a great panther," Triel prompted.

"Magnificent cat," Jarlaxle agreed, "the property of one Drizzt Do'Urden, if I have read the history of the renegade correctly. Guenhwyvar, by name, taken from the corpse of Masoj Hun'ett after Drizzt slew Masoj in battle."

"I heard that the panther, this Guenhwyvar, was on the Isle of Rothé," Triel clarified impatiently.

"Indeed," replied the mercenary. He slid a metallic whistle out from under his cloak and held it before his eyes. "On the isle, then dissolved into an insubstantial mist."

"And the summoning device?"

"You have Drizzt, my dear Triel," Jarlaxle replied calmly. "Neither I nor any of my band got anywhere near the renegade except in battle. And, in case you've never witnessed Drizzt Do'Urden in battle, let me assure you that my soldiers had more on their minds than picking that one's pockets!"

Triel's expression grew suspicious.

"Oh, one lesser soldier did go to the fallen renegade," Jarlaxle clarified, as though he had forgotten that one minor detail. "But he took no figurine, no summoning device at all, from Drizzt, I assure you."

"And neither you nor any of your soldiers happened to find the onyx figurine?"

"No."

Again, the crafty mercenary had spoken nothing but the truth, for Artemis Entreri was not, technically, a soldier of Bregan D'aerthe.

Triel's spell told her that Jarlaxle's words had been correct, but all reports claimed that the panther had been about on the isle and House Baenre's soldiers had not been able to locate the valuable figurine. Some thought it might have flown from Drizzt when he had gone over the ledge, landing somewhere in the murky water. Magical detection spells hadn't located it, but that could be readily explained by the nature of Donigarten. Calm on the surface, the dark lake was well known for strong undercurrents, and for darker things lurking in the deep.

Still, the Baenre daughter was not convinced about either the female or the panther. Jarlaxle had beaten her this time, she knew, but she trusted in her reports as much as she didn't trust in the mercenary.

Her ensuing expression, a pout so uncommon to the proud Baenre daughter, actually caught Jarlaxle off guard.

"The plans proceed," Triel said suddenly. "Matron Baenre has brought together a high ritual, a ceremony that will be heightened now that she has secured a most worthy sacrifice."

Jarlaxle considered the words carefully, and the weight with which Triel had spoken them. Drizzt, the initial link to Mithral Hall, had been delivered, but Matron Baenre still planned to proceed, with all speed, to the conquest of Mithral Hall. What would Lolth think of all this? the mercenary had to wonder.

"Surely your matron will take the time to consider all options," Jarlaxle replied calmly.

"She nears her death," Triel snapped in reply. "She is hungry for the conquest and will not allow herself to die until it has been achieved."

Jarlaxle nearly laughed at that phrase, "will not allow herself to die," then he considered the withered matron mother. Baenre should have died centuries ago, and yet she somehow lived on. Perhaps Triel was right, the mercenary mused. Perhaps Matron Baenre understood that the decades were finally catching up with her, so she would push on to the conquest without regard for consequences. Jarlaxle loved chaos, loved war, but this was a matter that required careful thinking. The mercenary truly enjoyed his life in Menzoberranzan. Might Matron Baenre be jeopardizing that existence?

"She thinks Drizzt's capture a good thing," Triel went on, "and it is— indeed it is! That renegade is a sacrifice long overdue the Spider Queen."

"But . . ." Jarlaxle prompted.

"But how will the alliance hold together when the other matron mothers

learn that Drizzt is already taken?" Triel pointed out. "It is a tentative thing, at best, and more tentative still if some come to believe that Lolth's sanction of the raid is no more, that the main goal in going to the surface has already been achieved."

Jarlaxle folded his fingers in front of him and paused for a long while. She was wise, this Baenre daughter, wise and as experienced in the ways of the drow as any in the city—except for her mother and, perhaps, Jarlaxle. But now she, with so much more to lose, had shown the mercenary something he had not thought of on his own, a potentially serious problem.

Trying vainly to hide her frustration, Triel spun away from the desk and marched across the small room, hardly slowing as she plunged straight into the unconventional portal, almost an interplanar goo that made her walk along a watery corridor for many steps—though the door seemed to be only several inches thick—before exiting between two smirking Bregan D'aerthe guardsmen in a corridor.

A moment later, Jarlaxle saw the heated outline of a drow hand against his almost translucent door, the signal that Triel was gone from the complex. A lever under the top of the mercenary's desk opened seven different secret doors—from the floor and the walls—and out stepped or climbed several dark elves and one human, Artemis Entreri.

"Triel heard reports of the female on the isle," Jarlaxle said to the drow soldiers, his most trusted advisors. "Go among the ranks and learn who, if any, betrayed us to the Baenre daughter."

"And kill him?" asked one eager drow, a vicious specimen whose skills Jarlaxle valued when conducting interrogations.

The mercenary leader put a condescending look over the impetuous drow, and the other Bregan D'aerthe soldiers followed suit. Tradition in the underground band did not call for the execution of spies, but rather the subtle manipulation. Jarlaxle had proven many times that he could get as much done, plant as much disinformation, with an enemy informant as with his own spies and, to disciplined Bregan D'aerthe, any plant that Triel had in place among the ranks would be a benefit.

Without needing to speak another word to his well-trained and well-practiced advisors, Jarlaxle waved them away.

"This adventure grows more fun by the hour," the mercenary remarked to Entreri when they were gone. He looked the assassin right in the eye. "Despite the disappointments."

The remark caught Entreri off guard. He tried to decipher what Jarlaxle might be talking about.

"You knew that Drizzt was in the Underdark, knew even that he was close to Menzoberranzan and soon to arrive," the mercenary began, though that statement told Entreri nothing enlightening.

"The trap was perfectly set and perfectly executed," the assassin argued, and Jarlaxle couldn't really disagree, though several soldiers were wounded and four had died. Such losses had to be expected when dealing with one as fiery as Drizzt. "I was the one who brought Drizzt down and captured Catti-brie," Entreri pointedly reminded him.

"Therein lies your error," Jarlaxle said with an accusing snicker.

Entreri eyed him with sincere confusion.

"The human woman called Catti-brie followed Drizzt down here, using Guenhwyvar and this," he said, holding up the magical, heart-shaped locket. "She followed blindly, by all reasoning, through twisting caverns and terrible mazes. She could never hope to retrace her steps."

"She will not likely be leaving," Entreri added dryly.

"Therein lies your error," Jarlaxle repeated. His smile was wide, and now Entreri was beginning to catch on.

"Drizzt Do'Urden alone could have guided you from the depths of the Underdark," Jarlaxle told him plainly. The mercenary tossed the locket to Entreri. "Feel its warmth," he explained, "the warmth of the warrior's blood coursing through the veins of Drizzt Do'Urden. When it cools, then know that Drizzt is no more, and know that your sunlight world is lost to you forever.

"Except for an occasional glance, perhaps, when Mithral Hall is taken," Jarlaxle added with a sly wink.

Entreri resisted the impulse to leap over the desk and murder the mercenary—mostly because he suspected that another lever under that desktop would open seven other trap doors and bring Jarlaxle's closest, closest advisors storming upon him. But truly, after that initial moment, the assassin was more intrigued than angered, both by Jarlaxle's sudden proclamation that he would never see the surface world, and by the thought that Drizzt Do'Urden could have led him out of the Underdark. Thinking, still holding the locket, the assassin started for the door.

"Did I mention that House Horlbar has begun its inquiry into the death of Jerlys?" Jarlaxle queried at his back, stopping the assassin in midstride. "They have even approached Bregan D'aerthe, willing to pay dearly for information. How ironic, wouldn't you agree?"

Entreri did not turn about. He simply walked to the door and pushed out of the room. It was more food for thought.

Jarlaxle, too, was thinking—thinking that this entire episode might become more delicious yet. He thought that Triel had pointed out some snares that Matron Baenre, blinded by her lust for power, would never notice. He thought most of all that the Spider Queen, in her love of chaos, had placed him in a position to turn the world of Menzoberranzan upon its head.

Matron Baenre had her own agenda, and Triel certainly had hers, and now Jarlaxle was solidifying one of his own, for no better reason than the onslaught of furious chaos, from which the cunning mercenary always seemed to emerge better off than before.

✕ ✕ ✕ ✕ ✕

The semiconscious Drizzt did not know how long the punishment had gone on. Vendes was brilliant at her cruel craft, finding every sensitive area on the hapless prisoner and beating it, gouging, it, raking it with wickedly tipped instruments. She kept Drizzt on the verge of unconsciousness, never allowing him to black out completely, kept him feeling the excruciating pain.

Then she left, and Drizzt slumped low on his shackles, unable to comprehend the damage the hard-edged rings were doing to his wrists. All the ranger wanted at the terrible time was to fall away from the world, from his pained body. He could not think of the surface, of his friends. He remembered that Guenhwyvar had been on the island, but could not concentrate enough to remember the significance of that.

He was defeated; for the first time in his life, Drizzt wondered if death would be preferable to life.

He felt someone grab roughly at his hair and yank his head back. He tried to see through his blurry and swollen eyes, for he feared that wicked Vendes had returned. The voices he heard, though, were male.

A flask came up against his lips, and his head was yanked hard to the side, angled so that the liquid would pour down his throat. Instinctively, thinking this some poison, or some potion that would steal his free will, Drizzt resisted. He spat out some of the liquid, but got his head slammed hard against the wall for the effort, and more of the sour-tasting stuff rolled down his throat.

Drizzt felt burning throughout his body, as though his insides were on fire. In what he believed were his last gasps of life, he struggled fiercely against the unyielding chains, then fell limp, exhausted, expecting to die.

The burn became a tingling, sweet sensation; Drizzt felt stronger suddenly, and his vision returned as the swelling began to subside from his eyes.

The Baenre brothers stood before him.

"Drizzt Do'Urden," Dantrag said evenly. "I have waited many years to meet you."

Drizzt had no reply.

"Do you know me? Of me?" Dantrag asked.

Again Drizzt did not speak, and this time his silence cost him a slap across the face.

"Do you know of me?" Dantrag asked more forcefully.

Drizzt tried hard to remember the name Matron Baenre had tagged on this one. He knew Berg'inyon from their years together at the Academy and on patrol, but not this one; he couldn't remember the name. He did understand that this one's ego was involved, and that it would be wise to appease that false pride. He studied the male's outfit for just a moment, drawing what he hoped to be the correct conclusion.

"Weapons master of House Baenre," he slurred, blood following every word from his battered mouth. He found that the sting of those wounds was not so great now, as though they were quickly healing, and he began to understand the nature of that potion that had been forced down his throat.

"Zaknafein told you, then, of Dantrag," the male reasoned, puffing out his chest like a barnyard rooster.

"Of course," Drizzt lied.

"Then you know why I am here."

"No," Drizzt answered honestly, more than a little confused.

Dantrag looked over his own shoulder, drawing Drizzt's gaze across the room to a pile of equipment—Drizzt's equipment!—stacked neatly in a far corner.

"For many years I desired a fight with Zaknafein," Dantrag explained, "to prove that I was the better. He was afraid of me and would not come out of his hiding hole."

Drizzt resisted the urge to scoff openly; Zaknafein had been afraid of no one.

"Now I have you," Dantrag went on.

"To prove yourself?" Drizzt asked.

Dantrag lifted a hand, as if to strike, but held his temper in check.

"We fight, and you kill me, and what does Matron Baenre say?" Drizzt asked, understanding Dantrag's dilemma. He had been captured for greater reasons than to appease the pride of an upstart Baenre child. It all seemed like such a game suddenly—a game that Drizzt had played before. When his sister had come to Mithral Hall and captured him, part of her deal with her

associate was to let the man, Artemis Entreri, have his personal fight with Drizzt, for no better reason than to prove himself.

"The glory of my victory will forestall any punishments," Dantrag replied casually, as though he honestly believed the claim. "And perhaps I will not kill you. Perhaps I will maim you and drag you back to your chains so that Vendes can continue her play. That is why we gave you the potion. You will be healed, brought to the brink of death, and healed again. It will go on for a hundred years, if that is Matron Baenre's will."

Drizzt remembered the ways of his dark people and did not doubt the claim for a minute. He had heard whispers of captured nobles, taken in some of the many interhouse wars, who were kept for centuries as tortured slaves of the victorious houses.

"Do not doubt that our fight will come, Drizzt Do'Urden," Dantrag said. He put his face right up to Drizzt's. "When you are healed and able to defend yourself." Faster than Drizzt's eyes could follow, Dantrag's hands came up and slapped him alternately on both cheeks. Drizzt had never seen such speed before and he marked it well, suspecting that he would one day witness it again under more dangerous circumstances.

Dantrag spun on his heels and walked past Berg'inyon, toward the door. The younger Baenre merely laughed at the hanging prisoner and spat in Drizzt's face before following his brother.

✕ ✕ ✕ ✕ ✕

"So beautiful," the bald mercenary remarked, running his slender fingers through Catti-brie's thick tangle of auburn hair.

Catti-brie did not blink; she just stared hard at the dimly lit, undeniably handsome figure. There was something different about this drow, the perceptive young woman realized. She did not think that he would force himself on her. Buried within Jarlaxle's swashbuckling facade was a warped sense of honor, but a definite code nonetheless, somewhat like that of Artemis Entreri. Entreri had once held Catti-brie as a prisoner for many days, and he had not placed a hand on her except to prod her along the necessary course.

So it was with Jarlaxle, Catti-brie believed, hoped. If the mercenary truly found her attractive, he would probably try to woo her, court her attention, at least for a while.

"And your courage cannot be questioned," Jarlaxle continued in his uncomfortably perfect surface dialect. "To come alone to Menzoberranzan!" The mercenary shook his head in disbelief and looked to Entreri, the only other person in the small, square room. "Even Artemis Entreri had to be coaxed here, and would leave, no doubt, if he could find the way.

"This is not a place for surface-dwellers," Jarlaxle remarked. To accentuate his point, the mercenary jerked his hand suddenly, again taking the Cat's Eye circlet from Catti-brie's head. Blackness, deeper than even the nights in the lowest of Bruenor's mines, enveloped her, and she had to fight hard to keep a wave of panic from overwhelming her.

Jarlaxle was right in front of her. She could feel him, feel his breath, but all she saw was his red-glowing eyes, sizing her up in the infrared spectrum. Across the room, Entreri's eyes likewise glowed, and Catti-brie did not understand how he, a human, had gained such vision.

She dearly wished that she possessed it as well. The darkness continued to overwhelm her, to swallow her. Her skin felt extra sensitive; all her senses were on their very edge.

She wanted to scream, but would not give her captors the satisfaction.

Jarlaxle uttered a word that Catti-brie did not understand, and the room was suddenly bathed in soft blue light.

"In here, you will see," Jarlaxle said to her. "Out there, beyond your door, there is only darkness." He teasingly held the circlet before Catti-brie's longing gaze, then dropped it into a pocket of his breeches.

"Forgive me," he said softly to Catti-brie, taking her off her guard. "I do not wish to torment you, but I must maintain my security. Matron Baenre desires you—quite badly I would guess, since she keeps Drizzt as a prisoner—and knows that you would be a fine way to gnaw at his powerful will."

Catti-brie did not hide her excitement, fleeting hope, at the news that Drizzt was alive.

"Of course they have not killed him," the mercenary went on, speaking as much to Entreri, the assassin realized, as to Catti-brie. "He is a valuable prisoner, a wellspring of information, as they say on the surface."

"They will kill him," Entreri remarked—somewhat angrily, Catti-brie had the presence of mind to note.

"Eventually," Jarlaxle replied, and he chuckled. "But both of you will probably be long dead of old age by then, and your children as well. Unless they are half-drow," he added slyly, tossing a wink at Catti-brie.

She resisted the urge to punch him in the eye.

"It's a pity, really, that events followed such a course," Jarlaxle continued. "I did so wish to speak with the legendary Drizzt Do'Urden before Baenre got him. If I had that spider mask in my possession, I would go to the Baenre compound this very night, when the priestesses are at the high ritual, and sneak in

for a talk with him. Early in the ceremony, of course, in case Matron Baenre decides to sacrifice him this very night. Ah, well." He ended with a sigh and a shrug and ran his gentle fingers through Catti-brie's thick hair one final time before he turned for the door.

"I could not go anyway," he said to Entreri. "I must meet with Matron Ker Horlbar to discuss the cost of an investigation."

Entreri only smiled in response to the pointedly cruel remark. He rose as the mercenary passed, fell in behind Jarlaxle, then stopped suddenly and looked back to Catti-brie.

"I think I will stay and speak with her," the assassin said.

"As you will," the mercenary replied, "but do not harm her. Or, if you do," he corrected with another chuckle, "at least do not scar her beautiful features."

Jarlaxle walked out of the room and closed the door behind, then let his magical boots continue to click loudly as he walked along the stone corridor, to let Entreri be confident that he had gone. He felt in his pocket as he went, and smiled widely when he discovered, to no surprise, that the circlet had just been taken.

Jarlaxle had sown the seeds of chaos; now he could sit back and watch the fruit of his labors grow.

21

THE LAYERS
STRIPPED AWAY

Catti-brie and Entreri spent a long moment staring at each other, alone for the first time since her capture, in the small room at Bregan D'aerthe's secret complex. By the expression on Entreri's face, Catti-brie knew that he was up to something.

He held his hand up before him and shifted his fingers, and the Cat's Eye agate dropped to the end of its silver chain.

Catti-brie stared at it curiously, unsure of the assassin's motives. He had stolen it from Jarlaxle's pocket, of course, but why would he risk a theft from so dangerous a dark elf?

"Ye're as much a prisoner as I am," Catti-brie finally reasoned. "He's got ye caught here to do his bidding."

"I do not like that word," Entreri replied, "prisoner. It implies a helpless state, and I assure you, I am never helpless."

He was nine parts bravado, one part hope, Catti-brie knew, but she kept the thought to herself.

"And what are ye to do when Jarlaxle finds it missing?" she asked.

"I shall be dancing on the surface by that time," the assassin replied coolly.

Catti-brie studied him. There it was, spoken plainly and clearly, beyond intrigue. But why the circlet? she continued to wonder, and then she grew suddenly afraid. Entreri may have decided that its starlight was preferable to, or complementary to, his infravision. But he would not have told her that he meant to go if he meant to leave her behind—alive.

"Ye do not need the thing," Catti-brie reasoned, trying to keep her voice steady. "Ye've been given the infravision and can see yer way well enough."

"But you need it," Entreri said, tossing the circlet to the young woman. Catti-brie caught it and held it in her hands, trying to weigh the consequences of putting it on.

"I cannot lead ye to the surface," she said, thinking that the assassin had miscalculated. "I found me way down only because I had the panther and the locket showing me the way to follow Drizzt."

The assassin didn't blink.

"I said I cannot lead ye out o' here," Catti-brie reiterated.

"Drizzt can," Entreri said. "I offer you a deal, one that you are in no position to refuse. I will get both you and Drizzt out of Menzoberranzan, and you two will escort me back to the surface. Once there, we go our separate ways, and may they stay separate through all eternity."

Catti-brie took a long moment to digest the startling proposition. "Ye're thinking that I'm to trust ye?" she asked, but Entreri didn't answer, didn't have to answer. Catti-brie sat imprisoned in a room surrounded by fierce drow enemies, and Drizzt's predicament was likely even worse. Whatever the evil Entreri might offer her, it could be no worse than the alternatives.

"What about Guenhwyvar?" Catti-brie asked. "And me bow?"

"I've the bow and quiver," Entreri answered. "Jarlaxle has the panther."

"I'll not leave without Guenhwyvar," Catti-brie said.

Entreri looked at her incredulously, as if he thought she were bluffing.

Catti-brie threw the circlet to his feet. She hopped up on the edge of a small table and crossed her arms defiantly over her chest.

Entreri looked down to the item, then to Catti-brie. "I could make you leave," he promised.

"If ye think ye could, then ye're thinking wrong," Catti-brie answered. "I'm guessing that ye'll need me help and cooperation to get through this place, and I'm not to give it to ye, not for meself and not for Drizzt, without the cat.

"And know ye that Drizzt will agree with me choice," Catti-brie went on, hammering home the point. "Guenhwyvar's a friend to us both, and we're not for leaving friends behind!"

Entreri hooked his toe under a loop in the circlet and casually flipped it across the room to Catti-brie, who caught it once more and, this time, put it on her head. Without another word, the assassin motioned for the woman to sit tight, and he abruptly left the room.

The single guard outside Jarlaxle's private room showed little interest in the approaching human; Entreri practically had to prod the drow to get his attention. Then the assassin pointed to the strange, flowing door and asked, "Jarlaxle?"

The soldier shook his head.

Entreri pointed again to the watery door, his eyes suddenly popping wide with surprise. When the soldier leaned over to see what was wrong, the assassin grabbed him across the shoulders and heaved him through the portal, both of them slipping through, into the watery corridor. Entreri tugged and twisted in a slow-motion wrestling match with the surprised drow. He was bigger than this one, and equally agile, and gradually made progress in moving the guard along.

They plunged out the other side, falling into Jarlaxle's room. The drow went for his sword, but Entreri's left hook staggered him. A quick combination of punches followed, and when the drow went down to one knee, the assassin's foot slammed hard against his cheek.

Entreri half-dragged, half-carried the drow to the side of the room, where he slammed him against the wall. He slugged him several times to make sure that he would offer no further resistance. Soon he had the dark elf helpless, down on his knees, barely conscious, with his hands tied behind his back and his mouth tightly gagged. He pinned the drow against the wall and felt about for a releasing mechanism. The door to a secret cubby slid open, and Entreri forced the drow inside.

Entreri considered whether or not to kill this one. On the one hand, if he killed the drow, there would be no witnesses and Jarlaxle would have to spend some time figuring out who had committed the crime. Something held Entreri's dagger hand in check, though, some instinct that told him to proceed with this operation cleanly, with no losses to Bregan D'aerthe.

It was all too easy, Entreri realized when he found not only the figurine of Guenhwyvar, but Catti-brie's magical mask as well, waiting for him—yes, waiting for him!—on Jarlaxle's desk. Entreri picked them up gingerly, looking for some devious traps nearby and checking to make sure that these were the genuine items.

Something strange was going on.

Entreri considered the not-so-subtle hints that Jarlaxle had been dropping, the fact that the mercenary had taken him to Sorcere and conveniently showed him the way to the spider mask. He reached into a pocket and took out the magical locket of Alustriel, the homing beacon to Drizzt Do'Urden that Jarlaxle had casually tossed to him. Jarlaxle had even managed to slip in the proper time for the attempt, the early hours of the high ritual being celebrated at House Baenre this very night.

What was it all about? Entreri wondered. Jarlaxle had some private agenda, one that apparently went against House Baenre's designs on Mithral Hall.

Standing there in the mercenary's office, it seemed obvious to Entreri that Jarlaxle had set him up as a pawn.

Entreri clutched the locket tightly, then thrust it back into his pocket. Very well, he decided. He would be an effective pawn indeed.

Twenty minutes later, Entreri, using the magical mask to appear as a drow soldier, and Catti-brie moved quietly and swiftly along the winding ways of Menzoberranzan, cutting a northeastern path along the stalagmite mounds, toward the higher level of Tier Breche and the drow Academy.

⚔ ⚔ ⚔ ⚔ ⚔

He saw again the tiered steps of the great dwarven Undercity, the heart of Mithral Hall. He imagined the entryway from the western gate, through Keeper's Dale, and pictured again the great chasm known as Garumn's Gorge.

Drizzt fought hard to warp those images, to distort the truth about Mithral Hall, but the details were so clear to him! It was as if he were there again, walking freely beside Bruenor and the others. In the throes of the mind flayer's hypnosis, Drizzt found himself overwhelmed. He had no more barriers to stack against the mental intrusion of Matron Baenre's pet, no more willpower against the mental giant.

As the images came to Drizzt, he felt them stripped away, mentally scraped from his brain, like so much food for the wretched illithid. Each intrusion burned painfully, shot electrical shocks along the synaptical connections of the drow ranger's mind.

Finally Drizzt felt the creature's insidious tentacles loosening their grip on the skin of his forehead, and he slumped, his mind a jumble of confusing images and his head throbbing with agony.

"We have gained some information this day," he heard the distant, watery voice say.

Gained some information . . .

The words rang over and over ominously in Drizzt's mind. The illithid and Matron Baenre were still talking, but he was not listening, concentrating on those three words, remembering the implications of those three terrible words.

Drizzt's lavender orbs slipped open, but he kept his head bowed, covertly peeking at Methil. The creature had its back to him, was only a couple of feet away.

The illithid now knew part of the layout of Mithral Hall, and its continuous intrusions into Drizzt's mind would soon show it the entire complex.

Drizzt could not let that happen; slowly the drow's hands clenched more tightly on the chains.

Drizzt's bare foot came up, his heel slamming the wretched creature's spongy head. Before Methil could move away, the ranger wrapped his legs about Methil's neck in a choke hold and began thrashing back and forth, trying to snap the thing's neck.

Drizzt felt the tentacles probing for his skin, felt them boring into his legs, but he fought away his revulsion and thrashed wildly. He saw wicked Vendes coming around the side and knew what would come, but he concentrated on his task. For the sake of his friends, Methil had to be killed!

The illithid threw its weight straight back, trying to confuse Drizzt and break the hold, but the skilled drow ranger turned with the move and Methil fell to the ground, half slumped against the wall and half held aloft by Drizzt's strong hold. Drizzt heaved him up and slammed him back, releasing the ineffective choke. Illithids were not physically imposing creatures, and Methil raised his three-fingered hands pitifully, trying to fend the sudden barrage of stomping feet.

Something hard slammed Drizzt at the base of his ribs, stealing his breath. He stubbornly continued to stomp, but was slammed again, then a third time and a fourth.

Hanging limply from the chains, the ranger tried to curl up to protect the area as Vendes hammered away. Drizzt thought that he was surely dead when he looked into the furious eyes of wicked Duk-Tak, which were filled with a mixture of venom and hatred and ecstacy, as she was allowed to vent that perpetual fury.

She stopped, sooner than Drizzt dared to hope, and calmly walked away, leaving Drizzt hanging from the shackles, trying to curl but unable to find the strength.

Methil had joined Matron Baenre, who sat comfortably on her driftdisk, and was looking back at Drizzt with his pupilless, milky white eyes.

Drizzt knew that the next time the illithid encroached on his mind, Methil would go out of his way to make the pain even more intense.

"No potion for him," Matron Baenre instructed Dantrag, standing impassively by the door. Dantrag followed his mother's gaze to several flasks along the wall to Drizzt's left and nodded.

"*Dobluth,*" she said to Drizzt, using the derisive drow word for "outcast." "The high ritual will be better served with our knowledge that you are here in agony." She nodded to Vendes, who wheeled about, hurling a small dart as she turned.

It caught Drizzt in the stomach, and he felt a small but stinging pinch. Then his entire belly felt as if it had ignited into roaring fires. He gagged, tried to scream, then sheer agony gave him the strength to curl up. The change in posture didn't help. The magical little dart continued to pump its droplets of poison into him, continued to burn at his insides.

Through tear-filled eyes, Drizzt saw the driftdisk slide from his cell, Vendes and Methil obediently following Matron Baenre. Dantrag, expressionless, remained leaning against the doorjamb for some time, then walked over near Drizzt.

Drizzt forced himself to stop screaming, and merely groaned and grunted through gritted teeth with the weapons master standing so close to him.

"You are a fool," Dantrag said. "If your attempts force my mother to kill you before I get the chance, I promise you that I will personally torture and slaughter every living creature that calls itself a friend of Drizzt Do'Urden!"

Again with speed that defied Drizzt's vision, Dantrag smacked Drizzt across the face. The ranger hung limp for just a second, then was forced to curl up again as the fiery explosions of the poisoned dart erupted across his stomach.

⚔ ⚔ ⚔ ⚔ ⚔

Out of sight, around the corner at the base of the wide stairs leading to Tier Breche, Artemis Entreri tried hard to recall an image of Gromph Baenre, the archmage of the city. He had seen Gromph only a few times, mostly while spying for Jarlaxle. Jarlaxle had thought that the archmage was shortening the nights in Menzoberranzan by lighting the lingering heat fires in the time clock of Narbondel a few instants too soon, and was interested in what the dangerous wizard might be up to, and so he had sent Entreri to spy on the drow.

Entreri's cloak changed to the flowing robes of the wizard; his hair became thicker and longer, a great white mane, and subtle, barely visible wrinkles appeared about his eyes.

"I cannot believe ye're trying this," Catti-brie said to him when he moved out of the shadows.

"The spider mask is in Gromph's desk," the assassin answered coldly, not thrilled with the prospects either. "There is no other way into House Baenre."

"And if this Gromph is sitting at his desk?"

"Then you and I will be scattered all over the cavern," Entreri answered gruffly, and he swept by the young woman, grabbed her hand, and pulled her up the wide stairway.

Entreri was counting as much on luck as on skill. He knew that Sorcere, the school of wizards, was full of reclusive masters who generally stayed out of each other's way, and he could only hope that Gromph, though only a male, had been invited to House Baenre's high ritual. The walls of the secretive place were protected against scrying and against teleportation, and if his disguise worked against whatever magical barriers might be in place, he should be able to get in and out of Gromph's room without too much interference. The city's archmage was known as a surly one, with a violent temper; no one got in Gromph's way.

At the top of the stairway, on the level of Tier Breche, the companions saw the three structures of the drow Academy. To their right was the plain, pyramidal structure of Melee-Magthere, the school of fighters. Directly ahead loomed the most impressive structure, the great spider-shaped building of Arach-Tinilith, the school of Lolth. Entreri was glad that he did not have to try to enter either of those buildings. Melee-Magthere was a place of swarming guardsmen and tight control, and Arach-Tinilith was protected by the high priestesses of Lolth, working in concert for the good of their Spider Queen. Only the gracefully spired structure to the left, Sorcere, was secretive enough to penetrate.

Catti-brie pulled her arm away and nearly bolted in sheer terror. She had no disguise and felt totally vulnerable up here. The young woman found her courage, though, and did not resist when Entreri roughly grabbed her arm once more and tugged her along at a great pace.

They walked into Sorcere's open front doorway, where two guards promptly blocked their way. One started to ask Entreri a question, but the assassin slapped him across the face and pushed past, hoping that Gromph's cruel reputation would get them through.

The bluff worked, and the guards went back to their posts, not even daring to mutter to themselves until the archmage was far away.

Entreri remembered the twisting ways perfectly and soon came to the plain wall flanking Gromph's private chambers. He took a deep breath and looked to his companion, silently reiterating his feelings that if Gromph was behind this door, they were both surely dead.

"Kolsen'shea orbb," the assassin whispered. To Entreri's relief, the wall began to stretch and twist, becoming a spiderweb. The strands rotated, leaving the hole and revealing the soft blue glow, and Entreri quickly—before he lost his nerve—rushed through and pulled Catti-brie in behind him.

Gromph was not inside.

Entreri made for the dwarf bone desk, rubbing his hands together and

blowing in them before reaching for the appropriate drawer. Catti-brie, meanwhile, intrigued by the obviously magical paraphernalia, walked about, eyeing parchments—from a distance—even going over to one ceramic bottle and daring to pop off its cork.

Entreri's heart leaped into his throat when he heard the archmage's voice, but he relaxed when he realized that it came from the bottle.

Catti-brie looked at the bottle and the cork curiously, then popped the cork back on, eliminating the voice. "What was that?" she asked, not understanding a word of the Drow language.

"I know not," Entreri replied harshly. "Do not touch anything!"

Catti-brie shrugged as the assassin went back to his work on the desk, trying to make sure that he uttered the password for the drawer perfectly. He recalled his conversation with Jarlaxle, when the mercenary had given him the word. Had Jarlaxle been honest, or was this whole thing part of some elaborate game? Had Jarlaxle baited him to this place, so that he might speak some false word, open the drawer, and destroy himself and half of Sorcere? It occurred to Entreri that Jarlaxle might have put a phony replica of the spider mask in the drawer, then tricked Entreri into coming here and setting off Gromph's powerful wards, thus destroying the evidence.

Entreri shook the disturbing thoughts away. He had committed himself to this course, had convinced himself that his attempt to free Drizzt was somehow part of the framework of Jarlaxle's grand plans, whatever they might be, and he could not surrender to his fears now. He uttered the phrase and pulled open the drawer.

The spider mask was waiting for him.

Entreri scooped it up and turned to Catti-brie, who had filled the top of a small hourglass with fine white sand and was watching it slip away with the moments. Entreri leaped from the dwarf bone desk and scrambled across the room, tipping the item to the side.

Catti-brie eyed him curiously.

"I was keeping the time," she said calmly.

"This is no timepiece!" the assassin roughly explained. He tipped the hourglass upside down and carefully removed the sand, replacing it in its packet and gently resealing it. "It is an explosive, and when the sand runs out, all the area bursts into flame. You must not touch anything!" he scolded harshly. "Gromph will not even know that we have been here if all is in proper order." Entreri looked around at the jumbled room as he spoke. "Or, at least, in proper disorder. He was not here when Jarlaxle returned the spider mask."

Catti-brie nodded and appeared genuinely ashamed, but it was only a facade. The young woman had suspected the general, if not the exact, nature of the hourglass all along, and would not have let the sand run out. She had only started it running to get some confirmation from the worldly Entreri.

The two quickly departed the wizard's room and Sorcere. Catti-brie did not let on that she had several more of those dangerous hourglasses, and their corresponding packets of detonating sand, tucked into a belt pouch.

22

BREAK-IN

Qu'ellarz'orl, the plateau occupied by some of the proudest noble houses, was
strangely quiet. Entreri, appearing as a common drow soldier again, and
Catti-brie made their silent and inconspicuous way along the great mushroom
grove, toward the twenty-foot-high spiderweb fence surrounding the Baenre
compound.

Panic welled in both the companions and neither said a thing, forced themselves to concentrate on the stakes in this game: ultimate victory or ultimate
loss.

Crouched in the shadows behind a stalagmite, the two watched as a grand
procession, led by several priestesses sitting atop blue-glowing driftdisks, made
its way through the open compound and toward the great doors of the huge
central chapel. Entreri recognized Matron Baenre and knew that some of
the others near her were probably her daughters. He watched the many disks
curiously, coming to understand that matron mothers of other houses were
in the procession.

It was a high ritual, as Jarlaxle had said, and Entreri snickered at how completely the sly mercenary had arranged all of this.

"What is it?" Catti-brie asked, not understanding the private joke.

Entreri shook his head and scowled, indicating that the troublesome young
woman should shut her mouth. Catti-brie bit her bottom lip and did not spew
the many venomous replies she had in mind. She needed Entreri now, and he
needed her; their personal hatred would have to wait.

And wait is exactly what Catti-brie and Entreri did. They squatted behind
the mound for many minutes as the long procession gradually disappeared

into the domed chapel. Entreri figured that many more than a thousand drow, maybe even two thousand, had gone into the structure, and few soldiers, or lizard-riders, could now be seen from his position.

Another benefit of their timing soon showed itself as songs to Lolth filtered out of the chapel's doors, filling the air about the compound.

"The cat?" Entreri whispered to Catti-brie.

Catti-brie felt the statuette in her pouch and considered the question, then looked doubtfully at the Baenre web fence. "When we get over," she explained, though she had no idea of how Entreri meant to pass that seemingly impenetrable barrier. The strands of the fence were as thick as Catti-brie's forearm.

Entreri nodded his agreement and took out the black velvet spider mask and slipped it over his head. Catti-brie couldn't contain a shudder as she regarded the assassin, his head now resembling some grotesque caricature of a huge spider.

"I will warn you only once," the assassin whispered. "You are a merciful one, foolishly so, but there is no place for mercy in the realm of the drow. Do not think to wound or knock unconscious any opponents we cross. Go for the kill."

Catti-brie didn't bother to reply, and if Entreri could see into the fires raging inside the young woman, he would not have bothered to utter the remark.

He motioned for her to follow, then picked his careful way from shadow to shadow to the base of the fence.

Entreri touched the strands tentatively, making certain that his fingers would not stick, then he took a firm hold and bade Catti-brie to climb on his back.

"Take care that you do not touch the fence!" he warned. "Else I will have to remove whatever limb you have stuck."

Catti-brie gingerly took hold of the evil man, wrapping her arms about his chest, one over one shoulder, the other under Entreri's arm. She clasped her hands tightly and squeezed with all her strength.

Entreri was not a big man, not forty pounds heavier than Catti-brie herself, but he was strong, his muscles honed for fighting, and he easily began his ascent, keeping his body as far from the dangerous fence as possible so that the young woman's hands did not get entangled. The trickiest part came at the top of the barrier, particularly when Entreri spotted a couple of lizard-riding soldiers approaching.

"Do not even breathe," he warned Catti-brie, and he inched along the top rim of the fence to take as much cover as possible in the shadows of an anchoring stalagmite post.

If there had been no lights in the Baenre compound, the two surely would been caught, their warm forms showing distinctively against the cooler stone of the mound. But lights were on, including many burning torches, and the Baenre soldiers were not using their infravision as they walked their posts. They passed by the fence no more than a dozen feet from the two intruders, but so adept at hiding in the shadows was Artemis Entreri that they never noticed the strange jut in the previously smooth stalagmite.

When they were gone, Entreri pulled himself to a standing position atop the fence and twisted to the side, so that Catti-brie could brace herself against the mound. He had only intended to take a short rest, but the young woman, desperate to be on with things, unexpectedly shifted off his back, onto the mound, and half slid, half climbed down its back side, coming to a roll in the Baenre compound.

Entreri hustled down the fence to join her, snapped off the mask, and glared at her, thinking her actions rash and stupid.

Catti-brie did not retreat from that look, just eyed the hated assassin dangerously and mouthed, "Where?"

Entreri slipped a hand into one pocket and felt for the magical locket, then turned about, facing different directions until the item seemed most warm. He had guessed Drizzt's location before the locket had even confirmed it: the great mound, the best guarded position in the entire compound.

They could only hope that most of Baenre's elite soldiers were attending the high ritual.

Crossing the compound to the elaborate structure was not difficult, for few guards were apparent, the shadows were many, and the singing emanating from the chapel amply covered any noise. No house would expect an attack, or dare to invoke the Spider Queen's anger by launching an attack, during a high ritual, and since the only possible threat to House Baenre was from another drow house, security in the compound was not at its highest point.

"In there," Entreri whispered as he and Catti-brie came flat against the walls flanking the doorway to the huge, hollowed stalagmite. Gently, Entreri touched the stone door to try to discern any traps—though he figured that any traps would be magical in nature and he would find them when they blew up in his face). To his surprise, the portal suddenly rose, disappearing into a crack in the top of the jamb and revealing a narrow, dimly lit corridor.

He and Catti-brie exchanged doubtful looks, and after a long, silent pause, both stepped in together—and both nearly fell over with relief when they realized that they were still alive in the corridor.

Their relief was not long-lived, however, for it was stolen by a guttural call, a question, perhaps. Before the pair could decipher any of the words, the form of a huge, muscular humanoid, easily seven feet tall and as wide as the five-foot corridor, stepped into the other end, almost completely stealing the diminutive light. The creature's sheer bulk, and its distinctive, bull-like head, revealed its identity.

Catti-brie nearly jumped out of her boots when the door slid closed behind her.

The minotaur grunted the question again, in the drow tongue.

"He's asking for a password," Entreri whispered to Catti-brie. "I think."

"So give it to him."

Easier said than done, Entreri knew well, for Jarlaxle had never mentioned any password to the inner Baenre structures. Entreri would have to take issue with the mercenary over that small slip, he decided—if he ever got the chance.

The monstrous minotaur advanced a threatening step, waving a spiked adamantite rod out in front of it.

"As if minotaurs aren't formidable enough without giving them drow-made weapons," Entreri whispered to Catti-brie.

Another step put the minotaur barely ten feet from the companions.

"Usstan belbol . . . usstan belbau ulu . . . dos," Entreri stuttered, and he jingled a pouch on his belt. *"Dosst?"*

The minotaur stopped its advance and screwed up its bullish features.

"What did you say?" Catti-brie whispered.

"I have no idea," Entreri admitted, though he thought he had mentioned something about a gift.

A low snarl emitted from the increasingly impatient minotaur guard's mouth.

"Dosst?" Catti-brie asked boldly, holding out her bow in one hand and trying to appear cheerful. She smiled widely and bobbed her head stupidly, as though offering the bow, all the while slipping her other hand inside the folds of her traveling cloak, feeling for an arrow in the quiver at her hip.

"Dosst?" she asked again, and the minotaur poked itself in the chest with a huge, stubby finger.

"Yeah, yerself!" Catti-brie growled, and out snapped the arrow, fitted to the string and fired before the stupid minotaur even got its back down. The arrow slammed into the monster's chest and sent it staggering backward.

"Use yer finger to fill the hole!" Catti-brie roared, fitting another arrow. "And how many fingers ye got?"

She glanced quickly to Entreri, who was staring at her dumbfoundedly.

Catti-brie laughed at him and put another arrow into the monster's chest, driving it back several more steps, where it toppled into the wider room beyond the corridor. When it fell, more than half a dozen other minotaurs were ready to take its place.

"You are crazy!" Entreri shouted at the woman.

Not bothering to answer, Catti-brie slammed an arrow into the closest minotaur's belly. It doubled over in pain and was plowed under by its charging comrades.

Entreri drew out his blades and met the charge, realizing that he had to keep the giants away from Catti-brie so that she might utilize her bow. He met the first minotaur two steps in from the end of the corridor, throwing his sword up to deflect a blow from the creature's spiked rod—and the assassin's whole side tingled with numbness from the sheer weight of the blow).

Much quicker than the lumbering giant, Entreri countered with three rapid dagger strikes to the monster's midsection. Down swooped the spiked rod, and, though his sword intercepted the blow, Entreri had to spin a complete circuit to absorb the shock and get out of harm's way.

He came around with his sword leading, its green-glowing point cutting a neat line under the minotaur's jaw, slicing through bone and the creature's cowlike tongue.

Blood spewed from the beast's mouth, but it swung again, forcing Entreri back.

A silver streak stole the sight from both combatants as Catti-brie's arrow flew over the engaged minotaur's shoulder to drive into the thick skull of the next creature in line.

Entreri could only hope that the minotaur was similarly blinded as he made his desperate rush, jabbing viciously with his dagger, cutting his sword in a brutal downward slash. He scored lightning-fast hit after hit on the stunned and wounded beast, and his sight returned as the minotaur slumped down in front of him.

Entreri didn't hesitate. He sprang right atop the thing's back, then leaped farther along to the back of the next dead beast, using its bulk to bring him up even with the next monster in line. His sword beat the minotaur to the attack, scoring a solid hit on the creature's shoulder. Entreri thought this one an easy kill as its weapon arm inevitably slumped useless at its side, but he had never fought the likes of a bull-headed minotaur before, and his surprise was complete when the creature snapped a head butt that caught him in the chest.

The minotaur jerked to the side and began a charge across the room, still carrying the assassin between its horns.

"Oh, damn," Catti-brie muttered as she saw the line between her and the remaining monsters suddenly open. She dropped to one knee and began frantically tearing out her arrows and launching them down the corridor.

The blinding barrage dropped one, then two minotaurs, but the third in line grabbed the falling second and hoisted it up as a shield. Catti-brie managed to skip an arrow off that one's thick head, but it did no real damage and the minotaur rapidly closed.

The young woman fired off one more shot, as much to blind the monsters as in any hope of stopping the charge, then she dived to the floor and boldly scrambled ahead, sliding aside the trampling legs.

The minotaur crashed hard into the outer door. Holding its dead comrade in front of it, it could not tell that Catti-brie had slipped away, and it heaved the huge corpse back from the wall and slammed it in again repeatedly.

Still on the floor, Catti-brie had to pick her way past three sets of treelike legs. All three minotaurs were roaring, offering some cover, for they thought that the one in front was squashing the puny woman.

She almost made it.

The last minotaur in line felt a brush against its leg and looked down, then bellowed and grabbed its spiked rod in both hands.

Catti-brie rolled to her back, her bow coming out in front. Somehow she got off a shot, knocking the creature back for just an instant. The woman instinctively threw her feet straight up and over her, launching herself into a backward roll.

The blinded minotaur's rod took a fair-sized chunk out of the stone floor an inch below Catti-brie's angled back.

Catti-brie came right to her feet, facing the beast. She whipped her bow across in front of her and spun away, stumbling out of the corridor.

⚔ ⚔ ⚔ ⚔ ⚔

The breath was taken from his body with the impact. The minotaur wrapped its good arm about Entreri's waist, holding him steady, and hopped back, obviously meaning to slam the assassin into the wall once more. Just a few feet away, another minotaur cheered its winning comrade on.

Entreri's dagger arm pumped wildly, futilely trying to penetrate the beast's thick skull.

The assassin felt as though his backbone had shattered when they hit the wall a second time. He forced himself to see through the pain and the fear, forced himself to take a quick survey of his situation. A cool head was the

fighter's best advantage, Entreri knew, and his tactics quickly changed. Instead of just smashing the dagger down against solid bone, he placed its tip on the flesh between the creature's bull horns, then ran it down the side of the minotaur's face, applying equal pressure to slide it and push it in.

They hit the wall again.

Entreri held his hand steady, confident that the dagger would do its work. At first, the blade slipped evenly, not able to penetrate, but then it found a fleshy spot and Entreri immediately changed its angle and plunged it home.

Into the minotaur's eye.

The assassin felt the hungry dagger grab at the creature's life force, felt it pulse, sending waves of strength up his arm.

The minotaur shuddered for a long while, holding steady against the wall. Its watching comrade continued to cheer, thinking that it was making mush of the human.

Then it fell dead, and Entreri, light-footed, hit the ground running, coming up into the other's chest before it could react. He launched a one-two-three combination, sword-dagger-sword, in the blink of an eye.

The surprised minotaur fell back, but Entreri paced it, keeping his dagger firmly embedded, drawing out, feeding on this one's energy as well. The dying creature tried a lame swing with its club, but Entreri's sword easily parried.

And his dagger feasted.

⋈ ⋈ ⋈ ⋈ ⋈

She came into the small room running, spun a half-circle as she fell to one knee. There was no need to aim, Catti-brie knew, for the bulk of the pursuing minotaurs fully filled the corridor.

The closest one was not at full speed, fortunately, having an arrow driven halfway through its inner thigh. The wounded minotaur was a stubborn one, though, taking brutal hit after hit and still coming on.

Behind the beast, the next minotaur screamed frantically for the third, the one pressing a corpse against the wall, to go the other way. But minotaurs were never known for intelligence, and the last in line insisted that it had the human pinned and squashed.

The last arrow was point blank, its tip, as it left Taulmaril, only half a foot from the charging creature's nose. It split the nostrils and the skull, nearly halving the stubborn minotaur's head. The creature was dead instantly, but its momentum carried it on, bowling over Catti-brie.

She wasn't badly injured, but there was no way that she could extract her body and bow in time to stop the second charging minotaur, just coming out of the corridor.

A sliding figure cut across the monster's path, slashing and jabbing, and when the blur had passed, the minotaur stood in a crouch and grabbed at its torn knees. It lumbered to the side in pursuit of this newest foe, but Entreri spun up to his feet and easily danced away.

He ran to the center of the room, behind a black marble pillar, and the minotaur followed, leaning forward. Entreri went around, and the minotaur, thinking quickly—for a minotaur—allowed itself to fall into a staggered run, hooked one arm about the pillar, and used its momentum to whip around.

Entreri had thought quicker. As soon as he knew that he was out of the minotaur's line of sight, he stopped his rush about the pillar and took a couple of steps back. The spinning minotaur rolled right in between the assassin and the pillar, affording Entreri a dozen clean jabs at its side and back.

Artemis Entreri never needed that many.

⚔ ⚔ ⚔ ⚔ ⚔

The minotaur hoisted its dead companion and jumped back three steps, then roared ahead, slamming the thing against the outer stone door.

An enchanted arrow sizzled into its back.

"Huh?" it asked and tried to turn.

A second arrow blew into its side, collapsing a lung.

"Huh?" it asked breathlessly, stupidly, finally turning enough to see Catti-brie, standing at the end of the corridor, grim-faced and with that wicked bow out in front of her.

The third arrow blew into the side of the minotaur's face. The beast took a step forward, but the fourth arrow slammed it in the chest, knocking it back against its dead comrade.

"Huh?"

It got hit five more times—and didn't feel any of them—before Entreri could get to Catti-brie and tell her that the fight was over.

"We are fortunate that there were no drow about," the assassin explained, looking nervously to the twelve doors and alcoves lining this circular room. He felt for the locket in his pouch, then turned to the floor-to-ceiling central pillar.

Without a word of explanation, the assassin ran to the pillar. Sensitive fingers rubbed against its smooth surface.

"What do ye know?" Catti-brie asked when Entreri's hands stopped moving and he turned and smiled her way. She asked again and, in response, the assassin pushed on the stone, and a portion of the marble slid away, revealing that this pillar was hollow. Entreri went in, pulling Catti-brie along with him, and the door closed of its own accord behind them.

"What is it?" Catti-brie demanded, thinking that they had just gone into a closet. She looked to the hole in the ceiling to her left, and the one in the floor to her right.

Entreri didn't answer. Following the locket's pull, he inched over to the hole in the floor, then crouched to one knee and peered down it.

Catti-brie slid down beside him, looking to him curiously when she saw no ladder. Then she looked around the unremarkable marble room, searching for some place to set a rope.

"Perhaps there is a foothold," Entreri remarked, and he slid over the edge, easing himself down the shaft. His expression became incredulous as he felt the weight lifted from his body, felt himself floating in midair.

"What is it?" Catti-brie asked impatiently, seeing the amazed look.

Entreri lifted his hands from the floor, held them wide, and smiled smugly as he gently descended. Catti-brie was into the hole right behind him, floating freely, gently descending through the darkness. Catti-brie noticed Entreri below her, replacing the magical mask of disguise now, and concentrating.

"You are my prisoner," the assassin said coldly, and for an instant, Catti-brie did not understand, thought that Entreri had double-crossed her. As she came down to the floor beside him, the assassin motioned for Taulmaril, and she recognized his intentions.

"The bow," Entreri said impatiently.

Catti-brie stubbornly shook her head, and the assassin knew her better than to argue the point. He moved to the closest wall and began feeling about, and soon had the door to this level open. Two drow males were waiting for them, hand-crossbows up and ready, and Catti-brie wondered if she had been wise in holding fast to her bow.

How quickly those crossbows—and two drow jaws—dropped when the guards saw Triel Baenre standing before them!

Entreri roughly grabbed Catti-brie and pulled her forward.

"Drizzt Do'Urden!" he cried in Triel's voice.

The guards wanted no argument with the eldest Baenre daughter. Their orders said nothing about escorting Triel, or anyone other than Matron Baenre, to the valuable Drizzt, but their orders had mentioned nothing about any human female prisoners. One scrambled ahead, while the other rushed to grab Catti-brie.

The young woman slumped, dropping her bow, and forcing one of the dark elves and Entreri to support her, one under each arm. The other drow quickly retrieved Taulmaril, and Catti-brie couldn't help a slight wince in seeing the magnificent weapon in the hands of an evil creature.

They walked along a dark corridor, past several iron-bound doors. The drow in front stopped before one of these and took out a tiny rod. He rubbed it down a metal plate beside the door handle, then tapped the plate twice. The door popped open.

The leading drow started to turn, smiling as though he was grateful to please Triel. Entreri's hand slapped across his mouth, jerking his head back and to the side, and the assassin's dagger hand followed swiftly, the blade plunging through the stunned drow's throat.

Catti-brie's assault was not as skilled, but even more brutal. She pivoted on one foot, her other leg flying high to slam the drow in the belly as they crashed against the wall. Catti-brie hopped back half a step and snapped her head forward, her forehead splattering the drow's delicate nose.

A flurry of punches followed, another knee to the belly, and Catti-brie wrestled her opponent into the room. She came up behind the drow, lifting him from the floor, with her arms wrapped under the drow's armpits and her fingers clenched tightly behind his neck.

The drow thrashed wildly but could not break the hold. Entreri was in by then, and had dropped the corpse to the side.

"No mercy!" Catti-brie growled through clenched teeth.

Entreri calmly walked over. The drow kicked out, banging his foot off Entreri's blocking forearm.

"Triel!" the confused soldier cried.

Entreri stepped back, smiled, and took off the mask, and as an expression of horror widened over the helpless drow's face, Entreri whipped a dagger into his heart.

Catti-brie felt the dark elf jerk, then go limp. A sick feeling washed over her, but it did not take hold as she glanced to the side and saw Drizzt, beaten and chained. He hung from the wall, groaning and trying futilely to curl up into a ball. Catti-brie dropped the dead drow to the floor and ran to her dear friend, immediately noticing the small but obviously wicked dart protruding from his stomach.

"I've got to take it!" she said to Drizzt, hoping that he would agree. He was beyond reason, though; she didn't think he even realized that she was in the room.

Entreri came up beside her. He gave only a slight glance at the dart, more concerned with the bindings holding Drizzt.

With a quick puff of steadying breath, Catti-brie took hold of the nasty dart and tugged it free.

Drizzt curled and gave a sharp cry of pain, then fell limp, unconscious.

"There are no locks to pick!" Entreri snarled, seeing that the shackles were solid rings.

"Move away," came Catti-brie's instructions as she ran out from the wall. When Entreri turned to regard her, he saw the woman lifting her deadly bow and promptly skittered to the side.

Two shots took out the chains, and Drizzt fell, to be caught by Entreri. The wounded ranger somehow managed to open one swollen eye. He could hardly comprehend what was happening, didn't know if these were friends or foes.

"The flasks," he begged.

Catti-brie looked about and spotted the rows of bottles resting against the wall. She rushed over, found a full one, and brought it to Drizzt.

"He should not be alive," Entreri reasoned when she came up with the foul-smelling liquid. "His scars are too many. Something has sustained him."

Catti-brie looked doubtfully at the flask.

The assassin followed her gaze and nodded. "Do it!" he commanded, knowing that they would never get Drizzt out of the Baenre compound in this condition.

Catti-brie shoved the flask against Drizzt's lips and forced his head back, compelled him to take a huge swallow. He sputtered and spat, and for a moment, the young woman feared that she had poisoned or drowned her dearest friend.

"How are you here?" Drizzt asked, both eyes suddenly wide, as the strength began to flow through his body. Still, the drow could not support himself and his breath was dangerously shallow.

Catti-brie ran over to the wall and came back with several more flasks, sniffing them first to make sure that they smelled the same, then pouring them down Drizzt's throat. In just a few minutes, the ranger was standing solidly, looking more than a little amazed to see his dearest friend and his worst enemy standing before him side by side.

"Your equipment," Entreri remarked, roughly turning Drizzt about to see the pile.

Drizzt looked more to Entreri than to the pile, wondering what macabre game the evil assassin was playing. When Entreri noticed the expression, the two enemies locked unblinking stares.

"We've not the time!" Catti-brie called harshly.

"I thought you dead," Drizzt said.

"You thought wrong," Entreri answered evenly. Never blinking, he stepped past Drizzt and lifted the suit of chain, holding it out for the following drow.

"Watch the corridor," Entreri said to Catti-brie. The young woman turned that way just as the iron-bound door swung in.

Turned that way to look down the length of Vendes Baenre's wand.

PART FIVE

C ourage.

In any language, the word has a special ring to it, as much, I suspect, from the reverent way in which it is spoken as from the actual sounds of the letters. Courage. The word evokes images of great deeds and great

EYE OF A WARRIOR

character: the grim set of the faces of men defending their town's walls from raiding goblins; the resilience of a mother caring for young children when all the world has seemingly turned hostile. In many of the larger cities of the Realms, young waifs stalk the streets, without parents, without homes. Theirs is a unique courage, a braving of hardships both physical and emotional.

I suspect that Artemis Entreri fought such a battle in the mud-filled lanes of Calimport. On one level, he certainly won, certainly overcame any physical obstacles and rose to a rank of incredible power and respect.

On another level, Artemis Entreri surely lost. What might he have been, I often wonder, if his heart had not been so tainted? But I do not mistake my curiosity for pity. Entreri's odds were no greater than my own. He could have won out over his struggles, in body and in heart.

I thought myself courageous, altruistic, when I left Mithral Hall determined to end the threat to my friends. I thought I was offering the supreme sacrifice for the good of those dear to me.

When Catti-brie entered my cell in House Baenre, when, through half-closed eyes, I glimpsed her fair and deceivingly delicate features, I learned the truth. I did not understand my own motivations when I walked from Mithral Hall. I was too full of unknown grief to recognize my own resignation. I was not courageous when I walked into the Underdark, because, in the deepest corner of my heart, I felt as if I had nothing to lose. I had not allowed myself to grieve for Wulfgar, and that emptiness stole my will and my trust that things could be put aright.

Courageous people do not surrender hope.

Similarly, Artemis Entreri was not courageous when he came with Catti-brie to rescue me. His actions were wrought of sheer desperation, for if he remained in Menzoberranzan, he was surely doomed. Entreri's goals, as always, were purely selfish. By his rescue attempt he made a conscious choice that coming after me was his best chance for survival. The rescue was an act of calculation, not of courage.

By the time Catti-brie had run out of Mithral Hall in pursuit of her foolish drow friend, she had honestly overcome her grief for Wulfgar. The grieving process had come full circle for Catti-brie, and her actions were motivated only by loyalty. She had everything to lose, yet had gone alone into the savage Underdark for the sake of a friend.

I came to understand this when first I looked into her eyes in the dungeons of House Baenre. I came to understand fully the meaning of the word courage.

And I came, for the first time since Wulfgar fell, to know inspiration. I had fought as the hunter, savagely, mercilessly, but it wasn't until I looked again upon my loyal friend that I regained the eyes of the warrior. Gone was my resignation and acceptance of fate; gone was my belief that all would be right if House Baenre got its sacrifice—gave my heart to Lolth.

In that dungeon, the healing potions returned strength to my battered limbs; the sight of grim, determined Catti-brie returned strength to my heart. I vowed then that I would resist, that I would fight the overwhelming events, and would fight to win.

When I saw Catti-brie, I remembered all that I had to lose.

—Drizzt Do'Urden

23

ÐUK-TAK

She reached for an arrow, then shifted her bow out in front of her in defense as a glob of greenish goo erupted from the wand and flew at her.

Catti-brie's bow was suddenly tight against her chest, and she was flying, to smack hard against the wall. One arm was pinned tightly against her chest, the other tightly to her hip, and she could not move her legs. She could not even fall from the wall!

She tried to call out, but her jaw would not work, and one eye would not open. She could see, barely, with the other eye, and she somehow managed to continue to draw breath.

Entreri spun about, sword and dagger coming to the ready. He dived to the side, to the middle of the room, in front of Catti-brie, when he saw the three drow females enter, two of them aiming loaded hand-crossbows his way.

The agile assassin rolled back to his feet and started forward, rising up as if he would leap into his attackers. Then he dived low, sword leading.

The skilled drow females held their shots through the assassin's feint, then brought their hands in line. The first dart hit Entreri's shoulder and jolted him more than he would have expected. Suddenly, his momentum was stolen and he was standing straighter. Black arcs of electricity, writhing like sparking tentacles, shot out from the dart, burning him, jolting him back a few steps.

The second dart got him in the belly and, though the initial hit did not pain the assassin too greatly, a huge electrical blast followed, hurling him backward to the floor. His sword went flying, narrowly missing the trapped Catti-brie.

Entreri came to a stop at the young woman's feet. He still clutched his jeweled dagger, and thought immediately that he might have to throw the thing. But he could only watch in astonishment as the fingers of that hand twitched involuntarily, his grasp on the dagger weakening. He willed his arm to heave the blade, but his muscles would not respond, and the dagger soon toppled out of his trembling hand.

He lay on the stone at Catti-brie's feet, confused and scared. For the first time in his life, those finely honed warrior muscles would not answer his call.

It was the third female, in the middle of the trio, that held Drizzt's attention: Vendes Baenre, Duk-Tak, his merciless torturer for all these long days. Drizzt stood very still, holding the coat of chain mail in front of him, not even daring to blink. The females flanking the cruel Baenre daughter put away their hand-crossbows and drew two shining swords each.

Drizzt expected to be blown away, or held by some magical intrusion, as Vendes quickly chanted under her breath.

"Valiant friends," the wicked noble remarked sarcastically, using perfect surface Common.

Drizzt understood the nature of her spell then, a dweomer that allowed her to communicate with Entreri and Catti-brie.

Entreri's mouth moved weirdly, and the expression on his face revealed what he was trying to say more than any decipherable words. "High ritual?"

"Indeed," Vendes replied. "My mother and sisters, and many visiting matron mothers, are gathered in the chapel. I was excused from the initial ceremonies and was instructed to bring Drizzt Do'Urden in to them later." She eyed Drizzt and seemed perfectly content. "I see that your friends have saved me the trouble of forcing the healing potions down your throat.

"Did you really expect to so easily walk into House Baenre, steal our most valuable prisoner, and walk out?" Vendes asked Entreri. "You were seen before you ever crossed the web fence—and there will be inquiries as to how you got your unclean hands on my brother's mask! Gromph, or perhaps that dangerous Jarlaxle, will have many questions to answer.

"I am surprised at you, too, assassin," she went on. "Your reputation precedes you—I would have expected a better performance. Did you not understand the significance of mere males guarding our prized catch?"

She looked to Drizzt and shook her head. "Those pretend guards I put in place were expendable, of course," she said. Drizzt made no move, showed no reply in his features. He felt the strength returning to him as the healing potions did their work, but that strength would make little difference, he realized, facing the likes of Vendes and two supremely armed and trained females. The ranger looked to his coat of armor disdainfully—it would do him little good held in his hands.

Entreri's mind was working more clearly now, but his body was not. The electrical impulses continued, defeating any coordinated attempt at movement. He did manage to drop one hand into his pouch, though, in response to something Vendes had said, some hint at fleeting hope.

"We suspected that the human woman was alive," Vendes explained, "in the clutches of Jarlaxle, most likely—and we hardly hoped that she would be so easily delivered to us."

Entreri had to wonder if Jarlaxle had double-crossed him. Had the mercenary concocted this elaborate plan for no better reason than to deliver Catti-brie to House Baenre? It made no sense to Entreri—but little about Jarlaxle's actions these last hours made sense to him.

The mention of Catti-brie brought a measure of fire to Drizzt's eyes. He couldn't believe that the young woman was here, in Menzoberranzan, that she had risked so much to come after him. Where was Guenhwyvar? he wondered. And had Bruenor or Regis come along beside Catti-brie?

He winced as he eyed the young woman, wrapped in greenish goo. How vulnerable she seemed, how utterly helpless.

The fires burned brighter in Drizzt's lavender eyes when he returned his gaze to Vendes. Gone was his fear of his torturer; gone was his resignation about how things had to end.

In one swift motion, Drizzt dropped the suit of armor and snapped out his scimitars.

On a nod from Vendes, the two females were on Drizzt, one circling to each side. One tapped her sword against Twinkle's curving blade, indicating that Drizzt should drop the weapon. He looked down to Twinkle, and all logic told him to comply.

He spun the scimitar in a wild arc instead, swishing the female's sword aside. His second blade came up suddenly, defeating a thrust from the other side before it ever began.

"O fool!" Vendes cried at him in obvious glee. "I do so wish to see you fight, Drizzt Do'Urden—since Dantrag is so intent on slaughtering you!"

The way she said it made Drizzt wonder who Vendes would want to win that potential fight. He had no time to ponder the continuing intrigue of the chaotic world, though, not with two drow females pressing him so.

Vendes reverted to the drow language then, commanding her soldiers to beat Drizzt fiercely, but not to kill him.

Drizzt turned a sudden spin, like a screw, his blades weaving a dangerous pattern on all sides. He came out of it suddenly, viciously, snapping a thrust at the female on his left. He scored a minor hit, doing no real damage against the fabulous drow armor—armor that Drizzt was not wearing.

That point was driven home by the tip of a sword that then nicked Drizzt from the right. He grimaced and pivoted back, his backhanded cut taking the sword away before it could do any real damage.

⚔ ⚔ ⚔ ⚔ ⚔

Entreri prayed that Vendes was as intent on the fight as her soldiers, for every movement he made seemed so very clumsy and obvious. Somehow, he managed to get the spider mask out of his pouch and over his trembling hand, and then he reached up and grabbed Catti-brie's belt.

His trembling fingers could not support the hold, though, and he fell back to the floor.

Vendes glanced casually his way, snickered—apparently not noticing the mask—and turned back to the fight.

Entreri sat half-propped by the wall, trying to find some inner control to ward off the nasty drow enchantment, but all his efforts proved useless; his muscles continued their involuntary twitching.

⚔ ⚔ ⚔ ⚔ ⚔

Swords cut in at Drizzt from every angle. One drew a line on his cheek, stinging him painfully. The skilled females, working perfectly in concert, kept him pinned near the corner, gave him no room to maneuver. Still, Drizzt's parrying work was excellent, and Vendes applauded his outstanding, if futile, efforts.

Drizzt knew that he was in serious trouble. Unarmored and still weak—though the magical potions continued to flow through his veins—he had few tricks that could get him past so powerful a tandem.

A sword cut low; Drizzt hopped the blade. Another chopped down, from the other side, but Drizzt, crouching as he leaped, got Twinkle up to deflect it. His other scimitar snapped back and forth in front of him, defeating the two middle-height attacks, one from each female, and completing the four-parry.

But Drizzt could not counter with any offensive routines as the relentless barrage continued, forcing him back on his heels, forcing him to react in awkward angles.

He hopped and ducked, spun his blades this way and that, and somehow managed to keep those stinging swords from cutting any deep holes in his vulnerable body, though the minor hits were beginning to add up.

The ranger glanced forlornly at Catti-brie, terrified at the prospects of what she would soon face.

✕ ✕ ✕ ✕ ✕

Entreri continued to wage his futile war, then finally slumped low, defeated, thinking that he could not possibly fight his way past the powerful enchantment.

But the assassin had not survived the streets of dangerous Calimport, had not risen to a position of leadership in the evil underworld of the southern city, by accepting defeat. He changed his thinking, decided that he had to work within the parameters offered to him.

Entreri's arm shot up above him. His fingers did not grasp—he did not try to grasp—but rather, he slapped his arm hard against the binding goo.

That was all the grip he would need.

With tremendous effort, Entreri coiled his stuck arm and pulled himself halfway up beside the trapped woman.

Catti-brie was watching him, helpless and hopeless, having no idea what he meant to do. She even winced and tried to duck—though of course her head would not move an inch—as the assassin's free arm swung about, as though she feared that he meant to strike her.

It was not the jeweled dagger perched in that free hand, though, but the spider mask, and Catti-brie began to understand as it came over the very top of her head. It wouldn't slip down very far at first, blocked by the binding goo, but that greenish sludge instantly began to give way to the item's mighty magic.

Catti-brie was fully blinded as a wave of goo, then the bottom lip of the spider mask, covered her one free eye.

A moment later, her other eye blinked open.

✕ ✕ ✕ ✕ ✕

Sparks flew as the battle intensified, the females pressing more fiercely against the stubborn defenses of the renegade male.

"Be done with it!" impatient Vendes growled. "Take him down, that we might drag him to the chapel, that he might bear witness as we sacrifice the foolish woman to Lolth!"

Of all the things that Vendes could have said, of all the threats that she could have then laid upon Drizzt Do'Urden, none would have been so foolish. The notion of Catti-brie, dear and innocent Catti-brie, being given to the horrid, wretched Spider Queen was too much for Drizzt's sensibilities to bear.

No longer was he Drizzt Do'Urden, for his rational identity was replaced by the welling urges of the primal hunter, the savage.

The female on his left came with another measured counter, but the one on his right struck more daringly, one of her swords thrusting far beyond the tip of Drizzt's blocking scimitar.

It was a cunning move, but in the heightened sensibilities of the hunter, that thrusting sword seemed to move almost in slow motion. Drizzt let the tip get within a few inches of his vulnerable abdomen before the blade in his left hand slashed across, deflecting the sword out wide, crossing under his upraised arm as his other scimitar worked against the female's second sword.

His scimitars then crossed in a powerful diagonal parry, alternating their targets, his left arm shooting across and up, his right across and down.

He dived to his knees, straight ahead, using his closest enemy's body to prevent the other female from hitting him. In came his right hand, deftly turning the blade so that it slashed against the outside of his opponent's knee, buckling the leg. Drizzt punched out with his left, connecting on the female's belly and throwing her back over that collapsing leg.

Still on his knees, the ranger spun desperately, hacking across with his left as the other female rushed in on him.

She was too high. The scimitar took one sword out wide, but the other sword poked lower.

The hunter's second scimitar intercepted it and turned it aside, though it slashed Drizzt's skin and nicked a rib.

Back and forth went the parries and thrusts, the hunter feeling no pain from this newest and most serious wound. It seemed impossible to Vendes, but Drizzt managed to get a foot under him and was soon standing even with her skilled soldier.

The other female writhed on the ground, clutching her blasted leg and tucking her arm tightly over her slashed belly.

"Enough!" Vendes cried, holding her wand Drizzt's way. She had enjoyed the spectacular battle, but had no intention of losing any females.

"Guenhwyvar!" came a shrill cry.

Vendes looked to the side, to the human woman—wearing the spider mask!—crouching low, away from the binding goo. Catti-brie charged out from the wall, dropping the magical figurine and scooping up a certain dagger as she went.

Instinctively, Vendes loosed another gob of goo, but it seemed to pass right through the charging woman to splat harmlessly against the wall.

Somewhat disoriented and certainly off balance, Catti-brie simply dived forward, dagger out. She managed to nick Vendes' hand, but the parrying wand rushed across and turned the deadly blade before it could dig in.

Catti-brie crashed heavily into the drow's thighs, and both females went sprawling, the woman trying to hold on, and Vendes kicking and scrambling fiercely to get away.

× × × × ×

Drizzt's scimitars banged against the remaining female's swords so rapidly that it sounded like one long, scraping ring. She kept up with his fury for a few moments, to her credit, but gradually her parries came later and later against the barrage of thrusts and cuts.

A sword snapped up to her right, defeating Twinkle. Her second sword turned up and out to take the second thrusting scimitar to the side.

But the second scimitar was not really thrusting, and it was the female's sword that went out. She recognized the feint and halted her own weapon's progress, bringing it right back in.

She was too late. Drizzt's scimitar plunged through the fine mesh armor. He was open to any counter, but the female had no strength, no life, left as the wicked scimitar jabbed at her heart. She shuddered as Drizzt withdrew the blade.

× × × × ×

A flurry of punches battered Catti-brie's head as she hugged tightly to the vicious drow's legs. The spider mask had turned about, and Catti-brie could not see, but she realized that if Vendes had a weapon handy, she would be in trouble.

Blindly, Catti-brie reached up with one hand, trying to grab at a drow wrist. Vendes was too quick for the move, though, and not only got her arm out of the way, but wriggled one leg free as well. She coiled and kicked, and Catti-brie nearly swooned.

Vendes pushed powerfully against her, slipping free, then Catti-brie was scrambling, trying to catch up to the suddenly receding legs. The young woman hesitated for just an instant, to pull the troublesome mask from her face, then cried out in denial as she saw Vendes's feet slipping too far from her grasp. The Baenre daughter quickly regained her footing and ran from the room.

Catti-brie could easily fathom the consequences of letting this one get away. Stubbornly, she put her arms under her and started to rise, but was pushed back to the floor by a gentle hand as someone came over her. She saw the bare feet of Drizzt Do'Urden hit the stone floor in front of her, in full pursuit.

Drizzt twisted weirdly as he came into the corridor. He threw himself backward and to the floor so fiercely that Catti-brie feared he had been clotheslined. She understood the move as Drizzt's own doing, though, as a gob of greenish goo flew harmlessly above him.

A twisting roll realigned Drizzt and put his feet back under him, and he shot off like a springing cat.

And a springing cat, Guenhwyvar, followed, leaping over Catti-brie and into the corridor, turning so perfect an angle, the instant the paws touched the stone, that Catti-brie had to blink to make sure she was not seeing things.

"Nau!" came the doomed drow's cry of protest from out in the corridor. The warrior whom Vendes had tortured, had beaten without mercy, was upon her, his eyes raging with fires of vengeance.

Guenhwyvar came right behind, desperate to help Drizzt, but in the instant it took the cat to reach the fighting, a scimitar had already plunged deep into Vendes's stomach.

⚔ ⚔ ⚔ ⚔ ⚔

A groan from the side refocused Catti-brie's attention. She spotted the wounded female crawling for her dropped weapons.

Catti-brie scrambled immediately, staying on the floor, and wrapped her legs about the drow's neck, squeezing with all her strength. Both ebon-skinned hands came up to tear at her, to punch at her. But then the female calmed, and Catti-brie thought she had surrendered—until she noticed the drow's lips moving.

She was casting a spell!

Purely on instinct, Catti-brie poked her finger repeatedly into the drow's eyes. The chant became cries of pain and protest, and they became no more than a wheeze as Catti-brie clamped her legs down tighter.

Catti-brie hated this with all her generous heart. The killing revolted her, especially a fight such as this, where she would have to watch for agonizing seconds, minutes perhaps, while she suffocated her opponent.

She spied Entreri's dagger not far away and grabbed it. Tears of rage and innocence lost filled her blue eyes as she brought the deadly blade to bear.

✕ ✕ ✕ ✕ ✕

Guenhwyvar skidded to a stop, and Drizzt roughly retracted the embedded blade and took a step back.

"*Nau?*" stunned Vendes repeated, the drow word for "no." Vicious Duk-Tak seemed little to Drizzt then, almost pitiful. She was doubled over in pain, trembling violently.

She fell over at Drizzt's feet. Her mouth moved, forming the denying word one last time, but no sound came from her breathless lips and the red glow left her eyes forever.

24

HEAD FIRST

Drizzt came back into his cell to see Catti-brie still lying on the stone floor, holding the spider mask and gasping heavily as she tried to steady her breathing. Behind her, Entreri hung awkwardly by one arm, twisted and stuck to the gooey wall.

"This'll get him down," Catti-brie explained, tossing the mask to Drizzt.

Drizzt caught the mask but made no move, having much more on his mind than freeing the assassin.

"Regis told me," Catti-brie explained, though that point seemed obvious enough. "I made him tell me."

"You came alone?"

Catti-brie shook her head, and for a moment Drizzt nearly swooned, thinking that another of his friends might be in peril, or might be dead. But Catti-brie motioned to Guenhwyvar, and the ranger breathed a sigh of relief.

"You are a fool," Drizzt replied, his words wrought of sheer incredulity and frustration. He scowled fiercely at Catti-brie, wanting her to know that he was not pleased.

"No more than yerself," the young woman answered with a wistful smile, a smile that stole the scowl from Drizzt's face. The dark elf couldn't deny his joy at seeing Catti-brie again, even in this dangerous circumstance.

"Are ye wanting to talk about it now?" Catti-brie asked, smiling still. "Or are ye wanting to wait until we're back in Mithral Hall?"

Drizzt had no answer, just shook his head and ran a hand through his thick mane. He looked to the spider mask then, and to Entreri, and his scowl returned.

"We've a deal," Catti-brie quickly put in. "He got me to ye, and said he'd get us both out, and we're to guide him back to the surface."

"And once there?" Drizzt had to ask.

"Let him go his way, and we're to go our own," Catti-brie answered firmly, as though she needed to hear the strength of her voice for the sake of her own resolve.

Again Drizzt looked doubtfully from the mask to the assassin. The prospects of setting Artemis Entreri free on the surface did not sit well in the noble ranger's gut. How many would suffer for Drizzt's actions now? How many would again be terrorized by the darkness that was Artemis Entreri?

"I gave me word," Catti-brie offered in the face of her friend's obvious doubts.

Drizzt continued to ponder the consequences. He couldn't deny Entreri's potential value on the ensuing journey, particularly the fight they would likely face in getting out of the Baenre complex. Drizzt had fought beside the assassin before on similar occasions, and together they had been nothing short of brilliant.

Still . . .

"I came in good faith," Entreri stuttered through chattering, barely controlled teeth. "I saved . . . I . . . saved that one." His free arm twitched out as though to indicate Catti-brie, but it jerked suddenly, violently, and banged against the wall instead.

"I'll have your word then," Drizzt offered, moving toward the man. He meant to go on and exact a promise from Entreri that his evil deeds would be at an end, even that once on the surface he would willingly stand trial for his dark past. Entreri saw it coming clearly, though, and cut Drizzt short, his rising anger giving him temporary control over his uncooperative muscles.

"Nothing!" he snarled. "You have what I offered to her!"

Drizzt immediately looked back to Catti-brie, who was up and moving for her bow.

"I gave me word," she replied, more emphatically, matching his doubtful stare.

"And we are running . . . short . . . of time," Entreri added.

The ranger moved the last two steps swiftly and plopped the mask over Entreri's head. The man's arm slid out of the goo and he dropped to the floor, unable to gain enough control to even stand. Drizzt went for the remaining potion bottles, hoping that they might restore the assassin's muscle control. He still wasn't wholly convinced that showing Entreri back to the surface was the right choice, but he decided that he couldn't wait around and debate the issue. He would free Entreri, and together the three and Guenhwyvar would try to escape the compound and the city. Other problems would have to be dealt with later.

It would all be moot, after all, if the potion's healing magic did not help the assassin, for Drizzt and Catti-brie surely could not carry the man out of there.

But Entreri was standing again before he had even finished his first draw on the ceramic flask. The effects of the dart were temporary and fast fading, and the revitalizing potion spurred the recovery even more quickly.

Drizzt and Catti-brie shared another flask, and Drizzt, after strapping on his armor, belted on two of the six remaining and gave two each to his companions.

"We have to go back out of Baenre's great mound," Entreri said, readying himself for the journey. "The high ritual is still in progress, no doubt, but if the slain minotaurs on the higher level have been discovered, then we'll likely find a host of soldiers waiting for us."

"Unless Vendes, in her arrogance, came down here alone," Drizzt replied. His tone, and the assassin's responding stare revealed that neither of them thought that possibility likely.

"Head first," Catti-brie offered. Both her companions looked to her, not understanding.

"The dwarven way," the young woman explained. "When ye've a back to yer wall, ye put yer head down low and let it lead."

Drizzt looked to Guenhwyvar, to Catti-brie and her bow, to Entreri and his deadly blades, and to his own scimitars—how convenient for cocky Dantrag, in anticipation of his fight with the captured ranger, to have placed all of Drizzt's items so near at hand! "They may have us cornered," Drizzt admitted, "but I doubt that they understand what it is they have cornered!"

※ ※ ※ ※ ※

Matron Baenre, Matron Mez'Barris Armgo, and K'yorl Odran stood in a tight triangle atop the central altar of House Baenre's immense chapel. Five other matron mothers, rulers of the fourth- to eighth-ranking houses of the city, formed a ring about the trio. This elite group, Menzoberranzan's ruling council, met often in the small, secret room used as council chambers, but not in centuries had they come together in prayer.

Matron Baenre felt truly at the pinnacle of her power. She had brought them together, one and all, had banded the eight ruling houses in an alliance

that would force all of Menzoberranzan to follow Matron Baenre's lead to Mithral Hall. Even vicious K'yorl, so resistant to the expedition and the alliance, now seemed honestly caught up in the budding frenzy. Earlier in the ceremony, K'yorl, with no prompting, had offered to go along personally on the attack, and Mez'Barris Armgo—not wanting the ruler of the house ranked behind her own to shine darker in Matron Baenre's eyes—had immediately offered likewise.

Lolth was with her, Matron Baenre believed with all of her evil heart. The others believed that Lolth was with the withered matron mother, too, and, thus, the alliance had been firmly joined.

Matron Baenre did well to hide her smile through the next portions of the ceremony. She tried hard to be patient with Vendes. She had sent her daughter to get Drizzt, after all, and Vendes was experienced enough in the ways of drow rituals to understand that the renegade might not survive the ceremony. If Vendes took a few torturing liberties with the prisoner now, Matron Baenre could not fault her. Baenre did not plan to sacrifice Drizzt at the ceremony. She had many games left to play with that one, and dearly wanted to give Dantrag his chance to outshine all other weapons masters in Menzoberranzan. But these religious frenzies had a way of deciding their own events, Baenre knew, and if the situation demanded that Drizzt be given over to Lolth, then she would eagerly wield the sacrificial dagger.

The thought was not an unpleasant one.

⚔ ⚔ ⚔ ⚔ ⚔

At the front of the circular structure, beside the great doors, Dantrag and Berg'inyon found themselves faced with equally difficult choices. A guard sneaked in, whispering word that some commotion had occurred at the great mound, that several minotaurs were rumored killed, and that Vendes and her escort had gone to the lower levels.

Dantrag looked down the rows of seated dark elves, to the raised central dais. All of his other sisters were down there, and his elder brother, Gromph, as well—though he didn't doubt that Gromph would have eagerly accepted the excuse to be out of that female-dominated scene). The high ritual was a ceremony of emotional peaks and valleys, and the ruling matron mothers, turning faster and faster circles on the dais, slapping their hands together and chanting wildly, were surely heading for a peak.

Dantrag looked into the waiting gaze of Berg'inyon, the younger Baenre obviously at a loss as to how they should proceed.

The weapons master moved out of the main hall, taking the guard and Berg'inyon with him. Behind them there came a succession of crescendos as the frenzied cheers mounted.

Go to the perimeter, Dantrag's hands flashed to Berg'inyon, for he would have had to shout to be heard. *See that it is secure.*

Berg'inyon nodded and moved off down the bending corridor, to one of the secret side doors, where he had left his lizard mount.

Dantrag took a quick moment to check his own gear. Likely, Vendes had the situation—if there even was a situation—well under control, but deep inside, Dantrag almost hoped that she did not, hoped that his fight with Drizzt would be thrust upon him. He felt his sentient sword's agreement with that thought, felt a wave of vicious hunger emanate from the weapon.

Dantrag let his thoughts continue down that path. He would carry the slain renegade's body in to his mother at the high ritual, would let her and the other matron mothers—and Uthegental Armgo, who sat in the audience—witness the result of his prowess.

The thought was not an unpleasant one.

⚔ ⚔ ⚔ ⚔ ⚔

"Head first," Catti-brie mouthed silently as the companions came up into the main level within the marble cylinder. Guenhwyvar crouched in front of her, ready to spring; Drizzt and Entreri stood to either side of the cat, weapons drawn. Catti-brie bent back Taulmaril.

A high-ranking drow soldier, a female, stood right before the opening as the marble door slid aside. Wide went her red eyes, and she threw her hands up before her.

Catti-brie's arrow blew right through the meager defense, blew right through the female, and took down the drow behind her as well. Guenhwyvar leaped in the arrow's wake, easily clearing the two falling dark elves and barreling into a host of others, scattering them all across the circular room.

Out went Drizzt and Entreri, one on either side of the opening, their flashing weapons leading. They came back into Catti-brie's line of sight almost immediately, both of them bearing suddenly blood-stained blades.

Catti-brie fired again, right between them, pounding a hole in the fleshy drow wall blocking the entrance to the exit corridor. Then she leaped out, between her companions, with Drizzt and Entreri doing equally brilliant sword work on either side of her. She fired again, nailing a drow to one of the side doors in the circular room. Entreri's dagger bit hard into a drow heart;

Drizzt's scimitars crossed up an opponent's attack routine, then countered, one over the other in opposing, diagonal, downward swipes, drawing a neat **X** on the drow's throat.

But this was Guenhwyvar's show. Inside the crowded room, nothing in all the world could have created more general havoc and panic than six hundred pounds of snarling, clawing fury. Guenhwyvar dashed this way and that, swiping one drow on the backside, tripping up another with a bite to the ankle. The cat actually killed no dark elves in that wild rush through the room and into the corridor, but left many wounded, and many more fleeing, terrified, in its wake.

Catti-brie was first into the corridor.

"Shoot the damned door!" Entreri cried to her, but she needed no prodding and put the first and second arrows away before the assassin even finished the command. Soon she could hardly even see the door for the blazing shower of sparks igniting all about it—but what she could make out continued to appear solid.

"Open, oh, open!" the young woman shouted, thinking that they were going to be trapped in the corridor. Once the chaos in the room behind them subsided, their enemies would overwhelm them. Just to accentuate Catti-brie's fears, the corridor suddenly went black.

Good fortune alone saved them, for the woman's next shot struck one of the opening mechanisms within the door, and up it slid. Still running blindly, Catti-brie stumbled out into the Baenre compound, Drizzt and Entreri, and then Guenhwyvar, coming fast behind.

They saw the streaks of glowing house emblems, leaving a residual trail of light as several lizard-riders swarmed to the area of the commotion. The companions had to make their choice immediately, as crossbow quarrels clicked off the stone around them. Entreri took up the lead. His first thought was to go for the fence, but he realized that the three of them, with only one spider mask, could not get past that barrier in time. He ran to the right, around the side of the great mound. It was an uneven wall, for the structure was really a tight cluster of several huge stalagmites. Catti-brie and Drizzt came right behind, but Guenhwyvar pivoted completely about just outside the doorway, and rushed back in, scattering the closest pursuing dark elves.

Entreri's mind worked furiously, trying to remember the general layout of the huge compound, trying to discern how many guards were likely on duty, and where they were all normally located. The immense house grounds covered nearly half a mile in one direction and a quarter of a mile in the other, and many of the guards, if Entreri chose correctly, would never get near the fighting.

It seemed as if all the drow of the house were about them now, though, a mounting frenzy on all sides of the escaping prisoners.

"There's nowhere to go!" Catti-brie cried. A javelin slammed the stone just above her head, and she swung about, Taulmaril ready. The enemy dark elf was already moving, diving out of sight behind a mound near the fence, but Catti-brie let fly anyway. The magical arrow skipped off the stone and slammed the fence, disintegrating into a tremendous shower of silver and purple sparks. For a moment, the woman dared to hope that luck had shown her a way to blow through the barrier, but when the sparks cleared, she realized that the strand of the mighty fence wasn't even scratched.

Catti-brie hesitated for a moment to consider the shot, but Drizzt slammed roughly against her back, forcing her to run on.

Around another bend went the assassin, only to find that many drow were coming at them from the other direction. With enemies so close, to run out into the open compound would have been suicide, and they could go neither forward nor back the way they had come. Entreri rushed forward anyway, then cut a sharp right, leaping up onto the mound, onto a narrow, ascending walkway used mostly by the goblin slaves the Baenre family had put to work sculpting the outside of the gorgeous palace.

The ledge was not difficult for the assassin, who was used to running along the high, narrow gutters of the great houses of southern cities. Neither was it difficult for Drizzt, so agile and balanced. If Catti-brie had found the time to pause a moment and consider her course, though, she likely would not have been able to go on. They were running up a path a foot and a half wide, open on one side—to an increasingly deep drop—and with an uneven wall on the other. But the dark elves were not far behind, and none of the fugitives had time to consider his or her course. Catti-brie not only paced Entreri step for step, but she managed to fire off a couple of shots into the compound below, just to keep her enemies scrambling for cover.

Entreri thought that they had met an obstacle when he rounded a bend to find two stupidly staring goblin workers. The terrified slaves wanted no part of any fight, though, and they dived over the edge of the walkway, sliding the bumpy ride down the side of the mound.

Around the next bend the assassin spotted a wide and decorated balcony, five feet to the side of the continuing walkway. Entreri leaped onto it, seeing a better carved stairway ascending from that point.

As soon as he landed, two dark elves burst out of doors set in the back of the balcony, against the mound. A silver-streaking arrow greeted the first, blowing her back into the carved room, and Entreri made short work of the

other, finishing her before Drizzt and Catti-brie had even leaped across to join him.

Then came Guenhwyvar, the panther flying past the three surprised companions to take up the lead along the stairway.

Higher and higher went the companions, fifty feet, a hundred feet, two hundred feet, off the ground. Huffing and puffing, the tired group ran on, having no choice. Finally, after they had put a thousand feet below them, the huge stalagmite became a stalactite, and the stair gave way to horizontal walkways, connecting many of the larger hanging stones over the Baenre compound.

A group of drow charged along the walkway from the other direction, cutting off the companions. The dark elves fired their hand-crossbows as they came, into the great panther as Guenhwyvar flattened its ears and charged. Darts stung the cat, pumping their poison, but Guenhwyvar would not be stopped. Realizing this, the trailing members of the group turned and fled, and some of those caught too close to the cat simply leaped over the side of the railed walkway, using their innate powers of levitation to keep them aloft.

Catti-brie immediately hit one of them with an arrow, the force of the impact spinning the dying drow over and over in midair, to hang grotesquely at a diagonal, upside-down angle, lines of his blood running freely from the wound to scatter like rain on the stone floor many hundreds of feet below. The other levitating dark elves, realizing how vulnerable they were, quickly dropped from sight.

Guenhwyvar buried the remaining elves on the walkway. Entreri came right behind and finished off those wounded drow left broken in the fierce panther's wake. Entreri looked back to his companions and gave a determined shout, seeing running room ahead of them.

Catti-brie responded in kind, but Drizzt kept silent. He knew better than the others how much trouble he and his friends were really in. Many of the Baenre drow could likely levitate, an ability that Drizzt had for some reason lost after he had spent some time on the surface. The Baenre soldiers would be up all along the walkways before long, hiding among the stalactites with their hand-crossbows ready.

The walkway came to another stalactite and split both ways around the structure. Guenhwyvar went left, Entreri right.

Suspecting an ambush, the assassin rushed around the bend in a slide on his knees. A single drow was waiting for him, arm extended. The dark elf snapped the hand-crossbow down as soon as she saw the assassin coming in low. She fired but missed, and Entreri's sword punctured her side. Up came the assassin in a flourish. Having no time for any extended battles, Entreri used his prodding sword as leverage and heaved the female over the railing.

Drizzt and Catti-brie heard a roar and saw a dark elf, swatted by the panther, go tumbling away on the left as well. Catti-brie started that way to follow, but heard a whistle from behind and looked over her shoulder just as Drizzt's tattered green cloak waved in the air. The woman reflexively ducked, then stood staring at a crossbow dart that had tangled up in the thick cloth, a crossbow dart that had been aimed at the back of her head.

Drizzt dropped the cloak and skipped to Catti-brie's side, affording her a fine view of the walkway behind them and the group of drow fast approaching.

On the narrow walkway, there was no better weapon in all the world than Taulmaril.

Streak after streak flashed down the length, killing and wounding several drow. Catti-brie thought she could keep up the attack indefinitely, until all the pursuing enemies were slain, but suddenly Drizzt grabbed her by the shoulders and heaved her to the side, falling flat with her under him halfway around the round stalactite.

A lightning bolt slammed the stone, right where they had been standing, showering them both with multicolored sparks.

"Damn wizard!" the fiery woman shouted. She came up on one knee and fired again, thinking she had located the mage. Her arrow dived for the approaching group, but hit some magical barrier and exploded into nothingness.

"Damn wizard!" Catti-brie cried again, then she was running, pulled on by Drizzt.

The walkway beyond the stalactite was clear, and the companions far outdistanced those pursuing, as the dark elves had to be wary of any ambush near the pillar.

Many intersecting walkways, a virtual maze above the great compound, presented themselves, and very few Baenre soldiers were anywhere to be seen. Again it seemed as though the friends had some running room, but where could they go? The entire cavern of Menzoberranzan was opened wide before them, below them, but the walkways ended far short of the perimeter of the Baenre compound in every direction, and few stalactites hung low enough to join with the great stalagmite mounds that might have offered them a way to get back to the ground.

Guenhwyvar, apparently sharing those confused thoughts, fell back into the group, and Entreri again took up the lead. He soon came to a fork in the

walkway and looked back to Drizzt for guidance, but the drow only shrugged. Both of the seasoned warriors realized that the defenses were fast organizing around them.

They came to another stalactite pillar and followed a ringing walkway ascending its curving side. They found a door, for this one pillar was hollowed, but there was only a single, empty room inside—no place to hide. At the top of the ascending ring, the bridging walkways continued on in two directions. Entreri started left, then stopped abruptly and fell flat to his back.

A javelin soared just over him, hitting and sinking into the stone stalactite right in front of Catti-brie's face. The young woman stared at it as writhing black tentacles arched along its quivering length, crackling and biting at the rock. Catti-brie could only imagine what pains that evil—looking enchantment might cause.

"Lizard-riders," Drizzt whispered into her ear, pulling her along once more. Catti-brie looked all about for a shot and heard the scuttling feet of subterranean lizards as they ran along the cavern's ceiling. But in the dimly lit view afforded her by her magical circlet, she made out no clear targets.

"Drizzt Do'Urden!" came a cry from a lower, parallel walkway. Drizzt stopped and looked that way, to see Berg'inyon Baenre on his lizard, hanging under the closest edge of the stone walkway and readying a javelin. The young Baenre's throw was remarkable, given the distance and his curious angle, but still the weapon fell short.

Catti-brie responded with a shot as the rider darted back under the stone bridge, her arrow skimming the stone and flying freely to the ground so very far below.

"That was a Baenre," Drizzt explained to her, "a dangerous one indeed!"

"Was," Catti-brie replied evenly, and she took up her bow and fired again, this time aiming for the center of the lower bridge. The magical arrow burrowed through the stone, and there came a shriek.

Berg'inyon fell free from below the bridge, and his dead lizard tumbled after. Out of the companions' sight, the young noble enacted his levitational powers and turned about in the air, slowly descending to the cavern floor.

Drizzt kissed Catti-brie on the cheek in admiration of the remarkable shot. Then they ran on, after Entreri and Guenhwyvar. Around the next stalactite, the two saw Entreri and the cat bury another dark elf.

It all seemed so hopeless, though, to no avail. They could keep scoring minor victories for hours on end and not deplete the resources of House Baenre. Even worse, sooner or later the compound's defense would organize fully, and the matron mother and high priestesses, and probably more than a few powerful wizards as well, would come out of the domed chapel to join in the chase.

They climbed a walkway ringing another stalactite, going to the highest worked levels of the cavern. Still there were drow above them, they knew, hiding in the shadows, on their lizard mounts, carefully picking their shots.

Guenhwyvar stopped suddenly and sprang straight up, disappearing into a cluster of hanging stones fully twenty-five feet above the walkway. Back down came the mighty panther, raking and gouging the lizard it brought along. The two crashed to the stone walkway, rolling and biting, and for a moment, Drizzt thought that Guenhwyvar would surely go over the side.

Entreri skidded to a stop a safe distance from the battling beasts, but the ranger sprang beyond him, putting his scimitars to deadly work on the entangled lizard.

Catti-brie had wisely kept her stare upward, and when a drow drifted slowly out of the stalactite cluster, Taulmaril was waiting. The dark elf fired his hand-crossbow and missed, the quarrel skipping off the bridge behind her; Catti-brie responded and blew the tip off a stalactite just to the side of the drow.

The drow realized immediately that he could not win against the woman and that deadly bow. He scrambled along the stalactites, kicking off them and flying along the cavern's ceiling. Another arrow cracked into the stone, not so far behind, and then another blew out the hanging stone right in front of him, just as he went to grab at it.

The levitating drow was stuck with no handholds, hanging in midair twenty feet up and now a few dozen feet to the side of the walkway. He should have released his levitation spell and dropped for the ground, recalling the magical energies when he was far below Catti-brie's level. He went up instead, seeking the safety of the nooks in the uneven ceiling.

Catti-brie took deadly aim and let fly. The streaking arrow drove right through the doomed drow and thundered up into the ceiling above, disappearing into the stone. A split second later, there came another explosion from above, from somewhere above the cavern roof.

Catti-brie stared curiously, trying to decipher the meaning of that second blast.

THE DESPERATE RUN

Matron Baenre swelled with pride as the ritual continued, undisturbed by the events in the compound. She did not know that Dantrag and Berg'inyon had gone out from the chapel, did not know that her vicious Duk-Tak was dead, slain by the very renegade Matron Baenre hoped to soon present before the other ruling matron mothers.

All that Matron Baenre knew was the sweet taste of power. She had brought together the most powerful alliance in recent drow history, with herself at its head. She had outmaneuvered K'yorl Odran, always a clever one, and had virtually cowed Mez'Barris Armgo, the second most influential drow in all the city. Lolth was smiling brightly on the matron mother of House Baenre, she believed.

All she heard was the singing, and not the sounds of battle, and all she saw, looking up, was the magnificent illusion of the Spider Queen, going through its perpetual shift from arachnid to drow and back to arachnid. How could she, or any of the others, watching that specter with similar awe, know of the raging fight nearly a thousand feet above the roof of that domed chapel, along the bridged stalactites of House Baenre?

✕ ✕ ✕ ✕ ✕

"A tunnel!" Catti-brie cried to Drizzt. She grabbed him by the shoulder and turning him toward the still-levitating dead drow.

Drizzt looked at her as though he did not understand.

"Up above!" she cried. Catti-brie brought her bow up and fired again into the general area. The arrow slammed into the base of a stalactite, but did not go through.

"It's up there, I tell ye!" the young woman exclaimed. "Another tunnel, above the cavern!"

Drizzt looked doubtfully to the area. He did not question Catti-brie's claim, but he had no idea of how they might get to this supposed tunnel. The closest walkway was fully a dozen feet from the area, and to get to that walkway, though it was barely thirty feet away from and a few feet higher than their current position, the companions would have to take a roundabout route, many hundreds of yards of running.

"What is it?" cried Entreri, rushing back to join his hesitating companions. Looking past them, back down the walkway, the assassin saw the forms of many gathering drow.

"There may be a tunnel above us," Drizzt quickly explained.

Entreri's scowl showed that he hardly believed the information valuable, but his doubts only spurred Catti-brie on. Up came her bow and off flew the arrows, one after another, all aimed for the base of that stubborn stalactite.

A fireball exploded on their walkway, not far behind them, and the whole bridge shuddered as the metal and stone in the area of the blast melted and shifted, threatening to break apart.

Catti-brie spun about and let fly two quick shots, killing one drow and driving the others back behind the protection of the closest supporting stalactite. From somewhere in the darkness ahead, Guenhwyvar growled and crossbows clicked.

"We must be off!" Entreri prodded them, grabbing Drizzt and trying to tug him on. The ranger held his ground, though, and watched with faith as Catti-brie turned again to the side and fired another of her arrows. It smacked solidly into the weakened stone.

The targeted stalactite groaned in protest and slipped down on one side to hang at an awkward angle. A moment later, it fell free into the far drop below. For a moment, Drizzt thought that it might hit the purple-glowing chapel dome, but it smashed to the stone floor a short distance away, shattering into a thousand pieces.

Drizzt, his ears keen, widened his eyes as he focused on the hole, a flicker of hope evident in his expression. "Wind," he explained breathlessly. "Wind from the tunnel!"

It was true. An unmistakable sound of rushing wind emanated from the hole in the ceiling as the air pressure in the caves above adjusted to match the air pressure in the great cavern.

"But how are we to get there?" Catti-brie asked.

Entreri, convinced now, was already fumbling with his pack. He took out a length of rope and a grappling hook and soon had the thing twirling above him. With one shot, he hooked it over the bridge nearest the tunnel. Entreri rushed to the nearest railing of his own walkway and tied off the rope, and Drizzt, without the slightest hesitation, hopped atop the cord and gingerly began to walk out. The agile drow picked up speed as he went, gaining confidence.

That confidence was shattered when an evil dark elf suddenly appeared. Coming out of an invisibility enchantment, he slashed at the rope with his fine-edged sword.

Drizzt dropped flat to the rope and held on desperately. Two cuts sliced it free of the grappling hook, and Drizzt swung down like a pendulum, rocking back and forth ten feet below his companions on the walkway.

The enemy drow's smug smile was quickly wiped away by a silver-streaking arrow.

Drizzt started to climb, then stopped and flinched as a dart whistled past. Another followed suit, and the drow looked down to see a handful of soldiers approaching, levitating up and firing as they came.

Entreri tugged fiercely at the rope, trying to help the ranger back to the walkway. As soon as Drizzt grabbed the lip, the assassin pulled him over, then took the rope from him. He looked at it doubtfully, wondering how in the Nine Hells he was supposed to hook it again over the distant walkway without the grappling hook. Entreri growled determinedly and made the cord into a lasso, then turned to search for a target.

Drizzt threw one knee over the bridge and tried to get his feet under him, just as a thunderous blast struck the walkway right below them. Both the ranger and Catti-brie were knocked from their feet. Drizzt fell again, to hang by his fingertips, and the stone under Catti-brie showed an unmistakable crack.

A crossbow quarrel hit the stone right in front of the drow's face; another popped against the bottom of his boot but did not get through. Then Drizzt was glowing, outlined by distinctive faerie fire, making him an even easier target.

The ranger looked down to the approaching dark elves and called upon his own innate abilities, casting a globe of darkness in front of them. Then he pulled himself up over the lip of the bridge, to find Catti-brie exchanging volleys with the dark elves behind them on the walkway, and Entreri pulling in the thrown lasso, cursing all the while.

"I've no way to hook it," the assassin growled, and he didn't have to spell out the implications. Drow were behind them and below them, inevitably working their way toward the band. The walkway, weakened by the magical assaults, seemed not so secure anymore, and, just to seal their doom, the companions saw Guenhwyvar rushing back to them, apparently in full retreat.

"We're not to surrender," Catti-brie whispered, her eyes filled with determination. She put another arrow back down the walkway, then fell to her belly and hooked her arms over the lip. The ascending drow wizard was just coming through Drizzt's darkness globe, a wand pointed for the walkway.

Catti-brie's arrow hit that wand squarely, split it apart, then gashed the drow's shoulder as it whistled past him. His scream was more of terror than of pain as he regarded his shattered wand, as he considered the release of magical energy that would follow. With typical drow loyalty, the wizard threw the wand below him, into the darkness and into the midst of his rising comrades. He urged his levitation on at full speed to get away from the unseen, crackling lightning balls, and heard the horrified calls of his dying companions.

He should have looked up instead, for he never knew what hit him as Catti-brie's next arrow shattered his backbone. That threat eliminated, or at least slowed, the young woman went back up to her knees and opened up another barrage on the stubborn dark elves behind her on the walkway. Their hand-crossbows couldn't reach Catti-brie, and they couldn't hope to hurl their javelins that far, but the woman knew that they were up to something, plotting some way to cause havoc.

Guenhwyvar was no ordinary panther; it possessed an intelligence far beyond the norm of its feline kind. Coming fast toward the cornered companions, Guenhwyvar quickly discerned their troubles and their hopes. The panther was sorely wounded, carrying a dozen poisoned crossbow darts in its hide as it ran, but its fierce loyalty was fully with Drizzt.

Entreri fell back and cried aloud as the cat suddenly rushed up and bit the rope from his hand. The assassin went immediately for his weapons, thinking that the cat meant to attack him, but Guenhwyvar skidded to a stop—knocking both Entreri and Drizzt several feet back—turned a right angle, and leaped away, flying through the air.

Guenhwyvar tried to stop, claws raking over the top of the target walkway's smooth stone. The cat's momentum was too great, though, and Guenhwyvar, still clamping tightly to the rope, pitched over the far side, coming to a jerking stop at the rope's end, some twenty feet below the bridge.

More concerned for the cat than for himself, Drizzt instinctively sprang onto the taut rope and ran across, without regard for the fact that Guenhwyvar's hold was tentative at best.

Entreri grabbed Catti-brie and pulled her over, motioning for her to follow the drow.

"I cannot walk a tightrope!" the desperate woman explained, eyes wide with horror.

"Then learn!" the assassin roughly replied, and he pushed Catti-brie so hard that she nearly fell right over the side of the walkway. Catti-brie put one foot up on the rope and started to shift her weight to it, but she fell back immediately, shaking her head.

Entreri leaped past her, onto the rope. "Work your bow well!" he explained. "And be ready to untie this end!"

Catti-brie did not understand, but had no time to question as Entreri sped off, walking as surefootedly along the hemp bridge as had Drizzt. Catti-brie fired down the walkway behind her, then had to spin about and fire the other way, ahead, at those drow who had been pursuing Guenhwyvar.

She had no time to aim either way as she continued to turn back and forth, and few of her arrows hit any enemies at all.

Catti-brie took a deep breath. She sincerely lamented the future she would never know. But she followed the sigh with a resigned but determined smile. If she was going down, then Catti-brie had every intention of taking her enemies down with her, had every intention of offering Drizzt his freedom.

⚔ ⚔ ⚔ ⚔ ⚔

Some of those inside the great Baenre chapel had heard and felt the stalactite crash on the compound's floor, but only slightly, since the chapel's walls were of thick stone and two thousand drow voices within the place were lifted in frantic song to Lolth.

Matron Baenre was notified of the crash several moments later, when Sos'Umptu, her daughter in charge of chapel affairs, found the opportunity to whisper to her that something might be amiss out in the compound.

It pained Matron Baenre to interrupt the ceremony. She looked around at the faces of the other matron mothers, her only possible rivals, and remained convinced that they were now wholly committed to her and her plan. Still, she gave Sos'Umptu permission to send out—discreetly—a few members of the chapel elite guard.

Then the first matron mother went back to the ceremony, smiling as though nothing out of the ordinary—except, of course, this extraordinary gathering—was going on. So secure was Matron Baenre in the power of her house that her only fears at that time were that something might disturb the sanctity of the ceremony, something might lessen her in the eyes of Lolth.

She could not imagine the antics of the three fugitives and the panther far, far above.

⚔ ⚔ ⚔ ⚔ ⚔

Hanging low over the bridge, coaxing his dear, wounded companion, Drizzt did not hear Entreri touch down on the stone behind him.

"There is nothing we can do for the cat!" the assassin said roughly, and Drizzt spun about, noticing immediately that Catti-brie was in dire straits across the way.

"You left her!" the ranger cried.

"She could not cross!" Entreri spat back in his face. "Not yet!" Drizzt, consumed by rage, went for his blades, but Entreri ignored him and focused back on Catti-brie, who was kneeling on the stone, fumbling with something that the assassin could not discern.

"Untie the rope!" Entreri called. "But hold fast as you do and swing out!"

Drizzt, thinking himself incredibly stupid for not understanding Entreri's designs, released his grip on his weapon hilts and dived down to help Entreri brace the hemp. As soon as Catti-brie untied the other end, six hundred pounds of pressure—from the falling panther—would yank the rope. Drizzt held no illusions that he and Entreri could hold the panther aloft for more than a short while, but they had to make the tug on the other end of the rope less violent, so that Catti-brie would be able to hold on.

The young woman made no immediate move for the rope, despite Entreri's screams and the dark elves approaching from both sides. Finally she went for it, but came up immediately and cried out, "Suren it's too tight!"

"Damn, she has no blade," Entreri groaned, realizing his mistake.

Drizzt drew out Twinkle and skipped back atop the rope, determined to die beside his dear Catti-brie. But the young woman hooked Taulmaril over her shoulder and leaped out onto the tentative bridge, wearing an expression of sheer terror. She came across hanging under the hemp, hands and knees locked tight. Ten feet out, then fifteen, halfway to her friends.

The dark elves closed quickly, seeing that no more of those wicked arrows would be coming at them. The lead drow were nearly up to the rope, hand-crossbows coming up, and Catti-brie would be an easy target indeed!

But then the dark elves in front skidded to a sudden stop and began scrambling to get away, some leaping off the bridge.

Drizzt did not understand what he was seeing, and had no time to sort it out as a ball of fire exploded on the other walkway, right between the converging groups of dark elves. Walls of flame rolled out at Drizzt, and he fell back, throwing his hands up in front of him.

A split second later, Entreri cried out and the rope, burned through on the other walkway, began to whip past them, with Guenhwyvar more than balancing Catti-brie's weight.

Entreri and Drizzt were quick enough to dive and grab at the rope when it stopped flying past, when valiant Guenhwyvar, understanding that Catti-brie would be knocked from her tentative grasp as she collided with the side of the walkway, let go and plummeted into the darkness.

The bridge across the way creaked apart and fell, crashing against one levitating drow who had survived the wand explosion, and dropping those dark elves remaining on the platform. Most of those still alive could levitate, and would not fall to their deaths, but the explosion had certainly bought the companions precious time.

Catti-brie, her face red from the heat and small flames dancing along her cloak, kept the presence of mind to reach up and grab Drizzt's offered hand.

"Let Guen go!" she pleaded breathlessly, her lungs pained by the heat, and Drizzt understood immediately. Still holding fast to the woman's hand, the ranger fished the figurine out of Catti-brie's pouch and called for Guenhwyvar to be gone. He could only hope that the magic took hold before the panther hit the floor.

Then the ranger heaved Catti-brie up to the walkway and wrapped her in a tight hug. Entreri, meanwhile, had retrieved the grappling hook and was tying it off. A deft shot put the thing through the hole Catti-brie had created by blasting away the stalactite.

"Go!" the assassin said to Drizzt, and the drow was off, climbing hand over hand as Entreri anchored the rope around the metal railing. Catti-brie went next, not nearly as fast as Drizzt, and Entreri shouted curses at her, thinking that her slowness would allow their enemies to catch up with them.

Drizzt could already see dark elves levitating up from the cavern floor beneath his newest position, though it would take them many minutes to get that high.

"It is secured!" Drizzt called from the tunnel above—and all were indeed relieved to learn that there truly was a tunnel up above, and not just a small cubby!

Entreri let go of his hold, then sprang onto the rope as it swung directly under the hole.

Drizzt pulled Catti-brie in and considered the climbing man. He could cut the rope and drop Entreri to his death, and surely the world would have been a better place without the assassin. But honor held Drizzt to his word, to Catti-brie's word. He could not dispute the assassin's daring efforts to get them all this far, and he would not now resort to treachery.

He grabbed Entreri when the man got close and hauled him in. Holding Taulmaril, Catti-brie went back to the hole, looking for any dark elves that might be on their way. Then she noticed something else: the purple faerie fire of the great, domed chapel, almost directly below her position. She thought of the expression on the faces of those drow at the high ritual inside if Guenhwyvar had crashed through that roof—and that notion led her mind to other ideas. She smiled wickedly as she looked again to the dome, and to the ceiling above it.

The tunnel was natural and uneven, but wide enough for the three to walk abreast. A flash stole the darkness up ahead, telling the companions that they were not alone.

Drizzt ran ahead, scimitars in hand, thinking to clear the way. Entreri moved to follow, but hesitated, seeing that Catti-brie was inexplicably going back the other way.

"What are you about?" the assassin demanded, but the woman didn't answer. She merely fitted an arrow to her bow as she measured her steps.

She fell back and cried out as she crossed a side passage and a drow soldier leaped out at her, but before he got his sword in line, a hurled dagger sank into his rib cage. Entreri rushed in, meeting the next drow in line, calling for Catti-brie to run back the other way, to join Drizzt.

"Hold them!" was all the explanation the young woman offered, and she continued on in the opposite direction.

"Hold them?" Entreri echoed. He cut down the second drow in line and engaged the third as two others ran off the way they had come.

⚔ ⚔ ⚔ ⚔ ⚔

Drizzt careened around a bend, even leaped onto the curving wall to keep his desperate speed.

"Valiant!" came a greeting call, spoken in the Drow tongue, and the ranger slowed and stopped when he saw Dantrag and Berg'inyon Baenre sitting casually atop their lizard mounts in the middle of the passage.

"Valiant attempt!" Dantrag reiterated, but his smile mocked the whole escape, made Drizzt feel that all their efforts had done no more good than offer amusement to the cocky weapons master and his unbeatable charge.

CATTI-BRIE'S SURPRISE

I thought that your lizard was shot out from under you," Drizzt remarked, trying to sound confident in the face of his disappointment.

Berg'inyon steeled his red-glowing gaze upon the impetuous renegade and did not respond.

"A fine shot," Dantrag agreed, "but it was only a lizard, after all, and well worth the entertainment you and your pitiful friends have provided." Dantrag casually reached over and took the long death lance from his brother's hand. "Are you ready to die, Drizzt Do'Urden?" he asked as he lowered the deadly tip.

Drizzt crouched low, feeling his balance, and crossed his scimitars in front of him. Where were Catti-brie and Entreri? he wondered, and he feared that they had met resistance—Dantrag's soldiers?—back in the corridor.

Despair washed over him suddenly with the thought that Catti-brie might already be dead, but the ranger pushed it away, reminded himself to trust her, to trust that she could take care of herself.

Dantrag's lizard leaped ahead, then skittered sideways along a wall. Drizzt had no idea of which way the creature would veer when it came near him. Back to the floor? Higher on the wall? Or might it turn right up onto the ceiling and carry its hanging rider right above the target?

Dantrag knew that Drizzt had been on the surface, where there were no ceilings, for many years—did he think the last choice the most devious?

Drizzt started toward the opposite wall, but fell to his knees instead at the same instant that Dantrag coaxed his fast-running, sticky-footed mount up to the ceiling. The tip of the long lance just missed the ducking ranger's head, and Drizzt leaped up as the rider passed, grabbing at the weapon's shaft.

He felt a sting in his lower back, and turned to see Berg'inyon sitting calmly atop his mount, reloading his hand-crossbow.

"It does not have to be a fair fight, Drizzt Do'Urden!" Dantrag explained with a laugh. He swung his well-trained mount about, brought it back to the floor, and lowered the lance once more.

⚔ ⚔ ⚔ ⚔ ⚔

Sword and dagger flashed wildly as Entreri tried to finish the stubborn dark elf. This one was a skilled fighter, though, and his parries were fast and on target. Behind the drow, the other dark elves were steadily inching toward Entreri, gaining confidence as they watched their companion hold the assassin's devilish attacks at bay.

"What are you doing?" Entreri demanded of Catti-brie, seeing her kneeling beside a large mound of rock. The woman stood up and fired an arrow into the stone, then a second, then dropped back to her knees.

"What are you doing?" Entreri demanded more emphatically.

"Stop yer whining and be done with the drow," Catti-brie snarled back, and Entreri regarded her incredulously, suddenly not so sure of what to make of this surprising creature. Almost as an afterthought, Catti-brie tossed the onyx panther figurine to the floor. "Come back, Guenhwyvar," she said too calmly. "Me heroic companion's needing yer help."

Entreri growled and went at his opponent with renewed fury—just the effect conniving Catti-brie had hoped for. His sword went into a circular movement, and his jeweled dagger poked in behind it at every opportunity.

The dark elf called out something, and one of those nearest him mustered some courage and came forward to join the combatants. Entreri growled and reluctantly fell back a step, across the corridor.

A streaking arrow cut in front of the assassin, stealing his sight, and when his vision returned, he faced only one drow again, and those others watching from behind, in the side passage, were long gone.

Entreri put a sarcastic glance at Catti-brie, but she was firing into the stone again—and talking to the returned panther—and did not hear.

⚔ ⚔ ⚔ ⚔ ⚔

Drizzt felt the burn of drow poison in his back, but felt, too, the tingling of the recently quaffed healing potions. He started to swoon—purposely—and heard Dantrag laughing at him, mocking him. The predictable click of

Berg'inyon's crossbow sounded, and Drizzt fell right to the stone, the dart arcing over him and stealing the mirth from the smug weapons master as it skipped off the stone not so far from Dantrag's head.

Dantrag's charge was on before Drizzt was fully back to his feet, the weapons master coming straight at him this time. Drizzt fell to one knee, shot back up, and spun away, frantically batting at the dangerous and enchanted lance as it passed just under his high-flying arm. Dantrag, incredibly fast, snapped off a backhanded slap into Drizzt's face as he passed. Drizzt, both his blades intent on keeping the lance at bay, could not respond.

Back came the weapons master, impossibly quick, and Drizzt had to dive to the side as the mighty lance scratched a deep line into the stone. Drizzt reversed his direction immediately, hoping to score a hit as the lance went past, but again Dantrag was too quick, snapping out his own sword and not only deflecting Drizzt's lunge, but countering with a slapping strike against the side of Drizzt's outstretched hand. And then the sword went back into its sheath, too fast for Drizzt to follow the move.

Around wheeled the lizard, going up on a wall for this pass and sending Drizzt into a frantic roll back the other way.

"How long, Drizzt Do'Urden?" the cocky weapons master asked, knowing that Drizzt, with all his frantic dodging had to be tiring.

Drizzt growled and could not disagree, but as he rose from the floor, turning to follow the lizard's progress, the ranger saw a glimmer of hope from the corner of his eye: the welcome face of a certain black panther as it bounded around the corridor's bend.

Dantrag was just turning his mount about for a fifth pass when Guenhwyvar barreled in. Over went the lizard, with Dantrag strapped in for the ride. The weapons master managed to somehow get loose of his bindings as the beasts continued to roll, and he came up, quite shaken, facing the ranger.

"Now the fight is fair," Drizzt declared.

A crossbow quarrel whistled past Dantrag, and past Drizzt's blocking scimitar, to score a hit on the ranger's shoulder.

"Hardly," Dantrag corrected, his smile returning. Faster than Drizzt's eye could follow, he snapped his two swords from their sheaths and began his measured advance. In his head his sentient sword, hungering for this fight perhaps more than the weapons master himself, telepathically agreed.

Hardly.

✕ ✕ ✕ ✕ ✕

"What are you about?" Entreri screamed when Guenhwyvar bounded past him, giving no apparent regard to his opponent. The flustered assassin took out his frustration on the lone drow facing him, hitting the unfortunate soldier with a three-cut combination that left him off balance and with one of his arms severely bleeding. Entreri probably could have finished the fight right then, except that his attention was still somewhat focused on Catti-brie.

"I'm just digging holes," the young woman said, as though that should explain everything. Several more bow shots followed in rapid succession, chipping away at the hard stone of an enormous stalactite. One arrow went through then, back into the cavern below.

"There is fighting ahead," Entreri called. "And dark elves will soon be floating through that hole in the ceiling."

"Then be done with yer work!" Catti-brie shouted at him. "And be leaving me to me own!"

Entreri bit back his next retort, gnawed on his lips instead, and determined that if he was alive when this was all over, Catti-brie would wish that she was not.

The drow facing the assassin came on suddenly, thinking that his opponent was distracted and thinking to score a quick victory. But Entreri's sword snapped left, right, and straight ahead, batting aside both weapons and scoring a minor hit, again on the bleeding arm.

⚔ ⚔ ⚔ ⚔ ⚔

They were no more than a tumbling ball of fur and scales, Guenhwyvar and the subterranean lizard locked in a raking, biting jumble. With its longer neck, the lizard had its head far to the side, biting at Guenhwyvar's flank, but Guenhwyvar stubbornly kept a firm hold on the base of the lizard's neck. More deadly still, the panther's claws were inside the lizard's reach, affording Guenhwyvar a distinct advantage as they rolled. The panther's front claws kept a tight and steady hold, while Guenhwyvar's rear legs tucked in close and began a vicious kicking rake, tearing at the reptilian beast.

Victory was at hand for the beleaguered panther, but then Guenhwyvar felt a wicked sting in the back, the sting of a sword.

The panther whipped its maw about in a frenzy, tearing out a chunk of the lizard's shoulder, but the pain brought blackness, and Guenhwyvar, already battered from the run along the walkways, had to give in, had to melt away into an insubstantial mist and follow the tunnel back to the Astral Plane.

The torn lizard rolled about on the stone, bleeding from its neck and sides, its belly hanging free of its skin. It crept away as swiftly as it could, seeking a hole in which to crawl.

Berg'inyon paid it no heed. He simply sat back on his own mount and watched the impending battle with more than a passing interest. He started to load his hand-crossbow, but changed his mind and just sat back.

It occurred to Berg'inyon then that he stood only to gain, no matter who won this contest.

Hands out, his sword blades resting across his shoulders, the weapons master casually walked up to stand before Drizzt. He started to say something, so Drizzt thought, when a sword abruptly whipped out. Drizzt heaved his own weapon up to block, heard the ring of steel on steel, then Dantrag sliced out with his second blade, and punched ahead with the hilt of his first.

Drizzt could hardly register the moves. He got Twinkle up in time to block the second blade, and got punched solidly in the face. Then he was struck in the face a second time as Dantrag's other hand flew up, too quick for Drizzt to catch.

What magic did this drow possess? Drizzt wondered, for he did not believe that anyone could move so quickly.

The razorlike edge of one of Dantrag's swords began to glow a distinct line of red, though it seemed no more than a dull blur to Drizzt as the weapons master continued his lightning-fast routines. Drizzt could only react to each move, snap his blades this way and that and take some relief in hearing the ring of steel. All thoughts of countering the moves were gone; Drizzt could hope only that Dantrag would quickly tire.

But Dantrag smiled, realizing that Drizzt, like any other drow, could not move fast enough to effectively counter.

Twinkle caught a slice coming in at Drizzt's left; Dantrag's other sword, the glowing one, arced out wide to the right, and Drizzt was somewhat off balance as his second scimitar rushed, tip straight up, to block. The sword connected on the scimitar near its tip, and Drizzt knew that he hadn't the strength to fully stop that blow with that difficult angle. He dived straight down as his blade inevitably tipped in, and the sword swished above his head, went right across as Drizzt spun away, to slash against—and cut deeply into!—the stone wall.

Drizzt nearly screamed aloud at the incredible edge that weapon displayed, to cut stone as easily as if it had been a wall of Bruenor Battlehammer's favorite smelly cheese!

"How long can you continue?" Dantrag asked him, mocked him. "Already your moves are slowing, Drizzt Do'Urden. I will have your head soon." In stalked the confident weapons master, even more confident now that he had seen the legendary renegade in battle.

Drizzt had been caught by surprise, back on his heels and fearful of the consequences of his loss. He forced himself to realize that now, forced himself to fall into a meditative trance, purely focused on his enemy. He could not continue to react to Dantrag's flashing movements; he had to look deeper, to understand the methods of his cunning and skilled adversary, as he had when Dantrag had first charged on the lizard. Drizzt had known the charging Dantrag would go to the ceiling, because he had managed to understand the situation through the weapons master's eyes.

And so it went now. Dantrag came with a left, right, left, left, thrust combination, but Drizzt's blades were in line for the parry every time, Drizzt actually beginning the blocks before Dantrag had begun the attacks. The weapons master's attacks were not so different from Zaknafein's during all those years of training. While Dantrag moved faster than any drow Drizzt had ever encountered, the ranger began to suspect that Dantrag could not improvise in the middle of any moves.

He caught a high-riding sword, spun a complete circuit to whip Twinkle across and knock away the predictable thrust of the second. It was true, Drizzt then knew; Dantrag was as much a prisoner of his own speed as were his opponents.

In came a vicious thrust, but Drizzt was already down on his knees, one scimitar snapping up above his head to keep Dantrag's weapon riding high. The weapons master's second strike was on the way, but it fell a split second after Twinkle had reached out and cut a fine line on the side of Dantrag's shin, forcing the Baenre into a hopping retreat instead.

With a growl of rage, the weapons master bore right back in, slapping at Drizzt's blades, slowly working them up high. Drizzt countered every move, falling in line with the attack patterns. At first, the ranger's mind worked ahead to find an effective counterstrike, but then Drizzt understood Dantrag's aim in this routine, a scenario that Drizzt had played out before with his father.

Dantrag could not know—only Drizzt and Zaknafein knew—that Drizzt had found the solution to this usually unbeatable offense.

Up higher went the scimitars, Dantrag moving under them and in. The attack was called double-thrust-low, wherein the aim was to get your opponent's weapons up high, then step back suddenly and come straight in with both your own blades.

Drizzt hopped back and snapped his crossed scimitars down atop the flying blades, the only parry against the cunning move, the cross-down. But Drizzt was countering even as he blocked, shifting his weight to his lead foot as his back foot kicked out, between his scimitar hilts, between Dantrag's surprised eyes.

He connected squarely on the weapons master's face, staggering Dantrag back several steps. Drizzt sprang right ahead, all over the stunned drow in a wild flurry. Now he was forcing the moves, striking repeatedly so that his opponent could not again gain the offensive, could not use that unbelievable speed to its fullest advantage.

Now it was Dantrag who was reacting to Drizzt's blinding attacks, scimitars snapping in at him from every conceivable angle. Drizzt didn't know how long he could keep up the wild flurry, but he understood that he could not allow Dantrag to regain the offensive, could not allow Dantrag to again put him back on his heels.

To Dantrag's credit, he managed to keep his balance well enough to defeat the attacks, and the weapons master dodged aside whenever a scimitar slipped through. Drizzt noticed that only Dantrag's hands seemed possessed of that impossible speed; the rest of the drow's body moved well, perfectly balanced, as would be expected of a Baenre weapons master. But, ultimately, except for the hands, Dantrag moved no faster than Drizzt could move.

Twinkle went straight in. Dantrag's sword banged against its side. Sly Drizzt twisted the scimitar, used its curving blade to roll it over the weapons master's sword and bite at his arm.

Dantrag leaped back, trying to break the clinch, but Drizzt paced him, scimitars waving. Again, then a third time, Drizzt turned Dantrag's perfect parries into minor hits, the fluid motions of his curving blades trapping the straight blocks of the swords.

Could Dantrag anticipate Drizzt's moves as well as Drizzt had anticipated the weapons master's? Drizzt wondered with more than a little sarcasm, and he sublimated his wicked smile. Straight ahead went Twinkle, and out snapped the blocking sword, the only possible defense. Drizzt started to twist the blade, and Dantrag started to retract the arm.

But Drizzt stopped suddenly and reversed the flow, Twinkle shooting across faster than Dantrag could react. The deadly scimitar gashed deeply into the weapons master's other forearm, poking it out wide, then came back across, Drizzt stepping into the move so that his extended blade slashed a tight line across Dantrag's belly.

Wincing in pain, the weapons master managed to leap back from his deadly adversary. "You are good," he admitted, and though he tried to keep his confident facade, Drizzt could tell by the quiver in his voice that the last hit had been serious.

Dantrag smiled unexpectedly. "Berg'inyon!" he called, looking to the side. His eyes widened indeed when he saw that his brother was no longer there.

"He wishes to be the weapons master," Drizzt reasoned calmly.

Dantrag roared in outrage and leaped ahead, his attacks coming in rapid fire, suddenly stealing the offensive.

⚔ ⚔ ⚔ ⚔ ⚔

Up flashed the sword and in stepped the furious assassin, his jeweled dagger drinking eagerly of his opponent's lifeblood. Entreri jerked the weapon once, then again, then stepped back and let the dead drow fall to the stone.

The assassin kept the presence of mind to immediately jump to the side of the passage, and shook his head helplessly as several darts knocked against the corridor wall opposite the opening.

Entreri turned to the still-kneeling Catti-brie and demanded again to know what she was up to.

The auburn-haired woman, so deceptively innocent-looking, smiled widely and held up the last of the loaded hourglasses, then put it into one of her arrow-blasted holes.

The blood drained from the assassin's face as he realized how Catti-brie had blown up the walkway back in the cavern, as he realized what she was doing now.

"We should be running," Catti-brie remarked, coming up from her crouch, Taulmaril in hand.

Entreri was already moving, not even looking down the side corridor as he passed it.

Catti-brie came right behind, actually laughing. She paused long enough at the hole in the floor, leading back into the main cavern, to shout out to those levitating dark elves drifting up toward her that they weren't likely to enjoy the reception.

⚔ ⚔ ⚔ ⚔ ⚔

Thrust left, thrust right, down-cut left, down-cut right. Dantrag's attack came brutally swift and hard, but Drizzt's scimitars were in place for the parries and blocks, and again the cunning ranger used a third

weapon—his boot—to counter. He snapped his foot up to slam the weapons master's already wounded belly.

Dantrag couldn't stop from lurching over, and then he was back on the defensive again, reacting desperately as Drizzt relentlessly waded in.

Around the bend came Entreri. "Run on!" he cried, and though the assassin needed Drizzt for his ultimate escape, he did not dare to stop and pull the ranger along.

Catti-brie came next, just in time to see Drizzt's scimitars flash straight ahead, to be taken out wide and held by Dantrag's blocking swords. Up came Drizzt's knee, quicker than Dantrag's, as the two inevitably moved together, and in a sudden explosion of agony, the wounded weapons master understood that he could not hold Drizzt back.

Drizzt turned Twinkle over the blocking sword and put it in line for Dantrag's ribs, then the two seemed to pause for an instant, eye to eye.

"Zaknafein would have defeated you," the ranger promised grimly, and he plunged Twinkle deep into Dantrag's heart.

Drizzt turned to Catti-brie, trying to fathom the level of terror apparent in her wide eyes.

Then she was coming at him, weirdly, and it took the ranger a moment to even realize that she was off her feet, propelled by the shock wave of an explosion.

SORTING IT OUT

It creaked and groaned in protest, shock waves and searing flames melting its hold on the cavern ceiling. Then it fell, like a great spear, whistling along its thousand-foot descent.

Helpless and horrified, those dark elves levitating nearby watched it fly past.

Inside the domed chapel, the ceremony continued undisturbed.

A female soldier, an elite guard of House Baenre but certainly no noble, rushed up to the central dais, screaming wildly. At first, Matron Baenre and the others thought her caught up in the outrageous frenzy, an all-too-common sight in the out-of-control drow rituals. Gradually they came to understand that this soldier was screaming cries of warning.

Seven matron mothers turned suddenly suspicious gazes on Matron Baenre, and even her own daughters did not know what she was about.

Then the stalactite hit.

✕ ✕ ✕ ✕ ✕

Drizzt caught Catti-brie in midair, then he, too, was flying. He rolled over as the two touched down, burying the young woman under him protectively.

They were both screaming, but neither heard anything beyond the thunderous roar of the widening fireball. Drizzt's back warmed, and his cloak ignited in several places as the very edge of the firestorm rolled over him.

Then it was done as quickly as it had begun. Drizzt rolled off Catti-brie, scrambled to get out of his burning cloak, and rushed to get to his still-down

companion, fearing that she had been knocked unconscious, or worse, in the explosion.

Catti-brie opened a blue eye and flashed a wistful, mischievous smile.

"I'm betting that the way is clear behind us," she smirked and Drizzt nearly laughed aloud. He scooped her up in his arms and hugged her tightly, feeling in that instant as though they might actually be free once more. He thought of the times to come in Mithral Hall, times that would be spent beside Bruenor and Regis and Guenhwyvar, and, of course, Catti-brie.

Drizzt could not believe all that he had almost thrown away.

He let Catti-brie go for a moment and rushed back around the bend, just to confirm that all those drow pursuing them were gone.

"Hello," Catti-brie whispered under her breath, looking down to a magnificent sword lying next to the fallen weapons master. Catti-brie gingerly picked the weapon up, confused as to why an evil drow noble would wield a sword whose hilt was sculpted in the shape of a unicorn, the symbol of the goodly goddess Mielikki.

"What have you found?" Drizzt asked, returning calmly.

"I think that this one'd suit yerself," Catti-brie remarked, holding up the weapon to display the unusual pommel.

Drizzt stared at the sword curiously. He had not noticed that hilt in his fight with Dantrag, though he certainly remembered that blade as the one that had so easily cut through the stone wall. "You keep it," he offered with a shrug. "I favor the scimitar, and if that is truly a weapon of Mielikki, then she would be pleased to have it on the hip of Catti-brie."

Catti-brie saluted Drizzt, smiled widely, and slipped the sword into her belt. She turned about, hearing Entreri's return, as Drizzt bent over Dantrag's body and quietly slipped the bracers off the dead drow's wrists.

"We cannot delay!" the obviously flustered assassin snapped. "All of Menzoberranzan knows of us now, and a thousand miles will not be enough ground between me and that wretched city."

For perhaps the first time, Drizzt found that he completely agreed with the assassin.

Belted as it was on the hip of the human woman was not exactly what the sentient Khazid'hea had in mind. The sword had heard much talk of Drizzt Do'Urden and, upon Dantrag's defeat, had altered the appearance of its magical pommel so that it might rest in the grasp of the legendary warrior.

Drizzt hadn't taken the bait, but the sword that had rightfully earned the name Cutter could wait.

⚔ ⚔ ⚔ ⚔ ⚔

The going was smooth, with no pursuit evident for the rest of that day and long into the night. Finally the group had no choice but to stop and rest, but it was a fitful and nervous time indeed.

So it went for three days of running, putting the miles behind them. Drizzt kept the lead, and kept the companions far from Blingdenstone, fearful of involving the svirfnebli in any of this incredible and dangerous web. He could not understand why lizard-riding drow patrols had not overtaken them, could hardly believe that scores of dark elves were not crouched in corridors behind them, or on their flanks, waiting to spring an ambush.

Thus, Drizzt was not surprised to see a familiar, outrageous dark elf standing in the middle of the corridor, wide-brimmed hat in hand, waiting to greet him and his fleeing companions.

Catti-brie, still seething, still on her warrior's edge, brought Taulmaril up immediately. "Ye're not for running free this time," she muttered under her breath, remembering how the crafty Jarlaxle had eluded them after the fight in Mithral Hall.

Entreri grabbed the arrow before Catti-brie had bent the bow, and the young woman, seeing that Drizzt was making no move to go for his weapons, did not continue.

"Please, dear and beautiful woman," the mercenary said to her. "I have only come out to say farewell."

His words grated on Catti-brie's nerves, but at the same time, she could not deny that Jarlaxle had treated her with dignity, had not abused her when she had been his helpless prisoner.

"From my perspective, that would seem a strange thing," Drizzt remarked, taking care to keep his voice calm. He felt in the pouch for the onyx figurine, but took little comfort in its presence, knowing that if he found the need to summon Guenhwyvar, they would all likely die. Both Drizzt and Entreri, understanding the methods of Bregan D'aerthe and the precautions of its elusive leader, knew that they were surrounded by skilled warriors in over-whelming numbers.

"Perhaps I was not so opposed to your escape, Drizzt Do'Urden, as you seem to think," Jarlaxle replied, and there was no doubt in anyone's mind that he had aimed that remark directly at Artemis Entreri.

Entreri did not seem surprised by the claim. Everything had fallen neatly into place for the assassin—Catti-brie's circlet and the locket that helped to locate Drizzt; the spider mask; Jarlaxle's references to the vulnerability

of House Baenre during the high ritual; even the panther figurine, waiting for him to take it, on Jarlaxle's desk. He did not know how purposeful and involved Jarlaxle had been in arranging things, but he certainly understood that the mercenary had anticipated what might come to pass.

"You betrayed your own people," the assassin said.

"My own people?" Jarlaxle balked. "Define that term, people." Jarlaxle paused a few moments, then laughed, hearing no answer to his request. "I did not cooperate with the plans of one matron mother," he corrected.

"The first matron mother," Entreri put in.

"For now," the mercenary added with a wistful smile. "Not all the drow of Menzoberranzan were so pleased by the alliance Baenre had formed—not even all of Matron Baenre's own family."

"Triel," Entreri said, more to Drizzt than to the mercenary.

"Among others," said Jarlaxle.

"What're the two talking about?" Catti-brie whispered to Drizzt, who only shrugged, not understanding the larger picture.

"We are discussing the fate of Mithral Hall," Jarlaxle explained to her. "I commend your aim, dear and beautiful lady." He swept into a graceful bow that, for some reason, made Catti-brie more than a little uncomfortable.

Jarlaxle looked to Drizzt. "I would pay dearly for a glimpse of the expressions worn by those matron mothers inside the Baenre chapel when your lovely companion's stalactite spear plunged through the roof!"

Both Drizzt and Entreri turned to stare at Catti-brie, who just shrugged and smiled innocently.

"You didn't kill many drow," Jarlaxle quickly added. "Only a handful in the chapel, and no more than two dozen throughout your entire escape. House Baenre will recover, though it may take a while to figure out how to extract your handiwork from their no-longer-perfectly-domed ceiling! House Baenre will recover."

"But the alliance," Drizzt remarked, beginning to understand why no drow other than Bregan D'aerthe had come into the tunnels in pursuit.

"Yes, the alliance," Jarlaxle replied, offering no explanation. "In truth, the alliance to go after Mithral Hall was dead the minute that Drizzt Do'Urden was taken captive."

"But the questions!" Jarlaxle continued. "So many to be answered. That is why I have come out, of course."

The three companions looked to each other, not understanding what the mercenary might be hinting at.

"You have something that I must return," Jarlaxle explained, looking directly at Entreri. He held out his empty hand. "You will turn it over."

"And if we don't?" Catti-brie demanded fiercely.

Jarlaxle laughed.

The assassin immediately produced the spider mask. Of course Jarlaxle would need to put it back in Sorcere, else he would be implicated in the escape.

Jarlaxle's eyes gleamed when he saw the item, the one piece left to put into his completed puzzle. He suspected that Triel Baenre had watched Entreri and Catti-brie's every step when they had gone into Sorcere to pilfer the thing. Jarlaxle's actions in guiding the assassin to the mask, though, in precipitating the escape of Drizzt Do'Urden, were perfectly in line with the eldest Baenre daughter's desires. He took faith that she would not betray him to her mother.

If he could just get that mask back into Sorcere—no difficult feat—before Gromph Baenre realized that it was missing . . .

Entreri looked to Drizzt, who had no answers, then tossed the mask to Jarlaxle. Almost as an afterthought, the mercenary reached up and took a ruby pendant off his neck.

"It is not so effective against drow nobles," he explained dryly, and threw it unexpectedly to Drizzt.

Drizzt's hand snapped out, too soon, and the pendant, Regis's pendant, slapped against the ranger's forearm. Quick as could be, Drizzt snapped his hand back in, catching the thing before it had fallen half an inch.

"Dantrag's bracers," Jarlaxle said with a laugh as he noticed the ranger's covered wrist. "I had suspected as much of them. Fear not, for you will get used to them, Drizzt Do'Urden, and then how much more formidable you will be!"

Drizzt said nothing, but didn't doubt the mercenary's words.

Entreri, not yet free of his rivalry with Drizzt, eyed the ranger dangerously, not the least bit pleased.

"And so you have defeated Matron Baenre's plans," Jarlaxle went on grandly, sweeping into another bow. "And you, assassin, have earned your freedom. But look ever over your shoulders, daring friends, for the memories of dark elves are long and the methods of dark elves are devious."

There came an explosion, a blast of orange smoke, and when it cleared, Jarlaxle was gone.

"And good riddance to ye," Catti-brie muttered.

"As I will say to you when we part company on the surface," Entreri promised grimly.

"Only because Catti-brie gave you her word," Drizzt replied, his tone

equally grave. He and Entreri locked uncompromising stares, looks of pure hatred, and Catti-brie, standing between them, felt uncomfortable indeed.

With the immediate threat of Menzoberranzan apparently behind them, it seemed as though the old enemies had become enemies again.

EPILOGUE

The companions did not go back to the cave beyond Dead Orc Pass. With Guenhwyvar's guidance, they came into the tunnels far beneath Mithral Hall, and Entreri knew the way well enough from there to guide them back to the tunnels connecting to the lower mines. The assassin and the ranger parted company on the same ledge where they had once battled, under the same starry sky they had seen the night of their duel.

Entreri walked off along the ledge, pausing a short distance away to turn and regard his hated rival.

"Long, too, is my own memory," he remarked, referring to Jarlaxle's parting words. "And are my methods less devious than those of the drow?"

Drizzt did not bother to respond.

"Suren I'm cursing me own words," Catti-brie whispered to Drizzt. "I'd be liking nothing better than to put an arrow through that one's back!"

Drizzt hooked his arm over the young woman's shoulder and led her back into the tunnels. He would not disagree that Catti-brie's shot, if taken, would have made the world a better place, but he was not afraid of Artemis Entreri anymore.

Entreri had a lot on his mind, Drizzt knew. The assassin hadn't liked what he had seen in Menzoberranzan, such a clear mirror to his own dark soul, and he would be long in recovering from his emotional trials, long in turning his thoughts back to a drow ranger so very far away.

Less than an hour later, the two friends came upon the site of Wulfgar's death. They paused and stood before it for a long while, silently, arm in arm.

By the time they turned to leave, a score of armed and armored dwarves

had appeared, blocking every exit with engines of war.

"Surrender or be squished!" came the cry, followed by howls of surprise when the two intruders were recognized. In rushed the dwarven soldiers, surrounding, mobbing the pair.

"Take them to the watch commander!" came a call, and Drizzt and Catti-brie were shuffled off at breakneck speed, along the winding ways and through the formal entrance to the tunnels of Mithral Hall. A short distance from there, they found the aforementioned commander, and the two friends were as startled to see him in that position as Regis was to see them.

"The commander?" was Catti-brie's first words as she looked again at her little friend. Regis bounded over and leaped into her arms, at the same time throwing an arm about Drizzt's neck.

"You're back!" he cried repeatedly, his cherubic features beaming brightly.

"Commander?" Catti-brie asked again, no less incredulously.

Regis gave a little shrug. "Somebody had to do it," he explained.

"And he's been doing it fine by me own eyes," said one dwarf. The other bearded folk in the room promptly agreed, putting a blush on the halfling's deceivingly dimpled face.

Regis gave a little shrug, then kissed Catti-brie so hard that he bruised her cheek.

⚔ ⚔ ⚔ ⚔ ⚔

Bruenor sat as if turned to stone, and the other dwarves in his audience hall, after giving their hearty welcomes to Catti-brie, wisely departed.

"I bringed him back," the young woman began matter-of-factly when she and her father were alone, trying to sound as if nothing spectacular had occurred. "And suren yer eyes should feast on the sights of Menzoberranzan!"

Bruenor winced; tears welled in his blue-gray eye. "Damned fool girl," he uttered loudly, stealing Catti-brie's cavalier attitude. She had known Bruenor since her earliest recollections, but she wasn't sure if the dwarf was about to hug her or throttle her.

"Damned fool yerself," she responded with characteristic stubbornness.

Bruenor leaped forward and lifted his hand. He had never before hit his adopted daughter, but only managed to stop himself at the last moment now.

"Damned fool yerself!" Catti-brie said again, as if daring Bruenor to strike her. "Sitting here wallowing in something that ye cannot change, when them things that are needing changing go merrily along their way!"

Bruenor turned away.

"Do ye think I'm missing Wulfgar any less than yerself?" Catti-brie went on, grabbing his shoulder—though she could not begin to turn the solid dwarf). "Do ye think Drizzt's missing him less?"

"And he's a fool, too!" Bruenor roared, spinning about to eye her squarely. For just a fleeting instant, Catti-brie saw that old spark, that old fire, burning in the dwarf's moist eye.

"And he'd be the first to agree with ye," Catti-brie replied, and a smile widened on her fair face. "And so are we all at times. But it's a friend's duty to help when we're being fools."

Bruenor gave in, offered the hug that his dear daughter desperately needed. "And Drizzt could never be asking for a better friend than Catti-brie," he admitted, burying his words in the young woman's neck, wet with an old dwarf's tears.

⚔ ⚔ ⚔ ⚔ ⚔

Outside Mithral Hall, Drizzt Do'Urden sat upon a stone, heedless of the stinging wind heralding the onslaught of winter, basking in the dawn he thought he would never see.

SIEGE OF DARKNESS

THE LEGEND OF DRIZZT, BOOK IX

By all appearances, she was too fair a creature to be walking through the swirling sludge of this smoky layer of the Abyss. Too beautiful, her features were sculpted fine and delicate, her shining ebony skin giving her the appearance of animated artwork, an obsidian sculpture come to life.

The monstrous things around her, crawling slugs and bat-winged denizens, monitored her every move, watched her carefully, cautiously. Even the largest and strongest of them,

PROLOGUE

gigantic fiends that could sack a fair-sized city, kept a safe distance, for appearances could be deceiving. While this fine-featured female seemed delicate, even frail by the standards of the gruesome monsters of the Abyss, she could easily destroy any one, any ten, any fifty, of the fiends now watching her.

They knew it, too, and her passage was unhindered. She was Lolth, the Spider Queen, goddess of the drow, the dark elves. She was chaos incarnate, an instrument of destruction, a monster beneath a delicate facade.

Lolth calmly strolled into a region of tall, thick mushrooms clustered on small islands amid the grimy swirl. She walked from island to island without concern, stepping so lightly about the slurping sludge that not even the bottoms of her delicate black slippers were soiled. She found many of this level's strongest inhabitants, even true tanar'ri fiends, sleeping amid those mushroom groves, and rudely roused them. Inevitably, the irritable creatures came awake snarling and promising eternal torture, and just as inevitably, they were much relieved when Lolth demanded of them only a single answer to a single question.

"Where is he?" she asked each time, and though none of the monsters knew of the great fiend's exact location, their answers led Lolth on, guided her until at last she found the beast she was looking for, a huge bipedal tanar'ri with a canine maw, the horns of a bull, and tremendous, leathery wings folded behind its huge body. Looking quite bored, it sat in a chair it had carved from one of the mushrooms, its grotesque head resting on the upraised palm of one hand. Dirty, curved claws scratched rhythmically against its pallid cheek. In its other hand the beast held a many-tongued whip and every so often, snapped it around, lashing at the side of the mushroom chair, where crouched the unfortunate lesser creature it had selected for torture during this point of eternity.

The smaller denizen yelped and whined pitifully, and that drew another stinging crack of the merciless fiend's whip.

The seated beast grunted suddenly, head coming up alert, red eyes peering intently into the smoky veil swirling all around the mushroom throne. Something was about, it knew, something powerful.

Lolth walked into view, not slowing in the least as she regarded this monster, the greatest of this area.

A guttural growl escaped the tanar'ri's lips, lips that curled into an evil smile, then turned down into a frown as it considered the pretty morsel walking into its lair. At first, the fiend thought Lolth a gift, a lost, wandering dark elf far from the Material Plane and her home. It didn't take the fiend long to recognize the truth of this one, though.

It sat up straight in its chair. Then, with incredible speed and fluidity for one its size, it brought itself to its full height, twelve feet, and towered over the intruder.

"Sit, Errtu," Lolth bade it, waving her hand impatiently. "I have not come to destroy you."

A second growl issued from the proud tanar'ri, but Errtu made no move for Lolth, understanding that she could easily do what she had just claimed she had not come here to do. Just to salvage a bit of his pride, Errtu remained standing.

"Sit!" Lolth said suddenly, fiercely, and Errtu, before he registered the movement, found himself back on the mushroom throne. Frustrated, he took up his whip and battered the sniveling beast that groveled at his side.

"Why are you here, drow?" Errtu grumbled, his deep voice breaking into higher, crackling whines, like fingernails on slate.

"You have heard the rumblings of the pantheon?" Lolth asked.

Errtu considered the question for a long moment. Of course he had heard that the gods of the Realms were quarreling, stepping over each other in intrigue-laden power grabs and using intelligent lesser creatures as pawns in their private games. In the Abyss, this meant that the denizens, even greater tanar'ri such as Errtu, were often caught up in unwanted political intrigue.

Which was exactly what Errtu figured, and feared, was happening here.

"A time of great strife is approaching," Lolth explained. "A time when the gods will pay for their foolishness."

Errtu chuckled, a grating, terrible sound. Lolth's red-glowing gaze fell over him scornfully.

"Why would such an event displease you, Lady of Chaos?" the fiend asked.

"This trouble will be beyond me," Lolth explained, deadly serious, "beyond us all. I will enjoy watching the fools of the pantheon jostled about, stripped of their false pride, some perhaps even slain, but any worshipped being who is not cautious will find herself caught in the trouble."

"Lolth was never known for caution," Errtu put in dryly.

"Lolth was never a fool," the Spider Queen quickly replied.

Errtu nodded but sat quietly for a moment on his mushroom throne, digesting it all. "What has this to do with me?" he asked finally, for tanar'ri were not worshipped, and thus, Errtu did not draw his powers from the prayers of any faithful.

"Menzoberranzan," Lolth replied, naming the fabled city of drow, the largest base of her worshippers in all the Realms.

Errtu cocked his grotesque head.

"The city is in chaos already," Lolth explained.

"As you would have it," Errtu put in, and he snickered. "As you have arranged it."

Lolth didn't refute that. "But there is danger," the beautiful drow went on. "If I am caught in the troubles of the pantheon, the prayers of my priestesses will go unanswered."

"Am I expected to answer them?" Errtu asked incredulously.

"The faithful will need protection."

"I cannot go to Menzoberranzan!" Errtu roared suddenly, his outrage, the outrage of years of banishment, spilling over. Menzoberranzan was a city of Faerûn's Underdark, the great labyrinth beneath the world's surface. but though it was separated from the region of sunlight by miles of thick rock, it was still a place of the Material Plane. Years ago, Errtu had been on that plane, at the call of a minor wizard, and had stayed there in search of Crenshinibon, the Crystal Shard, a mighty artifact, relic of a past and greater age of sorcery. The great tanar'ri had been so close to the relic! He had entered the tower it had created in its image, and had worked with its possessor, a pitiful human who would have died soon enough, leaving the fiend to his coveted treasure. But then Errtu had met a dark elf, a renegade from Lolth's own flock, from Menzoberranzan, the city she now apparently wanted him to protect!

Drizzt Do'Urden had defeated Errtu and to a tanar'ri, a defeat on the Material Plane meant a hundred years of banishment in the Abyss.

Now Errtu trembled visibly with rage, and Lolth took a step backward, preparing herself in case the beast attacked before she could explain her offer. "You cannot go," she agreed, "but your minions can. I will see that a gate is kept open, if all the priestesses of my domain must tend it continually."

Errtu's thunderous roar drowned out the words.

Lolth understood the source of that agony. A fiend's greatest pleasure was to walk loose on the Prime Material Plane, to challenge the weak souls and weaker bodies of the various races. Lolth understood, but she did not sympathize. Evil Lolth never sympathized with any creature.

"I cannot deny you!" Errtu admitted, and his great, bulbous, bloodshot eyes narrowed wickedly.

His statement was true enough. Lolth could enlist his aid simply by offering him his very existence in return. The Spider Queen was smarter than that, however. If she enslaved Errtu and was, indeed, as she expected, caught up in the coming storm, Errtu might escape her capture or, worse, find a way to strike back at her. Lolth was malicious and merciless in the extreme, but she was, above all else, intelligent. She had in her possession honey for this fly.

"This is no threat," she said honestly to the fiend. "This is an offer."

Errtu did not interrupt, still, the bored and outraged fiend trembled on the edge of catastrophe.

"I have a gift, Errtu," she purred, "a gift that will allow you to end the banishment Drizzt Do'Urden has placed on you."

The tanar'ri did not seem convinced. "No gift," he rumbled. "No magic can break the terms of banishment. Only he who banished me can end the indenture."

Lolth nodded her agreement. Not even a goddess had the power to go against that rule. "But that is exactly the point!" the Spider Queen exclaimed. "This gift will make Drizzt Do'Urden want you back on his plane of existence, back within his reach."

Errtu did not seem convinced.

In response, Lolth lifted one arm and clamped her fist tightly, and a signal, a burst of multicolored sparks and a rocking blast of thunder, shook the swirling sludge and momentarily stole the perpetual gray of the dismal level.

Forlorn and beaten, head down—for it did not take one such as Lolth very long to sunder the pride—he walked from the fog. Errtu did not know him, but understood the significance of this gift.

Lolth clamped her fist tight again, another explosive signal sounded, and her captive fell back into the veil of smoke.

Errtu eyed the Spider Queen suspiciously. The tanar'ri was more than a little interested, of course, but he realized that most everyone who had ever trusted the diabolical Lolth had paid greatly for their foolishness. Still, this bait was too great for Errtu to resist. His canine maw turned up into a grotesque, wicked smile.

"Look upon Menzoberranzan," Lolth said, and she waved her arm before the thick stalk of a nearby mushroom. The plant's fibers became glassy, reflecting the smoke, and a moment later, Lolth and the fiend saw the city of drow. "Your role in this will be small, I assure you," Lolth said, "but vital. Do not fail me, great Errtu!"

It was as much a threat as a plea, the fiend knew.

"The gift?" he asked.

"When things are put aright."

Again a suspicious look crossed Errtu's huge face.

"Drizzt Do'Urden is a pittance," Lolth said. "Daermon N'a'shezbaernon, his family, is no more, so he means nothing to me. Still, it would please me to watch great and evil Errtu pay back the renegade for all the inconveniences he has caused."

Errtu was not stupid, far from it. What Lolth was saying made perfect sense, yet he could not ignore the fact that it was Lolth, the Spider Queen, the Lady of Chaos, who was making these tempting offers.

Neither could he ignore the fact that her gift promised him relief from the interminable boredom. He could beat a thousand minor fiends a day, every day, torture them and send them crawling pitifully into the muck. But if he did that for a million days, it would not equal the pleasure of a single hour on the Material Plane, walking among the weak, tormenting those who did not deserve his vengeance.

The great tanar'ri agreed.

PART ONE

I watched the preparations unfolding at Mithral Hall, preparations for war, for, though we, especially Catti-brie, had dealt House Baenre a stinging defeat back in Menzoberranzan, none of us doubted that the dark elves might come our way once more. Above all else, Matron Baenre was likely angry, and having spent my youth in Menzoberranzan, I knew it was not a good thing to make an enemy of the first matron mother.

RUMBLES OF DISCORD

Still, I liked what I was seeing here in the dwarven stronghold. Most of all, I enjoyed the spectacle of Bruenor Battlehammer.

Bruenor! My dearest friend. The dwarf I had fought beside since my days in Icewind Dale—days that seemed very long ago indeed! I had feared Bruenor's spirit forever broken when Wulfgar fell, that the fire that had guided this most stubborn of dwarves through seemingly insurmountable obstacles in his quest to reclaim his lost homeland had been forever doused. Not so, I learned in those days of preparation. Bruenor's physical scars were deeper now—his left eye was lost, and a bluish line ran diagonally across his face, from forehead to jawbone—but the flames of spirit had been rekindled, burning bright behind his good eye.

Bruenor directed the preparations, from agreeing to the fortification designs being constructed in the lowest tunnels to sending out emissaries to the neighboring settlements in search of allies. He asked for no help in the decision-making, and needed none, for this was Bruenor, Eighth King of Mithral Hall, a veteran of so many adventures, a dwarf who had earned his title.

His grief was gone, and he was king again, to the joy of his friends and subjects. "Let the damned drow come!" Bruenor growled quite often, and always he nodded in my direction if I was about, as if to remind me that he meant no personal insult.

In truth, that determined war cry from Bruenor Battlehammer was among the sweetest things I had ever heard.

What was it, I wondered, that had brought the grieving dwarf from his despair? And it wasn't just Bruenor. All around me I saw an excitement, in the dwarves, in Catti-brie, even in Regis, the halfling known more for preparing for lunch and nap than for war. I felt it, too. That tingling anticipation, that camaraderie that had me and all the others patting each other on the back, offering praises for the simplest of additions to the common defense, and raising our voices together in cheer whenever good news was announced.

What was it? It was more than shared fear, more than giving thanks for what we had while realizing that it might soon be stolen away. I didn't understand it then, in that time of frenzy, in that euphoria of frantic preparations. Now, looking back, it is an easy thing to recognize.

It was hope.

To any intelligent being, there is no emotion more important than hope. Individually or collectively, we must hope that the future will be better than the past, that our offspring, and theirs after them, will be a bit closer to an ideal society, whatever our perception of that might be. Certainly a warrior barbarian's hope for the future might differ from the ideal fostered in the imagination of a peaceful farmer. And a dwarf would not strive to live in a world that resembled an elf's ideal! But the hope itself is not so different. It is at those times when we feel we are contributing to that ultimate end, as it was in Mithral Hall when we believed the battle with Menzoberranzan would soon come—that we would defeat the dark elves and end, once and for all, the threat from the Underdark city—we feel true elation.

Hope is the key. The future will be better than the past, or the present. Without this belief, there is only the self-indulgent, ultimately empty striving of the present, as in drow society, or simple despair, the time of life wasted in waiting for death.

Bruenor had found a cause—we all had—and never have I been more alive than in those days of preparation in Mithral Hall.

—Drizzt Do'Urden

I

DIPLOMACY

Her thick auburn hair bouncing below her shoulders, Catti-brie worked furiously to keep the drow's whirling scimitars at bay. She was a solidly built woman, a hundred and thirty pounds of muscles finely toned from living her life with Bruenor's dwarven clan. Catti-brie was no stranger to the forge or the sledge.

Or the sword, and this new blade, its white-metal pommel sculpted in the likeness of a unicorn's head, was by far the most balanced weapon she had ever swung. Still, Catti-brie was hard-pressed, indeed, overmatched, by her opponent this day. Few in the Realms could match blades with Drizzt Do'Urden, the drow ranger.

He was no larger than Catti-brie, a few pounds heavier perhaps, with his tight-muscled frame. His white hair hung as low as Catti-brie's mane and was equally thick, and his ebony skin glistened with streaks of sweat, a testament to the young woman's prowess.

Drizzt's two scimitars crossed in front of him—one of them glowing a fierce blue even through the protective padding that covered it—then went back out wide, inviting Catti-brie to thrust straight between.

She knew better than to make the attempt. Drizzt was too quick, and could strike her blade near its tip with one scimitar, while the other alternately parried low, batting the opposite way near the hilt. With a single step diagonally to the side, following his closer-parrying blade, Drizzt would have her beaten.

Catti-brie stepped back instead, and presented her sword in front of her. Her deep blue eyes peeked out around the blade, which had been thickened with heavy material, and she locked stares with the drow's lavender orbs.

"An opportunity missed?" Drizzt teased.

"A trap avoided," Catti-brie was quick to reply.

Drizzt came ahead in a rush, his blades crossing, going wide, and cutting across, one high and one low. Catti-brie dropped her left foot behind her and fell into a crouch, turning her sword to parry the low-rushing blade, dipping her head to avoid the high.

She needn't have bothered, for the cross came too soon, before Drizzt's feet had caught up to the move, and both his scimitars swished through the air, short of the mark.

Catti-brie didn't miss the opening, and darted ahead, sword thrusting.

Back snapped Drizzt's blades, impossibly fast, slamming the sword on both its sides. But Drizzt's feet weren't positioned correctly for him to follow the move, to go diagonally ahead and take advantage of Catti-brie's turned sword.

The young woman went ahead and to the side instead, sliding her weapon free of the clinch and executing the real attack, the slash at Drizzt's hip.

Drizzt's backhand caught her short, drove her sword harmlessly high.

They broke apart again, eyeing each other, Catti-brie wearing a sly smile. In all their months of training, she had never come so close to scoring a hit on the agile and skilled drow.

Drizzt's expression stole her glory, though, and the drow dipped the tips of his scimitars toward the floor, shaking his head in frustration.

"The bracers?" Catti-brie asked, referring to the magical wrist bands, wide pieces of black material lined with gleaming mithral rings. Drizzt had taken them from Dantrag Baenre, the deposed weapons master of Menzoberranzan's First House, after defeating Dantrag in mortal combat. Rumors said those marvelous bracers allowed Dantrag's hands to move incredibly fast, giving him the advantage in combat.

Upon battling the lightning-quick Baenre, Drizzt had come to believe those rumors, and after wearing the bracers in sparring for the last few tendays, he had confirmed their abilities. But Drizzt wasn't convinced that the bracers were a good thing. In the fight with Dantrag, he had turned Dantrag's supposed advantage against the drow, for the weapons master's hands moved too quickly for Dantrag to alter any started move, too quickly for Dantrag to improvise if his opponent made an unexpected turn. Now, in these sparring exercises, Drizzt was learning that the bracers held another disadvantage.

His feet couldn't keep up with his hands.

"Ye'll learn them," Catti-brie assured.

Drizzt wasn't so certain. "Fighting is an art of balance and movement," he explained.

"And faster ye are!" Catti-brie replied.

Drizzt shook his head. "Faster are my hands," he said. "A warrior does not win with his hands. He wins with his feet, by positioning himself to best strike the openings in his opponent's defenses."

"The feet'll catch up," Catti-brie replied. "Dantrag was the best Menzoberranzan had to offer, and ye said yerself that the bracers were the reason."

Drizzt couldn't disagree that the bracers greatly aided Dantrag, but he wondered how much they would benefit one of his skill, or one of Zaknafein's, his father's, skill. It could be, Drizzt realized, that the bracers would aid a lesser fighter, one who needed to depend on the sheer speed of his weapons. But the complete fighter, the master who had found harmony between all his muscles, would be put off balance. Or perhaps the bracers would aid someone wielding a heavier weapon, a mighty warhammer, such as Aegis-fang. Drizzt's scimitars, slender blades of no more than two pounds of metal, perfectly balanced by both workmanship and enchantment, weaved effortlessly, and even without the bracers, his hands were quicker than his feet.

"Come on then," Catti-brie scolded, waving her sword in front of her, her wide blue eyes narrowing intently, her shapely hips swiveling as she fell into a low balance.

She sensed her chance, Drizzt realized. She knew he was fighting at a disadvantage and finally sensed her chance to pay back one of the many stinging hits he had given her in their sparring.

Drizzt took a deep breath and lifted the blades. He owed it to Catti-brie to oblige, but he meant to make her earn it!

He came forward slowly, playing defensively. Her sword shot out, and he hit it twice before it ever got close, on its left side with his right hand, and on its left side again, bringing his left hand right over the presented blade and batting it with a downward parry.

Catti-brie fell with the momentum of the double block, spinning a complete circle, rotating away from her adversary. When she came around, predictably, Drizzt was in close, scimitars weaving.

Still the patient drow measured his attack, did not come too fast and strong. His blades crossed and went out wide, teasing the young woman.

Catti-brie growled and threw her sword straight out again, determined to find that elusive hole. And in came the scimitars, striking in rapid succession, again both hitting the left side of Catti-brie's sword. As before, Catti-brie spun to the right, but this time Drizzt came in hard.

Down went the young woman in a low crouch, her rear grazing the floor, and she skittered back. Both of Drizzt's blades swooshed through the air above and before her, for again his cuts came before his feet could rightly respond and position him.

Drizzt was amazed to find that Catti-brie was no longer in front of him.

He called the move the "Ghost Step," and had taught it to Catti-brie only a tenday earlier. The trick was to use the opponent's swinging weapon as an optical shield, to move within the vision-blocked area so perfectly and quickly that your opponent would not know you had come forward and to the side, that you had, in fact, stepped behind his leading hip.

Reflexively, the drow snapped his leading scimitar straight back, blade pointed low, for Catti-brie had gone past in a crouch. He beat the sword to the mark, too quickly, and the momentum of his scimitar sent it sailing futilely in front of the coming attack.

Drizzt winced as the unicorn-handled sword slapped hard against his hip.

For Catti-brie, the moment was one of pure delight. She knew, of course, that the bracers were hindering Drizzt, causing him to make mistakes of balance—mistakes that Drizzt Do'Urden hadn't made since his earliest days of fighting—but even with the uncomfortable bracers, the drow was a powerful adversary, and could likely defeat most swordsmen.

How delicious it was, then, when Catti-brie found her new sword slicing in unhindered!

Her joy was stolen momentarily by an urge to sink the blade deeper, a sudden, inexplicable anger focused directly on Drizzt.

"Touch!" Drizzt called, the signal that he had been hit, and when Catti-brie straightened and sorted out the scene, she found the drow standing a few feet away, rubbing his sore hip.

"Sorry," she apologized, realizing she had struck far too hard.

"Not to worry," Drizzt replied slyly. "Surely your one hit does not equal the combined pains my scimitars have caused you." The dark elf's lips curled up into a mischievous smile. "Or the pains I will surely inflict on you in return!"

"Me thinking's that I'm catching ye, Drizzt Do'Urden," Catti-brie answered calmly, confidently. "Ye'll get yer hits, but ye'll take yer hits as well!"

They both laughed at that, and Catti-brie moved to the side of the room and began to remove her practice gear.

Drizzt slid the padding from one of his scimitars and considered those last words. Catti-brie was indeed improving, he agreed. She had a warrior's heart, tempered by a poet's philosophy, a deadly combination indeed. Catti-brie, like Drizzt, would rather talk her way out of a battle than wage it, but when the avenues of diplomacy were exhausted, when the fight became a matter of survival, then the young woman would fight with conscience clear and passion heated. All her heart and all her skill would come to bear, and in Catti-brie, both of those ingredients were considerable.

And she was barely into her twenties! In Menzoberranzan, had she been a drow, she would be in Arach-Tinilith now, the school of Lolth, her strong morals being assaulted daily by the lies of the Spider Queen's priestesses. Drizzt shook that thought away. He didn't even want to think of Catti-brie in that awful place. Suppose she had gone to the drow school of fighters, Melee-Magthere, instead, he mused. How would she fare against the likes of young drow?

Well, Drizzt decided, Catti-brie would be near the top of her class, certainly among the top ten or fifteen percent, and her passion and dedication would get her there. How much could she improve under his tutelage? Drizzt wondered, and his expression soured as he considered the limitations of Catti-brie's heritage. He was in his sixties, barely more than a child by drow standards, for they could live to see seven centuries, but when Catti-brie reached his tender age, she would be old, too old to fight well.

That notion pained Drizzt greatly. Unless the blade of an enemy or the claws of a monster shortened his life, he would watch Catti-brie grow old, would watch her pass from this life.

Drizzt looked at her now as she removed the padded baldric and unclasped the metal collar guard. Under the padding above the waist, she wore only a simple shirt of light material. It was wet with perspiration now and clung to her.

She was a warrior, Drizzt agreed, but she was also a beautiful young woman, shapely and strong, with the spirit of a foal first learning to run and a heart filled with passion.

The sound of distant furnaces, the sudden, increased ringing of hammer on steel, should have alerted Drizzt that the room's door had opened, but it simply didn't register in the distracted drow's consciousness.

"Hey!" came a roar from the side of the chamber, and Drizzt turned to see Bruenor storm into the room. He half expected the dwarf, Catti-brie's adoptive, overprotective, father, to demand what in the Nine Hells Drizzt was looking at, and Drizzt's sigh was one of pure relief when Bruenor, his fiery red beard foamed with spittle, instead took up a tirade about Settlestone, the barbarian settlement south of Mithral Hall.

Still, the drow figured he was blushing—and hoped that his ebon-hued skin would hide it—as he shook his head, ran his fingers through his white hair to brush it back from his face, and likewise began to remove the practice gear.

Catti-brie walked over, shaking her thick auburn mane to get the droplets out. "Berkthgar is being difficult?" she reasoned, referring to Berkthgar the Bold, Settlestone's new chieftain.

Bruenor snorted. "Berkthgar can't be anything but difficult!"

Drizzt looked up at beautiful Catti-brie. He didn't want to picture her growing old, though he knew she would do it with more grace than most.

"He's a proud one," Catti-brie replied to her father, "and afraid."

"Bah!" Bruenor retorted. "What's he got to be afraid of? Got a couple hunnerd strong men around him and not an enemy in sight."

"He is afraid he will not stand well against the shadow of his predecessor," Drizzt explained, and Catti-brie nodded.

Bruenor stopped in midbluster and considered the drow's words. Berkthgar was living in Wulfgar's shadow, in the shadow of the greatest hero the barbarian tribes of faraway Icewind Dale had ever known. The man who had killed Dracos Icingdeath, the white dragon; the man who, at the tender age of twenty, had united the fierce tribes and shown them a better way of living.

Bruenor didn't believe any human could shine through the spectacle of Wulfgar's shadow, and his resigned nod showed that he agreed with, and ultimately accepted, the truth of the reasoning. A great sadness edged his expression and rimmed his steel-gray eyes, as well, for Bruenor could not think of Wulfgar, the human who had been a son to him, without that sadness.

"On what point is he being difficult?" Drizzt asked, trying to push past the difficult moment.

"On the whole damned alliance," Bruenor huffed.

Drizzt and Catti-brie exchanged curious expressions. It made no sense, of course. The barbarians of Settlestone and the dwarves of Mithral Hall already were allies, working hand in hand, with Bruenor's people mining the precious mithral and shaping it into valuable artifacts, and the barbarians doing the bargaining with merchants from nearby towns, such as Nesmé on the Trollmoors, or Silverymoon to the east. The two peoples, Bruenor's and Wulfgar's, had fought together to clear Mithral Hall of evil gray dwarves, the duergar, and the barbarians had come down from their homes in faraway Icewind Dale, resolved to stay, only because of this solid friendship and alliance with Bruenor's clan. It made no sense that Berkthgar was being difficult, not with the prospect of a drow attack hanging over their heads.

"He wants the hammer," Bruenor explained, recognizing Drizzt and Catti-brie's doubts.

That explained everything. The hammer was Wulfgar's hammer, mighty Aegis-fang, which Bruenor himself had forged as a gift for Wulfgar during the years the young man had been indentured to the red-bearded dwarf. During those years, Bruenor, Drizzt, and Catti-brie had taught the fierce young barbarian a better way.

Of course Berkthgar would want Aegis-fang, Drizzt realized. The war-hammer had become more than a weapon, had become a symbol to the hearty men and women of Settlestone. Aegis-fang symbolized the memory of Wulfgar, and if Berkthgar could convince Bruenor to let him wield it, his stature among his people would increase tenfold.

It was perfectly logical, but Drizzt knew Berkthgar would never, ever convince Bruenor to give him the hammer.

The dwarf was looking at Catti-brie then, and Drizzt, in regarding her as well, wondered if she was thinking that giving the hammer to the new barbarian leader might be a good thing. How many emotions must be swirling in the young woman's thoughts! Drizzt knew. She and Wulfgar were to have been wed. They had grown into adulthood together and had learned many of life's lessons side by side. Could Catti-brie now get beyond that, beyond her own grief, and follow a logical course to seal the alliance?

"No," she said finally, resolutely. "The hammer he cannot have."

Drizzt nodded his agreement, and was glad that Catti-brie would not let go of her memories of Wulfgar, of her love for the man. He, too, had loved Wulfgar, as a brother, and he could not picture anyone else, neither Berkthgar nor the god Tempus himself, carrying Aegis-fang.

"Never thought to give it to him," Bruenor agreed. He wagged an angry fist in the air, the muscles of his arm straining with the obvious tension. "But if that half-son of a reindeer asks again, I'll give him something else, don't ye doubt!"

Drizzt saw a serious problem brewing. Berkthgar wanted the hammer, that was understandable, even expected, but the young, ambitious barbarian leader apparently did not appreciate the depth of his request. This situation could get much worse than a strain on necessary allies, Drizzt knew. This could lead to open fighting between the peoples, for Drizzt did not doubt Bruenor's claim for a moment. If Berkthgar demanded the hammer as ransom for what he should give unconditionally, he'd be lucky to get back into the sunshine with his limbs attached.

"Me and Drizzt'll go to Settlestone," Catti-brie offered. "We'll get Berkthgar's word and give him nothing in return."

"The boy's a fool!" Bruenor huffed.

"But his people are not foolish," Catti-brie added. "He's wanting the hammer to make himself more the leader. We'll teach him that asking for something he cannot have will make him less the leader."

Strong, and passionate, and so wise, Drizzt mused, watching the young woman. She would indeed accomplish what she had claimed. He and Catti-brie would go to Settlestone and return with everything Catti-brie had just promised her father.

The drow blew a long, low sigh as Bruenor and Catti-brie moved off, the young woman going to retrieve her belongings from the side of the room. He watched the renewed hop in Bruenor's step, the life returned to the fiery dwarf. How many years would King Bruenor Battlehammer rule? Drizzt wondered. A hundred? Two hundred?

Unless the blade of an enemy or the claws of a monster shortened his life, the dwarf, too, would watch Catti-brie grow old and pass away.

It was an image that Drizzt, watching the light step of this spirited young foal, could not bear to entertain.

⚔ ⚔ ⚔ ⚔ ⚔

Khazid'hea, or Cutter, rested patiently on Catti-brie's hip, its moment of anger passed. The sentient sword was pleased by the young woman's progress as a fighter. She was able, no doubt, but still Khazid'hea wanted more, wanted to be wielded by the very finest warrior.

Right now, that warrior seemed to be Drizzt Do'Urden.

The sword had gone after Drizzt when the drow renegade had killed its former wielder, Dantrag Baenre. Khazid'hea had altered its pommel, as it usually did, from the sculpted head of a fiend—which had lured Dantrag—to one of a unicorn, knowing that was the symbol of Drizzt Do'Urden's goddess. Still, the drow ranger had bade Catti-brie take the sword, for he favored the scimitar.

Favored the scimitar!

How Khazid'hea wished that it might alter its blade as it could the pommel! If the weapon could curve its blade, shorten and thicken it . . .

But Khazid'hea could not, and Drizzt would not wield a sword. The woman was good, though, and getting better. She was human, and would not likely live long enough to attain as great a proficiency as Drizzt, but if the sword could compel her to slay the drow . . .

There were many ways to become the best.

✕ ✕ ✕ ✕ ✕

Matron Baenre, withered and too old to be alive, even for a drow, stood in the great chapel of Menzoberranzan's First House, her House, watching the slow progress as her slave workers tried to extract the fallen stalactite from the roof of the dome-shaped structure. The place would soon be repaired, she knew. The rubble on the floor had already been cleared away, and the bloodstains of the dozen drow killed in the tragedy had long ago been scoured clean.

But the pain of that moment, of Matron Baenre's supreme embarrassment in front of every important matron mother of Menzoberranzan, in the very moment of the first matron mother's pinnacle of power, lingered. The spearlike stalactite had cut into the roof, but it might as well have torn Matron Baenre's own heart. She had forged an alliance between the warlike Houses of the drow city, a joining solidified by the promise of new glory when the drow army conquered Mithral Hall.

New glory for the Spider Queen. New glory for Matron Baenre.

Shattered by the point of a stalactite, by the escape of that renegade Drizzt Do'Urden. To Drizzt she had lost her eldest son, Dantrag, perhaps the finest weapons master in Menzoberranzan. To Drizzt she had lost her daughter, wicked Vendes. And most painful of all to the old wretch, she had lost to Drizzt and his friends the alliance, the promise of greater glory. For when the matron mothers, the rulers of Menzoberranzan and priestesses all, had watched the stalactite pierce the roof of this chapel, this most sacred place of Lolth, at the time of high ritual, their confidence that the goddess had sanctioned both this alliance and the coming war had crumbled. They had left House Baenre in a rush, back to their own houses, where they sealed their gates and tried to discern the will of Lolth.

Matron Baenre's status had suffered greatly.

Even with all that had happened, though, the first matron mother was confident she could restore the alliance. On a necklace around her neck she kept a ring carved from the tooth of an ancient dwarven king, one Gandalug Battlehammer, patron of Clan Battlehammer, founder of Mithral Hall. Matron Baenre owned Gandalug's spirit and could exact answers from it about the ways of the dwarven mines. Despite Drizzt's escape, the dark elves could go to Mithral Hall, could punish Drizzt and his friends.

She could restore the alliance, but for some reason that Matron Baenre did not understand, Lolth, the Spider Queen herself, held her in check. The yochlol, the handmaidens of Lolth, had come to Baenre and warned her to forego the alliance and instead focus her attention on her family, to secure her House defenses. It was a demand no priestess of the Spider Queen would dare disobey.

She heard the harsh clicking of hard boots on the floor behind her and the jingle of ample jewelry, and she didn't have to turn around to know that Jarlaxle had entered.

"You have done as I asked?" she questioned, still looking at the continuing work on the domed ceiling.

"Greetings to you as well, First Matron Mother," the always sarcastic male replied. That turned Baenre to face him, and she scowled, as she and so many other of Menzoberranzan's ruling females scowled when they looked at the mercenary.

He was swaggering—there was no other word to describe him. The dark elves of Menzoberranzan, particularly the lowly males, normally donned quiet, practical clothes, dark-hued robes adorned with spiders or webs, or plain black jerkins beneath supple chain mail armor, and almost always, both male and female drow wore camouflaging *piwafwis*, dark cloaks that could hide them from the probing eyes of their many enemies.

Not so with Jarlaxle. His head was shaven and always capped by an outrageous wide-brimmed hat feathering the gigantic plume of a diatryma bird. In lieu of a cloak or robe, he wore a shimmering cape that flickered through every color of the spectrum, both in light and under the scrutiny of heat-sensing eyes looking in the infrared range. His sleeveless vest was cut high to show the tight muscles of his stomach, and he carried an assortment of rings and necklaces, bracelets, even anklets, that chimed gratingly—but only when the mercenary wanted them to. Like his boots, which had sounded so clearly on the hard chapel floor, the jewelry could be silenced completely.

Matron Baenre noted that the mercenary's customary eye patch was over his left eye this day, but what, if anything, that signified, she could not tell.

For who knew what magic was in that patch, or in those jewels and those boots, or in the two wands he wore tucked under his belt, and the fine sword he kept beside them? Half those items, even one of the wands, Matron Baenre believed, were likely fakes, with little or no magical properties other than, perhaps, the ability to fall silent. Half of everything Jarlaxle did was a bluff, but half of it was devious and ultimately deadly.

That was why the swaggering mercenary was so dangerous.

That was why Matron Baenre hated Jarlaxle so, and why she needed him so. He was the leader of Bregan D'aerthe, a network of spies, thieves,

and killers, mostly rogue males made Houseless when their families had been wiped out in one of the many interhouse wars. As mysterious as their dangerous leader, Bregan D'aerthe's members were not known, but they were indeed very powerful—as powerful as most of the city's established Houses—and very effective.

"What have you learned?" Matron Baenre asked bluntly.

"It would take me centuries to spew it all," the cocky rogue replied.

Baenre's red-glowing eyes narrowed, and Jarlaxle realized she was not in the mood for his flippancy. She was scared, he knew, and considering the catastrophe at the high ritual, rightly so.

"I find no conspiracy," the mercenary honestly admitted.

Matron Baenre's eyes widened, and she swayed back on her heels, surprised by the straightforward answer. She had enacted spells that would allow her to detect any outright lies the mercenary spoke, of course. And of course, Jarlaxle would know that. Those spells never seemed to bother the crafty mercenary leader, who could dance around the perimeters of any question, never quite telling the truth, but never overtly lying.

This time, though, he had answered bluntly, and right to the heart of the obvious question. And as far as Matron Baenre could tell, he was telling the truth.

Baenre could not accept it. Perhaps her spell was not functioning as intended. Perhaps Lolth had indeed abandoned her for her failure, and was thus deceiving her now concerning Jarlaxle's sincerity.

"Matron Mez'Barris Armgo," Jarlaxle went on, referring to the matron mother of Barrison del'Armgo, the city's Second House, "remains loyal to you, and to your cause, despite the . . ." He fished around for the correct word. "The disturbance," he said at length, "to the high ritual. Matron Mez'Barris is even ordering her garrison to keep on the ready in case the march to Mithral Hall is resumed. And they are more than eager to go, I can assure you, especially with . . ." The mercenary paused and sighed with mock sadness, and Matron Baenre understood his reasoning.

Logically, Mez'Barris would be eager to go to Mithral Hall, for with Dantrag Baenre dead, her own weapons master, mighty Uthegental, was indisputably the greatest in the city. If Uthegental could get the rogue Do'Urden, what glories House Barrison del'Armgo might know!

Yet that very logic, and Jarlaxle's apparently honest claim, flew in the face of Matron Baenre's fears, for without the assistance of Barrison del'Armgo, no combination of Houses in Menzoberranzan could threaten House Baenre.

"The minor shuffling among your surviving children has commenced, of course," Jarlaxle went on. "But they have had little contact, and if any of them plan to move against you, it will be without the aid of Triel, who has been kept busy in the Academy since the escape of the rogue."

Matron Baenre did well to hide her relief at that statement. If Triel, the most powerful of her daughters, and certainly the one most in Lolth's favor, was not planning to rise against her, a coup from within seemed unlikely.

"It is expected that you will soon name Berg'inyon as weapons master, and Gromph will not oppose," Jarlaxle remarked.

Matron Baenre nodded her agreement. Gromph was her elderboy, and as Archmage of Menzoberranzan, he held more power than any male in the city—except for, perhaps, sly Jarlaxle. Gromph would not disapprove of Berg'inyon as weapons master of House Baenre. The ranking of Baenre's daughters seemed secure as well, she had to admit. Triel was in place as Mistress Mother of Arach-Tinilith in the Academy, and though those remaining in the House might squabble over the duties and powers left vacant by the loss of Vendes, it didn't seem likely to concern her.

Matron Baenre looked back to the spike Drizzt and his companions had put through the ceiling, and was not satisfied. In cruel and merciless Menzoberranzan, satisfaction and the smugness that inevitably accompanied it too often led to an untimely demise.

2

The Gutbuster Brigade

We're thinking we'll need the thing?" Catti-brie asked as she and Drizzt made their way along the lower levels of Mithral Hall. They moved along a corridor that opened wide to their left, into the great tiered cavern housing the famed dwarven Undercity.

Drizzt paused and regarded her, then went to the left, drawing Catti-brie behind him. He stepped through the opening, emerging on the second tier up from the huge cavern's floor.

The place was bustling, with dwarves running every which way, shouting to be heard over the continual hum of great pumping bellows and the determined ring of hammer on mithral. This was the heart of Mithral Hall, a huge, open cavern cut into gigantic steps on both its east and west walls, so that the whole place resembled an inverted pyramid. The widest floor area was the lowest level, between the gigantic steps, housing the huge furnaces. Strong dwarves pulled carts laden with ore along prescribed routes, while others worked the many levers of the intricate ovens, and still others tugged smaller carts of finished metals up to the tiers. There the various craftsman pounded the ore into useful items. Normally, a great variety of goods would be produced here—fine silverware, gem-studded chalices, and ornate helmets—gorgeous but of little practical use. Now, though, with war hanging over their heads, the dwarves focused on weapons and true defensive armor. Twenty feet to the side of Drizzt and Catti-brie, a dwarf so soot-covered that the color of his beard was not distinguishable leaned another iron-shafted, mithral-tipped ballista bolt against the wall. The dwarf couldn't even reach the top of the eight-foot spear, but he regarded its barbed and many-edged tip and chuckled. No doubt he enjoyed a fantasy concerning its flight and little drow elves all standing in a row.

On one of the arcing bridges spanning the tiers, perhaps a hundred and fifty feet up from the two friends, a substantial argument broke out. Drizzt and Catti-brie could not make out the words above the general din, but they realized that it had to do with plans for dropping that bridge, and most of the other bridges, forcing any invading dark elves along certain routes if they intended to reach the complex's higher levels.

None of them, not Drizzt, Catti-brie, or any of Bruenor's people, hoped it would ever come to that.

The two friends exchanged knowing looks. Rarely in the long history of Mithral Hall had the Undercity seen this kind of excitement. It bordered on frenzy. Two thousand dwarves rushed around, shouting, pounding their hammers, or hauling loads that a mule wouldn't pull.

All of this because they feared the drow were coming.

Catti-brie understood then why Drizzt had detoured into this place, why he had insisted on finding the halfling Regis before going to Settlestone, as Bruenor had bade them.

"Let's go find the sneaky one," she said to Drizzt, having to yell to be heard. Drizzt nodded and followed her back into the relative quiet of the dim corridors. They moved away from the Undercity then, toward the remote chambers where Bruenor had told them they could find the halfling. Silently they moved along—and Drizzt was impressed with how quietly Catti-brie had learned to move. Like him, she wore a fine mesh armor suit of thin but incredibly strong mithral rings, custom fitted to her by Buster Bracer, the finest armorer in Mithral Hall. Catti-brie's armor did little to diminish the dwarf's reputation, for it was so perfectly crafted and supple that it bent with her movements as easily as a thick shirt.

Like Drizzt's, Catti-brie's boots were thin and well worn but to the drow's sharp ears, few humans, even so attired, could move so silently. Drizzt subtly eyed her in the dim, flickering light of the widely spaced torches. He noted that she was stepping like a drow, the ball of her foot touching down first, instead of the more common human heel-toe method. Her time in the Underdark, chasing Drizzt to Menzoberranzan, had served her well.

The drow nodded his approval but made no comment. Catti-brie had already earned her pride points this day, he figured. No sense in puffing up her ego any more.

The corridors were empty and growing increasingly dark. Drizzt did not miss this point. He even let his vision slip into the infrared spectrum, where

the varying heat of objects showed him their general shapes. Human Catti-brie did not possess such Underdark vision, of course, but around her head she wore a thin silver chain, set in its front with a green gemstone streaked by a single line of black: a cat's eye agate. It had been given to her by Lady Alustriel herself, enchanted so that its wearer could see, even in the darkest, deepest tunnels, as though she were standing in an open field under a starry sky.

The two friends had no trouble navigating in the darkness, but still, they were not comfortable with it. Why weren't the torches burning? they each wondered. Both had their hands close to weapon hilts. Catti-brie wished she had brought Taulmaril the Heartseeker, her magical bow, with her.

A tremendous crash sounded, and the floor trembled under their feet. Both were down in a crouch, and Drizzt's scimitars appeared in his hands so quickly that Catti-brie didn't even register the movement. At first the young woman thought the impossibly fast maneuver the result of the magical bracers, but in glancing at Drizzt, she realized he wasn't even wearing them. She likewise drew her sword and took a deep breath, privately scolding herself for thinking she was getting close in fighting skill to the incredible ranger. Catti-brie shook the thought aside—no time for it now—and concentrated on the winding corridor ahead. Side by side, she and Drizzt slowly advanced, looking for shadows where enemies might hide and for lines in the wall that would indicate cunning secret doors to side passages. Such ways were common in the dwarven complex, for most dwarves could make them, and most dwarves, greedy by nature, kept personal treasures hidden away. Catti-brie did not know this little-used section of Mithral Hall very well. Neither did Drizzt.

Another crash came, and the floor trembled again, more than before, and the friends knew they were getting closer. Catti-brie was glad she had been training so hard, and gladder still that Drizzt Do'Urden was by her side.

She stopped moving, and Drizzt did likewise, turning to regard her.

"Guenhwyvar?" she silently mouthed, referring to Drizzt's feline friend, a loyal panther that the drow could summon from the Astral Plane.

Drizzt considered the suggestion for a moment. He tried not to summon Guenhwyvar too often now, knowing there might soon be a time when the panther would be needed often. There were limits on the magic. Guenhwyvar could only remain on the Prime Material Plane for half a day out of every two.

Not yet, Drizzt decided. Bruenor had not indicated what Regis might be doing down here, but the dwarf had given no hint that there might be danger. The drow shook his head slightly, and the two moved on, silent and sure.

A third crash came, followed by a groan.

"Yer head, ye durned fool!" came a sharp scolding. "Ye gots to use yer stinkin' head!"

Drizzt and Catti-brie straightened immediately and relaxed their grips on their weapons. "Pwent," they said together, referring to Thibbledorf Pwent, the outrageous battlerager, the most obnoxious and bad-smelling dwarf south of the Spine of the World—and probably north of it, as well.

"Next ye'll be wantin' to wear a stinkin' helmet!" the tirade continued.

Around the next bend, the two companions came to a fork in the corridor. To the left, Pwent continued roaring in outrage, and to the right was a door with torchlight showing through its many cracks. Drizzt cocked his head, catching a slight and familiar chuckle that way.

He motioned for Catti-brie to follow and went through the door without knocking. Regis stood alone inside, leaning on a crank near the left-hand wall. The halfling's smile lit up when he saw his friends, and he waved one hand high to them—relatively high, for Regis was small, even by halfling standards, his curly brown hair barely topping three feet. He had an ample belly, though it seemed to be shrinking of late, as even the lazy halfling took seriously the threat to this place that had become his home.

He put a finger over pursed lips as Drizzt and Catti-brie approached, and he pointed to the "door" before him. It didn't take either of the companions long to understand what was transpiring. The crank next to Regis operated a sheet of heavy metal that ran along runners above and to the side of the door. The wood of the door could hardly be seen now, for the plate was in place right before it.

"Go!" came a thunderous command from the other side, followed by charging footsteps and a grunting roar, then a tremendous explosion as the barreling dwarf hit, and of course bounced off, the barricaded portal.

"Battlerager training," Regis calmly explained.

Catti-brie gave Drizzt a sour look, remembering what her father had told her of Pwent's plans. "The Gutbuster Brigade," she remarked, and Drizzt nodded, for Bruenor had told him, too, that Thibbledorf Pwent meant to train a group of dwarves in the not-so-subtle art of battleraging, his personal Gutbuster Brigade, highly motivated, skilled in frenzy, and not too smart.

Another dwarf hit the barricaded door, probably headfirst, and Drizzt understood how Pwent meant to facilitate the third of his three requirements for his soldiers.

Catti-brie shook her head and sighed. She did not doubt the military value of the brigade—Pwent could outfight anyone in Mithral Hall, except for

Drizzt and maybe Bruenor, but the notion of a bunch of little Thibbledorf Pwents running around surely turned her stomach!

Behind the door, Pwent was thoroughly scolding his troops, calling them every dwarven curse name, more than a few that Catti-brie, who had lived among the clan for more than a score of years, had never heard, and more than a few that Pwent seemed to be making up on the spot, such as "mule-kissin', flea-sniffin', water-drinkin', who-thinks-ye-squeeze-the-durned-cow-to-get-the-durned-milk, lumps o' sandstone."

"We are off to Settlestone," Drizzt explained to Regis, the drow suddenly anxious to be out of there. "Berkthgar is being difficult."

Regis nodded. "I was there when he told Bruenor he wanted the warhammer." The halfling's cherubic face turned up into one of his common, wistful smiles. "I truly believed Bruenor would cleave him down the middle!"

"We're needing Berkthgar," Catti-brie reminded the halfling.

Regis pooh-poohed that thought away. "Bluffing," he insisted. "Berkthgar needs us, and his people would not take kindly to his turning his back on the dwarves who have been so good to his folk."

"Bruenor would not really kill him," Drizzt said, somewhat unconvincingly. All three friends paused and looked to each other, each considering the tough dwarf king, the old and fiery Bruenor returned. They thought of Aegis-fang, the most beautiful of weapons, the flanks of its gleaming mithral head inscribed with the sacred runes of the dwarven gods. One side was cut with the hammer and anvil of Moradin the Soulforger, the other with the crossed axes of Clanggedon, dwarven god of battle, and both were covered perfectly by the carving of the gem within the mountain, the symbol of Dumathoin, the Keeper of Secrets. Bruenor had been among the best of the dwarven smiths, but after Aegis-fang, that pinnacle of creative triumph, he had rarely bothered to return to his forge.

They thought of Aegis-fang, and they thought of Wulfgar, who had been like Bruenor's son, the tall, fair-haired youth for whom Bruenor had made the mighty hammer.

"Bruenor *would* really kill him," Catti-brie said, echoing the thoughts of all three.

Drizzt started to speak, but Regis stopped him by holding up a finger.

" . . . now get yer head lower!" Pwent was barking on the other side of the door. Regis nodded and smiled and motioned for Drizzt to continue.

"We thought you might—"

Another crash sounded, then another groan, followed by the flapping of dwarven lips as the fallen would-be battlerager shook his head vigorously.

"Good recovery!" Pwent congratulated.

"We thought you might accompany us," Drizzt said, ignoring Catti-brie's sigh of disgust.

Regis thought about it for a moment. The halfling would have liked to get out of the mines and stretch in the sunshine once more, though the summer was all but over and the autumn chill already began to nip the air.

"I have to stay," the unusually dedicated halfling remarked. "I've much to do."

Both Drizzt and Catti-brie nodded. Regis had changed over the last few months, during the time of crisis. When Drizzt and Catti-brie had gone to Menzoberranzan—Drizzt to end the threat to Mithral Hall, Catti-brie to find Drizzt—Regis had taken command to spur grieving Bruenor into preparing for war. Regis, who had spent most of his life finding the softest couch to lie upon, had impressed even the toughest dwarf generals, even Thibbledorf Pwent, with his fire and energy. Now the halfling would have loved to go, both of them knew, but he remained true to his mission.

Drizzt looked hard at Regis, trying to find the best way to make his request. To his surprise, the halfling saw it coming, and immediately Regis's hands went to the chain around his neck. He lifted the ruby pendant over his head and casually tossed it to Drizzt.

Another testament to the halfling's growth, Drizzt knew, as he stared down at the sparkling ruby affixed to the chain. This was the halfling's most precious possession, a powerful charm Regis had stolen from his old guild master in far-off Calimport. The halfling had guarded it, coveted it, like a mother lion with a single cub, at least until this point.

Drizzt continued to look at the ruby, felt himself drawn by its multiple facets, spiraling down to depths that promised . . .

The drow shook his head and forced himself to look away. Even without one to command it, the enchanted ruby had reached out for him! Never had he witnessed such a powerful charm. And yet, Jarlaxle, the mercenary, had given it back to him, had willingly swapped it when they had met in the tunnels outside Menzoberranzan after Drizzt's escape. It was unexpected and important that Jarlaxle had given it back to Drizzt, but what the significance might be, Drizzt had not yet discerned.

"You should be careful before using that on Berkthgar," Regis said, drawing Drizzt from his thoughts. "He is proud, and if he figures out that sorcery was used against him, the alliance may indeed be dissolved."

"True enough," Catti-brie agreed. She looked to Drizzt.

"Only if we need it," the drow remarked, looping the chain around his

neck. The pendant settled near his breast and the ivory unicorn head, symbol of his goddess, that rested there.

Another dwarf hit the door and bounced off, then lay groaning on the floor.

"Bah!" they heard Pwent snort. "Ye're a bunch o' elf-lickin' pixies! I'll show ye how it's done!"

Regis nodded—that was his cue—and immediately began to turn the crank, drawing the metal plate out from behind the portal.

"Watch out," he warned his two companions, for they stood in the general direction of where Pwent would make his door-busting entrance.

"I'm for leaving," Catti-brie said, starting for the other, normal, door. The young woman had no desire to see Pwent. Likely, he would pinch her cheek with his grubby fingers and tell her to "work on that beard" so that she might be a beautiful woman.

Drizzt didn't take much convincing. He held up the ruby, nodded a silent thanks to Regis, and rushed out into the hall after Catti-brie.

They hadn't gone a dozen steps when they heard the training door explode, followed by Pwent's hysterical laughter and the admiring "oohs" and "aahs" of the naive Gutbuster Brigade.

"We should send the lot of them to Menzoberranzan," Catti-brie said dryly. "Pwent'd chase the whole city to the ends of the world!"

Drizzt—who had grown up among the unbelievably powerful drow Houses and had seen the wrath of the high priestesses and magical feats beyond anything he had witnessed in his years on the surface—did not disagree.

⚔ ⚔ ⚔ ⚔ ⚔

Councilor Firble ran a wrinkled hand over his nearly bald pate, feeling uncomfortable in the torchlight. Firble was a svirfneblin, a deep gnome, eighty pounds of wiry muscles packed into a three-and-a-half-foot frame. Few races of the Underdark could get along as well as the svirfnebli, and no race, except perhaps the rare pech, understood the ways of the deep stone so well.

Still, Firble was more than a bit afraid now, out in the—hopefully—empty corridors beyond the borders of Blingdenstone, the city that was his home. He hated the torchlight, hated any light, but the orders from King Schnicktick were final and unarguable: no gnome was to traverse the corridors without a burning torch in his hand.

No gnome except for one. Firble's companion this day carried no torch, for he possessed no hands. Belwar Dissengulp, Most Honored Burrow Warden of Blingdenstone, had lost his hands to drow, to Drizzt Do'Urden's brother Dinin, many years before. Unlike so many other Underdark races, though, the svirfnebli were not without compassion, and their artisans had fashioned marvelous replacements of pure, enchanted mithral: a block-headed hammer capping Belwar's right arm and a two-headed pickaxe on his left.

"Completed the circuit, we have," Firble remarked. "And back to Blingdenstone we go!"

"Not so!" Belwar grumbled. His voice was deeper and stronger than those of most svirfnebli, and was fitting, considering his stout, barrel-chested build.

"There are no drow in the tunnels," Firble insisted. "Not a fight in three tendays!"

It was true enough. After months of battling drow from Menzoberranzan in the tunnels near Blingdenstone, the corridors had gone strangely quiet. Belwar understood that Drizzt Do'Urden, his friend, had somehow played a part in this change, and he feared that Drizzt had been captured or killed.

"Quiet, it is," Firble said more softly, as if he had just realized the danger of his own volume. A shudder coursed the smaller svirfneblin's spine. Belwar had forced him out here—it was his turn in the rotation, but normally one as experienced and venerable as Firble would have been excused from scouting duties. Belwar had insisted, though, and for some reason Firble did not understand, King Schnicktick had agreed with the most honored burrow warden.

Not that Firble was unaccustomed to the tunnels. Quite the contrary. He was the only gnome of Blingdenstone with actual contacts in Menzoberranzan, and was more acquainted with the tunnels near the drow city than any other deep gnome. That dubious distinction was causing Firble fits these days, particularly from Belwar. When a disguised Catti-brie had been captured by the svirfnebli, and subsequently recognized as no enemy, Firble, at great personal risk, had been the one to show her quicker, secret ways into Menzoberranzan.

Now Belwar wasn't worried about any drow in the tunnels, Firble knew. The tunnels were quiet. The gnome patrols and other secret allies could find no hint that any drow were about at all, not even along the dark elves' normal routes closer to Menzoberranzan. Something important had happened in the drow city, that much was obvious, and it seemed obvious, too, that Drizzt and that troublesome Catti-brie were somehow involved. That was the real reason Belwar had forced Firble out here, Firble knew, and he shuddered again to think that was why King Schnicktick had so readily agreed with Belwar.

"Something has happened," Belwar said, unexpectedly playing his cards, as though he understood Firble's line of silent reasoning. "Something in Menzoberranzan."

Firble eyed the most honored burrow warden suspiciously. He knew what would soon be asked of him, knew that he would soon be dealing with that trickster Jarlaxle again.

"The stones themselves are uneasy," Belwar went on.

"As if the drow will soon march," Firble interjected dryly.

"*Cosim camman denoctusd*," Belwar agreed, in an ancient svirfneblin saying that translated roughly into "the settled ground before the earthquake," or, as it was more commonly known to surface dwellers, "the calm before the storm."

"That I meet with my drow informant, King Schnicktick desires," Firble reasoned, seeing no sense in holding back the guess any longer. He knew he would not be suggesting something that Belwar wasn't about to suggest to him.

"*Cosim camman denoctusd*," Belwar said again, with increased determination. Belwar, Schnicktick, and many others in Blingdenstone were convinced that the drow would soon march in force. Though the most direct tunnels to the surface, to where Drizzt Do'Urden called home, were east of Blingdenstone, beyond Menzoberranzan, the drow first would have to set out west, and would come uncomfortably close to the gnome city. So unsettling was that thought that King Schnicktick had ordered scouting parties far to the east and south, as far from home and Menzoberranzan as the svirfnebli had ever roamed. There were whispers of deserting Blingdenstone altogether, if the rumors proved likely and a new location could be found. No gnome wanted that, Belwar and Firble perhaps least of all. Both were old, nearing their second full century, and both were tied, heart and soul, to this city called Blingdenstone.

But among all the svirfnebli, these two understood the power of a drow march, understood that if Menzoberranzan's army came to Blingdenstone, the gnomes would be obliterated.

"Set up the meeting, I will," Firble said with a resigned sigh. "He will tell me little, I do not doubt. Never does he, and high always is the price!"

Belwar said nothing, and sympathized little for the cost of such a meeting with the greedy drow informant. The most honored burrow warden understood that the price of ignorance would be much higher. He also realized that Firble understood, as well, and that the councilor's apparent resignation was just a part of Firble's bluster. Belwar had come to know Firble well, and found that he liked the oft-complaining gnome.

Now Belwar, and every other svirfneblin in Blingdenstone, desperately needed Firble and his contacts.

3

AT PLAY

Drizzt and Catti-brie skipped down the rocky trails, weaving in and out of boulder tumbles as effortlessly and spiritedly as two children at play. Their trek became an impromptu race as each hopped breaks in the stone, leaped to catch low branches, then swung down as far as the small mountain trees would carry them. They came onto one low, level spot together, where each leaped a small pool—though Catti-brie didn't quite clear it—and split up as they approached a slab of rock taller than either of them. Catti-brie went right and Drizzt started left, then changed his mind and headed up the side of the barrier instead.

Catti-brie skidded around the slab, pleased to see that she was first to the other side.

"My lead!" she cried, but even as she spoke she saw her companion's dark, graceful form sail over her head.

"Not so!" Drizzt corrected, touching down so lightly that it seemed as if he had never been off the ground. Catti-brie groaned and kicked into a run again, but pulled up short, seeing that Drizzt had stopped.

"Too fine a day," the dark elf remarked. Indeed, it was as fine a day as the southern spur of the Spine of the World ever offered once the autumn winds began to blow. The air was crisp, the breeze cool, and puffy white clouds—gigantic snowballs, they seemed—raced across the deep blue sky on swift mountain winds.

"Too fine for arguing with Berkthgar," Catti-brie added, thinking that was the direction of the drow's statement. She bent a bit and put her hands to her thighs for support, then turned her head back and up, trying to catch

her breath.

"Too fine to leave Guenhwyvar out of it!" Drizzt clarified happily.

Catti-brie's smile was wide when she looked down to see Drizzt take the onyx panther figurine out of his backpack. It was among the most beautiful of artworks Catti-brie had ever seen, perfectly detailed to show the muscled flanks and the true, insightful expression of the great cat. As perfect as it was, though, the figurine paled beside the magnificent creature that it allowed Drizzt to summon.

The drow reverently placed the item on the ground before him. "Come to me, Guenhwyvar," he called softly. Apparently the panther was eager to return, for a gray mist swirled around the item almost immediately, gradually taking shape and solidifying.

Guenhwyvar came to the Material Plane with ears straight up, relaxed, as though the cat understood from the inflections of Drizzt's call that there was no emergency, that she was being summoned merely for companionship.

"We are racing to Settlestone," Drizzt explained. "Do you think you can keep pace?"

The panther understood. A single spring from powerful hind legs sent Guenhwyvar soaring over Catti-brie's head, across the twenty-foot expanse to the top of the rock slab she and Drizzt had just crossed. The cat hit the rock's flat top, backpedaled, and spun to face the duo. Then for no other reason than to give praise to the day, Guenhwyvar reared and stood tall in the air, a sight that sent her friends' hearts racing. Guenhwyvar was six hundred pounds, twice the size of an ordinary panther, with a head almost as wide as Drizzt's shoulders, a paw that could cover a man's face, and spectacular, shining green eyes that revealed an intelligence far beyond what an animal should possess. Guenhwyvar was the most loyal of companions, an unjudging friend, and every time Drizzt, Catti-brie, Bruenor, or Regis, looked at the cat, their lives were made just a bit warmer.

"Me thinking's that we should get a head start," Catti-brie whispered mischievously.

Drizzt gave a slight, inconspicuous nod, and they broke together, running full-out down the trail. A few seconds later they heard Guenhwyvar roar behind them, still from atop the slab of rock. The trail was relatively clear and Drizzt sprinted out ahead of Catti-brie, though the woman, young and strong, with a heart that would have been more appropriate in the chest of a sturdy dwarf, could not be shaken.

"Ye're not to beat me!" she cried, to which Drizzt laughed. His mirth disappeared as he rounded a bend to find that stubborn and daring Catti-brie had taken a somewhat treacherous shortcut, light-skipping over a patch of broken and uneven stones, to take an unexpected lead.

Suddenly this was more than a friendly competition. Drizzt lowered his head and ran full-out, careening down the uneven ground so recklessly that he was barely able to avoid smacking face first into a tree. Catti-brie paced him, step for step, and kept her lead.

Guenhwyvar roared again, and they knew they were being mocked.

Sure enough, barely a few seconds later, a black streak rebounded off a wall of stone to Drizzt's side, crossing level with the drow's head. Guenhwyvar cut back across the trail between the two companions, and passed Catti-brie so quickly and so silently that she hardly realized she was no longer leading.

Sometime later, Guenhwyvar let her get ahead again, then Drizzt took a treacherous shortcut and slipped into the front—only to be passed again by the panther. So it went, with competitive Drizzt and Catti-brie working hard, and Guenhwyvar merely hard at play.

The three were exhausted—at least Drizzt and Catti-brie were; Guenhwyvar wasn't even breathing hard—when they broke for lunch on a small clearing, protected from the wind by a high wall on the north and east, and dropping off fast in a sheer cliff to the south. Several rocks dotted the clearing, perfect stools for the tired companions. A grouping of stones was set in the middle as a fire pit, for this was a usual campsite of the oft-wandering drow.

Catti-brie relaxed while Drizzt brought up a small fire. Far below she could see the gray plumes of smoke rising lazily into the clear air from the houses of Settlestone. It was a sobering sight, for it reminded the young woman, who had spent the morning at such a pace, of the gravity of her mission and of the situation. How many runs might she, Drizzt, and Guenhwyvar share if the dark elves came calling?

Those plumes of smoke also reminded Catti-brie of the man who had brought the tough barbarians to this place from Icewind Dale, the man who was to have been her husband. Wulfgar had died trying to save her, had died in the grasp of a yochlol, a handmaiden of evil Lolth. Both Catti-brie and Drizzt had to bear some responsibility for that loss, yet it wasn't guilt that pained the young woman now, or that pained Drizzt. He, too, had noticed the smoke and had taken a break from his fire-tending to watch and contemplate.

The companions did not smile now, for simple loss, because they had taken so many runs just like this one, except that Wulfgar had raced beside them, his long strides making up for the fact that he could not squeeze through breaks that his two smaller companions could pass at full speed.

"I wish . . . " Catti-brie said, and the words resonated in the ears of the similarly wishing dark elf.

"Our war, if it comes, would be better fought with Wulfgar, son of Beornegar, leading the men of Settlestone," Drizzt agreed, and what both he and Catti-brie silently thought was that all their lives would be better if Wulfgar were alive.

There. Drizzt had said it openly, and there was no more to say. They ate their lunch silently. Even Guenhwyvar lay very still and made not a sound.

Catti-brie's mind drifted from her friends, back to Icewind Dale, to the rocky mountain, Kelvin's Cairn, dotting the otherwise flat tundra. It was so similar to this very place. Colder, perhaps, but the air held the same crispness, the same clear, vital texture. How far she and her friends, Drizzt and Guenhwyvar, Bruenor and Regis, and of course, Wulfgar, had come from that place! And in so short a time! A frenzy of adventures, a lifetime of excitement and thrills and good deeds. Together they were an unbeatable force.

So they had thought.

Catti-brie had seen the emotions of a lifetime, indeed, and she was barely into her twenties. She had run fast through life, like her run down the mountain trails, free and high-spirited, skipping without care, feeling immortal.

Almost.

AT THE SEAMS

A conspiracy?" the drow's fingers flashed, using the silent hand code of the dark elves, its movements so intricate and varied that nearly every connotation of every word in the drow language could be represented.

Jarlaxle replied with a slight shake of his head. He sighed and seemed sincerely perplexed—a sight not often seen—and motioned for his cohort to follow him to a more secure area.

They crossed the wide, winding avenues of Menzoberranzan, flat, clear areas between the towering stalagmite mounds that served as homes to the various drow families. Those mounds, and a fair number of long stalactites leering down from the huge cavern's ceiling, were hollowed out and sculpted with sweeping balconies and walkways. The clusters within each family compound were often joined by high bridges, most shaped to resemble spiderwebs. And on all the houses, especially those of the older and more established families, the most wondrous designs were highlighted by glowing faerie fire, purple and blue, sometimes outlined in red and not so often, in green. Menzoberranzan was the most spectacular of cities, breathtaking, surreal, and an ignorant visitor—who would not be ignorant, or likely even alive, for long!—would never guess that the artisans of such beauty were among the most malicious of Toril's races.

Jarlaxle moved without a whisper down the darker, tighter avenues surrounding the lesser Houses. His focus was ahead and to the sides, his keen eye—and his eye patch was over his right eye at the time—discerning the slightest of movements in the most distant shadows.

The mercenary leader's surprise was complete when he glanced back at his

companion and found, not M'tarl, the lieutenant of Bregan D'aerthe he had set out with, but another, very powerful, drow.

Jarlaxle was rarely without a quick response, but the specter of Gromph Baenre, Matron Baenre's elderboy, the archmage of Menzoberranzan, standing so unexpectedly beside him, surely stole his wit.

"I trust that M'tarl will be returned to me when you are finished," Jarlaxle said, quickly regaining his seldom-lost composure.

Without a word, the archmage waved his arm, and a shimmering green globe appeared in the air, several feet from the floor. A thin silver cord hung down from it, its visible end barely brushing the stone floor.

Jarlaxle shrugged and took up the cord, and as soon as he touched it, he was drawn upward into the globe, into the extradimensional space beyond the shimmering portal.

The casting was impressive, Jarlaxle decided, for he found within not the usual empty space created by such an evocation, but a lushly furnished sitting room, complete with a zombielike servant that offered him a drink of fine wine before he ever sat down. Jarlaxle took a moment to allow his vision to shift into the normal spectrum of light, for the place was bathed in a soft blue glow. This was not unusual for wizards, even drow wizards accustomed to the lightless ways of the Underdark, for one could not read scrolls or spellbooks without light!

"He will be returned if he can survive where I put him long enough for us to complete our conversation," Gromph replied. The wizard seemed not too concerned, as he, too, came into the extradimensional pocket. The mighty Baenre closed his eyes and whispered a word, and his *piwafwi* cloak and other unremarkable attire transformed. Now he looked the part of his prestigious station. His flowing robe showed many pockets and was emblazoned with sigils and runes of power. As with the House structures, faerie fire highlighted these runes, though the archmage could darken the runes with a thought, and his robe would be more concealing than the finest of *piwafwis*. Two brooches, one a black-legged, red-bodied spider, the other a shining green emerald, adorned the magnificent robe, though Jarlaxle could hardly see them, for the old wizard's long white hair hung down the side of his head and in front of his shoulders and chest.

With his interest in things magical, Jarlaxle had seen the brooches on the city's previous archmage, though Gromph had held the position longer than most of Menzoberranzan's drow had been alive. The spider brooch allowed the archmage to cast the lingering heat enchantment into Narbondel, the pillar clock of Menzoberranzan. The heat would rise to the tip of the clock over a twelve-hour period, then diminish back toward the base in a like amount of time, until the stone was again cool, a very obvious and effective clock for heat-sensing drow eyes.

The other brooch gave Gromph perpetual youth. By Jarlaxle's estimation, this one had seen the birth and death of seven centuries, yet so young did he appear that it seemed he might be ready to begin his training at the drow Academy!

Not so, Jarlaxle silently recanted in studying the wizard. There was an aura of power and dignity about Gromph, reflected clearly in his eyes, which showed the wisdom of long and often bitter experience. This one was cunning and devious, able to scrutinize any situation immediately, and in truth, Jarlaxle felt more uncomfortable and more vulnerable standing before Gromph than before Matron Baenre herself.

"A conspiracy?" Gromph asked again, this time aloud. "Have the other Houses finally become fed up with my mother and banded together against House Baenre?"

"I have already given a full accounting to Matron—"

"I heard every word," Gromph interrupted, snarling impatiently. "Now I wish to know the truth."

"An interesting concept," Jarlaxle said, smiling wryly at the realization that Gromph was truly nervous. "Truth."

"A rare thing," Gromph agreed, regaining his composure and resting back in his chair, his slender fingers tapping together before him. "But a thing that sometimes keeps meddling fools alive."

Jarlaxle's smile vanished. He studied Gromph intently, surprised at so bold a threat. Gromph was powerful—by all measures of Menzoberranzan, the old wretch was as powerful as any male could become. But Jarlaxle did not operate by any of Menzoberranzan's measures, and for the wizard to take such a risk as to threaten Jarlaxle . . .

Jarlaxle was even more surprised when he realized that Gromph, mighty Gromph Baenre, was beyond nervous. He was truly scared.

"I will not even bother to remind you of the value of this 'meddling fool,' " Jarlaxle said.

"Do spare me."

Jarlaxle laughed in his face.

Gromph brought his hands to his hips, his outer robes opening in front with the movement and revealing a pair of wands set under his belt, one on each hip.

"No conspiracy," Jarlaxle said suddenly, firmly.

"The truth," Gromph remarked in dangerous, low tones.

"The truth," Jarlaxle replied as straightforwardly as he had ever spoken. "I have as much invested in House Baenre as do you, Archmage. If the lesser Houses were banding against Baenre, or if Baenre's daughters plotted her demise, Bregan D'aerthe would stand beside her, at least to the point of giving her fair notice of the coming coup."

Gromph's expression became very serious. What Jarlaxle noted most was that the elderboy of House Baenre had taken no apparent notice of his obvious—and intentional—slip in referring to Matron Baenre as merely "Baenre." Errors such as that often cost drow, particularly male drow, their lives.

"What is it then?" Gromph asked, and the very tone of the question, almost an outright plea, caught Jarlaxle off his guard. Never before had he seen the archmage, or heard of the archmage, in so desperate a state.

"You sense it!" Gromph snapped. "There is something wrong about the very air we breathe!"

For centuries untold, Jarlaxle silently added, a notion he knew he would be wise to keep to himself. To Gromph he offered only, "The chapel was damaged."

The archmage nodded, his expression turning sour. The great domed chapel of House Baenre was the holiest place in the entire city, the ultimate shrine to Lolth. In perhaps the most terrible slap in the face the Spider Queen had ever experienced, the renegade Do'Urden and his friends had, upon their escape, dropped a stalactite from the cavern's roof that punctured the treasured dome like a gigantic spear.

"The Spider Queen is angered," Gromph remarked.

"I would be," Jarlaxle agreed.

Gromph snapped an angry glare over the smug mercenary. Not for any insult he had given Lolth, Jarlaxle understood, but simply because of his flippant attitude.

When that glare had no more effect than to bring a smile to Jarlaxle's lips, Gromph sprang from his chair and paced like a caged displacer beast. The zombie host, unthinking and purely programmed, rushed over, drinks in hand.

Gromph growled and held his palm upraised, a ball of flame suddenly appearing atop it. With his other hand Gromph placed something small and red—it looked like a scale—into the flame and began an ominous chant.

Jarlaxle watched patiently as Gromph played out his frustration, the mercenary preferring that the wizard aim that retort at the zombie and not at him.

A lick of flame shot out from Gromph's hand. Lazily, determinedly, like a snake that had already immobilized its prey with poison, the flame wound around the zombie, which, of course, neither moved nor complained. In mere seconds, the zombie was engulfed by this serpent of fire. When Gromph casually sat again, the burning thing followed its predetermined course back to stand impassively. It made it back to its station, but soon crumbled, one of its legs consumed.

"The smell . . . " Jarlaxle began, putting a hand over his nose.

"Is of power!" Gromph finished, his red eyes narrowing, the nostrils of his thin nose flaring. The wizard took a deep breath and basked in the stench.

"It is not Lolth who fosters the wrongness of the air," Jarlaxle said suddenly, wanting to steal the obviously frustrated wizard's bluster and be done with Gromph and out of this reeking place.

"What do you know?" Gromph demanded, suddenly very anxious once more.

"No more than you," Jarlaxle replied. "Lolth is likely angry at Drizzt's escape, and at the damage to the chapel. You above all can appreciate the importance of that chapel." Jarlaxle's sly tone sent Gromph's nostrils flaring once more. The mercenary knew he had hit a sore spot, a weakness in the archmage's armored robes. Gromph had created the pinnacle of the Baenre chapel, a gigantic, shimmering illusion hovering over the central altar. It continually shifted form, going from a beautiful drow female to a huge spider and back again. It was no secret in Menzoberranzan that Gromph was not the most devout of Lolth's followers, no secret that the creation of the magnificent illusion had spared him his mother's unmerciful wrath.

"But there are too many things happening for Lolth to be the sole cause," Jarlaxle went on after savoring the minor victory for a moment. "And too many of them adversely affect Lolth's own base of power."

"A rival deity?" Gromph asked, revealing more intrigue than he intended. "Or an underground revolt?" The wizard sat back suddenly, thinking he had hit upon something, thinking that any underground revolt would certainly fall into the domain of a certain rogue mercenary leader.

But Jarlaxle was in no way cornered, for if either of Gromph's suspicions had any basis, Jarlaxle did not know of it.

"Something," was all the mercenary replied. "Something perhaps very dangerous to us all. For more than a score of years, one House or another has, for some reason, overestimated the worth of capturing the renegade Do'Urden, and their very zeal has elevated his stature and multiplied the troubles he has caused."

"So you believe all of this is tied to Drizzt's escape," Gromph reasoned.

"I believe many matron mothers will believe that," Jarlaxle was quick to reply. "And, thus, Drizzt's escape will indeed play a role in what is to come. But I have not said, and do not believe, that what you sense is amiss is the result of the renegade's flight from House Baenre."

Gromph closed his eyes and let the logic settle. Jarlaxle was right, of course. Menzoberranzan was a place so wound up in its own intrigue that truth mattered less than suspicion, that suspicion often became a self—fulfilling prophecy, and thus, often created truth.

"I may wish to speak with you again, mercenary," the archmage said quietly, and Jarlaxle noticed a door near where he had entered the extradimensional pocket. Beside it the zombie still burned, now just a crumpled, blackened ball of almost bare bone.

Jarlaxle started for the door.

"Alas," Gromph said dramatically, and Jarlaxle paused. "M'tarl did not survive."

"A pity for M'tarl," Jarlaxle added, not wanting Gromph to think that the loss would in any way wound Bregan D'aerthe.

Jarlaxle went out the door, down the cord, and slipped away silently into the shadows of the city, trying to digest all that had occurred. Rarely had he spoken to Gromph, and even more rarely had Gromph requested, in his own convoluted way, the audience. That fact was significant, Jarlaxle realized. Something very strange was happening here, a slight tingle in the air. Jarlaxle, a lover of chaos—mostly because, within the swirl of chaos, he always seemed to come out ahead—was intrigued. What was even more intriguing was that Gromph, despite his fears and all that he had to lose, was also intrigued!

The archmage's mention of a possible second deity proved that, showed his entire hand. For Gromph was an old wretch, despite the fact that he had come as far in life as any male drow in Menzoberranzan could hope to climb.

No, not despite that fact, Jarlaxle silently corrected himself. Because of that fact. Gromph was bitter, and had been so for centuries, because, in his lofty view of his own worth, he saw even the position of archmage as pointless, as a limit imposed by an accident of gender.

The greatest weakness in Menzoberranzan was not the rivalry of the various Houses, Jarlaxle knew, but the strict matriarchal system imposed by Lolth's followers. Half the drow population was subjugated merely because they had been born male.

That was a weakness.

And subjugation inevitably bred bitterness, even—especially!—in one who had gone as far as Gromph. Because from his lofty perch, the archmage could clearly see how much farther he might possibly go if he had been born with a different set of genitals.

Gromph had indicated he might wish to speak with Jarlaxle again, and Jarlaxle had the feeling he and the bitter mage would indeed meet, perhaps quite often. He spent the next twenty steps of his walk back across Menzoberranzan wondering what information Gromph might extract from poor M'tarl, for of course the lieutenant was not dead—though he might soon wish he were.

Jarlaxle laughed at his own foolishness. He had spoken truly to Gromph, of course, and so M'tarl couldn't reveal anything incriminating. The mercenary sighed. He wasn't used to speaking truthfully, wasn't used to walking where there were no webs.

That notion dismissed, Jarlaxle turned his attention to the city. Something was brewing. Jarlaxle, the ultimate survivor, could sense it, and so could Gromph. Something important would occur all too soon, and what the mercenary needed to do was figure out how he might profit from it, whatever it might be.

CATTI-BRIE'S CHAMPION

Drizzt called Guenhwyvar to his side when the companions came down to the lower trails. The panther sat quietly, expecting what was to come.

"Ye should bring the cat in," Catti-brie suggested, understanding Drizzt's intent. The barbarians, though they had come far from their tundra homes and their secluded ways, remained somewhat distrustful of magic, and the sight of the panther always unnerved more than a few of Berkthgar's people, and didn't sit so well with Berkthgar himself.

"It is enough for them that I will enter their settlement," Drizzt replied.

Catti-brie had to nod in agreement. The sight of Drizzt, of a dark elf, one of a race noted for magic and evil, was perhaps even more unnerving to the Northmen than the panther. "Still, it'd teach Berkthgar good if ye had the cat sit on him for a while," she remarked.

Drizzt chuckled as he conjured an image of Guenhwyvar stretching comfortably on the back of the large, wriggling man. "The folk of Settlestone will grow accustomed to the panther as they did to my own presence," the drow replied. "Think of how many years it took Bruenor to become comfortable around Guenhwyvar."

The panther gave a low growl, as if she understood their every word.

"It wasn't the years," Catti-brie returned. "It was the number of times Guen pulled me stubborn father's backside out of a hot fire!"

When Guenhwyvar growled again, both Drizzt and Catti-brie had a good laugh at surly Bruenor's expense. The mirth subsided as Drizzt took out the figurine and bade Guenhwyvar farewell, promising to call the panther back as soon as he and Catti-brie were on the trails once more, heading back to Mithral Hall.

The formidable panther, growling low, walked in circles around the figurine. Gradually those growls diminished as Guenhwyvar faded into gray mist, then into nothing at all.

Drizzt scooped up the figurine and looked to the plumes of smoke rising from nearby Settlestone. "Are you ready?" he asked his companion.

"He'll be a stubborn one," Catti-brie admitted.

"We just have to get Berkthgar to understand the depth of Bruenor's distress," Drizzt offered, starting off again for the town.

"We just have to get Berkthgar to imagine Bruenor's axe sweeping in for the bridge of his nose," Catti-brie muttered. "Right between the eyes."

Settlestone was a rocky, windswept cluster of stone houses set in a vale and protected on three sides by the climbing, broken sides of the towering mountains known as the Spine of the World. The rock structures, resembling houses of cards against the backdrop of the gigantic mountains, had been built by the dwarves of Mithral Hall, by Bruenor's ancestors, hundreds of years before, when the place had been called Dwarvendarrow. It had been used as a trading post by Bruenor's people and was the only place for merchants to peek at the wonders that came from Mithral Hall, for the dwarves did not wish to entertain foreigners in their secret mines.

Even one who did not know the history of Dwarvendarrow would reason that this place had been constructed by the bearded folk. Only dwarves could have imbued the rocks with such strength, for, though the settlement had been uninhabited for centuries, and though the wind sweeping down the channel of the tall mountain walls was unrelenting, the structures had remained. In setting the place up for their own use, Wulfgar's people had no more a task than to brace an occasional wall, sweep out the tons of pebbles that had half buried some of the houses, and flush out the animals that had come to live there.

So it was a trading post again, looking much as it had in the heyday of Mithral Hall, but now called Settlestone and now used by humans working as agents for the busy dwarves. The agreement seemed sound and profitable to both parties, but Berkthgar had no idea of how tentative things had suddenly become. If he did not relent on his demand to carry Aegis-fang, both Drizzt and Catti-brie knew, Bruenor would likely order the barbarian and his people off the land.

The proud barbarians would never follow such a command, of course. The land had been granted, not loaned.

The prospect of war, of Bruenor's people coming down from the mountains and driving the barbarians away, was not so outlandish.

All because of Aegis-fang.

"Wulfgar would not be so glad to know the source of the arguing," Catti-brie remarked as she and Drizzt neared the settlement. " 'Twas he who bringed them all together. Seems a pity indeed that it's his memory threatening to tear them apart."

A pity and a terrible irony, Drizzt silently agreed. His steps became more determined. Put in that light, this diplomatic mission took on even greater significance. Suddenly Drizzt was marching to Settlestone for much more than a petty squabble between two unyielding rulers. The drow was going for Wulfgar's honor.

As they came down to the valley floor, they heard chanting, a rhythmic, solemn recitation of the deeds of a legendary warrior. They crossed into the empty ways, past the open house doors that the hearty folk never bothered to secure. Both knew where the chanting was coming from, and both knew where they would find the men, women, and children of Settlestone.

The only addition the barbarian settlers had made to the town was a large structure that could fit all four hundred people of Settlestone and a like number of visitors. Hengorot, "the Mead Hall," it was called. It was a solemn place of worship, of valor recalled, and ultimately of sharing food and drink.

Hengorot wasn't finished. Half its long, low walls were of stone, but the rest was enclosed by deerskin canopies. That fact seemed fitting to Drizzt, seemed to reflect how far Wulfgar's people had come, and how far they had to go. When they had lived on the tundra of Icewind Dale, they had been nomadic, following the reindeer herd, so all their houses had been of skin, which could be packed up and taken with the wandering tribe.

No longer were the hearty folk nomads; no longer was their existence dependent on the reindeer herd. It was an unreliable source that often led to warring between the various tribes, or with the folk of Ten-Towns, on the three lakes, the only non-barbarians in Icewind Dale.

Drizzt was glad to see the level of peace and harmony that the northmen had attained, but still it pained him to look at the uncompleted part of Hengorot, to view the skins and remember, too, the sacrifices these people had made. Their way of life, which had survived for thousands of years, was no more. Looking at this construction of Hengorot, a mere shade of the glories the mead hall had known, looking at the stone that now enclosed this proud people, the drow could not help but wonder if this way was indeed "progress."

Catti-brie, who had lived most of her young life in Icewind Dale, and who had heard countless tales of the nomadic barbarians, had understood the loss all along. In coming to Settlestone, the barbarians had given away a measure of their freedom and more than a bit of their heritage. They were richer now, far richer than they could have ever dreamt, and no longer would a harsh winter threaten their very existence. But there had been a price. Like the stars. The stars were different here beside the mountains. They didn't come down to the flat horizon, drawing a person's soul into the heavens.

With a resigned sigh, a bit of her own homesickness for Icewind Dale, Catti-brie reminded herself of the pressing situation. She knew that Berkthgar was being stubborn, but knew, too, how pained the barbarian leader was over Wulfgar's fall, and how pained he must be to think that a dwarf held the key to the warhammer that had become the most honored weapon in his tribe's history.

Never mind that the dwarf had been the one to forge that weapon; never mind that the man who had carried it to such glory had, in fact, been like that dwarf's son. To Berkthgar, Catti-brie knew, the lost hero was not the son of Bruenor, but was Wulfgar, son of Beornegar, of the Tribe of the Elk. Wulfgar of Icewind Dale, not of Mithral Hall. Wulfgar, who epitomized all that had been respected and treasured among the barbarian people. Perhaps most of all, Catti-brie appreciated the gravity of the task before them.

Two tall, broad-shouldered guards flanked the skin flap of the mead hall's opening, their beards and breath smelling more than a little of thick mead. They bristled at first, then moved hastily aside when they recognized the visitors. One rushed to the closest end of the long table set in the hall's center to announce Drizzt and Catti-brie, listing their known feats and their heritage—Catti-brie's at least, for Drizzt's heritage would not be a source of glory in Settlestone.

Drizzt and Catti-brie waited patiently at the door with the other man, who easily outweighed the two of them put together. Both of them focused on Berkthgar, seated halfway down the table's right-hand side, and he inevitably looked past the man announcing the visitors to stare back at them.

Catti-brie thought the man a fool in his argument with Bruenor, but neither she nor Drizzt could help but be impressed by the giant barbarian. He was nearly as tall as Wulfgar, fully six and a half towering feet, with broad shoulders and hardened arms the size of a fat dwarf's thighs. His brown hair was shaggy, hanging low over his shoulders, and he was beginning a beard for winter, the thick tufts on his neck and cheeks making him appear all the more fierce and imposing. Settlestone's leaders were picked in contests of strength, in matches of fierce battle, as the barbarians had selected their leaders through their history. No man in Settlestone could defeat Berkthgar—Berkthgar the Bold, he was called—and yet, because of that fact, he lived, more than any of the others, in the shadow of a dead man who had become legend.

"Pray, join us!" Berkthgar greeted warmly, but the set of his expression told the two companions that he had been expecting this visit, and was not so thrilled to see them. The chieftain focused particularly on Drizzt, and Catti-brie read both eagerness and trepidation in the large man's sky-blue eyes.

Stools were offered to Drizzt and Catti-brie—a high honor for Catti-brie, for no other woman was seated at the table, unless upon the lap of a suitor. In Hengorot, and in all this society, the women and children, save for the older male children, were servants. They hustled now, placing mugs of mead before the newest guests.

Both Drizzt and Catti-brie eyed the drinks suspiciously, knowing they had to keep their heads perfectly clear, but when Berkthgar offered a toast to them and held his own mug high, custom demanded they likewise salute. And in Hengorot, one simply did not sip mead!

Both friends downed their mugs to rousing cheers, and both looked to each other despairingly as another full mug quickly replaced the emptied one.

Unexpectedly, Drizzt rose and deftly hopped up on the long table.

"My greetings to the men and women of Settlestone, to the people of Berkthgar the Bold!" he began, and a chorus of deafening cheers went up, roars for Berkthgar, the focus of the town's pride. The huge, shaggy-haired man got slapped on the back a hundred times in the next minute, but not once did he blink, and not once did he take his suspicious gaze from the dark elf.

Catti-brie understood what was going on here. The barbarians had come to grudgingly accept Drizzt, but still he was a scrawny elf, and a dark elf on top of it all! The paradox was more than a little uncomfortable for them. They saw Drizzt as weak—probably no stronger than some of their hearty womenfolk—and yet they realized that not one of them could defeat the drow in combat. Berkthgar was the most uncomfortable of all, for he knew why Drizzt and Catti-brie had come, and he suspected this issue about the hammer would be settled between him and Drizzt.

"Truly we are grateful, nay, thrilled, at your hospitality. None in all the Realms can set a table more inviting!" Again the cheers. Drizzt was playing them well, and it didn't hurt that more than half of them were falling-down drunk.

"But we cannot remain for long," Drizzt said, his voice suddenly solemn. The effect on those seated near the drow was stunning, as they seemed to sober immediately, seemed to suddenly grasp the weight of the drow's visit.

Catti-brie saw the sparkle of the ruby pendant hanging around Drizzt's neck, and she understood that though Drizzt wasn't actively using the enchanting gem, its mere presence was as intoxicating as any amount of thick mead.

"The heavy sword of war hangs over us all," Drizzt went on gravely. "This is the time of allian—"

Berkthgar abruptly ended the drow's speech by slamming his mug on the table so brutally that it shattered, splattering those nearby with golden-brown mead and glass fragments. Still holding the mug's handle, the barbarian leader unsteadily clambered atop the table to tower over the dark elf.

In the blink of an eye, Hengorot hushed.

"You come here claiming alliance," the barbarian leader began slowly. "You come asking for alliance." He paused and looked around at his anxious people for dramatic effect. "And yet you hold prisoner the weapon that has become a symbol of my people, a weapon brought to glory by Wulfgar, son of Beornegar!"

Thunderous cheers erupted, and Catti-brie looked up to Drizzt and shrugged helplessly. She always hated it when the barbarians referred to Wulfgar by his legacy, as the son of Beornegar. For them to do so was an item of pride, and pride alone never sat well with the pragmatic woman.

Besides, Wulfgar needed no claim of lineage to heighten his short life's achievements. His children, had he sired any, would have been the ones to rightfully speak of their father.

"We are friends of the dwarf king you serve, dark elf," Berkthgar went on, his booming voice resonating off the stone sections of Hengorot's walls. "And we ask the same of Bruenor Battlehammer, son of Bangor, son of Garumn. You shall have your alliance, but not until Aegis-fang is delivered to me.

"I am Berkthgar!" the barbarian leader bellowed.

"Berkthgar the Bold!" several of the man's advisors quickly piped in, and another chorus went up, a toast of mugs lifted high to the mighty chieftain of Settlestone.

"Bruenor would sooner deliver his own axe," Drizzt replied, thoroughly fed up with Berkthgar's glories. The drow understood then that he and Catti-brie had been expected in Settlestone, for Berkthgar's little speech, and the reaction to it, had been carefully planned, even rehearsed.

"And I do not think you would enjoy the way he would deliver that axe,"

the drow finished quietly, when the roaring had died away. Again came the hush of expectation, for the drow's words could be taken as a challenge, and Berkthgar, blue eyes squinting dangerously, seemed more than ready to pick up the gauntlet.

"But Bruenor is not here," the barbarian leader said evenly. "Will Drizzt Do'Urden champion his cause?"

Drizzt straightened, trying to decide the best course.

Catti-brie's mind, too, was working fast. She held little doubt that Drizzt would accept the challenge and put Berkthgar down at once, and the men of Settlestone surely would not tolerate that kind of embarrassment.

"Wulfgar was to be my husband!" she yelled, rising from her chair just as Drizzt was about to respond. "And I am the daughter of Bruenor—by rights, the princess of Mithral Hall. If anyone here is to champion my father's cause—"

"You will name him," Berkthgar reasoned.

"I will *be* . . . *her*," Catti-brie replied grimly.

Roars went up again, all around the mead hall, and more than a few women at the back of the room tittered and nodded hopefully.

Drizzt didn't seem so pleased, and the look he put over Catti-brie was purely plaintive, begging her to calm this situation before things got fully out of hand. He didn't want a fight at all. Neither did Catti-brie, but the room was in a frenzy then, with more than half the voices crying for Berkthgar to "Fight the woman!" as though Catti-brie's challenge had already been launched.

The look that Berkthgar put over Catti-brie was one of pure outrage.

She understood and sympathized with his predicament. She had meant to go on and explain that she would be Bruenor's only champion, if there was to be a champion, but that she had not come here to fight. Events had swept her past that point, however.

"Never!" Berkthgar roared above the din, and the room calmed somewhat, eager cries dying away to whispers. "Never have I battled a woman!"

That's an attitude Berkthgar had better overcome soon, Drizzt thought, for if the dark elves were indeed marching to Mithral Hall, there would be little room for such inhibitions. Females were typically the strongest of drow warriors, both magically and with weapons.

"Fight her!" cried one man, obviously very drunk, and he was laughing as he called, and so, too, were his fellows around him.

Berkthgar looked from the man to Catti-brie, his huge chest heaving as he tried to take in deep breaths to calm his rage.

He could not win, Catti-brie realized. If they fought, he could not win, even if he battered her. To the hearty men of Settlestone, even lifting a weapon against her would be considered cowardly.

Catti-brie climbed onto the table and gave a slight nod as she passed in front of Drizzt. Hands on hips—and her hip out to the side to accentuate her feminine figure—she gave a wistful smile to the barbarian leader. "Not with weapons, perhaps," she said. "But there are other ways a man and woman might compete."

All the room exploded at that comment. Mugs were lifted so forcefully in toast that little mead remained in them as they came back down to the eager mouths of the men. Several in the back end of Hengorot took up a lewd song, clapping each other on the back at every crescendo.

Drizzt's lavender eyes grew so wide that they seemed as if they would simply roll out of their sockets. When Catti-brie took the moment to regard him, she feared he would draw his weapons and kill everyone in the room. For an instant, she was flattered, but that quickly passed, replaced by disappointment that the drow would think so little of her.

She gave him a look that said just that as she turned and jumped down from the table. A man nearby reached out to catch her, but she slapped his hands away and strode defiantly for the door.

"There's fire in that one!" she heard behind her.

"Alas for poor Berkthgar!" came another rowdy cry.

On the table, the stunned barbarian leader turned this way and that, purposely avoiding the dark elf's gaze. Berkthgar was at a loss. Bruenor's daughter, though a famed adventurer, was not known for such antics. But Berkthgar was also more than a little intrigued. Every man in Settlestone considered Catti-brie, the princess of Mithral Hall, the fairest prize in all the region.

"Aegis-fang will be mine!" Berkthgar finally cried, and the roar behind him, and all around him, was deafening.

The barbarian leader was relieved to see that Drizzt was no longer facing him, was no longer anywhere in sight, when he turned back. One great leap had taken the dark elf from the table, and he strode eagerly for the door.

Outside Hengorot, in a quiet spot near an empty house, Drizzt took Catti-brie by the arm and turned her to face him. She expected him to shout at her, even expected him to slap her.

He laughed at her instead.

"Clever," Drizzt congratulated. "But can you take him?"

"How do ye know that I did not mean what I said?" Catti-brie snapped in reply.

"Because you have more respect for yourself than that," Drizzt answered without hesitation.

It was the perfect answer, the one Catti-brie needed to hear from her friend, and she did not press the point further.

"But can you take him?" the drow asked again, seriously. Catti-brie was good, and getting better with every lesson, but Berkthgar was huge and tremendously strong.

"He's drunk," Catti-brie replied. "And he's slow, like Wulfgar was before ye showed him the better way o' fighting." Her blue eyes, rich as the sky just before the dawn, sparkled. "Like ye showed me."

Drizzt patted her on the shoulder lightly, understanding then that this fight would be as important to her as it was to Berkthgar. The barbarian came storming out of the tent then, leaving a horde of sputtering comrades leering out of the open flap.

"Taking him won't be half the trouble as figuring out how to let him keep his honor," Catti-brie whispered.

Drizzt nodded and patted her shoulder again, then walked away, going in a wide circuit around Berkthgar and back toward the tent. Catti-brie had taken things into hand, he decided, and he owed her the respect to let her see this through.

The barbarians fell back as the drow came into the tent and pointedly closed the flap, taking one last look at Catti-brie as he did, to see her walking side by side with Berkthgar—and he so resembled huge Wulfgar from the back!—down the windswept lane.

For Drizzt Do'Urden, the image was not a pleasant one.

⚔ ⚔ ⚔ ⚔ ⚔

"Ye're not surprised?" Catti-brie asked as she removed the practice padding from her backpack and began sliding it over the fine edge of her sword. She felt a twinge of emotion as she did so, a sudden feeling of disappointment, even anger, which she did not understand.

"I did not believe for a moment that you had brought me out here for the reason you hinted at," Berkthgar replied casually. "Though if you had—"

"Shut yer mouth," Catti-brie sharply interrupted.

Berkthgar's jaw went firm. He was not accustomed to being talked to in that manner, particularly not from a woman. "We of Settlestone do not cover our blades when we fight," he said boastfully.

Catti-brie returned the barbarian leader's determined look, and as she did, she slid the sword back out from its protective sheath. A sudden rush of elation washed over her. As with the earlier feeling, she did not understand it, and so she thought that perhaps her anger toward Berkthgar was more profound than she had dared to admit to herself.

Berkthgar walked away then, to his house, and soon returned wearing a smug smile and a sheath strapped across his back. Above his right shoulder Catti-brie could see the hilt and crosspiece of his sword—a crosspiece nearly as long as her entire blade!—and the bottom portion of the sheath poked out below Berkthgar's left hip, extending almost to the ground.

Catti-brie watched, awestruck, wondering what she had gotten herself into, as Berkthgar solemnly drew the sword to the extent of his arm. The sheath had been cut along its upper side after a foot of leather so that the barbarian could then extract the gigantic blade.

And gigantic indeed was Berkthgar's flamberge! Its wavy blade extended over four feet, and after that came an eight-inch ricasso between the formal crosspiece and a second, smaller one of edged steel.

With one arm, muscles standing taut in ironlike cords, Berkthgar began spinning the blade, creating a great "whooshing" sound in the air above his head. Then he brought its tip to the ground before him and rested his arm on the crosspiece, which was about shoulder height to his six-and-a-half-foot frame.

"Ye meaning to fight with that, or kill fatted cows?" Catti-brie asked, trying hard to steal some of the man's mounting pride.

"I would still allow you to choose the other contest," Berkthgar replied calmly.

Catti-brie's sword snapped out in front of her, at the ready, and she went down in a low, defensive crouch.

The barbarian hooted and went into a similar pose, but then straightened, looking perplexed. "I cannot," Berkthgar began. "If I were to strike you even a glancing blow, King Battlehammer's heart would break as surely as would your skull."

Catti-brie came forward suddenly, jabbing at Berkthgar's shoulder and tearing a line in his furred jerkin.

He looked down at the cut, then his eyes came slowly back to regard Catti-brie, but other than that, he made no move.

"Ye're just afraid because ye're knowing that ye can't move that cow-killer fast enough," the young woman taunted.

Berkthgar blinked very slowly, exaggerated the movement as if to show how boring he thought this whole affair was. "I will show you the mantle where Bankenfuere is kept," he said. "And I will show you the bedding before the mantle."

"The thing's better for a mantle than a swordsman's hands!" Catti-brie growled, tired of this one's juvenile sexual references. She sprang ahead again and slapped the flat of her blade hard against Berkthgar's cheek, then jumped back, still snarling. "If ye're afraid, then admit it!"

Berkthgar's hand went immediately to his wound, and when it came away, the barbarian saw that his fingers were red with blood. Catti-brie winced at that, for she hadn't meant to hit him quite so hard.

Subtle were the intrusions of Khazid'hea.

"I am out of patience with you, foolish woman," snarled the barbarian, and up came the tip of tremendous Bankenfuere, the Northern Fury.

Berkthgar growled and leaped ahead, both hands on the hilt this time as he swung the huge blade across in front of him. He attacked with the flat of his blade, as had Catti-brie, but the young woman realized that would hardly matter. Getting hit by the flat of that tremendous flamberge would still reduce her bones to mush!

Catti-brie wasn't anywhere near Berkthgar at that point, the woman in fast retreat—and wondering again if she was in over her head—as soon as the sword went up. The flamberge curled in an arc back over, left to right, then came across a second time, this cut angling down. Faster than Catti-brie expected, Berkthgar reversed the flow, the blade swishing horizontally again, this time left to right, then settled back at the ready beside the barbarian's muscular shoulder.

An impressive display indeed, but Catti-brie had watched the routine carefully, no longer through awestruck eyes, and she noticed more than a few holes in the barbarian's defenses.

Of course, she had to be perfect in her timing. One slip, and Bankenfuere would turn her into worm food.

On came Berkthgar, with another horizontal cut, a predictable attack, for there were only so many ways one could maneuver such a weapon! Catti-brie fell back a step, then an extra step just to make sure, and darted in behind the lumbering sweep of the blade, looking to score a hit on the barbarian's arm. Berkthgar was quicker than that, though, and he had the blade coming around and over so fast that Catti-brie had to abort the attack and scramble hard just to get out of the way.

Still, she had won that pass, she figured, for now she had a better measure of Berkthgar's reach. And by her thinking, every passing moment favored her, for she saw the sweat beading on the drunken barbarian's forehead, his great chest heaving just a bit more than before.

"If ye do other things as poorly as ye fight, then suren I'm glad I chose this contest," Catti-brie said, a taunt that sent proud Berkthgar into another wild-swinging tirade.

Catti-brie dodged and scrambled as Bankenfuere came across in several titanic, and ultimately futile, swipes. Across it came again, the barbarian's fury far from played out, and Catti-brie leaped back. Around and over went the blade, Berkthgar charging ahead, and Catti-brie went far out to the side, just ahead as the great sword came whipping down and across.

"I shall catch up to you soon enough!" Berkthgar promised, turning square to the young woman and whipping his mighty blade left to right once more, bringing it to the ready beside his right shoulder.

Catti-brie started in behind the cut, taking a long stride with her right foot, extending her sword arm toward Berkthgar's exposed hip. She dug her left foot in solidly, though, and had no intention of continuing the move. As soon as Bankenfuere came across to intercept, Catti-brie leaped back, pivoted on her anchor leg, and rushed in behind the blade, going for Berkthgar's right hip instead, and scored a nasty, stinging hit.

The barbarian growled and spun so forcefully that he nearly overbalanced.

Catti-brie stood a few feet away, crouched low, ready. There was no doubt that swinging the heavy weapon was beginning to take a toll on the man, especially after his generous swallows of mead.

"A few more passes," Catti-brie whispered, forcing herself to be patient.

And so she played on as the minutes passed, as Berkthgar's breathing came as loudly as the moaning wind. Through each attack, Catti-brie confirmed her final routine, one that took advantage of the fact that Berkthgar's huge blade and thick arms made a perfect optical barricade.

⚔ ⚔ ⚔ ⚔ ⚔

Drizzt suffered through the half-hour of rude comments.

"Never has he lasted this long!" offered one barbarian.

"Berkthgar the Brauzen!" cried another, the barbarian word for stamina.

"Brauzen!" all the rowdy men shouted together, lifting their mugs in cheer. Some of the women in the back of Hengorot tittered at the bawdy display, but most wore sour expressions.

"Brauzen," the drow whispered, and Drizzt thought the word perfectly fitting for describing his own patience during those insufferably long minutes.

As angry as he was at the rude jokes at Catti-brie's expense, he was more fearful that Berkthgar would harm her, perhaps defeat her in battle and take her in other ways.

Drizzt worked hard to keep his imagination at bay. For all his boasting, for all of his people's boasting, Berkthgar was an honorable man. But he was drunk . . .

I will kill him, Drizzt decided, and if anything the drow feared had come to pass, he indeed would cut mighty Berkthgar down.

It never got to that point, though, for Berkthgar and Catti-brie walked back into the tent, looking a bit ruffled, the barbarian's stubbly beard darkened in one area with some dried blood, but otherwise seeming okay.

Catti-brie winked subtly as she passed the drow.

Hengorot fell into a hush, the drunken men no doubt expecting some lewd tales of their leader's exploits.

Berkthgar looked to Catti-brie, and she wouldn't blink.

"I will not carry Aegis-fang," the barbarian leader announced.

Moans and hoots erupted, as did speculation about who won the "contest."

Berkthgar blushed, and Drizzt feared there would be trouble.

Catti-brie went up on the table. "Not a better man in Settlestone!" she insisted.

Several barbarians rushed forward to the table's edge, willing to take up that challenge.

"Not a better man!" Catti-brie growled at them, her fury driving them back.

"I'll not carry the warhammer, in honor of Wulfgar," Berkthgar explained. "And for the honor of Catti-brie."

Blank stares came back at him.

"If I am to properly suit the daughter of King Bruenor, our friend and ally," the barbarian leader went on, and Drizzt smiled at that reference, "then it is my own weapon, Bankenfuere, that must become legend." He held high the huge flamberge, and the crowd roared with glee.

The issue was ended, the alliance sealed, and more mead was passed around before Catti-brie even got down from the table, heading for Drizzt. She stopped as she walked beside the barbarian leader, and gave him a sly look.

"If ye ever openly lie," she whispered, taking care that no one could hear, "or if ye ever even hint that ye bedded me, then be knowin' that I'll come back and cut ye down in front o' all yer people."

Berkthgar's expression grew somber at that, and even more somber as he turned to watch Catti-brie depart, to see her deadly drow friend standing easily, hands on scimitar hilts, his lavender eyes telling the barbarian in no uncertain terms his feelings for Catti-brie. Berkthgar didn't want to tangle with Catti-brie again, but he would rather battle her a hundred times than fight the drow ranger.

"You'll come back and cut him down?" Drizzt asked as they exited the town, revealing to Catti-brie that his keen ears had caught her parting words with the barbarian.

"Not a promise I'd ever want to try," Catti-brie replied, shaking her head. "Fighting that one when he's not so full o' mead would be about the same as walking into the cave of a restless bear."

Drizzt stopped abruptly, and Catti-brie, after taking a couple more steps, turned around to regard him.

He stood pointing at her, smiling widely. "I have done that!" he remarked, and so Drizzt had yet another tale to recount as the two—and three, for Drizzt was quick to recall Guenhwyvar—made their way along the trails, back into the mountains.

Later, as the stars twinkled brightly and the campfire burned low, Drizzt sat watching Catti-brie's prone form, her rhythmic breathing telling the drow that she was fast asleep.

"You know I love her," the drow said to Guenhwyvar.

The panther blinked her shining green eyes, but otherwise did not move.

"Yet, how could I?" Drizzt asked. "And not for the memory of Wulfgar," he quickly added, and he nodded as he heard himself speak the words, knowing that Wulfgar, who loved Drizzt as Drizzt loved him, would not disapprove.

"How could I ever?" the drow reiterated, his voice barely a whisper.

Guenhwyvar issued a long, low growl, but if it had any meaning, other than to convey that the panther was interested in what the drow was saying, it was lost on Drizzt.

"She will not live so long," Drizzt went on quietly. "I will still be a young drow when she is gone." Drizzt looked from Catti-brie to the panther, and a new insight occurred to him. "You must understand such things, my eternal friend," the drow said. "Where will I fall in the span of your life? How many others have you kept as you keep me, my Guenhwyvar, and how many more shall there be?"

Drizzt rested his back against the mountain wall and looked to Catti-brie, then up to the stars. Sad were his thoughts, and yet, in many ways, they were comforting, like an eternal play, like emotions shared, like memories of Wulfgar. Drizzt sent those thoughts skyward, into the heavenly canopy,

letting them break apart on the ceaseless and mournful wind.

His dreams were full of images of friends, of Zaknafein, his father, of Belwar, the svirfneblin gnome, of Captain Deudermont, of the good ship *Sea Sprite*, of Regis and Bruenor, of Wulfgar, and most of all, of Catti-brie.

It was as calm and pleasant a sleep as Drizzt Do'Urden had ever known.

Guenhwyvar watched the drow for some time, then rested her great feline head on wide paws and closed her green eyes. Drizzt's comments had hit the mark, except, of course, his intimation that her memory of him would be inconsequential in the centuries ahead. Guenhwyvar had indeed come to the call of many masters, most goodly, some wicked, in the past millennium, and even beyond that. Some the panther remembered, some not, but Drizzt . . .

Forever would Guenhwyvar remember the renegade dark elf, whose heart was so strong and so good and whose loyalty was no less than the panther's own.

PART TWO

Forever after, the bards of the Realms called it the Time of Troubles, the time when the gods were kicked out of the heavens, their avatars walking among the mortals. The time when the Tablets of Fate were stolen, invoking the wrath of Ao, Overlord of the Gods, when magic went awry, and when, as a consequence, social and religious hierarchies, so often based on magical strength, fell into chaos.

THE ONSET OF CHAOS

I have heard many tales from fanatical priests of their encounters with their particular avatars, frenzied stories from men and women who claim to have looked upon their deities. So many others came to convert to a religion during this troubled time, likewise claiming they had seen the light and the truth, however convoluted it might be.

I do not disagree with the claims, and would not openly attack the premise of their encounters. I am glad for those who have found enrichment amidst the chaos; I am glad whenever another person finds the contentment of spiritual guidance.

But what of faith?

What of fidelity and loyalty? Complete trust?

Faith is not granted by tangible proof. It comes from the heart and the soul. If a person needs proof of a god's existence, then the very notion of spirituality is diminished into sensuality and we have reduced what is holy into what is logical.

I have touched the unicorn, so rare and so precious, the symbol of the goddess Mielikki, who holds my heart and soul. This was before the onset of the Time of Troubles, yet were I of a like mind to those who make the claims of viewing avatars, I could say the same. I could say that I have touched Mielikki, that she came to me in a magical glade in the mountains near Dead Orc Pass.

The unicorn was not Mielikki, and yet it was, as is the sunrise and the seasons, as are the birds and the squirrels, and the strength of a tree that has lived through the dawn and death of centuries. As are the leaves, blowing on autumn winds and the snow piling deep in cold mountain vales. As are the smell of a crisp night, the twinkle of the starry canopy, and the howl of a distant wolf.

No, I'll not argue openly against one who has claimed to have seen an avatar, because that person will not understand that the mere presence of such a being undermines the very purpose of, and value of, faith. Because if the true gods were so tangible and so accessible, then we would no longer be independent creatures set on a journey to find the truth, but merely a herd of sheep needing the guidance of a shepherd and his dogs, unthinking and without the essence of faith.

The guidance is there, I know. Not in such a tangible form, but in what we know to be good and just. It is our own reactions to the acts of others that show us the value of our own actions, and if we have fallen so far as to need an avatar, an undeniable manifestation of a god, to show us our way, then we are pitiful creatures indeed.

The Time of Troubles? Yes. And even more so if we are to believe the suggestion of avatars, because truth is singular and cannot, by definition, support so many varied, even opposing manifestations.

The unicorn was not Mielikki, and yet it was, for I have touched Mielikki. Not as an avatar, or as a unicorn, but as a way of viewing my place in the world. Mielikki is my heart. I follow her precepts because, were I to write precepts based on my own conscience, they would be the same. I follow Mielikki because she represents what I call truth.

Such is the case for most of the followers of most of the various gods, and if we looked more closely at the pantheon of the Realms, we would realize that the precepts of the "goodly" gods are not so different. It is the worldly interpretations of those precepts that vary from faith to faith.

As for the other gods, the gods of strife and chaos, such as Lolth, the Spider Queen, who possesses the hearts of those priestesses who rule Menzoberranzan . . .

They are not worth mentioning. There is no truth, only worldly gain, and any religion based on such principles is, in fact, no more than a practice of self-indulgence and in no way a measure of spirituality. In worldly terms, the priestesses of the Spider Queen are quite formidable; in spiritual terms, they are empty. Thus, their lives are without love and without joy.

So tell me not of avatars. Show me not your proof that yours is the true god. I grant you your beliefs without question and without judgment, but if you grant me what is in my heart, then such tangible evidence is irrelevant.

—Drizzt Do'Urden

WHEN MAGIC
WENT AWRY

Berg'inyon Baenre, weapons master of the First House of Menzoberranzan, put his twin swords through a dizzying routine, blades spinning circuits in the air between him and his opponent, an insubordinate drow common soldier.

A crowd of the Baenre House guard, highly trained though mostly males, formed a semicircle around the pair, while other dark elves watched from high perches, tightly saddled astride sticky-footed, huge subterranean lizards, the beasts casually standing along the vertical slopes of nearby stalactites or towering stalagmite mounds.

Though few thought him as good a swordsman as his brother Dantrag had been, the soldiers cheered every time Berg'inyon scored a minor hit or parried a fast-flying counter.

Berg'inyon noticed a reluctance in ther praise, though, and knew the source. He had been the leader of the Baenre lizard riders, the most elite grouping of the male House guards, for many years. But with Dantrag slain, he had become the House weapons master as well. Berg'inyon felt the intense pressure of his dual stations, felt his mother's scrutinizing gaze on his every movement and every decision. He did not doubt that his own actions had intensified as a rcsult. How many fights had he begun, how many punishments had he exacted on his subordinates, since Dantrag's death?

The common drow came ahead with a weak thrust that almost slipped past distracted Berg'inyon's defenses. A sword came up and around at the last moment to drive the enemy's blade aside.

Berg'inyon heard the sudden hush behind him at the near miss, understood

that several of the soldiers back there—perhaps all of them—hoped his enemy's next thrust would be quicker, too quick.

The weapons master growled low and came ahead in a flurry, spurred on by the hatred of those around him, of those under his command. Let them hate him! he decided. But while they did, they must also respect him—no, not respect, Berg'inyon decided. They must fear him.

He came forward one step, then a second, his swords snapping alternately, left and right, and each being cleanly picked off. The give and take had become common, with Berg'inyon coming ahead two steps, then retreating. This time, though, the Baenre did not retreat. He shuffled forward two more steps, his swords snapping as his opponent's blades rushed for the parry.

Berg'inyon had the lesser drow up on his heels, so the young Baenre rushed ahead again. His opponent was quick enough with his swords to turn the expected thrusts, but he could not retreat properly, and Berg'inyon was up against him in a clinch, their blades joined to either side, down low, by the hilt.

There was no real danger here—it was more like a break in the battle—but Berg'inyon realized something his opponent apparently did not. With a growl, the young Baenre heaved his off-balance opponent away. The drow skidded back a couple of steps, brought his swords up immediately to fend off any pursuit.

None came; it seemed a simple break of the clinch.

Then the backpedaling drow bumped into the House Baenre fence.

In the city of Menzoberranzan, there was perhaps nothing as spectacular as the twenty-foot-high, web-designed fence ringing House Baenre, anchored on the various stalagmite mounds that ringed the compound. Its silvery metallic cords, thick as a dark elf's leg, were wound into beautiful, symmetrical designs, as intricate as the work of any spider. No weapon could cut through it, no magic, save a single item that Matron Baenre possessed, could get one over it, and the simplest touch or brush against one of those enchanted strands would hold fast a titan.

Berg'inyon's opponent hit the fence hard with the flat of his back. His eyes went wide as he suddenly realized the young Baenre's tactics, as he saw the faces of those gathered brighten in approval of the vicious trick, as he saw devious and wicked Berg'inyon calmly approach.

The drow fell away from the fence and rushed out to meet the weapons master's advance.

The two went through a fast series of attacks and parries, with stunned

Berg'inyon on the defensive. Only through his years of superior training was the drow noble able to bring himself back even against his surprising opponent.

Surprising indeed, as every drow face, and all the whispers, confirmed.

"You brushed the fence," Berg'inyon said.

The drow soldier did not disagree. The tips of his weapons drooped as Berg'inyon's drooped, and he glanced over his shoulder to confirm what he, and all the others, knew could not be.

"You hit the fence," Berg'inyon said again, skeptically, as the drow turned back to face him.

"Across the back," he agreed.

Berg'inyon's swords went into their respective scabbards and the young Baenre stormed past his opponent, to stand right before the enchanted web. His opponent and all the other dark elves followed closely, too intrigued to even think of continuing the fight.

Berg'inyon motioned to a nearby female. "Rest your sword against it," he bade her.

The female drew her blade and laid it across one of the thick strands. She looked to Berg'inyon and around to all the others, then easily lifted the blade from the fence.

Another drow farther down the line dared to place his hand on the web. Those around him looked at him incredulously, thinking him dangerously daring, but he had no trouble removing himself from the metal.

Panic rushed through Berg'inyon. The fence, it was said, had been a gift from Lolth herself in millennia past. If it was no longer functioning, it might well mean that House Baenre had fallen out of the Spider Queen's favor. It might well mean that Lolth had dropped House Baenre's defense to allow for a conspiracy of lower Houses.

"To your posts, all of you!" the young Baenre shouted, and the gathered dark elves, sharing Berg'inyon's reasoning and his fears, did not have to be told twice.

Berg'inyon headed for the compound's great central mound to find his mother. He crossed paths with the drow he had just been fighting, and the commoner's eyes widened in sudden fear. Normally Berg'inyon, honorable only by the low standards of dark elves, would have snapped his sword out and through the drow, ending the conflict. Caught up in the excitement of the fence's failure, the commoner was off his guard. He knew it, too, and he expected to be killed.

"To your post," Berg'inyon said to him, for if the young Baenre's suspicions

proved correct, that a conspiracy had been launched against House Baenre and Lolth had deserted them, he would need every one of the House's twenty-five hundred soldiers.

⚔ ⚔ ⚔ ⚔ ⚔

King Bruenor Battlehammer had spent the morning in the upper chapel of Mithral Hall, trying to sort out the new hierarchy of priests within the complex. His dear friend Cobble had been the reigning priest, a dwarf of powerful magic and deep wisdom.

That wisdom hadn't gotten poor Cobble out of the way of a nasty drow spell, though, and the cleric had been squashed by a falling wall of iron.

There were more than a dozen remaining acolytes in Mithral Hall. They formed two lines, one on each side of Bruenor's audience chair. Each priest was anxious to impress his—or, in the case of Stumpet Rakingclaw, her—king.

Bruenor nodded to the dwarf at the head of the line to his left. As he did, he lifted a mug of mead, the holy water this particular priest had concocted. Bruenor sipped, then drained the surprisingly refreshing mead in a single swallow as the cleric stepped forward.

"A burst of light in honor of King Bruenor!" the would-be head priest cried, and he waved his arms and began a chanting prayer to Moradin, the Soulforger, god of the dwarves.

"Clean and fresh, and just the slightest twinge of bitterness," Bruenor remarked, running a finger along the rim of the emptied mug and sucking on it, that he might savor the last drop. The scribe directly behind the throne noted every word. "A hearty bouquet, properly curling nose hairs," Bruenor added. "Seven."

The eleven other clerics groaned. Seven on a scale of ten was the highest grade Bruenor had given any of the five samples of holy water he had already taste-tested.

If Jerbollah, the dwarf now in a frenzy of spellcasting, could perform as well with magic, he would be difficult to beat for the coveted position.

"And the light shall be," Jerbollah cried, the climax of his spell, "red!"

There came a tremendous popping noise, as if a hundred dwarves had just yanked their fingers from puckered mouths. And . . . nothing.

"Red!" Jerbollah cried in delight.

"What?" demanded Bruenor, who, like those dwarves beside him, saw nothing different about the lighting in the chapel.

"Red!" Jerbollah said again, and when he turned around, Bruenor and the others understood. Jerbollah's face was glowing a bright red—literally, the confused cleric was seeing the world through a rose-colored veil.

Frustrated Bruenor dropped his head into his palm and groaned.

"Makes a good batch o' holy water, though," one of the dwarves nearby remarked, to a chorus of snickers.

Poor Jerbollah, who thought his spell had worked brilliantly, did not understand what was so funny.

Stumpet Rakingclaw leaped forward, seizing the moment. She handed her mug of holy water to Bruenor and rushed out before the throne.

"I had planned something different," she explained quickly, as Bruenor sipped, then swallowed the mead—and the dwarf king's face brightened once more as he declared this batch a nine. "But a cleric of Moradin, of Clanggedon, who knows battle best of all, must be ready to improvise!"

"Do tell us, O Strumpet!" one of the other dwarves roared, and even Bruenor cracked a smile as the laughter exploded around him.

Stumpet, who was used to the nickname and wore it like a badge of honor, took no offense. "Jerbollah called for red," she explained, "so red it shall be!"

"It already *is* red," insisted Jerbollah, who earned a slap on the head from the dwarf behind him for his foolishness.

The fiery young Stumpet ruffled her short red beard and went into a series of movements so exaggerated that it seemed as if she had fallen into convulsions.

"Move it, Strumpet," a dwarf near the throne whispered, to renewed laughter.

Bruenor held up the mug and tapped it with his finger. "Nine," he reminded the wise-cracking dwarf. Stumpet was in the clear lead. If she pulled off her spell where Jerbollah had failed, she would be almost impossible to beat, which would make her the wisecracking dwarf's superior.

The dwarf behind the humbled jokester slapped him on the back of the head.

"Red!" Stumpet cried with all her might.

Nothing happened.

A few snickers came from the line, but in truth, the gathered dwarves were more curious than amused. Stumpet was a powerful spellcaster and should have been able to throw some light, whatever color, into the room. The feeling began to wash over them all—except Jerbollah, who insisted that his spell had worked perfectly—that something might be wrong.

Stumpet turned back to the throne, confused and embarrassed. She started to say something, to apologize, when a tremendous explosion rocked the

ground so violently that she and half the other dwarves in the room were knocked from their feet.

Stumpet rolled and turned, looking back to the empty area of the chapel. A ball of blue sparks appeared from nowhere, hovered in the air, then shot straight for a very surprised Bruenor. The dwarf king ducked and thrust his arm up to block, and the mug that held Stumpet's batch of holy water shattered, sheared off at the handle. A blue storm of raging sparks burst from the impact, sending dwarves scurrying for cover.

More sparking bursts ignited across the room, glowing balls zipping this way and that, thunderlike booms shaking the floor and walls.

"What in the Nine Hells did ye do?" the dwarf king, a little curled-up ball on his great chair, screamed at poor Stumpet.

The female dwarf tried to respond, tried to disclaim responsibility for this unexpected turn, but a small tube appeared in midair, generally pointed her way, and fired multicolored balls that sent Stumpet scrambling away.

It went on for several long, frightening minutes, dwarves diving every which way, sparks seeming to follow them wherever they hid, burning their backsides and singeing their beards. Then it was over, as suddenly as it had begun, leaving the chapel perfectly quiet and smelling of sulphur.

Gradually Bruenor straightened in his chair and tried to regain some of his lost dignity.

"What in the Nine Hells did ye do?" he demanded again, to which poor Stumpet merely shrugged. A couple of dwarves managed a slight laugh at that.

"At least it's still red," Jerbollah remarked under his breath, but loud enough to be heard. Again he was slapped by the dwarf behind him.

Bruenor shook his head in disgust, then froze in place as two eyeballs appeared in the air before him, scrutinizing him ominously.

Then they dropped to the floor and rolled around haphazardly, coming to rest several feet apart.

Bruenor looked on in disbelief as a spectral hand came out of the air and herded the eyeballs close together and turned them so that they were both facing the dwarf king once more.

"Well, that's never happened before," said a disembodied voice.

Bruenor jumped in fright, then settled and groaned yet again. He hadn't heard that voice in a long time, but never would he forget it. And it explained so much about what was going on in the chapel.

"Harkle Harpell," Bruenor said, and whispers ignited all around him, for most of the other dwarves had heard Bruenor's tales of Longsaddle, a town to the west of Mithral Hall, home of the legendary, eccentric wizard clan, the Harpells. Bruenor and his companions had passed through Longsaddle, had toured the Ivy Mansion, on their way to find Mithral Hall. It was a place the dwarf, no fan of wizardly magic, would never forget, and never remember fondly.

"My greetings, King Bruenor," said the voice, emanating from the floor right below the steadied eyeballs.

"Are ye really here?" the dwarf king asked.

"Hmmm," groaned the floor. "I can hear both you and those who are around me at the Fuzzy Quarterstaff," Harkle replied, referring to the tavern at the Ivy Mansion, back in Longsaddle. "Just a moment, if you please."

The floor "Hmmmm'd" several more times, and the eyeballs blinked once or twice, perhaps the most curious sight Bruenor had ever seen, as an eyelid appeared from nowhere, covered the ball momentarily, then disappeared once more.

"It seems that I'm in both places," Harkle tried to explain. "I'm quite blind back here—of course, my eyes are there. I wonder if I might get them back . . ." The spectral hand appeared again, groping for the eyeballs. It tried to grasp one of them securely, but only wound up turning the ball around on the floor.

"Whoa!" shouted a distressed Harkle. "So that is how a lizard sees the world! I must note it . . ."

"Harkle!" Bruenor roared in frustration.

"Oh, yes, yes, of course," replied Harkle, coming to what little senses he possessed. "Please excuse my distraction, King Bruenor. This has never happened before."

"Well it's happened now," Bruenor said dryly.

"My eyes are there," Harkle said, as though trying to sort things out aloud. "But, of course, I will be there as well, quite soon. Actually, I had hoped to be there now, but didn't get through. Curious indeed. I could try again, or could ask one of my brothers to try—"

"No!" Bruenor bellowed, cringing at the thought that other Harpell body parts might soon rain down on him.

"Of course," Harkle agreed after a moment. "Too dangerous. Too curious. Very well, then. I come in answer to your call, friend dwarf king!"

Bruenor dropped his head into his palm and sighed. He had feared those very words for more than two tendays now. He had sent an emissary to Longsaddle for help in the potential war only because Drizzt had insisted.

To Bruenor, having the Harpells as allies might eliminate the need for enemies.

"A tenday," Harkle's disembodied voice said. "I will arrive in a tenday!" There came a long pause. "Err, umm, could you be so kind as to keep my eyeballs safe?"

Bruenor nodded to the side, and several dwarves scrambled ahead, curious and no longer afraid of the exotic items. They battled to scoop up the eyes and finally sorted them out, with two different dwarves each holding one—and each taking obvious pleasure in making faces at the eye.

Bruenor shouted for them to quit playing even before Harkle's voice screamed in horror.

"Please!" pleaded the somewhat absent mage. "Only one dwarf to hold both eyes." Immediately the two dwarves clutched their prizes more tightly.

"Give 'em to Stumpet!" Bruenor roared. "She started this whole thing!"

Reluctantly, but not daring to go against an order from their king, the dwarves handed the eyeballs over.

"And do please keep them moist," Harkle requested, to which, Stumpet immediately tossed one of the orbs into her mouth.

"Not like that!" screamed the voice. "Oh, not like that!"

"I should get them," protested Jerbollah. "My spell worked!" The dwarf behind Jerbollah slapped him on the head.

Bruenor slumped low in his chair, shaking his head. It was going to be a long time in putting his clerical order back together, and longer still would be the preparations for war when the Harpells arrived.

Across the room, Stumpet, who, despite her antics, was the most level-headed of dwarves, was not so lighthearted. Harkle's unexpected presence had deflected the other apparent problems, perhaps, but the weird arrival of the wizard from Longsaddle did not explain the happenings here. Stumpet, several of the other clerics, and even the scribe realized that something was very wrong.

✖ ✖ ✖ ✖ ✖

Guenhwyvar was tired by the time she, Drizzt, and Catti-brie came to the high pass leading to Mithral Hall's eastern door. Drizzt had kept the panther on the Material Plane longer than usual, and though it was taxing, Guenhwyvar was glad for the stay. With all the preparations going on in the deep tunnels below the dwarven complex, Drizzt did not get outside much, and consequently, neither did Guenhwyvar.

For a long, long time, the panther figurine had been in the hands of various drow in Menzoberranzan, and thus, the panther had gone centuries without seeing the out-of-doors on the Material Plane. Still, the out-of-doors was where Guenhwyvar was most at home, where natural panthers lived, and where the panther's first companions on the Material Plane had lived.

Guenhwyvar had indeed enjoyed this romp along mountain trails with Drizzt and Catti-brie, but now was the time to go home, to rest again on the Astral Plane. For all their love of companionship, neither the drow nor the panther could afford that luxury now, with so great a danger looming, an impending war in which Drizzt and Guenhwyvar would likely play a major role, fighting side by side.

The panther paced around the figurine, gradually diminished, and faded to an insubstantial gray mist.

⚔ ⚔ ⚔ ⚔ ⚔

Gone from the material world, Guenhwyvar entered a long, low, winding tunnel, the silvery path that would take her back to the Astral Plane. The panther loped easily, not eager to be gone and too tired to run full out. The journey was not so long anyway, and always uneventful.

Guenhwyvar skidded to a stop as she rounded one long bend, her ears falling flat.

The tunnel ahead was ablaze.

Diabolical forms, fiendish manifestations that seemed unconcerned with the approaching cat, leaped from those flames. Guenhwyvar padded ahead a few short strides. She could feel the intense heat, could see the fiery fiends, and could hear their laughter as they continued to consume the circular tunnel's walls.

A rush of air told Guenhwyvar that the tunnel had been ruptured, somewhere in the emptiness between the planes of existence. Fiery fiends were pulled into elongated shapes then sucked out. The remaining flames danced wildly, leaping and flickering, seeming to go out altogether, then rising together in a sudden and violent surge. The wind came strong at Guenhwyvar's back, compelling the panther to go forward, compelling everything in the tunnel to fly out through the breach, into nothingness.

Guenhwyvar knew instinctively that if she succumbed to that force, there would be no turning back, that she would become a lost thing, helpless, wandering between the planes.

The panther dug in her claws and backpedaled slowly, fighting the fierce wind every inch of the way. Her black coat ruffled up, sleek fur turning the wrong way.

One step back.

The tunnel was smooth and hard, and there was little for panther claws to dig against. Guenhwyvar's paws pedaled more frantically, but inevitably the cat began to slide forward toward the flames and the breach.

⚔ ⚔ ⚔ ⚔ ⚔

"What is it?" Catti-brie asked, seeing Drizzt's confusion as he picked up the figurine.

"Warm," Drizzt replied. "The figurine is warm."

Catti-brie's expression likewise crinkled with confusion. She had a feeling of sheer dread then, a feeling she could not understand. "Call Guen back," she prompted.

Drizzt, equally fearful, was already doing exactly that. He placed the figurine on the ground and called out to the panther.

⚔ ⚔ ⚔ ⚔ ⚔

Guenhwyvar heard the call, and wanted desperately to answer it, but now the cat was close to the breach. Wild flames danced high, singeing the panther's face. The wind was stronger than ever, and there was nothing, nothing at all, for Guenhwyvar to hold on to.

The panther knew fear, and the panther knew grief. Never again would she come to Drizzt's call; never again would she hunt beside the ranger in the forests near Mithral Hall or race down a mountain with Drizzt and Catti-brie.

Guenhwyvar had known grief before, when some of her previous masters had died. This time, though, there could be no replacement for Drizzt. And none for Catti-brie or Regis, or even Bruenor, that most frustrating of creatures, whose love and hate relationship with Guenhwyvar had provided the panther with many hours of teasing enjoyment.

Guenhwyvar remembered the time Drizzt had bade her lie atop sleeping Bruenor and nap. How the dwarf had roared!

Flames bit at Guenhwyvar's face. She could see through the breach now, see the emptiness that awaited her.

Somewhere far off, beyond the shield of the screeching wind, came Drizzt's call, a call the cat could not answer.

Baenre's Fault

Uthegental Armgo, the patron and weapons master of Barrison del'Armgo, Second House of Menzoberranzan, was not Jarlaxle's favorite drow. In fact, Jarlaxle wasn't certain that this one was truly a drow at all. Standing near six feet, with a muscled torso that weighed close to two hundred pounds, Uthegental was the largest dark elf in Menzoberranzan, one of the largest of the normally slender race ever seen in the Underdark. More than size distinguished the fierce weapons master, though. While Jarlaxle was considered eccentric, Uthegental was simply frightening. He cropped his white hair short and spiked it with the thick, gelatinous extract gained by boiling rothé udders. A mithral ring was stuck through Uthegental's angular nose, and a golden pin protruded through each cheek.

His weapon was a trident, black like the fine-fitting mail of jointed plates he wore, and a net—magical, so it was said—hung on his belt, within easy reach.

Jarlaxle was glad that at least Uthegental wasn't wearing his war paint this day, zigzagging streaks of some dye the mercenary did not know that showed yellow and red in both the normal and infrared spectrums. It was common knowledge in Menzoberranzan that Uthegental, in addition to being patron to Matron Mother Mez'Barris, was the consort of many Barrison del'Armgo females. The Second House considered him breeding stock, and the thought of dozens of little Uthegentals running around brought a sour expression to Jarlaxle's face.

"The magic is wild, yet I remain strong!" the exotic weapons master growled, his perpetually furrowed brow making him even more imposing. He held one iron-muscled arm to the side and tightened his biceps as he crooked his elbow, the rock-hard muscles of his arm standing high and proud.

Jarlaxle took a moment to remind himself where he was, in the midst of his own encampment, in his own room and seated behind his own desk, secretly surrounded by a dozen highly skilled and undeniably loyal soldiers of Bregan D'aerthe. Even without the concealed allies, Jarlaxle's desk was equipped with more than a few deadly traps for troublesome guests. and of course, Jarlaxle was no minor warrior himself. A small part of him—a *very* small part of him—wondered how he might measure up in battle against Uthegental.

Few warriors, drow or otherwise, could intimidate the mercenary leader, but he allowed himself a bit of humility in the face of this maniac.

"*Ultrin Sargtlin!*" Uthegental went on, the drow term for "Supreme Warrior," a claim that seemed secure within the city with Dantrag Baenre dead. Jarlaxle often imagined the battle that most of Menzoberranzan's dark elves thought would one day be waged by bitter rivals Uthegental and Dantrag.

Dantrag had been the quicker—quicker than anyone—but with his sheer strength and size, Uthegental had rated as Jarlaxle's favorite in such a contest. It was said that when he went into his battle rage, Uthegental possessed the strength of a giant, and this fearsome weapons master was so tough that when he battled lesser creatures, such as goblin slaves, he always allowed his opponent to swing first, and never tried to parry the attack, accepting the vicious hit, reveling in the pain, before tearing his enemy limb from limb and having the choicest body parts prepared for his supper.

Jarlaxle shuddered at the notion, then put the image from his mind, reminding himself that he and Uthegental had more important business.

"There is no weapons master, no drow at all, in Menzoberranzan to stand against me," Uthegental continued his boasting, for no reason that Jarlaxle could discern beyond the savage's overblown sense of pride.

He went on and on, as was his way, and while Jarlaxle wanted to ask him if there was a point to it all, he kept silent, confident that the emissary from the Second House would eventually get around to a serious discussion.

Uthegental stopped his mounting tirade suddenly, and his hand shot out, snatching from the top of the desk a gem that the mercenary used as a paper-weight. Uthegental muttered some word that Jarlaxle did not catch, but the mercenary's keen eye did note a slight flicker in the huge drow's brooch, the House emblem of Barrison del'Armgo. Uthegental then held the gem aloft and squeezed it with all his strength. The muscles in his sculpted arm strained and bulged, but the gem held firm.

"I should be able to crush this," Uthegental growled. "Such is the power, the magic, that I have been Lolth-blessed with!"

"The gem would not be worth as much when reduced to powder," Jarlaxle replied dryly. What was Uthegental's point? he wondered. Of course, something strange was going on with magic all over the city. Now Jarlaxle better understood Uthegental's earlier boasting. The exotic weapons master was indeed still strong, but not *as* strong, a fact that apparently worried Uthegental more than a little.

"Magic is failing," the weapons master said, "failing everywhere. The priestesses kneel in prayer, sacrifice drow after drow, and still nothing they do brings Lolth or her handmaidens to them. Magic is failing, and it is Matron Baenre's fault!"

Jarlaxle took note of the way Uthegental seemed to repeat things. Probably to remind himself of what he was talking about, the mercenary mused, and his sour expression aptly reflected his opinion of Uthegental's intellect. Of course, Uthegental would never catch the subtle indication.

"You cannot know that," the mercenary replied. Uthegental's accusation no doubt came from Matron Mez'Barris herself. Many things were coming clear to the mercenary now, mostly the fact that Mez'Barris had sent Uthegental to feel out Bregan D'aerthe, to see if the time was ripe for a coup against Baenre. Uthegental's words could certainly be considered damning, but not against Barrison del'Armgo, for their weapons master was always running off at the mouth, and never with anything complimentary to anyone but himself.

"It was Matron Baenre who allowed the rogue Do'Urden to escape," Uthegental bellowed. "It was she who presided over the failed high ritual! Failed, as magic is failing."

Say it again, Jarlaxle thought, but wisely kept that derisive reply silent. The mercenary's frustration at that moment wasn't simply with the ignorance revealed by Uthegental. It was with the fact that Uthegental's reasoning was common all over the city. To Jarlaxle's thinking, the dark elves of Menzoberranzan continually limited themselves by their blind insistence that everything was symptomatic of a deeper meaning, that the Spider Queen had some grand design behind their every movement. In the eyes of the priestesses, if Drizzt Do'Urden denied Lolth and ran away, it was only because Lolth wanted House Do'Urden to fall and wanted the challenge of recapturing him presented to the other ambitious Houses of the city.

It was a limiting philosophy, one that denied free will. Certainly Lolth might play a hand in the hunt for Drizzt. Certainly she might be angered by the disruption of the high ritual, if she even bothered to take note of the event! But the reasoning that what was happening now was completely tied to that one event—ultimately a minor one in the five-thousand year history of Menzoberranzan—was a view of foolish pride, wherein the dwellers of Menzoberranzan seemed to think that all the multiverse revolved around them.

"Why then is all magic failing every House?" Jarlaxle asked Uthegental. "Why not just House Baenre?"

Uthegental briskly shook his head, not even willing to consider the reasoning. "We have failed Lolth and are being punished," he declared. "If only *I* had met the rogue instead of pitiful Dantrag Baenre!"

Now that was a sight Jarlaxle would wish to see! Drizzt Do'Urden battling Uthegental. The mere thought of it sent a tingle down the mercenary's spine.

"You cannot deny that Dantrag was in Lolth's favor," Jarlaxle reasoned, "while Drizzt Do'Urden most certainly was not. How, then, did Drizzt win?"

Uthegental's brow furrowed so fiercely that his red-glowing eyes nearly disappeared entirely, and Jarlaxle quickly reassessed the prudence of pushing the brute along that line of reasoning. It was one thing to back Matron Baenre; it was another to shake the foundation for one religion-blinded slave's entire world.

"It will sort itself out properly," Jarlaxle assured. "In all of Arach-Tinilith, in all of the Academy, and in every chapel of every House, prayers are being offered to Lolth."

"Their prayers are not being answered," Uthegental promptly reminded. "Lolth is angry with us and will not speak with us until we have punished those who have wronged her."

Their prayers were not being answered, or their prayers were not even being heard, Jarlaxle thought. Unlike most of the other typically xenophobic drow in Menzoberranzan, the mercenary was in touch with the outside world. He knew from his contacts that Blingdenstone's svirfneblin priests were having equal difficulty in their communion, that the deep gnomes' magic had also gone awry. Something had happened to the pantheon itself, Jarlaxle believed, and to the very fabric of magic.

"It is not Lolth," he said boldly, to which Uthegental's eyes went wide. Understanding exactly what was at stake here, the entire hierarchy of the city and perhaps the lives of half of Menzoberranzan's drow, Jarlaxle pressed ahead. "Rather, it is not *solely* Lolth. When you go back into the city, consider Narbondel," he said, referring to the stone pillar clock of

Menzoberranzan. "Even now, in what should be the cool dark of night, it glows brighter and hotter than ever before, so hot that its glow can even be viewed without the heat-sensing vision, so hot that any drow near the pillar cannot even allow their vision to slip into the heat-sensing spectrum, lest they be blinded.

"Yet Narbondel is enchanted by a wizard, and not a priestess," Jarlaxle went on, hoping that dim Uthegental would follow the reasoning.

"You doubt that Lolth could affect the clock?" the weapons master growled.

"I doubt she would!" Jarlaxle countered vehemently. "The magic of Narbondel is separate from Lolth, has always been separate from Lolth. Before Gromph Baenre, some of the previous archmages of Menzoberranzan were not even followers of Lolth!" He almost added that Gromph wasn't so devout, either, but decided to keep that bit of information back. No sense in giving the desperate Second House additional reasons to think that House Baenre was even more out of the Spider Queen's favor.

"And consider the faerie fires highlighting every structure," Jarlaxle continued. He could tell by the angle of Uthegental's furrowed brow that the brute was suddenly more curious than outraged—not a common sight. "Blinking on and off, or winking out altogether. Wizard's faerie fire, not the magic of a priestess, and decorating every House, not just House Baenre. Events are beyond us, I say, and beyond the high ritual. Tell Matron Mez'Barris, with all my respect, that I do not believe Matron Baenre can be blamed for this, and I do not believe the solution will be found in a war against the First House. Not unless Lolth herself sends us a clear directive."

Uthegental's expression soon returned to its normal scowl. Of course this one was frustrated, Jarlaxle realized. The most intelligent drow of Menzoberranzan, the most intelligent svirfnebli of Blingdenstone, were frustrated, and nothing Jarlaxle might say would change Uthegental's mind, or the war-loving savage's desire to attack House Baenre. But Jarlaxle knew he didn't have to convince Uthegental. He just had to make Uthegental say the right things upon his return to House Barrison del'Armgo. The mere fact that Mez'Barris sent so prominent an emissary, her own patron and weapons master, told Jarlaxle she would not lead a conspiracy against Baenre without the aid of, or at least the approval of, Bregan D'aerthe.

"I go," Uthegental declared, the most welcome words Jarlaxle had heard since the brute had entered his encampment.

Jarlaxle removed his wide-brimmed hat and ran his hands over his bald

pate as he slipped back comfortably in his chair. He could not begin to guess the extent of the events. Perhaps within the apparent chaos of the fabric of reality, Lolth herself had been destroyed. Not such a bad thing, Jarlaxle supposed.

Still, he hoped things would sort themselves out soon, and properly, as he had indicated to Uthegental, for he knew this request—and it was a request—to go to war would come again, and again after that, and each time, it would be backed by increasing desperation. Sooner or later, House Baenre would be attacked.

Jarlaxle thought of the encounter he had witnessed between Matron Baenre and K'yorl Odran, matron mother of House Oblodra, the city's third, and perhaps most dangerous House, when Baenre had first begun to put together the alliance to send a conquering army to Mithral Hall. Baenre had dealt from a position of power then, fully in Lolth's favor. She had openly insulted K'yorl and the Third House and forced the unpredictable matron mother into her alliance with bare threats.

K'yorl would never forget that, Jarlaxle knew, and she could possibly be pushing Mez'Barris Armgo in the direction of a war against House Baenre.

Jarlaxle loved chaos, thrived amidst confusion, but this scenario was beginning to worry him more than a little.

⚔ ⚔ ⚔ ⚔

Contrary to the usually correct mercenary's belief, K'yorl Odran was not nudging Matron Mez'Barris into a war against House Baenre. Quite the opposite, K'yorl was working hard to prevent such a conflict, meeting secretly with the matron mothers of the six other ruling Houses ranked below House Baenre—except for Ghenni'tiroth Tlabbar, Matron of House Faen Tlabbar, the Fourth House, whom K'yorl could not stand and would not trust. It wasn't that K'yorl had forgiven Matron Baenre for the insult, and it wasn't that K'yorl was afraid of the strange events. Far from it.

If it hadn't been for their extensive scouting network beyond House Oblodra and the obvious signs such as Narbondel and the winking faerie fire, the members of the Third House wouldn't even have known that anything was amiss. For the powers of House Oblodra came not from wizardly magic, nor from the clerical prayers to the Spider Queen. The Oblodrans were psionicists. Their powers were formed by internal forces of the mind, and thus far, the Time of Troubles had not affected them.

K'yorl couldn't let the rest of the city know that. She had the score of priestesses under her command hard at work, forcing the psionic equivalent of faerie fire highlighting her house to blink, as were the other houses. And to Mez'Barris and the other matron mothers, she seemed as agitated and nervous as they.

She had to keep a lid on things; she had to keep the conspiracy talk quieted. For when K'yorl could be certain that the loss of magic was not a devious trick, her family would strike—alone. She might pay House Faen Tlabbar back first, for all the years she had spent watching their every ambitious move, or she might strike directly against wretched Baenre.

Either way, the wicked matron mother meant to strike alone.

⚔ ⚔ ⚔ ⚔ ⚔

Matron Baenre sat stiffly in a chair on the raised and torch-lit central dais in the great chapel of her house. Her daughter Sos'Umptu, who served as caretaker to this most holy of drow places, sat to her left, and Triel, the eldest Baenre daughter and matron mistress of the drow Academy, was on her right. All three stared upward, to the illusionary image Gromph had put there, and it seemed strangely fitting that the image did not continue its shape-shifting, from drow to arachnid and back again, but rather, had been caught somewhere in the middle of the transformation and suspended there, like the powers that had elevated House Baenre to its preeminent position.

Not far away, goblin and minotaur slaves continued their work in repairing the dome, but Matron Baenre had lost all hope that putting her chapel back together would right the strange and terrible events in Menzoberranzan. She had come to believe Jarlaxle's reasoning that something larger than a failed high ritual and the escape of a single rogue was involved here. She had come to believe that what was happening in Menzoberranzan might be symptomatic of the whole world, of the whole multiverse, and that it was quite beyond her understanding or her control.

That didn't make things easier for Matron Baenre. If the other Houses didn't share those beliefs, they would try to use her as a sacrifice to put things aright. She glanced briefly at both her daughters. Sos'Umptu was among the least ambitious drow females she had ever known, and Baenre didn't fear much from that one. Triel, on the other hand, might be more dangerous. Though she always seemed content with her life as matron mistress of the Academy, a position of no minor importance, it was widely accepted that Triel, the eldest daughter, would one day rule the First House.

Triel was a patient one, like her mother, but like her mother, she was also

calculating. If she became convinced that it was necessary to remove her mother from the throne of House Baenre, that such an act would restore the Baenre name and reputation, then she would do so mercilessly.

That is why Matron Baenre had recalled her from the Academy to a meeting and had located that meeting within the chapel. This was Sos'Umptu's place, Lolth's place, and Triel would not dare strike out at her mother here.

"I plan to issue a call from the Academy that no House shall use this troubled time to war against another," Triel offered, breaking the virtual silence—for none of the Baenres had taken note of the hammering and groaning from the slaves working on the curving roof a mere hundred feet away. None of them took note even when a minotaur casually tossed a goblin to its death, for no better reason than enjoyment.

Matron Baenre took a deep breath and considered the words, and the meaning behind the words. Of course Triel would issue such a plea. The Academy was perhaps the most stabilizing force in Menzoberranzan. But why had Triel chosen this moment to tell her mother? Why not just wait until the plea was presented openly and to all?

Was Triel trying to reassure her? Matron Baenre wondered. Or was she merely trying to put her off her guard?

The thoughts circled in Matron Baenre's mind, ran around and collided with one another, leaving her in a trembling, paranoid fit. Rationally, she understood the self-destructive nature of trying to read things into every word, of trying to outguess those who might be less than enemies, who might even be allies. But Matron Baenre was growing desperate. A few tendays before, she had been at the pinnacle of her power, had brought the city together beneath her in readiness for a massive strike at the dwarven complex of Mithral Hall, near the surface.

How fast it had been taken away, as fast as the fall of a stalactite from the ceiling of the cavern above her treasured chapel.

She wasn't done yet, though. Matron Baenre had not lived through more than two thousand years to give up now. Damn Triel, if she was indeed plotting to take the throne. Damn them all!

The matron mother clapped her hands together sharply, and both her daughters started with surprise as a bipedal, man-sized monstrosity popped into view, standing right before them, draped in tremendous flowing crimson robes. The creature's purplish head resembled that of an octopus, except that only four skinny tentacles waved from the perimeter of its round, many-toothed orifice, and its eyes were pupilless and milky white.

The illithid, or mind flayer, was not unknown to the Baenre daughters. Far from it, El-Viddenvelp, or Methil, as he was commonly called, was Matron Baenre's advisor and had been at her side for many years. Recovered from their startlement, both Sos'Umptu and Triel turned curious stares to their surprising mother.

My greetings to you Triel, the illithid imparted telepathically. and *of course, to you, Sos'Umptu, in this, your place.*

Both daughters nodded and conjured similar mental replies, knowing that Methil would catch the thoughts as clearly as if they had spoken them aloud.

"Fools!" Matron Baenre shouted at both of them. She leaped from her chair and spun around, her withered features fierce. "How are we to survive this time if two of my principle commanders and closest advisors are such fools?"

Sos'Umptu was beside herself with shame, wrought of confusion. She even went so far as to cover her face with the wide sleeve of her thick purple-and-black robe.

Triel, more worldly-wise than her younger sister, initially felt the same shock, but quickly came to understand her mother's point. "The illithid has not lost its powers," she stated, and Sos'Umptu peeked curiously from above her arm.

"Not at all," Matron Baenre agreed, and her tone was not happy.

"But then we have an advantage," Sos'Umptu dared to speak. "For Methil is loyal enough," she said bluntly. There was no use in masking her true feelings behind words of half-truth, for the illithid would read her mind anyway. "And he is the only one of his kind in Menzoberranzan."

"But not the only one who uses such powers!" Matron Baenre roared at her, causing her to shrink back in her chair once more.

"K'yorl," Triel gasped. "If Methil has use of his powers . . ."

"Then so do the Oblodrans," Baenre finished grimly.

They exercise their powers continually, Methil telepathically confirmed to all three. *The highlights of House Oblodra would not be winking were it not for the mental commands of K'yorl's coven.*

"Can we be certain of this?" Triel asked, for there seemed no definite patterns in the failing of magic, just a chaotic mess. Perhaps Methil had not yet been affected, or did not even know that he had been affected. And perhaps Oblodra's faerie fire highlights, though different in creation than the fires glowing around the other houses, were caught in the same chaos.

Psionic powers can be sensed by psionic creatures, Methil assured her. *The Third House teems with energy.*

"And K'yorl gives the appearance that this is not so," Matron Baenre added in a nasty tone.

"She wishes to attack by surprise," Triel reasoned.

Matron Baenre nodded grimly.

"What of Methil?" Sos'Umptu offered hopefully. "His powers are great."

"Methil is more than a match for K'yorl," Matron Baenre assured her daughter, though Methil was silently doing the same thing, imparting a sense of undeniable confidence. "But K'yorl is not alone among the Oblodrans with her psionic powers."

"How many?" Triel wanted to know, to which Matron Baenre merely shrugged.

Many, Methil's thoughts answered.

Triel was thinking it, so she knew that Methil was hearing it, and so she said it aloud, suspiciously. "And if the Oblodrans do come against us, which side will Methil take?"

Matron Baenre was, for an instant, shocked by her daughter's boldness, but she understood that Triel had little choice in divulging her suspicions.

"And will he bring in his allies from the illithid cavern not far away?" Triel pressed. "Surely if a hundred illithids came to our side in this, our time of need . . ."

There was nothing from Methil, not a hint of telepathic communication, and that was answer enough for the Baenres.

"Our problems are not the problems of the mind flayers," Matron Baenre said. It was true enough, and she knew so. She had tried to enlist the illithids in the raid on Mithral Hall, promising them riches and a secure alliance, but the motivations of the otherworldly, octopus-headed creatures were not the same as those of the dark elves, or of any race in all the Underdark. Those motivations remained beyond Matron Baenre's understanding, despite her years of dealing with Methil. The most she could get from the illithids for her important raid was Methil and two others agreeing to go along in exchange for a hundred kobolds and a score of drow males, to be used as slaves by the illithid community in their small cavern city.

There was little else to say. The House guards were positioned at full readiness. Every spare drow was in prayer for help from the Spider Queen. House Baenre was doing everything it could to avert disaster, and yet, Matron Baenre did not believe they would succeed. K'yorl had come to her unannounced on several occasions, had gotten past her magical fence and past the many magical wards set around the complex. The matron mother of House Oblodra had done so only to taunt Baenre, and in truth, had little power remaining to

do anything more than that by the time her image was revealed to Baenre. But what might K'yorl accomplish with those magical guards down? Baenre had to wonder. How could Matron Baenre resist the psionicist without countering magic of her own?

Her only defense seemed to be Methil, a creature she neither trusted nor understood.

She did not like the odds.

8
Magical
Manifestations

Guenhwyvar knew pain, knew agony beyond anything the panther had ever felt. But more than that, the panther knew despair, true despair. Guenhwyvar was a creature formed of magic, the manifestation of the life-force of the animal known on Toril as the panther. The very spark of existence within the great panther depended on magic, as did the conduit that allowed Drizzt and the others before him to bring Guenhwyvar to the Prime Material Plane.

Magic having unraveled; the fabric that wove the universal Weave into a mystical and predictable pattern was torn.

The panther knew despair.

Guenhwyvar heard Drizzt's continued calling, begging. The drow knew the cat was in trouble, and his voice reflected that desperation. In his heart, so connected with his panther companion, Drizzt Do'Urden understood that Guenhwyvar would soon be lost to him forever.

The chilling thought gave the panther a moment of renewed hope and determination. Guenhwyvar focused on Drizzt, conjured an image of the pain she would feel if she could never again return to her beloved master. Growling low in sheer defiance, the panther scraped her back legs so force-fully that more than one claw hooked on the smooth, hard surface and was subsequently yanked out.

The pain did not stop the panther, not when Guenhwyvar measured it against the reality of slipping forward into those flames, of falling out of the tunnel, the only connection to the material world and Drizzt Do'Urden.

The struggle went on for more time than any creature should have resisted. But though Guenhwyvar had not slid any closer to the breach, neither had the panther earned back any ground toward her pleading master.

Finally, exhausted, Guenhwyvar gave a forlorn, helpless look over her shoulder. Her muscles trembled, then gave way.

The panther was swept to the fiery breach.

✕ ✕ ✕ ✕ ✕

Matron Baenre paced the small room nervously, expecting a guard to run in at any moment with news that the compound had been overrun, that the entire city had risen against her House, blaming her for the troubles that had befallen them.

Not so long ago, Baenre had dreamt of conquest, had aspired to the pinnacle of power. Mithral Hall had been within her grasp, and even more than that, the city seemed ready to fall into step behind her lead.

Now she believed she could not hold on to even her own House, to the Baenre empire that had stood for five thousand years.

"Mithral Hall," the wicked drow growled in a damning curse, as though that distant place had been the cause of it all. Her slight chest heaving with forced gasps of air, Baenre reached with both hands to her neck and tore free the chain that lay there.

"Mithral Hall!" she shouted into the ring-shaped pendant, fashioned from the tooth of Gandalug Battlehammer, the patron of Bruenor's clan, the real link to that surface world. Every drow, even those closest to Matron Baenre, thought Drizzt Do'Urden was the catalyst for the invasion, the excuse that allowed Lolth to give her blessing to the dangerous attempt at a conquest so near the surface.

Drizzt was but a part of the puzzle, and a small part, for this little ring was the true impetus. Sealed within it was the tormented spirit of Gandalug, who knew the ways of Mithral Hall and the ways of Clan Battlehammer. Matron Baenre had taken the dwarf king herself centuries before, and it was only blind fate that had brought a renegade from Menzoberranzan in contact with Bruenor's clan, blind fate that had provided an excuse for the conquest Matron Baenre had desired for many, many decades.

With a shout of outrage, Baenre hurled the tooth across the room, then fell back in shock as the item exploded.

Baenre stared blankly into the room's corner as the smoke cleared away, at the naked dwarf kneeling there. The matron mother pulled herself to her feet, shaking her head in disbelief, for this was no summoned spirit, but Gandalug's physical body!

"You dare to come forth?" Baenre screamed, but her anger masked her fear. When she had previously called Gandalug's physical form forth from the extradimensional prison, he was never truly whole, never corporeal—and never naked. Looking at him now, Baenre knew Gandalug's prison was gone, that Gandalug was returned exactly as he had been the moment Baenre had captured him, except for his clothes.

The battered old dwarf looked up at his captor, his tormentor. Baenre had spoken in the drow tongue, and of course, Gandalug hadn't understood a word. That hardly mattered, though, for the old dwarf wasn't listening. He was, in fact, beyond words.

Struggling, growling, with every pained movement, Gandalug forced his back to straighten, then put one, then the other, leg under him and rose determinedly. He understood that something was different. After centuries of torment and mostly emptiness, a fugue state in a gray void, Gandalug Battlehammer felt somehow different, felt whole and real. Since his capture, the old dwarf had lived a surreal existence, had lived a dream, surrounded by vivid, frightening images whenever this old wretch had called him forth, encompassed by interminable periods of nothingness, where place and time and thought were one long emptiness.

But now . . . now Gandalug felt different, felt even the creaks and pains of his old bones. And how wonderful those sensations were!

"Go back!" Baenre ordered, this time in the tongue of the surface, the language she always used to communicate with the old dwarf. "Back to your prison until I call you forth!"

Gandalug looked around, to the chain lying on the floor, the tooth ring nowhere in sight.

"I'm not fer tinkin' so," the old dwarf remarked in his heavy, ancient dialect, and he advanced a step.

Baenre's eyes narrowed dangerously. "You dare?" she whispered, drawing forth a slender wand. She knew how dangerous this one could be, and thus she wasted no time in pointing the item and reciting an arcane phrase, meaning to call forth a stream of webbing that would engulf the dwarf and hold him fast.

Nothing happened.

Gandalug took another step, growling like a hungry animal with every inch.

Baenre's steely-eyed gaze fell away, revealing her sudden fear. She was a creature weaned on magic, who relied on magic to protect her and to vanquish her enemies. With the items she possessed—which she carried with her at all times—and her mighty spell repertoire, she could fend off nearly any enemy, could likely crush a battalion of toughened dwarven fighters. But without those items, and with no spells coming to her call, Matron Baenre was a pitiful, bluffing thing, withered and frail.

It wouldn't have mattered to Gandalug had a titan been standing before him. For some reason he could not understand, he was free of the prison, free and in his own body, a sensation he had not felt in two thousand years.

Baenre had other tricks to try, and in truth, some of them, like the pouch that carried a horde of spiders that would rush to her call, had not yet fallen into the chaotic and magical web that was the Time of Troubles. She couldn't chance it, though. Not now, not when she was so very vulnerable.

She turned and ran for the door.

The corded muscles of Gandalug's mighty legs tightened, and the dwarf sprang, clearing the fifteen feet to get to the door before his tormentor.

A fist slammed Baenre's chest, stealing her breath, and before she could respond, she was up in the air, twirling around over the enraged dwarf's head.

Then she was flying, to crash and crumple against the wall across the room.

"I'm to be rippin' yer head off," Gandalug promised as he steadily advanced.

The door burst open, and Berg'inyon rushed into the room. Gandalug spun to face him as Berg'inyon drew his twin blades. Startled by the sight—how had a dwarf come into Menzoberranzan, into his own mother's private chambers?—Berg'inyon got the blades up just as Gandalug grabbed them, one in each hand.

Had the enchantment still been upon the weapons master's fine blades, they would have cut cleanly through the tough dwarven flesh. Even without the enchantment, the magic lost in the swirl of chaos, the swords dug deeply.

Gandalug hardly cared. He heaved Berg'inyon's arms out wide, the slender drow no match for his sheer strength. The dwarf whipped his head forward, crashing it into Berg'inyon's supple armor, slender rings that also relied on enchantment for their strength.

Gandalug repeated the movement over and over, and Berg'inyon's grunts fast became breathless gasps. Soon the young Baenre was out on his feet, hardly conscious as Gandalug yanked the swords from his hands. The dwarf's head came in one more time, and Berg'inyon, no longer connected to, and thus supported by, the dwarf, fell away.

Still ignoring the deep cuts on his hands, Gandalug threw one of

Berg'inyon's swords to the side of the room, took the other properly in hand, and turned on Matron Baenre, who was still sitting against the wall, trying to clear her thoughts.

"Where's yer smile?" the dwarf taunted, stalking in. "I'm wantin' a smile on yer stinkin' face when I hold yer head up in me hand fer all t'see!"

The next step was the dwarf king's last, as an octopus-headed monstrosity materialized before him, its grotesque tentacles waving his way.

A stunning blast of mental energy rolled Gandalug over, and he nearly dropped the sword. He shook his head fiercely to keep his wits about him.

He continued to growl, to shake his hairy head, as a second blast, then a third, assaulted his sensibilities. Had he held that wall of rage, Gandalug might have withstood even these, and even the two subsequent attacks from Methil. But that rage melted into confusion, which was not a powerful enough feeling to defeat the mighty illithid's intrusions.

Gandalug didn't hear the drow-made sword fall to the stone, didn't hear Matron Baenre call out for Methil and for the recovering Berg'inyon, as she instructed the pair not to kill the dwarf.

Baenre was scared, scared by these shifts in magic that she could not understand. But that fear did not prevent her from remembering her wicked self. For some unexplained reason, Gandalug had become alive again, in his own body and free of the apparently disintegrated ring.

That mystery would not prevent Baenre from paying this one back for the attack and the insult. Baenre was a master at torturing a spirit, but even her prowess in that fine art paled beside her abilities to torture a living creature.

⚔ ⚔ ⚔ ⚔ ⚔

"Guenhwyvar!" The figurine was wickedly hot now, but Drizzt held on stubbornly, pressed it close to his chest, his heart, though wisps of smoke were running up from the edge of his cloak and the flesh of his hands was beginning to blister.

He knew, and he would not let go. He knew that Guenhwyvar would be gone from him forever, and like a friend hugging close a dying comrade, Drizzt would not let go, would be there to the end.

His desperate calls began to lessen, not from resignation, but simply because his voice could not get past the lump of grief in his throat. Now his fingers, too, were burning, but he would not let go.

Catti-brie did it for him. On a sudden, desperate impulse, the young woman, herself torn with the pain of grief, grabbed roughly at Drizzt's arm and slapped hard the figurine, knocking it to the ground.

Drizzt's startled expression turned to one of outrage and denial, like the final burst of rage from a mother as she watched her child's casket lowered into the grave. For the moment the figurine hit the ground, Catti-brie drew Khazid'hea from its sheath and leaped to the spot. Up went the sword, over her head, its fine edge still showing the red line of its enchantment.

"No!" Drizzt cried, lunging for her.

He was too late. Tears rimming her blue eyes, her thoughts jumbled, Catti-brie found the courage for a last, desperate try, and she brought the mighty blade to bear. Khazid'hea could cut through stone, and so it did now, at the very instant that Guenhwyvar went through the breach.

There came a flash, and a throbbing pain, a pulsating magic, shot up Catti-brie's arm, hurling her backward and to the ground. Drizzt skidded, pivoted, and ducked low, shielding his head as the figurine's head fell free, loosing a line of raging fire far out into the air.

The flames blew out a moment later and a thick gray smoke poured from the body of the broken figurine. Gradually Drizzt straightened from his defensive crouch and Catti-brie came back to her senses, both to find a haggard-looking Guenhwyvar, the panther's thick coat still smoking, standing before them.

Drizzt dived to his knees and fell over the panther, wrapping Guenhwyvar in a great hug. They both crawled their way to Catti-brie, who was still sitting on the ground, laughing and sobbing though she was weak from the impact of the magic.

"What have you done?" Drizzt asked her.

She had no immediate answers. She did not know how to explain what had happened when Khazid'hea struck the enchanted figurine. She looked to the blade now, lying quiet at her side, its edge no longer glowing and a burr showing along its previously unblemished length.

"I think I've ruined me sword," Catti-brie replied softly.

⚔ ⚔ ⚔ ⚔ ⚔

Later that same day, Drizzt lounged on the bed in his room in the upper levels of Mithral Hall, looking worriedly at his panther companion. Guenhwyvar was back, and that was a better thing, he supposed, than what his instincts had told him would have happened had Catti-brie not cut the figurine.

A better thing, but not a good thing. The panther was weary, resting by the hearth across the small room, head down and eyes closed. That nap would not suffice, Drizzt knew. Guenhwyvar was a creature of the Astral Plane and could truly rejuvenate only among the stars. On several occasions necessity had prompted Drizzt to keep Guenhwyvar on the Material Plane for extended periods, but even a single day beyond the half the cat usually stayed left Guen exhausted.

Even now the artisans of Mithral Hall, dwarves of no small skill, were inspecting the cut figurine, and Bruenor had sent an emissary out to Silverymoon, seeking help from Lady Alustriel, as skilled as any this side of the great desert Anauroch in the ways of magic.

How long would it take? Drizzt wondered, unsure if any of them could repair the figurine. How long could Guenhwyvar survive?

Unannounced, Catti-brie burst through the door. One look at her tear-streaked face told Drizzt that something was amiss. He rolled from the bed to his feet and stepped toward the mantle, where his twin scimitars hung.

Catti-brie intercepted him before he had completed the step and wrapped him in a powerful hug that knocked them both to the bed.

"All I ever wanted," she said urgently, squeezing tight.

Drizzt likewise held on, confused and overwhelmed. He managed to turn his head so he could look into the young woman's eyes, trying to read some clues.

"I was made for ye, Drizzt Do'Urden," Catti-brie said between sobs. "Ye're all that's been in me thoughts since the day we met."

It was too crazy. Drizzt tried to extract himself, but he didn't want to hurt Catti-brie and her hold was simply too strong and desperate.

"Look at me," she sobbed. "Tell me ye feel the same!"

Drizzt did look at Catti-brie, as deeply as he had ever studied the beautiful young woman. He did care for her—of course he did. He did love her, and had even allowed himself a fantasy or two about this very situation.

But now it seemed simply too weird, too unexpected and with no introduction. He got the distinct feeling that something was out of sorts with the woman, something crazy, like the magic all around them.

"What of Wulfgar?" Drizzt managed to say, though the name got muffled as Catti-brie pressed tightly, her hair thick against Drizzt's face. The poor drow could not deny the woman's allure, the sweet scent of Catti-brie's hair, the warmth of her toned body.

Catti-brie's head snapped as if he had hit her. "Who?"

It was Drizzt's turn to feel as if he had been slapped.

"Take me," Catti-brie implored.

Drizzt's eyes couldn't have gone any wider without falling out of their sockets.

"Wield me!" she cried.

"Wield me?" Drizzt echoed under his breath.

"Make me the instrument of your dance," she went on. "Oh, I beg! It is all I was made for, all I desire." She stopped suddenly and pushed back to arm's length, staring wide-eyed at Drizzt as though some new angle had just popped into her head. "I am better than the others," she promised slyly.

What others? Drizzt wanted to scream, but by this point, the drow couldn't get any words out of his slack-jawed mouth.

"As are yerself," Catti-brie went on. "Better than that woman, I'm now knowing!"

Drizzt had almost found his center again, had almost regained control enough to reply, when the weight of that last statement buried him. Damn the subtlety! the drow determined, and he twisted and pulled free, rolling from the bed and springing to his feet.

Catti-brie dived right behind, wrapped herself around one of his legs, and held on with all her strength.

"Oh, do not deny me, me love!" she screamed, so urgently that Guenhwyvar lifted her head from the hearth and gave a low growl. "Wield me, I'm begging! Only in yer hands might I be whole!"

Drizzt reached down with both hands, meaning to extract his leg from the tight grip. He noticed something then, on Catti-brie's hip, that gave him pause, that stunned him and explained everything all at once.

He noticed the sword Catti-brie had picked up in the Underdark, the sword that had a pommel shaped into the head of a unicorn. Only it was no longer a unicorn.

It was Catti-brie's face.

In one swift movement, Drizzt drew the sword out of its sheath and tugged free, hopping back two steps. Khazid'hea's red line, that enchanted edge, had returned in full and beamed now more brightly than ever before. Drizzt slid back another step, expecting to be tackled again.

There was no pursuit. The young woman remained in place, half sitting, half kneeling on the floor. She threw her head back as if in ecstacy. "Oh, yes!" she cried.

Drizzt stared down at the pommel, watched in blank amazement as it shifted from the image of Catti-brie's face back into a unicorn. He felt an overwhelming warmth from the weapon, a connection as intimate as that of a lover.

Panting for breath, the drow looked back to Catti-brie, who was sitting straighter now, looking around curiously.

"What're ye doing with me sword?" she asked quietly. Again she looked around the room, Drizzt's room, seeming totally confused. She would have asked, "And what am I doing here?" Drizzt realized, except that the question was already obvious from the expression on her beautiful face.

"We have to talk," Drizzt said to her.

9

IMPLICATIONS

It was rare that both Gromph and Triel Baenre would be in audience with their mother at the same time, rarer still that they would be joined by Berg'inyon, Sos'Umptu, and the two other notable Baenre daughters, Bladen'Kerst and Quenthel. Six of the seven sat in comfortable chairs around the dais in the chapel. Not Bladen'Kerst, though. Ever seeming the caged animal, the most sadistic drow in the First House paced in circles, her brow furrowed and thin lips pursed. She was the second oldest daughter behind Triel and should have been out of the house by this time, perhaps as a matron in the Academy, or even more likely, as a matron mother of her own, lesser, House. Matron Baenre had not allowed that, however, fearing that her daughter's simple lack of civility, even by drow standards, would disgrace House Baenre.

Triel looked up and shook her head disdainfully at Bladen'Kerst every time she passed. She rarely gave Bladen'Kerst any thought. Like Vendes Baenre, her younger sister who had been killed by Drizzt Do'Urden during the escape, Bladen'Kerst was an instrument of her mother's torture and nothing more. She was a buffoon, a showpiece, and no real threat to anyone in House Baenre above the rank of common soldier.

Quenthel was quite a different matter, and in the long interludes between Bladen'Kerst's passing, Triel's stern and scrutinizing gaze never left that one.

And Quenthel returned the look with open hostility. She had risen to the rank of high priestess in record time and was reputed to be in Lolth's highest favor. Quenthel held no illusions about her tentative position. Had it not been for that fact of favor, Triel would have obliterated her long ago. For

Quenthel had made no secret of her ambitions, which included the stepping stone as matron mistress of Arach-Tinilith, a position Triel had no intention of abandoning.

"Sit down!" Matron Baenre snapped finally at the annoying Bladen'Kerst. One of Baenre's eyes was swollen shut and the side of her face still showed the welt where she had collided with the wall. She was not used to carrying such scars, nor were others used to seeing her that way. Normally a spell of healing would have cleaned up her face, but these were not normal times.

Bladen'Kerst stopped and stared hard at her mother, focusing on those wounds. They carried a double-edged signal. First, they showed that Baenre's powers were not as they should be, that the matron mother, that all of them, might be very vulnerable. Second, coupled with the scowl that perpetually clouded the worried matron mother's features, those wounds reflected anger.

Anger overweighed the perceived, and likely temporary, vulnerability, Bladen'Kerst wisely decided, and sat down in her appointed chair. Her hard boot, unusual for drow, but effective for kicking males, tapped hard and urgently on the floor.

No one paid her any attention, though. All of them followed Matron Baenre's predictable, dangerous gaze to Quenthel.

"Now is not the time for personal ambitions," Matron Baenre said calmly, seriously.

Quenthel's eyes widened as though she had been caught completely off guard.

"I warn you," Matron Baenre pressed, not the least deterred by the innocent expression.

"As do I!" Triel quickly and determinedly interjected. She wouldn't usually interrupt her mother, knew better than that, but she figured that this matter had to be put down once and for all, and that Baenre would appreciate the assistance. "You have relied on Lolth's favor to protect you these years. But Lolth is away from us now, for some reason that we do not understand. You are vulnerable, my sister, more vulnerable than any of us."

Quenthel came forward in her seat, even managed a smile. "Would you chance that Lolth will return to us, as we both know she shall?" the younger Baenre hissed. "And what might it be that drove the Spider Queen from us?" As she asked the last question, her gaze fell over her mother, as daring as anyone had ever been in the face of Matron Baenre.

"Not what you assume!" Triel snapped. She had expected Quenthel to try to lay blame on Matron Baenre's lap. The removal of the matron mother could only benefit ambitious Quenthel and might indeed restore some prestige to the fast-falling House. In truth, even Triel had considered that course, but she had subsequently dismissed it, no longer believing that Matron Baenre's recent failures had anything to do with the strangeness going on around them. "Lolth has fled every House."

"This goes beyond Lolth," Gromph, the wizard whose magic came from no god or goddess, added pointedly.

"Enough," said Baenre, looking around alternately, her stare calming her children. "We cannot know what has brought about the events. What we must consider is how those events will affect our position."

"The city desires a *pera'dene*," Quenthel reasoned, the drow word for scapegoat. Her unblinking stare at Baenre told the matron mother who she had in mind.

"Fool!" Baenre snapped into the face of that glare. "Do you think they would stop with *my* heart?"

That blunt statement caught Quenthel off guard.

"For some of the lesser Houses, there never has been and never will be a better opportunity to unseat this House," Matron Baenre went on, speaking to all of them. "If you think to unseat me, then do so, but know that it will do little to change the rebellion that is rising against us." She huffed and threw her arms up helplessly. "Indeed, you would only be aiding our enemies. I am your tie to Bregan D'aerthe, and know that our enemies have also courted Jarlaxle. And *I* am Baenre! Not Triel, and not Quenthel. Without me, you all would fall to chaos, fighting for control, each with your own factions within the House guard. Where will you be when K'yorl Oblodra enters the compound?"

It was a sobering thought. Matron Baenre had passed word to each of them that the Oblodrans had not lost their powers, and all the Baenres knew the hatred the Third House held for them.

"Now is not the time for personal ambitions," Matron Baenre reiterated. "Now is the time for us to hold together and hold our position."

The nods around her were sincere, Baenre knew, though Quenthel was not nodding. "You should hope that Lolth does not come back to me before she returns to you," the ambitious sister said boldly, aiming the remark squarely at Triel.

Triel seemed unimpressed. "You should hope that Lolth comes back at all," she replied casually, "else I will tear off your head and have Gromph place it atop Narbondel, that your eyes may glow when the day is full."

Quenthel went to reply, but Gromph beat her to it.

"A pleasure, my dear sister," he said to Triel. There was no love lost between the two, but while Gromph was ambivalent toward Triel, he perfectly hated Quenthel and her dangerous ambitions. If House Baenre fell, so, too, would Gromph.

The implied alliance between the two elder Baenre children worked wonders in calming the upstart younger sister, and Quenthel said not another word the rest of the meeting.

"May we speak now of K'yorl, and the danger to us all?" Matron Baenre asked.

When no dissenting voices came forth—and if there had been, Baenre likely would have run out of patience and had the speaker put to a slow death—the matron mother took up the issue of House defense. She explained that Jarlaxle and his band could still be trusted, but warned that the mercenary would be one to change sides if the battle was going badly for House Baenre. Triel assured them all that the Academy remained loyal, and Berg'inyon's report of the readiness of the House guard was beaming.

Despite the promising news and the well-earned reputation of the Baenre garrison, the conversation ultimately came down to the only apparent way to fully fend off K'yorl and her psionic family. Berg'inyon, who had taken part in the fight with the dwarf Gandalug, voiced it first.

"What of Methil?" he asked. "And the hundred illithids he represents? If they stand with us, the threat from House Oblodra seems minor."

The others nodded their agreement with the assessment, but Matron Baenre knew that such friends as mind flayers could not be counted on. "Methil remains at our side because he and his people know we are the keystone of security for his people. The illithids do not number one one-hundredth the drow in Menzoberranzan. That is the extent of their loyalty. If Methil comes to believe that House Oblodra is the stronger, he will not stand beside us." Baenre gave an ironic, seemingly helpless chuckle.

"The other illithids might even side with K'yorl," she reasoned. "The wretch is akin to them with her powers of the mind. Perhaps they understand one another."

"Should we speak so bluntly?" Sos'Umptu asked. She looked about the dais, concerned, and the others understood that she feared Methil might even be among them, invisibly, hearing every word, reading their every thought.

"It does not matter," Matron Baenre replied casually. "Methil already knows my fears. One cannot hide from an illithid."

"Then what are we to do?" Triel asked.

"We are to muster our strength," Baenre replied determinedly. "We are to show no fear and no weakness. And we are not to do anything that might push

Lolth further from us." She aimed that last remark at the rivals, Quenthel and Triel, particularly at Triel, who seemed more than ready to use this Lolth-absent time to be rid of her troublesome sister.

"We must show the illithids we remain the power in Menzoberranzan," Baenre went on. "If they know this, then they will side with us, not wanting House Baenre to be weakened by K'yorl's advances."

"I go to Sorcere," said Gromph, the archmage.

"And I to Arach-Tinilith," added a determined Triel.

"I make no illusions about friendship among my rivals," Gromph added. "But a few promises of repayment when issues sort themselves out will go far in finding allies."

"The students have been allowed no contact outside the school," Triel put in. "They know of the problems in general, of course, but they know nothing of the threat to House Baenre. In their ignorance, they remain loyal."

Matron Baenre nodded to both of them. "And you will meet with the lower Houses that we have established," she said to Quenthel, a most important assignment. A large portion of House Baenre's power lay in the dozen minor Houses that former Baenre nobles had come to head. So obviously a favorite of Lolth's, Quenthel was the perfect choice for such an assignment.

Her expression revealed that she had been won over—more by Triel and Gromph's threats, no doubt, than by the tidbit that had just been thrown her way.

The most important ingredient in squashing the rivalries, Baenre knew, was to allow both Triel and Quenthel to save face and feel important. Thus, this meeting had been a success and all the power of House Baenre would be coordinated into a single defensive force.

Baenre's smile remained a meager one, though. She knew what Methil could do, and suspected that K'yorl was not so much weaker. All of House Baenre would be ready, but without the Lolth-given clerical magic and Gromph's wizardly prowess, would that be enough?

⚔ ⚔ ⚔ ⚔ ⚔

Just off Bruenor's audience hall on the top level of Mithral Hall was a small room that the dwarf king had set aside for the artisans working on repairing the panther figurine. Inside was a small forge and delicate tools, along with dozens of beakers and flasks containing various ingredients and salves.

Drizzt was eager indeed when he was summoned to that room. He'd gone there a dozen times a day, of course, but without invitation, and every time to

find dwarves huddled over the still-broken artifact and shaking their bearded heads. A tenday had passed since the incident, and Guenhwyvar was so exhausted that she could no longer stand, could barely lift her head from her paws as she lay in front of the hearth in Drizzt's room.

The waiting was the worst part.

Now, though, Drizzt had been called into the room. He knew that an emissary had arrived that morning from Silverymoon. He could only hope that Alustriel had some positive solutions to offer.

Bruenor was watching his approach through the open door of the audience chamber. The red-bearded dwarf nodded and poked his head to the side, and Drizzt cut the sharp corner, pushing open the door without bothering to knock.

It was among the most curious of sights that Drizzt Do'Urden had ever witnessed. The broken—still broken!—figurine was on a small, round table. Regis stood beside it, working furiously with a mortar and pestle, mushing some blackish substance.

Across the table from Drizzt stood a short, stout dwarf, Buster Bracer, the noted armorer, the one, in fact, who had forged Drizzt's own supple chain mail, back in Icewind Dale. Drizzt didn't dare greet the dwarf now, fearing to upset his obvious concentration. Buster stood with his feet wide apart. Every so often, he took an exaggerated breath, then held perfectly steady, for in his hands, wrapped in wetted cloth of the finest material, he held . . . eyeballs.

Drizzt had no idea of what was going on until a voice, a familiar, bubbly voice, startled him from his shock.

"Greetings, O One of the Midnight Skin!" the disembodied wizard said happily.

"Harkle Harpell?" Drizzt asked.

"Could it be anyone else?" Regis remarked dryly.

Drizzt conceded the point. "What is this about?" he asked, pointedly looking toward the halfling, for he knew that any answer from Harkle would likely shed more dimness on the blurry situation.

Regis lifted the mixing bowl a bit. "A poultice from Silverymoon," he explained hopefully. "Harkle has overseen its mixing."

"Overseen," the absent mage joked, "which means they held my eyes over the bowl!"

Drizzt didn't manage a smile, not with the head of the all-important figurine still lying at the sculpted body's feet.

Regis snickered, more in disdain than humor. "It should be ready," he explained. "But I wanted you to apply it."

"Drow fingers are so dexterous!" Harkle piped in.

"Where are you?" Drizzt demanded, impatient and unnerved by the outrageous arrangement.

Harkle blinked, those eyelids appearing from thin air. "In Nesmé," he mage replied. "We will be passing north of the Trollmoors soon."

"And to Mithral Hall, where you will be reunited with your eyes," Drizzt said.

"I am *looking* forward to it!" Harkle roared, but again he laughed alone.

"He keeps that up and I'm throwin' the damned eyes into me forge," Buster Bracer growled.

Regis placed the bowl on the table and retrieved a tiny metal tool. "You'll not need much of the poultice," the halfling said as he handed the delicate instrument to Drizzt. "And Harkle has warned us to try to keep the mixture on the outside of the joined pieces."

"It is only a glue," the mage's voice added. "The magic of the figurine will be the force that truly makes the item whole. The poultice will have to be scraped away in a few day's time. If it works as planned, the figurine will be . . ." He paused, searching for the word. "Will be healed," he finished.

"If it works," Drizzt echoed. He took a moment to feel the delicate instrument in his hands, making sure that the burns he had received when the figurine's magic had gone awry were healed, making sure that he could feel the item perfectly.

"It will work," Regis assured.

Drizzt took a deep, steadying breath and picked up the panther head. He stared into the sculpted eyes, so much like Guenhwyvar's own knowing orbs. With all the care of a parent tending its child, Drizzt placed the head against the body and began the painstaking task of spreading the gluelike poultice around its perimeter.

More than two hours passed before Drizzt and Regis exited the room, moving into the audience hall where Bruenor was still meeting with Lady Alustriel's emissary and several other dwarves.

Bruenor did not appear happy, but Drizzt noted he seemed more at ease than he had since the onset of this strange time.

"It ain't a trick o' the drow," the dwarf king said as soon as Drizzt and Regis approached. "Or the damned drow are more powerful than anyone ever thought! It's all the world, so says Alustriel."

"Lady Alustriel," corrected the emissary, a very tidy-looking dwarf dressed in flowing white robes and with a short and neatly trimmed beard.

"My greetings, Fredegar," Drizzt said, recognizing Fredegar Rockcrusher, better known as Fret, Lady Alustriel's favored bard and advisor. "So at last you have found the opportunity to see the wonders of Mithral Hall."

"Would that the times were better," Fret answered glumly. "Pray tell me, how fares Catti-brie?"

"She is well," Drizzt answered. He smiled as he thought of the young woman, who had returned to Settlestone to convey some information from Bruenor.

"It ain't a trick o' the drow," Bruenor said again, more emphatically, making it clear that he didn't consider this the proper time and place for such light and meaningless conversation.

Drizzt nodded his agreement—he had been assuring Bruenor that his people were not involved all along. "Whatever has happened, it has rendered Regis's ruby useless," the drow said. He reached over and lifted the pendant from the halfling's chest. "Now it is but a plain, though undeniably beautiful, stone. And the unknown force has affected Guenhwyvar, and reached all the way to the Harpells. No magic of the drow is this powerful, else they would have long ago conquered the surface world."

"Something new?" Bruenor asked.

"The effects have been felt for several tendays now," Fret interjected. "Though only in the last couple of tendays has magic become so totally unpredictable and dangerous."

Bruenor, never one to care much for magic, snorted loudly.

"It's a good thing, then!" he decided. "The damned drow're more needin' magic than are me own folk, or the men o' Settlestone! Let all the magic drain away, I'm sayin', and let the drow come on and play!"

Thibbledorf Pwent nearly jumped out of his boots at that thought. He leaped over to stand before Bruenor and Fret, and slapped one of his dirty, smelly hands across the tidy dwarf's back. Few things could calm an excited battlerager, but Fret's horrified, then outraged, look did just that, surprising Pwent completely.

"What?" the battlerager demanded.

"If you ever touch me again, I will crush your skull," Fret, who wasn't half the size of powerful Pwent, promised in an even tone, and for some inexplicable reason, Pwent believed him and backed off a step.

Drizzt, who knew tidy Fret quite well from his many visits to Silverymoon, understood that Fret couldn't stand ten seconds in a fight against Pwent—unless the confrontation centered around dirt. In that instance, with Pwent messing up Fret's meticulous grooming, Drizzt would put all of his coin on Fret, as sure a bet as the drow would ever know.

It wasn't an issue, though, for Pwent, boisterous as he was, would never do anything against Bruenor, and Bruenor obviously wanted no trouble with an emissary, particularly a dwarven emissary from friendly Silverymoon. Indeed, all in the room had a good laugh at the confrontation, and all seemed more relaxed at the realization that these strange events were not connected to the mysterious dark elves.

All except for Drizzt Do'Urden. Drizzt would not relax until the figurine was repaired, its magic restored, and poor Guenhwyvar could return to her home on the Astral Plane.

10

THE THIRD HOUSE

It wasn't that Jarlaxle, who always thought ahead of others, hadn't been expecting the visit, it was simply the ease with which K'yorl Odran entered his camp, slipped past his guards and walked right through the wall of his private chambers, that so unnerved him. He saw her ghostly outline enter and fought hard to compose himself as she became more substantial and more threatening.

"I had expected you would come many days ago," Jarlaxle said calmly.

"Is this the proper greeting for a matron mother?" K'yorl asked.

Jarlaxle almost laughed, until he considered the female's stance. Too at ease, he decided, too ready to punish, even to kill. K'yorl did not understand the value of Bregan D'aerthe, apparently, and that left Jarlaxle, the master of bluff and the player of intrigue, at somewhat of a disadvantage.

He came up from his comfortable chair, stepped out from behind his desk, and gave a low bow, pulling his wide-brimmed and outrageously plumed hat from his head and sweeping it across the floor. "My greetings, K'yorl Odran, Matron Mother of House Oblodra, Third House of Menzoberranzan. Not often has my humble home been so graced . . ."

"Enough," K'yorl spat, and Jarlaxle came up and replaced the hat. Never taking his gaze from the female, never blinking, the mercenary went back to his chair and flopped down comfortably, putting both his boots atop his desk with a resounding slam.

It was then Jarlaxle felt the intrusion into his mind, a deeply unsettling probe into his thoughts. He quickly dismissed his many curses at the failure of conventional magic—usually his enchanted eye patch would have protected him from such a mental intrusion—and used his wits instead. He focused his gaze on K'yorl, pictured her with her clothes off, and filled his mind with thoughts so base that the matron mother, in the midst of serious business, lost all patience.

"I could have the skin flailed from your bones for such thoughts," K'yorl informed him.

"Such thoughts?" Jarlaxle said as though he had been wounded. "Surely you are not intruding on my mind, Matron K'yorl! Though I am but a male, such practices are surely frowned on. Lolth would not be pleased."

"Damn Lolth," K'yorl growled, and Jarlaxle was stunned that she had put it so clearly, so bluntly. Of course everyone knew that House Oblodra was not the most religious of drow Houses, but the Oblodrans had always kept at least the pretense of piety.

K'yorl tapped her temple, her features stern. "If Lolth was worthy of my praise, then she would have recognized the truth of power," the matron mother explained. "It is the mind that separates us from our lessers, the mind that should determine order."

Jarlaxle offered no response. He had no desire to get into this argument with so dangerous and unpredictable a foe.

K'yorl did not press the point, but simply waved her hand as if throwing it all away. She was frustrated, Jarlaxle could see, and in this one frustration equated with danger.

"It is beyond the Spider Queen now," K'yorl said. "I am beyond Lolth. And it begins this day."

Jarlaxle allowed a look of surprise to cross his features.

"You expected it," K'yorl said accusingly.

That was true enough—Jarlaxle had wondered why the Oblodrans had waited this long with all the other Houses so vulnerable—but he would not concede the point.

"Where in this does Bregan D'aerthe stand?" K'yorl demanded.

Jarlaxle got the feeling that any answer he gave would be moot, since K'yorl was probably going to tell *him* exactly where Bregan D'aerthe stood. "With the victors," he said cryptically and casually.

K'yorl smiled in salute to his cleverness. "I will be the victor," she assured him. "It will be over quickly, this very day, and with few drow dead."

Jarlaxle doubted that. House Oblodra had never shown any regard for life, be it drow or otherwise. The drow numbers within the Third House were small mainly because the wild clan members killed as often as they bred. They were renowned for a game that they played, a challenge of the highest stakes called *Khaless*—ironically, the drow word for trust. A globe of darkness and magical silence would be hung in the air above the deepest point in the chasm called the Clawrift. The competing dark elves would then levitate into the globe and there, unable to see or hear, it would become a challenge of simple and pure courage.

The first one to come out of the globe and back to secure footing was the loser, so the trick was to remain in the globe until the very last second of the levitation enchantment.

More often than not, both stubborn competitors would wait too long and would plunge to their demise.

Now K'yorl, merciless and ultimately wicked, was trying to assure Jarlaxle that the drow losses would be kept at a minimum. By whose standard? the mercenary wondered, and if the answer was K'yorl's, then likely half the city would be dead before the end of the day.

There was little Jarlaxle could do about that, he realized. He and Bregan D'aerthe were as dependent on magic as any other dark elf camps, and without it he couldn't even keep K'yorl out of his private chamber—even his private thoughts!

"This day," K'yorl said again, grimly. "And when it is done, I will call for you, and you will come."

Jarlaxle didn't nod, didn't answer at all. He didn't have to. He could feel the mental intrusion again, and knew that K'yorl understood him. He hated her, and hated what she was about to do, but Jarlaxle was ever pragmatic, and if things went as K'yorl predicted, then he would indeed go to her call.

She smiled again and faded away. Then, like a ghost, she simply walked through Jarlaxle's stone wall.

Jarlaxle rested back in his chair, his fingers tapping nervously together. He had never felt so vulnerable, or so caught in the middle of an uncontrollable situation. He could get word to Matron Baenre, of course, but to what gain? Even House Baenre, so vast and proud, could not stand against K'yorl when her magic worked and theirs did not. Likely, Matron Baenre would be dead soon, and all her family with her, and where would the mercenary hide?

He would not hide, of course. He would go to K'yorl's call.

Jarlaxle understood why K'yorl had paid him the visit and why it was important to her, who seemed to have everything in her favor, to enlist him in her court. He and his band were the only drow in Menzoberranzan with any true ties outside the city, a crucial factor for anyone aspiring to the position of first matron mother—not that anyone other than Matron Baenre had aspired to that coveted position in close to a thousand years.

Jarlaxle's fingers continued tapping. Perhaps it was time for a change, he thought. He quickly dismissed that hopeful notion, for even if he was right, this change did not seem for the better. Apparently, though, K'yorl believed that the situation with conventional magic was a temporary thing, else she would not have been so interested in enlisting Bregan D'aerthe.

Jarlaxle had to believe, had to pray, that she was right, especially if her coup succeeded—and the mercenary had no reason to believe it would not. He would not survive long, he realized, if First Matron Mother K'yorl, a drow he hated above all others, could enter his thoughts at will.

⚔ ⚔ ⚔ ⚔ ⚔

She was too beautiful to be drow, seemed the perfection of drow features to any, male or female, who looked at her. It was this beauty alone that held in check the deadly lances and crossbows of the House Baenre guard and made Berg'inyon Baenre, after one glance at her, bid her enter the compound.

The magical fence wasn't working and there were no conventional gates in the perimeter of the Baenre household. Normally, the spiderweb of the fence would spiral out, opening a wide hole on command, but now Berg'inyon had to ask the drow to climb over.

She said not a word, but simply approached the fence. Spiral wide it did, one last gasp of magic before this creature, the avatar of the goddess who had created it.

Berg'inyon led the way, though he knew beyond doubt that this one needed no guidance. He understood that she was heading for the chapel—of course she would be heading for the chapel!—so he instructed some of his soldiers to find the matron mother.

Sos'Umptu met them at the door of the chapel, the place that was in her care. She protested for an instant, but just for an instant.

Berg'inyon had never seen his devoted sister so flustered, had never seen her jaw go slack for lack of strength. She fell away from them, to her knees.

The beautiful drow walked past her without a word. She turned sharply—Sos'Umptu gasped—and put her glare over Berg'inyon as he continued to follow.

"You are just a male," Sos'Umptu whispered in explanation. "Be gone from this holy place."

Berg'inyon was too stricken to reply, to even sort out how he felt at that moment. He never turned his back, just gave a series of ridiculous bows, and verily fell through the chapel's door, back out into the courtyard.

Both Bladen'Kerst and Quenthel were out there, but the rest of the group that had gathered in response to the whispered rumors had wisely been dispersed by the sisters.

"Go back to your post," Bladen'Kerst snarled at Berg'inyon. "Nothing has happened!" It wasn't so much a statement as a command.

"Nothing has happened," Berg'inyon echoed, and that became the order of the day, and a wise one, Berg'inyon immediately realized. This was Lolth herself, or some close minion. He knew this in his heart.

He knew it, and the soldiers would whisper it, but their enemies must not learn of this!

Berg'inyon scrambled across the courtyard, passed the word, the command that "nothing had happened." He took up a post that allowed him an overview of the chapel and was surprised to see that his ambitious sisters dared not enter, but rather paced around the main entrance nervously.

Sos'Umptu came out as well and joined their parade. No words were openly exchanged—Berg'inyon didn't even notice any flashes of the silent hand code—as Matron Baenre hustled across the courtyard. She passed by her daughters and scurried into the chapel, and the pacing outside began anew.

For Matron Baenre it was the answer to her prayers and the realization of her nightmares all at once. She knew immediately who and what it was that sat before her on the central dais. She knew, and she believed.

"If I am the offending person, then I offer myself . . ." she began humbly, falling to her knees as she spoke.

"*Wael!*" the avatar snapped at her, the drow word for fool, and Baenre hid her face in her hands with shame.

"*Usstan'sargh wael!*" the beautiful drow went on, calling Matron Baenre an arrogant fool. Baenre trembled at the verbal attack, thought for a moment that she had sunk lower than her worst fears, that her goddess had come personally for no better reason than to shame her to death. Images of her tortured body being dragged through the winding avenues of Menzoberranzan flashed in her mind, thoughts of herself as the epitome of a fallen drow leader.

Yet thoughts such as that were exactly what this creature who was more than a drow had just berated her about, Matron Baenre suddenly realized. She dared look up.

"Do not place so much importance on yourself," the avatar said calmly.

Matron Baenre allowed herself to breathe a sigh of relief. Then this wasn't about her, she understood. All of this, the failure of magic and prayer, was beyond her, beyond all the mortal realms.

"K'yorl has erred," the avatar went on, reminding Baenre that while these catastrophic events might be above her, their ramifications most certainly were not.

"She has dared to believe that she can win without your favor," Matron Baenre reasoned, and her surprise was total when the avatar scoffed at the notion.

"She could destroy you with a thought."

Matron Baenre shuddered and lowered her head once more.

"But she has erred on the side of caution," the avatar went on. "She delayed her attack, and now, when she decided that the advantage was indeed hers to hold, she has allowed a personal feud to delay her most important strike even longer."

"Then the powers have returned!" Baenre gasped. "You are returned."

"*Wael!*" the frustrated avatar screamed. "Did you think I would not return?" Matron Baenre fell flat to the floor and groveled with all her heart.

"The Time of Troubles will end," the avatar said a moment later, calm once more. "And you will know what you must do when all is as it should be."

Baenre looked up just long enough to see the avatar's narrow-eyed glare full upon her. "Do you think I am so resourceless?" the beautiful drow asked.

A horrified expression, purely sincere, crossed Baenre's face, and she began to numbly shake her head back and forth, denying she had ever lost faith.

Again, she lay flat out, groveling, and stopped her prayers only when something hard hit the floor beside her head. She dared to look up, to find a lump of yellow stone, sulphur, lying beside her.

"You must fend off K'yorl for a short while," the avatar explained. "Go join the matron mothers and your eldest daughter and son in the meeting room. Stoke the flames and allow those I have enlisted to come through to your side. Together we will teach K'yorl the truth of power!"

A bright smile erupted on Baenre's face with the realization that she was not out of Lolth's favor, that her goddess had called on her to play a crucial role in this crucial hour. The fact that Lolth had all but admitted she was still rather impotent did not matter. The Spider Queen would return, and Baenre would shine again in her devious eyes.

By the time Matron Baenre mustered the courage to come off the floor, the beautiful drow had already exited the chapel. She crossed the compound without interference, walked through the fence as she had done at her arrival, and disappeared into the shadows of the city.

⚔ ⚔ ⚔ ⚔ ⚔

As soon as she heard the awful rumor that House Oblodra's strange psionic powers had not been too adversely affected by whatever was happening to other magic, Ghenni'tiroth Tlabbar, the matron mother of Faen Tlabbar, Menzoberranzan's Fourth House, knew she was in dire trouble. K'yorl Odran hated the tall, slender Ghenni'tiroth above all others, for Ghenni'tiroth had made no secret of the fact that she believed Faen Tlabbar, and not Oblodra, should rank as Menzoberranzan's Third House.

With almost eight hundred drow soldiers, Faen Tlabbar's number nearly doubled that of House Oblodra, and only the little understood powers of K'yorl and her minions had kept Faen Tlabbar back.

How much greater those powers loomed now, with all conventional magic rendered unpredictable at best!

Throughout it all, Ghenni'tiroth remained in the House chapel, a relatively small room near the summit of her compound's central stalagmite mound. A single candle burned upon the altar, shedding minimal light by surface standards, but serving as a beacon to the dark elves whose eyes were more accustomed to blackness. A second source of illumination came from the room's west-facing window, for even from halfway across the city, the wild glow of Narbondel could be clearly seen.

Ghenni'tiroth showed little concern for the pillar clock, other than the significance it now held as an indicator of their troubles. She was among the most fanatical of Lolth's priestesses, a drow female who had survived more than six centuries in unquestioning servitude to the Spider Queen. But she was in trouble now, and Lolth, for some reason she could not understand, would not come to her call.

She reminded herself constantly to keep fast her faith as she knelt and huddled over a platinum platter, the famed Faen Tlabbar Communing Plate. The heart of the latest sacrifice, a not-so-insignificant drow male, sat atop it, an offering to the goddess who would not answer Ghenni'tiroth's desperate prayers.

Ghenni'tiroth straightened suddenly as the heart rose from the bloody platter, came up several inches and hovered in midair.

"The sacrifice is not sufficient," came a voice behind her, a voice she had dreaded hearing since the advent of the Time of Troubles.

She did not turn to face K'yorl Odran.

"There is war in the compound," Ghenni'tiroth stated more than asked.

K'yorl scoffed at the notion. A wave of her hand sent the sacrificial organ flying across the room.

Ghenni'tiroth spun around, eyes wide with outrage. She started to scream out the drow word for sacrilege, but stopped, the sound caught in her throat, as another heart floated in the air, from K'yorl toward her.

"The sacrifice was not sufficient," K'yorl said calmly. "Use this heart, the heart of Fini'they."

Ghenni'tiroth slumped back at the mention of the obviously dead priestess, her second in the House. Ghenni'tiroth had taken in Fini'they as her own daughter when Fini'they's family, a lower-ranking and insignificant House, had been destroyed by a rival House. Insignificant indeed had been Fini'they's House—Ghenni'tiroth could not even remember its proper name—but Fini'they had not been so. She was a powerful priestess, and ultimately loyal, even loving, to her adopted mother.

Ghenni'tiroth leaned back further, horrified, as her daughter's heart floated past and settled with a sickening wet sound on the platinum platter.

"Pray to Lolth," K'yorl ordered.

Ghenni'tiroth did just that. Perhaps K'yorl had erred, she thought. Perhaps in death Fini'they would prove most helpful, would prove a suitable sacrifice to bring the Spider Queen to the aid of House Faen Tlabbar.

After a long and uneventful moment, Ghenni'tiroth became aware of K'yorl's laughter.

"Perhaps we are in need of a greater sacrifice," the wicked matron mother of House Oblodra said slyly.

It wasn't difficult for Ghenni'tiroth, the only figure in House Faen Tlabbar greater than Fini'they, to figure out who K'yorl was talking about.

Secretly, barely moving her fingers, Ghenni'tiroth brought her deadly, poisoned dagger out of its sheath under the concealing folds of her spider-emblazoned robes. "Scrag-tooth," the dagger was called, and it had gotten a younger Ghenni'tiroth out of many situations much like this.

Of course, on those occasions, magic had been predictable, reliable, and those opponents had not been as formidable as K'yorl. Even as Ghenni'tiroth locked gazes with the Oblodran, kept K'yorl distracted while she subtly shifted her hand, K'yorl read her thoughts and expected the attack.

Ghenni'tiroth shouted a command word, and the dagger's magic functioned, sending the missile shooting out from under her robes directly at the heart of her adversary.

The magic functioned! Ghenni'tiroth silently cheered. But her elation faded quickly when the blade passed right through the specter of K'yorl Odran to embed itself uselessly in the fabric of a tapestry adorning the room's opposite wall.

"I do so hope the poison does not ruin the pattern," K'yorl, standing far to the left of her image, remarked.

Ghenni'tiroth shifted about and turned a steely-eyed gaze at the taunting creature.

"You cannot outfight me, you cannot outthink me," K'yorl said evenly. "You cannot even hide your thoughts from me. The war is ended before it ever began."

Ghenni'tiroth wanted to scream out a denial, but found herself as silent as Fini'they, whose heart lay on the platter before her.

"How much killing need there be?" K'yorl asked, catching Ghenni'tiroth off her guard. The matron of Faen Tlabbar turned a suspicious, but ultimately curious, expression toward her adversary.

"My House is small," K'yorl remarked, and that was true enough, unless one counted the thousands of kobold slaves said to be running around the tunnels along the edges of the Clawrift, just below House Oblodra. "And I am in need of allies if I wish to depose that wretch Baenre and her bloated family."

Ghenni'tiroth wasn't even conscious of the movement as her tongue came out and licked her thin lips. There was a flicker of hope.

"You cannot beat me," K'yorl said with all confidence. "Perhaps I will accept a surrender."

That word didn't sit well with the proud leader of the Third House.

"An alliance then, if that is what you must call it," K'yorl clarified, recognizing the look. "It is no secret that I am not on the best of terms with the Spider Queen."

Ghenni'tiroth rocked back on her legs, considering the implications. If she helped K'yorl, who was not in Lolth's favor, overcome Baenre, then what would be the implications to her House if and when everything was sorted out?

"All of this is Baenre's fault," K'yorl remarked, reading Ghenni'tiroth's every thought. "Baenre brought about the Spider Queen's abandonment," K'yorl scoffed. "She could not even hold a single prisoner, could not even conduct a proper high ritual."

The words rang true, painfully true, to Ghenni'tiroth, who vastly preferred Matron Baenre to K'yorl Odran. She wanted to deny them, and yet, that surely meant her death and the death of her House, since K'yorl held so obvious an advantage.

"Perhaps I will accept a surren—" K'yorl chuckled wickedly and caught herself in midsentence. "Perhaps an alliance would benefit us both," she said instead.

Ghenni'tiroth licked her lips again, not knowing where to turn. A glance at Fini'they's heart did much to convince her, though. "Perhaps it would," she said.

K'yorl nodded and smiled again that devious and infamous grin that was known throughout Menzoberranzan as an indication that K'yorl was lying.

Ghenni'tiroth returned the grin—until she remembered who it was she was dealing with, until she forced herself, through the temptation of the teasing bait that K'yorl had offered, to remember the reputation of this most wicked drow.

"Perhaps not," K'yorl said calmly, and Ghenni'tiroth was knocked backward suddenly by an unseen force, a physical though invisible manifestation of K'yorl's powerful will.

The matron of Faen Tlabbar jerked and twisted, heard the crack of one of her ribs. She tried to call out against K'yorl, to cry out to Lolth in one final, desperate prayer, but found her words garbled as an invisible hand grasped tightly on her throat, cutting off her air.

Ghenni'tiroth jerked again, violently, and again, and more cracking sounds came from her chest, from intense pressure within her torso. She rocked backward and would have fallen to the floor except that K'yorl's will held her slender form fast.

"I am sorry Fini'they was not enough to bring in your impotent Spider Queen," K'yorl taunted, brazenly blasphemous.

Ghenni'tiroth's eyes bulged and seemed as if they would pop from their sockets. Her back arched weirdly, agonizingly, and gurgling sounds continued to stream from her throat. She tore at the flesh of her own neck, trying to grasp the unseen hand, but only drew lines of her own bright blood.

Then there came a final crackle, a loud snapping, and Ghenni'tiroth resisted no more. The pressure was gone from her throat, for what good that did her. K'yorl's unseen hand grabbed her hair and yanked her head forward so that she looked down at the unusual bulge in her chest, beside her left breast.

Ghenni'tiroth's eyes widened in horror as her robes parted and her skin erupted. A great gout of blood and gore poured from the wound, and Ghenni'tiroth fell limply, lying sidelong to the platinum plate.

She watched the last beat of her own heart on that sacrificial platter.

"Perhaps Lolth will hear this call," K'yorl remarked, but Ghenni'tiroth could no longer understand the words.

K'yorl went to the body and retrieved the potion bottle that Ghenni'tiroth carried, that all House Faen Tlabbar females carried. The mixture, a concoction that forced passionate servitude of drow males, was a potent one—or would be, if conventional magic returned. This bottle was likely the

most potent, and K'yorl marked it well for a certain mercenary leader.

K'yorl went to the wall and claimed Scrag-tooth as her own.

To the victor . . .

With a final look to the dead matron mother, K'yorl called on her psionic powers and became less than substantial, became a ghost that could walk through the walls and past the guards of the well-defended compound. Her smile was supreme, as was her confidence, but as Lolth's avatar had told Baenre, Odran had indeed erred. She had followed a personal vengeance, had struck out first against a lesser foe.

Even as K'yorl drifted past the structures of House Faen Tlabbar, gloating over the death of her most hated enemy, Matrons Baenre and Mez'Barris Armgo, along with Triel and Gromph Baenre and the matron mothers of Menzoberranzan's fifth through eighth Houses, were gathered in a private chamber at the back of the Qu'ellarz'orl, the raised plateau within the huge cavern that held some of the more important drow Houses, including House Baenre. The eight of them huddled, each to a leg, around the spider-shaped brazier set upon the small room's single table. Each had brought their most valuable of flammable items, and Matron Baenre carried the lump of sulphur that the avatar had given her.

None of them mentioned, but all of them knew, that this might be their only chance.

II

TRUMP

Normally it pleased Jarlaxle to be in the middle of such a conflict, to be the object of wooing tactics by both sides in a dispute. This time, though, Jarlaxle was uneasy with the position. He didn't like dealing with K'yorl Odran on any account, as friends, and especially not as enemies, and he was uneasy with House Baenre being so desperately involved in any struggle. Jarlaxle simply had too much invested with Matron Baenre. The wary mercenary leader usually didn't count on anything, but he had fully expected House Baenre to rule in Menzoberranzan until at least the end of his life, as it had ruled since the beginning of his life and for millennia before that.

It wasn't that Jarlaxle held any special feelings toward the city's First House. It was just that Baenre offered him an anchor point, a measure of permanence in the continually shifting power struggles of Menzoberranzan.

It would last forever, so he had thought, but after talking with K'yorl—how he hated that one!—Jarlaxle wasn't so sure.

K'yorl wanted to enlist him, most likely wanted Bregan D'aerthe to serve as her connection with the world beyond Menzoberranzan. They could do that, and do it well, but Jarlaxle doubted that he, who always had a private agenda, could remain in K'yorl's favor for long. At some point, sooner or later, she would read the truth in his mind, and she would dispatch and replace him.

That was the way of the drow.

✗ ✗ ✗ ✗ ✗

The fiend was gargantuan, a gigantic, bipedal, doglike creature with four muscled arms, two of which ended in powerful pincers. How it entered Jarlaxle's private cave, along the sheer facing of the Clawrift, some hundred yards below and behind the compound of House Oblodra, none of the drow guards knew.

"*Tanar'ri!*" The warning word, the name of the greatest creatures of the Abyss, known in all the languages of the Realms, was passed in whispers and silent hand signals all through the complex, and the reaction to it was uniformly one of horror.

Pity the two drow guards who first encountered the towering, fifteen-foot monster. Loyal to Bregan D'aerthe, courageous in the belief that others would back their actions, they commanded the great beast to halt, and when it did not, the drow guards attacked.

Had their weapons held their previous enchantment, they might have hurt the beast somewhat. But magic had not returned to the Material Plane in any predictable or reliable manner. Thus, the tanar'ri, too, was deprived of its considerable spell repertoire, but the beast, four thousand pounds of muscle and physical hazards, hardly needed magical assistance.

The two drow were summarily dismembered, and the tanar'ri walked on, seeking Jarlaxle, as Errtu had bade it.

It found the mercenary leader, along with a score of his finest soldiers, around the first bend. Several drow leaped forward to the defense, but Jarlaxle, better understanding the power of this beast, held them at bay, was not so willing to throw away drow lives.

"Glabrezu," he said with all respect, recognizing the beast.

Glabrezu's canine maw curled up in a snarl, and its eyes narrowed as it scrutinized Jarlaxle, privately confirming that it had found the correct dark elf.

"*Baenre cok diemrey nochtero,*" the tanar'ri said in a growl, and without waiting for a response, the gigantic beast lumbered about and waddled away, crouching low so that its head did not scrape the corridor's high ceiling.

Again, several brave, stupid drow moved as if to pursue, and again Jarlaxle, smiling now more widely than he had in many tendays, held them back. The tanar'ri had spoken in the language of the lower planes, a language that Jarlaxle understood perfectly, and it had spoken the words Jarlaxle had longed to hear.

The question was clear on the expressions of all the unnerved drow standing beside him. They did not understand the language and wanted desperately to know what the tanar'ri had said.

"*Baenre cok diemrey nochtero,*" Jarlaxle explained to them. "House Baenre will prevail."

His wry smile, filled with hope, and the eager way he clenched his fists, told his soldiers that such a prediction was a good thing.

✕ ✕ ✕ ✕ ✕

Zeerith Q'Xorlarrin, matron mother of the Fifth House, understood the significance of the makeup of the gathering. Triel and Gromph Baenre attended primarily to fill the two vacant spots at the spider-shaped brazier. One of those places rightfully belonged to K'yorl, and since they were gathered to fend off K'yorl, as the avatar of the Spider Queen had bade them, she hadn't been invited.

The other vacant place, the one filled by Gromph, was normally reserved for Zeerith's closest drow friend, Matron Mother Ghenni'tiroth Tlabbar. None had said it aloud, but Zeerith understood the significance of the Baenre son's presence and of the matron mother's failure to appear.

K'yorl hated Ghenni'tiroth—that was no secret—and so Ghenni'tiroth had been left open as a sacrifice to delay the intrusions of House Oblodra. These other supposed allies and the goddess they all served had allowed Zeerith's best friend to perish.

That thought bothered the matron mother for a short while, until she came to realize that she was the third highest-ranking drow in the meeting chamber. If the summoning was successful, if K'yorl and House Oblodra were beaten back, then the hierarchy of the ruling Houses would surely shift. Oblodra would fall, leaving vacant the third place, and since Faen Tlabbar was suddenly without a proper matron mother, it was feasible that House Xorlarrin could leap past it into that coveted spot.

Ghenni'tiroth had been given as a sacrifice. Zeerith Q'Xorlarrin smiled widely.

Such were the ways of the drow.

Into the brazier went Gromph's prized spider mask, a most magical item, the only one in all of Menzoberranzan that could get someone over the House Baenre web fence. The flames shot into the air, orange and angry green.

Mez'Barris nodded to Baenre, and the withered old matron mother tossed in the lump of sulphur that the avatar had given her.

If a hundred excited dwarves had pumped a huge bellows, their fire would not have been more furious. The flames shot straight up in a multicolored column that held the eight watchers fast with its unholy glory.

"What is this?" came a question from the front of the room, near the only door. "You dare hold a meeting of council without informing House Oblodra?"

Matron Baenre, at the head of the table and thus, with her back directly to K'yorl, held up her hand to calm the others gathered around the spider brazier. Slowly she turned to face that most hated drow, and the two promptly locked vicious stares.

"The executioner does not invite her victim to the block," Baenre said evenly. "She takes her there, or lures her in."

Baenre's blunt words made more than a few of the gathered drow uneasy. If K'yorl had been handled more tactfully, some of them might have escaped with their lives.

Matron Baenre knew better, though. Their only hope, her only hope, was to trust the Spider Queen, to believe with all their hearts that the avatar had not steered them wrongly.

When K'yorl's first wave of mental energy rolled over Baenre, she, too, began to foster some doubts. She held her ground for some seconds, a remarkable display of will, but then K'yorl overwhelmed her, pushed her back against the table. Baenre felt her feet coming from the floor, felt as if a gigantic, unseen hand had reached out and grabbed her and was now edging her toward the flames.

"How much grander the call to Lolth will be," K'yorl shrieked happily, "when Matron Baenre is added to the flames!"

The others in the room, particularly the other five matron mothers, did not know how to react. Mez'Barris put her head down and quietly began muttering the words of a spell, praying that Lolth would hear her and grant her this.

Zeerith and the others watched the flames. The avatar had told them to do this, but why hadn't an ally, a tanar'ri or some other fiend, come through?

⚔ ⚔ ⚔ ⚔ ⚔

In the sludge-filled Abyss, perched atop his mushroom throne, Errtu greatly enjoyed the chaotic scene. Even through the scrying device Lolth had prepared for him, the great tanar'ri could feel the fears of the gathered worshippers and could taste the bitter hatred on the lips of K'yorl Odran.

He liked K'yorl, Errtu decided. Here was one of his own heart, purely and deliciously wicked, a murderess who killed for pleasure, a player of intrigue for no better reason than the fun of the game. The great tanar'ri wanted to watch K'yorl push her adversary into the pillar of flame.

But Lolth's instructions had been explicit, and her bartered goods too tempting for the fiend to pass up. Amazingly, given the state of magic at the time, the gate was opening, and opening wide.

Errtu had already sent one tanar'ri, a giant glabrezu, through a smaller gate to act as messenger, but that gate, brought about by the avatar herself, had been tenuous and open for only a fraction of a moment. Errtu had not believed the feat could be duplicated, not now.

The notion of magical chaos gave the fiend a sudden inspiration. Perhaps the old rules of banishment no longer applied. Perhaps he himself might walk through this opening gate, onto the Material Plane once more. Then he would not need to serve as Lolth's lackey; then he might find the renegade Do'Urden on his own, and after punishing the drow, he could return to the frozen Northland, where the precious Crenshinibon, the legendary Crystal Shard, lay buried!

The gate was opened. Errtu stepped in.

And was summarily rejected, pushed back into the Abyss, the place of his hundred-year banishment.

Several fiends stalked by the great tanar'ri, sensing the opening, heading for the gate, but snarling Errtu, enraged by the defeat, held them back.

Let this wicked drow, K'yorl, push Lolth's favored into the flames, the wretched Errtu decided. The gate would remain open with the sacrifice, might even open wider.

Errtu did not like the banishment, did not like being lackey to any being. Let Lolth suffer; let Baenre be consumed, and only then would he do as the Spider Queen had asked!

⚔ ⚔ ⚔ ⚔ ⚔

The only thing that saved Baenre from exactly that fate was the unexpected intervention of Methil, the illithid. The glabrezu had gone to Methil after visiting Jarlaxle, bringing the same prediction that House Baenre would prevail, and Methil, serving as ambassador of his people, made it a point to remain on the winning side.

The illithid's psionic waves disrupted K'yorl's telepathic attack, and Matron Baenre slumped back to the side of the table.

K'yorl's eyes went wide, surprised by the defeat—until Methil, who had been standing invisibly and secretly at Matron Baenre's side, came into view.

Wait for this to end, K'yorl's thoughts screamed at the octopus-headed creature. *See who wins and decide where your alliances lie.*

Methil's assurance that he already knew the outcome did not disturb K'yorl half as much as the sight of the gigantic, batlike wing that suddenly extended from the pillar of flame: a tanar'ri—a true tanar'ri!

Another glabrezu hopped out of the fire to land on the floor between Baenre and her adversary. K'yorl hit it with a psionic barrage, but she was no match for such a creature, and she knew it.

She took note that the pillar was still dancing wildly, that another fiend was forming within the flames. Lolth was against her! she suddenly realized. All the Abyss seemed to be coming to Matron Baenre's call!

K'yorl did the only thing she could, became insubstantial once more and fled across the city, back to her house.

Fiends rushed through the open gate, a hundred of them, and still more. It went on for more than an hour, the minions of Errtu, and thus, the minions of Lolth, coming to the call of the desperate matron mothers, swooping across the city in frenzied glee to surround House Oblodra.

Smiles of satisfaction, even open cheers, were exchanged in the meeting room at the back of the Qu'ellarz'orl. The avatar had done as promised, and the future of Lolth's faithful seemed deliciously dark once more.

Of the eight gathered, only Gromph wore a grin that was less than sincere. Not that he wanted House Oblodra to win, of course, but the male held no joy at the thought that things might soon be as they had always been, that he, for all his power and devotion to the ways of magic, would, above all else, be a mere male once more.

He took some consolation, as the flames died away and the others began to exit, in noticing that several of the offered items, including his prized spider mask, had not been consumed by the magical flames. Gromph looked to the door, to the matron mothers and Triel, and they were so obsessed with the spectacle of the fiends that they took no notice of him at all.

Quietly and without attracting attention, the covetous drow wizard replaced his precious item under the folds of his robe, then added to his collection some of the most prized artifacts of Menzoberranzan's greatest Houses.

PART THREE

RESOLUTION

How I wanted to go to Catti-brie after I realized the dangers of her sword! How I wanted to stand by her and protect her! The item had possessed her, after all, and was imbued with a powerful and obviously sentient magic.

Catti-brie wanted me by her side—who wouldn't want the supportive shoulder of a friend with such a struggle looming?—and yet she did not want me there, could not have me there, for she knew this battle was hers to fight alone.

I had to respect her conclusion, and in those days when the Time of Troubles began to end and the magics of the world sorted themselves out once more, I came to learn that sometimes the most difficult battles are the ones we are forced not to fight.

I came to learn then why mothers and fathers seldom have fingernails and often carry an expression of forlorn resignation. What agony it must be for a parent in Silverymoon to be told by her offspring, no longer a child, that he or she has decided to head out to the west, to Waterdeep, to sail for adventure along the Sword Coast. Everything within that parent wants to yell out "Stay!" Every instinct within that parent wants to hug the child close, to protect that child forever. And yet, ultimately, those instincts are wrong.

In the heart, there is no sting greater than watching the struggles of one you love, knowing that only through such strife will that person grow and recognize the potential of his or her existence. Too many thieves in the Realms believe the formula for happiness lies in an unguarded treasure trove. Too many wizards seek to circumvent the years of study required for true power. They find a spell on a scroll or an enchanted item that is far beyond their understanding, yet they try it anyway, only to be consumed by the powerful magic. Too many priests in the Realms, and too many religious sects in general, ask of themselves and of their congregations only humble servitude.

All of them are doomed to fail in the true test of happiness. There is one ingredient missing in stumbling upon an unguarded treasure hoard; there is one element absent when a minor wizard lays his hands on an archmage's staff; there is one item unaccounted for in humble, unquestioning, and unambitious servitude.

A sense of accomplishment.

It is the most important ingredient in any rational being's formula of happiness. It is the element that builds confidence and allows us to go on to other, greater tasks. It is the item that promotes a sense of self-worth, that allows any person to believe there is value in life itself, that gives a sense of purpose to bolster us as we face life's unanswerable questions.

So it was with Catti-brie and her sword. This battle had found her, and she had determined to fight it. Had I followed my protective instincts, I would have refused to aid her in taking on this quest.

My protective instincts told me to go to Bruenor, who would have surely ordered the sentient sword destroyed. By doing that, or taking any other course to prevent Catti-brie's battle, I would have, in effect, failed to trust in her, failed to respect her individual needs and her chosen destiny, and thus, I would have stolen a bit of her freedom. That had been Wulfgar's single failure. In his fears for the woman he so dearly loved, the brave and proud barbarian had tried to smother her in his protective hug.

I think he saw the truth of his error in the moments before his death. I think he remembered then the reasons he loved Catti-brie: her strength and independence. How ironic it is that our instincts often run exactly opposite from what we truly desire for those we love.

In the situation I earlier named, the parents would have to let their child go to Waterdeep and the Sword Coast. And so it was with Catti-brie. She chose to take her sword, chose to explore its sentient side, perhaps at great personal risk. The decision was hers to make, and once she had made it, I had to respect it, had to respect her. I didn't see her much over the next couple of tendays, as she waged her private battle.

But I thought of her and worried for her every waking moment, and even in my dreams.

—Drizzt Do'Urden

12
WORTH THE TROUBLES

I have tricked tanar'ri to go to your city, Menzoberranzan, and soon I must force them back," the great Errtu roared. "And I cannot even go to this place and join in their havoc, or even to retrieve them!" The balor sat on his mushroom throne, watching the scrying device that showed him the city of drow. Earlier, he was receiving fleeting images only, as this magic, too, struggled against the effects of the strange time. The images had been coming more strongly lately, though, and now the mirrorlike surface was uncloudy, showing a clear scene of House Oblodra, wedged between the fingers of the Clawrift. Fiends great and minor stalked and swooped around the walled compound, banging strong fists against the stone, hurling threats and missiles of rock. The Oblodrans had buttoned the place up tightly, for even with their psionic powers, and the fact that the fiends' magic fared no better than anyone else's, the otherworldly beasts were simply too physically strong, their minds too warped by evil to be much affected by telepathic barrages.

And they were backed by a united army of drow, lying in wait behind the fiendish lines. Hundreds of crossbows and javelins were pointed House Oblodra's way. Scores of drow riding sticky-footed subterranean lizards stalked the walls and ceiling near the doomed house. Any Oblodran that showed her face would be hit by a barrage from every angle.

"Those same fiends are preventing the Third House from being attacked," Errtu snarled at Lolth, reminding the Spider Queen whose army was in control here. "Your minions fear my minions, and rightly so!"

The beautiful drow, back in the Abyss once more, understood that Errtu's outburst was one part outrage and nine parts bluster. No tanar'ri ever had to be "tricked" into going to the Material Plane, where it might wreak havoc. That was their very nature, the most profound joy in their miserable existence.

"You ask much, Lady of Spiders," Errtu grumbled on.

"I give much in return," Lolth reminded him.

"We shall see."

Lolth's red-glowing eyes narrowed at the tanar'ri's continuing sarcasm. The payment she had offered Errtu, a gift that could potentially free the fiend from nearly a century more of banishment, was no small thing.

"The four glabrezu will be difficult to retrieve," Errtu went on, feigning exasperation, playing this out to the extreme. "They are always difficult!"

"No more so than a balor," Lolth said in blunt response. Errtu turned on her, his face a mask of hatred.

"The Time of Troubles nears its end," Lolth said calmly into that dangerous visage.

"It has been too long!" Errtu roared.

Lolth ignored the tone of the comment, understanding that Errtu had to act outraged and overburdened to prevent her from concluding that the tanar'ri owed her something more. "It has been longer to my eyes than to your own, fiend," the Spider Queen retorted.

Errtu muttered a curse under his smelly breath.

"But it nears its end," Lolth went on, quietly, calmly. Both she and Errtu looked to the image on the scrying surface just as a great winged tanar'ri soared up out of the Clawrift, clutching a small, wriggling creature in one of its great fists. The pitiful catch could not have been more than three feet tall and seemed less than that in the massive fiend's clutches. It wore a ragged vest that did not hide its rust-colored scales, a vest made even more ragged from the tearing of the tanar'ri's clawed grasp.

"A kobold," Errtu remarked.

"Known allies of House Oblodra," Lolth explained. "Thousands of the wretches run the tunnels along the chasm walls."

The flying tanar'ri gave a hoot, grasped the kobold with its other clawed hand as well, and ripped the squealing thing in half.

"One less ally of House Oblodra," Errtu whispered, and from the pleased look on the balor's face, Lolth understood Errtu's true feelings about this whole event. The great tanar'ri was living vicariously through his minions, was watching their destructive antics and feeding off the scene.

It crossed Lolth's mind to reconsider her offered gift. Why should she repay the fiend for doing something it so obviously wanted to do?

The Spider Queen, never a fool, shook the thoughts from her mind. She had nothing to lose in giving Errtu what she had promised. Her eyes were set on the conquest of Mithral Hall, on forcing Matron Baenre to extend her grasp so that the city of drow would be less secure, and more chaotic, more likely to see interhouse warfare. The renegade Do'Urden was nothing to her, though she surely wanted him dead.

Who better to do that than Errtu? Lolth wondered. Even if the renegade survived the coming war—and Lolth did not believe he would—Errtu could use her gift to force Drizzt to call him from his banishment, to allow him back to the Material Plane. Once there, the mighty balor's first goal would undoubtedly be to exact vengeance on the renegade. Drizzt had beaten Errtu once, but no one ever defeated a balor the second time around.

Lolth knew Errtu well enough to understand that Drizzt Do'Urden would be far luckier indeed if he died swiftly in the coming war.

She said no more about the payment for the fiend's aid, understanding that in giving it to Errtu, she was, in effect, giving herself a present. "When the Time of Troubles has passed, my priestesses will aid you in forcing the tanar'ri back to the Abyss," Lolth said.

Errtu did not hide his surprise well. He knew that Lolth had been planning some sort of campaign, and he assumed his monstrous minions would be sent along beside the drow army. Now that Lolth had clearly stated her intentions, though, the fiend recognized her reasoning. If a horde of tanar'ri marched beside the drow, all the Realms would rise against them, including goodly creatures of great power from the upper planes.

Also, both Lolth and Errtu knew well that the drow priestesses, powerful as they were, would not be able to control such a horde once the rampage of warfare had begun.

"All but one," Errtu corrected.

Lolth eyed him curiously.

"I will need an emissary to go to Drizzt Do'Urden," the fiend explained. "To tell the fool what I have, and what I require in exchange for it."

Lolth considered the words for a moment. She had to play this out carefully. She had to hold Errtu back, she knew, or risk complicating what should be a relatively straightforward conquest of the dwarven halls, but she could not let the fiend know her army's destination. If Errtu thought Lolth's minions would soon put Drizzt Do'Urden, the great fiend's only chance at getting back to the Material Plane anytime soon, in jeopardy, he would covertly oppose her.

"Not yet," the Spider Queen said. "Drizzt Do'Urden is out of the way, and there he shall stay until my city is back in order."

"Menzoberranzan is never in order," Errtu replied slyly.

"In relative order," Lolth corrected. "You will have your gift when I give it, and only then will you send your emissary."

"Lady of Spiders . . ." The balor growled threateningly.

"The Time of Troubles nears its end," Lolth snapped in Errtu's ugly face. "My powers return in full. Beware your threats, balor, else you shall find yourself in a more wretched place than this!"

Her purplish black robes flying furiously behind her, the Spider Queen spun around sharply and moved off, swiftly disappearing into the swirling mist. She smirked at the proper ending to the meeting. Diplomacy went only so far with chaotic fiends. After reaching a point, the time inevitably came for open threats.

Errtu slumped back on his mushroom throne in the realization that Lolth was in full command of this situation. She held the link for his minions to the Material Plane, and she held the gift that might allow Errtu to end his banishment. On top of all of that, Errtu did not doubt the Spider Queen's claims that the pantheon was at last sorting itself out. And if the Time of Troubles was indeed a passing period, and Lolth's powers returned in full, she was far beyond the balor.

Resignedly, Errtu looked back to the image on the scrying surface. Five more kobolds had been pulled up from the Clawrift. They huddled together in a tight group while a host of fiends circled around them, teasing them, tormenting them. The great balor could smell their fear, could taste this torturous kill as sweetly as if he were among those circling fiends.

Errtu's mood brightened immediately.

✕ ✕ ✕ ✕ ✕

Belwar Dissengulp and a score of svirfnebli warriors sat on a ledge, overlooking a large chamber strewn with boulders and stalactites. Each held a rope—Belwar's was fastened through a loop on his belt and a mushroom-hide strap set over his pickaxe hand—that they might rappel quickly to the floor. For down below, the gnomish priests were at work, drawing runes of power on the floor with heated dyes and discussing the prior failures and the most effective ways they might combine their powers, both for the summoning, and in case the summoning, as had happened twice already, went bad.

The gnomish priests had heard the call of their god, Segojan, had sensed the returning of priestly magic. For the svirfnebli, no act could greater signify the end of this strange period, no act could better assure them that all was right once more, than the summoning of an elemental earth giant. This was

their sphere, their life, and their love. They were attuned to the rock, at one with the stone and dirt that surrounded their dwellings. To call an elemental forth, to share in its friendship, would satisfy the priests that their god was well. Anything less would not suffice.

They had tried several times. The first summoning had brought forth nothing, not a even trembling in the ground. The second, third, and fourth had raised tall stone pillars, but they had shown no signs of animation. Three of the stalagmite mounds in this very chamber were testaments to those failures.

On the fifth try, an elemental had come forth, and the gnomish priests had rejoiced—until the monster turned on them in rage, killing a dozen gnomes before Belwar and his troupe had managed to break it apart. That failure was perhaps the very worst thing that could befall the gnomes, for they came to believe not only that Segojan was out of their reach, but that, perhaps, he was angry with them. They had tried again—and again the elemental came forth only to attack them.

Belwar's defenses were better in place that sixth time, as they were now, and the stone-limbed monster was beaten back quickly, with no loss of svirfnebli.

After that second disaster, Belwar had asked that the priests wait a while before trying again, but they had refused, desperate to find Segojan's favor, desperate to know that their god was with them. Belwar was not without influence, though, and he had gone to King Schnicktick and forced a compromise.

Five days had passed since that sixth summoning, five days wherein the gnomish priests and all of Blingdenstone had prayed to Segojan, had begged him to no longer turn against them.

Unknown to the svirfnebli, those five days had also seen the end of the Time of Troubles, the realignment and correction of the pantheon.

Belwar watched now as the robed priests began their dance around the rune-emblazoned circle they had drawn on the ground. Each carried a stone, a small green gem previously enchanted. One by one, they placed a gem on the perimeter of the circle and crushed it with a huge mallet. When that was completed, the high priest walked into the circle, to its very center, placed his gem on the ground, and crying out a word of completion, smashed it under his mithral mallet.

For a moment there was only silence, then the ground began to tremble slightly. The high priest rushed out of the circle to join his huddling companions.

The trembling increased, multiplied. A large crack ran around the circumference of the enchanted area, separating that circle from the rest of the chamber. Inside the circle, rock split apart, and split again, rolling and roiling into a malleable mud.

Bubbles grew and blew apart with great popping sounds, and the whole chamber warmed.

A great head—a huge head!—poked up from the floor.

On the ledge, Belwar and his cohorts groaned. Never had they seen so tremendous an elemental! Suddenly, they were all plotting escape routes rather than attack routes.

The shoulders came forth from the floor, an arm on each side—an arm that could sweep the lot of the priests into oblivion with a single movement. Curious looks mixed with trepidation on the faces of priests and warriors alike. This creature was not like any elemental they had ever seen. Though its stone was smoother, with no cracks showing, it appeared more unfinished, less in the image of a bipedal creature. Yet, at the same time, it exuded an aura of sheer power and completion beyond anything the gnomes had ever known.

"The glory of Segojan are we witnessing!" one gnome near Belwar squealed in glee.

"Or the end of our people," Belwar added under his breath so that none would hear.

By the girth of the head and shoulders, the gnomes expected the monster to rise twenty feet or more, but when the trembling stopped and all was quiet again, the creature barely topped ten feet—not as tall as many of the elementals even single svirfneblin priests had previously summoned. Still, the gnomes had no doubt that this was a greater achievement, that this creature was more powerful than anything they had ever brought forth. The priests had their suspicions—so did Belwar, who had lived a long time and had listened carefully to the legends that gave his people their identity and their strength.

"Entemoch!" the most honored burrow warden gasped from his perch, and the name, the name of the Prince of Earth Elementals, was echoed from gnome to gnome.

Another name predictably followed, the name of Ogremoch, Entemoch's evil twin, and it was spoken sharply and with open fear. If this was Ogremoch and not Entemoch, then they all were doomed.

The priests fell to their knees, trembling, paying homage, hoping beyond hope that this was indeed Entemoch, who had always been their friend.

Belwar was the first down from the ledge, hitting the ground with a grunt and running off to stand before the summoned creature.

It regarded him from on high, made no move, and offered no sign as to its intentions.

"Entemoch!" Belwar shouted. Behind him, the priests lifted their faces. Some found the courage to stand and walk beside the brave burrow warden.

"Entemoch!" Belwar called again. "Answered our call, you have. Are we to take this as a sign that all is right with Segojan, that we are in his favor?"

The creature brought its huge hand to the floor, palm up, before Belwar. The burrow warden looked to the high priest standing at his right.

The priest nodded. "To trust in Segojan is our duty," he said, and he and Belwar stepped onto the hand together.

Up they rose, coming to a stop right before the behemoth's face. And they relaxed and were glad, for they saw compassion there, and friendship. This was indeed Entemoch, they both knew in their hearts, and not Ogremoch, and Segojan was with them.

The elemental prince lifted its hand above its head and melted back into the ground, leaving Belwar and the high priest in the center of the circle, perfectly reformed.

Cheers resounded through the chamber, and more than one rough-hewn svirfneblin face was streaked with tears. The priests patted themselves on the back, congratulated themselves and all the gnomes of Blingdenstone. They sang praises to King Schnicktick, whose guidance had led them to this pinnacle of svirfneblin achievement.

For at least one of them, Belwar, the celebration was short-lived. Their god was back with them, it seemed, and their magic was returning, but what did that mean for the drow of Menzoberranzan? the most honored burrow warden wondered. Was the Spider Queen, too, returned? And the powers of the drow wizards as well?

Before all of this had begun, the gnomes had come to believe, and not without reason, that the drow were planning for war. With the onset of this chaotic time, that war had not come, but that was reasonable, Belwar knew, since the drow were more dependent on magic than were the gnomes. If things were indeed aright once more, as the arrival of Entemoch seemed to indicate, then Blingdenstone might soon be threatened.

All around the most honored burrow warden, gnomish priests and warriors danced and cried out for joy. How soon, he wondered, might those cries be screams of pain or shrieks of grief?

13
REPAIRING THE DAMAGE

"Delicately!" Fret whispered harshly, watching Drizzt's hands as the drow scraped and chipped away the dried salve around the neck of the panther figurine. "Oh, do be careful!"

Of course Drizzt was being careful! As careful as the drow had ever been in any task. As important as the figurine appeared to be to Fret, it was a hundred times more important to Drizzt, who treasured and loved his panther companion. Never had the drow taken on a more critical task, not with his wits or his weapons. Now he used the delicate tool Fret had given him, a slender silver rod with a flattened and slightly hooked end.

Another piece of salve fell away—almost a half inch along the side of the panther's neck was clear of the stuff. And clear of any crack, Drizzt noted hopefully. So perfectly had the salve bonded the onyx figurine that not a line could be seen where the break had been.

Drizzt sublimated his excitement, understanding that it would inevitably lead him to rush in his work. He had to take his time. The circumference of the figurine's neck was no more than a few inches, but Drizzt fully expected, and Fret had agreed with the estimate, that he would spend the entire morning at his work.

The drow ranger moved back from the figurine so that Fret could see the cleared area. The tidy dwarf nodded to Drizzt after viewing it, even smiled hopefully. Fret trusted in Lady Alustriel's magic and her ability to mend a tragedy.

With a pat on Drizzt's shoulder, the dwarf moved aside and Drizzt went back to work, slowly and delicately, one tiny fleck at a time.

By noon, the neck was clear of salve. Drizzt turned the figurine over in his hands, studying the area where the break had been, seeing no indication, neither a crack nor any residue from the salve, that the figurine had been damaged. He clasped the item by the head and after a deep, steadying breath, dared to hold it aloft, with all the pressure of its weight centered on the area of the cut.

It held fast. Drizzt shook his hand, daring it to break apart, but it did not.

"The bonding will be as strong as any other area on the item," Fret assured the drow. "Take heart that the figurine is whole once more."

"Agreed," Drizzt replied, "but what of its magic?"

Fret had no answer.

"The real challenge will be in sending Guenhwyvar home to the Astral Plane," the drow went on.

"Or in calling the panther back," Fret added.

That notion stung Drizzt. The tidy dwarf was right, he knew. He might be able to open a tunnel to allow Guenhwyvar to return home, only to have the panther lost to him forever. Still, Drizzt entertained no thoughts of keeping the cat beside him. Guenhwyvar's condition had stabilized—apparently the panther could indeed remain on the Material Plane indefinitely—but the great cat was not in good health or good spirits. While she seemed no longer in danger of dying, Guenhwyvar roamed around in a state of perpetual exhaustion, muscles slack along her once sleek sides, eyes often closed as the panther tried to find desperately needed sleep.

"Better to dismiss Guenhwyvar to her home," Drizzt said determinedly. "Surely my life will be diminished if I cannot recall Guenhwyvar, but better that than the life Guenhwyvar must now endure."

They went together, the figurine in hand, to Drizzt's room. As usual, Guenhwyvar lay on the rug in front of the hearth, absorbing the heat of the glowing embers. Drizzt didn't hesitate. He marched right up before the panther—who lifted her head sluggishly to regard him—and placed the figurine on the floor before her.

"Lady Alustriel, and good Fret here, have come to our aid, Guenhwyvar," Drizzt announced. His voice quivered a bit as he tried to continue, as the realization hit him that this might be the last time he ever saw the panther.

Guenhwyvar sensed that discomfort and with great effort, managed to sit up, putting her head in line with kneeling Drizzt's face.

"Go home, my friend," Drizzt whispered, "go home."

The panther hesitated, eyeing the drow intently, as if trying to discern the source of Drizzt's obvious unease. Guenhwyvar, too, got the feeling—from

Drizzt and not from the figurine, which seemed whole to the panther once more—that this might be a final parting of dear friends.

But the cat had no control in the matter. In her exhausted state, Guenhwyvar could not have ignored the call of the magic if she tried. Shakily, the cat got to her feet and paced around the figurine.

Drizzt was both thrilled and scared when Guenhwyvar's form began to melt away into gray mist, then into nothing at all.

When the cat was gone, Drizzt scooped up the figurine, taking heart that he felt no warmth coming from it, that apparently whatever had gone wrong the last time he tried to send Guenhwyvar home was not happening again. He realized suddenly how foolish he had been, and looked at Fret, his violet orbs wide with shock.

"What is it?" the tidy dwarf asked.

"I have not Catti-brie's sword!" Drizzt whispered harshly. "If the path is not clear to the Astral Plane . . ."

"The magic is right once more," Fret replied at once, patting his hand soothingly in the air, "in the figurine and in all the world around us. The magic is right once more."

Drizzt held the figurine close. He had no idea of where Catti-brie might be, and knew she had her sword with her. All he could do, then, was sit tight, wait, and hope.

⚔ ⚔ ⚔ ⚔ ⚔

Bruenor sat on his throne, Regis beside him, and the halfling looking much more excited than the dwarf king. Regis had already seen the guests that would soon be announced to Bruenor, and curious Regis was always happy to see the extraordinary Harpells of Longsaddle. Four of them had come to Mithral Hall, four wizards who might play an important role in defending the dwarven complex—if they didn't inadvertently take the place down instead.

Such were the risks of dealing with the Harpells.

The four stumbled into the throne room, nearly running down the poor dwarf who had first entered to announce them. There was Harkle, of course, wearing a bandage around his face, for his eyes were already in Mithral Hall. Guiding him was fat Regweld, who had ridden into the outer hall on a curious mount, the front of which resembled a horse and the back of which had hind legs and a back end more akin to a frog. Regweld had appropriately named the thing Puddlejumper.

The third Harpell Bruenor and Regis did not know, and the wizard did not

offer his name. He merely growled low and nodded in their direction.

"I am Bella don DelRoy Harpell," announced the fourth, a short and quite beautiful young woman, except that her eyes did not look in the same direction. Both orbs were green, but one shined with a fierce inner light, while the other was dulled over and grayish. With Bella, though, that seemed to only add to her appearance, to give her fine features a somewhat exotic look.

Bruenor recognized one of the given names, and understood that Bella was probably the leader of this group. "Daughter of DelRoy, leader of Longsaddle?" the dwarf asked, to which the petite woman dipped low in a bow, so low that her bright blond mane nearly swept the floor.

"Greetings from Longsaddle, Eighth King of Mithral Hall," Bella said politely. "Your call was not unheeded."

A pity, Bruenor thought, but he remained tactfully quiet.

"With me are—"

"Harkle and Regweld," Regis interrupted, knowing the two quite well from a previous stay in Longsaddle. "Well met! And it is good to see that your experiments in crossbreeding a horse and a frog came to fruition."

"Puddlejumper!" the normally forlorn Regweld happily replied.

That name promised a sight that Regis would like to see!

"I am the daughter of DelRoy," Bella said rather sharply, eyeing the halfling squarely. "Please do not interrupt again, or I shall have to turn you into something Puddlejumper would enjoy eating."

The sparkle in her good green eye as she regarded Regis, and the similar glint in the halfling's gray orbs, told Regis that the threat was a hollow one. He heeded it anyway, suddenly anxious to keep on Bella's good side. She wasn't five feet tall, the halfling realized, and a bit on the heavy side, somewhat resembling a slightly larger version of Regis himself—except that there was no mistaking her feminine attributes. At least, not for Regis.

"My third companion is Bidderdoo," Bella went on.

The name sounded curiously familiar to both Bruenor and Regis, and came perfectly clear when Bidderdoo answered the introduction with a bark.

Bruenor groaned; Regis clapped and laughed aloud. When they had gone through Longsaddle, on their way to find Mithral Hall, Bidderdoo, through use of a bad potion, had played the role of the Harpell family dog.

"The transformation is not yet complete," Bella apologized, and she gave Bidderdoo a quick backhand on the shoulder, reminding him to put his tongue back in his mouth.

Harkle cleared his throat loudly and fidgeted about.

"Of course," Bruenor said immediately, taking the cue. The dwarf gave a sharp whistle, and one of his attendants came out of a side room, carrying the disembodied eyes, one in each hand. To his credit, the dwarf tried to keep them as steady as possible, and aimed them both in Harkle's direction.

"Oh, it is so good to see myself again!" the wizard exclaimed, and he spun around. Following what he could see, he started for himself, or for his eyes, or for the back wall, actually, and the door he and his companions had already come through. He cried out, "No, no!" and turned a complete circle, trying to get his bearing, which wasn't an easy thing while viewing himself from across the room.

Bruenor groaned again.

"It is so confusing!" an exasperated Harkle remarked as Regweld grabbed him and tried to turn him aright.

"Ah, yes," the wizard said, and turned back the wrong way once more, heading for the door.

"The other way!" frustrated Regweld cried.

Bruenor grabbed the dwarven attendant and took the eyes, turning them both to look directly into his own scowling visage.

Harkle screamed.

"Hey!" Bruenor roared. "Turn around."

Harkle calmed himself and did as instructed, his body facing Bruenor once more.

Bruenor looked to Regis, snickered, and tossed one of the eyes Harkle's way, then followed it a split second later with the other, snapping his wrist so the thing spun as it soared through the air.

Harkle screamed again and fainted.

Regweld caught one of the eyes; Bidderdoo went for the other with his mouth. Luckily, Bella cut him off. She missed though, and the eye bounced off her arm, fell to the floor, and rolled around.

"That was very naughty, King Dwarf!" the daughter of DelRoy scolded. "That was . . ." She couldn't maintain the facade, and was soon laughing, as were her companions—though Bidderdoo's chuckles sounded more like a growl. Regis joined in, and Bruenor, too, but only for a second. The dwarf king could not forget the fact that these bumbling wizards might be his only magical defense against an army of dark elves.

It was not a pleasant thought.

✕ ✕ ✕ ✕ ✕

Drizzt was out of Mithral Hall at dawn the next morning. He had seen a campfire on the side of the mountain the night before and knew it was Catti-brie's. He still had not tried calling Guenhwyvar back and resisted the urge now, reminding himself to take on one problem at a time.

The problem now was Catti-brie, or, more specifically, her sword.

He found the young woman as he came around a bend in the path, crossing into the shadow between two large boulders. She was almost directly below him, on a small, flat clearing overlooking the wide, rolling terrain east of Mithral Hall. With the rising sun breaking the horizon directly before her, Drizzt could make out only her silhouette. Her movements were graceful as she walked through a practice dance with her sword, waving it in slow, long lines before and above her. Drizzt rested and watched approvingly of both the grace and perfection of the woman's dance. He had shown her this, and as always, Catti-brie had learned well. She could have been his own shadow, Drizzt realized, so perfect and synchronous were her movements.

He let her continue, both because of the importance of this practice and because he enjoyed watching her.

Finally, after nearly twenty minutes, Catti-brie took a deep breath and held her arms out high and wide, reveling in the rising sun.

"Well done," Drizzt congratulated, walking down to her.

Catti-brie nearly jumped at the sound, and she spun around, a bit embarrassed and annoyed, to see the drow.

"Ye should warn a girl," she said.

"I came upon you quite by accident," Drizzt lied, "but fortunately it would seem."

"I seen the Harpells go into Mithral Hall yesterday," Catti-brie replied. "Have ye speaked with them?"

Drizzt shook his head. "They are not important right now," he explained. "I need only to speak with you."

It sounded serious. Catti-brie moved to slide her sword into its scabbard, but Drizzt's hand came out, motioning for her to stop.

"I have come for the sword," he explained.

"Khazid'hea?" Catti-brie asked, surprised.

"What?" asked the even more surprised drow.

"That is its name," Catti-brie explained, holding the fine blade before her, its razor-sharp edge glowing red once more. "Khazid'hea."

Drizzt knew the word, a drow word! It meant "to cut," or "cutter," and seemed an appropriate name indeed for a blade that could slice through solid stone. But how could Catti-brie know it? the drow wondered, and his face asked the question as plainly as words ever could.

"The sword told me!" Catti-brie answered.

Drizzt nodded and calmed. He shouldn't have been so surprised—he knew the sword was sentient, after all.

"Khazid'hea," the drow agreed. He drew Twinkle from its sheath, flipped it over in his hand, and presented it, hilt-first, to Catti-brie.

She stared at the offering blankly, not understanding.

"A fair exchange," Drizzt explained, "Twinkle for Khazid'hea."

"Ye favor the scimitar," Catti-brie said.

"I will learn to use a scimitar and sword in harmony," Drizzt replied. "Accept the exchange. Khazid'hea has begged that I be its wielder, and I will oblige. It is right that the blade and I are joined."

Catti-brie's look went from surprise to incredulity. She couldn't believe Drizzt would demand this of her! She had spent days—tendays!—alone in the mountains, practicing with this sword, connecting with its unnatural intelligence, trying to establish a bond.

"Have you forgotten our encounter?" Drizzt asked, somewhat cruelly. Catti-brie blushed a deep red. Indeed, she had not forgotten, and never would, and what a fool she felt when she realized how she—or at least how her sword, using her body—had thrown herself at Drizzt.

"Give me the sword," Drizzt said firmly, waving Twinkle's hilt before the stunned young woman. "It is right that we are joined."

Catti-brie clutched Khazid'hea defensively. She closed her eyes then, and seemed to sway, and Drizzt got the impression she was communing with the blade, hearing its feelings.

When she opened her eyes once more, Drizzt's free hand moved for the sword, and to the drow's surprise and satisfaction, the sword tip came up suddenly, nicking his hand and forcing him back.

"The sword does not want ye!" Catti-brie practically growled.

"You would strike me?" Drizzt asked, and his question calmed the young woman.

"Just a reaction," she stammered, trying to apologize.

Just a reaction, Drizzt silently echoed, but exactly the reaction he had hoped to see. The sword was willing to defend her right to wield it; the sword had rejected him in light of its rightful owner.

In the blink of an eye, Drizzt flipped Twinkle over and replaced it on his belt. His smile clued Catti-brie to the truth of the encounter.

"A test," she said. "Ye just gave me a test!"

"It was necessary."

"Ye never had any mind to take Khazid'hea," the woman went on, her volume rising with her ire. "Even if I'd taken yer offer . . ."

"I would have taken the sword," Drizzt answered honestly. "And I would have placed it on display in a secure place in the Hall of Dumathoin."

"And ye would have taken back Twinkle," Catti-brie huffed. "Ye lyin' drow!"

Drizzt considered the words, then shrugged and nodded his agreement with the reasoning.

Catti-brie gave an impertinent pout and tossed her head, which sent her auburn mane flying over her shoulder. "The sword just knows now that I'm the better fighter," she said, sounding sincere.

Drizzt laughed aloud.

"Draw yer blades, then!" Catti-brie huffed, falling back into a ready posture. "Let me show ye what me and me sword can do!"

Drizzt's smile was wide as his scimitars came into his hands. These would be the last and most crucial tests, he knew, to see if Catti-brie had truly taken control of the sword.

Metal rang out in the clear morning air, the two friends hopping about for position, their breath blowing clouds in the chill air. Soon after the sparring had begun, Drizzt's guard slipped, presenting Catti-brie with a perfect strike.

In came Khazid'hea, but it stopped far short, and the young woman jumped back. "Ye did that on purpose!" she accused, and she was right, and by not going for a vicious hit, she and her sword had passed the second test.

Only one test to go.

Drizzt said nothing as he went back into his crouch. He wasn't wearing the bracers, Catti-brie noticed, and so he wouldn't likely be off balance. She came on anyway, gladly and fiercely, and put up a fine fight as the sun broke clear of the horizon and began its slow climb into the eastern sky.

She couldn't match the drow, though, and in truth, hadn't seen Drizzt fight with this much vigor in a long time. When the sparring ended, Catti-brie was sitting on her rump, a scimitar resting easily atop each of her shoulders and her own sword lying on the ground several feet away.

Drizzt feared that the sentient sword would be outraged that its wielder had been so clearly beaten. He stepped away from Catti-brie and went to Khazid'hea first, bending low to scoop it up. The drow paused, though, his hand just an inch from the pommel.

No longer did Khazid'hea wear the pommel of a unicorn, nor even the fiendish visage it had taken when in the hands of Dantrag Baenre. That pommel resembled a sleek feline body now, something like Guenhwyvar running flat out, legs extended front and back. More important to Drizzt, though, there was a rune inscribed on the side of that feline, the twin mountains, symbol of Dumathoin, the dwarven god, Catti-brie's god, the Keeper of Secrets Under the Mountain.

Drizzt picked up Khazid'hea, and felt no enmity or any of the desire the sword had previously shown him. Catti-brie was beside him, then, smiling in regard to his obvious approval of her choice for a pommel.

Drizzt handed Khazid'hea back to its rightful owner.

14
THE WRATH OF LOLTH

Baenre felt strong again. Lolth was back, and Lolth was with her, and K'yorl Odran, that wretched K'yorl, had badly erred. Always before, the Spider Queen had kept House Oblodra in her favor, even though the so-called "priestesses" of the House were not pious and sometimes openly expressed their disdain for Lolth. These strange powers of the Oblodrans, this psionic strength, had intrigued Lolth as much as it had frightened the other Houses in Menzoberranzan. None of those Houses wanted a war against K'yorl and her clan, and Lolth hadn't demanded one. If Menzoberranzan was ever attacked from the outside, particularly from the illithids, whose cavern lair was not so far away, K'yorl and the Oblodrans would be of great help.

But no more. K'yorl had crossed over a very dangerous line. She had murdered a matron mother, and while that in itself was not uncommon, she had intended to usurp power from Lolth's priestesses, and not in the name of the Spider Queen.

Matron Baenre knew all of this, felt the will and strength of Lolth within her. "The Time of Troubles has passed," she announced to her family, to everyone gathered in her house, in the nearly repaired chapel.

Mez'Barris Armgo was there as well, in a seat of honor on the central dais, at Matron Baenre's personal invitation.

Matron Baenre took the seat next to the matron mother of the Second House as the gathered crowd exploded in cheers, and led by Triel, in song to the Spider Queen.

Ended? Mez'Barris asked of Baenre, using the silent hand code, for they could not have been heard above the roar of two thousand Baenre soldiers.

The Time of Troubles has ended, Baenre's delicate fingers responded.

Except for House Oblodra, Mez'Barris reasoned, to which Baenre only chuckled wickedly. It was no secret in Menzoberranzan that House Oblodra was in serious trouble. No secret indeed, for the tanar'ri and other fiends continued to circle the Oblodran compound, plucking kobolds from the ledges along the Clawrift, even attacking with abandon any Oblodran who showed herself.

K'yorl will be forgiven? Mez'Barris asked, popping up her left thumb at the end of the code to indicate a question.

Matron Baenre shook her head once briskly, then pointedly looked away, to Triel, who was leading the gathering in rousing prayers to the Spider Queen.

Mez'Barris tapped a long, curving fingernail against her teeth nervously, wondering how Baenre could be so secure in this decision. Did Baenre plan to go after House Oblodra alone, or did she mean to call Barrison del'Armgo into yet another alliance? Mez'Barris did not doubt that her House and House Baenre could crush House Oblodra, but she wasn't thrilled at the prospect of tangling with K'yorl and those unexplored powers.

Methil, invisible and standing off to the side of the dais, read the visiting matron mother's thoughts easily, and in turn, imparted them to Matron Baenre.

"It is the will of Lolth," Matron Baenre said sharply, turning back to regard Mez'Barris. "K'yorl has denounced the Spider Queen, and thus, she will be punished."

"By the Academy, as is the custom?" Mez'Barris asked, and hoped.

A fiery sparkle erupted behind Matron Baenre's red-glowing eyes. "By me," she answered bluntly, and turned away again, indicating that Mez'Barris would garner no further information.

Mez'Barris was wise enough not to press the point. She slumped back in her chair, trying to sort out this surprising, disturbing information. Matron Baenre had not declared that an alliance of Houses would attack Oblodra; she had declared a personal war. Did she truly believe she could defeat K'yorl? Or were those fiends, even the great tanar'ri, more fully under her control than Mez'Barris had been led to believe? That notion scared the matron mother of Barrison del'Armgo more than a little, for, if it were true, what other "punishments" might the angry and ambitious Matron Baenre hand out?

Mez'Barris sighed deeply and let the thoughts pass. There was little she could do now, sitting in the chapel of House Baenre, surrounded by two thousand Baenre soldiers. She had to trust in Baenre, she knew.

No, she silently corrected herself, not trust, never that. Mez'Barris had

to hope Matron Baenre would think she was more valuable to the cause—whatever it might now be—alive than dead.

⚔ ⚔ ⚔ ⚔ ⚔

Seated atop a blue-glowing driftdisk, Matron Baenre herself led the procession from House Baenre, down from the Qu'ellarz'orl and across the city, her army singing Lolth's praises every step. The Baenre lizard riders, Berg'inyon in command, flanked the main body, sweeping in and around the other House compounds to ensure that no surprises would block the trail.

It was a necessary precaution whenever the first matron mother went out, but Matron Baenre did not fear any ambush, not now. With the exception of Mez'Barris Armgo, no others had been told of the Baenre march, and certainly the lesser Houses, either alone or in unison, would not dare to strike at the First House unless the attack had been perfectly coordinated.

From the opposite end of the great cavern came another procession, also led by a Baenre. Triel, Gromph, and the other mistresses and masters of the drow Academy came from their structures, leading their students, every one. Normally it was this very force, the powerful Academy, that exacted punishment on an individual House for crimes against Menzoberranzan, but this time Triel had informed her charges that they would come only to watch, to see the glory of Lolth revealed.

By the time the two groups joined the gathering already in place at the Clawrift, their numbers had swelled five times over. Nobles and soldiers from every House in the city turned out to watch the spectacle as soon as they came to understand that House Baenre and House Oblodra would finish this struggle once and for all.

When they arrived before the front gates of House Oblodra, the Baenre soldiers formed a defensive semicircle behind Matron Baenre, shielding her, not from K'yorl and the Odran family, but from the rest of the gathering. There was much whispering, drow hands flashed frantically in heated conversations, and the fiends, understanding that some calamity was about to come, whipped into a frenzy, swooping across the Oblodran compound, even exercising their returned magic with an occasional bolt of blue-white lightning or a fireball.

Matron Baenre let the display continue for several minutes, realizing the terror it caused within the doomed compound. She wanted to savor this moment above all others, wanted to bask in the smell of terror emanating from the compound of that most hated family.

Then it was time to begin—or to finish, actually. Baenre knew what she must do. She had seen it in a vision during the ceremony preceding the war, and despite the doubts of Mez'Barris when she had shared it with her, Baenre held faith in the Spider Queen, held faith that it was Lolth's will that House Oblodra be devoured.

She reached under her robes and produced a piece of sulphur, the same yellow lump the avatar had given her to allow the priestesses to open the gate to the Abyss in the small room at the back of the Qu'ellarz'orl. Baenre thrust her hand skyward, and up into the air she floated. There came a great crackling explosion, a rumble of thunder.

All was suddenly silent, all eyes turned to the specter of Matron Baenre, hovering twenty feet off the cavern floor.

Berg'inyon, responsible for his mother's security, looked to Sos'Umptu, his expression sour. He thought his mother was terribly vulnerable up there.

Sos'Umptu laughed at him. He was not a priestess; he could not understand that Matron Baenre was more protected at that moment than at any other time in her long life.

"K'yorl Odran!" Baenre called, and her voice seemed magnified, like the voice of a giant.

⚔ ⚔ ⚔ ⚔ ⚔

Locked in a room in the highest level of the tallest stalagmite mound within the Oblodran compound, K'yorl Odran heard Baenre's call, heard it clearly. Her hands gripped tight on her throne's carved marble arms. She squeezed her eyes shut, as she ordered herself to concentrate.

Now, above any other time, K'yorl needed her powers, and now, for the first time, she could not access them! Something was terribly wrong, she knew, and though she believed that Lolth must somehow be behind this, she sensed, as many of the Spider Queen's priestesses had sensed when the Time of Troubles had begun, that this trouble was beyond even Lolth.

The problems had begun soon after K'yorl had been chased back to her house by the loosed tanar'ri. She and her daughters had gathered to formulate an attack plan to drive off the fiends. As always with the efficient Oblodran meetings, the group shared its thoughts telepathically, the equivalent of holding several understandable conversations at once.

The defense plan was coming together well—K'yorl grew confident that the tanar'ri would be sent back to their own plane of existence, and when that was accomplished, she and her family could go and properly punish

Matron Baenre and the others. Then something terrible had happened. One of the tanar'ri had thrown forth a blast of lightning, a searing, blinding bolt that sent a crack running along the outer wall of the Oblodran compound. That in itself was not so bad; the compound, like all the Houses of Menzoberranzan, could take a tremendous amount of punishment, but what the blast, what the return of magical powers, signified, was disastrous to the Oblodrans.

At that same moment, the telepathic conversation had abruptly ended, and try as they may, the nobles of the doomed House could not begin it anew.

K'yorl was as intelligent as any drow in Menzoberranzan. Her powers of concentration were unparalleled. She felt the psionic strength within her mind, the powers that allowed her to walk through walls or yank the beating heart from an enemy's chest. They were there, deep in her mind, but she could not bring them forth. She continued to blame herself, her lack of concentration in the face of disaster. She even punched herself on the side of the head, as if that physical jarring would knock out some magical manifestation.

Her efforts were futile. As the Time of Troubles had come to its end, as the tapestry of magic in the Realms had rewoven, many rippling side-effects had occurred. Throughout the Realms, dead magic zones had appeared, areas where no spells would function, or, even worse, where no spells would function as intended. Another of those side-effects involved psionic powers, the magiclike powers of the mind. The strength was still there, as K'yorl sensed, but bringing forth that strength required a different mental route than before.

The illithids, as Methil had informed Matron Baenre, had already discerned that route, and their powers were functioning nearly as completely as before. But they were an entire race of psionicists, and a race possessed of communal intelligence. The illithids had already made the necessary adjustments to accessing their psionic powers, but K'yorl Odran and her once powerful family had not.

So the matron of the Third House sat in the darkness, eyes squeezed tightly shut, concentrating. She heard Baenre's call, knew that if she did not go to Baenre, Baenre would soon come to her.

Given time, K'yorl would have sorted through the mental puzzle. Given a month, perhaps, she would have begun to bring forth her powers once more.

K'yorl didn't have a month; K'yorl didn't have an hour.

⚔ ⚔ ⚔ ⚔ ⚔

Matron Baenre felt the pulsing magic within the lump of sulphur, an inner heat, fast-building in intensity. She was amazed as her hand shifted, as the sulphur implored her to change the angle.

Baenre nodded. She understood then that some force from beyond the Material Plane, some creature of the Abyss, and perhaps even Lolth herself, was guiding the movement. Up went her hand, putting the pulsing lump in line with the top level of the highest tower in the Oblodran compound.

"Who are you?" she asked.

I am Errtu, came a reply in her mind. Baenre knew the name, knew the creature was a balor, the most terrible and powerful of all tanar'ri. Lolth had armed her well!

She felt the pure malice of the connected creature building within the sulphur, felt the energy growing to where she thought the lump would explode, probably bringing Errtu to her side.

That could not happen, of course, though she did not know it.

It was the power of the artifact itself she felt, that seemingly innocuous piece of sulphur, imbued with the magic of Lolth, wielded by the highest priestess of the Spider Queen in all of Menzoberranzan.

Purely on instinct, Baenre flattened her hand, and the sulphur sent forth a line of glowing, crackling yellow light. It struck the wall high on the Oblodran tower, the very wall between K'yorl and Baenre. Lines of light and energy encircled the stalagmite mound, crackling, biting into the stone, stealing the integrity of the place.

The sulphur went quiet again, its bolt of seemingly live energy freed, but Baenre did not lower her hand and did not take her awestruck stare from the tower wall.

Neither did the ten thousand dark elves that stood behind her. Neither did K'yorl Odran, who could suddenly see the yellow lines of destruction as they ate their way through the stone.

All in the city gasped as one as the tower's top exploded into dust and was blown away.

There sat K'yorl, still atop her black marble throne, suddenly in the open, staring down at the tremendous gathering.

Many winged tanar'ri swooped around the vulnerable matron mother, but they did not approach too closely, wisely fearing the wrath of Errtu should they steal even a moment of his fun.

K'yorl, always proud and strong, rose from her throne and walked to the edge of the tower. She surveyed the gathering, and so respectful were many drow, even matron mothers, of her strange powers, that they turned away when they felt her scrutinizing gaze on them, as though she, from on high, was deciding who she would punish for this attack.

Finally K'yorl's gaze settled on Matron Baenre, who did not flinch and did not turn away.

"You dare!" K'yorl roared down, but her voice seemed small.

"*You* dare!" Matron Baenre yelled back, the power of her voice echoing off the walls of the cavern. "You have forsaken the Spider Queen."

"To the Abyss with Lolth, where she rightly belongs!" stubborn K'yorl replied, the last words she ever spoke.

Baenre thrust her hand higher and felt the next manifestation of power, the opening of an interplanar gate. No yellow light came forth, no visible force at all, but K'yorl felt it keenly.

She tried to call out in protest, but could say nothing beyond a whimper and a gurgle as her features suddenly twisted, elongated. She tried to resist, dug her heels in, and concentrated once more on bringing forth her powers.

K'yorl felt her skin being pulled free of her bones, felt her entire form being stretched out of shape, elongated, as the sulphur pulled at her with undeniable strength. Stubbornly she held on through the incredible agony, through the horrible realization of her doom. She opened her mouth, wanting to utter one more damning curse, but all that came out was her tongue, pulled to its length and beyond.

K'yorl felt her entire body stretching down from the tower, reaching for the sulphur and the gate. She should have been dead already.

Matron Baenre held her hand steady, but could not help closing her eyes, as K'yorl's weirdly elongated form suddenly flew from the top of the broken tower, soaring straight for her.

Several drow, Berg'inyon included, screamed, others gasped again, and still others called to the glory of Lolth, as K'yorl, stretched and narrowed so that she resembled a living spear, entered the sulphur, the gate that would take her to the Abyss, to Errtu, Lolth's appointed agent of torture.

Behind K'yorl came the fiends, with a tremendous fanfare, roaring and loosing bolts of lightning against the Oblodran compound, igniting balls of exploding fire and other blinding displays of their power. Compelled by Errtu, they stretched and thinned and flew into the sulphur, and Matron Baenre held on against her terror, transforming it into a sensation of sheer power.

In a few moments, all the fiends, even the greatest tanar'ri, were gone. Matron Baenre felt their presence still, transformed somehow within the sulphur.

Suddenly, it was quiet once more. Many dark elves looked to each other, wondering if the punishment was complete, wondering if House Oblodra would be allowed to survive under a new leader. Nobles from several different Houses flashed signals to each other expressing their concern that Baenre would now put one of her own daughters in command of the Third House, further sealing her ultimate position within the city.

But Baenre had no such thoughts. This was a punishment demanded by Lolth, a complete punishment, as terrible as anything that had ever been exacted on a House in Menzoberranzan. Again heeding the telepathic instructions of Errtu, Matron Baenre hurled the throbbing piece of sulphur into the Clawrift, and when cheers went up around her, the dark elves thinking the ceremony complete, she raised her arms out wide and commanded them all to witness the wrath of Lolth.

They felt the first rumblings within the Clawrift beneath their feet. A few anxious moments passed, too quiet, too hushed.

One of K'yorl's daughters appeared on the open platform atop the broken tower. She ran to the edge, calling, pleading, to Matron Baenre. A moment later, when Baenre gave no response, she happened to glance to the side, to one of the fingerlike chasms of the great Clawrift.

Wide went her eyes, and her scream was as terrified as any drow had ever heard. From the higher vantage point offered by her levitation spell, Matron Baenre followed the gaze and was next to react, throwing her arms high and wide and crying out to her goddess in ecstacy. A moment later, the gathering understood.

A huge black tentacle snaked over the rim of the Clawrift, wriggling its way behind the Oblodran compound. Like a wave, dark elves fell back, stumbling all over each other, as the twenty-foot-thick monstrosity came around the back, along the side, and along the front wall, back toward the chasm.

"Baenre!" pleaded the desperate, doomed Oblodran.

"You have denied Lolth," the first matron mother replied calmly. "Feel her wrath!"

The ground beneath the cavern trembled slightly as the tentacle, the angry hand of Lolth, tightened its grasp on the Oblodran compound. The wall buckled and collapsed as the thing began its steady sweep.

K'yorl's daughter leaped from the tower as it, too, began to crumble. She cleared the tentacle, and was still alive, though broken, on the ground when a group of dark elves got to her. Uthegental Armgo was among that group, and the mighty weapons master pushed aside the others, preventing them from finishing the pitiful creature off. He hoisted the Odran in his powerful arms,

and through bleary eyes, the battered female regarded him, even managed a faint smile, as though she expected he had come out to save her.

Uthegental laughed at her, lifted her above his head and ran forward, heaving her over the side of the tentacle, back into the rolling rubble that had been her house.

The cheers, the screams, were deafening, and so was the rumble as the tentacle swept all that had been House Oblodra, all the structures and all the drow, into the chasm.

15

GREED

The mercenary shook his bald head, as defiant an act as he had ever made against Matron Baenre. At this moment, so soon after the first matron mother's awesome display of power, and given the fact that she was obviously in the Spider Queen's highest favor, Jarlaxle's questioning of her plans seemed even more dangerous.

Triel Baenre sneered at Jarlaxle, and Berg'inyon closed his eyes. Neither of them really wanted to see the useful male beaten to death. Wicked Bladen'Kerst, though, licked her lips anxiously and gripped the five-headed tentacle whip tied on her hip, hoping that her mother would allow her the pleasure.

"I fear it is not the time," Jarlaxle said openly, bluntly.

"Lolth instructs me differently," Baenre replied, and she seemed quite cool and calm, given the defiance of a mere male.

"We cannot be certain that our magic will continue to work as we expect," Jarlaxle reasoned.

Baenre nodded, and the others then realized, to their absolute surprise, that their mother was glad the mercenary was taking a negative role. Jarlaxle's questions were pertinent, and he was, in fact, helping Baenre sort through the details of her proposed new alliance and the march to Mithral Hall.

Triel Baenre eyed her mother suspiciously as all of this sank in. If Matron Baenre had received her instructions directly from the Spider Queen, as she had openly stated, then why would she want, or even tolerate, defiance or questioning at all? Why would Matron Baenre need to have these most basic questions concerning the wisdom of the march answered?

"The magic is secure," Baenre replied.

Jarlaxle conceded the point. Everything he had heard, both within and beyond the drow city, seemed to back that claim. "You will have no trouble forming an alliance after the spectacle of House Oblodra's fall. Matron Mez'Barris Armgo has been supportive all along, and no matron mother would dare even hint that she fears to follow your lead."

"The Clawrift is large enough to hold the rubble of many Houses," Baenre said dryly.

Jarlaxle snickered. "Indeed," he said. "And indeed this is the time for alliance, for whatever purpose that alliance must be formed."

"It is time to march to Mithral Hall," Baenre interrupted, her tone one of finality, "time to rise up from despair and bring higher glories to the Spider Queen."

"We have suffered many losses," Jarlaxle dared to press. "House Oblodra and their kobold slaves were to lead the attack, dying in the dwarven traps set for drow."

"The kobolds will be brought up from their holes in the Clawrift," Baenre assured him.

Jarlaxle didn't disagree, but he knew the tunnels below the rim of the chasm better than anyone, now that all of House Oblodra was dead. Baenre would get some kobolds, several hundred perhaps, but House Oblodra could have provided many thousand.

"The city's hierarchy is in question," the mercenary went on. "The Third House is no more, and the fourth is without its matron mother. Your own family still has not recovered from the renegade's escape and the loss of Dantrag and Vendes."

Baenre suddenly sat forward in her throne. Jarlaxle didn't flinch, but many of the Baenre children did, fearing that their mother understood the truth of the mercenary's last statement, and that Baenre simply would not tolerate any bickering between her surviving children as they sorted out the responsibilities and opportunities left open by the loss of their brother and sister.

Baenre stopped as quickly as she had started, standing before the throne. She let her dangerous gaze linger over each of her gathered children, then dropped it fully over the impertinent mercenary. "Come with me," she commanded.

Jarlaxle stepped aside to let her pass, and obediently and wisely fell into step right behind her. Triel moved to follow, but Baenre spun around, stopping her daughter in her tracks. "Just him," she growled.

A black column centered the throne room, and a crack appeared along its seemingly perfect and unblemished side as Baenre and the mercenary approached. The crack widened as the cunning door slid open, allowing the two to enter the cylindrical chamber within.

Jarlaxle expected Baenre to yell at him, or to talk to him, even threaten him, once the door closed again, separating them from her family. But the matron mother said nothing, just calmly walked over to a hole in the floor. She stepped into the hole, but did not fall, rather floated down to the next lower level, the great Baenre mound's third level, on currents of magical energy. Jarlaxle followed as soon as the way was clear, but still, when he got to the third level, he had to hurry to keep up with the hustling matron mother, gliding through the floor once more, and again, and again, until she came to the dungeons beneath the great mound.

Still she offered not a word of explanation, and Jarlaxle began to wonder if he was to be imprisoned down here. Many drow, even drow nobles, had found that grim fate. It was rumored that several had been kept as Baenre prisoners for more than a century, endlessly tortured, then healed by the priestesses, that they might be tortured again.

A wave of Baenre's hand sent the two guards standing beside one cell door scrambling for cover.

Jarlaxle was as relieved as curious when he walked into the cell behind Baenre to find a curious, barrel-chested dwarf chained to the far wall. The mercenary looked back to Baenre, and only then did he realize she was not wearing one of her customary necklaces, the one fashioned of a dwarf's tooth.

"A recent catch?" Jarlaxle asked, though he suspected differently.

"Two thousand years," Baenre replied. "I give to you Gandalug Battlehammer, patron of Clan Battlehammer, founder of Mithral Hall."

Jarlaxle rocked back on his heels. He had heard the rumors, of course, that Baenre's tooth pendant contained the soul of an ancient dwarf king, but never had he suspected such a connection. He realized then, suddenly, that this entire foray to Mithral Hall was not about Drizzt Do'Urden, that the renegade was merely a connection, an excuse, for something Baenre had desired for a very long time.

Jarlaxle looked at Baenre suddenly, curiously. "Two thousand years?" he echoed aloud, while he silently wondered just how old this withered drow really was.

"I have kept his soul through the centuries," Baenre went on, eyeing the old dwarf directly. "During the time Lolth could not hear our call, the item was destroyed and Gandalug came forth, alive again." She walked over, put

her snarling visage right up to the battered, naked dwarf's long, pointed nose, and put one hand on his round, solid shoulder. "Alive, but no more free than he was before."

Gandalug cleared his throat as if he meant to spit on Baenre. He stopped, though, when he realized that a spider had crawled out of the ring on her hand, onto his shoulder, and was now making its way along his neck.

Gandalug understood that Baenre would not kill him, that she needed him for her proposed conquest. He did not fear death, but would have preferred it to this torment and weighed against the realization that he might unwittingly aid in the fall of his own people. Baenre's gruesome mind flayer had already scoured Gandalug's thoughts more than once, taking information that no beatings could ever have extracted from the stubborn old dwarf.

Rationally, Gandalug had nothing to fear, but that did little to comfort him now. Gandalug hated spiders above all else, hated and feared them. As soon as he felt the hairy, crawly thing on his neck, he froze, eyes unblinking, sweat beading on his forehead.

Baenre walked away, leaving her pet spider on the dwarf's neck. She turned to Jarlaxle again, a supreme look on her face, as though Gandalug's presence should make all the difference in the world to the doubting mercenary.

It didn't. Jarlaxle never once doubted that Menzoberranzan could defeat Mithral Hall, never once doubted that the conquest would be successful. But what of the aftermath of that conquest? The drow city was in turmoil. There would soon be a fierce struggle, perhaps even an open war, to fill the vacancy left by both House Oblodra's demise and the death of Ghenni'tiroth Tlabbar. Living for centuries on the edge of disaster with his secretive band, the mercenary understood the perils of overextending his grab for power, understood that if one stretched his forces too far, they could simply collapse.

But Jarlaxle knew, too, that he would not convince Matron Baenre. So be it, he decided. Let Baenre march to Mithral Hall with no further questions from him. He would even encourage her. If things went as she planned, then all would be the better for it.

If not . . .

Jarlaxle didn't bother to entertain those possibilities. He knew where Gromph stood, knew the wizard's frustration and the frustrations of Bregan D'aerthe, a band almost exclusively male. Let Baenre go to Mithral Hall, and if she failed, then Jarlaxle would take Baenre's own advice and "rise up from despair."

Indeed.

16

OPEN HEARTS

Drizzt found her on the same east-facing plateau where she had practiced all those tendays, the very spot where she had at last gained control of her strong-willed sword. Long shadows rolled out from the mountains, the sun low in the sky behind them. The first stars shone clearly, twinkling above Silverymoon, and Sundabar to the east beyond that.

Catti-brie sat unmoving, legs bent and knees pulled in tightly to her chest. If she heard the approach of the almost silent drow, she gave no indication, just rocked gently back and forth, staring into the deepening gloom.

"The night is beautiful," Drizzt said, and when Catti-brie did not jump at the sound of his voice, he realized she had recognized his approach. "But the wind is chill."

"The winter's coming in full," Catti-brie replied softly, not taking her gaze from the darkened eastern sky.

Drizzt sought a reply, wanted to keep talking. He felt awkward here, strangely so, for never in the years he had known Catti-brie had there been such tension between them. The drow walked over and crouched beside Catti-brie, but did not look at her, as she did not look at him.

"I'll call Guenhwyvar this night," Drizzt remarked.

Catti-brie nodded.

Her continued silence caught the drow off guard. His calling of the panther, for the first time since the figurine was repaired, was no small thing. Would the figurine's magic work properly, enabling Guenhwyvar to return to his side? Fret had assured him it would, but Drizzt could not be certain,

could not rest easily, until the task was completed and the panther, the healed panther, was back beside him.

It should have been important to Catti-brie as well. She should have cared as much as Drizzt cared, for she and Guenhwyvar were as close as any. Yet she didn't reply, and her silence made Drizzt, anger budding within him, turn to regard her more closely.

He saw tears rimming her blue eyes, tears that washed away Drizzt's anger, that told him that what had happened between himself and Catti-brie had apparently not been so deeply buried. The last time they had met, on this very spot, they had hidden the questions they both wanted to ask behind the energy of a sparring match. Catti-brie's concentration had to be complete on that occasion, and in the days before it, as she fought to master her sword, but now that task was completed. Now, like Drizzt, she had time to think, and in that time, Catti-brie had remembered.

"Ye're knowin' it was the sword?" she asked, almost pleaded.

Drizzt smiled, trying to comfort her. Of course it had been the sentient sword that had inspired her to throw herself at him. Fully the sword, only the sword. But a large part of Drizzt—and possibly of Catti-brie, he thought in looking at her—wished differently. There had been an undeniable tension between them for some time, a complicated situation, and even more so now, after the possession incident with Khazid'hea.

"Ye did right in pushing me away," Catti-brie said, and she snorted and cleared her throat, hiding a sniffle.

Drizzt paused for a long moment, realizing the potential weight of his reply. "I pushed you away only because I saw the pommel," he said, and that drew Catti-brie's attention from the eastern sky, made her look at the drow directly, her deep blue eyes locking with his violet orbs.

"It was the sword," Drizzt said quietly, "only the sword."

Catti-brie didn't blink, barely drew breath. She was thinking how noble this drow had been. So many other men would not have asked questions, would have taken advantage of the situation. And would that have been such a bad thing? the young woman had to ask herself now. Her feelings for Drizzt were deep and real, a bond of friendship and love. Would it have been such a bad thing if he had made love to her in that room?

Yes, she decided, for both of them, because, while it was her body that had been offered, it was Khazid'hea that was in control. Things were awkward enough between them now, but if Drizzt had relented to the feelings that Catti-brie knew he held for her, if he had not been so noble in that strange situation and had given in to the offered temptation, likely neither of them would have been able to look the other in the eye afterward.

Like they were doing now, on a quiet plateau high in the mountains, with a chill and crisp breeze and the stars glowing ever more brightly above them.

"Ye're a good man, Drizzt Do'Urden," the grateful woman said with a heartfelt smile.

"Hardly a man," Drizzt replied, chuckling, and glad for the relief of tension.

Only a temporary relief, though. The chuckle and the smile died away almost immediately, leaving them in the same place, the same awkward moment, caught somewhere between romance and fear.

Catti-brie looked back to the sky, and Drizzt did likewise.

"Ye know I loved him," the young woman said.

"You still do," Drizzt answered, and his smile was genuine when Catti-brie turned back again to regard him.

She turned away almost at once, looked back to the bright stars and thought of Wulfgar.

"You would have married him," Drizzt went on.

Catti-brie wasn't so sure of that. For all the true love she held for Wulfgar, the barbarian carried around the weight of his heritage and a society that valued women not as partners, but as servants. Wulfgar had climbed above many of the narrow-thinking ways of his tribal people, but as his wedding to Catti-brie approached, he had become more protective of her, to the point of being insulting. That, above anything else, proud and capable Catti-brie could not tolerate.

Her doubts were clear on her face, and Drizzt, who knew her better than anyone, read them easily.

"You would have married him," he said again, his firm tone forcing Catti-brie to look back to him.

"Wulfgar was no fool," Drizzt went on.

"Don't ye be blamin' it all on Entreri and the halfling's gem," Catti-brie warned. After the threat of the drow hunting party had been turned away, after Wulfgar's demise, Drizzt had explained to her, and to Bruenor, who perhaps more than anyone else needed to hear the justification, that Entreri, posing as Regis, had used the hypnotic powers of the ruby pendant on Wulfgar. Yet that theory could not fully explain the barbarian's outrageous behavior, because Wulfgar had started down that path long before Entreri had even arrived at Mithral Hall.

"Surely the gem pushed Wulfgar further," Drizzt countered.

"Pushed him where he wanted to go."

"No." The simple reply, spoken with absolute surety, almost caught Catti-brie off guard. She cocked her head to the side, her thick auburn hair cascading over one shoulder, waiting for the drow to elaborate.

"He was scared," Drizzt went on. "Nothing in the world frightened mighty Wulfgar more than the thought of losing his Catti-brie."

"*His* Catti-brie?" she echoed.

Drizzt laughed at her oversensitivity. "His Catti-brie, as he was your Wulfgar," he said, and Catti-brie's smirk fell away as fully as her trap of words.

"He loved you," Drizzt went on, "with all his heart." He paused, but Catti-brie had nothing to say, just sat very still, very quiet, hearing his every word. "He loved you, and that love made him feel vulnerable, and frightened him. Nothing anyone could do to Wulfgar, not torture, not battle, not even death, frightened him, but the slightest scratch on Catti-brie would burn like a hot dagger in his heart.

"So he acted the part of the fool for a short while before you were to be wed," Drizzt said. "The very next time you saw battle, your own strength and independence would have held a mirror up to Wulfgar, would have shown him his error. Unlike so many of his proud people, unlike Berkthgar, Wulfgar admitted his mistakes and never made them again."

As she listened to the words of her wise friend, Catti-brie remembered exactly that incident, the battle in which Wulfgar had been killed. Those very fears for Catti-brie had played a large part in the barbarian's death, but before he was taken from her, he had looked into her eyes and had indeed realized what his foolishness had cost him, had cost them both.

Catti-brie had to believe that now, recalling the scene in light of the drow's words. She had to believe that her love for Wulfgar had been real, very real, and not misplaced, that he was all she had thought him to be.

Now she could. For the first time since Wulfgar's death, Catti-brie could remember him without the pangs of guilt, without the fears that, had he lived, she would not have married him. Because Drizzt was right; Wulfgar would have admitted the error despite his pride, and he would have grown, as he always had before. That was the finest quality of the man, an almost childlike quality, that viewed the world and his own life as getting better, as moving toward a better way in a better place.

What followed was the most sincere smile on Catti-brie's face in many, many months. She felt suddenly free, suddenly complete with her past, reconciled and able to move forward with her life.

She looked at the drow, wide-eyed, with a curiosity that seemed to surprise

Drizzt. She could go on, but exactly what did that mean?

Slowly, Catti-brie began shaking her head, and Drizzt came to understand that the movement had something to do with him. He lifted a slender hand and brushed some stray hair back from her cheek, his ebony skin contrasting starkly with her light skin, even in the quiet light of night.

"I do love you," the drow admitted. The blunt statement did not catch Catti-brie by surprise, not at all. "As you love me," Drizzt went on, easily, confident that his words were on the mark. "And I, too, must look ahead now, must find my place among my friends, beside you, without Wulfgar."

"Perhaps in the future," Catti-brie said, her voice barely a whisper.

"Perhaps," Drizzt agreed. "But for now . . ."

"Friends," Catti-brie finished.

Drizzt moved his hand back from her cheek, held it in the air before her face, and she reached up and clasped it firmly.

Friends.

The moment lingered, the two staring, not talking, and it would have gone on much, much longer, except that there came a commotion from the trail behind them, and the sound of voices they both recognized.

"Stupid elf couldn't do this inside!" blustered Bruenor.

"The stars are more fitting for Guenhwyvar," huffed Regis breathlessly. Together they crashed through a bush not far behind the plateau and stumbled and skidded down to join their two friends.

"Stupid elf?" Catti-brie asked her father.

"Bah!" Bruenor snorted. "I'm not for saying . . ."

"Well, actually," Regis began to correct, but changed his mind when Bruenor turned his scarred visage the halfling's way and growled at him.

"So ye're right and I said stupid elf!" Bruenor admitted, speaking mostly to Drizzt, as close to an apology as he ever gave. "But I've got me work to do." He looked back up the trail, in the direction of Mithral Hall's eastern door. "Inside!" he finished.

Drizzt took out the onyx figurine and placed it on the ground, purposely right before the dwarf's heavy boots. "When Guenhwyvar is returned to us, I will explain how inconvenienced you were to come and witness her return," Drizzt said with a smirk.

"Stupid elf," Bruenor muttered under his breath, and he fully expected that Drizzt would have the cat sleep on him again, or something worse.

Catti-brie and Regis laughed, but their mirth was strained and nervous, as Drizzt called quietly for the panther. The pain they would have to bear if the magic of the figurine had not healed, if Guenhwyvar did not return to them,

would be no less to the companions than the pain of losing Wulfgar.

They all knew it, even surly, blustery Bruenor, who to his grave would deny his affection for the magical panther. Silence grew around the figurine as the gray smoke came forth, swirled, and solidified.

Guenhwyvar seemed almost confused as she regarded the four companions standing around her, none of them daring to breathe.

Drizzt's grin was the first and the widest, as he saw that his trusted companion was whole again and healed, the black fur glistening in the starlight, the sleek muscles taut and strong.

He had brought Bruenor and Regis out to witness this moment. It was fitting that all four of them stood by when Guenhwyvar returned.

More fitting would it have been had the sixth companion, Wulfgar, son of Beornegar, joined them on that plateau, in the quiet night, under the stars, in the last hours of Mithral Hall's peace.

PART FOUR

THE DROW MARCH

I noticed something truly amazing, and truly heartwarming, as we, all the defenders of Mithral Hall and the immediate region, neared the end of preparations, neared the time when the drow would come.

I am drow. My skin proves that I am different. The ebony hue shows my heritage clearly and undeniably. And yet, not a glare was aimed my way, not a look of consternation from the Harpells and the Longriders, not an angry word from volatile Berkthgar and his warrior people. And no dwarf, not even General Dagna, who did not like anyone who was not a dwarf, pointed an accusing finger at me.

We did not know why the drow had come, be it for me or for the promise of treasure from the rich dwarven complex. Whatever the cause, to the defenders, I was without blame. How wonderful that felt to me, who had worn the burden of self-imposed guilt for many months, guilt for the previous raid, guilt for Wulfgar, guilt that Catti-brie had been forced by friendship to chase me all the way to Menzoberranzan.

I had worn this heavy collar, and yet those around me who had as much to lose as I placed no burden on me.

You cannot understand how special that realization was to one of my past. It was a gesture of sincere friendship, and what made it all the more important is that it was an unintentional gesture, offered without thought or purpose. Too often in the past, my "friends" would make such gestures as if to prove something, more to themselves than to me. They could feel better about themselves because they could look beyond the obvious differences, such as the color of my skin.

Guenhwyvar never did that. Bruenor never did that. Neither did Catti-brie or Regis. Wulfgar at first despised me, openly and without excuse, simply because I was drow. They were honest, and thus, they were always my friends. But in the days of preparation for war, I saw that sphere of friendship expand many times over. I came to know that the dwarves of Mithral Hall, the men and women of Settlestone, and many, many more, truly accepted me.

That is the honest nature of friendship. That is when it becomes sincere, and not self-serving. So in those days, Drizzt Do'Urden came to understand, once and for all, that he was not of Menzoberranzan.

I threw off the collar of guilt. I smiled.

—Drizzt Do'Urden

BLINGÐENSTONE

They were shadows among the shadows, flickering movements that disappeared before the eye could take them in. And there was no sound. Though three hundred dark elves moved in formation, right flank, left flank, center, there was no sound.

They had come to the west of Menzoberranzan, seeking the easier and wider tunnels that would swing them back toward the east and all the way to the surface, to Mithral Hall. Blingdenstone, the city of svirfnebli, whom the drow hated above all others, was not so far away, another benefit of this roundabout course.

Uthegental Armgo paused in one small, sheltered cubby. The tunnels were wide—uncomfortably so. Svirfnebli were tacticians and builders, and in a fight they would depend on formations, perhaps even on war machines, to compete with the more stealthy and individual-minded drow. The widening of these particular tunnels was no accident, Uthegental knew, and no result of nature. This battlefield had long ago been prepared by his enemies.

So where were they? Uthegental had come into their domain with three hundred drow, his group leading an army of eight thousand dark elves and thousands of humanoid slaves. And yet, though Blingdenstone itself could not be more than a twenty minute march from his position—and his scouts were even closer than that—there had been no sign of svirfnebli.

The wild patron of Barrison del'Armgo was not happy. Uthegental liked things predictable, at least as far as enemies were concerned, and had hoped that he and his warriors would have seen some action against the gnomes by now. It was no accident that his group, that he, was at the forefront of the drow

army. That had been a concession by Baenre to Mez'Barris, an affirmation of the importance of the Second House. But with that concession came responsibility, which Matron Mez'Barris had promptly dropped on Uthegental's sturdy shoulders. House Barrison del'Armgo needed to come out of this war with high glory, particularly in light of Matron Baenre's incredible display in the destruction of House Oblodra. When this business with Mithral Hall was settled, the rearrangement of the pecking order in Menzoberranzan would likely begin. Interhouse wars seemed unavoidable, with the biggest holes to be filled those ranks directly behind Barrison del'Armgo.

Thus had Matron Mez'Barris promised full fealty to Baenre, in exchange for being personally excused from the expedition. She remained in Menzoberranzan, solidifying her House's position and working closely with Triel Baenre in forming a web of lies and allies to insulate House Baenre from further accusations. Baenre had agreed with Mez'Barris's offer, knowing that she, too, would be vulnerable if all did not go well in Mithral Hall.

With the matron mother of his House back in Menzoberranzan, the glory of House Barrison del'Armgo was Uthegental's to find. The fierce warrior was glad for the task, but he was edgy as well, filled with nervous energy, wanting a battle, any battle, that he might whet his appetite for what was to come, and might wet the end of his wicked trident with the blood of an enemy.

But where were the ugly little svirfnebli? he wondered. The marching plan called for no attack on Blingdenstone proper—not on the initial journey, at least. If there was to be an assault on the gnome city, it would come on the return from Mithral Hall, after the main objective had been realized. Uthegental had been given permission to test svirfneblin defenses, though, and to skirmish with any gnomes he and his warriors found out in the open tunnels.

Uthegental craved that, and had already determined that if he found and tested the gnome defenses and discovered sufficient holes in them, he would take the extra step, hoping to return to Baenre's side with the head of the svirfneblin king on the end of his trident.

All glory for Barrison del'Armgo.

One of the scouts slipped back past the guards, moved right up to the fierce warrior. Her fingers flashed in the silent drow code, explaining to her leader that she had gone closer, much closer, had even seen the stairway that led up to the level of Blingdenstone's massive front gates. But no sign had she seen of the svirfnebli.

It had to be an ambush. Every instinct within the seasoned weapons master told Uthegental that the svirfnebli were lying in wait, in full force. Almost any other dark elf, a race known for caution when dealing with others—mostly because the drow knew they could always win such encounters if they struck at the appropriate time—would have relented. In truth, Uthegental's mission, a scouting expedition, was now complete, and he could return to Matron Baenre with a full report that she would be pleased to hear.

But fierce Uthegental was not like other drow. He was less than relieved, was, in fact boiling with rage.

Take me there, his fingers flashed, to the surprise of the female scout.

You are too valuable, the female's hands replied.

"All of us!" Uthegental roared aloud, his volume surprising every one of the many dark elves around him. But Uthegental wasn't startled, and did not relent. "Send the word along every column," he went on, "to follow my lead to the very gates of Blingdenstone!"

More than a few drow soldiers turned nervous looks to each other. They numbered three hundred, a formidable force, but Blingdenstone held many times that number, and svirfnebli, full of tricks with the stone and often allied with powerful monsters from the Plane of Earth, were not easy foes. Still, not one of the dark elves would argue with Uthegental Armgo, especially since he alone knew what Matron Baenre expected of this point group.

And so they arrived in full, at the stairway and up it they climbed, to the very gates of Blingdenstone—gates that a drow engineer found devilishly trapped, with the entire ceiling above them rigged to fall if they were opened. Uthegental called to a priestess that had been assigned to his group.

You can get one of us past the barrier? his fingers asked her, to which she nodded.

Uthegental's stream of surprises continued when he indicated he would personally enter the svirfneblin city. It was an unheard-of request. No drow leader ever went in first. That's what commoners were for.

But again, who would argue with Uthegental? In truth, the priestess really didn't care if this arrogant male got torn apart. She began her casting at once, a spell that would make Uthegental as insubstantial as a wraith, would make his form melt away into something that could slip through the slightest cracks. When it was done, the brave Uthegental left without hesitation, without bothering to leave instructions in the event that he did not return.

Proud and supremely confident, Uthegental simply did not think that way.

A few minutes later, after passing through the empty guard chambers, crisscrossed with cunningly built trenches and fortifications, Uthegental became only the second drow, after Drizzt Do'Urden, to glance at the

rounded, natural houses of the svirfnebli and the winding, unremarkable ways that composed their city. How different Blingdenstone was from Menzoberranzan, built in accord with what the gnomes had found in the natural caverns, rather than sculpted and reformed into an image that a dark elf would consider more pleasing.

Uthegental, who demanded control of everything around him, found the place repulsive. He also found it, this most ancient and hallowed of svirfneblin cities, deserted.

Belwar Dissengulp stared out from the lip of the deep chamber, far to the west of Blingdenstone, and wondered if he had done right in convincing King Schnicktick to abandon the gnomish city. The most honored burrow warden had reasoned that, with magic returned, the drow would surely march for Mithral Hall, and that course, Belwar knew, would take them dangerously close to Blingdenstone.

Though he had little difficulty in convincing his fellows that the dark elves would march, the thought of leaving Blingdenstone, of simply packing up their belongings and deserting their ancient home, had not settled well. For more than two thousand years the gnomes had lived in the ominous shadow of Menzoberranzan, and more than once had they believed the drow would come in full war against them.

This time was different, Belwar reasoned, and he had told them so, his speech full of passion and carrying the weight of his relationship with the renegade drow from that terrible city. Still, Belwar was far from convincing Schnicktick and the others until Councilor Firble piped in on the burrow warden's side.

It was indeed different this time, Firble had told them with all sincerity. This time, the whole of Menzoberranzan would band together, and any attack would not be the ambitious probing of a single House. This time the gnomes, and anyone else unfortunate enough to fall in the path of the drow march, could not depend on interhouse rivalries to save them. Firble had learned of House Oblodra's fall from Jarlaxle. An earth elemental sent secretly under Menzoberranzan and into the Clawrift by svirfneblin priests confirmed it and the utter destruction of the Third House. Thus, when, at their last meeting, Jarlaxle hinted "it would not be wise to harbor Drizzt Do'Urden," Firble, with his understanding of drow ways, reasoned that the dark elves would indeed march for Mithral Hall, in a force unified by the fear of the one who had so utterly crushed the Third House.

And so, on that ominous note, the svirfnebli had left Blingdenstone, and Belwar had played a critical role in the departure. That responsibility weighed heavily on the burrow warden now, made him second-guess the reasoning that had seemed so sound when he had thought danger imminent. Here to the west the tunnels were quiet, and not eerily so, as though enemy dark elves were slipping from shadow to shadow. The tunnels were quiet with peace; the war Belwar had anticipated seemed a thousand miles or a thousand years away.

The other gnomes felt it, too, and Belwar had overheard more than one complaining that the decision to leave Blingdenstone had been, at best, foolish.

Only when the last of the svirfnebli had left the city, when the long caravan had begun its march to the west, had Belwar realized the gravity of the departure, realized the emotional burden. In leaving, the gnomes were admitting to themselves that they were no match for the drow, that they could not protect themselves or their homes from the dark elves. More than a few svirfnebli, Belwar perhaps most among them, were sick about that fact. Their illusions of security, of the strength of their shamans, of their very god figure, had been shaken, without a single drop of spilled svirfneblin blood.

Belwar felt like a coward.

The most honored burrow warden took some comfort in the fact that eyes were still in place in Blingdenstone. A friendly elemental, blended with the stone, had been ordered to wait and watch, and to report back to the svirfneblin shamans who had summoned it. If the dark elves did come in, as Belwar expected, the gnomes would know of it.

But what if they didn't come? Belwar wondered. If he and Firble were wrong and the march did not come, then what loss had the svirfnebli suffered for the sake of caution?

Could any of them ever feel secure in Blingdenstone again?

⚔ ⚔ ⚔ ⚔ ⚔

Matron Baenre was not pleased at Uthegental's report that the gnomish city was deserted. As sour as her expression was, though, it could not match the open wrath showing on the face of Berg'inyon, at her side. His eyes narrowed dangerously as he considered the powerful patron of the Second House, and Uthegental, seeing a challenge, more than matched that ominous stare.

Baenre understood the source of Berg'inyon's anger, and she, too, was not pleased by the fact that Uthegental had taken it upon himself to enter

Blingdenstone. That act reflected clearly the desperation of Mez'Barris. Obviously Mez'Barris felt vulnerable in the shadows of Matron Baenre's display against Oblodra, and thus she had placed a great weight upon Uthegental's broad shoulders.

Uthegental marched for the glory of Barrison del'Armgo, Matron Baenre knew, marched fanatically, along with his force of more than three hundred drow warriors.

To Berg'inyon, that was not a good thing, for he, and not Matron Baenre, was in direct competition with the powerful weapons master.

Matron Baenre considered all the news in light of her son's expression, and in the end, she thought Uthegental's daring a good thing. The competition would push Berg'inyon to excellence. And if he failed, if Uthegental was the one who killed Drizzt Do'Urden—for that was obviously the prize both sought—even if Berg'inyon was killed by Uthegental, then so be it. This march was greater than House Baenre, greater than anyone's personal goals—except, of course, for Matron Baenre's own.

When Mithral Hall was conquered, whatever the cost to her son, she would be in the highest glory of the Spider Queen, and her House would be above the schemes of the others, if all the others combined their forces against her!

"You are dismissed," Baenre said to Uthegental. "Back to the forefront."

The spike-haired weapons master smiled wickedly and bowed, never taking his eyes from Berg'inyon. Then he spun on his heel to leave, but spun again immediately as Baenre addressed him once more.

"And if you chance to come upon the tracks of the fleeing svirfnebli," Baenre said, and she paused, looking from Uthegental to Berg'inyon, "do send an emissary to inform me of the chase."

Berg'inyon's shoulders slumped even as Uthegental's grin, showing those filed, pointy teeth, widened so much that it nearly took in his ears. He bowed again and ran off.

"The svirfnebli are mighty foes," Baenre said offhandedly, aiming the remark at Berg'inyon. "They will kill him and all of his party." She didn't really believe the claim, had made it only for Berg'inyon's sake. In looking at her wise son, though, she realized he didn't believe it either.

"And if not," Baenre said, looking the other way, to Quenthel, who stood by impassively, appearing quite bored, and to Methil, who always seemed quite bored, "the gnomes are not so great a prize." The matron mother's gaze snapped back over Berg'inyon. "We know the prize of this march," she said, her voice a feral snarl. She didn't bother to mention that her ultimate goal and Berg'inyon's goal were not the same.

The effect on the young weapons master was instantaneous. He snapped back to rigid attention, and rode off on his lizard as soon as his mother waved her hand to dismiss him.

Baenre turned to Quenthel. *See that spies are put among Uthegental's soldiers,* her fingers subtly flashed. Baenre paused a moment to consider the fierce weapons master, and to reflect on what he would do if such spies were discovered. *Males,* Baenre added to her daughter, and Quenthel agreed.

Males were expendable.

Sitting alone as her driftdisk floated amidst the army, Matron Baenre turned her thoughts to more important issues. The rivalry of Berg'inyon and Uthegental was of little consequence, as was Uthegental's apparent disregard for proper command. More disturbing was the svirfneblin absence. Might the wicked gnomes be planning an assault on Menzoberranzan even as Baenre and her force marched away?

It was a silly thought, one Matron Baenre quickly dismissed. More than half the dark elves remained in Menzoberranzan, under the watchful eyes of Mez'Barris Armgo, Triel, and Gromph. If the gnomes attacked, they would be utterly destroyed, more to the Spider Queen's glory.

But even as she considered those city defenses, the thought of a conspiracy against her nagged at the edges of Baenre's consciousness.

Triel is loyal and in control, came a telepathic assurance from Methil, who remained not so far away and was reading Baenre's every thought.

Baenre took some comfort in that. Before she had left Menzoberranzan, she had bade Methil to scour her daughter's reactions to her plans, and the illithid had come back with a completely positive report. Triel was not pleased by the decision to go to Mithral Hall. She feared her mother might be overstepping her bounds, but she was convinced, as most likely were all the others, that, in the face of the destruction of House Oblodra, Lolth had sanctioned this war. Thus, Triel would not head a coup for control of House Baenre in her mother's absence, would not, in any way, go against her mother at this time.

Baenre relaxed. All was going according to design, and it was not important that the cowardly gnomes had fled.

All was going even better than design, Baenre decided, for the rivalry between Uthegental and Berg'inyon would provide much entertainment. The possibilities were intriguing. Perhaps if Uthegental killed Drizzt, and killed Berg'inyon in the process, Matron Baenre would force the spike-haired savage into House Baenre to serve as her own weapons master. Mez'Barris would not dare protest, not after Mithral Hall was conquered.

18
Uneasy Gatherings

Even now is Regweld, who shall lead us, meeting with Bruenor, who is king," said a rider, a knight wearing the most unusual of armor. There wasn't a smooth spot on the mail; it was ridged and buckled, with grillwork pointing out at various angles, its purpose to turn aside any blows, to deflect rather than absorb.

The man's fifty comrades—a strange-looking group indeed—were similarly outfitted, which could be readily explained by looking at their unusual pennant. It depicted a stick-man, his hair straight up on end and arms held high, standing atop a house and throwing lightning bolts to the sky—or perhaps he was catching lightning hurled down at him from the clouds—one could not be sure. This was the banner of Longsaddle and these were the Longriders, the soldiers of Longsaddle, a capable, if eccentric, group. They had come into Settlestone this cold and gloomy day, chasing the first flakes of the first snow.

"Regweld shall lead *you*," answered another rider, tall and sure on his saddle, carrying the scars of countless battles. He was more conventionally armored, as were his forty companions, riding under the horse-and-spear banner of Nesmé, the proud frontier town on the edge of the dreaded Trollmoors. "But not *us*. We are the Riders of Nesmé, who follow no lead but our own!"

"Just because you got here first doesn't mean you pick the rules!" whined the Longrider.

"Let us not forget our purpose," intervened a third rider, his horse trotting up, along with two companions, to greet the newest arrivals. When he came closer, the others saw from his angular features, shining golden hair, and similarly colored eyes that he was no man at all, but an elf, though tall for one of his race. "I am Besnell of Silverymoon, come with a hundred soldiers from Lady Alustriel. We shall each find our place when battle is joined, though if there is to be any leader among us, it shall be me, who speaks on behalf of Alustriel."

The man from Nesmé and the man from Longsaddle regarded each other helplessly. Their respective towns, particularly Nesmé, were surely under the shadow of Silverymoon, and their respective rulers would not challenge Alustriel's authority.

"But you are not in Silverymoon," came a roaring reply from Berkthgar, who had been standing in the shadows of a nearby doorway, listening to the argument, almost hoping it would erupt into something more fun than bandied words. "You are in Settlestone, where Berkthgar rules, and in Settlestone, you are ruled by Berkthgar!"

Everyone tensed, particularly the two Silverymoon soldiers flanking Besnell. The elven warrior sat quietly for a moment, eyeing the huge barbarian as Berkthgar, his gigantic sword strapped across his back, steadily and calmly approached. Besnell was not overly proud, and his rank alone in the Silverymoon detachment proved that he never let pride cloud good judgment.

"Well spoken, Berkthgar the Bold," he politely replied. "And true enough." He turned to the other two mounted leaders. "We have come from Silverymoon, and you from Nesmé, and you from Longsaddle, to serve in Berkthgar's cause, and in the cause of Bruenor Battlehammer."

"We came to Bruenor's call," grumbled the Longrider, "not Berkthgar's."

"Would you then take your horse into the dark tunnels beneath Mithral Hall?" reasoned Besnell, who understood from his meetings with Berkthgar and Catti-brie that the dwarves would handle the underground troubles, while the riders would join with the warriors of Settlestone to secure the outlying areas.

"His horse and he might be underground sooner than he expects," Berkthgar piped in, an open threat that shook the Longrider more than a little.

"Enough of this," Besnell was quick to interject. "We have all come together as allies, and allies we shall be, joined in a common cause."

"Joined by fear," the Nesmé soldier replied. "We in Nesmé once met Bruenor's . . ." He paused, looking to the faces of the other leaders, then to his own grim men for support, as he searched for the proper words. "We have met King Bruenor's dark-skinned friend," he said finally, his tone openly derisive. "What good might come from association with evil drow?"

The words had barely left his mouth before Berkthgar was upon him, reaching up to grab him by a crease in his armor and pull him low in the saddle, that he might look right into the barbarian's snarling visage. The nearby Nesmé soldiers had their weapons out and ready, but so, too, did Berkthgar's people, coming out of every stone house and around every corner.

Besnell groaned and the Longriders, every one, shook their heads in dismay.

"If ever again you speak ill of Drizzt Do'Urden," Berkthgar growled, caring nothing of the swords and spears poised not so far away, "you will offer me an interesting choice. Do I cut you in half and leave you dead on the field, or do I bring you in to Drizzt, that he might find the honor of severing your head himself?"

Besnell walked his horse right up to the barbarian and used its heavy press to force Berkthgar back from the stunned Nesmé soldier.

"Drizzt Do'Urden would not kill the man for his words," Besnell said with all confidence, for he had met Drizzt on many occasions during the dark elf's frequent visits to Silverymoon.

Berkthgar knew the elf spoke truly, and so the barbarian leader relented, backing off a few steps.

"Bruenor would kill him," Berkthgar did say, though.

"Agreed," said Besnell. "And many others would take up arms in the dark elf's defense. but as I have said, enough of this. All joined, we are a hundred and ninety calvary, come to aid in the cause." He looked all around as he spoke and seemed taller and more imposing than his elven frame would normally allow. "A hundred and ninety come to join with Berkthgar and his proud warriors. Rarely have four such groups converged as allies. The Longriders, the Riders of Nesmé, the Knights in Silver, and the warriors of Settlestone, all joined in common cause. If the war does come—and looking at the allies I have discovered this day, I hope it does—our deeds shall be echoed throughout the Realms! And let the drow army beware!"

He had played perfectly on the pride of all of them, and so they took up the cheer together, and the moments of tension were passed. Besnell smiled and nodded as the shouts continued, but he understood that things were not as solid and friendly as they should be. Longsaddle had sent fifty soldiers, plus a handful of wizards, a very great sacrifice from the town that, in truth, had little stake in Bruenor's well-being. The Harpells looked more to the west, to Waterdeep, for trade and alliance, than to the east, and yet they had come to Bruenor's call, including their leader's own daughter.

Silverymoon was equally committed, both by friendship to Bruenor and

Drizzt and because Alustriel was wise enough to understand that if the drow army did march to the surface, all the world would be a sadder place. Alustriel had dispatched a hundred knights to Berkthgar, and another hundred rode independently, skirting the eastern foothills below Mithral Hall, covering the more rugged trails that led around Fourthpeak's northern face, to Keeper's Dale in the west. All told, there were two hundred mounted warriors, fully two-fifths of the famed Knights in Silver, a great contingent and a great sacrifice, especially with the first winds of winter blowing cold in the air.

Nesmé's sacrifice was less, Besnell understood, and likely the Riders of Nesmé's commitment would be too. This was the town with the most to lose, except of course for Settlestone, and yet Nesmé had spared barely a tenth of its seasoned garrison. The strained relations between Mithral Hall and Nesmé were no secret, a brewing feud that had begun before Bruenor had ever found his homeland, when the dwarf and his fellow companions had passed near Nesmé. Bruenor and his friends had saved several riders from marauding bog blokes, only to have the riders turn on them when the battle had ended. Because of the color of Drizzt's skin and the reputation of his heritage, Bruenor's party had been turned away, and though the dwarf's outrage had been later tempered somewhat by the fact that soldiers from Nesmé had joined in the retaking of Mithral Hall, relations had remained somewhat strained.

This time the expected opponents were dark elves and no doubt, that fact alone had reminded the wary men of Nesmé of their distrust for Bruenor's closest friend. But at least they had come, and forty were better than none, Besnell told himself. The elf had openly proclaimed Berkthgar the leader of all four groups, and so it would be—though, if and when battle was joined, each contingent would likely fall into its own tactics, hopefully complementing each other—but Besnell saw a role for himself, less obvious, but no less important. He would be the peacemaker. He would keep the factions in line and in harmony.

If the dark elves did come, his job would be much easier, he knew, for in the face of so deadly an enemy, petty grievances would fast be forgotten.

⚔ ⚔ ⚔ ⚔ ⚔

Belwar didn't know whether to feel relief or fear when word came from the spying elemental that the drow, a single drow at least, had indeed gone into Blingdenstone, and that a drow army had marched past the deserted city, finding the tunnels back to the east, the route to Mithral Hall.

The most honored burrow warden sat again in his now customary perch,

staring out at the empty tunnels. He thought of Drizzt, a dear friend, and of the place the dark elf now called home. Drizzt had told Belwar of Mithral Hall when he had passed through Blingdenstone on his way to Menzoberranzan several months earlier. How happy Drizzt had been when he spoke of his friends, this dwarf named Bruenor, and the human woman, Catti-brie, who had crossed through Blingdenstone on Drizzt's heels, and had, according to later reports, aided in Drizzt's wild escape from the drow city.

That very escape had facilitated this march, Belwar knew, and yet the gnome remained pleased that his friend had gotten free of Matron Baenre's clutches. Now Drizzt was home, but the dark elves were going to find him.

Belwar recalled the true sadness in Drizzt's lavender eyes when the drow had recounted the loss of one of his surface-found friends. What tears might Drizzt know soon, the gnome wondered, with a drow army marching to destroy his new home?

"Decisions we have to make," came a voice behind the sturdy gnome. Belwar clapped his mithral "hands" together, more to clear his thoughts than anything else, and turned to face Firble.

One of the good things that had come from all of this confusion was the budding friendship between Firble and Belwar. As two of the older svirf-nebli of Blingdenstone, they had known each other, or of each other, a very long time, but only when Belwar's eyes—because of his friendship with Drizzt—had turned to the world outside the gnomish city had Firble truly come into his life. At first the two seemed a complete mismatch, but both had found strength in what the other offered, and a bond had grown between them—though neither had as yet openly admitted it.

"Decisions?"

"The drow have passed," said Firble.

"Likely to return."

Firble nodded. "Obviously," the round-shouldered councilor agreed. "King Schnicktick must decide whether we are to return to Blingdenstone."

The notion hit Belwar like the slap of a cold, wet towel. Return to Blingdenstone? Of course they were to return to their homes! the most honored burrow warden's thoughts screamed out at him. Any other option was too ridiculous to entertain. But as he calmed and considered Firble's grim demeanor, Belwar began to see the truth of it all. The drow would be back, and if they had made a conquest near or at the surface, a conquest of Mithral Hall, as most believed was their intention, then there would likely remain an open route between Menzoberranzan and that distant place, a route that passed too close to Blingdenstone.

"Words, there are, and from many with influence, that we should go farther west, to find a new cavern, a new Blingdenstone," Firble said. From his tone it was obvious the little councilor was not thrilled at that prospect.

"Never," Belwar said unconvincingly.

"King Schnicktick will ask your opinion in this most important matter," Firble said. "Consider it well, Belwar Dissengulp. The lives of us all may hinge on your answer."

A long, quiet moment passed, and Firble gave a curt nod and turned to leave.

"What does Firble say?" Belwar asked before he could scurry off.

The councilor turned slowly, determinedly, staring Belwar straight in the eye. "Firble says there is only one Blingdenstone," he answered with more grit than Belwar had ever heard, or ever expected to hear, from him. "To leave as the drow pass by is one thing, a good thing. To stay out is not so good."

"Worth fighting for are some things," Belwar added.

"Worth dying for?" Firble was quick to put in, and the councilor did turn and leave.

Belwar sat alone with his thoughts for his home and for his friend.

19

IMPROVISING

Catti-brie knew as soon as she saw the dwarf courier's face, his features a mixture of anxiety and battle-lust. She knew, and so she ran off ahead of the messenger, down the winding ways of Mithral Hall, through the Undercity, seeming almost deserted now, the furnaces burning low. Many eyes regarded her, studied the urgency in her stride, and understood her purpose. She knew, and so they all knew.

The dark elves had come.

The dwarves guarding the heavy door leading out of Mithral Hall proper nodded to her as she came through. "Shoot straight, me girl!" one of them yelled at her back, and though she was terribly afraid, though it seemed as if her worst nightmare was about to come true, that brought a smile to her face.

She found Bruenor, Regis beside him, in a wide cavern, the same chamber where the dwarves had defeated a goblin tribe not so long ago. Now the place had been prepared as the dwarf king's command post, the central brain for the defense of the outer and lower tunnels. Nearly all tunnels leading to this chamber from the wilds of the Underdark had been thoroughly trapped or dropped altogether, or were now heavily guarded, leaving the chamber as secure a place as could be found outside Mithral Hall proper.

"Drizzt?" Catti-brie asked.

Bruenor looked across the cavern, to a large tunnel exiting into the deeper regions. "Out there," he said, "with the cat."

Catti-brie looked around. The preparations had been made; everything had been set into place as well as possible in the time allowed. Not so far away,

Stumpet Rakingclaw and her fellow clerics crouched and knelt on the floor, lining up and sorting dozens of small potion bottles and preparing bandages, blankets, and herbal salves for the wounded. Catti-brie winced, for she knew that all those bandages and more would be needed before this was finished.

To the side of the clerics, three of the Harpells—Harkle, Bidderdoo, and Bella don DelRoy—conferred over a small, round table covered with dozens of maps and other parchments.

Bella looked up and motioned to Bruenor, and the dwarf king rushed to her side.

"Are we to sit and wait?" Catti-brie asked Regis.

"For the time," the halfling answered. "But soon Bruenor and I will lead a group out, along with one of the Harpells, to rendezvous with Drizzt and Pwent in Tunult's Cavern. I'm sure Bruenor means for you to come with us."

"Let him try to stop me," Catti-brie muttered under her breath. She silently considered the rendezvous. Tunult's Cavern was the largest chamber outside Mithral Hall, and if they were going to meet Drizzt there, instead of some out-of-the-way place—and if the dark elves were indeed in the tunnels near Mithral Hall—then the anticipated battle would come soon. Catti-brie took a deep breath and took up Taulmaril, her magical bow. She tested its pull, then checked her quiver to make sure it was full, even though the enchantment of the quiver ensured that it was always full.

We are ready, came a thought in her mind, a thought imparted by Khazid'hea, she knew. Catti-brie took comfort in her newest companion. She trusted the sword now, knew that it and she were of like mind. And they were indeed ready. They all were.

Still, when Bruenor and Bidderdoo walked away from the other Harpells, the dwarf motioning to his personal escorts and Regis and Catti-brie, the young woman's heart skipped a few beats.

✕ ✕ ✕ ✕ ✕

The Gutbuster Brigade rambled and jostled, bouncing off walls and each other. Drow in the tunnels! They had spotted drow in the tunnels, and now they needed a catch or a kill.

To the few dark elves who were indeed so close to Mithral Hall, forward scouts for the wave that would follow, the thunder of Pwent's minions seemed almost deafening. The drow were a quiet race, as quiet as the Under-dark itself, and the bustle of surface-dwelling dwarves made them think that a thousand fierce warriors were giving chase. So the dark elves fell back, stretched their

lines thin, with the more-important females taking the lead in the retreat and the males forced to hold the line and delay the enemy.

First contact was made in a narrow but high tunnel. The Gutbusters came in hard and fast from the east, and three drow, levitating among the stalactites, fired hand-crossbows, putting poison-tipped darts into Pwent and the two others flanking him in the front rank.

"What!" the battlerager roared, as did his companions, surprised by the sudden sting. The ever wary Pwent, cunning and comprehending, looked around, then he and the other two fell to the floor.

With a scream of surprise, the rest of the Gutbusters turned around and fled, not even thinking to recover their fallen comrades.

Kill two. Take one back for questioning, the most important of the three dark elves signaled as he and his companions began floating back to the floor.

They touched down lightly and drew out fine swords.

Up scrambled the three battleragers, their little legs pumping under them in a wild flurry. No poison, not even the famed drow sleeping poison, could get through the wicked concoctions this group had recently imbibed. Gutbuster was a drink, not just a brigade, and if a dwarf could survive the drink itself, he wouldn't have to worry much about being poisoned—or being cold—for some time.

Closest to the dark elves, Pwent lowered his head, with its long helmet spike, and impaled one elf through the chest, blasting through the fine mesh of drow armor easily and brutally.

The second drow managed to deflect the next battlerager's charge, turning the helmet spike aside with both his swords. But a mailed fist, the knuckles devilishly spiked with barbed points, caught the drow under the chin and tore a gaping hole in his throat. Fighting for breath, the drow managed to score two nasty hits on his opponent's back, but those two strikes did little in the face of the flurry launched by the wild-eyed dwarf.

Only the third drow survived the initial assault. He leaped high in the air, enacting his levitation spell once more, and got just over the remaining dwarf's barreling charge—mostly because the dwarf slipped on the slick blood of Thibbledorf Pwent's quick kill.

Up went the drow, into the stalactite tangle, disappearing from sight.

Pwent straightened, shaking free of the dead drow. "That way!" he roared, pointing farther along the corridor. "Find an open area o' ceiling and take up a watch! We're not to let this one get away!"

Around the eastern bend came the rest of the Gutbusters, whooping and shouting, their armor clattering, the many creases and points on each suit grating and squealing like fingernails on slate.

"Take to lookin'!" Pwent bellowed, indicating the ceiling, and all the dwarves bobbed about eagerly.

One screeched, taking a hand-crossbow hit squarely in the face, but that shout of pain became a cry of joy, for the dwarf had only to backtrack the angle to spot the floating drow. Immediately a globe of darkness engulfed that area of the stalactites, but the dwarves now knew where to find him.

"Lariat!" Pwent bellowed, and another dwarf pulled a rope from his belt and scrambled over to the battlerager. The end of the rope was looped and securely tied in a slip knot, and so the dwarf, misunderstanding Pwent's intent, put the lasso twirling over his head and looked to the darkened area, trying to discern his best shot.

Pwent grabbed him by the wrist and held fast, sending the rope limply to the floor. "Battlerager lariat," Pwent explained.

Other dwarves crowded around, not knowing what their leader had in mind. Smiles widened on every face as Pwent slipped the loop over his foot, tightened it around his ankle, and informed the others that it would take more than one of them to get this drow-catcher flying.

Every eager dwarf grabbed the rope and began tugging wildly, doing no more than to knock Pwent from his feet. Gradually, sobered by the threats of the vicious battlerager commander, they managed to find a rhythm, and soon had Pwent skipping around the floor.

Then they had him up in the air, flying wildly, round and round. But too much slack was given the rope, and Pwent scraped hard against one of the corridor walls, his helmet spike throwing a line of bright sparks.

This group learned fast, though—considering that they were dwarves who spent their days running headlong into steel-reinforced doors—and they soon had the timing of the spin and the length of the rope perfect.

Two turns, five turns, and off flew the battlerager, up into the air, to crash among the stalactites. Pwent grabbed onto one momentarily, but it broke away from the ceiling and down the dwarf and stone tumbled.

Pwent hit hard, then bounced right back to his feet.

"One less barrier to our enemy!" one dwarf roared, and before the dazed Pwent could protest, the others cheered and tugged, bringing the battlerager lariat to bear once more.

Up flew Pwent, to similar, painful results, then a third time, then a fourth, which proved the charm, for the poor drow, blind to the scene, finally dared to come out into the open, edging his way to the west.

He sensed the living lariat coming and managed to scramble behind a long, thin stalactite, but that hardly mattered, for Pwent took the stone out cleanly, wrapped his arms around it, and around the drow behind it, and drow, dwarf, and stone fell together, crashing hard to the floor. Before the drow could recover, half the brigade had fallen over him, battering him into unconsciousness.

It took them another five minutes to get the semiconscious Pwent to let go of the victim.

They were up and moving, Pwent included, soon after, having tied the drow, ankles and wrists to a long pole, supported on the shoulders of two of the group. They hadn't even cleared the corridor, though, when the dwarves farthest to the west, the two Pwent had sent to watch, took up a cry of "Drow!" and spun around at the ready.

Into the passage came a lone, trotting dark elf, and before Pwent could yell out "Not that one!" the two dwarves lowered their heads and roared in.

In a split second, the dark elf cut left, back to the right, spun a complete circuit to the right, then went wide around the end, and the two Gutbusters stumbled and slammed hard into the wall. They realized their foolishness when the great panther came by an instant later, following her drow companion.

Drizzt was back by the dwarves' side, helping them to their feet. "Run on," he whispered, and they paused at the warning long enough to hear the rumble of a not-so-distant charge.

Misunderstanding, the Gutbusters smiled widely and prepared to continue their own charge to the west, headlong into the approaching force, but Drizzt held them firmly.

"Our enemies are upon us in great numbers," he said. "You will get your fight, more than you ever hoped for, but not here."

By the time Drizzt, the two dwarves, and the panther caught up to Pwent, the noise of the coming army was clearly evident.

"I thought ye said the damned drow moved silent," Pwent remarked, double-stepping beside the swift ranger.

"Not drow," Drizzt replied. "Kobolds and goblins."

Pwent skidded to an abrupt halt. "We're runnin' from stinkin' kobolds?" he asked.

"Thousands of stinking kobolds," Drizzt replied evenly, "and bigger monsters, likely with thousands of drow behind them."

"Oh," answered the battlerager, suddenly out of bluster.

In the familiar tunnels, Drizzt and the Gutbusters had no trouble keeping ahead of the rushing army. Drizzt took no detours this time, but ran straight to the east, past the tunnels the dwarves had rigged to fall.

"Run on," the drow ordered the assigned trap-springers, a handful of dwarves standing ready beside cranks that would release the ropes supporting the tunnel structure. Each of them in turn stared blankly at the surprising command.

"They're coming," one remarked, for that is exactly why these dwarves were out in the tunnels.

"All you will catch is kobolds," Drizzt, understanding the drow tactics, informed them. "Run on, and let us see if we cannot catch a few drow as well."

"But none'll be here to spring the traps!" more than one dwarf, Pwent among them, piped in.

Drizzt's wicked grin was convincing, so the dwarves, who had learned many times to trust the ranger, shrugged and fell in line with the retreating Gutbusters.

"Where're we runnin' to?" Pwent wanted to know.

"Another hundred strides," Drizzt informed him. "Tunult's Cavern, where you will get your fight."

"Promises, promises," muttered the fierce Pwent.

Tunult's Cavern, the most open area this side of Mithral Hall, was really a series of seven caverns connected by wide, arching tunnels. Nowhere was the ground even; some chambers sat higher than others, and more than one deep fissure ran across the floors.

Here waited Bruenor and his escorts, along with nearly a thousand of Mithral Hall's finest fighters. The original plan had called for Tunult's Cavern to be set up as an outward command post, used as a send-off point to the remaining, though less direct, tunnels after the drow advance had been stopped cold by the dropped stone.

Drizzt had altered that plan, and he rushed to Bruenor's side, conferring with the dwarf king, and with Bidderdoo Harpell, a wizard that the drow was surely relieved to find.

"Ye gave up the trap-springing positions!" Bruenor bellowed at the ranger as soon as he understood that the tunnels beyond were still intact.

"Not so," Drizzt replied with all confidence. Even as his gaze led Bruenor's toward the eastern tunnel, the first of the kobold ranks rushed in, pouring like water behind a breaking dam into the waiting dwarves. "I merely got the fodder out of the way."

The Battle of Tunult's Cavern

20

The confusion was immediate and complete, kobolds swarming in by the dozens, and tough dwarves forming into tight battle groups and rushing fast to meet them.

Catti-brie put her magical bow up and fired arrow after arrow, aiming for the main entrance. Lightning flashed with each shot as the enchanted bolt sped off, crackling and sparking every time it skipped off a wall. Kobolds went down in a line, one arrow often killing several, but it hardly seemed to matter, so great was the invading throng.

Guenhwyvar leaped away, Drizzt quick-stepping behind. A score of kobolds had somehow wriggled past the initial fights and were bearing down on Bruenor's position. A shot from Catti-brie felled one; Guenhwyvar's plunge scattered the rest; and Drizzt, moving quicker than ever, slipped in, stabbed one, pivoted and spun to the left, launching the blue-glowing Twinkle against the attempted parry of another. Had Twinkle been a straight blade, the kobold's small sword would have deflected it high, but Drizzt deftly turned the curving weapon over in his hand and slightly altered the angle of his attack. Twinkle rolled over the kobold's sword and dived into its chest.

The drow had never stopped his run and now skittered back to the right and slid to one knee. Across came Twinkle, slapping against one kobold blade, driving it hard into a second. Stronger than both the creatures combined, and with a better angle, Drizzt forced their swords and their defense high, and his second scimitar slashed across the other way, disemboweling one and taking the legs out from under the other.

"Damn drow's stealing all the fun," Bruenor muttered, running to catch up to the fray. Between Drizzt, the panther, and Catti-brie's continuing barrage, few of the twenty kobolds still stood by the time he got there, and those few had turned in full flight.

"Plenty more to kill," Drizzt said into Bruenor's scowl, recognizing the sour look.

A line of silver-streaking arrow cut between them as soon as the words had left the drow's mouth. When the spots cleared from before their eyes, the two turned and regarded the scorched and dead kobolds taken down by Catti-brie's latest shot.

Then she, too, was beside them, Khazid'hea in hand, and Regis, holding the little mace Bruenor had long ago forged for him, was beside her. Catti-brie shrugged as her friends regarded the change in weapon, and looking around, they understood her tactics. With more kobolds pouring in, and more dwarves coming out of the other chambers to meet the charge, it was simply too confusing and congested for the woman to safely continue with her bow.

"Run on," Catti-brie said, a wistful smile crossing her fair features.

Drizzt returned the look, and Bruenor, even Regis, had a sparkle in his eye. Suddenly it seemed like old times.

Guenhwyvar led their charge, Bruenor fighting hard to keep close to the panther's tail. Catti-brie and Regis flanked the dwarf, and Drizzt, speeding and spinning, flanked the group, first on the left, then on the right, seeming to be wherever battle was joined, running too fast to be believed.

⚔ ⚔ ⚔ ⚔ ⚔

Bidderdoo Harpell knew he had erred. Drizzt had asked him to get to the door, to wait for the first drow to show themselves inside the cavern and launch a fireball back down the tunnel, where the flames would burn through the supporting ropes and drop the stone.

"Not a difficult task," Bidderdoo had assured Drizzt, and so it should not have been. The wizard had memorized a spell that could put him in position, and knew others to keep him safely hidden until the blast was complete. So when all around him had run off to join in the fracas, they had gone reassured that the traps would be sprung, that the tunnels would be dropped, and that the tide of enemies would be stemmed.

Something went wrong. Bidderdoo had begun casting the spell to get him to the tunnel entrance, had even outlined the extradimensional portal that would reopen at the desired spot, but then the wizard had seen a group of kobolds, and they had seen him. This was not hard to do, for Bidderdoo,

a human and not blessed with sight that could extend into the infrared spectrum, carried a shining gemstone. Kobolds were not stupid creatures, not when it came to battle, and they recognized this seemingly out-of-place human for what he was. Even the most inexperienced of kobold fighters understood the value of getting to a wizard, of forcing a dangerous spellcaster into melee combat, keeping his hands tied up with weapons rather than often explosive components.

Still, Bidderdoo could have beaten their charge, could have stepped through the dimensions to get to his appointed position.

For seven years, until the Time of Troubles, Bidderdoo Harpell had lived with the effects of a potion gone awry, had lived as the Harpell family dog. When magic went crazy, Bidderdoo had reverted to his human form—long enough, at least, to get the necessary ingredients together to counteract the wild potion. Soon after, Bidderdoo had gone back to his flea-bitten self, but he had helped his family find the means to get him out of the enchantment. A great debate had followed in the Ivy Mansion as to whether they should "cure" Bidderdoo or not. It seemed that many of the Harpells had grown quite fond of the dog, more so than they had ever loved Bidderdoo as a human.

Bidderdoo had even served as Harkle's seeing-eye dog on a long stretch of the journey to Mithral Hall, when Harkle had no eyes.

But then magic had straightened out, and the debate became moot, for the enchantment had simply gone away.

Or had it? Bidderdoo had held no doubts about the integrity of his cure until this very moment, until he saw the kobolds approaching. His upper lip curled back in an open snarl. He felt the hair on the back of his neck bristling and felt his tailbone tighten—if he still had a tail, it would be straight out behind him!

He started down into a crouch, and noticed only then that he had not paws, but hands, hands that held no weapons. He groaned, for the kobolds were only ten feet away.

The wizard went for a spell instead. He put the tips of his thumbs together, hands out wide to each side, and chanted frantically.

The kobolds came in, straight ahead and flanking, and the closest of them had a sword high for a strike.

Bidderdoo's hands erupted in flame, jets of scorching, searing fire, arcing out in a semicircle.

Half a dozen kobolds lay dead, and several others blinked in amazement through singed eyelashes.

"Hah!" Bidderdoo cried, and snapped his fingers.

The kobolds blinked again and charged, and Bidderdoo had no spells quick enough to stop them.

× × × × ×

At first the kobolds and goblins seemed a swarming, confused mass, and so it remained for many of the undisciplined brawlers. But several groups had trained for war extensively in the caverns beneath the complex of House Oblodra. One of these, fifty strong, formed into a tight wedge, three large kobolds at the tip and a tight line running back and wide to each side.

They entered the main chamber, avoided combat enough to form up, and headed straight to the left, toward the looming entrance of one of the side caverns. Mostly the dwarves avoided them, with so many other easier kills available, and the kobold group almost got to the side chamber unscathed.

Coming out of that chamber, though, was a group of a dozen dwarves. The bearded warriors hooted and roared and came on fiercely, but the kobold formation did not waver, worked to perfection as it split the dwarven line almost exactly in half, then widened the gap with the lead kobolds pressing to the very entrance of the side chamber. A couple of kobolds went down in that charge, and one dwarf died, but the kobold ranks tightened again immediately, and those dwarves caught along the inside line, caught between the kobolds and the main cavern's low sloping wall, found themselves in dire straights indeed.

Across the way, the "free" half of the dwarven group realized their error, that they had taken the kobolds too lightly and had not expected such intricate tactics. Their kin would be lost, and there was nothing they could do to get through this surprisingly tight, disciplined formation—made even tighter by the fact that, in going near the wall, the kobolds went under some low-hanging stalactites.

The dwarves attacked fiercely anyway, spurred on by the cries of their apparently doomed companions.

Guenhwyvar was low to the ground, low enough to skitter under any stalactites. The panther hit the back of the kobold formation in full stride, blasting two kobolds away and running over a third, claws digging in for a better hold as the cat crossed over.

Drizzt came in behind, sliding to one knee again and killing two kobolds in the first attack routine. Beside him charged Regis, no taller than a kobold and fighting straight up and even against one.

With his great, sweeping style of axe-fighting, Bruenor found the tight quarters uncomfortable at best. Even worse off was Catti-brie, not as agile or quick as Drizzt. If she went down to one knee, as had the drow, she would be at a huge disadvantage indeed.

But standing straight, a stalactite in her face, she wasn't much better off.

Khazid'hea gave her the answer.

It went against every instinct the woman had, was contrary to everything Bruenor—who had spent much of his life repairing damaged weapons—had taught her about fighting. but hardly thinking, Catti-brie clasped her sword hilt in both hands and brought the magnificent weapon streaking straight across, up high.

Khazid'hea's red line flashed angrily as the sword connected on the hanging stone. Catti-brie's momentum slowed, but only slightly, for Cutter lived up to its name, shearing through the rock. Catti-brie jerked to the side as the sword exited the stalactite, and she would have been vulnerable in that instant—except that the two kobolds in formation right before her were suddenly more concerned that the sky was falling.

One got crushed under the stalactite, and the other's death was just as quick, as Bruenor, seeing the opening, rushed in with an overhead chop that nearly took the wretched thing in half.

Those dwarves that had been separated on the outside rank took heart at the arrival of so powerful a group, and they pressed the kobold line fiercely, calling out to their trapped companions to "hold fast!" and promising that help would soon arrive.

Regis hated to fight, at least when his opponent could see him coming. He was needed now, though. He knew that, and would not shirk his responsibilities. Beside him, Drizzt fought from his knees. How could the halfling, who would have to get up on his tiptoes to bang his head on a stalactite, justify standing behind his drow friend this time?

Both hands on his mace handle, Regis went in fiercely. He smiled as he actually scored a hit, the well-forged weapon crumbling a kobold arm.

Even as that opponent fell away, though, another squeezed in and struck, its sword catching Regis under his upraised arm. Only fine dwarven armor saved him—he made a note to buy Buster Bracer a few large mugs of mead if he ever got out of this alive.

Tough was the dwarven armor, but the kobold's head was not as tough, as the halfling's mace proved a moment later.

"Well done," Drizzt congratulated, his battle ebbing enough for him to witness the halfling's strike.

Regis tried to smile, but winced instead at the pain of his bruised ribs.

Drizzt noted the look and skittered across in front of Regis, meeting the charge as the kobold formation shifted to compensate for the widening breach. The drow's scimitars went into a wild dance, slashing and chopping, often banging against the low-hanging stalactites, throwing sparks, but more often connecting on kobolds.

To the side, Catti-brie and Bruenor had formed up into an impromptu alliance, Bruenor holding back the enemy, while Catti-brie and Cutter continued to clear a higher path, dropping the hanging stones one at a time.

Across the way, though, the dwarves remained sorely pressed, with two down and the other five taking many hits. None of the friends could get to them in time, they knew, none could cross through the tight formation.

None except Guenhwyvar.

Flying like a black arrow, the panther bored on, running down kobold after kobold, shrugging off many wicked strikes. Blood streamed from the panther's flanks, but Guenhwyvar would not be deterred. She got to the dwarves and bolstered their line, and their cheer at her appearance was of pure delight and salvation.

A song on their lips, the dwarves fought on, the panther fought on, and the kobolds could not finish the task. With the press across the way, the formation soon crumbled, and the dwarven group was reunited, that the wounded could be taken from the cavern.

Drizzt and Catti-brie's concern for Guenhwyvar was stolen by the panther's roar, and its flight, as Guenhwyvar led the five friends off to the next place where they would be needed most.

※ ※ ※ ※ ※

Bidderdoo closed his eyes, wondering what mysteries death would reveal.

He hoped there would be some, at least.

He heard a roar, then a clash of steel in front of him. Then came a grunt, and the sickening thud of a torn body slapping against the hard floor.

They are fighting over who gets to kill me, the mage thought.

More roars—dwarven roars!—and more grunts; more torn bodies falling to the stone.

Bidderdoo opened his eyes to see the kobold ranks decimated, to see a handful of the dirtiest, smelliest dwarves imaginable hopping up and down around him, pointing this way and that, as they of the Gutbuster Brigade tried to figure out where they might next cause the most havoc.

Bidderdoo took a moment to regard the kobolds, a dozen corpses that had

been more than killed. "Shredded," he whispered, and he nodded, deciding that was a better word.

"Ye're all right now," said one of the dwarves—Bidderdoo thought he had heard this one's name as Thibbledorf Pwent or some such thing—not that anyone named Bidderdoo could toss insults regarding names. "And me and me own're off!" the wild battlerager huffed.

Bidderdoo nodded, then realized he still had a serious problem. He had only prepared for one spell that could open such a dimensional door, and that one was wasted, the enchantment expired as he had battled with the kobolds.

"Wait!" he screamed at Pwent, and he surprised himself, and the dwarf, for along with his words came out a caninelike yelp.

Pwent regarded the Harpell curiously. He hopped up right before Bidderdoo and cocked his head to the side, a movement exaggerated by the tilting helmet spike.

"Wait. Pray, do not run off, good and noble dwarf," Bidderdoo said sweetly, needing assistance.

Pwent looked around and behind, as if trying to figure out who this mage was talking to. The other Gutbusters were similarly confused, some standing and staring blankly, scratching their heads.

Pwent poked a stubby, dirty finger into his own chest, his expression showing that he hardly considered himself "good and noble."

"Do not leave me," Bidderdoo pleaded.

"Ye're still alive," Pwent countered. "And there's not much for killin' over here." As though that were explanation enough, the battlerager spun and took a stride away.

"But I've failed!" Bidderdoo wailed, and a howl escaped his lips at the end of the sentence.

"Ye've fail-doooo?" Pwent asked.

"Oh, we are all do-oooo-omed!" the howling mage went on dramatically. "It's too-oooo far."

All the battleragers were around Bidderdoo by this point, intrigued by the strange accent, or whatever it was. The closest enemies, a band of goblins, could have attacked then, but none wanted to go anywhere near this wild troupe, a point made especially clear with the last group of kobolds lying in bloody pieces around the area.

"Ye better be quick and to the point," Pwent, anxious to kill again, barked at Bidderdoo.

"Oooo."

"And stop the damned howlin'!" the battlerager demanded.

In truth, poor Bidderdoo wasn't howling on purpose. In the stress of the situation, the mage who had lived so long as a dog was unintentionally recalling the experience, discovering once more those primal canine instincts. He took a deep breath and pointedly reminded himself he was a man, not a dog. "I must get to the tunnel entrance," he said without a howl, yip, or yelp. "The drow ranger bade me to send a spell down the corridor."

"I'm not for carin' for wizard stuff," Pwent interrupted, and turned away once more.

"Are ye for droppin' the stinkin' tunnel on the stinkin' drow's 'eads?" Bidderdoo asked in his best battlerager imitation.

"Bah!" Pwent snorted, and all the dwarven heads were bobbing eagerly around him. "Me and me own'll get ye there!"

Bidderdoo took care to keep his visage stern, but silently thought himself quite clever for appealing to the wild dwarves' hunger for carnage.

In the blink of a dog's eye, Bidderdoo was swept up in the tide of running Gutbusters. The wizard suggested a roundabout route, skirting the left-hand, or northern, side of the cavern, where the fighting had become less intense.

Silly mage.

The Gutbuster Brigade ran straight through, ran down kobolds and the larger goblins who had come in behind the kobold ranks. They almost buried a couple of dwarves who weren't quick enough in diving aside; they bounced off stalagmites, ricocheting and rolling on. Before Bidderdoo could even begin to protest the tactic, he found himself nearing the appointed spot, the entrance to the tunnel.

He spent a brief moment wondering which was faster, a spell opening a dimensional door or a handful of battle-hungry battleragers. He even entertained the creation of a new spell, *Battlerager Escort*, but he shook that notion away as a more immediate problem, a pair of huge, bull-headed minotaurs and a dark elf behind them, entered the cavern.

"Defensive posture!" cried Bidderdoo. "You must hold them off! Defensive posture!"

Silly mage.

The closest two Gutbusters flew headlong, diving into the feet of the towering, eight-foot monsters. Before they even realized what had hit them, the minotaurs were falling forward. Neither made it unobstructed to the ground, though, as Pwent and another wild-eyed dwarf roared in, butting the minotaurs head-to-head.

A globe of darkness appeared behind the tumble, and the drow was nowhere to be seen.

Bidderdoo wisely began his spellcasting. The drow were here! Just as Drizzt had figured, the dark elves were coming in behind the kobold fodder. If he could get the fireball away now, if he could drop the tunnel . . .

He had to force the words through a guttural, instinctual growl coming from somewhere deep in his throat. He had the urge to join the Gutbusters, who were all clamoring over the fallen minotaurs, taking the brutes apart mercilessly. He had the urge to join in the feast.

"The feast?" he asked aloud.

Bidderdoo shook his head and began again, concentrating on the spell. Apparently hearing the wizard's rhythmic cadence, the drow came out of the darkness, hand-crossbow up and ready.

Bidderdoo closed his eyes, forced the words to flow as fast as possible. He felt the sting of the dart, right in the belly, but his concentration was complete and he did not flinch, did not interrupt the spell.

His legs went weak under him. He heard the drow coming, imagined a shining sword poised for a killing strike.

Bidderdoo's concentration held. He completed the dweomer, and a small, glowing ball of fire leaped out from his hand, soared through the darkness beyond, down the tunnel.

Bidderdoo teetered with weakness. He opened his eyes, but the cavern around him was blurry and wavering. Then he fell backward, felt as though the floor were rushing up to swallow him.

Somewhere in the back of his mind he expected to hit the stone hard, but then the fireball went off.

Then the tunnel fell.

21
ONE FOR THE GOOD GUYS

A heavy burden weighed on the most honored burrow warden's strong shoulders, but Belwar did not stoop as he marched through the long, winding tunnels. He had made the decision with a clear mind and definite purpose, and he simply refused to second-guess himself all the way to Mithral Hall.

His opponents in the debate had argued that Belwar was motivated by personal friendship, not the best interests of the svirfnebli. Firble had learned that Drizzt Do'Urden, Belwar's drow friend, had escaped Menzoberranzan, and the drow march, by all indications, was straight for Mithral Hall, no doubt motivated in part by Lolth's proclaimed hatred of the renegade.

Would Belwar lead Blingdenstone to war, then, for the sake of a single drow?

In the end, that vicious argument had been settled not by Belwar, but by Firble, another of the oldest svirfnebli, another of those who had felt the pain most keenly when Blingdenstone had been left behind.

"A clear choice we have," Firble had said. "Go now and see if we can aid the enemies of the dark elves, or a new home we must find, for the drow will surely return, and if we stand, we stand alone."

It was a terrible, difficult decision for the council and for King Schnicktick. If they followed the dark elves and found their suspicions confirmed, found a war on the surface, could they even count on the alliance of the surface dwarves and the humans, races the deep gnomes did not know?

Belwar assured them they could. With all his heart, the most honored burrow warden believed that Drizzt, and any friends Drizzt had made, would not let him down. And Firble, who knew the outside world so well—but was,

by his own admission, somewhat ignorant of the surface—agreed with Belwar, simply on the logic that any race, even not-so-intelligent goblins, would welcome allies against the dark elves.

So Schnicktick and the council had finally agreed, but like every other decision of the ultimately conservative svirfnebli, they would go only so far. Belwar could march in pursuit of the drow, and Firble with him, along with any gnomes who volunteered. They were scouts, Schnicktick had emphasized, and no marching army. The svirfneblin king and all those who had opposed Belwar's reasoning were surprised to find how many volunteered for the long, dangerous march. So many, in fact, that Schnicktick, for the simple sake of the city operation, had to limit the number to fifteen score.

Belwar knew why the other svirfnebli had come, and knew the truth of his own decision. If the dark elves went to the surface and overwhelmed Mithral Hall, they would not allow the gnomes back into Blingdenstone. Menzoberranzan did not conquer, then leave. No, it would enslave the dwarves and work the mines as its own, then pity Blingdenstone, for the svirfneblin city would be too close to the easiest routes to the conquered land.

So though all of these svirfnebli, Belwar and Firble included, were marching farther from Blingdenstone than they had ever gone before, they knew that they were, in effect, fighting for their homeland.

Belwar would not second-guess that decision, and keeping that in mind, his burden was lessened.

⚔ ⚔ ⚔ ⚔ ⚔

Bidderdoo put the fireball far down the tunnel, but the narrow ways could not contain the sheer volume of the blast. A line of fire rushed out of the tunnel, back into the cavern, like the breath of an angry red dragon, and Bidderdoo's own clothes lit up. The mage screamed—as did every dwarf and kobold near him, as did the next line of minotaurs, rushing down for the cavern, as did the skulking dark elves behind them.

In the moment of the wizard's fireball, all of them screamed, and just as quickly, the cries went away, extinguished, overwhelmed, by hundreds of tons of dropping stone.

Again the backlash swept into the cavern, a blast so strong that the gust of it blew away the fires licking at Bidderdoo's robes. He was flying suddenly, as were all those near him, flying and dazed, pelted with stone, and extremely lucky, for none of the dropping stalactites or the heavy stone displaced in the cavern squashed him.

The ground trembled and bucked. One of the cavern walls buckled, and one of the side chambers collapsed. Then it was done, and the tunnel was gone, just gone, as though it had never been there, and the chamber that had been named for the dwarf Tunult seemed much smaller.

Bidderdoo pulled himself up from the piled dust and debris shakily and brushed the dirt from his glowing gemstone. With all the dust in the air, the light from the enchanted stone seemed meager indeed. The wizard looked at himself, seeing more skin than clothing, seeing dozens of bruises and bright red on one arm, under the clinging dust, where the fires had gotten to his skin.

A helmet spike, bent slightly to the side, protruded from a pile not far away. Bidderdoo was about to speak a lament for the battlerager, who had gotten him to the spot, but Pwent suddenly burst up from the dust, spitting pebbles and smiling crazily.

"Well done!" the battlerager roared. "Do it again!"

Bidderdoo started to respond, but then he swooned, the insidious drow poison defeating the momentary jolt of adrenaline. The next thing the unfortunate wizard knew, Pwent was holding him up and he was gagging on the most foul-tasting concoction ever brewed. Foul but effective, for Bidderdoo's grogginess was no more.

"Gutbuster!" Pwent roared, patting the trusty flask on his broad belt.

As the dust settled, the bodies stirred, one by one. To a dwarf, the Gutbuster Brigade, tougher than the stone, remained, and the few kobolds that had survived were cut down before they could plead.

The way the cavern had collapsed, with the nearest side chamber gone, and the wall opposite that having buckled, this small group found itself cut off from the main force. They weren't trapped, though, for one narrow passage led to the left, back toward the heart of Tunult's Cavern. The fighting in there had resumed, so it seemed from the ring of metal and the calls of both dwarves and kobolds.

Unexpectedly, Thibbledorf Pwent did not lead his force headlong into the fray. The passage was narrow at this end, and seemed to narrow even more just a short way in, so much so that Pwent didn't even think they could squeeze through. Also, the battlerager spotted something over Bidderdoo's shoulder, a deep crack in the wall to the side of the dropped tunnel. As he neared the spot, Pwent felt the stiff breeze rushing out of the crack, as the air pressure in the tunnels beyond adjusted to the catastrophe.

Pwent hooted and slammed the wall below the crack with all his strength. The loose stone gave way and fell in, revealing a passageway angling into the deeper corridors beyond.

"We should go back and report to King Bruenor," Bidderdoo reasoned, "or go as far as the tunnel takes us, to let them know we are in here, that they might dig us out."

Pwent snorted. "Wouldn't be much at scoutin' if we let this tunnel pass," he argued. "If the drow find it, they'll be back quicker than Bruenor's expectin'. Now that's a report worth givin'!"

In truth, it was difficult for the outrageous dwarven warrior to ignore those tempting sounds of battle, but Pwent found his heart seeking the promise of greater enemies, of drow and minotaurs, in the open corridors the other way.

"And if we get stuck in that tunnel there," Pwent continued, pointing back toward what remained of Tunult's Cavern, "the damned drow'll walk right up our backs!"

The Gutbuster Brigade formed up behind their leader, but Bidderdoo shook his head and squeezed into the passage. His worst fears were quickly realized, for it did indeed narrow, and he could not get near the open area beyond, where the fighting continued, could not even get close enough to hope to attract attention above the tumult of battle.

Perhaps he had a spell that would aid him, Bidderdoo reasoned, and he reached into an impossibly deep pocket to retrieve his treasured spellbook. He pulled out a lump of ruffled pages, smeared and singed, many with ink blotched from the intense heat. The glue and stitches in the binding, too, had melted, and when Bidderdoo held the mess up, it fell apart.

The wizard, breathing hard suddenly, feeling as if the world were closing in on him, gathered together as many of the parchments as he could and scrambled back out of the passageway, to find, to his surprise and relief, Pwent and the others still waiting for him.

"Figgered ye'd change yer mind," the battlerager remarked, and he led the Gutbuster Brigade, plus one, away.

✕ ✕ ✕ ✕ ✕

Fifty drow and an entire minotaur grouping, Quenthel Baenre's hands flashed, and from the sharp, jerking movements, her mother knew she was outraged.

Fool, Matron Baenre mused. She wondered then about her daughter's heart for this expedition. Quenthel was a powerful priestess, there could be no denying that, but only then did the withered old matron mother realize that young Quenthel had never really seen battle. House Baenre had not warred in many hundreds of years, and because of her accelerated education through the

Academy, Quenthel had been spared the duties of escorting scouting patrols in the wild tunnels outside Menzoberranzan.

It struck Baenre then that her daughter had never even been outside the drow city.

The primary way to Mithral Hall is no more, Quenthel's hands went on. *And several paralleling passages have fallen as well. And worse*, Quenthel stopped abruptly, had to pause and take a deep breath to steady herself. When she began again, her face was locked in a mask of anger. *Many of the dead drow were females, several powerful priestesses and one a high priestess.*

Still the movements were exaggerated, too sharp and too quick. Did Quenthel really believe this conquest would be easy? Baenre wondered. Did she think no drow would be killed?

Baenre wondered, and not for the first time, whether she had erred in bringing Quenthel along. Perhaps she should have brought Triel, the most capable of priestesses.

Quenthel studied the hard look that was coming at her and understood that her mother was not pleased. It took her a moment to realize she was irritating Baenre more than the bad report would warrant.

"The lines are moving?" Baenre asked aloud.

Quenthel cleared her throat. "Bregan D'aerthe has discovered many other routes," she answered, "even corridors the dwarves do not know about, which come close to tunnels leading to Mithral Hall."

Matron Baenre closed her eyes and nodded, approving of her daughter's suddenly renewed optimism. There were indeed tunnels the dwarves did not know about, small passages beneath the lowest levels of Mithral Hall lost as the dwarves continued to shift their mining operations to richer veins. Old Gandalug knew those ancient, secret ways, though, and with Methil's intrusive interrogation, the drow knew them as well. These secret tunnels did not actually connect to the dwarven compound, but wizards could open doors where there were none, and illithids could walk through stone and could take drow warriors with them on their psionic journeys.

Baenre's eyes popped open. "Word from Berg'inyon?" she asked.

Quenthel shook her head. "He exited the tunnels, as commanded, but we have not heard since."

Baenre's features grew cross. She knew that Berg'inyon was outwardly pouting at being sent outside. He led the greatest cohesive unit of all, numerically speaking, nearly a thousand drow and five times that in goblins and kobolds, with many of the dark elves riding huge lizards. But Berg'inyon's duties, though vital to the conquest of Mithral Hall, put him on the mountainside outside the dwarven complex. Very likely, Drizzt Do'Urden would be inside, in the lowest tunnels, working in an environment more suited to a dark elf. Very likely, Uthegental Armgo, not Berg'inyon, would get first try at the renegade.

Baenre's scowl turned to a smile as she considered her son and his tantrum when she had given him his assignment. Of course he had to act angry, even outraged. Of course he had to protest that he, not Uthegental, should spearhead the assault through the tunnels. But Berg'inyon had been Drizzt's classmate and primary rival in their years at Melee-Magthere, the drow school for fighters. Berg'inyon knew Drizzt perhaps better than any living drow in Menzoberranzan. And Matron Baenre knew Berg'inyon.

The truth of it was, Berg'inyon didn't want anything to do with the dangerous renegade.

"Search out your brother with your magic," Baenre said suddenly, startling Quenthel. "If he continues his obstinacy, replace him."

Quenthel's eyes widened with horror. She had been with Berg'inyon when the force had exited the tunnels, crossing out onto a ledge on a mountain overlooking a deep ravine. The sight had overwhelmed her, had dizzied her, and many other drow as well. She felt lost out there, insignificant and vulnerable. This cavern that was the surface world, this great chamber whose black dome sparkled with pinpoints of unknown light, was too vast for her sensibilities.

Matron Baenre did not appreciate the horrified expression. "Go!" she snapped, and Quenthel quietly slipped away.

She was hardly out of sight before the next reporting drow stepped before Baenre's blue-glowing driftdisk.

Her report, of the progress of the force moving secretly in the lower tunnels, was better, but Baenre hardly listened. To her, these details were fast becoming tedious. The dwarves were good, and had many months to prepare, but in the end, Matron Baenre did not doubt the outcome, for she believed that Lolth herself had spoken to her. The drow would win, and Mithral Hall would fall.

She listened to the report, though, and to the next, and the next, and the next after that, a seemingly endless stream, and forced herself to look interested.

STAR LIGHT, STAR BRIGHT

From her high perch, her eyesight enhanced by magical dweomers, they seemed an army of ants, swarming over the eastern and steepest side of the mountain, filling every vale, clambering over every rock. Filtering behind in tight formations came the deeper blackness, the tight formations of drow warriors.

Never had the Lady of Silverymoon seen such a disconcerting sight, never had she been so filled with trepidation, though she had endured many wars and many perilous adventures. Alustriel's visage did not reflect those battles. She was as fair as any woman alive, her skin smooth and pale, almost translucent, and her hair long and silvery—not gray with age, though she was indeed very old, but lustrous and rich, the quiet light of night and the sparkling brightness of stars all mixed together. Indeed, the fair lady had endured many wars, and the sorrow of those conflicts was reflected in her eyes, as was the wisdom to despise war.

Across the way toward the southern face, around the bend of the conical mountain, Alustriel could see the banners of the gathered forces, most prominent among them the silver flag of her own knights. They were proud and anxious, Alustriel knew, because most of them were young and did not know grief.

The Lady of Silverymoon shook away the disconcerting thoughts and focused on what likely would transpire, what her role might be.

The bulk of the enemy force was kobolds, and she figured that the huge barbarians and armored riders should have little trouble in scattering them.

But how would they fare against the drow? Alustriel wondered. She brought her flying chariot in a wide loop, watching and waiting.

⚔ ⚔ ⚔ ⚔ ⚔

Skirmishes erupted along the point line, as human scouts met the advancing kobolds.

At the sound of battle, and with reports filtering back, Berkthgar was anxious to loose his forces, to charge off to fight and die with a song to Tempus on his lips.

Besnell, who led the Knights in Silver, was a tempered fighter, and more the strategist. "Hold your men in check," he bade the eager barbarian. "We will see more fighting this night than any of us, even Tempus, your god of battle, would enjoy. Better that we fight them on ground of our choosing." Indeed, the knight had been careful in selecting that very ground, and had argued against both Berkthgar and King Bruenor himself to win over their support for his plan. The forces had been broken into four groups, spaced along the south side of the mountain, Fourthpeak, which held both entrances to Mithral Hall. Northwest around the mountain lay Keeper's Dale, a wide, deep, rock-strewn, and mist-filled valley wherein lay the secret western door to the dwarven complex.

From the soldiers' positions northeast around the mountain, across wide expanses of open rock and narrow, crisscrossing trails, lay the longer, more commonly used path to Mithral Hall's eastern door.

Bruenor's emissaries had wanted the force to split, the riders going to defend Keeper's Dale and the men of Settlestone guarding the eastern trails. Besnell had held firm his position, though, and had enlisted Berkthgar by turning the situation back on the proud dwarves, by insisting that they should be able to conceal and defend their own entrances. "If the drow know where the entrances lie," he had argued, "then that is where they will expect resistance."

Thus, the south side of Fourthpeak was chosen. Below the positions of the defenders the trails were many, but above them the cliffs grew much steeper, so they expected no attack from that direction. The defenders' groups were mixed according to terrain, one position of narrow, broken trails exclusively barbarians, two having both barbarians and riders, and one, a plateau above a wide, smooth, gradually inclined rock face, comprised wholly of the Riders of Nesmé.

Besnell and Berkthgar watched and waited now from the second position.

They knew the battle was imminent. The men around them could feel the hush, the crouch of the approaching army. The area lower on the mountain, to the east, exploded suddenly in bursts of shining light as a rain of enchanted pellets, gifts from dwarven clerics, came down from the barbarians of the first defense.

How the kobolds scrambled! As did the few dark elves among the diminutive creatures' front ranks. Those monsters highest on the face, near the secret position, were overwhelmed, a horde of mighty barbarians descending over them, splitting them in half with huge swords and battle-axes, or simply lifting the kobolds high over head and hurling them down the mountainside.

"We must go out and meet them!" Berkthgar roared, seeing his kin engaged. He raised huge Bankenfuere high into the air. "To the glory of Tempus!" he roared, a cry repeated by all those barbarians on the second position, and those on the third as well.

"So much for ambush," muttered Regweld Harpell, seated on his horse-frog, Puddlejumper. With a nod to Besnell, for the time drew near, Regweld gave a slight tug on Puddlejumper's rein and the weird beast croaked out a guttural whinny and leaped to the west, clearing thirty feet.

"Not yet," Besnell implored Berkthgar, the barbarian's hand cupping a dozen or so of the magic light-giving pellets. The knight pointed out the movements of the enemy force below, explained to Berkthgar that, while many climbed up to meet the defenders holding the easternmost position, many, many more continued to filter along the lower trails to the west. Also, the light was not so intense anymore, as dark elves used their innate abilities to counter the stingingly bright enchantments.

"What are you waiting for?" Berkthgar demanded.

Besnell continued to hold his hand in the air, continued to delay the charge.

To the east, a barbarian screamed as he saw that his form was outlined suddenly by blue flames, magical fires that did not burn. They weren't truly harmless, though, for in the night, they gave the man's position clearly away. The sound of many crossbows clicked from somewhere below, and the unfortunate barbarian cried out again and again, then he fell silent.

That was more than enough for Berkthgar, and he hurled out the pellets. His nearby kin did likewise, and this second section of the south face brightened with magic. Down charged the men of Settlestone, to Besnell's continuing dismay. The riders should have gone down first, but not yet, not until the bulk of the enemy force had passed.

"We must," whispered the knight behind the elven leader from Silverymoon, and Besnell quietly nodded. He surveyed the scene for just a moment. Berkthgar and his hundred were already engaged, straight down the face, with no hope of linking up with those brave men holding the high ground in the east. Despite his anger at the impetuous barbarian, Besnell marveled at Berkthgar's exploits. Mighty Bankenfuere took out three kobolds at a swipe, launching them, whole or in parts, high into the air.

"The light will not hold," the knight behind Besnell remarked.

"Between the two forces," Besnell replied, speaking loud enough so that all those riders around him could hear. "We must go down at an angle, between the two forces, so that the men in the east can escape behind us."

Not a word of complaint came back to him, though his chosen course was treacherous indeed. The original plan had called for the Knights in Silver to ride straight into the enemy, both from this position and the next position to the west, while Berkthgar and his men linked behind them, the whole of the defending force rolling gradually to the west. Now Berkthgar, in his bloodlust, had abandoned that plan, and the Knights in Silver might pay dearly for the act. But neither man nor elf complained.

"Keep fast your pellets," Besnell commanded, "until the drow counter what light is already available."

He reared his horse once, for effect.

"For the glory of Silverymoon!" he cried.

"And the good of all good folk!" came the unified response.

Their thunder shook the side of Fourthpeak, resonated deep into the dwarven tunnels below the stone. To the blare of horns, down they charged, a hundred riders, lances low, and when those long spears became entangled or snapped apart as they skewered the enemy, out came flashing swords.

More deadly were the sturdy mounts, crushing kobolds under pounding hooves, scattering and terrifying kobolds and goblins and drow alike, for these invaders from the deepest Underdark had never seen such a cavalry charge.

In mere minutes the enemy advance up the mountain was halted and reversed, with only a few of the defenders taken down. And as the dark elves continued to counter the light pellets, Besnell's men countered their spells with still more light pellets.

But the dark force continued its roll along the lower trails, evidenced by the blare of horns to the west, the calls to Tempus and to Longsaddle, and the renewed thunder as the Longriders followed the lead of the Knights in Silver.

The first real throw of magic led the charge from that third position, a lightning bolt from Regweld that split the darkness, causing more horror than destruction.

Surprisingly, there came no magical response from the drow, other than minor darkness spells or faerie fire limning selected defenders.

The remaining barbarian force did as the plan had demanded, angling between the Longriders and the area just below the second position, linking up, not with the Knights in Silver, as was originally planned, but with Berkthgar and his force.

⚔ ⚔ ⚔ ⚔ ⚔

High above the battle, Alustriel used all her discipline and restraint to hold herself in check. The defenders were, as expected, slicing the kobold and goblin ranks to pieces, killing the enemy in a ratio far in excess of fifty to one.

That number would have easily doubled had Alustriel loosed her magic, but she could not. The drow were waiting patiently, and she respected the powers of those evil elves enough to know that her first attack might be her only one.

She whispered to the enchanted horses pulling the aerial chariot and moved lower, nodding grimly as she confirmed that the battle was going as anticipated. The slaughter high on the south face was complete, but the dark mass continued to flow below the struggle to the west.

Alustriel understood that many drow were among the ranks of that lower group.

The chariot swooped to the east, swiftly left the battle behind, and the Lady of Silverymoon took some comfort in the realization that the enemy lines were not so long, not so far beyond the easternmost of the defensive positions.

She came to understand why when she heard yet another battle, around the mountain, to the east. The enemy had found Mithral Hall's eastern door, had entered the complex, and was battling the dwarves within!

Flashes of lightning and bursts of fire erupted within the shadows of that low door, and the creatures that entered were not diminutive kobolds or stupid goblins. They were dark elves, many, many dark elves.

She wanted to go down there, to rush over the enemy in a magical, explosive fury, but Alustriel had to trust in Bruenor's people. The tunnels had been prepared, she knew, and the attack from outside the mountain had been expected.

Her chariot flew on, around to the north, and Alustriel thought to complete the circuit, to cut low through Keeper's Dale in the east, where the other allies, another hundred of her Knights in Silver, waited.

What she saw did not settle well, did not comfort her.

The northern face of Fourthpeak was a treacherous, barren stretch of virtually unclimbable rock faces and broken ravines that no man could pass.

Virtually unclimbable, but not to the sticky feet of giant subterranean lizards.

Berg'inyon Baenre and his elite force, the four hundred famed lizard riders of House Baenre, scrambled across that northern facing, making swift progress to the west, toward Keeper's Dale.

The waiting knights had been positioned to shore up the final defenses against the force crossing the southern face. Their charge, if it came, would be to open up the last flank, to allow Besnell, the Longriders, and the men of Nesmé and Settlestone to get into the dale, which was accessible through only one narrow pass.

The lizard-riders would get there first, Alustriel knew, and they outnumbered the waiting knights—and they were drow.

✕ ✕ ✕ ✕ ✕

The easternmost position was surrendered. The barbarians, or what remained of their ranks, ran fast to the west, crossing behind the Knights in Silver to join Berkthgar.

After they had crossed, Besnell turned his force to the west as well, pushing Berkthgar's force, which had swelled to include nearly every living warrior from Settlestone, ahead.

The leader of the Knights in Silver began to think that Berkthgar's error would not be so devastating, that the retreat could proceed as planned. He found a high plateau and surveyed the area, nodding grimly as he noted that the enemy force below had rolled around the first three positions.

Besnell's eyes widened, and he gasped aloud as he realized the exact location of the leading edge of that dark cloud. The Riders of Nesmé had missed their call! They had to get down the mountainside quickly, to hold that flank, and yet, for some reason, they had hesitated and the leading edge of the enemy force seemed beyond the fourth, and last, position.

Now the Riders of Nesmé did come, and their full-out charge down the smoothest stone of the south face was indeed devastating, the forty horsemen trampling thrice that number of kobolds in mere moments.

But the enemy had that many to spare, Besnell knew, and many more beyond that. The plan had called for an organized retreat to the west, to Keeper's Dale, even in through Mithral Hall's western door if need be.

It was a good plan, but now the flank was lost and the way to the west was closed.

Besnell could only watch in horror.

PART FIVE

OLD KINGS AND OLD QUEENS

They came as an army, but not so. Eight thousand dark elves and a larger number of humanoid slaves, a mighty and massive force, swarmed toward Mithral Hall.

The descriptions are fitting in terms of sheer numbers and strength, and yet "army" and "force" imply something more, a sense of cohesion and collective purpose. Certainly the drow are among the finest warriors in the Realms, trained to fight from the youngest age, alone or in groups, and certainly the purpose seems clear when the war is racial, when it is drow battling dwarves. Yet, though their tactics are perfect, groups working in unison to support each other, that cohesion among drow ranks remains superficial.

Few, if any, dark elves of Lolth's army would give her or his life to save another, unless she or he was confident that the sacrifice would guarantee a place of honor in the afterlife at the Spider Queen's side. Only a fanatic among the dark elves would take a hit, however minor, to spare another's life, and only because that fanatic thought the act in her own best interest. The drow came crying for the glory of the Spider Queen, but in reality, they each were looking for a piece of her glory.

Personal gain was always the dark elves' primary precept.

That was the difference between the defenders of Mithral Hall and those who came to conquer. That was the one hope of our side when faced with such horrendous odds, outnumbered by skilled drow warriors!

If a single dwarf came to a battle in which his comrades were being overrun, he would roar in defiance and charge in headlong, however terrible the odds. Yet if we could catch a group of drow, a patrol, perhaps, in an ambush, those supporting groups flanking their unfortunate comrades would not join in unless they could be assured of victory.

We, not they, had true collective purpose. We, not they, understood cohesion, fought for a shared higher principle, and understood and accepted that any sacrifice we might make would be toward the greater good.

There is a chamber—many chambers, actually—in Mithral Hall, where the heroes of wars and past struggles are honored. Wulfgar's hammer is there; so was the bow—the bow of an elf—that Catti-brie put into service once more. Though she has used the bow for years, and has added considerably to its legend, Catti-brie refers to it still as "the bow of Anariel," that long-dead elf. If the bow is put into service again by a friend of Clan Battlehammer centuries hence, it will be called "the bow of Catti-brie, passed from Anariel."

There is in Mithral Hall another place, the Hall of Kings, where the busts of Clan Battlehammer's patrons, the eight kings, have been carved, gigantic and everlasting.

The drow have no such monuments. My mother, Malice, never spoke of the previous matron mother of House Do'Urden, likely because Malice played a hand in her mother's death. In the Academy, there are no plaques of former mistresses and masters. Indeed, as I consider it now, the only monuments in Menzoberranzan are the statues of those punished by Baenre, of those struck by Vendes and her wicked whip, their skin turned to ebony, that they might then be placed on display as testaments of disobedience on the plateau of Tier Breche outside the Academy.

That was the difference between the defenders of Mithral Hall and those who came to conquer. That was the one hope.

–Drizzt Do'Urden

23

POCKETS OF POWER

Bidderdoo had never seen anything to match it. Literally, it was raining kobolds and pieces of kobolds all around the terrified Harpell as the Gutbuster Brigade went into full battle lust. They had come into a small, wide chamber and found a force of kobolds many times their own number. Before Bidderdoo could suggest a retreat—or a "tactical flanking maneuver," as he planned to call it, because he knew the word "retreat" was not in Thibbledorf Pwent's vocabulary—Pwent had led the forthright charge.

Poor Bidderdoo had been sucked up in the brigade's wake, the seven frenzied dwarves blindly, happily, following Pwent's seemingly suicidal lead right into the heart of the cavern. Now it was a frenzy, a massacre the likes of which the studious Harpell, who had lived all his life in the sheltered Ivy Mansion—and a good part of that as a family dog—could not believe.

Pwent darted by him, a dead kobold impaled on his helmet spike and flopping limply. Arms wide, the battlerager leaped into a group of kobolds and pulled as many in as possible, hugging them tightly. Then he began to shake, to convulse so violently that Bidderdoo wondered if some agonizing poison had found its way into the dwarf's veins.

Not so, for this was controlled insanity. Pwent shook, and the nasty ridges of his armor took the skin from his hugged enemies, ripped and tore them. He broke away—and three kobolds fell dying—with a left hook that brought his mailed, spiked gauntlet several inches into the forehead of the next unfortunate enemy.

Bidderdoo came to understand that the charge was not suicidal, that the

Gutbusters would win easily by overwhelming the greater numbers with sheer fury. He also realized, suddenly, that the kobolds learned fast to avoid the furious dwarves. Six of them bypassed Pwent, giving the battlerager a respectfully wide berth. Six of them swung around and bore down on the one enemy they could hope to defeat.

Bidderdoo fumbled with the shattered remains of his spellbook, flipping to one page where the ink had not smeared so badly. Holding the parchment in one hand, his other hand straight out in front of him, he began a fast chant, waggling his fingers.

A burst of magical energy erupted from each of his fingertips, green bolts rushing out, each darting and weaving to unerringly strike a target.

Five of the kobolds fell dead, and the sixth came on with a shriek, its little sword rushing for Bidderdoo's belly.

The parchment fell from the terrified Harpell's hand. He screamed, thinking he was about to die, and reacted purely on instinct, falling forward over the blade, angling his chest down so that he buried the diminutive kobold beneath him. He felt a burning pain as the small creature's sword cut into his ribs, but there was no strength behind the blow and the sword did not dig in deeply.

Bidderdoo, so unused to combat, screamed in terror. And the pain, the pain . . .

Bidderdoo's screams became a howl. He looked down and saw the thrashing kobold, and saw more clearly the thrashing kobold's exposed throat.

Then he tasted warm blood and was not repulsed.

Growling, Bidderdoo closed his eyes and held on. The kobold stopped thrashing.

After some time, the poor Harpell noticed that the sounds of battle had ended around him. He gradually opened his eyes, turned his head slightly to look up at Thibbledorf Pwent, standing over him and nodding his head.

Only then did Bidderdoo realize he had killed the kobold, had bitten the thing's throat out.

"Good technique," Pwent offered, and started away.

✕ ✕ ✕ ✕ ✕

While the Gutbuster Brigade's maneuvers were loud and straightforward, wholly dependent on savagery, another party's were a dance of stealth and ambush. Drizzt and Guenhwyvar, Catti-brie, Regis, and Bruenor moved silently from one tunnel to another, the drow and panther leading.

Guenhwyvar was the first to detect an approaching enemy, and Drizzt quickly relayed the signals when the panther's ears went flat.

The five worked in unison, setting up so that Catti-brie, with her deadly bow, would strike first, followed by the panther's spring, the drow's impossibly fast rush into the fray, and Bruenor's typically dwarven roaring charge. Regis always found a way to get into the fight, usually moving in behind to slam a drow backside or a kobold's head with his mace when one of his friends became too closely pressed.

This time, though, Regis figured to stay out of the battle altogether. The group was in a wide, high corridor when Guenhwyvar, nearing a bend, fell into a crouch, ears flat. Drizzt slipped into the shadows of an alcove, as did Regis, while Bruenor stepped defensively in front of his archer daughter, so that Catti-brie could use the horns of his helmet to line up her shot.

Around the corner came the enemy, a group of minotaurs and drow, five of each, running swiftly in the general direction of Mithral Hall.

Catti-brie wisely went for the drow. There came a flash of silver, and one fell dead.

Guenhwyvar came out hard and fast, burying another dark elf, clawing and biting and rolling right away to bear down on a third drow.

A second flash came, and another elf fell dead.

But the minotaurs came on hard, and Catti-brie would get no third shot. She went for her sword as Bruenor roared and rushed out to meet the closest monster.

The minotaur lowered its bull-like head, and Bruenor dropped his notched battle-axe right behind him over his head, holding the handle tightly in both hands.

In came the minotaur, and over came the axe. The crack sounded like the snapping of a gigantic tree.

Bruenor didn't know what hit him. Suddenly he was flying backward, bowled over by six hundred pounds of minotaur.

⚔ ⚔ ⚔ ⚔

Drizzt came out spinning and darting. He hit the first minotaur from the side, a scimitar cutting deep into the back of the creature's thigh, stopping its charge. The ranger spun away and went down to one knee, jabbing straight ahead with Twinkle, hooking the tip of the blue-glowing scimitar over the next monster's kneecap.

The minotaur howled and half-fell, half-dived right for Drizzt, but the drow's feet were already under him, already moving, and the brute slammed hard into the stone.

Drizzt turned back for Catti-brie and Bruenor and the two remaining brutes bearing down on his friends. With incredible speed, he caught up to them almost immediately and his scimitars went to work on one, again going for the legs, stopping the charge.

But the last minotaur caught up to Catti-brie. Its huge club, made of hardened mushroom stalk, came flying around, and Catti-brie ducked fast, whipping her sword above her head.

Khazid'hea sliced right through the club, and as the minotaur stared at the remaining piece dumbfoundedly, Catti-brie countered with a slashing backhand.

The minotaur looked at her curiously. She could not believe she had missed.

⚔ ⚔ ⚔ ⚔ ⚔

Regis watched from the shadows, knowing he was overmatched by any enemy in this fight. He tried to gauge his companions, though, wanting to be ready if needed. Mostly he watched Drizzt, mesmerized by the sheer speed of the drow's charges and dodges. Drizzt had always been quick afoot, but this display was simply amazing, the ranger's feet moving so swiftly that Regis could hardly distinguish them. More than once, Regis tried to anticipate Drizzt's path, only to find himself looking where the drow was not.

For Drizzt had cut to the side, or reversed direction altogether, more quickly than the halfling would have believed possible.

Regis finally just shook his head and filed his questions away for another time, reminding himself that there were other, more important considerations. He glanced around and noticed the last of the enemy drow slipping to the side, out of the way of the panther.

⚔ ⚔ ⚔ ⚔ ⚔

The last drow wanted no part of Guenhwyvar, and was glad indeed that the woman with the killing bow was engaged in close combat. Two of his dark elf companions lay dead from arrows, a third squirmed around on the floor, half her face torn away by the panther's claws, and all five minotaurs were down or engaged. The fourth drow had run off, back around the bend, but that wicked panther was only a couple of strides behind, and the hiding dark elf knew his companion would be down in a matter of moments.

Still, the drow hardly cared, for he saw Drizzt Do'Urden, the renegade, the most hated. The ranger was fully engaged and vulnerable, working furiously to finish the three minotaurs he had wounded. If this drow could seize the opportunity and get Drizzt, then his place of glory, and his House's glory, would be sealed. Even if he was killed by Drizzt's friends, he would have a seat of honor beside Lolth, the Spider Queen.

He loaded his most potent dart, a bolt enchanted with runes of fire and lightning, onto his heavy, two-handed crossbow, an unusual weapon indeed for dark elves, and brought the sights in line.

Something hit the crossbow hard from the side. The drow pulled the trigger instinctively, but the bolt, knocked loose, went nowhere but down, exploding at his feet. The jolt sent him flying, and the puff of flame singed his hair and momentarily blinded him.

He rolled over on the floor and managed to get out of his burning *piwafwi*. Dazed, he noticed a small mace lying on the floor, then saw a small, plump hand reaching down to pick it up. The drow tried to react as the bare feet, hairy on top—something the Underdark drow had never seen before—steadily approached.

Then all went dark.

⚔ ⚔ ⚔ ⚔ ⚔

Catti-brie cried out and leaped back, but the minotaur did not charge. Rather, the brute stood perfectly still, eyeing her curiously.

"I didn't miss," Catti-brie said, as if her denial of what seemed obvious would change her predicament. To her surprise, she found she was right.

The minotaur's left leg, severed cleanly by Khazid'hea's passing, caved in under it, and the brute fell sidelong to the floor, its lifeblood pouring out unchecked.

Catti-brie looked to the side to see Bruenor, grumbling and groaning, crawling out from under the minotaur he had killed. The dwarf hopped to his feet, shook his head briskly to clear away the stars, then stared at his axe, hands on hips, head shaking in dismay. The mighty weapon was embedded nearly a foot deep in the minotaur's thick skull.

"How in the Nine Hells am I going to get the damned thing out?" Bruenor asked, looking at his daughter.

Drizzt was done, as was Regis, and Guenhwyvar came back around the corner, dragging the last of the dark elves by the scruff of his broken neck.

"Another win for our side," Regis remarked as the friends regrouped.

Drizzt nodded his agreement but seemed not so pleased. It was a small thing they were doing, he knew, barely scratching at the surface of the force that had come to Mithral Hall. And despite the quickness of this latest encounter, and of the three before it, the friends had been, ultimately, lucky. What would have happened had another group of drow or minotaurs, or even kobolds, come around the corner while the fight was raging?

They had won quickly and cleanly, but their margin of victory was a finer line and a more tentative thing than the rout would indicate.

"Ye're not so pleased," Catti-brie said quietly to the ranger as they started off once more.

"In two hours we have killed a dozen drow, a handful of minotaurs and a score of kobold fodder," Drizzt replied.

"With thousands more to go," the woman added, understanding Drizzt's dismay.

Drizzt said nothing. His only hope, Mithral Hall's only hope, was that they and other groups like them would kill enough drow to take the heart from their enemy. Dark elves were a chaotic and supremely disloyal bunch, and only if the defenders of Mithral Hall could defeat the drow army's will for the war did they have a chance.

Guenhwyvar's ears went flat again, and the panther slipped silently into the darkness. The friends, feeling suddenly weary of it all, moved into position and were relieved indeed when the newest group rambled into sight. No drow this time, no kobolds or minotaurs. A column of dwarves, more than a score, hailed them and approached. This group, too, had seen battle since the fight in Tunult's Cavern. Many showed fresh wounds, and every dwarven weapon was stained with enemy blood.

"How fare we?" Bruenor asked, stepping to the front.

The leader of the dwarven column winced, and Bruenor had his answer. "They're fightin' in the Undercity, me king," said the dwarf. "How they got into the place, we're not for knowin'! And fightin' too, in the upper levels, by all reports. The eastern door's been breached."

Bruenor's shoulders visibly slumped.

"But we're holdin' at Garumn's Gorge!" the dwarf said with more determination.

"Where're ye from and where're ye going?" Bruenor wanted to know.

"From the last guard room," the dwarf explained. "Come out in a short circuit to find yerself, me king. Tunnels're thick with drow scum, and glad we be to see ye standing!" He pointed behind Bruenor, then jabbed his finger to the left. "We're not so far, and the way's still clear to the last guard room . . ."

"But it won't be for long," another dwarf piped in glumly.

"And clear all the way to the Undercity from there," the leader finished.

Drizzt pulled Bruenor to the side and began a whispered conversation. Catti-brie and Regis waited patiently, as did the dwarves.

" . . . keep searching," they heard Drizzt say.

"Me place is with me people!" Bruenor roughly replied. "And yer own is with me!"

Drizzt cut him short with a long stream of words. Catti-brie and the others heard snatches such as "hunting the head" and "roundabout route," and they knew Drizzt was trying to convince Bruenor to let him continue his hunt through the outer, lower tunnels.

Catti-brie decided then and there that if Drizzt and Guenhwyvar were to go on, she, with her Cat's Eye circlet, which Alustriel had given her to allow her to see in the dark, would go with him. Regis, feeling unusually brave and useful, silently came to the same conclusion.

Still, the two were surprised when Drizzt and Bruenor walked back to the group.

"Get ye to the last guard room, and all the way to the Undercity if need be," Bruenor commanded the column leader.

The dwarf's jaw dropped with amazement. "But, me king," he sputtered.

"Get ye!" Bruenor growled.

"And leave yerself alone out here?" the stunned dwarf asked.

Bruenor's smile was wide and wicked as he looked from the dwarf to Drizzt, to Catti-brie, to Regis, and to Guenhwyvar, then finally, back to the dwarf.

"Alone?" Bruenor replied, and the other dwarf, knowing the prowess of his king's companions, conceded the point.

"Get ye back and win," Bruenor said to him. "Me and me friends got some huntin' to do."

The two groups split apart once more, both grimly determined, but neither overly optimistic.

Drizzt whispered something to the panther, and Guenhwyvar took up the lead as before. To this point, the companions had been lying in wait for every enemy group that came their way, but now, with the grim news from the Undercity and the eastern door, Drizzt changed that tactic. If they could not avoid the small groups of drow and other monsters, then they would fight, but otherwise, their path now was more direct. Drizzt wanted to find the priestesses—and he knew it had to be priestesses—who had led this march. The dwarves' only chance was to decapitate the enemy force.

And so the companions were now, as Drizzt had quietly put it to Bruenor, "hunting the head."

Regis, last in line, shook his head and looked more than once back the way the dwarven column had marched. "How do I always get myself into this?" the halfling whispered. Then, looking at the backs of his hearty, sometimes reckless friends, he knew he had his answer.

Catti-brie heard the halfling's resigned sigh, understood its source, and managed to hide her smile.

24

FIERY FURY

Alustriel watched from her high perch as the southern face of Fourthpeak flickered with light that seemed to be blinking like the stars above. The exchange of enchanted pellets from the defenders and countering dark magic from the invaders was furious. As she brought her chariot around the southwestern cliffs, the Lady of Silverymoon grew terribly afraid, for the defenders had been pushed into a U formation, surrounded on all sides by goblins, kobolds, and fierce drow warriors.

Still, the forces of the four armies fought well, practically back to back, and their line was strong. No great number could strike at them from the gap at the top of the U, the logical weak spot, because of the almost sheer cliffs, and the defenders were tightly packed enough along the entire line to hold against any concentrated assaults.

Even as Alustriel fostered that thought, her hopes were put to the test. A group of goblins, led by huge bugbears, seven-foot, hairy versions of goblins, formed into a tight diamond and spearheaded into the defenders' eastern flank.

The line wavered, and Alustriel almost revealed herself with a flurry of explosive magic.

But amidst the chaos and the press rose one sword above all others, one song above all others.

Berkthgar the Bold, his wild hair flying, sang to Tempus with all his heart, and Bankenfuere hummed as it swept through the air. Berkthgar ignored the lesser goblins and charged straight for the bugbears, and each mighty swipe cut one of them down. The leader of Settlestone took a vicious hit, and another, but no hint of pain crossed his stern visage or slowed his determined march.

Those bugbears who escaped the first furious moments of the huge man's assault fled from him thereafter, and with their leaders so terrified, the goblins quickly lost heart for the press and the diamond disintegrated into a fleeing mob.

Many would be the songs to celebrate Berkthgar, Alustriel knew, but only if the defenders won. If the dark elves succeeded in their conquest, then all such heroics would be lost to the ages, all the songs would be buried beneath a black veil of oppression. That could not happen, the Lady of Silverymoon decided. Even if Mithral Hall were to fall this night, or the next, the war would not be lost. All of Silverymoon would mobilize against the drow, and she would go to Sundabar, in the east, to Citadel Adbar, stronghold of King Harbromme and his dwarves, and all the way to Waterdeep, on the Sword Coast, to muster the necessary forces to push the drow back to Menzoberranzan!

This war was not lost, she reminded herself, and she looked down at the determined defenders, holding against the swarm, fighting and dying.

Then came the tragedy she had expected and feared all along: the magical barrage, bursts of fireballs and lightning, lines of consuming magical energy and spinning bolts of destruction.

The assault focused on the southwestern corner of the U, blew apart the ranks of the Riders of Nesmé, consuming horse and man alike. Many humanoid slaves fell as well, mere fodder and of no concern to the wicked drow wizards.

Tears streamed down Alustriel's face as she watched that catastrophe, as she heard the agonized cries of man and beast and saw that corner of the mountain become charred under the sheer power of the barrage. She berated herself for not foreseeing this war, for underestimating the intensity of the drow march, for not having her army fully entrenched, warriors, wizards, and priests alike, in the defense of Mithral Hall.

The massacre went on for many seconds, seeming like hours to the horrified defenders. It went on and on, the explosions and the cries.

Alustriel found her heart again and looked for the source, and when she saw it, she came to realize that the dark elf wizards, in their ignorance of the surface world, had erred.

They were concentrated within a copse of thick trees, under cover and hurling out their deadly volley of spells.

Alustriel's features brightened into a wicked smile, a smile of vengeance, and she cut her chariot across at a sharp angle, swooping down the mountainside from on high, flying like an arrow for the heart of her enemies.

The drow had erred; they were in the trees.

As she crossed the northern edge of the battlefield, Alustriel cried out a command, and her chariot, and the team of enchanted horses that pulled it, ignited into bright flames.

Below her she heard the cries of fear, from friend and enemy alike, and she heard the trumpets from the Knights in Silver, who recognized the chariot and understood that their leader had come.

Down she streaked, a tremendous fireball leading the way, exploding in the heart of the copse. Alustriel sped right to the trees' edge, then banked sharply and rushed along the thick line, the flames of her chariot igniting branches wherever she passed.

The drow wizards had erred!

She knew the dark elves had likely set up wards against countering magic—perhaps even over themselves—that would defeat even the most intense fires, but they did not understand the flammable nature of trees. Even if the fire did not consume them, the flames would blind them and effectively put them out of the fighting.

And the smoke! The thick copse was damp from previous rains and frost, and billowing black clouds thickened the air. Even worse for the drow, the wizards countered as they had always countered fire, with spells creating water. So great was their response, that the flames would have been quenched, except that Alustriel did not relent, continued to rush around the copse, even cut into the copse wherever she found a break. No water, not the ocean itself, could extinguish the fires of her enchanted chariot. As she continued to fuel the flames, the drenching spells by the wizards added steam to the smoke, thickened the air so that the dark elves could not see at all and could not breathe.

Alustriel trusted in her horses, extensions of her will, to understand her intent and keep the chariot on course, and she watched, her spells ready, for she knew the enemy could not remain within the copse. As she expected, a drow floated up through the trees, rising above the inferno, levitating into the air and trying to orient himself to the scene beyond the copse.

Alustriel's lightning bolt hit him in the back of the head and sent him spinning over and over, and he hung, upside down and dead, until his own spell expired, dropping him back into the trees.

Even as she killed that wizard, though, a ball of flame puffed in the air right before the chariot, and the speeding thing, and Alustriel with it, plunged right through. The Lady of Silverymoon was protected from the flames of her own spell, but not so from the fireball, and she cried out and came through pained, her face bright from burn.

⚔ ⚔ ⚔ ⚔

Higher up the mountainside, Besnell and his soldiers witnessed the attack against Alustriel. The elf steeled his golden eyes, and his men cried out in outrage. If their earlier exploits had been furious, they were purely savage now, and Berkthgar's men, fighting beside them, needed no prodding.

Goblins and kobolds, bugbears and orcs, even huge minotaurs and skilled drow, died by the score in the next moments of battle.

It hardly seemed to matter. Whenever one died, two took its place, and though the knights and the barbarians could have cut through the enemy lines, there was nowhere for them to go.

Farther to the west, his own Longriders similarly pressed, Regweld understood their only hope. He leaped Puddlejumper to a place where there were no enemies and cast a spell to send a message to Besnell.

To the west! the wizard implored the knight leader.

Then Regweld took up the new lead and turned his men and the barbarians closest to them westward, toward Keeper's Dale, as the original plan had demanded. The drow wizards had been silenced, momentarily at least, and now was the only chance Regweld would have.

A lightning bolt split the darkening air. A fireball followed, and Regweld followed that, leaping Puddlejumper over the ranks of his enemies and loosing a barrage of magical missiles below him as he flew.

Confusion hit the enemy ranks, enough so that the Longriders, men who had fought beside the Harpells for all their lives and understood Regweld's tactics, were able to slice through, opening a gap.

Beside them came many of the Settlestone warriors and the few remaining horsemen from Nesmé. Behind them came the rest of the barbarian force and the Knights in Silver, mighty Berkthgar bringing up the rear, almost single-handedly keeping the pursuing monsters at bay.

The defenders punched through quickly, but found their momentum halted as another force, mostly drow, cut across in front, forming thick ranks.

Regweld continued his magical barrage, charged ahead with Puddlejumper, expecting to die.

And so he would have, except that Alustriel, forced away from the copse by the increasingly effective counters of the drow wizards, rushed back up the mountainside, right along the dark elf line, low enough so that the drow who did not flee were trampled and burned by her fiery passing.

Besnell and his men galloped to the front of the fleeing force, cried out to Alustriel and for the good of all goodly folk, and plunged into the confusion of the drow ranks, right into the flaming chariot's charred wake.

Many more men died in those few moments of hellish fighting, many men and many drow, but the defenders broke free to the west, ran and rode on, and found the path into Keeper's Dale before the enemy could block it.

Above the battle once more, Alustriel slumped with exhaustion. She had not launched so concentrated a barrage of magic in many, many years, and had not engaged so closely in any conflict since the days before she had come to rule Silverymoon. Now she was tired and wounded, burned and singed, and she had taken several hits by sword and by quarrel as she had rushed along the drow ranks. She knew the disapproval she would find when she returned to Silverymoon, knew that her advisors, and the city's council, and colleagues from other cities, would think her rash, even stupid. Mithral Hall was a minor kingdom not worth her life, her detractors would say. To take such risks against so deadly an enemy was foolish.

So they would say, but Alustriel knew better, knew that the freedoms and rights that applied to Silverymoon were not there simply because of her city's size and strength. They applied to all, to Silverymoon, to Waterdeep, and to the smallest of kingdoms that so desired them, because otherwise the values they promoted were meaningless and selfish.

Now she was wounded, had nearly been killed, and she called off her chariot's flames as she rose high into the sky. To show herself so openly would invite a continuing magical attack that would likely destroy her. She was sorely wounded, she knew, but Alustriel was smiling. Even if she died this night, the Lady of Silverymoon would die smiling, because she was following her heart. She was fighting for something bigger than her life, for values that were eternal and ultimately right.

She watched with satisfaction as the force, led by Besnell and her own knights, broke free and sped for Keeper's Dale, then she climbed higher into the cold sky, angling for the west.

The enemy would pursue, and more enemies were coming fast around the north, and the battle had only just begun.

✕ ✕ ✕ ✕ ✕

The Undercity, where two thousand dwarves often labored hard at their most beloved profession, had never seen such bustle and tumult as this day.

Not even when the shadow dragon, Shimmergloom, and its host of evil gray dwarves had invaded, when Bruenor's grandfather had been king, had the Undercity been engulfed in such a battle.

Goblins and minotaurs, kobolds and wicked monsters that the dwarves could not name flooded in from the lower tunnels and through the floor itself, areas that had been breached by the magic of the illithids. And the drow, scores of dark elves, struggled and battled along every step and across the wide floor, their dance a macabre mix of swirling shadows in the glow of the many low-burning furnaces.

Still, the main tunnels to the lower levels had not been breached, and the greatest concentration of enemies, particularly the drow force, remained outside Mithral Hall proper. Now the dark elves who had gained the Undercity meant to open that way, to link up with the forces of Uthegental and Matron Baenre.

And the dwarves meant to stop them, knowing that if that joining came to pass, then Mithral Hall would be lost.

Lightning flashed, green and red and sizzling black bolts from below, from the drow, and it was answered from above by Harkle and Bella don DelRoy.

The lowest levels began to grow darker as the drow worked their magic to gain a favorable battlefield.

The fall of light pellets upon the floor sounded like a gentle rain as Stumpet Rakingclaw and her host of dwarven priests countered the magic, brightening the area, loading spell after spell, stealing every shadow from every corner. Dwarves could fight in the dark, but they could fight in the light as well, and the drow and other creatures from the Underdark were not so fond of brightness.

One group of twenty dwarves formed a tight formation on the wide floor and rolled over a band of fleeing goblins. Their boots sounded like a heavy, rolling wheel, a general din, mowing over whatever monster dared to stay in their path.

A handful of dark elves fired stinging crossbow quarrels, but the dwarves shook off the hits—and, since their blood ran thick with potions to counter any poisons, they shook off the infamous drow sleeping drug as well.

Seeing that their attack was ineffective, the drow scattered, and the dwarven wedge rolled toward the next obstacle, two strange-looking creatures that the bearded folk did not know, two ugly creatures with slimy heads that waved tentacles where the mouths should have been, and with milky white eyes that showed no pupils.

The dwarven wedge seemed unstoppable, but when the illithids turned their way and loosed their devastating mental barrage, the wedge wobbled and fell apart, stunned dwarves staggering aimlessly.

"Oh, there they are!" Harkle squealed from the third tier of the Undercity, more than sixty feet from the floor.

Bella don DelRoy's face crinkled with disgust as she looked at mind flayers for the first time. She and Harkle had expected the creatures. Drizzt had told them about Matron Baenre's "pet." Despite her disgust, Bella, like all Harpells, was more curious than afraid. The illithids had been expected—she just hadn't expected them to be so damned ugly!

"Are you sure of this?" the diminutive woman asked Harkle, who had devised the strategy for fighting the squishy-headed things. Her good eye revealed her true hopes, though, for while she talked to Harkle, it remained fixated on the ugly illithids.

"Would I have gone to all the trouble of learning to cast from the different perspective?" Harkle answered, seeming wounded by her doubts.

"Of course," Bella replied. "Well, those dwarves do need our help."

"Indeed."

A quick chant by the daughter of DelRoy brought a shimmering blue, door-shaped field right before the two wizards.

"After you," Bella said politely.

"Oh, rank before beauty," Harkle answered, waving his hand toward the door, indicating that Bella should lead.

"No time for wasting!" came a clear voice behind them, and surprisingly strong hands pressed against both Bella and Harkle's hips, heaving them both for the door. They went through together, and Fret, the tidy dwarf, pushed in right behind them.

The second door appeared on the floor, between the illithids and their stunned dwarven prey, and out popped the three dimensional travelers. Fret skidded to the side, trying to round up the vulnerable dwarves, while Harkle and Bella don DelRoy mustered their nerve and faced the octopus-headed creatures.

"I understand your anger," Harkle began, and he and his companion shuddered as a wave of mental energy rolled across their chests and shoulders and heads, leaving a wake of tingles.

"If I were as ugly as you . . ." Harkle continued, and a second wave came through.

". . . I would be mean, too!" Harkle finished, and a third blast of energy came forth, followed closely by the illithids. Bella screamed and Harkle nearly fainted as the monstrous things pushed in close, tentacles latching onto cheeks and chins. One went straight up Harkle's nose, in search of brain matter to devour.

"You are sure?" Bella cried out.

But Harkle, deep in the throes of his latest spell, didn't hear her. He didn't struggle against the illithid, for he didn't want the thing to jostle him too severely. It was hard enough to concentrate with wriggling tentacles burrowing under the skin of his face!

Those tentacles swelled now, extracting their prize.

An unmistakably sour look crossed the normally expressionless features of both the creatures.

Harkle's hands came up slowly, palms down, his thumbs touching and his other fingers spread wide. A flash of fire erupted from his hands, searing the confused illithid, burning its robes. It tried to pull away, and Harkle's facial skin bulged weirdly as the tentacles began to slide free.

Harkle was already moving with his next spell. He reached into his robes and extracted a dart, a leaf that had been mushed to powder, and a stringy, slimy thing, a snake's intestine, and squashed them all together as he completed the chant.

From that hand came forth a small bolt, shooting across the two feet to stick into the still-burning illithid's belly.

The creature gurgled something indecipherable and finally fell away, stumbling, grasping at its newest wound, for while the fires still nipped at it in places, this newest attack hurt more.

The enchanted bolt pumped acid into its victim.

Down went the illithid, still clutching at the leaking bolt. It had underestimated its enemy, and it telepathically sent that very message to its immediate companion, who already understood their error, and to Methil, deep in the caverns beside Matron Baenre.

Bella couldn't concentrate. Though her spell of polymorph had been perfect, her brain safely tucked away where the illithid could not find it, she simply couldn't concentrate with the squiggly tentacles probing around her skull. She berated herself, told herself that the daughter of DelRoy should be more in control.

She heard a rumbling sound, a cart rolling near, and opened her eyes to see Fret push the cart right up behind the illithid, a host of drow in pursuit. Holding his nerve, the tidy dwarf leaped atop the cart and drew out a tiny silver hammer.

"Let her go!" Fret cried, bringing the nasty little weapon to bear. To the dwarf's surprise, and disgust, his hammer sank into the engaged illithid's bulbous head and ichor spewed forth, spraying the dwarf and staining his white robes.

Fret knew the drow were bearing down on him. He had resolved to make one attack on the illithid, then turn in defense against the dark elves. But all plans flew away in the face of that gory mess, the one thing that could bring the tidy dwarf into full battle rage.

No woodpecker ever hit a log as rapidly. Fret's hammer worked so as to seem a blur, and each hit sent more of the illithid's brain matter spraying, which only heightened the tidy dwarf's frenzy.

Still, that would have been the end of Fret, of all of them, had not Harkle quickly enacted his next spell. He focused on the area in front of the charging drow, threw a bit of lard into the air, and called out his next dweomer.

The floor became slick with grease, and the charge came to a stumbling, tumbling end.

Its head smashed to dripping pulp, the illithid slumped before Bella, the still-clinging tentacles bringing her low as well. She grabbed frantically at those tentacles and yanked them free, then stood straight and shuddered with pure revulsion.

"I told you that was the way to fight mind flayers!" Harkle said happily, for it had been his plan every step of the way.

"Shut up," Bella said to him, her stomach churning. She looked all around, seeing enemies closing in from many directions. "And get us out of here!" she said.

Harkle looked at her, confused and a bit wounded by her disdain. The plan had worked, after all!

A moment later, Harkle, too, became more than a little frightened, as he came to realize that he had forgotten that last little detail, and had no spells left that would transport them back to the higher tiers.

"Ummm," he stammered, trying to find the words to best explain their dilemma.

Relieved he was, and Bella, too, when the dwarven wedge reformed around them, Fret joining the ranks.

"We'll get ye back up," the leader of the grateful dwarves promised, and on they rolled, once more burying everything in their path.

Even more destructive now was their march, for every so often a blast of lightning or a line of searing fire shot out from their ranks as Harkle and Bella joined in the fun.

Still, Bella remained uncomfortable and wanted this all to end so that she could return to her normal physiology. Harkle had studied illithids intently, and knew as much about them as perhaps any wizard in all the Realms. Their mentally debilitating blasts were conical, he had assured her, and so, if he and she could get close, only the top half of their bodies would be affected.

Thus they had enacted the physical transformation enchantment, wherein Harkle and Bella appeared the same, yet had transfigured two areas of their makeup, their brains and their buttocks.

Harkle smiled at his cleverness as the wedge rolled on. Such a transformation had been a delicate thing, requiring many hours of study and preparation. But it had been worth the trouble, every second, the Harpell believed, recalling the sour looks on the ugly illithid faces!

$$\times \quad \times \quad \times \quad \times \quad \times$$

The rumbles from the collapse of the bridges, and of all the antechambers near Garumn's Gorge, were felt in the lowest tunnels of Mithral Hall, even beyond, in the upper passages of the wild Underdark itself. How much work Bruenor's people would have if ever they tried to open the eastern door again!

But the drow advance had been stopped, and was well worth the price. For now General Dagna and his force of defenders were free to go.

But where? the tough, battle-hardened dwarf wondered. Reports came to him that the Undercity was under full attack, but he also realized that the western door, near Keeper's Dale, was vulnerable, with only a few hundred dwarves guarding the many winding tunnels and with no provisions for such catastrophic measures as had been taken here in the east. The tunnels in the west could not be completely dropped; there had not been time to rig them so.

Dagna looked around at his thousand troops, many of them wounded, but all of them eager for more battle, eager to defend their sacred homeland.

"The Undercity," the general announced a moment later. If the western door was breached, the invaders would have to find their way through, no easy task considering the myriad choices they would face. The fighting had already come to the Undercity, so that was where Dagna belonged.

Normally it would have taken many minutes, a half hour or more, for the dwarves to get down to the fighting, even if they went the whole way at a full charge. But this, too, had been foreseen, so Dagna led his charges to the appointed spot, new doors that had been cut into the walls connecting to chimneys running up from the great furnaces. As soon as those doors were opened, Dagna and his soldiers heard the battle, so they went without delay,

one after another, onto the heavy ropes that had been set in place.

Down they slid, fearlessly, singing songs to Clanggedon. Down they went, hitting the floor at a full run, rushing out of the warm furnaces and right into the fray, streaming endlessly, it seemed, as were the drow coming in from the lower tunnels.

The fighting in the Undercity grew ever furious.

25

KEEPER'S DALE

Berg'inyon's force swept into Keeper's Dale, the sticky-footed lizards making trails where none could be found. They came down the northern wall like a sheet of water, into the misty valley, ominous shadows slipping past tall pillars of stone.

Though it was warmer here than on the open northern face, the drow were uncomfortable. There were no formations like this in the Underdark, no misty valleys, except those filled with the toxic fumes of unseen volcanoes. Scouting reports had been complete, though, and had specifically outlined this very spot, the doorstep of Mithral Hall's western door, as safe for passage. Thus, the Baenre lizard riders went into the valley without question, fearing their own volatile matron mother more than any possible toxic fumes.

As they entered the vale, they heard the fighting on the southern side of the mountain. Berg'inyon nodded when he took the moment to notice that the battle was coming closer—all was going as planned. The enemy was in retreat, no doubt, being herded like stupid rothé into the valley, where the slaughter would begin in full.

The moving shadows that were Berg'inyon's force slipped quietly through the mist, past the stone sentinels, trying to get a lay of the valley, trying to find the optimum ambush areas.

Above the mist, a line of fire broke the general darkness of the night sky, streaking fast and angling into the vale. Berg'inyon watched it, as did so many, not knowing what it might be.

As she crossed above the force, Alustriel loosed the last barrage of her magic, a blast of lightning, a rain of greenish pulses of searing energy, and a shower of explosive fireballs that liquified stone.

The alert dark elves responded before the chariot crossed over the northern lip of the vale, hit back with enchanted crossbow quarrels and similar spells of destruction.

The flames of the chariot flared wider, caught in the midst of a fireball, and the whole of the cart jerked violently to the side as a line of lightning blasted against its base.

Alustriel's magic had killed more than a few, and taken the mounts out from under many others, but the real purpose in the wizard's passing had been the part of decoy, for every drow eye was turned heavenward when the second battalion of the Knights in Silver joined the fray, charging through Keeper's Dale, horseshoes clacking deafeningly on the hard stone.

Lances lowered, the knights barreled through the initial ranks of drow, running them down with their larger mounts.

But these were the Baenre lizard riders, the most elite force in all of Menzoberranzan, a complement of warriors and wizards that did not know fear.

Silent commands went out from Berg'inyon, passed from waggling fingers to waggling fingers. Even after the surprise barrage from the sky and the sudden charge of the force that the drow did not know were in Keeper's Dale, the dark elf ranks outnumbered the Knights in Silver by more than three to one. Had those odds been one-to-one, the Knights in Silver still would have had no chance.

The tide turned quickly, with the knights, those who were not taken down, inevitably falling back and regrouping into tight formations. Only the mist and the unfamiliar terrain prevented the slaughter from being wholesale; only the fact that the overwhelming drow force could not find all the targets allowed the valiant knights to continue to resist.

Near the rear of the dark elf ranks, Berg'inyon heard the commotion as one unfortunate human got separated and confused, galloping his mount unintentionally toward the north, away from his comrades.

The Baenre son signaled for his personal guards to follow him, but to stay behind, and took up the chase, his great lizard slinking and angling to intercept. He saw the shadowy figure—and what a magnificent thing Berg'inyon thought the rider to be, so high and tall on his powerful steed.

That image did not deter the weapons master of Menzoberranzan's First House. He came around a pillar of stone, just to the side of the knight, and called out to the man.

The great horse skidded and stopped, the knight wheeling it around to face Berg'inyon. He said something Berg'inyon could not understand, some proclamation of defiance, no doubt, then lowered his long lance and kicked his horse into a charge.

Berg'inyon leveled his own mottled lance and drove his heels into the lizard's flanks, prodding the beast on. He couldn't match the speed of the knight's horse, but the horse couldn't match the lizard's agility. As the opponents neared, Berg'inyon swerved aside, brought his lizard right up the side of a thick stone pillar.

The knight, surprised by the quickness of the evasion, couldn't bring his lance out fast enough for an effective strike, but as the two passed, Berg'inyon managed to prod the running horse in the flank. It wasn't a severe hit, barely a scratch, but this was no ordinary lance. The ten-foot pole that Berg'inyon carried was a devilish death lance, among the most cunning and wicked of drow weapons. As the lance tip connected on the horseflesh, cutting through the metal armor the beast wore as though it were mere cloth, dark, writhing tentacles of black light crawled down its length.

The horse whinnied pitifully, kicked and jumped and came to a skidding stop. Somehow the knight managed to hold his seat.

"Run on!" he cried to his shivering mount, not understanding. "Run on!"

The knight suddenly felt as though the horse was somehow less substantial beneath him, felt the beast's ribs against his calves.

The horse threw its head back and whinnied again, an unearthly, undead cry, and the knight blanched when he looked into the thing's eyes, orbs that burned red with some evil enchantment.

The death lance had stolen the creature's life-force, had turned the proud, strong stallion into a gaunt, skeletal thing, an undead, evil thing. Thinking quickly, the knight dropped his lance, drew his huge sword, and sheared off the monster's head with a single swipe. He rolled aside as the horse collapsed beneath him, and came to his feet, hopping around in confusion.

Dark shapes encircled him, and he heard the hiss of nearby lizards, sucking sounds as sticky feet came free of stone.

Berg'inyon Baenre approached slowly. He, too, lowered his lance. A flick of his wrist freed him from his binding saddle, and he slid off his mount, determined to test one of these surface men in single combat, determined to show those drow nearby the skill of their leader.

Out came the weapons master's twin swords, sharp and enchanted, among the very finest of drow weapons.

The knight, nearly a foot taller than this adversary, but knowing the

reputation of dark elves, was rightfully afraid. He swallowed that fear, though, and met Berg'inyon head-on, sword against sword.

The knight was good, had trained hard for all of his adult life, but if he trained for all of his remaining years as well, they would not total the decades the longer-living Berg'inyon had spent with the sword.

The knight was good. He lived for almost five minutes.

⚔ ⚔ ⚔ ⚔ ⚔

Alustriel felt the chill, moist air of a low cloud brush her face, and it brought her back to consciousness. She moved quickly, trying to right the chariot, and felt the bite of pain all along her side.

She had been hit by spell and by weapon, and her burned and torn robes were wet with her own blood.

What would the world think if she, the Lady of Silverymoon, died here? she wondered. To her haughty colleagues, this was a minor war, a battle that had no real bearing on the events of the world, a battle, in their eyes, that Alustriel of Silverymoon should have avoided.

Alustriel brushed her long, silvery hair—hair that was also matted with blood—back from her beautiful face. Anger welled within her as she thought of the arguments she had fought over King Bruenor's request for aid. Not a single advisor or councilor in Silverymoon, with the exception of Fret, wanted to answer that call, and Alustriel had to wage a long, tiresome battle of words to get even the two hundred Knights in Silver released to Mithral Hall.

What was happening to her own city? the lady wondered now, floating high above the disaster of Fourthpeak. Silverymoon had earned a reputation as the most generous of places, as a defender of the oppressed, champion of goodness. The knights had gone off to war eagerly, but they weren't the problem, and had never been.

The problem, the wounded Alustriel came to realize, was the comfortably entrenched bureaucratic class, the political leaders who had become too secure in the quality of their own lives. That seemed crystal clear to Alustriel now, wounded and fighting hard to control her enchanted chariot in the cold night sky above the battle.

She knew the heart of Bruenor and his people; she knew the goodness of Drizzt, and the value of the hearty men of Settlestone. They were worth defending, Alustriel believed. Even if all of Silverymoon were consumed in the war, these people were worth defending, because, in the end, in the annals future historians would pen, that would be the measure of Silverymoon. That generosity would be the greatness of the place, would be what set Silverymoon apart from so many other petty kingdoms.

But what was happening to her city? Alustriel wondered, and she came to understand the cancer that was growing amidst her own ranks. She would go back to Silverymoon and purge that disease, she determined, but not now.

Now she needed rest. She had done her part, to the best of her abilities, and perhaps at the price of her own life, she realized as another pain shot through her wounded side.

Her colleagues would lament her death, would call it a waste, considering the minor scale of this war for Mithral Hall.

Alustriel knew better, knew how she, like her city, would be ultimately judged.

She managed to bring the chariot crashing down to a wide ledge, and she tumbled out as the fiery dweomer dissipated into nothingness.

The Lady of Silverymoon sat there against the stone, in the cold, looking down on the distant scramble far below her. She was out of the fight, but she had done her part.

She knew she could die with no guilt weighing on her heart.

⚔ ⚔ ⚔ ⚔ ⚔

Berg'inyon Baenre rode through the ranks of lizard-mounted drow, holding high his twin bloodstained swords. The dark elves rallied behind their leader, filtered from obelisk to obelisk, cutting the battlefield in half and more. The mobility and speed of the larger horses favored the knights, but the dark elves' cunning tactics were quick to steal that advantage.

To their credit, the knights were killing drow at a ratio of one to one, a remarkable feat considering the larger drow numbers and the skill of their enemies. Even so, the ranks of knights were being diminished.

Hope came in the form of a fat wizard riding a half-horse, half-frog beastie and leading the remnants of the defenders of the southern face, hundreds of men, riding and running—from battle and into battle.

Berg'inyon's force was fast pushed across the breadth of Keeper's Dale, back toward the northern wall, and the defending knights rode free once more.

But in came the pursuit from the south, the vast force of drow and humanoid monsters. In came those dark elf wizards who had survived Alustriel's conflagration in the thick copse.

The ranks of the defenders quickly sorted out, with Berkthgar's hearty warriors rallying behind their mighty leader and Besnell's knights linking with

the force that had stood firm in Keeper's Dale. Likewise did the Longriders fall into line behind Regweld, and the Riders of Nesmé—both of the survivors— joined their brethren from the west.

Magic flashed and metal clanged and man and beast screamed in agony. The mist thickened with sweat, and the stone floor of the valley darkened with blood.

The defenders would have liked to form a solid line of defense, but to do so would leave them terribly vulnerable to the wizards, so they had followed savage Berkthgar's lead, had plunged into the enemy force headlong, accepting the sheer chaos.

Berg'inyon ran his mount halfway up the northern wall, high above the valley, to survey the glorious carnage. The weapons master cared nothing for his dead comrades, including many dark elves, whose broken bodies littered the valley floor.

This fight would be won easily, Berg'inyon thought, and the western door to Mithral Hall would be his.

All glory for House Baenre.

※ ※ ※ ※ ※

When Stumpet Rakingclaw came up from the Undercity to Mithral Hall's western door, she was dismayed—not by the reports of the vicious fighting out in Keeper's Dale, but by the fact that the dwarven guards had not gone out to aid the valiant defenders.

Their orders had been explicit: they were to remain inside the complex, to defend the tighter tunnels, and if the secret door was found by the enemy and the defenders were pushed back, the dwarves were prepared to drop those tunnels near the door. Those orders, given by General Dagna, Bruenor's second in command, had not foreseen the battle of Keeper's Dale.

Bruenor had appointed Stumpet as High Cleric of Mithral Hall, and had done so publicly and with much fanfare, so that there would be no confusion concerning rank once battle was joined. That decision, that public ceremony, gave Stumpet the power she needed now, allowed her to change the orders, and the five hundred dwarves assigned to guard the western door, who had watched with horror the carnage from afar, were all too happy to hear the new command.

There came a rumbling beneath the ground in all of Keeper's Dale, the grating of stone against stone. On the northern side of the valley, Berg'inyon held tight to his sticky-footed mount and hoped the thing wouldn't be shaken from the wall. He listened closely to the echoes, discerning the pattern, then looked to the southeastern corner of the valley.

A glorious, stinging light flashed there as the western door of Mithral Hall slid open.

Berg'inyon's heart skipped a beat. The dwarves had opened the way!

Out they came, hundreds of bearded folk, rushing to their allies' aid, singing and banging their axes and hammers against their shining shields, pouring from the door that was secret no more. They came up to, and beyond, Berkthgar's line, their tight battle groups slicing holes in the ranks of goblin and kobold and drow alike, pushing deeper into the throng.

"Fools!" the Baenre weapons master whispered, for even if a thousand, or two thousand dwarves came into Keeper's Dale, the course of the battle would not be changed. They had come out because their morals demanded it, Berg'inyon knew. They had opened their door and abandoned their best defenses because their ears could not tolerate the screams of men dying in their defense.

How weak these surface dwellers were, the sinister drow thought, for in Menzoberranzan courage and compassion were never confused.

The furious dwarves came into the battle hard, driving through drow and goblins with abandon. Stumpet Rakingclaw, fresh from her exploits in the Undercity, led their charge. She was out of light pellets but called to her god now, enacting enchantments to brighten Keeper's Dale. The dark elves quickly countered every spell, as the dwarf expected, but Stumpet figured that every drow concentrating on a globe of darkness was out of the fight, at least momentarily. The magic of Moradin, Dumathoin, and Clanggedon flowed freely through the priestess. She felt as though she was a pure conduit, the connection to the surface for the dwarven gods.

The dwarves rallied around her loud prayers as she screamed to her gods with all her heart. Other defenders rallied around the dwarves, and suddenly they were gaining back lost ground. Suddenly the idea of a single line of defense was not so ridiculous.

High on the wall across the way, Berg'inyon chuckled at the futility of it all. This was a temporary surge, he knew, and the defenders of the western door had come together in one final, futile push. All the defense and all the defenders, and Berg'inyon's force still outnumbered them several times over.

The weapons master coaxed his mount back down the wall, gathered his elite troops around him, and determined how to turn back the momentum. When Keeper's Dale fell, so, too, would the western door.

And Keeper's Dale would fall, Berg'inyon assured his companions with all confidence, within the hour.

26

SNARL AGAINST SNARL

The main corridors leading to the lower door of Mithral Hall had been dropped and sealed, but that had been expected by the invading army. Even with the largest concentration of drow slowed to a crawl out in the tunnels beyond the door, the dwarven complex was hard pressed. And though no reports had come to Uthegental about the fighting outside the mountain, the mighty weapons master could well imagine the carnage on the slopes, with dwarves and weakling humans dying by the score. Both doors of Mithral Hall were likely breached by now, Uthegental believed, with Berg'inyon's lizard riders flooding the higher tunnels.

That notion bothered the weapons master of Barrison del'Armgo more than a little. If Berg'inyon was in Mithral Hall, and Drizzt Do'Urden was there, the renegade might fall to the son of House Baenre. Thus Uthegental and the small band of a half-dozen elite warriors he took in tow now sought the narrow ways that would get them to the lowest gate of Mithral Hall proper. Those tunnels should be open, with the dark elves filtering out from the Undercity to clear the way.

The weapons master and his escort came into the cavern that had previously served as Bruenor's command post. It was deserted now, with only a few parchments and scraps from clerical preparations to show that anyone had been in the place. After the fall of the tunnels and the collapse of portions of Tunult's Cavern—and many side tunnels, including the main one that led back to this chamber—Bruenor's lower groups apparently had been scattered, without any central command.

Uthegental passed through the place, hardly giving it a thought. The drow band moved swiftly down the corridors, staying generally east, silently following the weapons master's urgent lead. They came to a wide fork in the trail and noticed the very old bones of a two-headed giant lying against the wall—ironically, a kill Bruenor Battlehammer had made centuries before. Of more concern, though, was the fork in the tunnel.

Frustrated at yet another delay, Uthegental sent scouts left and right, then he and the rest of his group went right, the more easterly course.

Uthegental sighed, relieved that they had at last found the lower door, when his scout and another drow, a priestess, met him a few moments later.

"Greetings, Weapons master of the Second House," the priestess greeted, affording mighty Uthegental more respect than was normally given to mere males.

"Why are you out in the tunnels?" Uthegental wanted to know. "We are still far from the Undercity."

"Farther than you think," the priestess replied, looking disdainfully back toward the east, down the long tunnel that ended at the lower door. "The way is not clear."

Uthegental issued a low growl. Those dark elves should have taken the Undercity by now, and should have opened the passages. He stepped by the female, his pace revealing his anger.

"You'll not break through," the priestess assured him, and he spun around, scowling as though she had slapped him in the face.

"We have been striking at the door for an hour," the priestess explained. "And we shall spend another tenday before we get past that barricade. The dwarves defend it well."

"*Ultrin sargtlin!*" Uthegental roared, his favorite title, to remind the priestess of his reputation. Still, despite the fact that Uthegental had earned that banner of "Supreme Warrior," the female did not seem impressed.

"A hundred drow, five wizards, and ten priestesses have not breached the door," she said evenly. "The dwarves strike back against our magic with great spears and balls of flaming pitch. And the tunnel leading to the door is narrow and filled with traps, as well defended as House Baenre itself. Twenty minotaurs went down there, and those dozen that stumbled past the traps found hearty dwarves waiting for them, coming out of concealment from small, secret cubbies. Twenty minotaurs were slain in the span of a few minutes.

"You'll not break through," the priestess said again, her tone matter-of-fact and in no way insulting. "None of us will unless those who have entered the dwarven complex strike at the defenders of the door from behind."

Uthegental wanted to lash out at the female, mostly because he believed her claim.

"Why would you wish to enter the complex?" the female asked unexpectedly, slyly.

Uthegental eyed her with suspicion, wondering if she was questioning his bravery. Why wouldn't he want to find the fighting, after all?

"Whispers say your intended prey is Drizzt Do'Urden," the priestess went on.

Uthegental's expression shifted from suspicion to intrigue.

"Other whispers say the renegade is in the tunnels outside Mithral Hall," she explained, "hunting with his panther and killing quite a few drow."

Uthegental ran a hand through his spiked hair and looked back to the west, to the wild maze of tunnels he had left behind. He felt a surge of adrenaline course through his body, a tingling that tightened his muscles and set his features in a grim lock. He knew that many groups of enemies were operating in the tunnels outside the dwarven complex, scattered bands fleeing the seven-chambered cavern where the first battle had been fought. Uthegental and his companions had met and slain one such group of dwarves on their journey to this point.

Now that he thought about it, it made sense to Uthegental that Drizzt would be out here as well. It was very likely the renegade had been in the battle in the seven-chambered cavern, and if that was true, then why would Drizzt flee back into Mithral Hall?

Drizzt was a hunter, a former patrol leader, a warrior that had survived a decade alone with his magical panther in the wild Underdark—no small feat, and one that even Uthegental respected.

Yes, now that the priestess had told him the rumor, it made perfect sense to Uthegental that Drizzt Do'Urden would be out there, somewhere back in the tunnels to the west, roaming and killing. The weapons master laughed loudly and started back the way he had come, offering no explanation.

None was needed, to the priestess or to Uthegental's companions, who fell into line behind him.

The weapons master of the Second House was hunting.

⚔ ⚔ ⚔ ⚔ ⚔

"We are winning," Matron Baenre declared.

None of those around her—not Methil or Jarlaxle, not Matron Zeerith Q'Xorlarrin, of the Fourth House, or Auro'pol Dyrr, matron mother of House

Agrach Dyrr, now the Fifth House, not Bladen'Kerst or Quenthel Baenre—argued the blunt statement.

Gandalug Battlehammer, dirty and beaten, his wrists bound tightly by slender shackles so strongly enchanted that a giant could not break them, cleared his throat, a noise that sounded positively gloating. There was more bluster than truth in the dwarf's attitude, for Gandalug carried with him a heavy weight. Even if his folk were putting up a tremendous fight, dark elves had gotten into the Undercity. And they had come to that place because of Gandalug, because of his knowledge of the secret ways. The old dwarf understood that no one could withstand the intrusions of an illithid, but the guilt remained, the notion that he, somehow, had not been strong enough.

Quenthel moved before Bladen'Kerst could react, smacking the obstinate prisoner hard across the back, her fingernails drawing lines of blood.

Gandalug snorted again, and this time Bladen'Kerst whacked him with her five-tonged snake-headed whip, a blow that sent the sturdy dwarf to his knees.

"Enough!" Matron Baenre growled at her daughters, a hint of her underlying frustration showing through.

They all knew—and it seemed Baenre did as well, despite her proclamation—that the war was not going according to plan. Jarlaxle's scouts had informed them of the bottleneck near Mithral Hall's lowest door, and that the eastern door from the surface had been blocked soon after it was breached, at a cost of many drow lives. Quenthel's magical communications with her brother told her that the fighting was still furious on the southern and western slopes of Fourthpeak, and that the western door from the surface had not yet been approached. And Methil, who had lost his two illithid companions, had telepathically assured Matron Baenre that the fight for the Undercity was not yet won, not at all.

Still, there was a measure of truth in Baenre's prediction of victory, they all knew, and her confidence was not completely superficial. The battle outside the mountain was not finished, but Berg'inyon had assured Quenthel that it soon would be—and given the power of the force that had gone out beside Berg'inyon, Quenthel had no reason to doubt his claim.

Many had died in these lower tunnels, but most of the losses had been humanoid slaves, not dark elves. Now those dwarves who had been caught outside their complex after the tunnel collapse had been forced into tactics of hunt and evade, a type of warfare that surely favored the stealthy dark elves.

"All the lower tunnels will soon be secured," Matron Baenre elaborated, a statement made obvious by the simple fact that this group, which would risk no encounters, was on the move once more. The elite force surrounding Baenre was responsible for guiding and guarding the first matron mother. They would not allow Baenre any advancement unless the area in front of them was declared secure.

"The region above the ground around Mithral Hall will also be secured," Baenre added, "with both surface doors to the complex breached."

"And likely dropped," Jarlaxle dared to put in.

"Sealing the dwarves in their hole," Matron Baenre was quick to respond. "We will fight through this lower door, and our wizards and priestesses will find and open new ways into the tunnels of the complex, that we might filter among our enemy's ranks."

Jarlaxle conceded the point, as did the others, but what Baenre was talking about would take quite a bit of time, and a drawn out siege had not been part of the plan. The prospect did not sit well with any of those around Matron Baenre, particularly the other two matron mothers. Baenre had pressured them to come out, so they had, though their Houses, and all the city, was in a critical power flux. In exchange for the personal attendance of the matron mothers in the long march, House Xorlarrin and House Agrach Dyrr had been allowed to keep most of their soldiers at home, while the other Houses, particularly the other ruling Houses, had sent as much as half their complement of dark elves. For the few months that the army was expected to be away, the fourth and fifth Houses seemed secure.

But Zeerith and Auro'pol had other concerns, worries of power struggles within their families. The hierarchy of any drow House, except perhaps for Baenre, was always tentative, and the two matron mothers knew that if they were away for too long, they might return to find they had been replaced.

They exchanged concerned looks now, doubting expressions that ever observant Jarlaxle did not miss.

Baenre's battle group moved along on its slow and determined way, the three matron mothers floating atop their driftdisks, flanked by Baenre's two daughters—dragging the dwarf—and the illithid, who seemed to glide rather than walk, his feet hidden under his long, heavy robes. A short while later, Matron Baenre informed them that they would find an appropriate cavern and set up a central throne room, from which she could direct the continuing fight.

It was another indication that the war would be a long one, and again Zeerith and Auro'pol exchanged disconcerted looks.

Bladen'Kerst Baenre narrowed her eyes at both of them, silently threatening.

Jarlaxle caught it all, every connotation, every hint of where Matron Baenre might find her greatest troubles.

The mercenary leader bowed low and excused himself, explaining that he would join up with his band and try to garner more timely information.

Baenre waved her hand, dismissing him without a second thought. One of her escorts was not so casual.

You and your mercenaries will flee, came an unexpected message in Jarlaxle's mind.

The mercenary's own thoughts whirled in a jumble, and caught off guard, he couldn't avoid sending the telepathic reply that the notion of deserting the war had indeed crossed his mind. As close to desperation as he had ever been, Jarlaxle looked back over his shoulder at the expressionless face of the intruding illithid.

Beware of Baenre should she return, Methil imparted casually, and he continued on his way with Baenre and the others.

Jarlaxle paused for a long while when the group moved out of sight, scrutinizing the emphasis of the illithid's last communication. He came to realize that Methil would not inform Baenre of his wavering loyalty. Somehow, from the way the message had been given, Jarlaxle knew that.

The mercenary leaned against a stone wall, thinking hard about what his next move should be. If the drow army stayed together, Baenre would eventually win—that much he did not doubt. The losses would be greater than anticipated—they already had been—but that would be of little concern once Mithral Hall was taken, along with all its promised riches.

What, then, was Jarlaxle to do? The disturbing question was still bouncing around the mercenary's thoughts when he found some of his Bregan D'aerthe lieutenants, all bearing news of the continuing bottleneck near the lower door, and information that even more dark elves and slaves were being killed in the outer tunnels, falling prey to roving bands of dwarves and their allies.

The dwarves were defending, and fighting, well.

Jarlaxle made his decision and relayed it silently to his lieutenants in the intricate hand code. Bregan D'aerthe would not desert, not yet. But neither would they continue to spearhead the attack, risking their forward scouts.

Avoid all fights, Jarlaxle's fingers flashed, and the gathered soldiers nodded their accord. *We stay out of the way, and we watch, nothing more.*

Until Mithral Hall is breached, one of the lieutenants reasoned back.

Jarlaxle nodded. *Or until the war becomes futile*, his fingers replied, and from his expression, it was obvious the mercenary leader did not think his last words ridiculous.

⚔ ⚔ ⚔ ⚔ ⚔

Pwent and his band rambled through tunnel after tunnel, growing frustrated, for they found no drow, or even kobolds, to slam.

"Where in the Nine Hells are we?" the battlerager demanded. No answer came in reply, and when he thought about it, Pwent really couldn't expect one. He knew these tunnels better than any in his troupe, and if he had no idea where they were, then certainly the others were lost.

That didn't bother Pwent so much. He and his furious band really didn't care where they were as long as they had something to fight. Lack of enemies was the real problem.

"Start to bangin'!" Pwent roared, and the Gutbusters ran to the walls in the narrow corridor and began slamming hammers against the stone, causing such a commotion that every creature within two hundred yards would easily be able to figure out where they were.

Poor Bidderdoo Harpell, swept up in the wake of the craziest band of suicidal dwarves, stood in the middle of the tunnel, using his glowing gem to try to sort through the few remaining parchments from his blasted spellbook, looking for a spell, any spell—though preferably one that would get him out of this place!

The racket went on for several minutes, and frustrated, Pwent ordered his dwarves to form up, and off they stormed. They went under a natural archway, around a couple of bends in the passage, then came upon a wider and squarer way, a tunnel with worked stone along its walls and an even floor. Pwent snapped his fingers, realizing that they had struck out to the west and south of Mithral Hall. He knew this place, and knew that he would find a dwarven defensive position around the next corner. He bobbed around in the lead, and scrambled over a barricade that reached nearly to the ceiling, hoping to find some more allies to "enlist" into his terror group. As he crested the wall, Pwent stopped short, his smile erased.

Ten dwarves lay dead on the stone floor, amidst a pile of torn goblins and orcs.

Pwent fell over the wall, landed hard, but bounced right back to his feet. He shook his head as he walked among the carnage. This position was strongly fortified, with the high wall behind, and a lower wall in front, where the corridor turned a sharp corner to the left.

Mounted against that left-hand wall, just before the side tunnel, was a curious contraption, a deadly dwarven side-slinger catapult, with a short, strong arm that whipped around to the side, not over the top, as with conventional catapults. The arm was pulled back now, ready to fire, but Pwent noticed immediately that all the ammunition was gone, that the valiant dwarves had held out to the last.

Pwent could smell the remnants of that catapult's missiles and could see flickering shadows from the small fires. He knew before he peeked around the bend that many, many dead enemies would line the corridor beyond.

"They died well," the battlerager said to his minions as they and Bidderdoo crossed the back wall and walked among the bodies.

The charge around the corner came fast and silent, a handful of dark elves rushing out, swords drawn.

Had Bidderdoo Harpell not been on the alert—and had he not found the last remaining usable page of his spellbook—that would have been the swift end of the Gutbuster Brigade, but the wizard got his spell off, enacting a blinding—to the drow—globe of brilliant light.

The surprised dark elves hesitated just an instant, but long enough for the Gutbusters to fall into battle posture. Suddenly it was seven dwarves against five dark elves, the element of surprise gone. Seven battleragers against five dark elves, and what was worse for the drow, these battleragers happened to be standing among the bodies of dead kin.

They punched, kicked, jumped, squealed, and head-butted with abandon, ignoring any hits, fighting to make their most wild leader proud. They plowed under two of the drow, and one dwarf broke free, roaring as he charged around the bend.

Pwent got one drow off to the side, caught the dark elf's swinging sword in one metal gauntlet and punched straight out with the other before the drow could bring his second sword to bear.

The drow's head verily exploded under the weight of the spiked gauntlet, furious Pwent driving his fist right through the doomed creature's skull.

He hit the drow again, and a third time, then tossed the broken body beside the other four dead dark elves. Pwent looked around at his freshly bloodied troops, noticed at once that one was missing, and noticed, too, that Bidderdoo was trembling wildly, his jowls flapping noisily. The battlerager would have asked the wizard about it, but then the cry of agony from down the side corridor chilled the marrow in even sturdy Thibbledorf Pwent's bones. He leaped to the corner and looked around.

The carnage along the length of the fifty-foot corridor was even more tremendous than Pwent had expected. Scores of humanoids lay dead, and

several small fires still burned, so thick was the pitch from the catapult missiles along the floor and walls.

Pwent watched as a large form entered the other end of the passage, a shadowy form, but the battlerager knew it was a dark elf, though certainly the biggest he had ever seen. The drow carried a large trident, and on the end of the trident, still wriggling in the last moments of his life, was Pwent's skewered Gutbuster. Another drow came out behind the huge weapons master, but Pwent hardly noticed the second form, and hardly cared if a hundred more were to follow.

The battlerager roared in protest, but did not charge. In a rare moment where cleverness outweighed rage, Pwent hopped back around the corner.

"What is it, Most Wild Battlerager?" three of the Gutbusters yelled together.

Pwent didn't answer. He jumped into the basket of the side-slinger and slashed his spiked gauntlet across the trigger rope, cutting it cleanly.

Uthegental Armgo had just shaken free the troublesome kill when the side-slinger went off, shooting the missile Pwent down the corridor. The weapons master's eyes went wide; he screamed as Pwent screamed. Suddenly Uthegental wished he still had the dead dwarf handy, that he might use the body as a shield. Purely on instinct, the warrior drow did the next best thing. He grabbed his drow companion by the collar of his *piwafwi* and yanked him in front.

Pwent's helmet spike, and half his head, blasted the unfortunate dark elf, came through cleanly enough to score a hit on Uthegental as well.

The mighty weapons master extracted himself from the tumble as Pwent tore free of the destroyed drow. They came together in a fit of fury, rage against rage, snarl against snarl, Pwent scoring several hits, but Uthegental, so strong and skilled, countering fiercely.

The butt of the trident slammed Pwent's face, and his eyes crossed. He staggered backward and realized, to his horror, that he had just given this mighty foe enough room to skewer him.

A silver beast, a great wolf running on its hind legs, barreled into Uthegental from the side, knocking him back to the floor.

Pwent shook his head vigorously, clearing his mind, and regarded the newest monster with more than a little apprehension. He glanced back up the corridor to see his Gutbusters approaching fast, all of them pointing to the wolf and howling with glee.

"Bidderdoo," Pwent mumbled, figuring it out.

Uthegental tossed the werewolf Harpell aside and leaped back to his feet.

Before he had fully regained his balance, though, Pwent sprang atop him.

A second dwarf leaped atop him, followed by a third, a fourth, the whole of the Gutbuster Brigade.

Uthegental roared savagely, and suddenly, the drow possessed the strength of a giant. He stood tall, dwarves hanging all over him, and threw his arms out wide, plucking dwarves and hurling them as though they were mere rodents.

Pwent slammed him in the chest, a blow that would have killed a fair-sized cow.

Uthegental snarled and gave the battlerager a backhand slap that launched Pwent a dozen feet.

"Ye're good," a shaky Pwent admitted, coming up to one knee as Uthegental stalked in.

For the first time in his insane life—except, perhaps, for when he had inadvertently battled Drizzt—Thibbledorf Pwent knew he was outmatched—knew that his whole brigade was outmatched!—and thought he was dead. Dwarves lay around groaning and none would be able to intercept the impossibly strong drow.

Instead of trying to stand, Pwent cried out and hurled himself forward, scrambling on his knees. He came up at the last second, throwing all of his weight into a right hook.

Uthegental caught the hand in midswing and fully halted Pwent's momentum. The mighty drow's free hand closed over Pwent's face, and Uthegental began bending the poor battlerager over backward.

Pwent could see the snarling visage through the wide-spread fingers. He somehow found the strength to lash out with his free left, and scored a solid hit on the drow's forearm.

Uthegental seemed not to care.

Pwent whimpered.

The weapons master threw his head back suddenly.

Pwent thought the drow meant to issue a roar of victory, but no sound came from Uthegental's mouth, no noise at all, until a moment later when he gurgled incoherently.

Pwent felt the drow's grip relax, and the battlerager quickly pulled away. As he straightened, Pwent came to understand. The silver werewolf had come up behind Uthegental and had bitten the drow on the back of the neck. Bidderdoo held on still, all the pressure of his great maw crushing the vertebrae and the nerves.

The two held the macabre pose for many heartbeats, and all the conscious Gutbusters gathered around them marveled at the strength of Bidderdoo's

mouth, and at the fact that this tremendous drow warrior was still holding his feet.

There came a loud crack, and Uthegental jerked suddenly, violently. Down he fell, the wolf atop him, holding fast.

Pwent pointed to Bidderdoo. "I got to get him to show me how he did that," the awe-stricken battlerager remarked.

Bidderdoo, clamped tightly on his kill, didn't hear.

27
THE LONGEST NIGHT

Belwar heard the echoes, subtle vibrations in the thick stone that no surface dweller could ever have noticed. The other three hundred svirfnebli heard them as well. This was the way of the deep gnomes—in the deeper tunnels of the Underdark, they often communicated by sending quiet vibrations through the rock. They heard the echoes now, constant echoes, not like the one huge explosion they had heard a couple of hours before, the rumbling of an entire network of tunnels being dropped. The seasoned svirfnebli fighters considered the newest sound, a peculiar rhythm, and they knew what it meant. Battle had been joined, a great battle, and not so far away.

Belwar conferred with his commanders many times as they inched through the unfamiliar terrain, trying to follow the strongest vibrations. Often one of the svirfnebli on the perimeter, or at the point of the group, would tap his hammer slightly on the stone, trying to get a feel for the density of the rock. Echo hunting was tricky because the density of the stone was never uniform, and vibrations were often distorted. Thus, the svirfnebli, arguably the finest echo followers in all the world, found themselves more than once going the wrong way down a fork in the trail.

A determined and patient bunch, though, they stayed with it, and after many frustrating minutes, a priest named Suntunavick bobbed up to Belwar and Firble and announced with all confidence that this was as close to the sound as these tunnels would allow them to get.

The two followed the priest to the exact spot, alternately putting their ears against the stone. Indeed the noise beyond was loud, relatively speaking.

And constant, Belwar noted with some confusion, for this was not the echoing of give-and-take battle, not the echoes they had heard earlier, or at least, there was more to the sound than that.

Suntunavick assured the burrow warden this was the correct place. Mixed in with this more constant sound was the familiar rhythm of battle joined.

Belwar looked to Firble, who nodded, then to Suntunavick. The burrow warden poked his finger at the spot on the wall, then backed away, so Suntunavick and the other priests could crowd in.

They began their chanting, a grating, rumbling, and apparently wordless sound, and every once in a while one of the priests would throw a handful of some mudlike substance against the stone.

The chanting hit a crescendo. Suntunavick rushed up to the wall, his hands straight out in front of him, palms pressed tightly together. With a cry of ecstacy, the little gnome thrust his fingers straight into the stone. Then he groaned, his arm and shoulder muscles flexing as he pulled the wall apart, opened it as though it were no more solid than a curtain of heavy fabric.

The priest jumped back, and so did all the others, as the echo became a roar and a fine spray, the mist of a waterfall, came in on them.

"The surface, it is," Firble muttered, barely able to find his breath.

And so it was, but this deluge of water was nothing like any of the gnomes had pictured the surface world, was nothing like the descriptions in the many tales they had heard of the strange place. Many in the group harbored thoughts of turning back then and there, but Belwar, who had spoken with Drizzt not so long ago, knew something here was out of the ordinary.

The burrow warden hooked a rope from his belt with his pick-axe hand and held it out to Firble, indicating that the councilor should tie it around his waist. Firble did so and took up the other end, bracing himself securely.

With only the slightest of hesitation, the brave Belwar squeezed through the wall, through the veil of mist. He found the waterfall, and a ledge that led him around it, and Belwar gazed upon stars.

Thousands of stars!

The gnome's heart soared. He was awed and frightened all at once. This was the surface world, that greatest of caverns, under a dome that could not be reached.

The moment of pondering, of awe, was short-lived, defeated by the clear sounds of battle. Belwar was not in Keeper's Dale, but he could see the light of the fight, flames from torches and magical enchantments, and he could hear the ring of metal against metal and the familiar screams of the dying.

With Belwar in their lead, the three hundred svirfnebli filtered out of the caverns and began a quiet march to the east. They came upon many areas that seemed impassable, but a friendly elemental, summoned by gnomish priests, opened the way. In but a few minutes, the battle was in sight, the scramble within the misty vale, of armor-clad horsemen and lizard-riding drow, of wretched goblins and kobolds and huge humans more than twice the height of the tallest svirfneblin.

Now Belwar did hesitate, realizing fully that his force of three hundred would plunge into a battle of thousands, a battle in which the gnomes had no way of discerning who was winning.

"It is why we have come," Firble whispered into the burrow warden's ear.

Belwar looked hard at his uncharacteristically brave companion.

"For Blingdenstone," Firble said.

Belwar led the way.

⚔ ⚔ ⚔ ⚔ ⚔

Drizzt held his breath, they all did, and even Guenhwyvar was wise enough to stifle an instinctive snarl.

The five companions huddled on a narrow ledge in a high, wide corridor, while a column of drow, many drow, marched past, a line that went on and on and seemed as if it would never end.

Two thousand? Drizzt wondered. Five thousand? He had no way of guessing. There were too many, and he couldn't rightly stick his head out and begin a count. What Drizzt did understand was that the bulk of the drow force had linked together and was marching with a singular purpose. That could mean only that the way had been cleared, at least to Mithral Hall's lower door. Drizzt took heart when he thought of that door, of the many cunning defenses that had been rigged in that region. Even this mighty force would be hard-pressed to get through the portal; the tunnels near the lower door would pile high with bodies, drow and dwarf alike.

Drizzt dared to slowly shift his head, to look past Guenhwyvar, tight against the wall beside him, to Bruenor, stuck uncomfortably between the panther's rear end and the wall. Drizzt almost managed a smile at the sight, and at the thought that he had better move quickly once the drow column passed, for Bruenor would likely heave the panther right over the lip of the ledge, taking Drizzt with her.

But that smile did not come to Drizzt, not in the face of his doubts. Had he done right in leading Bruenor out here? he wondered, not for the first time. They could have gone back to the lower door with the dwarves they had met hours before; the king of Mithral Hall could be in place among his army.

Drizzt did not underestimate how greatly Bruenor's fiery presence would bolster the defense of that lower door, and the defense of the Undercity. Every dwarf of Mithral Hall would sing a little louder and fight with a bit more heart in the knowledge that King Bruenor Battlehammer was nearby, joining in the cause, his mighty axe leading the way.

Drizzt's reasoning had kept Bruenor out, and now the drow wondered if his action had been selfish. Could they even find the enemy leaders? Likely the priestesses who had led this army would be well hidden, using magic from afar, directing their forces with no more compassion than if the soldiers were pawns on a gigantic chess board.

The matron mother, or whoever was leading this force, would take no personal risks, because that was the drow way.

Suddenly, up there and crouched on that ledge, Drizzt Do'Urden felt very foolish. They were hunting the head, as he had explained to Bruenor, but that head would not be easy to find. and given the size of the force that was marching along below them, toward Mithral Hall, Drizzt and Bruenor and their other companions would not likely get anywhere near the dwarven complex anytime soon.

The ranger put his head down and blew a deep, silent breath, composing himself, reminding himself he had taken the only possible route to winning the day, that though that lower door would not be easily breached, it would eventually come down, whether or not Bruenor Battlehammer was among the defenders. But out here now, with so many drow and so many tunnels, Drizzt began to appreciate the enormity of the task before him. How could he ever hope to find the leaders of the drow army?

What Drizzt did not know was that he was not the only one on a purposeful hunt.

⚔ ⚔ ⚔ ⚔ ⚔

"No word from Bregan D'aerthe."

Matron Baenre sat atop her driftdisk, digesting the words and the meaning behind them. Quenthel started to repeat them, but a threatening scowl from her mother stopped her short.

Still the phrase echoed in Matron Baenre's mind. "No word from Bregan D'aerthe."

Jarlaxle was lying low, Baenre realized. For all his bravado, the mercenary leader was, in fact, a conservative one, very cautious of any risks to the band he had spent centuries putting together. Jarlaxle hadn't been overly eager to march to Mithral Hall, and had, in fact, come along only because he hadn't really been given a choice in the matter.

Like Triel, Baenre's own daughter and closest advisor, the mercenary had hoped for a quick and easy conquest and a fast return to Menzoberranzan, where so many questions were still to be answered. The fact that no word had come lately from the Bregan D'aerthe scouts could be coincidence, but Baenre suspected differently. Jarlaxle was lying low, and that could mean only that he, with the reports that he was constantly receiving from the sly scouts of his network, believed the momentum halted, that he, like Baenre herself, had come to the conclusion that Mithral Hall would not be easily swept away.

The withered old matron mother accepted the news stoically, with confidence that Jarlaxle would be back in the fold once the tide turned again in the dark elves' favor. She would have to come up with a creative punishment for the mercenary leader, of course, one that would let Jarlaxle know the depth of her dismay without costing her a valuable ally.

A short while later, the air in the small chamber Baenre had come to use as her throne room began to tingle with the budding energy of an enchantment. All in the room glanced nervously around and breathed easier when Methil stepped out of thin air into the midst of the drow priestesses.

His expression revealed nothing, just the same passive, observant stare that always came from one of Methil's otherworldly race. Baenre considered that always unreadable face the most frustrating facet of dealing with the illithids. Never did they give even the subtlest clue of their true intentions.

Uthegental Armgo is dead, came a thought in Baenre's mind, a blunt report from Methil.

Now it was Baenre's turn to put on a stoic, unrevealing facade. Methil had given the disturbing thought to her and to her alone, she knew. The others, particularly Zeerith and Auro'pol, who were becoming more and more skittish, did not need to know the news was bad, very bad.

The march to Mithral Hall goes well, came Methil's next telepathic message. The illithid shared it with all in the room, which Matron Baenre realized by the suddenly brightening expressions. *The tunnels are clear all the way to the lower door, where the army gathers and prepares.*

Many nods and smiles came back at the illithid, and Matron Baenre did not have any more trouble than Methil in reading the thoughts behind those expressions. The illithid was working hard to bolster morale—always a tentative thing in dealing with dark elves. but like Quenthel's report, or lack of report, from Bregan D'aerthe, the first message the illithid had given echoed in Baenre's thoughts disconcertingly. Uthegental Armgo was dead! What might the soldiers of Barrison del'Armgo, a significant force vital to the cause, do when they discovered their leader had been slain?

And what of Jarlaxle? Baenre wondered. If he had learned of the brutish weapons master's fall, that would certainly explain the silence of Bregan D'aerthe. Jarlaxle might be fearing the loss of the Barrison del'Armgo garrison, a desertion that would shake the ranks of the army to its core.

Jarlaxle does not know, nor do the soldiers of the Second House, Methil answered her telepathically, obviously reading her thoughts.

Still Baenre managed to keep up the cheery—relatively speaking—front, seeming thrilled at the news of the army's approach to the lower door. She clearly saw a potential cancer growing within her ranks, though, a series of events that could destroy the already shaky integrity of her army and her alliances, and could cost her everything. She felt as though she were falling back to that time of ultimate chaos in Menzoberranzan just before the march, when K'yorl seemed to have the upper hand.

The destruction of House Oblodra had solidified the situation then, and Matron Baenre felt she needed something akin to that now, some dramatic victory that would leave no doubts in the minds of the rank and file. Foster loyalty with fear. She thought of House Oblodra again and toyed with the idea of a similar display against Mithral Hall's lower door. Baenre quickly dismissed it, realizing that what had happened in Menzoberranzan had been a one-time event. Never before—and likely never again—and certainly not so soon afterward!—had Lolth come so gloriously and so fully to the Material Plane. On the occasion of House Oblodra's fall, Matron Baenre had been the pure conduit of the Spider Queen's godly power.

That would not happen again.

Baenre's thoughts swirled in a different direction, a more feasible trail to follow. *Who killed Uthegental?* she thought, knowing that Methil would "hear" her.

The illithid had no answer, but understood what Baenre was implying. Baenre knew what Uthegental had sought, knew the only prize that really mattered to the mighty weapons master. Perhaps he had found Drizzt Do'Urden.

If so, that would mean Drizzt Do'Urden was in the lower tunnels, not behind Mithral Hall's barricades.

You follow a dangerous course, Methil privately warned, before Baenre could even begin to plot out the spells that would let her find the renegade.

Matron Baenre dismissed that notion with hardly a care. She was the first matron mother of Menzoberranzan, the conduit of Lolth, possessed of powers that could snuff the life out of any drow in the city, any matron mother, any wizard, any weapons master, with hardly an effort. Baenre's course now was indeed dangerous, she agreed—dangerous for Drizzt Do'Urden.

⚔ ⚔ ⚔ ⚔ ⚔

Most devastating was the dwarven force and the center of the blocking line, a great mass of pounding, singing warriors, mulching goblins and orcs under their heavy hammers and axes, leaping in packs atop towering minotaurs, their sheer weight of numbers bringing the brutes down.

But all along the eastern end of Keeper's Dale, the press was too great from every side. Mounted knights rushed back and forth across the barbarian line, bolstering the ranks wherever the enemy seemed to be breaking through, and with their timely support, the line held. Even so, Berkthgar's people found themselves inevitably pushed back.

The bodies of kobolds and goblins piled high in Keeper's Dale; a score dying for every defender. But the drow could afford those losses, had expected them, and Berg'inyon, sitting astride his lizard, calmly watching the continuing battle from afar along with the rest of the Baenre riders, knew that the time for slaughter grew near. The defenders were growing weary, he realized. The minutes had turned into an hour, and that into two, and the assault did not diminish.

Back went the defending line, and the towering eastern walls of Keeper's Dale were not so far behind them. When those walls halted the retreat, the drow wizards would strike hard. Then Berg'inyon would lead the charge, and Keeper's Dale would run even thicker with the blood of humans.

⚔ ⚔ ⚔ ⚔ ⚔

Besnell knew they were losing, knew that a dozen dead goblins were not worth the price of an inch of ground. A resignation began to grow within the elf, tempered only by the fact that never had he seen his knights in finer form. Their tight battle groups rushed to and fro, trampling enemies, and though every man was breathing so hard he could barely sing out a war song, and every horse was lathered in thick sweat, they did not relent, did not pause.

Grimly satisfied, and yet terribly worried—and not just for his own men, for Alustriel had made no further appearance on the field—the elf turned his attention to Berkthgar, then he was truly amazed. The huge flamberge, Bankenfuere, hummed as it swept through the air, each cut obliterating any

enemies foolish enough to stand close to the huge man. Blood, much of it his own, covered the barbarian from head to toe, but if Berkthgar felt any pain, he did not show it. His song and his dance were to Tempus, the god of battle, and so he sang, and so he danced, and so his enemies died.

In Besnell's mind, if the drow won here and conquered Mithral Hall, one of the most tragic consequences would be that the tale of the exploits of mighty Berkthgar the Bold would not leave Keeper's Dale.

A tremendous flash to the side brought the elf from his contemplations. He looked down the line to see Regweld Harpell surrounded by a dozen dead or dying, flaming goblins. Regweld and Puddlejumper were also engulfed by the magical flames, dancing licks of green and red, but the wizard and his extraordinary mount did not seem bothered and continued to fight without regard for the fires. Indeed, those fires engulfing the duo became a weapon, an extension of Regweld's fury when the wizard leaped Puddlejumper nearly a dozen yards, to land at the feet of two towering minotaurs. Red and green flames became white hot and leaped out from the wizard's torso, engulfing the towering brutes. Puddlejumper hopped straight up, bringing Regweld even with the screaming minotaurs' ugly faces. Out came a wand, and green blasts of energy tore into the monsters.

Then Regweld was gone, leaping to the next fight, leaving the minotaurs staggering, flames consuming them.

"For the good of all goodly folk!" Besnell cried, holding his sword high. His battle group formed beside him, and the thunder of the charge began anew, this time barreling full stride through a mass of kobolds. They scattered the beasts and came into a thicker throng of larger enemies, where the charge was stopped. Still atop their mounts, the Knights in Silver hacked through the morass, bright swords slaughtering enemies.

Besnell was happy. He felt a satisfaction coursing through his body, a sensation of accomplishment and righteousness. The elf believed in Silverymoon with all his heart, believed in the precept he yelled out at every opportunity.

He was not sad when a goblin spear found a crease at the side of his breast-plate, rushed in through his ribs, and collapsed a lung. He swayed in his saddle and somehow managed to knock the spear from his side.

"For the good of all goodly folk!" he said with all the strength he could muster. A goblin was beside his mount, sword coming in.

Besnell winced with pain as he brought his own sword across to block. He felt weak and suddenly cold. He hardly registered the loss as his sword slipped from his hand to clang to the ground.

The goblin's next strike cut solidly against the knight's thigh, the drow-made weapon tearing through Besnell's armor and drawing a line of bright blood.

The goblin hooted, then went flying away, broken apart by the mighty sweep of Bankenfuere.

Berkthgar caught Besnell in his free hand as the knight slid off his mount. The barbarian felt somehow removed from the battle at that moment, as though he and the noble elf were alone, in their own private place. Around them, not so far away, the knights continued the slaughter and no monsters approached.

Berkthgar gently lowered Besnell to the ground. The elf looked up, his golden eyes seeming hollow.

"For the good of all goodly folk," Besnell said, his voice barely a whisper, but by the grace of Tempus, or whatever god was looking over the battle of Keeper's Dale, Berkthgar heard every syllable.

The barbarian nodded and silently laid the dead elf's head on the stone.

Then Berkthgar was up again, his rage multiplied, and he charged headlong into the enemy ranks, his great sword cutting a wide swath.

✕ ✕ ✕ ✕ ✕

Regweld Harpell had never known such excitement. Still in flames that did not harm him or his horse-frog, but attacked any that came near, the wizard single-handedly bolstered the southern end of the defending line. He was quickly running out of spells, but Regweld didn't care, knew that he would find some way to make himself useful, some way to destroy the wretches that had come to conquer Mithral Hall.

A group of minotaurs converged on him, their great spears far out in front to prevent the fires from getting at them.

Regweld smiled and coaxed Puddlejumper into another flying leap, straight up between the circling monsters, higher than even minotaurs and their long spears could reach.

The Harpell let out a shout of victory, then a lightning bolt silenced him.

Suddenly Regweld was free-flying, spinning in the air, and Puddlejumper was spinning the other way just below him.

A second thundering bolt came in from a different angle, and a third, forking so that it hit both the wizard and his strange mount.

They were each hit again, and again after that as they tumbled, falling very still upon the stone.

The drow wizards had joined the battle.

The invaders roared and pressed on, and even Berkthgar, outraged by the valiant elf's death, could not rally his men to hold the line. Drow lizard riders filtered in through the humanoid ranks, their long lances pushing the mounted knights inevitably back, back toward the blocking wall.

⚔ ⚔ ⚔ ⚔ ⚔

Berg'inyon was among the first to see the next turn of the battle. He ordered a rider up the side of a rock pillar, to gain a better vantage point, then turned his attention to a group nearby, pointing to the northern wall of the valley.

Go up high, the weapons master's fingers signaled to them. *Up high and around the enemy ranks, to rain death on them from above when they are pushed back against the wall.*

Evil smiles accompanied the agreeing nods, but a cry from the other side, from the soldier Berg'inyon had sent up high, stole the moment.

The rock pillar had come to life as a great elemental monster. Berg'inyon and the others looked on helplessly as the stone behemoth clapped together great rock arms, splattering the drow and his lizard.

There came a great clamor from behind the drow lines, from the west, and above the thunder of the svirfneblin charge was heard a cry of "Bivrip!" the word Belwar Dissengulp used to activate the magic in his crafted hands.

⚔ ⚔ ⚔ ⚔ ⚔

It was a long time before Berkthgar and the other defenders at the eastern end of Keeper's Dale even understood that allies had come from the west. Those rumors eventually filtered through the tumult of battle, though, heartening defender and striking fear into invader. The goblins and dark elves engaged near that eastern wall began to look back the other way, wondering if disaster approached.

Now Berkthgar did rally what remained of the non-dwarven defenders: two-third of his barbarians, less than a hundred Knights in Silver, a score of Longriders, and only two of the men from Nesmé. Their ranks were depleted, but their spirit returned, and the line held again, even made progress in following the dwarven mass back out toward the middle of Keeper's Dale.

Soon after, all semblance of order was lost in the valley. No longer did lines of soldiers define enemies. In the west, the svirfneblin priests battled drow wizards, and Belwar's warriors charged hard into drow ranks. They were the bitterest of enemies, ancient enemies, drow and svirfnebli. No less could be said on the eastern side of the valley, where dwarves and goblins hacked away at each other with abandon.

It went on through the night, a wild and horrible night. Berg'inyon Baenre engaged in little combat and kept the bulk of his elite lizard riders back as well, using his monstrous fodder to weary the defense. Even with the unexpected arrival of the small but powerful svirfneblin force, the drow soon turned the tide back their way.

"We will win," the young Baenre promised those soldiers closest to him. "And what defense might be left in place beyond the western door of the dwarven complex?

28
DIVINATION

Quenthel Baenre sat facing a cubby of the small chamber's wall, staring down into a pool of calm water. She squinted as the pool, a scrying pool, brightened, as the dawn broke on the outside world, not so far to the east of Fourthpeak.

Quenthel held her breath, though she wanted to cry out in despair.

Across the small chamber, Matron Baenre was similarly divining. She had used her spells to create a rough map of the area, and to enchant a single tiny feather. Chanting again, Baenre tossed the feather into the air above the spread parchment and blew softly.

"Drizzt Do'Urden," she whispered in that breath, and she puffed again as the feather flopped and flitted down to the map. A wide, evil grin spread across Baenre's face when the feather, the magical pointer, touched down, its tip indicating a group of tunnels not far away.

It was true, Baenre knew then. Drizzt Do'Urden was indeed in the tunnels outside Mithral Hall.

"We leave," the matron mother said suddenly, startling all in the quiet chamber.

Quenthel looked back nervously over her shoulder, afraid that her mother had somehow seen what was in her scrying pool. The Baenre daughter found that she couldn't see across the room, though, for the view was blocked by a scowling Bladen'Kerst, glaring down at her, and past her, at the approaching spectacle.

"Where are we to go?" Zeerith, near the middle of the room, asked aloud, and from her tone, it was obvious she was hoping Matron Baenre's scrying had found a break in the apparent stalemate.

Matron Baenre considered that tone and the sour expression on the other matron mother's face. She wasn't sure whether Zeerith, and Auro'pol, who was similarly scowling, would have preferred to hear that the way was clear into Mithral Hall, or that the attack had been called off. Looking at the two of them, among the very highest-ranking commanders of the drow army, Baenre couldn't tell whether they preferred victory or retreat.

That obvious reminder of how tentative her alliance was angered Baenre. She would have liked to dismiss both of them, or, better, to have them executed then and there. But Baenre could not, she realized. The morale of her army would never survive that. Besides, she wanted them, or at least one of them, to witness her glory, to see Drizzt Do'Urden given to Lolth.

"You shall go to the lower door, to coordinate and strengthen the attack," Baenre said sharply to Zeerith, deciding that the two of them standing together were becoming too dangerous. "And Auro'pol shall go with me."

Auro'pol didn't dare ask the obvious question, but Baenre saw it clearly anyway from her expression.

"We have business in the outer tunnels," was all Matron Baenre would offer.

Berg'inyon will soon see the dawn, Quenthel's fingers motioned to her sister.

Bladen'Kerst, always angry, but now boiling with rage, turned away from Quenthel and the unwanted images in the scrying pool and looked back to her mother.

Before she could speak, though, a telepathic intrusion came into her mind, and into Quenthel's. *Do not speak ill of other battles*, Methil imparted to them both. *Already, Zeerith and Auro'pol consider desertion.*

Bladen'Kerst considered the message and the implications and wisely held her information.

The command group split apart, then, with Zeerith and a contingent of the elite soldiers going east, toward Mithral Hall, and Matron Baenre leading Quenthel, Bladen'Kerst, Methil, half a dozen skilled Baenre female warriors, and the chained Gandalug off to the south, in the direction of the spot indicated by her divining feather.

✕ ✕ ✕ ✕ ✕

On another plane, the gray mists and sludge and terrible stench of the Abyss, Errtu watched the proceedings in the glassy mirror Lolth had created on the side of the mushroom opposite his throne.

The great balor was not pleased. Matron Baenre was hunting Drizzt Do'Urden, Errtu knew, and he knew, too, that Baenre would likely find the renegade and easily destroy him.

A thousand curses erupted from the tanar'ri's doglike maw, all aimed at Lolth, who had promised him freedom—freedom that only a living Drizzt Do'Urden could bestow.

To make matters even worse, a few moments later, Matron Baenre was casting yet another spell, opening a planar gate to the Abyss, calling forth a mighty glabrezu to help in her hunting. In his twisted, always suspicious mind, Errtu came to believe that this summoning was enacted only to torment him, to take one of his own kind and use the beast to facilitate the end of the pact. That was the way with tanar'ri, and with all the wretches of the Abyss, Lolth included. These creatures were without trust for others, since they, themselves, could not be trusted by any but a fool. And they were an ultimately selfish lot, every one. In Errtu's eyes, every action revolved around him, because nothing else mattered, and thus, Baenre summoning a glabrezu now was not coincidence, but a dagger jabbed by Lolth into Errtu's black heart.

Errtu was the first to the opening gate. Even if he was not bound to the Abyss by banishment, he could not have gone through, because Baenre, so skilled in this type of summoning, was careful to word the enchantment for a specific tanar'ri only. But Errtu was waiting when the glabrezu appeared through the swirling mists, heading for the opened, flaming portal.

The balor leaped out and lashed out with his whip, catching the glabrezu by the arm. No minor fiend, the glabrezu moved to strike back, but stopped, seeing that Errtu did not mean to continue the attack.

"It is a deception!" Errtu roared.

The glabrezu, its twelve-foot frame hunched low, great pincers nipping anxiously at the air, paused to listen.

"I was to come forth on the Material Plane," Errtu went on.

"You are banished," the glabrezu said matter-of-factly.

"Lolth promised an end!" Errtu retorted, and the glabrezu crouched lower, as if expecting the volatile fiend to leap upon him.

But Errtu calmed quickly. "An end, that I might return, and bring forth behind me an army of tanar'ri." Again Errtu paused. He was improvising now, but a plan was beginning to form in his wicked mind.

Baenre's call came again, and it took all the glabrezu's considerable willpower to keep it from leaping through the flaring portal.

"She will allow you only one kill," Errtu said quickly, seeing the glabrezu's hesitance.

"One is better than none," the glabrezu answered.

"Even if that one prevents my freedom on the Material Plane?" Errtu asked. "Even if it prevents me from going forth, and bringing you forth as my general, that we might wreak carnage on the weakling races?"

Baenre called yet again, and this time it was not so difficult for the glabrezu to ignore her.

Errtu held up his great hands, indicating that the glabrezu should wait here a few moments longer, then the balor sped off, into the swirl, to retrieve something a lesser fiend had given him not so long ago, a remnant of the Time of Troubles. He returned shortly with a metal coffer and gently opened it, producing a shining black sapphire. As soon as Errtu held it up, the flames of the magical portal diminished, and almost went out altogether. Errtu was quick to put the thing back in its case.

"When the time is right, reveal this," the balor instructed, "my general."

He tossed the coffer to the glabrezu, unsure, as was the other fiend, of how this would all play out. Errtu's great shoulders ruffled in a shrug then, for there was nothing else he could do. He could prevent this fiend from going to Baenre's aid, but to what end? Baenre hardly needed a glabrezu to deal with Drizzt Do'Urden, a mere warrior.

The call from the Material Plane came yet again, and this time the glabrezu answered, stepping through the portal to join Matron Baenre's hunting party.

Errtu watched in frustration as the portal closed, another gate lost to the Material Plane, another gate that he could not pass through. Now the balor had done all he could, though he had no way of knowing if it would be enough, and he had so much riding on the outcome. He went back to his mushroom throne then, to watch and wait.

And hope.

⚔ ⚔ ⚔ ⚔ ⚔

Bruenor remembered. In the quiet ways of the tunnels, no enemies to be seen, the eighth king of Mithral Hall paused and reflected. Likely the dawn was soon to come on the outside, another crisp, cold day. But would it be the last day of Clan Battlehammer?

Bruenor looked to his four friends as they took a quick meal and a short rest. Not one of them was a dwarf, not one.

And yet, Bruenor Battlehammer could not name any other friends above these four: Drizzt, Catti-brie, Regis, and even Guenhwyvar. For the first time, that truth struck the dwarf king as curious. Dwarves, though not xenophobic, usually stayed to their own kind. Witness General Dagna, who, if given his way, would kick Drizzt out of Mithral Hall and would take Taulmaril away from Catti-brie, to hang the bow once more in the Hall of Dumathoin. Dagna didn't trust anyone who was not a dwarf.

But here they were, Bruenor and his four non-dwarven companions, in perhaps the most critical and dangerous struggle of all for the defense of Mithral Hall.

Surely their friendship warmed the old dwarf king's heart, but reflecting on that now did something else as well.

It made Bruenor think of Wulfgar, the barbarian who had been like his own son, and who would have married Catti-brie and become his son-in-law, the unlikely seven-foot prince of Mithral Hall. Bruenor had never known such grief as that which bowed his strong shoulders after Wulfgar's fall. Though he should live for more than another century, Bruenor had felt close to death in those tendays of grieving, and had felt as if death would be a welcome thing.

No longer. He missed Wulfgar still—forever would his gray eye mist up at the thought of the noble warrior—but he was the eighth king, the leader of his proud, strong clan. Bruenor's grief had passed the point of resignation and had shifted into the realm of anger. The dark elves were back, the same dark elves who had killed Wulfgar. They were the followers of Lolth, evil Lolth, and now they meant to kill Drizzt and destroy all of Mithral Hall, it seemed.

Bruenor had wetted his axe on drow blood many times during the night, but his rage was far from sated. Indeed, it was mounting, a slow but determined boil. Drizzt had promised they would hunt the head of their enemy, would find the leader, the priestess behind this assault. It was a promise Bruenor needed to see the drow ranger keep.

He had been quiet through much of the fighting, even in preparing for the war. Bruenor was quiet now, too, letting Drizzt and the panther lead, finding his place among the friends whenever battle was joined.

In the few moments of peace and rest, Bruenor saw a wary glance come his way more than once and knew that his friends feared he was brooding again, that his heart was not in the fight. Nothing could have been farther from the truth. Those minor skirmishes didn't matter much to Bruenor. He could kill a hundred—a thousand!—drow soldiers, and his pain and anger would not relent. If he could get to the priestess behind it all, though, chop her down and decapitate the drow invading force . . .

Bruenor might know peace.

The eighth king of Mithral Hall was not brooding. He was biding his time and his energy, coming to a slow boil. He was waiting for the moment when revenge would be most sweet.

✕ ✕ ✕ ✕ ✕

Baenre's group, the giant glabrezu in tow, had just begun moving again, the matron mother guiding them in the direction her scrying had indicated, when Methil telepathically informed her that matrons Auro'pol and Zeerith had been continually entertaining thoughts of her demise. If Zeerith couldn't find a way through Mithral Hall's lower door, she would simply organize a withdrawal. Even now, Auro'pol was considering the potential for swinging the whole army around and leaving Matron Baenre dead behind them, according to Methil.

Do they plot against me? Baenre wanted to know.

No, Methil honestly replied, *but if you are killed, they will be thrilled to turn back for Menzoberranzan without you, that a new hierarchy might arise.*

In truth, Methil's information was not unexpected. One did not have to read minds to see the discomfort and quiet rage on the faces of the matron mothers of Menzoberranzan's fourth and Fifth Houses. Besides, Baenre had suffered such hatred from her lessers, even from supposed allies such as Mez'Barris Armgo, even from her own daughters, for all her long life. That was an expected cost of being the first matron mother of chaotic and jealous Menzoberranzan, a city continually at war with itself.

Auro'pol's thoughts were to be expected, but the confirmation from the illithid outraged the already nervous Matron Baenre. In her twisted mind, this was no ordinary war, after all. This was the will of Lolth, as Baenre was the Spider Queen's agent. This was the pinnacle of Matron Baenre's power, the height of Lolth-given glory. How dare Auro'pol and Zeerith entertain such blasphemous thoughts? the first matron mother fumed.

She snapped an angry glare over Auro'pol, who simply snorted and looked away—possibly the very worst thing she could have done.

Baenre issued telepathic orders to Methil, who in turn relayed them to the glabrezu. The driftdisks, side by side, were just following Baenre's daughters around a bend in the tunnel when great pincers closed around Auro'pol's slender waist and yanked her from her driftdisk, the powerful glabrezu easily holding her in midair.

"What is this?" Auro'pol demanded, squirming to no avail.

"You wish me dead," Baenre answered.

Quenthel and Bladen'Kerst rushed back to their mother's side, and both were stunned that Baenre had openly moved against Auro'pol.

"She wishes me dead," Baenre informed her daughters. "She and Zeerith believe Menzoberranzan would be a better place without Matron Baenre."

Auro'pol looked to the illithid, obviously the one who had betrayed her. Baenre's daughters, who had entertained similar treasonous thoughts on more than one occasion during this long, troublesome march, looked to Methil as well.

"Matron Auro'pol bears witness to your glory," Quenthel put in. "She will witness the death of the renegade and will know that Lolth is with us."

Auro'pol's features calmed at that statement, and she squirmed again, trying to loosen the tanar'ri's viselike grip.

Baenre eyed her adversary dangerously, and Auro'pol, cocky to the end, matched the intensity of her stare. Quenthel was right, Auro'pol believed. Baenre needed her to bear witness. Bringing her into line behind the war would solidify Zeerith's loyalty as well, so the drow army would be much stronger. Baenre was a wicked old thing, but she had always been a calculating one, not ready to sacrifice an inch of power for the sake of emotional satisfaction. Witness Gandalug Battlehammer, still alive, though Baenre certainly would have enjoyed tearing the heart from his chest many times during the long centuries of his imprisonment.

"Matron Zeerith will be glad to hear of Drizzt Do'Urden's death," Auro'pol said, and lowered her eyes respectfully. The submissive gesture would suffice, she believed.

"The head of Drizzt Do'Urden will be all the proof Matron Zeerith requires," Baenre replied.

Auro'pol's gaze shot up, and Baenre's daughters, too, looked upon their surprising mother.

Baenre ignored them all. She sent a message to Methil, who again relayed it to the glabrezu, and the great pincers began to squeeze around Auro'pol's waist.

"You cannot do this!" Auro'pol objected, gasping for every word. "Lolth is with me! You weaken your own campaign!"

Quenthel wholeheartedly agreed, but kept silent, realizing the glabrezu still had an empty pincer.

"You cannot do this!" Auro'pol shrieked. "Zeerith will . . ." Her words were lost to pain.

"Drizzt Do'Urden killed you before I killed Drizzt Do'Urden," Matron Baenre explained to Auro'pol. "Perfectly believable, and it makes the renegade's death all the sweeter." Baenre nodded to the glabrezu, and the pincers closed, tearing through flesh and bone.

Quenthel looked away, but wicked Bladen'Kerst watched the spectacle with a wide smile.

Auro'pol tried to call out once more, tried to hurl a dying curse Baenre's way, but her backbone snapped and all her strength washed away. The pincers snapped shut, and Auro'pol Dyrr's body fell apart to the floor.

Bladen'Kerst cried out in glee, thrilled by her mother's display of control and power. Quenthel, though, was outraged. Baenre had stepped over a dangerous line. She had killed a matron mother, and had done so to the detriment of the march to Mithral Hall, purely for personal gain. Wholeheartedly devoted to Lolth, Quenthel could not abide such stupidity, and her thoughts were similar indeed to those that had gotten Auro'pol Dyrr chopped in half.

Quenthel snapped a dangerous glare over Methil, realizing the illithid was reading her thoughts. Would Methil betray her next?

She narrowed her thoughts into a tight focus. *It is not Lolth's will!* her mind screamed at Methil. *No longer is the Spider Queen behind my mother's actions.*

That notion held more implications for Methil, the illithid emissary to Menzoberranzan, not to Matron Baenre, than Quenthel could guess, and her relief was great indeed when Methil did not betray her.

⚔ ⚔ ⚔ ⚔ ⚔

Guenhwyvar's ears flattened, and Drizzt, too, thought he heard a slight, distant scream. They had seen no one, enemies or friends, for several hours, and the ranger believed that any group of dark elves they now encountered would likely include the high priestess leading the army.

He motioned for the others to move with all caution, and the small band crept along, Guenhwyvar leading the way. Drizzt fell into his Underdark instincts now. He was the hunter again, the survivor who had lived alone for a decade in the wilds of the Underdark. He looked back at Bruenor, Regis, and Catti-brie often, for, though they were moving with all the stealth they could manage, they sounded like a marching army of armored soldiers to Drizzt's keen ears. That worried the drow, for he knew their enemies would be far quieter. He considered going a long way ahead with Guenhwyvar, taking up the hunt alone.

It was a passing thought. These were his friends, and no one could ever ask for finer allies.

They slipped down a narrow, unremarkable tunnel and into a chamber that

opened wide to the left and right, though the smooth wall directly opposite the tunnel was not far away. The ceiling here was higher than in the tunnel, but stalactites hung down in several areas, nearly to the floor in many places.

Guenhwyvar's ears flattened again, and the panther paused at the entrance. Drizzt came beside her and felt the same tingling sensation.

The enemy was near, very near. That warrior instinct, beyond the normal senses, told the drow ranger the enemy was practically upon them. He signaled back to the three trailing, then he and the panther moved slowly and cautiously into the chamber, along the wall to the right.

Catti-brie came to the entrance next and fell to one knee, bending back her bow. Her eyes, aided by the Cat's Eye circlet, which made even the darkest tunnels seem bathed in bright starlight, scanned the chamber, searching among the stalactite clusters.

Bruenor was soon beside her, and Regis came past her on the left. The halfling spotted a cubby a few feet along the wall. He pointed to himself, then to the cubby, and he inched off toward the spot.

A green light appeared on the wall opposite the door, stealing the darkness. It spiraled out, opening a hole in the wall, and Matron Baenre floated through, her daughters and their prisoner coming in behind her, along with the illithid.

Drizzt recognized the withered old drow and realized his worst fears, knew immediately that he and his friends were badly overmatched. He thought to go straight for Baenre, but realized that he and Guenhwyvar were not alone on this side of the chamber. From the corner of his wary eye Drizzt caught some movement up among the stalactites.

Catti-brie fired a silver-streaking arrow, practically point-blank. The arrow exploded into a shower of multicolored, harmless sparks, unable to penetrate the first matron mother's magical shields.

Regis went into the cubby then and cried out in sudden pain as a ward exploded. Electricity sparked around the halfling, sending him jerking this way and that, then dropping him to the floor, his curly brown hair standing straight on end.

Guenhwyvar sprang to the right, burying a drow soldier as she floated down from the stalactites. Drizzt again considered going straight for Baenre, but found himself suddenly engaged as three more elite Baenre guards rushed out of hiding to surround him. Drizzt shook his head in denial. Surprise now worked against him and his friends, not for them. The enemy had expected them, he knew, had hunted them even as they had hunted the enemy. And this was Matron Baenre herself!

"Run!" Drizzt cried to his friends. "Flee this place!"

29
KING AGAINST QUEEN

The long night drifted into morning, with the dark elves once again claiming the upper hand in the battle for Keeper's Dale. Berg'inyon's assessment of the futility of the defense, even with the dwarven and svirfneblin reinforcements, seemed correct as the drow ranks gradually engulfed the svirf-nebli, then pushed the line in the east back toward the wall once more.

But then it happened.

After an entire night of fighting, after hours of shaping the battle, holding back the wizards, using the lizard riders at precise moments and never fully committing them to the conflict, all the best laid plans of the powerful drow force fell apart.

The rim of the mountains east of Keeper's Dale brightened, a silvery edge that signaled the coming dawn. For the drow and the other monsters of the Underdark, that was no small event.

One drow wizard, intent on a lightning bolt that would defeat the nearest enemies, interrupted his spell and enacted a globe of darkness instead, aiming it at the tip of the sun as it peeked over the horizon, thinking to blot out the light. The spell went off and did nothing more than a put a black dot in the air a long way off, and as the wizard squinted against the glare, wondering what he might try next, those defenders closest charged in and cut him down.

Another drow battling a dwarf had his opponent all but beaten. So intent was he on the kill that he hardly noticed the coming dawn—until the tip of the sun broke the horizon, sending a line of light, a line of agony, to sensitive drow eyes. Blinded and horrified, the dark elf whipped his weapons in a frenzy, but he never got close to hitting the mark.

Then he felt a hot explosion across his ribs.

All these dark elves had seen things in the normal spectrum of light before, but not so clearly, not in such intense light, not with colors so rich and vivid. They had heard of the terrible sunshine—Berg'inyon had witnessed a dawn many years before, had watched it over his shoulder as he and his drow raiding party fled back for the safe darkness of the lower tunnels. Now the weapons master and his charges did not know what to expect. Would the infernal sun burn them as it blinded them? They had been told by their elders that it would not, but had been warned they would be more vulnerable in the sunlight, that their enemies would be bolstered by the brightness.

Berg'inyon called his forces into tight battle formations and tried to regroup. They could still win, the weapons master knew, though this latest development would cost many drow lives. Dark elves could fight blindly, but what Berg'inyon feared here was more than a loss of vision. It was a loss of heart. The rays slanting down from the mountains were beyond his and his troops' experience. And as frightening as it had been to walk under the canopy of unreachable stars, this event, this sunrise, was purely terrifying.

Berg'inyon quickly conferred with his wizards, tried to see if there was some way they could counteract the dawn. What he learned instead distressed him as much as the infernal light. The drow wizards in Keeper's Dale had eyes also in other places, and from those far-seeing mages came the initial whispers that dark elves were deserting in the lower tunnels, that those drow who had been stopped in the tunnels near the eastern door had retreated from Mithral Hall and had fled to the deeper passages on the eastern side of Fourthpeak. Berg'inyon understood that information easily enough; those drow were already on the trails leading back to Menzoberranzan.

Berg'inyon could not ignore the reports' implications. Any alliance between dark elves was tentative, and the weapons master could only guess at how widespread the desertion might be. Despite the dawn, Berg'inyon believed his force would win in Keeper's Dale and would breach the western door, but suddenly he had to wonder what they would find in Mithral Hall once they got there.

Matron Baenre and their allies? King Bruenor and the renegade, Drizzt, and a host of dwarves ready to fight? The thought did not sit well with the worried weapons master.

Thus, it was not greater numbers that won the day in Keeper's Dale. It was not the courage of Berkthgar or Besnell, or the ferocity of Belwar and his gnomes, or the wisdom of Stumpet Rakingclaw. It was the dawn and the distrust among the enemy ranks, the lack of cohesion and the very real fear that supporting forces would not arrive, for every drow soldier, from Berg'inyon to the lowest commoner, understood that their allies would think nothing of leaving them behind to be slaughtered.

Berg'inyon Baenre was not questioned by any of his soldiers when he gave the order to leave Keeper's Dale. The lizard riders, still more than three hundred strong, rode out to the rough terrain of the north, their sticky-footed mounts leaving enemies and allies alike far behind.

The very air of Keeper's Dale tingled from the tragedy and the excitement, but the sounds of battle died away to an eerie stillness, shattered occasionally by a cry of agony. Berkthgar the Bold stood tall and firm, with Stumpet Rakingclaw and Terrien Doucard, the new leader of the Knights in Silver, flanking him, and their victorious soldiers waiting, tensed, behind them.

Ten feet away, Belwar Dissengulp stood point for the depleted svirfneblin ranks. The most honored burrow warden held his strong arms out before him, cradling the body of noble Firble, one of many svirfnebli who had died this day, so far from, but in defense of, their home.

They did not know what to make of each other, this almost-seven-foot barbarian, and the gnome who was barely half his height. They could not talk to each other, and had no comprehensible signs of friendship to offer.

They found their only common ground among the bodies of hated enemies and beloved friends, piled thick in Keeper's Dale.

Faerie fire erupted along Drizzt's arms and legs, outlining him as a better target. He countered by dropping a globe of darkness over himself, an attempt to steal the enemy's advantage of three-to-one odds.

Out snapped the ranger's scimitars, and he felt a strange urge from one, not from Twinkle, but from the other blade, the one Drizzt had found in the lair of the dragon Dracos Icingdeath, the blade that had been forged as a bane to creatures of fire.

The scimitar was hungry. Drizzt had not felt an urge from it since . . .

He parried the first attack and groaned, remembering the other time his scimitar had revealed its hunger, when he had battled the balor Errtu. Drizzt knew what this meant.

Baenre had brought friends.

Catti-brie fired another arrow, straight at the withered old matron mother's laughing visage. Again the enchanted arrow merely erupted into a pretty display of useless sparks. The young woman turned to flee, as Drizzt had ordered. She grabbed her father, meaning to pull him along.

Bruenor wouldn't budge. He looked to Baenre and knew she was the source. He looked at Baenre and convinced himself that she had personally killed his boy. Then Bruenor looked past Baenre, to the old dwarf. Somehow Bruenor knew that dwarf. In his heart, the eighth king of Mithral Hall recognized the patron of his clan, though he could not consciously make the connection.

"Run!" Catti-brie yelled at him, taking him temporarily from his thoughts. Bruenor glanced at her, then looked behind, back down the tunnel.

He heard fighting in the distance, from somewhere behind them.

Quenthel's spell went off then, and a wall of fire sprang up in the narrow tunnel, cutting off retreat. That didn't bother determined Bruenor much, not now. He shrugged himself free of Catti-brie's hold and turned back to face Baenre—in his own mind, to face the evil dark elf who had killed his boy.

He took a step forward.

Baenre laughed at him.

⚔ ⚔ ⚔ ⚔ ⚔

Drizzt parried and struck, then, using the cover of the darkness globe, quick-stepped to the side, too quickly for the dark elf coming in at his back to realize the shift. She bored in and struck hard, hitting the same drow that Drizzt had just wounded, finishing her.

Hearing the movement, Drizzt came right back, both his blades whirling. To the female's credit, she registered the countering move in time to parry the first attack, the second and the third, even the fourth.

But Drizzt did not relent. He knew his fury was a dangerous thing. There remained one more enemy in the darkness globe, and for Drizzt to press against a single opponent so forcefully left him vulnerable to the other. But the ranger knew, too, that his friends sorely needed him, that every moment he spent engaged with these warriors gave the powerful priestesses time to destroy them all.

The ranger's fifth attack, a wide-arcing left, was cleanly picked off, as was the sixth, a straightforward right thrust. Drizzt pressed hard, would not relinquish the offensive. He knew, and the female knew, that her only hope would be in her lone remaining ally.

A stifled scream, followed by the growl of a panther ended that hope.

Drizzt's fury increased, and the female continued to fall back, stumbling now in the darkness, suddenly afraid. And in that moment of fear, she banged her head hard against a low stalactite, an obstacle her keen drow senses should have detected. She shook off the blow and managed to straighten her posture, throwing one sword out in front to block another of the ranger's furious thrusts.

She missed.

Drizzt didn't, and Twinkle split the fine drow armor and dived deep into the female's lung.

Drizzt yanked the blade free and spun around.

His darkness globe went away abruptly, dispelled by the magic of the waiting tanar'ri.

※ ※ ※ ※ ※

Bruenor took another step, then broke into a run. Catti-brie screamed, thinking him dead, as a line of fire came down on him.

Furious, frustrated, the young woman fired her bow again, and more harmless sparks exploded in the air. Through the tears of outrage that welled in her blue eyes she hardly noticed that Bruenor had shrugged off the stinging hit and broke into a full charge again.

Bladen'Kerst stopped the dwarf, enacting a spell that surrounded Bruenor in a huge block of magical, translucent goo. Bruenor continued to move, but so slowly as to be barely perceptible, while the three drow priestesses laughed at him.

Catti-brie fired again, and this time her arrow hit the block of goo, diving in several feet before stopping and hanging uselessly in place above her father's head.

Catti-brie looked to Bruenor, to Drizzt and the horrid, twelve-foot fiend that had appeared to the right, and to Regis, groaning and trying to crawl at her left. She felt the heat as fires raged in the tunnel behind her, heard the continuing battle back, that way which she did not understand.

They needed a break, a turn in the tide, and Catti-brie thought she saw it then, and a moment of hope came to her. Finished with the kill, Guenhwyvar growled and crouched, ready to spring upon the tanar'ri.

That moment of hope for Catti-brie was short-lived, for as the panther sprang out, one of the priestesses casually tossed something into the air, Guenhwyvar's way. The panther dissipated into gray mist in midleap and was gone, sent back to the Astral Plane.

"And so we die," Catti-brie whispered, for this enemy was too strong. She dropped Taulmaril to the floor and drew Khazid'hea. A deep breath steadied her, reminded her that she had run close to death's door for most of her adult life. She looked to her father and prepared to charge, prepared to die.

A shape wavered in front of the block of goo, between Catti-brie and Bruenor, and the look of determination on the young woman's face turned to one of disgust as a gruesome, octopus-headed monster materialized on this side of the magical block, calmly walking—no, floating—toward her.

Catti-brie raised her sword, then stopped, overwhelmed suddenly by a psionic blast, the likes of which she had never known.

Methil waded in.

✕ ✕ ✕ ✕ ✕

Berg'inyon's force pulled up and regrouped when they had cleared Keeper's Dale completely, had left the din of battle far behind and were near the last run for the tunnels back to the Underdark. Dimensional doors opened near the lizard riders, and drow wizards—and those other dark elves fortunate enough to have been near the wizards when the spells were enacted—stepped through. Stragglers, infantry drow and a scattering of humanoid allies, struggled to catch up, but they could not navigate the impossible terrain on this sign of the mountain. And they were of no concern to the Baenre weapons master.

All those who had escaped Keeper's Dale looked to Berg'inyon for guidance as the day brightened around them.

"My mother was wrong," Berg'inyon said bluntly, an act of blasphemy in drow society, where the word of any matron mother was Lolth-given law.

Not a drow pointed it out, though, or raised a word of disagreement. Berg'inyon motioned to the east, and the force lumbered on, into the rising sun, miserable and defeated.

"The surface is for surface-dwellers," Berg'inyon remarked to one of his advisors when she walked her mount beside his. "I shall never return."

"What of Drizzt Do'Urden?" the female asked, for it was no secret that Matron Baenre wanted her son to slay the renegade.

Berg'inyon laughed at her, for not once since he had witnessed Drizzt's exploits at the Academy had he entertained any serious thoughts of fighting the renegade.

✕ ✕ ✕ ✕ ✕

Drizzt could see little beyond the gigantic glabrezu, and that spectacle was enough, for the ranger knew he was not prepared for such a foe, knew that the mighty creature would likely destroy him.

Even if it didn't defeat him, the glabrezu would surely hold him up long enough for Matron Baenre to kill them all!

Drizzt felt the savage hunger of his scimitar, a blade forged to kill such beasts, but he fought off the urge to charge, knew that he had to find a way around those devilish pincers.

He noted Guenhwyvar's futile leap and disappearance. Another ally lost.

The fight was over before it had begun, Drizzt realized. They had killed a couple of elite guards and nothing more. They had walked headlong into the pinnacle of Menzoberranzan's power, the most high priestesses of the Spider Queen, and they had lost. Waves of guilt washed over Drizzt, but he dismissed them, refused to accept them. He had come out, and his friends had come beside him, because this had been Mithral Hall's only chance. Even if Drizzt had known that Matron Baenre herself was leading this march, he would have come out here, and would not have denied Bruenor, Regis, and Catti-brie the opportunity to accompany him.

They had lost, but Drizzt meant to make their enemy hurt.

"Fight on, demon spawn," he snarled at the glabrezu, and he fell into a crouch, waving his blades, eager to give his scimitar the meal it so greatly desired.

The tanar'ri straightened and held out a curious metal coffer.

Drizzt didn't wait for an explanation, and almost unintentionally destroyed the only chance he and his friends had, for as the tanar'ri moved to open the coffer, Drizzt, with the enchanted ankle bracers speeding his rush, yelled and charged, right past the lowered pincers, thrusting his scimitar into the fiend's belly.

He felt the surge of power as the scimitar fed.

⚔ ⚔ ⚔ ⚔ ⚔

Catti-brie was too confused to strike, too overwhelmed to even cry out in protest as Methil came right up to her and the wretched tentacles licked her face. Then, through the confusion, a single voice, the voice of Khazid'hea, her sword, called out in her head.

Strike!

She did, and though her aim was not perfect, Khazid'hea's wicked edge hit Methil on the shoulder, nearly severing the illithid's arm.

Out of her daze, Catti-brie swept the tentacles from her face with her free hand.

Another psionic wave blasted her, crippling her once more, stealing her strength and buckling her legs. Before she went down, she saw the illithid jerk weirdly, then fall away, and saw Regis, staggering, his hair still dancing wildly. The halfling's mace was covered in blood, and he fell sidelong, over the stumbling Methil.

That would have been the end of the illithid, especially when Catti-brie regained her senses enough to join in, except that Methil had anticipated such a disaster and had stored enough psionic energy to get out of the fight. Regis lifted his mace for another strike, but felt himself sinking as the illithid dissipated beneath him. The halfling cried out in confusion, in terror, and swung anyway, but his mace clanged loudly as it hit only the empty stone floor beneath him.

⚔ ⚔ ⚔ ⚔ ⚔

It all happened in a mere instant, a flicker of time in which poor Bruenor had not gained an inch toward his taunting foes.

The glabrezu, in pain greater than anything it had ever known, could have killed Drizzt then. Every instinct within the wicked creature urged it to snap this impertinent drow in half. Every instinct except one: the fear of Errtu's reprisal once the tanar'ri got back to the Abyss—and with that vile scimitar chewing away at its belly, the tanar'ri knew it would soon make that trip.

It wanted so much to snap Drizzt in half, but the fiend had been sent here for a different reason, and evil Errtu would accept no explanations for failure. Growling at the renegade Do'Urden, taking pleasure only in the knowledge that Errtu would soon return to punish this one personally, the glabrezu reached across and tore open the shielding coffer, producing the shining black sapphire.

The hunger disappeared from Drizzt's scimitar. Suddenly, the ranger's feet weren't moving so quickly.

Across the Realms, the most poignant reminder of the Time of Troubles were the areas known as dead zones, wherein all magic ceased to exist. This sapphire contained within it the negative energy of such a zone, possessed the antimagic to steal magical energy, and not Drizzt's scimitars or his bracers, not Khazid'hea or the magic of the drow priestesses, could overcome that negative force.

It happened for only an instant, for a consequence of revealing that sapphire was the release of the summoned tanar'ri from the Material Plane, and the departing glabrezu took with it the sapphire.

For only an instant, the fires stopped in the tunnel behind Catti-brie. For only an instant, the shackles binding Gandalug lost their enchantment. For only an instant, the block of goo surrounding Bruenor was no more.

For only an instant, but that was long enough for Gandalug, teeming with centuries of rage, to tear his suddenly feeble shackles apart, and for Bruenor to surge ahead, so that when the block of goo reappeared, he was beyond its influence, charging hard and screaming with all his strength.

Matron Baenre had fallen unceremoniously to the floor, and her driftdisk reappeared when magic returned, hovering above her head.

Gandalug launched a backhand punch to the left, smacking Quenthel in the face and knocking her back against the wall. Then he jumped to the right and caught Bladen'Kerst's five-headed snake whip in his hand, taking more than one numbing bite.

The old dwarf ignored the pain and pressed on, barreling over the surprised Baenre daughter. He reached around her other shoulder and caught the handle of her whip in his free hand, then pulled the thing tightly against her neck, strangling her with her own wicked weapon.

They fell in a clinch.

⚔ ⚔ ⚔ ⚔ ⚔

In all the Realms there was no creature more protected by magic than Matron Baenre, no creature shielded from blows more effectively, not even a thick-scaled ancient dragon. But most of those wards were gone now, taken from her in the moment of antimagic. And in all the Realms there was no creature more consumed by rage than Bruenor Battlehammer, enraged at the sight of the old, tormented dwarf he knew he should recognize. Enraged at the realization that his friends, that his dear daughter, were dead, or soon would be. Enraged at the withered drow priestess, in his mind the personification of the evil that had taken his boy.

He chopped his axe straight overhead, the many-notched blade diving down, shattering the blue light of the driftdisk, blowing the enchantment into nothingness. Bruenor felt the burn as the blade hit one of the few remaining magical shields, energy instantly coursing up the weapon's head and handle, into the furious king.

The axe went from green to orange to blue as it tore through magical

defense after magical defense, rage pitted against powerful dweomers. Bruenor felt agony, but would admit none.

The axe drove through the feeble arm that Baenre lifted to block, through Baenre's skull, through her jawbone and neck, and deep into her frail chest.

✕ ✕ ✕ ✕ ✕

Quenthel shook off Gandalug's heavy blow and instinctively moved for her sister. Then, suddenly, her mother was dead and the priestess rushed back toward the wall instead, through the green-edged portal, back into the corridor beyond. She dropped some silvery dust as she passed through, enchanted dust that would dispel the portal and make the wall smooth and solid once again.

The stone spiraled in, fast transforming back into a solid barrier.

Only Drizzt Do'Urden, moving with the speed of the enchanted anklets, got through that opening before it snapped shut.

✕ ✕ ✕ ✕ ✕

Jarlaxle and his lieutenants were not far away. They knew that a group of wild dwarves and a wolfman had met Baenre's other elite guards in the tunnels across the way, and that the dwarves and their ally had overwhelmed the dark elves and were fast bearing down on the chamber.

From a high vantage point, looking out from a cubby on the tunnel behind that chamber, Jarlaxle knew the approaching band of furious dwarves had already missed the action. Quenthel's appearance, and Drizzt's right behind her, told the watching mercenary leader the conquest of Mithral Hall had come to an abrupt end.

The lieutenant at Jarlaxle's side lifted a hand-crossbow toward Drizzt, and seemed to have a perfect opportunity, for Drizzt's focus was solely on the fleeing Baenre daughter. The ranger would never know what hit him.

Jarlaxle grabbed the lieutenant's wrist and forced the arm down. Jarlaxle motioned to the tunnels behind, and he and his somewhat confused, but ultimately loyal, band slipped silently away.

As they departed, Jarlaxle heard Quenthel's dying scream, a cry of "Sacrilege!" She was yelling out a denial, of course, in Drizzt Do'Urden's—her killer's—face, but Jarlaxle realized she could just as easily, and just as accurately, have been referring to him.

So be it.

⚔ ⚔ ⚔ ⚔ ⚔

The dawn was bright but cold, and it grew colder still as Stumpet and Terrien Doucard, of the Knights in Silver, made their way up the difficult side of Keeper's Dale, climbing hand over hand along the almost vertical wall.

"Ye're certain?" Stumpet asked Terrien, a half-elf with lustrous brown hair and features too fair to be dimmed by even the tragedy of the last night.

The knight didn't bother to reply, other than with a quick nod, for Stumpet had asked the question more than a dozen times in the last twenty minutes.

"This is the right wall?" Stumpet asked, yet another of her redundant questions.

Terrien nodded. "Close," he assured the dwarf.

Stumpet came up on a small ledge and slid over, putting her back against the wall, her feet hanging over the two-hundred-foot drop to the valley floor. She felt she should be down there in the valley, helping tend to the many, many wounded, but if what the knight had told her was true, if Lady Alustriel of Silverymoon had fallen up here, then this trip might be the most important task Stumpet Rakingclaw ever completed in her life.

She heard Terrien struggling below her and bent over, reaching down to hook the half-elf under the shoulder. Stumpet's powerful muscles corded, and she easily hoisted the slender knight over the ledge, guiding him into position beside her against the wall. Both the half-elf and the dwarf breathed heavily, puffs of steam filling the air before them.

"We held the dale," Stumpet said cheerily, trying to coax the agonized expression from the half-elf's face.

"Would the victory have been worth it if you had watched Bruenor Battlehammer die?" the half-elf replied, his teeth chattering a bit from the frigid air.

"Ye're not for knowing that Alustriel died!" Stumpet shot back, and she pulled the pack from her back, fumbling around inside. She had wanted to wait a while before doing this, hopefully to get closer to the spot where Alustriel's chariot had reportedly gone down.

She took out a small bowl shaped of silvery mithral and pulled a bulging waterskin over her head.

"It is probably frozen," the dejected half-elf remarked, indicating the skin.

Stumpet snorted. Dwarven holy water didn't freeze, at least not the kind Stumpet had brewed, dropping in a little ninety-proof to sweeten the mix. She popped the cork from the waterskin and began a rhythmic chant as she

poured the golden liquid into the mithral bowl. She was lucky—she knew that—for though the image her spells brought forth was fuzzy and brief, an area some distance away, she knew this region, and knew where to find the indicated ledge.

They started off immediately at a furious and reckless pace, Stumpet not even bothering to collect her bowl and skin. The half-elf slipped more than once, only to be caught by the wrist by Stumpet's strong grasp, and more than once Stumpet found herself falling, and only the quick hands of Terrien Doucard, deftly planting pitons to secure the rope between them, saved her.

Finally, they got to the ledge and found Alustriel lying still and cold. The only indication that her magical chariot had ever been there was a scorch mark where the thing had crashed, on the floor of the ledge and against the mountain wall. Not even debris remained, for the chariot had been wholly a creation of magic.

The half-elf rushed to his fallen leader and gently cradled Alustriel's head in one arm. Stumpet whipped out a small mirror from her belt pouch and stuck it in front of the lady's mouth.

"She's alive!" the dwarf announced, tossing her pack to Terrien. The words seemed to ignite the half-elf. He gently laid Alustriel's head to the ledge, then fumbled in the pack, tearing out several thick blankets, and wrapped his lady warmly, then began briskly rubbing Alustriel's bare, cold hands. All the while, Stumpet called upon her gods for spells of healing and warmth, and gave every ounce of her own energy to this wondrous leader of Silverymoon.

Five minutes later, Lady Alustriel opened her beautiful eyes. She took a deep breath and shuddered, then whispered something neither Stumpet nor the knight could hear, so the half-elf leaned closer, put his ear right up to her mouth.

"Did we hold?"

Terrien Doucard straightened and smiled widely. "Keeper's Dale is ours!" he announced, and Alustriel's eyes sparkled. Then she slept, peacefully, confident that this furiously working dwarven priestess would keep her warm and well, and she was confident that, whatever her own fate, the greater good had been served.

For the good of all goodly folk.

EPILOGUE

Berg'inyon Baenre was not surprised to find Jarlaxle and the soldiers of Bregan D'aerthe waiting for him far below the surface, far from Mithral Hall. As soon as he had heard reports of desertion, Berg'inyon realized that the pragmatic mercenary was probably among those ranks of drow fleeing the war.

Methil had informed Jarlaxle of Berg'inyon's approach, and the mercenary leader was indeed surprised to find that Berg'inyon, the son of Matron Baenre, the weapons master of the First House, had also run off in desertion. The mercenary had figured that Berg'inyon would fight his way into Mithral Hall and die as his mother had died.

Stupidly.

"The war is lost," Berg'inyon remarked. Unsure of himself, he looked to Methil, for he hadn't anticipated that the illithid would be out here, away from the matriarch. The illithid's obvious wounds, one arm hanging limply and a large hole on the side of his octopus head, grotesque brain matter oozing out, caught Berg'inyon off guard as well, for he never expected that anyone could catch up to Methil and harm him so.

"Your mother is dead," Jarlaxle replied bluntly, drawing the young Baenre's attention from the wounded illithid. "As are your two sisters and Auro'pol Dyrr."

Berg'inyon nodded, seeming hardly surprised.

Jarlaxle wondered whether he should mention that Matron Baenre was the one who had murdered the latter. He held the thought in check, figuring he might be able to use that little bit of information against Berg'inyon at a later time.

"Matron Zeerith Q'Xorlarrin led the retreat from Mithral Hall's lower door," the mercenary went on.

"And my own force caught up to those drow who tried, and failed, to get in the eastern door," Berg'inyon added.

"And you punished them?" Jarlaxle wanted to know, for he was still unsure of Berg'inyon's feelings about all of this, still unsure if he and his band were about to fight yet another battle down here in the tunnels.

Berg'inyon scoffed at the notion of punishment, and Jarlaxle breathed a little easier.

Together, they marched on, back for the dark and more comfortable ways of Menzoberranzan. They linked with Zeerith and her force soon after, and many other groups of dark elves and humanoids fell into line as the days wore on. In all, more than two thousand drow, a fourth of them Baenre soldiers, had died in the assault on Mithral Hall, and twice that number of humanoid slaves had been killed, most outside the mountain, on Fourthpeak's southern slopes and in Keeper's Dale. And a like number of humanoids had run off after the battles, fleeing to the surface or down other corridors, taking their chances in the unknown world above or in the wild Underdark rather than return to the tortured life as a slave of the drow.

Things had not gone as Matron Baenre had planned.

Berg'inyon fell into line as the quiet force moved away, letting Zeerith control the procession.

"Menzoberranzan will be many years in healing from the folly of Matron Baenre," Jarlaxle remarked to Berg'inyon later that day, when he came upon the young weapons master alone in a side chamber as the army camped in a region of broken caves and short, connecting tunnels.

Berg'inyon didn't disagree with the statement and showed no anger at all. He understood the truth of Jarlaxle's words, and knew that much trouble would befall House Baenre in the days ahead. Matron Zeerith was outraged, and Mez'Barris Armgo and all the other matron mothers would be, too, when they learned of the disaster.

"The offer remains," Jarlaxle said, and he left the chamber, left Berg'inyon alone with his thoughts.

House Baenre would likely survive, Berg'inyon believed. Triel would assume its rulership, and though they had lost five hundred skilled soldiers, nearly two thousand remained, including more than three hundred of the famed lizard riders. Matron Baenre had built a huge network of allies outside the House as well, and even this disaster, and the death of Baenre, would not likely topple the First House.

There would indeed be trouble, though. Matron Baenre was the solidifying force. What might House Baenre expect from troublesome Gromph with her gone?

And what of Triel? Berg'inyon wondered. Where would he fit into his sister's designs? Now she would be free to raise children of her own and bring them into power. The first son born to her would either be groomed as the House wizard or as a candidate for Berg'inyon's position as weapons master.

How long, then, did Berg'inyon have? Fifty years? A hundred? Not long in the life span of a dark elf.

Berg'inyon looked to the archway, to the back of the departing mercenary, and considered carefully Jarlaxle's offer for him to join Bregan D'aerthe.

⚔ ⚔ ⚔ ⚔ ⚔

Mithral Hall was a place of mixed emotions: tears for the dead and cheers for the victory. All mourned Besnell and Firble, Regweld Harpell and so many others who had died valiantly. And all cheered for King Bruenor and his mighty friends, for Berkthgar the Bold, for Lady Alustriel, still nursing her grievous wounds, and for Stumpet Rakingclaw, hero of both the Undercity and Keeper's Dale.

And all cheered most of all for Gandalug Battlehammer, the patron of Clan Battlehammer, returned from the grave, it seemed. How strange it was for Bruenor to face his own ancestor, to see the first bust in the Hall of Kings come to life!

The two dwarves sat side by side in the throne room on the upper levels of the dwarven complex, flanked by Alustriel—with Stumpet kneeling beside the Lady of Silverymoon's chair, nagging her to rest!—on the right and Berkthgar on the left.

The celebration was general throughout the dwarven complex, from the Undercity to the throne room, a time of gathering, and of parting, a time when Belwar Dissengulp and Bruenor Battlehammer finally met. Through the magic of Alustriel, an enchantment that sorted out the language problems, the two were able to forge an alliance between Blingdenstone and Mithral Hall that would live for centuries, and they were able to swap tales of their common drow friend, particularly when Drizzt was wandering around, just far enough away to realize they were talking about him.

"It's the damned cat that bothers me," Bruenor huffed on one occasion, loud enough so that Drizzt would hear.

The drow sauntered over, put a foot on the raised dais that held the thrones,

and leaned forward on his knee, very close to Belwar. "Guenhwyvar humbles Bruenor," Drizzt said in the Drow tongue, a language Belwar somewhat understood, but which was not translated by Alustriel's spell for Bruenor. "She often uses the dwarf for bedding."

Bruenor, knowing they were talking about him, but unable to understand a word, hooted in protest—and protested louder when Gandalug, who also knew a bit of the Drow tongue, joined in the conversation and the mirth.

"But suren the cat's not fer using me son's son's son's son's son's son's son's 'ead fer a piller!" the old dwarf howled. "Too hard it be. Too, too!"

"By Moradin, I should've left with the damned dark elves," a defeated Bruenor grumbled.

That notion sobered old Gandalug, took the cheer from his face in the blink of an eye.

Such was the celebration in Mithral Hall, a time of strong emotions, both good and bad.

Catti-brie watched it all from the side, feeling removed and strangely out of place. Surely she was thrilled at the victory, intrigued by the svirfnebli, whom she had met once before, and even more intrigued that the patron of her father's clan had been miraculously returned to the dwarven complex he had founded. Along with those exciting feelings, though, the young woman felt a sense of completion. The drow threat to Mithral Hall was ended this time, and new and stronger alliances would be forged between Mithral Hall and all its neighbors, even Nesmé. Bruenor and Berkthgar seemed old friends now—Bruenor had even hinted on several occasions that he might be willing to let the barbarian wield Aegis-fang.

Catti-brie hoped that would not come to pass, and didn't think it would. Bruenor had hinted at the generous offer mostly because he knew it wouldn't really cost him anything, Catti-brie suspected. After Berkthgar's exploits in Keeper's Dale, his own weapon, Bankenfuere, was well on its way as a legend among the warriors of Settlestone.

No matter what Berkthgar's exploits might be, Bankenfuere would never rival Aegis-fang, in Catti-brie's mind.

Though she was quiet and reflective, Catti-brie was not grim, not maudlin. Like everyone else in Mithral Hall, she had lost some friends in the war. But like everyone else, she was battle-hardened, accepting the ways of the world and able to see the greater good that had come from the battle. She laughed when a group of svirfnebli practically pulled out what little hair they had, so frustrated were they in trying to teach a group of drunken dwarves how to hear vibrations in the stone. She laughed louder when Regis bopped into the throne room, pounds of food tucked under each arm and already so stuffed that the buttons on his waistcoat were near bursting.

And she laughed loudest of all when Bidderdoo Harpell raced past her, Thibbledorf Pwent scrambling on his knees behind the wizard, begging Bidderdoo to bite him!

But there remained a reflective solitude behind that laughter, that nagging sense of completion that didn't sit well on the shoulders of a woman who had just begun to open her eyes to the wide world.

⚔ ⚔ ⚔ ⚔ ⚔

In the smoky filth of the Abyss, the balor Errtu held his breath as the shapely drow, the delicate disaster, approached his mushroom throne.

Errtu didn't know what to expect from Lolth; they had both witnessed the disaster.

The balor watched as the drow came through the mist, the prisoner, the promised gift, in tow. She was smiling, but on the face of the Lady of Chaos, one could never hope to guess what that meant.

Errtu sat tall and proud, confident he had done as instructed. If Lolth tried to blame him for the disaster, he would argue, he determined, though if she had somehow found out about the antimagic stone he had sent along with the glabrezu . . .

"You have brought my payment?" the balor boomed, trying to sound imposing.

"Of course, Errtu," the Spider Queen replied.

Errtu cocked his tremendous, horned head. There seemed no deception in either her tone or her movements as she pushed the prisoner toward the gigantic, seated balor.

"You seem pleased," Errtu dared to remark.

Lolth's smile nearly took in her ears, and Errtu understood. She was pleased! The old wretch, the most wicked of the wicked, was glad of the outcome. Matron Baenre was gone, as was all order in Menzoberranzan. The drow city would know its greatest chaos now, thrilling interhouse warfare and a veritable spiderweb of intrigue, layer upon layer of lies and treachery, through each of the ruling Houses.

"You knew this would happen from the beginning!" the balor accused.

Lolth laughed aloud. "I did not anticipate the outcome," she assured Errtu. "I did not know Errtu would be so resourceful in protecting the one who might end his banishment."

The balor's eyes widened, and his great leathery wings folded close around him, a symbolic, if ineffective, movement of defense.

"Fear not, my fiendish ally," Lolth cooed. "I will give you a chance to redeem yourself in my eyes."

Errtu growled low. What favor did the Spider Queen now want from him?

"I will be busy these next decades, I fear," Lolth went on, "in trying to end the confusion in Menzoberranzan."

Errtu scoffed. "Never would you desire such a thing," he replied.

"I will be busy watching the confusion then," Lolth was willing to admit. Almost as an afterthought, she added, "And watching what it is you must do for me."

Again came that demonic growl.

"When you are free, Errtu," Lolth said evenly, "when you have Drizzt Do'Urden entangled in the tongs of your merciless whip, do kill him slowly, painfully, that I might hear his every cry!" The Spider Queen swept hers arms up then and disappeared with a flurry of crackling black energy.

Errtu's lip curled up in an evil smile. He looked to the pitiful prisoner, the key to breaking the will and the heart of Drizzt Do'Urden. Sometimes, it seemed, the Spider Queen did not ask for much.

⚔ ⚔ ⚔ ⚔ ⚔

It had been two tendays since the victory, and in Mithral Hall the celebration continued. Many had left—first the two remaining men from Nesmé and the Longriders, along with Harkle and Bella don DelRoy—though Pwent finally convinced Bidderdoo to stick around for a while. Then Alustriel and her remaining Knights in Silver, seventy-five warriors, began their journey back to Silverymoon with their heads held high, the lady ready to meet the challenges of her political rivals head-on, confident that she had done right in coming to King Bruenor's aid.

The svirfnebli were in no hurry to leave, though, enjoying the company of Clan Battlehammer, and the men of Settlestone vowed to stay until the last of Mithral Hall's mead was drained away.

Far down the mountain from the dwarven complex, on a cold, windy plain, Catti-brie sat atop a fine roan—one of the horses that had belonged to a slain Silverymoon knight. She sat quietly and confidently, but the sting in her heart as she looked up to Mithral Hall was no less acute. Her eyes scanned the trails to the rocky exit from the mountains, and she smiled, not surprised, in seeing a rider coming down.

"I knew ye'd follow me down here," she said to Drizzt Do'Urden when the ranger approached.

"We all have our place," Drizzt replied.

"And mine's not now in Mithral Hall," Catti-brie said sternly. "Ye'll not change me mind!"

Drizzt paused for a long while, studying the determined young woman. "You've talked with Bruenor?" he asked.

"Of course," Catti-brie retorted. "Ye think I'd leave me father's house without his blessings?"

"Blessings he gave grudgingly, no doubt," Drizzt remarked.

Catti-brie straightened in her saddle and locked her jaw firmly. "Bruenor's got much to do," she said. "And he's got Regis and yerself . . ." She paused and held that thought, noticing the heavy pack strapped behind Drizzt's saddle. "And Gandalug and Berkthgar beside him," she finished. "They've not even figured which is to rule and which is to watch, though I'm thinking Gandalug's to let Bruenor remain king."

"That would be the wiser course," Drizzt agreed.

A long moment of silence passed between them.

"Berkthgar talks of leaving," Drizzt said suddenly, "of returning to Icewind Dale and the ancient ways of his people."

Catti-brie nodded. She had heard such rumors.

Again came that uncomfortable silence. Catti-brie finally turned her eyes away from the drow, thinking he was judging her, thinking, in her moment of doubt, that she was being a terrible daughter to Bruenor, terrible and selfish. "Me father didn't try to stop me," she blurted with a tone of finality, "and yerself cannot!"

"I never said I came out to try to stop you," Drizzt calmly replied.

Catti-brie paused, not really surprised. When she had first told Bruenor she was leaving, that she had to go out from Mithral Hall for a while and witness the wonders of the world, the crusty dwarf had bellowed so loudly that Catti-brie thought the stone walls would tumble in on both of them.

They had met again two days later, when Bruenor was not so full of dwarven holy water, and to Catti-brie's surprise and relief, her father was much more reasonable. He understood her heart, he had assured her, though his gruff voice cracked as he delivered the words, and he realized she had to follow it, had to go off and learn who she was and where she fit in the world. Catti-brie had thought the words uncharacteristically understanding and philosophical of Bruenor, and now, facing Drizzt, she was certain of their source. Now she knew who Bruenor had spoken to between their meetings.

"He sent ye," she accused Drizzt.

"You were leaving and so was I," Drizzt replied casually.

"I just could not spend the rest o' me days in the tunnels," Catti-brie said, suddenly feeling as if she had to explain herself, revealing the guilt that had weighed heavily on her since her decision to leave home. She looked all around, her eyes scanning the distant horizon. "There's just so much more for me. I'm knowing that in me heart. I've known it since Wulfgar . . ."

She paused and sighed and looked to Drizzt helplessly.

"And more for me," the drow said with a mischievous grin, "much more."

Catti-brie glanced back over her shoulder, back to the west, where the sun was already beginning its descent.

"The days are short," she remarked, "and the road is long."

"Only as long as you make it," Drizzt said to her, drawing her gaze back to him. "And the days are only as short as you allow them to be."

Catti-brie eyed him curiously, not understanding that last statement.

Drizzt was grinning widely as he explained, as full of anticipation as was Catti-brie. "A friend of mine, a blind old ranger, once told me that if you ride hard and fast enough to the west, the sun will never set for you."

By the time he had finished the statement, Catti-brie had wheeled her roan and was in full gallop across the frozen plain toward the west, toward Nesmé and Longsaddle beyond that, toward mighty Waterdeep and the Sword Coast. She bent low in the saddle, her mount running hard, her cloak billowing and snapping in the wind behind her, her thick auburn hair flying wildly.

Drizzt opened a belt pouch and looked at the onyx panther figurine. No one could ask for better companions, he mused, and with a final look to the mountains, to Mithral Hall, where his friend was king, the ranger kicked his stallion into a gallop and chased after Catti-brie.

To the west and the adventures of the wide world.

PASSAGE TO DAWN

THE LEGEND OF DRIZZT Book X

She was beautiful, shapely, and pale-skinned with thick, lustrous hair cascading halfway down her naked back. Her charms were offered openly, brazenly, conveyed to him at the end of a gentle touch. So gentle. Little brushing fingers of energy tickled his chin, his jawbone, his neck.

Every muscle of his body tensed and he fought for control, battled the seductress with every bit of will-power remaining in him after so many years.

PROLOGUE

He didn't even know why he resisted anymore, didn't consciously remember what offerings of the other world, the real world, might be fueling his stubbornness. What were "right" and "wrong" in this place? What might be the price of pleasure?

What more did he have to give?

The gentle touch continued, soothing his trembling muscles, raising goose bumps across his skin wherever those fingers brushed. Calling to him. Bidding him to surrender.

Surrender.

He felt his willpower draining away, argued against his stubbornness. There was no reason to resist. He could have soft sheets and a comfortable mattress. The smell—the awful reek so terrible that even years had not allowed him to get used to it—could be taken away. She could do that with her magic. She had promised him.

Falling fast, he half-closed his eyes and felt the touch continuing, felt it more keenly than before.

He heard her snarl, a feral, bestial sound.

Now he looked past her. They were on the lip of a ridge, one of countless ridges across the broken, heaving ground that trembled as if it were a living thing, breathing, laughing at him, mocking him. They were up high. He knew that. The ravine beyond the ridge was wide, and yet he could not see more than a couple of feet beyond the edge. The landscape was lost in the perpetual swirling grayness, the smoky pall.

The Abyss.

Now it was his turn to growl, a sound that was not feral, not primal, but one of rationale, of morality, of that tiny spark that remained in him of who he had been. He grabbed her hand and forced it away, turning it, twisting it. Her strength in resisting confirmed his memories, for it was supernatural, far beyond what her frame should have allowed.

Still, he was the stronger and he forced the hand away, turned it about, then set his stare upon her.

Her thick hair had shifted a bit, and one of her tiny white horns had poked through.

"Do not, my lover," she purred. The weight of her plea nearly broke him. Like her physical strength, her voice carried more than was natural. Her voice was a conduit of charms, of deceit, of the ultimate lie that was all this place.

A scream erupted from his lips and he heaved her backward with all his strength, hurled her from the ridge.

Huge batlike wings unfolded behind her and the succubus hovered, laughing at him, her open mouth revealing horrid fangs that would have punctured his neck. She laughed and he knew that although he had resisted, he had not won, could never win. She had almost broken him this time, came closer to it than the last, and would be closer still the next. And so she laughed at him, mocked him. Always mocking him!

He realized that it had been a test, always a test. He knew who had arranged it and was not surprised when the whip tore into his back, laying him low. He tried to take cover, felt the intense heat building all around him, but knew that there was no escape.

A second snapping had him crawling for the ledge. Then came a third lash, and he grabbed on to the lip of the ridge, screamed, and pulled himself over, wanting to pitch into the ravine, to splatter his corporeal form against the rocks. Desperate to die.

Errtu, the great balor, twelve feet of smoking deep red scales and corded muscles, casually walked to the edge and peered over. With eyes that had seen through the mists of the Abyss since the dawn of time, Errtu sought out the falling form, then reached out to him.

He was falling slower. Then he was not falling at all. He was rising, caught in a telekinetic web, reeled in by the master. The whip was waiting and the next lash sent him spiraling, mercifully, into unconsciousness.

Errtu did not retract the whip's cords. The balor used the same telekinetic energy to wrap them about the victim, binding him fast. Errtu looked back to the hysterical succubus and nodded. She had done well this day.

Drool slipped over her bottom lip at the sight of the unconscious form. She wanted to feast. In her eyes, the table was set and waiting. A flap of her wings brought her back to the ledge and she approached cautiously, seeking some way through the balor's defenses.

Errtu let her get close, so close, then gave a slight tug on the whip. His victim flopped away weirdly, jumping past the balor's perpetual flames. Errtu shifted a step to the side, putting his bulk between the victim and the succubus.

"I must," she whined, daring to move a bit closer, half-walking and half-flying. Her deceivingly delicate hands reached out and grasped at the smoky air. She trembled and panted.

Errtu stepped aside. She inched closer.

The balor was teasing her, she knew, but she could not turn away, not with the sight of this helpless one.

She whined, knowing she was going to be punished, but she could not stop.

Taking a slightly roundabout route, she walked past the balor. She whined again, her feet digging a firm hold that she might rush to the prone victim and taste of him at least once before Errtu denied her.

Out shot Errtu's arm, holding a sword that was wrought of lightning. He lifted it high and uttered a command and the ground jolted with the strength of a thunderstroke.

The succubus waited and leaped away, running for the ledge and then flying off of it, shrieking all the while. Errtu's lightning hit her in the back and sent her spinning, and she was far below the edge of the ridge before she regained control.

Back on the ledge, Errtu gave her not another thought. The balor was thinking of his prisoner, always of his prisoner. He enjoyed tormenting the wretch, but had to continually sublimate his bestial urges. He could not destroy this one, could not break him too far, else the victim would hold no value for the balor. This was but one being, and measured against the promise of freedom to walk again on the Prime Material Plane, that did not seem so much.

Only Drizzt Do'Urden, the renegade dark elf, the one who had banished Errtu to a hundred years in the Abyss, could grant that freedom. The drow would do that, Errtu believed, in exchange for the wretch.

Errtu turned his horned, apelike head to look over one massive shoulder. The fires that surrounded the balor burned low now, simmering as was Errtu's rage. Patience, the balor reminded himself. The wretch was valuable and had to be preserved.

The time was coming, Errtu knew. He would speak with Drizzt Do'Urden before another year had passed on the Material Plane. Errtu had made contact with the witch, and she would deliver his message.

Then the balor, one of the true tanar'ri, among the greatest denizens of the lower planes, would be free. Then Errtu could destroy the wretch, could destroy Drizzt Do'Urden, and could destroy every being that loved the renegade drow.

Patience.

PART ONE

Six years. Not so long in the life span of a drow, and yet, in counting the months, the tendays, the days, the hours, it seemed to me as if I had been away from Mithral Hall a hundred times that number. The place was removed, another lifetime, another way of life, a mere stepping stone to . . .

To what? To where?

My most vivid memory of

WIND AND SPRAY

Mithral Hall is of riding away from the place with Catti-brie at my side, is the view in looking back over the plumes of smoke rising from Settlestone to the mountain called Fourthpeak. Mithral Hall was Bruenor's kingdom, Bruenor's home, and Bruenor was among the most dear of friends to me. But it was not my home, had never been so.

I couldn't explain it then, and still cannot. All should have been well there after the defeat of the invading drow army. Mithral Hall shared prosperity and friendship with all of the neighboring communities, was part of an assortment of kingdoms with the power to protect their borders and feed their poor.

All of that, but still Mithral Hall was not home.

Not for me, and not for Catti-brie. Thus had we taken to the road, riding west to the coast, to Waterdeep.

I never argued with Catti-brie—though she had certainly expected me to—concerning her decision to leave Mithral Hall. We were of like minds. We had never really set down our hearts in the place; we had been too busy, in defeating the enemies who ruled there, in reopening the dwarven mines, in traveling to Menzoberranzan and in battling the dark elves who had come to Mithral Hall. All that completed, it seemed time to settle, to rest, to tell and to lengthen tales of our adventures. If Mithral Hall had been our home before the battles, we would have remained. After the battles, after the losses . . . for both Catti-brie and Drizzt Do'Urden, it was too late. Mithral Hall was Bruenor's place, not ours. It was the war-scarred place where I had to again face the legacy of my dark heritage. It was the beginning of the road that had led me back to Menzoberranzan.

It was the place where Wulfgar had died.

Catti-brie and I vowed that we would return there one day, and so we would, for Bruenor was there, and Regis. But Catti-brie had seen the truth. You can never get the smell of blood out of the stones. If you were there when that blood was spilled, the continuing aroma evokes images too painful to live beside.

Six years, and I have missed Bruenor and Regis, Stumpet Rakingclaw, and even Berkthgar the Bold, who rules Settlestone. I have missed my journeys to wondrous Silverymoon, and watching the dawn from one of Fourthpeak's many rocky perches. I ride the waves along the Sword Coast now, the wind and spray in my face. My ceiling is the rush of clouds and the canopy of stars; my floor is the creaking boards of a swift, well-weathered ship, and beyond that, the azure blanket, flat and still, heaving and rolling, hissing in the rain and exploding under the fall of a breaching whale.

Is this my home? I know not. Another stepping stone, I would guess, but whether there really is a road that would lead me to a place called home, I do not know.

Nor do I think about it often, because I've come to realize that I do not care. If this road, this series of stepping stones, leads nowhere, then so be it. I walk the road with friends, and so I have my home.

—Drizzt Do'Urden

I

THE SEA SPRITE

Drizzt Do'Urden stood on the very edge of the beam, as far forward as he could go, one hand grasping tight the guide rope of the flying jib. This ship was a smooth runner, perfect in balance and ballast and with the best of crews, but the sea was rough this day and the *Sea Sprite* cut and bounced through the rolls at full sail, throwing a heavy spray.

Drizzt didn't mind. He loved the feel of the spray and the wind, the smell of the brine. This was freedom, flying, skimming the water, skipping the waves. Drizzt's thick white hair flipped in the breeze, billowing like his green cape behind him, drying almost as fast as the water soaked it. Splotches of white caked salt could not lessen the luster of his ebony skin, which glistened with wetness. His violet eyes sparkled with joy as he squinted at the horizon and caught a fleeting glimpse of the sails of the ship they pursued.

Pursued and would catch, Drizzt knew, for there was no ship north of Baldur's Gate that could outrun Captain Deudermont's *Sea Sprite*. She was a three-masted schooner, new in design, light, sleek, and full of sail. The square-rigged caravel they were chasing could put up a fair run in a straight line, but anytime the bulkier vessel altered its course even the slightest bit, the *Sea Sprite* could angle inside it, gaining ground. Always gaining ground.

That was what she was meant to do. Built by the finest engineers and wizards of Waterdeep, funded by the lords of that city, the schooner was a pirate chaser. How thrilled Drizzt had been to discover the good fortunes of his old friend, Deudermont, with whom he had sailed all the way from Waterdeep to Calimshan in pursuit of Artemis Entreri when the assassin had captured Regis the halfling. That journey, particularly the fight in Asavir's

Channel when Captain Deudermont had won—with no small help from Drizzt and his companions—against three pirate ships, including the flagship of the notorious Pinochet, had caught the attention of sailors and merchants all along the Sword Coast. When the Lords of Waterdeep had completed this schooner, they had offered it to Deudermont. He loved his little two-master, the original *Sea Sprite,* but no seaman could resist this new beauty. Deudermont had accepted a commission in their service and they had granted him the right to name the vessel and allowed him to handpick his crew.

Drizzt and Catti-brie had arrived in Waterdeep sometime after that. When the *Sea Sprite* next put in to the grand harbor of the seaport, and Deudermont found his old friends, he promptly made room for them among his crew of forty. That was six years and twenty-seven voyages ago. Among those who monitored the shipping lanes of the Sword Coast, particularly among the pirates themselves, the schooner had become a scourge. Thirty-seven victories, and still she sailed.

Now number thirty-eight was in sight.

The caravel had noticed them, from too far away to see the flag of Waterdeep. That hardly mattered, for no other ship in the region carried the distinctive design of the *Sea Sprite,* the three masts of billowing triangular, lateen sails. Up came the caravel's square rigs, and so the chase was on in full.

Drizzt was at the point, one foot on the lion-headed ram, loving every second. He felt the sheer power of the sea bucking beneath him, felt the spray and the wind. He heard the music, loud and strong, for several of the *Sea Sprite*'s crewmen were minstrels and whenever the chase was on, they took up their instruments and played rousing songs.

"Two thousand!" Catti-brie yelled down from the crow's nest. It was a measure of the distance yet to gain. When her estimate got down to five hundred, the crew would move to their battle posts, three going to the large ballista mounted on a pivot atop the flying deck in the *Sea Sprite*'s stern, two going to the smaller, swiveling crossbows mounted to the forward corners of the bridge. Drizzt would join Deudermont at the helm, coordinating the close combat. The drow's free hand slipped to the hilt of one of his scimitars at the thought. The *Sea Sprite* was a vicious foe from a distance. It had crack archers, a skilled ballista team, a particularly nasty wizard, an evoker full of fireballs and lightning bolts, and of course, Catti-brie with her deadly bow, Taulmaril the Heartseeker. But it was in close, when Drizzt and his panther companion—Guenhwyvar—and the other skilled warriors could get across, that the *Sea Sprite* was truly deadly.

"Eighteen hundred!" came Catti-brie's next call. Drizzt nodded at the

confirmation of their speed, though the gain was truly startling. The *Sea Sprite* was running faster than ever. Drizzt had to wonder if her keel was even getting wet!

The drow dropped a hand into his pouch, feeling for the magical figurine that he used to summon the panther from the Astral Plane, wondering if he should even call to Guenhwyvar this time. The panther had been aboard for much of the last tenday, hunting the hundreds of rats that threatened the ship's food stores, and was likely exhausted.

"Only if I need you, my friend," Drizzt whispered. The *Sea Sprite* cut hard to starboard and Drizzt had to take up the guide rope in both hands. He steadied himself and remained silent, his gaze to the horizon, to the square-rigged ship growing larger by the minute. Drizzt felt deep within himself, mentally preparing for the coming battle. He immersed himself in the hiss and splash of the water below him, in the rousing music cutting the wind, and in Catti-brie's calls.

Fifteen hundred, a thousand.

"Black cutlass, lined in red!" the young woman shouted down when, thanks to her spyglass, she was able to discern the design on the snapping flag of the caravel.

Drizzt didn't know the insignia, didn't care about it. The caravel was a pirate ship, one of the many who had overstepped their bounds near Waterdeep's harbors. As in any waters with trading routes, there had always been pirates on the Sword Coast. Until the last few years, though, the pirates had been somewhat civil, following specific codes of conduct. When Deudermont had defeated Pinochet in Asavir's Channel, he had subsequently let the pirate go free. That was the way, the unspoken agreement.

No longer was that the case. The pirates of the north had become bolder and more vicious. Ships were no longer simply looted, but the crews, particularly if any females were aboard, were tortured and murdered. Many ruined hulks had been found adrift in the waters near Waterdeep. The pirates had crossed the line.

Drizzt, Deudermont, and all the *Sea Sprite*'s crew, were being paid handsomely for their work, but down to every last man and woman—with the possible exception of the wizard, Robillard—they weren't chasing pirates for the gold.

They were fighting for the victims.

"Five hundred!" Catti-brie called down.

Drizzt shook himself from his trance and looked to the caravel. He could see the men on her decks now, scrambling, preparing for the fight, an army of ants. The *Sea Sprite*'s crew was outnumbered, possibly two to one, Drizzt realized, and the caravel was heavily armed. She carried a fair-sized catapult on her stern deck, and probably a ballista beneath that, ready to shoot out from the open windows.

The drow nodded and turned back to the deck. The crossbows fixed on the bridge and the ballista was manned. Many of the crew lined the rail, testing the pull of their longbows. The minstrels played on as they would right up until the boarding began. High above the deck, Drizzt spotted Catti-brie, Taulmaril in one hand, her spyglass in the other. He whistled to her and she gave a quick wave in response, her excitement obvious.

How could it be otherwise? The chase, the wind, the music, and the knowledge that they were doing good work here. Smiling widely, the drow skittered back along the beam and then the rail, joining Deudermont at the wheel. He noticed Robillard the wizard, looking bored as usual, sitting on the edge of the poop deck. Every so often he waved one hand in the direction of the mainmast. Robillard wore a huge ring on that hand, a silver band set with a diamond, and its sparkle now came from more than a reflection of the light. With every gesture from the wizard, the ring loosed its magic, sending a strong gust of wind into the already straining sails. Drizzt heard the creak of protest from the mainmast and understood their uncanny speed.

"Carrackus," Captain Deudermont remarked as soon as the drow was beside him. "Black cutlass outlined in red."

Drizzt looked at him curiously, not knowing the name.

"Used to sail with Pinochet," Deudermont explained. "First mate on the pirate's flagship. He was among those we battled in Asavir's Channel."

"Captured?" Drizzt asked.

Deudermont shook his head. "Carrackus is a scrag, a sea troll."

"I do not remember him."

"He has a penchant for staying out of the way," Deudermont replied. "Likely he dived overboard, taking to the depths as soon as Wulfgar turned us about to ram his ship."

Drizzt remembered the incident, the incredible pull of his strong friend that nearly turned the original *Sea Sprite* on its stern, right into the faces of so many surprised pirates.

"Carrackus was there, though," Deudermont continued. "By all reports, it was he who rescued Pinochet's wounded ship when I set him adrift outside of Memnon."

"And is the scrag allied with Pinochet still?" Drizzt asked.

Deudermont nodded grimly. The implications were obvious. Pinochet

couldn't come after the troublesome *Sea Sprite* personally because in return for his freedom he had sworn off vengeance against Deudermont. The pirate had other ways of repaying enemies. He had many allies like Carrackus who were not bound by his personal oath.

Drizzt knew at that moment that Guenhwyvar would be needed and he took the intricate figurine from his pouch. He studied Deudermont carefully. The man stood tall and straight, slender but well-muscled, his gray hair and beard neatly trimmed. He was a refined captain, his dress impeccable, as at home in a grand ball as on the open sea. Now his eyes, so light in hue that they seemed to reflect the colors about them rather than to possess any color of their own, revealed his tension. Rumors had followed the *Sea Sprite* for many months that the pirates were organizing against the vessel. With confirmation that this caravel was allied with Pinochet, Deudermont believed that this might be more than a chance crossing.

Drizzt glanced back at Robillard, who was up on one knee now, arms outstretched and eyes closed, deep in meditation. Now the drow understood the reason Deudermont had put them at such a reckless speed.

A moment later, a wall of mist rose around the *Sea Sprite,* dimming the view of the caravel, which was now barely a hundred yards away. A loud splash to the side told them that the catapult had begun firing. A moment later, a burst of fire erupted in the air before them, dissipating into a cloud of hissing steam as they and their defensive mist wall streamed through it.

"They've a wizard," Drizzt remarked.

"Not surprising," Deudermont was quick to reply. He looked back to Robillard. "Keep your measures defensive," he ordered. "We can take them with ballista and bow!"

"All the fun for you," Robillard called back dryly.

Deudermont managed a smile, despite his obvious tension.

"Bolt!" came a cry, several cries, from forward. Deudermont instinctively spun the wheel. The *Sea Sprite* leaned into the leeward turn so deeply that Drizzt feared they would capsize.

At the same moment, Drizzt heard a rush of wind to his right as a huge ballista bolt ripped past, snapping a line, skipping off the edge of the poop deck right beside a surprised Robillard and rebounding to tear a small hole in the crossjack—the sail on the mizzenmast.

"Secure that line," Deudermont instructed coolly.

Drizzt was already going that way, his feet moving impossibly fast. He got the snapping line in hand and quickly tied it off, then got to the rail as the *Sea Sprite* straightened. He looked to the caravel, now barely fifty yards ahead and to starboard. The water between the two ships rolled wildly. Whitecaps spit water that was blown into mist, caught in a tremendous wind.

The crew of the caravel didn't understand, and so they put their bows in line and began firing, but even the heaviest of their crossbow quarrels was turned harmlessly aside as it tried to cut through the wall of wind that Robillard had put between the ships.

The archers of the *Sea Sprite,* accustomed to such tactics, held their shots. Catti-brie was above the wind wall as was the archer poised in the crow's nest of the other ship—an ugly seven-foot-tall gnoll with a face that seemed more canine than human.

The monstrous creature loosed its heavy arrow first, a fine shot that sank the bolt deep into the mainmast, inches below Catti-brie's perch. The gnoll ducked below the wooden wall of its own crow's nest, readying another arrow.

No doubt the dumb creature thought itself safe, for it didn't understand Taulmaril.

Catti-brie took her time, steadied her hand as the *Sea Sprite* closed.

Thirty yards.

Her arrow went off like a streak of lightning, trailing silver sparks and blasting through the feeble protection of the caravel's crow's nest as though it were no stronger than a sheet of old parchment. Splinters and the unfortunate lookout were thrown high into the air. The doomed gnoll gave a shriek, bounced off the crossbeam of the caravel's mainmast, and spun head over heels to splash into the sea, quickly left behind by the speeding ships.

Catti-brie fired again, angling down, concentrating on the catapult crew. She hit one man, a half-orcish brute by the looks of him, but the catapult launched its load of burning pitch.

The caravel's gunners hadn't properly compensated for the sheer speed of the *Sea Sprite* and the schooner crossed under the pitch and was long gone by the time it hit the water, hissing in protest.

Deudermont brought the schooner alongside the caravel, barely twenty yards of water between them. Suddenly the water in that narrow channel stopped its wind-whipped turmoil and the archers of the *Sea Sprite* let fly many of their arrows that sported small gobs of flaming pitch.

Catti-brie let fly for the catapult itself this time, her enchanted arrow blasting a deep crack along the machine's throwing beam. *Sea Sprite*'s deadly ballista drove a heavy bolt right into the caravel's hull at sea level.

Deudermont spun the wheel to port, angling away, satisfied with the pass. More missiles, many flaming, soared between the ships before Robillard

created a wall of blocking mist behind the *Sea Sprite*'s stern.

The caravel's wizard put a lightning bolt right into the mist. Though the energy was dispersed somewhat, it crackled all about the edges of the *Sea Sprite*, knocking several men to the deck.

Drizzt, leaning far over the rail and straining to watch the caravel's deck with his hair flying wildly from the energy of the lightning bolt, spotted the wizard, amidships, near the mainmast. Before the *Sea Sprite*, now running perpendicular to the pirate ship, was too far away, the drow called upon his innate powers, summoned a globe of impenetrable darkness and dropped it over the man.

He clenched his fist when he saw the globe moving along the caravel's deck, for he had hit the mark and the globe's magic had caught the wizard. It would follow and blind him, until he found some way to counter the magic. Even more than that, the ten-foot ball of blackness marked the dangerous wizard clearly.

"Catti-brie!" Drizzt cried.

"I have him!" she replied, and Taulmaril sang out, once and then again, sending two streaks into that ball of blackness.

Still it continued its run. Catti-brie hadn't dropped the wizard, but surely she and Drizzt had given the man something to think about!

A second ballista bolt soared out from the *Sea Sprite*, cutting across the bow of the caravel, and then a fireball from Robillard exploded high in the air before the rushing ship. The caravel, not agile and no longer equipped with an able wizard, rushed right into the explosions. As the fireball disappeared, both masts of the square-rigger were tipped in flames, giant candles on the open sea.

The caravel tried to respond with its catapult, but Catti-brie's arrows had done their work and the throwing beam split apart as soon as the crew cranked too much tension on it.

Drizzt rushed back to the wheel. "One more pass?" he asked Deudermont.

The Captain shook his head. "Time for only one," he explained. "And no time to stop and board."

"Two thousand yards! Two ships!" Catti-brie called out.

Drizzt looked at Deudermont with sincere admiration. "More of Pinochet's allies?" he asked, already knowing the answer.

"That caravel alone could not defeat us," the seasoned captain coolly added. "Carrackus knows that and so would Pinochet. She was to lead us in."

"But we were too fast for that tactic," Drizzt reasoned.

"Are you ready for a fight?" Deudermont asked slyly.

Before the drow could even answer, Deudermont pulled hard and the *Sea Sprite* leaned into a starboard turn until it came about to face the slowed caravel. The square-sailed ship's topmasts were burning and half her was crew busy trying to repair the rigging, to at least keep her under half-sail. Deudermont angled his ship to intercept, to cut across the prow, in what the archers called a "bow rake."

And the wounded caravel couldn't maneuver out of harm's way. Her wizard, though blinded, had kept the presence of mind to put up a wall of thick mist, the standard and effective defensive seaboard tactic.

Deudermont measured his angle carefully, wanting to turn the *Sea Sprite* right against the edge of that mist and the whipping water, to get as close to the caravel as he could. This was their last pass, and it had to be devastating or else the caravel would be able to limp into the fight with its sister ships, which were closing fast.

There came a flash on the square-rigged ship's deck, a spark of light that countered Drizzt's darkness spell.

From her high perch above the defensive magic, Catti-brie saw it. She was already training on the darkness when the wizard emerged. The robed man went immediately into a chant, meaning to hurl a devastating spell in the path of the *Sea Sprite* before she could cross the caravel's bow, but only a couple of words had escaped his lips when he felt a tremendous thump against his chest and heard the planks of the ship's deck splinter behind him. He looked down at the blood beginning to pour onto the decking and realized that he was sitting, then lying, and all the world grew dark.

The wall of mist the wizard had put up fell away.

Robillard saw it, recognized it, and clapped his hands and sent twin bolts of lightning slashing across the caravel's deck, slamming the masts and killing many pirates. The *Sea Sprite* crossed in front of the caravel, and the archers let fly. So, too, did the ballista crew, but they did not hurl a long spear this time. They used a shortened and unbalanced bolt, trailing a chain lined with many-pronged grapnels. The contraption twirled as it flew, entangling many lines, fouling up the caravel's rigging.

Another missile, a living missile, six hundred pounds of sleek and muscled panther, soared from the *Sea Sprite* as she crossed by and caught the caravel's beam.

"Are you ready, drow?" Robillard called, seeming excited for the first time this fight.

Drizzt nodded and motioned to his fighting companions, the score of

veterans who comprised the *Sea Sprite*'s crack boarding crew. They scrambled toward the wizard from all sections of the ship, dropping their bows and drawing out weapons for close melee. By the time Drizzt, leading the rush, got near to Robillard, the wizard already had a shimmering field—a magical door—on the deck beside him. Drizzt didn't hesitate, charging right through, scimitars in hand. One of them, Twinkle, glowed a fierce blue.

Out the other end of Robillard's magical tunnel he came, arriving in the midst of many surprised pirates aboard the caravel. Drizzt slashed left and right, clearing a hole in their ranks, and he darted through, his feet a blur. He turned sharply, fell to the side and rolled as one archer shot harmlessly above him. He came back to his feet, darted straight for the bowman and cut him down.

More of the *Sea Sprite*'s warriors poured through the gate and the middle of the caravel erupted in wild battle.

The confusion on the caravel's bow was no less as Guenhwyvar, all teeth and claws she seemed, slashed and tore through the mass of men who wanted nothing more than to be away from this mighty beast. Many were pulled down under those powerful claws, and several others simply turned to the side and leaped overboard, ready to take their chances with the sharks.

Again the *Sea Sprite* bent low in the water, Deudermont pulling her hard to port, angling away from the caravel and turning to meet the charge of the coming duo head-on. The tall captain smiled as he heard the fighting on the ship behind him, confident in his boarding party, though they were still likely outnumbered two to one.

The dark elf and his panther tended to even such odds.

From her high perch, Catti-brie picked several more shots, each one taking down a strategically-placed pirate archer, and one driving through a man to kill the pirate goblin sitting next to him!

Then the young woman turned her attention away from the caravel, looking forward in order to direct the *Sea Sprite*'s movements.

Drizzt ran and rolled, leaped in confusing spins and always came down with his scimitars angled for an enemy's most vital areas. Under his boots, he wore bands of gleaming mithral rings secured around black material, enchanted for speed. Drizzt had taken these from Dantrag Baenre, a famed drow weaponmaster. Dantrag had used them as bracers to speed his hands, but Drizzt understood the truth of the items. On his ankles, they allowed the drow to run and dart like a wild hare.

He used them now, along with his amazing agility, to confuse the pirates, to keep them unsure of where he was, or where they could next expect him to be. Whenever one of them guessed wrong and was caught off guard, Drizzt seized the opportunity and came in hard, scimitars slashing away. He made his way generally forward, seeking to join up with Guenhwyvar, the fighting companion who knew him best and complimented his every move.

He didn't quite get there. The rout on the caravel was nearly complete, many pirates dead, others throwing down their weapons, or throwing themselves overboard in sheer desperation. One of the crew, the most seasoned and most fearsome, a personal friend of Pinochet, wasn't so quick to surrender.

He emerged from his cabin under the forward bridge, his body bent over because the low construction of the ship would not accommodate his ten-foot height. He wore only a sleeveless red vest and short breeches, which barely covered his scaly green skin. Limp hair the color of seaweed hung below his broad shoulders. He carried no weapon fashioned on a smithy's anvil but his dirty claws and abundant teeth seemed deadly enough.

"So the rumors were true, dark elf," he said in a wet, bubbly voice. "You have returned to the sea."

"I do not know you," Drizzt said, skidding to a stop a cautious distance from the scrag. He guessed the pirate to be Carrackus, the sea troll Deudermont had spoken of, but could not be sure.

"I know you!" the scrag growled. He charged, his clawed hands slashing for Drizzt's head.

Three quick steps brought Drizzt out of the monster's path. The drow dropped to one knee and spun about, both scimitars slashing across, blades barely an inch apart.

More agile than Drizzt expected, the opponent turned the opposite way and twirled, pulling in his trailing leg. The drow's scimitars barely nicked the monster as they passed.

The scrag charged, meaning to bury Drizzt where he knelt, but again the drow was too quick for such a straightforward tactic. He came up to his feet and started left, then, as the scrag took the bait and began to turn, Drizzt came back fast to the right, underneath the monster's swinging arm.

Twinkle stabbed a hip and Drizzt's other blade followed with a deep cut along the scrag's side.

Drizzt accepted the backhand his opponent launched his way, knowing that the off-balance scrag couldn't put much of its formidable strength and weight behind it. The long and skinny arm thudded off the drow's shoulder and then off his parrying blades as he spun to face the lurching brute.

Now it was Drizzt's turn to charge, lightning fast and straight ahead. He slid Twinkle under the elbow of the outstretched scrag arm, drawing a deep

gash and then hooked the fine-edged and curving blade underneath the hanging flap of skin. His other scimitar poked for the scrag's chest, slipped past the frantic block of the other arm.

There was only one way for the off-balance monster to move. Drizzt knew that, anticipated the scrag's retreat perfectly. The drow secured his grip on Twinkle, even braced his shoulder against the weapon's hilt to hold it firm. The scrag roared in agony and dived back and to the side, directly opposite the angle of Twinkle's nasty bite. The sickly flesh peeled from the scrag's arm, all the way from its biceps to its wrist. The torn lump fell to the deck with a sickening thud.

His black eyes filled with outrage and hatred. The scrag looked down to the exposed bone, to the writhing lump of troll flesh on the deck. And finally, to Drizzt, who stood casually, scimitars crossed down low in front of him.

"Damn you, Drizzt," the monstrous pirate growled.

"Strike your colors," Drizzt ordered.

"You think you have won?"

In response, Drizzt looked down to the slab of meat.

"It will heal, foolish dark elf!" the pirate insisted.

Drizzt knew that the scrag spoke truly. Scrags were close relatives of trolls, horrid creatures renowned for their regenerative powers. A dead dismembered troll could come back together.

Unless . . .

Drizzt called upon his innate abilities once more, that small part of magic inherent in the dark elf race. A moment later, purplish flames climbed the towering scrag's form, licking at green scales. This was only faerie fire, harmless light the dark elves could use to outline their opponents. It had no power to burn, nor could it prevent the regenerative process of a troll.

Drizzt understood that, but he was betting the monster did not.

The scrag's gruesome features twisted in an expression of sheer horror. He flailed his good arm, beat it against his leg and hip. The stubborn purple flames would not relent.

"Strike your colors and I will release you of the flames that your wounds might heal," Drizzt offered.

The scrag snapped a look of pure hatred at the drow. He took a step forward, but up came Drizzt's scimitars. He decided he didn't want to feel their bite again, especially if the flames prevented him from healing!

"We will meet again!" the scrag promised. The creature wheeled about to see dozens of faces—Deudermont's crew and captured pirates—staring at him in disbelief. He howled and charged across the deck, scattering those in the way of the furious rush. The pirate leaped from the rail, back to the sea, back to his true home where he might heal.

So quick was Drizzt that he got across the deck and managed yet another hit on him before the scrag got off the rail. The drow had to stop there, unable to pursue and fully aware that the sea troll would indeed regenerate to complete health.

He hadn't even gotten a curse of frustration out of his mouth when he saw a fast movement to his side, a rush of black. Guenhwyvar leaped past Drizzt, flew out from the rail, and splashed into the sea right behind the troll.

The panther disappeared under the azure blanket and the rough and choppy waves quickly covered any indication that the scrag and the cat had gone in.

Several of the *Sea Sprite*'s boarding party peered intently over the rail, worried for the panther who had become such a friend to them.

"Guenhwyvar is in no danger," Drizzt reminded them, producing the figurine and holding it high so that all could see. The worse the scrag could do was send the panther back to the Astral Plane, where the cat would heal any wounds and be ready to return to Drizzt's next call. Still, the drow's expression was not bright as he considered the spot where Guenhwyvar had gone in, as he considered that the panther might be in pain.

The deck of the captured caravel went perfectly quiet, save the creaking of the old vessel's timbers.

An explosion to the south turned all heads, all eyes strained to perceive tiny sails, still far away. One of the pirate ships had turned away. The other caravel burned while the *Sea Sprite* literally sailed circles about her. Flash after flash of silver streaking arrows came from the *Sea Sprite*'s crow's nest, battering the hull and masts of the damaged, seemingly helpless ship.

Even from this great distance, the people on the captured caravel could see the pirate flag go down the mainmast, colors struck in surrender.

That brought a cheer from the *Sea Sprite*'s boarding party, a rousing yell that was halted abruptly by churning waters just off the side of the caravel. They saw green scales and black fur tumbling in the turmoil. A scrag arm floated out from the mass, and Drizzt was able to sort the confusing scene out enough to realize that Guenhwyvar had gotten onto the scrag's back. Her forelegs were tight about the monster's shoulders, her back legs were kicking, raking wildly, and the panther's powerful jaws were clamped tight onto the back of the scrag's neck.

Dark blood stained the sea, mixing with torn pieces of the pirate's flesh and bone. Soon enough, Guenhwyvar sat still, teeth and claws securely in place on the back of the dead, floating scrag.

"Better fish the thing out," one of the *Sea Sprite*'s boarding party remarked, "or we'll be growing a whole crew o' stinking trolls!"

Men arrived at the rail with long gaff hooks and began the gruesome task of hauling in the carcass. Guenhwyvar got back to the caravel easily enough, clambering over the rail and then giving a good shake, spraying water on all those nearby.

"Scrags don't heal if they're out o' the sea," a man remarked to Drizzt. "We'll haul this one up the yardarm to dry, then burn the damned thing."

Drizzt nodded. The boarding party knew their duty well enough. They would organize and supervise the captured pirates, freeing the rigging and getting the caravel as seaworthy as possible for the trip back to Waterdeep.

Drizzt looked to the southern horizon and saw the *Sea Sprite* returning. The damaged pirate ship limped alongside.

"Thirty-eight and thirty-nine," the drow muttered.

Guenhwyvar gave a low growl in reply and shook vigorously again, soaking her dark elf companion.

2
THE FIRST MESSENGER

Captain Deudermont seemed out of place indeed as he strolled down Dock Street, the infamous, rough and tumble avenue that lined Waterdeep Harbor. His clothes were fine and perfectly tailored to his tall and thin frame, his posture was perfect, and his hair and goatee meticulously groomed. All about him, the scurvy sea dogs who had put in for their tendays ashore staggered out of taverns, reeking of ale, or fell down unconscious in the dust. The only thing protecting them from the many robbers lurking in the area was the fact that they had no coin or valuables to steal.

Deudermont ignored the sights, and didn't fancy himself any better than those sea dogs. In fact, there was an aspect of their way of life that intrigued the gentlemanly captain, an honesty that mocked the pretentious courts of nobles.

Deudermont pulled his layered cloak tighter about his neck, warding off the chill night breeze that blew in off the harbor. Normally one would not walk alone down Dock Street, not even in the light of noonday, but Deudermont felt secure. He carried his decorated cutlass at his side, and knew how to use it well. Even more than that, the word had been passed through every tavern and every pier in Waterdeep that the *Sea Sprite*'s captain had been afforded the personal protection of the Lords of Waterdeep, including some very powerful wizards who would seek out and destroy anyone bothering the captain or his crew while they were in port. Waterdeep was the *Sea Sprite*'s haven, and so Deudermont thought nothing of walking alone down Dock Street. He was more curious than fearful when a wrinkled old man, bone skinny and barely five feet tall, called to him from the edge of an alleyway.

Deudermont stopped and looked about. Dock Street was quiet, except for the overspill of sound from the many taverns and the groan of old wood against the incessant sea breeze.

"Ye's is Doo-dor-mont-ee, asin't yer?" the old seabones called softly, a whistle accompanying each syllable. He smiled widely, almost lewdly, showing but a couple of crooked teeth set in black gums.

Deudermont stopped and eyed the man patiently, silently. He felt no compulsion to answer the question.

"If ye be," the man wheezed, "then oi've got a bit o' news for yer. A warnin' from a man yer's is rightly fearin'."

The captain stood tall and impassive. His face showed none of the questions that raced about in his mind. Who would he be afraid of? Was the old dog talking of Pinochet? That seemed likely, especially considering the two caravels the *Sea Sprite* had escorted into Waterdeep Harbor earlier that tenday. But few in Waterdeep had any contact with the pirate, whose domain was much farther to the south, south of Baldur's Gate even, in the straights near the Moonshae Isles.

But who else might the man be talking about?

Smiling still, the sea dog motioned for Deudermont to come to the alley. The captain didn't move as the old man turned and took a step in.

"Well, be yer fearin' old Scaramundi?" the sea dog whistled.

Deudermont realized it could be a disguise. Many of the greatest assassins in the Realms could look as helpless as this one, only to put a poisoned dagger into their victim's chest.

The sea dog came back to the entrance to the alley, then walked right out into the middle of the street toward Deudermont.

No disguise, the captain told himself, for it was too complete, too perfect. Besides, he recollected that he had seen this same old man before, usually sitting right near to this very same alleyway, which probably served as his home.

What then? Might there be an ambush set down that alley?

"Have it yer own way then," the old man wheezed as he threw up one hand. He leaned heavily on his walking stick and started back to the alley, grumbling. "Just a messenger, I be, and not fer carin' if yer hears the news or not!"

Deudermont cautiously looked all around again. Seeing nobody nearby, and no likely hiding spots for an ambush party, he moved to the mouth of the alleyway. The old sea dog was ten short paces in, at the edge of the slanting shadows cast by the building to the right, and barely visible in the dimness. He laughed and coughed and moved in yet another step.

One hand on the hilt of his cutlass, Deudermont cautiously approached, scanning carefully before each step. The alleyway seemed empty enough.

"Far enough!" Deudermont said suddenly, stopping the sea dog in his tracks. "If you have news for me, then speak it, and speak it now."

"Some things shouldn't be said too loudly," the old man replied.

"Now," Deudermont insisted.

The salty sea dog smiled widely and coughed, perhaps laughing. He ambled back a few steps, stopping barely three feet from Deudermont.

The smell of the man nearly overwhelmed the captain, who was accustomed to powerful body odors. There wasn't much opportunity to bathe on a ship at sea and the *Sea Sprite* was often out for tendays, even months, at a time. Still, the combination of cheap wine and old sweat gave this one a particularly nasty flavor that made Deudermont scrunch up his face, even put a hand over his nose to try to intercept some of the fumes.

The sea dog, of course, laughed hysterically at that.

"Now!" the captain insisted.

Even as the word left Deudermont's lips, the sea dog reached out and caught him by the wrist. Deudermont, not afraid, turned his arm, but the old man held on stubbornly.

"I want you to tell me of the dark one," the sea dog said, and it took Deudermont a moment to realize that the man's dockside accent was gone.

"Who are you?" Deudermont insisted, and he tugged fiercely, to no avail. Only then did Deudermont realize the truth of the superhuman grip. He might as well have been pulling against one of the great fog giants that lived on the reef surrounding Delmarin Island, far to the south.

"The dark one," the old man repeated. With hardly any effort, he yanked Deudermont deeper into the alleyway.

The captain went for his cutlass, and though the old man held Deudermont's right hand fast, he could fight fairly well with his left. It was somewhat awkward extracting the curving blade from its sheath with that hand, and before the cutlass came fully free, the old man's free hand shot forward, open-palmed, to slam Deudermont in the face. He flew backward, crashing against the wall. Keeping his wits about him, he drew out the blade, transferred it to his now-free right hand, and slashed hard at the ribs of the approaching sea dog.

The fine cutlass gashed deep into the sea dog's side, but he didn't even flinch. Deudermont tried to block the next slap, and the next after that, but his defenses simply were not strong enough. He tried to get his cutlass in line to parry, but the old man slapped it away, sent it spinning from his hand,

then resumed the battering. Open palms came in with the speed of a striking snake, heavy blows that knocked Deudermont's head tilting, and he would have fallen, except that the old man grabbed him by the shoulder and held him fast.

Through bleary eyes, Deudermont peered at his foe. Confusion crossed his stern features as his enemy's face began to melt away and then to reform.

"The dark one?" he, *it,* asked again, and Deudermont hardly heard the voice, his voice, so dumbfounded was he at the spectacle of his own face leering back at him.

⚔ ⚔ ⚔ ⚔ ⚔

"He should be here by now," Catti-brie remarked, leaning on the bar.

She was growing impatient, Drizzt realized, and not because Deudermont was late—the captain was often detained at one function or another in Waterdeep—but because the sailor on the other side of her, a short and stocky man with a thick beard and curly hair, both the color of a raven's wing, kept bumping into her. He apologized each time, looking over his shoulder to regard the beautiful woman, often winking and always smiling.

Drizzt turned so that his back was against the waist-high bar. The Mermaid's Arms was nearly empty this night. The weather had been fine and most of the fishing and merchant fleets were out. Still, the place was loud and rowdy, full of sailors relieving months of boredom with drink, companionship, bluster, and even fisticuffs.

"Robillard," Drizzt whispered, and Catti-brie turned and followed the drow's gaze to see the wizard slipping through the crowd, moving to join them at the bar.

"Good evening," the wizard said without much enthusiasm. He didn't look at the companions as he spoke, and didn't wait for the bartender to come near, merely waggled his fingers and a bottle and a glass magically came to his place. The bartender started to protest, but a pile of copper pieces appeared in his hand. The bartender shook his head with disdain, never caring much for the *Sea Sprite*'s wizard and his arrogant antics, and moved away.

"Where is Deudermont?" Robillard asked. "Squandering my pay, no doubt."

Drizzt and Catti-brie exchanged smiles wrought of continued disbelief. Robillard was among the most distant and caustic men either of them had ever known, more grumpy even than General Dagna, the surly dwarf who served as Bruenor's garrison commander at Mithral Hall.

"No doubt," Drizzt replied.

Robillard turned to regard him with an accusing, angry glare.

"Of course, Deudermont's one to steal from us all the time," Catti-brie added. "Takes a fancy to the finest o' ladies and the finest o' wine, and is free with what's not his to be free with."

A growl escaped Robillard's thin lips and he pushed off the bar and walked away.

"I'd like to know that one's tale," Catti-brie remarked.

Drizzt nodded his accord, his eyes never leaving the departing wizard's back. Indeed, Robillard was a strange one, and the drow figured that something terrible must have happened to him somewhere in his past. Perhaps he had unintentionally killed someone, or had been rejected by a true love. Perhaps he had seen too much of wizardry, had looked into places where a man's eyes were not meant to go.

Catti-brie's simple spoken thought had sparked a sudden interest within Drizzt Do'Urden. Who was this Robillard, and what precipitated his perpetual boredom and anger?

"Where is Deudermont?" came a question from the side, breaking Drizzt's trance. He turned to see Waillan Micanty, a lad of barely twenty winters, with sandy-colored hair, cinnamon eyes, and huge dimples that always showed because Waillan never seemed to stop smiling. He was the youngest of the *Sea Sprite*'s crew, younger even than Catti-brie, but with an uncanny eye on the ballista. Waillan's shots were fast becoming legend, and if the young man lived long enough, he would no doubt assemble quite a reputation along the Sword Coast. Waillan Micanty had put one ballista bolt through the window of a pirate captain's quarters at four hundred yards and had skewered the pirate captain as the man was buckling on his cutlass. The momentum of the heavy spear had hurled the pirate right through his closed cabin door and out onto the deck. The pirate ship struck her colors immediately, the capture ended before the fighting had really even begun.

"We are expecting the man," Drizzt answered, his mood brightening simply at the sight of the beaming young man. Drizzt couldn't help but notice the contrast between this youngster and Robillard, who was probably the oldest of the crew, except for Drizzt.

Waillan nodded. "Should be here by now," he remarked under his breath, but the drow's keen ears caught every word.

"You are expecting him?" Drizzt was quick to ask.

"I need to speak with him," Waillan admitted, "about a possible advance on earnings." The young man blushed deep red and moved close to Drizzt so that Catti-brie could not hear. "A lady friend," he explained.

Drizzt found his smile widening even more. "The captain is overdue," he said. "I'm sure he will not be much longer."

"He was less than a dozen doors down when I last saw him," Waillan said. "Near to the Foggy Haven and heading this way. I thought he'd beat me here."

For the first time, Drizzt grew a bit concerned. "How long ago was that?"

Waillan shrugged. "I been here since the fight before," he said.

Drizzt turned and leaned back against the bar. He and Catti-brie exchanged concerned looks this time, for many minutes had passed since the previous two fights. There wasn't much to interest the captain between the Mermaid's Arms and the place Waillan spoke of, certainly nothing that should have detained Deudermont for this long.

Drizzt sighed and took a long swallow of the water he was drinking. He looked to Robillard, now sitting by himself, though a table not far from the man held open chairs beside the four that were occupied by members of the *Sea Sprite*'s crew. Drizzt wasn't too concerned. Perhaps Deudermont had forgotten some business, or had simply changed his mind about coming to the Mermaid's Arms this night. But still, Dock Street in Waterdeep was a dangerous place, and the drow ranger's sixth sense, that warrior instinct, told him to be wary.

⚔ ⚔ ⚔ ⚔ ⚔

Deudermont, practically senseless, did not know how long the beating went on. He was lying on the cold ground now, that much he knew. The thing, whatever it was, having assumed his exact form, clothing, even weapons, was sitting on his back. The physical torture was not so great anymore, but even worse than the beating, the captain felt the creature within his mind, probing his thoughts, gaining knowledge that it could no doubt use against his friends.

You will taste fine, Deudermont heard in his thoughts. *Better than the old Scaramundi.*

Despite the unreality of it all, the lack of true sensation, the captain felt his stomach churning. He believed he knew, in that distant corner of consciousness, what monster had come to him. Dopplegangers were not common in the Realms, but the few who had made themselves known had certainly caused enough havoc to secure the wretched reputation of the alien race.

Deudermont felt himself being lifted from the ground. So strong was the grasp of the creature that the captain felt as if he were weightless, simply floating to his feet. He was spun around to face the thing, to face himself, and he expected then to be devoured.

"Not yet," the creature replied to his unspoken fears. "I need your thoughts, good Captain Deudermont. I need to know enough about you and your ship to sail it out of Waterdeep Harbor, far to the west and far to the south, to an island that few know, but many speak of."

The thing's smile was tantalizing and Deudermont had just focused fully on it when the creature's head shot forward, its forehead slamming him in the face, knocking him senseless. Some time later—he did not know how many seconds might have passed—Deudermont felt the cold ground against his cheek once more. His hands were tightly bound behind his back, his ankles likewise strapped, and a tight gag was about his mouth. He managed to turn his head enough to see the creature, wearing his form still, bending over a heavy iron grate.

Deudermont could hardly believe the strength of the thing as it lifted that sewer covering, a mass of metal that had to weigh near to five hundred pounds. The creature casually leaned it against the wall of a building, then turned and grabbed Deudermont, dragging him to the opening and unceremoniously dropping him in.

The stench was awful, worse than the captain would have expected even from a sewer, and when he managed to shift about and get his face out of the muck, he understood the source.

Scaramundi, it had to be Scaramundi, lay beside him, caked in blood, more than half of his torso torn away, eaten by the creature. Deudermont jumped as the sewer grate clanked back into place, and then he lay still, horrified and helpless, knowing that he would soon share the same grisly fate.

3
THE MESSAGE, SUBTLY TOLD

Some time later, Drizzt was beginning to worry. Robillard had already left the Mermaid's Arms, disgusted that his captain, as he had put it, "couldn't be counted on." Waillan Micanty was still at the bar beside Drizzt, though the young man had taken up a conversation with another sailor on the other side of him.

Drizzt, his back to the bar, continued to survey the crowd, perfectly at ease among the sailors. It hadn't always been so. Drizzt had come through Waterdeep only twice before he and Catti-brie had left Mithral Hall, first on his way to Calimport chasing Entreri, and on the return trip, when he and his friends were making their way back to reclaim Mithral Hall. Drizzt had made that first passage through the city in disguise, using a magical mask to appear as a surface elf. The second journey through, made without the mask, had been a trickier proposition. The *Sea Sprite* had put into Waterdeep Harbor in early morning but at Deudermont's request, Drizzt and his friends had waited until after dark to leave the city for the road to the east.

Upon his return to Waterdeep with Catti-brie six years ago, Drizzt had dared to walk openly as a drow. It had been an uncomfortable experience, eyes were upon him every step, and more than one ruffian had challenged him. Drizzt had avoided those challenges, but knew that sooner or later, he would have to fight, or even worse, he would be slain from afar, likely by a hidden bowman, for no better reason than the color of the skin.

Then the *Sea Sprite* had put in and Drizzt had found Deudermont, his old friend and a man of considerable reputation among the docks of the great city. Soon after, Drizzt had become widely accepted in Waterdeep, particularly all along Dock Street, because of his personal reputation, spread in no small way by Captain Deudermont. Wherever the *Sea Sprite* docked, it was made clear that Drizzt Do'Urden, this most unusual of dark elves, was a member of her heroic crew. Drizzt's road had been easier, had even become comfortable.

And through it all, Catti-brie and Guenhwyvar had been beside him. He looked to them now, the young woman sitting at a table with two of the *Sea Sprite*'s crew, the great panther curled up on the floor about her legs. Guenhwyvar had become a mascot to the patrons of the Mermaid's Arms, and Drizzt was glad that he could sometimes call in the cat, not for battle, but simply for companionship. Drizzt wondered which reason would hold this day. Catti-brie had requested the panther, saying her feet were cold, and Drizzt had agreed, but in the back of the drow's mind was the realization that Deudermont might be in trouble. Guenhwyvar might be needed for more than companionship.

The drow surely relaxed a moment later, blew out a deep sigh of relief as Captain Deudermont walked into the Mermaid's Arms, glanced around, then focused on Drizzt and sidled up to the bar.

"Calimshan wine," the doppleganger said to the bartender, for it had scoured Deudermont's mind and knew that to be the man's customary drink. In the short time they had spent together, the doppleganger had learned much of Captain Deudermont and of the *Sea Sprite.*

Drizzt turned about and leaned over the bar. "You are late," he remarked, trying to feel the captain out, trying to discern if there had been any trouble.

"A minor problem," the impostor assured him.

"What is it, Guen?" Catti-brie asked softly as the panther's head came up, the cat looking in the direction of Drizzt and Deudermont, her ears flattened against her head and a low growl resonating from her strong body. "What do ye see?"

Guenhwyvar continued to watch the pair closely, but Catti-brie dismissed the cat's temperament, figuring there must be a rat or the like in the far corner beyond Drizzt and the captain.

"Caerwich," the impostor announced to Drizzt.

The ranger regarded the man curiously. "Caerwich?" he echoed. Drizzt knew the name. Every sailor along the Sword Coast knew the tiny island, even if it was too small and remote to appear on the vast majority of nautical charts.

"We must put out at once for Caerwich," the impostor explained, looking Drizzt directly in the eye. So perfect was the disguise of the doppleganger that

Drizzt hadn't the slightest idea that anything was amiss.

Still, the request sounded strange to Drizzt. Caerwich was a shipboard story, a tale of a haunted island that played home to a blind witch. Many doubted its existence, though some sailors claimed to have visited the place. Certainly Drizzt and Deudermont had never spoken of it. For the captain to announce that they must go there caught the drow completely by surprise.

Again Drizzt studied Deudermont, this time noting the man's stiff mannerisms, noting how uncomfortable Deudermont seemed in this place, which had always been his favorite among the taverns of Dock Street. Drizzt believed something had unnerved Deudermont. Whatever had delayed his arrival at the Mermaid's Arms—Drizzt figured it to be a visit by one of Waterdeep's secretive lords, perhaps even mysterious Khelben—had upset Deudermont greatly. Perhaps Deudermont's announcement wasn't so out of place. Many times in the last six years, the *Sea Sprite,* the tool of Waterdeep's Lords, had been assigned private, unusual missions, and so the drow accepted the information without question.

What both Drizzt and the doppleganger hadn't counted on was Guenhwyvar, who crouched so low that her belly brushed against the floor as she inched for Deudermont's back, her ears flat.

"Guenhwyvar!" Drizzt scolded.

The doppleganger spun about, putting its back to the wooden bar just as Guenhwyvar charged in, coming up high and pinning the creature to the bar. Had the doppleganger kept its wits and played the innocent victim, it might have talked its way out of the predicament. But the creature recognized Guenhwyvar, or at least the fact that this panther was not of the Prime Material Plane. And if the doppleganger instinctively recognized that about the panther, it figured the panther would recognize the same.

Purely on instinct, the creature batted Guenhwyvar with its forearm, the weight of the blow launching the six-hundred pound cat halfway across the wide room.

No human could do that, and when the impostor looked again at Drizzt, it found that the drow had his scimitars in hand.

"Who are you?" Drizzt demanded.

The creature hissed and grabbed at the blades, catching one. Drizzt struck, tentatively and with the flat of his free blade, for he feared that this might be Deudermont under some type of enchantment. He smacked the impostor on the side of the neck.

The creature caught the blade in its open hand, and it rushed forward and bowled Drizzt aside.

The rest of those in the tavern were up then, most thinking it one of the typical fights. But the crew of the *Sea Sprite,* particularly Catti-brie, realized the absolute strangeness of the scene.

The doppleganger made for the door, slapping aside the one confused sailor, one of the *Sea Sprite*'s crewmen, who stood in its way.

Catti-brie had her bow ready, and she put an arrow, trailing silvery sparks, into the wall right beside the creature's head. The doppleganger spun to face her, hissed loudly, and was subsequently buried by six hundred pounds of flying panther. This time Guenhwyvar recognized the strength of her foe and by the time the two had sorted out their tumble, the great cat was sitting on the doppleganger's back, her powerful jaws clamped tight on the nape of the thing's neck. Drizzt was there in an instant, followed closely by Catti-brie, Waillan Micanty and the rest of the crew, and more than a few curious onlookers, including the proprietor of the Mermaid's Arms, who wanted to get a look at the damage from that enchanted arrow.

"What are you?" Drizzt demanded, grabbing the impostor by the hair and turning its head so that he could look into its face. Drizzt rubbed his free hand across the thing's cheek, looking for makeup, but found none. He barely got his fingers away before the doppleganger bit at them.

Guenhwyvar growled and tightened her jaws, forcing the creature's face to slam hard back into the floor.

"Go and check out Dock Street!" Drizzt called to Waillan. "Near to where you last saw the captain!"

"But . . ." Waillan protested, pointing to the prone form.

"This is not Captain Deudermont," Drizzt assured him. "This is not even human!"

Waillan motioned to several of the *Sea Sprite*'s crew and headed out, followed by many other sailors who called themselves friends of the apparently missing captain.

"And call for the Watch!" Drizzt yelled after them, referring to the famed Waterdeep patrols. "Be ready with your bow," Drizzt said to Catti-brie and she nodded and fitted another arrow to the bowstring.

Working with Guenhwyvar, the drow managed to get the doppleganger fully subdued and standing against a wall. The bartender offered some heavy rope, and they tightly bound the doppleganger's hands behind its back.

"I ask you one more time," Drizzt began threateningly. The creature merely spat in his face and began laughing, a diabolical sound indeed.

The drow did not respond with force, just stared hard at this impostor. Truly Drizzt's heart was low then, for the way the impostor looked at him, laughed

at him, only at him, sent a shiver along his spine. He wasn't afraid for his own safety, never that, but he feared that his past had caught up with him once again, that the evil powers of Menzoberranzan had found him here in Waterdeep, and that the good Captain Deudermont had fallen because of him.

If true, it was more than Drizzt Do'Urden could bear.

"I offer your life in exchange for Captain Deudermont," the drow said.

"It's not your place to be bargaining with the . . . whatever it might be," remarked one sailor whom Drizzt did not know. The drow, scowling fiercely, turned to face the man, who went silent and backed away, having no desire to invoke the wrath of a dark elf, especially one of Drizzt's fighting reputation.

"Your life for Deudermont," Drizzt said again to the doppleganger. Again came that diabolical laughter and the creature spat in Drizzt's face.

Left, right, left came Drizzt's open palms in rapid succession, battering the creature's face. The last punch bent the thing's nose, but it reformed, right before Drizzt's eyes, to perfectly resemble the unmarred nose of Captain Deudermont.

That image, combined with the continuing laughter, sent ripples of rage through the drow and he slugged the impostor with all his strength.

Catti-brie wrapped her arms about Drizzt and pulled him away, though the mere sight of her reminded Drizzt of who he was and shamed him for his rash, out-of-control actions.

"Where is he?" Drizzt demanded, and when the creature continued to taunt him, Guenhwyvar came up on her hind legs, resting one forepaw on each shoulder, and putting her snarling visage barely an inch from the doppleganger's face. That quieted the creature, for it knew that Guenhwyvar recognized the truth of its existence, and knew that the angry panther could utterly destroy it.

"Get a wizard," one sailor offered suddenly.

"Robillard!" exclaimed another, the last of the Sea Sprite's crew, besides Drizzt and Catti-brie, in the tavern. "He'll know how to get the information out of this thing."

"Go," Catti-brie agreed, and the man rushed out.

"A priest," offered another man. "A priest will better deal with . . ." The man paused, not knowing what to make of this impostor.

Through it all, the doppleganger remained passive, matching Guenhwyvar's stare but making no threatening moves.

The crewman had barely exited the tavern when he was passed by another of the Sea Sprite's hands, heading back in with the news that Deudermont had been found.

Out they went, Drizzt shoving the doppleganger along, Guenhwyvar on the other side of the creature and Catti-brie behind it, her bow up and ready, an arrow tip nearly touching the back of the thing's head. They came into the alley even as the sewer grate was being pried open, one sailor promptly dropping into the smelly hole to help his captain out.

Deudermont eyed the doppleganger, eyed the perfect image of himself, with open contempt. "You may as well assume your natural form," he said to the thing. Drawing himself up straight, he brushed off some of the muck, regaining his dignity in an instant. "They know who I am, and know what you are."

The doppleganger did nothing. Drizzt kept Twinkle tight against the side of its neck, Guenhwyvar remained alert on the other side, and Catti-brie went over to Deudermont, supporting the injured man.

"Might I lean on your bow?" the captain asked, and Catti-brie, with hardly a thought, quickly handed it over.

"Must be a wizard," Deudermont said to Drizzt, though the captain suspected differently. The injured Deudermont took the offered bow and leaned on it heavily. "If he utters a single, uncalled for syllable, slash his throat," he instructed.

Drizzt nodded and pressed Twinkle a bit closer. Catti-brie moved to take Deudermont's arm, but he waved her ahead, then followed closely.

× × × × ×

Far away, on a smoky layer of the Abyss, Errtu watched the unfolding scene with pure delight. The trap had been set, not as the great tanar'ri had expected when he had sent the doppleganger to Waterdeep, but set anyway, and perhaps more deliciously, more unexpectedly, more chaotically.

Errtu understood Drizzt Do'Urden well enough to know that the mention of Caerwich was all the bait that was needed. Something awful had happened to them that night and they would not let it pass, would go willingly to the mentioned island and discover the source.

The mighty fiend was having more fun than he had known in years. Errtu could have delivered the message to Drizzt more easily, but this intrigue—the doppleganger, the blind witch who waited at Caerwich—was the fun of it all.

The only thing that would be more fun for Errtu was tearing Drizzt Do'Urden apart, little piece by little piece, devouring his flesh before his very eyes.

The balor howled at that thought, figuring that it would soon enough come to pass.

⚔ ⚔ ⚔ ⚔ ⚔

Deudermont straightened as much as possible and continued to wave away any offered help. The captain put on a good face, and stayed close behind Catti-brie as she moved slowly toward the alley exit, toward Drizzt and Guenhwyvar and the captured doppleganger.

Deudermont watched that strange creature most carefully of all. He understood the evil of the thing, had felt it up close. Deudermont hated the thing for the beating it had given him, but in assuming the captain's form, the thing had violated him in a way that he could not tolerate. Looking at the creature now, as it wore the features of the *Sea Sprite*'s Captain, Deudermont could barely keep his anger in check. He kept very close to Catti-brie, watching, anticipating.

Near to Dock Street, Drizzt stood quietly beside the bound impostor. The drow and the many crewmen nearby were focused on the injured captain, and none of them noticed as the creature began to shift its malleable form once more, reshaping its arms so that they slipped and twisted free of the bonds.

Drizzt just got his second scimitar out after the creature suddenly shoved him aside. The doppleganger bolted for the alley's exit with Guenhwyvar close behind. Wings sprouted from the doppleganger's back and it leaped high, meaning to fly off into the night.

Guenhwyvar charged and sprang mightily in pursuit while Captain Deudermont slipped an arrow from the quiver on Catti-brie's hip. The woman, sensing the theft, spun about as the bow came up. She cried out, fell to the side and Deudermont let fly.

The doppleganger was more than twenty feet off the ground by the time Guenhwyvar began her leap, but still the great panther caught up to the flying monster, her jaws catching a firm hold on the creature's ankle. That limb shifted and reformed immediately, making the panther's grasp tentative. Then came the silver-streaking arrow, slamming the doppleganger square in the back, right between the wings.

Down came Guenhwyvar, landing lightly on padded paws, and down came the doppleganger, dead before it ever hit the ground.

Drizzt was there in an instant, the others rushing to catch up with him.

The creature began to shift its form again. Its newest features melted away, to be replaced by a humanoid appearance the likes of which none of the gathering had ever seen. Its skin was perfectly smooth, the fingers of its slender hand showing no distinguishable grooves. It was completely hairless, and everything about it seemed perfectly unremarkable. It was a lump of humanoid-shaped clay and nothing more.

"Doppleganger," Deudermont remarked. "It would seem that Pinochet is not pleased by our latest exploits."

Drizzt nodded, allowing himself to agree with the captain's reasoning. This incident wasn't about him, wasn't about who he was and where he came from.

He had to believe that.

$$\times \ \times \ \times \ \times \ \times$$

Errtu thoroughly enjoyed the spectacle, and was glad that he would not have to pay off his hired master of disguise. It bothered the fiend for a moment that his guide for the *Sea Sprite*'s voyage to the virtually unchartered island had just gone away, but the balor held his faith. The seeds had been sown. The doppleganger had teased Deudermont about the destination, and Drizzt had heard the exact name of the island and would pass it on to the captain. The balor knew neither were cowards, both were resourceful and curious.

Errtu knew Drizzt and Deudermont would find their way to Caerwich and the blind seer who held the fiend's message. Soon enough.

4
UNASKED FOR
"ASSISTANCE"

The *Sea Sprite* put back out two tendays later, her course south. Captain Deudermont explained that they had business pending in Baldur's Gate, one of the largest ports on the Sword Coast, about halfway between Waterdeep and Calimshan. No one questioned Deudermont openly, but many felt that he seemed on edge, almost indecisive, a mannerism they had never experienced with the confident captain before.

That demeanor changed four days out of Waterdeep Harbor, when the *Sea Sprite's* lookout caught sight of a square-rigger sporting a deck covered with sailors. Caravels were ordinarily crewed by forty to fifty men. A pirate ship, wanting to attack swiftly with overwhelming odds, and then bring the booty quickly to shore, might carry three times that number. Pirate ships didn't carry cargo, they carried warriors.

If Deudermont had seemed indecisive before, not so now. Up came the *Sea Sprite's* sails to full. Catti-brie hooked Taulmaril over her shoulder and began the climb to the crow's nest, and Robillard was ordered to take his place on the poop deck and to use his magic to further fill the sails. But the natural wind was already strong from the northwest, from astern it already filled the sails of both the *Sea Sprite* and the running pirate ship, and the chase would be a long one.

At center deck, the ship's musicians took up a rousing tune, and Drizzt came back from the forward beam earlier than usual to stand beside Deudermont at the wheel.

"Where will we tow her once captured?" the drow asked, a usual question on the high seas. They were still closer to Waterdeep than to Baldur's Gate, but the wind was from the north generally, favoring a southern course.

"Orlumbor," Deudermont answered without hesitation.

Drizzt was surprised by that. Orlumbor was a rocky, windswept island halfway between Waterdeep and Baldur's Gate, an independent city-state, lightly populated and hardly equipped to hold a caravel full of pirates.

"Will the shipwrights even take her?" the drow asked doubtfully.

Deudermont nodded, his face stern. "Orlumbor owes much to Waterdeep," he explained. "They will hold her until another ship of Waterdeep arrives to tow her away. I will instruct Robillard to use his powers to contact the Lords of Waterdeep."

Drizzt nodded. It seemed perfectly logical, yet perfectly out of place. The drow understood now that this was no ordinary run for the normally patient *Sea Sprite*. Never before had Deudermont left off a captured ship and crew for another to pick up in his wake. Time had never seemed an issue out here, amidst the steady and eternal roll of the sea. The *Sea Sprite* would normally run until she found a pirate ship, snag her or sink her, then return to one of the friendly ports and hand her over, however long that might take.

"Our business in Baldur's Gate must be urgent," the drow remarked, cocking a suspicious eye the captain's way.

Deudermont turned to look at him directly, to stare long and hard at Drizzt for the first time this voyage. "We are not going to Baldur's Gate," he admitted.

"Then where?" Drizzt's tone showed that he was not surprised by that revelation.

The captain shook his head and turned his stare forward, adjusting the wheel slightly to keep them in line with the running caravel.

Drizzt accepted that. He knew that Deudermont had graced him by even admitting that they would not sail for Baldur's Gate. He also knew that the captain would confide in him as Deudermont needed. Their business now at hand was the pirate ship, still far ahead, her square sails barely visible on the blue line of the horizon.

"More wind, wizard!" Deudermont casually called back to Robillard, who grunted and waved his hand at the captain. "We'll not catch her before dusk unless we have more wind."

Drizzt offered a smile to Deudermont, then made his way forward, back to the beam, to the smell and the spray, to the hissing sound of the *Sea Sprite*'s run, to the solitude he needed to think and to prepare.

They ran for three hours before the caravel was close enough for Catti-brie, in the crow's nest with her spyglass, to even confirm that it was indeed a

pirate ship. The day was long then, the sun halfway from peak to the western horizon, and the chasers knew they would be cutting this one close. If they couldn't catch the pirate ship before sunset, she would sail off into the darkness. Robillard had some spells to try to keep track of her movements, but the pirate ship no doubt had a wizard of her own, or a cleric, at least. Though neither would likely be very powerful, certainly not as accomplished as Robillard, such tracking spells were easily defeated. Also, pirates never ventured too far from their secret ports, and the *Sea Sprite* certainly couldn't chase this one all the way home, where her friends might be waiting.

Deudermont didn't seem overly concerned. They had lost pirates to the night before, and would again. There would always be another outlaw to chase. But Drizzt, keeping a covert eye on the captain, never remembered seeing him quite this casual. Obviously, it had something, or everything, to do with the incident in Waterdeep and the mysterious destination that Deudermont would not discuss.

The drow tightened his hold on the line of the flying jib and sighed. Deudermont would tell him in his own time.

The wind lessened and the *Sea Sprite* made up some ground. It seemed as though this pirate ship might not get away after all. The band of minstrels, which had broken up during the long and tedious middle hours of the chase, came back together again and took up the tune. Drizzt knew that soon the pirates would hear the music, it would reach to them across the waves, a harbinger of their doom.

Now things seemed back to normal, more relaxed despite the fact that a battle seemed imminent. Drizzt tried to convince himself that Deudermont was calm because he had known they would catch the pirate ship. Everything was back to normal.

"Spray astern!" came a cry, turning all hands about.

"What is that?" more than one voice cried. Drizzt looked to Catti-brie, who had her spyglass aimed behind the *Sea Sprite*, and was shaking her head curiously.

The drow skittered along the rail, pulling up to a halt amidships, and leaning out to catch his first glimpse of the unknown pursuer. He saw a high wedge of spray, the spray the giant dorsal fin of a killer whale might make if any whale in all the world could move so quickly. But this was no natural animal, Drizzt knew instinctively, and so did everyone else aboard the *Sea Sprite*.

"She's going to ram!" warned Waillan Micanty, near to the ballista mounted on the ship's stern. Even as he spoke, the strange rushing pursuer veered to starboard and cut by the *Sea Sprite* as though she was standing still.

No whale, Drizzt realized as the creature, or whatever it was, plowed past, twenty yards from the *Sea Sprite,* but close enough to lift a wall of water against the side of the schooner. The drow thought he saw a form inside that spray, a human form.

"It's a man!" Catti-brie called from above, confirming Drizzt's suspicions.

All the crew watched in disbelief as the speeding creature rushed away from the *Sea Sprite,* closing the ground to the caravel.

"A wizard?" Deudermont asked Robillard.

Robillard shrugged, as did all of the others nearby, none of them having any explanation whatsoever. "The more important question," the wizard finally said, "would be to inquire as to the loyalty of this newcomer. Friend, or foe?"

Apparently, those on the caravel didn't know the answer to that either, for some stared silently from the rail, while others picked up crossbows. The pirate ship's catapult crew even launched a ball of flaming pitch at the newcomer, but he was moving too fast for them to gauge the distance and the missile hissed harmlessly into the surf. Then the rushing man moved up alongside the caravel, easily outpacing her. The wake diminished and then disappeared in an instant, to reveal a robed man wearing a heavy pack and standing atop the waves, waving his arms frantically and calling out. He was too far from the *Sea Sprite* now for any of the crew to make out exactly what he was saying.

"Suren he's to casting a spell!" Catti-brie yelled down from the crow's nest. "He's—" She stopped abruptly, drawing a concerned look from Drizzt, and though the drow couldn't make her out clearly from his angle so far below, he could tell that she was confused and could see that she was shaking her head, as if in denial of something.

Those on the deck of the *Sea Sprite* struggled to figure out exactly what was going on. They saw a flurry of activity near the rail facing the man as he stood upon the water. They heard shouts and the clicking sound of crossbows firing, but if any bolts struck the man, he did not show it.

Suddenly, there came a tremendous flash of fire that dissipated immediately into a huge cloud of thick fog, a ball of white where the caravel had been. And it was growing! Soon the cloud covered the water-walking spellcaster as well, and spread out thick and wide. Deudermont kept his course straight and fast, but when he finally neared the location, he had to slow to a drifting crawl, not daring to enter the unexplained bank. Frustrated, cursing under his breath, Deudermont turned the *Sea Sprite* broadside to the misty veil.

All hands stood ready along the rail. The heavy mounted crossbows were

armed and ready, as was the ballista on the *Sea Sprite*'s stern deck.

Finally, the fog began to lift, to roll back under the press of the stiff breeze. A ghostly figure appeared just within the veil, standing on the water, chin in palm, looking disconcertingly at the spot where the caravel had been.

"Ye're not to believe this," Catti-brie called down to Drizzt, a groan accompanying her words.

Indeed, Drizzt did not, for he also came to recognize the unexpected arrival. He noted the carmine robe, decorated with wizardly runes and outrageous images. These were stick figures, actually, depicting wizards in the throes of spellcasting, something an aspiring wizard the ripe age of five might draw in a play spellbook. Drizzt also recognized the hairless, almost childish face of the man—all dimples and huge blue eyes—and the brown hair, long and straight, pulled back tight behind the man's ears so that they stood out from his head at almost right angles.

"What is it?" Deudermont asked the drow.

"Not what," Drizzt corrected. "But who." The drow gave a short laugh and shook his head in disbelief.

"Who then?" Deudermont demanded, trying to sound stern though Drizzt's chuckles were both comforting and infectious.

"A friend," Drizzt replied, and he paused and looked up at Catti-brie. "Harkle Harpell of Longsaddle."

"Oh, no," Robillard groaned from behind them. Like every wizard in all the Realms, Robillard had heard the tales of Longsaddle and the eccentric Harpell family, the most unintentionally dangerous group of wizards ever to grace the multiverse.

As the moments passed and the fog cloud continued to dissipate, Deudermont and his crew relaxed. They had no idea of what had happened to the caravel until the cloud was nearly gone, for then they spotted the pirate ship, running fast, far, far away. Deudermont almost called for full sails, meaning to give chase once more, but he looked to the lowering sun, gauged the distance between his ship and his adversary, and decided that this one had gotten away.

The wizard, Harkle Harpell, was in clear sight now, just a dozen yards or so beyond the *Sea Sprite*'s starboard bow. Deudermont gave the wheel over to a crewman and walked with Drizzt and Robillard to the closest point. Catti-brie came down the mainmast to join them.

Harkle stood impassively, chin in hand, staring at the spot where the caravel had been. He rolled with the swells, up high and down low, and continually tapped his foot upon the sea. It was a strange sight, for the water moved away from him, his water-walking enchantment preventing his foot from actually making any contact with the salty liquid.

Finally, Harkle looked back at the *Sea Sprite,* at Drizzt and the others. "Never thought of that," he admitted, shaking his head. "Aimed the fireball too low, I suppose."

"Wonderful," Robillard muttered.

"Are you coming aboard?" Deudermont asked the man, and the question, or the sudden realization that he was not aboard any ship, seemed to break Harkle from his trance.

"Ah, yes!" he said. "Actually a good idea. Glad I am that I found you." He pointed down at his feet. "I do not know how much longer my spell—"

As he spoke the words, the spell apparently expired, for under he went, plop, into the sea.

"Big surprise," remarked Catti-brie, moving to the rail to join the others.

Deudermont called for poles to fish the wizard out, then looked to his friends in disbelief. "He came out on the high seas with such a tentative enchantment?" the captain asked incredulously. "He might never have found us, or any other friendly ship, and then . . ."

"He is a Harpell," Robillard answered as though that should explain everything.

"Harkle Harpell," Catti-brie added, her sarcastic tone accentuating the wizard's point.

Deudermont just shook his head, taking some comfort in the fact that Drizzt, standing beside him, was obviously enjoying all of this.

5

A Passing Thought

Wrapped in a blanket, his robes hanging on the mast high above him to dry in the wind, the waterlogged wizard sneezed repeatedly, spraying those around him. He simply couldn't contain himself and got Deudermont right in the face when the captain came up for an introduction.

"I give to you one Harkle Harpell of Longsaddle," Drizzt said to Deudermont. Harkle extended his hand, and the blanket fell away from him. The skinny wizard scrambled to retrieve it, but was too late.

"Get this one a meal," Catti-brie snickered from behind. "Suren he could use a bit o'meat on that bum."

Harkle blushed a deep red. Robillard, who had already met the Harpell, just walked away, shaking his head and suspecting that exciting times were yet to come.

"What brings you here," Deudermont asked, "so far from shore, on the open seas?"

Harkle looked to Drizzt. "I came on invitation," he said at length, seeming somewhat perturbed when the drow made no move to answer for him.

Drizzt eyed him curiously.

"I did!" protested the wizard. "On your word." He spun about to regard Catti-brie. "And yours!"

Catti-brie looked to Drizzt, who shrugged and held his hands out to the sides, having no idea of what Harkle might be talking about.

"Oh, well, well, well, a fine 'hello,' I suppose," the exasperated wizard stammered. "But then, I expected it, though I hoped a drow elf would have a longer memory. What do you say to someone you meet again after a century?

Couldn't remember his name, could you? Oh, no, no. That would be too much trouble."

"What are you talking about?" Drizzt had to ask. "I remember your name."

"And a good thing, too!" Harkle roared. "Or I would really be mad!" He snapped his fingers indignantly in the air, and the sound sobered him. He stood for a long moment, seeming thoroughly confused, as though he had forgotten what in the world he was talking about.

"Oh, yes," Harkle said at length and looked straight at Drizzt. The wizard's stern expression soon softened to one of curiosity.

"What are you talking about?" Drizzt asked again, trying to prompt Harkle.

"I do not know," the wizard admitted.

"You were telling me what brought you out here," Deudermont put in.

Harkle snapped his fingers again. "The spell, of course!" he said happily.

Deudermont sighed. "Obviously, it was a spell," the captain began slowly, trying to find a path that would garner some useful information from the rambling mage.

"Not 'a' spell," Harkle retorted. "*The* spell. My new spell, the fog of fate."

"The fog of fate?" Deudermont echoed.

"Oh, very good spell," Harkle began excitedly. "Expedites things, you know. Get on with your life and all that. Shows you where to go. Puts you there even, I think. But it doesn't tell you why." The wizard moved one hand up to tap at his chin, and his blanket slipped down again, but he didn't seem to notice. "I should work on that part. Yes, yes, then I would know why I was here."

"Ye're not even knowin'?" Catti-brie asked, and she faced the rail, even leaned over it somewhat, so she wouldn't have to look at Harkle's bony buttocks.

"Answering an invitation, I suppose," Harkle replied.

Catti-brie's expression was purely doubtful, as was Drizzt's.

"It's true!" Harkle protested vehemently. "Oh, so convenient of you to forget. Shouldn't say things you don't mean, I say! When you, both of you"—he looked from one to the other, waggling his finger—"passed through Longsaddle six years ago, you mentioned that you hoped our paths might cross once more. 'If ever you find yourself near to us.' That is exactly what you said!"

"I do not—" Drizzt began, but Harkle waved him silent, then rushed to the oversized pack he had carried with him, which was drying on the deck. His blanket slipped down farther, but the wizard was too consumed by his task to notice. Catti-brie didn't bother to look away, she just snickered and shook her head.

Harkle pulled a small flask from his pack, retrieved his blanket for modesty's sake, and bounced back over to stand before Drizzt. Snapping his fingers defiantly in the air before the drow, the wizard popped off the cork.

From the flask came a voice, Catti-brie's own voice. "If you ever find yerself near to us," she said, "do look in."

"So there," Harkle said in superior tones as he plopped the cork back into place. He stood for a long moment, hands on hips, until Drizzt's smile became inviting. "And just where are we?" the wizard asked, turning to Deudermont.

The captain looked to the drow ranger, and Drizzt could offer only a shrug in reply. "Come, and I will show you," Deudermont said, leading the wizard toward his cabin. "And I will get you some proper clothes to wear until your robes have dried."

When the two were gone, Catti-brie, walked back over to her friend. Robillard stood not so far away, glaring at them both.

"Pray we find no more pirates to fight until we can be rid of our cargo," the wizard said.

"Harkle will try to help," Catti-brie replied.

"Pray hard," Robillard muttered and walked away.

"You should be more careful of what you say," Drizzt remarked to Catti-brie.

"Could have been yer own voice just as well as me own," the young woman shot back. "And besides, Harkle did try to help in the fight."

"It could as easily have been us he engulfed, in stream or in fire," Drizzt promptly reminded her.

Catti-brie sighed and had no words to reply. They turned to the door of Deudermont's cabin, where the captain stood with Harkle, about to enter.

"So that was the fog of fate you cast at our pirate friends, eh?" Deudermont asked, trying to sound impressed.

"Huh?" Harkle answered. "That? Oh, no, no, that was a fireball. I am good at casting those!" The Harpell paused and lowered his eyes, following Deudermont inside. "Except that I aimed too low," Harkle admitted quietly.

Catti-brie and Drizzt looked to each other, then to Robillard. "Pray," all three whispered in unison.

⚔ ⚔ ⚔ ⚔ ⚔

Drizzt and Catti-brie dined privately with Deudermont that night, the captain seeming more animated than he had since they had put out from Waterdeep. The two friends tried to apologize for Harkle's arrival several times, but Deudermont brushed such thoughts away, even hinted that he was not so upset about the Harpell's arrival.

Finally Deudermont sat back in his chair, wiped his neatly groomed goatee with a satin napkin and stared hard at the two friends, who fell silent, understanding that the captain had something important to tell them.

"We are not in this area by chance," Deudermont admitted bluntly.

"And not going to Baldur's Gate," reasoned Drizzt, who had suspected all along. The *Sea Sprite* was supposedly running to Baldur's Gate, but Deudermont hadn't been careful about staying close to the coast, the more direct route, the safer route, and the route most likely to allow them to find and capture pirates.

Again there ensued a long pause, as though the captain had to settle things in his own mind before admitting them openly. "We're turning west for Mintarn," Deudermont said.

Catti-brie's jaw dropped open.

"A free port," Drizzt reminded, and warned. The island of Mintarn had a well-earned reputation as a haven for pirates and other fugitives, a rough and tumble place. How might the *Sea Sprite,* the hunter of justice, be received in such a port?

"A free port," Deudermont agreed. "Free for pirates and free for the *Sea Sprite,* in need of information."

Drizzt didn't openly question the captain, but his doubting expression spoke volumes.

"The Lords of Waterdeep have given the *Sea Sprite* over to me completely," Deudermont said, somewhat harshly. "She's my ship, under my word alone. I can take her to Mintarn, to the Moonshaes, all the way to Ruathym, if I so please, and let no one question me!"

Drizzt sat back in his seat, stung by the harsh words and surprised that Deudermont, who had professed to be his friend, had so treated him as a subordinate.

The captain winced openly at the sight of the drow's disappointment. "My pardon," he said quietly.

Drizzt came forward in his seat, leaning his elbows on the table to bring himself closer to Deudermont. "Caerwich?" he asked.

Deudermont eyed him directly. "The doppleganger spoke of Caerwich, and so to Caerwich I must go."

"And do ye not think ye'll be sailing right into a trap?" Catti-brie put in. "Going right where they're wanting ye to go?"

"Who?" Deudermont asked.

"Whoever sent the doppleganger," Catti-brie reasoned.

"Who?" Deudermont asked again.

Catti-brie shrugged. "Pinochet?" she queried. "Or mighten it be some other pirate that's had his fill o' the *Sea Sprite?*"

Deudermont leaned back in his seat again, as did Drizzt, all three sitting in silence for several long moments. "I cannot, nor do I believe that you can, continue to sail up and down the Sword Coast as though nothing at all has happened," the captain explained. Drizzt closed his lavender eyes, expecting this answer and agreeing with the logic. "Someone powerful, for doppleganger hirelings are neither common nor cheap, desires my demise and the end of the *Sea Sprite,* and I intend to find out who it might be. I've never run from a fight, nor has my crew, and any who are not prepared to go to Caerwich may disembark in Mintarn and catch a sail back to Waterdeep, paid by my own coffers."

"Not a one will go," Catti-brie admitted.

"Yet we do not even know if Caerwich truly exists," Drizzt remarked. "Many claim to have been there, but these are the tales of seagoing men, tales too often exaggerated by drink or by bluster."

"So we must find out," Deudermont said with a tone of finality. Neither Drizzt nor Catti-brie, both willing to face trouble head-on, offered a word of disagreement. "Perhaps it is not such a bad thing that your wizard friend arrived," the captain went on. "Another wizard knowledgeable in the mystical arts might help us to sort through this mystery."

Catti-brie and Drizzt exchanged doubtful looks. Captain Deudermont obviously didn't know Harkle Harpell! They said no more about it, though, and finished the meal discussing more pertinent matters of the everyday handling of the ship and crew. Deudermont wanted to go to Mintarn, so Drizzt and Catti-brie would follow.

After the meal, the two friends strolled out onto the nearly deserted deck of the schooner, walking under a canopy of brilliant stars.

"Ye were relieved at the captain's tale," Catti-brie remarked.

After a moment of surprise, Drizzt nodded.

"Ye thought the attack in Waterdeep had to do with yerself, and not with Deudermont or the *Sea Sprite,*" Catti-brie went on.

The drow simply stood and listened, for, as usual, the perceptive young woman had hit his feelings exactly, had read him like an open book.

"Ye'll always be fearing that every danger comes from yer home," Catti-brie said, moving to the rail and looking over at the reflection of the stars in the rolling waters.

"I have made many enemies," Drizzt replied as he joined her.

"Ye've left them buried in yer tracks," Catti-brie said with a laugh.

Drizzt shared in that chuckle, and had to admit that she was right. This time, he believed, it wasn't about him. For several years now, he had been a player in the larger drama of the world. The personal element of the danger that had followed him every step since his initial departure from Menzoberranzan seemed a thing of the past. Now, under the stars and with Catti-brie beside him, thousands of miles and many years from Menzoberranzan, Drizzt Do'Urden felt truly free, and carefree. He did not fear the trip to Mintarn, or to any mysterious island beyond that, whatever the rumors of haunts might be. Never did Drizzt Do'Urden fear danger. He lived on the edge willingly, and if Deudermont was in trouble, then Drizzt was more than ready to take up his scimitars.

As was Catti-brie, with her bow, Taulmaril, and the magnificent sword, Khazid'hea, always ready at her hip. As was Guenhwyvar, ever-faithful companion. Drizzt did not fear danger; only guilt could bend his stoic shoulders. This time, it seemed, he carried no guilt, no responsibility for the attack and for the *Sea Sprite*'s chosen course. He was a player in Deudermont's drama, a willing player.

He and Catti-brie basked in the wind and the spray, watched the stars silently for hours.

6

THE NOMADS

Kierstaad, son of Revjak, knelt on the soft turf, his knee denting the ground. He was not tall by the standards of the Icewind Dale nomads, barely topping six feet, and was not as muscular as most. His hair was long and blond, his eyes the color of the sky on the brightest of days, and his smile, on those rare occasions that he displayed it, beamed from a warm soul.

Across the flat tundra Kierstaad could see the snow-capped top of Kelvin's Cairn. It was the lone mountain in the thousand square miles of the land called Icewind Dale, the windswept strip of tundra between the Sea of Moving Ice and the northwestern spur of the Spine of the World mountains. If he were to move but a few miles toward the mountain, Kierstaad knew that he would see the tips of the masts of the fishing ships sailing Lac Dinneshere, second largest of the three lakes in the region.

A few miles to a different world, Kierstaad realized. He was just a boy, really, having seen only seventeen winters. But in that time, Kierstaad had witnessed more of the Realms and of life than most in the world would ever know. He had traveled with many warriors to the call of Wulfgar, from Icewind Dale to a place called Settlestone, far, far away. He'd celebrated his ninth birthday on the road, removed from his family. At the age of eleven, the young barbarian lad had battled goblins, kobolds, and drow elves, fighting beside Berkthgar the Bold, leader of Settlestone. It was Berkthgar who had decided that the time had come for the barbarian peoples to return to Icewind Dale—their ancestral home—and the ways of their forebears.

Kierstaad had seen so much, had lived two different lives, it seemed, in two different worlds. Now he was a nomad, a hunter out on the open tundra, approaching his eighteenth birthday and his first solitary hunt. Looking at Kelvin's Cairn, though, and knowing of the fishing ships on Lac Dinneshere, on Maer Dualdon to the west, and on Redwaters to the south, Kierstaad realized how narrow his existence had truly become, and how much wider was the world—a world just a few short miles from where he now knelt. He could picture the markets in Bryn Shander, the largest of the ten towns surrounding the lakes. He could imagine the multicolored garments, the jewels, the excitement, as the merchant caravans rolled in with the spring, the southerners bartering for the fine scrimshaw carved from the head bone of the three lakes' abundant knucklehead trout.

Kierstaad's own garments were brown, like the tundra, like the reindeer he and his people hunted, like the tents they lived in.

Still, the young man's sigh was not a lament for what was lost to him, but rather a resignation that this was now his way, the way of his ancestors. There was a simple beauty to it, Kierstaad had to admit, a toughness, too, that hardened the body and the soul. Kierstaad was a young man, but he was wise beyond his years. A family trait, so it was said, for Kierstaad's father, Revjak, had led the unified tribes after Wulfgar's departure. Calm and always in control, Revjak hadn't left Icewind Dale to go to war in Mithral Hall, explaining that he was too old and set in his ways. Revjak had stayed on with the majority of the barbarian people, solidifying the alliance between the nomadic tribes, and also strengthening the ties with the folk of Ten-Towns.

Revjak hadn't been surprised, but was pleased at the return of Berkthgar, of Kierstaad—his youngest child—and of all the others. Still, with that return came many questions concerning the future of the nomadic tribes and the leadership of the barbarian people.

"More blood?" came a question, drawing the young man from his contemplations. Kierstaad turned to see the other hunters, Berkthgar among them, moving up behind him.

Kierstaad nodded and pointed to the red splotch on the brown ground. Berkthgar had speared a reindeer, a fine throw from a great distance, but only had wounded the beast, and it had taken flight. Always efficient, particularly when dealing with this animal that gave to them so very much, the hunters had rushed in pursuit. They would not wound an animal to let it die unclaimed. That was not their way. It was, according to Berkthgar, "the wasting way of the men who lived in Ten-Towns, or who lived south of the Spine of the World."

Berkthgar walked up beside the kneeling young man, the tall leader

locking his own stare on distant Kelvin's Cairn. "We must catch up to the beast soon," Berkthgar stated. "If it gets too close to the valley, the dwarves will steal it."

There were a few nods of agreement and the hunting party started off at a swift pace. Kierstaad lagged behind this time, his steps weighed by his leader's words. Ever since they had left Settlestone, Berkthgar had spoken ill of the dwarves, the folk who had been their friends and allies, Bruenor's folk, who had fought in a war of good cause beside the barbarians. What had happened to the cheers of victory? His most vivid memory of the short couple of years in Settlestone was not of the drow war, but of the celebration that had followed, a time of great fellowship between the dwarves, the curious svirfneblin, and the warriors who had joined in the cause from several of the surrounding villages.

How had that all changed so dramatically? Barely a tenday on the road out of Settlestone, the story of the barbarian existence there had begun to change. The good times were no longer spoken of, replaced by tales of tragedy and hardship, of the barbarians lowering their spirits to menial tasks not fit for the Tribe of the Elk, or the Tribe of the Bear, or any of the ancestral tribes. Such talk had continued all the way around the Spine of the World, all the way back to Icewind Dale, and then, gradually, it had died away.

Now, with rumors that the several score of the dwarves had returned to Icewind Dale, Berkthgar's critical remarks had begun anew. Kierstaad understood the source. The rumors said that Bruenor Battlehammer himself, the Eighth King of Mithral Hall, had returned. Shortly after the drow war, Bruenor had given the throne back over to his ancestor, Gandalug, Patron of Clan Battlehammer, who had returned from centuries of magical imprisonment at the hands of the drow elves. Even at the height of their alliance, relations between Berkthgar and Bruenor had been strained, for Bruenor had been the adoptive father of Wulfgar, the man who stood tallest in the barbarians' legends. Bruenor had forged mighty Aegis-fang, the warhammer which, in the hands of Wulfgar, had become the most honored weapon of all the tribes.

But then, with Wulfgar gone, Bruenor would not give Aegis-fang over to Berkthgar.

Even after his heroic exploits in the battle of Keeper's Dale against the drow, Berkthgar had remained in Wulfgar's shadow. It seemed to perceptive Kierstaad, that the leader had embarked on a campaign to discredit Wulfgar, to convince his proud people that Wulfgar was wrong, that Wulfgar was not a strong leader, that he was even a traitor to his people and their gods. Their old life, so said Berkthgar, one of roaming the tundra and living free of any bonds, was the better way.

Kierstaad liked his life on the tundra, and wasn't certain that he disagreed with Berkthgar's observations concerning which was the more honorable lifestyle. But the young man had grown up admiring Wulfgar, and Berkthgar's words about the dead leader did not sit well with him.

Kierstaad looked to Kelvin's Cairn as he ran along the soft, spongy ground, and wondered if the rumors were true. Had the dwarves returned, and if so, was King Bruenor with them?

And if he was, could it be possible that he brought with him Aegis-fang, that most powerful of warhammers?

Kierstaad felt a tingle at that thought, but it was lost a moment later when Berkthgar spotted the wounded reindeer and the hunt was on in full.

$$\times \quad \times \quad \times \quad \times \quad \times$$

"Rope!" Bruenor bellowed, hurling to the floor the twine the shopkeeper had offered him. "Thick as me arm, ye durned orc-brain! Ye thinking that I'm to hold up a tunnel with that?"

The flustered shopkeeper scooped up the twine and rambled away, grumbling with every step.

Standing at Bruenor's left, Regis gave the dwarf a scowl.

"What?" demanded the red-bearded dwarf, leaping to face the portly halfling directly. There weren't many people that the four-and-a-half foot dwarf could look down on, but Regis was one of them.

Regis ran both his plump hands through his curly brown hair and chuckled. "It is good that your coffers run deep," the halfling said, not afraid of blustery Bruenor in the least. "Otherwise Maboyo would throw you out into the street."

"Bah!" the dwarf snorted, straightening his lopsided, one-horned helmet as he turned away. "He's needing the business. I got mines to reopen, and that's meaning gold for Maboyo."

"Good thing," Regis muttered.

"Keep flapping yer lips," Bruenor warned.

Regis looked up curiously, his expression one of blank amazement.

"What?" Bruenor insisted, turning to face him.

"You *saw* me," Regis breathed. "And you just saw me again."

Bruenor started to reply, but the words got caught in his throat. Regis was standing on Bruenor's left, and Bruenor had lost his left eye in a fight

in Mithral Hall. After the war between Mithral Hall and Menzoberranzan, one of the most powerful priests of Silverymoon had cast healing spells over Bruenor's face, which was scarred from forehead, down diagonally across the eye, to the left side of his jaw. The wound was an old one by that point, and the cleric had predicted that his work would do little more than cosmetic repair. Indeed, it took several months for a new eye to appear, deep within the folds of the scar, and some time after that for the orb to grow to full size.

Regis pulled Bruenor closer. Unexpectedly, the halfling covered Bruenor's right eye with one hand, pointed a finger of his other hand, and jabbed it at the dwarf's left eye.

Bruenor jumped and caught the poking hand.

"You can see!" the halfling exclaimed.

Bruenor grabbed Regis in a tight hug, even swung him completely about. It was true, the dwarf's sight had returned in his left eye!

Several other patrons in the store watched the emotional outburst, and as soon as Bruenor became aware of their stares, and even worse, their smiles, he dropped Regis roughly back to the floor.

Maboyo arrived then, his arms full with a coil of heavy rope. "Will this meet your desires?" he asked.

"It's a start," Bruenor roared at him, the dwarf turning suddenly sour again. "I need another thousand feet."

Maboyo stared at him.

"Now!" Bruenor roared. "Ye get me the rope or I'm out for Luskan with enough wagons to keep me and me kin supplied for a hunnerd years!"

Maboyo stared a moment longer, then gave up and headed for his storeroom. He had known the dwarf meant to clean him out of many items as soon as Bruenor had entered his store with a heavy purse. Maboyo liked to dole out supplies slowly, over time, making each purchase seem precious and extracting as much gold from the customer as possible. Bruenor, the toughest bargainer this side of the mountains, didn't play that game.

"Getting back your vision didn't do much to improve your mood," Regis remarked as soon as Maboyo was out of sight.

Bruenor winked at him. "Play the game, Rumblebelly," the dwarf said slyly. "Suren this one's glad we're back. Doubles his business."

True enough, Regis understood. With Bruenor and two hundred of Clan Battlehammer back in Icewind Dale, Maboyo's store—the largest and best-stocked in all of Bryn Shander, in all of Ten-Towns—stood to do well.

Of course, that meant Maboyo would have to put up with the surliest of customers. Regis chuckled privately at the thought of the battles the shop-keeper and Bruenor would fight, just as it had been nearly a decade before, when the rocky valley just south of Kelvin's Cairn chimed with the ringing of dwarven hammers.

Regis spent a long while staring at Bruenor. It was good to be home.

PART TWO

We are the center. In each of our minds—some may call it arrogance, or selfishness—we are the center, and all the world moves about us, and for us, and because of us. This is the paradox of community, the one and the whole, the desires of the one often in direct conflict with the needs of the whole. Who among us has not wondered if all the world is no more than a personal dream?

THE FOG OF FATE

I do not believe that such thoughts are arrogant or selfish. It is simply a matter of perception; we can empathize with someone else, but we cannot truly see the world as another person sees it, or judge events as they affect the mind and the heart of another, even a friend.

But we must try. For the sake of all the world, we must try. This is the test of altruism, the most basic and undeniable ingredient for society. Therein lies the paradox, for ultimately, logically, we each must care more about ourselves than about others, and yet, if, as rational beings we follow that logical course, we place our needs and desires above the needs of our society, and then there is no community.

I come from Menzoberranzan, city of drow, city of self. I have seen that way of selfishness. I have seen it fail miserably. When self-indulgence rules, then all the community loses, and in the end, those striving for personal gains are left with nothing of any real value.

Because everything of value that we will know in this life comes from our relationships with those around us. Because there is nothing material that measures against the intangibles of love and friendship.

Thus, we must overcome that selfishness and we must try; we must care. I saw this truth plainly following the attack on Captain Deudermont in Waterdeep. My first inclination was to believe that my past had precipitated the trouble, that my life course had again brought pain to a friend. I could not bear this thought. I felt old and I felt tired. Subsequently learning that the trouble was possibly brought on by Deudermont's old enemies, not my own, gave me more heart for the fight.

Why is that? The danger to me was no less, nor was the danger to Deudermont, or to Catti-brie, or any of the others about us.

Yet my emotions were real, very real, and I recognized and understood them, if not their source. Now, in reflection, I recognize that source, and take pride in it. I have seen the failure of self-indulgence, and I have run from such a world. I would rather die because of Deudermont's past than have him die because of my own. I would suffer the physical pains, even the end of my life. Better that than watch one I love suffer and die because of me. I would rather have my physical heart torn from my chest, than have my heart of hearts, the essence of love, the empathy and the need to belong to something bigger than my corporeal form, destroyed.

They are a curious thing, these emotions. How they fly in the face of logic, how they overrule the most basic instincts. Because, in the measure of time, in the measure of humanity, we sense those self-indulgent instincts to be a weakness, we sense that the needs of the community must outweigh the desires of the one. Only when we admit to our failures and recognize our weaknesses can we rise above them.

Together.

—Drizzt Do'Urden

MINTARN

It took some effort for Drizzt to spot the panther. The island of Mintarn, four hundred miles southwest of Waterdeep, was cloaked in thick trees, and Guenhwyvar was perfectly blended, reclining on a branch twenty feet from the ground, camouflaged so well that a deer might walk right under the cat, never realizing its doom.

Guenhwyvar was not hunting deer this day. The *Sea Sprite* had put into port barely two hours before, flying no flag, no colors at all, and with her name covered by tarps. The three-masted schooner was likely recognizable, though, for she was unique along the Sword Coast, and many of the rogues now visiting the free port had run from her in the past. So it was that Drizzt, Catti-brie, and Deudermont had been approached soon after they had entered the Freemantle, a tavern just off the docks.

Now they waited for their contact, half expecting an ambush in the thick woods barely a hundred yards from the town common.

There and then, Deudermont could truly appreciate the value of such loyal and powerful friends. With Drizzt and Catti-brie, and ever-alert Guenhwyvar keeping watch, the captain feared no ambush, not if all the pirates of the Sword Coast rose against him! Without these three around him, Deudermont would have been terribly vulnerable. Even Robillard, undeniably powerful but equally unpredictable, could not have afforded the captain such comfort. More than their skill, Deudermont trusted in these three for their loyalty. They'd not desert him, not one of them, no matter the risk.

Guenhwyvar's ears flattened and the panther gave a low growl, a sound the other three felt in their bellies rather than heard with their ears.

Drizzt went into a low crouch and scanned the region, he pointed east and north, then slipped into the shadows, silent as death. Catti-brie moved behind a tree and fixed an arrow to Taulmaril's bowstring. She tried to follow Drizzt's movements, using them to discern the approach of their contact, but the drow was gone. It seemed he had simply vanished soon after he had entered the thick growth. As it turned out, she didn't need Drizzt's movements as a guide, for their visitors were not so adept at traveling silently and invisibly through the woods.

Deudermont stood calmly in the open, his hands folded behind his back. Every now and then he brought out one hand to adjust the pipe that hung in his mouth. He, too, sensed the proximity of other men, several men, taking up positions in the woods about him.

"You do not belong here," came an expected voice from the shadows. The speaker, a tiny man with small dark eyes and huge ears poking out from under his bowl-cut brown hair, had no idea that he had been spotted twenty steps from his current position, which was still more than a dozen yards from the captain. He did not know that his seven companions, too, were known to Drizzt and Catti-brie, and especially to Guenhwyvar. The panther was a moving shadow among the branches, positioning herself close enough to get to four of the men with a single leap.

Off to the speaker's left side, one of his companions spotted Catti-brie and brought his own bow up, putting an arrow in line with the woman. He heard a rustle, but before he could react, a dark form rushed past him. He gave a short yelp, fell back, and saw the forest green of a cape swish past. Then the form was gone, leaving the man stunned and unharmed.

"Brer'Cannon?" the man addressing Deudermont asked, and there came rustling from several positions.

"I'm all right," a shaken Brer'Cannon replied quickly, straightening himself and trying to understand what that pass had been about. He figured it out when he at last looked back to his bow and saw that the bowstring had been cut. "Damnation," Brer'Cannon muttered, scanning the brush frantically.

"I am not accustomed to speaking with shadows," Deudermont called out clearly, his voice unshaken.

"You are not alone," the speaker replied.

"Nor are you," Deudermont said without hesitation. "So do come out and let us be done with this business—whatever business you might have with me."

More rustling came from the shadows, and more than one whispering voice told the speaker, a man named Dunkin, to go talk to the *Sea Sprite*'s captain.

At last, Dunkin mustered the courage to stand up and come forward, taking one step and looking all around, then another step and looking all around. He walked right under Guenhwyvar and didn't know it, which brought a smile to Deudermont's lips. He walked within three feet of Drizzt and didn't know it, but he did spot Catti-brie, for the woman was making no real effort to conceal herself behind the tree just to the side of the small clearing where Deudermont stood.

Dunkin fought hard to regain his composure and his dignity. He walked to within a few paces of the tall captain and straightened himself. "You do not belong here," he said in a voice that cracked only once.

"It was my understanding that Mintarn was a free port," Deudermont replied. "Free for scalawags only?"

Dunkin pointed a finger and started to reply, but the words apparently did not suffice and he stopped after uttering only a meaningless grunt.

"I have never known of any restrictions placed on vessels desiring to dock," Deudermont went on. "Surely my ship is not the only one in Mintarn Harbor flying no colors and with her name covered." The last statement was true enough. Fully two-thirds of all the vessels that put into the free port did so without any open identification.

"You are Deudermont and your ship is the *Sea Sprite*, out of Waterdeep," Dunkin said, his tone accusing. He tugged at his ear as he spoke, a nervous tick, the captain reasoned.

Deudermont shrugged and nodded.

"A law ship," Dunkin went on, finding some courage at last. He let go of his ear. "Pirate hunter, and here, no doubt, to—"

"Do not presume to know my intentions," Deudermont interrupted sharply.

"The *Sea Sprite*'s intentions are always known," Dunkin retorted, his voice equally firm. "She's a pirate hunter, and yes, there are indeed pirates docked in Mintarn, including one you chased this very tenday."

Deudermont's expression grew stern. He understood that this man was an official of Mintarn, an emissary from his tyrancy, Tarnheel Embuirhan, himself. Tarnheel had made his intentions of keeping Mintarn in line with its reputation as a free port quite clear to all the lords along the Sword Coast. Mintarn was not a place to settle vendettas, or to chase fugitives.

"If we came in search of pirates," Deudermont said bluntly, "the *Sea Sprite* would have come in under the flag of Waterdeep, openly and without fear."

"Then you admit your identity," accused Dunkin.

"We hid it only to prevent trouble for your port," Deudermont replied easily. "If any of the pirates now in Mintarn Harbor sought retribution, we would have had to sink them, and I am certain that your overlord would not approve of so many wrecks under the waves of his harbor. Is that not exactly why he sent you to find me in the Freemantle, and why he bade you to come out here with your bluster?"

Dunkin again seemed to not be able to find the words to reply.

"And you are?" Deudermont asked, prompting the nervous man.

Dunkin straightened once more, as if remembering his station. "Dunkin Tallmast," he said clearly, "emissary of His Tyrancy, Lord Tarnheel Embuirhan of the free port of Mintarn."

Deudermont considered the obviously phoney name. This one had probably crawled onto Mintarn's docks years ago, running from another scalawag, or from the law, and over time had found his way into Tarnheel's island guard. Dunkin was not a great choice as an emissary, Deudermont realized. Not practiced in diplomacy and not long on courage. But the captain refused to underestimate Tarnheel, reputably a proficient warrior who had kept the relative peace on Mintarn for many years. Dunkin was no imposing diplomat, but Tarnheel had probably decided that he would be the one to meet with Deudermont for a reason, possibly to make the *Sea Sprite*'s captain understand that he and his ship were not considered very important to his tyrancy.

Diplomacy was a curious game.

"The *Sea Sprite* has not sailed in to engage with any pirates," Deudermont assured the man. "Nor in search of any man who might be in hiding on Mintarn. We have come to take on provisions, and in search of information."

"About a pirate," Dunkin reasoned, seeming not pleased.

"About an island," Deudermont replied.

"A pirate island?" Dunkin retorted, and again his tone made the question seem more of an accusation.

Deudermont pulled the pipe from his mouth and stared hard at Dunkin, answering the question without uttering a word.

"It is said that nowhere in all the Realms can a greater concentration of the most seasoned sea dogs be found than on Mintarn," Deudermont began at length. "I seek an island that is as much legend as truth, an island known to many through tales, but to only a few by experience."

Dunkin didn't reply, and didn't seem to have any idea of what Deudermont might be talking about.

"I will make you a deal," the captain offered.

"What have you to bargain with?" Dunkin replied quickly.

"I, and all of my crew, will remain on the *Sea Sprite,* quietly, and far out in the harbor. Thus will the peace of Mintarn remain secure. We have no intention of hunting any on your island, even known outlaws, but many might seek us out, foolishly thinking the *Sea Sprite* vulnerable while in port."

Dunkin couldn't help but nod. Back in the Freemantle, he had already heard whispers hinting that several of the ships now in port were not pleased to see the *Sea Sprite,* and might join together against her.

"We will remain out of the immediate dock area," Deudermont said again, "and you, Dunkin Tallmast, will find for me the information I desire." Before Dunkin could respond, Deudermont tossed him a pouch full of gold coins. "Caerwich," the captain explained. "I want a map to Caerwich."

"Caerwich?" Dunkin echoed skeptically.

"West and south, by tales I've heard," Deudermont replied.

Dunkin gave a sour look and moved to toss the coins back, but Deudermont raised a hand to stop him. "The Lords of Waterdeep will not be pleased to learn that Mintarn's hospitality was not extended to one of their ships," the captain was quick to point out. "If you are not a free port for the legal ships of Waterdeep, then you proclaim yourself an open haven only to outlaws. Your Lord Tarnheel will not be pleased at the results of such a proclamation."

It was as close to a threat as Deudermont wanted to get, and he was much relieved when Dunkin clutched the bag of coins tightly once more.

"I will speak with his tyrancy," the short man asserted. "If he agrees . . ." Dunkin let it go at that, waving his hand.

Deudermont popped the pipe back into his mouth and nodded to Catti-brie, who came out of hiding, her bow relaxed, all arrows replaced in her quiver. She never blinked as she walked past Dunkin, and he matched her stare.

His resolve melted a moment later, though, when Drizzt slipped out of the brush to the side. And if the sight of a drow elf wasn't enough to fully unnerve the man, surely the sudden presence of a six-hundred pound black panther dropping to the ground barely five feet to Dunkin's side, was.

⚔ ⚔ ⚔ ⚔ ⚔

Dunkin rowed out to the *Sea Sprite* the very next day. Despite the fact that Deudermont welcomed him warmly, he came aboard tentatively, as though he was in awe of this vessel that was so fast becoming a legend along the Sword Coast.

They greeted Dunkin on the open deck, in full view of the crew. Guenhwyvar was at rest in her astral home, but Robillard and Harkle joined the others this time, standing together, and Drizzt thought that a good thing. Perhaps Robillard, an adept wizard, could keep Harkle's powers under control, the drow reasoned. And perhaps Harkle's perpetual smile would rub off on the grumpy Robillard!

"You have my information?" Deudermont asked, coming right to the point. The *Sea Sprite* had sat calm and undisturbed thus far, but Deudermont held no illusions about their safety in Mintarn Harbor. The captain knew that no less than a dozen ships now in port desired their demise, and the sooner the schooner was out of Mintarn, the better.

Dunkin motioned to the door to the captain's private quarters.

"Out here," Deudermont insisted. "Give it over and be gone. I've not the time for any delays, and I need no privacy from my crew."

Dunkin looked around and nodded, having no desire to debate the point.

"The information?" Deudermont asked.

Dunkin started, as if surprised. "Ah, yes," he stuttered. "We have a map, but it's not too detailed. And we cannot be sure, of course, for the island you seek might be no more than legend, and then, of course, there would be no correct map."

His humor was not appreciated, he soon realized, and so he calmed himself and cleared his throat.

"You have my gold," Deudermont said after yet another long pause.

"His tyrancy wishes a different payment," Dunkin replied. "More than the gold."

Deudermont's eyes narrowed dangerously. He put his pipe in his mouth deliberately and took a long, long draw.

"Nothing so difficult," Dunking was quick to assure. "And my lord offers more than a simple map. You'll need a wizard or a priest to create a hold large enough to carry ample supplies."

"That would be us," Harkle put in, draping an arm over Robillard's shoulders as he spoke, then quickly withdrawing it upon seeing the grumpy wizard's threatening scowl.

"Ah, yes, but no need, no need," Dunkin blurted. "For his tyrancy has a most wonderful chest, a magical hold, it is, and he will give it to you on loan, along with the map, for the pouch of gold, which was not so much, and one other little favor."

"Speak it," demanded Deudermont, growing weary of the cryptic game.

"Him," said Dunkin, pointing to Drizzt.

Only Drizzt's quick reaction, lifting a blocking arm, kept Catti-brie from leaping forward and punching the man.

"Him?" Deudermont asked incredulously.

"Just to meet with the drow," Dunkin quickly explained, realizing that he was treading on dangerous ground here. The water was cold about Mintarn and the man had no desire for a long swim back to shore.

"A curiosity piece?" Catti-brie snapped, pushing against Drizzt's blocking arm. "I'll give ye something for yer stupid tyrant!"

"No, no," Dunkin tried to explain. He never would have gotten the words out of his mouth, would have been tossed overboard for simply making the seemingly absurd request, had not Drizzt intervened, a calming voice that revealed no offense taken.

"Explain your lord's desire," the drow said quietly.

"Your reputation is considerable, good drow," Dunkin stammered. "Many pirates limping into Mintarn speak of your exploits. Why, the main reason that the *Sea Sprite* has not been . . ." He stopped and glanced nervously at Deudermont.

"Has not been attacked in Mintarn Harbor," Deudermont finished for him.

"They wouldn't dare come out and face you," Dunkin dared to finish, looking back to Drizzt. "My lord, too, is a warrior of no small reputation."

"Damn," Catti-brie muttered, guessing what was to come, and Drizzt, too, could see where this speech was leading.

"Just a contest," Dunkin finished. "A private fight."

"For no better reason than to prove who is the better," Drizzt replied distastefully.

"For the map," Dunkin reminded him. "And the chest, no small reward." After a moment's thought, he added, "You will have those whether you win or lose."

Drizzt looked at Catti-brie, then to Deudermont, then to all the crew, who were making no effort anymore to disguise the fact that they were listening intently to every word.

"Let us be done with it," the drow said.

Catti-brie grabbed him by the arm, and when he turned to face her, he realized that she did not approve.

"I cannot ask you to do such a thing," Deudermont said.

Drizzt looked at him directly, and with a smile. "Perhaps my own curiosity over who is the better fighter is no less than Tarnheel's," he said, looking back to Catti-brie, who knew him and knew his motivations better than that.

"Is it any different than your own fight with Berkthgar over Aegis-fang before the dark elves came to Mithral Hall?" Drizzt asked simply.

True enough, Catti-brie had to admit. Before the drow war, Berkthgar had threatened to break the alliance with Bruenor unless the dwarf turned Aegis-fang over to him, something Bruenor would never do. Catti-brie had gone to Settlestone and had ended the debate by defeating Berkthgar in the challenge of single combat. In light of that memory, and the drow's duty now, she let go of Drizzt's arm.

"I will return presently," Drizzt promised, following Dunkin to the rail, and then into the small boat.

Deudermont, Catti-brie, and most of the other crewmen, watched them row away, and Catti-brie noticed the sour expression on the captain's face, as though Deudermont was somewhat disappointed, something the perceptive young woman understood completely.

"He's not wanting to fight," she assured the captain.

"He is driven by curiosity?" Deudermont asked.

"By loyalty," Catti-brie answered. "And nothing more. Drizzt is bound by friendship to ye and to the crew, and if a simple contest against the man will make for an easier sail, then he's up to the fight. But there's no curiosity in Drizzt. No stupid pride. He's not for caring who's the better at swordplay."

Deudermont nodded and his expression brightened. The young woman's words confirmed his belief in his friend.

The minutes turned into an hour, then into two, and the conversation on the *Sea Sprite* gradually shifted away from Drizzt's confrontation to their own situation. Two ships, square-riggers both, had sailed out of Mintarn. Neither had gone out into the open sea, but rather, had turned into the wind just beyond the harbor, tacking and turning so that they remained relatively still.

"Why don't they just drop their anchors?" Waillan asked a crewman who was standing near him on the poop deck, just behind the *Sea Sprite*'s deadly ballista.

Catti-brie and Deudermont, near the center of the ship, overheard the remark and looked to each other. Both knew why.

A third ship put up her lower sails and began to drift out in the general direction of the *Sea Sprite*.

"I'm not liking this," Catti-brie remarked.

"We may have been set up," Deudermont replied. "Perhaps Dunkin informed our sailor friends here that the *Sea Sprite* would be without a certain dark elf crewman for a while."

"I'm for the nest," Catti-brie said. She slung Taulmaril over her shoulder and started up the mainmast.

Robillard and Harkle came back on deck then, apparently aware of the potentially dangerous situation. They nodded to Deudermont and moved astern, beside Waillan and his ballista crew.

Then they waited, all of them. Deudermont watched the creeping movements of the three ships carefully, and then a fourth pushed off from Mintarn's long docks. Possibly they were being encircled, the captain knew, but also he knew that the *Sea Sprite* could put up anchor and be out to sea in mere minutes, especially with Robillard's magic aiding the run. And all the while, between the ballista and the archers, particularly Catti-brie and that devastating bow of hers, the *Sea Sprite* could more than match any barrage they offered.

Deudermont's primary concern at that moment was not for his ship, but for Drizzt. What fate might befall the drow if they had to leave him behind?

That notion disappeared, but a new fear materialized when Catti-brie, spyglass in hand, yelled down that Drizzt was on his way back. Deudermont and many others followed the woman's point and could just make out the tiny rowboat in front and to starboard of the third ship drifting out of the harbor.

"Robillard!" Deudermont yelled.

The wizard nodded and peered intently to spot the craft. He began casting a spell immediately, but even as the first words left his mouth, a catapult on the third pirate ship let fly, dropping a bail of pitch into the water right beside the rowboat, nearly capsizing her.

"Up sails!" Deudermont cried. "Weigh anchor!"

Catti-brie's bow hummed, streaking arrow after arrow back toward the drifting caravel, though the ship was still more than three hundred yards away.

All the harbor seemed to come to life immediately. The two ships farther out put up full sails and began their turn to catch the wind, the third ship launched another volley at the rowboat, and the sails of the fourth ship, indeed a part of the conspiracy, unfurled.

Before Robillard's spell began its effect, a third ball of pitch hit just behind the rowboat, taking part of her stern with her. Still, the enchantment caught the tiny craft, a directed wave of water grabbing at her and speeding her suddenly in the direction of the *Sea Sprite*. Drizzt put up the now-useless oars while Dunkin bailed frantically, but even though they made great progress toward the schooner, the damaged rowboat could not stay afloat long enough to get to the *Sea Sprite*'s side.

Robillard recognized that fact and as the craft floundered, the wizard dispelled his magic, else Drizzt and Dunkin would have been drowned beneath the enchanted wave.

Deudermont's mind worked furiously, trying to measure the distance and the time before the pirates would catch them. He figured that as soon as the sails were up, he would have to turn the *Sea Sprite* in toward the harbor, for he would not leave Drizzt behind, no matter the risk.

His calculations quickly shifted when he saw that Drizzt, Dunkin in tow, was swimming furiously toward the ship.

Dunkin was even more surprised by this turn of events than was Deudermont. When the rowboat went under, the man's first instinct told him to get away from the drow. Drizzt's carried twin scimitars and wore a suit of chain mail. Dunkin wore no encumbering equipment and figured that the drow would cling to him and likely drown them both. To Dunkin's surprise, though, Drizzt could not only stay above the water, but could swim impossibly fast.

The chain mail was supple, cunningly forged of the finest materials and to drowlike design by Buster Bracer of Clan Battlehammer, one of the finest smithies in all the Realms. And Drizzt wore enchanted anklets, allowing him to kick his feet incredibly fast. He caught up to Dunkin and dragged the man out in the direction of the *Sea Sprite* almost immediately, closing nearly a quarter of the distance before the startled man even gained his wits enough about him to begin swimming on his own.

"They are coming fast!" Waillan cried happily, thinking his friend would make it.

"But they lost the chest!" Robillard observed, pointing to the floundering rowboat. Right behind the wreckage and coming faster still was the third pirate ship, her sails now full of wind.

"I will get it!" cried Harkle Harpell, wanting desperately to be of some use. The wizard snapped his fingers and began an enchantment, as did Robillard, realizing that they had to somehow slow the pursuing caravel if Drizzt was to have any chance of making it to the *Sea Sprite*.

Robillard stopped his casting almost immediately, though, and looked to Harkle curiously.

Robillard's eyes widened considerably as he considered a fish that appeared suddenly on the deck at Harkle's feet. "No!" he cried, reaching for the Harpell, figuring out what type of spell Harkle had enacted. "You cannot cast an extra dimension on an item enchanted with an extra dimension!"

Robillard had guessed correctly. Harkle was trying to pull in the sinking magical chest by creating an extra-dimensional gate in the region where the

rowboat and the chest went down. It was a good idea, or would have been, except that the chest Tarnheel had promised to the *Sea Sprite* was a chest of holding—a contained extra-dimensional space that could hold much more volume than would be indicated by the item's size and weight. The problem was that extra-dimensional spells and items did not usually mesh correctly. Throwing a bag of holding into a chest of holding, for example, could tear a rift in the multiverse, spewing everything nearby into the Astral Plane, or even worse, into the unknown space between the planes of existence.

"Oops," Harkle apologized, realizing his error and trying to let go of his enchantment.

Too late. A huge wave erupted right in the area where the rowboat had gone down, rocking the approaching caravel and rolling into Drizzt and Dunkin, hurling them toward the *Sea Sprite*. The water churned and danced, then began to roll, forming a giant whirlpool.

"Sail on!" Deudermont cried as ropes were thrown out to Drizzt and Dunkin. "Sail on, for all our lives!"

The sails fell open, and crewmen immediately pulled to put them against the wind. At once the *Sea Sprite* lurched and rolled away, gliding swiftly out of the harbor.

Things were not as easy for the pursuing caravel. The pirate ship tried to tack and turn, but was too close to the mounting whirlpool. She crested the lip and was pulled sideways violently, many of her crew being tossed overboard into the turmoil. Around she went, once and then twice. Those aboard the *Sea Sprite* watched her sails diminish as she sank lower and lower into the spin.

But other than horrified Harkle, the eyes of those on the *Sea Sprite* had to go outward, to the two vessels lying in wait. Robillard called up a mist, understanding that Deudermont's intent was not to engage, but to slip by, out into the open waters. Waillan's crew fired at will, as did the archers, while several crewmen, Deudermont among them, hauled Drizzt and a very shaken Dunkin Tallmast aboard.

"Sealed," Drizzt said to Deudermont with a wry smile, producing a capped scroll tube that obviously contained the map to Caerwich.

Deudermont clapped him on the shoulder and turned to go to the wheel. Both surveyed the situation, and both figured that the *Sea Sprite* would have little trouble slipping through this trap.

The situation looked bright, to those looking forward. But hanging over the stern rail, Harkle Harpell could only watch in dismay. Rationally, he knew that his unintentional catastrophe had probably saved Drizzt and the other man in the rowboat, and probably would make the *Sea Sprite*'s run all the easier, but the gentle Harkle could not suffer the sights of the turmoil within the whirlpool and the screams of the drowning men. He muttered, "oh, no," over and over, searched his mind for some spell that might help the poor men of the caravel.

But then, almost as suddenly as it had appeared, the whirlpool dissipated, the water flattening to perfect, glassy calm. The caravel remained, hanging so low to the side that her sails nearly touched the water.

Harkle breathed a deep sigh of relief and thanked whatever gods might be listening. The water was full of sailors, but they all seemed close enough to get to the swamped hull.

Harkle clapped his hands happily and ran down from the poop deck, joining Deudermont and Drizzt by the wheel. The engagement was on in full by then, with the two square-riggers trading shots with the *Sea Sprite,* though none of the three were close enough to inflict any real damage.

Deudermont eyed Harkle curiously.

"What?" asked the flustered mage.

"Have you any more fireballs in you?" Deudermont asked.

Harkle paled. So soon after the horror of the whirlpool, he really didn't have the heart to burn up another vessel. But that wasn't what sly Deudermont had in mind.

"Put one in the water between our enemies," the captain explained, then looked to Drizzt. "I'll run for the mist and swing to port, then we'll have time to contend with only one of the pirate ships up close."

Drizzt nodded. Harkle brightened, and was more than happy to comply. He waited for Deudermont's signal, then skipped a fireball just under the waves. There came a flash and then a thick cloud of steam.

Deudermont headed straight for it, and the square-riggers predictably turned to cut off such an escape. Soon before plunging into the mist, Deudermont cut hard to port, skimming the cloud and angling outside the pirate ship farthest to the left.

They would pass close, but that didn't bother Deudermont much, not with the *Sea Sprite*'s speed and Robillard's magical defenses.

An explosion soon changed Deudermont's mind, a heavy ball of iron shearing through Robillard's defensive shields and snipping through a fair amount of rigging as well.

"They've got a smokepowder gun!" Harkle roared.

"A what?" Drizzt and Deudermont asked at the same time.

"Arquebus," Harkle whimpered, and his hands began spinning large circles in the air. "Big arquebus."

"A what?" the two asked again.

Harkle couldn't begin to explain, but his horrified expression spoke volumes. Smokepowder was a rare and dangerous thing, a fiendish concoction of Gondish priests that used sheer explosive energy to launch missiles from metal barrels, and oftentimes, to inadvertently blow apart the barrels. "One in ten," was the saying among those who knew smokepowder best, meaning that one in ten attempts to fire would likely blow up in your face. Harkle figured these pirates must truly despise the *Sea Sprite* to risk such a dangerous attack.

But still, even if the one in ten rule held true, nine in ten could take the *Sea Sprite* out of the water!

Harkle knew that he had to act as the seconds passed, as the others, even Robillard, looked on helplessly, not understanding what they were suddenly up against. Smokepowder was more common in the far eastern reaches of the Realms, and had even been used in Cormyr, so it was said. Of course, there were rumors that it had surfaced just a bit on the Sword Coast, mostly aboard ships. Harkle considered his options, considered the volume of smokepowder and its volatility, considered the weapons he had at his disposal.

"A metal cylinder!" Catti-brie called down from the crow's nest, spotting the targeting gun through the steam.

"With bags near to it?" Harkle cried back.

"I cannot see!" Catti-brie called, for the cloud continued to drift and to obscure her vision of the pirate ship's deck.

Harkle knew that time was running out. The smokepowder cannon wasn't very accurate, but it didn't have to be, for one of its shots could take down a mast, and even a glancing hit on the hull would likely blow a hole large enough to sink the schooner.

"Aim for it!" Harkle cried out. "For the cylinder and the decking near to it!"

Catti-brie was never one to trust in Harkle Harpell, but his reasoning then seemed unusually sound. She put up Taulmaril and sent off an arrow, then another, thinking to disable the crew near to the cylinder, if not take out the weapon itself. Through the fog, she saw the sparks as one enchanted arrow skipped off the cylinder, then heard a cry of pain as she nailed one of the gunners.

The *Sea Sprite* ran on, nearing the pirate ship. Harkle bit at his fingernails. Dunkin, who also knew of smokepowder guns, tugged at his large ears.

"Oh, turn away the ship," Harkle bade Deudermont. "Too close, too close. They'll fire it off again right into our faces, and knock us under the waves."

Deudermont didn't know how to respond. He had already learned that Robillard's magic couldn't stop the smokepowder weapon. Indeed, when the captain glanced back to Robillard, he found the wizard frantically creating gusts of wind to speed their passage, apparently with no intent of even trying to stop a second shot. Still, if the captain tried to turn to port, he would likely be in range of that weapon for some time, and if he tried to veer to starboard, he might not be able to even get past the pirate ship and into the cloud, might ram the ship head-on. Even if they could then defeat the crew of this ship, her two remaining friends would have little trouble in overcoming the *Sea Sprite*.

"Get the wizard and get to them," Deudermont said to Drizzt. "And get the cat. We need you now, my friend!"

Drizzt started to move, but Harkle, spotting the light of a torch near to where Catti-brie had pointed out the cylinder, shouted out "no time!" and dived flat to the deck.

From on high, Catti-brie saw the torch, and with its light, she also saw the large sacks that Harkle had inquired about. She instinctively aimed for the torchbearer, thinking to slow the smokepowder crew, but then took a chance and agreed with Harkle, shifting her aim slightly and letting fly, straight for the pile of sacks on the pirate's decking.

Her arrow streaked in the instant before the man put the torch to the cannon, as the *Sea Sprite* was running practically parallel to the pirate ship. It was just an instant, but in that time, the torchbearer was foiled, was blown into the air as the streaking arrow sliced into the sacks of volatile smokepowder.

The pirate ship nearly stood straight up on end. The fireball was beyond anything Harkle, or even Robillard, had ever seen, and the sheer concussion and flying debris nearly cleaned the *Sea Sprite*'s deck of standing crewmen, and tore many holes in the schooner's lateen sails.

The *Sea Sprite* lurched wildly, left and right, before Deudermont could regain his senses and steady the wheel. But she plowed on, leaving the trap behind.

"By the gods," Catti-brie muttered, truly horrified, for where the pirate square-rigger had been, there was now only flotsam and jetsam, splinters, charred wood, and floating bodies.

Drizzt, too, was stunned. Looking on the carnage, he thought he was previewing the end of the world. He had never seen such devastation, such complete carnage, not even from a powerful wizard. Enough smokepowder could flatten a mountain, or a city. Enough smokepowder could flatten all the world.

"Smokepowder?" he said to Harkle.

"From Gondish priests," the wizard replied.

"Damn them all," muttered Drizzt, and he walked away.

Later that day, as the crew worked to repair the tears in the sails, Drizzt and Catti-brie took a break and leaned on the rail of the schooner's bow, looking down at the empty water and considering the great distance they had yet to travel.

Finally Catti-brie couldn't stand the suspense any longer. "Did ye beat him?" she asked.

Drizzt looked at her curiously, as though he didn't understand.

"His tyrancy," Catti-brie explained.

"I brought the map," Drizzt replied, "and the chest, though it was lost."

"Ah, but Dunkin promised it whether ye won or lost," the young woman said slyly.

Drizzt looked at her. "The contest was never important," he said. "Not to me."

"Did ye win or lose?" Catti-brie pressed, not willing to let the drow slip out of this one.

"Sometimes it is better to allow so important a leader and valuable an ally to retain his pride and his reputation," Drizzt replied, looking back to the sea, then to the mizzenmast, where a crewman was calling for some assistance.

"Ye let him beat ye?" Catti-brie asked, not seeming pleased by that prospect.

"I never said that," Drizzt replied.

"So he beat ye on his own," the young woman reasoned.

Drizzt shrugged as he walked away toward the mizzenmast to help out the crewman. He passed by Harkle and Robillard, who were coming forward, apparently meaning to join Drizzt and Catti-brie at the rail.

Catti-brie continued to stare at the drow as the wizards walked up. The woman did not know what to make of Drizzt's cryptic answers. Drizzt had let Tarnheel win, she figured, or at least had allowed the man to fight him to a draw. For some reason the young woman did not understand, she didn't want to think that Tarnheel had actually beaten Drizzt. She didn't want to think that anyone could beat Drizzt.

Both Robillard and Harkle were smiling widely as they considered the young woman's expression.

"Drizzt beat him," Robillard said at last.

Startled, Catti-brie turned to the wizard.

"That is what you were wondering about," Robillard reasoned.

"We watched it all," Harkle said. "Oh, of course we did. A good match." Harkle went into a fighting crouch, his best imitation of Drizzt in combat, which of course seemed a mockery to Catti-brie. "He started left," Harkle began, making the move, "then ran to the right so quickly and smoothly that Tarnheel never realized it."

"Until he got hit," Robillard interjected. "His tyrancy was still swinging forward, attacking a ghost, I suppose."

That made sense to Catti-brie. The move they had just described was called "the ghost step."

"He learned better, he did!" howled Harkle.

"Suffice it to say that his tyrancy will not be sitting down anytime soon," Robillard finished, and the two wizards exploded into laughter, as animated as Catti-brie had ever seen Robillard.

The young woman went back to the rail as the two walked away, howling still. Catti-brie was smiling too. She now knew the truth of Drizzt's claims that the fight wasn't important to him. She'd make certain that she teased the drow about it in the days to come. She also was smiling because Drizzt had won.

For some reason, that was very important to Catti-brie.

8

SEA TALK

Repairs continued on the *Sea Sprite* for two days, preventing her from putting up her sails in full. Even so, with the strong breeze rushing down from the north, the swift schooner made fine speed southward, her sails full of wind. In just over three days, she ran the four hundred miles from Mintarn to the southeasternmost point of the great Moonshae Isles, and Deudermont turned her to the west, due west, for the open sea, running just off the southern coast of the Moonshaes.

"We'll run for two days with the Moonshaes in sight," Deudermont informed the crew.

"Are you not making for Corwell?" Dunkin Tallmast, who always seemed to be asking questions, was quick to interrupt. "I think I should like to be let off at Corwell. A beautiful city, by all accounts." The little man's cavalier attitude was diminished considerably when he began tugging at his ear, that nervous tick that revealed his trepidation.

Deudermont ignored the pesty man. "If the wind holds, tomorrow, mid-morning, we'll pass a point called Dragon Head," he explained. "Then we'll cross a wide harbor and put in at a village, Wyngate, for our last provisions. Then it's the open sea, twenty days out, I figure, twice that without the wind."

The seasoned crew understood it would be a difficult journey, but they bobbed their heads in accord, not a word of protest from the lot of them—with one exception.

"Wyngate?" Dunkin protested. "Why, I'll be a month in just getting out of the place!"

"Whoever said that you were leaving?" Deudermont asked him. "We shall put you off where we choose . . . after we return."

That shut the man up, or at least changed his train of thought, for before Deudermont could get three steps away, Dunkin shouted at him. "*If* you return, you mean!" he called. "You have lived along the Sword Coast all your stinking life. You know the rumors, Deudermont."

The captain turned slowly, ominously, to face the man. Both were quite conscious of the murmurs Dunkin's words had caused, a ripple of whispers all across the schooner's deck.

Dunkin did not look at Deudermont directly, but scanned the deck, his wry smile widening as he considered the suddenly nervous crew. "Ah," he moaned suspiciously. "You haven't told them."

Deudermont didn't blink.

"You wouldn't be leading them to an island of legend without telling them all of the legend?" Dunkin asked in sly tones.

"The man enjoys intrigue," Catti-brie whispered to Drizzt.

"He enjoys trouble," Drizzt whispered back.

Deudermont spent a long moment studying Dunkin, the captain's stern gaze gradually stealing the little man's stupid grin. Then Deudermont looked to Drizzt—he always looked to Drizzt when he needed support—and to Catti-brie, and neither seemed to care much for Dunkin's ominous words. Bolstered by their confidence, the captain turned to Harkle, who seemed distracted, as usual, as though he hadn't even heard the conversation. The rest of the crew, at least those near to the wheel, had heard, and Deudermont noted more than one nervous movement among them.

"Tell us what?" Robillard asked bluntly. "What is the great mystery of Caerwich?"

"Ah, Captain Deudermont," Dunkin said with a disappointed sigh.

"Caerwich," Deudermont began calmly, "may be no more than a legend. Few claim to have been there, for it is far, far away from any civilized lands."

"That much, we already know," Robillard remarked. "But if it is just a legend and we sail empty waters until we are forced to return, then that bodes no ill for the *Sea Sprite*. What is it that this insignificant worm hints at?"

Deudermont looked hard at Dunkin, wanting at that moment to throttle the man. "Some of those who have been there," the captain began, choosing his words carefully, "claim that they witnessed unusual visions."

"Haunted!" Dunkin interrupted dramatically. "Caerwich is a haunted island," he proclaimed, dancing around to cast a wild-eyed stare at each of the crewmen near to him. "Ghost ships and witches!"

"Enough," Drizzt said to the man.

"Shut yer mouth," Catti-brie added.

Dunkin did shut up, but he returned the young woman's stare with a superior look, thinking he had won the day.

"They are rumors," Deudermont said loudly. "Rumors I would have told you when we reached Wyngate, but not before." The captain paused and looked around once more, this time his expression begging friendship and loyalty from the men who had been with him so very long. "I would have told you," he insisted, and everyone aboard, except perhaps for Dunkin, believed him.

"This sail is not for Waterdeep, nor against any pirates," Deudermont went on. "It is for me, something I must do because of the incident on Dock Street. Perhaps the *Sea Sprite* sails into trouble, perhaps to answers, but I must go, whatever the outcome. I would not force any of you to go along. You signed on to chase pirates, and in that regard, you have been the finest crew any captain could wish for."

Again came a pause, a long one, with the captain alternately meeting the gaze of each man, and of Catti-brie and Drizzt, last of all.

"Any who do not wish to sail to Caerwich may disembark at Wyngate," Deudermont offered. It was an extraordinary offer that widened the eyes of every crewman. "You will be paid for your time aboard the *Sea Sprite,* plus a bonus from my personal coffers. When we return . . ."

"If you return," Dunkin put in, but Deudermont simply ignored the troublemaker.

"When we return," Deudermont said again, more firmly, "we will pick you up at Wyngate. There will be no questions of loyalty asked, and no retribution by any who voyaged to Caerwich."

Robillard snorted. "Is not every island haunted?" he asked with a laugh. "If a sailor were to believe every whispered rumor, he'd not dare sail the Sword Coast at all. Sea monsters off of Waterdeep! Coiled serpents of Ruathym! Pirates of the Nelanther!"

"That last one's true enough!" one sailor piped in, and everyone gave a hearty laugh.

"So it is!" Robillard replied. "Seems some of the rumors might be true."

"And if Caerwich is haunted?" another sailor asked.

"Then we'll dock in the morning," Waillan answered, hanging over the rail of the poop deck, "and put out in the afternoon."

"And leave the night for the ghosts!" yet another man finished, again to hearty laughter.

Deudermont was truly appreciative, especially to Robillard, from whom the captain had never expected such support. When the roll was subsequently called, not a single one of the *Sea Sprite*'s crew meant to get off at Wyngate.

Dunkin listened to it all in sheer astonishment. He kept trying to put in some nasty flavoring to the rumors of haunted Caerwich, tales of decapitation and the like, but he was shouted or laughed down every time.

Neither Drizzt nor Catti-brie was surprised by the unanimous support for Deudermont. The *Sea Sprite*'s crew, they both knew, had been together long enough to become true friends. These two companions had enough experience with friendship to understand loyalty.

"Well, I mean to get off at Wyngate," a flustered Dunkin said at last. "I'll not follow any man to haunted Caerwich."

"Who ever offered you such a choice?" Drizzt asked him.

"Captain Deudermont just said . . ." Dunkin started, turning to Deudermont and pointing an accusing finger the captain's way. The words stuck in his throat, though, for Deudermont's sour expression explained that the offer wasn't meant for him.

"You cannot keep me here!" Dunkin protested. "I am the emissary of his tyrancy. I should have been released in Mintarn."

"You would have been killed in Mintarn Harbor," Drizzt reminded him.

"You will be released in Mintarn," Deudermont promised.

Dunkin knew what that meant.

"When we might have a proper inquiry as to your part in the attempted ambush of the *Sea Sprite*," Deudermont went on.

"I did nothing!" Dunkin cried, tugging his ear.

"It is convenient that so soon after you informed me that Drizzt's presence aboard the *Sea Sprite* was preventing any pirate attacks, you arranged to take Drizzt from our decks," Deudermont said.

"I was almost killed by that very ambush!" Dunkin roared in protest. "If I had known that the scalawags were after you, I never would have rowed out into the harbor."

Deudermont looked to Drizzt.

"True enough," the drow admitted.

Deudermont paused a moment, then nodded. "I find you innocent," he said to Dunkin, "and agree to return you to Mintarn after our journey to Caerwich."

"You will pick me back up at Wyngate, then," Dunkin reasoned, but Deudermont shook his head.

"Too far," the captain replied. "None of my crew will disembark at Wyngate.

And now that I must return to Mintarn, I will return from Caerwich by a northerly route, passing north of the Moonshaes."

"Then let me off at Wyngate and I'll find a way to meet you in a northern town of the Moonshaes," Dunkin offered.

"Which northern town?" Deudermont asked him.

Dunkin had no answers.

"If you wish to leave, you may get off at Wyngate," Deudermont offered. "But I cannot guarantee your passage back to Mintarn from there." With that, Deudermont turned and walked to his cabin. He entered without looking back, leaving a frustrated Dunkin standing droop-shouldered by the wheel.

"With your knowledge of Caerwich, you will be a great asset to us," Drizzt said to the man, patting him on the shoulder. "Your presence would be appreciated."

"Ah, come along then," Catti-brie added. "Ye'll find a bit o' adventure and a bit o' friendship. What more could ye be asking for?"

Drizzt and Catti-brie walked away, exchanging hopeful smiles.

"I am new to this, too," Harkle Harpell offered to Dunkin. "But I am sure that it will be fun." Smiling, bobbing his head stupidly, the dimpled wizard bounded away.

Dunkin moved to the rail, shaking his head. He did like the *Sea Sprite,* he had to admit. Orphaned at a young age, Dunkin had taken to sea as a boy and had subsequently spent the bulk of his next twenty years as a hand on pirate vessels, working among the most ruthless scalawags on the Sword Coast. Never had he seen a ship so full of comradery, and their escape from the pirate ambush in Mintarn had been positively thrilling.

He had been nothing but a complaining fool over the last few days, and Deudermont had to know of his past, or at least to suspect that Dunkin had done some pirating in his day. Yet the captain was not treating him as a prisoner, and by the words of the dark elf, they actually wanted him to go along to Caerwich.

Dunkin leaned over the rail, took note of a school of bottle-nosed dolphins dancing in the prow waves and lost himself in thought.

⚔ ⚔ ⚔ ⚔ ⚔

"You're thinking about them again," came a voice behind the sullen dwarf. It was the voice of Regis, the voice of a friend.

Bruenor didn't answer. He stood on a high spot along the rim of the dwarven valley, four miles south of Kelvin's Cairn, a place known as Bruenor's

Climb. This was the dwarf king's place of reflection. Though this column of piled stones was not high above the flat tundra, barely fifty feet up, every time he climbed the steep and narrow trail it seemed to Bruenor as though he was ascending to the very stars.

Regis huffed and puffed as he clambered up the last twenty feet to stand beside his bearded friend. "I do love it up here at night," the halfling remarked. "But there will not be much night in another month!" he continued happily, trying to bring a smile to Bruenor's face. His observation was true enough. Far, far in the north, Icewind Dale's summer days were long indeed, but only a few hours of sun graced the winter sky.

"Not a lot o' time up here," Bruenor agreed. "Time I'm wantin' to spend alone." He turned to Regis as he spoke, and even in the darkness, the halfling could make out the scowling visage.

Regis knew the truth of that expression. Bruenor was more bark than bite.

"You would not be happy up here alone," the halfling countered. "You would think of Drizzt and Catti-brie, and miss them as much as I miss them, and then you would be a veritable growling yeti in the morning. I cannot have that, of course," the halfling said, waggling a finger in the air. "In fact, a dozen dwarves begged me to come out here and keep up your cheer."

Bruenor huffed, but had no reasonable response. He turned away from Regis, mostly because he did not want the halfling to see the hint of a smile turning up the corners of his mouth. In the six years since Drizzt and Catti-brie had gone away, Regis had become Bruenor's closest friend, though a certain dwarven priestess named Stumpet Rakingclaw had been almost continually by Bruenor's side, particularly of late. Giggled whispers spoke of a closer bond growing between the dwarf king and the female.

But it was Regis who knew Bruenor best, Regis who had come out here when, Bruenor had to admit, he truly needed the company. Since the return to Icewind Dale, Drizzt and Catti-brie had been on the old dwarf's mind almost continually. The only things that had saved Bruenor from falling into a deep depression had been the sheer volume of work in trying to reopen the dwarven mines, and Regis, always there, always smiling, always assuring Bruenor that Drizzt and Catti-brie would return to him.

"Where do you think they are?" Regis asked after a long moment of silence.

Bruenor smiled and shrugged, looking to the south and west, and not at the halfling. "Out there," was all that he replied.

"Out there," Regis echoed. "Drizzt and Catti-brie. And you miss them, as do I." The halfling moved closer, put a hand on Bruenor's muscled shoulder.

"And I know that you miss the cat," Regis said, once again drawing the dwarf from dark thoughts.

Bruenor looked at him and couldn't help but grin. The mention of Guenhwyvar reminded Bruenor not only of all the conflict between himself and the panther, but also that Drizzt and Catti-brie, his two dear friends, were not alone and were more than able to take care of themselves.

The dwarf and halfling stood for a long time that night, in silence, listening to the endless wind that gave the dale its name and feeling as though they were among the stars.

⚔ ⚔ ⚔ ⚔ ⚔

The gathering of supplies went well at Wyngate and the *Sea Sprite,* fully provisioned and fully repaired, put out and soon left the Moonshaes far behind.

The winds diminished greatly, though, just a day off the western coast of the Moonshaes. They were out in the open ocean with no land in sight.

The schooner could not be completely calmed, not with Robillard aboard. But still, the wizard's powers were limited. He could not keep the sails full of wind for very long, and settled for a continual fluttering that moved the ship along slowly.

Thus the days passed, uneventful and hot, the *Sea Sprite* rolling in the ocean swells, creaking, and swaying. Deudermont ordered strict rationing three days out of Wyngate, as much to slow the rising incidents of seasickness as to preserve the food stores. At least the crew wasn't worried about pirates. Few other ships came out this far, certainly no cargo or merchant vessels, nothing lucrative enough to keep a pirate happy.

The only enemies were the seasickness, the sunburn, and the boredom of days and days of nothing but the flat water.

They found some excitement on the fifth day out. Drizzt, on the forward beam, spotted a tail fin, the dorsal fin of a huge shark, running parallel to the schooner. The drow yelled up to Waillan, who was in the crow's nest at the time.

"Twenty footer!" the young man called back down, for from his high vantage point, he could make out the shadow of the great fish.

All of the crew came on deck, yelling excitedly, taking up harpoons. Any thoughts they might have had of spearing the fish dissolved into understandable fear, though, as Waillan continued to call down numbers, as they all came to realize that the shark was not alone. The counts varied—many of the dorsal fins were hard to spot amidst the suddenly churning water—but Waillan's estimate, undoubtedly the most accurate, put the school at several hundred.

Several hundred! And many of them were nearly as large as the one Drizzt had spotted. Words of excitement were fast replaced by prayers.

The shark school stayed with the *Sea Sprite* throughout the day and night. Deudermont figured that the sharks did not know what to make of the vessel, and though no one spoke the words, all were thinking along the same lines, hoping that the voracious fish didn't mistake the *Sea Sprite* for a running whale.

The next morning, the sharks were gone, as suddenly and inexplicably as they had come. Drizzt spent the better part of the morning walking the rails of the ship, even climbing up the mainmast to the crow's nest a few times. The sharks were gone, just gone.

"They're not answering to us," Catti-brie remarked late that morning, meeting Drizzt as he came down the mast from one of his skyward jaunts. "Never that. Suren they're moving in ways they know, but we cannot."

It struck Drizzt as a simple truth, a plain reminder of how unknown the world about him really was, even to those, like Deudermont, who had spent the bulk of their lives on the sea. This watery world, and the great creatures that inhabited it, moved to rhythms that he could never truly understand. That realization, along with the fact that the horizon from every angle was nothing but flat water, reminded Drizzt of how small they really were, of how overwhelming nature could be.

For all his training, for all his fine weapons, for all his warrior heart, the ranger was a tiny thing, a mere speck on a blue-green tapestry.

Drizzt found that notion unsettling and comforting all at once. He was a small thing, an insignificant thing, a single swallow to the fish that had easily paced the *Sea Sprite*. And yet, he was a part of something much bigger, a single tile on a mosaic much huger than his imagination could even comprehend.

He draped an arm comfortably across Catti-brie's shoulder, connected himself to the tile that complimented his own, and she leaned against him.

✕ ✕ ✕ ✕ ✕

The winds picked up the next day, and the schooner rushed on, to the applause of every crewman. Robillard's mirth disappeared soon after, though. The wizard had spells to tell of impending weather, and he informed Deudermont that the new winds were the forerunners of a substantial storm.

What could they do? There were no ports nearby, no land at all, and so Deudermont ordered everything battened down as much as was possible.

What followed was among the worst nights of Catti-brie's life. It was as bad as any storm anyone aboard the schooner had ever suffered. Deudermont and the forty crewmen huddled belowdecks as the *Sea Sprite* rode out the storm, the long and slender ship tossing about wildly, nearly going over more than once.

Robillard and Harkle worked frantically. Robillard was on the deck for most of the storm, sometimes having to take cover below and view the deck through a magical, disembodied eye. All the while, he enacted spells to try and counter the fierce winds. Harkle, with Guenhwyvar and a handful of crewmen beside him, scrambled about on all fours in the lowest hold, dodging rats and shifting crates of foodstuff as they inspected the hull. The Harpell had a spell to keep the area well lit, and others that could enlarge wood to seal cracks. The crewmen carried tarred lengths of rope that they hammered in between any leaking boards.

Catti-brie was too sick to move—so were many others. The tossing got so bad at one point that many of the crew had to tie themselves down to stop from bouncing off the walls or crushing each other. Poor Dunkin got the worst of it. In one particularly bad roll, the small man, reaching at the time for an offered length of rope, went flying head over heels and slammed into a beam so violently that he dislocated a shoulder and broke his wrist.

There was no sleep that night aboard the *Sea Sprite*.

The ship was listing badly to port the next morning, but she was still afloat and the storm had passed without a single loss of life. The crew, those who were able, worked through the morning, trying to get up a single sail.

About midday, Catti-brie called down from the crow's nest, reporting that the air was alive with birds to the north and west. Deudermont breathed a deep sigh of relief. He had feared that the storm had blown them off course and that they would not be able to recover in time to put in at the Gull Rocks, the last charted islands on the way to Caerwich. As it was, they were well to the south of their intended course, and had to work frantically, particularly poor Robillard and Harkle. Both of the wizards had bluish bags under their eyes that showed their exhaustion from both the physical and magical strain.

Somehow, the *Sea Sprite* managed to veer enough to get to the rocks. The place was aptly named. The Gull Rocks were no more than a series of barren stones, most smaller than the *Sea Sprite,* many large enough for only two or three men to stand upon. A couple of the rocks were substantial, one nearly a mile across, but even these large ones were more white than gray, thick with guano. As the *Sea Sprite* neared the cluster, thousands and thousands of seagulls, a veritable cloud of them, fluttered in the air all about her, squawking angrily at the intrusion to this, their private domain.

Deudermont found a little inlet where the water was more calm, where repairs could be done in peace, and where each of the crew could take turns off of the ship, to calm their churning stomachs, if nothing else.

Later on that day, at the highest point on the Gull Rocks, perhaps fifty feet above sea level, Deudermont stood with Drizzt and Catti-brie. The Captain was looking south using the spyglass, though he obviously expected to find nothing but flat water.

It had taken them nearly two tendays to cover the five hundred miles from the westernmost spur of the Moonshaes to the Gull Rocks, nearly double the time Deudermont had expected. Still, the captain remained confident that the provisions would hold and they would find their way to Caerwich. Nothing much had been said about the island since the *Sea Sprite* had put out of Wyngate. Nothing openly, at least, for Drizzt had overheard the nervous whispers of many of the crew, talk of ghosts and the like.

"Five hundred behind us and five hundred to go," Deudermont said, the spyglass to his eye and his gaze to the south and west. "There is an island not far south of here where we might gain more provisions."

"Do we need them?" Drizzt asked.

"Not if make good speed to Caerwich, and good speed on the return," Deudermont replied.

"What're ye thinking then?" Catti-brie asked.

"I grow weary of delays, and weary of the journey," Deudermont replied.

"That's because yer fearin' what's at its end," Catti-brie reasoned bluntly. "Who's for knowin' what we'll find in Caerwich, if even there is a Caerwich?"

"She's out there," the captain insisted.

"We can always stop at this other island on our return," Drizzt offered. "Certainly we've enough provisions to get to Caerwich."

Deudermont nodded. They would make straight for Caerwich then, the last leg of their journey out. The captain knew the stars—that was all he would have available to take him from the Gull Rocks to Caerwich. He hoped that the map Tarnheel had provided was accurate.

He hoped that Caerwich truly existed.

And still, a part of him hoped that it did not.

9

CAERWICH

H ow small is this island of Caerwich?" Catti-brie asked Deudermont.
Another tenday of sailing had slipped past, this one uneventfully. Another
tenday of emptiness, of solitude, though the schooner was fully crewed and
there were few places where someone could be out of sight of everyone else.
That was the thing about the open ocean, you were never physically alone,
yet all the world seemed removed. Catti-brie and Drizzt had spent hours
together, just standing and watching, each lost, drifting on the rolls of the
azure blanket, together and yet so alone.

"A few square miles," the captain answered absently, as though the response
was an automatic reflex.

"And ye're thinkin' to find it?" An unmistakable edge showed in the woman's
voice, drawing a lazy stare from Drizzt, as well as from Deudermont.

"We found the Gull Rocks," Drizzt reminded Catti-brie, trying to brighten
her mood though he, too, was getting that unmistakable edge of irritation to
his voice. "They are not much larger."

"Bah, they're known to all," Catti-brie retorted. "A straight run west."

"We know where we are, and where we must go," Deudermont insisted.
"There is the matter of the map. We're not sailing blindly."

Catti-brie glanced over her shoulder and cast a scowl at Dunkin, the
provider of the map, who was hard at work scrubbing the poop deck. The
woman's sour expression alone answered Deudermont's claim, told the captain
how reliable she believed that map might be.

"And the wizards have new eyes that see far," Deudermont said. True
enough, Catti-brie realized, though she wondered how reliable the "eyes" in

question might be. Harkle and Robillard had taken some birds from the Gull Rocks, and claimed that they could communicate with them through use of their magic. The gulls would help, the two wizards declared, and each day, they set them flying freely, ordering them to report back with their findings. Catti-brie hadn't thought much about the wizards and in truth, all but two of the ten birds they had taken had not returned to the *Sea Sprite*. Catti-brie figured the birds had more likely flown all the way back to the Gull Rocks, probably laughing at the bumbling wizards all the way.

"The map is all we have had since we left Mintarn," Drizzt said softly, trying to erase the young woman's fears and the anger that was plain upon her fair, sunburned features. He sympathized with Catti-brie, because he was sharing those negative thoughts. They had all known the odds, and thus far, the journey had not been so bad—certainly not as bad as it might have been. They had been out for several tendays, most of that time on the open ocean, yet they had not lost a single crewman and their stores, though low, remained sufficient. Thank Guenhwyvar and Harkle for that, Drizzt thought with a smile, for the panther and the wizard had cleared the ship of the bulk of her pesky rats soon after they had departed from Wyngate.

But still, despite the logical understanding that the journey was on course and going well, Drizzt could not help the swells of anger that rose up in him. It was something about the ocean, he realized, the boredom and the solitude. Truly the drow loved sailing, loved running the waves, but too long in the open ocean, too long in looking at emptiness as profound as could be found in all the world, grated on his nerves.

Catti-brie walked away, muttering. Drizzt looked to Deudermont, and the experienced captain's smile relieved the drow of a good measure of his worry.

"I have seen it before," Deudermont said quietly to him. "She will relax as soon as we sight Mintarn, or as soon as we make the decision to turn back to the east."

"You would do that?" Drizzt asked. "You would forsake the words of the doppleganger?"

Deudermont thought long and hard on that one. "I have come here because I believe it to be my fate," he answered. "Whatever the danger that is now pursuing me, I wish to meet it head-on and with my eyes wide open. But I'll not risk my crew more than is necessary. If our food stores become too diminished to safely continue, we will turn back."

"And what of the doppleganger?" Drizzt asked.

"My enemies found me once," Deudermont replied casually, and truly the

man was a rock for Drizzt and for all the crew, something solid to hold onto in a sea of emptiness. "They will find me again."

"And we will be waiting," Drizzt assured him.

✕ ✕ ✕ ✕ ✕

As it turned out, the wait, for Caerwich at least, was not a long one. Less than an hour after the conversation, Harkle Harpell bounded out of Deudermont's private quarters, clapping his hands excitedly.

Deudermont was the first to him, followed closely by a dozen anxious crewmen. Drizzt, at his customary spot on the forward beam, came to the rail of the flying bridge to survey the gathering. He realized what was going on immediately, and he glanced upward, to Catti-brie, who was peering down intently from the crow's nest.

"Oh, what a fine bird, my Reggie is!" Harkle beamed.

"Reggie?" Deudermont, and several others nearby, asked.

"Namesake of Regweld, so fine a wizard! He bred a frog with a horse— no easy feat that! Puddlejumper, he called her. Or was it Riverjumper? Or maybe . . ."

"Harkle," Deudermont said dryly, his tone bringing the wizard from the rambling confusion.

"Oh, of course," babbled Harkle. "Yes, yes, where was I? Oh, yes, I was telling you about Regweld. What a fine man. Fine man. He fought valiantly in Keeper's Dale, so say the tales. There was one time . . ."

"Harkle!" Now there was no subtle coercion in Deudermont's tone, just open hostility.

"What?" the wizard asked innocently.

"The damned seagull," Deudermont growled. "What have you found?"

"Oh, yes!" Harkle replied, clapping his hands. "The bird, the bird. Reggie. Yes, yes, fine bird. Fastest flyer of the lot."

"Harkle!" a score of voices roared in unison.

"We have found an island," came a reply from behind the flustered Harpell. Robillard stepped onto the deck and appeared somewhat bored. "The bird returned this day chattering about an island. Ahead and to port, and not so far away."

"How large?" Deudermont asked.

Robillard shrugged and chuckled. "All islands are large when seen through the eyes of a seagull," he answered. "It could be a rock, or it could be a continent."

"Or even a whale," Harkle piped in.

It didn't matter. If the bird had indeed spotted an island out here, out where the map indicated that Caerwich should be, then Caerwich, it must be!

"You and Dunkin," Deudermont said to Robillard, and he motioned to the wheel. "Get us there."

"And Reggie," Harkle added happily, pointing to the seagull, which had perched on the very tip of the mainmast, right above Catti-brie's head.

Drizzt saw a potential problem brewing, given the bird's position, the woman's sour mood and the fact that she had her bow with her. Fortunately, though, the bird flew off at Harkle's bidding without leaving any presents behind.

Had it not been for that bird, the *Sea Sprite* would have sailed right past Caerwich, within a half mile of the place without ever sighting it. The island was circular, resembling a low cone, and was just a few hundred yards in diameter. It was perpetually shrouded in a bluish mist that looked like just another swell in the sea from only a short distance away.

As the schooner approached that mist, drifting quietly at half sail, the wind turned colder and the sun seemed somehow less substantial. Deudermont did a complete circle of the island, but found no particularly remarkable place, nor any area that promised an easy docking.

Back in their original spot, Deudermont took the wheel from Dunkin and turned the *Sea Sprite* straight toward Caerwich, slowly slipping her into the mist.

"Ghost wind," Dunkin remarked nervously, shuddering in the sudden chill. "She's a haunted place, I tell you." The small man tugged at his ear ferociously, suddenly wishing that he had gotten off the schooner at Wyngate. Dunkin's other ear got tugged as well, but not by his own hand. He turned about to look eye to eye with Drizzt Do'Urden. They were about the same height, with similar builds, though Drizzt's muscles were much more finely honed. But at that moment, Drizzt seemed much taller to poor Dunkin, and much more imposing.

"Ghost wi—" Dunkin started to say, but Drizzt put a finger to his lips to silence him.

Dunkin leaned heavily on the rail and went silent.

Deudermont ordered the sails lower still and brought the schooner to a creeping drift. The mist grew thick about them and something about the way the ship was handling, something about the flow of the water beneath them, told the captain to be wary. He called up to Catti-brie, but she had no answers for him, more engulfed by blinding mist than he.

Deudermont nodded to Drizzt, who rushed off to the forward beam and crouched low, marking their way. The drow spotted something a moment later, and his eyes widened.

A pole was sticking out of the water, barely fifty yards ahead of them.

Drizzt eyed it curiously for just an instant, then recognized it for what it was: the top of a ship's mast.

"Stop us!" he yelled.

Robillard was into his spellcasting before Deudermont agreed to heed the warning. The wizard sent his energy out directly in front of the *Sea Sprite,* brought up a ridgelike swell of water that halted the ship's drifting momentum. Down came the *Sea Sprite's* sails, and down dropped the anchor with a splash that seemed to echo ominously about the decks for many seconds.

"How deep?" Deudermont asked the crewmen manning the anchor. The chain was marked in intervals, allowing them to gauge the depth when they put the anchor down.

"A hundred feet," one of them called back a moment later.

Drizzt rejoined the captain at the wheel. "A reef, by my guess," the drow said, explaining his call for a stop. "There is a hulk in the water barely two ship-lengths ahead of us. She's fully under, except for the tip of her mast, but standing straight. Something brought her down in a hurry."

"Got her bottom torn right off," Robillard reasoned.

"I figure us to be a few hundred yards from the beach," Deudermont said, peering hard into the mist. He looked to the stern. The *Sea Sprite* carried two small rowboats, one hanging on either side of the poop deck.

"We could circle again," Robillard remarked, seeing where the captain's reasoning was leading. "Perhaps we will find a spot with a good draw."

"I'll not risk my ship," Deudermont replied. "We will go in using the rowboat," he decided. He looked to a group of nearby crewmen. "Drop one," he instructed.

Twenty minutes later, Deudermont, Drizzt, Catti-brie, the two wizards, Waillan Micanty, and a very reluctant and very frightened Dunkin glided away from the *Sea Sprite,* filling their rowboat so completely that its rim was barely a hand above the dark water. Deudermont had left specific instructions with those remaining on the *Sea Sprite.* The crew was to put back out of the mist a thousand yards and wait for their return. If they had not returned by nightfall, the *Sea Sprite* was to move out away from the island, making one final run at Caerwich at noon the next day.

After that, if the rowboat had not been spotted, she was to sail home.

The seven moved away from the *Sea Sprite,* Dunkin and Waillan on the oars and Catti-brie peering over the prow, expecting to find a reef at any moment. Farther back, Drizzt knelt beside Deudermont, ready to point out the mast he had spotted.

Drizzt couldn't find it.

"No reef," Catti-brie said from the front. "A good and deep draw, by me own guess." She looked back to Drizzt and especially to Deudermont. "Ye might've bringed her in right up to the damned beach," she said.

Deudermont looked to the drow, who was scanning the mist hard, wondering where that mast had gone to. He was about to restate what he had seen when the rowboat lurched suddenly, her bottom scraping on the rocks of a sharp reef.

They bumped and ground to a halt. They might have gotten hung up there, but a spell from Robillard brought both wizards, Deudermont, and Catti-brie floating above the creaking planks of the boat, while Drizzt, Dunkin, and Waillan cautiously brought the lightened boat over.

"All the way in?" Drizzt remarked to Catti-brie.

"It wasn't there!" the young woman insisted. Catti-brie had been a lookout for more than five years, and was said to have the best eyes on the Sword Coast. So how, she wondered, had she missed so obvious a reef, especially when she was looking for exactly that?

A few moments later, Harkle, at the very stern of the rowboat, gave a startled cry and the others turned to see the mast of a ship sticking out of the water right beside the seated wizard.

Now the others, especially Drizzt, were having the same doubts as Catti-brie. They had practically run over that mast, so why hadn't they seen it?

Dunkin tugged furiously at his ear.

"A trick of the fog," Deudermont said calmly. "Bring us around that mast." The command caught the others off guard. Dunkin shook his head, but Waillan slapped him on the shoulder.

"Hard on the oar," Waillan ordered. "You heard the captain."

Catti-brie hung low over the side of the rowboat, curious to learn more about the wreck, but the mist reflected in the water, leaving her staring into a gray veil whose secrets she could not penetrate. Finally, Deudermont gave up on gathering any information out here, and commanded Waillan and Dunkin to put straight in for the island.

At first, Dunkin nodded eagerly, happy to get off the water. Then, as he considered their destination, he alternated pulls on the oar with pulls on his ear.

The surf was not strong, but the undertow was and it pulled back against

the rowboat's meager progress. The island was soon in sight, but it seemed to hang out there, just beyond their grasp, for many moments.

"Pull hard!" Deudermont ordered his rowers, though he knew that they were doing exactly that, were as anxious as he to get this over with. Finally, the captain looked plaintively to Robillard, and the wizard, after a resigned sigh, stuck his hand into his deep pockets, seeking the components for a helpful spell.

Still up front, Catti-brie peered hard through the mist, studying the white beach for some sign of inhabitants. It was no good. The island was too far away, given the thick fog. The young woman looked down instead, into the dark water.

She saw candles.

Catti-brie's face twisted in confusion. She looked up and rubbed her eyes, then looked back to the water.

Candles. There could be no mistake about it. Candles . . . *under the water.*

Curious, the woman bent lower and looked more closely, finally making out a form holding the closest light.

Catti-brie fell back, gasping. "The dead," she said, though she couldn't get more than a whisper out of her mouth. Her sharp movements alone had caught the attention of the others, and then she hopped right to her feet, as a bloated and blackened hand grabbed the rim of the rowboat.

Dunkin, looking only at Catti-brie, screamed as she drew out her sword. Drizzt got to his feet and scrambled to get by the two oarsmen.

Catti-brie saw the top of the ghost's head come clear of the water. A horrid, skeletal face rose to the side of the boat.

Khazid'hea came down hard, hitting nothing but the edge of the boat and driving right through the planking until it was at water level.

"What are you doing?" Dunkin cried. Drizzt, at Catti-brie's side, wondered the same thing. There was no sign of any ghost, there was just Catti-brie's sword wedged deeply into the planking of the rowboat.

"Get us in!" Catti-brie yelled back. "Get us in!"

Drizzt looked at her hard, then looked all around. "Candles?" he asked, noticing the strange watery lights.

That simple word sparked fear in Deudermont, Robillard, Waillan, and Dunkin, sailors all, who knew the tales of sea ghosts, lying in wait under the waves, their bloated bodies marked by witchlight candles.

"How pretty!" said an oblivious Harkle, looking overboard.

"Get us to the beach!" Deudermont cried, but he needn't have bothered, for

Waillan and Dunkin were pulling with all of their strength.

Robillard was deep into spellcasting. He summoned a wave right behind the small craft and the rowboat was lifted up and sent speeding toward shore. The jolt of the sudden wave knocked Catti-brie to the deck and nearly sent Drizzt right over.

Harkle, entranced by the candles, wasn't so fortunate. As the wave crested, coming right over the tide line, he tumbled out.

The rowboat shot ahead, sliding hard onto the beach.

In the surf, ten yards offshore, a drenched Harkle stood up.

A dozen grotesque and bloated forms stood up around him.

"Oh, hello . . ." the friendly Harpell started, and then his eyes bulged and nearly rolled from their sockets.

"Eeyah!" Harkle screamed, plowing through the undertow and toward the shore.

Catti-brie was already up and in position, lifting Taulmaril and fitting an arrow. She took quick aim and let fly.

Harkle screamed again as the arrow streaked right past him. Then he heard the sickening thump and splash as an animated corpse hit the water, and understood that he was not the woman's target.

Another arrow followed closely, taking out the next nearest zombie. Harkle, as he came to more shallow water, tore himself free of grabbing weeds and quickly outdistanced the other monsters. He had just cleared the water, putting a few feet of moist sand behind him, when he heard the roar of flames and glanced back to see a curtain of fire separating him from the water, and from the zombies.

He ran the rest of the way up the beach to join the other six by the rowboat and expressed his thanks to Robillard, shaking the wizard so hard that he broke the man's concentration.

The curtain of blocking fire fell away. Where there had been ten zombies, there were now a score, and more were rising from the water and the weeds.

"Well done," Robillard said dryly.

Catti-brie fired again, blasting away another zombie.

Robillard waggled the fingers of one hand and a bolt of green energy erupted from each of them, soaring down the beach. Three hit one zombie in rapid succession, dropping it to the water. Two sped past, burning into the next monster in line and likewise sending it down.

"Not very creative," Harkle remarked.

Robillard scowled at him. "You can do better?"

Harkle snapped his fingers indignantly, and so the challenge was on.

Drizzt and the others stood back, weapons ready, but knowing better than to charge down at their foes in the face of wizardly magic. Even Catti-brie, after a couple of more shots, lowered her bow, giving the competing spell-casters center stage.

"A Calimshan snake charmer taught me this one," Harkle proclaimed. He tossed a bit of twine into the air and chanted in a cracking, high-pitched voice. A line of seaweed came alive to his call, rose up like a serpent and immediately wrapped itself about the nearest zombie, yanking the thing down under the surf.

Harkle smiled broadly.

Robillard snorted derisively. "Only one?" he asked, and he launched himself into the throes of another spell, spinning, dancing, and tossing flakes of metal into the air. Then he stopped and pivoted powerfully, hurling one hand out toward the shore. Shards of shining, burning metal flew out, gained a momentum all their own, and sent a barrage into the zombies' midst. Several were hit, the ignited metals clinging to them stubbornly, searing through the weeds and the remnants of clothing, through rotted skin and bone alike.

A moment later, a handful of the gruesome zombies tumbled down.

"Oh, simple evocation," Harkle chided and he answered Robillard's spell by pulling out a small metal rod and pointing it toward the water.

Seconds later, a lightning bolt blasted forth. Harkle aimed it at the water and the bolt blasted in, spreading wide in a circular pattern, engulfing many monsters.

How weird, even funny, that sight appeared! Zombie hair popped up straight and the stiff-moving things began a strange, hopping dance, turning complete circles, rolling this way and that before spinning down under the waves.

When it was over, the zombie ranks had been cut in half, though more were rising stubbornly all along the beach.

Harkle smiled widely and snapped his fingers again. "Simple evocation," he remarked.

"Indeed," muttered Robillard.

Catti-brie had eased her bowstring by this point, and was smiling, sincerely amused, as she regarded her companions. Even Dunkin, so terrified a moment before, seemed ready to laugh aloud at the spectacle of the battling wizards. In looking at the pair, Deudermont was glad, for he feared that the sight of such horrid enemies had defeated his team's heart for this search.

It was Robillard's turn and he focused on a single zombie that had cleared the water and was ambling up the beach. He used no material components this time, just chanted softly and waved his arms in specific movements. A line of fire rushed out from his pointing finger, reaching out to the unfortunate target monster and then shrouding it in flames, an impressive display that fully consumed the creature in but a few moments. Robillard, concentrating deeply, then shifted the line of fire, burning away a second monster.

"The scorcher," he said when the spell was done. "A remnant from the works of Agannazar."

Harkle snorted. "Agannazar was a minor trickster!" he declared, and Robillard scowled.

Harkle reached into a pocket, pulling forth several components. "Dart," he explained, lifting the item. "Powdered rhubarb and the stomach of an adder."

"Melf!" Robillard cried happily.

"Melf indeed!" echoed Harpell. "Now there was a wizard!"

"I know Melf," said Robillard.

Harkle stuttered and stopped his casting. "How old are you?" he asked.

"I know Melf's work," Robillard clarified.

"Oh," said Harkle and he went back to casting.

To prove his point, Robillard reached into his own pocket and produced a handful of beads that smelled of pine tar. Harkle caught the aroma, but paid it little heed as he was in the throes of the final runes of his own spell by then.

The dart zipped out from Harkle's hand, rocketing into the belly of the closest zombie. Immediately it began to pump forth acid, boring an ever-widening hole right through the creature. The zombie grasped futilely at the wound, even bent low as if it meant to peer right through itself.

Then it fell over.

"Melf!" Harkle proclaimed, but he quieted when he looked back to Robillard and saw tiny meteors erupting from the wizard's hand, shooting out to blast mini-fireballs among the zombie ranks.

"Better Melf," Harkle admitted.

"Enough of this foolishness," Captain Deudermont put in. "We can simply run up off the beach. I doubt they will pursue." Deudermont's voice trailed away as he realized that neither wizard was paying him much heed.

"We are not on the ship," was all that indignant Robillard would reply. Then to Harkle, he said, "Do you admit defeat?"

"I have not yet begun to boom!" declared the obstinate Harpell.

Both launched themselves into spells, among the most powerful of their considerable repertoires. Robillard pulled out a tiny bucket and shovel, while Harkle produced a snakeskin glove and a long, painted fingernail.

Robillard cast first, his spell causing a sudden and violent excavation right at the feet of the closest zombies. Beach sand flew wildly. The monsters walked right into the pit, falling from sight. Robillard shifted his angle and muttered a single word, and another pit began, not far to the side of the first.

"Dig," he muttered to Harkle, between chants.

"Bigby," Harkle countered. "You know of Bigby?"

Robillard blanched despite his own impressive display. Of course he knew of Bigby! He was one of the most powerful and impressive wizards of all time, on any world.

Harkle's spell began as a gigantic disembodied hand. It was transparent and hovered over the beach, in the area near Robillard's first pit. Robillard looked hard at the hand. Three of the fingers were extended, pointing toward the hole, but the middle finger was curled back and under the thumb.

"I have *improved* on Bigby," Harkle boasted. A zombie ambled between the gigantic hand and the hole.

"Doink!" commanded the Harpell and the hand's middle finger popped out from underneath the thumb, slamming the zombie on the side of the head and launching it sideways into the pit.

Harkle turned a smug smile at Robillard. "Bigby's Snapping Digits," he explained. He focused his thoughts on the hand again, and it moved to his will, gliding all along the beach and "doinking" zombies whenever they came within range.

Robillard didn't know whether to roar in protest or howl in laughter. The Harpell was good, he had to admit, very good. But Robillard wasn't about to lose this one. He took out a diamond, a gem that had cost him more than a thousand gold pieces. "Otiluke," he said defiantly, referring to yet another of the legendary and powerful wizards whose works were the staples of a magician's studies. Now it was Harkle's turn to blanch, for he had little knowledge of the legendary Otiluke.

When Robillard considered that diamond, and the quickly diminishing ranks of their monstrous adversaries, he had to wonder if it was really worth the price. He snapped his fingers with a revelation, popped the diamond back into his pocket and took out a thin sheet of crystal instead.

"Otiluke," he said again, choosing another variation of the same spell. He cast the spell and immediately, all along the beach, the surf simply froze, locking fast in the thick ice those zombies who had not yet come out of the water.

"Oh, well done," Harkle admitted as Robillard slapped his hands together in a superior motion, wiping himself clean of the zombies and of Harkle. The spells had cleared the beach of enemies, and so the fight was apparently over.

But Harkle couldn't let Robillard have the last word, not that way. He looked to the zombies struggling in the ice, and then glowered at Robillard. Deliberately, he reached into his deepest pocket and pulled forth a ceramic flask. "Super heroism," he explained. "You have perhaps heard of Tenser?"

Robillard put a finger to pursed lips. "Oh, yes," he said a moment later. "Of course, crazy Tenser." Robillard's eyes went wide as he considered the implications. Tenser's most renowned spell reportedly transformed a wizard into a warrior for a short duration—a berserk warrior!

"Not the Tenser!" Robillard yelled, tackling Harkle where he stood, pinning the man down before he could pop the cork off the potion flask.

"Help me!" Robillard begged, and the others were there in a moment. The battle, and the contest, was at its end.

They pulled themselves together and Deudermont announced that it was time to get off the beach.

Drizzt motioned to Catti-brie and immediately moved out front, more than ready to be on the move. The woman didn't immediately follow. She was too intent on the continuing, now-friendly, exchange between the wizards. Mostly, she was watching Robillard, who seemed much more animated and happy. She thought perhaps Harkle Harpell was indeed having a positive effect on the man.

"Oh, that digging spell worked so very well with my Bigby variation," she heard Harkle say. "You really must teach it to me. My cousin, Bidderdoo, he is a werewolf, and he has this habit of burying everything about the yard—bones, wands, and the like. The dig spell will help me to recover . . ."

Catti-brie shook her head and rushed to catch up with Drizzt. She skidded to an abrupt stop, though, and looked back to the rowboat. More particularly, she looked back to Dunkin Tallmast, who was seated in the beached craft, shaking his head back and forth. Catti-brie motioned to the others and they all went back to the man.

"I wish to go back to the boat," Dunkin said sternly. "One of the wizards can get me there." As he spoke, the man was clutching the rail so tightly that the knuckles on both his hands had whitened for lack of blood.

"Come along," Drizzt said to him.

Dunkin didn't move.

"You have been given a chance to witness what few men have ever seen," the ranger said. As he spoke, Drizzt took out the panther figurine and dropped it on the sand.

"You know more about Caerwich than any other aboard the *Sea Sprite,*"

Deudermont added. "Your knowledge is needed."

"I know little," Dunkin retorted.

"But still more than any other," Deudermont insisted.

"There is a reward for your assistance," Drizzt went on, and Dunkin's eyes brightened for an instant—until the drow explained what he meant by the word "reward."

"Who knows what adventure we might find here?" Drizzt said excitedly. "Who knows what secrets might be unveiled to us?"

"Adventure?" Dunkin asked incredulously, looking to the carnage along the beach, and to the zombies still frozen in the water. "Reward?" he added with a chuckle. "Punishment, more likely, though I have done nothing to harm you, any of you!"

"We are here to unveil a mystery," Drizzt said, as though that fact should have piqued the man's curiosity. "To learn and to grow. To live as we discover the secrets of the world about us."

"Who wants to know?" Dunkin snapped, deflating the drow and dismissing his grandiose speech. Waillan Micanty, inspired by the drow's words, had heard enough of the whining little man. The young sailor moved to the side of the beached rowboat, tore Dunkin's hands free of the rail and dragged the man onto the sand.

"I could have done that with much more flair," Robillard remarked dryly.

"So could Tenser," said Harkle.

"*Not* the Tenser," Robillard insisted.

"Not the Tenser?"

"Not the Tenser," Robillard reiterated, in even tones of finality. Harkle whimpered a bit, but did not respond.

"Save your magic," Waillan said to both of them. "We may need it yet."

Now it was Dunkin's turn to whine.

"When this is over, you will have a tale to widen the eyes of every sailor who puts in at Mintarn Harbor," Drizzt said to the small man.

That seemed to calm Dunkin somewhat, until Catti-brie added, "If ye live."

Drizzt and Deudermont both scowled at her, but the woman merely grinned innocently and walked away.

"I will tell his tyrancy," Dunkin threatened, but no one was listening to him anymore.

Drizzt called to Guenhwyvar and when the panther came onto the beach, the seven adventurers gathered around Deudermont. The captain drew a rough outline of the island in the sand. He put an *X* on the area indicating their beach, then another one outside his drawing, to show the location of the *Sea Sprite.*

"Ideas?" he asked, looking particularly at Dunkin.

"I've heard people speak of 'the Witch of the Moaning Cave,' " the small man offered sheepishly.

"There might be caves along the coast," Catti-brie reasoned. "Or up here." She put her finger down onto Deudermont's rough drawing, indicating the one mountain, the low cone that comprised the bulk of Caerwich.

"We should search inland before we put back out into the sea," Deudermont reasoned, and none of them had to follow his gaze to the frozen zombies to be reminded of the dangers along the shore of Caerwich. And so off they trudged, inland, through a surprisingly thick tangle of brush and huge ferns.

Almost as soon as they had left the openness of the beach behind, sounds erupted all about them—the hoots and whistles of exotic birds, and throaty howling calls that none of them had heard before. Drizzt and Guenhwyvar took up the point and flanks, moving off to disappear into the tangle without a sound.

Dunkin groaned at this, not liking the fact that his immediate group had just become smaller. Catti-brie chuckled at him, drawing a scowl. If only Dunkin knew how much safer they were with the drow and his cat moving beside them.

They searched for more than an hour, then took a break in a small clearing halfway up the low conical mountain. Drizzt sent Guenhwyvar off alone, figuring that the cat could cover more ground in the span of their short break than they would search out the rest of the day.

"We will come down the back side of the cone, then move southward, all the way around and back to the boat," Deudermont explained. "Then back up and over the cone, and then to the north."

"We may have walked right past the cave without ever seeing it," Robillard grumbled. It was true enough, they all knew, for the tangle was so very thick and dark, and the mist had not diminished in the least.

"Well, perhaps our two wizards could be of use," Deudermont said sarcastically, "if they hadn't been so absorbed in wasting their spells to prove a point."

"There were enemies to strike down," Harkle protested.

"I could've cut 'em down with me bow," said Catti-brie.

"And wasted arrows!" Harkle retorted, thinking he had her in a logic trap.

Of course, the others all knew, Catti-brie's quiver was powerfully enchanted.

"I don't run out of arrows," she remarked, and Harkle sat back down.

Drizzt interrupted then, abruptly, by hopping to his feet and staring hard into the jungle. His hand went to the pouch that held the onyx figurine.

Catti-brie jumped to her feet, taking up Taulmaril, and the others followed suit.

"Guenhwyvar?" the woman asked.

Drizzt nodded. Something had happened to the panther, but he wasn't sure of what that might be. On a hunch, he took out the figurine, placed it on the ground, and called to the panther once more. A moment later, the gray mist appeared, and then took form, Guenhwyvar pacing nervously about the drow.

"There's two of them things?" Dunkin asked.

"Same cat," Catti-brie explained. "Something sent Guen home."

Drizzt nodded and looked to Deudermont. "Something that Guenhwyvar could find again," he reasoned.

Off they went, through the tangle, following Guenhwyvar's lead. Soon they came to the northern slopes of the cone, and behind a curtain of thick hanging moss, they found a dark opening. Drizzt motioned to Guenhwyvar, but the panther would not go in.

Drizzt eyed her curiously.

"I'm going back to the boat," Dunkin remarked. He took a step away, but Robillard, tired of the man's foolishness, drew out a wand and pointed it right between Dunkin's eyes. The wizard said not a word, he didn't have to.

Dunkin turned back to the cave.

Drizzt crouched near to the panther. Guenhwyvar would not enter the cave, and the drow had no idea of why that might be. He knew that Guenhwyvar was not afraid. Might there be an enchantment on the area that prevented the panther from entering?

Satisfied with that explanation, Drizzt drew out Twinkle, the fine scimitar glowing its customary blue, and motioned for his friends to wait. He slipped past the mossy curtain, waited a moment so that his eyes could adjust to the deeper gloom, then moved in.

Twinkle's light went away. Drizzt ducked to the side, behind the protection of a boulder. He realized that he was not moving as quickly as expected, his enchanted anklets were not aiding him.

"No magic," he reasoned, and then it seemed perfectly clear to him why Guenhwyvar would not enter. The drow turned to go back out, but found his impatient friends already slipping in behind him. Both Harkle and Robillard wore curious expressions. Catti-brie squinted into the gloom, one hand fiddling with the suddenly useless cat's eye pendant strapped to her forehead.

"I have forgotten all of my spells," Harkle said loudly, his voice echoing off the bare wall of the large cave. Robillard slapped his hand over Harkle's mouth.

"Sssssh!" the calmer wizard hissed. When he thought about what Harkle had said, though, Robillard had his own outburst. "As have I!" he roared, and then he slapped his hand over his own mouth.

"No magic in here," Drizzt told them. "That is why Guenhwyvar could not enter."

"Might be that is what sent the cat home," Catti-brie added.

The discussion ended abruptly, and all heads swung about to regard Waillan as the light of a makeshift torch flared brightly.

"I'll not walk in blindly," the young sailor explained, holding high the burning branches he had strapped together.

None of them could argue. Just the few feet they had gone past the cave's entrance had stolen most of the light, and their senses hinted to them that this was no small place. The cave felt deep, and cool. It seemed as if the sticky humidity of the island air had been left behind outside.

As they moved in a bit farther, the torchlight showed them that their senses were telling the truth. The cave was large and roughly oval in shape, perhaps a hundred feet across at its longest point. It was uneven, with several different levels across its broken floor and gigantic stalactites leering down at them.

Drizzt was about to suggest a systematic exploration, when a voice cut the stillness.

"Who would seek my sight?" came a cackle from the rear of the cave, where there appeared to be a rocky tier a dozen feet above the party's present level. All of the group squinted through the gloom. Catti-brie tightened her grip on Taulmaril, wondering how effective the bow might be without its magic.

Dunkin turned back for the door, and out came Robillard's wand, though the wizard's gaze was firmly set ahead, upon the tier of boulders. The small man hesitated, then realized that Robillard had no power against him, not in here.

"Who would seek my sight?" came the cackling question again.

Dunkin bolted out through the moss.

As one, the group looked back to the exit.

"Let him go," Deudermont said. The captain took the torch from Waillan and moved forward slowly, the other five following in his wake. Drizzt, ever cautious, moved to the shadows offered by the side wall of the cave.

The question came a third time, in rehearsed tones as though the witch

was not unaccustomed to visits by sailors. She showed herself to them then, moving out between a tumble of boulders. The hag was old, ancient, wearing a tattered black shift and leaning heavily on a short and polished staff. Her mouth was open—she seemed to be gasping for breath—showing off a single, yellow tooth. Her eyes, appearing dull even from a distance, did not blink.

"Who will bear the burden of knowledge?" she asked. She kept her head turned in the general direction of the five for a short while, then broke into cackling laughter.

Deudermont held his hand up, motioning for the others to halt, then boldly stepped forward. "I will," he announced. "I am Deudermont of the *Sea Sprite,* come to Caerwich . . ."

"Go back!" the hag yelled at him so forcefully that the captain took a step backward before he realized what he was doing. Catti-brie bent her bow a bit more, but kept it low and unthreatening.

"This is not for you, not for any man!" the hag explained. All eyes shifted to regard Catti-brie.

"It is for two, and only two," the hag went on, her croaking voice rhythmic, as though she was reciting a heroic poem. "Not for any man, or any male whose skin browns under the light of the sun."

The obvious reference sent Drizzt's shoulders slumping. He came out of the shadows a moment later, and looked to Catti-brie, who seemed as crestfallen as he in the sudden realization that this was, after all, about Drizzt once more. Deudermont had almost been killed in Waterdeep, and that the *Sea Sprite* and her crew were in peril, a thousand miles from their usual waters, because of his legacy.

Drizzt sheathed his blades and walked over to Catti-brie, and together they moved past the startled captain, and out in front to face the blind witch.

"My greetings, renegade of Daermon N'a'shezbaernon," the blind witch said, referring to Drizzt's ancient family name, a name that few outside of Menzoberranzan would know. "And to you, daughter of a dwarf, who hurled the mightiest of spears!"

That last sentence caught the pair off guard, and confused them for just a moment, until they realized the reference. The witch must be speaking of the stalactite that Catti-brie had dropped, the great "spear" that drove through the dome of House Baenre's chapel! This was about them, about Drizzt's past, and the enemies they thought they had left behind.

The blind hag motioned for them to come closer, and so they did, walking with as much heart as they could muster. They were barely ten feet from the ugly woman when they stopped. They were several feet below her as well, a fact that made her— someone who knew what she should not have known— seem all the more imposing. The crone pulled herself up as high as she could, showing great effort in trying to straighten her bowed shoulders, and aligned her sightless orbs straight with those of Drizzt Do'Urden.

Then she recited, quietly and quickly, the verse Errtu had given her:

> *No path by chance but by plot,*
> *Further steps along the road of his father's ghost.*
> *The traitor to Lolth is sought*
> *By he who hates him most.*
>
> *The fall of a house, the fall of a spear,*
> *Puncture the Spider Queen's pride as a dart.*
> *And now a needle for Drizzt Do'Urden to wear*
> *'Neath the folds of his cloak, so deep in his heart.*
>
> *A challenge, renegade of renegade's seed,*
> *A golden ring thee cannot resist!*
> *Reach, but only when the beast is freed*
> *From festering in the swirl of Abyss.*
>
> *Given to Lolth and by Lolth given*
> *That thee might seek the darkest of trails.*
> *Presented to one who is most unshriven*
> *And held out to thee, for thee shall fail!*
> *So seek, Drizzt Do'Urden, the one who hates thee most.*
> *A friend, and too, a foe, made in thine home that was first.*
> *There thee will find one feared a ghost*
> *Bonded by love and by battle's thirst.*

The blind hag stopped abruptly, her sightless eyes lingering, her entire body perfectly still, as though the recital had taken a great deal of her strength. Then she drifted back between the stones, moving out of sight.

Drizzt hardly noticed her, just stood, shoulders suddenly slumped, strength sapped by the impossible possibility. "Given to Lolth," he muttered helplessly, and only one more word could he speak, "Zaknafein."

10

KIERSTAAD'S HEART

They came out of the cave to find Guenhwyvar sitting calmly atop a pinned Dunkin. Drizzt waved the cat off the man and they departed.

Drizzt was hardly conscious of the journey back across the island to the rowboat. He said nothing all the way, except to dismiss Guenhwyvar back to her astral home as soon as they realized that they would face no resistance on the beach this time. The ice was gone and so were the zombies. The others, respecting the drow's mood, understanding the unnerving information the hag had given him, remained quiet as well.

Drizzt repeated the blind seer's words over and over in his mind, vainly trying to commit them to memory. Every syllable could be a clue, Drizzt realized, every inflection might offer him some hint as to who might be holding his father prisoner. But the words had come too suddenly, too unexpectedly.

His father! Zaknafein! Drizzt could hardly breathe as he thought of the sudden possibility. He remembered their many sparring matches, the years they had spent in joyful and determined practice. He remembered the time when Zaknafein had tried to kill him, and he loved his father even more for that, because Zaknafein had come after him only in the belief that his beloved Drizzt had gone over to the dark ways of the drow.

Drizzt shook the memories from his mind. He had no time for nostalgia when he had to focus on the task so suddenly at hand. As great as was his elation at the thought that Zaknafein might be returned to him, so was his trepidation. Some powerful being, either a matron mother, or perhaps even Lolth herself, held the secret, and the hag's words implicated Catti-brie as well as Drizzt. The ranger cast a sidelong glance at Catti-brie, who was lost in apparently similar contemplations. The hag had intimated that all of this, the attack in Waterdeep and the journey to this remote island, had been arranged by a powerful enemy who sought revenge not only upon Drizzt, but upon Catti-brie.

Drizzt slowed and let the others get a few steps ahead as they dragged the rowboat to the surf. He released Catti-brie from his gaze, and momentarily at least, from his thoughts, going back to privately reciting the hag's verse. The best thing he could do for Catti-brie, and for Zaknafein, was to memorize it, all of it, as exactly as possible. Drizzt understood that consciously, but still, the possibility that Zaknafein might be alive, overwhelmed him, and all the verses seemed fuzzy, a distant dream that the ranger fought hard to recollect. Drizzt was not alert as they splashed back off the beach of Caerwich. His eyes focused only on the swish of the oars under the dark water, and so intent was he that if a horde of zombies had risen up against them from the water, Drizzt would have been the last to draw a weapon.

As it turned out, they got back to the *Sea Sprite* without incident and Deudermont, after a quick check with Drizzt to assure that they were done with their business on the island, wasted no time in putting the ship back out to sea. Deudermont called for full sails the moment they got out of the enveloping fog of Caerwich, and the swift schooner soon put the misty island far, far behind. Only after Caerwich was out of sight did Deudermont call Drizzt, Catti-brie, and the two wizards into his private quarters for a discussion of what had just transpired.

"You knew what the old witch was speaking about?" the captain asked Drizzt.

"Zaknafein," the drow replied without hesitation. He noticed that Catti-brie's expression seemed to cloud over. The woman had been tense all the way back from the cave, almost giddy, but it seemed to Drizzt that she was now merely crestfallen.

"And our course now?" Deudermont asked.

"Home, and only home," Robillard put in. "We have no provisions, and we still have some damage to repair from the storm that battered us before we made the Gull Rocks."

"After that?" the captain wanted to know, looking directly at Drizzt as he asked the question.

Drizzt was warmed by the sentiment, by the fact that Deudermont was deferring to his judgment. When the drow gave no immediate response, the captain went on.

" 'Seek the one who hates you most,' the witch said," Deudermont reasoned. "Who might that be?"

"Entreri," Catti-brie answered. She turned to a surprised Deudermont. "Artemis Entreri, a killer from the southlands."

"The same assassin we once chased all the way to Calimshan?" Deudermont asked.

"Our business with that one never seems to be finished," Catti-brie explained. "He's hating Drizzt more than any—"

"No," Drizzt interrupted, shaking his head, running a hand through his thick white hair. "Not Entreri." The drow understood Artemis Entreri quite well, too well. Indeed Entreri hated him, or had once hated him, but their feud had been more propelled by blind pride, the assassin's need to prove himself the better, than by any tangible reason for enmity. After his stay in Menzoberranzan, Entreri had been cured of that need, at least somewhat. No, this challenge went deeper than the assassin. This had to do with Lolth herself, and involved not only Drizzt, but Catti-brie, and the dropping of the stalactite mount into the Baenre chapel. This pursuit, this proverbial golden ring, was based in pure and utter hatred.

"Who then?" Deudermont asked after a lengthy silence.

Drizzt could not give a definite answer. "A Baenre, most likely," he replied. "I have made many enemies. There are dozens in Menzoberranzan who would go to great lengths to kill me."

"But how do you know it is someone from Menzoberranzan?" Harkle interjected. "Do not take this the wrong way, but you have made many enemies on the surface as well!"

"Entreri," Catti-brie said again.

Drizzt shook his head. "The hag said, 'A foe made in the home that was first,' " Drizzt explained. "An enemy from Menzoberranzan."

Catti-brie wasn't sure that Drizzt had correctly repeated the witch's exact words, but the evidence seemed irrefutable.

"So where to start?" Deudermont, playing the role of moderator and nothing more, asked them all.

"The witch spoke of otherworldly influence," Robillard reasoned. "She mentioned the Abyss."

"Lolth's home," Drizzt added.

Robillard nodded. "So we must get some answers from the Abyss," the wizard reasoned.

"Are we to sail there?" Deudermont scoffed.

The wizard, more knowledgeable in such matters, merely smiled and shook his head. "We must bring a fiend to our world," he explained, "and extract information from it. Not so difficult or unusual a task for those practiced in the art of sorcery."

"As you are?" Deudermont asked him.

Robillard shook his head and looked to Harkle.

"What?" the distracted Harpell said dumbly as soon as he noticed every gaze upon him. The wizard was deep in thought, also trying to reconstruct the blind witch's verse, though from his vantage point in the cave, he hadn't heard every word.

"As you are," Robillard explained, "practiced in matters of sorcery."

"Me?" he squeaked. "Oh, no. Not allowed at the Ivy Mansion, not for twenty years. Too many problems. Too many fiends walking around eating Harpells!"

"Then who will get us the answers?" Catti-brie asked.

"There are wizards in Luskan who practice sorcery," Robillard offered, "as do some priests in Waterdeep. Neither will come cheaply."

"We have the gold," Deudermont said.

"That is the ship's gold," Drizzt put in. "For all crew of the *Sea Sprite*."

Deudermont waved a hand at him as he spoke, the captain shaking his head with every syllable. "Not until Drizzt Do'Urden and Catti-brie came aboard have we enjoyed such a business and such a profit," he told the drow. "You are a part of the *Sea Sprite*, a member of her crew, and all will donate their share as you would donate yours to help another."

Drizzt could find no argument against that offer, but he did note a bit of grumbling when Robillard added, "Indeed."

"Waterdeep or Luskan, then?" Deudermont asked Robillard. "Do I sail north of the Moonshaes, or south?"

"Waterdeep," Harkle unexpectedly answered. "Oh, I would choose the priest," the wizard explained. "A goodly priest. Better with fiends than a wizard because the wizard might have other duties or questions he wishes to ask of the beast. Not good to get a fiend too involved, I say."

Drizzt, Catti-brie, and Deudermont looked at the man curiously, trying to decipher what he was talking about.

"He is right," the *Sea Sprite*'s wizard quickly explained. "A goodly priest will stick to the one task, and we can be sure that such a person will call to a fiend only to better the cause of good, of justice." He looked at Drizzt as he said this, and the drow got the feeling that Robillard was suddenly questioning the wisdom of this search, the wisdom of following the blind witch's words. Questioning the course, and perhaps, Drizzt realized, the motive.

"Freeing Zaknafein from the clutches of Lolth, or of a matron mother would be a just act," Drizzt insisted, a bit of anger seeping into the edges of his voice.

"Then a goodly priest is our best choice," the *Sea Sprite's* wizard replied casually, no apologies forthcoming.

⚔ ⚔ ⚔ ⚔ ⚔

Kierstaad looked into the black, dead eyes of the reindeer lying still, so very still, upon the flat tundra, surrounded by the colorful flowers that rushed to bloom in Icewind Dale's short summer. He had killed the deer cleanly with one throw of his great spear.

Kierstaad was glad of that. He felt little remorse at the sight of the magnificent beast, for the survival of his people depended upon the success of the hunt. Not a bit of this proud animal would be wasted. Still, the young man was glad that the kill, his *first* kill, had been clean. He looked into the eyes of the dead animal and gave thanks to its spirit.

Berkthgar came up behind the young hunter and patted him on the shoulder. Kierstaad, too overwhelmed by the spectacle, by the sudden realization that in the eyes of the tribe he was no more a boy, hardly noticed as the huge man strode past him, a long knife in hand.

Berkthgar crouched beside the animal and shifted its legs out of the way. His cut was clean and perfect, long practiced. Only a moment later, he turned about and stood up, holding his bloody arms out to Kierstaad, holding the animal's heart.

"Eat it and gain the deer's strength and speed," the barbarian leader promised.

Kierstaad took the heart tentatively and brought it near to his lips. This was part of the test, he knew, though he had no idea that this would be expected of him. The gravity in Berkthgar's voice was unmistakable, he could not fail. No more a boy, he told himself. Something savage welled in him at the smell of the blood, at the thought of what he must do.

"The heart holds the spirit of the deer," another man explained. "Eat of that spirit."

Kierstaad hesitated no longer. He brought the blackish-red heart to his lips and bit deeply. He was hardly conscious of his next actions, of devouring the heart, of bathing in the spirit of the slain deer. Chants rose around him, the hunters of Berkthgar's party welcoming him to manhood.

No more a boy.

Nothing more was expected of Kierstaad. He stood impassively to the side while the older hunters cleaned and dressed the reindeer. This was indeed the better way for he and his people, living free of the bonds of wealth and the ties to others. In that, at least, Kierstaad knew that Berkthgar was right. Yet, the young man continued to bear no ill will toward the dwarves or the folk of Ten-Towns, and had no intention of allowing any lies to diminish his respect for Wulfgar, who had done so much good for the tribes of Icewind Dale.

Kierstaad looked to the harvesting of the reindeer, so complete and perfect. No waste and no disrespect for the proud animal. He looked to his own bloody hands and arms, felt a line of blood running down his chin to drip onto the spongy soil. This was his life, his destiny. Yet what did that mean? More war with Ten-Towns, as had happened so many times in the past? And what of relations with the dwarves who had returned to their mines south of Kelvin's Cairn?

Kierstaad had listened to Berkthgar throughout the last few tendays. He had heard Berkthgar arguing with Revjak, Kierstaad's father and the accepted leader of the Tribe of the Elk, at present the one remaining tribe on Icewind Dale's tundra. Berkthgar would break away, Kierstaad thought as he looked at the gigantic man. Berkthgar would take the other young warriors with him and begin anew the Tribe of the Bear, or one of the other ancestral tribes. Then the tribal rivalry that had for so long been a way of life for Icewind Dale's barbarians would begin anew. They would fight for food or for good ground as they wandered the tundra.

It was one possibility only, Kierstaad reasoned, trying to shake the disturbing thoughts away. Berkthgar wanted to be the complete leader, wanted to emulate and then surpass the legend of Wulfgar. He could not do that if he splintered the remaining barbarians, who in truth were not yet numerous enough to support any separate tribes of any real power.

Wulfgar had united the tribes.

There were other possibilities, but as he thought about it, none of them sat well with him.

Berkthgar looked up from the kill, smiling widely, accepting Kierstaad fully and with no ulterior motives. Yet Kierstaad was the son of Revjak, and it seemed to him now that Berkthgar and his father might be walking a troubled course. The leader of a barbarian tribe could be challenged.

That notion only intensified when the successful hunting party neared the deerskin tent encampment of the tribe, only to intercept one Bruenor Battlehammer and another dwarf, the priestess Stumpet Rakingclaw.

"You do not belong here!" Berkthgar immediately growled at the dwarven leader.

"Well met to yerself too," Stumpet, never the one to sit back and let others speak for her, snarled at Berkthgar. "Ye're forgettin' Keeper's Dale, then, as we've heard ye were?"

"I do not speak to females on matters of importance," Berkthgar said evenly.

Bruenor moved quickly, extending an arm to hold the outraged Stumpet back. "And I'm not for talking with yerself," Bruenor replied. "Me and me cleric have come to see Revjak, the leader of the Tribe of the Elk."

Berkthgar's nostrils flared. For a moment, Kierstaad and the others expected him to hurl himself at Bruenor, and the dwarf, bracing himself and slapping his many-notched axe across his open palm, apparently expected it, too.

But Berkthgar, no fool, calmed himself. "I, too, lead the hunters of Icewind Dale," he said. "Speak your business and be gone!"

Bruenor chuckled and walked past the proud barbarian, moving into the settlement. Berkthgar howled and leaped, landing right in Bruenor's path.

"Ye led in Settlestone," the red-bearded dwarf said firmly. "And ye might be leadin' here. Then again, ye might not. Revjak was king when we left the dale and Revjak's king still, by all word I'm hearing." Bruenor's judging gray eyes never left Berkthgar as he walked past the huge man once more.

Stumpet turned up her nose and didn't bother to eye the giant barbarian.

For Kierstaad, who liked Bruenor and his wild clan, it was a painful meeting.

× × × × ×

The wind was light, the only sound the creaking timbers of the *Sea Sprite* as it glided quietly eastward on calm waters. The moon was full and pale above them as it crossed a cloudless sky.

Catti-brie sat on the raised platform of the ballista, huddled near to a candle, every so often jotting something down on parchment. Drizzt leaned on the rail, his parchment rolled and in a pocket of his cloak. On Deudermont's wise instructions, all six who had been in the blind witch's cave were to write down the poem as they remembered it. Five of them could write, an extraordinary percentage. Waillan, who was not skilled with letters would dictate his recollection to both Harkle and Robillard, who would separately pen the words, hopefully without any of their own interpretations.

It hadn't taken Drizzt long to write down the verse, at least the parts he remembered most clearly, the parts he considered vital. He understood that every word might provide a necessary clue, but he was simply too excited, too overwhelmed to pay attention to minute details. In the poem's second line, the witch had spoken of Drizzt's father, and had intimated at Zaknafein's survival several times thereafter. That was all that Drizzt could think of, all that he could hope to remember.

Catti-brie was more diligent, her written record of the verse far more complete. But she, too, had been overwhelmed and surprised, and simply couldn't be certain of how accurate her recording might be.

"I would have liked to share a night such as this with him," Drizzt said, his voice shattering the stillness so abruptly that the young woman nearly jabbed her quill through the fragile parchment. She looked up to Drizzt, whose eyes were high, his gaze focused on the moon.

"Just one," the drow went on. "Zaknafein would have loved the surface night."

Catti-brie smiled, not doubting the claim. Drizzt had spoken to her many times about his father. Drizzt's soul was the legacy of his father's, not of his evil mother's. The two were alike, in combat and in heart, with the notable exception that Drizzt had found the courage to walk away from Menzoberranzan, whereas Zaknafein had not. He had remained with the evil dark elves and had eventually come to be sacrificed to the Spider Queen.

"Given to Lolth and by Lolth given."

The true line came suddenly to Catti-brie. She whispered it once aloud, hearing the ring and knowing it to be exact, then went back to her parchment and located the line. She had written, "for" instead of "to," which she quickly corrected.

Every little word could be vital.

"I suspect that the danger I now face is beyond anything we have ever witnessed," Drizzt went on, talking to himself as much as to Catti-brie.

Catti-brie didn't miss his use of the personal pronoun, instead of the collective. She too was involved, a point that she was about to make clear, but another line came to her, jogged by Drizzt's proclamation.

"That thee might seek the darkest of trails."

Catti-brie realized that was the next line and her quill went to work. Drizzt was talking again, but she hardly heard him. She did catch a few words, though, and she stopped writing, her gaze lifting from the parchment to consider the drow. He was speaking again of going off alone!

"The verse was for us two," Catti-brie reminded him.

"The dark trail leads to my father," Drizzt replied, "a drow you have never met."

"Yer point being?" Catti-brie asked.

"The trail is for me to walk . . ."

"With meself," Catti-brie said determinedly. "Don't ye be doing that again!" she scolded. "Ye walked off once on me, and nearly brought ruin upon yerself and us all for yer stupidity!"

Drizzt swung about and eyed her directly. How he loved this woman! He knew that he could not argue the point with her, knew that whatever arguments he might present, she would defeat them, or simply ignore them.

"I'm going with ye, all the way," Catti-brie said, no compromise in her firm tone. "And me thinkin's that Deudermont and Harkle, and maybe a few o' the others're coming along, too. And just ye try to stop us, Drizzt Do'Urden!"

Drizzt began to reply, but changed his mind. Why bother? He would never talk his friends into letting him walk this dark course alone. Never.

He looked back out to the dark sea and to the moon and stars, his thoughts drifting back to Zaknafein and the "golden ring," the witch had held out to him.

"It will take at least two tendays to get back to port," he lamented.

"Three, if the wind doesn't come up strong," Catti-brie put in, her focus never leaving the all-important parchment.

Not so far away, on the main deck just below the rail of the poop deck, Harkle Harpell rubbed his hands eagerly. He shared Drizzt's lament that all of this would take so very long, and had no stomach for another two or three tendays of rolling about on the empty water.

"The fog of fate," he mouthed quietly, thinking of his new, powerful spell, the enchantment that had brought him out to the *Sea Sprite* in the first place. The opportunity seemed perfect for him to energize his new spell once more.

BREWING STORM

Revjak's smile widened nearly enough to take in his ears when he saw that the rumors were true, that Bruenor Battlehammer had returned to Icewind Dale. The two had lived side by side for the first forty years of Revjak's life, but during that time the barbarian had little experience with Bruenor, other than as enemies. But then Wulfgar had united the nomadic tribes and cast them into the war as allies of the folk of Ten-Towns and the dwarves of Clan Battlehammer against evil Akar Kessel and his goblinoid minions.

On that occasion, less than a decade before, Revjak had come to appreciate the strength and fortitude of Bruenor and of all the dwarves. In the few tendays that had followed, before Bruenor and Wulfgar had set out to find Mithral Hall, Revjak had spent many days with Bruenor and had forged a fast friendship. Bruenor was going to leave, but the rest of Clan Battlehammer would remain in Icewind Dale until Mithral Hall was found, and Revjak had taken on the responsibility of tightening the friendship between the giant barbarians and the diminutive dwarves. He had done such a fine job that many of his people, Berkthgar included, had opted to go south with Clan Battlehammer to join in the fight to reclaim Mithral Hall, and there they had stayed for several years.

It seemed to wise Revjak that Berkthgar had forgotten all of that, for when the giant warrior entered the tent to join in the meeting with Bruenor and Stumpet, his face was locked in a deep and unrelenting scowl.

"Sit, Berkthgar," Revjak bade the man, motioning to a spot beside him.

Berkthgar held out his hand, indicating that he would remain standing. He

was trying to be imposing, Revjak knew, towering over the seated dwarves. If hardy Bruenor was bothered at all, though, he didn't show it. He reclined comfortably on the thick blanket of piled skins so that he did not have to crook his neck to look up at the standing Berkthgar.

"Ye're still looking like yer last meal didn't taste so good," the dwarf remarked to Berkthgar.

"Why has a king come so far from his kingdom?" Berkthgar retorted.

"No more a king," Bruenor corrected. "I gived that back to me great-great-great-great grandfather."

Revjak looked at the dwarf curiously. "Gandalug?" he asked, remembering the improbable story Berkthgar had told him of how Bruenor's ancestor, the original Patron of Clan Battlehammer and the founder of Mithral Hall, had returned from the dead as a prisoner of the drow elves.

"The same," Stumpet answered.

"Yerself can call me prince," Bruenor said to Berkthgar, who huffed and looked away.

"Thus you have returned to Icewind Dale," Revjak intervened, before the discussion could turn ugly. It seemed to the barbarian leader that Bruenor did not appreciate the level of antipathy Berkthgar had cultivated for the dwarves—either that, or Bruenor simply didn't care. "You're here to visit?"

"To stay," Bruenor corrected. "The mines are being opened as we sit here talkin'. Cleaning out the things that've crawled in and fixing the supports. We'll be taking ore in a tenday and hammering out goods the day after that."

Revjak nodded. "Then this is a visit for purposes of business," he reasoned.

"And for friendship," Bruenor was quick to reply. "Better if the two go together, I say."

"Agreed," Revjak said. He looked up to notice that Berkthgar was chewing hard on his lip. "And I trust that your clan will be fair with its prices for goods that we need."

"We've got the metal, ye've got the skins and the meat," Bruenor answered.

"You have nothing that we need," Berkthgar interjected suddenly and vehemently. Bruenor, smirking, looked up at him. After returning the look for just a moment, Berkthgar looked directly to Revjak. "We need nothing from the dwarves," the warrior stated. "All that we need is provided by the tundra."

"Bah!" Bruenor snorted. "Yer stone speartips bounce off good mail!"

"Reindeer wear no mail," Berkthgar replied dryly. "And if we come to war with Ten-Towns and the allies of Ten-Towns, our strength will put the stone tips through anything a dwarf can forge."

Bruenor sat up straight and both Revjak and Stumpet tensed, fearing that the fiery red-bearded dwarf would pounce upon Berkthgar for such an open threat.

Bruenor was older and wiser than that, though, and he looked instead to Revjak. "Who's speaking for the tribe?" the dwarf asked.

"I am," Revjak stated firmly, looking directly at Berkthgar.

Berkthgar didn't blink. "Where is Aegis-fang?" the giant man asked.

There it was, Bruenor thought, the point of it all, the source of the argument from the very beginning. Aegis-fang, the mighty warhammer forged by Bruenor himself as a gift to Wulfgar, the barbarian lad who had become as his son.

"Did you leave it in Mithral Hall?" Berkthgar pressed, and it seemed to Bruenor that the warrior hoped the answer would be yes. "Is it hanging useless as an ornament on a wall?"

Stumpet understood what was going on here. She and Bruenor had discussed this very point before they had set out on the return to Icewind Dale. Berkthgar would have preferred it if they had left Aegis-fang in Mithral Hall, hundreds and hundreds of miles away from Icewind Dale. So far away, the weapon would not have cast its shadow over him and his own great sword, Bankenfuere, the Northern Fury. Bruenor would hear nothing of such a course, though. Aegis-fang was his greatest accomplishment, the pinnacle of his respectable career as a weaponsmith, and even more importantly, it was his only link to his lost son. Where Bruenor went, Aegis-fang went, and Berkthgar's feelings be damned!

Bruenor hedged for a moment on the question, as if he was trying to figure out the best tactical course. Stumpet was not so ambivalent. "The hammer's in the mines," she said determinedly. "Bringed by Bruenor, who made it."

Berkthgar's scowl deepened and Stumpet promptly attacked.

"Ye just said the dale'll give ye all ye're needin'," the priestess howled. "Why're ye caring for a dwarf-made hammer, then?"

The giant barbarian didn't reply, but it seemed to both Bruenor and Revjak as if Stumpet was gaining the upper hand here.

"Of course that own sword ye wear strapped to yer back was not made in the dale," she remarked. "Ye got it in trade, and it, too, was probably made by dwarves!"

Berkthgar laughed at her, but there was no mirth in Revjak's tent, for his laugh seemed more of threat than of mirth.

"Who are these dwarves who call themselves our friends?" Berkthgar asked. "And yet they will not give over to the tribe a weapon made legendary by one of the tribe."

"Yer talk is getting old," Bruenor warned.

"And you are getting old, dwarf," Berkthgar retorted. "You should not have returned." With that, Berkthgar stormed from the tent.

"Ye should be watchin' that one," Bruenor said to Revjak.

The barbarian leader nodded. "Berkthgar has been caught in a web spun of his own words," he replied. "And so have many others, mostly the young warriors."

"Always full o' fight," Bruenor remarked.

Revjak smiled and did not disagree. Berkthgar was indeed one to be watched, but in truth, there was little Revjak could do. If Berkthgar wanted to split the tribe, enough would agree and follow him so that Revjak could not stop him. And even worse, if Berkthgar demanded the Right of Challenge for the leadership of the united tribe, he would have enough support so that Revjak would find it difficult to refuse.

Revjak was too old to fight Berkthgar. He had thought the ways of the barbarians of Icewind Dale changed when Wulfgar had united the tribes. That is why he had accepted the offered position as leader when Wulfgar had left, though in the past such a title could be earned only by inheritance or by combat, by deed or by blood.

Old ways died hard, Revjak realized, staring at the tent flap through which Berkthgar had departed. Many in the tribe, especially those who had returned from Mithral Hall, and even a growing number of those who had remained with Revjak waxed nostalgic for the freer, wilder days gone by. Revjak often happened upon conversations where older men retold tales of the great wars, the unified attack upon Ten-Towns, wherein Wulfgar was captured by Bruenor.

Their nostalgia was misplaced, Revjak knew. In the unified attack upon Ten-Towns, the warriors had been so completely slaughtered that the tribes had barely survived the ensuing winter. Still, the stories of war were always full of glory and excitement, and never words of tragedy. With the excitement of Berkthgar's return along with the return of Bruenor and the dwarves, many remembered too fondly the days before the alliance.

Revjak would indeed watch Berkthgar, but he feared that to be all he could do.

✕ ✕ ✕ ✕ ✕

Outside the tent, another listener, young Kierstaad, nodded his agreement with Bruenor's warning. Kierstaad was truly torn, full of admiration for Berkthgar but also for Bruenor. At that moment though, little of that greater struggle entered into the young man's thoughts.

Bruenor had confirmed that Aegis-fang was in the dale!

⚔ ⚔ ⚔ ⚔ ⚔

"Might be the same storm that hit us near the Gull Rocks," Robillard remarked, eyeing the black wall that loomed on the eastern horizon before the *Sea Sprite*.

"But stronger," Deudermont added. "Taking power from the water." They were still in the sunshine, six days out from Caerwich, with another eight to the Moonshaes, by Deudermont's figuring.

The first hints of a head wind brushed against the tall captain's face, the first gentle blows of the gales that would soon assault them.

"Hard to starboard!" Deudermont yelled to the sailor at the wheel. "We shall go north around it, north around the Moonshaes," he said quietly, so that only Robillard could hear. "A straighter course to our port."

The wizard nodded. He knew that Deudermont did not want to turn to the north, where the wind was less predictable and the waters choppier and colder, but he understood that they had little choice at this point. If they tried to dodge the storm to the south, they would wind up near the Nelanther, the Pirate Isles, a place the *Sea Sprite*, such a thorn in the side of the pirates, did not want to be.

So, north they would go, around the storm, and around the Moonshaes. That was the hope, anyway. In looking at the wall of blackness, often creased by a shot of lightning, Robillard was not sure they could run fast enough.

"Do go and fill our sails with your magical wind," Deudermont bade him, and the captain's quiet tone showed that he obviously shared the wizard's trepidation.

Robillard moved to the rail of the poop deck and sat down, slipping his legs under the rail so that he was facing the mainmast. He held his left hand up toward the mast and called on the powers of his ring to create a gust of wind. Such a minor enchantment would not tax the powers of the wizard's mighty ring, and so Robillard enacted it again and again, filling the sails, launching the *Sea Sprite* on a swift run.

Not swift enough. The black wall closed in on them, waves rocking the *Sea Sprite* and soon turning her ride into more of a bounce than a run. A grim

choice lay before Deudermont. He could either drop the sails and batten every-thing down in an attempt to ride out the storm, or keep up the run, skirting the edge of the storm in a desperate attempt to slip off to the north of it.

"Luck be with us," the captain decided, and he tried the run, keeping the sails full until, at last, the storm engulfed them.

She was among the finest ships ever built, crewed by a handpicked group of expert sailors that now included two powerful wizards, Drizzt, Catti-brie, and Guenhwyvar, and she was captained by one of the most experienced and well-respected seamen anywhere along the Sword Coast. Great indeed were the powers of the *Sea Sprite* when measured by the standards of man, but tiny she seemed now in the face of the sheer weight of nature. They tried to run, but like a skilled hunter, the storm closed in.

Guide ropes snapped apart and the mast itself bent for the strain. Robillard tried desperately to counter, so did Harkle Harpell, but even their combined magic could not save the mainmast. A crack appeared along the main vertical beam, and the only thing that saved it was the snapping of the horizontal guide beam.

Out flapped the sail, knocking one man from the rigging to splash into the churning sea. Drizzt moved immediately, yelling to Guenhwyvar, calling the panther to his side and then sending her over the rail in search of the sailor. Guenhwyvar didn't hesitate—they had done this before. Roaring all the way, the cat splashed into the dark water and disappeared immediately.

Rain and hail pelted them, as did the walls of waves that splashed over the bow. Thunder boomed all about the tossing ship, more than one bolt of lightning slamming into the tall masts.

"I should have stopped the run sooner!" Deudermont cried, and though he screamed with all his strength, Drizzt, standing right beside him, could barely hear him over the roar of the wind and the pounding of the thunder.

The drow shook his head. The ship was nearly battened down, most of the crew had gone below, and still the *Sea Sprite* was being tossed wildly. "We are on the edges because of the run," the drow said firmly. "If you had stopped earlier, we would be in the heart of the storm and surely doomed!"

Deudermont heard only a few of the words, but he understood the gist of what his dark elven friend was trying to communicate. Grateful, he put a hand on Drizzt's shoulder, but suddenly went flying away, slamming hard against the rail and nearly toppling over, as a huge wave nearly lay the *Sea Sprite* down on her side.

Drizzt caught up to him in an instant, the drow's enchanted bracers and sheer agility allowing him to navigate on the rocking deck. He helped the captain to his feet and the two struggled for the hatch.

Deudermont went down first, Drizzt stopping to survey the deck, to make sure that everyone else had gone below. Only Robillard remained, wedged in with his thighs pressing against the rail, cursing the storm and throwing magical gusts into the teeth of the raging wind. The wizard noticed that Drizzt was looking at him, and he waved the drow away, then pointed to his ring, reminding Drizzt that he had enough magical power to save himself.

As soon as he got into the cramped deck below, Drizzt took out the panther figurine. He had to hope that Guenhwyvar had found the sailor and had him in her grasp, for if he waited any longer, the man would surely be drowned anyway. "Go home, Guenhwyvar," he said to the statue.

He wanted to call Guenhwyvar back almost immediately, to find out if the man had been saved, but a wave slammed the ship and the figurine flew off into the darkness. Drizzt scrambled, trying to follow its course, but it was too cramped and too dark.

In the blackness belowdecks, the terrified crew had no way of really knowing if this was the same storm that had battered them before. If it was, then it had indeed intensified, for this time, the *Sea Sprite* was tossed about like a toy. Water washed over them from every crack in the deck above, and only their frantic bailing, coordinated and disciplined despite the darkness and the terror, kept the ship afloat. It went on for more than two hours, two horrible gut-wrenching hours, but Drizzt's estimate of the value of Deudermont's run was accurate. The *Sea Sprite* was on the fringe of the storm, not in its heart. No ship in all the Realms could have survived this storm in full.

Then all went quiet, except for the occasional thunder boom, growing ever more distant. The *Sea Sprite* was listing badly to port, but she was up.

Drizzt was the first on deck, Deudermont right behind him. The damage was extensive, especially to the mainmast.

"Can we repair her?" Drizzt asked.

Deudermont didn't think so. "Not without putting into port," he replied, not bothering to mention the fact that the nearest port might be five hundred miles away.

Catti-brie came up soon after, bearing the onyx figurine. Drizzt wasted no time in calling to the panther, and when the cat came on deck, she was escorted by a very sorry-looking sailor.

"There is a tale for your grandchildren," Deudermont said in a chipper voice to the man, clapping him on the shoulder and trying to keep up the morale of those near him. The stricken sailor nodded sheepishly as two other crewmen helped him away.

"So fine a friend," Deudermont remarked to Drizzt, indicating Guen-hwyvar. "The man was surely doomed."

Drizzt nodded and dropped a hand across Guenhwyvar's muscled flank. Never did he take the cat's friendship for granted.

Catti-brie watched the drow's actions intently, understanding that saving the sailor was important to Drizzt for reasons beyond the drow's altruistic demeanor. Had the sailor drowned, that would have been one more weight of guilt laid across the shoulders of Drizzt Do'Urden, one more innocent sacrificed because of the ranger's dark past.

But that had not come to pass, and it seemed for a moment as if the *Sea Sprite* and all of her crew had survived. That happy notion fell away a moment later, though, when Harkle bounded over, asking a simple, but poignant question. "Where is Robillard?"

All eyes turned to regard the forward rail of the poop deck, to see that the rail had split apart in precisely the spot where Drizzt had last seen the wizard.

Drizzt's heart nearly failed him and Catti-brie rushed to the rail and began surveying the empty water.

Deudermont didn't seem so upset. "The wizard has ways to escape the storm," the captain assured the others. "It has happened before."

True enough, Drizzt and Catti-brie realized. On several occasions Robillard had left the *Sea Sprite* by use of his magic in order to attend a meeting of his guild in Waterdeep, even though the ship was sailing waters hundreds of miles removed from that city at the time.

"He cannot drown," Deudermont assured them. "Not while he wears that ring."

Both the friends seemed satisfied with that. Robillard's ring was of the Elemental Plane of Water, a powerfully enchanted device that gave the wizard many advantages on the sea, no matter the strength of a storm. He might have been hit by lightning, or might have been knocked unconscious, but more likely, he had been swept away from the *Sea Sprite* and forced to use his magic to get clear of the storm long before the ship ever did.

Catti-brie continued her scan, and Drizzt joined her.

Deudermont had other business to attend to, he had to figure out how he was going to get the *Sea Sprite* into a safe port. They had weathered the storm and survived, but that might prove to be a temporary reprieve.

Harkle, in watching the captain's movements and in surveying the extensive damage to the schooner, knew it too. He moved quietly to Deudermont's cabin, hiding his eagerness until he was safely locked away. Then he rubbed his hands together briskly, his smile wide, and took out a leather book.

Glancing around to ensure that no one was watching, Harkle opened a magical tome, one of the components he needed for his newest, and perhaps most powerful spell. Most of the pages were blank—all of them had been blank until Harkle had first cast his fog of fate. Now the first few pages read as a journal of Harkle's magical ride to join the *Sea Sprite,* and he was glad to see, of his continuing experiences with the ship. To his absolute amazement, for he hadn't dared look so extensively at the journal before, even the blind seer's poem was there, word for word.

The fog of fate was working still, Harkle knew, for neither he nor any other man had penned a single word into the journal. The continuing enchantment of the spell was recording the events!

This exceeded Harkle's wildest expectations for the fog of fate. He didn't know how long this might continue, but he understood that he had stumbled onto something very special here. And something that needed a little boost. The *Sea Sprite* was dead in the water, and so was the quest that had apparently befallen Drizzt and Catti-brie, and by association, Harkle. Harkle wasn't one to be patient, not now. He waved his hand over the first of the many blank pages, chanting softly. He reached into a pouch and produced some diamond dust, sprinkling it sparingly onto the first of the still-blank pages.

Nothing happened.

Harkle continued for nearly an hour, but when he emerged from the cabin, the *Sea Sprite* was still listing, still drifting aimlessly.

Harkle rubbed the stubble on his unshaven face. Apparently, the spell needed more work.

⚔ ⚔ ⚔ ⚔ ⚔

Robillard stood on top of the rolling water, tapping his foot impatiently. "Where is that brute?" he asked, referring to the water elemental monster he had summoned to his aid. He had sent the creature in search of the *Sea Sprite,* but that had been many minutes ago.

Finally, the azure blanket before the wizard rolled up and took on a roughly humanoid shape. Robillard gurgled at it, asking the creature in its own watery language if it had found the ship.

It had, and so the wizard bade the elemental to take him to it. The creature held out a huge arm. It appeared watery, but was in truth much more substantial than any normal liquid. When the wizard was comfortably in place, the monster whisked him away with the speed of a breaking wave.

12

THE FOG OF FATE

The crew worked through the afternoon, but they seemed to be making little progress on the extensive damage the ship had taken. They could hoist one of the sails, the mizzensail, but they couldn't control it to catch the wind, or to steer the ship in any desired direction.

Thus was their condition when Catti-brie called out an alert from the crow's nest. Deudermont and Drizzt rushed side by side to see what she was calling about, both fearing that it might be a pirate vessel. If that was the case, damaged as she was and without Robillard, the proud *Sea Sprite* might be forced to surrender without a fight.

No pirate blocked their path, but directly ahead loomed a curtain of thick fog. Deudermont looked up to Catti-brie, and the young woman, having no explanation, only shrugged in reply. This was no usual occurrence. The sky was clear, except for this one fog bank, and the temperature had been fairly constant.

"What would cause such a mist?" Drizzt asked Deudermont.

"Nothing that I know of," the captain insisted. "Man some oars!" he yelled out to the crew. "Try to put up a sail. Let us see if we can navigate around it."

By the time Deudermont turned his attention back to the sea before them, however, he found Drizzt shaking his head doubtfully, for the fog already loomed much nearer. It was not stationary.

"It is approaching us," the captain breathed in disbelief.

"Swiftly," Drizzt added, and then the drow, with his keen ears, heard the chuckle of Harkle Harpell and knew in his heart that this was the wizard's work. He turned in time to see the man disappearing through the hatch belowdecks, and started to follow. Drizzt stopped before he reached the hatch, though, hearing Deudermont's gasp and the nervous cries of many crewmen.

Catti-brie scrambled down the rigging. "What is it?" she asked, near desperation.

Into the gray veil they went. The sound of splashing water went away, as did any sensation of movement. Crewmen huddled together and many drew out their weapons, as if expecting some enemy to climb aboard from the dark mist.

It was Guenhwyvar who gave Drizzt the next clue of what might be going on. The panther came to Drizzt's side, ears flattened, but her expression and demeanor showing more curiosity than fear.

"Dimensional," the drow remarked.

Deudermont looked at him curiously.

"This is Harkle's doing," Drizzt said. "The wizard is using his magic to get us off the open sea."

Deudermont's face brightened at that notion, so did Catti-brie's—at least until both of them took a moment to consider the source of their apparent salvation.

Catti-brie looked out at the thick fog. Suddenly, drifting in a damaged ship across empty waters did not seem like such a bad thing.

⚔ ⚔ ⚔ ⚔ ⚔

"What do you mean?" Robillard roared. He slapped his hands together fiercely and translated his question into the watery, gurgling language of the water elemental.

The reply came without hesitation, and Robillard knew enough of such a creature to understand that it had the means to know the truth of the matter. This one had been cooperative, as elemental creatures go, and Robillard did not believe that it was lying to him.

The *Sea Sprite* was gone, vanished from the sea.

Robillard breathed a sigh of relief when he heard the next reply, that the ship had not sunk, had simply drifted out of the waters.

"Harkle Harpell," the wizard reasoned aloud. "He has gotten them into a port. Well done!" Robillard considered his own situation then, alone and so far from land. He commanded the elemental to keep him moving in a generally easterly direction, and explained that he would need the creature until the next dawn. Then he took out his spellbook, a fabulous leatherbound

and watertight work, and moved its golden tassel bookmark to the page containing his teleportation spell.

Then the wizard sat back and relaxed. He needed to sleep, to gather his strength and his energy. The elemental would see to his safety for now, and in the morning he would use his spell to put him in his private room in the guild hall in Waterdeep. Yes, the wizard decided, it had been a difficult and boring few tendays, and now was a good time for some restful shore leave.

Deudermont would just have to catch up with him later.

× × × × ×

The *Sea Sprite* drifted in a surreal stillness, no sound of water or wind, for many minutes. The fog was so thick about them that Drizzt had to hang very low over the rail to even see the water. He didn't dare reach out and touch that gray liquid, not knowing what Harkle's spell, if this was indeed Harkle's spell, might be doing.

At last they heard a splash, the lap of a wave against the prow of the ship. The fog began to thin almost immediately, but though they couldn't see their surroundings, everyone on board sensed that something had changed.

"The smell," Catti-brie remarked, and the heads of all those near her bobbed in agreement. Gone was the salty aroma, so thick that it left a taste in your mouth, replaced by a crisp summer scent, filled with trees, flowers, and the slick feel of an inlet swamp. The sounds, too, had changed, from the empty, endless whistle of the wind and the muted splashes of deep water to the gentle lapping of lesser waves and the trilling of . . .

"Songbirds?" Drizzt asked.

The fog blew away, and all of the crew breathed a sigh of relief, for they were near to land! To the left loomed a small island, tree-covered, centered by a small castle and dotted with large mansions. A long bridge stretched in front of the *Sea Sprite,* reaching from the island to the shore, to the docks of a fair-sized, walled town. Behind the town, the ground sloped up into tall mountains, a landmark that no sailor could miss, but that Deudermont did not know. Many boats were about, though none much bigger than the rowboats the *Sea Sprite* carried astern. All the crews stood, staring blankly at the magnificent sailing ship.

"Not Waterdeep," Deudermont remarked. "Nor anywhere near to the city that I know of."

Drizzt surveyed the area, studying the coastline that curled back behind them. "Not the open sea," he replied.

"A lake," Catti-brie reasoned.

All three of them looked at each other for a moment, then yelled out, "Harkle!" in unison. The Harpell, expecting the call, scrambled out of the hatch and bounded right up beside them, his expression full of cheer.

"Where are we?" Deudermont demanded.

"Where the fates wanted us to be," the mage said mysteriously, waving his arms, the voluminous sleeves of his robe flying wide.

"I'm thinking ye'll have to do better than that," Catti-brie put in dryly.

Harkle shrugged and lowered his arms. "I do not know for sure, of course," he admitted. "The spell facilitates the move—not a random thing—but wherever that might be, I cannot tell."

"The spell?" Deudermont asked.

"The fog of fate," Drizzt answered before Harkle could. "The same spell that brought you to us."

Harkle nodded through the drow's every word, his smile wide, his expression one of pride and accomplishment.

"You put us in a lake!" Deudermont roared angrily.

Harkle stammered for a reply, but a call from the water cut the private conversation short. "Yo ho, *Sea Sprite!*"

The four went to the rail, Drizzt pulling the hood of his cloak over his head. He didn't know where they were, or what reception they might find, but he felt it likely that the greeting would be less warm if these sailors discovered that the *Sea Sprite* carried a drow elf.

A fair-sized fishing boat had pulled up alongside, its crew of six studying the schooner intently. "You've seen battle," an old graybeard, seeming to be the skipper of the fishing boat, reasoned.

"A storm," Deudermont corrected. "As fierce a blow as I've ever known."

The six fishermen exchanged doubting looks. They had been on the water every day for the last month and had seen no storms.

"Far from here," Deudermont tried to explain, recognizing the doubting expressions.

"How far can you get?" the old graybeard asked, looking about at the ever-present shoreline.

"Ye'd be surprised," Catti-brie answered, casting a sidelong glance at the blushing Harkle.

"Where did you put in?" the graybeard asked.

Deudermont held his hands out wide. "We are the *Sea Sprite*, out of Waterdeep."

The doubting expressions turned into open smirks. "Waterdeep?" the graybeard echoed.

"Are we in another world?" Catti-brie whispered to Drizzt, and the drow found it hard to honestly comfort her, especially with Harkle Harpell behind it all.

"Waterdeep," Deudermont said evenly, seriously, with as much conviction as he could muster.

"You're a long way from home, captain," another of the fishermen remarked. "A thousand miles."

"Fifteen hundred," the graybeard corrected.

"And all of it land," another added, laughing. "Have you wheels on the *Sea Sprite?*" That brought a chuckle from the six and from several other crews of boats moving close to investigate.

"And a team of horses I'd like to see," a man on another boat put in, drawing more laughter.

Even Deudermont managed a smile, relieved that he and his ship were apparently still in the Realms. "Wizard's work," he explained. "We sailed the Sea of Swords, five hundred miles southwest of the Moonshaes, when the storm found us and left us drifting. Our wizard"—Deudermont looked over to Harkle— "cast some enchantment to get us into port."

"He missed," howled a man.

"But he got us off of the open sea," Deudermont said when the laughter died away. "Where we surely would have perished. Pray tell me, good sailors, where are we?"

"This is Impresk Lake," the graybeard replied, then pointed to shore, to the walled town. "Carradoon."

Deudermont didn't recognize the names.

"Those are the Snowflakes," the skipper continued, indicating the mountains.

"South," Catti-brie said suddenly. All eyes turned to her. "We are far south of Waterdeep," she said. "And if we sailed south from the lake, we'd get to the Deepwash, then to Vilhon Reach in the Inner Sea."

"You have the place," the graybeard announced. "But you'd not draw enough water to get that ship to Shalane Lake."

"And unless you've wings with those wheels, you won't be sailing over the Cloven Mountains!" the man beside the graybeard roared. But the laughter was subdued now, all the sailors, on the *Sea Sprite* and on the fishing boats, digesting the gravity of the situation.

Deudermont blew a long sigh and looked to Harkle, who cast his gaze to the deck. "We'll worry about where we are going later," Deudermont said. "For now, the task is to repair the *Sea Sprite*." He turned to the graybeard. "I fear that your lake hasn't enough draw," he said. "Is there a long wharf, where we might put in for repairs?"

The skipper pointed to Carradoon Island, and one long dock jutting out in the direction of the *Sea Sprite.*

"The draw is deeper on the northern side of the island," the man next to him remarked.

"But the long dock is privately owned," a third fisherman put in.

"We'll get permission to put her in," the graybeard said firmly.

"But the task is not so easy," Deudermont interjected. "We've not the sails, nor the steering to navigate. And I do not know these waters, obviously."

"Put out some lines, Captain . . ."

"Deudermont," the *Sea Sprite*'s captain replied. "Captain Deudermont."

"My name's Terraducket," the graybeard said. "Well met." He signaled to all the other boats as he spoke, and already they were swarming about the *Sea Sprite,* trying to get in position.

"We'll get you in to the docks, and Carradoon has a fair number of shipwrights to help in your repairs," Terraducket went on. "Even on that mast, though we'll have to find a tall tree indeed to replace it! Know that it will cost you a fair number of stories about your sailing adventures on the Sea of Swords, if I know my fellows!"

"We've a fair number to tell!" Deudermont assured him.

The ropes went out and the fishing fleet put in line and began to guide and tow the great schooner.

"The brotherhood of sailors extends to those upon the lakes," Drizzt remarked.

"So it would seem," Deudermont agreed. "If we had crew to replace, I'd know where to begin my search." The captain looked over to Harkle, who was still staring forlornly at the deck. "You did well, Master Harpell," Deudermont said, and the wizard's face brightened as he looked up at the man. "We would have perished in the uncharted waters so far from the Moonshaes, and now we shall live."

"But on a lake," Harkle replied.

Deudermont waved that notion away. "Robillard will find us, and the two of you will find a way to put us back where we belong, I do not doubt. For now, my ship and my crew are safe, and that is all that matters. Well done!"

Harkle verily glowed.

"But why are we here?" Catti-brie had to ask.

"The fog of fate," Drizzt and Harkle said in unison.

"And that means that there is something here that we need," the wizard went on.

"Need for what?" Catti-brie asked.

"For the quest, of course!" Harkle roared. "That is what this is all about, is it not?" He looked around as if that should explain everything, but saw that the stares coming back at him were not looks of comprehension. "Before the storm, we were heading for . . ."

"Waterdeep," Deudermont answered. "Your spell has not put us closer to Waterdeep."

Harkle waved his hands frantically. "No, no," he corrected. "Not for Waterdeep, but for a priest, or perhaps a wizard, in Waterdeep."

"And you think that we're more likely to find a spellcaster of the power we need here than in Waterdeep?" Drizzt asked incredulously. "In this tiny town so far from home?"

"Good Captain Terraducket," Harkle called.

"Here," came the reply from farther away than before, for Terraducket's fishing boat had moved forward to join in the towing line.

"We seek a priest," Harkle said. "A very powerful priest . . ."

"Cadderly," Terraducket interrupted without hesitation. "Cadderly Bonaduce. You'll not find a more powerful priest in all the Realms!" Terraducket boasted, as if this Cadderly was the property of all of Carradoon.

Harkle cast a superior glance at his friends. "Fog of fate," he remarked.

"And where might we find this Cadderly?" Deudermont asked. "In Carradoon?"

"No," came Terraducket's reply. "Two day's march out, into the mountains, in a temple called the Spirit Soaring."

Deudermont looked to Harkle, no more doubting questions coming to surface.

Harkle clapped his hands together. "Fog of fate!" he said again. "Oh, and it all fits so well," he said excitedly, as though another thought had just popped into his head.

"Fits like the *Sea Sprite* in a lake," Catti-brie put in sarcastically, but Harkle just ignored her.

"Don't you see?" the wizard asked them all, excited once more and flapping those winglike arms. "*Sea Sprite* and Spirit Soaring. SS and SS, after all! And fog of fate, FF."

"I'm needin' a long sleep," Catti-brie groaned.

"And HH!" Harkle bellowed. Drizzt looked at him curiously. "Harkle Harpell!" the excited wizard explained, then he poked a finger the drow's way.

"And DD for Drizzt Do'Urden! FF for fog of fate, and SS and SS, HH and DD! And you . . ." he pointed at Catti-brie.

"Doesn't work," the young woman assured him.

"Doesn't matter," Drizzt added. Deudermont was biting hard on his lip, trying not to steal Harkle's moment of glory with a burst of laughter.

"Oh, there's something in the letters," Harkle said, speaking to himself more than to the others. "I must explore this!"

"Explore yer mind," Catti-brie said to him, and then she added under her breath, so that only Drizzt and Deudermont could hear, "Better take a big lantern and a dwarf's cave pack."

That brought a snicker.

"But your father!" Harkle yelled suddenly, leaping at Catti-brie. She barely held back from slugging him, so great was her surprise.

"Me father?" she asked.

"BB!" Harkle, Drizzt, and Deudermont all said together, the drow and the captain feigning excitement.

Catti-brie groaned again.

"Yes, yes. Bruenor Battlehammer," Harkle said to himself, and started walking away. "BB. Oh, I must explore the correlation of the letters, yes, I must."

"While ye're thinkin' on it, find the correlation of BF," Catti-brie said to him. The distracted wizard nodded and rambled along, making a straight path to Deudermont's private quarters, which Harkle had practically taken over.

"BF?" the captain asked Catti-brie.

"Babbling fool," she and Drizzt replied together, drawing yet another laugh from those nearby. Still, neither Drizzt nor Catti-brie, Deudermont nor any of the others could dismiss the fact that the "babbling fool" had apparently saved the *Sea Sprite,* and had put them closer to their goal.

PART THREE

They are the absolutes, the pantheon of ideals, the goodly gods and the evil fiends, forever locked in the struggle for the souls of the mortals. The concept that is Lolth is purely evil; that of Mielikki, purely good. As opposite as black and white, with no shades of gray in between.

THE NATURE OF EVIL

Thus are the concepts, good and evil. Absolute, rigid. There can be no justification for a truly evil act. There are no shades of gray. While an act of good often brings personal gain, the act itself is absolute as its measure is based on intent. This is epitomized by our beliefs in the pantheon, but what of the mortal races, the rational beings—the humans and the races of elvenkind and dwarvenkind, the gnomes and the halflings, the goblinoids and giantkin? Here the question muddles, the absolutes blend.

To many, the equation is simple: I am drow, drow are evil, thus I am evil.

They are wrong. For what is a rational being if not a choice? And there can be no evil, nor any good, without intent. It is true that in the Realms there are races and cultures, particularly the goblinoids, which show a general weal of evil, and those, such as the surface elves, which lean toward the concept of good. But even in these, which many consider personifications of an absolute, it is the individual's intents and actions that ultimately decide. I have known a goblin who was not evil, and I am a drow who has not succumbed to the ways of his culture. Still, few drow and fewer goblins can make such claims, and so the generalities hold.

Most curious and most diverse among the races are the humans. Here the equation and the expectations muddle most of all. Here perception reins supreme. Here intent is oft hidden, secret. No race is more adept than humans at weaving a mask of justification. No race is more adept than humans at weaving a mask of excuses, at ultimately claiming good intent. And no race is more adept at believing its own claims. How many wars have been fought, man against man, with both armies espousing that god, a goodly god, was on their side and in their hearts?

But good is not a thing of perception. What is "good" in one culture cannot be "evil" in another. This might be true of mores and minor practices, but not of virtue. Virtue is absolute.

It must be. Virtue is the celebration of life and of love, the acceptance of others and the desire to grow toward goodness, toward a better place. It is the absence of pride and envy, the willingness to share our joys and to bask in the accomplishments of others. It is above justification because it is what truly lies in each and every heart. If a person does an evil act, then let him weave his mask, but it will not hide the truth, the absolute, from what is naked within his own heart.

There is a place within each of us where we cannot hide from the truth, where virtue sits as judge. To admit the truth of our actions is to go before that court, where process is irrelevant. Good and evil are intents, and intent is without excuse.

Cadderly Bonaduce went to that place as willingly and completely as any man I have known. I recognize that growth within him, and see the result, the Spirit Soaring, most majestic and yet most humble of human accomplishments.

Artemis Entreri will go to that place. Perhaps not until the moment of his death, but he will go, as we all must eventually go, and what agony he will realize when the truth of his evil existence is laid bare before him. I pray that he goes soon, and my hope is not born of vengeance, for vengeance is an empty prayer. May Entreri go of his own volition to that most private place within his heart to see the truth and thus, to correct his ways. He will find joy in his penance, true harmony that he can never know along his present course.

I go to that place within my heart as often as I am able in order to escape the trap of easy justification. It is a painful place, a naked place, but only there might we grow toward goodness. Only there, where no mask can justify, might we recognize the truth of our intents, and thus, the truth of our actions. Only there, where virtue sits as judge, are heroes born.

—Drizzt Do'Urden

13
THE SPIRIT SOARING

Drizzt, Catti-brie, Deudermont, and Harkle encountered no trouble as they left Carradoon for their trek into the Snowflake Mountains. The drow kept the cowl of his cloak pulled low, and everyone in town was so excited by the presence of the schooner that none paid too much attention to the group as they departed.

Once they got past the gate, the foursome found the going easy and safe. Guided around any potential problems by the drow ranger, they found nothing remarkable, nothing exciting.

Given what they had all been through over the last few tendays, that was just the way they wanted it.

They chatted easily, mostly with Drizzt explaining to them the nature of the wildlife about them—which birds went with which chatter, and how many deer had made the beds of flattened needles near to one grove of pines. Occasionally the conversation drifted to the task at hand, to the blind seer's poem. This put poor Harkle in quite a predicament. He knew that the others were missing obvious points, possibly critical points in the verse, for with his journal, he had been able to scrutinize the poem thoroughly. The wizard wasn't sure how much he could intervene, though. Fog of fate had been created as a passive spell, a method for Harkle to facilitate, and then witness dramatic unfolding events. If he became an active participant in those events by letting another of the players in this drama glance at his enchanted journal, or by using what the journal had shown to him, he would likely ruin the spell.

Certainly Harkle could use his other magical abilities if fate led them to battle, and certainly he could use his intuition, as in the discussion on the *Sea*

Sprite when they had first agreed that they needed to see a sorcerer or a priest. But direct intervention, using information given by the facilitation of the spell, would alter the future perhaps, and thus defeat the intentions of fate. Harkle's spell had never been created for such a purpose; the magic had its edges. Poor Harkle didn't know how far he could push that boundary. In living his forty years surrounded by wizards at least as outrageous as he, he understood all too well the potentially grave side effects of pushing magic too far.

So Harkle let the other three babble through their discussions of the poem, nodding his head and agreeing with whatever seemed to be the most accepted interpretation of any given line. He avoided any direct questions, though his halfhearted shrugs and mumbled responses brought many curious looks.

The trails climbed higher into the mountains, but the going remained easy, for the path was well-worn and oft-traveled. When the foursome came out from under the gloom of the mountain canopy, off the path and onto a flat meadow near to the edge of one steep drop, they understood why.

Drizzt Do'Urden had seen the splendors of Mithral Hall, so had Catti-brie. With his magic, Harkle Harpell had visited many exotic places, such as the Hosttower of the Arcane in Luskan. Deudermont had sailed the Sword Coast from Waterdeep to exotic Calimport. But none of those places had ever taken the breath from any of the four like the sight before them now.

It was called the Spirit Soaring, a fitting name indeed for a gigantic temple—a cathedral—of soaring towers and flying buttresses, of great windows of colored glass and a gutter system finished at every corner with an exotic gargoyle. The lowest edges of the cathedral's main roof were still more than a hundred feet from the ground, and three of the towers climbed to more than twice that height.

The Baenre compound was larger, of course, and the Hosttower was more obviously a free-flowing creation of magic. But there was something more solemn about this place, more reverent and holy. The stone of the cathedral was gray and brown, unremarkable really, but it was the construction of that stone, the earthly, and even greater, strength of the place that gave them awe. It was as though the cathedral's roots were deep in the mountains and its soaring head touched the heavens themselves.

A beautiful melody, a voice rich and sweet, wafted out of the temple, reverberated off the stones. It took the four a moment to even realize that it was a voice, a human voice, for the Spirit Soaring seemed to have a melody all its own.

The grounds were no less spectacular. A grove of trees lined a cobblestone walk that led up to the temple's massive front doors. Outside that perfectly straight tree line was a manicured lawn, thick and rich, bordered by

perfectly-shaped hedgerows and filled with various flower beds, all red and pink, purple and white. Several leafy bushes dotted the lawn as well, and these had been shaped to resemble various woodland animals—a deer and a bear, a huge rabbit and a group of squirrels.

Catti-brie blinked several times when she spotted the gardener, the most unusual dwarf she, who had been raised by dwarves, had ever seen. She poked Drizzt, pointing out the little fellow, and the others noticed, too. The gardener saw them, and began bobbing their way, smiling widely.

His beard was green—green!—split in half and pulled back over his large ears, then twisted with his long green hair into a single braid that dangled more than halfway down his back. He wore a thin sleeveless robe, pale green in color, that hung halfway to the knee, leaving bare his bowed legs, incredibly hairy and powerfully muscled. Bare too were the dwarf's large feet, except for the thin straps of his open-toed sandals.

He cut an intersecting course, coming onto the cobblestones thirty feet ahead of the foursome. There he skidded to a stop, stuck two fingers in his mouth, looked back over his shoulder and gave a shrill whistle.

"What?" came a call a moment later. A second dwarf, this one looking more like what the foursome would expect, rose up from the shade of the tree closest to the temple door. He had broad, square shoulders and a yellow beard. Dressed all in brown, he wore a huge axe strapped on his back and a helmet adorned with deer antlers.

"I told ye I'd help ye!" the yellowbeard roared. "But ye promised me sleep time!" Then this second dwarf noticed the foursome and he stopped his tirade immediately and bobbed down the path toward the group.

The green-bearded dwarf got there first. He said not a word, but gave a dramatic bow, then took up Catti-brie's hand and kissed it. "Hee hee hee," he squeaked with a blush, moving in turn from Catti-brie to Deudermont, to Drizzt, to . . .

Back to Drizzt, where the little one ducked low, peeking up under the full hood.

The drow obliged him, pulling back the hood and shaking out his thick white mane. First meetings were always difficult for Drizzt, especially so far from those places where he was known and accepted.

"Eek!" the little one squealed.

"A stinkin' drow!" roared the yellowbeard, running down the path, tearing the axe off of his back as he came.

Drizzt wasn't surprised, and the other three were more embarrassed than startled.

936

The greenbeard continued to hop up and down and point, benign enough, but the yellowbeard took a more direct and threatening course. He brought his axe up high over his head and bore down on Drizzt like a charging bull.

Drizzt waited until the last possible second, then, using the magical anklets and his honed reflexes, he simply sidestepped. The yellowbeard stumbled as he passed, running headlong into the tree behind the drow.

The greenbeard looked to the other dwarf, then to Drizzt, seeming for a moment as if he, too, meant to charge. Then he looked back to the other dwarf, noting the axe now stuck in the tree. He walked toward the yellowbeard, bracing himself and slapping the dwarf hard on the side of the head.

"A stinkin' drow!" the yellowbeard growled, taking one hand from his axe handle to fend off the continuing slaps. Finally he managed to yank his axe free, but when he leaped about, he found three of the four, the drow included, standing impassively. The fourth, though, the auburn-haired woman, held a bow taut and ready.

"If we wanted ye dead, we'd've cut ye down afore ye got up from yer nap," she said.

"I mean no ill," Drizzt added. "I am a ranger," he said, mostly to the greenbeard, who seemed the more levelheaded of the two. "A being of the forest, as are you."

"Me brother's a druid," the yellowbeard said, trying to appear firm and tough, but seeming rather embarrassed at the moment.

"Doo-dad!" the greenbeard agreed.

"Druid dwarf?" Catti-brie asked. "I've lived most o' me life with dwarves, and have never heared of a druid among the race."

Both dwarves cocked their heads curiously. Surely the young woman sounded dwarfish with her rough accent.

"What dwarves might that be?" the yellowbeard asked.

Catti-brie lowered Taulmaril. "I am Catti-brie," she said. "Adopted daughter of Bruenor Battlehammer, Eighth King of Mithral Hall."

The eyes of both dwarves popped open wide, and their mouths similarly dropped open. They looked hard at Catti-brie, then at each other, back to Catti-brie, and back to each other. They bumped their foreheads together, a firm, smacking sound, then looked back to Catti-brie.

"Hey," the yellowbeard howled, poking a stubby finger Drizzt's way. "I heared o' ye. Ye're Drizzt Dudden."

"Drizzt Do'Urden," the drow corrected, giving a bow.

"Yeah," the yellowbeard agreed. "I heared o' ye. Me name's Ivan, Ivan Bouldershoulder, and this is me brother, Pikel."

"Me brudder," the greenbeard agreed, draping an arm across Ivan's sturdy shoulders.

Ivan glanced back over his shoulder, to the deep cut he had put in the tree. "Sorry about me axe," he said. "I never seen a drow elf."

"Ye come to see the cathedr . . . the catheter . . . the cathe . . . the durned church?" Ivan asked.

"We came to see a man named Cadderly Bonaduce," Deudermont answered. "I am Captain Deudermont of the *Sea Sprite,* sailing out of Waterdeep."

"Ye sailed across land," Ivan said dryly.

Deudermont had his hand up to wave away that expected response before the dwarf ever began it.

"We must speak with Cadderly," Deudermont said. "Our business is most urgent."

Pikel slapped his hands together, put them aside his tilted head, closed his eyes and gave a snore.

"Cadderly's takin' his nap," Ivan explained. "The little ones wear him out. We'll go and see Lady Danica and get ye something to eat." He winked at Catti-brie. "Me and me brother're wanting to hear more about Mithral Hall," he said. "Word says an old one's running the place since Bruenor Battlehammer packed up and left."

Catti-brie tried to hide her surprise, even nodded as though she was not surprised by what Ivan had to say. She glanced at Drizzt, who had no response. Bruenor had left? Suddenly both of them wanted to sit and talk with the dwarves as well. The meeting with Cadderly could wait.

The inside of the Spirit Soaring was no less majestic and awe-inspiring than the outside. They entered the main area of the cathedral, the central chapel, and though there were at least a score of people within, so large was the place that the four strangers each felt alone. All of them found their eyes inevitably moving up, up to the soaring columns, past several ledges lined with decorated statues, past the glow coming in through the stained glass windows, to the intricately carved vaulting of the ceiling more than a hundred feet above them.

When he finally managed to move the stricken four through the main area, Ivan took them through a side door, into rooms more normally sized. The construction of the place, the sheer strength and detail of the place, continued to overwhelm them. No supporting arch or door was without decoration, and one door they went through was so covered in runes and sculptures that Drizzt believed he could stand and study it for hours and hours without seeing every detail, without deciphering every message.

Ivan knocked on a door, then paused for an invitation to enter. When it came, he swung the door open. "I give ye Lady Danica Bonaduce," the dwarf said importantly, motioning for the others to follow.

They started in, Deudermont in the lead, but the captain stopped short, was nearly tripped, as two young children, a boy and a girl, cut across his path. Seeing the stranger, both skidded to a halt. The boy, a sandy-haired lad with almond-shaped eyes, opened his mouth and pointed straight at the drow.

"Please excuse my children," a woman across the room said.

"No offense taken," Drizzt assured her. He bent to one knee, and motioned the pair over. They looked to each other for support, then moved cautiously to the drow, the boy daring to reach up and touch Drizzt's ebony skin. Then he looked at his own fingers, as if to see if some of the coloring had rubbed off.

"No black, Mum," he said, looking to the woman and holding up his hand. "No black."

"Hee hee," Pikel chuckled from the back.

"Get the brats outa here," Ivan whispered to his brother.

Pikel pushed through so that the children could see him, and their faces brightened immediately. Pikel stuck a thumb into each ear and waggled his fingers.

"Oo, oi!" the children roared in unison, and they chased "Uncle Pike" from the room.

"Ye should be watching what me brother's teaching them two," Ivan said to Danica.

She laughed and rose from her chair to greet the visitors. "Surely the twins are better off for having a friend such as Pikel," she said. "And such as Ivan," she graciously added, and the tough-as-iron dwarf couldn't hide a blush.

Drizzt understood that the woman was a warrior simply by the way she walked across the room, lightly, silently, in perfect balance through the complete motion of every step. She was slight of build, a few inches shorter than Catti-brie and no more than a hundred and ten pounds, but every muscle was honed and moved in harmony. Her eyes were even more exotic than those of her children, almond-shaped and rich brown, full of intensity, full of life. Her hair, strawberry blond and as thick as the drow's white mane, bounced gaily about her shoulders as though the abundance of energy that flowed within this woman could not be contained.

Drizzt looked from Danica to Catti-brie, saw a resemblance there in spirit, if not in body.

"I give ye Drizzt Dudden," Ivan began, pulling the deer-antlered helmet from his head. "Catti-brie, daughter of Bruenor of Mithral Hall, Captain

Deudermont of the *Sea Sprite,* outa Waterdeep, and . . ." The yellow-bearded dwarf stopped and looked curiously at the skinny wizard. "What'd ye say yer name was?" he asked.

"Harpell Harkle . . . er, Harkle Harpell," Harkle stuttered, obviously enchanted by Danica. "Of Longsaddle."

Danica nodded. "Well met," she said to each of them in turn, ending with the drow.

"Drizzt Do'Urden," the ranger corrected.

Danica smiled.

"They came to speak to Cadderly," Ivan explained.

Danica nodded. "Go and wake him," she said, still holding Drizzt's hand. "He will not want to miss an audience with such distinguished visitors."

Ivan hopped away, rambling down the hallway.

"Ye've heared of us?" Catti-brie asked.

Danica looked at her and nodded. "Your reputation precedes you," she assured the young woman. "We have heard of Bruenor Battlehammer and the fight to reclaim Mithral Hall."

"And the war with the drow elves?" Drizzt asked.

Danica nodded. "In part," she replied. "I hope that before you leave you will find the time to tell us the story in full."

"What do ye know o' Bruenor's leavin'?" Catti-brie asked bluntly.

"Cadderly knows more of that than I," Danica replied. "I have heard that Bruenor abdicated his reclaimed throne to an ancestor."

"Gandalug Battlehammer," Drizzt explained.

"So it is said," Danica went on. "But where the king and the two hundred loyal to him went, that I do not know."

Drizzt and Catti-brie exchanged glances, both having a fair guess as to where Bruenor might have gone.

Ivan returned then, along with an old, but sprightly man dressed in a tan-white tunic and matching trousers. A light blue silken cape was pulled back from his shoulders, and a wide-brimmed hat, blue and banded in red topped his head. At the front center of the hat band sat a porcelain and gold pendant that depicted a candle burning above an eye, which all of the four recognized as the holy symbol of Deneir—the god of literature and art.

The man was of average height, around six feet, and was muscular, despite his advanced age. His hair, what was left of it, was mostly silver in hue, with a hint of brown. Something about his appearance seemed strangely out of place to the companions. Drizzt finally recognized it to be the man's eyes, striking gray orbs that seemed full of sparkle, the eyes of a younger man.

"I am Cadderly," he said warmly with a humble bow. "Welcome to the Spirit Soaring, the home of Deneir and of Oghma, and of all the goodly gods. You have met my wife, Danica?"

Catti-brie looked from the old Cadderly, to Danica, who could not have been much older than Catti-brie, certainly not yet out of her twenties.

"And yer twins," Ivan added with a smirk, eyeing Catti-brie as she studied Danica. It seemed to perceptive Drizzt and Deudermont that the dwarf was familiar with such confusion upon such an introduction, a fact that led them both to think that Cadderly's advanced age was no natural thing.

"Ah, yes, the twins," Cadderly said, shaking his head and unable to contain a smirk at the mere thought of his boisterous legacy.

The wise priest studied the expressions of the four, appreciating their gracious withholding of the obvious questions. "Twenty-nine," he remarked offhandedly. "I am twenty-nine years old."

"Thirty in two tendays," Ivan added. "Though ye're not looking a day over a hunnerd and six!"

"It was the task of building the cathedral," Danica explained, and there was just a hint of sorrow and anger in her controlled tones. "Cadderly gave to the place his life force, a choice he made for the glory of his god."

Drizzt looked long and hard at the young woman, the dedicated warrior, and he understood that Danica, too, had been forced into a great sacrifice because of Cadderly's choice. He sensed an anger within her, but it was buried deep, overwhelmed by her love for this man and her admiration for his sacrifice.

Catti-brie didn't miss any of it. She, who had lost her love, surely empathized with Danica, and yet, she knew that this woman was undeserving of any sympathy. In those few sentences of explanation, in the presence of Cadderly and of Danica, and within the halls of this most reverent of structures, Catti-brie understood that to give sympathy to Danica would belittle the sacrifice, would diminish what Cadderly had accomplished in exchange for his years.

The two women looked into each other's eyes, locking gazes, Danica's exotic almond-shaped orbs and Catti-brie's large eyes, the richest shade of blue. Catti-brie wanted to say, "At least you have your lover's children," wanted to explain to Danica the emptiness of her own loss, with Wulfgar gone before . . .

Before so much, Catti-brie thought with a sigh.

Danica knew the story, and simply in sharing that long look with Catti-brie, she understood and appreciated what was in the woman's heart.

The eight—for Pikel soon returned, explaining that the children were sleeping in the gardens and being watched over by several priests—spent the next two hours exchanging tales. Drizzt and Cadderly seemed kindred spirits and indeed, had shared many adventures. Both had faced a red dragon and lived to tell the tale, both had overcome legacies of their past. They hit it off splendidly, as did Danica and Catti-brie, and though the dwarven brothers wanted to hear more of Mithral Hall, they found it hard in cracking into the conversation between the women, and the one between Drizzt and Cadderly. Gradually they gave up, and spent their time engaged with Harkle. He had been to Mithral Hall and had participated in the drow war, and turned out to be quite the storyteller, highlighting his tales with minor illusions.

Deudermont felt strangely removed from it all. He found himself missing the sea and his ship, longing to sail again out of Waterdeep Harbor to chase pirates on the open waters.

It might have gone on for all of the afternoon, except that a priest knocked on the door, informing Danica that the children were awake. The woman started to leave with the dwarves, but Drizzt stopped her. He took out the panther figurine and called to Guenhwyvar.

That set Ivan back on his heels! Pikel squealed, too, but in glee, the dwarfish druid always willing to meet with such a magnificent animal, despite the fact that the animal could tear the features from his face.

"The twins will enjoy their time with Guenhwyvar," the drow explained.

The great cat ambled out of the room, Pikel in close pursuit, grabbing the panther's tale that Guenhwyvar might pull him along.

"Not as much as me brother," Ivan, still a bit shaken, remarked.

Danica was going to ask the obvious question of safety, but she held the thought in check, realizing that if the panther wasn't to be trusted, Drizzt would never have brought it in. She smiled and bowed graciously, then left with Ivan. Catti-brie would have gone, but Drizzt's posture, suddenly formal, told her that it was time to speak of business.

"You have not come here merely to exchange tales, fine though they may be," Cadderly said, and he sat up straight, folding his hands in front of him, ready to hear their most important story in full.

Deudermont told it, Drizzt and Catti-brie adding in points they thought necessary, and Harkle constantly highlighting the story with remarks that really had nothing to do with anything as far as the other four could tell.

Cadderly confirmed that he had read of Caerwich and the blind seer. "She speaks in riddles that are not always what they seem," he warned.

"So we have heard," Deudermont agreed. "But this is one riddle my friends cannot ignore."

"If the seer spoke truthfully, then a friend lost, my father Zaknafein, is in the clutches of an evil being," Drizzt explained. "A minion of Lolth, perhaps, or a matron mother of one of Menzoberranzan's ruling houses."

Harkle bit hard on his lip. He saw a mistake here, but had to consider the limitations of his spell. He had read the blind seer's poem, word by word, at least a score of times, committing it fully to memory. But that was privileged information, beyond the scope of his spell. The fog of fate facilitated what would be, but if Harkle used the information that the spell privately gave to him, then he might be altering fate. What that might mean, catastrophe or better conclusion, the wizard could only guess.

Cadderly nodded, not disagreeing with Drizzt's reasoning, but wondering where he might fit in all of this, wondering what role the visitors expected him to play.

"I expect it is a handmaiden," Drizzt went on. "An extraplanar being of the Abyss."

"You wish me to use my powers to confirm this," Cadderly reasoned. "Perhaps to bring forth the beast that you might bargain or battle for your father's soul."

"I understand the depth of my request," Drizzt said firmly. "A yochlol is a powerful being . . ."

"I learned long ago not to fear evil," Cadderly calmly assured him.

"We have gold," Deudermont offered, thinking the price would be high.

Drizzt knew better. In the short time he had been with Cadderly, the drow understood the man's heart and motivations. Cadderly would not take gold, would take no payment at all. He was not surprised when Cadderly answered simply, "One soul is worth saving."

14

THE FLUSTERED WIZARD

Where's Deudermont?" Catti-brie asked of Harkle when the wizard stumbled into a small side room where the young woman was sitting with Drizzt.

"Oh, out and about, out and about," the distracted Harpell replied. There were two chairs in the room, both set before a large window that looked out over the majestic Snowflakes. Drizzt and Catti-brie occupied these, half-facing each other and half-looking out to the beautiful view. The dark elf reclined, his feet up on the window's wide sill. Harkle considered the scene for just a moment, then seemed to collect his wits and moved right between the two. He motioned Drizzt to take his feet away, then hopped up to sit on the window sill.

"Do join us," Catti-brie said with obvious sarcasm—obvious to Drizzt at least, for Harkle smiled dumbly.

"You were discussing the poem, of course," the wizard reasoned. It was partially true. Drizzt and Catti-brie were talking as much about the news that Bruenor had left Mithral Hall as about the all-important poem.

"Of course you were," Harkle said. "That is why I have come."

"Have you deciphered any more of the verse?" Drizzt asked, not too hopeful. The drow liked Harkle, but had learned not to expect too much from the wizard. Above all else, Harkle and his kin were unpredictable sorts, oftentimes of great help, as in the fight for Mithral Hall, and at other times more a detriment than an advantage.

Harkle recognized the drow's ambivalent tone, and he found that he wanted to prove himself at that moment, wanted to tell the drow all of the information in his magical journal, to recite the poem word by word, exactly as the seer had told it. Harkle bit back the words, though, fearful of the limitations of his spell and the potential consequences.

"We're thinking it's Baenre," Catti-brie said. "Whoever's holding the Baenre throne, I mean. 'Given to Lolth and by Lolth given,' is what she said, and who better than the one sitting on Baenre's throne for the Spider Queen to give such a gift?"

Harkle nodded, letting Drizzt take up the thought, but believing that they were slipping off track.

"Catti-brie thinks that it is Baenre, but the seer spoke of the Abyss, and that makes me believe that Lolth has engaged a handmaiden," said Drizzt.

Harkle bit hard on his lip and nodded unconvincingly.

"Cadderly has an informant in the Abyss," Catti-brie added. "An imp, or something akin to that. He'll summon the beastie and try to find us a name."

"But I fear that my road . . ." Drizzt began.

"Our road," Catti-brie corrected, so firmly that Drizzt had to concede the point.

"I fear that our road will once again lead to Menzoberranzan," Drizzt said with a sigh. He didn't want to go back there, that much was obvious, but it was clear also that the ranger would charge headlong into the accursed city for the sake of a friend.

"Why there?" Harkle asked, his voice almost frantic. The wizard saw where the seer's poem had guided Drizzt, and knew that the second line, the one concerning Drizzt's father's ghost, had forced the ranger to think of Menzoberranzan as the source of it all. There were references in the poem to Menzoberranzan, but there was one word in particular that led Harkle to believe that the drow city was not their ultimate goal.

"We have already discussed that," Drizzt replied. "Menzoberranzan would seem to be the dark road the seer spoke of."

"You think it is a handmaiden?" Harkle asked Drizzt.

The drow half-nodded, half-shrugged.

"And you agree?" Harkle questioned Catti-brie.

"Might be that it is," Catti-brie replied. "Or might be a matron mother. That'd be me own guess."

"Aren't handmaidens female?" Harkle's question seemed irrelevant.

"All of Lolth's closest minions are female," Catti-brie replied. "That's why the Spider Queen's one to be fearin'," she added with a wink, trying to break some of the tension.

"As are all of the matron mothers," Harkle reasoned.

Drizzt looked to Catti-brie, neither of them quite understanding what the unpredictable wizard might be getting at.

Harkle flapped his arms suddenly, looking as if he was about to burst. He hopped down from the window, nearly overturning Drizzt in his chair. "She said *he!*" the flustered wizard cried. "The blind hag said *he!* 'The traitor to Lolth is sought by *he* who hates him most!' " Harkle stopped and gave a great, exasperated sigh. Then there came a hissing sound and a line of gray smoke began wafting out of his pocket.

"Oh, by the gods," the wizard moaned.

Drizzt and Catti-brie both jumped to their feet, more because of the wizard's surprisingly acute reasoning than because of the present smoky spectacle.

"What foe, Drizzt?" Harkle pressed with all urgency, the wizard suddenly suspecting that his time was short.

"He," Catti-brie echoed over and over, trying to jog her memory. "Jarlaxle?"

" 'Who is most unshriven,' " Harkle reminded her.

"Not the mercenary, then," said Drizzt, for he had come to the conclusion that Jarlaxle was not as evil as many. "Berg'inyon Baenre, perhaps. He has hated me since our days in the Academy."

"Think! Think! Think!" Harkle shouted as a great gout of smoke rose up from his pocket.

"What are you burning?" Catti-brie demanded, trying to pull the Harpell around so that she could better see. To her surprise and horror, her hand went right through the wizard's suddenly-less-than-corporeal form.

"Never mind that!" Harkle snapped at her. "Think, Drizzt Do'Urden. What foe, who is most unshriven, who festers in the swirl of Abyss and hates you above all? What beast must be freed, that only you can free?" Harkle's voice seem to trail away as his form began to fade.

"I have exceeded the limits of my spell," the wizard tried to explain to his horrified companions. "And so I am out of it, I fear, sent away . . ."

Harkle's voice came back strong, unexpectedly. "What beast, Drizzt? What foe?" And then he was gone, simply gone, leaving Drizzt and Catti-brie standing and staring blankly in the small room.

That last call, as Harkle faded from view, reminded Drizzt of another time when he had heard such a distant cry.

"Errtu," the drow whispered breathlessly. He shook his head even as he spoke the obvious answer, for, though Harkle's reasoning seemed sound, it didn't make sense to Drizzt, not in the context of the poem.

"Errtu," Catti-brie echoed. "Suren that one's hating ye above all, and Lolth'd likely know him, or know of him."

Drizzt shook his head. "It cannot be, for never did I meet the tanar'ri in Menzoberranzan, as the blind seer declared."

Catti-brie thought on that one for a moment. "She never said Menzoberranzan," the woman replied. "Not once."

"In the home that was . . ." Drizzt began to recite, but he nearly gagged on the words, on the sudden realization that his interpretation of their meaning might not be correct.

Catti-brie caught it, too. "Ye never called that place yer home," she said. "And ye often told me that yer first home was . . ."

"Icewind Dale," Drizzt said.

"And it was there that ye met Errtu, and made o' him an enemy," Catti-brie reasoned, and Harkle Harpell seemed a wise man indeed at that moment.

Drizzt winced, remembering well the power and wickedness of the evil balor. It pained the ranger to think of Zaknafein in Errtu's clutches.

⚔ ⚔ ⚔ ⚔ ⚔

Harkle Harpell lifted his head from his huge desk and stretched with a great yawn.

"Oh, yes," he said, recognizing the pile of parchments spread on the desk before him. "I was working on my spell."

Harkle sorted them out and studied them more closely.

"My new spell!" he cried in glee. "Oh, it is finally completed, the fog of fate! Oh, joy, oh happy day!" The wizard leaped up from his chair and twirled about the room, his voluminous robes flying wide. After so many months of exhausting research, his new spell was finally complete. The possibilities rolled through Harkle's mind. Perhaps the fog of fate would take him to Calimshan, on an adventure with a pasha, perhaps to Anauroch, the great desert, or perhaps even to the wastelands of Vaasa. Yes, Harkle would like to go to Vaasa and the rugged Galena Mountains.

"I will have to learn more of the Galenas and have them fully in mind when I cast the spell," he told himself. "Yes, yes, that's the trick." With a snap of his fingers, the wizard rushed to his desk, carefully sorted and arranged the many parchments of the long and complicated spell and placed them in a drawer. Then he rushed out, heading for the library of the Ivy Mansion, to gather information on Vaasa and neighboring Damara, the famed Bloodstone Lands. He could hardly keep his balance, so excited was he about what he believed to

be the initial casting of his new spell, the culmination of months of labor.

For Harkle had no recollection of the true initial casting. All of the last few tendays had been erased from his mind as surely as the pages of the enchanted journal that accompanied the spell were now blank once more. As far as Harkle knew, Drizzt and Catti-brie were sailing off the coast of Waterdeep, in a pirate hunting ship whose name he did not know.

⚔ ⚔ ⚔ ⚔ ⚔

Drizzt stood beside Cadderly in a square room, gorgeously decorated, though not a single piece of furniture was in it. The walls were all of polished black stone, bare, except for twisted iron wall sconces, one set in the exact center of each wall. The torches in these were not burning, not in the conventional sense. They were made of black metal, not wood, each with a crystal ball set at its top. The light—it seemed that Cadderly could conjure whatever colored light he chose—emanated from the balls. One was glowing red now, another yellow, and two green, giving the room a strange texture of colors and depth, with some hues seeming to penetrate more deeply into the glassy surface of the polished walls than others.

All of that held Drizzt's attention for a while, an impressive spectacle indeed, but it was the floor that most amazed the dark elf, who had seen so many amazing sights in his seven decades of life. The perimeter of the floor was black and glassy, like the walls, but the bulk of the floor area was taken up by a mosaic, a double-lined circle. The area between the lines, about a foot wide, was filled with arcane runes. A sign was etched inside, its starlike tips touching the innermost circle. All of these designs had been cut into the floor, and were filled with crushed gemstones of various colors. There was an emerald rune beside a ruby star, both of which were between the twin diamond lines of the outer circles.

Drizzt had seen rooms like this in Menzoberranzan, though certainly not as fabulously made. He knew its function. Somehow it seemed out of place to him in this most goodly of structures, for the twin circles and the sign were used for summoning otherworldly creatures, and because those runes that decorated the edges were of power and protection, the creatures summoned were not likely of a goodly weal.

"Few are allowed to enter this place," Cadderly explained, his voice grave. "Just myself, Danica, and Brother Chaunticleer among the residents of the library. Any guests that require the services of this place must pass the highest of scrutiny."

Drizzt understood that he had just been highly complimented, but that did not dissuade the many questions that bobbed about in his thoughts.

"There are reasons for such callings," Cadderly went on, as if reading the drow's mind. "Sometimes the cause of good can be furthered only by dealing with the agents of evil."

"Is not the summoning of a tanar'ri, or even a minor fiend, in itself an act of evil?" Drizzt asked bluntly.

"No," Cadderly replied. "Not in here. This room is perfect in design and blessed by Deneir himself. A fiend called is a fiend trapped, no more a threat in here than if the beast had remained in the Abyss. As with all questions of good and evil, the intent of the calling is what determines its value. In this case, we have discovered that a soul undeserving of such torture has fallen into the hands of a fiend. We may retrieve that soul only by dealing with the fiend. What better place and better way?"

Drizzt could accept that, especially now, when the stakes were so high and so personal.

"It is Errtu," the drow announced with confidence. "A balor."

Cadderly nodded, not disagreeing. When Drizzt had informed him of his new suspicions given his talk with Harkle Harpell, Cadderly had called upon a minor fiend, a wicked imp, and had sent it on a mission seeking confirmation of the drow's suspicions. Now he meant to call back the imp and get his answers.

"Brother Chaunticleer communed with an agent of Deneir this day," Cadderly remarked.

"And the answer?" the ranger asked, though Drizzt was a bit surprised by the apparent route Chaunticleer had taken.

"No agent of Deneir could give such an answer," Cadderly replied at once, seeing that the drow's reasoning was off course. "No, no, Chaunticleer desired information about our missing wizard friend. Fear not, for Harkle Harpell, it seems, is back at the Ivy Mansion in Longsaddle. We have ways of contacting him, even of retrieving him, if you so desire."

"No!" Drizzt blurted, and he looked away, a bit embarrassed by his sudden outburst. "No," he repeated more quietly. "Harkle Harpell has certainly done enough already. I would not endanger him in this issue that does not truly concern him."

Cadderly nodded and smiled, understanding the truth of the drow's hesitance. "Shall I call now to Druzil, that we might get our answer?" he asked, though he didn't even wait for a response. With a word to each sconce, Cadderly turned all the lights in the room to a velvety purple hue. A second

chant made the designs in the floor glow eerily.

Drizzt held his breath, never comfortable in the midst of such a ceremony. He hardly listened as Cadderly began a soft, rhythmic chant, rather he focused on the glowing runes, concentrated on his suspicions and on the possibilities the future might hold.

After several minutes there came a sharp hissing sound in the middle of the circles, and then an instant of blackness as the fabric of the planes tore asunder. A sharp crackle ended both the hissing and the tear, leaving a very angry looking bat-winged and dog-faced imp sitting on the floor, cursing and spitting.

"Well, greetings my dear Druzil," Cadderly said cheerily, which of course made the wicked imp, the unwilling servant, grumble all the more. Druzil hopped to his feet, his small horns hardly reaching the height of Drizzt's knee, and folded his leathery wings about him.

"I wanted you to meet my friend," Cadderly said casually. "I haven't yet decided whether or not I will have him cut you into little pieces with those fine blades of his."

The evil gaze from Druzil's black eyes locked onto Drizzt's lavender orbs. "Drizzt Do'Urden," the imp spat. "Traitor to the Spider Queen."

"Ah, good," Cadderly said, and his tone told the imp that he had unwitting-ly offered up a bit of information by admitting his recognition of the drow. "You know of him, thus you have spoken with some fiend who knows the truth."

"You desired a specific answer, and only one," Druzil rasped. "And promised a year of peace from you in return!"

"So I did," Cadderly admitted. "And have you my answer?"

"I pity you, foolish drow," Druzil said, staring again intently at Drizzt. "I pity you and laugh at you. Foolish drow. The Spider Queen cares little for you now, because she has given out your punishment as a reward to one who helped her in the Time of Troubles."

Drizzt pulled his gaze from Druzil to regard Cadderly, the old priest standing perfectly calm and collected.

"I pity any who so invokes the rage of a balor," Druzil went on, giving a wicked little laugh.

Cadderly saw that the imp's attitude was difficult for Drizzt, who was under such intense stress from this all. "The balor's name!" the priest demanded.

"Errtu!" Druzil barked. "Mark it well, Drizzt Do'Urden!"

Fires simmered behind Drizzt's lavender eyes, and Druzil could not bear their scrutiny.

The imp snapped his evil gaze over Cadderly instead. "A year of peace, you promised," he rasped.

"Years are measured in different ways," Cadderly growled back at him.

"What treachery—" Druzil started to say, but Cadderly slapped his hands together, uttering a single word, and two black lines, rifts in the fabric of the planes, appeared, one on either side of the imp, and came together as forcefully as Cadderly's hands came together. With a boom of thunder and a waft of smoke, Druzil was gone.

Cadderly immediately brightened the light in the room, and remained quiet for some time, regarding Drizzt, who stood with his head bowed, digesting the confirmation.

"You should utterly destroy that one," the drow said at length.

Cadderly smiled widely. "Not so easy a task," he admitted. "Druzil is a manifestation of evil, a type more than an actual being. I could tear apart his corporeal body, but that merely sends him back to the Abyss. Only there, in his smoking home, could I truly destroy Druzil, and I have little desire to visit the Abyss!" Cadderly shrugged, as if it really mattered very little. "Druzil is harmless enough," the priest explained, "because I know him, know of him, know where to find him, and know how to make his miserable life more miserable still if the need arises."

"And now we know that it is truly Errtu," Drizzt said.

"A balor," Cadderly replied. "A mighty foe."

"A foe in the Abyss," said Drizzt. "A place where I also have no desire to ever go."

"We still need answers," Cadderly reminded. "Answers that Druzil would not be able to provide."

"Who, then?"

"You know," Cadderly answered quietly.

Drizzt did know, but the thought of summoning in the fiend Errtu was not a pleasant one to Drizzt.

"The circle will hold the balor," Cadderly assured him. "You do not have to be here when I call to Errtu."

Drizzt waved that notion away before Cadderly ever finished the sentence. He would be there to face the one who hated him most, and who apparently held captive a friend.

Drizzt gave a deep sigh. "I believe that the prisoner the hag spoke of is Zaknafein, my father," he confided to the priest, for he found that he truly trusted Cadderly. "I am not yet certain of how I feel about that."

"Surely it torments you to think your father in such foul hands," Cadderly

replied. "And surely it thrills you to think that you might meet with Zaknafein once more."

Drizzt nodded. "It is more than that," he said.

"Are you ambivalent?" Cadderly asked, and Drizzt, caught off his guard by the direct question, cocked his head and studied the old priest. "Did you close that part of your life, Drizzt Do'Urden? And now are you afraid because it might again be opened?"

Drizzt shook his head without hesitation, but it was an unconvincing movement. He paused a long while, then sighed deeply. "I am disappointed," the drow admitted. "In myself, for my selfishness. I want to see Zaknafein again, to stand beside him and learn from him and listen to his words." Drizzt looked up at Cadderly, his expression truly serene. "But I remember the last time I saw him," he said, and he told Cadderly then of that final meeting.

Zaknafein's corpse had been animated by Matron Malice, Drizzt's mother, and then imbued with the dead drow's spirit. Bound in servitude to evil Malice, working as her assassin, Zaknafein had then gone out into the Underdark in search of Drizzt. At the critical moment, the true Zaknafein had broken through the evil matron mother's will for a fleeting moment, had shone forth once again and spoken to his beloved son. In that moment of victory, Zaknafein's spirit had proclaimed its peace, and Zaknafein had destroyed his own animated corpse instead, freeing Drizzt and freeing himself from the grasp of evil Malice Do'Urden.

"When I heard the blind hag's words and spent the time to consider them, I was truly sorry," Drizzt finished. "I believed that Zaknafein was free of them now, free of Lolth and all the evil, and sitting in a place of just rewards for the truth that was always in his soul."

Cadderly put a hand on Drizzt's shoulder.

"To think that they had captured him once again . . ."

"But that may not be the case," Cadderly said. "And if it is true, then hope is not lost. Your father needs your help."

Drizzt set his jaw firmly and nodded. "And Catti-brie's help," he replied. "She will be here when we call to Errtu."

15
DARKNESS INCARNATE

His smoking bulk nearly filled the circle. His great leathery wings could not extend to their fullest, else they would have crossed the boundary line where the fiend could not pass. Errtu clawed at the stone and issued a guttural growl, threw back his huge and ugly head and laughed maniacally. Then the balor suddenly calmed, and looked forward, his knowing eyes boring into the gaze of Drizzt Do'Urden.

Many years had passed since Drizzt had looked upon mighty Errtu, but the ranger surely recognized the fiend. His ugly face seemed a cross between a dog and an ape, and his eyes—especially those eyes—were black pits of evil, sometimes wide with outrage and red with flame, sometimes narrowed, slanted, intense slits promising hellish tortures. Yes, Drizzt remembered Errtu well, remembered their desperate fight on the side of Kelvin's Cairn those years before.

The ranger's scimitar, the one he had taken from the white dragon's lair, seemed to remember the fiend, too, for Drizzt felt it calling to him, urging him to draw it forth and strike at the balor again that it might feed upon Errtu's fiery heart. That blade had been forged to battle creatures of fire, and seemed particularly eager for the smoking flesh of a fiend.

Catti-brie had never seen such a beast, darkness incarnate, evil embodied, the most foul of the foul. She wanted to take up Taulmaril and shoot an arrow into the beast's ugly face, and yet she feared that to do so would loose wicked Errtu upon them, something the young woman most certainly did not desire.

Errtu continued to chuckle, then with terrifying speed, the great fiend

lashed out toward Drizzt with its many-thonged whip. The weapon snapped forward, then stopped fast in midair, as though it had hit a wall, and indeed it had.

"You cannot send your weapons, your flesh, or your magic through the barrier, Errtu," Cadderly said calmly—the old priest seemed not shaken in the least by the true tanar'ri.

Errtu's eyes narrowed wickedly as the balor dropped his gaze over Cadderly, knowing that it was the priest who had dared to summon the balor. Again came that rumbling chuckle and flames erupted at Errtu's huge, clawed feet, burning white and hot, blazing so high that they nearly blocked the companions' view of the balor. The three friends squinted against the intense, stinging heat. At last, Catti-brie fell away with a shout of warning, and Drizzt heeded that call, went with her. Cadderly remained in place, though, standing impassively, confident that the rune-etched circles would stop the fires. Sweat beaded on his face, droplets falling from his nose.

"Desist!" Cadderly yelled above the crackle. Then he recited a string of words in a language that neither Drizzt nor Catti-brie had ever heard before, an arcane phrase that ended with the name of Errtu, spoken emphatically.

The balor roared as if in pain, and the fire walls fell away to nothingness.

"I will remember you, old man," the great balor promised. "When I walk again on the plane that is your world."

"Do pay me a visit," Cadderly replied evenly. "It would be my pleasure to banish you back to the filth where you truly belong."

Errtu said no more, but growled and focused once more upon the renegade drow, the most-hated Drizzt Do'Urden.

"I have him, drow," the fiend teased. "In the Abyss."

"Who?" Drizzt demanded, but the balor's response was yet another burst of maniacal laughter.

"Who do you have, Errtu?" Cadderly asked firmly.

"No questions must I answer," the balor reminded the priest. "I have him, that you know, and the one way you have of getting him back is to end my banishment. I will take him to this, your land, Drizzt Do'Urden, and if you want him, then you must come and get him!"

"I will speak with Zaknafein!" Drizzt yelled, his hand going to the hilt of his hungry scimitar. Errtu mocked him, laughed at him, thoroughly enjoying the spectacle of Drizzt's frustration. It was just the beginning of the drow's torment.

"Free me!" the fiend roared, silencing the questions. "Free me now! Each day is an eternity of torture for my prisoner, your beloved fa—" Errtu stopped abruptly, letting the teasing word hang in the air. The balor waggled a finger at Cadderly. "Have I been tricked?" Errtu said, feigning horror. "Almost did I answer a question, something that is not required of me."

Cadderly looked to Drizzt, understanding the ranger's dilemma. The priest knew that Drizzt would willingly leap into the circle and fight Errtu here and now for the sake of his lost father, of a friend, or of any goodly person, but to free the fiend seemed a desperate and dangerous act to the noble drow, a selfish act for the sake of his father that might jeopardize so many others.

"Free me!" roared the balor, his thunderous voice echoing about the chamber.

Drizzt relaxed suddenly. "That I cannot do, foul beast," he said quietly, shaking his head, seeming to gain confidence in his decision with every passing second.

"You fool!" Errtu roared. "I will flail the skin from his bones! I will eat his fingers! And I will keep him alive, I promise, alive and conscious through it all, telling him before each torture that you refused to help him, that you caused his doom!"

Drizzt looked away, relaxed no more, his breathing coming in hard, angry gasps. He knew the truth of Zaknafein, though, understood his father's heart, and knew that the weaponmaster would not wish Drizzt to free Errtu, whatever the cost.

Catti-brie took Drizzt's hand, as did Cadderly.

"I'll not tell you what to do, good drow," the old priest offered, "but if the fiend imprisons a soul undeserving of such a fate, then it is our responsibility to save . . ."

"But at what price?" Drizzt said desperately. "At what cost to the world?"

Errtu was laughing again, wildly. Cadderly turned to quiet the fiend, but Errtu spoke first. "You know, priest," the fiend accused. "You know!"

"What does the ugly thing mean?" Catti-brie asked.

"Tell them," Errtu bade Cadderly, who seemed uncomfortable for the first time.

Cadderly looked at Drizzt and Catti-brie and shook his head.

"Then I shall tell them!" Errtu shouted, the balor's tremendous, throaty voice echoing again about the stone room, paining their ears.

"You shall be gone!" Cadderly promised, and he began a chant. Errtu jerked suddenly, violently, then seemed smaller, seemed as if he was falling back in on himself.

"I am free now!" the balor proclaimed.

"Wait," Drizzt bade Cadderly, and the priest obeyed.

"I shall go where I please, foolish Drizzt Do'Urden! By your will I have touched the ground of the Prime Material Plane, and thus my banishment is at its end. I can return to the call of any!"

Cadderly began his chant again, more urgently, and Errtu began to fade away.

"Come to me, Drizzt Do'Urden," the balor's now-distant voice beckoned. "If you would see him again. I'll not come for you."

Then the fiend was gone, leaving the three companions exhausted in the empty room. Most weary among them was Drizzt, who slumped back against the wall, and it seemed to the others as if the solid stone was the only thing keeping the weary ranger on his feet.

"Ye didn't know," Catti-brie reasoned, understanding the guilt that so weighed on her friend's shoulders. She looked to the old priest who hardly seemed bothered by the revelations.

"Is it true?" Drizzt asked Cadderly.

"I cannot be certain," the priest replied. "But I believe that our summoning of Errtu to the Prime Material Plane might have indeed ended the balor's banishment."

"And ye knew it all along," Catti-brie said in accusing tones.

"I suspected," Cadderly admitted.

"Then why did you let me call to the beast?" Drizzt asked, completely surprised. He would never have figured that Cadderly would end the banishment of such an evil monster. When he looked at the old priest now, though, it seemed to Drizzt as if Cadderly wasn't bothered in the least.

"The fiend, as is always the case with such denizens, can get to the Prime Material Plane only with assistance from a priest or a wizard," Cadderly explained. "Any of that ilk who so desired such a beast could find many, many waiting for their call, even other balors. The freeing of Errtu, if indeed Errtu is free, is not so much a travesty."

Put in that context, it made sense to Drizzt and to Catti-brie. Those who desired to call a fiend to their service would find no shortage, for the Abyss was full of powerful denizens, all eager to come forth and wreak havoc among the mortals.

"The thing I fear," Cadderly admitted, "is that this particular balor hates you above all, Drizzt. He may, despite his last words, seek you out if he ever gets back to our world."

"Or I will seek out Errtu," Drizzt replied evenly, unafraid, and that brought a smile to Cadderly's lips. It was just the response he had hoped to hear from the courageous drow. Here was a mighty warrior in the war for good, Cadderly knew. The priest held great faith that if such a battle were to come about, Drizzt and his friends would prevail, and the torment of Drizzt's father would come to an end.

⚔ ⚔ ⚔ ⚔ ⚔

Waillan Micanty and Dunkin Tallmast arrived at the Spirit Soaring later that day, and found Captain Deudermont outside the structure, relaxing in the shade of a tree, feeding strange nuts to a white squirrel.

"Percival," Deudermont explained to the two men, holding his hand out to the squirrel. As soon as Percival snatched the treat, Deudermont pointed out Pikel Bouldershoulder, hard at work as always, tending his many gardens. "Pikel over there informs me that Percival is a personal friend of Cadderly's."

Waillan and Dunkin exchanged doubting looks, neither having a clue as to what Deudermont might be talking about.

"It is not important," the captain remarked, rising to his feet and brushing the twigs from his trousers. "What news on the *Sea Sprite?*"

"The repairs are well underway," replied Waillan. "Many of Carradoon's fishermen have joined in to help. They have even found a tree suitable to replace the mast."

"A friendly lot, these men of Carradoon," Dunkin put in.

Deudermont regarded Dunkin for a while, pleased at the subtle changes he had witnessed in the man. This was not the same surly and conniving emissary who had first come to the *Sea Sprite* in the name of Lord Tarnheel Embuirhan in search of Drizzt Do'Urden. The man was a fine sailor and a fine companion according to Waillan, and Deudermont planned to offer him a full-time position as a crewman aboard the *Sea Sprite* as soon as they figured out how to get the ship back in the Sea of Swords where she belonged.

"Robillard is in Carradoon," Waillan said unexpectedly, catching the captain off guard, though Deudermont never doubted that the wizard had survived the storm and would eventually find them. "Or he was. He might have gone back to Waterdeep by now. He says that he can get us back where we belong."

"But it will cost us," added Dunkin. "For the wizard will need help from his brotherhood, an exceptionally greedy lot, by Robillard's own admission."

Deudermont wasn't very concerned about that. The Lords of Waterdeep would likely reimburse any expenses. The captain did note Dunkin's use of the word "us," and that pleased him more than a little.

"Robillard said that it would take him some time to organize it all," Waillan

finished. "But we're two tendays from repairing the *Sea Sprite* in any case, and with the help, it's easier fixing her here than in Waterdeep."

Deudermont only nodded. Pikel came bobbing over then, stealing the attention of Waillan and Dunkin. That was fine with Deudermont. The details of returning the *Sea Sprite* where she belonged would work themselves out, he did not doubt. Robillard was a competent and loyal wizard. But the captain saw a parting of the ways in his immediate future, for two friends—three, counting Guenhwyvar—wouldn't likely go back with the ship, or if they did, they wouldn't likely remain with her for long.

16

THE BAIT

Icewind Dale," Drizzt said, before the three had even left the room of summoning.

Cadderly looked surprised, but as soon as Catti-brie heard the words, she understood what Drizzt was talking about and agreed with his reasoning. "Ye're thinking that the fiend'll go after the crystal shard," she explained, more for Cadderly's sake than for any need of confirmation.

"If ever Errtu does get back to our world, then he will certainly go for the artifact," Drizzt replied.

Cadderly knew nothing about this crystal shard they referred to, but he realized that the pair believed they were on to something important. "You are sure of this?" he asked Drizzt.

The drow nodded. "When first I met Errtu, it was on a windswept mountain above the Spine of the World, in the place called Kelvin's Cairn in Icewind Dale," he explained. "The fiend had come to the call of the wizard who possessed Crenshinibon—the crystal shard—a most powerful artifact of evil."

"And where is this artifact?" Cadderly asked, suddenly seeming quite concerned. The priest had some experience in dealing with evil artifacts, had once put his own life and the lives of those he loved in jeopardy for the sake of destroying such an item.

"Buried," Catti-brie replied. "Buried under a mountain o' snow and rock by an avalanche down the side o' Kelvin's Cairn." She looked more at Drizzt than the priest as she spoke, her expression showing that she was beginning to doubt the drow's reasoning.

"The item is sentient," the ranger reminded her. "A malignant tool that will not accept such solitude. If Errtu gets back to our world, he will go to Icewind Dale in search of Crenshinibon, and if he is near to the thing, it will call out to him."

Cadderly agreed. "You must destroy this crystal shard," he said so determinedly that he caught them by surprise. "That is paramount."

Drizzt wasn't sure that he agreed with that priority, not with his father apparently held prisoner by the balor. But he did agree that the world would be a better place without the likes of Crenshinibon.

"How does one destroy so powerful an artifact?" the ranger dared to ask.

"I do not know. Each artifact has specific ways in which it may be undone," Cadderly replied. "A few years ago, when I was young, it was asked by my god to destroy the Ghearufu, a sentient and evil thing. I had to seek . . . to demand assistance from a great red dragon."

"A few years ago when I was young," Catti-brie repeated under her breath, so that neither of the others could hear.

"Thus I put it upon you now to find and destroy Crenshinibon, this artifact that you call the crystal shard."

"I'm not knownin' any dragons," Catti-brie remarked dryly.

Drizzt actually did know of another red, but he kept that quiet, having no desire to face the great wyrm called Hephaestus again and hoping that Cadderly would offer an alternative.

"When you have the item in your possession and Errtu is dealt with, then bring it back to me," Cadderly said. "Together, with the guidance of Deneir, we will discover how the crystal shard might be destroyed."

"Ye make it sound so easy," Catti-brie added, and again, her tone was ripe with sarcasm.

"Hardly," Cadderly said. "But I hold fast my faith. Would it please you more if I said 'if' instead of 'when' ? "

"I'm gettin' yer point," Catti-brie replied.

Cadderly smiled broadly and draped an arm about the young woman's sturdy shoulders. Catti-brie didn't shy away from that embrace in the least, finding that she truly liked the priest. There was nothing about Cadderly that made her uncomfortable, except perhaps the casual way in which Cadderly dealt with such powers as Errtu and the crystal shard. Now that was confidence!

"We can't be gettin' the crystal shard out from under the pile," Catti-brie reasoned to Drizzt.

"Likely, it will find its own way out," Cadderly said. "Likely, it already has."

"Or Errtu will discover it," said Drizzt.

"So we're to go to Icewind Dale and wait?" Catti-brie huffed, suddenly realizing the depth of the task before them. "Ye're wanting to sit and serve as guardians? For how many centuries?"

Drizzt also wasn't pleased by the prospect, but the responsibility seemed clear to him, now that Errtu was apparently freed. The thought of seeing Zaknafein again would hold the drow even if it meant centuries of servitude.

"We will take it as the fates give it to us," Drizzt told Catti-brie. "We have a long road ahead of us, and yes, perhaps a long wait after that."

"There is a temple of Deneir in Luskan," Cadderly interjected. "That is near to this place called Icewind Dale, is it not?"

"The closest city south of the mountains," Drizzt replied.

"I can get you there," Cadderly said. "Together the three of us can walk the wind to Luskan."

Drizzt considered the prospects. It was nearly midsummer and many merchants would be on their way through Luskan, bound for Ten-Towns to trade for the valuable knucklehead trout scrimshaw. If Cadderly could get them to Luskan quickly, they would have little trouble in joining a caravan to Icewind Dale.

Only then did Drizzt realize yet another obstacle. "What of our friends?" he asked.

Catti-brie and Cadderly looked to each other. In the excitement, they had both nearly forgotten about Deudermont and the stranded *Sea Sprite*.

"I cannot take so many," Cadderly admitted. "And certainly, I cannot take a ship!"

Drizzt thought it over for a moment. "But we must go," he said to Catti-brie.

"I'm thinking that Deudermont's to like sailin' on a lake," Catti-brie retorted sarcastically. "Not many pirates about, and if he opened the *Sea Sprite*'s sails wide, then suren he'd find himself a mile into the stinkin' woods!"

Drizzt seemed to deflate under the weight of her honest words. "Let us go and find the captain," he replied. "Perhaps we will retrieve Harkle Harpell. He put the *Sea Sprite* in Impresk Lake, let him get her back where she belongs!"

Catti-brie mumbled something under her breath, her tone too low for Drizzt to decipher the actual words. He knew what she thought of Harkle though, and could imagine them readily enough.

The three found Deudermont, Waillan and Dunkin sitting with Ivan and Pikel along the walk outside of the Spirit Soaring's front doors. Deudermont told them the news of Robillard and the plan to get back where they belonged,

which came as a great relief to both Drizzt and Catti-brie. The two looked to each other, and Deudermont knew them well enough to understand the gist of what was going on.

"You are leaving us," he reasoned. "You cannot wait the two or three tendays it will take Robillard to facilitate our return."

"Cadderly can get us to Luskan," Drizzt replied. "In less than two or three tendays, I hope to be in Ten-Towns."

The news put a pall on the previously lighthearted conversation. Even Pikel, who hardly knew what the others were talking about, issued a long and forlorn, "Ooooo."

Deudermont tried to find a way out of this, but he recognized the inevitable. His place was with the *Sea Sprite,* and given the high stakes, Drizzt and Catti-brie had no choice but to follow the words of the blind seer. Besides, Deudermont had not missed their expressions when Ivan had informed them that Bruenor had left Mithral Hall. Drizzt said he was going back to Ten-Towns, to Icewind Dale, and that was likely where Bruenor had gone.

"Perhaps if we get back to the Sword Coast before the weather turns toward winter, I'll sail the *Sea Sprite* around the bend and into the Sea of Moving Ice," Deudermont said, his way of bidding his friends farewell. "I would like to visit this Icewind Dale."

"My home," Drizzt said solemnly.

Catti-brie nodded to Drizzt and to Deudermont. She was never comfortable with good-byes and she knew that was exactly what this was.

It was time to go home.

THE FEEL OF POWER

Stumpet Rakingclaw plodded through the snow halfway up the side of Kelvin's Cairn. The dwarf knew that her course was risky, for the melt in Icewind Dale was on in full and the mountain was not so high that its temperature remained below the point of freezing. The dwarf could feel the wetness seeping through her thick leather boots, and more than once she heard telltale rumblings of the complaining snow.

The stubborn dwarf plowed on, thrilled by the potential danger. The whole slope could go tumbling down—avalanches were not uncommon on Kelvin's Cairn, where the melt came fast. Stumpet felt like a true adventurer at that moment, braving ground she believed no one had trod in many years. She knew little of the region's history, for she had gone to Mithral Hall along with Dagna and the thousands from Citadel Adbar and had been too busy working in the mines to pay attention to the stories the members of Clan Battlehammer told of Icewind Dale.

Stumpet did not know the story of the most famous avalanche on this very mountain. She did not know that Drizzt and Akar Kessel had waged their last battle here before the ground had fallen out from under them, burying Kessel.

Stumpet stopped and reached into a pouch, producing a bit of lard. She uttered a minor enchantment and touched the lard to pursed lips, enacting a spell to help her ward off the chill. The season was fast turning to summer down below, but the wind up here was cold still and the dwarf was wet. Even as she finished, she heard another rumble and looked up to the mountain's peak, which was still two hundred feet away. For the first time she wondered if she could really get there.

Kelvin's Cairn was certainly not a large mountain. If it had been near Adbar, Stumpet's birthplace, or near Mithral Hall, it wouldn't even have been called a mountain at all. It was just a hillock, a thousand-foot-high clump of rock. But out here on the flat tundra, it seemed a mountain, and Stumpet Rakingclaw was a dwarf who considered the challenge of climbing to be the primary purpose of any mountain. She knew that she could have waited until late summer, when there would have been little snow remaining on Kelvin's Cairn and the ground would be more accessible, but the dwarf had never been known for her patience. Anyway, the mountain wouldn't be much of a challenge without the dangerous, shifting snow.

"Don't ye be falling on me," Stumpet said to the mountain. "And don't ye take me all the way back down!"

She spoke too loudly and as if in answer, the mountain gave a tremendous groan. Suddenly Stumpet was sliding backward.

"Oh, damn ye!" she cursed, taking up her huge pick, looking for a hold. She tumbled over backward, but kept herself oriented enough to dodge a jutting stone and to set her pick firmly into its side. Her muscles strained as the snow washed past, but it was not too deep and the force of it not too strong.

A moment later all was quiet again, save the distant echoes, and Stumpet pulled herself out of the giant snowball that she and the supporting rock had become.

Then she noticed a curious shard of ice lying on the now bare ground. Coming free of the snow pile, the dwarf gave the strangely shaped item little thought. She moved up to a spot of bare ground and brushed herself off as thoroughly as possible before the snow could melt on her and further wet her already sopping clothing.

Her eyes kept roving back to the crystal. It didn't seem so extraordinary, just a hunk of ice. And yet, the dwarf got the distinct feeling deep in her gut that it was more than that.

For a few moments, Stumpet managed to fend off the unreasonable urges and concentrate on getting herself ready to continue her climb.

The piece of crystal kept calling to her, just below her conscious level, beckoning her to pick it up.

Before she realized what she was doing, she had the item in hand. Not ice, she realized immediately, for it was warm to the touch, warm and somehow comforting. She held it up to the light. It appeared to be a square-sided icicle, barely a foot long. Stumpet paused and removed her gloves.

"Crystal," she muttered in confirmation, for the warm item did not have the slick feel of ice. Stumpet closed her eyes, concentrating on her tactile sense, trying to feel the true temperature of the item.

"Me spell," the dwarf whispered, thinking she had figured out the mystery. She chanted again, dispelling the magic she had just enacted to fend off the cold.

Still the crystal shard felt warm. Stumpet rubbed her hands across its side and its warmth spread out even to her wet toes.

The dwarf scratched the stubble on her chin and looked around to see if anything else might have dislodged in the small avalanche. She was thinking clearly now, reasoning through this unexpected mystery. But all she saw was white, gray, and brown, the unremarkable tapestry that was Kelvin's Cairn. That didn't deter her suspicions. Again she held the crystal shard aloft, watching the play of sunlight through its depths.

"A magical ward against the cold," she said aloud. "A merchant brought ye on a trip to the dale," she reasoned. "Might be that he was seeking some treasure up here, or just that he came up here to get a better look around, thinking that ye'd protect him. And from the cold, ye did," she reasoned confidently, "but not from the snowfall that buried him!"

There, she had it figured out. Stumpet felt herself lucky indeed to have found such a useful item in the empty wasteland that was Kelvin's Cairn. She looked to the south, where the tall peaks of the Spine of the World, perpetually covered in snow, loomed in a gray mist. Suddenly, the dwarven priestess was thinking of where this crystal shard might take her. What mountain would be beyond her if she carried such protection? She could climb them all in a single journey, and her name would be revered among the dwarves!

Already Crenshinibon, the crystal shard, the sentient and insidious artifact was at work, imparting subtle promises of Stumpet's deepest desires upon her. Crenshinibon recognized this wielder, not only a dwarf, but a dwarven priestess, and was not pleased. Dwarves were a stubborn and difficult lot, and resistant to magic. But still, the most evil of artifacts was glad to be out of the snow, glad that someone had returned to Kelvin's Cairn to bear Crenshinibon away.

The crystal shard was back among the realm of the living now, back where it might cause more havoc.

※ ※ ※ ※ ※

He crept along the tunnels, measuring his steps by the rhythmic pounding of dwarven hammers. The fit of the tight place was not comfortable, not for

one used to the stars as his ceiling, and tall Kierstaad sometimes had to get down on his knees to pass through low archways.

Hearing footsteps, he paused at one corner and flattened himself as much as possible against the wall. He was unarmed, but he would not be welcomed here in the dwarven mines, not after Bruenor's unsavory encounter with Berkthgar. Kierstaad's father, Revjak, had been better in dealing with the dwarf, welcoming Bruenor's return, but even in that meeting, the strain had been obvious. Berkthgar and his followers were putting tremendous pressure on Revjak for a complete return to the ancient ways of mistrusting anyone who was not of the tribe. Revjak was wise enough to know that if he fought Berkthgar too boldly on this issue, he might lose control of the tribe altogether.

Kierstaad saw it, too, and his feelings were mixed. He remained loyal to his father, and believed that the dwarves were his friends, but Berkthgar's arguments were convincing. The ancient ways—the hunt across the tundra, the prayers to the spirits of those animals who were taken—seemed so refreshing to the young man who had spent the last few years of his life dealing with wretched merchants or battling dark elves.

The approaching dwarves turned away at the intersection, never noticing Kierstaad, and the barbarian breathed easier. He paused a moment to get his bearings, recalling which tunnels he had already passed through and where he believed the personal quarters of the leader would be. Many of the dwarves were out of the mines this day, having gone to Bryn Shander to collect the supplies Bruenor had purchased. Those remaining were in the deeper tunnels, eagerly opening up veins of precious minerals.

Kierstaad encountered no others as he made his way, often backtracking, sometimes going in circles. At last he came to a small corridor with two doors on either side and another at the very end. The first room seemed very undwarflike. Plush carpets and a bed stacked high with mattresses and higher still with warm comforters told the barbarian who it was that used this room.

"Regis," Kierstaad said with a soft chuckle, nodding as he spoke the name. The halfling was supposedly everything the barbarian people despised, lazy, fat, gluttonous, and worst of all, sneaky. Yet, Kierstaad's smile—and the smiles of many other barbarians—had widened every time Regis had come bobbing into Settlestone. Regis was the only halfling Kierstaad had ever met, but if "Rumblebelly," as many called him, was indicative of the race, Kierstaad thought that he would like to meet many more. Gently he closed the door, with one last smirk at the pile of mattresses—Regis often boasted that he could make himself comfortable any place, at any time.

Indeed.

Both rooms across the hall were unoccupied, each holding a single bed more suited to a human than a dwarf. This, too, Kierstaad understood, for it was no secret that Bruenor hoped that Drizzt and Catti-brie would someday return to his side.

The end of the hall was likely a sitting room, the barbarian reasoned. That left one door, the door to the chambers of the dwarven king. Kierstaad moved slowly, tentatively, fearing that a cunning trap had been set.

He cracked open the door, just an inch. No pits opened below his feet, no stones fell from the ceiling onto his head. Gaining confidence, the young barbarian pushed the door wide.

Bruenor's room, there could be no doubt. A scattering of parchments sat atop a wooden desk across the way, extra clothes were piled nearly as high as Kierstaad in one corner. The bed was not made, was a tumble of blankets and pillows.

Kierstaad hardly noticed any of it. The moment the door had opened, his eyes had fixed upon a single object set on the wall at the head of Bruenor's bed.

Aegis-fang. Wulfgar's warhammer.

Hardly breathing, Kierstaad crossed the small room to stand beside the mighty weapon. He saw the gorgeous runes etched into its gleaming mithral head—the twin mountains, the symbol of Dumathoin, dwarven god and keeper of secrets. Looking closer, Kierstaad made out portions of another rune buried under the twin mountain disguise. So perfect was the overlay that he could not determine what it might be. He knew the legend of Aegis-fang, though. Those hidden runes were the marks of Moradin, the Soul Forger, greatest of the dwarven gods on one side, and the axe of Clangeddin, the dwarven battle god, on the other.

Kierstaad stood for a long time, staring, thinking of the legend that was Wulfgar, thinking of Berkthgar and Revjak. Where would he fit in? If the conflict exploded between the former leader of Settlestone and the current leader of the Tribe of the Elk, what role might Kierstaad play?

A greater one, he knew, if he held Aegis-fang in his hands. Hardly considering the movement, Kierstaad reached out and clasped the warhammer, lifting it from its hooks.

How heavy it seemed! Kierstaad brought it in close, then, with great effort, lifted it above his head.

It banged against the low ceiling, and the young man nearly fell sidelong as it bounced out too wide for him to properly control its momentum. When he at last regained his balance, Kierstaad laughed at his foolishness. How could

he hope to wield mighty Aegis-fang? How could he hope to follow in the giant footsteps of mighty Wulfgar?

He brought the fabulous warhammer in close to his chest again, wrapping his arms about it reverently. He could feel its strength, its perfect balance, could almost feel the presence of the man who had wielded it so long and so well.

Young Kierstaad wanted to be like Wulfgar. He wanted to lead the tribe in his own vision. He didn't agree with Wulfgar's course any more than he now agreed with Berkthgar's, but there was a place in between, a compromise that would give the barbarians the freedom of the old ways and the alliances of the new. With Aegis-fang in hand, Kierstaad felt as if he could do that, could take control and lead his people on the best possible course.

The young barbarian shook his head and laughed again, mocking himself and his grand dreams. He was barely more than a boy, and Aegis-fang was not his to wield. That thought made the young man glance back over his shoulder, to the open door. If Bruenor returned and found him in here holding the warhammer, the taciturn dwarf would likely cut him in half.

It wasn't easy for Kierstaad to replace the hammer on its hooks, and it was harder still for him to leave the room. But he had no choice. Empty-handed, he quietly and cautiously snuck back out of the tunnels, back under the open sky, and ran all the way back to his tribe's encampment, some five miles across the tundra.

⚔ ⚔ ⚔ ⚔ ⚔

The dwarf reached as high as she possibly could, her stubby fingers brushing aside the crusty snow and grasping desperately at the rock. The last ledge, the doorway to the top, the very top.

Stumpet groaned and strained, knowing it to be an impossible obstacle, knowing that she had overreached her bounds and was surely destined to fall thousands of feet to her death.

But then, somehow, she found the strength. Her fingers latched on firmly and she pulled with all her might. Little legs kicked and scraped at the rock, and suddenly she was over, onto the flat plateau at the top of the tallest mountain in all the world.

The resilient dwarf stood tall on that high place and surveyed the scene below her, the world conquered. She noted the crowds then, thousands and thousands of her bearded minions, filling all the valleys and all the trails. They were cheering, bowing before her.

Stumpet came awake drenched in sweat. It took her several moments to orient herself, to realize that she was in her own small room in the dwarven mines in Icewind Dale. She gave a slight smile as she recalled the vivid dream, the breathtaking last surge that got her over the top. But that smile was lost in confusion as she considered the subsequent scene, the cheering dwarves.

"Why'd I go and dream that?" Stumpet wondered aloud. She never climbed for glory, simply for the personal satisfaction that conquering a mountain gave to her. Stumpet didn't care what others thought of her climbing prowess, and she rarely even told anyone where she was going, where she had been, or whether or not the climb had been a success.

The dwarf wiped her forehead and slipped back to her hard mattress, the images of the dream still vividly clear in her mind. A dream or a nightmare? Was she lying to herself about the truth of why she climbed? Was there indeed a measure of personal satisfaction, a feeling of superiority, when she conquered a mountain? And if that was the case, then was that feeling a measure of superiority not only over the mountain, but over her fellow dwarves?

The questions nagged the normally-unshakable cleric, the usually humble priestess. Stumpet hoped the thoughts weren't true. She thought more of herself, her true self, than to be concerned with such pettiness. After a long while of tossing and turning, the dwarf finally fell back to sleep.

⚔ ⚔ ⚔ ⚔ ⚔

No more dreams came to Stumpet that long night. Crenshinibon, resting in a locker at the foot of the dwarf's bed, sensed Stumpet's dismay and realized that it had to be careful in imparting such dreams. This dwarf was not an easy one to entice. The artifact had no idea of what treasures it could promise to weaken the will of Stumpet Rakingclaw.

Without those insidious promises, the crystal shard could grab no firm hold over the dwarf. But if Crenshinibon became more overt, more forceful, it could tip Stumpet off to the truth of its origins and its designs. And certainly the artifact did not want to arouse the suspicions of one who could call upon the powers of goodly gods, perhaps even learning the secrets of how to destroy Crenshinibon!

The crystal shard closed in its magic, kept its sentient thoughts deep within its squared sides. Its long wait was not quite over, it realized, not while it was in the hands of this one.

PART FOUR

I remember well that occasion when I returned to Menzoberranzan, the city of my birth, the city of my childhood. I was floating on a raft across the lake of Donigarten when the city came into view, a sight I had feared and longed for at the same time. I did not ever want to return to Menzoberranzan, and yet, I had to wonder what

ICEWIND DALE

going there would feel like. Was the place as bad as my memories told me?

I remember well that moment when we drifted past the cavern's curving wall, the sculpted stalagmites coming into view.

It was a disappointment.

I did not feel any anger, nor any awe. No warmth of nostalgia, true or false, washed over me. I did not dwell in the memories of my childhood, not even in the memories of my good times with Zaknafein.

All that I thought of in that critical moment was the fact that there were lights burning in the city, an unusual and perhaps significant event. All that I thought of was my critical mission, and how I must move fast to get the job done. My fears, for indeed they remained, were of a rational nature. Not the impulsive and unreasonable fears wrought of childhood memories, but the very real trepidations that I was walking into the lair of a powerful enemy.

Later, when the situation allowed, I reflected on that moment, confused as to why it had been so disappointing, so insignificant. Why hadn't I been overwhelmed by the sight of the city that had been my home for the first three decades of my life?

Only when I turned around the northwestern corner of the Spine of the World mountain range, back into Icewind Dale, did I realize the truth. Menzoberranzan had been a place along my journey, but not a home, never a home. As the blind seer's riddle had inferred, Icewind Dale had been my home that was first. All that had come before, all that had led to that windswept and inhospitable place—from Menzoberranzan, to Blingdenstone, to the surface, even to the enchanted grove of my ranger mentor, Montolio DeBrouchee—had been but a road, a path to follow.

These truths came clear to me when I turned that corner, facing the dale for the first time in a decade, feeling the endless wind upon my face, the same wind that had always been there and that gave the place its name.

It is a complicated word: home. It carries varied definitions to nearly every person. To me, home is not just a place, but a feeling, a warm and comfortable sensation of control. Home is where I need make no excuses for my actions or the color of my skin, where I must be accepted because this is my place. It is both a personal and a shared domain, for it is the place a person most truly belongs, and yet it is so only because of those friends around him.

Unlike my first glimpse of Menzoberranzan, when I looked upon Icewind Dale I was filled with thoughts of what had been. There were thoughts of sitting on the side of Kelvin's Cairn, watching the stars and the fires of the roaming barbarian tribes, thoughts of battling tundra yeti beside Bruenor. I remembered the dwarf's sour expression when he licked his axe and first learned that the brains of a tundra yeti tasted terrible! I remembered my first meeting with Catti-brie, my companion still. She was but a girl then, a trusting and beautiful spirit, wild in nature yet always sensitive.

I remembered so very much, a veritable flood of images, and though my mission on that occasion was no less vital and pressing than the one that had taken me to Menzoberranzan, I thought nothing of it, didn't consider my course at all.

At that moment, it simply didn't matter. All that I cared about was that I had come home.

—Drizzt Do'Urden

18
WALKING THE WIND

Drizzt and Catti-brie accompanied Deudermont, Waillan, and Dunkin back to Carradoon to say their farewells to the crewmen they had worked beside for more than five years, friends all. Drizzt was impatient and didn't want to delay his return to Icewind Dale any longer than necessary, but this short trip was important. It was a fond farewell with promises that they would meet again.

The two friends—Drizzt called in Guenhwyvar later—dined with Deudermont and Robillard that night. Robillard, seeming more animated and friendly than usual, promised to use his magic to whisk them back to the Spirit Soaring, to get them on their way.

"What?" the wizard asked as the other three exchanged knowing glances and grins, all of them thinking exactly the same thing.

Robillard had changed in the last few tendays, especially since the wild battle on the beach of Caerwich. The fact was, Harkle had rubbed off on him.

"What?" Robillard demanded again, more forcefully.

Deudermont laughed and lifted his glass of wine in a toast. "To Harkle Harpell," the captain said, "and the good he has left in his wake!"

Robillard snorted, ready to remind them that the *Sea Sprite* was locked tight in a lake hundreds of miles from the Sword Coast. But as he considered the continuing smirks on his companions' faces, the wary wizard realized the truth of Deudermont's toast, realized that it was aimed at him.

Robillard's first instinct was to yell out a protest, perhaps even to rescind his offer to take Drizzt and Catti-brie back to the cathedral. But they were right, the wizard finally had to admit to himself, and so he lifted his glass. Though he kept quiet, Robillard was thinking that maybe he would go to the famed Ivy Mansion in Longsaddle and pay his eccentric friend a visit.

It was difficult for Drizzt, Catti-brie, and Deudermont to say good-bye. They shared hugs and promised that they would meet again, but they all knew the depth of the task facing Drizzt and Catti-brie. There was a very real possibility that neither of them would ever leave Icewind Dale alive.

They all knew this, but none of them mentioned that possibility, acting as though this was merely a short interruption to their friendship.

※ ※ ※ ※ ※

Twenty minutes later, Drizzt and Catti-brie were back at the Spirit Soaring. Robillard said his farewells, and then disappeared in a flash of magical energy.

Ivan, Pikel, and Danica greeted them. "Cadderly's gettin' ready," the stout, yellow-bearded dwarf remarked. "Takes the old man longer, ye know!"

"Hee hee hee," Pikel piped in.

Danica feigned a protest, but in truth—and Catti-brie saw it—she was glad that the dwarves continued to taunt Cadderly's advanced age. They did it only because they believed that the priest was growing stronger, even younger, and their taunts were filled with hope, not malice.

"Come," Danica bade Catti-brie. "We have not had enough time together." The woman cast a sour look at Ivan and Pikel, bobbing along on their heels. "Alone," she finished pointedly.

"Ooooo," moaned Pikel.

"Does he always do that?" Drizzt asked Ivan, who sighed and nodded.

"Ye think ye got long enough to tell me o' Mithral Hall?" Ivan asked. "I heared o' Menzoberranzan, but I'm not for believing what I heared."

"I will tell what I may," Drizzt replied. "And you will indeed have a difficult time in believing many of the splendors I describe."

"And what of Bruenor?" Ivan added.

"Booner!" put in the excited Pikel.

Ivan slapped his brother on the back of the head. "We'd go with ye, elf," the yellow-bearded dwarf explained, "but we've got chores to do here right now. Takin' care o' the twins and all that, and me brother with his gardens." As soon as he mentioned Pikel, Ivan turned fast to regard his brother, as if expecting another silly remark. Pikel did seem like he wanted to say something, but he began to whistle instead. When Ivan turned back to Drizzt, the drow had to shake his head and bite his lip. For, in looking over the yellow-

bearded Ivan, Drizzt caught the face, thumbs in ears, fingers wagging, tongue stuck out to its limits, that Pikel offered.

Ivan spun back, but Pikel was standing calm again, whistling away. They went through three more such exchanges before Ivan finally gave up.

Drizzt had known these two for only two days, but he was thinking that they were grand fun, and he was imagining the good times the Bouldershoulders would inflict on Bruenor if ever they met!

✕ ✕ ✕ ✕ ✕

For Danica and Catti-brie, that last hour together was much more serious and controlled. They went to Danica and Cadderly's private quarters, a grouping of five rooms near the rear of the great structure. They found Cadderly in the bedroom, praying and preparing, so they quietly left him alone.

Their talk at first was general in nature, Catti-brie telling of her past, of how she had been orphaned when very young and then taken under the wing of Bruenor, to be raised among the dwarves of Clan Battlehammer. Danica spoke of her training in the teachings of Grandmaster Penpahg D'Ahn. She was a monk, a disciplined warrior, not so unlike Catti-brie.

Catti-brie wasn't used to dealing with women of her own age and of a similar mind. She liked it, though, liked Danica quite a bit, and could imagine a great friendship between the two if time and the situation would permit. In truth, the situation was also awkward for Danica, her life had been no easier and her contact with women of her own age no more common.

They spoke of the past and finally, of the present, of their hopes for the future.

"Do you love him?" Danica dared to ask, referring to the dark elf.

Catti-brie blushed, and really had no answer. Of course she loved Drizzt, but she didn't know if she loved him in the way that Danica was speaking of. Drizzt and Catti-brie had agreed to put off any such feelings, but now, with Wulfgar gone for so many years and Catti-brie approaching the age of thirty, the question was beginning to resurface.

"He is a handsome one," Danica remarked, giggling like a little girl.

Indeed, that's what Catti-brie felt like, reclining on the wide davenport in Danica's sitting room: a girl. It was like being a teenager again, thinking of love and of life, allowing herself to believe that her biggest problem was in trying to decide if Drizzt was handsome or not.

Of course, the weight of reality for both these women was fast to intrude, fast to steal the giggles. Catti-brie had loved and lost, and Danica, with two young children of her own, had to face the possibility that her husband, unnaturally aged by the creation of the Spirit Soaring, would soon be gone.

The conversation gradually shifted, then died away, and then Danica sat quiet, staring intently at Catti-brie.

"What is it?" Catti-brie wanted to know.

"I am with child," Danica said, and Catti-brie knew at once that she was the first person the monk had told, even before Cadderly.

Catti-brie waited a moment, waited to see the smile widen on Danica's face to make sure that, for the young monk, being pregnant was indeed a good thing, and then she grinned broadly and wrapped Danica in a tight hug.

"Do not say anything to Cadderly," Danica begged. "I've already planned how I will tell him."

Catti-brie sat back. "And yet ye told me first," she said, the gravity of that reality evident in her solemn tones.

"You are leaving," Danica answered matter-of-factly.

"But ye hardly know o' me," Catti-brie reminded her.

Danica shook her head, her strawberry blonde hair flying wide and her exotic almond-shaped eyes locking fast with Catti-brie's deep blue eyes. "I know you," Danica said softly.

It was true enough, and Catti-brie felt that she knew Danica as well. They were much alike, and both came to realize that they would miss each other a great deal.

They heard Cadderly stirring in the room next door. It was almost time to go.

"I will come back here someday," Catti-brie promised.

"And I will visit Icewind Dale," Danica responded.

Cadderly entered the room and told them that it was time for Catti-brie and Drizzt to leave. He smiled warmly, and was gracious enough to say nothing of the moisture that rimmed the eyes of the two young women.

⚔ ⚔ ⚔ ⚔ ⚔

Cadderly, Drizzt, and Danica stood atop the highest tower of the Spirit Soaring, nearly three hundred feet above the ground, the wind whipping against their backs.

Cadderly chanted quietly for some time, and gradually, both friends began to feel lighter, somehow less substantial. Cadderly grabbed a hand of each and continued his chant, and the threesome faded away. Ghostlike, they walked off the tower top with the wind.

All the world sped past, blurry, in a fog, a dreamlike vision. Neither Drizzt nor Catti-brie knew how long they were flying, but dawn was breaking along the eastern horizon when they slowed and then stopped, becoming more substantial again.

They were in the city of Luskan, along the northernmost stretch of the Sword Coast, just south of the western lip of the Spine of the World mountains and barely two hundred miles, by horse or by foot, from Ten-Towns.

Cadderly didn't know the city, but the priest's aim was perfect and the three came out of their enchantment right in front of the temple of Deneir. Cadderly was well received by his fellow priests. He quickly secured rooms for his friends and while they were sleeping, went out with one of the Luskan priests to make the arrangements for Drizzt and Catti-brie to hook up with a caravan heading for Icewind Dale.

It was easier than Cadderly expected, and that made him glad, for he feared that Drizzt's heritage would outweigh any words he might offer. But Drizzt was known among many of the merchants in Luskan, as was Catti-brie, and their fighting prowess would be a welcome addition to any caravan traveling north to the dangerous land that was Icewind Dale.

The two were awake when Cadderly got back to the Deneirian temple, speaking with the other priests and gathering supplies for the long road ahead. Drizzt accepted one gift reverently, a pair of waterskins filled with blessed water from the temple's font. The drow didn't see any practical use for the water, but the significance that a human priest of a goodly god had given it to him, a drow elf, was not lost on him.

"Your fellows are a good lot," Drizzt remarked to Cadderly, when he, the old priest, and Catti-brie were at last alone. Cadderly had already explained the provisions that had been made, including the time and place, where Drizzt and Catti-brie were to meet with the caravan. The merchants were putting out this very day, giving the pair less than an hour to get out on the road. They knew that this was yet another parting.

"They do Deneir proud," Cadderly agreed.

Drizzt was busy with his pack then, and so Catti-brie quietly pulled Cadderly aside. Her thoughts were on Danica, her friend.

Cadderly smiled warmly, seeming to understand what this private conversation might be about.

"Ye've got many responsibilities," Catti-brie began.

"My god is not so demanding," Cadderly said coyly, for he knew that Catti-brie was not speaking of his duties to Deneir.

"I'm meaning the twins," Catti-brie whispered. "And Danica."

Cadderly nodded. No argument there.

Catti-brie paused for a long while, seeming to struggle with the words. How might she put things so as not to insult the old priest?

"Ivan told me something about yer . . . condition," Catti-brie admitted.

"Oh?" Cadderly replied. He wasn't going to make this easy for the young woman.

"The dwarf says ye expected to die as soon as the Spirit Soaring was completed," Catti-brie explained. "Says ye looked like ye would, too."

"I felt like I would," Cadderly admitted. "And the visions I had of the cathedral made me believe that to be the truth."

"That was more than a year ago," Catti-brie remarked.

Cadderly nodded again.

"The dwarf says ye look like ye're getting younger," Catti-brie pressed. "And stronger."

Cadderly's smile was wide. He understood that Catti-brie was looking out for Danica's interests and her apparently deep friendship with his wife warmed his heart profoundly. "I cannot be certain of anything," he said to her, "but the dwarf's observations seem to be accurate. I am stronger now, much stronger and more energetic than when the cathedral was first completed." Cadderly reached up and pulled straight a few strands of hair, mostly gray, but with several sandy-colored strands mixed in. "Brown hairs," the old priest went on. "It was white, all white, when first the cathedral was completed."

"Ye're gettin' younger!" Catti-brie proclaimed with much enthusiasm.

Cadderly blew a long and deep sigh, and then, couldn't help but nod. "So it would seem," he admitted.

"I cannot be sure of anything," he said as if he was afraid of speaking his hopes out loud. "The only explanation that I can figure is that the visions shown to me—visions of my impending death—and the fatigue I felt at the completion of the Spirit Soaring were a test of my ultimate loyalty to the precepts and commandments of Deneir. I honestly expected to die as soon as the first service in the new cathedral was completed, and indeed, when it was done, a great weariness overcame me. I went to my room—I was practically carried by Danica and Ivan—and went to sleep, expecting to never again open my eyes upon this world. I accepted that." He paused and closed his eyes, recalling that fateful date.

"But now," Catti-brie prompted.

"Perhaps Deneir tested me, tested my loyalty," Cadderly said. "It might be that I passed that test, and so now my god has chosen to spare me."

"If he's a goodly god, then the choice is made," Catti-brie said firmly. "No

good god'd take ye from Danica and the twins, and . . ." She paused and bit her lip, not wanting to give away Danica's secret.

"Deneir is a goodly god," Cadderly replied with equal determination. "But you speak of the concerns of mortals and we cannot understand Deneir's will or his ways. If Deneir takes me from Danica and my children, then that does not make him anything less than the goodly god that he truly is."

Catti-brie shook her head and didn't seem convinced.

"There are higher meanings and higher principles than we humans can understand," Cadderly said to her. "I hold faith that Deneir will do what is ultimately right by his needs and his designs, which outweigh my own."

"But ye hope it's true," Catti-brie said, her tone showing the words to be an accusation. "Ye hope ye get young again, as young as yer bride, that ye might live out yer life beside her and with yer kids!"

Cadderly laughed aloud. "True enough," he finally admitted, and Catti-brie was appeased.

So was Drizzt, listening in with those keen drow ears of his, only half his attention focused upon the task of packing his haversack.

Catti-brie and Cadderly shared a hug, and then the old priest, who seemed not so old, went to Drizzt and offered a sincere handshake. "Bring to me the artifact, this crystal shard," Cadderly said. "Together we will discover a way to rid the world of its evil.

"And bring your father as well," Cadderly went on. "I feel that he would enjoy a stay at the Spirit Soaring."

Drizzt gripped Cadderly's hand all the tighter, thankful for the priest's confidence that he would succeed. "The artifact will give me . . . give us," he corrected, looking to Catti-brie, "the excuse we need to make the journey back to Carradoon."

"A journey I must make now," Cadderly said, and so he left the pair.

They said nothing when they were alone, just went about finishing their preparations for the road.

The road home.

19
And All the World Is Theirs

Revjak knew that it would come to this, had guessed it as soon as he had realized that Berkthgar did not mean to split off from the Tribe of the Elk to recreate one of the other tribes.

So now Revjak stood facing the brutish barbarian within a ring of all their people. Everyone in the tribe knew what was to come, but it had to be done properly, by the rules of ancient traditions.

Berkthgar waited for the gathering to quiet. He could be patient because he knew that the whispers were leaning in his favor, that the arguments for his ascension were gaining momentum. Finally, after what seemed to Revjak to be many minutes, the crowd went silent.

Berkthgar lifted his arms high to the sky, his hands reaching wide. Behind him, strapped diagonally across his back, loomed Bankenfuere, his huge flamberge. "I claim the Right of Challenge," the huge barbarian declared.

A chorus of cheers rose up, not a strong as Berkthgar would have liked, but showing that he had quite a bit of support.

"By what birthright do you make such a claim?" Revjak responded properly.

"Not by blood," Berkthgar promptly answered, "but by deed!" Again came the cheers from the younger man's supporters.

Revjak shook his head. "There is no reason, if blood does not demand a challenge," he protested, and his supporters, though not as vocal as Berkthgar's, gave their own burst of cheering. "I have led in peace and in strength," Revjak finished firmly, a claim that was all too true.

"As have I!" Berkthgar was quick to interrupt. "In Settlestone, so far from

our home. I have brought our people through war and peace, and have led the march all the way back to Icewind Dale, our home!"

"Where Revjak is King of the Tribe of the Elk," the older man put in without hesitation.

"By what birthright?" Berkthgar demanded.

Revjak had a problem here, and he knew it.

"What birthright does Revjak, son of Jorn the Red, who was not a king, claim?" Berkthgar asked slyly.

Revjak had no answer.

"The position was given to you," Berkthgar went on, telling a tale that was nothing new to his people, but from a slightly different perspective than they normally heard. "It was handed to you, through no challenge and no right, by Wulfgar, son of Beornegar."

Kierstaad watched it all from the sidelines. At that moment, the young man came to understand the real reason why Berkthgar had launched a campaign to discredit Wulfgar. If the legend of Wulfgar still loomed larger than life to the barbarians, then his father's claim as king would be strong indeed. But with Wulfgar somewhat discredited . . .

"Who rightly claimed the kingship from Heafstaag, who was by birthright, rightly king," Revjak reasoned. "How many here," he asked the general gathering, "remember the battle wherein Wulfgar, son of Beornegar, became our king?"

Many heads bobbed, mostly of the older folk who had remained in Icewind Dale through all the years.

"I, too, remember the battle." Berkthgar growled defiantly. "And I do not doubt Wulfgar's claim, nor all the good he did for my people. But you have no claim of blood, no more than my own, and I would lead, Revjak. I demand the Right of Challenge!"

The cheers were louder than ever.

Revjak looked to his son and smiled. He could not avoid Berkthgar's claim, no more than he could possibly defeat the huge man in combat. He turned back to Berkthgar. "Granted," he said, and the cheers were deafening then, from both Berkthgar's supporters and Revjak's.

"In five hours, before the sun runs low along the horizon," Berkthgar began.

"Now," Revjak said unexpectedly.

Berkthgar eyed the man, trying to discern what trick he might be pulling. Normally a Right of Challenge would be answered later in the day on which it was made, after both combatants had the time to prepare themselves mentally and physically for the combat.

Berkthgar narrowed his blue eyes and all the crowd hushed in anticipation. A smile widened on the huge man's face. He didn't fear Revjak,
not now, not ever. Slowly, the huge man's hand went up over his shoulder,
grasping the hilt of Bankenfuere, drawing the massive blade up from its
scabbard. That sheath had been cut along its top edge so that Berkthgar
could draw the weapon quickly. He did so, hoisting the heavy blade high
into the sky.

Revjak took up his own weapon, but to his observant and worried son, he
did not seem ready for combat.

Berkthgar approached cautiously, feeling the balance of Bankenfuere with
every step.

Then Revjak held up his hand and Berkthgar stopped, waiting.

"Who among us hopes for Revjak to win?" he asked, and a loud cheer of
many voices went up.

Thinking the question to be no more than a ruse to lower his confidence,
Berkthgar issued a low growl. "And who would see Berkthgar, Berkthgar the
Bold, as King of the Tribe of the Elk?"

The cheer was louder still, obviously so.

Revjak moved right up to his opponent, unthreateningly, one hand up and
his axe's head low to the ground. "The challenge is answered," he said, and he
dropped his weapon to the ground.

All eyes widened in disbelief, Kierstaad's perhaps widest of all. This was
dishonor! This was cowardice among the barbarians!

"I cannot defeat you, Berkthgar," Revjak explained, speaking loudly so that
all would hear. "Nor can you defeat me."

Berkthgar scowled mightily. "I could cut you in half!" he declared, taking
up his sword in both hands so powerfully that Revjak half expected him to
do so right then and there.

"And our people would suffer the consequences of your actions," Revjak
said quietly. "Whoever might win the challenge would be faced with two
tribes, not one, split apart by anger and wanting revenge." He looked to the
general gathering again, speaking to all his people. "We are not strong enough
yet to support that," he said. "Whether we are to strengthen the friendship
with Ten-Towns and the dwarves who have returned, or whether we are to
return to our ways of old, we must do so together, as one!"

Berkthgar's scowl did not relent. Now he understood. Revjak could not
defeat him in combat—they both knew that—so the wily older man had
usurped the very power of the challenge. Berkthgar truly wanted to cut him
in half, but how could he take any actions against the man?

"As one," Revjak repeated, and he held out his hand, bidding his opponent to clasp his wrist.

Berkthgar was wild with rage. He hooked his foot under Revjak's dropped axe and sent it spinning across the circle. "Yours is the way of the coward!" he roared. "You have proven that this day!" Up went Berkthgar's huge arms, up and out wide as if in victory.

"I have no claim of blood!" Revjak yelled, commanding attention. "Nor do you! The people must decide who will rule and who will step aside."

"The challenge is of combat!" Berkthgar retorted.

"Not this time!" Revjak shot back. "Not when all the tribe must suffer your foolish pride." Berkthgar moved again as if to strike, but Revjak ignored him and turned to the gathering. "Decide!" he commanded.

"Revjak!" yelled one man, but his voice was buried by a band of young warriors who cried out for Berkthgar. They, in turn, were outdone by a large group calling for Revjak. And so it went, back and forth, mounting cries. Several fights broke out, weapons were drawn.

Through it all, Berkthgar glowered at Revjak, and when the older man matched that intense stare, Berkthgar merely shook his head in disbelief. How could Revjak have done such dishonor to their people?

But Revjak held faith in his choice. He was not afraid to die, never that, but he truly believed that a fight between himself and Berkthgar would split the tribe and bring hardship to both groups. This was the better way, as long as things didn't get out of hand.

And they seemed to be heading in just that direction. Both sides continued to yell out, but now each cry was accompanied by a lifting of sword and axe, open threats.

Revjak watched the crowd carefully, measuring the support for him and for Berkthgar. Soon enough he understood and admitted the truth.

"Stop!" he commanded at the top of his voice, and gradually, the shouting match did diminish.

"With all your strength, who calls out for Berkthgar?" Revjak asked.

A great roar ensued.

"And who for Revjak?"

"Revjak who would not fight!" Berkthgar quickly added, and the cheers for the son of Jorn were not as loud, or as enthusiastic.

"Then it is settled," Revjak said, more to Berkthgar than to the crowd. "And Berkthgar is King of the Tribe of the Elk."

Berkthgar could hardly believe what had just transpired. He wanted to strike down the wily older man. This was to be his day of glory, a victory of mortal combat, as had been the way since the dawn of the tribes. But how could he do that? How could he slay an unarmed man, one who had just proclaimed him as the leader of all his people?

"Be wise, Berkthgar," Revjak said quietly, moving close, for the buzz of the astonished gathering was loud indeed. "Together we will discover the true way for our people, what is best for our future."

Berkthgar shoved him aside. "I will decide," he corrected loudly. "I need no advice from a coward!"

He walked out of the circle then, his closest supporters falling in line behind him.

Stung by the rejection of his offer, but not really surprised, Revjak took comfort in the fact that he had tried his best to do what was right for his people. That counted little, though, when the man looked upon his son, who had just completed the rights of passage into manhood.

Kierstaad's expression was one of disbelief, even of shame.

Revjak lifted his head high and walked over to the young man. "Understand," he commanded. "This is the only way."

Kierstaad walked away. Logic might have shown him the truth of his father's bravery this day, but logic played a very minor role in the young man's consciousness. Kierstaad felt ashamed, truly ashamed, and he wanted nothing more than to run away, out onto the open tundra, to live or to die.

It hardly seemed to matter.

⚔ ⚔ ⚔ ⚔ ⚔

Stumpet sat on the very highest peak of Kelvin's Cairn, which seemed an easy climb to her. Her waking thoughts, like most of her dreams, were now squarely focused on the south, on the towering peaks of the Spine of the World. Fleeting images of glory and of victory raced through the dwarf's mind. She pictured herself standing atop the tallest mountain, surveying all the world.

The impracticality of the image, the sheer irrationality of it, did not make its way into Stumpet Rakingclaw's conscious thoughts. The constant barrage of images, the stream of delusion, began to erode the normally pragmatic dwarf's rational sensibilities. For Stumpet, logic was fast losing to desires, desires that were not truly her own.

"I'm on me way, towering peaks," the dwarf said suddenly, addressing those distant mountains. "And not a one o' ye's big enough to keep me down!"

There, she had said it aloud, had proclaimed her course. She immediately began gathering together her things, then swung herself over the edge of the

peak and began her scramble to the mountain's base.

In her haversack, Crenshinibon verily purred with elation. The powerful artifact still had no designs on making Stumpet Rakingclaw its wielder. The sentient crystal shard knew the stubbornness of this one, despite the delusions it had gradually enacted over the dwarf. Even worse, Crenshinibon understood Stumpet's place in her society, as a priestess of Moradin, the Soul Forger. Thus far, the artifact had managed to generally sidetrack any of Stumpet's attempts at communing with her god, but sooner or later, the dwarf would seek that higher level, and would likely learn the truth of the "warming stick" that she kept in her pack.

So Crenshinibon would use her to get away from the dwarves, to escape to the wilds of the Spine of the World, where it might find a troll, a giant, or perhaps even a dragon to serve as its wielder.

Yes, a dragon, Crenshinibon hoped. The artifact would like to work in collusion with a dragon!

Oblivious to such wishes, even to the fact that her "warming stick" could wish at all, poor Stumpet cared only about conquering the mountain range. And even she wasn't sure of why she cared.

※ ※ ※ ※ ※

On the very first night of his rule, Berkthgar began to reveal the precepts that the barbarians of Icewind Dale would follow, a way of life such as they had lived until only a decade hence, before Wulfgar had defeated Heafstaag.

All contact with the folk of Ten-Towns was ordered to stop, and on pain of death, no barbarian was to speak with Bruenor Battlehammer or any of the bearded folk.

"And if one of the bearded folk is found in need on the open tundra," Berkthgar said, and it seemed to Kierstaad that the man was looking directly at him as he spoke, "leave him to die!"

Later that night, Kierstaad sat alone under the wide canopy of stars, a tortured soul. Now he understood what his father had tried to do that afternoon. Revjak could not defeat Berkthgar, everyone knew that, and so the older man had tried to work out a compromise, one that would benefit all the barbarians. In his mind, Kierstaad realized that Revjak's abdication when the majority favored Berkthgar was a wise, even courageous thing to do, but in his heart and in his gut, the young man still felt the shame of his father's unwillingness to fight.

Better if Revjak had taken up his axe and died at Berkthgar's hands, Kierstaad believed, or at least a part of him believed. That was the way of their people, the ancient and sacred way. What might Tempus, the god of the barbarians, the god of battle, think of Revjak this day? What place in the afterworld might a man such as Revjak, who refused honest and rightful combat, find?

Kierstaad put his head in his hands. Not only was his father dishonored, but so were he and his family.

Perhaps he should proclaim allegiance to Berkthgar and reject his father. Berkthgar, who had been with Kierstaad all the years in Settlestone, who had been beside Kierstaad when the young man had made his first hunting kill on the open tundra, would welcome such support. He would see it, no doubt, as a solidification of his position as leader.

No. He could not abandon his father, however angry he might be. He would take up his weapon against Berkthgar if need be, and kill the man or die in order to restore his family's honor. He would not desert his father.

That option also seemed ridiculous to the young man, and he sat alone, overwhelmed, under the vastness of Icewind Dale's canopy, a tortured soul.

20

EARNING THEIR PAY

Both Drizzt and Catti-brie had become quite proficient at riding horses on their trip from Mithral Hall to Waterdeep. But that had been six years before, and the only thing the companions had ridden since then were waves. By the time the caravan got around the western edge of the Spine of the World, five days out from Luskan, the two had settled back into the rhythm, though both had painful sores on their legs and buttocks.

They were at the lead, far ahead of the caravan when they reached the dale.

Reached the dale!

Drizzt was about to call for Catti-brie to slow up, but she, as awestruck as the drow, was pulling tight her reigns before he ever began the command.

They were home, truly home, within a hundred miles of the place where they had first met and where their lives and their most important friendships had been shaped and forged. All the memories washed over them at that moment as they looked across the windswept tundra, heard that forlorn moan, the incessant call of the winds blowing off the glaciers to the north and east. The icewind that gave the dale its name.

Catti-brie wanted to say something to Drizzt, something profound and meaningful, and he fostered the same desires. Neither could find the words. They were too overwhelmed by simply seeing the spectacle of Icewind Dale again.

"Come along," Drizzt said finally. The drow looked back over his shoulder, to see the six wagons of the caravan gaining ground, then looked ahead, to the beautiful and wonderful emptiness that was Icewind Dale. Kelvin's Cairn was not in sight, was still too far away, but it would not be long.

Suddenly the drow desperately wanted to see that mountain again! How many hours and days had he spent on the side of that rocky place?

How many times had he sat upon the barren stones of Kelvin's Cairn, looking at the stars and at the twinkling campfires of the distant barbarian encampments?

He started to tell Catti-brie to begin moving, but again, the woman seemed to share his thoughts, for she set her mount off and running before he could get his own horse moving.

Something else struck Drizzt Do'Urden then, another memory of Icewind Dale, a warning from his ranger sensibilities that this was not a safe place. Turning the final corner around the Spine of the World had put them truly in the wilderness again, where fierce tundra yeti and tribes of wild goblins roamed. He didn't want to steal the moment from Catti-brie, not yet, but he hoped that she was sharing his thoughts once again.

Unwary people did not survive long in the unforgiving land called Icewind Dale.

They met up with no trouble that day or the next, and were on the road early before the dawn, making great progress. The mud from the spring thaw had dried and the ground was solid and flat beneath them, the wagon wheels turning easily.

The sun came up in their faces, stinging their eyes, particularly Drizzt's lavender orbs, designed by heredity for the lightless Underdark. Even after more than two decades on the surface, after six years of sailing the bright waters of the Sea of Swords, Drizzt's sensitive eyes had not fully adjusted to the surface light. He didn't mind the sting, though, reveled in it, greeting the bright dawn with a smile, using the light as a reminder of how far he had come.

Later that morning, when the sun climbed high in the clear southeastern sky and the horizon before them became distinct and perfectly clear, they caught what Drizzt claimed to be their first true sight of the area that had been their home, a single flash that Drizzt decided had to be a reflection of the sun off the crystalline snow topping Kelvin's Cairn.

Catti-brie was not so sure of that. Kelvin's Cairn was not so high, and they were still two days of hard riding away. She didn't express any doubts, though, hoping that the drow was right. She wanted to be home!

As did Drizzt, and their pace quickened, became so great that they left the wagons even farther behind. Finally, reason and a terse call from the driver of the lead wagon reminding them of their duty, slowed them down. The pair exchanged knowing smiles.

"Soon," Drizzt promised.

The pace was still swift, for a short while. Then, Drizzt began to slow his horse, glancing all around, sniffing the air.

That was all the warning Catti-brie needed. She brought her horse to a trot and scanned the ground.

Everything seemed unremarkable to Drizzt. The ground was flat, brown and gray, and unbroken. He could see nothing unusual, and could hear nothing save the *clip-clop* of hooves on the hard ground and the moan of the wind. He could smell nothing other than the wet scent that Icewind Dale's summer wind always carried. But that did not allow the drow to sit easier on his mount. No signs, but that was the way with monsters in the dale.

"What do ye know?" Catti-brie whispered finally.

Drizzt continued to look about. There was about a hundred yards between them and the wagons, and the distance was fast closing. Still, Drizzt's eyes told him nothing, nor did his keen ears, nor even his sense of smell. But that sixth warrior sense knew better, knew that he and Catti-brie had missed something, had passed something by.

Drizzt took the onyx figurine from his pouch and softly called to Guenhwyvar. As the mist grew and the panther took shape, the drow motioned for Catti-brie to ready her bow, which she was already doing, and then to circle back toward the wagons, flanking right while he flanked out to the left.

The young woman nodded. The hairs on the back of her neck were tingling, her warrior instincts yelling at her to be ready. She had an arrow on Taulmaril, holding the weapons easily in one hand while her other guided the horse.

Guenhwyvar came onto the tundra with her ears flat, knowing from both the secretive tone of Drizzt's call and her own incredible senses that enemies were about. The cat looked right to Catti-brie, then left to Drizzt, then padded silently up the middle, ready to spring to the aid of either.

Noticing the movement of his point guards, and then the presence of the panther, the lead driver slowed his wagon, then called for a general halt. Drizzt held high a scimitar, showing his agreement with the stop.

Now far to the right, Catti-brie was the first to spot an enemy. It was deep into the soil, just the top of its shaggy brown head visible, poking from a hole. A tundra yeti, the fiercest hunter of Icewind Dale. Shaggy brown in the summer, snow white in the winter, tundra yetis were known to be masters of camouflage. Catti-brie nodded at that assessment, almost in appreciation of their skills. She and Drizzt, no novices, had walked their mounts right past the beasts, oblivious to the danger. This was Icewind Dale, the young woman promptly reminded herself. Merciless and unforgiving of the smallest error.

But the error this time was the yeti's, Catti-brie decided grimly, lifting her bow. Off streaked an arrow, hitting the unsuspecting beast right in the back of the head. It lurched forward, rebounded back violently, then slumped dead in its hole.

A split second later, the very ground seemed to explode as half a dozen yetis leaped up from similar trenches. They were powerful, shaggy beasts, looking like a cross between a human and a bear—and indeed, the lore of Icewind Dale's barbarian tribes claimed that they were exactly that!

Back behind Drizzt and Catti-brie, right in the middle of the flanking pair, Guenhwyvar hit one beast in full stride. She knocked it back into its hole, the panther's momentum carrying her in right behind it.

The yeti grabbed on with all its might, thinking to squeeze the life from the cat, but Guenhwyvar's powerful rear legs raked at the beast and held it at bay.

Meanwhile, Drizzt went into a full gallop, racing right beside one spinning yeti and double slashing at it with his scimitars as he held fast to his mount with his strong legs.

The bloodied beast fell away, roaring and howling in protest, and Drizzt, bearing down on a second yeti, paid it no more heed. This second yeti was ready for him, and even worse, it was ready for his horse. Yetis had been known to stop a horse at full charge, breaking the animal's neck in the process.

Drizzt couldn't risk that. He angled his charge to the left of the yeti, then lifted his left leg over the saddle and dropped from his speeding mount into a run, his enchanted anklets allowing him to get his feet under him in but a few speedy strides.

He went by the surprised yeti in a wild, slashing blur, scoring several wicked hits before he was too far away to strike. Drizzt kept running, knowing that the yeti, far from finished, had turned in pursuit. When he had put enough ground between himself and the beast, he turned back, angling for another swift pass.

Then Catti-brie, too, went into a full gallop, using her legs to hold herself steady and she leaned low in the saddle, taking a bead on the next closest beast.

She fired, and missed, but had another arrow up and ready in an instant and fired again, taking the yeti in the hip.

The beast flailed at the arrow and spun in a circle, taking another arrow, and then another in the chest as it came around to face the closing woman. Still it was standing, stubbornly, as Catti-brie came upon it. Ready to improvise,

the woman hooked Taulmaril over the horn of her saddle and in one flashing motion, drew out Khazid'hea, her fabulous sword.

Catti-brie rambled past, swiping hard in a downward arc, the fine edge of Khazid'hea caving in the dying beast's skull, finishing the grim task. Down went the beast, its brain spilling from its skull onto the brown plain.

Catti-brie went right by the dying thing, replaced her sword and fired off her fifth shot with Taulmaril, this one popping into the shoulder of the next beast in line, dropping its arm lifeless to its side. Looking past the wounded yeti, Catti-brie saw the last of the yetis, which were closest to the lead wagons. In the distance she also noted the other caravan guards, a dozen sturdy fighters, riding hard to catch up to the battle.

"This fight's our own," the woman said quietly, determinedly, and as she closed on the wounded yeti, she hooked Taulmaril over the horn of her saddle and once more drew out Khazid'hea.

Still down in the tight hole, Guenhwyvar found her mighty claws gave her the advantage. The yeti tried to bite, but the panther was quicker, her neck more flexible. Guenhwyvar angled under the yeti's chin, her jaws snapping onto the shaggy neck.

Her claws kept up their raking motions, kept the yeti's considerable weapons at bay, while the deadly jaws clamped tight and suffocated the beast.

The panther came out of the hole as soon as the yeti had stopped its fighting. Guenhwyvar looked left and right, to Drizzt and Catti-brie. She issued a roar and raced right, where the situation seemed far more dangerous.

Drizzt was charging at the yeti he had wounded, but pulled up short, forcing the yeti, which had been ready to meet the charge, to overcompensate. It leaned too far forward. The drow's scimitars cut fast and hard, ripping into the yeti's hands, severing several of the beast's fingers.

The yeti howled and pulled in its arms. Drizzt, so impossibly quick, chased them back, snapping Twinkle into the yeti's upper arm, and scoring a hit down low, at the beast's waist, with his other blade. Then Drizzt went deftly out to the side, out of range before the beast could counter.

The yeti was not a stupid thing, not where combat was concerned, and it understood that it was overmatched. It turned to flee, long and loping strides that could outrun almost any man, or any elf.

But Drizzt wore the enchanted anklets, and he paced the beast easily. He was behind it and then beside it, scoring hit after hit, turning the dirty, shaggy coat bright red with spilling blood. The ranger knew the truth of tundra yetis, knew that they were not simple animal hunters. They were vicious monsters that murdered for sport as well as for food.

So he continued to pace it, would not let it flee, easily dodging the feeble attempts the beast made to strike at him, and scoring his own brutal hits repeatedly. Finally, the yeti pulled up and turned in a final, desperate rush.

Drizzt, too, charged, scimitars extended, one taking the yeti in the throat, the other in the belly.

Agile Drizzt came out the other side, right under the stumbling yeti's reaching arm. The drow skidded to a stop and banged his blades hard against the yeti's back, but the beast was already on the way down, already defeated. It fell headlong into the dirt.

Now it became a race between Catti-brie and the one remaining uninjured enemy to get to the yeti she had wounded in the arm.

Catti-brie won that race, and slashed hard as the yeti reached for her with its one working arm. Khazid'hea, fine-edged Khazid'hea, took that arm off cleanly, severing it at the shoulder.

The yeti went into a crazed dance, spinning all about and then toppling to the ground, its lifeblood gushing forth.

Catti-brie rushed away from it, not wanting to get caught up in that frenzied thrashing, and knowing that the fight was not yet won. She turned just in time to meet the charge of the last yeti, extending her sword and bracing herself.

The beast came straight in, arms out wide and extended.

Khazid'hea went right through its chest, but still its strong arms grasped Catti-brie's shoulders and its momentum barreled her over backward.

As she flew and fell, Catti-brie realized the danger of a five hundred pound yeti coming down atop her. Then, suddenly, she was still falling, but the yeti was gone, simply gone, its momentum reversed by the flying Guenhwyvar.

Catti-brie hit the ground hard, managed to roll to absorb some of the force, and then came back to her feet.

The fight was over, though, with Guenhwyvar's strong jaws clamped tight on the throat of the already dead yeti.

Catti-brie looked up from the cat, into the stare of blank amazement splayed across the faces of the other caravan guards.

Six dead tundra yetis in a matter of minutes.

Catti-brie couldn't restrain a smile, nor could Drizzt as he came up to join her, as the men turned their horses away, shaking their heads in disbelief.

According to Cadderly, Drizzt's reputation as a fighter had gotten them onto the caravan in the first place, and now, the pair realized, that reputation would spread wide among the merchants of Luskan. Would spread wide, as would the clear acceptance of this most unusual drow elf.

⚔ ⚔ ⚔ ⚔ ⚔

Soon after, the friends were back on their mounts and back in the lead.

"Three for me," Catti-brie remarked offhandedly.

Drizzt's lavender orbs narrowed as he considered her. He understood the game, had played it often with Wulfgar and even more so with Bruenor, during the days of their exploits.

"Two and a half," Drizzt corrected, remembering the panther's role in killing the last of the beasts.

Catti-brie did the math quickly in her head and then decided that there was no harm in giving the drow the argument, though she believed that the last yeti was dead before Guenhwyvar ever got to it. "Two and a half," she replied, "but only two for yerself!"

Drizzt couldn't suppress a chuckle.

"And only one and a half for the cat!" Catti-brie added with a superior snap of her fingers.

Guenhwyvar, loping along beside the horses, issued a growl, and both Catti-brie and Drizzt burst out in laughter, figuring that the too-intelligent panther had understood every word.

The caravan continued into Icewind Dale without further incident, arriving ahead of schedule in Bryn Shander, the primary marketplace in the dale and the largest of the ten towns that gave this region of the dale its name. Bryn Shander was a walled city, built upon low hills and circular in design. It was located near to the exact center of the triangle created by the three lakes of Maer Dualdon, Lac Dinneshere, and Redwaters. Bryn Shander was the only town of the ten without a fishing fleet, the staple of Ten-Towns' economy, and yet it was the most thriving of the cities, the home of the craftsmen and the merchants, the hub of politics in all the region.

Drizzt's welcome there was not friendly, even after he was formally intro-duced to the gate guards, and one of them admitted that he remembered the drow ranger from when he was a boy. Catti-brie was well received, though, quite well, particularly because her father had returned to the dale and all in the city were anxious for the precious metals to begin their flow from the dwarven mines.

Because his time of work for the caravan merchants was ended, Drizzt would not have even entered Bryn Shander. He meant to turn instead straight north for the dwarven valley. Before they could settle up with the caravan leaders inside the city gates, though, the companions were informed that

Cassius, the Spokesman of Bryn Shander had requested an audience with Catti-brie.

Though she was dirty from the long ride and wanted nothing more than to fall into a comfortable bed, Catti-brie could not refuse, but she insisted that Drizzt accompany her.

⚔ ⚔ ⚔ ⚔ ⚔

"It went well," the young woman remarked, later that day, when she and Drizzt left the spokesman's mansion.

Drizzt didn't disagree. Indeed it had gone better than Drizzt had expected, for Cassius remembered Drizzt Do'Urden well, and had greeted the drow with an unexpected smile. And now Drizzt was walking openly down the streets of Bryn Shander, suffering many curious looks, but no open hostility. Many, particularly the children, pointed and whispered, and Drizzt's keen ears caught words such as "ranger" and "warrior" more than once, always spoken with respect.

It was good to be home, so good that Drizzt almost forgot the desperate search that had brought him here. For a short while at least, the drow didn't have to think of Errtu and the crystal shard.

Before they reached the gate, another of Bryn Shander's residents came running up to them, hollering their names.

"Regis!" Catti-brie shouted, turning to see the three-and-a-half-foot halfling. His curly brown hair was bobbing, as was his ample belly as he huffed along.

"You were leaving without even a visit!" the halfling cried, finally catching up to the pair. He was immediately scooped up in a tight hug by a speechless Catti-brie. "No 'well met' for your old friend?" Regis asked, falling back to his feet.

"We thought you would be with Bruenor," Drizzt explained honestly, and Regis was not offended, for the explanation was simple and truly believable. Surely if Drizzt and Catti-brie had known that the halfling was in Bryn Shander, they would have gone straight to see him.

"I split my time between the mines and the city," Regis explained. "Somebody has to serve as ambassador between the merchants and that surly father of yours!"

Catti-brie gave him another hug.

"We have dined with Cassius," Drizzt explained. "It seems that not much has changed in Ten-Towns."

"Except for many of the people. You know the way of the dale. Most don't stay long, or don't live long."

"Cassius still rules in Bryn Shander," Drizzt remarked.

"And Jensin Brent speaks still for Caer-Dineval," Regis reported happily. That was good news for the companions, for Jensin Brent was among the heroes of the battle for Icewind Dale against Akar Kessel and the crystal shard. He was among the most reasonable politicians either of them had ever known.

"The good with the bad," Regis went on, "for Kemp remains in Targos."

"Tough old orc-kin," Catti-brie replied quietly.

"Tougher than ever," Regis said. "Berkthgar has returned as well."

Drizzt and Catti-brie nodded. Both had heard rumors to that effect.

"He's running with Revjak and the Tribe of the Elk," the halfling explained. "We hear little from them."

His tone told the pair that there was more to that tale.

"Bruenor paid Revjak a visit," Regis admitted. "It did not go well."

Drizzt knew Revjak, understood the wise man's soul. He knew Berkthgar, too, and it didn't take the drow long to surmise the source of the apparent problems.

"Berkthgar's never truly forgiven Bruenor," Regis said.

"Not the hammer again," said an exasperated Catti-brie.

Regis could offer no explanations, but Drizzt resolved then and there to pay the barbarians a visit of his own. Berkthgar was a noble and powerful warrior, but he could be a stubborn one, and the drow suspected that his old friend Revjak might be needing some support.

But that was business for another day. Drizzt and Catti-brie spent the night with Regis in his Bryn Shander residence, and then the three were out bright and early the next day, setting a swift pace due north for the dwarven mines.

They arrived before midday, and as they came down into the valley, an anxious Catti-brie, who had grown up in this very place, took the lead from Regis. The young woman needed no guide in this familiar setting. She went straight to the common entrance to the dwarven complex and went in without hesitation, stooping to get under the low frame so easily that it seemed as if she had never been away from the place.

She verily ran along the dimly lit corridors, pausing briefly with every dwarf she encountered—bearded folk whose faces inevitably beamed when they recognized that Catti-brie and Drizzt had returned. Conversations were polite, but very short, a well-wish from the dwarf, an inquiry by Catti-brie or Drizzt about where they might find Bruenor.

At last they came to the room where Bruenor was reportedly at work. They heard the hammer banging within. The dwarf was forging, a rare event over the last decade, since the creation of Aegis-fang.

Catti-brie cracked open the door. Bruenor had his back to her but she knew that it was him by the sturdy set of his shoulders, the wild red hair, and the helmet with one horn broken away. With the sound of his hammer and the roaring fire just to the side of him, he did not hear them enter.

The three walked right up to the oblivious dwarf and Catti-brie tapped him on the shoulder. He half-turned, hardly glancing her way.

"Get ye gone!" the dwarf grumbled. "Can't ye see I'm fixin' . . ."

Bruenor's words fell away in a profound swallow. He continued to stare straight ahead for a long moment as if he was afraid to look, afraid that the quick glimpse had deceived him.

Then the red-bearded dwarf did turn, and he nearly swooned at the sight of his daughter returned, and of his best friend, come home to him after six long years. He dropped his hammer right on top of his own foot, but he didn't seem to notice as he shuffled over a step and wrapped both Catti-brie and Drizzt in a hug so tight that they thought the powerful dwarf would surely snap their spines.

Gradually, Bruenor let Drizzt slip out of that hug, and he wrapped Catti-brie all the tighter, mumbling, "me girl," over and over again.

Drizzt took the opportunity to bring in Guenhwyvar from her astral home, and as soon as the dwarf finally sorted himself out from Catti-brie, the panther buried him, knocking him prone and standing triumphantly above him.

"Get the durned cat off o' me!" Bruenor roared, to which Guenhwyvar casually licked him full in the face.

"Oh, ye stupid cat," the dwarf complained, but there was no anger in Bruenor's voice. How could he possibly be angry with his two, no three, friends returned?

And how could that anger, if there had been any, have held up against the howls of laughter from Drizzt, Catti-brie, and Regis. A defeated Bruenor looked up to the cat, and it seemed to him as if Guenhwyvar was smiling.

The five companions spent the remainder of that day, long into the night, trading tales. Bruenor and Regis had little to say, other than to quickly retell their decision to leave Mithral Hall in Gandalug's hands and return to Icewind Dale.

Bruenor couldn't fully explain that choice—his choice, for Regis merely had followed along—but Drizzt could. When Bruenor's grief over the loss of Wulfgar and his elation about the victory over the dark elves had finally

dissipated, Bruenor had gotten restless, as had Catti-brie and Drizzt. The red-bearded dwarf was old, past two hundred, but not too old by the standards of the dwarven folk. He was not yet ready to settle down and live happily ever after. With Gandalug back in Mithral Hall, Bruenor, for once, could forget about responsibilities and consider his own feelings.

For their part, Drizzt and Catti-brie had much more to talk about, recounting tales of their pirate-chasing along the Sword Coast with Captain Deudermont. Bruenor, too, had sailed with the captain, though Regis did not know the man.

And the two had so many tales to tell! One battle after another—thrilling chases, music playing, and Catti-brie always straining to decipher the enemy's insignia from her high perch. When they got to the events of the last few tendays, though, Drizzt ended the recounting abruptly.

"And so it went," the drow said. "But even such times can become a hollow enjoyment. We both knew that it was time to come home, to find you two."

"How'd ye know where to find us?" he asked.

Drizzt stuttered over his answer for just a moment. "Why, that was how we knew it was time to come home," he lied. "We heard in Luskan that some dwarves had come through the city, returning to Icewind Dale. The rumors said that Bruenor Battlehammer was among them."

Bruenor nodded, though he knew that his friend was not telling him the truth, or at least, not all of it. Bruenor's party had purposely avoided Luskan, and though the people there certainly knew of the march, the dwarves had not "come through the city," as Drizzt had just claimed. The red-bearded dwarf said nothing, though, for he held faith that Drizzt would tell him the complete truth in good time.

He suspected that his friends had some monumental secret, and the dwarf figured that he knew what it was. How ironic, Bruenor privately considered, for a dwarf to have a drow elf for a son-in-law!

The group went quiet for a while, Drizzt and Catti-brie's tales having been told in full, at least, as in full as they were apparently going to be told at this sitting. Regis went out into the hall and returned in a moment with news that the sun was high in the eastern sky.

"Good food and warm beds!" Bruenor proclaimed, and so off they went, Drizzt dismissing Guenhwyvar and promising to recall the cat as soon as she was rested.

After the short sleep, they were back together—except for Regis, who considered anything less than ten hours too short—talking and smiling. Drizzt and Catti-brie revealed nothing new about the last few tendays of their

adventure, though, and Bruenor didn't press the point, holding faith in his dear friend and his daughter.

For that brief moment, at least, all the world seemed bright and carefree.

21
WHENEVER

Drizzt reclined in the shade on the smooth and slanted side of a boulder, crossing his hands behind his head and closing his eyes, enjoying the unusually warm day—for it did not often get so warm in Icewind Dale, even in late summer.

Though he was far from the entrance to the dwarven mines, Drizzt did not fear his lapse of readiness, for Guenhwyvar reclined nearby, always alert. The drow was just about asleep when the panther issued a low growl, her ears going flat.

Drizzt sat up, but then Guenhwyvar calmed, even rolled over lazily and he knew that whoever was approaching was no threat. A moment later, Catti-brie walked around a bend in the trail to join her friends. Drizzt was pleased to see her—Drizzt was always pleased to see her—but then he noted the troubled look upon her fair features.

She walked right up and sat down on the boulder beside the dark elf. "I'm thinking that we have to tell them," she said immediately, ending any suspense.

Drizzt understood exactly what she was talking about. When they had recounted their adventures to Bruenor, it had been Drizzt, and Drizzt alone, who had fabricated the ending tales, Catti-brie going conspicuously silent. She was uncomfortable in lying to her father. So was Drizzt, but the drow wasn't certain of what he might say to Bruenor to explain the events that had brought them to the dale. He did not want to inject any unnecessary tension and as far as he knew, it could be years, even decades, before Errtu found his way to them.

"Eventually," Drizzt replied to Catti-brie.

"Why're ye wanting to wait?" the woman asked.

Drizzt paused—good question. "We need more information," he explained at length. "We do not know whether Errtu means to come to the dale, and have no idea of when that might be. Fiends measure time differently than do we. A year is not so long to one of Errtu's race, nor is a century. I see no need to alarm Bruenor and Regis at this time."

Catti-brie thought on that for a long while. "How're ye thinking to get more information?" she asked.

"Stumpet Rakingclaw," Drizzt replied.

"Ye hardly know her."

"But I will get to know her. I know enough of her, of her exploits in Keeper's Dale and in Menzoberranzan against the invading dark elves, to trust in her power and her sense."

Catti-brie nodded—from everything she had heard of Stumpet Rakingclaw, the cleric was an excellent choice. Something else bothered Catti-brie, though, something that the drow had hinted at. She sighed deeply, and that told Drizzt what was on her mind.

"We have no way of knowing how long it will be," the drow ranger admitted.

"Then are we to become guardians for a year?" Catti-brie asked, rather sharply. "Or a hundred years?" She saw the drow's pained look and regretted the words as soon as she had spoken them. Surely it would be difficult for Catti-brie, lying in wait as the months rolled by for a fiend that might not even show up. But how much worse it must be for Drizzt! For Drizzt was not just waiting for Errtu, but for his father, his tortured father, and every day that passed meant another day that Zaknafein was in Errtu's evil clutches.

The woman bowed her head. "I'm sorry," she said. "I should've been thinkin' of yer father."

Drizzt put a hand on her shoulder. "Fear not," he replied, "I think of him constantly."

Catti-brie lifted her deep blue eyes to look deeply into the drow's lavender orbs. "We'll get him back," she promised grimly, "and pay Errtu for all the pain he's given yer father."

"I know," Drizzt said with a nod. "But there is no need to raise the alarm just yet. Bruenor and Regis have enough to concern them with winter fast approaching."

Catti-brie agreed and sat back on the warm stone. They would wait as long as they had to, and then let Errtu beware!

And so the friends fell into the routine of everyday life in Icewind Dale, working with the dwarves over the next couple of tendays. Drizzt secured a cave to serve as an outer camp for his many forays onto the open tundra, and Catti-brie spent quite a bit of time there as well, beside her friend, silently comforting him.

They spoke little of Errtu and the crystal shard, and Drizzt hadn't yet approached Stumpet, but the drow thought of the fiend, and more particularly, of the fiend's prisoner, almost constantly.

Simmering.

⚔ ⚔ ⚔ ⚔

"You must come quicker when I call to you!" the wizard growled, pacing anxiously about the room. He hardly seemed imposing to the twelve-foot glabrezu. The fiend had four arms, two ending with mighty hands and two with pincers that could snap a man in half.

"My fellows, they do not tolerate delays," the wizard went on. The glabrezu, Bizmatec, curled up his canine lips in a sly smile. This wizard, Dosemen of Sundabar, was all in disarray, battling hard to win a foolish contest against his fellow guild members. Perhaps he had erred in preparing the circle . . .

"Do I ask much of you?" Dosemen wailed. "Of course I do not! Just a few answers to minor questions, and I have given much in return."

"I do not complain," Bizmatec replied. While the fiend spoke, he scrutinized the circle of power, the only thing holding back the glabrezu's wrath. If Dosemen had not properly prepared the circle, Bizmatec meant to devour him.

"But neither do you give to me the answers!" Dosemen howled. "Now, I will ask once more, and you will have three hours, just three hours, to return with my answers."

Bizmatec heard the words distinctly, and considered their implications in a new and respectful light, for by that time, the fiend had come to know that the circle was complete and perfect. There could be no escape.

Dosemen began rattling off his seven questions, seven unimportant and obscure questions, worthless except that finding their answers was the contest the wizard's guild had begun. Dosemen's voice showed his urgency. He knew that at least three of his fellows had garnered several of the answers already.

Bizmatec was not listening, though, was trying to recall something he had heard in the Abyss, a proposition put forth by a tanar'ri much greater than he.

The glabrezu looked at the perfect circle again and scowled doubtfully, and yet, Errtu had said that the power of the summoner or the perfection of the magical binding circle was not an issue.

"Wait!" Bizmatec roared, and Dosemen, despite his confidence and his anger, fell back and fell silent.

"The answers you require will take many hours to discover," the fiend explained.

"I do not have many hours!" Dosemen retorted, gaining back a bit of his composure with his rising ire.

"Then I have for you an answer," the glabrezu replied with a sly and wicked grin.

"You just said . . ."

"I have no answers to your questions," Bizmatec quickly explained. "But I know of one who does, a balor."

Dosemen paled at the mention of the great beast. He was no minor wizard, practiced at summoning and confident of his magic circle. But a balor! Never had Dosemen tried to bring in such a beast. Balors, and by all accounts there were only a score or so, were the highest level of tanar'ri, the greatest of the terrors of the Abyss.

"You fear the balor?" Bizmatec teased.

Dosemen pulled himself up straight, remembering that he had to show confidence in the face of a fiend. Weakness of attitude bred weakness of binding, that was the sorcerer's creed. "I fear nothing!" the wizard declared.

"Then get your answers from the balor!" Bizmatec roared. "Errtu, by name."

Dosemen fell back another step at the sheer power of the glabrezu's roar. Then the wizard calmed considerably and stood staring. The glabrezu had just given him the name of a balor, openly and without a price. A tanar'ri's name was among its most precious commodities, for with that name, a wizard such as Dosemen could strengthen the binding of his call.

"How much do you desire defeating your rivals?" Bizmatec teased, snickering with each word. "Surely Errtu will show you the truth of your questions."

Dosemen thought on it for just a moment, then turned sharply upon Bizmatec. He was still leery about the prospects of bringing in a balor, but the carrot, his first victory in one of the guild's bi-annual contests, was too juicy to ignore. "Be gone!" he commanded. "I'll waste no more energy upon the likes of you."

The glabrezu liked hearing that promise. He knew that Dosemen was speaking only of wasting his energy upon Bizmatec for the time being. The

wizard had become quite a thorn to the glabrezu. But if the whispers filtering around the smoky layers of the Abyss concerning mighty Errtu were true, then Dosemen would soon enough be surprised and terrified by the ironic truth of his own words.

Back in the Abyss, the interplanar gate fast closing behind him, Bizmatec rushed to an area of gigantic mushrooms, the lair of mighty Errtu. The balor at first moved to destroy the fiend, thinking the glabrezu an invader, but when Bizmatec spouted his news, Errtu fell back on his mushroom throne, grinning from horn to horn.

"You gave the fool my name?" Errtu asked.

Bizmatec hesitated, but there seemed no anger in Errtu's voice, only eager anticipation. "By the instructions I heard . . ." the glabrezu began tentatively, but Errtu's cackling laughter stopped him.

"That is good," the balor said. Bizmatec relaxed considerably.

"But Dosemen is no minor wizard," Bizmatec warned. "His circle is perfect."

Errtu chuckled again as if that hardly mattered. Bizmatec was about to reiterate that point, figuring that the balor simply believed that he would find a flaw where the glabrezu had not, but Errtu moved first, holding forth a small black coffer.

"No circle is perfect," the balor remarked cryptically and with all confidence. "Now, come quickly. I have another task for you, a service of guarding my most valuable prisoner." Errtu slid from his throne and started away, but stopped, seeing that the glabrezu was hesitating.

"The rewards will be great, my general," Errtu promised. "Many days running free on the Prime Material Plane . . . many souls to devour."

No tanar'ri could resist that.

Dosemen's call came a short while later, and though it was weak, the wizard having already expended much of his magical energy in summoning Bizmatec, Errtu scooped up his precious coffer and was quick to respond. He followed the interplanar gate to Dosemen's room in Sundabar, and found himself, as Bizmatec had warned, standing in the middle of a perfectly ingrained circle of power.

"Close fast the gate!" the balor cried, his thunderous, grating voice reverberating off the stone walls of the room. "The baatezu might follow me through! Oh, fool! You have separated me from my minions, and now the beasts of doom will follow me through the gate! What will you do, foolish mortal, when the pit fiends enter your domain?"

As any wise wizard would, Dosemen was already frantically at work in closing the gate. Pit fiends! More than one? No circle, no wizard, could hold a balor and a pair or more of pit fiends. Dosemen chanted and worked his arms in concentric circles, throwing various material components into the air.

Errtu continued to feign rage and terror, watching the wizard and then looking back as if he was viewing the very gate he had come through. Errtu needed that gate closed, for any working magic would soon be dispelled, and if the gate was still empowered at the time, the balor would likely be sent back to the Abyss.

Finally, it was done, and Dosemen stood calm—as calm as a wizard could while looking into the half-ape, half-dog face of a balor!

"I have summoned you for a simple—" Dosemen began.

"Silence!" roared mighty Errtu. "You have summoned me because you were instructed to summon me!"

Dosemen eyed the beast curiously, then looked to his circle, his perfect circle. He had to hold faith, had to consider the balor's words as a bluff.

"Silence!" Dosemen yelled back, and because his circle was indeed perfect, and because he had summoned the tanar'ri correctly, using its true name, Errtu had to comply.

So the balor was silent as he produced the black coffer, holding it up for Dosemen to see.

"What is that?" the wizard demanded.

"Your doom," Errtu answered, and he was not lying. Grinning wickedly, the balor opened the coffer, revealing a shining black sapphire the size of a large man's fist, a remnant of the Time of Troubles. Contained within that sapphire was an energy of antimagic, for it was a piece of dead magic zone, one of the most important remnants of the days when the avatars of the gods walked the Realms. When the shielding coffer was opened, Dosemen's mental binding over Errtu was gone, and the wizard's circle, though its tracings remained perfect, was no longer a prison for the summoned fiend, no longer a deterrence, nor were any of the protection spells that the wizard had placed upon his person.

Errtu, too, had no magic that he could hurl in the face of that dead magic stone, but the powerful tanar'ri, a thousand pounds of muscle and catastrophe, hardly needed any.

⚔ ⚔ ⚔ ⚔ ⚔

Dosemen's fellow wizards entered his private room later that night, fearful for their guild-brother. They found a shoe, just one, and a splotch of dried blood.

Errtu, having replaced the sapphire in the coffer, which could shield even against such wicked antimagic, was far, far away by then, flying fast to the north and the west—to Icewind Dale, where Crenshinibon, an artifact that the balor had coveted through centuries, waited.

22
LIKE OLD TIMES

The ranger ran with the wind in his ears, that constant humming. It had shifted more from the north now, off the glaciers and the great bergs of the Sea of Moving Ice, as the season drifted away from summer, through the short fall and into the long and dark winter.

Drizzt knew this change on the tundra as well as any. He had lived in Icewind Dale for just a decade, but in that time he had come to know well the land and its ways. He could tell by the texture of the ground exactly what time of year it was to within a tenday. Now the ground was hardening once more, though there remained a bit of sliding under his moving feet, a subtle hint of mud below the dry surface, the last remnant of the short summer.

The ranger kept his cloak tight about his neck, warding off the chilly breeze. Though he was bundled, and though he could not hear much above the incessant moan of the wind, the drow was alert, always alert. Creatures venturing out onto the open plain of Icewind Dale who were not careful did not survive for long. Drizzt noted tracks of tundra yeti in several places. He also found one group of footprints close together, moving side by side, the way a goblin band might travel. He could read those prints, where they had come from and where they were going, and he had not come out from Kelvin's Cairn for any fight. He took special note of them now simply to avoid the creatures who had made them.

Soon Drizzt found the tracks he desired, two sets of prints from soft boots, man-sized, traveling slowly, as a hunter would stalk. He noted that the deepest depression by far was near the ball of the foot. Barbarians walked in a toe-heel manner, not the heel-toe stride used by most of the peoples of the

Realms. There could be no doubt now for the ranger. He had ventured near to the barbarian encampment the night before, meaning to go in and speak with Revjak and Berkthgar. Listening secretly from the darkness, however, the drow had discovered that Berkthgar intended to go out on a hunt the next day, alone with Revjak's son.

That news unsettled Drizzt at first—did Berkthgar mean to indirectly strike a blow at Revjak and kill the boy?

Drizzt had quickly dismissed that silly notion. He knew Berkthgar. For all their differences, the man was honorable and no murderer. More likely, Drizzt reasoned, Berkthgar was trying to win over the trust of Revjak's son, strengthening his base of power within the tribe.

Drizzt had stayed out of the encampment all the night, in the darkness, undetected. He had moved safely away before the dawn and had subsequently circled far to the north.

Now he had found the tracks, two men, side by side. They were an hour ahead of him, but moving as hunters, and so Drizzt was confident that he would find them in but a few minutes.

The ranger slowed his pace a moment later when he found that the tracks split, the smaller set going off to the west, the larger continuing straight north. Drizzt followed the larger, figuring them to be Berkthgar's, and a few minutes later, he spotted the giant barbarian, kneeling on the tundra, shielding his eyes and peering hard to the north and west.

Drizzt slowed and moved cautiously. He discovered that he was nervous at the sight of the imposing man. Drizzt and Berkthgar had argued many times in the past, usually when Drizzt was serving Bruenor as liaison to Settlestone, where Berkthgar ruled. This time was different, Drizzt realized. Berkthgar was back home now, needing nothing from Bruenor, and that might make the man more dangerous.

Drizzt had to find out. That was why he had come out from Kelvin's Cairn in the first place. He moved silently, step by step, until he was within a few yards of the still-kneeling, apparently oblivious barbarian.

"My greetings, Berkthgar," the ranger said. His sudden voice did not appear to startle the barbarian, and Drizzt believed that Berkthgar, so at home on the tundra, had sensed his approach.

Berkthgar rose slowly and turned to face the drow.

Drizzt looked to the west, to a speck on the distant tundra. "Your hunting partner?" he asked.

"Revjak's son, Kierstaad by name," Berkthgar replied. "A fine boy."

"And what of Revjak?" Drizzt asked.

Berkthgar paused a moment, jaw firm. "It was whispered that you had returned to the dale," he said.

"Is that a good thing in the eyes of Berkthgar?"

"No," came the simple reply. "The tundra is wide, drow. Wide enough so that we will not have to meet again." Berkthgar began to turn away, as if that was all that had to be said, but Drizzt wasn't ready to let things go just yet.

"Why would you desire that?" Drizzt asked innocently, trying to push Berkthgar into playing his hand openly. Drizzt wanted to know just how far the barbarians were moving away from the dwarves and the folk of Ten-Towns. Were they to become invisible partners sharing the tundra, or, as they once had been, sworn enemies?

"Revjak calls me friend," Drizzt went on. "When I left the dale those years ago, I named Revjak among those I would truly miss."

"Revjak is an old man," Berkthgar said evenly.

"Revjak speaks for the tribe."

"No!" Berkthgar's response came fast and sharp. Then he quickly calmed and his smile told Drizzt that the denial was true. "No more does Revjak speak for the tribe," Berkthgar went on.

"Berkthgar, then?" Drizzt asked.

The huge barbarian nodded, smiling still. "I have returned to lead my people," he said. "Away from the errors of Wulfgar and Revjak, back to the ways we once knew, when we were free, when we answered to no one but our own and our god."

Drizzt thought on that for a moment. The proud young man was truly deluding himself, the drow realized, for those old times that Berkthgar spoke of so reverently were not as carefree and wonderful as the huge man apparently believed. Those years were marked by war, usually between tribes competing for food that was often scarce. Barbarians starved to death and froze to death, and often wound up as meals for tundra yeti, or for the great white bears that also followed the reindeer herd along the coast of the Sea of Moving Ice.

That was the danger of nostalgia, Drizzt realized. One often remembered the good of the past while forgetting the troubles.

"Then Berkthgar speaks for the tribes," Drizzt agreed. "Will he lead them to despair? To war?"

"War is not always despair," the barbarian said coolly. "And do you forget so soon that following the course of Wulfgar led us to war with your own people?"

Drizzt had no response to that statement. It hadn't happened exactly like that, of course. The drow war was far more an accident of chance than of

anything Wulfgar had done. But still, the words were true enough, at least from Berkthgar's stilted perspective.

"And before that, Wulfgar's course led the tribes to war in helping to reclaim the throne for your ungrateful friend," Berkthgar pressed.

Drizzt glared hard at Berkthgar. Again the man's words were true, if stilted, and the drow realized that there was no practical response he could offer to sway Berkthgar.

They both noticed then that the speck on the tundra was larger now as Kierstaad approached.

"We have found the clean air of the tundra again," Berkthgar proclaimed before the lad arrived. "We have returned to the old ways, the better ways, and those do not allow for friendship with drow elves."

"Berkthgar forgets much," Drizzt replied.

"Berkthgar remembers much," the giant barbarian answered, and walked away.

"You would do well to consider the good that Wulfgar did for your people," Drizzt called after him. "Perhaps Settlestone was not the place for the tribe, but Icewind Dale is an unforgiving land, a land where allies are the most valuable assets for any man."

Berkthgar didn't slow. He came up to Kierstaad and walked right past the young man. Kierstaad turned and watched him for a short time, the young man quickly deciphering what had just happened. Then Kierstaad turned back to Drizzt and recognizing the drow, sprinted over to stand before him.

"Well met, Kierstaad," Drizzt said. "The years have done you well."

Kierstaad straightened a bit at that remark, thrilled to have Drizzt Do'Urden say anything complimentary to him. Kierstaad was just a boy of twelve when Drizzt left Mithral Hall, and so he did not know the drow very well. He knew of Drizzt, though, the legendary warrior. Once Drizzt and Catti-brie had come to Hengorot, the mead hall in Settlestone, and Drizzt had leaped upon the table, giving a speech that called for a strengthened alliance between the dwarves and the barbarians. By all the old ways that Berkthgar so often spoke of, no drow elf should have been allowed in Hengorot, and certainly none would have been shown any respect. But the mead hall showed respect to Drizzt Do'Urden that day, a testament to the drow's battle prowess.

Kierstaad could not forget, too, the stories his father had told him of Drizzt. In one particularly vicious battle with the folk of Ten-Towns, the barbarian warriors invading Ten-Towns were badly beaten, in no small part because of Drizzt Do'Urden. After that fight, the ranks of the barbarians were greatly diminished. With winter coming on, it seemed that many hardships would befall those who had survived the war, particularly the very young and the very old, for there simply were not enough hunters left alive to provide for all.

But the fresh carcasses of reindeer had been found along the trail as the nomadic barbarians had moved west with the herd, killed cleanly and left for the tribe. The work of Drizzt Do'Urden, Revjak and many of the elders agreed, the drow who had defended Ten-Towns against the barbarians. Revjak had never forgotten the significance of that act of kindness, nor had many of the older barbarians.

"Well met, to you," Kierstaad replied. "It is good that you have returned."

"Not everyone agrees with that view," Drizzt remarked.

Kierstaad snorted and shrugged noncommittally. "I am sure that Bruenor is glad to see the likes of Drizzt Do'Urden again," he said.

"And of Catti-brie," Drizzt added. "For she returned at my side."

Again the young man nodded and Drizzt could tell that he wanted to say something more profound than the polite conversation. He kept looking back over his shoulder, though, to the departing form of Berkthgar, his leader. His loyalties were obviously split.

Finally, Kierstaad sighed and turned to face the drow directly, the internal battle decided. "Many remember the truth of Drizzt Do'Urden," he said.

"And of Bruenor Battlehammer?"

Kierstaad nodded. "Berkthgar leads the tribe, by right of deed, but not all agree with his every word."

"Then let us hope that Berkthgar soon remembers that truth," Drizzt replied.

Kierstaad glanced back one more time, to see that Berkthgar had stopped and had turned to regard him. The young barbarian understood then what was expected of him, and he gave a quick nod to Drizzt, not even offering a parting word, and ran off to join the giant man.

Drizzt spent a long time considering the implications of that sight, the young man blindly running to Berkthgar's will, though he did not share many of his leader's views. Then Drizzt considered his own course. He had meant to go back to the encampment for a word with Revjak, but that seemed a useless, even dangerous proposition now.

Now that Berkthgar spoke for the tribe.

✕ ✕ ✕ ✕ ✕

While Drizzt was running north of Kelvin's Cairn, another traveler was traversing the tundra to the south of the mountain. Stumpet Rakingclaw

rambled on, her back bent for the weight of her huge pack, her eyes focused on that singular goal: the towering peaks of the Spine of the World.

Crenshinibon, hanging through a loop on the dwarf's belt, was silent and pleased. The artifact had invaded Stumpet's dreams every night. Its communications with the dwarf had been more subtle than was usual for the domineering artifact, for Crenshinibon held a healthy respect for this one, both dwarf and priestess of a goodly god. Gradually, over the tendays, Crenshinibon had worn away Stumpet's resistance, had slowly convinced the dwarf that this was not a foolishly dangerous trek, but rather a challenge to be met and conquered.

And so Stumpet had come out the previous day, striding determinedly to the south, weapon in hand and ready to meet any monsters, ready to climb any mountain.

She wasn't yet near the mountains, about halfway from Redwaters, the southernmost of the three lakes. Crenshinibon planned to remain silent. The artifact was a work of the ages and a few days meant nothing to it. When they got to the mountains, the wilderness, the artifact would find a more suitable wielder.

But then, unexpectedly, the crystal shard sensed a presence, powerful and familiar.

A tanar'ri.

Stumpet stopped her run a moment later, her face screwed up with curiosity as she considered the item on her belt. She felt the vibrations from it, as though it was a living thing. As she studied the item, she recognized those vibrations as a call.

"What then?" the dwarf asked, lifting the crystal shard from the loop. "What're ye about?"

Stumpet was still eyeing the shard when a ball of blackness swept out of the blue haze of the distant horizon, hearing the call now and speeding fast on leathery wings. Finally, the dwarf shrugged her shoulders. Not understanding, she replaced the shard, then looked up.

Too late.

Errtu came in hard and fast, overwhelming the dwarf before she could even lift her weapon. In mere seconds, the fiend held Crenshinibon in his clutches, a union both desired.

Stumpet, on the ground and dazed, her weapon knocked far from her hands, propped herself on her elbows and looked upon the tanar'ri. She started to call to her god, but Errtu would have none of that. He kicked her hard, launching her a dozen feet away and moved in for the torturous kill.

Crenshinibon stopped him. The artifact did not disdain brute force, nor did it hold any sympathy for the dwarf. But a simple reminder to Errtu that enemies such as Stumpet could be used to his advantage gave the fiend pause. Errtu knew nothing about Bruenor Battlehammer and the quest for Mithral Hall, knew nothing about the clan's departure from the dale, let alone their return. But the fiend did know of Drizzt's previous allegiance to the dwarves of Icewind Dale. If Drizzt Do'Urden was in the dale, or if he ever came back, he would likely once again befriend the dwarves that worked the mines south of the mountain called Kelvin's Cairn. This female, obviously, was of that clan.

Errtu towered over her, menacing her, preventing her from holding any concentration that she would need to cast a spell, or even to retrieve her weapon. The fiend held out one hand, on his second finger was a ring adorned with a blackish-purple gemstone. Errtu's black eyes blazed into orange flames as he began to chant in the guttural language of the Abyss.

The gemstone flared a purplish light that washed over Stumpet.

Suddenly Stumpet's perspective changed. She was no longer looking up at the fiend, but was rather looking down, on her own body! She heard Errtu's cackling laughter, sensed the approval of the crystal shard, and then watched helplessly as her form rose up from the ground and moved about, collecting the dropped items.

Zombielike, moving stiff-legged, the soulless dwarven body turned about and walked off to the north.

Stumpet's soul remained, trapped within the purplish gem, hearing the cackles, sensing the sentient waves that the evil artifact sent out to Errtu.

⚔ ⚔ ⚔ ⚔ ⚔

That same night, Drizzt and Catti-brie sat atop Bruenor's climb with the red-bearded dwarf and Regis, basking in the starlight. Both the dwarf and the halfling recognized the uneasiness of their companions, sensed that Drizzt and Catti-brie were keeping a secret.

Many times, the drow and the woman exchanged concerned looks.

"Well," Bruenor said at length, unable to bear the cryptic glances.

Catti-brie chuckled, the tension relieved by her father's acute observations. She and Drizzt had indeed taken Bruenor and Regis up here this night to discuss more than the beauty of the moon and stars. After long discussion, the drow had finally agreed with Catti-brie's reasoning that it would not be fair to keep their friends in the dark of their true reasons for returning to Icewind Dale.

And so Drizzt told the tale of his last few tendays aboard the *Sea Sprite,* of the attack on Deudermont in Waterdeep and the run to Caerwich, of the journey to Carradoon caused by Harkle's spell and the windwalk with Cadderly that had brought them to Luskan. He left nothing out, not even the remnants he could remember of the blind hag's poem and the intimations that his father was a prisoner of Errtu, the great tanar'ri.

Catti-brie interjected her thoughts often, mostly reassuring her father that a big part of the reason that they decided it was time to come home was because this was home, was because Bruenor was here, and Regis was here.

Silence fell over the four after Drizzt finished. All gazes fell over Bruenor, waiting for his response as though it was a judgment of them all.

"Ye durned elf!" he bellowed at last. "Ye're always bringing trouble! Know that ye make life interesting!"

After a short, strained laugh, Drizzt, Catti-brie, and Bruenor turned to hear what Regis had to say on the matter.

"I do have to widen my circle of friends," the halfling remarked, but like Bruenor's outrage, Regis's despair was a feigned thing.

Guenhwyvar roared in the night.

They were together again, the five friends, more than ready to face whatever odds, more than ready for battle.

They didn't know the depth of Errtu's terror, and didn't know that the fiend already had Crenshinibon in his evil clutches.

23
CRYSHAL-TIRITH

A whisper of sound, a ball of flying blackness against the dark night sky, the fiend rushed north, past the three lakes, past Kelvin's Cairn, across the open tundra and over the encampment of Berkthgar's people. Errtu meant to go to the farthest reaches of the tundra to set up his fortresses, but when he got to that point, to the edge of the Sea of Moving Ice, the fiend discovered a better and more forlorn landscape. Errtu, a creature of the fiery Abyss, was no friend of snow and ice, but the texture of the great icebergs clogging the waters—a mountain range built among defensible, freezing moats—showed him potential he could not resist.

Out swooped the tanar'ri, across the first and widest expanse of open water, setting on the side of the visible cone of the closest tall iceberg. He peered out through the darkness, first using his normal vision, then letting his eyes slip into the spectrum of heat. Predictably, a cold blackness reflected back at him from both the normal and the infrared spectrums, cold and dead.

The fiend started to move on again, but felt the will of Crenshinibon, asking him to look more closely.

Errtu expecting to find nothing, didn't understand the point to such scrutiny, but he continued his scan. He was surprised indeed when he did see a patch of warmer air rising from a hollow on the side of an iceberg perhaps a hundred yards away. That was too far for Errtu to make out any distinct forms so the great tanar'ri gave a short flap of his leathery wings and halved the gap.

Closer still the balor crept, until Errtu could discern that the heat was coming from a group of warm-blooded forms, huddled in a tight circle. A

more knowledgeable traveler of Icewind Dale would have thought them to be seals, or some other marine animal, but Errtu was not familiar with the creatures of the north and so he approached cautiously.

They were humanoid, man-sized, with long arms and large heads. Errtu thought that they were dressed in furs, until he got close enough to recognize that they were not dressed at all, but had their own coat of thick, shaggy fur covered with a filmy, oily sheen.

The beginnings of your army, came an intrusion into the balor's thoughts, as eager Crenshinibon renewed its quest for ever more power.

Errtu paused and considered that thought for some time. The fiend wasn't planning to raise an army, not here in this forlorn wilderness. He would remain in Icewind Dale for a short time only, long enough to discover if Drizzt Do'Urden was about, and long enough to destroy the drow ranger if he was. When that business was finished, Errtu planned to be long gone from the emptiness of the dale and into more hospitable, more thickly inhabited regions.

Crenshinibon's suggestions did not relent, and after awhile, the tanar'ri came to see a potential value of enslaving some of the area's creatures. Perhaps it would be wise to fortify his position with some expendable soldiers.

The balor chuckled wickedly and muttered a few words, a spell that would allow him to converse with the creatures in their own guttural and grunting language—if that's what their snorts and snarls could be called. Errtu called upon his magical abilities once again and disappeared, reappearing on the slope right behind and above the shaggy creatures' impromptu encampment. Now the balor had a better look at the beasts, about two-score of them, he figured. Their shaggy fur was white, their heads large, though virtually without any discernable forehead. They were strongly built and jostled each other roughly, each apparently trying to get closest to the center of the huddle, what Errtu figured to be the warmest spot.

They are yours! Crenshinibon declared.

Errtu agreed. He felt the power of the crystal shard, a dominating force indeed. The balor leaped up to his full twelve foot height atop the ridge and bellowed to the shaggy humanoids in their own tongue, Errtu declaring himself their god.

The camp disintegrated into pandemonium, creatures running all about, slamming into each other, falling over each other. Down swooped Errtu into their midst, and when they moved out from the towering fiend, encircling him cautiously, the balor brought up a ring of low, simmering fire, a personal perimeter.

Errtu held high his lightning bolt sword, commanding the creatures to kneel before him.

Instead, the shaggy beasts shoved one of their own, the largest of the group, forward.

Errtu understood the challenge. The large, shaggy creature bellowed a single threat, but the word was caught in its throat as the tanar'ri's other weapon, that wicked many-thonged whip, snapped out and wrapped about the beast's ankles. A half-hearted tug from the mighty fiend jerked the creature onto its back and Errtu casually pulled it in so that it lay, screaming in agony, in the fiend's ring of fire.

Errtu didn't kill the creature. He gave a rolling snap on his whip a moment later and the thing flew out of the flames and rolled about on the ice, whimpering.

"Errtu!" the tanar'ri proclaimed, his thunderous voice driving back the cowed creatures. Cowed, but not kneeling, Errtu realized, and so he took a different tactic. Errtu understood the basic, instinctual way of these tribal beasts. Scrutinizing them and their trinkets in the light of the fire, the balor realized that they were likely less civilized than the goblins he was more used to dealing with.

Cower them and reward them, Crenshinibon imparted, a strategy that Errtu already had well under way. The cowering was done. With a roar the fiend leaped away, soaring over the top of the berg and into the blackness of the night. Errtu heard the continuing grunts and whispers as he departed, and he smiled again, thinking himself clever, imagining the faces of the stupid brutes when he gave them their reward.

Errtu didn't have to fly far to figure out what that reward might entail. He saw the fin of a creature, a huge creature, poking from the black surface of the water.

It was a killer whale, though to Errtu, it was merely a big fish, merely some meat he might provide. Down swooped the fiend, diving fast onto the back of the behemoth. In one hand Errtu held his lightning sword, in the other, the crystal shard. Hard struck the sword, a mighty blow, but harder still came the assault from Crenshinibon, its power loosed for the first time in many years, a line of blazing white fire that tore through whale flesh as easily as a beacon cut through the night sky.

Just a few minutes later, Errtu returned to the encampment of the shaggy humanoids, dragging the dead whale behind him. He flopped the creature into the midst of the stunned humanoids, and once again proclaimed himself as their god.

The brutes fell over the slain whale, chopping wildly with crude axes, tearing flesh and guzzling blood, a grisly ceremony.

Just the way Errtu liked it.

Within the span of a few hours, Errtu and his new minions located a suitable ice floe to serve as their stronghold. Then Errtu used the powers of Crenshinibon once more, and the creatures, already falling into worship for the fiend, leaped about in circles, crying Errtu's name, falling to their faces and groveling.

For, Crenshinibon's greatest power was to enact an exact replica of itself, huge in proportion, a crystalline tower—Cryshal-Tirith. At Errtu's invitation, the creatures searched all about the base of the tower, but they saw no entrance—only extraplanar creatures could find the door to Cryshal-Tirith.

Errtu did just that, and entered. The fiend wasted no time in calling back to the Abyss, in opening a gate that Bizmatec could come through with the balor's helpless and tormented prisoner in tow.

"Welcome to my new kingdom," Errtu told the tortured soul. "You should like this place." With that, Errtu snapped his whip repeatedly, beating the prisoner unconscious.

Bizmatec howled with glee, knowing that the fun had just begun.

They settled into their new stronghold over the next few days, Errtu bringing in other minor fiends, a horde of wretched manes, and even conversing with another powerful true tanar'ri, a six-armed marilith, coaxing her to join in the play.

But Errtu's focus did not wander too far from his primary purpose. He didn't let the intoxication of such absolute power distract him from the truth of his minor conquest. Upon one wall of the tower's second level, there was set a mirror, a device for scrying, and Errtu perused it often, scouring the dale with his magical vision. Great indeed was Errtu's pleasure when he found that Drizzt Do'Urden was indeed in Icewind Dale.

The prisoner, always at Errtu's side, saw the specter of the drow elf, the human woman, a red-bearded dwarf, and a plump halfling as well, and his expression changed. His eyes brightened for the first time in many years.

"You will be valuable to me indeed," Errtu remarked, deflating any hope, reminding the prisoner that he was but a tool for the fiend, a piece of barter. "With you in hand, I will bring the drow to me, and destroy Drizzt Do'Urden before your very eyes before I destroy you as well. That is your fate and your doom." The fiend howled with ecstasy and whipped his prisoner again and again, driving him to the floor.

"And you will prove of value," the balor said to the large, purple stone set on his ring, the prison of poor Stumpet Rakingclaw's consciousness. "Your body, at least."

Trapped Stumpet heard the distant words, but the spirit of the priestess was caught in a gray void, an empty place where not even her god could hear her pleas.

⚔ ⚔ ⚔ ⚔ ⚔

Drizzt, Bruenor, and the others looked on in helpless amazement as Stumpet walked back into the dwarven mines that night, her expression blank, devoid of any emotion at all. She moved to the main audience hall on the uppermost level, and just stood in place.

"Her soul's gone," was Catti-brie's guess, and the others, in examining the dwarf, in trying to wake her from her stupor, even going so far as to slap her hard across the face, couldn't rightly disagree.

Drizzt spent a long while in front of the zombielike dwarf, questioning her, trying to wake her. Bruenor dismissed most of the others, allowing only his closest friends—and ironically, not one of these was a dwarf—to remain.

On impulse, the drow begged Regis to give him the precious ruby pendant, and Regis readily complied, slipping the enchanted item from around his neck and tossing it to the drow. Drizzt spent a moment marveling at the large ruby, its incessant swirl of little lights that could draw an unsuspecting onlooker far into its hypnotic depths. Drizzt then put the item right in front of the zombie dwarf's face and began talking to her softly, easily.

If she heard him at all, if she even saw the ruby pendant, she did not show it.

Drizzt looked back to his friends, as if to say something, as if to admit defeat, but then his expression brightened in recognition, just a flicker, before it went grave once more. "Has Stumpet been out on her own?" Drizzt asked Bruenor.

"Try to keep that one in one place," the dwarf replied. "She's always out—look at her pack. Seems to me that she was off again, heading for what's needin' climbing."

A quick look at Stumpet's huge pack confirmed the red-bearded dwarf's words. The haversack was stuffed with food and with pitons and rope, and other gear for scaling mountains.

"Has she climbed Kelvin's Cairn?" Drizzt asked suddenly, things finally falling into place.

Catti-brie gave a low groan, seeing where the drow was taking this.

"Had her eyes set on the place from the minute we walked into Ten-Towns," Bruenor proclaimed. "I think she got it, said she did anyway, not so long ago."

Drizzt looked to Catti-brie and the young woman nodded her agreement.

"What are you thinking?" Regis wanted to know.

"The crystal shard," Catti-brie replied.

They searched Stumpet carefully then, and subsequently went to her private quarters, tearing the place apart. Bruenor called for another of his priests, one who could detect magical auras, but the enhanced scan was similarly unsuccessful.

Not long after, they left Stumpet with the priest, who was trying an assortment of spells to awaken or at least comfort the zombielike dwarf. Bruenor expanded the search for the crystal shard to include every dwarf in the mines, two hundred industrious fellows.

Then all they could do was wait, and hope.

Bruenor was awakened late that night by the priest, the dwarf frantic that Stumpet had just walked away from him, was walking right out of the mines.

"Did ye stop her?" Bruenor was quick to ask, shaking off his grogginess.

"Got five dwarves holding her," the priest answered. "But she just keeps on walkin,' trying to push past 'em!"

Bruenor roused his three friends and together they rushed for the exit to the mines, where Stumpet was still plodding, bouncing off the fleshy barricade, but stubbornly walking right back into it.

"Can't wear her out, can't kill her," one of the blocking dwarfs lamented when he saw his king.

"Just hold her then!" Bruenor growled back.

Drizzt wasn't so sure of that course. He began to sense something here, and figured that it was more than coincidence. Somehow, the drow had the feeling that whatever had happened to Stumpet might be related to his return to Icewind Dale.

He looked to Catti-brie, seeing by her return gaze that she was sharing his feelings.

"Let us pack for the road," Drizzt whispered to Bruenor. "Perhaps Stumpet has something she wishes to show us."

Before the sun had begun to peek over the mountains in the east, Stumpet Rakingclaw walked out of the dwarven valley, heading north across the tundra, with Drizzt, Catti-brie, Bruenor, and Regis in tow.

Just as Errtu, watching from the scrying room of Cryshal-Tirith, had planned.

The fiend waved a clawed hand and the image in the mirror grew gray and indistinct, then washed away altogether. Errtu then went up into the tower's highest level, the small room in which the crystal shard hung, suspended in midair.

Errtu felt the curiosity of the item, for the fiend had developed quite an empathetic and telepathic bond with Crenshinibon. It sensed his delight, the fiend knew, and it wanted to know the source.

Errtu snickered at it and flooded the item with a barrage of incongruous images, defeating its mental intrusions.

Suddenly the fiend was hit with a shocking intrusion, a focused line of Crenshinibon's will that nearly tore the story of Stumpet from his lips. It took every ounce of mental energy the mighty balor could manage to resist that call, and even with that, Errtu found that he had not the strength to leave the room, and knew that he could not resist for long.

"You dare . . ." the fiend gasped, but the crystal shard's attack was undiminished.

Errtu continued a blocking barrage of meaningless thoughts, knowing his doom if Crenshinibon read his mind at that time. He gingerly reached around his hip, taking a small sack that he kept hooked and hanging from the lowest claw of his leathery wings.

In one fierce movement, Errtu brought the sack around and tore it apart, grabbing up the coffer and pulling it open, the black sapphire tumbling into his hand.

Crenshinibon's attack heightened, and the fiend's great legs buckled.

But Errtu had gotten close enough. "I am the master!" Errtu proclaimed, lifting the antimagic gemstone near to Crenshinibon.

The ensuing explosion hurled Errtu back against the wall, shook the tower and the iceberg to their very roots.

When the dust cleared, the antimagic gemstone was gone, simply gone, with barely a speck of useless powder to show that it had ever been there.

Never again do such a foolish thing! came a telepathic command from Crenshinibon, the artifact following up that order with promises of ultimate torture.

Errtu pulled himself up from the floor, simmering and delighted all at once. The bared power of Crenshinibon was great indeed for it to have so utterly destroyed the supremely unenchanted sapphire. And yet, that subsequent command Crenshinibon had hurled the balor's way was not so strong. Errtu knew that he had hurt the crystal shard, temporarily, most likely, but still something he had never wanted to do. It couldn't be avoided, the

fiend decided. He had to be in command here, not in the blind service of a magical item!

Tell me! the stubborn shard's intrusions came again, but as with the outrage over the fiend's game with the antimagic gemstone, the telepathic message carried little strength.

Errtu laughed openly at the suspended shard. "I am the master here, not you," the great balor declared, pulling himself up to his full height. His horns brushed the very top of the crystallizing tower. Errtu hurled the empty, shielding coffer at the crystal, missing the mark. "I will tell when it pleases me, and will tell only as much as pleases me!"

The crystal shard, most of its energy sapped by the close encounter with the devilish sapphire, could not compel the fiend to do otherwise.

Errtu left the room laughing, knowing that he was again in control. He would have to pay close heed to Crenshinibon, would have to gain the ultimate respect of the item in the days ahead. Crenshinibon would likely regain its sapped strength, and Errtu had no more antimagic gems to throw at the artifact.

Errtu would be in command, or they would work together. The proud balor could accept nothing less.

PART FIVE

MORTAL ENEMIES

Berkthgar was right.

He was right in returning his people to Icewind Dale, and even more so in returning to the ancient ways of their heritage. Life may have been easier in Settlestone for the barbarians, their material wealth greater by far. In Settlestone, they had more food and better shelter, and the security of allies all around them. But out here on the open tundra, running with the reindeer herd, was their god. Out here on the tundra, in the soil that held the bones of their ancestors, was their spirit. In Settlestone, the barbarians had been far richer in material terms. Out here they were immortal, and thus, richer by far.

So Berkthgar was right in returning to Icewind Dale, and to the old ways. And yet, Wulfgar had been right in uniting the tribes, and in forging alliances with the folk of Ten-Towns, especially with the dwarves. And Wulfgar, in inadvertently leading his people from the dale, was right in trying to better the lot of the barbarians, though perhaps they had gone too far from the old ways, the ways of the barbarian spirit.

Barbarian leaders come to power in open challenge, "by blood or by deed," and that, too, is how they lead. By blood, by the wisdom of the ages, by the kinship evoked in following the course of best intent. Or by deed, by strength and by sheer physical prowess. Both Wulfgar and Berkthgar claimed leadership by deed—Wulfgar by slaying Dracos Icingdeath, and Berkthgar by assuming the leadership of Settlestone after Wulfgar's death. There the resemblance ends, though, for Wulfgar had subsequently led by blood, while Berkthgar continues to lead by deed. Wulfgar always sought what was best for his people, trusting in them to follow his wise course, or trusting in them to disapprove and deny that course, showing him the folly of his way.

Berkthgar is possessed of no such trust, in his people or in himself. He leads by deed only, by strength and by intimidation. He was right in returning to the dale, and his people would have recognized that truth and approved of his course, yet never did he give them the chance.

Thus Berkthgar errs; he has no guidance for the folly of his way. A return to the old does not have to be complete, does not have to abandon that which was better with the new. As is often the case, the truth sits somewhere in the middle. Revjak knows this, as do many others, particularly the older members of the tribe. These dissenters can do nothing, though, when Berkthgar rules by deed, when his strength has no confidence and thus, no trust.

Many others of the tribe, the young and strong men mostly, are impressed by powerful Berkthgar and his decisive ways; their blood is high, their spirits soar.

Off the cliff, I fear.

The better way, within the context of the old, is to hold fast the alliances forged by Wulfgar. That is the way of blood, of wisdom.

Berkthgar leads by deed, not by blood. He will take his people to the ancient ways and ancient enemies.

His is a road of sorrow.

—Drizzt Do'Urden

24

STUMPET'S WALK

Drizzt, Catti-brie, Bruenor, and Regis paced Stumpet as she continued her trancelike trek across the tundra, heading to the north and east. Her line was straight, perfectly straight, as if she knew exactly where she was going, and she walked tirelessly for many hours.

"If she's meaning to walk all the day, we'll not pace her," Bruenor remarked, looking mostly at Regis, who was huffing and puffing, trying to catch his breath and trying to keep up.

"Ye could bring in the cat to pace her," Catti-brie offered to the ranger. "Then Guen could come back and show us the way."

Drizzt thought on that for just a moment, then shook his head. Guenhwyvar might be needed for more important reasons than trailing the dwarf, he decided, and he did not want to waste the panther's precious time on the Prime Material Plane. The drow considered tackling Stumpet and binding her, and he was explaining to Bruenor that they should do just that, when suddenly the dwarven priestess simply sat down on the ground.

The four companions surrounded her, fearing for her safety, fearing that they had come to the place Errtu desired. Catti-brie had Taulmaril in hand and ready, scanning the noonday skies for sight of the fiend.

But all was quiet, the skies perfectly blue and perfectly empty, save a few puffy clouds drifting fast on stiff winds.

✕ ✕ ✕ ✕ ✕

Kierstaad heard his father talking with some of the older men about the march of Bruenor and Drizzt. More pointedly the young man heard his father's concerns that the friends were walking into some trouble once more. That same morning, his father left the barbarian encampment along with a group of his closest friends. They were going hunting, so they said, but Kierstaad, wise beyond his years, knew better.

Revjak was following Bruenor.

At first, the young barbarian was sorely wounded that his father had not confided in him, had not asked him to go along. But when he considered Berkthgar, the huge man living always on the verge of outrage, Kierstaad came to realize that he didn't need that anymore. If Revjak had lost the glory of the Jorn family, then Kierstaad, Kierstaad the man, meant to reclaim it. Berkthgar's hold on the tribe was tightening and only an act of heroic proportions would garner Kierstaad the needed accolades for a right of challenge. He thought he knew how to do that, for he knew how his dead hero had done it. Now Wulfgar's own companions were out in the wild and in need of help, he believed.

It was time for Kierstaad to make a stand.

He arrived at the dwarven mines at midday, quietly slipping into the small tunnels. Again, the chambers were mostly empty, the dwarves, as always, busy with their mining and crafting. Their industry apparently even outweighed any concerns they might hold for the safety of their leader. At first this struck Kierstaad as odd, but then he came to realize that the dwarves' apparent ambivalence was merely a show of respect for Bruenor, who needed no watching after, and who had been, after all, often out on the road with his nondwarven friends.

Much more familiar with the place now, Kierstaad had little trouble in getting back to Bruenor's room. When he had Aegis-fang in his hands once more, the warhammer feeling so solid and comforting, his course was clear to him.

It was midafternoon when the young barbarian managed to get back out onto the open tundra, Aegis-fang in hand. By all accounts, Bruenor and his companions had half a day's lead on him, and Revjak had been on the march for nearly eight hours. But they were likely walking, Kierstaad knew, and he was young. He would run.

⚔ ⚔ ⚔ ⚔ ⚔

The reprieve lasted the remainder of the afternoon, until Stumpet just as suddenly and unexpectedly climbed back to her feet and plodded off across the

barren tundra, walking purposefully, though her eyes showed only a blank, unthinking gaze.

"Considerate fiend, givin' us a rest," Bruenor remarked sarcastically.

None of the others appreciated the humor—if Errtu had arranged the impromptu rest, then the balor likely knew exactly where they were.

That thought hung on them with every step, until something else caught Drizzt's attention soon after. He was flanking the group, running swiftly, moving from one side to the other in wide arcs. After some time, he paused and motioned for Bruenor to slide out to join him.

"We are being followed," the drow remarked.

Bruenor nodded. No novice to the tundra, the dwarf had sensed the unmistakable signs: a flitter of movement far to the side, the rush of tundra fowl startled by passage, but too far off to have been disturbed by the companions.

"Barbarians?" the dwarf asked, seeming concerned. Despite the recent troubles between the peoples, Bruenor hoped that it was Berkthgar and his tribesmen. At least then, the dwarf would know what problems he was getting!

"Whoever stalks us knows the tundra—few fowl have been roused, and not a deer has skittered away. Goblinoids could not be so careful and tundra yeti do not pursue, they ambush."

"Men, then," replied the dwarf. "And the only men knowing the tundra well enough'd be the barbarians."

Drizzt didn't disagree.

They parted then, Bruenor going back to Catti-brie and Regis to inform them of their suspicions, and Drizzt swinging in another wide, trotting arc. There really wasn't much they could do about the pursuit. The ground was simply too open and flat for any evasive actions. If it was the barbarians, then it was likely that Berkthgar's people were watching more for curiosity than for any threat. Confronting the barbarians might just put problems where there were none.

So the friends walked on, throughout the rest of the day, and long into the night, until Stumpet finally stopped again, unceremoniously dropping to the cold and hard ground. The companions immediately went to work in setting up a formal camp this time. They figured that their rest would last for several hours and understood that the summer was fast on the wane, the chills of winter beginning to sneak into Icewind Dale, particularly during the ever-lengthening night. Catti-brie draped a heavy blanket around Stumpet, though the entranced dwarf didn't seem to notice.

The quiet calm lasted a long hour.

"Drizzt?" Catti-brie whispered, but she realized as soon as she had spoken that the drow was not really asleep, was sitting motionless and with his eyes closed, but was very much alert and very much aware that a small avian form had silently glided above the camp. Perhaps it had been an owl—there were huge owls in Icewind Dale, though they were rarely seen.

Perhaps, but neither of them could afford to think that way.

The slight, barely perceptible flutter came again, to the north, and a shape darker than the night sky glided silently overhead.

Drizzt came up in a rush, scimitars sliding free of his belt. The creature reacted at once, giving a quick flap of its wings to lift it out of Drizzt's deadly reach.

But not out of Taulmaril's range.

A silver-streaking arrow cut the night and slammed into the creature, whatever it was, before it cleared the encampment. Multi-colored sparks lit up the area and Drizzt caught his first true vision of the invader, an imp, as it tumbled from the air, shaken, but not really hurt. It landed hard, rolled to a sitting position, then quickly hopped up, flapping batlike wings to get itself into the air once more before the deadly drow could close in.

Regis had a lantern lit and opened wide by then, and Bruenor and Drizzt flanked the creature, Catti-brie standing back, her bow at the ready.

"My master said you would do that," the imp rasped to Catti-brie. "Errtu protects me!"

"I still put ye out o' the air," the woman replied.

"Why are you here, Druzil?" Drizzt asked, for he surely recognized the imp, the same imp Cadderly had used at the Spirit Soaring to gather information.

"Ye're knowin' this thing?" Bruenor asked the drow.

Drizzt nodded, but didn't reply, too intent on Druzil to banter.

"It did not please Errtu to learn that I was the one who told Cadderly," Druzil snarled in explanation. "Errtu uses me now."

"Poor Druzil," Drizzt said with much sarcasm. "Yours is a difficult lot."

"Spare me your false pity," the imp rasped. "I do so love working for Errtu. When my master is done with you here, we will go to Cadderly next. Perhaps Errtu will even make the Spirit Soaring our fortress!" Druzil snickered with every word, obviously savoring the thought.

Drizzt could barely contain a snicker as well. He had been to the Spirit Soaring and understood its strength and its purity. No matter how powerful Errtu might be, no matter how numerous and strong his minions, the fiend would not defeat Cadderly, not there, in that house of Deneir, in that house of goodness.

"Ye admit then that Errtu's behind the march, and behind the troubles of the dwarf?" Catti-brie asked, indicating Stumpet.

Druzil ignored the women. "Fool!" the imp snapped at Drizzt. "Do you think my master even cares about the fodder in this forlorn place? No, Errtu stays only to meet with you, Drizzt Do'Urden, that you might pay for the troubles you have caused!"

Drizzt moved instinctively, a fast stride toward the imp. Catti-brie lifted her bow, and Bruenor, his axe.

But Drizzt calmed quickly, expecting more information, and he held his dangerous friends in check with an upraised hand.

"I offer a deal from Errtu," Druzil said, speaking to Drizzt only. "Your soul for the soul of the tormented one, and for the soul of the female dwarf."

The way the imp described Zaknafein as "the tormented one," surely stung Drizzt to his heart. For a moment, the temptation of the offered deal nearly overwhelmed him. He stood with his head down suddenly, his scimitar tips dipping toward the ground. He would be willing to sacrifice himself to save Zaknafein, surely, or to save Stumpet, for that matter. How could he ever do less?

But then it occurred to Drizzt that neither of them, Zaknafein nor Stumpet, would want him to, that neither of them would subsequently be able to live with such knowledge.

The drow exploded into action, too fast for Druzil to react. Twinkle sliced deeply into the imp's wing, and the other scimitar, the one forged to fight creatures of fire, scratched at the spinning imp's chest, drawing upon Druzil's life force even though it had not sunk in deeply.

Druzil managed to twirl away, and was about to say something in a last desperate act of defiance, but all of the imp's magical shield had been burned away by Catti-brie's first shot. Her second one, perfectly aimed, blew the imp right out of the sky.

Drizzt was to the spot in an instant, his scimitar moving immediately to cave in Druzil's head. The imp shuddered once, and then melted away into a black and acrid smoke.

"I do not deal with denizens of the lower planes," the drow ranger explained to a fast-closing Bruenor, who had not been quick enough to get into the fight.

Still, Bruenor dropped his heavy axe on the dead imp's head for good measure, before the corporeal form faded away altogether. "Good choice," the dwarf agreed.

Soon after, Regis was snoring contentedly, and Catti-brie was fast asleep. Drizzt did not sleep, preferring to keep a watchful eye over his friends, though even the wary drow expected no more trouble from Errtu that night. He paced a perimeter about the camp, scanning the horizons and more often than not, looking up to the bright stars, letting his heart fly with the freedom that was Icewind Dale. At that moment, under that spectacle of sheer beauty, Drizzt understood why he had truly returned, and why Berkthgar and the others from Settlestone had come running home.

"Ye're not to find many monsters peeking at us from behind the durned stars," came a gruff whisper from behind. Drizzt turned as Bruenor approached. The dwarf was already dressed in his battlegear, his one-horned helmet tilted to the side and his many-notched axe comfortably resting across his shoulder, in anticipation of the coming march.

"Balors can fly," Drizzt reminded him, though they both knew that Drizzt was not looking up at the sky in anticipation of any enemy.

Bruenor nodded and moved beside his friend. There ensued a long period of quiet, each of them alone in the wind, alone among the stars. Drizzt sensed Bruenor's somber mood and knew that the dwarf had come out of the camp for a reason, likely to tell him something.

"I had to come back," Bruenor said at length.

Drizzt looked to him and nodded, but Bruenor was still staring up at the sky.

"Gandalug's got Mithral Hall," Bruenor remarked, and it sounded to Drizzt as though the red-bearded dwarf was making excuses. "Rightfully his."

"And you have Icewind Dale," Drizzt added.

Bruenor turned to him then, as if he meant to protest, to further explain himself. One look into Drizzt's lavender orbs told the dwarf that he didn't have to. Drizzt understood him and understood his actions. He had to come back. That was all that he needed to say.

The pair spent the rest of the night standing in the chill wind, watching the stars, until dawn's first glow stole the majestic view, or rather, replaced it with yet another. Stumpet was up soon after, walking zombielike again. The pair roused Catti-brie and Regis. The friends went off in pursuit, together.

25

TO THE BERGS

Over a ridge, they saw the icebergs and shifting floes floating about in the dark waters of the Sea of Moving Ice. Logic told them that they should be nearing their goal, but all of them feared that Stumpet would keep moving, would pick her way across those treacherous expanses, from floe to floe, up and down the conical bergs. Crenshinibon was known to produce towers, and another of the artifact's names was Cryshal-Tirith, which literally translated from Elvish meant "crystal tower." A ridge blocked their view of the actual shoreline, but surely any tower before the sea would have been visible to them by this time.

Stumpet, seeming oblivious to it all, continued her march to the sea. She came over the ridge first, the friends rushing to keep close behind, when a barrage of icy snowballs assailed them all.

Drizzt went into a flurry, cut left and right, ducking and slapping away at the hurled missiles with his scimitars. Regis and Catti-brie fell flat to the ground, but the two dwarves, particularly poor Stumpet, who just continued her walking, got pummeled. Bloody welts rose on the priestess's face and she staggered more than once.

Catti-brie, recovered from the shock, put her feet under her and rushed ahead, tackling Stumpet and falling over her protectively.

The barrage stopped as abruptly as it had begun.

Drizzt had the onyx figurine on the ground in front of him, quietly calling in his panther ally. He saw the enemy then, they all did, though none of them knew what to make of the creatures. They came as ghosts, slipping from the white ice onto the still-brown shore so smoothly that they seemed part of the land. They were humanoid, bipedal, large, and strong and covered in shaggy white hair.

"I'd be mean too, if I was that ugly," Bruenor remarked, moving close to Drizzt so they could calculate their next move.

"You are," Regis said from his prone position.

Neither the drow nor the dwarf had the time or compunction to respond to the halfling. More and more enemies came off the icy sea—flanking left and right—two score, three, and still they came.

"I'm thinking we might want to turn about," Bruenor remarked.

Drizzt hated that thought, but it seemed their only choice. He and his friends could dole out considerable damage, had battled many mighty enemies, but no less than a hundred of these creatures faced them now. They were obviously not stupid beasts, moving in an organized and cunning fashion.

Guenhwyvar was there then, beside her master, ready to spring.

"Perhaps we can scare them off," Drizzt whispered to Bruenor, and with a word, he sent the cat springing away, a powerful rush straight ahead.

A hail of iceballs slapped against the panther's black sides, and even those creatures directly in Guenhwyvar's line did not retreat, did not waver at all. Two of them were buried where they stood, but a host of others closed in, whacking at the cat with heavy clubs. Soon it was Guenhwyvar who was in full retreat.

Catti-brie, meanwhile, had climbed up from Stumpet—who immediately rose and resumed her march until Regis likewise tackled her—and strung Taulmaril. She quickly surveyed the scene and sent fly an arrow, putting the bolt right between the wide-spread legs of the largest creature to the left of her. Again, the merciful Catti-brie wanted only to scare the things away, and was surprised by the savage response. The creature didn't flinch, as though it didn't care whether it lived or died, and it responded, as did a score of creatures near to it, by hurling iceballs at the woman.

Catti-brie dived and rolled, but got hit several times. One strike on the temple nearly knocked her senseless. She came up in a short run, getting to the side of Drizzt, Bruenor, and the returned panther.

"I'm thinking that our road just turned the other way," she remarked, rubbing the bruise on her forehead.

"A true warrior knows when to turn away," Drizzt agreed, but his eyes continued to scan the icebergs on the dark sea, looking for some hint of Cryshal-Tirith, some hint that Errtu was nearby.

"Would someone please tell that to the damned dwarf!" called a flustered Regis, holding fast to one of Stumpet's sturdy legs. The entranced priestess

merely walked along with him, dragging him across the tundra.

All about them, the creatures continued to flank, passing those nasty iceballs down the line for another barrage—one that the companions suspected would be accompanied by a wild charge.

They had to leave, but had not the time to drag Stumpet along with them. If she would not turn with them, surely she would be killed.

⚔ ⚔ ⚔ ⚔ ⚔

"You sent them out!" Errtu roared accusingly at the crystal shard as it hovered in midair in the highest room of the Cryshal-Tirith. From the scrying mirror, the mighty balor watched his minions, the taers, as they blocked the passage of Drizzt Do'Urden, something Errtu most certainly did not desire.

"Admit it!" the fiend bellowed.

You take dangerous chances concerning the rogue drow, came the telepathic reply. *I cannot allow that.*

"The taers are mine to command!" Errtu screamed. The fiend knew that he merely had to think of his responses and the sentient crystal shard would "hear" them, but Errtu needed to hear the sound of his own roar at that grim time, had to vent his outrage verbally.

"No matter," the fiend decided a moment later. "Drizzt Do'Urden is no small foe. He and his companions will chase off the taers. You have not stopped him!"

They are unthinking tools, came Crenshinibon's casual and confident reply. *They obey my command, and will fight to the death. Drizzt Do'Urden is stopped.*

Errtu didn't doubt the declaration. Crenshinibon, though it had certainly been weakened by its joust with the antimagic sapphire, was strong enough to dominate the stupid taers. And those creatures, more than a hundred in number, were too strong and too numerous for Drizzt and his friends to defeat. They might escape—the fleet-footed drow at least—but Stumpet was doomed, as was Bruenor Battlehammer and the chubby halfling.

Errtu considered swooping out of his tower then, or of using his magical abilities to get to that beach, to face off with the drow then and there.

Crenshinibon read his thoughts easily and the image in the scrying mirror disappeared as did Errtu's magical teleportation options, for the balor wasn't even sure of where that particular beach might be. He could take wing, of course, and he had a general idea of where Stumpet would make the Sea of Moving Ice, but he realized that by the time he arrived, Drizzt Do'Urden would likely be dead.

The fiend turned angrily on the crystal shard, and Crenshinibon met his rage with a stream of soothing thoughts, of promises of greater power and glory.

The sentient artifact didn't comprehend the level of Errtu's hatred, didn't understand that the fiend's most important reason for coming to the Prime Material Plane was to exact revenge on Drizzt Do'Urden.

Errtu, impotent and confused, stalked from the room.

⚔ ⚔ ⚔ ⚔ ⚔

"We cannot leave Stumpet," Catti-brie said, and of course, Drizzt and Bruenor agreed.

"Hit at them hard," the drow instructed. "Shoot your arrows to kill."

Even as he spoke the words, the iceball volley slapped in. Poor Stumpet got hit repeatedly, and Regis took one in the head and let go of the dwarf. She continued her slow walk until three missiles hit her simultaneously, dropping her to the ground.

Catti-brie killed two taers in rapid succession, then rushed after Drizzt, Bruenor, and Guenhwyvar as they charged to form a defensive ring about Stumpet and Regis. The taers were out of iceballs then, and on they came, fearlessly, brandishing clubs and howling like the north wind.

"There's only a hunnerd o' the durned things!" Bruenor blustered, hoisting his axe.

"And four of us!" yelled Catti-brie.

"Five," Regis corrected, stubbornly pulling himself to his feet.

Guenhwyvar roared. Catti-brie fired, killing yet another.

Take me in hand! came a desperate plea from Khazid'hea.

The woman sent off another arrow, and then the creatures were too close. She dropped her precious bow and drew out the eager Khazid'hea.

Drizzt cut in front of her, double-slashing a taer across the throat, falling into a spin to his knees and thrusting ahead with Twinkle, driving the curving blade deep into a creature's belly. His other scimitar slashed horizontally behind him, tripping up the next beast as it bore down on Catti-brie.

Her downward chop sent the sharp-edged Khazid'hea right through the thing's skull and halfway down its neck. But Catti-brie had to tear her sword free immediately, and Drizzt had to get back to his feet and go into yet another scrambling maneuver, for the throng swarmed about them, closing off any escape.

They knew they were doomed . . . until they heard the unified cry of "Tempus!"

Revjak and his twenty-five warriors came hard into the taer ranks, their huge weapons cutting a swath through the lines of surprised shaggy beasts.

Regis yelled out to their reinforcements, but was silenced by a taer club that slammed him on the shoulder, knocking the breath from him and sending him flying to the ground. Three of the creatures towered over him, ready to smash him down.

A flying Guenhwyvar slammed into them sidelong, the panther spinning about with all four paws raking wildly. A fourth taer slipped by the embattled three, seeking the prone halfling and the unconscious dwarven female lying beside him.

It met a growling Bruenor, or more particularly, Bruenor's chopping axe.

Dazed, Regis was glad to see the boots of Bruenor as the sturdy dwarf straddled him.

Now Drizzt and Catti-brie worked side by side, the two friends who had been together, fighting together, for so many years.

Catti-brie caught the club of one taer in her free hand and sent Khazid'hea in a short arc, severing the creature's other arm just below the shoulder. To her surprise and horror, though, the taer continued to press forward, and another creature came in right beside it, on Catti-brie's left. Struggling to keep her grip firm on the first creature's club, and with her sword all the way on the other side, the woman had no practical defense against the newcomer.

She screamed in defiance and slashed again with her sword, angling higher this time, cutting halfway through the neck of the creature she held. As she moved, Catti-brie closed her eyes, not wanting to see the incoming club.

Drizzt's scimitar came across and under Khazid'hea's high cut, the drow lurching violently to get his blade all the way past Catti-brie to intercept the club. The parry was perfect, as a surprised Catti-brie realized when she opened her eyes.

The woman didn't hesitate. Drizzt had to go back to the two taers he was battling, but his desperate parry had given Catti-brie the moment she needed. She twisted wildly to face this second taer, cutting her blade the rest of the way through the dead and falling creature's neck, and then using its momentum as it pulled free to thrust it straight ahead, right into this newest foe's chest.

The taer fell back, but two others took its place.

As the ground around Bruenor filled with piled bodies and severed limbs, the dwarf accepted hit after hit from the taer's clubs, belting the beasts with his mighty axe in exchange.

"Six!" he yelled as his axe dived into the sloped forehead of yet another creature, but his call was shortened as yet another beast slammed him in the back.

That one hurt, truly hurt, but Bruenor knew that he had to ignore the pain. Gasping as he turned, he launched his axe in a two-handed semicircle, chopping it deep into the side of the taer as if the creature were a tree.

The taer flew sidelong as the axe barreled in, then stood twisted over the blade, dying fast.

Bruenor heard the roar behind him and was glad to know that Guenhwyvar had untangled herself once more and was protecting his back.

Then he heard another cry, a call to the barbarian god, as Revjak and his warriors joined up with the companions. The ring around Regis and Stumpet was secure, and the defense was sturdy enough for Guenhwyvar to go out into the taer ranks, a muscled black ball of devastation. Drizzt and Catti-brie cut through the first line and then charged into the second.

In a matter of mere minutes, every taer was dead or downed with injuries too grievous for it to continue the battle, even though Crenshinibon's commands went on, unabated in their relentless brainwashing assault.

Stumpet had recovered enough by then to get back to her feet and to stubbornly resume her march.

Drizzt, down on one knee, trying to catch his breath, called to Revjak, and the barbarian immediately ordered two of his strongest men to surround the dwarf and lift her off the ground. Stumpet offered no resistance, just held steady, staring blankly ahead, her feet pumping futilely in the empty air.

The smile Drizzt and Revjak exchanged was cut short, though, by a familiar voice.

"Treason!" roared Berkthgar as he and his warriors, more than twice the number Revjak had brought out, surrounded the group.

"This keeps gettin' better and better," Catti-brie said dryly.

"The laws, Revjak!" Berkthgar blustered. "You knew them and you disobeyed!"

"To leave Bruenor and his fellows to die?" Revjak asked incredulously, showing no fear, though it seemed to the companions that battle might soon be joined once more. "Never would I follow such a command," Revjak went on confidently. The warriors with him, many of them nursing wounds from the taer fight, were unified in their agreement.

"Some of our people do not forget the friendship shown to us by Bruenor and Catti-brie, by Drizzt Do'Urden and all the others," the older man finished.

"Some of us do not forget the war with Bruenor's folk and the folk of Ten-Towns," Berkthgar retorted, and his warriors bristled.

"I've heared enough," Catti-brie whispered, and before Drizzt could stop her, she stalked across the open ground to stand right before the huge and imposing barbarian.

"Suren, ye've diminished," Catti-brie said defiantly.

Calls behind the barbarian leader hinted that he should slap the impertinent woman aside. Good sense held Berkthgar in check. For, not only was Catti-brie a formidable opponent, as he had learned personally back in Settlestone when she had defeated him in private combat, but she was backed by Drizzt and by Bruenor, neither of whom the barbarian wanted to face. If he put a hand on Catti-brie, Berkthgar understood that the only thing that would keep the drow ranger off of him would be Bruenor, beating Drizzt to the attack.

"All the respect I once had for ye," Catti-brie went on, and Berkthgar was surprised by the sudden change in her tone and the direction of her words. "Ye were the rightful leader after Wulfgar," she said sincerely. "By deed and by wisdom. Without yer guidance, the tribe would have been lost so far away in Settlestone."

"Where we did not belong!" Berkthgar was quick to respond.

"Agreed," said Catti-brie, again catching the man off guard, cutting inside the direction of his ire. "Ye did right in returning to the dale and to yer god, but not to the ancient enemies. Think on the truth o' me father, Berkthgar, and on the truth o' Drizzt."

"Both killers of my kin."

"Only when yer kin came to kill," Catti-brie said, not backing down an inch. "What cowards would they be if they did not defend their home and kin! Do ye begrudge them for fightin' better than yer own?"

Berkthgar's breath came in short, angry puffs. Drizzt saw it and was quick to join Catti-brie. He had heard the quiet conversation, every word, and he knew where to take it up from there.

"I know what you did," the drow said. Berkthgar stiffened, thinking the words to be an accusation.

"To gain control of the united tribe you had to discredit he who came before you. But I warn you, for the good of all in the dale, do not get caught up in your own half-truths. The name of Berkthgar is spoken of reverently in Mithral Hall, Silverymoon, Longsaddle, and Nesmé, even in Ten-Towns and the dwarven mines. Your exploits in Keeper's Dale will not be forgotten, though you seem to choose to forget the alliance and the good that Bruenor's folk have done. Look to Revjak now—we owe him our lives—and decide, Berkthgar, what course is best for you and your people."

Berkthgar was quiet then, and both Catti-brie and Drizzt knew that to be a good thing. He was not a stupid man, though often he let his emotions cloud his judgment. He did look at Revjak, and at the resolute warriors standing behind the older man, a bit battered, certainly outnumbered, and yet showing no fear. The most important point to the huge barbarian was that neither Drizzt nor Catti-brie was denying his claim of leadership. They were willing to work with him, so it seemed, and Catti-brie had even publicly compared him favorably to Wulfgar!

"And let the hammer stay with Bruenor, where it rightfully belongs," Catti-brie dared to press, as if she was reading Berkthgar's every thought. "Yer own sword is the weapon of yer tribe now, and its legend'll be no less than Aegis-fang's if Berkthgar chooses wisely."

That was bait that Berkthgar could not ignore. He visibly relaxed, so did the men following his every word, and Drizzt recognized that they had just passed an important test.

"You were wise in following Bruenor and his companions," Berkthgar said loudly to Revjak, as much an apology as anybody had ever heard the proud barbarian offer.

"And you were wrong in denying our friendship with Bruenor," Revjak replied. Drizzt and Catti-brie both tensed, wondering if Revjak had pushed a bit too hard, too fast.

But Berkthgar took no offense. He didn't respond to the charge. The barbarian didn't show that he agreed, but neither did he become defensive.

"Return with us now," he bade Revjak.

Revjak looked to Drizzt, then to Bruenor, knowing that they still needed his help. It was two of his men, after all, who were still holding Stumpet up in the air.

Berkthgar looked first to Revjak, then followed his gaze to Bruenor, and then looked past the dwarf and to the coast looming not so far away. "You are going out onto the Sea of Moving Ice?"

A frustrated Bruenor gave Stumpet a sidelong glance. "So it'd seem," the dwarf admitted.

"We cannot accompany you," Berkthgar said flatly. "And this is no choice of mine, but an edict of our ancestors. No tribesman may venture out onto the floating land."

Revjak had to nod his agreement. It was indeed an ancient edict, one put in for practicality because there was little to be gained and much to lose in venturing out onto the dangerous ice floes, the land of the white bear and the great whales.

"We would not ask for you to go," Drizzt quickly put in, and his companions seemed surprised by that. They were going off to fight a balor and all of his devious minions, and an army of powerful barbarians might come in handy! But Drizzt knew that Berkthgar would not go against that ancient rule, and he did not want Revjak to split any further from the leader, did not want to jeopardize the healing that had begun here. Also, none of Revjak's warriors had been killed against the taers, but that would not likely hold true if they followed Drizzt all the way to Errtu. Drizzt Do'Urden had enough blood on his hands already. For the drow ranger, this was a private battle. He would have preferred it to be him against Errtu, one against one, but he knew that Errtu would not be alone, and he could not deny his closest friends the chance to stand beside him as he would stand beside them.

"But ye admit that yer folk owe this much, at least, to Bruenor?" Catti-brie had to ask.

Again Berkthgar didn't openly answer, but his silence, his lack of protest, was all the confirmation that the woman needed to hear.

The companions bandaged up their bruises as well as possible, bid their farewells, and thanked the barbarians. Revjak's men put Stumpet down then, and she resumed her march. The companions plodded off after her.

The Tribe of the Elk turned south in a unified march, Berkthgar and Revjak walking side by side.

⚔ ⚔ ⚔ ⚔ ⚔

Sometime later, Kierstaad came upon the scene of a hundred taer bodies bloating in the afternoon sun. It didn't take the wily young barbarian long to figure out what had happened. Obviously the barbarians with his father had joined in the fight beside Bruenor's group, and so many different prints were to be found that Kierstaad understood that another group—certainly one led by Berkthgar—had also come upon the scene.

Kierstaad looked to the south, wondering if his father had been escorted back to the encampment as a prisoner. He almost turned then and ran off in pursuit, but the other tracks—the ones of two dwarves, a drow, a woman, a halfling, and a hunting cat—compelled him to the north.

Aegis-fang in hand, the young barbarian picked his way down to the cold coast and then out onto the broken trail of ice floes. He was breaking the ancient edicts of his people, he knew, but he dismissed that. In his mind and in his heart, he was following the footsteps of Wulfgar.

26

NOT BY SURPRISE

The glabrezu was adamant, not backing down from his story despite the mounting threats of a nervous and desperate Errtu.

"Drizzt Do'Urden and his friends have passed the taers," Bizmatec insisted once more, "leaving them dead and torn on the plain."

"You have seen this?" Errtu asked for the fifth time, the great balor clenching and unclenching his fist repeatedly.

"I have seen this," Bizmatec replied without hesitation, though the glabrezu did lean back warily from the balor. "The taers did not stop them, hardly slowed them. They are mighty indeed, these enemies you have chosen."

"And the dwarf?" Errtu asked, his frustration turning fast to eagerness. As he spoke, the balor tapped his bejeweled ring to show that he was referring to the imprisoned female dwarf.

"Leads them still," Bizmatec answered with a wicked smile, the glabrezu thrilled to see the eagerness, the sheer wickedness bringing the light back to Errtu's glowing eyes.

The balor left with a great flourish, a victorious spin and flap of leathery wings that got it to the landing of the crystalline tower's open first level. Up Errtu climbed, maddened by hunger, by desire to show Crenshinibon its failure.

"Errtu has put us in line with worthy enemies," Bizmatec remarked again, watching the balor's departure.

The other tanar'ri in the tower's lowest level, a six-armed woman with the lower torso of a snake, smirked, seeming truly unimpressed. There were no worthy enemies to be found among the mortals of the Prime Material Plane.

High above his minions, Errtu clambered into the small room at the tower's highest level. The fiend went to the narrow window first, peering out in the hopes that he might catch a glimpse of the approaching quarry. Errtu wanted to make a dramatic statement to Crenshinibon, but the fiend's excitement betrayed his thoughts to the sentient, telepathic artifact.

Your path remains one of danger, the crystal shard warned.

Errtu spun away from the window and issued a hearty, croaking laugh.

You must not fail, the artifact's telepathic message went on. *If you and yours are defeated, then defeated am I, placed in the hands of those who know my nature and . . .*

Errtu's continued laughter rebuked any more telepathic intrusions.

"I have met the likes of Drizzt Do'Urden before," the great balor said with a feral snarl. "He will know true sorrow and true pain before I release him into death! He will see the deaths of his beloved, of those who were foolish enough to accompany him and of he who I hold as prisoner." The great fiend turned back angrily toward the window. "What an enemy have you made, foolish drow rogue! Come to me now that I might exact my revenge and give to you the punishment you deserve!"

With that, Errtu kicked the small coffer still lying on the floor where the fiend had dropped it after the volatile reaction between the crystal shard and the antimagic sapphire. Errtu started to leave, but reconsidered for just a moment. He would be facing Drizzt and all of his companions soon, including the imprisoned priestess. If Stumpet came face to face with the fiend's entrapping gemstone, her spirit might find its way aback to her body.

Errtu pulled off his ring and showed it to Crenshinibon. "The dwarven priestess," the fiend explained. "This holds her spirit. Dominate her and lend what aid you may!"

Errtu dropped the ring to the floor and stormed from the chamber, back down to his minions to prepare for the arrival of Drizzt Do'Urden.

Crenshinibon felt keenly the tanar'ri's rage and the sheer wickedness that was mighty Errtu. Drizzt and his friends had gotten past the taers, so it seemed, but what were they compared to the likes of Errtu?

And Errtu, the crystal shard knew, had powerful allies lying in wait.

Crenshinibon was satisfied, was quite secure. And to the evil artifact, the thought of using Stumpet against the companions was certainly a pleasant one.

⚔ ⚔ ⚔ ⚔ ⚔

Stumpet continued her march across the treacherous and broken ice, leaping small gaps, sometimes splashing her feet into the icy water, but pulling them out with apparently no regard for the freezing wetness.

Drizzt understood the dangers of the water. He wanted to tackle Stumpet once more and pull off her boots, wrapping her feet in warm and dry blankets. The drow let it go. He figured that if frozen toes were the worst of their troubles, they would certainly be better off than he had hoped. Right now, the best thing he could do for Stumpet, for all of them, was to get to Errtu and get this grim business over with.

The drow kept one hand in his pocket as he marched, fingers feeling the intricate detailing of the onyx figurine. He had sent Guenhwyvar home shortly after the taer fight, giving the cat what little rest she might find before the next battle. Now, in looking around, the drow wondered about the wisdom of that decision, for he knew that he was out of place in this unfamiliar terrain.

The landscape seemed surreal, nothing but jagged white mounds, some as high as forty feet, and long sheets of flat whiteness, often cracked by zigzagging dark lines.

They were more than two hours off the beach, far out into the ice-clogged sea, when the weather turned. Dark and ominous clouds rose up, the wind bit harder, colder. Still they plodded on, crawling up the side of one conical iceberg, then sliding down the other side. They came into an area of more dark water and less ice, and there they caught their first sight of their goal, far away to the north and west. The crystalline tower gleamed above the berg cones, shining even in the dull gray daylight. There could be no doubt, for the tower was no natural structure, and though it appeared as if it was made of ice, it seemed unnatural and out of place among the hard and stark whiteness of the bergs.

Bruenor considered the sight and their present course, then shook his head. "Too much water," he explained, pointing to the west. "Should be going straight out that way."

By all appearances, it seemed as if the dwarf was right. They were traveling generally north, but the ice floes seemed more tightly packed to the west.

Their course was not for them to decide though, and Stumpet continued on her oblivious way to the north, where it seemed as if she would soon be stopped by a wide gap of open water.

Appearances could be deceiving in the surreal and unfamiliar landscape. A long finger of ice bridged that watery gap, turning them more directly toward the crystal tower. When they crossed over, they came into another region of

clogged icebergs, and looming before them, barely a quarter of a mile away, was Cryshal-Tirith.

Drizzt brought in Guenhwyvar once more. Bruenor knocked Stumpet down and sat on her, while Catti-brie scrambled up the tallest nearby peak to get a better feeling for the area.

The tower was on a large iceberg, set right in back of the thirty foot high conical tip of the natural structure. Catti-brie guessed she and her companions would cross onto the berg from the southwest, on a narrow strip of ice about a dozen feet wide. One other iceberg directly west of the tower, was close enough, perhaps, to make a leap onto the main area, but other than that, the fiend's fortress was surrounded by ocean.

Catti-brie marked one other point: a cave entrance on the southern face of the conical peak that was almost directly across from the tower on the other side of the berg. It was at least a man's height up from the wider flat area on the southern side of the berg, the area they would cross, the area that seemed as if it would soon become a killing ground. With a resigned sigh, the woman slid back down and reported it all to her friends.

"Errtu's minions will meet us soon after we cross the last stretch," Drizzt reasoned, and Catti-brie nodded with every word. "We will have to fight them all the way to the cave entrance, and even more so within."

"Let's get on with it, then," Bruenor grumbled. "Me durned feet're getting cold!"

Catti-brie looked to Drizzt, as though she wanted to hear some options. Few seemed apparent, though. Even if that leap was possible for Catti-brie, Drizzt, and Guenhwyvar, Bruenor, in his heavy armor, could not hope to make it, nor could Regis. And if they went that way, Stumpet—who could only walk—would be alone.

"I'll not be much good in a fight," Regis said quietly.

"That never stopped ye before!" Bruenor howled, misunderstanding. "Ye meanin' to sit here—"

Drizzt stopped the dwarf with an upraised hand, guessing that the remarkably resourceful halfling had something important and valuable in mind.

"If Guenhwyvar could get me across that gap, I might make it quietly to the tower," the halfling explained.

The faces of his companions brightened as they began to consider the possibilities.

"I have been in Cryshal-Tirith before," Regis went on. "I know how to get through the tower, and how to defeat the crystal shard if I make it." He looked to Drizzt as he said this and nodded. Regis had been with Drizzt on the plain north of Bryn Shander, when the drow had beaten Akar Kessel's tower.

"A desperate chance," Drizzt remarked.

"Yeah," Bruenor agreed dryly. "Not like walking into the middle of a tanar'ri horde."

That brought a chuckle—a strained one indeed—from the group.

"Let Stumpet up," Drizzt bade Bruenor. "She will take us in to whatever Errtu has planned. And you," he added, looking to the halfling, "may Gwaeron Windstrom, servant of Mielikki and patron of rangers, be with you on your journey. Guenhwyvar will get you across. Understand, my friend, that if you fail and Crenshinibon is not defeated, Errtu will be all the stronger!"

Regis nodded grimly, took a firm hold of the scruff on the back of Guenhwyvar's neck, and split apart from the group, thinking that his one chance would be to get to the iceberg quickly and secretly. He and the cat were soon out of sight, moving up and down across the rough terrain. Guenhwyvar did most of the work, her claws cutting deep into the ice, grabbing holds where she could find them. Regis merely kept his hold on her and tried to keep his legs moving quickly enough so that he would not be too much of a burden.

They nearly met with disaster coming down the slippery backside of one steep cone. Guenhwyvar dug in, but Regis stumbled and went down. His momentum as he slipped past the cat cost Guenhwyvar her tenuous hold. Down they careened, heading for the black water. Regis stifled a cry, but closed his eyes and expected to splash into his freezing doom.

Guenhwyvar caught a new hold barely inches from the deadly cold sea.

Shaken and bruised, the pair pulled themselves up and started off once more. Regis bolstered his resolve, burying his fears by reminding himself repeatedly of the importance of his mission.

⚔ ⚔ ⚔ ⚔ ⚔

The companions understood how very vulnerable they were as they crossed the last expanse of open ice to get to the huge iceberg that held Cryshal-Tirith. They sensed that they were being watched, sensed that something terrible was about to happen.

Drizzt tried to hurry Stumpet along. Bruenor and Catti-brie ran up ahead.

Errtu's minions were waiting, crouched within the cave entrance and behind the icy bluffs. Indeed the fiend was watching the group, as was Crenshinibon.

The artifact thought the balor a fool, risking so much for so little real gain. It used the gemstone ring to connect with Stumpet, to see through the imprisoned dwarf's eyes, to know exactly where the enemies were.

Suddenly, the very tip of Cryshal-Tirith glowed a fierce red, stealing the grayness of the approaching storm in a pinkish haze.

Catti-brie yelled to Drizzt, and Bruenor grabbed the woman and tugged her forward and to the ground.

Drizzt barreled into Stumpet, but merely bounced off. He skittered past—he had to move—then skidded, trying desperately to slow, as a line of blazing fire shot out from the tower's tip and sliced through the ice walk in front of the drow.

Thick steam engulfed the area and the stunned ranger. Drizzt could not fully stop and so he yelled out and charged ahead, leaping and rolling with all his strength.

Only good luck saved him. The line of fire halted abruptly from the tower, and then began again, this time over the standing dwarven priestess, cutting another line behind her. The force of the blow sent flecks of ice flying, thickened the steam. The now-severed floe, two hundred square feet of drifting ice, floated to the southeast, turning slowly as it drifted.

Stumpet had nowhere to go, so she merely stood perfectly still, her gaze impassive.

On the main iceberg, the three friends were up and running once more.

"Left!" Catti-brie called as a creature clambered over the ridge that was the side of the central cone. The woman nearly gagged on her word at the sight of the horrid thing, one of the least of the Abyss's creatures that were called manes. It was the dead spirit of a wretch from the Prime Material Plane. Pale white skin, bloated and overloaded with oozing liquids, hung in loose flaps along the thing's torso, and many-legged parasites clung to its hide. It was only three feet tall, Regis's size, but it sported long and obviously sharp claws and nasty teeth.

Catti-brie blew it away with a single silver-streaking arrow, but a group of its friends, showing no regard whatsoever for their safety, scrambled over the ridge right behind it.

"Left!" the woman cried again, but Drizzt and Bruenor could not afford to heed those words.

For many more manes had come ambling out of the cave entrance, barely thirty feet away, and two flying fiends, giant bugs that seemed a horrid cross between a human and a giant fly, came out above the horde.

Bruenor met the closest fiends with a vicious chop of his axe. The single stroke did the trick, but the destroyed fiend, rather than lie down dead, exploded into a puff of noxious, acidic fumes that burned at the dwarf's skin and lungs.

"Durned slime-orcs," the red-bearded dwarf grumbled, and he was not deterred, blasting away a second fiend, and then a third in rapid succession, filling the air about him with fumes.

Drizzt was hitting at manes and moving so quickly that the ensuing cloud of evil vapors did not even touch him. He had a line of them down, but then had to fall flat to avoid the low pass of one of the flying tanar'ri, chasme they were called.

By the time the drow regained his footing, a gang of manes had closed around him, reaching eagerly with their long and nasty claws.

Catti-brie nearly wretched again at the mere sight of the flying fiends. She had downed half a dozen manes already, but now she had to turn her attention to the horrible bugs.

She whirled and fired at the closest, nearly point-blank, and sighed with sincere relief as her arrow threw the fiend backward and to the ground.

Its companion, though was gone, simply disappeared in a display of fiendish magic.

It stood quietly behind Catti-brie.

⚔ ⚔ ⚔ ⚔ ⚔

Regis and Guenhwyvar saw the commotion, saw the lines of blazing white fire and heard the ensuing battle. They picked up their pace as much as possible, but the terrain was not favorable, not at all.

Again the halfling was merely holding on, letting Guenhwyvar tow him in full flight. Regis bumped and bounced, but didn't complain. Whatever his pains, he was certain that his friends were feeling worse.

⚔ ⚔ ⚔ ⚔ ⚔

"Behind ye!" Bruenor yelled, bursting free of the horde of manes. One of the wretched creatures clung fast to the dwarf, its claws deep into the back of his neck, but he hardly cared.

All that mattered was Catti-brie, and she was in dire trouble. The dwarf couldn't get to the fiend behind her, but the one she had hit was back up, walking this time, and was directly between Bruenor and his beloved daughter.

Not a good place to be.

Catti-brie spun on her heels as the chasme struck. She accepted the vicious hit on her shoulder and rolled with it, doing two complete somersaults across the ice before putting her feet back underneath her.

Bruenor's twirling axe hit the other chasme full force in the back, blasting it to the ground for the second time. Still the stubborn thing tried to rise, but the running dwarf summarily buried it, diving upon it and grabbing up his weapon. He tore the axe free and pounded away repeatedly, driving the chasme into the ice, splattering the white surface with green and yellow gore.

Still the other fiend hung on the back of the furious dwarf, scratching and biting. It was starting to do some real damage, but that ended as abruptly as the cut of a drow's scimitar.

The remaining chasme was airborne once more, and Catti-brie had her bow in line. She scored a brutal hit and the fiend had seen enough. It flew right past her and over the ridge, toward the back side of the glacier.

As she turned to follow its flight, Catti-brie had to lower her bow to a different target, one of the score of manes who, by this time, had come scrambling over the ridge.

The chasme under Bruenor seemed to deflate—there really was no other way to describe how the fiend's body flattened, like a waterskin emptying its contents.

Drizzt pulled the dwarf up and roughly turned him about. The immediate threat to Catti-brie had been halted, but they had lost ground and the horde of oozing manes had regrouped.

No matter for the two seasoned friends. A quick glance told them that Catti-brie had the group to the side under control and so they charged, side by side, tearing into the closest ranks of least tanar'ri.

Drizzt, with his deadly, slashing scimitars and his quick feet, made the most progress, slicing through reaching arms and dodging manes with abandon, laying six of them low in a matter of seconds. The drow hardly registered that his opponent had changed a moment later, until his wild swing was met, not by one, but by three separate ringing parries.

The horde thinned in this area, the lesser fiends giving a respectful distance to the six-armed monstrosity that now faced off against Drizzt Do'Urden.

Catti-brie saw the fight and recognized the drow's predicament. She rushed to her right, toward the shoreline, trying to get an angle for a shot, paying no heed to unblinking Stumpet on the drifting floe, now some forty feet out from the iceberg. Her wounded shoulder continued to pump out blood—nasty indeed was the strike of a chasme—but she couldn't stop and bandage it.

Down the woman skidded to one knee. The angle was difficult, especially with the active drow between her and the six-armed tanar'ri. But Catti-brie knew that Drizzt would want her to try, that he needed her to try. Up came Taulmaril, Catti-brie's fingers finding their hold on the string behind the arrow's fletchings.

"The drow cannot fight his own battles?" came a question behind the woman, a deep, throaty voice. "We must talk about that." It was the glabrezu, Bizmatec.

Catti-brie threw herself forward and ducked her shoulder, moving her arm out to full extension to protect the bow, and more particularly, to protect the integrity of the readied arrow. Agile Catti-brie fired off her shot before she even completed the spin, grimacing as her shoulder spouted a red stream. This newest opponent's expression went from amazement to agony as the silver-streaking arrow skipped off the inside of the glabrezu's huge thigh.

Catti-brie winced then, for the arrow continued out from the shore, skipping across the water and onto the drifting chunk of ice barely a few feet from oblivious Stumpet. The woman realized that she shouldn't have wasted the time to follow the arrow, though, for the twelve-foot glabrezu, all muscle and horrible pincers, roared in outrage and closed the gap to Catti-brie with one long stride.

In came a monstrous claw that could easily snap the woman in half, setting into place about Catti-brie's slender, vulnerable waist.

In one fluid motion, Catti-brie punched her hand between the bow and its string, reaching across her body and tearing Khazid'hea from its sheath. Catti-brie cried out and tried futilely to fall away, snapping off a weak backhand with the weapon, hoping to wedge the blade into the fiend's pincers and turn aside his attack.

Khazid'hea, so very sharp, hit the inside edge of the pincer and kept on going, slicing right through.

I feared I was forgotten! the sentient sword relayed to Catti-brie.

"Never that," the woman replied grimly.

Bizmatec howled again and brought his great arm snapping across, the remaining side of the pincers knocking Catti-brie flat to the ground. In stalked the glabrezu, lifting a huge foot to squash the woman.

Khazid'hea, coming up fast and sure, made the fiend reconsider the wisdom of that maneuver, and took one of the toes from Bizmatec's huge foot in the process.

Again the glabrezu howled in rage. Bizmatec hopped back and Catti-brie climbed to her feet, readying herself for the next assault.

The ensuing attack was not what the woman expected. Bizmatec loved to

toy with mortals, particularly humans, to torment them and finally, to tear them apart slowly, limb by limb. This one was too formidable for such tactics, the wounded tanar'ri decided, and so Bizmatec called upon magical powers.

Catti-brie felt her back foot slip out from under her, and when she tried to recover, she realized that she was no longer standing on the ice, was floating in the air.

"No, ye cheatin' dog-faced smoke-sucker!" Catti-brie protested, to no avail.

Bizmatec waved his huge hand and Catti-brie drifted by, ten feet in the air now, and moving out over the open water. The woman growled defiantly. Understanding what the fiend had in mind, she took up Khazid'hea in one hand, holding it more like a spear than a sword, and hurled it to the side, to the ice floe holding Stumpet. The sword hit the ice near to the dwarf, and sunk in to the hilt.

Catti-brie wasn't watching, was scrambling to regain her balance and to ready her bow. She did so, but Bizmatec merely laughed at her and released his magical energy.

Catti-brie splashed into the icy water, lost her breath immediately, and could feel her toes quickly going numb.

"Stumpet!" Catti-brie yelled to the dwarf, and Khazid'hea called out to the priestess as well, a mental plea for Stumpet to pull the sword from the ice. Stumpet stood impassively, perfectly oblivious to the threatening scene.

Bruenor knew what had happened to Catti-brie. The dwarf had seen her rise into the air, had heard the splash and her subsequent cries for Stumpet. Every paternal instinct within Bruenor told him to run from the fight and leap into the water after his dear daughter, and yet he knew that to be a foolhardy course. It would not only get him killed—for he cared little for personal safety where Catti-brie was concerned—but would doom his daughter as well. The only thing Bruenor could do for Catti-brie was win the fight quickly, and so the dwarf went at the manes with abandon, chopping enemies nearly in half with his mighty axe and screaming all the while. His progress was amazing and all the area near him was cloudy with puffs of yellowish gas.

Bruenor's fortune reversed in the flare of a sudden burst of fire. The dwarf fell back and yelped, stunned for a moment, his face red from the flash. He shook his head fiercely and came back to his senses as Bizmatec entered the fray, the huge fiend clubbing Bruenor on the head with what remained of his right claw, his left pincers going for the fast kill at the dwarf's throat.

Drizzt heard it all, the fate of both Catti-brie and Bruenor. The drow did not allow the intimations of guilt to creep into his senses. Long ago, Drizzt

Do'Urden had learned that he was not responsible for all of the sorrow in the world, and that his friends would follow the course of their own choosing. What Drizzt felt was outrage, pure and simple, and adrenaline coursed through his veins, carrying him to greater heights of battle.

But how could someone parry six attacks?

Twinkle went left, left, left, then back to the right, each swing picking off a rushing blade. Drizzt's other blade, verily pulsing with hunger, came in a vertical swipe, tip pointing to the ground, blocking two of the marilith's swords at once. Twinkle flew back the other way, angling up to block, and then turning down to intercept. Then the drow hopped as high as he could, purely on instinct, as the marilith half-spun, her green and scaly tail whipping past in an attempt to take the drow's feet out from under him.

Advantage gained, Drizzt hit the ground running, straight ahead, his scimitars flying out in front in a wild offensive flurry. But though he was inside the angles of the fiend's six swords, his attack was defeated as the marilith simply disappeared—pop!—and reappeared right behind him.

Drizzt knew enough about fiends to react to the move. As soon as his target vanished, he dived into a headlong roll, twisting as he came back to his feet. His hungry scimitar shot out to the side as he rose, cutting down a fiend that had ventured too near, but Drizzt hardly followed the attack, his quick feet already turning on the ice to reverse his direction, to get him back at the marilith.

Again came the ringing of parry and counter, sounding almost as a single, long wail, as eight blades wove a blurring dance of death.

It seemed almost a miracle, a virtual impossibility, but Drizzt scored the first hit, Twinkle taking the marilith in one of her numerous shoulders, rendering that arm useless.

And then there were five swords charging hard at the drow's face and he had to fall away.

※ ※ ※ ※ ※

Regis and Guenhwyvar made it at last to the narrowest point in the channel between the icebergs, and it seemed a desperate leap to the frightened halfling. Even worse, a new problem presented itself, for the area across from them was not an empty, secret run to the crystal tower, but was filling fast with wretched manes.

Regis would have turned back then, preferring to try and find his friends, or, if they were already gone, to turn tail and run, all the way back to the

tundra, all the way back to the dwarven mines. Images of coming back with an army of dwarves—of coming back *behind* an army of dwarves!—flitted through the halfling's mind, but it soon proved to be a moot notion.

Regis was holding fast to Guenhwyvar, and he soon realized that the dedicated panther had no intention of even slowing. The halfling grabbed all the tighter. He yelped in fear as the great cat jumped, soaring out over the black water, across the gap to skid hard on the ice, scattering the nearest group of manes. Guenhwyvar could have made short work of those horrid creatures, but the panther knew her mission and went at it with single-minded abandon. With Regis holding on desperately and howling in terror, Guenhwyvar ran on, cutting left and right, dodging manes and leaving them far behind. In a matter of seconds, the pair went over a ridge and came down into an empty little vale, right at the base of Cryshal-Tirith. The manes, apparently too stupid to follow prey that had gone out of sight, did not come in fast pursuit.

"I have to be insane," Regis whispered, looking again at the crystal tower that had served as a prison to him when Akar Kessel had invaded Icewind Dale. And Kessel, though a wizard, was but a man. This time a fiend, a great and powerful balor, controlled the crystal shard!

Regis could not see any door to the four-sided tower, as he knew he would not. An added defense of the tower was that Cryshal-Tirith's entrance was not visible to creatures of the plane of existence on which the tower stood, with the single exception of the crystal shard's wielder. Regis could not see the door, but Guenhwyvar, a creature of the Astral Plane, surely could.

Regis hesitated, managed to hold Guenhwyvar back for a moment. "There are guards," the halfling explained. He remembered the giant and powerful trolls that had been in the last Cryshal-Tirith, and imagined what monsters Errtu might have put in place.

Even as he spoke, the pair heard a buzzing sound and looked up. Regis nearly fainted dead away as a chasme swooped over the ridge and bore down on them.

⚔ ⚔ ⚔ ⚔ ⚔

Not bothered at all at being bonked on the head, Bruenor got his axe up to intercept the nipping pincer. The dwarf bolted ahead, or at least, he tried. When that attack didn't work, he wisely reversed his course and went into a quick tactical retreat.

"Bigger beastie, bigger target," Bruenor snarled, straightening the one-horned helmet on his head. He whipped his axe to the side, knocking back a pair of manes, then roared and charged straight in at Bizmatec, showing no fear whatsoever.

The four-armed glabrezu met the charge with a pounding half-claw and a pair of punching fists. Bruenor scored a hit, but got slugged twice in return. Dazed, the dwarf could only look on helplessly as the fiend's good pincer came rushing in again.

A silver streak passed right by the dwarf, the arrow hitting the fiend in his massive chest and driving Bizmatec back a staggering step.

There was Catti-brie, in the water still, thrashing about, bobbing high so that she could bring Taulmaril, which she had turned sidelong, free of the water long enough to get off a shot. Firing the bow at all was amazing, but for her to actually hit the mark . . .

Bruenor couldn't understand how she came high again, impossibly high, until the dwarf realized that Catti-brie had her foot on a submerged piece of ice. Up she went, letting fly another deadly arrow.

Bizmatec howled and staggered back another step.

Catti-brie howled, too, in glee, but hers was not a sincere cry. She was glad that she was exacting some revenge on the fiend, and glad that she was aiding her father, but she could not deny that her legs were already numb, that her shoulder continued to bleed, and that her time for this fight was not long. All around her, the black and cold water waited impatiently, a prowling animal waiting to gobble up the doomed woman.

Her third shot missed the mark, but it came close enough so that Bizmatec had to duck suddenly. The fiend twisted and bent low, then his eyes widened considerably when he realized that he had just put his forehead in perfect alignment with Bruenor's rushing axe.

The explosion dropped Bizmatec to his knees. The fiend felt the fierce yank as Bruenor tore his axe free. Then came another explosion and a silver streak to the side that blasted away the manes that were trying to come to the glabrezu's aid. Where was Errtu now? Then came a third hit, and the world was swirling, darkening, as the spirit of Bizmatec careened along the corridor that would take him back to the Abyss for a hundred years of banishment.

Bruenor came out from the black smoke, all that remained of the glabrezu, with renewed abandon, hacking at the fast-thinning ranks of manes, working his way to Drizzt. He couldn't actually see the drow, but he could hear the ring of steel, the impossibly fast repetition of blade striking blade.

He did manage to get a glimpse of Catti-brie, and his heart soared with hope, for his daughter had somehow splashed her way over to the same ice floe that bore Stumpet.

"Come on, dwarf," Bruenor muttered intensely. "Find yer god and save me girl!"

Stumpet didn't move as Catti-brie continued to flounder. The woman was too engaged, as was her father, to notice another large form making its way toward the battle, moving swiftly and gracefully across the ice.

⚔ ⚔ ⚔ ⚔ ⚔

From a short distance back within the cave opening, Errtu watched it all with pure enjoyment. The fiend felt no loss as Bizmatec was pounded away into nothingness, cared little for the chasme, and nothing at all for the manes. Even the marilith, in such desperate combat with Drizzt, merely concerned the balor because Errtu feared that she might kill the drow. As for the generals and his soldiers, they were replaceable, easily replaceable. There was no shortage of willing fiends waiting eagerly in the Abyss.

So let the companions win out here on the open berg, Errtu figured. Already the woman was out of the fight, and the dwarf was battered. And Drizzt Do'Urden, though he was fighting so very well, was surely tiring. By the time Drizzt got into the cave, he would likely be alone, and no single mortal, not even a drow elf, could stand up to the mighty balor.

The fiend smiled wickedly and watched the continuing fight. If the marilith gained too much of an advantage, Errtu would have to intervene.

⚔ ⚔ ⚔ ⚔ ⚔

Crenshinibon also viewed the battle with great interest. The crystal shard, intent on the main fight, was oblivious to the enemies who had come to Cryshal-Tirith's doorstep. Unlike Errtu, the artifact wanted the fight done with, wanted Drizzt and his friends simply destroyed before they ever got near the cave. Crenshinibon would have liked to send out another line of fire—the drow was a more stationary target now, locked in combat as he was—but the first such attack had severely weakened the shard. The encounter with the antimagic sapphire had taken a toll. Crenshinibon could only hope the damage would eventually heal.

For now, though . . .

The wicked artifact found a way. It reached out telepathically to the ring Errtu had left on the floor, to the trapped dwarf held within that gem prison.

On the ice floe, Stumpet finally moved, and Catti-brie, not understanding, smiled hopefully when she noticed the priestess's approach.

⚔ ⚔ ⚔ ⚔ ⚔

In the never-ending wars of the Abyss, the fiends known as mariliths have a reputation as generals, as the finest tacticians. But Drizzt soon realized that the creature with seven appendages was not so coordinated in her movements. The marilith's routines did not vary, simply because of the confusion any wielder would find in trying to coordinate the movements of six separate blades.

And so the drow was doing better, though his arms tingled with numbness from the sheer number of parries he had been through.

Left, left, then right went Twinkle, complimenting the up and down movements of the other scimitar, and Drizzt was quick to jump when the marilith's tail, predictably, came slashing around.

The fiend disappeared once more, and Drizzt decided to spin about. The marilith expected him to do that, he realized, and so he came straight ahead instead, and scored a vicious hit as the creature reappeared, exactly where she had just been.

"Oh, my son," the marilith said unexpectedly, falling back.

That gave Drizzt pause, but he was still in a ready crouch, still able to double-slash into gas the two manes that ventured near.

"Oh, my son," the fiend said again, in a voice that was so familiar to the beleaguered drow. "Can you not see through the disguise?" his enemy went on.

Drizzt sucked in a deep breath, trying not to look at the deep and bleeding slash he had put across the marilith's left breast, wondering suddenly if he had struck foolishly.

"It is Zaknafein," the creature went on. "A trick of Errtu, forcing me to fight against you . . . as Matron Malice did with Zin-carla!"

The words stunned Drizzt profoundly, locked his feet into place. His knees nearly buckled as the creature gradually shifted shape, went from a six-armed monstrosity to a handsome drow male, a male that Drizzt Do'Urden knew so very well.

Zaknafein!

"Errtu wants you to destroy me," the creature said. The marilith did well to hide a snicker. She had scoured Drizzt's thoughts to come up with this ploy, and had followed their ensuing course, letting Drizzt lead, every step. As soon as she had proclaimed this to be a trick of the balor, Drizzt had thought of Matron Malice, whoever that was, and of Zin-carla, whatever that was. The marilith was more than prepared to play along.

And it was working! Drizzt's scimitars sagged. "Fight him, my father!" Drizzt yelled. "Find your freedom, as you did from Malice!"

"He is strong," the marilith replied. "He . . ." The creature smiled, her two remaining weapons dipping low. "My son!" came the soothing, familiar voice.

Drizzt nearly swooned. "We must aid the dwarf," he started to say, willing to believe that this was indeed Zaknafein, and that his father could find his way out of Errtu's mental clutches.

Drizzt was willing to believe that, but his scimitar, forged to destroy such creatures of fire, most certainly was not. The scimitar could not "see" the marilith's illusion, could not hear the soothing voice.

Drizzt actually took a step to the side, toward Bruenor, when he recognized the continued throbbing, the unrelenting hunger, of that blade. He took another step, just to get his feet properly positioned, and then hurled himself at the illusion of his father, his rage doubling.

He was met by the five remaining blades as the marilith quickly resumed her more natural form, and the battle began anew.

Drizzt called upon his innate magic and limned the fiend with purplish faerie fire, but the marilith laughed and countered the magical energy, dousing the fire with a thought.

Drizzt heard the familiar shuffling behind him and immediately brought up a globe of impenetrable darkness, right over himself and the creature.

The marilith taunted him. "You think I cannot see?" the fiend roared gleefully. "I have lived longer in darkness than you, Drizzt Do'Urden!"

Her unabated attacks seemed to confirm her words. Sword rang out against scimitar, against scimitar, against scimitar, against . . . axe.

The creature didn't understand for a split second, a fatal hesitation. Suddenly she realized that Drizzt was no longer in front of her, but the drow's dwarven ally! And if Bruenor was in front . . .

The marilith reached into her innate magic once more, thinking to teleport away to safety.

Drizzt's strike came first, though, his hungry scimitar driving through the marilith's backbone.

His darkness globe went away then, and Bruenor, in front of the fiend, howled insanely as the tip of Drizzt's scimitar blasted out of the marilith's chest.

Drizzt held on, even managed a twist or two, as the scimitar fed, energy coursing along its blade and hilt.

The marilith spat curse after curse. She tried to attack Bruenor, but could not lift her arms as that wicked, cursed blade gulped at her life force, draining it away. The marilith was less substantial suddenly, her flesh melting away to smoky nothingness.

She promised Drizzt Do'Urden a thousand tortured deaths, promised that she would one day return to exact horrific revenge.

Drizzt had heard it all before.

"There's more and worse inside," Drizzt said to Bruenor when the business was finished.

Bruenor gave a quick look over his shoulder and saw Stumpet closing on his struggling daughter—what the dwarf thought to be a good thing. There was nothing more that Bruenor could do for her. "Let's go then!" he bellowed in reply.

Only a few manes remained—more were coming over the ridge from the back side of the iceberg—and the friends charged on, side by side. They blew away any of the meager resistance, went into the cave hard and fast, where the last group of manes waited, and were summarily destroyed.

The only light the companions had with them came from Drizzt's blades. Twinkle glowed its usual blue, while the other blade flared brightly, a different hue of blue. This scimitar glowed only in extreme cold, and it was glowing more fiercely after its most recent feast.

The cave seemed larger from the inside. The floor inside the entrance sloped down steeply to add to its depth, though the whole of the place was thick with icy stalagmites and stalactites, most reaching from floor to ceiling, which was now more than thirty feet above the pair.

When the fight was ended, Drizzt pointed across the way, to a steep incline, a path up the opposite wall, which ended on a landing that seemed to turn around a blocking sheet of thick ice.

They started across the jagged floor, but stopped when they heard the maniacal laughter. Errtu appeared, and cold became hot as the mighty balor loosed his devastating fire.

⚔ ⚔ ⚔ ⚔ ⚔

It was a simple case of underestimation. The chasme knew about the material world, had been here before, and understood what to expect from the creatures that lived here.

But Guenhwyvar was not of the material world, and was above what a normal cat could do.

The chasme rushed over the pair, thinking itself high enough to be safe.

Great indeed was the fiend's surprise when the mighty cat leaped straight up, crossing thirty feet in a mere instant, great claws hooking fast onto the buglike torso.

Down they went in a heap, Guenhwyvar raking wildly with her back legs, holding fast with her front and biting with all the considerable strength of her powerful jaws.

Regis looked to the rolling pair, quickly surmising that he could do little to help. He called repeatedly for Guenhwyvar, then looked about, seeing that some of the manes were fast returning, this time continuing over the ridge to close in.

"Hurry, Guenhwyvar!" the halfling cried, and the panther did just that, redoubling her devastating kicks.

Then it was Guenhwyvar alone on the ground, pulling herself from the fast-dissipating black smoke. The cat came right to Regis, and started for the door, but Regis, an idea popping into his head, tugged hard to stop her momentum.

"There's a window on the top floor!" the halfling explained, for he had no desire to fight his way through the tower's guardians, which might, he realized, include Errtu. He knew this was a desperate chance, for the window on Cryshal-Tirith's top floor was as often a portal to another place as a normal entrance or exit for the tower.

Guenhwyvar scanned the indicated area quickly, then changed direction. Regis went right onto the panther's back, fearing that he would slow the cat's desperate run if his legs could not keep up.

Up the side of the conical mound went Guenhwyvar. Claws digging in, legs churning with all her strength, she came to a relatively flat area, gained a burst of speed, and leaped out for the tower, for the small window.

The pair hit the side of Crenshinibon hard, Regis somehow scrambling over the panther to get his body through the narrow portal. He landed hard and rolled backward, finally putting his back to the wall. He started to call out for Guenhwyvar to come in.

But he heard the cat's roar, and then heard Guenhwyvar spring away from the tower's side, the panther going fast to the aid of her master.

That left Regis alone in the small room to face the crystal shard.

"Great," the terrified halfling said dryly.

SHOWDOWN

Drizzt and Bruenor quickly came to understand the absolutely unfavorable conditions in which they had met Errtu. The fiend's fires raged, turning the ice cave into a sloshing quagmire. Huge blocks fell from the ceiling, forcing the friends to dodge and twist, the cold water weighing them down.

Even worse, whenever the great balor moved away from the pair, taking away his fiendish heat, the water began to refreeze about Drizzt and Bruenor, slowing them.

Throughout the ordeal, they heard the taunting laughter of the mighty Errtu.

"What torment awaits you, Drizzt Do'Urden!" the fiend bellowed.

Drizzt heard the sudden splash behind him, felt the suddenly intense heat, and knew that the fiend had used his magic, had teleported to arrive right behind the drow. Drizzt started to turn, was quick enough to dodge, but the fiend merely stuck his lightning sword into the water behind the drow, and the energy released from the blade jolted Drizzt's every muscle.

Drizzt spun, gritted his teeth to prevent himself from biting off his own tongue. Around came Twinkle, a perfect parry, catching Errtu's second attack in mid-swing.

The fiend laughed all the louder as his devilish blade released another jolt, a burst of electrical energy that rushed through Drizzt's scimitar and into the drow, coursing down his body and popping his knees so painfully that he lost his balance and nearly lost consciousness.

He heard Bruenor's roar, and the sloshing as the dwarf pounded his way

toward him. The dwarf couldn't get there in time, Drizzt realized. Errtu's sudden assault had beaten him.

But suddenly, the fiend was gone, simply gone. It took Drizzt only a moment to understand that Errtu was playing with them! The fiend had waited all these years to exact revenge on Drizzt, and now the wicked balor was truly enjoying himself.

Bruenor skidded by as Drizzt regained his footing. The pair heard the sound of Errtu's taunting laughter once more, from across the way.

"Beware, for the fiend can appear wherever he chooses," Drizzt warned, and even as he spoke the words, he heard the crack of a whip and the cry of the dwarf. Drizzt spun about as Bruenor was tugged from his feet.

"Ye don't say?" the dwarf asked, scrambling furiously to get himself in line for a strike as Errtu jerked him backward, away from Drizzt.

Bruenor realized the depth of his troubles then, for in looking back, he saw a wall of fire looming before him, sizzling and sputtering as it turned the ice to steam. Behind it stood Errtu reeling him in with the whip, grinning wickedly.

Drizzt felt the strength drain from his body, and he knew how Errtu meant to torment him. Bruenor was doomed.

✕ ✕ ✕ ✕ ✕

Regis didn't know it, but his presence alone in that small room at the top of Cryshal-Tirith saved Catti-brie. Stumpet was near to her, at the edge of the ice. To Catti-brie's horror, the dwarf did not try to help her get her numbed form over the edge of the floe, but rather began pushing and kicking at her, trying to dislodge her and drop her back into the water.

Catti-brie fought back as fiercely as she could, but without firm footing and with her legs completely numb, she was losing the struggle.

But then Regis went into the tower, and the crystal shard had to release Stumpet from its domineering hold and concentrate on this newest threat.

Stumpet stopped fighting, went perfectly still. As soon as she realized the truth of the immobile dwarf, Catti-brie grabbed a hold on Stumpet's sturdy leg, using the dwarf's bulk to pull herself clear of the water.

After a considerable struggle, the woman managed to get shakily to her feet. Drizzt and Bruenor were gone by then, into the cave, but there remained manes to shoot, including a group that had leaped into the water and were thrashing about, gradually closing the gap to Catti-brie and Stumpet, the last remaining visible enemies.

Up came Taulmaril.

✕ ✕ ✕ ✕ ✕

Bruenor struggled with all his might. He grabbed on to the remaining stump of one destroyed stalagmite, but the icy thing was too slick for him to get a firm hold. It wouldn't have helped anyway, not with Errtu—so huge and strong—pulling against him. The dwarf howled in pain as his feet went into the fiendish fire.

Drizzt scrambled so fast that his feet slipped out from under him. He kept moving, though, churning his knees, banging them hard. The drow hardly cared for his pain. Bruenor needed him, that was all that mattered. He rushed with all speed, found a proper foothold amidst the quagmire, and shoved off, diving straight out, his arm extended and holding straight the ice-forged scimitar, sliding its curving blade right beside his friend.

In that area, Errtu's fires were extinguished, put out by the magic of the scimitar.

Both friends tried to rise, and both were blasted back to the wet ground as the balor plunged his lightning sword into the watery ice, taunting them all the while.

"Yes, a reprieve!" the fiend bellowed. "Well done, Drizzt Do'Urden, foolish drow. You have extended my pleasure, and for that—"

The fiend's sentence ended with a grunt as Guenhwyvar soared in, slamming Errtu hard, knocking him off-balance on the slick floor.

Drizzt was up and charging. Bruenor worked fast to untangle himself from the binding thongs of the fiend's whip. And Guenhwyvar raked wildly, biting and clawing.

Errtu knew the cat, had faced Guenhwyvar on that same occasion when Drizzt had banished him, and the balor felt the fool for not anticipating that the animal would soon arrive.

No matter, though, Errtu reasoned, and with a huge shrug of powerful muscles, the fiend launched the cat away.

In came Drizzt, his hungry scimitar thrusting for the fiend's belly.

Errtu's lightning sword swiped down in a parry, and that, too, was an attack, as the energy coursed from weapon to weapon, and subsequently into Drizzt, hurling him backward.

Bruenor was in fast and the dwarf's axe chopped hard into Errtu's leg. The fiend roared and swatted the dwarf, and Bruenor flew backwards. Out came the fiend's leathery wings, up he rose, above the reach of the mighty friends. Guenhwyvar leaped again, but Errtu caught her in mid-flight, locked her with

a telekinesis spell, as the glabrezu had done with Catti-brie.

Still, for Drizzt and Bruenor, shaking off their earlier wounds, Guenhwyvar was helping, was keeping the fiend's considerable magical energies engaged.

"Let my father go!" Drizzt cried out.

Errtu laughed at him, and the reprieve was at its end. Errtu's spell hurled the panther aside, and the fiend came on in all his wrath.

⚔ ⚔ ⚔ ⚔ ⚔

It was a small room, perhaps a dozen feet in diameter and with a domed ceiling reaching up to the tower's pinnacle. In the middle of the room, hanging in the empty air, loomed Crenshinibon, the crystal shard, the heart of the tower, pulsing with a pinkish-red color as though it were a living thing.

Regis glanced around quickly. He spotted the coffer lying on the floor—he knew it from somewhere, though he couldn't immediately place it—and the gem-studded ring, but what significance they held, the halfling could not be sure.

And he didn't have the time to figure it out. Regis had talked extensively with Drizzt after the fall of Kessel, and he knew well the technique the drow had used to defeat the tower on that occasion, simply by covering the pulsing shard with blocking flour. So it was with the halfling now as he pulled the small pack from his back and strode confidently in.

"Time to sleep," Regis taunted. He was almost right, but not in the manner he meant, for he was almost knocked unconscious. The halfling and Drizzt had erred. In the tower on the plain outside of Bryn Shander those years ago, Drizzt had covered not Crenshinibon, but one of the shard's countless images. On this occasion, it was the real crystal shard, the sentient and powerful artifact, serving as the tower's heart. Such a meager attack was defeated by a pulse of energy that disintegrated the flour as it descended, burned the sack in the halfling's hands, and hurled Regis hard against the far wall.

The dazed halfling groaned all the louder when the trap door in the room's floor flew open. The stench of trolls wafted in, followed closely by a huge and wide hand with sharpened claws and rubbery, putrid green skin.

⚔ ⚔ ⚔ ⚔ ⚔

Catti-brie could hardly feel her extremities, her teeth chattered uncontrollably and she knew that her bowstring was cutting deeply into her fingers, though she felt no pain there. She had to continue, for the sake of her father and of Drizzt.

Using solid Stumpet as a support, the young woman steadied herself and let fly an arrow, taking down the fiend closest to the cave entrance. Again and again, Catti-brie let fly, her enchanted quiver providing her with endless ammunition. She decimated most of the manes remaining on the ice beach, and blew away those coming over the ridge. She nearly shot Guenhwyvar, too, before she recognized the speeding cat. Her heart was lifted with some hope as the mighty panther rushed into the cave.

Soon all that remained of the manes were the few in the water, swimming fast for Catti-brie. Catti-brie worked frantically—most of her shots hit the mark—but one did get up on the ice floe, and came rushing in.

Catti-brie looked to her sword, buried to the hilt in the ice, and knew that she could not get to it in time. Instead, she used her bow like a club, whacking the fiend hard across the face.

The wretched thing skidded in, off-balance, and even as the two connected, Catti-brie snapped her forehead right into the ugly fiend's nose. Up came the tip of her bow, driving hard under the thing's saggy chin, poking through the oozing skin. The creature exploded into noxious gas, but it had done its work. The momentum of its rush, combined with the sudden gaseous cloud, sent Catti-brie moving backward, past the dwarf and into the water.

Up she came, gasping for breath, flailing with arms that she could not feel. Her legs were useless to her now. She managed somehow to grab on to the very edge of the ice floe, locking her fingers into a small crevice, for she knew that her strength was already going away. She cried out for Stumpet, but even those muscles of her mouth would not respond to her mind's command.

Catti-brie had survived the fiends, it seemed, only to be destroyed by the natural elements of Icewind Dale, the place she had called home for most of her life. That irony was not lost on her as all the world grew cold.

✕ ✕ ✕ ✕ ✕

Regis's back skimmed the curving ceiling as the nine-foot troll, the larger of the two that had entered the room, lifted him high into the air to look into its ghastly face. "Now youses goes into me belly!" the horrid thing proclaimed, opening wide its considerable maw.

The mere fact that the troll could speak gave Regis an idea, a desperate glimmer of hope.

"Wait!" he bade the creature, reaching under his tunic. "I have treasure to

offer." Out came the halfling's prized pendant, the magnificent, hypnotic ruby dancing on the end of the chain just inches from the startled, and suddenly intrigued, troll's eyes.

"This is only the beginning," Regis stammered, fighting hard to improvise for the consequences of failure were all too evident. "I have a mound of these—look at how wonderfully it spins, drawing your eyes . . ."

"Ere now, be ye to eats the thing or not?" the second troll demanded, shoving the first one hard. But that troll was caught fast by the charm, and was already thinking that it didn't want to share the booty with its companion.

Thus, the horrid thing was more than open to Regis's ensuing suggestion as the halfling casually glanced at the second troll and said, "Kill him."

Regis dropped hard to the floor, and was nearly squashed as the two trolls fell into a wild wrestling match. The halfling had to move fast, but what was he to do? His rolling evasion took him to the gem-studded ring, which he promptly pocketed, and to the open and empty coffer, which he suddenly recognized.

It was the same coffer the glabrezu had been carrying when Regis and his companions had come upon evil Matron Baenre in the tunnels under Mithral Hall, the same coffer that had held the stone—the black sapphire that had stolen away all the magic.

Regis scooped up the thing and dashed past the rolling trolls, bearing down fast on the crystal shard. A flood of mental images assaulted him then, nearly buckling his legs. The sentient artifact, sensing the danger, entered the halfling's mind, dominating poor Regis. Regis wanted to move forward, he really did, but his feet would not obey.

And then he wasn't sure that he wanted to move forward at all. Suddenly Regis had to wonder why he had wanted to destroy the crystal tower, the beautiful and marvelous structure. And why would he desire the destruction of Crenshinibon, the creator, when he might use the artifact to his own benefit?

What did Drizzt know anyway?

Though he was a confused and nearly lost soul at that point, the halfling thought to lift his own ruby pendant up before his eyes.

Immediately Regis found himself swirling into the item's depths, following the red flickers deeper and deeper. Most people got lost in that charm, but it was there, deep within the hypnosis of his gemstone, that Regis found himself.

He dropped the pendant chain and leaped forward, snapping the shielding coffer over Crenshinibon just as it released another pulse of deadly energy.

The coffer swallowed the item and its attack, and Regis plucked the shard out of the air.

Immediately the tower, the gigantic image of the crystal shard, began to shudder, the initial rumbles of its death throes.

"Oh, not again," the halfling muttered, for he had been through this before, and had escaped only with aid of Guenhwyvar, while Drizzt had escaped by . . .

Regis turned to the window, leaped up to its sill. He glanced back at the trolls, hugging instead of wrestling as their tower home shivered beneath them. In unison, they turned to regard the smiling halfling.

"Another day perhaps," Regis said to them, and then, without looking down, he leaped out. Twenty feet down, he hit the side of the iceberg cone, bouncing and sliding wildly to come to a sudden, jolting stop in the icy snow. The crystal tower crumbled around him, huge blocks narrowly missing the stunned and bruised halfling.

※ ※ ※ ※ ※

The earthquake on the iceberg brought a temporary halt to the fighting within the cave, a temporary reprieve for those being badly beaten by the powerful tanar'ri. But poor Bruenor, standing by the cave wall, fell down as a wide crack opened at his feet. Though the break wasn't very deep, barely to Bruenor's waist, when the shaking ended, the dwarf found himself wedged in tightly.

The loss of Crenshinibon did nothing to diminish Errtu's powers, and the obvious fall of the tower only heightened the balor's rage.

Guenhwyvar came flying back in at him, but the fiend skewered the cat in mid-flight with his mighty sword, holding Guenhwyvar aloft with one powerful hand.

Drizzt, on his knees in the slush, could only watch in horror as Errtu calmly stalked in, as the panther twitched and tried futilely to free herself, growling with agony.

It was over, Drizzt knew. All of it had come to a sudden, crashing end. He could not win out. He wished that Guenhwyvar could get off of that sword—if she did, Drizzt would send her over to Bruenor and then dismiss her. Hopefully she would take the dwarf with her to the relative safety of her astral home.

But that couldn't happen. Guenhwyvar twitched again and slumped, and then dissipated into gray smoke, her corporeal form defeated and sent away from the Prime Material Plane.

Drizzt pulled out the figurine. He knew that he could not recall the cat, not for some days. He heard the hiss as the fiend's fires neared him and were extinguished by his trusty blade, and he looked from the figurine to grinning Errtu, towering over him, barely five feet away.

"Are you ready to die, Drizzt Do'Urden?" the fiend asked. "Your father can see us, you know, and how pained he is that you will die slowly before me!"

Drizzt didn't doubt the words, and his rage came up in full. But it wouldn't help him, not this time. He was cold, weary, filled with sorrow, and defeated. He knew that.

⚔ ⚔ ⚔ ⚔ ⚔

Errtu's words were half true. The prisoner, behind a partially opaque wall of ice at the side of the cave's upper landing, could indeed see the scene, highlighted by the blue glow of Drizzt's scimitars and the orange flames near Errtu.

He clawed at the wall futilely. He cried as he had not cried in so many years.

⚔ ⚔ ⚔ ⚔ ⚔

"And what a fine pet your cat will make for me," Errtu teased.

"Never," the drow growled, and purely on impulse, Drizzt threw the figurine with all his might, back through the cave entrance. He didn't hear the splash, but he was confident that he had heaved it far enough to reach the sea.

"Well done, me friend," a grim Bruenor said from the side.

Errtu's grin became a grimace of outrage. Up came the deadly sword, hanging right over Drizzt's vulnerable head. The drow lifted Twinkle to block.

And then a hammer twirled in end over end to slam hard into the balor, accompanied by the hearty call of "Tempus!"

Without fear, Kierstaad rushed into the cave, skidding right through the breach in Errtu's flames caused by Drizzt's scimitar, skidding right into the face of the tanar'ri, and howling for Aegis-fang all the way. Kierstaad knew the hammer's legend, knew that it would return to his hands.

But it didn't. It was gone from the ground near the fiend, but for some reason that Kierstaad did not understand, it had not materialized in his waiting hands.

"It should have come back!" he cried in protest, to Bruenor mostly, and then Kierstaad was flying, slapped away by the fiend. He smacked hard into an ice mound, rolled off the thing and fell heavily, groaning, to the slushy floor.

"It should have come back," he said once more, before his consciousness drifted away.

⚔ ⚔ ⚔ ⚔ ⚔

Aegis-fang couldn't go back to Kierstaad, for it had returned to its rightful owner, to Wulfgar, son of Beornegar, watching the scene from behind an ice wall. Wulfgar had been Errtu's prisoner for six long years.

The feel of the weapon transformed Wulfgar, gave him back a measure of himself along with the familiarity of this warhammer, forged for him by the dwarf who loved him. He remembered so much at that moment, so much that he had, by necessity, forced himself to forget in the years of hopelessness.

Truly the strong barbarian was overwhelmed, but not so much so that he didn't think of the immediate need. He roared out to Tempus, his god—how good it felt to hear that name coming from his lips again!—and began taking down the wall with mighty chops of his powerful hammer.

⚔ ⚔ ⚔ ⚔ ⚔

Regis felt a call in his mind. At first he thought it to be the crystal shard, and then, when he convinced himself that the artifact was safely and completely locked away in the coffer, he guessed it to be the ruby pendant.

When that proved false, Regis finally discerned the source: the gemstone ring in his pocket. Regis took it out and stared hard at it. He feared that it was yet another manifestation of Crenshinibon and lifted his arm back to hurl it into the sea.

But then Regis recognized the little voice in his head.

"Stumpet?" he asked, curiously, peering hard into the stone. He moved as he spoke, coming to kneel right beside one of the broken tower blocks. Out came his little mace.

⚔ ⚔ ⚔ ⚔ ⚔

The thunder of the barbarian's hits shook the whole of the cave, so much so that a suddenly nervous Errtu could not help but look back. And when the balor did, Drizzt Do'Urden struck hard.

Twinkle gashed against the fiend's calf, while Drizzt launched his other blade higher, aiming for Errtu's groin. The scimitar's pointy tip dug in, and how Errtu howled! Again came that welcomed throbbing along Drizzt's arm as the scimitar fed on the fiend's life force.

But the turn in the battle was temporary. Errtu quickly slapped Drizzt away, then disappeared, coming back into view high among the icy fingers that hung down from the ceiling.

"Up, Bruenor," Drizzt called. "We have been given a reprieve, for Zaknafein will soon be among us."

The drow looked to the red-bearded dwarf as he spoke, and Bruenor had nearly wriggled his way out of the hole.

Up Drizzt scrambled, up and ready, but something about the look that came over Bruenor's face as the dwarf gazed to the side, weakened Drizzt's knees. He followed the dwarf's stare across the chamber, to the ice wall, where he expected to see Zaknafein.

He saw Wulfgar instead, with unkempt, wild hair and beard, but Wulfgar no doubt, hoisting Aegis-fang high and roaring with pure hatred.

"Me boy," was all the dwarf could whisper, and Bruenor slumped back into the hole.

Errtu went at Wulfgar hard, swooping in, his whip cracking and his sword blazing.

A hurled Aegis-fang nearly knocked the fiend from the air. Still the balor swept by, entangling Wulfgar's ankles with his whip and tugging the man from the ledge to send him bouncing among the ice mounds of the slushy floor.

"Wulfgar," Drizzt called out, and he winced as the man tumbled. It would take more than a fall to stop the tormented Wulfgar, now that he was among his friends, now that he held his mighty hammer. Up he sprang, roaring like some animal, and Aegis-fang, beautiful and solid Aegis-fang, was back in his hand.

Errtu went into a frenzy, determined to squash this minor uprising, to destroy all of Drizzt's friends, and then the drow himself. Balls of darkness appeared in the air, obscuring Wulfgar's vision as he tried to line up another throw. The fiend cracked his whip and zipped all about the cave, sometimes in swift flight, other times calling upon magic to teleport himself from place to place.

The chaos was complete, and every time Drizzt tried to get to Bruenor, Wulfgar, or even to fallen Kierstaad, there was Errtu, smacking him away. Always the drow parried the lightning sword, but each hit jolted him and hurt him. And every time, before Drizzt could begin to counter, Errtu was gone, simply gone, to wreak havoc in another part of the cave with another of the drow's friends.

✕ ✕ ✕ ✕ ✕

She wasn't cold anymore, was far beyond that simple sensation. Catti-brie was walking in darkness, fleeing the realm of mortals.

A strong hand grabbed her by the shoulder, the physical shoulder, bringing her senses back in tune with her corporeal body, and then she felt herself being lifted from the water.

And then . . . the woman felt warmth, magical warmth, seeping through her body, returning life where there was barely any.

Catti-brie's eyes fluttered open to see Stumpet Rakingclaw working furiously over her, calling upon the dwarven gods to breathe life back into this woman who had been as a daughter to Clan Battlehammer.

✕ ✕ ✕ ✕ ✕

Lightning simmered every time Errtu used that mighty sword. The rumbling of thunder and the fiend's victorious roars were matched by the beating of great leathery wings, the roars of Wulfgar to his battle god, and the cries of "Me boy!" from a wild-eyed, and still trapped Bruenor. Drizzt shouted, trying to bring some semblance of order to his companions, some common strategy that might corner and at last defeat wicked Errtu.

The fiend would have none of that. Errtu swooped and disappeared, struck fast and hard and was simply gone. Sometimes the balor hung up high amidst the stalactites, using his fires to loosen and drop the natural spikes at the companions scrambling below. Other times, Errtu had to come down to keep them apart, and even with the balor's tremendous efforts, Drizzt wove his way stubbornly toward Bruenor.

Wherever the fiend chose to appear, he could not remain in place and visible for very long. Even though the quagmire continued to slow any moves the drow might try, and even though the dwarf remained stuck in the stubborn crevice, the tormented prisoner, and his mighty hammer were always quick to the call. On several occasions Errtu vanished just an instant before Aegis-fang slammed into the wall, marking the spot where the fiend had been.

And so Errtu retained the upper hand, but in that craziness, the fiend could score no decisive hits.

It was time to win.

Bruenor was almost out of the crack, stuck by a single leg, when the mighty balor appeared, right behind him.

Drizzt, yelled out a warning, and purely on instinct, the dwarf whipped about, throwing himself as far into the fiend as possible, grabbing the balor's leg, wrenching his own knee in the process. Errtu's sword came swishing down, but Bruenor was in too close for it to cleave him. Still the dwarf was battered hard, and the energy jolt nearly popped his knees out of joint, especially the twisted one.

Bruenor grabbed on all the harder, knowing he could not hurt the balor, but hoping he could keep the fiend in place long enough for his friends to strike. His hair singed and his eyes stung as the fiend's fires came up, but they were gone in an instant and Bruenor knew that Drizzt was nearby.

Errtu's whip cracked, slowing the drow's approach. Drizzt went in a complete spin to dodge, skidding down to one knee, and he stumbled as he tried to get back to his feet.

The whip cracked again, but it could do little to slow the progress of twirling Aegis-fang. The hammer caught the balor on the side, slamming Errtu back against the ice wall, and the fiend's respect for the man that had been his prisoner soared. Errtu had been hit by Aegis-fang once already, when Kierstaad had entered the fray, and so he understood the power of the weapon. But that first throw could not prepare Errtu for the power that was Wulfgar. Kierstaad's throw had stung him, but Wulfgar's had truly hurt.

In came Drizzt, but the balor lashed out hard with his foot, tearing Bruenor from the crevice and launching the dwarf a dozen feet across the cave floor. The fiend used his magic to disappear immediately, and Drizzt went sliding into empty wall.

"Fools!" the balor bellowed from the cave's exit. "I will retrieve the crystal shard and meet with you again before you leave this sea. Know that you are doomed!"

Drizzt scrambled, Wulfgar tried to line up a parting shot, and even Bruenor worked hard to stagger back to his feet, but none of them would get to Errtu in time.

The fiend turned away from them and started to fly off, but his surprise was complete, his momentum fully halted, by a silver-streaking arrow that hit him right in the face.

Errtu howled and Wulfgar threw, the hammer smashing hard into the fiend, crushing bones.

Catti-brie let fly again, putting one right into his chest. The balor howled again and stumbled backward into the cave.

Bruenor hobbled toward him, catching his axe as Drizzt tossed it to him. He reversed his grip to add to the momentum of the throw and buried the many-notched blade deep into the fiend's backside.

Errtu howled and Catti-brie hit him again, right beside her last shot.

Drizzt was there, Twinkle striking hard. He plunged his other blade plunging deep into the fiend's side, right under Errtu's arm as the fiend tried to lift his own sword to fend off the drow. Then Wulfgar was there, pounding away beside his father. Catti-brie kept the exit blocked by a steady line of streaking arrows.

And Drizzt held on, leaving his gulping blade deep in the fiend's flesh, while Twinkle worked furiously, cutting wound after wound.

With a last burst of energy, Errtu turned about, throwing off Bruenor and Wulfgar, but not Drizzt. The mighty balor looked right into the drow's lavender eyes. Errtu was defeated—even then, the fiend could feel his corporeal form beginning to melt away—but this time, the balor meant to take Drizzt Do'Urden back to the abyss.

Up came the balor's sword and his free hand came across, accepting the sting as it connected with Twinkle, moving the blocking weapon aside.

Drizzt had no defense. He let go of his embedded scimitar and tried to fall away. Too late.

The lightning flared along the blade's edge as it slashed toward the drow's head.

A strong hand shot out before the horrified drow's eyes and caught the fiend by the wrist, somehow stopping the cut, somehow holding mighty Errtu at bay, the lightning weapon barely inches from the target. Errtu glanced across to see Wulfgar, mighty Wulfgar, teeth clenched and muscles standing out like steel cords. All the years of frustration were in that iron grip, all the horrors the young barbarian had known were transformed then into sheer hatred for the fiend.

There was no way that Wulfgar, or any man, could hold back Errtu, but Wulfgar denied that logic, that truth, with the stronger truth that he would not let Errtu hurt him anymore, would not let the fiend take Drizzt from his side.

Errtu shook his half-canine, half-ape head in disbelief. It could not be!

And yet it was. Wulfgar held him, and soon, the balor was gone, in a waft of smoke and a wail of protest.

The three friends fell together in a tearful hug, too overwhelmed to speak, to even stand, for many, many moments.

28
The Son of Beornegar

Catti-brie saw Regis stumbling his way over the ridge to the left of the cone. She saw Drizzt and Bruenor, leaning heavily on each other for support as they exited the cave. And she saw Kierstaad, being carried over the shoulder of . . .

Stumpet, with her spells of healing, had done much to bolster the woman, and so the dwarf was surprised when Catti-brie gave a stifled yelp and fell down her knees. The dwarven priestess looked to her with concern, then followed her blank stare across the way, recognizing the source immediately.

"Hey," Stumpet said, scratching her stubbly face, "is that. . ."

"Wulfgar," Catti-brie breathed.

Regis joined the four at the edge of the iceberg, and was similarly knocked off his feet when he saw who it was that they had rescued from the clutches of evil Errtu. The halfling squeaked repeatedly and launched himself into the barbarian's arms, and Wulfgar, on the slick ice and with Kierstaad on his shoulder, pitched over backward, nearly cracking his head.

The huge man didn't mind, though. Errtu and his wicked minions were gone and now was the time for celebration!

Almost.

Drizzt searched frantically along the stretch of the iceberg in front of the cave entrance, cursing himself repeatedly for losing faith in himself and his friends. He questioned Regis, then called out to Catti-brie and Stumpet, but none of them had seen it.

The figurine that allowed the drow to call to Guenhwyvar was gone, swallowed up in the dark sea.

With Drizzt in such a fit, Bruenor surveyed the situation and quickly took command, setting the friends to work. The first order of business was to get Catti-brie and Stumpet back to them—and fast, for Drizzt, Bruenor, and Wulfgar were wet and fast freezing, and Kierstaad needed immediate attention from the cleric.

On the ice floe, Stumpet pulled a grappling hook and heavy line from her pack, and with the practiced throw of a seasoned climber, put the hook on the iceberg barely ten feet from her companions. Bruenor secured it quickly, then went beside Wulfgar, who was already pulling hard to bring the floating ice to shore, and pulling all the harder as he looked upon Catti-brie, his love, the woman who was to be his wife all those years ago.

Drizzt was of little help. He knelt over the edge of the iceberg, put his scimitars into the water to try and illuminate it. "I need some protection so I can go down there!" the drow called to Stumpet, who was pulling on her end of the rope and trying to offer some words of comfort to the pained ranger.

Regis, standing beside Drizzt, shook his head knowingly. The halfling had put out a line of his own, weighted at the end. He had fifty feet of cord into the water and still had not felt bottom. Even if Stumpet could enact a spell to keep Drizzt warm and to allow him to breathe underwater, he could not go that deep for very long, and could not hope to find the black figurine in the dark water.

Catti-brie and Bruenor exchanged a quick hug at the shoreline—Stumpet went right to work on Kierstaad—and then the woman and Wulfgar squared off uncomfortably.

Truly the barbarian looked ragged, his blond hair flying wildly, his beard down to his chest, and a hollow look in his eyes. He was still huge, still so well-muscled, but a slackness had come into his limbs, more a loss of spirit than of girth, Catti-brie knew. But it was Wulfgar, and whatever scars Errtu had put on him seemed irrelevant to the woman at that moment.

Wulfgar's heart pounded in his still-massive chest. Catti-brie did not look so different at all. A bit thicker perhaps, but that sparkle remained in her deep blue eyes, that love of life and adventure, that spirit that could not be tamed.

"I thought ye . . ." Catti-brie began, but she stopped and took a deep, steadying breath. "I never once forgot ye."

Wulfgar grabbed her up in his arms, pulling her tight to him. He tried to talk to her, to explain that only thoughts of her had kept him alive during his ordeal. But he couldn't find the words, not a one, and so he just held her as tight as he could and they both let the tears come.

It was a heartwarming sight for Bruenor, for Regis, for Stumpet, and for

Drizzt, though the drow could not take the moment to consider and enjoy it. Guenhwyvar was gone from him, a loss as great as the loss of his father, as the loss of Wulfgar. Guenhwyvar had been his companion for so many years, often his only companion, his one true friend.

He could not say good-bye to her.

It was Kierstaad, coming out of his stupor with the help of some dwarven healing magic, who broke the spell. The barbarian understood the trouble they were still in, especially with the sky growing thick with moisture and with the short day fast on the wane. It was colder out here than on the tundra, much colder, and they had little materials to set and maintain a fire.

Kierstaad knew a different way to shelter them. Still on the ground, propped on his elbows, he took up the call from Bruenor and began directing the movements. Using Khazid'hea, Catti-brie cut out blocks of ice, and the others piled them as instructed, soon building a domelike structure—an ice hut.

Not a moment too soon, for the dwarven priestess was out of spells and the cold was creeping back into the companions. Soon after, the sky opened up, unleashing a driving sleet, and then later, a fierce snowstorm.

But inside the shelter, the companions were safe and warm.

Except for Drizzt. Without Guenhwyvar, the drow felt as if he would never be warm again.

⚔ ⚔ ⚔ ⚔ ⚔

The next dawn was dim and gray, the air even colder than the previous, freezing night. Even worse, the friends found that they were trapped, stranded, for the night winds had shifted the ice that gave this sea its appropriate name and their berg was too far from any others for them to get across.

Kierstaad, feeling much better, climbed to the top of the conical tip and took up his horn, blowing wildly.

But the only answer came in the form of echoes, bouncing back across the flatness of the dark sea from the numerous other ice mountains.

Drizzt spent the morning in prayer, to Mielikki and to Gwaeron Windstrom, seeking guidance from them, asking them to return to him his panther, his precious friend. He wanted Guenhwyvar to lift out of the sea, back into his arms, and prayed for just that, but Drizzt knew that it didn't work that way.

Then he had an idea. He didn't know if it was god-inspired or one of his own, and he didn't care. He went to Regis first, Regis who had carved so very many wonderful objects with the bone of knucklehead trout, Regis who had created the very unicorn that hung around Drizzt's neck.

The halfling cut an appropriate-sized block of ice and went to work, while Drizzt went to the back side of the iceberg, as far from the others as possible, and began to call.

Two hours later, the drow returned, a young seal flopping along behind him, a newfound friend. As a ranger, Drizzt knew animals, knew how to communicate with them in rudimentary terms, and knew which movements would frighten them, and which would give them confidence. He was pleased upon his return to see that Catti-brie and Bruenor, using a bow and a hastily-strung, makeshift net, had caught some fish, and the drow was quick to proffer one and toss it to the seal.

"Hey!" Bruenor howled in protest, and then the dwarf's face brightened. "Yeah," he said, rubbing his hands briskly together as he thought he understood the drow's intent, "fatten the thing up."

Drizzt's ensuing scowl, as serious as the drow had ever been, ended that train of thought.

The drow went to Regis next, and was amazed and thrilled by the halfling's work. Where there once had been an unremarkable block of ice there was now a near likeness, in size and shape, of the onyx figurine.

"If I had more time," Regis started to say, but Drizzt stopped him with a wave of his hand. This would suffice.

And so they began training the seal. Drizzt tossed the ice statue into the water, yelled, "Guen!" and Regis rushed to the edge of the iceberg and scooped out the figurine in the same net Bruenor had put together for fishing. When Regis turned net and statue over to Drizzt, the drow rewarded him with one of the fish. They repeated it over and over, and finally, Drizzt put the net in the seal's mouth, tossed the figurine into the water and yelled, "Guen!"

Sure enough, the clever creature snorted and plunged in, quickly retrieving the halfling's sculpture. Drizzt glanced around at his friends, daring a smile of hope as he tossed a fish to the eager seal.

They went at it for more than twenty minutes, with each successive throw going farther out into the black water. Every time, the seal retrieved it perfectly, and every time, was rewarded by excitement and more importantly, by a fish.

Then they needed a break, for the seal was tired and was no longer hungry.

The next few hours were terminally long for poor Drizzt. He sat in the ice hut, warming with his friends, while the others talked, mostly to Wulfgar, trying to bring the barbarian back to the world of the living.

It was painfully obvious to them all, especially to Wulfgar, that he had a long, long road yet to travel.

During that time, Kierstaad would occasionally go out onto the iceberg and blare his horn. The young barbarian was growing quite concerned, for if they were drifting away at all, it was farther out from the shore, and there seemed no way to navigate back to their homes. They could catch their fish, the dwarven priestess and the ice hut could do much to keep them warm, but out on the Sea of Moving Ice was no way to spend Icewind Dale's winter! Eventually, Kierstaad knew, a blizzard would catch up to them, burying them in their hut while they slept, or a hungry white bear would come calling.

Drizzt was back to his work with the seal that afternoon, ending by having Regis distract the seal, while the drow splashed the water and called out, pretending to toss in the statue.

In leaped the seal, excitedly, but that lasted only a few moments, and finally, the frustrated creature clambered back onto the iceberg, barking in protest.

Drizzt did not reward it.

The drow kept the seal inside the ice hut that night and most of the next morning. He needed the creature to be hungry, very hungry, for he knew that they were running out of time. He could only hope that the iceberg hadn't drifted too far from the statue.

After a couple of throws, the drow used the same distractions and sent the seal in on a futile hunt. A few minutes passed, and when it seemed as if the seal was growing frustrated, Drizzt secretly slipped the figurine into the water.

The happy seal spotted it and brought it out, and was rewarded.

"It doesn't sink," Regis remarked, guessing the problem. "We have to get the seal used to diving for it." Following the logic, they weighed down the statue with Stumpet's grappling hook, which was easily bent by Wulfgar. Drizzt was careful on the next couple of throws, making sure that the seal could follow the statue's descent. The cunning animal performed perfectly, gliding under the dark water, out of sight, and returning with the figurine in the net every time.

They tried the ruse again, distracting the seal, while Drizzt slapped the water, and all of them held their breath when the seal went far under.

It surfaced many, many yards from the iceberg, barked to Drizzt and then disappeared again. This happened many times.

And then the seal came up right near the iceberg, leaping with joy up beside the drow, its mission complete.

With Guenhwyvar's figurine in the net.

The friends took up a huge cheer, and Kierstaad blew furiously on his horn.

This time, the young barbarian's call was answered by more than echoes. Kierstaad looked to the others hopefully, then blew again.

Drifting through the misty sea came a single boat, Berkthgar standing tall atop its prow while a host of both dwarves and barbarians pulled with all their strength.

Kierstaad responded once more, and then handed his horn over to Wulfgar, who blew the strongest and clearest note ever heard in Icewind Dale.

From out on the dark water, Berkthgar looked upon him, and so did Revjak. It was a moment of confusion and then elation, even for proud Berkthgar.

⚔ ⚔ ⚔ ⚔ ⚔

On the night of their return to the dwarven mines, Drizzt retired with mixed emotions. He was so glad, impossibly thrilled, to have Wulfgar back at his side, and to have come away from an encounter with such powerful enemies with all of his friends, Guenhwyvar included, virtually unharmed.

But the drow could not help thinking about his father. For months he had pursued this course in the belief that it would lead to Zaknafein. He had built the fantasy of being with his father and mentor once more, and though he did not for a moment begrudge the fact that Errtu's prisoner was Wulfgar and not Zaknafein, he could not easily let go of those fantasies.

He went to sleep troubled, and in that sleep, the drow dreamed.

He was awakened in his room by a ghostly presence. He went for his scimitars, but then stopped abruptly and fell back on his bed, recognizing the spirit of Zaknafein.

"My son," the ghost said to him, and Zaknafein was smiling warmly, a proud father, a contented spirit. "All is well with me, better than you can imagine."

Drizzt couldn't find the words to reply, but his expression asked every question in his heart anyway.

"An old priest called me," Zaknafein explained. "He said that you needed to know. Fare well, my son. Keep close to your friends and to your memories, and know in your heart that we will meet again."

With that, the ghost was gone.

Drizzt remembered it all vividly the next morning, and he was indeed comforted. Logic told him that it had been a dream—until he realized that the ghost had been speaking to him in the drow tongue, and until he realized that the old priest Zaknafein had referred to could only be Cadderly.

Drizzt had already decided that he would be going back to the Spirit

Soaring after the winter, bearing the crystal shard— securely tucked into the shielding coffer—as he had promised.

As the days went by and the memory of his ghostly encounter did not fade, the drow ranger found true peace, for he came to understand and to believe that it had been no dream.

⚔ ⚔ ⚔ ⚔ ⚔

"They offered me the tribe," Wulfgar said to Drizzt. It was a crisp wintry morning outside the dwarven mines, more than two months after their return from the Sea of Moving Ice.

Drizzt considered the not-unexpected news and the healthier condition of his returned friend. Then he shook his head—Wulfgar had not yet recovered, and should not take on the burden of such responsibility.

"I refused," Wulfgar admitted.

"Not yet," Drizzt said comfortingly.

Wulfgar looked to the blue sky, the same color as his eyes, which were shining again after six years of darkness. "Not ever," he corrected. "That is not my place."

Drizzt wasn't sure that he agreed. He wondered how much of Wulfgar's refusal was fostered by the overwhelming adjustment the barbarian was trying to make. Even the simplest things in this life seemed unfamiliar to poor Wulfgar. He was awkward with everyone, especially Catti-brie, though Bruenor and Drizzt had little doubt that the spark was rekindling between the two.

"I will guide Berkthgar, though," Wulfgar went on. "And will accept no hostility between his people, my people, and the folk of Icewind Dale. We each have enough real enemies without creating more!"

Drizzt didn't argue that point.

"Do you love her?" Wulfgar asked suddenly, and the drow was off his guard.

"Of course I do," Drizzt responded truthfully. "As I love you, and Bruenor, and Regis."

"I would not interfere—" Wulfgar started to say, but he was stopped by Drizzt's chuckle.

"The choice is neither mine nor yours," the drow explained, "but Catti-brie's. Remember what you had, my friend, and remember what you, in your foolishness, nearly lost."

Wulfgar looked long and hard at his dear friend, determined to heed that wise advice. Catti-brie's life was Catti-brie's to decide and whatever, or whomever, she chose, Wulfgar would always be among friends.

The winter would be long and cold, thick with snow and mercifully uneventful. Things would not be the same between the friends, could never be after all they had experienced, but they would be together again, in heart and in soul. Let no man, and no fiend, ever try to separate them again!

✕ ✕ ✕ ✕ ✕

It was one of those perfect spring nights in Icewind Dale, not too cold, but with enough of a breeze to keep the skin tingling. The stars were bright and thick. Drizzt couldn't tell where the night sky ended and the dark tundra began. And it didn't matter to him, Bruenor, or Regis. Guenhwyvar was similarly content, prowling about on the lower rocks of Bruenor's Climb.

"They're friends again," Bruenor explained, speaking of Catti-brie and Wulfgar. "He's needin' her now, and she's helping to get him back."

"You do not forget six years of torment at the hands of a fiend like Errtu in short order," Regis agreed.

Drizzt smiled widely, thinking that his friends had found their place together once more. That notion, of course, led the drow to wonder about his own place.

"I believe that I can catch up with Deudermont in Luskan," he said suddenly, unexpectedly. "If not there, then certainly in Waterdeep."

"Ye durned elf, what're ye runnin' from this time?" the dwarf pressed.

Drizzt turned to regard him and laughed aloud. "I am not running from anything, good dwarf," the drow replied. "But I must, on my word and for the good of all, deliver the crystal shard to Cadderly at the Spirit Soaring, in faraway Carradoon."

"Me girl said that place was south o' Sundabar," Bruenor protested, thinking he had caught the drow in a lie. "Ye ain't for sailin' there!"

"Far south of Sundabar," Drizzt agreed, "but closer to Baldur's Gate than to Waterdeep. The *Sea Sprite* runs swiftly. Deudermont can get me much nearer to Cadderly."

Bruenor's bluster was defeated by the simple logic. "Durned elf," the dwarf muttered. "I'm not much for goin' back on a durned boat! But if we must . . ."

Drizzt looked hard at the dwarf. "You are coming?"

"You think we would stay?" Regis replied, and when Drizzt turned his startled gaze on the halfling, Regis promptly reminded him that it was he, and not Drizzt, who had captured Crenshinibon.

"Of course they're goin'," came a familiar voice from the darkness some distance below. "As are we!"

A moment later, Catti-brie and Wulfgar walked up the steep path to join their friends.

Drizzt looked to them all, one by one, then turned away to regard the stars.

"All my life, I have been searching for a home," the drow said quietly. "All my life, I have been wanting more than that which was offered to me, more than Menzoberranzan, more than friends who stood beside me out of personal gain. I always thought home to be a place, and indeed it is, but not in any physical sense. It is a place in here," Drizzt said, putting a hand to his heart and turning back to look upon his companions. "It is a feeling given by true friends.

"I know this now, and know that I am home."

"But ye're off to Carradoon," Catti-brie said softly.

"And so're we!" Bruenor bellowed.

Drizzt smiled at them, laughed aloud. "If circumstances will not allow me to remain at home," the ranger said firmly, "then I will simply take my home with me!"

From somewhere not so far away, Guenhwyvar roared. They would be out on the road, all six, before the next dawn.

CONTINUE YOUR ADVENTURE

The Dungeons & Dragons® Fantasy Roleplaying Game Starter Set has everything you need for you and your friends to start playing. Explore infinite universes, create bold heroes and prepare to begin– or rediscover– the game that started it all.

Watch Videos
Read Sample Chapters
Get product previews

Learn more about D&D® products
at
DungeonsandDragons.com

DUNGEONS & DRAGONS, D&D, WIZARDS OF THE COAST, and their respective logos are trademarks of Wizards of the Coast LLC in the U.S.A. and other countries. ©2011 Wizards.